THE
DECAMERON

ALSO BY WAYNE A. REBHORN

George Puttenham, *The Art of English Poesy: A Critical Edition* (with Frank Whigham)

Niccolò Machiavelli, *The Prince and Other Writings* (translation)

Sir Thomas More, *Utopia, Translated by Ralph Robinson, with The Life of Sir Thomas More by William Roper* (edition)

Renaissance Debates on Rhetoric (edition and translation)

The Emperor of Men's Minds: Literature and the Renaissance Discourse of Rhetoric (critical study)

Foxes and Lions: Machiavelli's Confidence Men (critical study)

Courtly Performances: Masking and Festivity in Castiglione's Book of the Courtier (critical study)

Giovanni Boccaccio

THE DECAMERON

Translated and with an Introduction by

WAYNE A. REBHORN

W. W. NORTON & COMPANY

New York • London

For information about permission to reproduce selections from this book,
write to Permissions, W. W. Norton & Company, Inc.,
500 Fifth Avenue, New York, NY 10110

For information about special discounts for bulk purchases, please contact
W. W. Norton Special Sales at specialsales@wwnorton.com or 800-233-4830

Manufacturing by RR Donnelley, Harrisonburg
Book design by Chris Welch Design
Production manager: Julia Druskin

Library of Congress Cataloging-in-Publication Data

Boccaccio, Giovanni, 1313–1375.
[Decameron. English]
The decameron / Giovanni Boccaccio ; Translated and with an
Introduction by Wayne A. Rebhorn. — First Edition.
pages cm
ISBN 978-0-393-06930-3 (hardcover)
1. Plague—Europe—History—Fiction. 2. Storytelling—Fiction.
I. Rebhorn, Wayne A., 1943– translator. II. Title.
PQ4272.E5A3613 2013
853.15—dc23
2013018804

W. W. Norton & Company, Inc.
500 Fifth Avenue, New York, N.Y. 10110
www.wwnorton.com

W. W. Norton & Company Ltd.
Castle House, 75/76 Wells Street, London W1T 3QT

2 3 4 5 6 7 8 9 0

For Marlette and Doug

My best readers

CONTENTS

THE DECAMERON

Day 1

Day 2

Day 3

Day 4

Day 5

Day 6

Day 7

house with a dagger in his hand, and her husband winds up escorting Leonetto home.

Day 8

Day 9

Day 10

daughter of a peasant. After he has had two children with her, he makes it look to her as though they have been put to death. Later on, pretending to have grown weary of her, he claims he has married another woman and arranges to have his own daughter brought home as though she were his bride, meanwhile having turned his wife out of doors wearing nothing but her shift. On finding that she has borne everything with patience, however, he takes her back home again, dearer to him than ever, shows her their grown-up children, and honors her as Marchioness and causes everyone else to do so as well.

INTRODUCTION

One of the most famous opening lines in Western literature is surely that of Dante's *Divine Comedy*: *Nel mezzo del cammin di nostra vita*. Dante records how, "in the middle of the journey of our life," he came to consciousness in a dark wood, having lost his way along the path that leads to salvation. After this beginning, the poet as wayfarer or pilgrim will travel from Hell through Purgatory until he finally winds up in Paradise and stands in the presence of God. Dante deliberately places his pilgrimage in his thirty-fifth year: his journey thus occurs at the biblical midpoint of his life, a key moment when he finds himself in between his own sinful past and his redeemed future. His epic poem of one hundred cantos is thus about being in the middle of things—and then, moving beyond.

Both Boccaccio and his greatest literary work, the *Decameron*, are also very much about being in the middle of things, albeit without the urge to transcendence we find in Dante. Boccaccio started composing his book just after the Black Death had struck Florence in 1348, and since he was born in 1313, he would have been thirty-five that year— *Nel mezzo del cammin di nostra vita*—just as Dante was when he woke up in the dark wood. But Boccaccio was in the middle of things in many other ways as well. Much of the first half of his life had been spent in Naples where he associated with the French-speaking Angevin court and where he produced a series of poems in an Italian decidedly medieval in character. Later, during the years when he was writing the *Decameron* in Florence, he met Francesco Petrarca—Petrarch—often regarded as the "father" of the Italian Renaissance. Under his influence, Boccaccio largely turned away from the vernacular and from medieval genres even as he was completing the *Decameron* and began producing scholarly works in Latin that looked forward to the new age that was about to dawn, to the Renaissance, with its investment, as the name suggests, in the "rebirth" of pagan antiquity in the modern world. In short, the *Decameron* was written at a time when, perhaps without knowing it, Boccaccio was at a turning point in his life, putting an end to his career as a medieval poet and beginning one as a Renaissance scholar.

If the *Decameron* comes in the middle of Boccaccio's life, that life itself occurs during an age in transition. The court culture of the late Middle Ages with its emphasis on knightly prowess, chivalry, and courtly love still had great prestige throughout Italy in the fourteenth century, but the burgeoning city-states clustered in the northern and central regions of the peninsula were fostering a secular culture in which knowledge of ancient Greece and Rome, the ability to speak in public forums with rhetorical effect, and a sophisticated grasp of the Latin tongue, as much as the military skills of the knight or warrior, were becoming the key to success and a means of personal self-definition. Nowhere was that transformation going on with more intensity than in Florence, a center of banking and the wool trade and, increasingly after the mid-fourteenth century, a place where ancient rhetoric and the study of the Greek and Latin classics held pride of place in the intellectual world. It was a city that would soon have chancellors, political figures, such as Coluccio Salutati and Leonardo Bruni, who were Latin scholars and authors as well. Florence became an important center of humanist learning: a center for the scholarly study of Latin and Greek, the recovery and editing of classical texts, and the teaching of Latin based on the language of Cicero and Vergil. Boccaccio, together with Petrarch, was right in the middle of this grand cultural shift.

Like its author, the *Decameron* straddles two ages without being fully part of either. With its heavy investment in the idealism of medieval romance and its celebration of virtues such as courtly love and magnanimity, the book reflects the culture that Boccaccio embraced during his youthful years in Naples and that he captured in the decidedly medieval works he wrote in the vernacular while he was living there and immediately after his return to Florence in the 1340s, works including romances, dream visions, and courtly debates about love. To be sure, there is another strand in the *Decameron* that is anything but courtly and romantic. While the tales sometimes put knights and ladies on display, they even more frequently celebrate the cunning, greed, lust, and energy of lower- and middle-class characters who play tricks on one another and often display great verbal wit in pursuit of food, money, and, especially, sex. This earthy aspect of Boccaccio's work is what he is most famous for—*boccaccesco* in Italian is a synonym for "licentious"—and it links him to the Middle Ages as well. For if the knightly romance was the high genre of that period, tales of lower-class characters engaging in farcical behavior were their comic counterpart. Scholars refer to those tales, using their French name, as *fabliaux* ("little fables or stories"), but it might be equally appropriate to call them what Boccaccio does, *novelle.*

While Boccaccio cultivates medieval genres such as the romance and the *novella* in his *Decameron,* he also anticipates the future, at least partially. Although he does not share the classicizing bent in it that would later define the cultural movement called humanism and that is central to any conception of the Renaissance, his book does look forward to several aspects of the age to come and is thus "in the middle," this time between two historical periods. In its emphasis on worldly pleasures, its embrace of sex and the body, and its investment in things material, the *Decameron* anticipates the increasingly worldly and secular side of the Renaissance. In addition, although there is very little in the book to suggest the notion of self-fashioning that most modern scholars think of as defining the Renaissance—very little to suggest that Boccaccio imagined human identity as something achieved through one's efforts rather than ascribed to one at birth—he is nevertheless intensely aware of the social mobility that was occurring in his world, and he repeatedly has his characters play roles and adopt different identities, however temporary they may be, creating and re-creating themselves in their clever verbal performances. The protagonist of the very first story, Ser Ciappelletto, is the "worst man who had ever been born" (see p. 26), but who manages to concoct a fictional autobiography—a self of sorts—in his final confession that dupes a gullible friar into taking him for a saint. Thus, while the *Decameron* gets produced in the middle of Boccaccio's career change from medieval vernacular poet to proto–Renaissance Latin scholar, it also takes a set of medieval genres and fills them with Renaissance themes and characters. In short, like its author and his age, Boccaccio's book is in the middle of things, and partly as a result, it turns into a masterpiece that is, perhaps confusingly at times, both medieval and Renaissance all at once.

Boccaccio in the Middle of Things

Boccaccio was born during the summer of 1313 in or near the Tuscan town of Certaldo outside of Florence (or possibly in Florence itself). A bastard, he was quickly legitimized by his father, a man from Certaldo named Boccaccino di Chellino, who had relocated to Florence around 1300 where he worked for the powerful banking firm owned by the Bardi family. Growing up in Florence, Boccaccio was encouraged to study Dante by the father of one of his closest friends, and he would be deeply influenced by Dante's works throughout his life. In fact, during his last years, when Boccaccio was in his most humanist, proto-Renaissance scholarly phase, committed as he was to the study of the classics, he demonstrated his continuing interest in his great Italian predecessor by undertaking a series of public lectures in Florence commenting on Dante's masterpiece. It should also be noted that he received a stipend from the city of Florence for this work, something he doubtless appreciated since he spent most of his adult life dealing with the problem of inadequate monetary resources.

Boccaccio's father went to Naples in 1326 to assume a position in the Bardi bank there, and his son accompanied him. After spending six unproductive years working in his father's bank, Boccaccio was allowed to enter the Neapolitan *Studium*, essentially the university, where he studied canon law. Although he was not taken with the profession and did not complete a degree, he did have an opportunity to deepen his knowledge of a variety of fields, including literature. The Kingdom of Naples, which included all of southern Italy, was ruled by Robert the

Wise (b. 1277, reigned 1309–43), a member of the Angevin dynasty that
controlled the area from 1266 until the middle of the fifteenth century.
Boccaccio gained entrance to Robert's feudal, French-speaking court
because of his father's high position in the Bardi bank, and it was here
that he formed a largely positive image of aristocratic life in the late
Middle Ages.

During his Neapolitan period, Boccaccio came into contact with a
number of important writers and scholars, and he himself produced
a number of substantial works in Italian, including: *La caccia di Diana*
(*Diana's Hunt*, 1334–37), a short mythological poem; *Il Filostrato* (the
title was thought to mean "the one cast down by love"; 1335–40), a long
romance in verse about frustrated love set during the Trojan War; *Il
Filocolo* (*The Labors of Love*, finished 1336–39), a prose romance on the
adventures of the French lovers Flor and Blanchefleur; and the *Teseida*
(*The Thesiad*, 1339–40), an epic also on the theme of unhappy love,
which was to form the basis for Chaucer's *The Knight's Tale*.

Boccaccio returned to Florence most likely in 1340–41, having been
preceded there by his father, who had stopped working for the Bardi
bank in 1338 and had apparently gone bankrupt. Boccaccio left Naples
with some reluctance, and wrote a letter to a powerful friend there,
the Florentine Niccolò Acciaiuoli, in August of 1341, unsuccessfully
attempting to obtain some sort of post in the court to enable his return.
Boccaccio remained in Florence with his father, an elderly widower, as
well as with two of the five illegitimate children he would sire during
the course of his life. (None of Boccaccio's children managed to survive into adulthood.) During this period in Florence, Boccaccio composed more works in the vernacular, such as the *Elegia di Madonna
Fiammetta* (*The Elegy of Madonna Fiammetta*, 1343–45) in which a
character named Panfilo, who would turn up later in the *Decameron*,
disparages the city of Florence, which is also attacked in the *Comedía
delle ninfe fiorentine* (*The Comedy of the Florentine Nymphs*, 1341–42), a
prose work with interspersed poems. Boccaccio produced an allegorical
poem, the *Amorosa visione* (*The Amorous Vision*, 1342), as well as a long
pastoral poem, the *Ninfale fiesolano* (*The Nymph of Fiesole*), probably in
1344–46 (there is some question as to whether he was the author). All

of these works exalt the power of love, but tend to be more allegorical in character than the ones he produced in Naples.

Political chaos in Florence led Boccaccio to move to Ravenna, where records place him in 1346. In 1348 Florence was struck by the worst plague in European history, which Boccaccio would use as a pretext to have the ten narrators of the *Decameron* flee the city and spend the better part of two weeks telling stories in the Tuscan countryside. Since the conventional definition of comedy in the Middle Ages was that such a work began in awful circumstances but ended in happier ones, Boccaccio's collection, like Dante's *Commedia*, was thus intended to be seen as a comedy. No hard evidence exists that Boccaccio was actually in Florence when the plague broke out—indeed, there are records of Boccaccio's having been in the town of Forlí in late 1347 and early 1348—and many elements in his description of the ravages of the disease come from the eighth-century *Historia Longobardorum* (*History of the Lombards*) by Paulus Diaconus ("Paul the Deacon"). However, his father, who was the minister of supply (*Ufficiale dell'Abbondanza*) and was in charge of organizing relief during the epidemic, may have communicated details about the disaster to him. Boccaccio's father died in 1349, though not from the plague, making Boccaccio the head of his family and leaving him in difficult economic circumstances.

Despite the criticisms of Florence that Boccaccio voiced in several of his works, the city had a profound influence on him. In the generation before his, the traditional, feudal nobility were banned from holding offices in the city and were forced to tear down the towers they had built as a way of asserting their dominance. Florence was an extraordinarily rich city at the time, but its political life was marked by constant struggles for wealth and power among different fractions of what we would call the middle class. The Florentine elite admired intelligence, imagination, and hard work, and a fair number of people in the city, including many who came there from the countryside around Florence, experienced some form of the social mobility that would become one of the defining features of the European Renaissance, even though they had not yet developed anything like an ideology of self-fashioning to define what that mobility meant. There was also, simultaneously, a great deal of hostility to *la gente nuova*, the "new people," the socially ambitious who sought to rise above what many thought was their proper station in life. If Boccaccio's *Decameron* reflects some of the aristocratic principles of the Neapolitan court, principles such as magnanimity and proper manners, which were adopted by the Florentine ruling class, at the same time his work also reflects the mercantile values of that class, its emphasis on the intelligence, the calculation, and the inventiveness needed to succeed in the world of commerce.

Boccaccio probably wrote the *Decameron* between 1349 and 1351 or 1352, although three of its tales had appeared earlier in his works (two in the *Filocolo* and one in the *Comedía*), and he may well have been assembling materials long before the advent of the plague in 1348. It is possible that he originally intended a collection of seventy stories told by seven young women, but he added three men and thirty more stories, then arranged for his ten narrators to tell their tales on ten separate days spread over a period of two weeks. (They take two pairs of Fridays and Saturdays off for religious observances and personal hygiene.) By thus increasing the number of stories to one hundred, Boccaccio made his text more closely resemble the *Divine Comedy* with its one hundred cantos. That resemblance was also enhanced by many textual references within the work to Dante's epic and by Boccaccio's expanding the materials in the frame immediately after Days 3 and 6, thus dividing the work into three large sections that might recall the three divisions of Dante's work. Of course, the *Decameron* is not about the spiritual journey of a pilgrim on his way to Paradise after passing through Hell and Purgatory. Its concern is with earthly matters, and it emphasizes the body and the body's pleasures. The very first sentence of Boccaccio's work does not place its author in a dark wood like Dante; instead, the *Decameron* begins by emphasizing the earthly and the human—as well as the humane: "It is a matter of humanity to show compassion for those who suffer" (see p. 1).

The *Decameron* marks a turning point in Boccaccio's career: this was virtually his last full engagement with a medieval vernacular genre (or set of genres), for after 1350 he was deeply involved in the proto-humanistic culture of the Renaissance. In October, he was sent to welcome Petrarch, the most famous man of letters in Italy, at the gates of Florence, and the two men quickly formed a close friendship while Petrarch was staying in Boccaccio's home. Nonetheless, Boccaccio regarded his friend as his intellectual superior and consistently referred to him as *magister* ("master," "teacher"). In March of 1351 Boccaccio was sent to Padua, where Petrarch was then staying, in an attempt— ultimately unsuccessful—to persuade him to come and live in the city from which he and his family had been exiled. Boccaccio's diplomatic failure did not prevent the two men from engaging in long discussions that may have influenced what Boccaccio said about the importance of poetry in the last two books of his *De genealogia deorum gentilium* (*On the Genealogy of the Pagan Gods*), an encyclopedic work on classi- cal mythology that was finished in 1360, but that Boccaccio revised throughout the rest of his life. Its defense of poetry in its last books has much in common with what Boccaccio wrote at the end of the *Decameron*, although the *Genealogy* sees the poet's role in much more purely didactic and moralistic terms.

After his life-changing encounter with Petrarch, Boccaccio wrote very little in Italian. There are a misogynistic diatribe called the *Cor- baccio* (*The Crow*), a consolatory letter to a friend, a little treatise in praise of Dante (*Trattatello in laude di Dante*, first edition in 1360), and his unfinished commentary on the *Divine Comedy* (*Esposizioni sopra la Comedía di Dante*, 1373–75). Some scholars think Boccaccio's commit- ment to Petrarchan classicism also entailed a commitment to a certain kind of antifeminine asceticism as well. Boccaccio's consolatory letter was written to Pino de' Rossi in 1361–62 after the addressee was ban- ished from Florence by the government because of his connection with an attempted coup d'état. Significantly, at this point Boccaccio gave his house in Florence to his brother Iacopo and retired to Certaldo where he lived for the remainder of his life.

Boccaccio had been very active as a diplomat during the 1350s, going on numerous missions for the Signoria, the governing body of the city, both inside and outside Italy. He met Petrarch again in 1359, and by 1360, like his friend, had decided to take holy orders. He also sought the patronage of Niccolò Acciaiuoli in the court of Naples once again, but he failed, for Acciaiuoli never really trusted him, labeling him *Johannes tranquillitatum*, "Fair-weather John," to suggest Boccaccio's supposed undependability in a political crisis—yet another reason for Boccaccio to retire to Certaldo in the early 1360s.

Inspired by Petrarch, Boccaccio advanced the cause of classical studies in the 1350s. He persuaded the Florentine government to establish a chair in Greek at the university in 1359–60, and he himself produced a variety of compendia in Latin based on his extensive reading of the classics. There is a view that Boccaccio's turn to humanist scholarship, didacticism, and a form of religious asceticism after 1350 meant that he came to look down on his earlier, more secular works in the vernacular. This is supposedly supported by an account in one of Petrarch's letters from 1362, which is a response to a lost letter from Boccaccio. In that letter Boccaccio purportedly said that he had been visited by a Carthusian monk who had brought him a warning that his death was imminent and that he should repent of his folly. This apparently prompted Boccaccio to consider destroying his earlier, "profane" works, including, of course, the *Decameron*. In his letter responding to this incident, Petrarch suggests that the two men were devoting somewhat more time to literature than they should have, but it ends with a suggestion that they should pool their libraries and live together, a suggestion that is hardly consistent with the idea that Boccaccio was about to burn his secular writings.

Although Boccaccio traveled a great deal in the 1360s, often going on diplomatic missions for the city of Florence just as he had in the 1350s, and managed to see Petrarch one last time in 1368, he had essentially retired to Certaldo. He worked there on revising his Latin works, and in 1370–71 he copied the entire *Decameron* out in his own hand, thus suggesting that whatever regrets he might have felt about this most "pagan" and licentious of his works, he remained deeply attached to it. This manuscript is known as the Hamilton codex and is in the Staatsbibliothek of Berlin. It is the basis for all modern editions of the work, although they also make use of a codex in Paris that includes a few minor additions to what is found in the Hamilton codex.

In 1373 the Florentine government invited Boccaccio to give a series of public lectures on Dante, but he only got as far as the seventeenth canto of the *Inferno* before he died. He was preceded in death the year before by Petrarch, whose passing he commemorated in a sonnet, the last poem in his *Rime* (*Poems*). Boccaccio was famously fat and suffered from a variety of illnesses in his last years, which finally led to his demise in Certaldo on December 21, 1375.

The *Decameron* in the Middle Ages

Boccaccio was probably thinking about creating a collection of tales united within a single framework as early as the *Filocolo* of the 1330s, in which characters debate various questions about love by telling tales on the subject. He had also had the nymphs provide accounts of their exploits in his *Comedia delle ninfe fiorentine* of 1341–42. And both his *Fiammetta* and this *Amorosa visione* have characters who talk about the notion of passing the hotter part of the day telling stories. All of this storytelling tends to occur in some sort of *locus amoenus,* a "pleasant place," that is, an ideal spot of natural harmony and pleasure, like the ones the company of young men and women in the *Decameron* find waiting for them in the countryside to which they flee in order to escape the ravages of the plague in Florence. Finally, Boccaccio's choice of a Hellenizing title for his work is consistent with such early efforts as the *Filostrato* and the *Teseida,* although his real model in this case was the *Hexaemeron* of Saint Ambrose, the theologian's pious elaboration of the six days of creation. Boccaccio's reference to this serious work by means of his title can only be said to be ironic.

There is no precedent in Italian literature for Boccaccio's use of a frame narrative to unify his collection. The only collection of stories to appear before his own was the anonymous *Novellino* from the late thirteenth century, and it is really a series of anecdotes told in a relatively simple style without any frame whatsoever. Boccaccio took material for several tales in the *Decameron* from this collection, but he elaborated on it considerably. He also drew on the French *fabliau,* as mentioned earlier, and on collections of edifying stories, *exempla,* such as the

Disciplina clericalis (*A School for Clerics*) by Peter Alphonsi (or Alfonsi) from the early fourteenth century, which contains some thirty-seven tales often derived from Middle Eastern and Asian sources. Moreover, Boccaccio had historical works he could draw on in both Latin and the vernacular, and there was classical literature as well, including a variety of texts by the Roman writers Ovid and Apuleius.

More important as influences on Boccaccio's work than all these were the collections of stories from Asia that had been circulating in translation throughout Europe since the early Middle Ages. Some, like the *Panchatantra* (*The Five Heads*), which was written in Sanskrit around 500 CE, involved the use of a frame narrative. Boccaccio probably knew this text, although in a Latin translation based on a Hebrew version (which was itself based on one in Arabic, which was in turn based on one in Persian). There was also a collection known as *The Seven Wise Masters*, in which seven advisors to an emperor tell him stories about the evil powers of women to nullify the plot of the empress who seeks to have the emperor's son put to death. This technique of fending off death by telling tales is generally applicable to the situation in the *Decameron*, and it appears in the most famous Eastern framed collection, *The Thousand and One Nights*, which Boccaccio probably did not know, as well as in the eighth and ninth books of Apuleius's *Metamorphoses*, or the *Golden Ass*, which he certainly did.

The *Decameron* actually has two frames. Around the stories themselves is the frame of the ten narrators and the world they inhabit; it describes the Florence that has been destroyed by the plague and the bucolic environments in which the group tells its tales. But that frame is surrounded in turn by one involving the author and his readers, a frame that might be called the "macrotext" in order to distinguish it from the other frame contained within it. Although Boccaccio identifies the audience of the macrotext specifically as women, it would perhaps be better to think of it as having multiple audiences consisting of both men and women since the macrotext really involves anyone who is reading the work. Boccaccio addresses this multiple audience on three distinct occasions: in his Preface, in the lengthy Introduction to Day 4, and in his Author's Conclusion. In the first of these he expresses his sympathy for women, who are trapped inside their houses and have no way of finding emotional relief when they are in love, and he dedicates his stories to their recreation, offering them as a form of vicarious relief. In the other two passages where Boccaccio addresses his audience directly, he adopts a witty, tongue-in-cheek tone as he defends the seriousness of his storytelling in the face of a variety of criticisms. Despite all his witty nonchalance, however, he is really arguing for the essential value of literature, and in particular for that of prose fiction. This is important because Boccaccio is one of the first writers in the West to see prose fiction as a serious, rather than marginalized and trivial, form of literature. Although Boccaccio is creating a surface of wit and banter in these passages, underneath it he is clearly quite earnest about the business of writing stories in the vernacular, no matter how little the world may think of such an enterprise.

To return to the frame story of the *Decameron*: the book begins with a description of the plague that feels powerfully real, no matter how much Boccaccio may have been indebted to written sources. There is a clear disconnect, however, between that description and the presentation of the ten young men and women who will narrate the one hundred stories: we have moved from the realm of history and fact to that of art and fiction. The storytellers do assemble in a real place, the Church of Santa Maria Novella, which was probably chosen because the last word in its name looks forward to the stories, the *novelle*, they would be telling. But the literary or fictional nature of Boccaccio's group of storytellers is dramatized by the numbers involved: there are ten of them in all, including seven women and three men. The number seven had many important associations in late medieval thinking, including the days of the week, the seven (known) planets, the seven virtues, and the seven liberal arts. Like seven, the number three could suggest the Trinity or the three Graces, and it was identified as the male number in some medieval numerological systems. Moreover, the number ten is the result of adding one, the number of unity or perfection or God, to nine, which was considered the "golden number" since, among other things, it was the result of multiplying three, the number of the Trinity, by itself, and thus, in a sense, perfecting it. This and other possible examples of number symbolism in the *Decameron* are clearly indebted not just to medieval thought in general, but also to Dante's practice in the *Divine Comedy*. His work consists of three canticles, which, in turn, are comprised of thirty-four cantos (an initial threshold canto plus thirty-three others) in *Inferno*, followed by thirty-three cantos each in *Purgatorio* and *Paradiso*. Dante's number symbolism ultimately points to the mysterious, mystical identity of God (one) with the other persons of the Trinity (three). The numbers used in Boccaccio's work may echo Dante's, but it would be hard to argue that they aim at such a spiritual end.

The fictional nature of the company of storytellers is also suggested by Boccaccio's refusal to call them by their real names and his giving them other, allegorical ones instead. Various scholars have tried to identify the real people supposedly hiding behind these masks, but with little success, and a variety of different allegories have been suggested for the division of the group into seven women and three men. (On this matter as well as the issue of number symbolism, see the first of the Headnotes following this Introduction.) Perhaps the most important thing Boccaccio is doing by inviting readers to think about the allegorical names of the ten narrators is preparing us to think in allegorical terms about the stories they will tell as well. Thinking in allegorical terms was, of course, the "default position" for readers in the Middle Ages, who had been trained since antiquity to think about the Bible as well as a wide variety of both secular and religious texts, that every narrative—if not everything in the universe—could and should be interpreted allegorically.

The unrealistic, fictional character of the storytellers is enhanced by Boccaccio's descriptions of the settings in which they tell their tales: they are all delightful places in the countryside in which nature has been carefully shaped by art. During their first day away from Florence, the group travels about two miles to Fiesole and installs itself in a little palace atop a hill. The palace has bedrooms adorned with fresh flowers and soft, comfortable beds; its water is pure; its cellars are stocked with the finest wine; and the food is excellent and abundant. More important, the palace also has a variety of gardens around it as well as a spacious, shaded meadow in which the group spends its first two afternoons telling stories. They then relocate to an equally attractive palace on Day 3, although the garden attached to it in which they tell their tales is surrounded by a wall and contains a little meadow with a fountain at its center. Not surprisingly, this walled garden is explicitly compared to the earthly paradise, although it is a distinctly artificial one, created by human beings, not by God.

The final relocation made by the group takes place on Day 7, when they go to the Valley of the Ladies. This ideal natural space may well be some version of Heaven, as several critics have suggested, but if so, it is the Heaven of Art itself, with all its vegetation growing in terraces arranged like tiers in an amphitheater as they descend toward the bottom of the valley. At its center there is a little lake of crystal-clear water, in which, at the end of Day 6, the ladies take a swim and in which the men do the same thing later on. This swimming can be read as a kind of ritual purification, for they all go to the valley the following day, Day 7, during which they will tell some of the most salacious tales in Boccaccio's book before returning to the palace they had stayed in on Days 3 to 6 and in whose walled garden they will tell the rest of their stories.

In short, Boccaccio uses the frame of the *Decameron* to transport his ten young men and women from plague-stricken Florence into a series of artificial paradise-like natural spaces in the country in which they amuse themselves by talking and singing and dancing, by eating and drinking, and, most memorably, by telling stories. Those stories are, of course, art on display, just as art is on display in all the "natural" locations where their storytelling takes place. The ten young men and women have achieved their own version of paradise, a kind of salvation, during their two weeks in the country, although the paradise and the salvation they achieve are the result of human effort, of art, and unlike Dante's, they have a decidedly earthly nature.

The *Decameron* in the Middle of the Plague

Boccaccio's framed collection of stories takes an actual event, the plague that invaded Europe in 1347–48 and carried off as much as a third of the population in some areas, and uses it as the catalyst for his ten young narrators to go out into the country and tell their tales. The plague has essentially destroyed the civilization of Florence. The social, political, and religious institutions and hierarchies that served to organize and direct people's life have all broken down. Laws have ceased to function, religious institutions failed to carry out their responsibilities, and the few servants left scarcely obey their masters (or are cared for by their masters in turn). As hierarchies collapse, the boundaries between people and things, the boundaries that provide essential definitions and distinctions, are effaced. People can enter others' houses with impunity; animals in the country wander out of their fields because their masters have died; and the boundaries of sexual propriety are crossed as women do not hesitate to expose themselves at times to their male servants. Even the dividing line between humans and animals is erased, as Boccaccio describes how a pair of pigs, tossing about the rags of a plague victim with their snouts, themselves succumb to the disease. In short, the structures that maintain society all seem to have crumbled.

Equally important, the affective bonds that hold people together in families, neighborhoods, political alliances, and the like have been destroyed by the plague. Families have been decimated by the disease, and Boccaccio reports with horror that family members no longer take care of one another. Many people retreat from social contact altogether by staying in their homes, and although others band together in groups to eat, drink, and be merry, we are told that such irresponsible socializing does not keep them from avoiding death. Perhaps most striking in this regard is the alteration in burial customs. Funerals are collective occasions that enable communities to manage the breach in society that has been opened up by death, but the sheer scope of the mortality caused by the plague has made funerals impossible. No longer do the female friends and relations of the deceased gather in the house to pay their last respects. No longer do the men gather to do so outside. Priests and mourners can scarcely be found to form a proper funeral cortege; the dead are carried on wooden planks instead of being borne to their grave sites on proper biers; a funeral procession for a single person is quickly made into one for a host of victims; and many of the dead are simply tossed into mass graves, like so much cargo piled up in a ship's hold. In short, one of the primary rituals that functions as the glue holding society together has been destroyed, turning Florence not only into a city whose structures have collapsed, but one in which people are fundamentally disconnected from one another.

Essentially, Florence has become a living Hell. People are trapped inside a city of the dead, forced to endure endless repetitions of the same sterile events that only provoke depression and despair. In this context, it is significant that Pampinea, the leader of Boccaccio's group of storytellers, proposes that she and her friends flee the city. She stresses the fact that they are doing the same things over and over again, as if their lives consisted of nothing except listening to the moans and groans of the dying, counting the number of corpses piling up, and experiencing the terror that they, too, might soon become victims of the disease. Of course, to be trapped in such a deadly vicious circle is precisely the punishment meted out to the damned in Dante's *Inferno*, who are condemned to repeat some allegorical version of their sins in one of the circles of Hell over and over again for all eternity, often enough by literally running around the circle to which they have been consigned.

It is with some relief for the reader—and for Boccaccio himself— that he finally describes how Pampinea and her friends come together one Tuesday morning and decide to flee the vicious circle of Florence's Hell by escaping into the countryside. Although they take pains to justify their flight, they hardly need to do so, for they have been abandoned by family and friends and servants, and the social structures that would normally provide stability in their lives have collapsed. A two-week escape to the country, with ten of the days involved being devoted to storytelling, thus seems like a perfectly reasonable decision. Their sojourn in the country will be more than a mere escape, of course; it will be a way for them to find some personal and intellectual, if not social and institutional, means to cope with the plague, perhaps a way for them to restore at least certain aspects of their city that has been turned into a living Hell.

The group takes a remarkable and unprecedented step when it goes off to the country, for it goes there to invent a life for itself to replace the

one it left behind. To be more precise: to compensate for the structures
and rituals that once organized life in Florence, the group creates a set
of artfully invented rituals or ritual-like activities for themselves. Of
course, throughout the Middle Ages, people would frequently step outside their normal social life in order to participate in rituals or ritual-
like activities. They would go on processions and pilgrimages, attend
religious services, and join in all the collective, often raucous festivities
sprinkled throughout the year from Christmas to carnival to All Hal-
lows' Eve. As people still do, they would enter what is usually spoken
of as a liminal (from Latin *limen*: "threshold") time and space separate
from that of their ordinary social world, even if nowadays it may be,
for instance, just the few special hours set aside for trick-or-treating on
Halloween. But the narrators of the *Decameron* are not participating
in a preestablished festivity of this sort, one whose rules were more or
less codified; they are inventing their own ritual-like activity out of
whole cloth.

The group thus begins the process by leaving their normal world and
going out into the country, but as we have noted, they do not exactly
enter the wilds of nature. Just as all ritual activities involve liminal
spaces, the group finds palaces to accommodate them and, more important, tells their tales in meadows and gardens attached to those palaces
that are likewise spaces situated betwixt and between, embracing both
nature and culture at the same time. The group then shapes its day by
altering the normal routines they would have followed back in Florence. They are, in fact, even more organized than they would have been
at home, perhaps in order to compensate for the utter chaos created
there by the plague. They also quickly create a temporary and unusual
sociopolitical structure for themselves that is quite different from that
of Florence. Although by coming with their servants they do retain at
least one aspect of their city's traditional hierarchy, they invent a kind
of revolving monarchy, naming a new king or queen for each day of
storytelling and passing the crown from one to the other until all ten
of them have had a chance to rule.

By spending so much time in one another's company, the group
restores something of the society that was destroyed in Florence.

Indeed, as they walk, and especially as they dance, they literally touch one another, restoring the contact that the plague had made far too dangerous. But it is by telling stories in particular that they create a sense of community, of shared values and pleasures, for their stories complement the structure their daily routine supplies and give a positive intellectual and emotional content to their experience. They serve to restore a kind of rationality (one of the verbs most frequently used for their storytelling is *ragionare*: to speak, discuss, or reason about) and a real feeling of compassion (many of their stories deliberately provoke that response and in some cases bring them close to tears). After all, rationality and compassion were lost in Florence when the Black Death descended on the city. As they tell their stories, the group sits in a symbolic circle: they turn their backs to the outside world and face one another, reinforcing their connectedness by looking at and listening to the other members of the group. If life back in Florence had become something like a vicious circle of Hell, the storytellers respond to this by creating a circle of their own, but one that affirms their personal health and social well-being and thus, in a sense, supplies a cure for the plague.

Participating in rituals impacts people, for by stepping outside their ordinary roles and abrogating the rules of society at least temporarily, they enter a liminal space and time that gives them a freedom, a license to engage in all sorts of normally unpermitted behaviors. Boccaccio's young men and women can thus tell stories that have made the *Decameron* synonymous with witty irreverence, mockery, and sexual license. Festive freedom also allows for a kind of stocktaking, enabling people to reflect on themselves and to clarify the nature of their social world. The experience may lead to nothing more than a reaffirmation of conventional structures and rules, but it can also enable the contemplation of alternatives. In other words, rituals and festivities have a creative potential that makes for the possibility—or at least the thought—of change. Such stocktaking, reflection, self-reflection, and potential thinking about alternatives are precisely what Boccaccio's group is doing—and it does so, of course, primarily by means of its artfully constructed stories.

Through their tales as well as through their interactions with one another, the storytellers of the *Decameron* are thus engaged in the project not just of restoring the Florence they have left behind—although they are certainly doing that—but of reimagining, however unconsciously and unprogrammatically, that society through their art. Although they all come from the same social class, they populate their stories with a wide range of individuals—aristocrats, merchants and tradesmen, artisans and peasants, women as well as men—and this cast of characters includes both Florentines and people from all over Italy as well as the rest of Europe and the Mediterranean basin. It may be misleading to speak of the narrators as "reimagining" the society they live in, for they do not construct some sort of blueprint for a brave new world to replace the Florence that has been ravaged by the plague. The *Decameron*, after all, is not *Utopia*; it is not a discursive exploration of social alternatives. Rather, through its stories, it implicitly offers alternatives to the moral and religious teachings of the Church, opens up new vistas of possibilities for women's as well as men's behavior, argues for the importance of the body and its pleasures, stresses the value of generosity and magnanimity, and celebrates intelligence in all its forms as essential for personal happiness as well as social survival. Clearly, the *Decameron* is not suggesting a full-scale social and religious reordering of society, let alone an economic or political one; it is not what one would call a revolutionary work. But it does take a small step in the direction of More's groundbreaking text, a text that would usher in the era of rethinking social norms and structures that we call the Renaissance.

Reimagining the world the storytellers live in is actually an entirely appropriate response to the plague's destruction of Florence. Although Boccaccio never uses a word such as "new" or "novel" to describe the Black Death itself, his description of it leaves no doubt that nothing like this has ever happened before, even if, ironically, his borrowing parts of his description of the plague from Paulus Diaconus suggests the devastation was by no means unprecedented. Nevertheless, the plague of 1347–48 was indeed unique, if only because of its severity and the widespread effects it had on Italy and on Europe generally.

This *new*, this unprecedented calamity, Boccaccio tells us in his Introduction, provokes the creation of all sorts of *new* customs in Florence, customs that largely seem inconsistent with any sort of social order. In this context, then, it makes perfect sense for the group of storytellers to find their own *new* solution to the problems the plague has produced, and it is especially fitting that their central activity is to tell stories, for "stories" in Italian is *novelle*, a word that derives from *nuovo*, "new," and that always has some sense that the story involved is new, different, unexpected, a notion enshrined as well in the idea of the "news," which would be another perfectly legitimate way to translate *novelle*. Moreover, Boccaccio's fiction is new in another remarkable way, for he deliberately breaks with the storytelling traditions of the Middle Ages by setting almost all his tales in real places and presenting real historical characters and, at times, events in them, even though their plots are, by and large, literary inventions. Reflecting the liminal world of the storytellers, those tales are thus also situated betwixt and between, hybrids that yoke together history and literature, always playing with the fact that both can be described by means of the same word, *story*.

The social rethinking done in the *Decameron* is most evident in its principal themes. To a certain extent, those themes may be found in the topics that the group selects to organize their individual days of storytelling. The principal ones are four in number, introduced more or less in this order: intelligence, Fortune, desire (or appetite), and magnanimity. In one way or another, however, each story in the *Decameron* can be said to be about one or more of these themes.

"Intelligence" is really a shorthand term for all the many different words Boccaccio uses in Italian to identify a range of mental attributes, from reason, prudence, and sound judgment through good sense, sagacity, and resourcefulness, down to ingenuity, cleverness, and trickery. From the very first day, which has no set topic for storytelling, intelligence manifests itself in the ability to speak well, in eloquence, and in a generally witty way with words. More important, intelligence enables people to create compelling fictions, to make up stories, that persuade others to do their bidding. It is thus essential to one's social survival, both a defensive resource to protect one from the depredations of the powerful, and an offensive weapon that is necessary if individuals are to get what they desire. To put it differently: intelligence is essential for reaching some sort of accommodation between the individual and society. In an ideal world, all people would possess it, and it would enable them to fulfill their desires while maintaining some sort of social order. But intelligence can also be used in purely self-interested ways that work against social harmony, and it can have a nasty, even sadistic edge. By the time his work is done, Boccaccio has let us see this dimension of intelligence as well.

Boccaccio's second main theme involves Fortune, a concept that had been around since Roman times and was even personified and turned into a goddess. Although it is an issue in practically every story in the *Decameron*, it is the specific focus of Day 2, standing, in essence, for all the uncertainties and vagaries and contingencies of the world. In a rigorously Christian theological scheme, such as Dante's, Fortune is God's servant, which means that everything that happens, whether for good or ill, must have some sort of divine sanction, even if human beings cannot see how that can be. There are moments in the *Decameron* when Fortune seems to function in this way, but in general, Fortune is a more secular matter in Boccaccio's work, the set of forces and circumstances that intelligence must deal with in its pursuit of human happiness. Sometimes Fortune is embodied in the irrational resistance and hostility and malice of people; sometimes it is just a matter of "dumb luck." In any case, it stands as a limit, reminding the reader that intelligence is not all powerful and that even the wisest and cleverest among us sometimes need a break.

When relying on their intelligence to deal with whatever Fortune may hand them, Boccaccio's characters typically place that intelligence in the service of desire, and in particular, sexual desire or appetite. Indeed, if Boccaccio has any axe to grind, it is with the Church and its teaching about sex, for he insists on the naturalness, the inescapability— and hence the goodness—of human beings' appetites, and in particular the one he calls love, which almost always has sexual desire at its core. Boccaccio actually mounts a defense of sexual desire in the Introduction to Day 4, not surprisingly by composing a little story to make his point. In most of Boccaccio's tales, desire is centrally concerned with the body and its pleasures, and *godere,* "to enjoy," not surprisingly, is a key verb throughout the *Decameron.* Even more important is *far festa,* a phrase with a large number of possible meanings: to make a fuss over someone, to greet someone with enthusiasm, to feel happy and flattered about something, to celebrate, to stage some sort of party or festivity, and to engage in a ritual celebration such as a wedding or a coronation. The phrase inevitably invokes the idea of carnival, with all its licentiousness, its satire of the conventional social order, its celebration of the body, and its investment in food, drink, sex, and things material. *Far festa* thus points to the importance of collective, communal activities, and accordingly, the comic endings that conclude so many of Boccaccio's stories invariably involve pairs of individuals, couples, who live "happily ever after," and who are often joined by entire communities participating in some final festivity that rounds off the tale.

Desire can also have insalubrious forms, for some of Boccaccio's characters are possessed by the urge to inflict harm and to humiliate others. Indeed, some of his most memorable characters get a certain satisfaction from deceiving or outwitting others, a sentiment that is not unrelated to sadism. Desire in all its forms is something that intelligence is primed to serve, but desire, like intelligence, can also be a threat both to people and to the society they live in. A balancing act of sorts is thus absolutely necessary, the *Decameron* seems to suggest, but how to achieve such a balancing act is never clearly defined, making desire a mixed affair, to say the least.

The last theme of general importance in the *Decameron* is that of magnanimity. This is introduced in several individual stories on Day 1, but it becomes the actual topic selected for the tenth and final day of the work, where it is offered as a corrective of sorts for the kinds of tales that were told on the preceding days. Magnanimity—variously called generosity, liberality, magnificence, and even compassion and humanity—is an aristocratic virtue that was largely embraced by members of the Florentine mercantile elite and that manifests itself in the bestowing of elaborate rewards on others. Although it is the specific topic of Day 10, the theme actually appears throughout the collection

whenever Boccaccio's characters, and especially members of the elite,
offer food or wealth or positions of social and political importance to
those below them. Predictably, Boccaccio's social inferiors often seem
to have "earned" those rewards by means of the intelligence they have
displayed in dealing with their superiors, an intelligence that those
superiors recognize even when they see themselves being manipulated
by it. Boccaccio's celebration of magnanimity in Day 10 is meant to
end his work on a high note and in a sense to return us to the very
beginning, for in being identified with both compassion and humanity, it deliberately recalls the opening words of Boccaccio's Preface, in
which he states that his purpose in writing the *Decameron* is his desire
to display his humanity by bestowing compassion on those who suffer.

The Structure of the *Decameron*: Betwixt and Between

The four principal themes of the *Decameron* are integrated into the
distinctive structure of Boccaccio's work. Critics have offered a number of different models for that structure, some of which present the
work as centered about Day 5, with its love stories featuring happy
endings, or about Days 5 and 6, the latter of which contains stories
about how people use witty quips to negotiate their relationships with
others. The Italian scholar Vittore Branca long ago suggested what I
think is a more compelling vision of the work's structure because it
accounts for the progressive nature of one's reading experience as one
moves through it from start to finish. In Branca's view, we begin with
stories primarily featuring people who often use their intelligence to
reprove the vices of the great on Day 1; confront Fortune on Days 2
and 3; deal with love in tragic and then comic modalities on the next
two days; focus on intelligence in various forms from Day 6 to Day 9;
and end with magnanimity on Day 10. Branca sees this movement as
constituting a cathartic experience by the time we are done. By contrast, Teodolinda Barolini has argued that the *Decameron* has a circu-
lar structure, emphasizing the fact that the storytellers journey away

from Florence to a set of locations increasingly distant from the city before they begin to retrace their steps, and that they tell tales designed to enable them to recuperate something of the rational control and human compassion the plague had destroyed back in Florence. She rightly emphasizes that many of the tales from Day 6 on are set in Florence as the group begins its return journey, and that the more realistic stories of Days 7, 8, and 9 concern people close to the storytellers in time and space, thus making the *novelle* told about them a little less like stories and a little more like news from home. Barolini's argument, however, like Branca's, fails to account for a crucial fact, namely that the intelligence on display in the tales of Day 6 is considerably more attractive than what one sees on Days 7, 8, and 9, nor does Barolini's claim that the group is making a gradual return to Florence in their stories deal with the fact that almost all of those on Day 10 are set elsewhere, sometimes in quite exotic, if not fantastic, locations. Following Branca's more "evolutionary" model for the structure of the *Decameron*, let me offer another view of what Boccaccio is trying to accomplish, a view that will finally stress the unresolved nature of his arguments and the open-ended character of his collection. In the last analysis, the *Decameron* leaves the reader betwixt and between on a variety of issues, in the midst of a muddle about them, although that muddle, like all muddles, nevertheless offers us important creative possibilities.

To understand what Boccaccio is attempting to do through the structure of his work, let us actually begin with the conclusion of Day 6 and with Dioneo, who has distinguished himself throughout the *Decameron* as the most irreverent and subversive of the storytellers. Dioneo has just been chosen king and is thus responsible for naming the topic for the stories to be told the next day. The topic he selects is the tricks that women play on their husbands for the sake of love or for their own preservation, and it instantly raises the hackles of the women in the group who reject it almost as soon as they hear it. By contrast, no such protest occurs on any other day, not even after Filostrato has proposed that on Day 4 the group tell stories about the "harsh topic" (see p. 308) of tragedy. Dioneo finally manages to persuade the ladies to accept what he wants, although they do so without much enthusiasm. In fact, their irritation with his topic is later confirmed by Lauretta, when she is named queen for the next day of storytelling and announces her new topic. She begins by insisting that she has every right to exact vengeance by having the group tell tales about the tricks husbands play on their wives, but she finally declares that she will rise above her feelings and have them tell a variety of stories about the tricks all kinds of people play on one another. The ladies' irritation may well seem somewhat mysterious, since the first six days of the *Decameron* contain many examples of women cleverly deceiving men, any number of whom are in fact their husbands. But there is a good reason for Dioneo's topic to irritate them, for it implicitly challenges a number of key assumptions on which the first six days of storytelling were based, effectively turning the whole world of the *Decameron* topsy-turvy.

Dioneo's topic actually entails at least three separate challenges. First—and most obviously—it contains an affront to conventional morality and social harmony: women's wit will achieve sexual satisfaction for them outside of marriage and at the expense of the men they deceive. Second, his topic is challenging to the group because it both appears to identify women rather than their lovers as the responsible agents in their illicit love affairs and deliberately portrays them as the antagonists of men—of their husbands—rather than as, say, the accomplices of their lovers. Finally, Dioneo's topic implicitly contains a distinctly antihierarchical element, insofar as Boccaccio's society thought of women as being socially, politically, intellectually—indeed, ontologically—inferior to men.

Dioneo underscores the antihierarchical character of his topic by deliberately identifying it with the servant girl Licisca who, at the start of Day 6, violently interrupts the pattern of decorous dining and dancing and storytelling established during the first five days of the *Decameron*. Uninvited, Licisca bursts into the space occupied by the group, scolding her fellow servant Tindaro, who comes with her but is scarcely permitted a word in his own defense, and calling him a fool for thinking that women are virgins when they marry. She then goes on to protest the fact that women should be controlled by men at all, and she proclaims it the right of every wife to play tricks on her husband. The key word she uses here is *beffe,* which means tricks, to be sure, but also implies scorn for the poor husband who has been deceived. In social terms Licisca is doubly disruptive both because of what she says and because of what she does, for she is a woman who speaks against a man and against male authority, and she is a servant who thrusts herself unbidden into the space of her social superiors. At the end of Day 6, when Dioneo, who has already taken Licisca's side in her dispute with Tindaro, chooses his topic for the next day's stories, he says he picks it precisely because of what Licisca said, thus essentially confirming the social and sexual inversion that her disruption entailed. Ironically, although the obstreperous Licisca is finally silenced, Dioneo's choice of a topic for Day 7 effectively gives Licisca—unruly servant and unruly woman—her voice back again, making her an invisible, disruptive presence throughout the stories to come.

Dioneo's challenge actually does more than irritate the women in the group; it provokes a succession of stories of trickery that surprisingly does not end with the seventh day, but continues on through the eighth, whose topic is, as has been noted, the tricks that all sorts of people play on one another. Such storytelling persists through the ninth day as well, even though this day has no specific topic and the storytellers are supposedly free to speak on any subject that interests them. This three-day torrent of tales radically alters the trajectory that the *Decameron* had established during its first six days, forcing the reader to reevaluate the meanings of intelligence and desire, which seemed, up to that point, key ingredients in the creation of a happy and productive society.

The structural pattern of the *Decameron* up until Day 7 was basically an alternating one. Thus, after having presented stories on the first day about characters who escaped from difficulties or reproved others by means of their intelligence and control of language, Boccaccio focused his second day on the irrational power symbolized by Fortune, which can defeat the cleverest plans of the cleverest tricksters, although Fortune turns out to be a rather benevolent deity when all is said and done. Underscoring the importance of intelligence in managing the social world, Boccaccio responds to the stories of the second day with those of the third in which he celebrates human beings' *industria,* that is, their ingenuity, resourcefulness, and industriousness, thus showing how intelligence, once again, is essential for social survival, achieving its ends despite the opposition of Fortune. On Day 4, Boccaccio turns his attention to tragedy, which is the result of the intolerance, perversity, and intransigent hatred inside some people that stands in the way of the protagonists' fulfilling their sexual desires and that no amount of intelligence can outmaneuver. By the next day, Boccaccio has turned from tragedy to comedy, to stories about love and desire fulfilled rather than lives sadly cut short. The *Decameron* then reaches a kind of climax on the sixth day, whose stories celebrate an ideal Florence made up of witty, clever citizens, whose intelligence is manifested in their *motti*— that is, their witty quips and clever repartee. In general, then, the first six days of the *Decameron* have a distinctive shape in which days stressing the limitations of intelligence alternate with those celebrating its capabilities, the latter outnumbering and containing those focused on the power of Fortune and human perversity. By the end of Day 6, it would seem as though Boccaccio has created a version of his own quite human and humane *Hexaemeron*. Like Saint Ambrose, whose work described the first six days of the creation of the world, Boccaccio has led his readers to the point of imagining something like a re-created Florence arising out of the chaos of the plague. Saint Ambrose fittingly stops at the sixth day, because God rested on the seventh. Boccaccio, by contrast, keeps on going—and that makes all the difference in the world.

The vision of a renewed Florence imagined during the first six days of the *Decameron* assumes that the potentially leveling power of intelligence does not pose a serious threat to the traditional, hierarchical social order. Indeed, the deliberately idealizing sixth day presents a range of witty characters, from the noblewoman of the first tale down to the rascally Frate Cipolla of the tenth, but in this version of an idealized Florence, the socially disruptive potential of wit is extremely qualified. In the first place, some of Boccaccio's "heroes" are, in fact, members of the social elite, the mercantile aristocracy, while others may be less elevated, but are still highly regarded writers and artists. More important, when members of the lower orders use their wits to defend themselves or to satisfy their desires on Day 6, their actions either have no real effect on the established social hierarchy, or actually serve to confirm it. For example, in the second story of the day, when the baker Cisti seemingly refuses to send some of his special wine as a gift to his social superior, Messer Geri Spina, Cisti's refusal is actually a rebuke directed at Messer Geri's servant who has come with an overly large container in order to have some of the wine for himself. His is no wine for servants, but for gentlemen, insists Cisti, thus defending the class hierarchy of Florentine society, which he reinforces at the end of the story by happily having an entire cask of the wine delivered directly to Messer Geri himself. In this connection, one should recall that the sixth day began with Boccaccio's group of storytellers carefully distinguishing itself from the lower orders represented by its servants, from Licisca and Tindaro, whose quarrel may have disrupted their peaceful order, but who were finally silenced by the reigning queen.

Dioneo's challenge and the torrent of stories starting on Day 7 about tricks people play on one another fundamentally challenges the assumption that intelligence will serve the interests of personal desire while preserving social harmony. Up through Day 6, when tricksters used their wits to satisfy their appetites, they seldom inflicted harm on—indeed, they often benefited—their dupes and thus reinforced or even enhanced the traditional social order. By contrast, on Days 7, 8, and 9 intelligence often serves as an instrument of antisocial malice and sadism. Of course, there was always a touch of sadistic pleasure in the tricksters' abuse of their dupes before then, but what is really striking about these three days is how often the sadistic element involved in the stories is either excessive, or gratuitous, or both. Thus, tricksters do not merely satisfy their desires by deceiving their dupes, but subject them to humiliation and even to physical harm. Perhaps the worst treatment accorded a dupe occurs in the seventh story of Day 8, the story of the scholar and the widow, who almost kill one another, playing tricks whose sole purpose is to inflict suffering and humiliation on their victim. Indeed, the group of storytellers finds this tale excessively harsh and says so. The essential point in such stories is that the dupes do not go away satisfied, albeit deceived, as they did repeatedly in the

first six days. Moreover, on these three days intelligence fails to gener-
ate the sort of positive, inclusive community one often saw in the first
half of the *Decameron*. When individuals do band together now, they
are groups of tricksters who do so in order to torment a dupe who is,
of necessity, rejected by, if not ejected from, the community involved.
In other words, they define themselves against others rather than with,
or by means of, them; the society they create is exclusive, not inclusive.
Significantly, in the ninth story of Day 8, the hapless dupe, who thinks
he is about to be initiated into a merry society of "privateers" led by a
pair of tricksters, winds up being ejected from it instead, unceremoni-
ously dumped into a ditch filled with excrement.

If Days 7, 8, and 9 expose the union of intelligence and social benevolence as an illusion, they similarly reveal that women, in particular,
use that intelligence to achieve what they desire by operating as men's
antagonists more than their allies and accomplices. Now they are
presented as betrayers who sell themselves for money, as corrupters
of their husbands who turn them into drunkards, as shrews who beat
their husbands and need beatings in return, and as sadists who derive
pleasure from the humiliation and suffering of their husbands and of
other men. Moreover, although women's sexuality was potentially a
problem for men during the first six days because of its abundance,
it is now frightening because it is associated with betrayal, pain, and
humiliation. Revealingly, in these tales women often wind up "on top,"
both literally at times, and figuratively more often, as they beat men or
arrange to have that beating done on their behalf, and expose them to
the jeers of others or even of an entire community. Not surprisingly,
as tales of trickery continue on Days 8 and 9, a number of them stress
the way men resort to force in order to maintain their dominance over
women, a theme that receives its purest expression in the ninth story of
Day 9, the story of the sage Solomon who has a husband domesticate
his shrewish wife by thrashing her mercilessly.

Finally, the stories of the seventh, eighth, and ninth days explode
the illusion that intelligence will necessarily help to preserve some version of the traditional hierarchical social order. To be sure, there are
many stories on those days in which social superiors put their nominal

inferiors—servants or wives—in their places, often resorting to force in order to do so. However, the more typical pattern on these days is to have characters at the same social level deceive one another or to have inferiors deceive their social superiors, such as when a pair of painters make a fool of a university-trained physician in one story, a Sicilian prostitute undoes a wealthy merchant, and wives repeatedly deceive and humiliate their husbands. Even though intelligence does not openly challenge the traditional social hierarchy in these stories, it almost always fails to confirm it. Instead, the world represented in them is essentially bipolar, divided between the witty and their prey. Social life is turned into a constant competition, which produces endlessly shifting hierarchies of tricksters and gulls so that one person's dupe today may well become someone else's con man tomorrow. Such a vision of human life hardly seems consistent with any sort of stable, traditional social order at all. If, on the upside, it suggests that some people are educable, in that fools can turn into tricksters, on the downside it suggests that even the wisest of tricksters can sometimes play the fool, with the result that society seems a free-for-all in which one can never afford to let down one's guard.

Dioneo's challenge and the stories it provokes have indeed turned the world of the *Decameron* topsy-turvy, leaving us as readers situated betwixt and between, in a conceptual muddle about how to judge the intelligence that once seemed so essential to the restoration of Florence. By proposing his topic for the seventh day, Dioneo has opened up a Pandora's box, prompting stories that relentlessly undermine the group's previous collective fantasy about the compatibility of human intelligence, sexual desire, and social happiness, a fantasy that turns out to be possible only if the hostility, competitiveness, and sexual fears and rivalries that galvanize intelligence into action are successfully hidden from sight, as they generally were throughout the first six days. What the stories of Days 7, 8, and 9 suggest is that a society based on intelligence placed in the service of desire may, in fact, be no society at all.

In response to the problematic nature of intelligence on these three days, Boccaccio has his narrators turn to an alternative principle, that of magnanimity, on the tenth and last day in an attempt to identify an unambiguously positive source of civilized values. Magnanimity is presented as being about bestowing things on others rather than taking things away from them, about repressing desire, including one's sexual appetites, rather than giving in to them. Magnanimity thus seems the missing ingredient needed to construct a truly civilized society, which is what the storytellers putatively aim to do during their retreat to the countryside from the plague-ridden city. For example, in one story the protagonist willingly renounces his claims on the woman he has long loved with desperation and restores her to the husband who has seemingly abandoned her, and in another, a king foregoes his desire for the young daughters of a former enemy in order to live up to the best image of himself, thus affirming a positive, ideal notion of kingship. And in the very last story of the collection, the famous tale of the patient Griselda, the heroine's self-abnegation takes the virtue of magnanimity to an ultimate—and perhaps unbelievable—level.

Precisely because it may well be unbelievable, however, this last example should give us pause. Although most readers who come away from the story feel that Griselda is the one who exemplifies magnanimity in acceding to her husband Gualtieri's every wish, it is more accurate to say that he, not she, is the example of magnanimity being offered the reader. For he initially displays his generosity by taking Griselda from abject poverty and making her his bride, and then, after he has deprived her of everything, including her children, has divorced her, and has sadistically ordered her to serve as an attendant on his new bride at their wedding, it turns out that he has not really taken anything away at all, her children are alive, and the girl he is to marry is actually Griselda's daughter, who is restored to her mother in a triumphant affirmation of her patience. In other words, it is Gualtieri who displays magnanimity in giving so much to Griselda both at the start of the story and then, again, at the end. The problem here is that in order to be magnanimous this second time, he had to take away what he originally bestowed on her, and his doing so—and the suffering that he inflicts on his victim—are the real focus of the story. His final act of generosity thus appears supplementary, gratuitous, and fundamentally incapable of compensating for the torment to which he subjected his wife over a number of years. The narrator of this story is, of course, Dioneo, whose tales almost always parody the ones that come before them, and Dioneo actually frames his story at the start by denouncing the *matta bestialità*, the "senseless brutality" (see p. 839), of Gualtieri and his sadistic project.

At the end of his story, Dioneo asks rhetorically whether anyone other than Griselda would have endured so cheerfully the trials to which Gualtieri subjected her, and then goes on to say that it would have served him right if his wife had been the kind of woman who, having been thrown out of his house wearing nothing but her shift, would have given herself to another man instead. Dioneo's comment underscores the unreality of Griselda's perfect patience as well as the sadism and cruelty involved in Gualtieri's behavior, and it suggests that a truer, more human, more natural emotion for her to have felt was not the self-abnegation involved in her submission to her husband's whims, but a desire for revenge that would have led her to betray him with another man. In other words, Dioneo's comment—like his entire story—leads us right back to the tales of Days 7, 8, and 9, tales in which human beings are not motivated by high-minded altruism and generosity, but selfish desires for money, sex, and power, coupled with a keen desire for revenge when those desires are thwarted. That, Dioneo is saying, is the human reality.

The qualified nature of magnanimity is reinforced by several aspects of the stories on Day 10. While a large number of the more realistic tales of Days 7, 8, and 9 are set in Florence, those of this day are located elsewhere, sometimes in Italian cities quite distant from Boccaccio's hometown, as well as in foreign countries such as Spain, in the ancient Roman Empire, and even in such exotic locales as Cathay and Egypt. Moreover, the somewhat unreal quality of these stories is documented by the extreme behavior of characters like Griselda and Gualtieri, among many others. Finally, there are two stories that actually take magic seriously, one of which has a magician create a spring garden in the midst of a cold, snowy January, while the other involves transporting its protagonist from Egypt back to his home in Italy overnight on a magic bed. Such displays of magic are designed to elicit a sense of wonder in the reader, as they do among the storytellers who are listening to them, but since Boccaccio has been consistently hostile toward any belief in the supernatural, often making such beliefs a defining feature of many of his most foolish characters, the seriousness with which magic seems to be taken on Day 10 can only serve to induce a certain skepticism on the part of any attentive reader.

In his proposed alternative ending to the last story of Day 10, Dioneo's emphasis on the reality of selfish human desire might also cause readers to rethink what the magnanimity celebrated on that day really entails. To be sure, the protagonists of the stories do make personal sacrifices, repressing their own desires and bestowing liberal rewards on others. And yet, when they do so, they usually stage their magnanimous acts in front of an audience, often before an entire community, clearly seeking to enhance their reputations by what they are doing. In other words, all of these characters may be exemplars of magnanimity and may thus be said to contribute to the well-being of their societies and even to be offering models for behavior within them, but they are also satisfying their own egotistical desires by their actions, seeking public admiration for their self-sacrifice and generosity. Being magnanimous may be allowing someone else to eat your cake, but you wind up getting a large—indeed, if I may put it this way, a generous—slice of it yourself.

Simply put: magnanimity in the *Decameron* is never a virtue practiced for its own sake, never an example of undiluted altruism, never the self-abnegation of the saint (Griselda aside, of course). Moreover, it always implicitly involves the actor's comparing himself to others and behaving the way he does in order to stand out from them. In other words, magnanimity contains an element of rivalry at its core. Nowhere is this aspect of the virtue clearer than in the third story of the day, the story of Nathan who has built a house on the major east-west road in Cathay and bestows such lavish hospitality on everyone who passes by that he achieves fame for possessing a degree of generosity that cannot be surpassed. When the wealthy young Mithridanes hears of it, he is immediately possessed by a rivalrous desire to outdo Nathan's magnanimity and appears to have matched it until an incident occurs that makes him feel he has fallen short. Filled with murderous rage, he instantly sets off for Cathay with every intention of making his magnanimity supreme in the world by killing his competitor. Nathan, having discovered the young man's intentions, actually invites his own death, with the result that Mithridanes is deeply shamed and eventually leaves Cathay, confessing that Nathan's generosity is simply beyond compare. What this story thus shows is that magnanimity may involve giving, but it is a deeply self-interested virtue, and that if it may confer benefits on others, it can also provoke feelings that could destroy any vestige of social harmony.

Although Boccaccio's narrators want to end the *Decameron* on a high note by telling stories about magnanimity on Day 10, clearly the situation here, like life itself, is more complicated than that. Magnanimity cannot simply serve, in and of itself, as a solution to the problem that desire, allied to intelligence, has created for social and sexual harmony on Days 7, 8, and 9. It offers a glimpse of a "better world" perhaps, but in many different ways it returns us to the world of the preceding three days, which definitively qualified the idealism of the first half of Boccaccio's work. Furthermore, the very principle of rivalry and individualistic competition that is a key component in the magnanimous acts performed on Day 10 appears to guide Boccaccio's narrators as well, albeit in a milder form, for as they tell their stories, they repeatedly attempt to surpass one another with the examples of magnanimity they describe. This rivalry among Boccaccio's storytellers is actually present in the *Decameron* from the start, although it largely remains implicit, visible chiefly in the "correction" that one storyteller may tacitly offer of the viewpoint contained in another's tale. This rivalry among the storytellers comes right out into the open on Day 10, revealing the competitive, egotistical drive animating them just as surely as it informs the displays of generosity they celebrate in their stories. As readers, we are thus left in a quandary, not sure just how to evaluate magnanimity, both admiring it as a virtue that can contribute to the happiness of society, and worrying about it as a potential source of friction and rivalry that can lead to the sadism of a Gualtieri or the murderous rage of a Mithridanes—or even to the unraveling of the very bonds that have kept the storytellers together during their two-week sojourn in the country.

Instructively, as Boccaccio's storytellers head back to Florence, they do not return with plans for building some brave new world, even though the social thinking they have done in their stories has opened up new ways for people to conceive of the traditional social order. Instead, as the men go off to pursue their different interests and the ladies assemble briefly once again in Santa Maria Novella before heading for their homes, they essentially return to the lives they used to lead. The things they value—the power of intelligence, the ability of wit to triumph over Fortune, the satisfaction of desire, the virtue of magnanimity—have all been celebrated in their stories, but also revealed as problematic in many different ways. All of their storytelling has helped them deal with the ruin of the plague by offering them the repeated experience of closure, of plots that have beginnings, middles, and ends, the kind of thing that stories can provide in a way that history, especially the seemingly unending sequence of terrifying experiences in plague-stricken Florence, cannot. But when they tell their one-hundredth tale, their two-week experience in the liminal space of their country gardens does not reach a conclusion; it simply comes to a stop. Or, rather, it stops in the middle of things, leaving us, like the storytellers, in the muddle that is life itself. In this respect, the most one can say is that their stories have given them—and us as readers—a chance to reflect on what makes society work and what does not. We never get beyond that liminal experience, beyond a feeling that we are still in a state betwixt and between. But in a sense, that is what great literary works—including Boccaccio's *Decameron*, of course—are truly all about.

Boccaccio and His *Decameron* as Galeotto

If Boccaccio, like Dante, places us in the middle of things, the alternative title he has chosen for his collection, *Prince Galeotto*, which appears in the rubric at the start of the Preface, also invites us to make yet another significant comparison between his work and the *Divine Comedy*. In the fifth canto the *Inferno*, Dante places two of the most famous lovers in world literature, Paolo and Francesca, in the circle of Hell reserved for the lustful. The pair fell in love because of a book, a book that contains a romantic story of courtly love and adultery. Francesca, who tells her sad tale to Dante, refuses to accept any responsibility for having been placed in Hell for her lust; instead, she blames the book she read, calling it a *Galeotto*. *Galeotto* is the Italian form of Gallehault, the name of a character in a French romance who acted as a go-between or pander for Guinevere and Lancelot. Clearly, Dante wants us to see the limited nature of Francesca's vision here. He also wants us to see that this is the wrong way to go about reading: one needs to move beyond the literal or fleshly level to the allegorical or spiritual one. Echoing Francesca—and Dante—Boccaccio says that his book, too, is a *Galeotto*. However, it is a *Galeotto* with a difference, for he offers it as a remedy to women in love who are confined to their homes, have no means of release for their frustrated desires, and may thus be able to find some sort of vicarious satisfaction in reading the stories Boccaccio has crafted. Since those stories are often about illicit love relationships, it would seem that Boccaccio is not condemning the natural appetites of his readers or urging them to transcend the world of the flesh by having recourse to an allegory that would lead them to more spiritual matters. If anything, Boccaccio's allegory takes them right back into the world again and to the pleasures and satisfactions it has to offer. If Dante's emphasis is on the life to come, as he makes his way from Hell to Purgatory to Paradise, Boccaccio's emphasis falls on our life in this world. When the transcendent is imagined, as it is in just a few tales, that sphere is always made to serve the interests of our mundane existence. Dante's concern for the afterlife led readers to call his work *La Divina Commedia*. It is thus no wonder that Italian critics have long insisted on labeling Boccaccio's *La Commedia Umana*, "The Human Comedy."

When Dante hears Francesca's story about her love for Paolo and the way a book served as the Galeotto or go-between in their love affair, his reaction to it is to faint. This dramatic response suggests that Dante may be overwhelmed by the fact that he, like Francesca, could face the fires of Hell because of his youthful desire for Beatrice. It could equally well be an expression of his fear that the love poetry he wrote for her might be regarded as having the same function that the book did for Francesca and her lover, in other words, that Dante's poems might be condemned as a Galeotto, too. If Dante faints in response to such an idea, Boccaccio, by contrast, remains clear-eyed and wide awake. He embraces the fact that his book may be an incentive to love, whether licit or illicit, and although he lays the responsibility for any unwholesome reactions off on his readers in his Author's Conclusion, even there he is still indulging in suggestive sexual innuendo, joking about how light he is to bear (by implication, in the act of making love) and how the women in his neighborhood have praised him for the sweetness of his tongue. Despite blaming his readers for any lascivious thoughts they might have had while reading the *Decameron*, he ends his book by being nothing less than a Galeotto, a go-between—a pander—inviting us to entertain lascivious thoughts with the very words he chooses.

A Galeotto or go-between: that is precisely what makes Boccaccio Boccaccio. We have seen him as a figure poised between two ages and two cultures, embracing a host of genres in his *Decameron*: some high, like the romances of Day 2 and the tragedies of Day 4; some low, like the *fabliau*-inspired *novelle*; some exalted, or seemingly so, as in the celebrations of wit on Day 6 and of magnanimity on Day 10; and many more throughout the work that are realistic and down to earth. A go-between, Boccaccio typically leaves us uncertain just how to interpret his stories in any ethical, let alone spiritual sense. If Dante may be said to be a go-between in the *Divine Comedy*, helping us to get from sin to grace, from an earth that may seem like Hell, to the joys of Heaven, Boccaccio keeps us in the middle of things, leaving us less than fully certain what to value or how to proceed. There is something we can say with a fair degree of certainty, however: Boccaccio does aim to make us more adept at judging, and hence at acting in the world, if only because we have had to face the interpretational challenges his collection poses. All literature actually functions as a kind of intermediary between us as readers and the author, and between us as readers and the world in which we will adapt our reading to the real-life situations we encounter. Boccaccio knows this truth only too well and underscores his knowledge for us right at the start by calling his book *Prince Galeotto*, Prince Go-Between, even Prince Pander. It could be nothing else.

Translating Boccaccio and His Styles: The Translator as Middleman

While my general goal as a translator, like that of all translators, is to make a text written in a foreign language and coming from a very distant culture comprehensible to modern readers of English, I also want them to appreciate something of the "strangeness" of this great classic work. The root meaning of "translate" is to take something across a border or boundary, thus bringing that which is foreign or strange from one language—and in this case, from a different age as well—into another. Translation makes strangers feel familiar, but a good one should also allow us to sense something of the alien in our midst. A good translator is, in short, a go-between or middleman, linking the foreign with the domestic, the strange with the familiar, while preventing the former from being completely absorbed into the latter. For me this has meant writing modern American English, but also: referring to time not by our modern system, but by the canonical hours, such as matins and vespers; calling the large meal Boccaccio's characters eat in midmorning not breakfast, as other translators have done, but dinner; retaining some Italian words that most readers would know, such as "piazza" (for "town square"); and keeping some titles and forms of address that really have no exact equivalent in modern English. As a translator my goals are clearly contradictory, indeed paradoxical. The work that I have produced is thus, to some extent, betwixt and between two worlds, the modern world of the English-speaking reader, and the late medieval world of the Italian-speaking author. It is more the first than the second, of course, but its strangeness is felt not just in those Italian words and names I have left in their original forms, but also because the modes of thought and the feelings of the characters, the ways they address one another, the times at which they take their meals, and a host of other details gives them a certain strangeness, albeit a strangeness that should not prevent us from responding to the humanity we share with them.

One of the things that separates them from us—that separates most characters in prose fiction before the nineteenth century from us—is the paucity of psychological detail Boccaccio supplies. Although we are occasionally told what characters are thinking, we mostly infer motives and feelings from what they say or do. Boccaccio has often been praised for the economy of his stories, for what they accomplish by way of characterization with relatively slender means, but this prevents us from reading his *novelle* the way we would a modern novel. His characters are typically filled with a desire for something, come up with a strategy to obtain it (often not sharing that strategy in advance with the reader), and then succeed (or fail) in their pursuit. There is nothing like the interior monologues or the psychological development we experience even within the limited space of the modern short story.

Translating Boccaccio is a challenge, and not just because he writes in a foreign language that is seven hundred years old—although I do not minimize the difficulties that those things present. Boccaccio is even more of a challenge because he actually writes in several distinct styles. Most of the narrative portions of his text are written in a very formal prose that is modeled on late medieval Latin. To capture this aspect of his style, I have tried to preserve his long, syntactically complicated sentences, although I have sometimes been forced to break them up in order to ensure that they are readable in English. In those lengthy sentences, Boccaccio typically connects elements together by means of a host of dependent conjunctions, and even more frequently by using past and present participial constructions, some of which I have retained, but most of which I felt had to be turned into clauses with active subjects and verbs. Moreover, those participial constructions make the reader work at determining how the various pieces of each sentence fit together, whether one idea precedes or follows another in time or serves as the cause or effect of something else. This has meant that sometimes I have simply broken his sentences apart, not because they threatened to become overly long, but because I felt a need to sort out temporal and causal sequences for the reader. Moreover, in Boccaccio's aesthetic, it was clearly acceptable to repeat a word, or various forms of a word, within the short space of just a sentence or two. Modern English style demands more variation, and thus, whereas Boccaccio was content to write *amare* ("to love"), to follow it in short order with *amato* ("beloved"), and then to speak of an *amatore* ("lover"), I have elected to supply variations, turning *amare*, "to love," for instance, sometimes into "to fall for" or "to become enamored of."

There is a sharp break in the *Decameron* between the more formal narrative portions of the text, whether they are being produced by Boccaccio or by his ten young storytellers, and the often quite informal, even colloquial language used by the characters, especially the lower-class characters, in the stories when they talk to one another. I have sought to capture this difference not only by reproducing the shorter sentences and simpler syntax that those characters employ when they speak, as opposed to the more complicated, formal language of the narrative portions of the text, but I have also allowed the characters to use contractions (e.g., can't) whereas I have completely avoided them in the more formal portions of the text. And I have even occasionally allowed the characters to speak in something close to slang (American slang, to be sure) where that seemed appropriate, although I have used slang terms such as "guy" and "buddy," which should not feel excessively colloquial. To give one striking example of this: *dir male* in Boccaccio's Italian means to speak badly, to say bad things, about someone or something; in the mouths of the two Florentine usurers who appear in the very first story of the collection, this seemed to me best translated as "to bad-mouth," a nice colloquial American expression that also does a good job of capturing the meaning of Boccaccio's phrase.

In general, I have kept the names for Boccaccio's characters in their original Italian forms. Giannotto is always Giannotto, never Little John, let alone Jehannot, as he is for some translators who turn Boccaccio's Italianized version of what is in at least one story set in France back into its French original. In a number of cases, the names given to characters are what might be called "speaking names," names that have particular meanings. One might argue that all names, however ordinary and "realistic," have such meanings: to call someone Giovanni, that is, John, always, at least potentially, evokes the author of one of the Gospels and of Revelation, with all that that might entail. For such names I have generally not supplied any annotation. However, in some cases the meaning of the name Boccaccio gives a character is so important for an understanding of the story that I have provided a gloss for it in a footnote, or in other cases, where that meaning is interesting but perhaps less essential, I have glossed it in an endnote. The protagonist of the last story of Day 6, for example, is named Cipolla, which means "Onion." I could have called him that, of course, but I chose to leave his Italian name in the original rather than rechristen him in English, although I then supplied the necessary translation (and explanation for the name) in a footnote. By contrast, with other characters, the meanings of whose names seemed less essential for the stories in question, I have restricted my gloss to an endnote. Thus, for Scannadio, a truly minor character, indeed a dead one, in the first story of Day 9, I confined my gloss ("he slits the throat of God") to an endnote. There are a few cases, however, where the name is a nickname that is intended to provoke laughter, and in those cases I have elected to turn it into English, lest the reader miss the joke involved. Thus Guccio Balena, Cipolla's exceedingly fat comic sidekick, becomes Guccio the Whale, which is what the word *balena* means. In this way I have tried to transmit to the reader something of the occasional playfulness and wit of Boccaccio's language, just as I have with, say, the endless comic insults that Boccaccio's clever tricksters direct at their usually uncomprehending dupes.

On occasion, I have sought to keep something of the regional inflection Boccaccio gives his prose in certain stories: the lilt of Venetian Italian when the comic cook Chichibio speaks in the fourth story of Day 6; or the French and Sicilian preference for "madama" over "madonna"— both mean "my lady"—as an honorific in several different stories. I also felt the need to make country people, whom Boccaccio's narrators generally look down on, sound the way they do in the stories, that is, to make them talk like bumpkins, since part of the comedy of the stories lies in the pleasure—a somewhat sadistic pleasure, to be sure—that one derives from laughing at them.

I had a crucial decision to make with regard to the poems. There are ten *canzoni*, or "songs," sung at the end of each of the ten days of the work, as well as another one in the seventh story of the last day. Rather than attempt to reproduce something like Boccaccio's rhyme scheme as well as his complicated use of varying meters, which would have forced me to depart drastically from his Italian, I elected only to keep the English equivalent of his meters, which vary from stanza to stanza and poem to poem, substituting the standard iambic pentameter for his hendecasyllabic lines and iambic trimeter for his *settenari*, or seven-syllable lines. My translations thus capture his meaning, while at least seeming like poetry because of their metrical regularity and because they duplicate the different line lengths of Boccaccio's poems on the page, even though they fail to rhyme. I have rendered them all in modern English, except for the poem that occurs in the seventh story of Day 10, which is deliberately written in an older style by Boccaccio; I consequently felt free to use a slightly archaic English in translating it. As for the verse that occasionally shows up in the stories and usually aims at some sort of comic effect or serves as a spell, I have tried to turn it into rhyme whenever possible, reproducing the effect of the original that way, but without ever sacrificing the sense.

Finally, one of the most interesting features of the style of Boccaccio's work is that although he frequently speaks of the "low" subject of sex, he never resorts to anything like low language in order to do so. Nevertheless, although Boccaccio's language remains proper in such cases, he compensates for this by supplying an endless series of metaphors and euphemisms that provide a double pleasure, in that we can enjoy the cleverness with which he comes up with a variety of "neutral" words to describe sexual organs and the act of making love, and yet we can experience a tiny vicarious sexual charge from knowing exactly what is being referred to. Thus, in the fourth story of Day 5, when Messer Lizio da Valbona goes out onto the balcony of his house one morning, he discovers that his daughter, who has begged to be allowed to spend the night there in order to hear the nightingale sing, is fast asleep in the arms of her lover, holding his "nightingale" in her hand. The reader's pleasure in the scene is doubled by the clever metamorphosis in the story by which a literal nightingale becomes a bird of a very different feather.

As far as "low" language is concerned, things are slightly different when it comes to the issue of scatology. To be sure, Boccaccio does not follow Dante's lead in the *Inferno* where, for instance, he uses an extremely vulgar word to describe at one point how flatterers are immersed in excrement for their sins, declaring that he cannot recognize one of them because his *"capo sì [era] di merda lordo"* (18.116: "head [was] so smeared with shit"). Such low words fit the low inhabitants of Hell, of course, so there is nothing arguably indecorous in Dante's using them at this juncture in his work. Boccaccio, by contrast, has recourse to a milder kind of scatological imagery in a very small number of his stories, and except in one instance, he directs it not at those who deserve eternal damnation, but at those who violate the rules of decorum by seeking to rise above their social station. The exception to this rule is the Venetian woman in the second tale of Day 4, who is duped thinking that the Angel Gabriel is in love with her. Informed of the angel's infatuation, the narrator says she went strutting around her house with her head so high in the air that "her shift did not reach down to cover her butt [*il cul*]" (see p. 324). Otherwise, there are only two other stories in which Boccaccio uses scatology and, in particular, references to *il culo,* which I have usually translated as "butt," but which, in other, less "proper" texts, might well be rendered as "ass."

Boccaccio marshals such scatology in the service of invective in the eighth story of Day 7 about a woman who cheats on her husband, a successful merchant, who has married into a socially superior family. The wife gets everyone to believe that her husband is at fault, prompting her mother to deliver a vicious attack on him as a "petty dealer in donkey droppings [*feccia d'asino*]" (see p. 570), one of those upstarts who have come up from the country and go around in cheap clothing and baggy breeches "with their quill pens stuck in their butts [*nel culo*]" (see p. 570). Finally, in what is the most scatological story—and one of the funniest—in the *Decameron,* the ninth story of Day 8, which

I have mentioned before, Boccaccio gives us a Bolognese doctor who has set up his practice in Florence and has an exaggerated sense of his knowledge, his social importance, and his sexual prowess. Two of Boccaccio's cleverest tricksters "punish" him for his arrogance by means of a mock initiation into their secret society, promising to bestow the "contessa di Civillari," the "Contessa di Crappa" (see p. 671), upon him as his mistress. The doctor does not know that "Civillari" was the name for a ditch in Florence in which all sorts of excrement were deposited, nor does he catch the play on *culo* when he is told that the Contessa is "the most beautiful thing to be found in "the whole *ass-sembly [il culattario]* of the human race" (see p. 671, my italics). The doctor's initiation reaches its comic conclusion when he is indeed dumped into a ditch and gets covered from head to toe in excrement.

These are virtually the only places in the *Decameron* where Boccaccio could be said to employ *parollacce*, "bad words," and they are relatively mild ones at that. He uses them to mock a simpleminded resident of Venice, Florence's great commercial rival, or to put social upstarts very much down in their place. Otherwise, Boccaccio's language in the *Decameron* is extraordinarily proper, although all the witty references to mortars and pestles, leeks and birds should leave no doubt in any reader's mind about the metaphorical meaning of those terms. If nothing else, by showing himself the master of euphemisms, Boccaccio reveals one last time just how artfully he can manipulate language. In this way, too, he ensures that his *Decameron* would still be read almost seven centuries after its creation, maintaining its place up to the present not just as one of the fundamental texts in the Italian literary tradition, but as one of the great works of world literature—even in translation.

HEADNOTES

1. The Names and Number of Boccaccio's Storytellers

The *Decameron* is narrated by ten young men and women. The women are introduced first in the frame narrative, toward the end of the Introduction. There are seven of them, and their names are all allegorical and literary, alluding to figures in the works of other poets as well as to those who appear in Boccaccio's earlier literary productions.

Pampinea means "the blooming one" and was used by Boccaccio in his youthful *Bucolicum carmen* (*Pastoral Poem*).

Fiammetta, "the little flame," was used repeatedly as the name for Boccaccio's beloved throughout his early works.

Filomena, meaning either "the beloved" or "the lover of song," was an even earlier name for Boccaccio's beloved.

Emilia, "the alluring one," also appeared in earlier works, such as his *Amorosa visione* (*Vision of Love*).

Lauretta, the diminutive of Laura, alludes to Petrarch's beloved in his great lyric collection, the *Canzoniere*, or *Rime sparse* (*Songbook, or Scattered Rhymes*), as well as to the laurel tree, whose leaves crowned the poet laureate.

Neifile means "the newly beloved" and may refer to the beloved typically celebrated by poets before Dante, such as Guido Cavalcanti, who wrote elevated lyrics in praise of their ladies in what became known as the *Dolce Stil Novo* ("Sweet New Style").

Elissa is another name for Dido, the tragic, love-struck queen of Vergil's *Aeneid*.

Encouraged perhaps by Boccaccio's insistence on the historical reality of these characters, as well as that of the three men soon to join them, scholars have attempted to identify the real women the names seem to allude to. They have not been successful. It is important to note that the number seven had many important associations in late medieval thinking, including the days of the week, the seven (known) planets, the seven virtues and vices, and the seven liberal arts. Moreover, the ladies' age limits of eighteen and twenty-seven are both multiples of nine, which was considered the "golden number" since, among other things, it was the result of multiplying three, the number of the Trinity, by itself, thus, in a sense, perfecting it. This and other possible examples of number symbolism in the *Decameron* are clearly indebted not just to medieval thought in general, but also to Dante's practice in the *Divine Comedy*.

Just as with the women, although it is impossible to determine the historical reality behind the names of the three men, those names also have allegorical significance.

Panfilo, "he who is made entirely of love," or "he who loves all," was used by Boccaccio in his earlier *Eclogues* and *Fiammetta*.

Filostrato was thought to mean "he who is cast down or overcome by love" (the true etymological meaning is "he who loves war"); it was an epithet used to identify the hero Troilo of Boccaccio's youthful *Il Filostrato,* which Chaucer translated as his *Troilus* and which helped shape Shakespeare's *Troilus and Cressida.* Since *Il Filostrato* was dedicated to a woman named Filomena, some critics think that she is the one with whom Filostrato is in love, while others think the woman is Fiammetta. Any such identification remains uncertain.

Dioneo ("lustful") was used by Boccaccio in several minor works and is derived from Dione, the mother of Venus.

Although they are linked to the seven young women by bonds of love or kinship, who is in love with or related to whom is never made clear. The number three, like seven, was also symbolic and could refer to the past, present, and future, or birth, life, and death, or the three Graces in classical mythology, or the Holy Trinity in a more specifically Christian context, although it is difficult to see the three men as being connected to most of these things. Three, however, was the male number, two the female, in some medieval numerological systems.

2. The Times of the Day and the Storytellers' Daily Routine

People in late medieval Italy told time according to the canonical hours, rather than using twenty-four-hour clocks. Although the exact names and number of the canonical hours shifted during the course of the Middle Ages, there were seven (or eight) of them by Boccaccio's time. At those times, church bells would be rung, and the religious would recite prayers. The hours included: matins, which, followed immediately by lauds, was celebrated before daybreak; prime, at sunrise; tierce, at midmorning; sext, at noon; nones, at midafternoon; vespers, at sunset; and compline, after dark. Since days were longer in the summer than the winter and matched nights in length only at the vernal and autumnal equinoxes, the duration of the hours varied throughout the year, being shorter in winter and longer in spring.

It is likely that the storytellers in the *Decameron* set out for the country several weeks after the plague struck Florence in March 1348 (it would continue to rage well into the summer), and since we are told that they try to avoid being out in the sun during the heat of the day, they are probably away from Florence in the month of April or, more likely, May, or even June. Thus, we should imagine that the sun is rising around 5:00 a.m. and setting sometime after 7:00 p.m. This would mean something like the following distribution of hours: matins and lauds would be celebrated before 5:00 a.m. at which time prime would occur; tierce would be around 8:30 or 9:00 a.m.; sext, at noon; nones, around 3:30 p.m.; vespers, around 7:30; and compline, after dark.

The company of storytellers thus rises around 5:00 a.m., occasionally having a little something by way of breakfast, after which they divert themselves by going for walks and the like. They then eat one of their two principal meals of the day in the midmorning or perhaps a little later. They are said to be dining after tierce, which means they would be going to the table between around 9:00 a.m. and 10:30 a.m. or so. This meal is not given an identifying name, and some translators and critics refer to it as breakfast. However, since medieval and Renaissance Italians and Europeans in general ate their main meal of the day in the late morning, dinner seems the much more appropriate label and has been used accordingly. Note that at the start of Day 3, the story-tellers move to a new palace in the country where they live until their final return to Florence. They have arisen at daybreak, eat nothing, and when they arrive at the palace after a relatively short walk, their steward greets them there with fine wine and *confetti*. I have translated *confetti* as "sweets" (instead of the slightly old-fashioned "sweetmeats"), which were candy-like confections originally made from honey and dried fruit as well as spices and, possibly, seeds or nuts. They were pro-duced by apothecaries and were thought to have restorative powers, as was wine, which is why the group is served some wine and sweets after having exerted themselves with their walk. Later, when they have finished exploring the walled garden attached to the palace, they then eat their main meal, as usual, sometime after tierce. The members of the company sleep during the middle of the day and then get up around nones, or 3:30 p.m., after which they tell their tales in the shade during the hottest part of the day. Once again, they set off walking in order to relax for a while before supper, which seems to occur shortly before vespers, or around 7:30 p.m. For this meal, Boccaccio does have a word, *cena*, or "supper," which he uses consistently throughout his text. Fol-lowing their meal, they dance and sing songs until after it has grown dark at which time they retire for the night.

3. Titles and Forms of Address

Frate: the English equivalent for this word when used alone is "friar," and I have translated it accordingly. However, when placed before a name, such as "Frate Rinaldo," I have elected to keep the Italian rather than write "Brother Rinaldo."

Madonna (Monna, Madama): this was the honorific title used for a woman with something like the equivalent of upper- or middle-class status. *Madonna* was sometimes shortened to *monna,* and *madama* was used in certain regions of Italy, such as Sicily, in place of *madonna.* When prefacing a name, I have elected to keep these terms. When used as a form of direct address without the individual's name, I have translated both as "my lady," which is close to the original Italian and avoids the anachronistic effect of "Madam," which is old fashioned and speaks to a more modern society with a self-consciously defined middle class or bourgeoisie.

Master: my translation of the Italian *maestro,* itself a version of the Latin *magister,* a title for someone with a university degree who practiced a profession or was empowered to teach. Since the English term has a long pedigree and is still employed to identify an expert, someone in charge, a teacher, and the like, I felt free to use it for *maestro.*

Messere (Ser): this was the honorific title used for a man with something like the equivalent of upper- or middle-class status (*ser* is short for *messere*); it was like addressing someone as "sir," but without the implication of aristocratic status. Since there was no concept of a middle class in Boccaccio's time, translating it as "Mister" would be anachronistic, and I have accordingly retained the Italian terms. When someone is simply addressed as *messere,* I have translated the word as "sir." In a number of the more satirical stories, *messer* is used before a character's title, as in *messer lo prete* ("Messer Priest"), and I have retained it there where it serves to underscore the satire, since the person in question is hardly deserving of the honor the honorific signifies.

Podestà: this was the title for the chief magistrate and administrative officer in the towns of northern and central Italy during the late Middle Ages. Since those cities were often riven by factions, the *podestà* was inevitably a titled foreigner who was appointed, usually for a short period of six months or so, because he would be impartial, and who theoretically derived his authority from the Holy Roman Emperor to whom the towns owed nominal allegiance. The *podestà* held court in his palace, and often had judges and magistrates who served under him and whom he brought from elsewhere. In Boccaccio's time, the authority of these figures was on the decline, and they were often intensely disliked by some of the residents in the cities where they served. Since there is no exact English equivalent for the word, I have usually retained the Italian form throughout the translation.

Signoria: this was the name for the ruling body of republican city-states in Italy during the Middle Ages and Renaissance. It comes from the word *signore*, which is the equivalent of the English "sir," and ultimately derives from the Latin *senex* ("elder").

THE
DECAMERON

Preface

Here begins the book called Decameron, *also known as* Prince Galeotto, *which contains one hundred stories told in ten days by seven ladies and three young men.*[*]

It is a matter of humanity to show compassion for those who suffer, and although it is fitting for everyone to do so, it is especially desirable in those who, having had need of comfort, have received it from others—and if anyone ever needed it or appreciated it or derived any pleasure from it, I am one of them.[1] For, from my earliest youth up to the present, I have been enflamed beyond measure by a most exalted, noble love, which, were I to describe it, might seem greater than what is suitable for one in my low condition. Although I was praised and held in high regard for that love by those discerning individuals to whose attention I had come, it was nevertheless extremely painful to endure, not because of the cruelty of my beloved lady, to be sure, but because of the enormous fire produced within me by my poorly regulated appetite, which never allowed me to rest content or stay within reasonable limits and often made me feel more pain than I should have. While I was suffering, the pleasant conversation and invaluable consolation certain friends provided gave me such relief that I am absolutely convinced they are the reason I did not die. But as it pleased Him who is infinite and who has decreed by immutable law that all earthly things must come to an end, my love abated in the course of time of its own

---

[*] The title of Boccaccio's work derives from Greek and means "ten days." Prince Galeotto (Gallehault, in French) is a character from Arthurian romance who served as a go-between in the love affair of Lancelot and Guinevere. On both the title and the alternative title, see the Introduction.

accord, although it had been more fervent than any other and could not
be altered or extinguished by the force of reason or counsel or public
shame or the harm it might cause. At present, love has left in my mind
only the pleasurable feeling that it normally gives to those who refrain
from sailing on its deepest seas. Thus, whereas it used to be painful,
now that all my suffering has been removed, I feel only the delightful
sensation that still remains.

⟦But although my pain has ceased, I have not forgotten the benefits
I once received from those who, because of the benevolence they felt
toward me, shared my heavy burden, nor will this memory ever fade in
me, I truly believe, until I myself am dead⟧ And since, in my opinion,
gratitude should be the most highly praised of all the virtues, while its
contrary is to be condemned, and since I do not wish to appear ungrateful, I have decided to use what little ability I have, now that I am free
of love, to try and provide some relief in exchange for that which I
received. And if I cannot provide it for those who aided me, since they,
thanks to their intelligence or their good luck, do not require it, I will
offer it to those who do. For, however slight my support—or comfort,
if you prefer—might be to the needy, I nevertheless feel that it should
be directed where it is more in demand, for there it will be more helpful and more appreciated.

Who will deny that it is much more fitting to give this aid, however
inadequate, to charming women than to men? Out of fear and shame,
women keep the flames of love hidden within their delicate breasts, and
as everyone knows who has had this experience, such fires have much
greater force than do those that burn out in the open. Restrained by
the desires, whims, and commands of their fathers, mothers, brothers, and husbands, most of the time women remain pent up within
the narrow confines of their rooms, and as they sit there in apparent
idleness, both yearning and not yearning at the same time, the varied
thoughts they mull over in their minds cannot always be happy ones.
And if, because of those thoughts, a fit of melancholy brought on by
their burning desire should take possession of their minds, it will inevitably remain there, causing them great pain, unless it is removed by

new interests.[2] Finally, women's powers of endurance are simply less than those of men.

As we can plainly see, this is not what happens to men who are in love. Should melancholy or burdensome thoughts afflict them, they have many ways to alleviate or remove them, for, if they wish, they never lack opportunities to get out of the house where they can see and hear all sorts of things going on, and where they can hawk, hunt or fish, go riding or gamble, or just attend to their business affairs. Each of these activities has the power to occupy a man's mind either wholly or in part and to free it from painful thoughts, at least for a while, after which, one way or another, either he will find consolation or the pain will subside.

Therefore, I wish, to some extent, to provide a remedy for the sins of Fortune, who has been more niggardly in providing support where there is less strength, as we see in the case of our delicate ladies. And so, I offer here a succor and refuge for those who are in love, whereas for those who are not, they can just make do with their needles, their spindles, and their wool winders. My plan is to recount one hundred stories, or fables, or parables, or histories, or whatever you wish to call them.[3] They were told over ten days, as will be seen, by an honorable company made up of seven ladies and three young men who came together during the time of the recent plague that was responsible for so many deaths. I will also include some little songs sung for their delight by the ladies I mentioned. In the stories, you will see many cases of love, both pleasing and harsh, as well as other adventures, which took place in both ancient and modern times. In reading them, the ladies of whom I have been speaking will be able to derive not only pleasure from the entertaining material they contain, but useful advice as well, for the stories will teach them how to recognize what they should avoid, and likewise, what they should pursue.[4] And I believe that as they read them, their suffering would come to an end. Should this occur—and may God grant that it should—let them thank Love who, in freeing me from his bonds, has granted me the ability to attend to their pleasures.

Day 1, Introduction

Here begins the first day of the Decameron, *in which the author explains how it came about that the individuals, who will soon make their appearance, were induced to come together in order to converse with one another, and how, under the rule of Pampinea, they speak on whatever topic each one finds most agreeable.*

Most gracious ladies, whenever I contemplate how compassionate you all are by nature, I recognize that, in your judgment, the present work will seem both somber and painful, for its opening contains the sad record of the recent, deadly plague, which inspired so much horror and pity in all who actually saw it or otherwise came to know of it. But I do not want you to be afraid of reading beyond this introduction, as though you would always be going forward amid continual sighs and tears. You will be affected by this horrific beginning no differently than travelers are by a steep and rugged mountain, for beyond it there lies a most beautiful and delightful plain, which will supply them with pleasure that matches the difficulty of both their ascent and their descent.[1] And thus, just as happiness at its limit turns into sadness, so misery is ended by the joy that follows it.

This brief pain—I call it brief because it is contained in just a few words—will be quickly followed by the sweetness and pleasure that I have just promised you and that such a beginning would not, perhaps, have led you to expect, had I not explained what is about to happen. And truly, if in all honesty I could have led you where I want to go by any route other than by such a difficult path as this one will be, I would have done so gladly. But because, without recalling these events, I could not explain the origins of the things you will read about later on, I have been forced by necessity, as it were, to write it all down.

Let me say, then, that one thousand, three hundred, and forty-eight years had passed since the fruitful Incarnation of the Son of God when the deadly plague arrived in the noble city of Florence, the most beautiful of any in Italy.[2] Whether it descended on us mortals through the influence of the heavenly bodies or was sent down by God in His righteous anger to chastise us because of our wickedness, it had begun some years before in the East, where it deprived countless beings of their lives before it headed to the West, spreading ever-greater misery as it moved relentlessly from place to place. Against it all human wisdom and foresight were useless. Vast quantities of refuse were removed from the city by officials charged with this function, the sick were not allowed inside the walls, and numerous instructions were disseminated for the preservation of health—but all to no avail. Nor were the humble supplications made to God by the pious, not just once but many times, whether in organized processions or in other ways, any more effective. For practically from the start of spring in the year we mentioned above, the plague began producing its sad effects in a terrifying and extraordinary manner. It did not operate as it had done in the East, where if anyone bled through the nose, it was a clear sign of inevitable death. Instead, at its onset, in men and women alike, certain swellings would develop in the groin or under the armpits, some of which would grow like an ordinary apple and others like an egg, some larger and some smaller. The common people called them *gavoccioli*, and within a brief space of time, these deadly, so-called *gavoccioli* would begin to spread from the two areas already mentioned and would appear at random over the rest of the body.* Then, the symptoms of the disease began to change, and many people discovered black or livid blotches on their arms, thighs, and every other part of their bodies, sometimes large and

---

Gavocciolo is a Tuscan word meaning a swelling or protuberance; it is a diminutive and derives from the late Latin *gaba* (Italian *gozzo*), meaning goiter, crop, throat, or even stomach. These swellings are called *bubboni* in modern Italian and buboes in English (from the Greek word for groin or gland), and it is from this term that we get the name of the sickness, the bubonic plague. It was also called the Black Death because of the black spots on the body that were due to internal bleeding and that Boccaccio will describe in the next sentence.

widely scattered, at other times tiny and close together. For whoever contracted them, these spots were a most certain sign of impending death, just as the *gavoccioli* had been earlier and still continued to be.

Against these maladies the advice of doctors and the power of medicine appeared useless and unavailing. Perhaps the nature of the disease was such that no remedy was possible, or the problem lay with those who were treating it, for their number, which had become enormous, included not just qualified doctors, but women as well as men who had never had any training in medicine, and since none of them had any idea what was causing the disease, they could hardly prescribe an appropriate remedy for it. Thus, not only were very few people cured, but in almost every case death occurred within three days after the appearance of the signs we have described, sometimes sooner and sometimes later, and usually without fever or any other complication. Moreover, what made this pestilence all the more virulent was that it was spread by the slightest contact between the sick and the healthy just as a fire will catch dry or oily materials when they are placed right beside it. In fact, this evil went even further, for not only did it infect those who merely talked or spent any time with the sick, but it also appeared to transfer the disease to anyone who merely touched the clothes or other objects that had been handled or used by those who were its victims.

What I have to tell is incredible, and if I and many others had not seen these things with our own eyes, I would scarcely dare to believe them, let alone write them down, no matter how trustworthy the person was who told me about them. Let me just say that the plague I have been describing was so contagious as it spread that it did not merely pass from one man to another, but we frequently saw something much more incredible, namely that when an animal of some species other than our own touched something belonging to an individual who had been stricken by the disease or had died of it, that animal not only got infected, but was killed almost instantly. With my own eyes, as I have just said, I witnessed such a thing on many occasions. One day, for example, two pigs came upon the rags of a poor man that had been thrown into the public street after he had died of the disease, and as they usually do, the pigs first poked at them with their snouts, after which they picked them up between their teeth and shook them against their jowls. Thereupon, within a short time, after writhing about as if they had been poisoned, both of them fell down dead on the ground, splayed out upon the rags that had brought about their destruction.

These things and many others like them, or even worse, caused all sorts of fears and fantasies in those who remained alive, almost all of whom took one utterly cruel precaution, namely, to avoid the sick and their belongings, fleeing far away from them, for in doing so they all thought they could preserve their own health.

Some people were of the opinion that living moderately and being abstemious would really help them resist the disease. They, therefore, formed themselves into companies and lived in isolation from everyone else. Having come together, they shut themselves up inside houses where no one was sick and they had ample means to live well, so that, while avoiding overindulgence, they still enjoyed the most delicate foods and the best wines in moderation. They would not speak with anyone from outside, nor did they want to hear any news about the dead and the dying, and instead, they passed their time playing music and enjoying whatever other amusements they could devise.

Others, holding the contrary opinion, maintained that the surest medicine for such an evil disease was to drink heavily, enjoy life's pleasures, and go about singing and having fun, satisfying their appetites by any means available, while laughing at everything and turning whatever happened into a joke. Moreover, they practiced what they preached to the best of their ability, for they went from one tavern to another, drinking to excess both day and night. They did their drinking more freely in private homes, however, provided that they found something there to enjoy or that held out the promise of pleasure. Such places were easy to find, because people, feeling as though their days were numbered, had not just abandoned themselves, but all their possessions, too. Most houses had thus become common property, and any stranger who happened upon them could treat them as if he were their rightful owner. And yet, while these people behaved like wild animals, they always took great care to avoid any contact at all with the sick.

In the midst of so much affliction and misery in our city, the respect for the reverend authority of the laws, both divine and human, had declined just about to the vanishing point, for, like everyone else, their officers and executors, who were not dead or sick themselves, had so few personnel that they could not fulfill their duties. Thus, people felt free to behave however they liked.

There were many others who took a middle course between the two already mentioned, neither restricting their diet so much as the first, nor letting themselves go in drinking and other forms of dissipation so much as the second, but doing just enough to satisfy their appetites. Instead of shutting themselves up, they went about, some carrying flowers in their hands, others with sweet-smelling herbs, and yet others with various kinds of spices. They would repeatedly hold these things up to their noses, for they thought the best course was to fortify the brain with such odors against the stinking air that seemed to be saturated with the stench of dead bodies and disease and medicine. Others, choosing what may have been the safer alternative, cruelly maintained that no medicine was better or more effective against the plague than flight. Convinced by this argument, and caring for nothing but themselves, a large number of both men and women abandoned their own city, their own homes, their relatives, their properties and possessions, and headed for the countryside, either that lying around Florence or, better still, that which was farther away. It was as if they thought that God's wrath, once provoked, did not aim to punish men's iniquities with the plague wherever it might find them, but would strike down only those found inside the walls of their city. Or perhaps they simply concluded that no one in Florence would survive and that the city's last hour had come.

Of the people holding these varied opinions, not all of them died, but, by the same token, not all of them survived. On the contrary, many proponents of each view got sick here, there, and everywhere. Moreover, since they themselves, when they were well, had set the example for those who were not yet infected, they, too, were almost completely abandoned by everyone as they languished away. And leaving aside the fact that the citizens avoided one another, that almost no one took care of his neighbors, and that relatives visited one another infrequently, if ever, and always kept their distance, the tribulation of the plague had put such fear into the hearts of men and women that brothers abandoned their brothers, uncles their nephews, sisters their brothers, and very often wives their husbands. In fact, what is even worse, and almost unbelievable, is that fathers and mothers refused to tend to their children and take care of them, treating them as if they belonged to someone else.

Consequently, the countless numbers of people who got sick, both men and women, had to depend for help either on the charity of the few friends they had who were still around, or on the greed of their servants, who would only work for high salaries out of all proportion to the services they provided. For all that, though, there were few servants to be found, and those few tended to be men and women of limited intelligence, most of whom, not trained for such duties, did little more than hand sick people the few things they asked for or watch over them as they died. And yet, while performing these services, they themselves often lost their lives along with their wages.

As a result of the abandonment of the sick by neighbors, friends, and family, and in light of the scarcity of servants, there arose a practice hardly ever heard of before, whereby when a woman fell ill, no matter how attractive or beautiful or noble, she did not object to having a man as one of her attendants, whether he was young or not. Indeed, if her infirmity made it necessary, she experienced no more shame in showing him every part of her body than she would have felt with a woman, which was the reason why those women who were cured were perhaps less chaste in the period that followed. Moreover, a great many people chanced to die who might have survived if they had had any sort of assistance. In general, between the inadequacy of the means to care for the sick, and the virulence of the plague, the number of people dying both day and night was so great that it astonished those who merely heard tell of it, let alone those who actually witnessed it.

As a result of the plague, it was almost inevitable that practices arose among the citizens who survived that went contrary to their original customs. It used to be the case, as it is again today, that the female relatives and next-door neighbors of a dead man would come to his house and mourn there with the women of the household, while his male neighbors and a fair number of other citizens would assemble in front of the house with his male relatives. After that, the clergymen would arrive, their number depending on the social rank of the deceased, who would then be carried on the shoulders of his peers, amid all the funeral pomp of candles and chants, to the church he had chosen before his death. As the ferocity of the plague began to increase, such practices all but disappeared in their entirety, while other new ones arose to take their place. For people did not just die without women around them, but many departed this life without anyone at all as a witness, and very few of them were accorded the pious lamentations and bitter tears of their families. On the contrary, in place of all the usual weeping, mostly there was laughing and joking and festive merrymaking—a practice that women, having largely suppressed their feminine piety, had mastered in the interest of preserving their health. Moreover, there were few whose bodies were accompanied to church by more than ten or twelve of their neighbors, nor were they carried on the shoulders of their honored and esteemed fellow citizens, but by a band of gravediggers, come up from the lower classes, who insisted on being called *sextons* and performed their services for a fee. They would shoulder the bier and quick-march it off, not to the church that the dead man had chosen before his demise, but in most cases, to the one closest by. They would walk behind four or six clergymen who carried just a few candles—and sometimes none at all—and who did not trouble themselves with lengthy, solemn burial services, but instead, with the aid of those *sextons*, dumped the corpse as quickly as they could into whatever empty grave they found.

The common people and most of those of the middling sort presented a much more pathetic sight, for the majority of them were constrained to stay in their houses either by their hope to survive or by their poverty. Confined thus to their own neighborhoods, they got sick every day by the thousands, and having no servants or anyone else to attend to their needs, they almost invariably perished. Many expired out in the public streets both day and night, and although a great many others died inside their houses, the stench of their decaying bodies announced their deaths to their neighbors well before anything else did. And what with these, plus the others who were dying all over the place, the city was overwhelmed with corpses.

For the most part, the neighbors of the dead always observed the same routine, prompted more by a fear of contamination from the decaying bodies than by any charity they might have felt. Either by themselves or with the aid of porters, whenever any could be found, they carried the bodies of the recently deceased out of their houses and put them down by the front doors, where anyone passing by, especially in the morning, could have seen them by the thousands. Then the bodies were taken and placed on biers that had been sent for, or for lack of biers, on wooden planks. Nor was it unusual for two or three bodies to be carried on a single bier, for on more than one occasion, they were seen holding a wife and a husband, two or three brothers, a father and a son, or other groups like that. And countless were the times when a couple of priests bearing a cross would go to fetch someone, and porters carrying three or four biers would fall in behind them, so that whereas the priests thought they had one corpse to bury, they would have six or eight, and sometimes more. Even so, however, there were no tears or candles or mourners to honor the dead; on the contrary, it had reached the point that people who died were treated the same way that goats would be treated nowadays. Thus, it is quite clear that things which the natural course of events, with its small, infrequent blows, could never teach the wise to bear with patience, the immensity of this calamity made even simple people regard with indifference.[3]

There was not enough consecrated ground to bury the enormous number of corpses that were being brought to every church every day at almost every hour, especially if they were going to continue the ancient custom of giving each one its own plot. So, when all the graves were full, enormous trenches were dug in the cemeteries of the churches, into which the new arrivals were put by the hundreds, stowed layer upon layer like merchandise in ships, each one covered with a little earth, until the top of the trench was reached.

But rather than go on recalling in elaborate detail all the miseries we experienced in the city, let me just add that the baleful wind blowing through it in no way spared the surrounding countryside. The fortified towns there fared just like the city, though on a smaller scale, and in the scattered villages and farms the poor, wretched peasants and their families died at all hours of the day and night. Without the aid of doctors or help from servants, they would expire along the roads and in their tilled fields and in their homes, dying more like animals than human beings. They, too, became as apathetic in their ways as the city dwellers were, neglecting their property and ignoring the work they had to do. Indeed, since they thought every day was going to be their last, they consumed what they already had on hand, neglecting what they might get in the future from their animals and fields and from all their past labors. Thus it came about that oxen, asses, sheep, goats, pigs, chickens, and even dogs, who are so loyal to men, were driven from their homes and left to roam freely through fields in which the wheat had not even been reaped, let alone gathered in. Nevertheless, many of the animals, as if they were rational beings, would eat well there during the day and then return home full at night, needing no shepherd to guide them.

To leave the countryside and return to the city: what more can be said except that the cruelty of the heavens—and perhaps, in some measure, that of men, too—was so great and so malevolent that from March to the following July, between the fury of the pestilence and the fact that many of the sick were poorly cared for or abandoned in their need because of the fears of those who were healthy, it has been reliably calculated that more than one hundred thousand human beings were deprived of their lives within the walls of the city of Florence, although before the outbreak of the plague perhaps no one would have thought it contained so many.*

---

*Boccaccio's estimate of the number of deaths due to the plague is somewhat exaggerated, perhaps for the sake of rhetorical effect. Historians, relying on various fourteenth-century chroniclers, think that about 60 percent of the population, or anywhere from fifty to eighty thousand people, perished in Florence and the surrounding countryside. Boccaccio's interest in rhetorical effect is also evident in the heightened language of the following paragraph.

Oh, how many great palaces, beautiful houses, and noble dwellings, once filled with lords and ladies and their retainers, were emptied of all their inhabitants, down to the last little serving boy! Oh, how many famous families, how many vast estates, how many notable fortunes were left without a legitimate heir! How many valiant men, how many beautiful women, how many lovely youths, whom Galen, Hippocrates, and Aesculapius—not to mention others—would have judged perfectly healthy, dined in the morning with their families, companions, and friends, only to have supper that evening with their ancestors in the next world![4]

Since my own grief will be increased if I continue to meditate any longer on so much misery, I want to pass over what I can suitably omit and tell what happened one Tuesday morning while our city was in these straits and had been practically deserted. As I later learned from a trustworthy person, seven young women, who had just attended divine services and who, in keeping with the requirements of the times, were dressed in mourning attire, found themselves in the venerable Church of Santa Maria Novella, which was otherwise almost empty. Each one was the friend, neighbor, or relative of one of the others, none had reached her twenty-eighth year or was under eighteen, and all were intelligent, wellborn, attractive, and graced with fine manners and marvelous honesty. I would tell you their real names, but there is a good reason that prevents me from doing so, which is that I do not want any of them to feel shame in the future because of the ensuing stories, which they either listened to or told themselves. For the rules concerning pleasure, which are rather strict today, were then, for the reasons I have already given, very lax, not just for women of their age, but even for those who were much older. Nor do I wish to supply the envious, who are ready to censure the most praiseworthy life, with material that might allow them to denigrate the honesty of these worthy ladies in any way by means of their filthy gossip. However, so that what each one said may be understood without confusion, I intend to identify them by means of names that are either wholly, or partially, adapted to their characters. We shall call the first of them, who was also the oldest, Pampinea, and the second Fiammetta; the third and

fourth, Filomena and Emilia; then let us say that the fifth is Lauretta
and the sixth Neifile; and to the last, not without reason, we will give
the name Elissa.*

By chance rather than some prior agreement, they had all come
together in one part of the church and were sitting down more or less
in a circle. After finishing their prayers, they heaved a deep sigh and
began talking among themselves about the terrible times they were
going through. After a while, when all the others had fallen silent,
Pampinea began to speak as follows:

"My dear ladies, we have all heard many times that there is no harm
in exercising our rights in an honest way. Now, every person on earth
has a natural right to maintain, preserve, and defend his life to the best
of his ability. In fact, the proof that we all take this for granted is that
men are judged innocent if they sometimes kill others in self-defense.
Thus, if the laws, to which the welfare of every human being has been
entrusted, concede such a thing, how can it be wrong, provided no one
is harmed, for us or for anyone else to use whatever remedies we can
find in order to preserve our lives? When I pause to consider what we
have been doing this morning as well as on previous mornings, and
when I think about the subjects we have discussed and what we have
had to say about them, I realize, just as you must realize, too, that each
of us fears for her life. I am not surprised by this, but considering that
we all have the natural feelings shared by women, what really does
surprise me is why you have not taken any steps to protect yourselves
from what each of you has a right to fear.

"Instead, here we sit, in my opinion, as if our sole purpose were to
count the number of corpses being carried to their graves, or to hear
whether the friars inside the church, whose numbers have practically
dwindled away to nothing, are chanting their offices at the specified
hours, or to exhibit, by means of our clothing, the quality and quantity of our miseries to anybody who might show up here. And if we go
outside, either we see the dead and the sick being carried everywhere
about us; or we see people, once condemned and sent into exile for

---

*On the names and the number of the seven women, see Headnote 1.

their misdeeds by the authority of the civil law, mocking that law as they rampage through the city committing acts of violence, knowing that those who enforce the law are either sick or dead; or we are tormented by the dregs of our city who, thirsting for our blood, call themselves *sextons* now and go about everywhere, both on horseback and on foot, singing scurrilous songs to add insults to our injuries. And all we ever hear is 'So-and-so is dead' and 'So-and-so is about to die.' If there were anyone left to grieve, we would hear nothing but doleful laments everywhere.

"And when we return home, I do not know whether you have the same experience that I do, but since, out of a large household of servants, there is no one left except my maid, I get so frightened that I feel as if all the hairs on my head were standing on end. And what terrifies me even more is that wherever I go in the house, wherever I pause for a moment, I see the shades of those who have passed away, and their faces are not the ones I was used to, but they have strange, horrible expressions on them that come from who knows where. For these reasons, whether I am here or outside or in my house, I am always anxious, and all the more so, because it seems to me that there is no one possessing sufficient means and having some place to go to, as we do, who is left in the city except us. And as for the few people still around, they make no distinction, as I have often heard and seen for myself, between what is honest and what is not, and prompted only by their appetites, they do what promises them the most pleasure, both day and night, alone and in groups. Moreover, I am not speaking only of laymen, but also of those cloistered in monasteries, who have convinced themselves that such wicked behavior is suitable for them and only improper for others. Breaking their vows of obedience, they have given themselves over to carnal pleasures, and in the belief that they will thereby escape death, they have become wanton and degenerate.

"And if this is so—and it most manifestly *is* so—then what are we doing here, what are we waiting for, what are we dreaming about? Why are we lazier and slower than all the other inhabitants of this city in providing for our safety? Do we consider ourselves less valuable than they are? Or do we believe that our lives, unlike those of others, are tied to our bodies by chains so strong that we need not worry about all these things that have the power to harm them? We are mistaken, we are deceived, what bestial stupidity for us to think this way! The clearest argument against us is the frequency with which we are forced to recall the names and conditions of the young men and women who have been struck down by this cruel pestilence.

"Although I do not know if things appear to you the way they do to me, for my part I have come to the conclusion that the best thing for us to do in our present situation would be to leave the city, just as many have done before us and many are still doing, lest we fall prey through timidity or complacency to what we might possibly avoid if we desired to do so. We should go and stay on one of our various country estates, shunning the wicked practices of others like death itself, but having as much fun as possible, feasting and making merry, without ever overstepping the bounds of reason in any way.

"There we will hear the little birds sing and see the hills and plains turning green, the fields full of wheat undulating like the sea, and thousands of kinds of trees. There we will have a clearer view of the heavens, for, even if they are sullen, they do not for all that deny us their eternal beauties, which are so much more attractive to look at than are the walls of our empty city. Moreover, the air is much fresher in the country, the necessities of life are more abundant, and the number of difficulties to contend with is smaller. Although the peasants are dying there in the same way that the city dwellers are here, our distress will be lessened if only because the houses and the people are fewer and farther between. Besides, if I am right, we will not be abandoning anyone here. Rather, we can truly say that we are the ones who have been abandoned, for our relatives, by dying or fleeing from death, have left us alone in the midst of this great affliction as if we were no kin of theirs. Nor will anyone reproach us if we adopt this plan, whereas if we do not, we will be facing sorrow and grief and possibly death itself.

"Consequently, if you please, I think it would be a good idea for us to do what I suggest, taking our maidservants with us and having everything we need sent after. We can live in one place today and another tomorrow, pursuing whatever pleasures and amusements the present times offer. And if death does not claim us before then, let us go on living this way until such time as we can perceive the end that Heaven has decreed for these events. Just remember that it is no less unseemly for us to go away and thus preserve our honor than for the great majority of the others to stay here and lose theirs."

Having listened to Pampinea, the other women not only applauded her advice, but were so eager to take it that they were already beginning to work out the details among themselves, as though they were going to get right up out of their seats and set off at once. But Filomena, who was very prudent, declared: "Ladies, although what Pampinea has argued is very well said, that is no reason for us rush into it, as you seem to want to do. Remember, we are all women, and every one of us is sufficiently adult to recognize how women, when left to themselves in a group, can be quite irrational, and how, without a man to look after them, they can be terribly disorganized. Since we are fickle, quarrelsome, suspicious, weak, and fearful, I am really worried that if we take no guide along with us other than ourselves, this company will fall apart much more quickly, and with much less to credit to ourselves, than would otherwise be the case. We would be well advised to deal with this problem before we start."

"It is certainly true," said Elissa, "that man is the head of woman, and without a man to guide us, only rarely does anything we do accord us praise.[5] But how are we to get hold of these men? As we all know, the majority of our male relatives are dead, and the others who remain alive not only have no idea where we are, but are fleeing in scattered little groups from exactly the same thing we seek to avoid ourselves. Nor would it be seemly for us to take up with those who are not our kin. Therefore, if self-preservation is the purpose of our flight, we must find a way to arrange things so that no matter where we go in quest of fun and relaxation, trouble and scandal do not follow us there."

The ladies were engaged in their discussion, when lo and behold, who should come into the church but three young men, though none so young as to be under twenty-five, in whom neither the horrors of the times, nor the loss of friends and relatives, nor fear for their own lives had been able to cool down, let alone extinguish, the love they felt. The first was named Panfilo, the second Filostrato, and the last Dioneo, all of them very pleasant and well bred.* In the midst of all this turbulence, they were seeking the solace, sweet beyond measure, of catching a glimpse of the ladies they loved, all three of whom just so happened to be among the seven previously mentioned, while several of the others were close relatives of one or another of the men. No sooner did they catch sight of the ladies than the ladies caught sight of them, whereupon Pampinea smiled and began: "Look how Fortune favors us right from the start in placing before us three discreet and worthy young men who will gladly guide us and serve us if we are not too proud to ask them to do so."

Neifile's entire face had turned scarlet with embarrassment because she was the object of one of the youths' affections. "Pampinea, for the love of God," she said, "be careful about what you are saying. I know for certain that nothing but good can be said of any one of them, and I believe they are more than competent to carry out this task. I also think they would provide good, honest company not only for us, but for many women more beautiful and finer than we are. But since it is perfectly obvious that they are in love with some of us here, I am afraid that if we were to take them with us, through no fault of theirs or of our own, we would be exposed to censure and disgrace."

"That really does not matter in the least," said Filomena. "If I live like an honest woman and my conscience is clear, let people say what they like to the contrary, for God and Truth will take up arms on my behalf. Now, if only they were disposed to accompany us, then we could truly claim, as Pampinea has said, that Fortune favors our plan."

Having heard what Pampinea had to say, the other ladies stopped talking and unanimously agreed that the men should be called over, told about their intentions, and asked if they would like to accompany them on their expedition. And so, without another word, Pampinea, who was related by blood to one of the men, got up and went over to where they stood gazing at the women. After giving them a cheerful greeting, Pampinea explained their plan and asked them on behalf of

---

*On the names and the number of the three men, see Headnote 1.

all the women if, in a spirit of pure, brotherly affection, they might be disposed to accompany them.

At first the young men thought they were being mocked, but when they saw that Pampinea was speaking in earnest, they replied happily that they were ready to go. In order to avoid delaying their project, they all made arrangements then and there for what they had to do before their departure. The next day, which was a Wednesday, after having carefully prepared everything they needed down to the last detail and sent it all on ahead to the place where they were going, they left the city at the crack of dawn and started on their way, the ladies traveling with a few of their maids, the three youths with three of their servants. Nor did they go more than two short miles from the city before they arrived at their first destination.

The place in question was some distance from any road, situated on a little mountain that was quite a pleasant sight to see with all its shrubs and trees decked out in their green foliage.[6] At the top there was a palace, built around a large, lovely courtyard, containing loggias, great halls, and bedchambers, all of which were beautifully proportioned and adorned with charming paintings of happy scenes. Surrounded by meadows and marvelous gardens, the palace had wells of the coolest water and vaulted cellars stocked with precious wines, wines more suitable for connoisseurs than for honest, sober ladies. When they got there, the company discovered to their great delight that the palace had been swept clean from top to bottom, the beds had been made up in their chambers, every room had been adorned with seasonal flowers, and the floors had been carpeted with rushes.

Soon after reaching the palace, they sat down, and Dioneo, who was the merriest of the young men and had the readiest wit, said: "Ladies, we have been led here more by your good sense than by our own foresight. Now, I do not know what you intend to do with all your troubles, but I left mine inside the city gates when I passed through them with you just a short while ago. Hence, you must either prepare to have fun and to laugh and sing along with me—as much as is consistent, of course, with your dignity—or you should give me leave to go back there to reclaim my troubles and stay in our afflicted city."

As though she, too, had gotten rid of such thoughts herself, Pampinea replied to him gaily: "Very well said, Dioneo. We should have fun while we are living here, for that is the very reason we fled our sorrows back there. But since things that lack order will not last long, and since I am the one who initiated the discussions that led to the formation of this fair company, I think that if we are to preserve our happiness, we have to choose a leader from among ourselves, someone whom we will honor and obey as our superior and whose every thought will be aimed at enabling us to pass our time together agreeably. Moreover, to allow us all to experience the heavy burden as well as the pleasure of being in command, and thereby to prevent those who are not in charge from envying the person who is, I think that the burden and the honor should be assigned to each of us in turn for just one day. The first ruler is someone we should all elect, but as for those who follow, the person who has been in charge on a particular day should, when the hour of vespers approaches, choose his or her successor.* Then this new ruler will be free to determine the place where we will go and to dictate the manner in which we are to live during the period of his or her reign."

They were all quite happy with Pampinea's proposal and unanimously elected her Queen for the first day, whereupon Filomena quickly ran over to a laurel tree, for she had often heard people say that its leaves were quite venerable and conferred great honor on those worthy individuals who were crowned with them. Having gathered a few branches, she made a magnificent garland of honor, which, during the time the company remained together, was placed on each person's head as a clear sign of royal sovereignty and authority.[7]

Once she had been crowned Queen, Pampinea summoned the servants of the three men as well as the women's maids, who were four in number. She then ordered everyone to be silent, and when they were, she said:

"So that I may begin by setting an example for you all that will allow our company to be able to live free from shame and will make our experience here an ever more orderly and pleasurable one for as long as we

---

*Vespers: evening. On the canonical hours, see Headnote 2.

choose to stay together, let me first appoint Parmeno, Dioneo's servant, as my steward and entrust him with the care and management of our entire household as well as everything pertaining to the service of our dining hall.[8] I want Sirisco, Panfilo's servant, to be our buyer and treasurer and to carry out Parmeno's orders. Tindaro, who is in Filostrato's service, shall take care of his master's bedchamber as well as those of the other two men whenever their own servants are prevented by their duties from doing so. My maid Misia will be in the kitchen full-time with Filomena's maid Licisca, where they will diligently prepare all the dishes ordered by Parmeno. We want Chimera, Lauretta's maid, and Stratilia, Fiammetta's, to act as the ladies' chambermaids and to clean all the places we frequent. Finally, if they wish to stay in our good graces, we desire and command all of the servants to take care that, no matter what they see or hear in their comings and goings, no news from the outside world should ever reach us unless that news is good."[9]

Having summarily given out her orders, which everyone commended, she rose gaily to her feet and declared: "Here there are gardens and meadows and lots of other truly delightful spots in which we are free to walk and enjoy ourselves. However, at the stroke of tierce, let us all return here so that we can eat while it is still cool."*

After the merry company was given leave to go by the Queen, the young men and their lovely companions set off on a leisurely walk through one of the gardens, talking of pleasant matters, making lovely garlands out of various types of foliage for one another, and singing songs of love. Then, when they had spent as much time there as the Queen had allotted them, they returned to their lodging where they found Parmeno had been quite diligent in carrying out his duties, for when they entered one of the great halls on the ground floor, they saw that tables had been set up, laid with the whitest tablecloths on which there were goblets gleaming like silver, and that the whole room had been adorned with broom blossoms. At the Queen's behest they rinsed their hands in water and went to sit in the places Parmeno had assigned them.

---

*Tierce: midmorning. On the canonical hours, see Headnote 2.

Exquisitely prepared dishes were brought in, the finest wines were at the ready, and without a sound the three servants began waiting on them. The entire company was delighted that everything was so beautiful and so well presented, and all through the meal there was a great deal of pleasant talk and much good cheer. As soon as the tables were cleared away, the Queen sent for musical instruments so that a few of their number who were well versed in music could play and sing, while all the rest, the ladies together with the young men, could dance a *carola*.* At her request, Dioneo took up a lute and Fiammetta a viol,[10] and the pair began playing a melodious dance tune together, whereupon the Queen, having sent the servants away to eat, formed a circle with the other ladies and the two young men, and all began dancing at a stately pace. After that, they sang a number of pleasant, happy little songs, and continued to entertain themselves in this manner until the Queen, thinking it was time for a nap, dismissed them. The three young men consequently retired to their bedchambers, which were separated from those of the ladies. There they found not merely that their beds had been neatly made, but that their rooms were as full of flowers as the hall had been, and the ladies made a similar discovery, whereupon the entire company undressed and lay down to rest.

Not long after nones had struck, the Queen got up and had the young men and all the other women awakened, declaring that it was harmful to sleep too much during the day.† They then went off to a little meadow where the grass, shaded everywhere from the sun, grew lush and green, and where, feeling a gentle breeze wafting over them, the Queen asked them to sit down in a circle on the green grass. She then spoke to them as follows:

"As you can see, the sun is high, the heat is intense, and nothing can be heard but the cicadas up in the olive trees. To take a walk and go somewhere else right now would be the height of folly, since it is so lovely and cool here, and besides, as you can see, there are boards set up for backgammon and chess. However, although we are free to

---

* *Carola*: a dance in which the dancers joined hands and moved in a clockwise direction, usually accompanied by music and the singing of the dancers themselves.

† Nones: midafternoon. On the canonical hours, see Headnote 2.

amuse ourselves in whatever way we like, if you would take my advice in this, we should not spend the hot part of the day playing games, for they necessarily leave one of the players feeling miffed, without giving that much pleasure either to his opponent or to those who are watching. Rather, we should tell stories, for even though just one person is doing the talking, all the others will still have the pleasure of listening. And by the time each one of you will have told his or her little tale, the sun will be setting, the heat will have abated, and we will be able to go and amuse ourselves wherever you choose. Now, if you like what I am proposing, let us put it into effect, but if you dislike it, since my only desire is to carry out your wishes, let us all go and spend our time doing whatever we please until the hour of vespers."

The entire company, the ladies and the young men alike, praised the idea of telling stories.

"Then, if that is your pleasure," said the Queen, "my wish is that, on this first day, we should all be free to speak on whatever topic each of us finds most agreeable."

Turning to Panfilo, who was seated to her right, the Queen graciously asked him to start things off with one of his stories. Upon hearing her command, Panfilo responded with alacrity, and as all the others listened, he began speaking as follows.

Day 1, Story 1

Ser Cepparello deceives a holy friar with a false confession and dies, and although he was one of the worst of men during his life, he is reputed after his death to be a saint and is called Saint Ciappelletto.[1]

Dearest ladies, it is fitting that everything man does should take as its origin the wonderful and holy name of Him who was the maker of all things. Thus, since I am the first and must begin our story-telling, I intend to start off with one of His marvelous works so that, once you have heard it, our hope in Him, as in that which is immutable, will be strengthened, and we will forever praise His name. Now, it is clear that the things of this world are all transitory and fading, so that both in themselves and in what they give rise to, they are filled with suffering, anguish, and toil, as well as being subject to countless dangers. We, who live in the midst of these things and are a part of them, would certainly not be able to resist and defend ourselves against them, if the special grace of God did not lend us strength and discernment. It is wrong to believe that this grace descends to us and enters us because of any merit of our own. Rather, it is sent by His loving kindness and is obtained through the prayers of those who, though mortal like us, truly followed His will while they were alive and now enjoy eternal bliss with Him. To them, as to advocates informed by experience of our frailty, we offer up prayers about our concerns, perhaps because we do not dare to present them personally before the sight of so great a judge. And yet in Him, who is generous and filled with pity for us, we perceive something more. Although human sight is not sharp enough to penetrate the secrets of the divine mind in any way, it sometimes happens that we are deceived by popular opinion into making someone

our advocate before Him in all His majesty whom He has cast into
eternal exile. And yet He, from whom nothing is hidden, pays more
attention to the purity of the supplicant than to his ignorance or to
the damned state of his intercessor, listening to those who pray as if
their advocate were actually blessed in His sight. All of this will appear
clearly in the tale I intend to tell—clearly, I say, not in keeping with
the judgment of God, but with that of men.

The story is told that Musciatto Franzesi, an extremely rich and celebrated merchant in France, who had been made a knight, was once
supposed to move to Tuscany with Lord Charles Sans Terre, the King
of France's brother, whom Pope Boniface had sent for and was encouraging to come.[2] Musciatto recognized that his affairs, as those of merchants often are, were tangled up here and there and could not be put
right quickly and easily, but he thought of a number of different people
to whom he could entrust them and thus found a way to take care of
everything. There was, however, one exception. He was unsure whom he
could leave behind to recover the loans he had made to quite a few people
in Burgundy. The reason for his uncertainty was that he had heard the
Burgundians were a quarrelsome lot, evil by nature and untrustworthy,
and he could think of no one he could rely on who would be sufficiently
wicked that his wickedness would match theirs. After he had given the
matter a great deal of thought, there came to mind a certain Ser Cepparello da Prato, who was often a guest in his house in Paris.[3] Because
the man was small of stature and dressed like a dandy, the French, not
knowing what "Cepparello" signified and thinking it meant "hat," that is,
"garland," in their language, called him, because he was small as we have
said, not Ciappello, but Ciappelletto. And so, he was called Ciappelletto
everywhere, while only a select few knew he was really Ser Cepparello.*

* Cepparello's first name is the diminutive (-ello) of Ciapo, short for Jacopo (James),
although Boccaccio plays with the fact that ceppo meant "log" or "stump." "Cepparello"
could thus be translated as "Little Log." The French-speaking Burgundians mistake his
name, thinking it sounds like their word for hat or garland, chapelet, and transform
it into the half-French, half-Italian Ciappelletto, "Little Garland." In the course of the
fourteenth century, chapelet also acquired the meaning of "rosary," so his name could
also mean "Little Rosary."

Let me tell you about the kind of life this Ciappelletto led. A notary, he would feel the greatest shame if even one of the very few legal documents he drew up was found to be other than false. He had composed as many of these phony ones as people requested, and he did so for free more willingly than someone else would have done for a sizable payment. Furthermore, he supplied false testimony with the greatest delight, whether it was asked for or not, and since people in France in those days placed the greatest trust in oaths, and since he did not care if his were false, he won a great many law cases through his wickedness whenever he was asked to swear upon his oath to tell the truth. Because it gave him real pleasure, he went to great lengths to stir up bad feelings, hatred, and scandals among friends and relations and everyone else, and the greater the evils he saw arise as a result, the greater his happiness. Invited to be an accomplice in a murder or some other criminal act, he would never refuse to go. Indeed, he would do so with a ready will and often found himself happily wounding or killing men with his own hands. He was the greatest blasphemer of God and the Saints, and since he would do so at the slightest provocation, he came off as the most irascible man alive. He never went to church and used abominable words to mock all its sacraments as being beneath contempt. On the other hand, he happily spent time in taverns and frequented other places of ill repute. Of women, he was as fond as dogs are of being beaten with a stick, and he took more delight in their opposite than any degenerate ever did. He would rob and steal with a conscience like that of a holy man giving alms. He was a total glutton and a great drinker, so much so that sometimes it would make him disgustingly ill. Plus, he was a devout cardsharp and gambled with loaded dice. But why do I lavish so many words on him? He was perhaps the worst man who had ever been born. For a long time his wickedness had preserved the wealth and rank of Messer Musciatto who often protected him from both private persons, who were frequently the victims of his abuse, and from the courts, which always were.

Thus, when this Ser Cepparello crossed the mind of Messer Musciatto, who was well acquainted with his life, he thought to himself that this would be just the man he needed to deal with the wickedness of the Burgundians. He therefore had Ciappelletto sent for and spoke to him as follows:

"Ser Ciappelletto, as you know, I am about to leave here for good, and since, among others, I have to deal with the Burgundians, who are full of tricks, I know of no one more qualified than you to recover my money from them. Since you're not doing anything at present, if you take care of this business for me, I intend to obtain the favor of the court for you here and to award you a fair portion of what you recover."

Ser Ciappelletto, who was indeed unemployed and in short supply of worldly goods, saw the man who had long been his refuge and defense about to depart, and so, without a moment's hesitation, constrained, as it were, by necessity, he made up his mind and said he would be more than willing to do what Musciatto wanted. The two of them then worked out the details of their agreement, and Ser Ciappelletto received Musciatto's power of attorney as well as letters of introduction from the King. Soon after Messer Musciatto's departure, Ciappelletto went off to Burgundy, where almost no one knew him. There, in a kind and gentle manner quite beyond his nature, as though he were holding back his wrath till the end, he began recovering Musciatto's money and taking care of what he had been sent to do.

Before long, while he was lodging in the house of two Florentine brothers who lent money at interest and who treated him with great respect out of love for Messer Musciatto, he happened to fall ill. The two brothers immediately sent for doctors and servants to take care of him and to provide him with everything he might need to recover his health. All their help was in vain, however, for, in the opinion of the doctors, the good man, who was already old and had lived a disorderly life, was going from bad to worse every day, as people did who had a fatal illness. The two brothers were very upset about this, and one day, right next to the bedroom in which Ser Ciappelletto lay sick, they began talking together.

"What are we going to do about this guy?" said the one of them to the other. "We've got a terrible mess on our hands on account of him, because if we kick him out of our house, as sick as he is, people would condemn us for doing it. Plus, they'd really think we're stupid since we didn't just take him in at first, but also went to great lengths to find servants and doctors for him, and now, although he couldn't have done anything to offend us, they see him suddenly kicked out of our house when he's deathly ill. On the other hand, he's been such a bad man that he won't want to make his confession or receive any of the sacraments of the Church, and if he dies without confession, no church will want to receive his body, and they'll wind up tossing him into some garbage pit like a dog.⁴ But if he goes ahead and makes his confession, the same thing will happen. Since his sins are so many and so horrible, no friar or priest will be willing or able to absolve him, and so, without absolution, he'll be tossed into a garbage pit just the same. And when that happens, the people of this town—both because of our profession, which they think is truly wicked and which they bad-mouth all day long, and because of their desire to rob us—well, they'll rise up and riot when they see it. And as they come running to our house, they'll be screaming, 'These Lombard dogs that the Church refuses to accept, we won't put up with them any longer!' And maybe they won't just steal our stuff, but on top of that, they'll take our lives. So, no matter how things work out, it'll be bad for us if this guy dies."

Ser Ciappelletto, who, as we said, was lying close to where they were talking, and whose hearing was sharp, as it often is in those who are sick, caught every word they were saying about him and reacted by sending for them to come to him.

"I don't want you to fear anything on my account," he told them, "or to be afraid you'll be harmed because of me. I heard what you were saying about me, and I'm very sure that the outcome will be exactly what you've predicted if things happen the way you've been imagining them. However, it's all going to turn out differently. I've done the Lord God so many injuries during my lifetime that doing Him one more at the hour of my death won't make a difference to Him one way or the other. So go and arrange for the holiest and worthiest friar you can find to come to me—if such a one exists—and leave everything to me, for I'm sure I can set both your affairs and my own in order so that all will be well and you'll be satisfied with the result."

Although the two brothers didn't derive much hope from this, they nevertheless went off to a monastery and asked for a wise and holy man to hear the confession of a Lombard who was sick in their house. They were assigned an elderly friar, a grand master of the Scriptures, who had lived a good and holy life and was a very venerable figure toward whom all the townspeople felt an immense special devotion, and they took this man back home with them.

When the friar reached the bedroom where Ser Ciappelletto was lying, he seated himself beside the sick man, and after speaking some words of comfort, asked him how much time had passed since he had made his last confession. Ser Ciappelletto, who had never been to confession, replied to him: "Father, it used to be my custom to go to confession at least once a week, without counting the many weeks in which I went more often. Since I've been sick for about a week now, the truth is that the suffering I've endured from my illness has been so great that it has prevented me from going to confession."

"My son," said the friar, "you've done well, and you should continue that practice in the future. Considering how often you've made your confession, I don't think it will be a lot of trouble for me to hear it and to examine you."

"Messer Friar," said Ser Ciappelletto, "don't speak like that. Although I've gone to confession many, many times, I've always had a longing to make a general confession of all the sins I could remember, starting from the day of my birth and coming right down to the present. Therefore, my good father, I beg you to examine me point by point about everything just as if I'd never been to confession. And don't be concerned about me because I'm sick, for I would much rather mortify this flesh of mine than indulge it by doing something that might lead to the perdition of my soul, which my Savior redeemed with His precious blood."[5]

These words pleased the holy man immensely and seemed to him to argue a well-disposed mind. Consequently, after commending Ser Ciappelletto warmly for making frequent confessions, he began by asking him if he had ever committed the sin of lust with a woman.[6]

"Father," Ser Ciappelletto replied with a sigh, "I'm ashamed to tell you the truth on this subject for fear I might be committing the sin of pride."

"Don't be afraid to speak," said the holy friar. "Telling the truth was never a sin either in confession or anywhere else."

"Since you give me such reassurance," said Ser Ciappelletto, "I'll go ahead and tell you: I'm as much a virgin today as when I came forth from my mama's body."

"Oh, God's blessings on you!" said the friar. "What a good man you've been! In fact, by acting as you have, you are all the more meritorious, because, if you had wanted to, you had more freedom to do the opposite than we and others like us do, since we are bound by the vows of religion."

Next, he asked Ciappelletto if he had displeased God through the sin of gluttony. Breathing a heavy sigh, Ser Ciappelletto replied that he had done so many times. For although it was his habit to fast on bread and water at least three days a week, in addition to doing so during the periods of fasting that devout people observed on holy days throughout the year, he had nevertheless drunk that water with as much delight and gusto as any great wine drinker ever drank his wine, and especially if he was exhausted from performing acts of devotion or making a pilgrimage. Moreover, he was often filled with a longing to have those little salads of baby field greens that women fix when they go to the country, and sometimes, as he ate them, doing so seemed better to him than it should have seemed to someone, like himself, who fasted out of piety, which was the precise reason why he was fasting.

"My son," replied the friar, "these sins are natural and quite trivial, so I don't want you to burden your conscience with them any more than necessary. No matter how truly holy a man may be, eating after a long fast and drinking after hard work will always seem good to him."

"Oh, father," said Ser Ciappelletto, "don't say that just to console me. Surely you must realize that I know how every act we perform in the service of God has to be done wholeheartedly and with an unspotted soul, and how anybody who does otherwise is committing a sin."

Feeling quite content, the friar said: "I am overjoyed that you think like this. It pleases me greatly that on this topic your conscience is pure and good. But tell me: have you committed the sin of avarice by desiring more than what was proper or by keeping what you should not have kept?"

"Father," said Ser Ciappelletto, "I don't want you to suspect me of this because I'm living in the house of these usurers. I'm not here to do business. On the contrary, I've come with the intention of admonishing and chastising them and of leading them away from their abominable moneymaking. What is more, I think I would have succeeded if God had not visited this tribulation upon me. Now, you should know that although my father left me a rich man, I gave away the greater part of what he had to charity after his death. Then, however, in order to sustain my life and to be able to aid Christ's poor, I've done a little bit of trading, and in doing so, I did indeed desire to make money. But I've always divided what I earned down the middle with God's poor, devoting my half to my needs, and giving the other half to them, and my Creator has aided me so well in this that my business has continually gotten better and better."

"Well done," said the friar. "But say, how often have you gotten angry?"

"Oh," said Ser Ciappelletto, "that's something, just let me tell you, that's happened to me a lot. For who could restrain himself, seeing the disgusting things men do all day long, neither observing God's commandments, nor fearing His chastisement? There've been many days when I would have preferred to die rather than live to listen to young people swearing and forswearing themselves, and to watch them pursuing vanities, frequenting taverns rather than going to church, and following the ways of the world rather than those of God."

"My son," said the friar, "this is righteous anger, and for my part, I cannot impose any penance on account of it. But was there ever a case in which your anger led you to commit murder or to hurl abuse at anyone or to do them any other sort of injury?"

Ser Ciappelletto answered him: "Alas, sir, how can you, who appear to be a man of God, speak such words? If I'd had even the teeniest little thought about doing any one of the things you've mentioned, do you think I'd believe that God would have shown me so much favor? Those are things that thugs and criminals would do, and whenever I've come upon a person of that sort, I've always said, 'Be gone! And may God convert you.'"

"God bless you, my son!" said the friar. "Now tell me: have you ever borne false witness against anyone or spoken ill of others or taken things from them without their permission?"

"Yes, sir," replied Ser Ciappelletto, "I really have spoken ill of others. Because once I had a neighbor who, without the least justification, was forever beating his wife, and so one time, I criticized him to his wife's family because of the great pity I felt for the wretched creature. Whenever he'd had too much to drink, God alone could tell you how he used to smack her around."

"Well, then," said the friar, "you tell me you've been a merchant. Have you ever deceived anyone, as merchants do?"

"Yes, sir, by gosh," replied Ser Ciappelletto, "but I don't know who he was, except that he was a man who brought me money he owed me for some cloth I'd sold him, and I put it in a box without counting it. Then, a good month later, I discovered that there were four more pennies in it than there should have been. Well, I kept them for an entire year with the intention of returning them to him, but when I never saw him again, I gave them away to charity."

"That was a trifle," said the friar, "and you did well to have acted as you did."

On top of this, the holy friar went on to ask him about many other things and got the same kind of reply in each case. But then, just as he was about to proceed to absolution, Ser Ciappelletto said: "I still have a sin or two more, sir, that I haven't told you about."

The friar asked him what they were, and Ciappelletto replied: "I remember how one Saturday I didn't show proper reverence for the Holy Sabbath because after nones I had my servant sweep the house."[7]

"Oh, my son," said the friar, "that's a trifle."

"No," said Ser Ciappelletto, "don't call it a trifle, for the Sabbath cannot be honored too much, seeing that it was on just such a day our Savior came back to life from the dead."

Then the friar asked: "Have you done anything else?"

"Yes, sir," replied Ser Ciappelletto. "Once, not thinking about what I was doing, I spat in the house of God."

The friar smiled and said: "My son, that's nothing to worry about. We, who are in holy orders, spit there all day long."

"And what you're doing is vile," said Ser Ciappelletto, "for nothing should be kept as clean as the Holy Temple in which we offer sacrifice to God."

In brief, he told the holy friar many things of this sort, until he finally began sighing and then burst into tears—for he was someone who knew only too well how to do this when he wanted to.

"My son," said the holy friar, "what's wrong?"

"Alas, sir," Ser Ciappelletto replied, "there's still one sin of mine remaining that I've never confessed because I feel so much shame in speaking about it. As you can see, every time I remember it, it makes me weep, and I think there can be no doubt that God will never have mercy on me because of it."

"Come on now, son," said the holy friar, "what are you talking about? If all the sins that have ever been committed by all of humanity, or that will be committed by them as long as the world lasts, were united in one single man, and yet he were as penitent and contrite as I see you are, then truly the benignity and mercy of God are so great that if that man were to confess them, he would be forgiven willingly. Therefore, don't be afraid to speak."

Ser Ciappelletto continued to weep violently as he replied: "Alas, father, my sin is so great that I can hardly believe God will ever pardon it unless you use your prayers on my behalf."

"Speak freely," said the friar, "for I promise I'll pray to God for you."

Ser Ciappelletto just kept on crying and refusing to talk about it, and the friar went on encouraging him to speak. Then, after Ser Ciappelletto had kept the friar in suspense with his weeping for a very long time, he heaved a great sigh and said: "Father, since you've promised to pray to God for me, I will tell you about it. You should know that when I was a little boy, I once cursed my mama." And having said this, he started weeping violently all over again.

"Oh, my son," said the friar, "does this seem such a great sin to you? Why, men curse God all day long, and yet He freely pardons anyone who repents of having cursed Him. And you don't think that He will pardon you for this? Don't weep and don't worry, for surely, even if you had been one of those who placed Him on the cross, He would pardon you because of the contrition I see in you."

"Alas, father," replied Ser Ciappelletto, "what are you saying? My sweet mama, who carried me in her body, day and night, for nine months, and who held me in her arms more than a hundred times—I was too wicked when I cursed her! My sin is too great! And if you don't pray to God for me, it will not be forgiven."

When the friar saw that there was nothing left to say to Ser Ciappelletto, he absolved him and gave him his blessing, taking him to be a very holy man, for he fully believed that what Ser Ciappelletto had said was true—and who would not have believed it, seeing a man at the point of death speak like that?

Then, after all this, the friar said to him: "Ser Ciappelletto, with the help of God you'll soon be well, but if it should happen that God calls that blessed, well-disposed soul of yours to Him, would you like to have your body buried at our monastery?"

"Yes, sir," replied Ser Ciappelletto. "In fact, I wouldn't want to be anywhere else, since you've promised to pray to God for me, not to mention the fact that I have always been especially devoted to your order. Therefore, when you return to your monastery, I beg you to have them send me that most true body of Christ that you consecrate upon the altar every morning, for, although I'm unworthy of it, I would like, with your permission, to partake of it, and afterward, to receive Holy Extreme Unction so that if I have lived a sinner, at least I may die a Christian."*

The holy man said he was greatly pleased that Ser Ciappelletto had spoken so well, and told him that he would arrange for the Host to be brought to him right away. And so it was.

---

*The "body of Christ" is the Host, the bread that is eaten during Communion. Extreme Unction is a sacrament of the Catholic Church administered to those who are on their deathbed.

The two brothers, who were afraid that Ser Ciappelletto was going to deceive them, had placed themselves near a partition that divided the room where he was lying from the one they were in, and as they eavesdropped, they were able to understand everything he said to the friar. Upon hearing him confess the things he had done, they sometimes had such a desire to laugh that they almost burst, and from time to time they would say to one another: "What kind of man is this, whom neither old age, nor sickness, nor the fear of death, which is imminent, nor the fear of God, before whose judgment he must stand in just a short while, could induce him to give up his wickedness and want to die any differently than he lived?" But, seeing as how he had spoken in such a way that he would be received for burial in a church, everything else was of no consequence to them.

A little later Ser Ciappelletto took Communion, and as his condition was rapidly deteriorating, he received Extreme Unction and then died just a little after vespers of the day on which he had made his good confession. Using Ser Ciappelletto's own money, the two brothers took care of all the arrangements necessary for him to be given an honorable burial, and sent word to the friars' house that they should come in the evening to perform the customary wake and take away the body in the morning.

The holy friar who had confessed Ser Ciappelletto, having heard that he had passed away, came to an understanding with the Prior of the monastery, and after the chapterhouse bell had been rung and the friars were gathered together, he explained to them how Ser Ciappelletto had been a holy man, according to what he had deduced from the confession he had heard. And in the hope that the Lord God was going to perform many miracles through Ser Ciappelletto, he persuaded the others to receive the body with the greatest reverence and devotion. The credulous Prior and the other friars agreed to this plan, and in the evening they all went to the room where Ser Ciappelletto's body was laid and held a great and solemn vigil over it. Then, in the morning, they got dressed in their surplices and copes, and with their books in their hands and the cross before them, they went for the body, chanting along the way, after which they carried it to their church with the greatest ceremony and solemnity, followed by almost all the people of the city, men and women alike. Once the body had been placed in the church, the holy friar who had confessed Ser Ciappelletto mounted the pulpit and began to preach marvelous things about him, about his life, his fasts, his virginity, his simplicity and innocence and sanctity, recounting, among other things, what he had confessed to him in tears as his greatest sin, and how he had scarcely been able to get it into his head that God would forgive him for it. After this, the holy friar took the opportunity to reprimand the people who were listening. "And you, wretched sinners," he said, "for every blade of straw your feet trip over, you blaspheme against God and His Mother and all the Saints in Paradise."

Besides this, the holy friar said many other things about Ser Ciappelletto's faith and purity, so that in short, by means of his words, which the people of the countryside believed absolutely, he managed to plant the image of Ser Ciappelletto so deeply inside the minds and hearts of everyone present that when the service was over, there was a huge stampede as the people rushed forward to kiss Ser Ciappelletto's hands and feet. They tore off all the clothing he had on, each one thinking himself blessed if he just got a little piece of it. Furthermore, the body had to be kept there all day long so that everyone could come to see him. Finally, when night fell, he was given an honorable burial in a marble tomb located in one of the chapels. The next day people immediately began going there to light candles and pray to him, and later they made vows to him and hung up ex-votos of wax in fulfillment of the promises they had made.* So great did the fame of Ciappelletto's holiness and the people's devotion to him grow that there was almost no one in some sort of difficulty who did not make a vow to him rather than to some other saint. In the end, they called him Saint Ciappelletto, as they still do, and claim that God has performed many miracles through him and will perform them every day for those who devoutly entrust themselves to him.

---

*An ex-voto is a votive offering (the phrase means "out of or because of a vow" in Latin).

Thus lived and died Ser Cepparello da Prato who, as you have heard, became a saint.[8] Nor do I wish to deny the possibility that he sits among the Blessed in the presence of God. For although his life was wicked and depraved, it is possible that at the very point of death he became so contrite that God took pity on him and accepted him into His kingdom. However, since this is hidden from us, what I will say in this case, on the basis of appearances, is that he is more likely in the hands of the Devil down in Hell than up there in Paradise. And if that is so, then we may recognize how very great God's loving kindness is toward us, in that He does not consider our sinfulness, but the purity of our faith, and even though we make our intercessor one of His enemies, thinking him His friend, God still grants our prayers as if we were asking a true saint to obtain His grace for us. And therefore, so that all of us in this merry company may, by His grace, be kept safe and sound during our present troubles, let us praise His name, which is what we began with, and venerate Him, commending ourselves to Him in our need, in the certain knowledge that we will be heard.

And at this point he fell silent.[9]

Day 1, Story 2

Abraham the Jew, urged on by Giannotto di Civignì, goes to the court of Rome, and after having seen the wickedness of the clergy, returns to Paris and becomes a Christian.[1]

The ladies laughed at parts of Panfilo's story while praising it in its entirety. They had given it their full attention, and once it came to an end, the Queen commanded Neifile, who was sitting next to Panfilo, to continue the order of the entertainment they had begun by telling a story of her own. Being no less endowed with courtly manners than beauty, Neifile replied gaily that she would do so with pleasure and began in this fashion:

In his storytelling Panfilo has shown us how the benevolence of God disregards our errors when they result from something we cannot understand, and in mine, I intend to show you how this same benevolence gives proof of its infallible truth by patiently enduring the faults of those who, although they ought to serve as true witnesses to it in both word and deed, do just the opposite. And I tell it in the hope that we will all put what we believe into practice with greater conviction.

I have heard it said, gracious ladies, that in Paris there once lived a great merchant, a good man named Giannotto di Civignì. Extremely honest and upright, he ran a flourishing cloth business and had the greatest friendship with a very rich Jew named Abraham who was likewise a merchant and an extremely upright and honest man.[2] Recognizing Abraham's honesty and upright character, Giannotto began to feel deep regret that the soul of such a worthy man, who was as good as he was wise, should go to perdition because of his lack of faith. And so, he started pleading with Abraham in an amiable manner to leave behind the errors of the Jewish faith and convert to the Christian truth, which, as something good and holy, was always prospering and increasing, as Abraham could see for himself, whereas clearly his own religion, by contrast, was on the decline and would come to nothing.

The Jew replied that he believed no faith to be either good or holy except the Jewish one, that having been born into it, he intended to live and die in it, and that nothing would ever make him abandon it. Nevertheless, Giannotto did not give up, and a few days later he addressed similar words to Abraham, speaking to him bluntly, as most merchants know how to do, and demonstrating to him how our faith is better than the Jewish one. Although the Jew was a grand master of the Jewish law, he actually began to find Giannotto's arguments compelling, either because he was moved by his great friendship with Giannotto, or perhaps because of the words that the Holy Spirit put into the mouth of that simple man. Still, however, the Jew clung stubbornly to his faith and would not allow himself to be converted.

The more obstinate he remained, the more Giannotto continued to entreat him, until the Jew was finally overcome by his continual insistence. "Look here, Giannotto," he said, "you'd like me to become a Christian. Well, I'm willing to do so, but on one condition: first, I want to go to Rome to see the man who you say is the Vicar of God on earth and to observe his life and habits, and likewise those of his brothers, the cardinals.[3] Then, if they seem to me to be such men that, between what you've said and what I'm able to observe about them for myself, I can see that your faith is better than mine—which is what you've been trying so hard to show me—I'll do what I've promised you. But if things should turn out differently, I'll remain the Jew that I am."

When Giannotto heard this, he was stricken with a deep sadness. "I've lost all the pains that I thought were so well taken," he said to himself. "I think I've converted him, and yet, if he goes to the court of Rome and sees the wicked and filthy lives of the clergy, not only won't he change from a Jew into a Christian, but if he had already become a Christian, he would, without fail, go back to being a Jew again."

Then, turning to Abraham, he said: "Come on, my friend, why do you want to go to all the trouble and expense you'll have in traveling from here to Rome? Not to mention the fact that both by sea and by land, the journey is filled with dangers for a rich man like you. Don't you think you'll find someone here to baptize you? And if, perhaps, you have doubts about the faith that I've explained to you, where are there more teachers and more learned men than right here who can answer your questions and tell you what you want to know?⁴ Therefore, in my opinion, your trip is unnecessary. Remember that the prelates there are just like the ones you've seen here over the years, although those there are admittedly better insofar as they are closer to the Chief Shepherd. So, my counsel is that you should save your energy now, and at some other time you should go on a pilgrimage to seek an indulgence, when I, perhaps, will be able to keep you company."

"Giannotto," the Jew replied, "I do believe everything you've been saying is true, but to sum it all up in a word: if you want me to do what you've begged me to do so often, I absolutely must go there. Otherwise, I shall do nothing about it."

Seeing his determination, Giannotto said: "Go, then, and good luck to you!" Meanwhile, he thought to himself that Abraham would never want to become a Christian once he had seen the court of Rome, but since there was nothing to be lost if he went there, Giannotto stopped arguing.⁵

Mounting his horse, the Jew set off as quickly as he could for the court of Rome, where, upon his arrival, he was given an honorable reception by his Jewish friends. He settled in, and without telling anyone why he had come, he began carefully scrutinizing the behavior of the Pope, the cardinals, the other prelates, and all their courtiers. Between what he himself observed—for he was a keenly perceptive man—and the information he obtained from others, he discovered that from the highest to the lowest, all of the clergy, unrestrained by any sense of shame or remorse, committed the sin of lust in great wickedness, and not just the natural variety, but also the sodomitical, such that the influence of whores and boys was of no little importance in obtaining great favors from them. Besides this, he saw clearly that the clergy were all gluttons, drunks, and sots, who, like brute beasts, served their bellies more than anything else except for their lust. On closer inspection, he also discovered that they were all so avaricious and moneygrubbing that they would as readily buy and sell human blood, that is to say the blood of Christians, as they would sacred objects, whether the sacraments or benefices were involved. In these matters they did more business and employed more middlemen than could be found in any Paris market, including that of the cloth trade. They gave the name of "procurement" to their buying and selling of Church offices, and of "daily rations" to their gluttony, as if, no matter what their words actually referred to, God could not understand the intentions in their wicked hearts, and would allow Himself to be deceived, just as men are, by the names that are given to things.[6] These failings, together with many others it is best to pass over in silence, were highly displeasing to the Jew, who was a sober and temperate man. When he finally felt that he had seen enough, he decided to return to Paris, which is just what he did.

Upon learning that Abraham had returned, Giannotto came to see him, thinking nothing less likely than that he had turned Christian. The two men greeted one another with the greatest warmth, and then, after letting him have a few days to rest, Giannotto asked him what he thought about the Holy Father and the cardinals and the other courtiers.

"I think they're a curse—which is what I wish God would pronounce on all of them!" the Jew promptly replied. "I'm telling you this, because, if I'm any kind of judge, I saw no holiness there, no devotion, no good works or models of life—or of anything else—in any member of the clergy. Instead, it seemed to me that lust, avarice, gluttony, fraud, envy, pride, and the like, and worse, if anything worse is possible, had such power over everyone that I consider the place a forge of diabolical works rather than divine ones. The way it looks to me, your Shepherd, and all of the others, too, are only interested in reducing the Christian religion to nothing and use all their wits and all their skill to drive it from the world, just when they should be serving as its foundation and support. Still, since I see that what they are trying to do hasn't happened, and the fact is that your religion is constantly growing and becoming more resplendent and illustrious, I think I'm right to conclude that the Holy

Spirit must indeed be its foundation and support, for it is truer and holier than any other.[7] Therefore, whereas I used to stand firm and unyielding against all your entreaties, refusing to become a Christian, now I tell you frankly that I wouldn't let anything get in the way of my becoming one. So, let's go to church, and there I'll have myself baptized according to the customary rites of your holy faith."

When Giannotto, who was expecting precisely the opposite conclusion, heard him say this, he was the happiest man there ever was, and off he went together with Abraham to Notre Dame de Paris where he asked the priests to baptize his friend. Once they learned that Abraham himself wanted it done, they performed the ceremony right away, and as Giannotto raised him from the sacred font, he named him Giovanni.* Giannotto then had the most learned men instruct him thoroughly about our faith, which he quickly mastered, and from that time on, Giovanni was not just a good and worthy man, but one who lived a holy life as well.

---

*By lifting Abraham up from the baptismal font and naming him Giovanni, Giannotto is acting as his godfather.

Day 1, Story 3

Melchisedech the Jew uses a story about three rings to avoid a very dangerous trap set for him by Saladin.[1]

After Neifile had fallen silent and everyone had finished praising her story, Filomena, at the Queen's command, began to speak as follows:

The story told by Neifile calls to mind one about the dangerous straits that a Jew once found himself in. Since we have already spoken quite well about God and the truth of our faith, no one should object if at this point we descend to worldly events and the deeds of men. Once you have heard the story I am going to tell you, perhaps you will become more cautious in responding to questions that are put to you.

It is a fact, my dear companions, that just as stupidity will often take a person from a state of happiness and cast him into the greatest misery, so intelligence will extricate him from the gravest dangers and lead him to a state of peace and perfect security. Now, it is so clear that stupidity leads people from happiness into misery that I feel no need to demonstrate the truth of that notion by means of a tale, especially since you can easily find a thousand examples of it every day. Instead, as I promised, by means of a little story, I will show you in brief how intelligence can be our salvation.

Although Saladin's talents were so great that they enabled him to rise from humble beginnings and become the Sultan of Babylon,* while helping him gain many victories over both Saracen and Christian kings, on one occasion he discovered himself in need of a large sum of money,

---

*Babylon: the medieval name for Cairo.

43

for his entire treasury had been used up in his wars and grand displays of munificence. Unable to see where he could get such a sum in short order, he happened to recall a rich Jew named Melchisedech who had a money-lending business in Alexandria.[2] Saladin thought this man might just be of service to him if he were willing to provide the money, but the Jew was so miserly he would never do so of his own free will, and Saladin was reluctant to use force. Since his needs were pressing, however, he racked his brains to find a way to get the Jew to be of service and finally decided to use force, but force disguised as reason.

Saladin sent for Melchisedech, and after having received him in an amicable manner, had the Jew sit down beside him. "You're a worthy man," said Saladin, "and many people have told me about your great wisdom and your deep knowledge of the ways of God. Consequently, I would gladly learn from you which of the three laws—the Jewish, the Saracen, or the Christian—you think to be the true one."

The Jew, who really was a wise man, knew only too well that Saladin was looking to catch him making some verbal slip in order to pick a quarrel with him, and he realized that if he praised one of the three more than the other two, he would enable Saladin to achieve his goal. Therefore, knowing that he needed a response that would enable him to avoid being caught, Melchisedech sharpened his wits, and in no time at all came up with just what he needed to say.

"My lord," he replied, "the question you've put to me is a beauty. However, if I'm to reveal to you what I think about it, I must first ask you to listen to the little story you're about to hear.

"Unless I'm mistaken, I remember having heard many times about how there was once a great and wealthy man who had a very beautiful, precious ring that was among the finest jewels in his treasury. Because of its value and its beauty, he wanted to do it the honor of leaving it in perpetuity to his descendants. Consequently, he announced that he would bequeath it to one of his sons, that whoever was discovered to have the ring in his possession should be considered his heir, and that all the others should honor and respect him as the head of the family.

"The son to whom he left the ring then made a similar arrangement for his descendants, doing exactly what his father had done, and thus the ring was passed down through many succeeding generations, ultimately arriving in the hands of a man who had three handsome, virtuous, very obedient sons, all of whom he loved equally. Since the three young men knew about the tradition of the ring, they were all eager to be singled out as the most honored heir and did their utmost to persuade their father, who was by now an old man, to leave them the ring when he died. The worthy man, who loved all his sons equally and could not make up his mind which one to bequeath it to, decided, after having promised it to each of them, that he would attempt to satisfy all three. Accordingly, he had a master craftsman secretly make two other rings that were so similar to the first that he himself, who had ordered them made, was scarcely able to identify the true one. Then, when he was dying, in private he gave each of his sons a ring of his own.

"After their father's death, they all claimed the inheritance and the title, while denying the claims of their brothers, and each one produced his ring as proof that he was right. But when they found the rings were so similar to one another that they could not tell which was the true one, the question of which son was their father's real heir was left pending. And so it still is to this day.

"Now, I say the same thing, my lord, about the three laws given by God the Father to the three peoples about whom you questioned me. Each one believes itself to be the rightful possessor of His inheritance, His true law, and His commandments, but as with the rings, the question of who is right is still pending."

Realizing that the Jew had cleverly figured out how to avoid the snare that was spread out before his feet, Saladin decided instead to say openly what it was he needed and to see if Melchisedech would be willing to be of service to him. And that is just what he did, while also admitting what he had planned to do if Melchisedech had not responded as discreetly as he had.

Melchisedech willingly gave Saladin every last bit of the money he asked for, which Saladin later paid back in full. What is more, Saladin bestowed the most lavish gifts on Melchisedech, became his lifelong friend, and kept him at his side in a lofty position of honor.

Day 1, Story 4

A monk, having committed a sin deserving the gravest punishment, escapes paying any penalty for it by justly rebuking his Abbot for the same fault.[1]

When she finished her story, Filomena fell silent. Dioneo was sitting next to her, and since he knew from the order they had established that it was his turn, he did not wait for a command from the Queen, but immediately began speaking as follows:

Dear ladies, if I have truly understood your scheme, our purpose here is to amuse ourselves by telling stories. Therefore, as long as we do nothing contrary to this, I think each of us is permitted to do what our Queen has said we could do just a little while ago, namely, to tell whatever stories we think will be the most amusing. Having now heard how Abraham saved his soul through the good advice of Giannotto di Civignì, and how Melchisedech used his wits to defend his wealth from Saladin's snares, I intend, without fear of your censure, to tell a brief tale about how cleverly a monk saved his body from the gravest punishment.[2]

In Lunigiana, a place not very far from here, there was a monastery that once contained more monks, not to mention more holiness, than it does today.[3] In it there was a young monk whose vigor and freshness neither fasts nor vigils were able to diminish. By chance, one day around noon, when all the others were sleeping and the young monk was walking all by himself about the church, which was in a very isolated location, he caught sight of an extremely beautiful young woman. Perhaps the daughter of one of the local laborers, she was going through the fields collecting greens of various sorts, and as soon as he laid eyes on her, he was fiercely assaulted by carnal desire.

The monk approached the girl and struck up a conversation with her. One thing led to another until they reached an understanding, after which, making sure no one noticed them, he took her with him back to his cell. As he was sporting with her, however, he got carried away by his inordinate desire and threw caution to the winds, with the result that the Abbot, who had gotten up from his nap and happened to be walking quietly past the monk's cell, heard the racket they were making together. In order to distinguish their voices better, the Abbot stealthily approached the entrance to the cell where he could listen to them. When he realized there was a woman inside, at first he was tempted to order them to open the door. But then he decided on a different approach, and returning to his room, he waited there for the monk to come out.

Although the monk was busy entertaining himself with the girl, to his very great pleasure and delight, he nevertheless suspected that something was up because he thought he heard the shuffling of feet in the corridor. Putting his eye to a tiny hole in the wall, he looked through it and saw the Abbot as clear as day, standing there listening. He realized that the Abbot must have discovered that the girl was in his cell, and he was, consequently, extremely anxious, afraid that he would be severely punished for what he had done. Without revealing his concern to the girl, he ran over a number of different options in his mind, looking for one that might save him. Suddenly, a new kind of trick occurred to him that would hit the target he was aiming at right in the center.

Pretending that he had had enough fun with the girl, the monk said to her: "I want to go and try to find a way for you to get out of here without being seen. Just stay put and keep quiet till I return." After leaving his cell and locking it behind him, however, he went straight to the Abbot's room and gave him the key, as the monks usually did when they went outside. Then, with a straight face, he said: "Sir, this morning I was not able to bring back all the wood that I had them cut. With your permission, I'd like to go to the forest and have it brought here."

Thinking that the monk did not know that he had been observed, the Abbot rejoiced at this turn of events, because it would give him a chance to inform himself more fully about the sin that the monk had committed. He gladly took the key and at the same time gave the monk permission to go. After watching him leave, the Abbot was faced with the decision of what to do next: whether to open the cell in the presence of all the others and let them see the monk's guilt, so that they would have no reason to grumble when he was punished, or rather, before doing that, to get the girl to give him an account of the affair. On reflecting that she might be a respectable woman or the daughter of some important man, and not wishing to shame such a lady by putting her on display in front of all the monks, he decided first to see who she was and then to make up his mind. He therefore went quietly to the cell, opened the door, and went in, locking the door behind him.

When the girl saw the Abbot, she was scared out of her wits and began crying for shame. Messer Abbot looked her over, and noticing how fresh and beautiful she was, he immediately felt, despite his years, the prickings of the flesh that burned in him as much as in the young monk.[4] "Well, why shouldn't I enjoy myself when I can?" he thought to himself. "After all, sorrow and suffering are always available around here whenever I want them. This gal's a beauty, and nobody really knows she's here. If I can get her to have some fun with me, I don't know why I shouldn't do it. Who is there to know? No one is ever going to find out about it, and 'a sin that's hidden is half forgiven.'[5] Since I may never have such an opportunity again, I think it the part of a wise man to get some benefit from gifts that God has given to others."

After these reflections, he completely changed the purpose he had originally had in going to the cell. Approaching the girl, he asked her not to cry and gently began sweet-talking her. As one word led to another, he managed to convey to her just what it was he wanted, and the girl, who was hardly made of iron or diamond, gave in very easily to his desires. Embracing her and kissing her repeatedly, he climbed into the monk's little bed with her. Then, perhaps out of regard for the heavy burden of his dignity and the tender years of the girl, or perhaps fearing that he might harm her because of his excessive corpulence, he did not get on top of her, but put her on top of him, and for a long time, amused himself with her.

The young monk had only pretended to go to the woods and had

hidden himself instead in the corridor. When he saw the Abbot enter
the cell alone, he felt pretty sure that his plan was going to succeed.
Indeed, when he saw the door being locked, he was absolutely certain
it would. Coming out from his hiding place, he quietly went up to a
hole in the wall through which he could see and hear what the Abbot
was up to.

Meanwhile, the Abbot, having decided that he had been with the
girl long enough, locked her in the cell and returned to his own room.
A bit later he heard the monk, who he thought was coming back from
the woods. In order to keep for himself alone the booty that both of
them had won, the Abbot decided to give the monk a good scolding
and then have him locked up. Accordingly, he had the monk summoned before him, put on a stern face, and after rebuking him severely,
ordered them to put him in prison.[6]

The monk responded with the greatest alacrity: "Master, I've not
yet been in the Order of Saint Benedict long enough to have learned
every particular detail of its rules. Up to now you hadn't shown me
how monks are supposed to support women just as they support fasts
and vigils. But now that you've shown me how, I promise you that if
you pardon me this time, I'll never sin that way again. On the contrary,
I'll always do exactly what I saw you doing."

The Abbot, who was a clever man, knew at once that the monk had
outsmarted him and had seen what he had done, and since he also
felt some degree of remorse because of his own guilt, he was ashamed
to inflict a punishment on the monk that he himself deserved just as
much. Consequently, he pardoned the monk and imposed a vow of
silence on him about what he had seen. Then they got the young girl out
of there quite unobtrusively—but you had better believe that afterward
they frequently had her back in again.

Day 1, Story 5

By means of a banquet consisting entirely of hens, plus a few sprightly little words, the Marchioness of Monferrato curbs the foolish love of the King of France.[1]

As the ladies listened to Dioneo's story, at first it made them feel a twinge of embarrassment, which manifested itself in their faces as a modest blush, but after a while, that was replaced by a malicious grin, and as they glanced back and forth at one another, they were scarcely able to keep from laughing. Nevertheless, once Dioneo had finished, they scolded him with a few gentle little words, making it clear that such stories were not the sort to be told in the presence of ladies. The Queen then turned to Fiammetta, who was seated next to Dioneo on the grass, and told her to take her turn. With a cheerful expression on her face, Fiammetta graciously began:

Whereas in men it is a sign of great wisdom to court women whose social position is higher than their own, women show how very discerning they are by means of their ability to protect themselves from the love of men stationed above them. For this reason, and also because I am quite pleased to see us using our stories to demonstrate the power of prompt and witty retorts, it occurred to me that I could use the story I have to tell in order to show you, lovely ladies, how a noble woman defended herself by both word and deed from that sort of love and dispelled it in her suitor as well.

The Marquis of Monferrato was a very worthy man who, as a Gonfalonier of the Church, had sailed across the seas leading a Christian army on a Crusade.[2] Some time after that, when people were talking one day about his merits at the court of Philippe le Borgne, who was himself preparing to leave France and join the Crusade, a knight remarked that there was no couple beneath the stars like the Marquis and his wife, for just as the Marquis was famed among knights for every virtue, so his wife was considered more beautiful and worthy of more respect than any other woman in the world. These words penetrated the heart of the French King so deeply that without his ever having seen her, he immediately began to love her with a passion, and decided that he would not set sail for the Crusade he was about to go on from any port except Genoa, because in traveling overland to that city he would have an honest excuse for going to see the Marchioness, and with the Marquis out of the way, he thought he would have a good opportunity to satisfy his desires.[3]

The King put his plan into effect, sending his men on ahead and setting out afterward himself with a small retinue, including a few noblemen. As he approached the territory of the Marquis, he sent word to the Marchioness a day in advance that she should expect him for dinner the next morning. Being both wise and prudent, the lady sent back a cheerful reply, saying that this would be an honor beyond any other and that he would be truly welcome. Then, however, she started wondering what it meant that such a great king would come to visit her when her husband was not at home. Nor did she deceive herself when she reached the conclusion that he had been drawn there by her reputation for beauty. Nevertheless, like the worthy woman she was, she prepared to receive him, and after having summoned the gentlemen who still remained in her court, she solicited their advice, after which she gave orders for all the necessary arrangements to be made, at the same time declaring that she would take care of the banquet and the details of the menu by herself. Then, without a moment's hesitation she had all the hens in the countryside rounded up and ordered her cooks to make a series of different dishes out of them for the royal feast.

The King arrived on the appointed day and was honorably and ceremoniously received by the lady. Now that he actually saw her, it seemed to him that her beauty, worth, and refinement went far beyond anything he had imagined on the basis of the knight's words. Awestruck, he complimented her lavishly, for he was even more inflamed with passion on finding that the lady transcended his expectations of her. After a short rest in his chambers, which were richly furnished in a manner appropriate for the reception of so great a king, it was time for dinner, and the King sat down at one table with the Marchioness, while the remaining guests were given seats of honor at the other tables according to their rank.

As he was served an elaborate series of dishes one after the other, all accompanied by the finest, most precious wines, the King gazed contentedly from time to time at the radiantly beautiful Marchioness, which filled him with the most intense pleasure. However, as one course succeeded another, he found himself increasingly baffled by the fact that, however different the preparations were, hens supplied the main ingredient in all of them. The King was well enough acquainted with that region to know that it had to have an abundant supply of game of all sorts, and by announcing his arrival to the lady in advance, he had given her plenty of time to organize a hunt. Nevertheless, although he was truly puzzled, he had no desire to do anything except to get her to say something about her hens. So, with a smile on his face, he turned to her and said: "My lady, are hens alone born in this country, and never any cocks at all?"

The Marchioness, who understood perfectly well what he was asking, realized that God had given her just the opportunity she desired to explain what she intended. Turning boldly to the King, she replied to his question: "No, my lord, although they differ from others somewhat in their rank and style of clothing, for all that, the females here are made the same way they are everywhere else."*

On hearing this, the King understood clearly the reason for the banquet of hens as well as the virtue concealed beneath the Marchioness's words. He realized that persuasion would be wasted on such a woman

---

*The Marchioness's remark needs interpretation. She may be saying that the King should not expect women in Monferrato, and especially her, to be unlike women elsewhere. In other words, they will be faithful to their husbands. There might also be an implied criticism of the King in her choice of "hens" for the banquet. On the equation of hens with women and cocks with men, see the supposedly deaf-mute Masetto's first words to the Abbess near the end of 3.1.

and that force was out of the question. And so, just as he had been foolishly inflamed because of her, he now decided wisely that, for the sake of his honor, his ill-conceived fire had to be extinguished. Fearing her retorts, he refrained from teasing her any further, and with all his hopes dashed, concentrated on eating his dinner. As soon as the meal was finished, in order to cover the dishonorable way he had come by means of a hasty departure, he thanked her for her hospitality, she wished him Godspeed, and off he went to Genoa.

Day 1, Story 6

By means of a fine quip a worthy man confounds the wicked hypocrisy of the religious.[1]

They all praised the Marchioness for her courage and the sprightly rebuke she gave to the King of France. Then, in keeping with the wishes of the Queen, Emilia, who was seated next to Fiammetta, boldly began to speak:

I, too, will not pass over in silence the way a worthy layman taunted an avaricious clergyman with a quip no less amusing than it was commendable.

Not so very long ago, my dear young ladies, there was in our city a Franciscan friar, who was an Inquisitor of Heretical Depravity.[2] Just like all the rest of them, he tried very hard to appear holy and tenderly devoted to the Christian religion, but was really as good an investigator of those whose purses were full as he was of those who were lacking in matters of faith. Thanks to his diligence, he chanced to find out about a good man, who had much more money than sense, and who one day, not because of any defect in his faith, but perhaps because he had become heated by drinking or too much joking around, foolishly remarked to a group of his friends that he had a wine so good that Christ himself would drink it.

When this remark was reported to the Inquisitor, and he found out that the man's estates were large and his purse was bulging, he came down on him *cum gladiis et fustibus** and hastily brought the

---

*"With swords and staves," a phrase from Matthew 26:47 that had become quasi-proverbial.

most serious action against him, thinking that the effect would not be a diminishing of the impiety of the accused so much as a lining of the Inquisitor's own pockets with florins, which is what, in fact, happened. Having issued a summons, the Inquisitor asked the man if the charges against him were true. The good man replied that they were and explained how it had all come about, at which point this most holy Inquisitor, a devotee of Saint John Golden-Beard,* said to him: "So, you've made Christ a drinker, have you, and a connoisseur of fine wines, as if He were Cinciglione or one of your other lushes and drunks and tavern crawlers?[3] And now you speak with humility and want to argue that the matter is completely trivial. But you are mistaken, and you deserve to be burned for it when we decide to take action against you, as we must."

With these words and a host of others, and with the most menacing look on his face, the Inquisitor spoke to the man as if he had been Epicurus himself denying the immortality of the soul.[4] In short, he terrified him so much that the good man was only able to persuade the Inquisitor to treat him with leniency by using certain go-betweens to grease his palms with a goodly amount of the fat of Saint John Golden-Mouth. Although Galen does not discuss such an ointment anywhere in his books on medicine, it is a very effective remedy against the pestilential avarice of the clergy and especially that of the Franciscans, who do not deign to touch money.[5] The man took this extremely efficacious ointment and applied it so generously that the fire he was threatened with was commuted by grace into the mere wearing of a cross as a kind of badge, as if he were about to be sent off on a Crusade. Indeed, to make the badge appear all the more beautiful, the friar ordered it to be yellow on a black background. Moreover, besides pocketing the money,

---

* Saint John Chrysostom (347–407), a Church father and interpreter of the Bible, who was Archbishop of Constantinople, was celebrated for his eloquence; his honorific last name means "golden mouth." However, in Boccaccio's age, the saint's name had become a byword for the avariciousness of the clergy. Since later in the story Boccaccio refers to him as Saint John Golden-Mouth, the reference to him here as Golden-Beard may be a mistake, or it may be a reference to Saint John the Baptist, the protector of Florence, whose bearded image was printed on the (golden) florin.

the friar had the man detained for many days, then ordered him to hear Mass every morning in Santa Croce as penance and to present himself before the friar at the dinner hour, after which he was free to do as he pleased the rest of the day.[6]

The man was performing his penance quite diligently, when one morning at Mass, as the Gospel was being sung, he happened to hear these words, "For every one, you shall receive a hundredfold, and shall inherit everlasting life."[7] With these words firmly implanted in his memory, at the usual hour he went as instructed to the Inquisitor whom he found eating his dinner. The Inquisitor asked him if he had heard Mass that morning, and he promptly replied, "Yes, Monsignor."

"Did you hear anything in it," asked the Inquisitor, "that raised doubts or that you wish to ask a question about?"

"I certainly have no doubts about any of the things I heard," said the good man. "On the contrary, I firmly believe them all to be true. I did hear one thing, though, that made me feel the greatest pity for you and your fellow friars, and I still feel sorry for you when I think about how wretched you're going to be in the next life."

"And what was the passage," asked the Inquisitor, "that moved you to feel pity for us?"

"Monsignor," the good man replied, "it was the passage from the Gospel that says, 'For every one, you shall receive a hundredfold.'"

"That passage is certainly true," said the Inquisitor, "but why did it move you to feel sorry for us?"

"Monsignor," replied the good man, "I will tell you. Every day since I started coming here, I've seen a crowd of poor people outside who were given sometimes one and sometimes two huge cauldrons of broth that you and the friars in this convent send them as leftovers. So, if each of you gets a hundredfold return on what you've given here, you're going to have so much of it up there that you'll all drown in it."[8]

All the others at the Inquisitor's table burst out laughing, but the Inquisitor, on hearing their guzzling hypocrisy rebuked, was furious, and were it not that he had already been discredited for what he had done, he would have come down on the man with another accusation because of the way his amusing quip had ridiculed him and those other lazy rogues. In a rage, then, the Inquisitor ordered the good man to go about his business as he pleased and never appear before him again.

Day 1, Story 7

With a story about Primasso and the Abbot of Cluny, Bergamino justly rebukes Messer Can della Scala for an unexpected fit of avarice.[1]

Emilia's story and her pleasant way of telling it moved the Queen and everyone else to laugh and to commend the original quip thought up by the "crusader." When the laughter subsided and everyone was quiet, Filostrato, whose turn had come to tell a story, began speaking in the following manner:

It is a fine thing, worthy ladies, to hit a target that never moves, but it is quasi-miraculous when some unexpected object appears all of a sudden and an archer hits it in a flash. The vicious and filthy life of the clergy is in many regards just such a fixed target of wickedness, so that it is not especially difficult for anyone so inclined to speak out, attack, and reproach them for it. Therefore, if the good man did well to rebuke the Inquisitor for the hypocritical charity of the friars, because they offered the poor what should have been given to the pigs or just thrown out, then I think the person of whom I shall speak, and of whom I was reminded by the last tale, is worthy of much more praise. For this man rebuked Messer Can della Scala, a great lord, for a sudden and atypical fit of avarice by telling a charming story in which he represented, through its characters, what he wanted to say about himself and his lord.[2] And the story goes as follows.

Practically everyone in the world knows of the great fame of Messer Can della Scala, a man whom Fortune favored in so many ways and who had the reputation of being one of the most distinguished and magnificent lords Italy has seen since the time of the Emperor Frederick II.[3] Messer Cane decided to stage a splendid festival in Verona, one that would be truly memorable, and he invited many people to it from all over, and especially court entertainers of every stripe. However, a sudden whim led him to change his mind, and after partially reimbursing his guests with token gifts, he sent them all away. Only one man remained behind, an entertainer named Bergamino, whose mastery of impromptu, yet polished speech was so impressive that you would only believe it if you heard him talk.[4] Since he had neither received a gift nor been given leave to depart, he hoped that this meant there was still some future benefit in store for him. However, the idea had somehow gotten itself into Messer Cane's head that anything he might give the man would be more surely wasted than if he had thrown it into the fire. Still, Messer Cane did not say anything to Bergamino about this, nor did he have anyone else do so.

After several days, Bergamino began to grow melancholy, for he was not sent for and asked to give a professional performance, and he realized he was using up all of his money just staying at the inn with his servants and horses. Nevertheless, he continued to wait, since it did not seem like a good idea for him to leave. In order to make an honorable appearance at the festival, he had brought with him three beautiful, expensive suits of clothes, which had been given to him by other lords, and since the innkeeper was asking to be paid, Bergamino started out by giving him one of them. Then, as the waiting continued a while longer, he was obliged, if he wanted to keep his room at the inn, to give him the second one. Finally, Bergamino started living off the third suit, having decided to stay until he saw how long it would last him and to go away after that.

Now, while he was consuming his third suit of clothes, he just happened to be standing one day by the table where Messer Cane was eating his dinner. Upon seeing Bergamino with a very melancholy look on his face, Messer Cane said, more to mock him than to be entertained by one of his witty remarks: "Bergamino, what's wrong? You look so melancholy. Tell us about it."

Without reflecting for more than a split second, yet speaking as though he had spent a great deal of time thinking about what he would say, Bergamino told this story, which fit his situation to a tee.

"My lord," he said, "let me begin by telling you about Primasso, a most worthy grammar master who had no equal at composing verse and was able to produce it with greater facility than anyone else.[5] His talents had made him so respected and so famous that even where he was not known by sight, there was almost no one who did not know him by name and reputation.

"Now it happened that one day when Primasso was in Paris, living in poverty—indeed, most of the time his livelihood depended on a talent that was little appreciated by those who had the means to help him— he heard mention of the Abbot of Cluny, a man who was thought to have so much income from his estates that he was the richest prelate, except for the Pope, in God's Church.[6] He heard people saying marvelous, magnificent things about the Abbot, such as how he was always holding court and how no one who went there was ever denied food and drink, provided he asked for them while the Abbot himself was dining.

"When Primasso heard these things, being a man who enjoyed associating with gentlemen and lords, he decided to go and see just how magnificent a lifestyle this Abbot had. He asked how far away the Abbot's residence was from Paris, and on being told that it was a distance of perhaps six miles, he calculated that he could get there by the dinner hour if he set out early in the morning. He was shown which road to take, but when he couldn't find anyone going in that direction, he was afraid that he might have the bad luck to get lost and wind up in a place where it would be difficult to find something to eat. Therefore, to be on the safe side, he decided to make sure he wouldn't lack for food by taking three loaves of bread with him, being convinced at the same time that he would always be able to find water to drink, even though it was not something he especially cared for.[7]

"Tucking the three loaves into his shirt, he started on his journey and made such progress that he arrived at the Abbot's residence before the dinner hour. Once inside, he went about inspecting everything, and when he discovered that a very large number of tables had been set, great preparations were under way in the kitchen, and many other things were being made ready for the meal, he said to himself: 'Truly, this man is as magnificent as people say he is.' For a while he just stood

there, watching intently everything that was going on, until it was time
to eat, at which point the Abbot's steward ordered water for all of them
to wash their hands and then seated them at the tables.

"By chance, Primasso was given a seat right opposite the doorway
through which the Abbot would pass when he entered the dining room.
They had a custom in his court of never putting wine or bread or anything else to eat or drink on the tables before the Abbot himself had
come in and sat down. Thus, when the tables were set, the steward sent
word to the Abbot, informing him that the food was ready and he could
come whenever he pleased. The Abbot had a servant open the door
so that he could enter the room, and as he walked in, looking straight
ahead of him, the very first man his eyes happened to light on was the
shabbily dressed Primasso, whom he did not recognize by sight. As he
stared at Primasso, a mean thought suddenly popped into his head,
the kind of thought he had never had before, and he said to himself:
'Just look at the guy I'm giving my food to!' Then, turning on his heels,
he ordered his servants to shut the door behind him, after which he
asked them if anyone recognized the ragamuffin who was seated at
the table directly opposite the entrance to the room. None of them,
however, knew who the man was.

"Primasso had worked up quite an appetite because of his walk, and
he wasn't in the habit of fasting, so after waiting a bit and seeing no sign
of the Abbot coming back, he took one of the three loaves he'd carried
with him out of his shirt and began to eat it. Meanwhile, the Abbot,
who had paused a moment, ordered one of his servants to go and see if
Primasso had left. The servant replied, 'No, sir. On the contrary, he's
eating some bread that he must have brought with him.' 'Well,' said the
Abbot, 'let him eat his own food, if he's got any, because he's not going
to eat any of ours today.'

"The Abbot would have preferred to have Primasso leave of his own
accord, for it seemed discourteous to send him away. By this time, Primasso had finished the first loaf, and there being no sign of the Abbot,
began to eat the second. This fact was likewise reported to the Abbot
who had sent a servant to see if the man had left. Finally, when the
Abbot still did not come, Primasso, who had polished off the second

loaf, started on the third. This fact was also reported to the Abbot, who, after pondering what it meant, said to himself, 'Now what's this strange thing that's gotten into me today? Why am I being such a miser? Why do I feel all this contempt? And for whom? I've given my food to anyone who wanted it for many years now without asking if he was a gentleman or a peasant, rich or poor, merchant or huckster. With my own eyes, I've seen any number of tramps devouring my food, and never once did I feel the way I do about this one. Since I would never have been afflicted with such stinginess by a man of no moment, this one, whom I've been regarding as a good-for-nothing, must really be somebody, for me to have set my heart against offering him my hospitality.'

"After these reflections, the Abbot really wanted to find out who the man might be, and when he discovered it was Primasso, who had come to see if what he had heard about the Abbot's magnificence were true, he felt a deep sense of shame, for he had long been aware of Primasso's reputation as a worthy man. Desirous of making amends, the Abbot contrived all sorts of ways to honor him, and after a dinner in keeping with Primasso's merits, he had him outfitted like a gentleman, provided him with money and a saddle horse, and told him he was free to come and go as he pleased.[8] More than satisfied, Primasso gave the Abbot the most heartfelt thanks, after which he returned to Paris on horseback, from which he had come on foot."

Messer Cane, a most perceptive lord, did not need an explanation to grasp what Bergamino meant, and with a broad smile said to him: "Bergamino, you've given an apt demonstration of the wrongs you've suffered, while at the same time showing us your virtues, my miserliness, and what it is you want from me. Honestly, never before have I been afflicted with the avarice I felt today on your account, but I will beat it away, using the stick you yourself have provided." Then, having paid off the innkeeper, Messer Cane had Bergamino dressed most nobly in one of his own suits of clothes, provided him with money and a saddle horse, and told him he was free to come and go as he pleased for the rest of his stay.

Day 1, Story 8

With sprightly words Guiglielmo Borsiere rebukes the avarice of Messer Ermino de' Grimaldi.[1]

Because she was sitting next to Filostrato, Lauretta knew it was her turn, and when everyone had finished praising Bergamino's resourcefulness, she did not wait for the Queen's command to speak, but gracefully began as follows:

The preceding story, my dear companions, prompts me to tell you how, in a similar way and with equally fruitful results, a worthy court entertainer attacked the cupidity of a very rich merchant. Although the gist of my story resembles that of the last one, that is no reason for you to find it less pleasing, especially considering the good that came out of it in the end.

In Genoa, quite some time ago, there lived a gentleman named Messer Ermino de' Grimaldi, whose was reputed by everyone, because of his immense wealth and enormous estates, to be the richest citizen in the Italy of his day. And just as he exceeded every other Italian in wealth, so in his avarice and stinginess he surpassed by far every other greedy, miserly person in the world. For not only did he keep his purse shut tight when it came to entertaining others, but also, contrary to the Genoese custom of dressing in style, he endured the greatest privations in order to spare himself any expense as far as his own person was concerned. Nor was he any different when it came to food and drink. Consequently, he lost the surname of Grimaldi, and everybody simply called him Ermino Miser instead.

In those days, while this man, who refused to spend money, was working away to increase his fortune, there arrived in Genoa a worthy court entertainer, a well-spoken man with elegant manners whose name was Guiglielmo Borsiere and who did not in the least resemble his present-day counterparts. For to the immense shame of those who nowadays, despite their corrupt and contemptible habits, claim the name and title of gentlemen and lords, these court entertainers of ours look more like asses who have not been brought up at court, but among the filthiest, scummiest, and vilest of men. In those days, it used to be their function, something to which they devoted all their energy, to make peace where quarrels or disputes had arisen among gentlemen, to arrange marriages, alliances, and friendships, to restore the spirits of the weary and entertain the court with splendid, elegant witticisms, and as fathers do, to criticize the defects of the wicked, all of which they did for the slenderest of rewards. Nowadays, they are determined to spend their time spreading gossip, sowing discord, talking of wicked and repulsive things, and what is worse, doing them in the presence of gentlemen. Or else they will accuse one another both justly and unjustly of wicked, shameful, and disgusting deeds, and will use false flattery to entice noble men to do things that are vile and evil. And the man whose words and deeds are the most abominable is the one who is held in the greatest esteem among them and is most honored and richly rewarded by the basest, most dissolute lords. This is the great shame of the modern world and deserves the most severe censure, and it offers us the clearest proof that the virtues have left us wretched mortals down here below, abandoning us to live our lives amid the dregs of vice.

But to return to where I started before my righteous indignation led me further astray than I intended to go, let me say that the Guiglielmo I spoke of was honored upon his arrival and given a warm welcome by all the gentlemen of Genoa. After having been in the city a few days and often heard people talk of Messer Ermino's miserliness and avarice, he was very interested in meeting the man. Messer Ermino had likewise heard about Guiglielmo Borsiere and about how worthy everyone considered him to be, and since he still had within him, despite his greed, a tiny spark of gentility, he received Guiglielmo with friendly words and a cheerful countenance, and then began a conversation with him on a variety of subjects. And as they chatted together, Messer Ermino led him and the other Genoese who were with him to a beautiful new house he had just had built for himself.

After Messer Ermino had shown Guiglielmo all around it, he said: "Well now, Messer Guiglielmo, as someone who's seen and heard a great deal, could you tell me about something that no one has ever seen so that I can have it painted in the great hall of this house of mine?"

After listening to his unseemly words, Guiglielmo replied: "Sir, I don't think I could tell you about anything that has never been seen before, unless it were a fit of sneezing or something like that. However, if you like, I could certainly tell you about something that I don't believe you yourself have ever seen."

"Ah," said Messer Ermino, not expecting the response he was going to get, "I beg you to tell me what that is."

Without skipping a beat, Guiglielmo replied: "Here have them paint Courtesy."*

When Messer Ermino heard that word, he instantly felt such a deep sense of shame that it completely transformed his character, making him into virtually the opposite of what he had been up to that time. "Messer Guiglielmo," he said, "I will have it painted in such a way that neither you nor anyone else will ever again have just cause to tell me that I have not seen and known it."

From that day forward, the word spoken by Guiglielmo had such a powerful effect that Ermino became the most liberal and affable of gentlemen, and for the rest of his life, he entertained foreigners as well as his fellow citizens more honorably than any other man in Genoa.

---

*Guiglielmo says *Cortesia*, which I could have rendered as "Liberality." In Boccaccio's time, however, "Courtesy" was an aristocratic virtue that was assumed to include generosity or liberality as one of its defining features.

Day 1, Story 9

The King of Cyprus, stung to the quick by a lady of Gascony, is transformed from a base coward into a man of courage.[1]

The Queen's final command was reserved for Elissa, who did not wait for it, but began in quite a festive manner:

It has often happened, young ladies, that a single word, frequently uttered spontaneously rather than *ex proposito*,* has managed to transform a person when all kinds of rebukes and frequent punishments could not. This is quite clear from the story told by Lauretta, and I, too, intend to demonstrate it to you by means of another one that is very short. For good stories can always be useful and should be listened to attentively no matter who the teller is.

Let me say, then, that in the time of the first King of Cyprus, after the Holy Land had been conquered by Godfrey of Bouillon, it happened that a noble lady from Gascony went on a pilgrimage to the Sepulcher,† and having arrived in Cyprus on her return journey, was raped there by a band of ruffians. Grieving inconsolably over what had happened, she decided to go and seek redress from the King. She was told, however, that her efforts would be wasted, because he was so fainthearted and of so little account that he not only permitted the wrongs done to others to go unpunished, but the shameful coward also allowed countless wrongs to be done to him. Indeed, if anyone was disgruntled for any reason, he would vent his feelings by insulting or shaming the King.

When the lady heard this, she despaired of being revenged, but then

---

* "On purpose."

† Sepulcher: the Holy Sepulcher, the putative burial place of Christ in Jerusalem.

she decided to console herself for her troubles by going and rebuking the King for his faintheartedness. Presenting herself before him in tears, she said to him:

"My lord, I do not come before you with the expectation of receiving any form of redress for the wrong that has been done to me. But in compensation for my injury, I beg you to teach me how you manage to endure the wrongs that I have been led to understand are done to you, so that I might learn from you how to bear my own with patience. For God knows, if I could, I'd gladly give them all to you, since you're so good at putting up with such things."

The King, who had been slow and dull up until that moment, seemed like a man who had been roused from sleep. The first thing he did was to punish severely the injury done to the lady, and from then on, he prosecuted to the utmost rigor of the law all those who offended in any way the honor of his crown.

Day 1, Story 10

Master Alberto da Bologna justly shames a woman who wanted to make him feel ashamed for loving her.[1]

When Elissa fell silent, the only one left to tell a story was the Queen, and so, with womanly grace, she began speaking as follows:

Worthy young ladies, just as heaven is decorated with stars on cloudless nights, and the green meadows are brightened with flowers in the spring, so good manners and pleasant conversation are adorned with clever quips. These, because they are brief, are much better suited to women than to men, whereas it is much less becoming for the former than the latter to give long, elaborate speeches, when they can be avoided. Yet nowadays, there is hardly a woman left who understands witticisms, or if she manages to do so, knows how to respond to them—a source of universal shame for all of us here and for every woman alive. That virtue was once lodged deep in our souls, but modern women have replaced it with the adorning of the body, so that those whose clothes have more colors and stripes and frills think they should be more highly respected and honored than the rest. They forget that if the only thing of consequence was what one wore or what one had on one's back, then far more could be put on the back of an ass than on any of theirs, and yet, no one would respect it as being anything more than an ass.

I am ashamed to say it, for I cannot condemn others without condemning myself, but these overdressed, dolled-up women in their heavy makeup just stand around like marble statues, mute and insensible, or if someone should happen to ask them a question, they respond in such a way that it would have been much better for them to have remained silent. Nevertheless, they are convinced that their inability to engage in conversation with gentlemen and ladies derives from the purity of their minds, and they have given the name of honesty to their dullness, as though the only honest women were those who speak to no one except their maids, their washerwomen, or their pastry cooks. But surely, if this had been Nature's intention, as they allow themselves to believe it is, Nature would have found some other way to limit their twittering.

In this as in other matters, the truth is that one must take into account the time, the place, and the person with whom one is convers- ing, for it sometimes happens that just when men and women think they will make another person blush by means of some clever little pleasantry, they find that they have not measured the powers of either party adequately, and the blush, which they intended for someone else, winds up on their face instead. Therefore, I want to use this, the last of today's stories, which it now falls to me to tell, in order to teach you how to protect yourselves and keep people from applying the proverb to you that one hears on everyone's lips, namely that in every situa- tion women always make the worst choice. Thus you will be able to show that you are different from other women not only because of your intrinsic nobility, but even more because of the excellence of your manners.

Not many years ago, a very distinguished doctor named Master Alberto, whose fame had spread around much of the world, was liv- ing in Bologna, where he may perhaps still be living today.[2] Although at the time he was an old man close to seventy, his heart was so noble that it could still burn in the flames of love, even though almost all the natural heat in his body was gone. During a festival one day, he saw a stunningly beautiful widow named, according to some, Malgherida dei Ghisolieri. He was instantly drawn to her, and just like a young man, he felt his aged breast burn with such fire that if he did not see the charming, delicate face of that lovely lady during the day, he was unable to get much sleep that night.[3] Consequently, he started spending time around the lady's house, going up and down the street in front of it, sometimes on foot and sometimes on horseback, as the spirit moved him. The lady figured out why he was coming there, as did her many friends and neighbors, and they would often joke among themselves to see a man of such great age and wisdom ensnared by love. It was as if they thought that love, the most delightful of the passions, could find a place to dwell only in the frivolous hearts of the young.

Master Alberto was still regularly passing by the house, when it just so happened on one particular holiday that the lady and her friends were sitting outside her door. Having caught sight of him in the distance coming toward them, they all decided, with the lady's approval, to receive him and entertain him honorably, but then to make fun of him because of this grand passion of his. So, what they did was to get up from their seats and invite him inside the house, leading him into a cool courtyard where they called for sweets and the choicest wines. Then, in the most elegant and politest terms, they asked him how he could have ever fallen in love with this beautiful young lady when he knew she was being courted by so many handsome, wellborn, lively young men.

On hearing himself mocked in so courteous a fashion, the doctor smiled broadly and replied: "My lady, the fact that I am in love should not provoke wonder in anyone who is wise, and especially not in you, considering how worthy you are of being loved. For although Nature deprives older men of the powers that are required for lovemaking, it does not deprive them of a ready will or keep them from understanding what they should love. On the contrary, they naturally know more about that subject since they have much more experience than young men do. Consequently, the hope that sustains an old man like me in loving you, despite your being courted by so many young ones, is something I've had the chance to observe often enough when I've been in places where ladies were making a light meal out of lupines and leeks. Now, although no part of the leek is any good, the part that is less objectionable and more pleasing to the palate is the head, and yet, led by some perverse appetite, you generally hold the head in your hands and eat the leaves, which are not only worthless, but also have an unpleasant taste. So, how am I to know, my lady, whether you don't do the same thing when you choose your lovers? If that's the case, then I'm the one you should choose, and all the others should be tossed away."

The noble lady, who along with the others was feeling rather embarrassed, said: "Master Alberto, you've given us a courteous and very sound reprimand for our presumptuousness. Nevertheless, your love is still very precious to me, as that of a wise and worthy man truly ought to be. And therefore, since I am yours, you should feel free, my honor aside, to ask of me whatever you wish."

The doctor then stood up with his companions, thanked her, and after taking his leave amid much laughter and merriment, departed. Thus, the lady, who thought she would gain a victory, underestimated the man she was making fun of and was herself defeated. And you, if you are wise, will be very careful to guard against following her lead.

Day 1, Conclusion

The sun was already sinking as vespers approached, and the heat had largely dissipated, when the young women and the three young men found that their storytelling had come to an end. Accordingly, the Queen addressed them in pleasant tones:

"Now, my dear companions, nothing remains for me to do during my reign today except to present you with a new Queen who will decide how her time and ours should be spent in honest pleasures tomorrow. And although my reign would seem to last until nightfall, I think this is the best hour for us to begin ruling from now on, so that we can make preparations for whatever topic the new Queen thinks appropriate for the next day. After all, those who do not set aside time for things beforehand will not be able to provide adequately for the future.[1] Therefore, in reverence for Him through Whom all things live, and for the sake of your pleasure, I say that the most prudent Filomena shall govern our realm on this, our second day."[2]

When she had finished speaking, she rose to her feet, and taking her garland of laurel, placed it reverently on Filomena, whom she and all the other ladies, and the men as well, hailed as their Queen, after which they happily pledged that they would obey her.

Blushing a bit because of her embarrassment at seeing herself crowned Queen, Filomena remembered the words spoken by Pampinea just a little earlier, and in order not to appear dull, she plucked up her courage and began by confirming the orders Pampinea had given. Then, seeing that they would continue to stay in their present lodging, she made arrangements for what they would eat the next morning as well as for their supper later that day, after which she spoke to them as follows:

"My dear, dear companions, although Pampinea, more out of kindness than because of my merits, has made me Queen over you, I am disinclined to rely on my judgment alone as to how we should spend our time, and instead, want us to make all our decisions together. In order to give you a chance to add things to my plan and to subtract things from it as you wish, let me briefly explain what I think we should do. Now, unless I am mistaken, the formalities observed by Pampinea today seem to me to have been both praiseworthy and delightful, and as long as they do not become tedious, either because we repeat them too often or for some other reason, in my judgment we should not make any changes.

"Given, then, the order that we have already begun to follow, we should get up now and go off in search of ways to amuse ourselves for a while. At about the time the sun is setting, we should eat our supper out of doors, after which we will have a few little songs and other entertainment until it is time for us to go to bed. Tomorrow morning, we will get up while it is still cool, and once again we will all go off and amuse ourselves in whatever ways we think best. Then, just as we did today, we will return at the appointed hour to eat and dance, and after we have arisen from our nap, we will come back here to tell stories, which always, in my opinion, provide us with a great deal of pleasure as well as profit.

"Speaking frankly, I wish to initiate a practice that Pampinea could not introduce because she was elected Queen so late, and that is, I want to restrict within definite limits the subject matter of the stories we are going to tell. This way, because the theme will be announced in advance, each of you will have time to think up a fine story to tell about the topic that has been proposed. And this, if you please, is what it shall be: since from the beginning of time men have been subject to the whims of Fortune, as they will be to the very end, each one of us should speak about people who, after suffering through many misfortunes, arrive at a happy end beyond anything they could have hoped for."

All of them, both the women and the men, praised this arrangement and agreed to abide by it, except for Dioneo, who said, when the rest were silent: "My lady, like everyone else, I, too, say that the order

you have established is quite pleasing and praiseworthy. But I beg you
to grant me a special favor, which I would like to see confirmed for as
long as this company stays together, namely, that if I do not want to
be, I will not be forced by our arrangement to tell a story on the theme
proposed, but can tell one on whatever topic I wish. Moreover, so that
no one thinks I want this favor because I am the kind of person who
does not have a lot of stories at hand, from now on I am willing always
to be the last one to speak."

With the consent of all the others, the Queen happily granted him
his wish, knowing that he was an entertaining and jovial person and
clearly perceiving that he was only asking for such a favor so that, if the
company ever got tired of talking on their chosen theme, he could cheer
them up with a tale that would make them laugh. Then she stood up,
and they all walked off at a leisurely pace toward a stream of crystal-
clear water, whose banks were lined with smooth stones and verdant
grasses, and that flowed down from a little mountain into the shade
of a thickly wooded valley. There, with their feet and arms bare, they
waded into the water and started playing all sorts of games with one
another. Later, as the time for supper drew near, they returned to the
palace where they ate together merrily.

When their meal was finished, they called for instruments, and
the Queen had them begin a dance, which Lauretta was to lead, while
Emilia would sing a song accompanied by Dioneo on the lute. Obedient to the Queen's command, Lauretta began dancing at once, while
Emilia sang the following song in amorous tones:

> I'm so enamored of my loveliness
> That I will never care for other loves
> Or ever feel desire for them.
> When in my looking glass I view myself,
> I see the good that makes the mind content,
> Nor can some new event or some old thought
> Serve to deprive me of such dear delight.
> What other pleasing object, then,

Could ever come in view
To fill my heart with new desire?
    This good will never flee when I desire
The consolation of its sight. Instead,
To my delight, it moves toward me
And is so sweet, I feel no words can say
What it may be, or if they could, be grasped
By any mortal living here
Who did not burn with similar desire.
    And as I gaze more fixedly at it,
My flame burns fiercer every hour.
To it I give myself, to it surrender,
Already tasting what it's promised me,
And hoping that a greater joy than this,
Whose equal no one ever felt,
May come from such desire for loveliness.[3]

Even though the words of the little song made some of them ponder its meaning, they all cheerfully joined together in singing the refrains. When they were done, they did a few little dances for a while, and then, a portion of the short night having already passed, the Queen was pleased to proclaim that the end of the first day had been reached. Having called for torches to be lit, she ordered them all to go to bed, and after returning to their rooms, that is what they did.

Day 2, Introduction

Here ends the First Day of the Decameron, *and the Second begins, in which, under the rule of Filomena, they speak of people who, after suffering through many misfortunes, arrive at a happy end beyond anything they could have hoped for.*

The sun had already brought in the new day, bathing everything in light, and the birds, singing their happy songs up among the green branches, were announcing its arrival to the ear, when the seven ladies and the three young men all arose at the same time and went out into the gardens. They amused themselves there for quite some time, walking at a leisurely pace from one spot to another on the grass and making lovely garlands for each other. Then, just as they had spent the preceding day, they spent this one, first eating and dancing while it was cool and later taking a nap that lasted until nones. After that, they got up, and at the Queen's request, went to a shady meadow where they sat down and arranged themselves around her in a circle. Radiantly beautiful, there the charming Filomena sat, crowned with her garland of laurel, and for a long while simply gazed at each member of the company in turn. Finally, she ordered Neifile to begin the day's storytelling with a tale of her own, and Neifile, far from making excuses, happily began to speak.

Day 2, Story 1

Pretending to be a cripple, Martellino makes it seem as though he is cured after having been placed on the body of Saint Arrigo. When his ruse is discovered, he is beaten and then arrested, and though in danger of being hanged, he gets off in the end.[1]

Dearest ladies, it often happens that those who try to make fools of others, and especially in matters worthy of reverence, wind up not only being made fools of themselves, but sometimes come to harm as well. Therefore, in obedience to the Queen's command, I will begin our storytelling on the chosen topic by telling you about what happened to a fellow citizen of ours who was at first quite unlucky, but wound up, beyond his wildest expectations, very happy indeed.

Not long ago there was a poor German named Arrigo living in Treviso, who worked as a porter, carrying heavy loads for anyone willing to pay, yet he was universally held to be a good man and was thought to have lived the most saintly of lives. Whether it was true or not, the Trevisans affirm that when he died, at the hour of his death all the bells of the Cathedral of Treviso began to ring even though no one was there pulling the ropes. Taking this to be a miracle, everyone said that Arrigo was a saint, and the entire populace of the city ran to the house in which his corpse was lying and carried it to the cathedral as if it were indeed the body of a saint. The lame, the crippled, and the blind were brought there, along with others suffering from all manner of illnesses and infirmities, in the belief that they would all be healed merely by touching his body.

In the midst of all this turmoil, with people coming and going, three of our fellow citizens happened to arrive in Treviso, the first named Stecchi, the second Martellino, and the third Marchese, all of whom

77

used to frequent various noblemen's courts, entertaining the spectators there by putting on disguises and using strange gestures and expressions to impersonate anyone they pleased. They had never been to Treviso before and were surprised to see everyone running about, but as soon as they learned the reason why, they were eager to go and see for themselves.

After they had deposited their belongings at an inn, Marchese said: "We may want to go and have a look at this saint, but for my part, I don't see how we're going to get to him because from what I've heard, the square is full of Germans as well as lots of armed men whom the ruler of the city has stationed there to prevent disturbances.[2] And besides that, the church is said to be so packed with people that no one else can get inside."

"Don't give up just for that," said Martellino, who was eager to see what was going on. "I'm certain I can find a way to reach the saint's body."

"How?" asked Marchese.

"I'll tell you how," Martellino replied. "I'm going to disguise myself like a cripple, and then, with you on one side and Stecchi on the other, you'll go along holding me up as if I couldn't walk on my own, pretending that you want to take me where I can be healed by the saint. Anybody seeing us will get out of the way and let us through."

Marchese and Stecchi liked the plan, so the three of them promptly left the inn, and as soon as they reached a deserted spot, Martellino twisted up not only his hands, fingers, arms, and legs, but his mouth, eyes, and entire face as well, making himself look so horrific that anyone who saw him would have believed his body was crippled and hopelessly paralyzed. When he was ready, Marchese and Stecchi picked him up, and with the most pitiful expressions on their faces, made their way to the church, humbly asking all those in front of them, for the love of God, to let them through. They got people to move out the way without difficulty, and in short, accompanied by shouts of "Make way! Make way!" and with all eyes turned to look at them, they managed to reach the spot where the body of Saint Arrigo had been placed. There some gentlemen standing around the body immediately grabbed Martellino and put him on top of it so that he might benefit from contact with its holiness.

For some time Martellino just lay there while everyone stared at him, waiting to see what would happen. Then, like the expert performer he was, he began his show, pretending to straighten one of his fingers, then a hand, then an arm, and so on, until he had unwound himself completely. When the people saw this, they made so much noise in praise of Saint Arrigo that a thunderclap could not have been heard over it.

By chance, there was a Florentine nearby who was well acquainted with Martellino, but who had failed to recognize him when they brought him in because he had disguised himself so well. But when he saw Martellino standing up straight, he recognized who it was and burst out laughing. "Goddamn the guy!" he said. "Who would've believed that when he came here he wasn't a real cripple?"

"What?" exclaimed several Trevisans who had overheard what he had said. "Do you mean to say he wasn't a cripple?"

"Heaven forbid!" the Florentine replied. "He's always stood as straight as any one of us. But as you've just seen, he knows better than anybody how to play these tricks and can disguise himself any way he wants to."

That was all they needed to hear. Forcing their way to the front, they shouted: "Seize the traitor, this guy who mocks God and the Saints. He wasn't a cripple; he just came here disguised as one to make fun of us and our saint." And so saying, they grabbed him and dragged him down from where he was standing. Holding him by the hair, they tore all the clothes off his back and started punching and kicking him. To Martellino it seemed as though everybody there had rushed up to join in the fray. "Mercy," he cried, "for the love of God!" But although he did his best to defend himself, it was no use, and the crowd on top of him just kept getting bigger and bigger.

When Stecchi and Marchese saw what was happening, they realized that things were not looking good, but since they feared for their own safety, they did not dare to help Martellino, and in fact, along with everyone else, they were screaming that he deserved to be killed. At the very same time, however, they were trying to think of a way to get him out of the people's hands, who would surely have slain him if, all of a sudden, a plan had not occurred to Marchese. Since the entire watch of the city was posted outside the church, he went as quickly as he could to the lieutenant who had been put in charge by the *podestà*,[3] and said to him, "Help me, for God's sake! There's a crook here who's cut my purse, and it had at least a hundred gold florins in it. Arrest him, please. I want to get my money back."

On hearing this, a good dozen watchmen immediately ran over to where the wretched Martellino was being given a thorough shellacking.[4] They had the greatest difficulty in the world forcing their way through the crowd, but they managed to get him away from them and dragged him off to the palace, all bruised and battered. Many who felt he had been mocking them followed him there, and when they heard that he had been arrested as a cutpurse, they all began saying that he had cut their purses, too, since they had no other warrant to make trouble for him. When the *podestà*'s judge, a tough customer himself, heard these accusations, he immediately took Martellino aside and began interrogating him. But Martellino answered back with smart talk, as though he thought his arrest were no big deal. This infuriated the judge, who had him tied to the strappado and given a series of good, hard jerks.[5] The judge's intention was to get Martellino to confess to what his accusers were saying and then to have him hanged.

When Martellino was down on the ground again, the judge asked him if what his accusers were saying against him was true. Since denials would have been useless, Martellino replied: "My lord, I'm ready to confess the truth. But first, make everyone who's accusing me say when and where I cut his purse, and then I'll tell you whether I did it or not."

"Good idea," said the judge and had a number of them brought forward. One said that his purse had been cut a week before, another six days, another four, and several, that very day.

When Martellino heard them, he said: "My lord, they're lying through their teeth, and I can prove it! The truth is that I've never set foot inside this town—and I wish I'd never done so—until just a little while ago, and the moment I arrived, I went to see the body of this saint, where I had the bad luck to get a thorough shellacking, as you can see for yourself. Everything I'm telling you can be verified by the gatekeeper, who keeps tabs on all the foreigners coming into the city, and you can check his register, and ask my innkeeper, too. And then, if you conclude that I'm telling you the truth, please don't have me tortured and put to death because of the accusations of these wicked men."

While things were in this state, word had reached Marchese and Stecchi that the judge was giving Martellino a very rough time and had already had him tortured on the strappado. "What a mess we've made of it," they said, terrified, to one another. "We've taken him out of the frying pan and thrown him into the fire." Proceeding with the utmost caution, they then located the innkeeper and explained to him what had happened. Once he stopped laughing, he took them to a certain Sandro Agolanti, who lived in Treviso and had great credit with the ruler of the city.[6] The innkeeper told Sandro the whole story and with the other two begged him to intervene on Martellino's behalf.

After a hearty laugh, Sandro went to the ruler and asked him to send for Martellino, which he did. The men who went to fetch him found him standing before the judge in nothing but his shirt, thoroughly terrified and dismayed because the judge would not listen to anything that was said in his defense. On the contrary, since the judge just happened to have some sort of grudge against Florentines, he was absolutely determined to have Martellino hanged, and until forced to do so, he stubbornly refused to release him. When Martellino stood before the ruler, he told him the whole story and begged him, as a special favor, to be allowed to leave, because, he said, until he was in Florence again, he would always feel he had a noose around his neck. The ruler laughed long and hard over his misadventures, and then had each one of the Florentines given a new suit of clothes. Thus, beyond anything they could have expected, all three of them escaped from their terrible ordeal and returned home safe and sound.

Day 2, Story 2

After being robbed, Rinaldo d'Asti turns up at Castel Guiglielmo, where he is given lodging by a widow, and then, after having recovered his possessions, returns home safe and sound.[1]

The ladies laughed heartily at Neifile's account of Martellino's misadventures, as did the young men, and especially Filostrato, who was sitting next to her and was then ordered by the Queen to continue the storytelling. Without a moment's hesitation, he began:

My fair ladies, the story that attracts my interest involves a mixture of piety, misfortune, and love. Perhaps all there is to say for it is that it will be profitable for those who hear it and especially for those who have wandered through the hazardous lands of love, where anyone who has not said the Prayer of Saint Julian over and over again will find bad lodging no matter how good his bed may be.[2]

During the rule of the Marquis Azzo da Ferrara, a merchant named Rinaldo d'Asti was returning home from Bologna where he had gone to take care of some business.[3] He had already left Ferrara behind and was riding toward Verona when he happened to run into some men who looked to him like merchants, but were actually bandits, a trio of wicked and particularly disreputable individuals. Rinaldo struck up a conversation with them and then foolishly decided to ride along in their company.

Seeing that Rinaldo was a merchant, the bandits guessed that he had money on him and decided they would rob him when the first opportunity presented itself. Meanwhile, to prevent him from getting suspicious, they assumed an air of modesty and propriety, and as they rode along, spoke with him only about matters involving honesty and trust, doing their best to make themselves seem humble and unthreatening. Since Rinaldo was traveling alone, accompanied by only a single servant on horseback, he concluded that his running into them was quite a stroke of good luck.

As they rode on, the conversation passed from one topic to another as it tends to do, until they got into a discussion of the prayers men say to God, at which point one of the three thieves addressed Rinaldo: "And you, my good sir, what prayer do you usually say when you're traveling?"

"To tell the truth," Rinaldo replied, "in such matters I'm pretty simple and down to earth, the old-fashioned kind of guy who'll tell you that two *soldi* are twenty-four *denari*,* and so, I don't have many prayers on hand. Still, when I'm traveling, it's always been my custom never to leave my lodging in the morning without saying an Our Father and a Hail Mary for the souls of Saint Julian's father and mother. After that, I pray to the saint himself and to God to send me good lodging on the night to come. During my travels I've spent a lot of days exposed to grave dangers, but I've escaped all of them and invariably found myself at night in a safe place where there was a comfortable inn. I therefore firmly believe that Saint Julian, in whose honor I always say my prayer, interceded with God to obtain this grace for me, and that if I fail to say that prayer in the morning, I doubt the day would go well for me or I'd arrive safely at night."

"And did you say it this morning?" asked the man who had questioned him.

"Yes, indeed," replied Rinaldo.

Then the bandit, who already knew what was going to happen, said to himself: "You're really going to need that prayer, because if our plan succeeds, I think you're going to find pretty bad lodging tonight."

"I've done a lot of traveling, too," he said to Rinaldo, "and although I've never recited that prayer, which I've heard many people praise, I myself have never wound up with a bad inn. Perhaps this evening you'll

* *Soldi* and *denari* were coins of the period, each *soldo* being worth twelve *denari* (*denaro* comes from the Latin *denarius*, which is usually translated as "penny"). What Rinaldo means is that he is the sort of man who "says what's what," or "calls them like he sees them."

be able to discover which of us finds the better one, you who have said the prayer, or I who have not. Truth to tell, though, instead of that one of yours, I do say the *Dirupisti* or the *'Ntemerata* or the *De profundis*, which are all very effective, or so my old grandmother used to tell me."*

As they continued on their way, talking with Rinaldo of this and that, the bandits were constantly on the lookout for a suitable time and place to carry out their evil plan. It was already getting late when they reached a river crossing beyond Castel Guiglielmo. Seeing that it was almost night and that the spot they had reached was deserted and out of the way, the three of them assaulted Rinaldo and robbed him, leaving him on foot with nothing but his shirt. Riding off, they said: "Now go and see if your Saint Julian will give you good lodging tonight; our saint is certainly going to provide them for us." And crossing the river, away they went.

When Rinaldo's coward of a servant saw him being attacked, instead of coming to his master's aid, he turned his horse around, and galloping off in the direction they had come from, did not stop until he reached Castel Guiglielmo. Since it was already evening when he entered the fortress, he went and found himself an inn for the night and never gave what had happened another thought.

Rinaldo, barefooted and wearing only his shirt, was at his wits' end, for night had already fallen, the cold was intense, and the heavy snow kept falling and falling. Shivering all over, his teeth chattering, he decided to look around for some sort of shelter where he could spend the night and not die from the cold. But since there had recently been a war in the surrounding countryside, everything had been burned to the ground, and there was no shelter to be found. Setting off at a trot because of the frigid temperature, Rinaldo headed in the direction of Castel Guiglielmo. He did not know whether his servant had fled there or elsewhere, but he thought that if he could just get inside, then perhaps God would send him some sort of relief. However, by the

---

*The bandit cites, with some inaccuracy in the second case, the openings of three medieval prayers: *Dirupisti* (from Psalm 116.16: "Thou hast loosed my bonds"), *O intemerata Virgo* ("O intact Virgin"), and *De profundis* (from Psalm 130.1: "Out of the depths have I cried").

middle of the night he was still a mile away, and when he finally did arrive, he could not get in because it was now so late that the gates had been locked and the drawbridges raised. Grief stricken and weeping inconsolably, he was looking around for a place where he could at least get out of the snow, when by chance he caught sight of a house jutting out from the top of the castle walls. He decided he would go there and take shelter under it until the morning. When he reached the spot and discovered that there was a locked door beneath the overhang, he gathered some straw together that was on the ground nearby and sat down on it in front of the door, repeatedly complaining to Saint Julian in sad and mournful tones and saying that this was not what he deserved for all his faith and devotion. Saint Julian was, however, keeping an eye on him and did not wait long to supply him with good lodging.

In that fortress there was a widow whose beauty surpassed that of all other women, and Marquis Azzo, having fallen passionately in love with her, had set her up, for his pleasure, in the very house under whose overhang Rinaldo had taken refuge. By chance, the Marquis had come to the fortress during the day with the intention of spending the night with her and had made secret arrangements to have a bath and a magnificent supper prepared in her house. But just when everything was ready and she was anticipating his arrival, a servant showed up at the town gates with a message for the Marquis requiring him to leave immediately, and he quickly rode off on his horse, having first sent word to the lady that she should not wait up for him. Rather disconsolate and not knowing quite what to do with herself, the lady finally decided to get into the bath prepared for the Marquis, after which she would eat supper and go to bed.

The bath she got into was located near the door next to which the wretched Rinaldo sat huddled together on the other side of the town wall. As the lady lay there, she could hear someone who was weeping and whose teeth were chattering so badly that he sounded as if he had been turned into a stork clacking its beak. She called her maid and said: "Go upstairs, take a look over the wall, and see who's on the other side of this door. Then find out who he is and what he's doing there."

The maid went, and thanks to the clear night air, she could see

Rinaldo sitting just as we said he was, barefooted, with nothing on but his shirt, and shivering violently. She asked him who he was, and Rinaldo, shaking so badly that he could scarcely pronounce the words, told her as quickly as he could who he was, how he had come there, and why. He then begged her in a pitiful voice to do whatever she could to prevent his being left there all night to die from the cold.

The maid, feeling quite sorry for him, returned and told her mistress everything, which moved her to feel sorry for Rinaldo as well. Recalling that she had the key to that door, which the Marquis sometimes used for his clandestine visits, she said: "Go and let him in, but do it quietly. We have this supper here with no one to eat it, and there's plenty of room to put him up."

The maid lavishly praised her lady for the humanity of her deed and then went directly to open the door for Rinaldo. Once they got him inside and saw that he was almost frozen to death, the lady said to him: "Quickly, my good man, get into this bath while it's still warm."

More than willing to get in, Rinaldo did not need a second invitation. There, as the heat of the bath succeeded in reviving him, he felt like a dead man who had come back to life. The lady then had him supplied with clothes that had once belonged to her recently deceased husband, and when Rinaldo put them on, he found that they fit as though they had been made to measure for him. While he waited for further instructions from the lady, he fell to thanking God and Saint Julian for having saved him from the horrible night he had been expecting and for leading him to what seemed like very good lodging, indeed.

Meanwhile, the lady had ordered her maid to light a great fire in one of her rooms and had gone off to take a short nap. When she returned, she asked at once how the gentleman was doing.

"He's dressed, my lady," her maid responded, "and he's oh so handsome and looks just like a proper gentleman."

"Well, go and call him," said the lady. "Tell him to come here and have some supper by the fire, since I know he hasn't had anything to eat."

When Rinaldo entered the room and saw the lady, who seemed from her appearance to be a person of quality, he greeted her respectfully and offered her his most sincere thanks for the kindness she had done him. Looking him over as he spoke, the lady concluded he was everything her maid had said he was, and after welcoming him cordially, she had him take a comfortable seat beside her by the fire and asked him to tell her all about the misfortune that had brought him there. In response, Rinaldo told her the whole story from beginning to end.

Since the lady had already learned something about what had happened because of the arrival of Rinaldo's servant at the fortress, she had no difficulty believing everything he said. In turn, she told him what she knew about his servant, adding that it would be easy to find him the next morning. But now that the table was set, they washed their hands, and at the lady's invitation, Rinaldo sat down and had supper with her.

Rinaldo was a fine, tall, handsome man in the prime of life, with impeccable manners, and as the lady repeatedly glanced over at him, she saw a lot there to like. Furthermore, since thoughts of the Marquis, who was to have come and slept with her that night, had already aroused her carnal appetite, after supper, she got up from the table and went to consult her maid, asking her if she thought it a good idea to make use of the gift that Fortune had sent her, seeing as how the Marquis had left her high and dry. The maid understood what her lady wanted and did everything she could to encourage her to go after it for all she was worth.

Consequently, the lady returned to the fire where she had left Rinaldo all alone, and as she looked at him, her eyes brimming with desire, she said: "Oh, Rinaldo, why are you so pensive? Don't you think you can find something to compensate for the loss of a horse and a few clothes? Relax and cheer up. I'd like you to feel you're right at home here. Actually, there's something more I want to say to you. Seeing you there in those clothes, I'm reminded so much of my late husband that I've wanted to give you a hug and a kiss at least a hundred times this evening. In fact, if I hadn't been afraid you'd dislike it, I would have done so for sure."

Upon hearing these words and seeing the gleam in the lady's eyes, Rinaldo, who was no fool, approached her with open arms. "My lady, I shall always have you to thank for my life," he said, "and when I consider the situation you've rescued me from, I think it would be very discourteous of me indeed not to try as hard as I can to do whatever gives you pleasure. So, come hug and kiss me to your heart's content, and I'll be more than happy to do the same in return."

After this, there was no need for them to go on talking. The lady, who was burning with amorous desire, immediately threw herself into his arms, and embracing him passionately, gave him a thousand kisses and received as many back from him. Then they got up from their seats and went off into the bedroom, where they lost no time getting into bed, and before the night was over, they had satisfied their desires to the fullest many times over.

As soon as dawn began to break, however, they arose in keeping with the lady's wishes, for she did not want anyone to get wind of what had happened. After giving Rinaldo some fairly shabby clothes, she filled his purse with money, telling him to keep it hidden, and then showed him which road he should take so that he could find his servant in the fortress. Finally, she let him out through the door by which he had entered, imploring him to keep their encounter a secret.

When it was broad daylight and the gates were open, Rinaldo entered the fortress, pretending he was coming from some distance away, and located his servant. Having put on some of his own clothes, which were in his saddlebags, he was about to mount his servant's horse when, by some divine miracle, the three bandits were brought to the fortress, having been arrested for some other crime they had committed shortly after they had robbed him the previous evening. They made a voluntary confession of what they had done, and as a result, Rinaldo got his horse, his clothes, and his money back, and wound up losing only a pair of garters, which the bandits could not account for.

Thus it was that Rinaldo, giving thanks to God and Saint Julian, mounted his horse and returned home safe and sound, whereas the next day the three bandits were left kicking their heels in the north wind.

Day 2, Story 3

Three young men squander their wealth and are reduced to poverty. Later, a nephew of theirs, returning home in despair, falls in with an Abbot who he discovers is really the daughter of the King of England. After she takes him as her husband, she makes up what his uncles lost and restores all of them to their proper social station.[1]

The young women and men listened with admiration to the adventures of Rinaldo d'Asti, praising his devotion and thanking God and Saint Julian who had come to his aid in the time of his greatest need. Nor, for that matter, did they think the lady a fool for knowing how to take advantage of the gift that God had sent to her house, although they did not say so openly. Meanwhile, as they were talking and snickering about the enjoyable night she had spent, Pampinea, finding herself right next to Panfilo and realizing that it had to be her turn to speak, as it just so happened to be, collected her thoughts and started pondering what she was going to say. Then, at the Queen's command, she began to speak in a confident and lively manner:

Worthy ladies, if you look carefully at the ways of Fortune, the more we talk about what she does, the more there is left to say. Nor is this surprising when you think about it, for all those things we foolishly call our own are really in her hands, and she transforms them according to her own inscrutable plan, constantly changing one thing into another and then changing it back again, without seeming to follow any order we can discern. Although this truth is clearly visible in everything that happens every day, and although it has also been borne out by some of our previous stories, nevertheless, as it pleases our Queen to have us speak about this topic, I will add to the tales already told one of my own, from which my listeners may possibly derive some benefit, but which I think they will certainly find enjoyable.

In our city there once lived a nobleman named Messer Tebaldo, who belonged to the Lamberti family according to what some people say, while others insist that he was one of the Agolanti, basing their argument on the fact that his sons later plied the very same trade that the Agolanti once did and that they continue to ply today.[2] But setting aside the question of which of the two families it was, I will just say that he was one of the richest noblemen of his day and that he had three sons, the first named Lamberto, the second Tedaldo, and the third Agolante. All of them had already become handsome, fashionable young men, the eldest not yet eighteen years old, when Messer Tebaldo died a very rich man and left them all his goods and property as his legitimate heirs.

When the young men found themselves in the possession of such vast wealth and so much property, they began spending recklessly and without restraint, heedless of everything except what gave them pleasure. They maintained a large household full of servants, kept a large number of fine horses, dogs, and birds, and held court continually, giving presents away and sponsoring tournaments. They engaged not only in activities befitting gentlemen, but also in anything else their youthful desires prompted them to do. They had not been leading this life for very long, however, when the fortune left them by their father dwindled away, and since they found their income no longer sufficient to meet their commitments, they began borrowing money and pawning their possessions, and as they sold one thing after another, they were scarcely aware that they were almost bankrupt until poverty finally opened their eyes, which wealth had always kept shut.

One day, therefore, Lamberto called the other two together, and contrasting their father's magnificent lifestyle with their own, he spoke of how much wealth they used to have and of how they had been impoverished by their prodigal spending. He did his best to encourage them to sell what little they had left and to go away before their destitution became even more apparent to everybody. They agreed to do so, and without saying good-bye to anyone, indeed, without any fanfare at all, they left Florence and did not stop until they reached England. There

they took a little house in London, and reducing their expenditures to
a minimum, devoted themselves to the business of lending money at
a high rate of interest. And in this Fortune was so favorable to them
that in just a few years they had accumulated a huge amount of money.[3]

Thanks to their new wealth, one after another they were able to
return to Florence where, after buying back most of their possessions
and purchasing many other things as well, all three of them got married. Since they still had their money-lending business in England, they
sent a young nephew of theirs named Alessandro to manage it while
the three of them remained in Florence. They had, however, forgotten
the condition their reckless spending had reduced them to before, and
despite the fact that all of them now had families, they began spending more extravagantly than ever. Offered lavish credit by all the merchants, they borrowed enormous sums of money, and for a few years
they managed to meet their expenses with the help of the funds sent to
them by Alessandro. He had begun making loans to various noblemen,
and those loans, secured by the noblemen's castles and the revenues
from their other properties, brought in a handsome profit.

The brothers were thus spending lavishly and relying as always on
England to enable them to borrow money whenever they needed it,
when, to everyone's surprise, a war broke out between the English King
and one of his sons.[4] It divided the entire island, some people siding with
the father and others with the son, the result of which was that all of the
noblemen's castles were taken from Alessandro and he was left with no
other source of income at all. Nevertheless, he remained on the island,
hoping from one day to the next that father and son would make peace
and that he would be able to recoup not just his capital, but the interest he had made as well. Meanwhile, back in Florence, since the three
brothers did not limit their excessive expenditures in any way, they had
to borrow more and more every day.

As the years passed, however, and the three brothers' expectations
were seen to bear no fruit, they not only lost their sources of credit,
but since those who had made them loans were demanding payment,
the three of them were arrested. Although all the brothers' possessions
were sold, the money raised did not suffice to pay off their debts, and

so they remained in prison for what they still owed, leaving their wives and infant children to wander the countryside in rags, some going to one place and some to another, with nothing but a lifetime of destitution to look forward to.

After waiting several years in England for a peace that never came, Alessandro concluded that staying there any longer was not only futile, but actually put his life in jeopardy, and decided to return to Italy. He set out all alone on his journey, and as he was leaving Bruges, he saw an Abbot, dressed in white, also leaving the city, accompanied by a group of monks and preceded by a host of servants and a large baggage train.[5] After them came two elderly knights, relatives of the King, whom Alessandro greeted as acquaintances and who readily welcomed him into their company.

As he traveled along with them, Alessandro made polite inquiries about the monks who were riding ahead with such a large retinue of servants, and asked the knights where they were going. "The person up front there," replied one of them, "is a young relation of ours who was recently appointed Abbot of one of the largest abbeys in England. And because he's under the legal age for someone to occupy such a high office, we're going to Rome with him in order to ask the Holy Father to grant him a dispensation because of his extreme youth and then to confirm him in office. But this isn't something you should talk about with anyone else."

As he traveled along, the Abbot occasionally rode ahead of his retinue and occasionally fell behind it, just as gentlemen do all the time when they are on the road. At one point he drew abreast with Alessandro, who was a handsome, exceedingly well-built young man, and seemed as polite, agreeable, and well mannered as a person could be. At first sight what presented itself before the Abbot's eyes gave him so much more pleasure than anything he had ever seen before that he called Alessandro to his side and struck up a pleasant conversation with him, asking him who he was, where he came from, and where he was going. Alessandro answered all the Abbot's questions, frankly explaining his situation and offering the Abbot his services, however slight they might be. As he listened to Alessandro's fine, precise manner of speaking, and observed his manners more closely, the Abbot, judging him to be a gentleman despite the base nature of his occupation, was all the more warmly attracted to him. Filled with pity for Alessandro because of his misfortunes, he comforted him with affectionate words, telling him not to give up hope, for if he were worthy, God would restore him to the position from which Fortune had cast him down and would perhaps raise him up to an even loftier one. Then, since they were all going in the direction of Tuscany, he asked Alessandro if he would like to join their party. Alessandro thanked him for his encouragement and said he was entirely at the Abbot's disposal.

As he traveled along, the Abbot, inspired by what he saw of Alessandro, felt new emotions coursing through his breast. A few days later, they happened to arrive at a small town, albeit one not well supplied with inns. When the Abbot declared that he wished to be put up there for the night, Alessandro had him dismount at the home of an innkeeper who was a close friend of his and arranged for a room to be prepared for him in the most comfortable part of the house. An experienced traveler, Alessandro had practically become the Abbot's majordomo by this time, and he did his best to find lodging for the entire company, some in one place and some in another. By the time he was done, it was quite late, the Abbot had eaten his supper, and everyone had gone to bed. Alessandro then asked the innkeeper where he could sleep himself.

"To be honest, I don't know," the innkeeper replied. "You can see we're completely full. I myself am going to have to sleep on some benches with my family. Still, in the Abbot's room there are some bins for storing grain. If you like, I can take you there and fix up some sort of bed for you to sleep on tonight as best you can."

"How am I going to squeeze into the Abbot's room?" asked Alessandro. "You know how tiny it is. It's so narrow that none of his monks could lie down in it. If I'd noticed the grain bins when the Abbot's bed curtains were drawn, I could have had some of his monks sleep in them, and I could have slept where they are now."

"Well, that's the way it is," the innkeeper replied. "You can pass a very good night in there if you want. The Abbot's asleep now, and all six curtains are drawn around his bed, so I'll be very quiet and just put down a nice little pallet for you to sleep on."

When Alessandro saw that all this could be done without disturbing the Abbot, he agreed to the plan and settled down there, making as little noise as possible.

The Abbot, however, was not sleeping, but was meditating intently on his new desires. He had overheard what the innkeeper and Alessandro were saying, and when he realized where Alessandro was going to sleep, he was quite delighted. "God has given me this opportunity," he said to himself, "and if I don't make use of it to satisfy my desires, it may be a long time before another one like this comes my way."

Determined to take his chances, the Abbot waited until everything had quieted down at the inn, and then he called to Alessandro in a low voice, inviting him to lie down beside him. Finally, after many polite refusals, Alessandro undressed and got into the bed. The Abbot put his hand on Alessandro's chest and then, to Alessandro's great astonishment, began touching him the way amorous young girls fondle their lovers, causing Alessandro to suspect that the Abbot was in the throes of some unnatural kind of passion. But either by intuition, or because of some movement on Alessandro's part, the Abbot immediately sensed what he was thinking and began to smile. Hastily removing the shirt he was wearing, he took Alessandro's hand and placed it on his chest.

"Alessandro," he said, "stop thinking such foolish thoughts. If you feel around here, you'll discover what it is I've been hiding."

Alessandro placed his hand on the Abbot's chest and discovered two small, round breasts, as firm and delicate as if they had been made of ivory. Upon feeling them, he knew right away that the Abbot was a woman, and without waiting for a further invitation, immediately embraced her. But as he tried for a kiss, she said to him:

"Wait. Before you come any closer, there's something I want to tell you. As you can see, I'm a woman, not a man. I left my home a virgin and was going to have the Pope arrange for my marriage. Now, I don't know whether it's your good luck or my misfortune, but when I saw you the other day, Love kindled such a fire in me that no woman has ever burned with so much passion for a man as I do for you. Therefore,

I've resolved to have you, rather than someone else, as my husband. But if you don't want me as your wife, you must leave here at once and go back to the place you just came from."[6]

Although Alessandro did not know who she was, he deduced from the size of her retinue that she was rich and noble, and he could see her stunning beauty for himself. Thus, without taking much time to think about her proposal, he replied that if she liked the idea, so did he. Then she sat up in the bed, and beneath a little painting representing Our Lord, she placed a ring in his hand and had him marry her with it. After that, they embraced, and for what remained of the night, they enjoyed themselves, to the immense satisfaction of both parties. The two of them then agreed on a plan of action, and at daybreak Alessandro arose and left the room the way he had come in, making sure no one found out where he had slept that night. Ecstatically happy, he set out again with the Abbot and his retinue, and many days later they finally arrived in Rome.

After they had been there a few days, the Abbot, accompanied only by the two knights and Alessandro, had an audience with the Pope. Having paid him their respects in the appropriate fashion, the Abbot began:

"Holy Father, as you yourself know better than anyone, a person who desires to live a good and honorable life should do his utmost to avoid any motive for behaving differently. Now, since I really do desire to live such a life, I fled here in secret, wearing only the clothes you see I have on, so that your Holiness could arrange for my marriage. I also brought along a substantial portion of the treasures belonging to my father who wanted me to marry the King of Scotland, who's a very elderly man, whereas I'm a young girl, as you can see.[7] Nevertheless, I did not flee because the King of Scotland is old, but because I feared that if I were married to him, the frailty of my youth would lead me to do something contrary to divine law and against the honor of my father's royal blood.

"This was my frame of mind on my way here, when God, who knows best what each one of us needs, was moved by His compassion to set before my eyes the man whom He chose to be my husband. And that man was this youth"—here she pointed to Alessandro—"whom you see beside me, someone whose character and manners make him a worthy match for a great lady, even though he may not be as pure blooded as a member of some royal family. He, therefore, is the one I've chosen, the only one I really want, and I will never accept another, no matter what my father or anyone else may think about it.

"Although the principal reason for my coming to Rome was thus removed, I still wanted to complete my journey in order to meet with your Holiness as well as to visit all the holiest and most venerable sites that abound in this city. But I also wanted to complete it so that through your good offices I could make public, before you and thus before all men, the marriage Alessandro and I have contracted in the sight of God alone. I beseech you that what has been pleasing to God and to me should also find favor with you, and I humbly beg you to bestow your blessing on us, for if we have that, then we may be more certain of God's approval, since you are His vicar, and we may live our lives together, to the glory not only of God but also of yourself, till death do us part."

Upon hearing that his wife was the daughter of the King of England, Alessandro was both astonished and filled with a marvelous feeling of joy deep down inside. By contrast, the two knights, even more aston- ished, were so furious that if they had been anywhere other than in the presence of the Pope, they would have done harm to Alessandro and perhaps to the lady as well. For his part, the Pope, too, was greatly astonished both at how the girl was dressed and at the choice she had made, but knowing that there was no turning back now, he decided to grant her request. First of all, since he knew the knights were angry, he pacified them and reconciled them with Alessandro and the lady, and he then gave orders for everything else that needed to be done.

The Pope arranged a magnificent ceremony, which all the cardinals as well as many other worthy gentlemen had been invited to attend, and when the appointed day arrived, he had the lady brought forth in their presence. She was wearing regal robes and appeared so beautiful and charming that she won the well-deserved praise of everyone there. Similarly, Alessandro came out in splendid attire, accompanied by the two knights, and to judge by his looks and bearing, he seemed more like a prince than a moneylender. With great solemnity, the Pope then had them go through the entire marriage ceremony from start to finish, following it with a magnificent wedding feast, after which he bestowed his blessings on them and gave them permission to go.

After they left Rome, both Alessandro and the lady wanted to go to Florence where, the news of their story having arrived ahead of them, they were received by the citizens with the highest honors. The three brothers were set free after the lady paid off their creditors, and she also arranged to have all their possessions restored to them and their wives. Then, as everyone wished them well, Alessandro and his lady left Florence and went to Paris, taking Agolante along with them, where they were honorably received by the King.

From there the two knights journeyed to England and worked on the King so effectively that he pardoned his daughter and arranged a most festive welcome for her and his son-in-law. A little later, he knighted Alessandro with great pomp and ceremony, and then made him the Earl of Cornwall. A most worthy and intelligent man, Alessandro made peace between father and son, which greatly benefited the island and thereby won him the love and favor of all its people. At the same time, Agolante recovered absolutely everything he was owed there, and after having been knighted by Earl Alessandro, he was able to return to Florence an immensely wealthy man. As for the Earl himself, he enjoyed a glorious life with his lady, and some people say that, with his intelligence and valor and the help of his father-in-law, he later conquered Scotland and was crowned its king.[8]

Day 2, Story 4

Landolfo Rufolo is impoverished, becomes a pirate, and is shipwrecked after being captured by the Genoese. He escapes, however, on a chest filled with very precious jewels, is cared for by a woman on Corfu, and finally returns home a rich man.[1]

Seated next to Pampinea, Lauretta saw that the glorious conclusion of the story had been reached, and so, without waiting any longer, she began to speak as follows:

Most gracious ladies, in my opinion none of Fortune's deeds appears greater than the spectacle of someone being taken from the depths of poverty and raised up to a kingly throne, which is what Pampinea's story has shown us happened to Alessandro. And since no one telling stories on our announced topic will be able to go beyond the extremes of high and low that she has described, I shall not feel any shame if I tell you a story that, while containing even greater misfortunes than hers did, does not come to so splendid a conclusion. When I consider the previous story, I realize that mine will be followed less attentively, but I will be excused since I simply cannot do any better.

The seacoast between Reggio and Gaeta is thought to be just about the most delightful part of Italy. Quite close to Salerno there is a stretch of it overlooking the sea, which the inhabitants call the Amalfi coast and which contains many small towns, adorned with gardens and fountains, where countless merchants live, as wealthy and enterprising a group as you will find anywhere. Among those small towns there is one called Ravello, and although many men living there today are very well off, the town used to count among its citizens a man named

Landolfo Rufolo who was really extraordinarily rich.[2] Not satisfied
with the wealth he had, however, he sought to double it, and as a result,
he came close to losing not just everything he possessed, but his very
own life in the bargain.

Having made all the necessary preliminary calculations that merchants typically make, he bought a very large ship, loaded it full of
merchandise of all sorts that he had purchased using his own money,
and sailed with it to Cyprus. There he discovered that other ships had
arrived with exactly the same kind of merchandise he had brought, so
that not only did he have to sell what he had for cheap, but by the end
he practically had to give it away in order to get rid of it, coming close
to being ruined as a result.

Being extremely distressed over what had happened, not knowing
what to do, and finding himself, one of the richest of men, virtually
impoverished, he finally decided he would either restore his losses by
means of piracy or die in the attempt. He was determined, having left
his home a rich man, not to return to it a poor one. And so, he located
a buyer for his boat, and with the money he got for it and from the sale
of his merchandise, he bought a small, fast pirate ship that he armed
as well as he could and equipped with everything else necessary for
such an enterprise. Then he dedicated himself to making other people's
property his own, and especially that belonging to the Turks.

In this undertaking, Fortune was much more favorable to him than
she had been when he was a merchant. Within the space of about a
year, he had captured and plundered so many Turkish ships that he not
only regained what he had lost in trading, but discovered that he had
more than doubled it. Chastened by the pain he had suffered before
from his losses, he reckoned he now had enough to avoid a repetition
of his former experience, and having persuaded himself to rest content
with what he had and not to seek anything more, he decided to take
his loot and return home.

Wary of commercial ventures, he did not bother to invest his money,
but had the crew put the oars into the water and set off at once for home
in the little boat with which he had gained his wealth. One evening,

after having come as far as the Archipelago,* he ran into a fierce south wind that was blowing head-on. With his little boat hardly able to make any progress against the heavy sea swells, he took shelter in a cove on the leeward side of a little island, where he intended to wait for better winds. He had only been there a short while when two large Genoese merchant ships returning from Constantinople struggled into the cove to escape the same storm Landolfo had fled. The crews on board the two ships recognized his little boat and had heard rumors about his fabulous wealth. Being greedy and rapacious by nature, they blocked his way out of the cove and made preparations to capture him. They put a party of men ashore, well armed with crossbows, positioning them so that anyone trying to get off the little boat would be shot with their arrows. Then they launched dinghies, by means of which, aided by the current, they drew up alongside Landolfo's little boat, and in short order they seized it and its entire crew without much of a struggle and without losing a single man themselves. They brought Landolfo, dressed in a ragged old doublet, aboard one of their ships, and after removing all the cargo from the boat, sent it to the bottom.

When the wind changed the next day, the two merchant ships set sail on a westerly course. They made good progress all day long, but in the evening a gale arose, producing high seas that separated the two ships from one another. By a stroke of bad luck, the ship on which the wretched, destitute Landolfo was sailing was taken by the winds and hurled with tremendous force onto the shoals off the island of Cephalonia, where it split apart and was smashed to bits, like a piece of glass shattered against a wall.[3] As usually happens in such cases, the sea was strewn with chests and planks and merchandise, and although the night was pitch black and there was an extremely heavy swell, the miserable wretches who had been on board, or at least those who knew how to swim, grabbed onto anything within reach that happened to float by.

Among those wretches was poor Landolfo, who had called on death repeatedly throughout the day, preferring to die rather than return home as poor as he was. Now that death was imminent, however, he

_____

* Archipelago: the medieval Greek name for the Aegean Sea.

was afraid, and like the others, he seized the first plank that floated his way, in the hope that if he put off drowning a while, God would somehow come to his rescue. Straddling the plank, he did his best to hold on till daybreak, despite being tossed hither and thither by sea and wind. When it was light, he took a look around, but all he could see was the clouds and the sea, and a chest that was bobbing on the waves. He was terrified because the chest would occasionally get close, and he was afraid he would be injured if it hit him. Although he did not have much strength left, he did his best to push it away with his hand whenever it came too near.

But as luck would have it, all of a sudden a violent gust of wind caused a sea swell that drove the chest right into the plank Landolfo was sitting on and turned it upside down. Losing his grip, he went under, and when he was able to swim back up, aided more by his terror than by his strength, he saw that the plank had floated some distance away. Fearing he would never be able to reach it, he made for the chest, which was quite close, got the upper part of his body onto the lid, and using his arms, did his best to hold it upright. And in this fashion, unable to eat because he had no food on him, forced to drink more than he would have wished, and unsure where he was because all he could see around him was water, he spent the whole of that day and the following night being tossed this way and that way by the sea.

By the next day Landolfo had almost turned into a sponge, when, either thanks to the benevolence of God or through the power of the wind, he reached the coast of the island of Corfu, still clinging to the chest, holding its edges tightly with both hands just as we see people do who are in danger of drowning. By chance, a poor little woman, who happened to be there cleaning and polishing her pots and pans in the sand and salt water, caught sight of him. At first she could not make out what sort of creature was approaching and ran back screaming in fear. Landolfo said nothing to her, for he was unable to speak and scarcely able to see. But as the sea brought him closer to the land, she began to make out the chest by its shape, and as she stared at it more intently, first she recognized a pair of arms stretched across it, then picked out a face, and finally realized just what it was.

Prompted by compassion, the woman waded out some distance into the sea, which had now become calm, seized Landolfo by the hair, and dragged him to the shore, chest and all. With some difficulty, she unhooked his hands from the chest, which she took and placed on the head of her young daughter, who was there with her, while she herself picked Landolfo up like a little child and carried him back to her village. Having put him into a hot bath, she rubbed and washed him in the warm water with such vigor that the bodily heat he had lost returned and he regained a portion of his former strength. When the time seemed right, she took him out and gave him some good wine and sweets to help him recuperate. For several days she did her best to take care of him until he fully recovered his strength and understood where he was. At that point, the good woman felt she ought to give him back his chest, which she had saved for him, and tell him it was time for him to fend for himself. And that is just what she did.

Landolfo remembered nothing about the chest, but accepted it anyway when the good woman presented it to him, thinking that it had to be worth enough to pay his expenses for a few days at least. When he found it to be very light, however, his hopes were seriously dampened. All the same, once the good woman was out of the house, he pried it open to see what it contained and found a great many precious stones inside, some of them loose and others in settings. Being quite knowledgeable on the subject of jewels, Landolfo realized from the moment he saw them that they were extremely valuable. This discovery really raised his spirits, and he praised God for not having decided to abandon him yet. Still, as a man whom Fortune had cruelly made her target twice already, he feared a third encounter and decided he would have to proceed with great caution if he wanted to bring those things home with him. So, he wrapped them up as carefully as he could in some old rags and told the good woman that he no longer needed the chest, and that she was welcome to keep it if she gave him a sack in its place.

The good woman was happy to make the exchange, and Landolfo, after thanking her profusely for all the help she had given him, slung the sack over his shoulder and departed, first taking a boat to Brindisi and from there traveling along the coastline until he finally arrived in

Trani, where he ran into some cloth merchants who turned out to be fellow townsmen.[4] Without mentioning the chest, he narrated all his adventures to them, moving them for the love of God, to give him a new suit of clothes. They also lent him a horse and found him an escort to take him all the way back to Ravello, to which he wanted to return at all costs.

Finding himself safe at home, Landolfo thanked God for having brought him that far and then opened up his little sack. Examining everything with greater care than he had done before, he discovered that the stones were so numerous and of such quality, that if he sold them for their fair market value, or even for less, he would still be twice as rich as he had been when he first set out. After he found a way to dispose of the jewels, he sent a tidy sum of money as payment for services rendered to the good woman in Corfu who had pulled him out of the sea, and he did something similar for the merchants in Trani who had given him the new clothes. Then, abandoning any thought of being a merchant, he kept the rest of the money and was able to live on it in becoming prosperity for the rest of his life.

Day 2, Story 5

Andreuccio da Perugia comes to buy horses in Naples where, during a single night, he is caught in three serious misadventures, manages to extricate himself from all of them, and returns home with a ruby.[1]

The stones found by Landolfo—began Fiammetta, for it was her turn to tell a story—reminded me of a tale that contains almost as many perils as the one narrated by Lauretta, but differs from hers in that the misadventures she recounted happened over the course of many years, whereas those in this tale, as you are about to hear, occurred in the space of a single night.[2]

According to what I have been told, there once lived in Perugia a young man named Andreuccio di Pietro, a horse trader by profession.* Having heard that horses were cheap in Naples, he put five hundred gold florins in his purse, and despite never having been away from home before, set off for that city with several other merchants. He arrived there one Sunday evening around vespers, and the next morning, following the directions given to him by his innkeeper, went to the marketplace. Although he saw quite a few horses there, many of which he liked, he was finally unable to conclude a single deal despite having made offers on a number of them. During the negotiations, in order to show that he had the wherewithal to make a purchase, he kept pulling out his purse full of florins in front of all the passersby, a sure sign of his inexperience and lack of caution.

While he was thus engaged in bargaining, with his purse on full

* Andreuccio's first name is a pet name and means something like "Little Andrew" in English, but it also could have the more general, symbolic meaning of "Man" or "Little Man" since its Greek root means "man."

display, a young Sicilian woman, who was not only very beautiful, but was willing to satisfy any man for a modest sum, happened to walk by. Although he took no notice of her, she caught sight of his purse and immediately said to herself: "Who'd be better off than I would be if that money were mine?" She then walked right on by him.

There was an old woman with her, however, also a Sicilian, and when she saw Andreuccio, she let her young companion go ahead while she herself ran up to him and gave him a warm embrace. On seeing this, the young woman did not say a thing, but simply stood off to the side, waiting for her companion. Andreuccio, having turned around and recognized the old woman, greeted her heartily and got her to promise him to come and see him at the inn. After a brief conversation with him, she went away, while Andreuccio returned to his trading, although he did not wind up buying anything that morning.

The young woman, who had initially seen Andreuccio's purse, had also noted the friendly greeting he had exchanged with her old companion, and since she was determined to figure out a way to get hold of his money, or at least some part of it, she cautiously began questioning her friend, asking her who he was, where he came from, what he was doing in Naples, and how she happened to know him. The old woman, who had lived with Andreuccio's father in Sicily for a long time, and later on in Perugia as well, gave her a full report about him, almost as good a one as he himself might have given, letting her know where he was staying and why he had come to Naples.

Now that she was fully informed about Andreuccio's family, down to the names of all his relatives, the cunning young woman devised a clever plan, based on what she had learned, to get the prize she desired. Upon returning home, she gave the old woman enough work to do for the rest of the day in order to keep her from going back to see Andreuccio. Then she took aside a young maidservant of hers, whom she had trained thoroughly for such purposes, and around the hour of vespers, sent her to the inn where Andreuccio was staying.

When the girl arrived there, she ran into him by chance, all alone, at the door and asked him if Andreuccio was in. When he told her he was that very man, she drew him aside and said: "Sir, there's a gentlewoman

in this city who would be happy to speak with you, if you please." When
he heard this, Andreuccio immediately assumed, looking himself over
from head to foot and thinking he was a pretty good-looking guy, that
the lady had to be in love with him—as if he were the only handsome
young man to be found in Naples at that time. So, without hesitation,
he told the girl he was ready to go and asked her where and when the
lady would speak with him.

"Whenever you wish to come, sir," said the girl, "she'll be there at
home, waiting for you."

Without mentioning anything to the people at the inn, Andreuccio
replied at once: "You go ahead and lead the way. I'll be coming right
behind you."

The girl led him to the woman's house in a quarter of the city called
Malpertugio* whose name alone reveals how honest a place it is.[3]
Knowing nothing about it, Andreuccio did not suspect a thing, but
believed he was going to meet a proper lady in a very respectable area of
the city. Thus, with the servant girl leading him, he entered her house
without a second thought. The girl had already called out to the lady,
saying, "Look, Andreuccio's here," and as he climbed the stairs, he saw
her come out on the landing to wait for him.

The woman was still young and rather tall, with a gorgeous face, and
her clothing and jewelry were all quite proper looking. As Andreuccio
approached her, she descended three steps to meet him with her arms
wide open. Clasping him about the neck, she stood there for some time
without saying anything as though she were overwhelmed by tender
feelings. Finally, as she wept, she kissed him on the forehead and said
in a broken voice: "O my Andreuccio, how happy I am to see you."

Marveling at her tender caresses, the dumbfounded Andreuccio
replied: "My lady, the pleasure is mine."

Taking him by the hand, she led him up to the main living room, and
from there, without uttering a word, she entered her bedroom, which
was redolent with the fragrance of roses and orange blossoms and other
lovely scents. In the room he could see a handsome curtained bed, a

---

*Malpertugio means "bad hole" and refers to a gap in the city's walls.

large number of dresses hanging up on pegs, as was the custom there, plus many other beautiful, luxurious furnishings. Judging by what he saw, Andreuccio, like the greenhorn he was, firmly believed that she was nothing less than a great lady.

She had him sit beside her on a chest at the foot of her bed and began speaking as follows:

"Andreuccio, I'm quite sure you're amazed at my embracing you like this and shedding all these tears, for you don't know me, and it may be that no one's ever mentioned me to you. But you're about to hear something that will probably make you even more amazed: the simple fact is that I'm your sister. For a long time I've wanted to meet all my brothers, and since God has now granted me the favor of allowing me to see one of them before I die, I can tell you that I'll die content when the hour arrives. But in case you've never heard anything about this before, let me tell you my story.

"Pietro, who is my father as well as yours, lived for a long time in Palermo, as I believe you may know. Being a good and amiable man, he was greatly loved by everyone who knew him there, and to this day he still is. Among the people who were attracted to him, no one loved him more than my mother, a gentlewoman who was at that time a widow. In fact, she loved him so much that she cast off her honor as well as her fear of her father and her brothers, and became so intimate with him that it led to the birth of the person you see before you.

"When I was still a little girl, Pietro was called away from Palermo and returned to Perugia on some business or other, leaving me behind with my mother, nor, from what I've been able to discover, did he ever think of me or of her again. This is why, if he were not my father, I'd reproach him bitterly, considering his ingratitude toward my mother, for she was moved by the most devoted love for him to put herself and all her worldly goods into his hands without otherwise knowing any- thing about him. I'll say nothing about the affection he ought to feel for me, his daughter, since I'm not the child of a serving maid or some low-class woman.

"But what's the point of all this? It's a whole lot easier to condemn wrongs done a long time ago than to right them now. In any case, what happened was that when I was a little girl, he left me in Palermo where I grew up and have spent most of my time until fairly recently. My mother, being a wealthy woman, arranged my marriage to a well-heeled gentleman from Agrigento, who, out of love for my mother and me, came to live in Palermo. He was a staunch supporter of the Guelfs and entered into secret negotiations with our King Charles, but King Frederick got wind of the plot before it could be carried out, and we had to flee Sicily just when I thought I was going to be the grandest lady ever on the island.[4] We carried away what few things we could—I say 'few' in comparison to the huge number of things we owned there— and leaving behind our lands and palaces, we became refugees in this country. Here we've found King Charles to be so grateful to us as to give us houses and lands in partial compensation for the losses we suf- fered on his account, and as you will soon see for yourself, he contin- ues to provide a substantial allowance for my husband, who is also, of course, your brother-in-law. So, that's how I came to be in Naples where, thanks more to God than to you, my sweet brother, I have met you at last."

Having said all this, she embraced him again, and weeping tenderly, once more kissed him on the forehead. She had recounted her fable in an orderly and artful manner, never stammering or stumbling over a word at any point, and for his part, Andreuccio not only remembered that his father really had been in Palermo, but knew from his own expe- rience how easily, and lightly, young men fall in love during their youth. So, what with her tender tears and embraces and the honest kisses she gave him, as Andreuccio listened to her, he was convinced that what she was saying was truer than truth. When she fell silent, he replied:

"My lady, don't take it too hard that I'm amazed by all this, for to tell the truth, up to now I've had no more knowledge of you than if you'd never existed. For whatever reason, my father never talked about your mother and you, or if he did, I never heard a word about it. But I'm all the more delighted to have found my sister here, because I'm completely on my own and was never expecting anything like this to happen. In fact, although I'm just a small-time merchant, I really can't imagine anyone, no matter how exalted his station, who wouldn't treasure you. There is one thing, however, that I'd ask you to clarify for me, please. How did you know I was here?"

"I was told about it this morning by a poor woman who often comes to see me," the lady replied, "because, according to what she tells me, she had spent a lot of time with our father in Palermo and Perugia. And if it had not seemed more honorable for you to make your way to me here, where you'd be at home, than for me to visit you in someone else's place, I would have come to see you long before now."

After saying this, she began inquiring about all his relatives individually by name, and as Andreuccio answered her questions one after the other, he came to believe even more firmly that which he should never have believed at all.

Since it was hot and they had been talking for a while, she sent for sweets and Greco wine, making sure that Andreuccio was given some of it to drink.[5] After that he wanted to leave because it was time for supper, but she would not hear of it, and making a show of being very upset, she threw her arms around his neck.

"Alas!" she said. "Now I see clearly how little you care for me. What else am I to think when you are with a sister of yours whom you've never seen before, and in her own house, where you should have been staying from the moment you arrived here, and yet you want to leave her in order to go get supper at some inn? Really! You are going to eat with me. And although my husband's away, which is something I regret very much, and although I'm just a woman, I'm still capable of showing you at least a little hospitality."

Not knowing what else to say to this, Andreuccio replied: "You are as precious to me as a sister should be, but if I don't go, they'll be waiting there the entire evening for me to come to supper, and I'll be behaving like a boor."

"God be praised!" she said. "As if I didn't have someone in the house who could be sent there to tell them not to expect you! But it would be a greater courtesy on your part, and no more than your duty, if you sent for your companions and told them to come here for supper.

Afterward, if you still wanted to leave, you could all go back together as a group."

Andreuccio replied that he did not want his companions there that evening, saying he would place himself at her disposal if that was what she wished. She pretended to send word to the inn not to expect him for supper, and then, after they had talked for quite some time, they sat down to a splendid meal, consisting of multiple courses, which she cleverly prolonged until night had fallen. When they got up from the table, Andreuccio indicated that he would have to go, but she said that under no circumstances would she permit it, because Naples was no place to wander about in at night, especially for a stranger. Furthermore, she said that when she had sent word to the inn not to expect him for supper, she had told them the same thing about his returning to sleep there.

Andreuccio believed everything she said, and since, in his deluded state, he was enjoying her company, he stayed put. After supper was over, she deliberately kept him talking and talking into the wee hours of the night, at which point she left him to sleep in her bedroom, with a little boy to attend him and show him where to find whatever he needed, while she herself went off into another bedroom with her maidservants.

The heat was intense, and so, as soon as Andreuccio was alone, he quickly stripped down to his doublet, removing his breeches and stockings and placing his clothes at the head of the bed. Then, feeling a natural urge to dispose of the extra load in his belly, he asked where he should do it, and the boy, motioning toward a door in one of the corners of the room, said: "Go in there." The unsuspecting Andreuccio did so and chanced to set his foot down on a plank that came away at its other end from the beam that supported it, so that it flew up into the air, flipped upside down, and went tumbling to the ground, taking Andreuccio along with it. Despite having fallen from quite a height, by the grace of God he did not get hurt, but he did get covered from head to toe with the muck that filled up the place where he fell.

To give you a better picture both of what had happened and of what is about to follow, let me describe what that place was like. In a narrow alleyway, such as we often see between two houses, they had taken some planks and nailed them to two beams stretching from one house to the other, and had put a place to sit on top of them. It was one of those planks that had fallen with Andreuccio to the bottom.*

Finding himself down there in the alley, Andreuccio bemoaned his bad luck and started calling for the boy. But the boy, as soon as he had heard Andreuccio fall, had gone scurrying off to tell the lady. She immediately ran into her bedroom and checked to see if Andreuccio's clothes were there. She found them, and with them all his money, which he had been so stupid as to carry on him because he did not trust anyone else with it. Now that this woman from Palermo, who had transformed herself into the sister of a man from Perugia, had gotten what she had set her snares for, she did not give him another thought, but quickly went and closed the door that he had passed through before his fall.

When the boy did not respond, Andreuccio started calling louder, but to no avail. Growing suspicious, he began to realize, now when it was too late, that he had been tricked, and having climbed over a little wall that closed the alley off from the street, he scrambled down to the ground and went up to the front door, which he recognized readily enough. There he remained for a long time, vainly calling out while he repeatedly shook and pounded on the door. Now he saw his misfortune clearly, and starting to weep, he said: "Alas, poor me! Look how little time it took me to lose five hundred florins, and a sister, too!"

After saying quite a bit more, he started to shout and to beat on the door all over again, keeping it up for so long that he awoke many of the people living nearby who got up out of bed because they could not stand the racket. One of the lady's maids, who looked very sleepy, came to the window and said, in a scolding voice: "Who's that knocking down there?"

* The streets in the oldest part of Naples form a grid that was laid out by Greek settlers when the city was originally founded (Naples comes from the Greek *Neapolis,* meaning "New City"). Those streets and the houses on them were very close together, so it is easy to imagine how the inhabitants in Boccaccio's time could put beams from one house to the next across a street in order to create something like an elevated outhouse.

"Oh," said Andreuccio, "don't you recognize me? I'm Andreuccio, Madama Fiordaliso's brother."*

"Listen, buddy," she replied, "if you've had too much to drink, go sleep it off, and come back tomorrow morning. I don't know any Andreuccio. You're talking nonsense. For goodness' sake, please go away and let us sleep."

"What," said Andreuccio, "you don't know what I'm talking about? Sure you do. But look, even if people from Sicily can forget the relatives they've just acquired in such a short space of time, at least give me the clothes I left there, and then, in God's name, I'll go away gladly."

"You must be dreaming, buddy," she said, scarcely able to keep from laughing.

As she said this, she simultaneously shut the window and went back inside, which made Andreuccio, who was now more certain than ever that he had lost everything, so upset that what had been intense anger before turned into a towering rage. Deciding that if he wanted to get his belongings back, force would be more effective than words had been, he got a large rock and began frantically beating on the door all over again, this time hitting it harder than ever. Disturbed by his hammering, many of the neighbors, who had been awakened and gotten up before, decided he was a troublemaker who had invented some story to make life difficult for the good lady there. Coming to their windows, they began to shout at him, like all the dogs in the neighborhood barking at a stray:

"You really ought to be ashamed of yourself, buddy, coming around at this hour to the homes of good women and talking this nonsense. For the love of God, please go away and let us sleep. If you have any business with her, come back tomorrow, and stop bothering us like this tonight."

Perhaps encouraged by these words, the good woman's pimp, who was inside the house and whom Andreuccio had neither seen nor heard, came to the window and said, in a horrible, rough, savage growl: "Who's that down there?"

---

*Fiordaliso (Fr. *fleur-de-lis*) means "lily," and may be a fictional name the lady has adopted.

Hearing that voice, Andreuccio raised his head and saw someone who, as far as he could tell, seemed like some sort of big shot. His face was covered with a thick, black beard, and he was yawning and rubbing his eyes as though he had been awakened from a deep sleep and had just gotten out of bed. Somewhat fearfully, Andreuccio replied: "I'm the brother of the lady who lives here."

But the man did not wait for Andreuccio to finish. Instead, more fiercely than before, he said: "I don't know what's keeping me from coming down there and beating you with a stick until you can't move any longer, you stupid, drunken ass. Nobody can get any sleep here tonight because of you." Then he turned around and went inside, locking the window behind him.

Some of the neighbors, who knew more about the kind of man he was, said to Andreuccio, speaking in a whisper: "For God's sake, buddy, take off, unless you want get yourself killed here tonight. For your own good, go away."

Terrified by the man's voice and appearance, and urged on by the advice of the neighbors, who seemed to speak to him out of charity, Andreuccio set off to return to the inn, feeling he was the most wretched man alive and filled with despair about the money he had lost. Not really sure where to go, he walked in the direction of the place from which he had come following the serving girl the previous day.

Disgusted by himself because of the stench he was giving off, he thought he would head for the sea where he could wash himself off, and so he made a turn to the left and went up a street called Ruga Catalana.[6] As he walked toward the upper part of the city, by chance he saw two men coming toward him with lanterns in their hands, and fearing that they were members of the watch or else men who might do him harm, he decided to avoid them and quietly took refuge in an abandoned hut he saw nearby. But the two men were headed for the same spot and also entered the hut. After they were inside, one of them put down the iron tools he had been carrying over his shoulders, and then the two of them began talking together as they inspected them.

Right in the middle of their discussion, the first one said: "What's going on here? That's the worst stench I think I've ever smelled."

Having said this, he lifted up his lantern a bit, and they caught sight of the wretched Andreuccio. Astonished by what they saw, they asked: "Who's that there?"

Andreuccio remained silent, but when they came closer to him with the light and asked him what he was doing there, covered in filth as he was, he told them the whole story of what had happened to him. The two of them, who could easily imagine where all this must have taken place, said to one another: "It must have happened at Boss But-tafuoco's house."[7]

Then they turned to Andreuccio, and one of them said: "Listen, buddy, you may have lost your money, but you should really thank God for the accident that happened to you when you fell down and couldn't get back into the house. Because if you hadn't fallen, you may rest assured that as soon as you were asleep, you would have been killed, and in that case you would have lost your life as well as your money. But what's the use of crying over it now? You have about as much chance of getting a penny of your money back as you have of plucking the stars out of the sky. And there's a very good chance you'll be killed if that guy ever finds out you've said a word about it."

When he had finished speaking, they had a brief discussion among themselves and then said to Andreuccio: "Look, we're feeling sorry for you, and since we were on our way to do a job, if you're willing to go along with us, we can pretty much guarantee that your share will amount to a lot more than what you've lost." Feeling desperate, Andreuccio responded that he was ready to go.

Earlier that day an archbishop from Naples named Messer Filippo Minutolo had been buried.[8] He had been interred in very expensive vestments and had a ruby on his finger worth more than five hundred gold florins, which was the booty the two of them were after. They communicated their plan to Andreuccio, and he, more avaricious than wise, set off with them. As they were on their way to the cathedral and Andreuccio was still smelling pretty awful, one of them said: "Couldn't we find a way for this guy to wash up a bit somewhere or other so he wouldn't stink so horribly?"

"Sure," said the other, "not far from here there's a well that always used to have a pulley and a large bucket. Let's go there and give him a quick wash."

When they reached the well, they found that the rope was still there, but someone had removed the bucket. The idea occurred to them of tying Andreuccio to the rope and lowering him into the well so that he could wash himself off down below. When he had finished washing, he was to give the rope a tug, and they would haul him up.

But as they were proceeding to do this and had just lowered him into the well, several members of the watch happened to show up. They were thirsty because of the heat and because they had just been chasing somebody, and they were coming to the well for a drink. When the pair caught sight of them, they immediately ran away, making their escape without being seen by the watchmen as they approached the well. Down at the bottom, Andreuccio had finished washing himself and gave a tug on the rope. The watchmen, who had put down their shields and weapons and taken off their surcoats, started to pull it up, thinking there was a bucket full of water hanging from it. When Andreuccio saw himself nearing the top of the well, he let go of the rope and used his hands to heave himself onto the rim. On seeing him appear all of a sudden, the terrified watchmen immediately let go of the rope and without saying a word began running away as fast as they could. Andreuccio was so surprised by this that if he had not held on tightly, he would have fallen back down to the bottom and been seriously injured or even killed himself. However, when he managed to get out of the well, he was even more surprised to discover the weapons, for he knew his companions had not brought them. Lamenting his misfortune and fearing lest something worse should occur, Andreuccio decided to leave without touching a thing. And so off he went, although he did not have the slightest idea where he was going.

As he was walking along, he happened to run into his two companions who were coming back to haul him out of the well. When they saw him, they were amazed and asked him who had pulled him up. Andreuccio replied that he did not know and gave them a detailed account of everything that had occurred, describing what he had found lying next to the well. They figured out what had really happened and had a good laugh as they told him why they had fled and who was responsible for having pulled him out of the well. Then, without wasting any more time talking, since it was already midnight, they made their way to the cathedral and got in without difficulty. Going up to the tomb, which was made of marble and was very large, they took out their iron bars and lifted its enormously heavy lid, propping it open just enough to allow a man to get inside.

This done, one of them asked: "Who's going to go in?"

"Not me," replied the other.

"Not me, either," said the first. "Let's have Andreuccio do it."

"No, I won't do it," said Andreuccio, at which point both of them then rounded on him and said:

"What do you mean you won't do it? I swear to God, if you don't, we're going to bash in your head with one of these rods, and we'll just keep on hitting you until you fall down and die."

The terrified Andreuccio climbed in, thinking to himself as he did so: "These guys are making me do this in order to trick me, because once I've handed them all the stuff from inside, they'll go off about their business, leaving me struggling to get out of the tomb, and I'll wind up with nothing." Consequently, he decided to make sure he got his own share first, and recalling what he had heard them saying about an expensive ring, as soon as he climbed down into the tomb, he took it off the Archbishop's finger and put it on his own. Then he gave them the Archbishop's crosier, miter, and gloves, and having stripped him of everything else down to his shirt, he passed it all out to his companions. When he said there was nothing left, they insisted the ring had to be there and told him to look all over for it. But he replied that he was unable to find it and kept them waiting quite some time as he made a show of searching for it. They were just as wily as Andreuccio, however, and while they went on telling him to look really hard for it, they seized the opportunity to pull out the prop that was holding up the lid. At that point they fled, leaving Andreuccio shut up inside the tomb.

When Andreuccio realized what had happened, you can imagine how he felt. Again and again he tried, first using his head and then his shoulders, to raise the lid, but he labored in vain, until finally, overcome by deep despair, he fainted and fell down on top of the Archbishop's corpse. Anyone seeing the two of them there would have had trouble telling which of the two, Andreuccio or the Archbishop, was really the dead man. When Andreuccio came to, he burst into a flood of tears, for he had no doubt that one of two ends was in store for him: either no one would come to open the tomb, and he would die there from hunger and from the stench, covered by the worms from the dead body, or else someone would come and find him inside, and then he would be hanged as a thief.

As these sad thoughts were going through Andreuccio's mind, making him feel terribly despondent, he heard a number of people talking to one another and moving about the church. He quickly concluded that they were coming to do just what he and his companions had already done, a realization that only increased his fears. But having opened the tomb and propped up the lid, they got into an argument about who was going to climb in. No one wanted to do it, until finally, after a long debate, a priest said: "What are you afraid of? Do you think he's going to eat you? The dead don't eat people. I'll go inside there myself." Having said this, he placed his chest on the rim of the tomb and swiveled around, turning his head to face out while thrusting his legs inside, ready to make his descent.

When Andreuccio saw this, he stood up, grabbed the priest by one of his legs, and pretended he was trying to pull him down into the tomb. The priest no sooner felt Andreuccio's hands than he let out an earsplitting scream and instantly hurled himself out of the tomb. This terrified all the others, and leaving the tomb wide open, they ran away as if they were being chased by a hundred thousand devils.

Happy beyond his wildest hopes when he saw what had happened, Andreuccio quickly threw himself out of the tomb and left the church by the way he had come in. Day was already starting to break as he went wandering aimlessly about with the ring on his finger. Eventually, he reached the waterfront where he stumbled upon his inn and discovered that his companions and the innkeeper had spent the entire night up, worried about what had become of him. After he told them what had happened, the innkeeper counseled him to leave Naples right away. Andreuccio did so at once and returned home to Perugia, having invested his money in a ring rather than in the horses he had set out to buy.

Day 2, Story 6

Having been separated from her two sons, Madama Beritola is discovered living on an island with two roebucks and is taken to Lunigiana, where one of her sons, who has entered the household of the lord she herself serves, is put in prison after sleeping with the lord's daughter. Following the Sicilian rebellion against King Charles, Madama Beritola recognizes her son, who marries the lord's daughter and is reunited with his brother, and all of them are restored to their elevated social positions.[1]

Both the ladies and the young men had a good laugh over Fiammetta's account of Andreuccio's adventures. Then Emilia, on seeing that the story was finished and being ordered to speak by the Queen, began as follows:

The vicissitudes of Fortune can be painful and distressing, but since it is the case that whenever we talk about them, our minds, which are easily lulled asleep by her more flattering visions, wake right up, I think no one, whether happy or miserable, should ever regret hearing about what she does. For from such stories, happy people will learn prudence, while those who are miserable will obtain some measure of consolation. Consequently, although many fine things have already been said on this subject, I intend to tell you a story about the vicissitudes of Fortune that is no less true than touching. And although it has a happy ending, the suffering involved was so great and lasted for such a long time that I can hardly believe it was ever really assuaged by the happiness that followed it.

Dearest ladies, you should know that Manfred, who was crowned King of Sicily after the death of the Emperor Frederick II, had in his entourage a nobleman from Naples named Arrighetto Capece whom he held in the highest esteem and who was married to a beautiful noblewoman, also from Naples, named Madama Beritola Caracciolo.[2] Arrighetto was the governor of the island when he learned that King Charles I had defeated and killed Manfred at Benevento, and that the entire kingdom had gone over to his side. Having little faith in the loyalty of the fickle Sicilians, and not wishing to become a subject of his lord's enemy, Arrighetto made plans to flee. But when the Sicilians found out about them, they promptly took him prisoner and turned him over to King Charles, along with many other followers and servants of King Manfred. Not long after that, King Charles had the entire island under his control.

In the midst of this great upheaval, not knowing what had become of Arrighetto, terrified by what had happened, and afraid for her honor, Madama Beritola left behind everything she had, and though pregnant and destitute, fled on a little boat to Lipari with her son Giuffredi, who was perhaps eight years old.[3] There she gave birth to a second male child whom she named The Outcast, and having hired a nurse, she embarked on a ship with them in order to return to her family in Naples.

But things did not work out as she planned, for the ship, which was bound for Naples, was driven by strong winds to the island of Ponza where they entered a little inlet to wait for good weather so that they could continue their voyage. Like the others on board, Madama Beritola disembarked on the island, seeking a remote, solitary spot where she could grieve, all alone, for her Arrighetto. She made this her daily routine, until one day, while she was engaged in her lamentations, a pirate galley turned up, taking the crew and passengers by surprise, and then sailed off after capturing all of them without a struggle.

When Madama Beritola had finished her daily lament, she returned to look for her sons on the beach as she was accustomed to do. On finding no one there, though initially perplexed, she quickly guessed what had happened and cast her eyes seaward, where she saw the galley, still not that far away, with the little ship in tow. Realizing only too well that she had now lost her sons as well as her husband, and seeing herself abandoned there, alone and destitute, without the slightest notion of

how she might ever locate any of them again, she collapsed on the beach
in a dead faint, the names of her husband and her sons still on her lips.

Since there was no one there to revive her with cold water or any
other remedy, her spirit wandered freely wherever it pleased until the
strength that had left her wretched body finally returned. As it did,
with it came more tears and lamentations as she called out over and
over again to her sons, searching high and low and looking in every last
cavern for them. But when she saw that all her efforts were in vain and
that night was falling, she began, prompted by some vague, instinctive
feeling of hope, to feel some concern for her own situation. Consequently, she left the beach and returned to the cave where she used to
go in order to weep and lament.

She had eaten nothing the previous evening, and a little after tierce
the next day, having spent the night in a state of both terror and indescribable sadness, Madama Beritola was driven by her hunger to start
grazing on the grass. After she had eaten what she could, she started
weeping again as she contemplated what was going to become of her.
In the midst of her sad musings, she saw a doe come and enter a nearby
cave, from which she emerged a little while later and ran off into the
woods. Madama Beritola got up and entered the cave from which the
doe had come, where she saw two roebucks that had perhaps been
born that very day and that seemed to her the sweetest, most darling
things in the world. Since her own milk was not yet dry after her recent
delivery, she picked them up tenderly and placed them at her breast.
They did not refuse what she offered, but suckled there as they would
have done with their own mother, and from then on made no distinction between her and the doe. Thus, the gentle lady felt that she had
found some company in that deserted place, and since she had become
as familiar with the doe as with the two roebucks, she resolved to live
and die there, grazing on the grass, drinking the water, and weeping
whenever she recalled her husband and her sons and her past life.

Living this way, the gentle lady had gradually become a wild thing
herself, when, a few months later, a little ship from Pisa happened to
be driven by a squall into the very inlet where she had first arrived

and where it remained for several days. On board there was a noble-man, one of the marquises of the Malaspina family, named Currado, who was returning home with his worthy wife, a truly devout lady, from a pilgrimage they had made to all the holy sites in the Kingdom of Apulia.[4] One day, in order to relieve their boredom, Currado, with his wife, some of his servants, and his dogs, set off for the interior of the island. Not far from where Madama Beritola was staying, the dogs began tracking the two roebucks, which had now grown quite large and were out grazing. Chased by the dogs, they fled right back to the very cave that sheltered Madama Beritola.

When she saw what was happening, she got up, grabbed a stick, and drove the dogs back. Currado and his wife, who were following the dogs, arrived on the scene and were amazed at what they saw, for Madama Beritola had gotten skinny and tan and shaggy, although for her part, she was even more amazed to see them. At her entreaty, Cur-rado called off his dogs, after which they persuaded her, with a good deal of coaxing, to tell them who she was and what she was doing there. She gave them a full account of her situation, explaining what had happened to her and finally revealing her fierce determination to remain on the island. As he heard her story, Currado, who had known Arrighetto Capece quite well, wept for pity, and then attempted, using every resource at his disposal, to talk her out of her wild plan, offering to take her back to her home, or alternatively, to bring her to his house where he would honor her as a sister and where she could stay until God might send her a better fortune. The lady was unmoved by his proposal, however, and so he left her to his wife, asking her to arrange for food to be brought there, and since Madama Beritola was in rags, to give the woman some of her own clothing to wear. In particular, he implored his wife to do everything she could to get the lady to come back with her.

Left alone with Madama Beritola, Currado's wife first wept many a tear over her misfortunes. Then she gave instructions for food and clothing to be brought, which she had the greatest difficulty convinc-ing Madama Beritola to accept. Finally, after many entreaties, with Madama Beritola insisting that she would not go to any place where people knew who she was, Currado's wife persuaded her to accompany them to Lunigiana. She was allowed to bring the two roebucks and the doe with her, for the doe had returned in the meantime and, to the great astonishment of the lady, had greeted Madama Beritola with the most lavish show of affection.

And so, when the weather turned fair again, Madama Beritola boarded the ship with Currado and his wife, taking the doe as well as the two roebucks with them, which led people to call Madama Beritola "Cavriuola," since few of them knew her real name.* Thanks to a favorable wind, they soon arrived at the mouth of the Magra, where they disembarked and went up to Currado's castle. There, dressed in widow's weeds, Madama Beritola began serving Currado's wife as an honest, humble, and obedient lady-in-waiting, while she continued to treat her roebucks with affection and always made sure they were being cared for.

The pirates, who had unwittingly left Madama Beritola behind when they had seized the ship at Ponza on which she had been traveling, took everyone else on board to Genoa with them. There, when the booty was being divided up by the galley's owners, by chance Madama Beritola's nurse and the two children, along with a number of goods, were assigned to a certain Messer Guasparrino Doria who sent her and the children to his house where he intended to employ them as slaves to do domestic chores.[5]

The nurse wept long and hard, grief stricken over the loss of her mistress and the terrible misfortune that had befallen her and the two children. Despite her low station in life, however, she was a sensible and prudent woman, and when she saw that tears were no help at all in gaining freedom for herself, let alone for the boys, she consoled herself as best she could. Taking stock of their situation, she concluded it was quite possible that the two boys might have problems if someone there chanced to recognize them. At the same time, she was hoping that sooner or later their fortune would change, in which case, provided they were still alive, they might be able to return to

* "Cavriuola" means "doe."

their former station in life. Consequently, she decided not to reveal who they were to anyone at all until the time was right, and to claim that they were her own children whenever she was asked about them. Although she did not bother to change the name of the younger one, she started calling the older one Giannotto di Procida instead of Giuffredi and took great pains to explain to him why she had changed his name and how dangerous it might be for him if he were recognized. Nor did she remind him of this just once, but repeated it so often and so persistently that, being an intelligent boy, he followed the instructions of his wise nurse to the letter. And so, for many years, the two lads, badly clothed and worse shod, lived with their nurse in Messer Guasparrino's house, patiently performing all the most menial tasks.

Giannotto, however, had more spirit than is typically found in a slave, and by the time he was sixteen, he had come to loathe the baseness of his servile condition so much that he left the service of Messer Guasparrino and enlisted on the galleys that went back and forth between Genoa and Alexandria, but despite traveling far and wide, he never managed to find any opportunity for advancement. Some three or four years after he had left Messer Guasparrino's and had grown into a tall, handsome young man, he learned that his father, whom he believed to be dead, was still alive, but was being held prisoner by King Charles. As he wandered from one place to the next, despairing of his fortune, he finally arrived in Lunigiana, where he chanced to enter the household of Currado Malaspina whom he served, to the latter's satisfaction, with great skill. Although he saw his mother occasionally, since she was a lady-in-waiting to Currado's wife, he never recognized her, any more than she recognized him, so much had age transformed both of them from what they had been like the last time they had seen one another.

While Giannotto was in Currado's service, it just so happened that one of his daughters, named Spina, having been left a widow by a certain Niccolò da Grignano, returned to her father's house.[6] A very beautiful and agreeable girl just a little over sixteen, she had the opportunity one day to look Giannotto over, as he did her, and the two of them fell passionately in love. Nor was it very long before their relationship was consummated, although as month after month went by and no one detected it, they grew overconfident and began behaving with less discretion than the situation warranted. One day, while out walking through a splendid, densely wooded forest, Giannotto and the girl pushed on ahead of the rest of their party. Then, when they thought they were quite a distance from the others, they found a pleasant, secluded spot, ringed round by trees and covered with grass and flowers, where they began making love. The fun they were having made them lose all track of time, and they had actually been there quite a while when they were surprised, first by the girl's mother, and then by Currado. Distressed beyond measure by what he saw, he had three of his servants seize the pair, and without offering a word of explanation, he had them bound and taken away to one of his castles. He then returned home, seething with rage and indignation, determined to have them ignominiously put to death.

The girl's mother was very upset and thought her daughter deserved the harshest of punishments for her lapse, but she had been able to glean Currado's intentions from the few words he had spoken and could not bear the thought of what he was going to do. So she hurried to catch up to her furious husband and began pleading with him not to rush headlong into becoming the murderer of his daughter in his old age, let alone to dirty his hands with the blood of a servant. He could find some other way to appease his anger, she insisted, such as throwing them into prison where they would have plenty of time to suffer and lament the sin they had committed. The saintly woman continued talking and arguing with Currado until she got him to change his mind about killing the pair. Instead, he ordered that they should be imprisoned in separate places where they would be closely guarded and given the minimum amount of food while enduring the maximum amount of discomfort, until such time as he decided otherwise about them. Currado's sentence was carried out, and you can imagine for yourself what their life in captivity was like, how there was continual weeping, and how their fasting went on far, far longer than necessary.

When Giannotto and Spina had already spent more than a year languishing in these wretched conditions and had been long forgotten by Currado, King Peter of Aragon, having entered into an agreement with Messer Gian di Procida, stirred up a rebellion in Sicily and took the island from King Charles.[7] Currado, who was a Ghibelline, rejoiced at the news.

When Giannotto heard about what had happened from one of the guards, he breathed a deep sigh and said: "Alas! For the last fourteen years I've traveled the world living a beggar's life waiting for this to happen, but now that it has, just to prove the vanity of my hopes, I find myself in prison, with death as my only hope of release."

"What's that?" said the jailor. "How could the affairs of great kings mean anything to you? What were you doing in Sicily?"

"It just about breaks my heart," replied Giannotto, "when I think about the position my father once had there. Even though I was just a little boy when I fled the island, I can still remember seeing him ruling over Sicily when King Manfred was alive."

"So, who was your father?" was the jailor's next question.

"My father's name," said Giannotto, "can now be safely revealed, since I find myself in precisely the sort of peril I feared I'd be in if I ever mentioned it. He was called—and if he's alive, he is still called—Arrighetto Capece, and my name's not Giannotto, but Giuffredi. Moreover, I have no doubt that if I were released, I could return to Sicily and occupy, even now, a position of the highest importance."

The worthy man did not ask any more questions, and as soon as he had an opportunity, he recounted the entire story to Currado. Although, as he listened, Currado put on a show of indifference for the jailor, afterward he went straight to Madama Beritola and asked her in a kindly manner if she and Arrighetto had ever had a son named Giuffredi. Dissolving in tears, the lady replied that if the older of her two sons were alive, this would indeed be his name, and he would be twenty-two years old.

When Currado heard this, he concluded that his prisoner had to be that same young man, and if so, it occurred to him that he could perform a grand act of clemency and at the same time remove his own shame as well as his daughter's by offering him her hand in marriage. He therefore had Giannotto brought to him in secret and interrogated him about every detail of his past life, and when he confirmed beyond any doubt that the young man truly was Giuffredi, the son of Arrighetto Capece, he said to him:

"Giannotto, you know both the nature and the magnitude of the injury you've done me in the person of my daughter. I treated you well, practically like a friend, and you should have been a dutiful servant and always done everything to promote and defend both my honor and that of my family. There are many men who would have put you to death ignominiously if you had done to them what you did to me, but my sense of clemency would not let me do it. Now, since what you say is true and you are indeed the son of a nobleman and a noblewoman, I would like, if this accords with your wishes, to put an end to your suffering and release you from your wretched captivity, at the same time restoring both your honor and my own. As you are aware, Spina, to whom you had a loving, but improper, attachment, is a widow with a dowry that is both substantial and secure. Moreover, you already know what kind of character she has and who her father and mother are. Of your present condition I will say nothing. Therefore, if you're amenable, I'm willing to transform your unchaste mistress into your chaste wife and to let you live here with her as long as you like as if you were my own son."

Although Giannotto's body had wasted away in prison, that experience had not diminished in any way the innate nobility of his spirit or the wholehearted love he bore his lady. Thus, even though he fervently desired what Currado was offering him and recognized that he was in the man's power, he would not debase in any way the thoughts his noble heart was prompting him to utter.

"Currado," he replied, "neither lust for power, nor desire for wealth, nor any other motive has ever led me, like some traitor, to plot against your life or your interests. I fell in love with your daughter, I love her now, and I will always love her, because I consider her worthy of my affection. Moreover, if, in the judgment of common people, I behaved less than honorably with her, the sin I committed is inseparable from youth, and in order to eradicate it, you would have to do away with youth itself. Indeed, it would not be judged so serious a sin as you and many others make it out to be if old men would just remember that they were young once and would measure other people's failings against their own, and their own against those of others. Finally, just remember: the person who committed this sin was your friend, not your enemy.[8]

"What you've just offered me is something I've wanted all along. Indeed, if I had thought you would have given your consent, I would have asked you for it a long time ago, and to have it now is all the more gratifying because I had almost no expectation of getting it. But if your words don't reflect your actual intentions, don't feed me with vain hopes, but have me taken right back to prison and torture me there as much as you like. But no matter what you do to me, I will always love Spina, and for her sake, I will always love and respect you as well."

As he listened in amazement, Currado was impressed by the nobil-ity of Giannotto's spirit and the fervor of his love, and held him in even higher esteem. He therefore stood up, embraced and kissed the young man, and without further ado gave orders to have Spina brought there in secret. She had become so thin and pale and weak in prison that she, like Giannotto, almost seemed to be another person. Still, in Currado's presence, and by mutual consent, they exchanged marriage vows according to our custom.[9]

A few days later, before anyone found out what had happened, Cur-rado, who had generously provided the couple with everything they could ever need or desire, decided it was time to bring joy to their two mothers. And so, having summoned his wife and Cavriuola, he turned to the latter and asked her: "What would you say, my lady, if I could arrange to have your elder son restored to you as the husband of one of my daughters?"

"The only thing I could say," Cavriuola replied, "would be that if I could possibly be more obliged to you than I am already, then I would feel myself even more in your debt, because you would be giving me something that is more precious to me than my very own life. Indeed, by returning him to me in the way you describe, you'd be restoring, in some measure, all my lost hopes." And at this point she fell silent and began weeping.

Then Currado asked the former: "And what would you think, wife, if I were to provide you with such a son-in-law?"

"If he were pleasing to you," she replied, "I would have no objection to his being a vagabond, let alone a man of noble birth."

"Within a few days, then," Currado declared, "I hope to make you both happy women."

When he saw that the two young people had recovered and looked like their old selves, he had them dressed in fine clothing. Then he asked Giuffredi: "Wouldn't it increase your happiness beyond what it is at present for you to see your mother here?"

"She has suffered through so many appalling misfortunes," Giuffredi replied, "that I can't believe she's still alive. But if she is, then it would be wonderful to see her, for with her advice I believe I might be able to recover a large portion of my estates in Sicily."

Currado had the two women summoned, and they both embraced the new bride with the most incredible warmth, while wondering what could have possibly inspired Currado to feel such benevolence that he would unite Giannotto with her in wedlock. Recalling Currado's earlier words, Madama Beritola began to stare at the young man, and as she did, some occult power awoke in her a recollection of the boyish features of her son's face. At that moment, without waiting for further proof, she ran to him and threw her arms about his neck. Her feelings of maternal joy and love were so intense that they did not merely prevent her from speaking, but overwhelmed her senses, and she collapsed in her son's arms as if she were dead. Giuffredi was filled with amazement, for he recalled how frequently he had seen her before then in that very castle without ever recognizing her. Yet now, all of a sudden, he knew instinctively that she was his mother, and reproaching himself for his past negligence, he wept as he held her in his arms and covered her with tender kisses. Shortly afterward, thanks to the compassionate care of Spina and Currado's wife, who applied cold water and other remedies of theirs, Madama Beritola regained her senses and embraced her son once again, weeping copiously and uttering many sweet terms of endearment. Filled with maternal affection, she kissed him a thousand times or more, while he embraced her and gazed at her in reverence.

When these chaste and joyful greetings had been repeated three or four times,[10] to the great satisfaction and approval of all the onlookers, they told one another all about their adventures. Since Currado had already informed his friends about the family alliance he had made and received their delighted approval, and he had, as well, arranged for a beautiful, sumptuous wedding feast to be prepared, at this point Giuffredi said to him:

"Currado, you have done so much for my happiness and have treated my mother honorably for such a very long time. Still, to use your good offices to the full, I would ask you to gladden the wedding feast, as well as my mother and myself, by sending for my brother. As I've told you already, he and I were taken by pirates acting for Messer Guasparrino Doria, who is keeping him as a slave in his house. And after that, would you also send someone to Sicily to bring us back a full report about the situation on the island and to find out whether my father Arrighetto is dead or alive, and if he is alive, to let us know how he's doing?"

Giuffredi's request pleased Currado, who immediately sent a number of his most discreet emissaries to Genoa and Sicily. The one who went to Genoa found Messer Guasparrino and entreated him earnestly on Currado's behalf to hand over The Outcast and his nurse, giving him a precise account of everything Currado had done for Giuffredi and his mother.

"It's true that I'd do anything in my power to please Currado," said Messer Guasparrino, who was greatly astonished by the story. "For the past fourteen years both the boy you're asking for and his mother have been in my house, and I will gladly send them to Currado. You should warn him, on my behalf, not to be too credulous, however, and not to fall for the tall tales made up by Giannotto, who now, you tell me, goes by the name of Giuffredi, for he's much more devious than Currado may realize."

When he had finished speaking and had arranged for the good man to be honorably entertained, Guasparrino sent for the nurse in secret and questioned her closely on the matter. She had heard about the rebellion in Sicily, and on learning that Arrighetto was alive, she cast off her former fear and told Messer Guasparrino the whole story, explaining as well her motives for what she had done. When he saw that the nurse's account corresponded exactly with that of Currado's emissary, he was inclined to believe what they were saying. Being an extremely astute man, he then continued his investigation by one means or another, finding more and more evidence that made the story seem increasingly credible. Ashamed now at having treated the boy in so base a manner, and well aware of who Arrighetto was and the important position he used to have, Messer Guasparrino made amends by offering the boy a wife in the person of his pretty little eleven-year-old daughter, together with a large dowry. After celebrating the marriage with a grand feast, he boarded a well-armed galley, together with his daughter, the boy, Currado's envoy, and the nurse, and they all sailed away to Lerici, where he was welcomed by Currado.[11] Then, with his entire entourage, he went to one of Currado's castles, which was not very far from there, where the great wedding feast was about to be held.

The joy they all experienced as they feasted together cannot be described in words, whether it is the joy that the mother felt upon seeing her son again, or that of the two brothers, or that of all three of them at the sight of their faithful nurse, or that which everyone experienced together with Messer Guasparrino and his daughter—which he fully reciprocated—or that which the whole company shared with Currado, his children, and his friends. And since it cannot be described, ladies, I leave it all to your imagination.

In order to make their joyous celebration complete, the good Lord, whose largess can be unlimited once he has begun to dispense it, saw to it that they received, in addition, the happy news that Arrighetto Capece was alive and well. For in the midst of their grand celebration, when the guests, both the men and the women, were still seated at the tables eating the first course, the emissary who had gone to Sicily arrived. Among other things, he recounted how, when the revolt against King Charles had broken out on the island, the people had stormed the prison where the King had ordered Arrighetto held captive. In a rage, they killed the guards and released Arrighetto, after which, since he had been the principal enemy of King Charles, they made him their captain, and following him as their leader, pursued and slaughtered the French. For this reason, Arrighetto came to stand in the very good graces of King Peter, who restored all his titles and possessions, with the result that he occupied once again a position of great dignity and authority.

The emissary added that Arrighetto, who had received him with the highest honors, was filled with indescribable joy at learning the news of his wife and child, for he had heard nothing about them since the time of his capture. Finally, to top it all off, the emissary said that Arrighetto was sending a brigantine with a number of gentlemen on board to come and fetch them, and that it was due to arrive very soon.

The emissary and his tale were received with great cheers and rejoicing, and Currado promptly set off with several of his friends to meet the gentlemen who were coming for Madama Beritola and Giuffredi. After greeting them warmly, he brought them back to the banquet, which was not yet half over.

Upon seeing them, the lady, Giuffredi, and all the others experienced a happiness that was simply unheard of. Before sitting down to eat, the gentlemen conveyed, as fully as possible, Arrighetto's warmest greetings and expressed his sincerest gratitude to Currado and his lady for the honors they had bestowed on his wife and son, adding that he placed himself and everything he had in his power at their disposal. Then the gentlemen turned to Messer Guasparrino, whose kindness had come as a surprise to them, and told him they were quite certain that when Arrighetto learned about everything he had done on behalf of The Outcast, Arrighetto's gratitude to him would match, if it did not surpass, his gratitude to Currado. This done, they were very happy to join the others in feasting with the two new brides and their spouses.

Currado's entertainment of his son-in-law and his other friends and relations did not stop with just that one day, but went on for many more. When it was over, and Madama Beritola and Giuffredi and all the others thought it was time to go, they wept many a tear as they bid farewell to Currado and his wife and Messer Guasparrino. They then boarded the brigantine and sailed away, taking Spina along with them.

Thanks to favorable winds, they soon reached Sicily, where Arrighetto, with a joy that could never be expressed in words, welcomed his two sons as well as the ladies, and there, it is believed, they all lived long, happy lives, ever grateful to the good Lord for the benefits they had received from Him.

Day 2, Story 7

The Sultan of Babylon sends one of his daughters to be married to the King of Algarve, and in a series of misadventures spanning a period of four years, she passes through the hands of nine men in various places, until she is finally restored to her father as a virgin and goes off, as she was doing at the start, to marry the King of Algarve.[1]

If Emilia's tale had gone on perhaps just a little bit longer, the pity the young ladies were feeling for Madama Beritola because of her misfortunes would have made them weep. But since the tale had come to an end, it was the Queen's pleasure to have Panfilo continue the storytelling. Most obedient, he began as follows:

It is difficult, charming ladies, for us to know what is truly in our best interest. For, as we have frequently observed, there are many who have thought that if only they were rich, they would be able to lead secure, trouble-free lives, and they have not just prayed to God for wealth, but have made every effort to acquire it, sparing themselves neither effort nor danger in the process. However, no sooner did they succeed than the prospect of a substantial legacy led to their being murdered by people who would never have considered harming them before then. Others have risen from low estate to the heights of power, passing through the dangers of a thousand battles and shedding the blood of their brothers and friends to get there, all because of their belief that to rule was felicity itself. And yet, as they could have seen and heard for themselves, it was a felicity fraught with endless cares and fears, and when it cost them their lives, they finally realized that at the tables of royalty chalices may contain poison, even though they are made of gold.[2] Again, there have been many who have ardently yearned for physical strength and beauty, while others have sought bodily ornaments with equal passion, only to discover that the things they unwisely desired were the cause of misery or even death.

But to avoid reviewing every conceivable human desire, let me simply affirm that no person alive can choose any one of them in complete confidence that it will remain immune from the vicissitudes of Fortune. Thus, if we wish to live upright lives, we should resign ourselves to acquiring and preserving whatever is bestowed on us by the One who alone knows what we need and has the ability to provide it for us. However, just as there are myriad ways in which men are driven to sin because of their desires, so you, gracious ladies, sin above all in one particular way, namely, in your desire to be beautiful, for finding that the attractions bestowed on you by Nature are insufficient, you make use of the most extraordinary art trying to improve on them. And therefore, I would like to tell you a tale about a Saracen girl's unfortunate beauty, which in the space of about four years turned her into a newlywed nine separate times.

A long time ago Babylon* was ruled a Sultan named Beminedab, in whose reign very little happened that went contrary to his wishes.[3] Among his many children of both sexes, he had a daughter named Alatiel who was at that time, according to what everyone said who saw her, the most beautiful woman in the world. The Sultan had been recently attacked by a huge army of Arabs, but thanks to the timely assistance of the King of Algarve, he had been able to defeat them decisively.[4] Consequently, when, as a special favor, the King asked to be given Alatiel as his wife, the Sultan agreed, and after having seen her aboard a well-armed, well-equipped ship and having provided her with an honorable escort of men and women as well as with many elegant and expensive trappings, he commended her to God's protection and sent her on her way.

When the sailors saw that the weather was favorable, they unfurled their sails into the wind, and for some while after leaving the port of Alexandria, their voyage prospered. One day, however, after they had

*Babylon: the medieval name for Cairo.

already passed Sardinia and seemed close to their journey's end, cross-winds suddenly arose that were so violent and buffeted the ship so badly that time and again not only the lady, but the crew thought they were done for. Nevertheless, they held out valiantly, and by marshaling all their skill and all their strength, they resisted the onslaught of the heavy seas for two days. As night approached for the third time since the start of the storm, however, not only did it not abate, but rather, it kept growing stronger, until they felt the ship beginning to break apart. Although they were not far to the north of Majorca, the sailors had no idea of their location, and because it was a dark night and the sky was covered with thick clouds, they were unable to determine their position either by using nautical instruments or by making visual observations.

It now became a case of every man for himself, and the officers, seeing no other means of escape, lowered a dinghy into the water and jumped into it, choosing to put their faith in it rather than in the foundering ship. Right behind them, however, came all the other men on board, leaping down into the boat one after the other, despite the fact that those who had gotten there first were trying, knife in hand, to fend them off. Although they all thought this was the way to escape death, they actually ran right into it, for the dinghy, not built to hold so many people in such weather, went down, taking everyone with it.

Meanwhile, the ship, though torn open and almost completely filled with water, was being blown swiftly along by a fierce wind that finally drove it aground on a beach on the island of Majorca. At this point the only people remaining on board were the lady and her female attendants, all of whom lay prostrate, looking as if they were dead, overcome by both the tempest and their fear. The ship's impetus had been so great that it had thrust itself deep into the sand almost a stone's throw from the shore, where, now that the wind could no longer make it budge, it remained all night long, relentlessly pounded by the sea.

By daybreak the tempest had calmed down considerably, and the lady, who was feeling half dead, raised her head and, weak though she was, began calling to her servants one after the other. She did so in vain, however, because they were too far away to hear her. Puzzled when she got no reply and could see no one about, she began to feel quite panic stricken, staggered to her feet, and finally discovered her ladies-in-waiting as well as all the other women lying about everywhere. As she went from one to the other, she called and shook them repeatedly. Few, however, showed any sign of life, most having died from a combination of terror and horrible stomach convulsions, a discovery that only served to intensify the lady's fears. Since she was all alone there and had no idea of her whereabouts, she felt a desperate need of assistance and prodded those who were still alive until she got them to their feet. But when she realized that no one knew where the men had gone and saw that the boat was stuck in the sand and full of water, she began weeping and wailing along with all the rest of them.

The hour of nones was already upon them before they saw anyone on the shore or elsewhere in the vicinity who might be moved to pity them and come to their assistance, for by chance, at that very hour, a nobleman named Pericone da Vislago, who was returning from one of his estates, happened to come riding by on horseback, accompanied by several of his servants.[5] The instant he saw the ship, he figured out what had happened and ordered one of his men to climb aboard without delay and to report what he discovered there. Although the servant had to struggle, he managed to get onto the ship, where he found the young noblewoman, frightened out of her wits, hiding with her few remaining companions under the end of the bowsprit. On seeing him, they started weeping and repeatedly begged him for mercy, although when they realized he could not understand them, nor they him, they tried to explain their misfortune by means of gestures.

Once he had assessed the situation to the best of his ability, the servant reported what he had discovered up there to Pericone, who promptly had his men bring the women down, along with the most valuable objects they could salvage from the ship. Then he escorted the women to one of his castles where he arranged for them to be fed and allowed to rest in order to restore their spirits. From their rich attire he deduced that he had stumbled across some great lady, and he quickly recognized which one she was by the deference that the other women paid to her alone. Although she was pallid and extremely disheveled because of her exhausting experiences at sea, her features still struck

Pericone as extremely beautiful, and for this reason he resolved on the spot to take her to wife if she had no husband, and if marriage were out of the question, to make her his mistress.

Quite a robust man with a commanding presence, Pericone had her waited on hand and foot, and when, after a few days, she had recovered completely, he found her to be more beautiful than he could have imagined. Although it pained him that they could not understand one another and he could not determine who she was, nevertheless, her beauty had set him all ablaze, and he tried, by means of pleasant, loving gestures, to coax her to give in to his desires without a struggle. But it was all in vain: she kept refusing to let him get on familiar terms with her, and in the meantime, Pericone's passion just got hotter and hotter.

The lady had no idea where she was, but she guessed, after having observed the local customs for a few days, that she was among Christians and in a place where she saw that there was little to be gained by revealing her identity, even if she had known how to do so. She recognized what was going on with Pericone, and although she concluded that eventually either force or love was going to make her satisfy his desires, nevertheless, she proudly resolved to rise above her wretched predicament. To her three remaining women, she gave orders never to reveal their identities to anyone unless they found themselves in a place where doing so would clearly help them gain their freedom. Beyond that, she implored them to preserve their chastity, declaring that she herself was determined to let no one except her husband ever enjoy her favors. Her women commended her resolve and said they would do their utmost to follow her instructions.

Pericone's passion was burning more fiercely from day to day, growing hotter and hotter as he got closer to the object of his desire and it was ever more firmly denied him. When he saw that his flattering her was getting him nowhere, he sharpened his wits and decided to make use of deception, keeping force in reserve as a last resort. On several occasions he had noticed that the lady liked wine, which she was unaccustomed to drinking because the laws of her religion forbade it, and by using it as Venus's assistant, he thought he would be able to have his way with her.[6] Thus, one evening, pretending not to care about the very thing for which she had shown such distaste, he arranged for a splendid supper in the manner of a holiday celebration, which the lady attended. Since the meal was graced with a wide array of dishes, he ordered the man who was serving her to give her a variety of different kinds of wine to drink with them. The man did his job extremely well, and the lady, caught off guard and carried away by the pleasures of drinking, consumed more wine than was consistent with her honor. Forgetting all the adversities she had been through, she became positively merry, and when she saw other women doing Majorcan dances, she herself did one in the Alexandrian manner.*

On seeing this, Pericone thought he was getting close to what he wanted, and calling for more food and drink, he prolonged the banquet into the wee hours of the night. Finally, after the guests were gone, he accompanied her, alone, to her bedroom. There, unhindered by any feeling of shame, and more heated by the wine than restrained by her sense of honor, she undressed in front of him as if he were one of her women, and got into bed. Pericone was not slow to follow her, and after extinguishing the lights, he quickly got in from the other side. Lying down beside her, he took her in his arms, and with no resistance whatsoever on her part, began playing the game of love with her. Up until that moment, she had no conception of the kind of horn men do their butting with, but once she did, she almost regretted not having given in to Pericone's solicitations. And from then on, she would no longer wait for an invitation to enjoy such sweet nights, but often issued the invitation herself, not by means of words, since she did not know how to make herself understood, but by means of actions.

Fortune, however, was not content to have made the wife of a king into the mistress of a lord, but was preparing a crueler alliance for the lady in place of the very pleasurable one she had with Pericone. For Pericone had a twenty-five-year-old brother named Marato, fair and fresh as a rose, who had seen the lady and felt powerfully attracted to her. As far as he could judge from her reactions, it seemed very likely to him that he stood in her good graces, and since he thought the only

---

*By "Alexandrian" is meant "Egyptian," presumably belly dancing.

thing between him and what he desired was the strict watch that Pericone kept over her, he devised a cruel plan that he quickly turned into a terrible reality.

There happened to be a ship down in the port just then that was loaded up with merchandise and bound for Chiarenza in Romania.* Although it had already hoisted sail, ready to depart with the first favorable wind, Marato made a deal with its two young Genoese masters for them to take himself and the lady on board the following night. With this out of the way, Marato made up his mind about how he would proceed, and as soon as night fell, he wandered unobserved over to Pericone's house, taking along with him several of his most trusted companions whom he had enlisted specifically to help him carry out his plan. Since Pericone had no reason to be on his guard, Marato was able to hide himself inside the house just as he had told his men he was going to do. Then, in the dead of night, he opened the door and led them to the room in which Pericone and the lady were sleeping. They slew Pericone in his bed and seized the lady, now wide awake and in tears, threatening to kill her if she made any noise. Then, after taking many of Pericone's most precious possessions, they left the house without being heard and hurried down to the harbor where Marato and the lady immediately boarded the ship while his companions returned to the city. The crew set sail, and with a good, fresh wind behind them, began their voyage.

The lady grieved bitterly over this second misfortune, just as she had over the first one, but Marato made good use of Saint Grows-in-the-Hand, God's gift to all of us, and began consoling her in such a way that she was soon on intimate terms with him and forgot all about Pericone. Things thus seemed to be going pretty well for her, but Fortune, not content it seems with the lady's previous tribulations, was already preparing her a new one. For what with her beauty, which was, as we have said many times before, quite stunning, and her extremely refined

*Boccaccio's "Romania" was the name given generally to the Byzantine (i.e., Eastern Roman) Empire, although the Peloponnesus, in which the port of Chiarenza (or Klarenza) is located, was more frequently called Morea, the term Byzantine Greeks used for the area.

manners, the two young masters of the ship contracted such a violent love for her that they forgot about everything else and sought only to serve her and provide for her pleasures, at the same time, however, making sure that Marato never caught on to what they were doing.

When they discovered they were both in love with her, they talked things over in secret and agreed to make the acquisition of her love a joint venture—as if love could be shared like merchandise or money. The fact that Marato kept a close watch on her hindered their plan, but one day, when the ship was sailing ahead at full speed and he stood at the stern gazing out to sea, never suspecting that there was a plot against him, they both crept up on him, grabbed him quickly from behind, and threw him into the water. By the time anyone noticed that he had fallen overboard, they were already more than a mile away. When the lady heard what had happened and realized that there was no way of going to his rescue, she began filling the ship once more with the sound of her mourning.

Her two lovers came straightway to console her, and with the aid of sweet words and the most extravagant promises, of which she understood very little, they worked at getting her to calm down. She was really lamenting her own misfortune more than the loss of Marato, and when, after their lengthy speeches, which they repeated twice over, she seemed much less distressed to them, the pair had a private discussion to decide who would be the first one to take her to bed with him. Each man wanted that honor, and failing to reach an agreement, they started a violent argument about it. Their words kept fanning the flames of their anger until they reached for their knives and in a fury hurled themselves at one another, and before any of the ship's crew could separate them, they had both been stabbed repeatedly. One of them died instantly from his wounds, and although the other survived, he was left with serious injuries to many parts of his body.

The lady was very upset over what had happened, for she could see that she was all alone there now, with no one to turn to for aid or advice, and she was terrified that the relations and friends of the two masters would take their anger out on her. However, partly because of the injured man's pleas on her behalf and partly because the ship quickly reached Chiarenza, she escaped the danger of being killed. Upon arriving, she disembarked with the injured man and went to stay with him at an inn, from which rumors of her stunning beauty spread throughout the city, eventually reaching the ears of the Prince of Morea who was living in Chiarenza at the time. He insisted on seeing her, and once he had, not only did he find that her beauty surpassed anything he had heard about it, but he immediately fell in love with her so passionately that he could think of nothing else.

Having learned about the circumstances of her arrival in the city, he saw no reason why he should not be able to have her, and in fact, while he was still trying to figure out a way to do so, the family of the injured man discovered what he was up to and sent the lady to him without a moment's hesitation. The Prince was absolutely delighted by this turn of events, as was the lady, who felt she had escaped a very dangerous situation indeed. Observing that she was endowed with refined manners as well as beauty, the Prince concluded, not having any other way to determine her identity, that she had to be a noblewoman, which had the effect of redoubling his love for her and led not only to his keeping her in high style, but to his treating her more like a wife than a mistress.

When the lady compared her present situation with the awful experiences she had been through, she considered herself pretty well off, and now that she had recovered fully and felt happy again, her beauty flowered to such an extent that all of Romania seemed to be talking about nothing else. And that is why the Duke of Athens, a handsome, well-built youth, who was a friend and relative of the Prince, was moved by a desire to see her. And so, under the pretext that he was just paying a visit to the Prince, as he used to do on occasion, he arrived in Chiarenza at the head of a splendid, noble retinue, and was received there with honor amid great rejoicing.[7]

A few days later, the two men fell to talking about the lady's beauty, and the Duke asked if she was really so marvelous an object as people said. "Far more so!" replied the Prince. "But rather than take my word for it, I'd prefer it if you judged with your own eyes."

The Prince invited the Duke to follow him, and together they went to the place where she was staying. Having already been informed of their approach, she welcomed them with the greatest civility, her face glowing with happiness. They had her sit down between them, but took no pleasure in conversing with her since she understood little or nothing of their language. Instead, as if she were some marvelous creature, they wound up simply gazing at her, and especially the Duke, who could hardly bring himself to believe she was a mere mortal. He did not realize he was drinking down the poison of Love through his eyes as he stared at her, and although he may have believed he could satisfy his desire simply by looking, the wretch was actually being caught up in the snare of her beauty and was falling passionately in love with her.[8] After he and the Prince had taken their leave and he had had some time for reflection, he concluded that the Prince was the happiest of men in having such a beautiful creature at his beck and call. Many and varied were his thoughts on the subject until his burning passion finally overcame his sense of honor, and he decided that, whatever the consequences, he would do everything in his power to deprive the Prince of that happiness and make it his own.

Determined to move with dispatch, he set aside all considerations of reason and justice, concentrating entirely on his treachery, and one day, in furtherance of his wicked plan, made arrangements with one of the Prince's most trusted servants, a man named Ciuriaci, to have his horses and baggage secretly readied for a sudden departure. When night fell, Ciuriaci, whom we just mentioned, silently let him and an accomplice, both fully armed, into the Prince's chamber. It was a very hot night, and while the lady lay sleeping, the Duke saw the Prince standing completely naked next to a window that faced the sea, enjoying a light breeze coming from that direction. The Duke, who had told his accomplice what to do ahead of time, stole quietly across the room to the window and thrust a dagger into the Prince's back with such force that it went straight through him, after which he quickly picked him up and hurled him out of the window. The palace stood high above the sea, and the window by which the Prince had been standing overlooked a cluster of houses that had been reduced to ruins by the pounding of the waves. People went there seldom, if ever, and consequently, as the

Duke had foreseen, no one noticed the Prince's body as it fell, for there was no one there to see it.

When the Duke's accomplice saw that the deed was done, he quickly took out a noose he had brought with him for the purpose, and while pretending to embrace Ciuriaci, threw it around his neck, and drew it so tight that the man could not make a sound. The Duke then came over, and together they strangled Ciuriaci before throwing him down where the Prince had just been thrown. Once this was done, and they were absolutely certain that neither the lady nor anyone else had heard them, the Duke took up a lantern, carried it over to the bed, and quietly took all the covers off of her as she lay there sound asleep. Looking her over from head to toe, he was enraptured, and if he had found her attractive when dressed, now that she was naked, his admiration knew no bounds. The flames of the Duke's desire were burning even more fiercely than before, and unperturbed by the crime he had just committed, he lay down beside her, his hands still bloody, and made love to her, while she, half asleep, thought he was the Prince.

After a while, having enjoyed himself to the limit with her, the Duke got up and summoned a few of his men whom he ordered to hold the lady in such a way that she could not make a sound and to carry her out through the secret door by which he had entered. Then, making as little noise as possible, they put her on a horse, and the Duke led them all in the direction of Athens. Since he already had a wife, however, he did not take this unhappiest of ladies to Athens itself, but to an extraordinarily beautiful villa he had, not far from the city, that overlooked the sea. There he kept her hidden away, but ordered that she be treated with respect and given everything she needed.

The next day the Prince's courtiers waited until nones for him to get up, but when they still heard no sound coming from his room, they pushed open the doors, which were unlocked, only to discover that no one was there. Working on the assumption that he had gone off somewhere in secret to spend a few days in the happy company of his beautiful mistress, they did not give the matter a second thought.

Things stood thus until the next day, when a madman, who had wandered into the ruins where the bodies of the Prince and Ciuriaci were lying, dragged Ciuriaci out by the rope around his neck, and walked about, pulling the body behind him. When people recognized who it was, they were dumbfounded and managed to coax the madman into taking them to the place from which he had brought the body. There, to the immense sorrow of the entire city, they found the dead Prince. After burying him with full honors, they opened an investigation to discover who was responsible for the heinous crime, and when they learned that the Duke of Athens, who had departed in secret, was nowhere to be found, they concluded correctly that he was the culprit and that he must have taken the lady away with him. After hastily choosing a brother of their dead Prince as their new ruler, they urged him with all the eloquence at their command to seek revenge. And when yet more evidence appeared, confirming that their suspicions were true, the new Prince summoned his friends, relations, and servants from various places to support his cause, quickly assembling a splendid, large, and powerful army, with which he set out to wage war against the Duke of Athens.

The moment the Duke heard what was happening, he, too, mobilized his entire army for his defense. Many noblemen came to his aid, including two who were sent by the Emperor of Constantinople, namely his son Constantine and his nephew Manuel, who arrived at the head of a fine large force.[9] They were warmly welcomed by the Duke, and even more so by the Duchess, who was Constantine's sister.

As war came closer day by day, the Duchess found a convenient moment to invite the two young men to her room, where she told them the entire story in great detail. Weeping copiously as she explained the causes of the war, she complained bitterly about the disrespect the Duke was showing her by having some woman as his mistress, whose existence he thought he was managing to keep hidden from her, and she begged them, for the sake of the Duke's honor and her own happiness, to take whatever measures were necessary to set things right. Since the young men already knew the whole story, they did not ask her very many questions, but did their best to comfort her and give her every reason to be hopeful. Then, after being informed as to where the lady was staying, they took their leave of her.

Since they had often heard the lady praised for her marvelous beauty, they were actually quite eager to see her and begged the Duke to present her to them. He promised he would, forgetting what had happened to the Prince for having done something similar. And the next morning, after arranging to have a magnificent banquet served in a lovely garden that was on the estate where the lady was staying, he took the two young men, along with a few other companions, to dine with her there. Sitting down next to her, Constantine stared at her in wonder, vowing to himself that he had never seen anything so lovely and that no one would blame the Duke, or anybody else, for resorting to treachery and other dishonest means in order to gain possession of so beautiful an object. And as he looked her over again and again, each time he admired her more than the time before, until finally the same thing happened to him that had happened to the Duke. As a result, by the time he left, he was so much in love with her that he abandoned any thought of going to war and concentrated on how he might take her away from the Duke, all the while doing a very good job of concealing his passion from everyone.

As Constantine was burning in this fire, the moment arrived to march against the Prince who had by now almost reached the Duke's territories. In accordance with their strategic plan, the Duke, Constantine, and all the others left Athens and went to take up positions along certain stretches of the frontier where they intended to block the Prince's advance. While they waited there for several days, Constantine, whose thoughts and feelings were entirely focused on the lady, fancied that since the Duke was no longer anywhere near her, he now had an excellent opportunity to get what he wanted. Pretending to be seriously ill in order to have a pretext for returning to Athens, he got permission from the Duke, handed his command over to Manuel, and went back to stay with his sister in the city. Several days later, after he got her talking about the disrespect she thought the Duke was showing her with his kept woman, he told her that if she wanted, he could certainly be of considerable assistance to her in this business, for he could have the woman removed from where she was staying and taken elsewhere. Thinking that Constantine was prompted by his love for her rather than for the lady, the Duchess said that it would please her very much, provided it was done in such a way that the Duke never found out she had given her consent to the scheme. Constantine reassured her completely on this point, and accordingly, the Duchess gave him permission to proceed in whatever way he thought best.

Constantine had a swift boat fitted out in secret, and one evening, after giving those of his men who were on board their instructions, he sent it to a spot near the garden on the estate where the lady was staying. Then, with another group of men, he went to her villa, where he was warmly received by her servants and by the lady herself, who at his request, went with him and his men to take a walk in the garden, accompanied by her servants.

Pretending he wanted to speak to her on behalf of the Duke, he led her down toward a gate overlooking the sea that had been unlocked earlier by one of his crew. There, at a given signal, the boat pulled up, and Constantine had his men seize her and quickly put her on board. Then he turned to her servants and said: "Don't anyone move or make a sound unless you want to be killed. My intention here is not to steal the Duke's mistress, but to take away the shame he's inflicted on my sister."

Seeing that no one dared to respond to him, he boarded the boat with his men, and sitting down beside the weeping lady, he ordered them to put their oars into the water and get under way. They did not row so much as fly along, arriving at Aegina just before dawn the next day.[10]

Disembarking there in order to rest, Constantine had his fun with the lady, who did nothing but lament her unlucky beauty. Then they boarded the boat once again and in just a few days reached Chios, where Constantine decided to put up, thinking he would be safe there both from his father's reprimands and from the possibility that someone might take away from him the lady he himself had stolen. For several days the beauty bewailed her misfortune, but eventually, thanks to Constantine's unremitting efforts to console her, she began to enjoy, as she had every other time, the lot that Fortune had assigned her.

This was the state of affairs when Osbech, at that time the King of the Turks, who was constantly at war with the Emperor, chanced to come to Smyrna, where he learned that Constantine was leading a dissolute life on Chios with some woman of his whom he had abducted and that he had consequently not bothered to set up any defenses there.[11] Arriving one night with a squadron of light warships, Osbech quietly entered the town with his men, capturing many people in their beds before they were even aware that the enemy was upon them, and killing those who awoke in time to run and get their weapons.[12] They then set fire to the town, loaded their booty and their prisoners onto the ships, and went back to Smyrna. Upon reviewing their spoils after their return, the young Osbech was delighted to discover the beautiful lady, whom he recognized as being the one he had captured in bed together with Constantine as they lay sleeping. He married her on the spot, and after the wedding spent the next several months very happily sleeping with her.

In the period before these events occurred, the Emperor had been negotiating a pact with Basano, the King of Cappadocia, to have his forces attack Osbech from one direction while the Emperor assaulted him from the other.[13] He had not yet brought their negotiations to a conclusion, however, because he would not agree to some of Basano's demands that he found quite unreasonable. But on hearing what had happened to his son, the Emperor was so distraught that he accepted the King of Cappadocia's terms at once and urged him to attack Osbech as soon as he possibly could, while he himself made preparations to come down on Osbech from the other direction.

When Osbech heard about all this, rather than let himself get caught in the middle between two powerful rulers, he assembled his army and marched against the King of Cappadocia, leaving the lovely lady at Smyrna under the protection of a loyal retainer and friend. Some time later, he confronted the King of Cappadocia and attacked him, but in the battle his army was defeated and put to flight, and he himself was killed. Unopposed, the victorious Basano then marched on Smyrna, and as he went, all the peoples along the way submitted to him as their conqueror.

The retainer in whose care Osbech had left the lovely lady, a man named Antioco, was so taken with her beauty that he betrayed the trust of his friend and master, and despite his advanced years, fell in love with her. It pleased her immensely that he knew her language, because for a number of years she had been forced to live as if she were a deaf-mute, incapable of understanding others or getting them to understand her. Spurred on by love, in the first few days Antioco began taking so many liberties with her that before long they had cast aside any concern for their master, who was away fighting in the war, and became not merely friends, but lovers who gave one another the greatest pleasure imaginable over and over again as they lay together between the sheets.

When they heard that Osbech had been defeated and killed, however, and that Basano was on his way, carrying everything before him, they were of one mind in deciding to leave rather than wait for his arrival. Taking with them a substantial quantity of Osbech's most valuable possessions, they fled together in secret to Rhodes, where they had not been very long before Antioco contracted a fatal illness.[14] At the time he happened to have a Cypriot merchant staying in his house, a very close friend whom he loved dearly, and as Antioco felt the end approaching, he decided to leave his friend both his possessions and his beloved lady. And so, when he felt his death was imminent, he summoned the two of them and said:

"I have no doubt that my strength is failing, which saddens me because my life has never been as happy as it's been of late. Truthfully, though, there's one thing that reconciles me to my death, and it's that since I'm going to die, I will do so in the arms of the two people I love more than anyone else in the world, that is, in your arms, my dear, dear friend, and in those of this lady, whom I've loved more than I love myself for as long as I've known her. But still, what really continues to trouble me is that when I die, she'll be left all alone here in a strange land, with no one to turn to for help or counsel. And this worry would weigh on me even more than it does if I didn't have you here, because I believe that, out of love for me, you will take good care of her just as you would of me. Consequently, in the event of my death, I commit her, together with all my worldly goods, to your charge, and I entreat you as earnestly as I can to make use of them in whatever way you think will offer my soul some measure of consolation. And as for you, my dearest lady, I beg you not to forget me after my death, for then I can boast up there that I have been loved down here by the most beautiful woman ever fashioned by Nature. And now, if both of you will just reassure me on these two points, you may have no doubt but that I will die content."

Both Antioco's merchant friend and the lady wept as they listened to his words, and when he was finished, they comforted him and swore on their honor to do what he requested if he should happen to die. And not long after this, he did, in fact, pass away, and they saw to it that he was given an honorable burial.

A few days later, when the Cypriot merchant had taken care of all his business in Rhodes, he decided to take ship on a Catalan merchant vessel then in port that was about to sail to Cyprus.[15] He asked the lady what she wanted to do, in light of the fact that he was compelled to return to Cyprus, and she replied that if he had no objection, she would gladly go with him, because she hoped that, out of love for Antioco, he would think of her like a sister and would treat her accordingly. The merchant said he would be happy to do whatever she wished, and in order to protect her from any harm that might befall her before they reached Cyprus, he told everyone she was his wife. When they got on board, they were, consequently, assigned a small cabin in the stern, and to ensure that their actions were consistent with their words, he slept in the same narrow little bunk with her. What happened next was something that neither one of them had intended when they left Rhodes. Stimulated by the darkness as well as by the warmth and comfort of the bed, which are forces not to be underestimated, they were both seized by the same desires, and forgetting all about the loyalty and love they owed Antioco, before long they were fondling one another, with the inevitable result that even before they reached Paphos, the Cypriot's hometown, they were sleeping together like a regular married couple.[16] Indeed, for quite some time after they reached their destination, she went on living with the merchant in his house.

By chance, a gentleman named Antigono happened to come to Paphos on some business or other at a time when the Cypriot merchant was away on a trading mission in Armenia. An elderly man, Antigono had acquired even more wisdom than years, albeit very little wealth in the process, because every time he had undertaken a commission in the service of the King of Cyprus, Fortune had always been his enemy.[17] One day, as he was passing by the house where the lovely lady was staying, he happened to catch sight of her at one of the windows. He just could not stop staring at her, not only because she was so beautiful, but also because he had a vague recollection that he had seen her at some other time, although he could by no means remember where that had been.

For a long while, the lovely lady had been Fortune's plaything, but the moment was approaching when her sufferings would be over. Observing Antigono, she recalled having seen him in Alexandria where he had served her father in a position of some importance, and all of a sudden she was filled with hope that there might be some possibility of her returning once more to her royal station with the help of this man's advice. Since her merchant was out of the way, she sent for the old counselor at the first opportunity, and when he arrived, she asked him shyly if he was, as she thought, Antigono di Famagosto. Antigono replied that he was, adding: "My lady, I think I've seen you before, but I can't, for the life of me, remember where. Please be good enough, therefore, unless you have some objection, to remind me who you are."

When the lady heard that he was indeed Antigono, to his complete astonishment she burst into tears and threw her arms about his neck. Then, after a moment, she asked him if he had ever seen her in Alexandria. The instant Antigono heard her question, he recognized that she was Alatiel, the Sultan's daughter, who everybody thought had died at sea. He tried to bow to her as court etiquette required, but she would not permit it, inviting him, instead, to sit down beside her for a while. When he was seated, he asked her with due reverence how and when and from where she had come to Cyprus, for all of Egypt was convinced that she had drowned at sea many years before.

"I really wish that had happened," replied the lady, "instead of my having led the sort of life I've led. Furthermore, I think my father would agree with me if he ever found out about it." Then, having said this, she began weeping prodigiously once again.

"My lady, don't distress yourself unnecessarily," said Antigono. "Tell me about your misfortunes, if you like, and about the life you've led. Perhaps things can be handled in such a way that, with God's help, we'll be able to find a solution for your problem."

"Antigono," said the lovely lady, "when I first saw you here, I felt I was looking at my own father, and although I could have concealed my identity from you, I was moved to reveal it by the same love and tender affection I am bound to feel for him. Actually, there are few people I would have been as happy to have seen here as I am to have seen you, and therefore, I'm going to reveal to you, as to a father, the story of my terrible misfortunes, which I've always kept hidden from everyone else. If, after you've heard it, you can see any means of restoring me to my pristine condition, I implore you to make use of it. If not, I beg you never to tell anyone that you've either seen me or heard anything about me."

This said, she gave him an account, without ever ceasing to weep, of everything that had happened to her from the day she was shipwrecked off Majorca up to the present moment. Her story made Antigono start weeping himself out of pity for her, and after pondering the matter awhile, he said: "My lady, since no one ever knew who you were during all your misadventures, have no doubt but that I can restore you, more precious than ever, first to your father and then, as his bride, to the King of Algarve."

Questioned by her as to how he would manage this, he explained in detail just what she had to do. Then, to prevent anything from happening that might cause a delay, Antigono returned at once to Famagosto where he presented himself before the King. "My lord," he said, "if it please you, you can do something at very little cost that will greatly redound to your honor, while simultaneously being of inestimable benefit to me, who have grown poor while I've been in your service."

When the King asked how this might be done, Antigono answered: "The beautiful young daughter of the Sultan, who was long thought to have drowned at sea, has turned up in Paphos. For many years she has suffered through extreme hardships in order to preserve her honor, and now she is living here in poverty and wants to return to her father. If it should be your pleasure to send her back to him under my escort, it would greatly enhance your honor and would mean a rich reward for me. It is, moreover, inconceivable that the Sultan would ever forget such a service."

Moved by regal feelings of magnanimity, the King said that it was indeed his pleasure to send the lady home, and he dispatched an honor guard to accompany her to Famagosto where he and the Queen received her with the most incredible pomp and circumstance. When they asked her about her adventures, she replied by recounting the whole story just as Antigono had taught her to tell it.

A few days later, at her request, the King sent her back to the Sultan under Antigono's protection and with a splendid retinue of distinguished gentlemen and ladies. No one need ask how warm a welcome she got there or how Antigono and her entire entourage were received. After letting her rest awhile, the Sultan wanted to know how it had come about that she was still alive, where she had been living for all that time, and why she had never sent him word about her situation.

The lady, who had memorized Antigono's instructions to the letter, answered the Sultan as follows: "Father, some twenty days after I left you, our ship foundered in a fierce storm and ran aground one night on some beach or other in the West near a place called Aigues-Mortes.[18] I never found out what happened to the men who were on board. All I do remember is that when dawn arrived, I felt as though I was rising from the dead and returning to life. Some peasants, who had spotted the wrecked ship, came running from all over to plunder it. When I was put ashore with two of my women, they were instantly snatched up by some young men who then fled, carrying them off in different directions, and I never discovered what became of them. As for me, although I tried to fight them off, two young men grabbed me and started to drag me away by my hair. I was weeping violently the whole time, but then, just as they started heading down a road in the direction of a very dense forest, four horsemen happened to come riding by, and the instant my abductors caught sight of them, they let go of me and immediately fled away.

"When they saw what was happening, the four horsemen, who seemed like persons of some authority, galloped over to me. They asked me a lot of questions, and I gave them a lot of answers, but it was impossible for us to understand one another. Then, after a long consultation among themselves, they put me on one of their horses and led me to a convent of women who practiced these men's religion. I have no idea what they said there, but the women gave me a very kind welcome and always treated me with respect. While I was in the convent, I joined them in reverently worshipping Saint Grows-in-the-Deep-Valley, to whom the women of that country are passionately devoted.[19] After I'd lived there awhile and had learned something of their language, they asked me who I was and what country I'd come from. Knowing where I was, I feared that if I told them the truth, they might expel me as an enemy to their religion, and so I replied that I was the daughter of an important nobleman of Cyprus, who had been sending me to be married in Crete when, unfortunately, we were driven onto their shores by a storm and shipwrecked.

"Fearful of a worse fate, I made a regular habit of observing their customs of every sort until, eventually, I was asked by the women's superior, whom they call their Abbess, whether I wanted to return to Cyprus, and I replied that there was nothing I desired more. Out of concern for my honor, however, she was unwilling to entrust me to just anyone coming to Cyprus, at least up until about two months ago, when certain French gentlemen, some of whom were related to the Abbess, arrived there with their wives. When she heard that they were going to Jerusalem to visit the Sepulcher, where the man they consider their God was buried after the Jews had killed Him, she placed me in their care and asked them to hand me over to my father in Cyprus.

"It would make too long a story if I were to describe how much I was honored and how warm a welcome I was given by these noblemen and their wives. Suffice it to say that we all took ship and in just a few days reached Paphos, where it suddenly hit me that I'd come to a place where I didn't know anyone and thus had no idea what to tell the noblemen who wanted to follow the venerable lady's instructions and hand me over to my father. Perhaps God took pity on me, however, for he arranged to have Antigono there on the shore at Paphos at the precise moment we were getting off the ship. I called out to him at

once, using our own language so as not to be understood by the noblemen and their wives, and told him to welcome me as his daughter. He
grasped my meaning instantly and made a tremendous fuss over me.
After entertaining those noblemen and their wives as well as his limited means allowed, he took me to the King of Cyprus, and I couldn't
begin to describe how much he honored me, not only with the welcome
he gave me there, but by sending me back here to you. If anything else
remains to be said, I leave it to Antigono, for he has heard me recount
my adventures time and time again."

"My lord," said Antigono, turning to the Sultan, "she has now told
you exactly the same story she's recounted to me many times and what
the noblemen who were accompanying her told me as well. There's only
one part that she's left out, which I think she omitted because it would
not be appropriate for her to talk about it, and that is how much praise
the gentlemen and ladies with whom she was traveling lavished on her
not just because of the honest life she'd led with the pious women, but
also because of her virtue and her laudable character. She also failed to
mention how all of them, the men as well as the women, grieved and
wept bitter tears when the time came to say farewell to her and place
her in my charge. Were I to recount in detail everything they told me
on this subject, I'd be talking not only all day, but all night, too. Let it
suffice for me to say just this much, that from what their words have
revealed to me, and from what I myself have been able to see, you may
boast of having a daughter who is far lovelier, chaster, and more courageous than that of any monarch wearing a crown today."

The Sultan was absolutely overjoyed to hear these things, and he
repeatedly asked God to grant him the grace to bestow proper rewards
on all those who had treated his daughter so honorably, and in particular on the King of Cyprus who had sent her home with such pomp
and ceremony. A few days later, having ordered the most lavish gifts
for Antigono, he gave him leave to return to Cyprus, sending letters
and special envoys along with him to convey his most sincere gratitude to the King for what he had done for his daughter. Then, since
he wanted to bring what he had started long before to its conclusion,
namely to make her the wife of the King of Algarve, he wrote to the

King, explaining everything that had happened, and adding that if he still wished to have her, he should send his envoys to fetch her. The King of Algarve was quite delighted by this proposition, sent an honorable escort for her, and gave her a joyous welcome. Thus, although she had slept with eight men perhaps ten thousand times, she not only came to the King's bed as if she were a virgin, but made him believe she really was one, and for a good many years after that, lived a perfectly happy life with him as his Queen. And that is the reason why we say:

A mouth that's been kissed never loses its charm,
But just like the moon, it's forever renewed.[20]

Day 2, Story 8

Having been falsely accused, the Count of Antwerp goes into exile and leaves his two children in different parts of England. When he later returns from Ireland in disguise and finds that they are doing well, he serves as a groom in the army of the King of France until his innocence is established and he is restored to his former station.[1]

The ladies sighed repeatedly over the lovely lady's various misadventures, but who knows what may have moved them to do so? Perhaps some of them sighed as much out of a desire for such frequent marriages as out of pity for Alatiel. However, setting this question aside for the present, after the group had finished laughing at Panfilo's last words, which indicated to the Queen that his tale was done, she turned to Elissa and ordered her to keep things going with a story of her own. Happy to oblige, Elissa began as follows:

The field in which we have been roaming today is so very wide that, as we go jousting there, every single one of us should be able to run the course not just once, but ten times or more, so abundantly has Fortune filled it with wonders and afflictions. But now, to choose just one story to recount from among an infinite number of them, let me tell you that when the power of the Holy Roman Empire had been transferred from France to Germany, the two countries became the bitterest of enemies, and a fierce, protracted war broke out between them.[2] In order both to defend their own country and to attack the Germans, the King of France and one of his sons mobilized all the military resources of their realm, including those of their retainers and relatives, and put an immense army in the field ready to move against the enemy. Before they proceeded any further, however, not wishing to leave their country ungoverned, they installed Gualtieri, the Count of Antwerp, as viceroy in their place. They knew he was both noble and wise as well as being one of their most loyal friends and retainers, and they also thought that although he was skilled in the art of war, he was less fit for its hardships than for handling more delicate matters. Thus, leaving him to govern the entire Kingdom of France, off they went on their campaign.

A prudent man, Gualtieri performed his duties in an orderly manner, always conferring with the Queen and her daughter-in-law about everything, for although they had been left in his care and under his jurisdiction, he nevertheless treated them with deference as if they were his lords and masters. This Gualtieri was about forty years old, very handsome in appearance, and as pleasant and well mannered as any nobleman could be. What is more, he was considered the best-dressed, the most elegant, and the most refined knight known in those times.

Gualtieri's wife had died, leaving him with just two small children, a boy and a girl, and one day, while the King of France and his son were away at the wars that have been referred to, and Gualtieri was holding court with the ladies I mentioned, discussing the affairs of the kingdom with them, the wife of the King's son happened to cast her eyes in his direction and found herself so passionately attracted by his good looks and fine manners that she secretly began to burn with the most fervent love for him. Considering that she herself was young and fresh, and he was wifeless, she thought it would be an easy matter to satisfy her desires, and since nothing stood in her way except shame, she decided to get rid of it and to reveal what she felt directly to him. And so, one day, when she was alone and the time seemed right, she sent for him on the pretext that she had a number of things she needed to discuss with him.

The Count, whose thoughts were all quite distant from those of the lady, came to her without delay. The two of them were quite alone in the room, and at her request the Count sat down beside her on a sofa. Twice he asked her why she had summoned him, and each time she remained silent, until finally, the love she felt forced her to speak. Blushing scarlet with shame, on the point of tears, she was trembling all over as she stammered out:

"Sweet friend and lord, O my dearest, since you are wise, you surely understand how frail men and women are, and how some, for any number of reasons, are frailer than others. That is why a just judge would never impose the same punishment on people of different social ranks for the same sin. For wouldn't everyone agree that if a poor man or woman, who has to work hard to earn enough for all the necessities of life, were to surrender to the promptings of Love, he or she would be considered more culpable than a rich woman who has ample leisure and possesses everything she needs to gratify her desires? Surely, I don't think anyone would dispute this. Therefore, in my opinion, the advantages the rich woman possesses should go a long way toward excusing her, should she, by chance, slip and fall in love. And if, in addition, she chose a wise and valiant lover on whom to bestow her favors, then she would need no excuse whatsoever.[3] Now, in my opinion, I meet both of these requirements, and since I have other reasons as well for falling in love, such as my youth and my husband's absence, it is only fitting that these things should come to my aid and defend my burning love in your sight. And if they have as much influence as they should have with wise men, then let me appeal to you for your counsel and assistance in what I'm about to ask you.

"The truth is that because of my husband's absence, I find myself unable to resist the promptings of the flesh and the power of Love, which are so irresistible that they will conquer even the strongest men, to say nothing of frail women, just as they always have. Living a life of ease, as you can see, with nothing to occupy my time, I have allowed myself to slip and can think of nothing but falling in love and the pleasures of the flesh. If people knew about this, I realize they would consider it dishonorable, but still, as long as it remains hidden, I don't think there's any harm in it, especially since Love has been very obliging to me and has not deprived me of my good judgment in choosing a lover. On the contrary, he actually enhanced it by showing me how worthy you are of being loved by a woman of my station. For unless I deceive myself, I think you're the most handsome, agreeable, refined, and prudent knight to be found anywhere in the Kingdom of France, and just as I can claim to have no husband here, so you, too, have no wife. In the name, therefore, of the immense love I feel for you, I implore you not to deny me your love in return, but to take pity on my youth, which is truly melting away for you like ice before a fire."

These words produced such an abundance of tears that even though she intended to go on pleading with him, she no longer had the ability to speak. Instead, very nearly overcome by emotion, she bowed her head, and still weeping, allowed it to rest on his breast. The Count was the most loyal of knights and began to upbraid her sternly for her insane passion, pushing her away as she tried to throw her arms about his neck. With many an oath, he swore that he would sooner allow himself to be drawn and quartered than permit such harm to be done to his lord's honor, either by himself or by anyone else.

No sooner did the lady hear this than she instantly forgot all about love, and burning now with savage fury, she said to him: "So, base knight, this is how my desire is going to be flouted by you? Since you want to be the cause of my death, I'll be the cause of yours, so help me God, or I'll have you driven from the face of the earth." Having said this, she tore at her hair with her hands until it was completely disheveled, ripped apart her clothes at her breast, and began screaming out loud: "Help, help! The Count of Antwerp is trying to rape me!"

When he saw what was happening, the Count was far more concerned about the envy of the courtiers than confident he could rely on his own clear conscience, for he feared that they would sooner believe the lady's wickedness than his claims of innocence. He therefore rushed out of the room, left the palace, and fled to his house where, without pausing for further reflection, he set his children on a horse, mounted one himself, and rode off toward Calais as quickly as possible.

At the sound of the lady's screams, many people came running, and when they saw her and heard what she was shouting about, not only did they believe everything she said, but they were now convinced that the Count had been using his charm and his refined manners all along for just this purpose. In a fury they rushed to his residence in order to arrest him, but failing to find him there, they ransacked the place and then razed it to the ground.[4] When the story, replete with all its sordid details, reached the King and his son in the field, they were absolutely furious and condemned the Count and his descendants to perpetual banishment, promising huge rewards to whoever would bring him back dead or alive.

Deeply troubled that by fleeing he had transformed himself from an innocent man into a guilty one, the Count reached Calais with his children, having managed to conceal his identity and avoid being recognized by anyone. He made a rapid crossing to England, where after dressing them all in shabby clothes, he proceeded toward London. Before entering the city, however, he spoke at some length with his two little children, stressing two things in particular: first, that they should be patient and endure the state of poverty in which, through no fault of their own, Fortune had placed not just them, but him as well; and second, that if they valued their lives, they should take every precaution not to reveal to anyone where they came from or whose children they were. The boy, named Luigi, was about nine years old, while the girl, named Violante, was about seven, but despite their tender age, they both understood their father's lessons perfectly, as they later demonstrated by means of their actions. To make things easier for them, the Count decided he needed to give them new names, and this he did, calling the boy Perotto and the girl Giannetta.[5] Once they reached London, they began to go about, dressed in their shabby clothes, begging for alms, just like the French tramps we see around here.

By chance, as the Count and his two children were begging one morning in front of a church, a great lady, who was the wife of one of the Marshals of the King of England, happened to come out and catch sight of them. On being asked where he hailed from and whether the children were his, the Count replied that he was from Picardy and that the two children were his indeed, but that he had had to flee with them because of a crime committed by a wicked elder son of his. The compassionate lady looked the girl over and was quite taken with her, for she was beautiful and charming and had an air of gentility about her.

"Good sir," said the lady, "if you would be willing to leave this little daughter of yours with me, I'd be happy to take her on, for she looks like a very nice child to me. And should she turn out to be an honest woman, I'll arrange a suitable marriage for her at the proper time."

This request was most gratifying to the Count, who promptly accepted it and handed his daughter over, albeit with tears in his eyes, warmly commending her to the lady's care. He was well aware of who the lady was, and now that he had found a good home for his daughter, he decided it was time to go. And so, he and Perotto begged their way across the island, a journey he found quite tiring since he was not used to traveling on foot, until they finally reached Wales, where another one of the King's Marshals had his residence. This nobleman lived in the grand manner, maintaining a large suite of retainers, and to his courtyard the Count, sometimes alone and sometimes with his son, would frequently go in order to get something to eat.

The Marshal, whom I mentioned, had several sons who, together with the sons of the local nobility, used to play children's games, such as running and jumping, in the courtyard. Gradually Perotto joined in, playing each of their games as skillfully as any one of them did, or even better. On several occasions the Marshal noticed this, and being taken with the boy's bearing and comportment, asked who he was. When he was informed that the boy was the son of a poor man who occasionally came there begging for alms, the Marshal sent someone to ask the Count to let him have the boy. Although the prospect of parting with his son was distressing, the Count, who had been praying to God for just such a thing, freely handed him over.

Having thus provided for his son and daughter, the Count saw no reason to stay in England any longer, and one way or another he managed to cross over to Ireland, where he landed at Strangford.[6] There he entered into the service of a knight, the vassal of a rural count, for whom he performed all the usual chores of a servant or a groom, and in that position, unrecognized by anyone, he remained, enduring great discomfort and hardship, for a very long time.

Meanwhile, back in London, Violante, now called Giannetta, had become a great favorite not only of the lady and her husband, with whom she was living, but of everyone else in the household, indeed of all the people who knew her, for as she grew up, her character developed so splendidly and she became so beautiful that she was a marvel to behold. Nor would anyone have denied, upon observing her comportment and her manners, that she deserved all the honor and wealth imaginable. Since receiving the girl from her father, the noblewoman had never been able to find out anything about him beyond what he had told her, and she now decided to arrange an honorable marriage for her in keeping with what she guessed the girl's social status might be. But God, who justly observes what people merit, decided things differently, for He knew that the girl was of noble birth, and through no fault of her own, was doing penance for the sins of another. Thus, we must believe that He, in His loving kindness, permitted events to take the course they did in order to keep the noble young lady from falling into the hands of some baseborn man.

The noblewoman with whom Giannetta was living had an only son whom she and his father loved very dearly, not just because he was their son, but also because his virtues and other meritorious qualities made him worthy of it, for he was exceptionally handsome, well mannered, courageous, and discreet. He was about six years older than Giannetta, and when he noticed how very beautiful and graceful she was, he fell so deeply in love with her that from then on he had eyes for no one but her. Because he suspected she was baseborn, however, he did not dare to ask his father and mother for permission to marry her. In fact, fearful of being reproached for falling in love with a commoner, he did his best to keep everything a secret, with the result that he was tormented by his feelings even more than if he had revealed them. Eventually, his suffering became so severe that it caused him to fall ill, and that most gravely. In an effort to cure him, a number of doctors were sent for, but despite their careful examination of one symptom after another, they were unable to diagnose his disease, and to a man they despaired of saving him. The youth's father and mother were so weighed down by grief and worry that they could not possibly have borne anything more, and they begged their son over and over again to tell them the cause of his illness. By way of answer to their piteous entreaties, he would only respond with sighs or tell them he felt he was wasting away.

One day it just so happened that a doctor, who was quite young, but deeply learned in his art, was seated beside him, holding his wrist in order to take his pulse, when for some reason or other Giannetta, who, for his mother's sake, had been devotedly caring for the youth, came into the room where he was lying. As soon as he saw her come in, he felt love's fire flare up in his heart, and although he neither spoke nor moved, his pulse began beating more strongly than usual. The doctor noticed this at once, but hid his surprise and remained silent, waiting to see how long it would last. As soon as Giannetta left the room, the rapid pulse returned to normal, leading the doctor to think that he may well have discovered part of the cause of the young man's illness. He waited for a while, and then, still holding the young man by the arm, he sent for Giannetta on the pretense that he wanted to ask her a question. She came right away, and no sooner did she enter the room, than the young man's pulse began pounding and only returned to normal after she left.

As a result, the doctor felt absolutely certain about his diagnosis, and having gotten to his feet, he took the young man's father and mother aside and said to them: "Your son's health doesn't depend on the remedies of physicians, but lies in Giannetta's hands. As I've learned from certain unmistakable signs, the young man is burning with love for her, although as far as I can tell, she herself is unaware of it. But now you yourselves must know what you have to do if you value his life."

On hearing this, the nobleman and his wife were relieved at having found a way to save their son, although they were distressed at the dubious prospect that in order to do so, they had to let him marry Giannetta. So, after the doctor had left, they went to see the sick young man.

"My son," said the lady, "I would never have believed you capable of desiring something and keeping it from me, especially when you see yourself wasting away because you can't get what you want. You may be quite sure—indeed, you should have known all along—that there's nothing I wouldn't do to make you happy, even if it were something less than honorable that I wouldn't do on my own account. However, despite your behaving as you have, it appears that the Lord God has decided to show you more mercy than you've shown yourself, and lest you die from your illness, He has revealed its cause to me, which is nothing other than the excessive love you feel for some young woman or other. This is something you really shouldn't be ashamed about revealing, since it's a normal experience for someone your age. Indeed, if you were not in love, I wouldn't think you were worth very much. So, instead of hiding things from me, my son, feel free to let me know what you want. Get rid of your melancholy and all those thoughts of yours that are causing this illness, and take heart. You may rest assured that there's nothing you can ask of me that I wouldn't do to make you happy, if it's in my power to do it, because you are more important to me than my own life. So, cast off your shame and your fear, and tell me if there's anything I can do to assist you with this love of yours. And if you don't find that I put my heart into it and work everything out for you, then you may consider me the cruelest mother who ever gave birth to a son."

As the young man listened to what his mother was saying, the first thing he felt was shame, but after reflecting that no one was in a better position than she was to procure his happiness, he overcame his embarrassment and said: "My lady, if I've kept my love a secret, it's only because I've noticed that most people, after reaching a certain age, refuse to remember they were ever young once themselves. But now that I see how understanding you are about all this, I will not deny that what you claim to have discovered is true. Moreover, I'll tell you who the girl is, but only on the condition that you'll do everything in your power to keep your promise and thus make it possible for me to regain my health."

Overly confident about an affair that was not going to turn out the way she thought it would, the lady replied eagerly that if he revealed his every wish to her, he should have no doubt but that she would immediately take steps to make sure he got what he wanted.

"My lady," said the youth, "I've been reduced to the condition you see me in because of the exalted beauty and exquisite manners of our Giannetta and also because of my own inability to make her notice my love for her, let alone make her feel pity for me, not to mention the fact that I've never dared to reveal these feelings to a single person. And unless you can find some way of making good on the promise you've given me, you may rest assured that my days are numbered."

"Oh, my son," said the lady with a smile, thinking this was a time to comfort him rather than scold him, "is this what you've made yourself sick about? Now don't you worry. Just leave everything to me, and you really are going to get better."

Filled with new hope, the youth very quickly showed signs of an enormous improvement, to the immense delight of his mother, who decided she would now attempt to make good on her promise. So, one day, she summoned Giannetta, and as if she were in jest, she asked the girl very courteously whether she had a lover.

"My lady," replied Giannetta, blushing all over, "it's neither expected nor proper for a poor maiden like me, who's been driven out of her home and lives in another's service, to be concerned with love."[7]

"Well," said the lady, "if you don't have a lover, we'd like to give you one, a man with whom you'll lead a merry life and enjoy your beauty even more. It's just not right for a lovely young lady like you to be without a lover."

"My lady," replied Giannetta, "from the moment you took me out of the poverty in which I was living with my father, you have raised me as your daughter, so in return, I really should do whatever you wish. But in this case not only will I never oblige you, but I think I am right in refusing to do so. If it's your pleasure to present me with a husband, then that's the man I intend to love, and no one else. For the only thing I have left that I've inherited from my ancestors is my honor, and I'm determined to safeguard and preserve it for as long as I live."

To the lady these words seemed to present a major obstacle to the plan she had devised as a way of keeping her promise to her son, although deep in her heart, like the wise woman she was, she praised the girl for her sentiments.

"Come on, Giannetta," she said. "What if His Royal Highness, the King, a gallant young knight, wanted to enjoy the love of a very beautiful girl like you, would you deny it to him?"

To this question, Giannetta promptly replied: "The King could take me by force, but he would never get my consent unless his intentions were honorable."

Knowing now what the girl's character was like, the lady did not say anything more on the subject, but decided to put her to the test.

She therefore told her son that as soon as he was well, she would put the girl in a bedroom with him where he could do his best to have his way with her, explaining that it seemed dishonorable for her to be pleading her son's cause like some procuress and soliciting her own lady-in-waiting for him.

This plan did not make the young man happy in the least, and his illness immediately took a terrible turn for the worse. Seeing this, the lady revealed her scheme to Giannetta, but discovered that she was more adamant than ever. She then told her husband what she had done, and although they found it quite disconcerting, they both reached the same conclusion and decided to let him marry her, preferring to have a live son with an unsuitable wife than a dead one with no wife at all. And so, though not without discussing the matter further among themselves, that is finally just what they did.

This made Giannetta very happy, and she thanked God with a devout heart for not having forgotten her, nor for all that did she ever reveal that she was anyone other than the daughter of a man from Picardy. After the young man got well, he celebrated his wedding, convinced he was the happiest man alive, and proceeded to have a very fine time with her indeed.

Meanwhile, back in Wales, Perotto, who continued living in the household of the Marshal of the King of England, had likewise grown up and had become one of his lord's favorites. As handsome and worthy a man as any on the island, he had no equal in all the land when it came to tournaments or jousting or other feats of arms, and as his fame grew, the name of Perotto the Picard came to be known everywhere.

And just as God had not forgotten his sister, so, too, He showed Himself to be mindful of Perotto. For a deadly plague visited that region, carrying off almost half of the population and causing the vast majority of those who were left to flee in terror to other parts, so that the country appeared to be completely deserted. In the midst of that devastation, Perotto's master, the Marshal, died, as did his wife and their son along with many of his brothers and grandchildren and other family members, leaving behind only a daughter of marriageable age and a handful of retainers, among them Perotto. Once the plague had spent some of its fury, the young woman, who knew Perotto to be a man of valor and discretion, responded to the advice and encouragement of her few remaining fellow countrymen by choosing him as her husband and making him the master of everything that had come to her by way of inheritance. Nor was it long before the King of England, having heard that the Marshal was dead and knowing the worth of Perotto the Picard, made him Marshal in the dead man's place.

And that, in short, is what happened to the two innocent children whom the Count of Antwerp had given away and thought he had lost forever.

More than eighteen years had passed since he had fled Paris, when the Count, who had been leading a miserable existence in Ireland and enduring all manner of hardships, realized that he had become an old man and was seized by a desire to find out, if possible, what had happened to his children. He could see for himself that his physical appearance was changed beyond all recognition from what it once had been, but because of his long years of hard work, he felt he was in better shape now than when he was young and living a life of leisure. And so, very poor and shabbily dressed, he left the person in whose household he had served for so many years, and went to England, returning to the place where he had parted from Perotto. To his great delight he discovered not only that his son was a handsome, healthy, sturdy young man, but also that he had become a marshal and a great lord. The Count did not want to make himself known, however, before finding out what had become of Giannetta.

Consequently, he set off on his journey again and did not stop until he reached London, where he made discreet inquiries about the lady with whom he had left Giannetta and about how his daughter was getting on there. When he found out that she had married the lady's son, he was overjoyed, and since he had now found his children alive and so well off, he concluded that all his past hardships were of little consequence. Eager to see his daughter again, he began hanging out near her house like a beggar, until one day he was spotted by Giachetto Lamiens—for that was the name of Giannetta's husband—who took pity on him, since he seemed so old and so poor, and Giachetto ordered one of his servants, for the love of God, to take him into the house and give him something to eat, which the servant did with a ready will.

Giannetta had borne her husband several boys and girls, of whom the eldest was no more than eight, and they were all the prettiest, most darling little children in the world. When they saw the Count eating, they gathered around him and made a fuss over him, as if moved by some hidden power that made them sense he was their grandfather. Since he knew they were his grandchildren, the Count did not hesitate to show his love for them and caress them, with the result that they were unwilling to leave him no matter how insistently their tutor kept calling them. Hearing the commotion, Giannetta left the room she was in and came to where the Count was eating. When she threatened to give the children a good spanking if they did not obey their tutor's commands, they started to cry and said that they wanted to stay with this worthy man who loved them more than their tutor did, at which both the lady and the Count burst out laughing.[8]

The Count had risen to his feet, not like a father getting up to greet his daughter, but like a poor man showing respect to a lady, and as soon as he set eyes on her, his heart was filled with a marvelous feeling of pleasure. She, however, utterly failed to recognize him, either then or later on, for he had changed remarkably from the way he used to be, having grown old and thin and gray. Indeed, with his beard and sun-darkened complexion, he did not look like the Count at all. When she saw that her children did not want to be parted from him, however, and cried when attempts were made to separate them, she told the tutor to let them stay there for a while.

While the children were with the worthy man, Giachetto's father, who felt only scorn for Giannetta, happened to return home. When the tutor told him what had occurred, he said: "Let them stay with him, goddamn them! They're just showing where they come from. Seeing as how they're descended from a tramp on their mother's side, it's no surprise they want to hang out with tramps."

When the Count overheard these words, he was deeply hurt, but he simply shrugged his shoulders and suffered this injury just as he had borne many others. Although Giachetto was displeased when he

learned about the fuss the children were making over the worthy man,
that is, over the Count, he loved them so much that rather than see
them cry, he gave instructions that if the worthy man were willing to
remain with them, he should be offered some job or other in the household. The Count replied that he would gladly stay on, but that the only
thing he knew how to do was to care for horses, which he had been
accustomed to handling his whole life. A horse was therefore assigned
to him, and when he had finished grooming it, he would occupy his
time by playing with the children.

While Fortune was leading the Count of Antwerp and his children
about in the manner just described, the King of France happened to die,
and his crown passed to his son, whose wife had been responsible for
the Count's banishment. The old King had negotiated a series of truces
with the Germans, and now that the last one had expired, the new King
opened hostilities again with renewed fury. The King of England, who
had recently become a relative of his, sent a large force to aid him under
the command of his Marshal, Perotto, and Giachetto Lamiens, the son
of his other Marshal. With the latter went the worthy man, that is, the
Count, who served as a groom in the army for quite some time without
ever being recognized by anyone, and like the capable man he was, he
did a great deal of good by giving advice and performing feats of arms,
in both cases going well beyond what was required of him.

During the war, the Queen of France happened to fall gravely ill,
and when she realized she was about to die, she repented of all her
sins and made a devout confession before the Archbishop of Rouen,
who was universally considered a very good and holy man. Among her
other sins, she told him about the great wrong done to the Count of
Antwerp because of her. Nor was she satisfied merely to tell this to the
Archbishop, but she gave a true account of everything that had happened in the presence of many other worthy men, beseeching them to
use their good offices with the King in order to have the Count restored
to his former position if he were alive, or if he were dead, to have his
children restored to theirs. Not long after this she died and was buried
with full honors.

When the King was told about the confession, he heaved many a sad sigh because of the injuries the worthy man had unjustly suffered. He then issued a proclamation, which was widely circulated, both throughout the army and elsewhere, stating that whoever provided information concerning the whereabouts of the Count of Antwerp or any of his children would receive a substantial reward for each member of the family who was found. It also said that because of the Queen's confession, the Count was now considered innocent of the crime for which he had gone into exile, and that the King intended to restore him not merely to his former position, but to give him an even higher one. The Count, who was still serving as a groom, heard rumors about the proclamation, and once he had confirmed that they were true, he went immediately to Giachetto and begged him to arrange a meeting with Perotto so that he could show the two of them what the King was looking for.

When the three had come together, the Count addressed Perotto, who was himself already thinking about revealing his identity.

"Perotto," said the Count, "Giachetto here is married to your sister, but he never received a dowry from her. Therefore, lest she remain without one, I think that he, and he alone, should get the great reward the King is offering. What I want him to do is to proclaim that you are the son of the Count of Antwerp, that his wife, Violante, is your sister, and that I myself am your father, the Count of Antwerp."

While Perotto was listening, he stared intently at the Count. All of a sudden, he recognized who it was, and dissolving in tears, he threw himself at the Count's feet. Embracing him, he cried: "O my father, I am so, so happy to see you here!"

Giachetto, who had also listened to the Count's words and seen Perotto's response, was overwhelmed by such a sense of wonder and at the same time by such joy that he scarcely knew what he should do. But being convinced that it was all true, and feeling deeply ashamed of the injurious words he had sometimes directed at the Count when he was a groom, he, too, fell down onto his knees, and weeping, humbly begged the Count's forgiveness for his past offenses. This the Count gave him most graciously after first having raised him to his feet.

When the three of them had finished recounting their various adventures to one another, weeping and laughing together for quite some time over them, Perotto and Giachetto offered to provide the Count a new suit of clothes. The latter would by no means permit it, however. On the contrary, the Count wanted Giachetto, once he was assured of getting the promised reward, to present him just as he was, in his groom's outfit, in order to make the King feel all the more shame over what had happened.

Therefore, accompanied by the Count and Perotto, Giachetto presented himself before the King and offered to produce the Count and his children, though only on the condition that in accordance with the terms of the proclamation, he should get the reward. The King immediately had it placed in its entirety before Giachetto's astonished eyes, telling him that he could take everything away with him as soon as he made good on his offer and truly showed them what he had promised. Giachetto then turned and made way for the Count, who had been his groom, and for Perotto.

"Behold, Your Majesty," he said, "here are the father and the son. The daughter, my wife, is not present, but, God willing, you will soon be seeing her."

Upon hearing this, the King stared at the Count, and even though his appearance was greatly altered, after looking at him for a while, the King managed to recognize him, at which point, his eyes brimming with tears, he raised the Count, who was kneeling, to his feet, and kissed and embraced him. After giving Perotto a very warm greeting, he ordered them to provide the Count immediately with clothes, servants, horses, and all the other trappings appropriate to one of his noble rank. This was no sooner said than done, and what is more, the King lavished the highest honors on Perotto and insisted on hearing every detail of his past adventures.[9]

As Giachetto accepted the three magnificent rewards for having produced the Count and his children, the Count said to him:

"Take these gifts as tokens of the munificence of His Royal Majesty, and remember to tell your father that your children, who are his grandchildren as well as mine, are not descended from some tramp on their mother's side."

Giachetto took away the gifts and sent for his wife and his mother to come to Paris. Perotto's wife came, too, and there they were all lavishly entertained by the Count, who, thanks to the King, had recovered everything he had once possessed and had been raised to a rank far higher than the one he used to hold. Then, with his leave, they all returned to their homes, while the Count himself spent the rest of his days in Paris, leading a life there more glorious than ever before.

Day 2, Story 9

Deceived by Ambruogiuolo, Bernabò of Genoa loses his money and orders his innocent wife to be killed. She escapes, however, and dressed like a man, enters the service of the Sultan. Having located the deceiver, she lures her husband to Alexandria, where Ambruogiuolo is punished and she dresses like a woman again, after which she and her husband, rich once more, return to Genoa.[1]

When Elissa had done her duty and finished her touching story, their Queen, the tall, lovely Filomena, who had the most pleasing and cheerful countenance of them all, spent a moment collecting her thoughts. Then she said: "We should honor our agreement with Dioneo, and seeing as how only he and I are left to speak, I will tell my story first, so that he can have the privilege he requested of being the last one to address us." And having thus spoken, she began as follows:

There is a certain proverb that you frequently hear among the common people: every deceiver will wind up beneath the foot of his dupe.[2] Although this might not seem amenable to rational argument, its truth can nevertheless be demonstrated by looking at actual cases. Therefore, dearest ladies, without departing from our chosen theme, at the same time I would like to prove to you that the proverb is as true as they say it is. At the same time, you should also find my story rewarding because it will teach you how to protect yourselves from deceivers.

A number of very important Italian merchants were once staying at the same inn in Paris, a city to which they used to go on one sort of business or another. One evening, after they had all had dined together quite cheerfully, they started talking about this and that, and as one subject led to another, they wound up discussing the wives they had left at home.

In jest, one of them remarked: "I don't know what mine is up to, but this much I do know: whenever I come across some attractive little gal here, I set the love I bear my wife to the side, and have as much fun with the one at hand as I can."

"I do exactly the same thing," replied a second man, "because whether or not I believe my wife is playing around, well, that what's she's going to be doing. It's a matter of tit for tat: when an ass bumps into a wall, the wall bumps him right back."*

A third, joining in, arrived at the same conclusion. In short, all of them seemed to agree that the wives they left behind were not letting a moment go to waste.

Only one man, a Genoese named Bernabò Lomellin, said the opposite, claiming that by God's special grace, he had a wife who was perhaps the most perfect in all of Italy and who possessed not just all the virtues that any woman should have, but even many of those that knights or squires must have.[3] Still quite young, she was physically attractive, lithe, and lively, nor was there any type of woman's work, such as silk embroidery and the like, that she could not do better than the other members of her sex. Moreover, he said it was impossible to find a squire, or servant as we would put it, who could wait at a gentleman's table better or more skillfully than she could, for she was a model of intelligence, discretion, and good manners. After this, he praised her for being better than any merchant at riding a horse, at falconry, and at reading and writing and doing accounts. Finally, after a number of other eulogies, he arrived at the topic they had been discussing and maintained with an oath that she was the most chaste and honest woman of all. Consequently, if he were away from home for ten years, or even for the rest of his life, he felt absolutely certain that she would never engage in those kinds of escapades with another man.

Among the merchants present at the discussion, there was a young man from Piacenza named Ambruogiuolo. Upon hearing the last words of praise Bernabò bestowed on his wife, he began roaring with

---

* This proverb amounts to saying something like "you always get as good as you give": when the ass bumps into the wall, he gets hurt by it in doing so. In other words, if you cheat on your wife, you can expect her to cheat on you—and vice versa.

laughter and jokingly asked him if the Emperor had granted this privilege to him and him alone.* Slightly irritated, Bernabò replied that he had been granted this boon not by the Emperor, but by God, who was just a bit more powerful than the Emperor.

"Bernabò," said Ambruogiuolo, "I have no doubt in the least that you believe what you're saying is the truth, but, from what I can see, you haven't gone very far in studying the nature of things, because if you had, I think you're sufficiently intelligent to have made certain observations that would have led you to be more cautious in discussing this topic. We've spoken very freely about our wives here, and lest you think ours are made of different stuff than yours is, I want to pursue this subject a bit further and make you see that we were moved to speak by what we actually know about their nature.

"It's always been my understanding that man is the noblest animal among all the mortal beings created by God and that woman comes right after him. Moreover, man is generally believed to be the more perfect of the two, as his actions also demonstrate. Now, if he's the more perfect of the two, then he must necessarily be endowed with more constancy, which is also confirmed by the fact that women are generally more fickle, the reasons for which have to do with certain physical factors I don't intend to get into at the present moment.

"So, if man has greater constancy and yet can't keep from giving in to his desire for any woman he finds attractive, let alone one who pursues him, and if he doesn't just desire her, but does everything he can to have her to himself, and if he finds himself in this predicament not just once a month but a thousand times a day, how can you hope that a woman, fickle by nature, would be able to resist the entreaties, the flattery, the gifts, and the thousand other tactics that a clever man who's in love with her has at his disposal? Do you think she can hold back? Although you may claim she could, I'm sure you don't believe it. In fact, you yourself told us that your wife is a woman, made of flesh and blood just like the rest, and if that's the case, she must feel the same desires as other women and have no more power to resist these natural urges

* The Emperor is the Holy Roman Emperor.

than they do. Thus, no matter how incredibly virtuous she may be, it's entirely possible that she'll do what they do, and whenever something is possible, one should never rule it out, let alone affirm its opposite, in such absolute terms as you are using."

"I'm a merchant, not a philosopher," replied Bernabò, "so I'll answer you like a merchant and say I recognize that what you're talking about can occur in the case of foolish women who have no sense of shame. But those who are wise are so solicitous of their honor that in defending it they actually become stronger than men, who generally don't much care about their own. And my wife is made of just that stuff."

"Truth to tell," said Ambruogiuolo, "if every time women indulged in such escapades, a horn, bearing witness to what they've done, were to grow out of their foreheads, I think very few would be inclined to act that way. However, not only don't they grow horns, but the wise ones don't leave a trace, not the slightest hint, of their activities behind. And since there's no shame or dishonor when the thing's not discovered, if women can keep it a secret, they'll do it, or they're fools if they don't. You can rest assured that the only chaste woman is either one who's never been propositioned or one who's had her own advances rebuffed.[4] Furthermore, although I know that both Nature and rational argument prove I'm right, I wouldn't be speaking about it as confidently as I've been doing, if I hadn't put it to the test myself on many occasions and with all sorts of women. In fact, let me tell you, if I were anywhere near this oh-so-saintly wife of yours, I don't think it would take me very long to lead her where I've already led the others."

"We could go on and on arguing like this," replied Bernabò, who was now quite angry. "First you'd speak, then I'd speak, and at the end, it would all amount to nothing. But since you say that all women are so compliant and that you're so clever, I am prepared, just to prove to you how honest my wife is, to let you cut off my head if you ever succeed in getting her to satisfy you that way. And if you don't, the only thing you'd forfeit would be a thousand gold florins."

"Bernabò," replied Ambruogiuolo, who had gotten heated himself during their discussion, "I have no idea what the point would be of shedding your blood, were I to win. But if you really want to see proof of what I've been arguing, go ahead and put up five thousand gold florins of yours, which must be worth a lot less to you than your head, against a thousand of mine. And although you did not fix a time limit, I'll undertake to go to Genoa and have my way with this wife of yours within three months from the day I leave here. Furthermore, as proof, I'll bring some of her most intimate possessions back with me, and I'll supply so many particular details that you yourself will have to confess it's all true—provided that you promise me, on your honor, neither to come to Genoa during this period nor to write a single word to her about what's going on."

Bernabò said he was quite pleased with this arrangement, and although the other merchants present, knowing that the affair could end in disaster, tried their best to prevent things from going any further, the feelings of the two men were so inflamed that they ignored the others' wishes and drew up a formal contract with their own hands that was binding on both of them.

Once their agreement was signed, while Bernabò stayed behind, Ambruogiuolo went off to Genoa by the quickest route possible. Having learned the name of the quarter where the lady lived, he spent a few days making very discreet inquiries about her habits, which only confirmed, and then some, what Bernabò had said about her, leading him to conclude that his undertaking was sheer folly. Nevertheless, he managed to get to know a poor woman who spent a lot of time in the house and of whom the lady was quite fond. Unable to persuade the woman by any other means, he bribed her with money to arrange to have him brought into the house inside a chest, specially designed by him for the purpose, and carried straight into the lady's bedroom. Following Ambruogiuolo's orders, the good woman pretended she had to go away for a few days and in the meantime, asked the lady to safeguard the chest, which thus remained where it was in her bedroom.

After nightfall, when Ambruogiuolo thought the lady was sleeping, he used certain tools he had with him to open the chest and quietly climbed out into the room. A light was burning, thanks to which he first observed the arrangement of the room, the paintings on the walls, and everything else of note that it contained, committing everything he had seen to memory. Next, he approached the bed, and finding that the lady and a little girl who slept with her were both sound asleep in it, he drew all the covers off of her and discovered that she was as beautiful naked as she was when fully dressed. He did not see, however, any special marks on her body that he could report on, except for a mole under her left breast that was surrounded by a few strands of fine, golden blonde hair. Having noted this, he quietly covered her up again, although she was so beautiful that he was seized by a desire, even at the risk of his life, to lie down beside her. But since he had heard how strict and severe she was about escapades of that sort, he decided not to take the chance.

After roaming around the bedroom at his leisure for the better part of the night, he took a purse and a gown out of one of her coffers, together with a couple of rings and belts, and stowed it all in his chest, after which he got back inside and closed it up just as it had been before. And in this way he spent two nights without the lady ever suspecting a thing. On the third day, the good woman, following her instructions, returned for the chest and took it back to the place where she had first picked it up. Ambruogiuolo got out, and after paying her what he had promised, he hurried back to Paris with all the things he had taken, arriving there well before his time was up.

Once back in the city, Ambruogiuolo summoned all the merchants who had been at the discussions when the wager was made, and in Bernabò's presence he announced that since he had made good on his boast, he was the winner. To prove what he said was true, he began by describing the arrangement of the bedroom and the paintings it contained, and then he showed them the things he had brought back with him, claiming that they had been given to him by the lady. Bernabò conceded that the bedroom looked just the way Ambruogiuolo said it did and granted as well that the things really did belong to his wife. But he noted that Ambruogiuolo could have learned about the arrangement of the room from one of the house servants and could have obtained the things in a similar manner. Thus, in his opinion, if Ambruogiuolo had nothing else to say, this evidence did not suffice for him to win the wager.

"All of this should truly be sufficient," replied Ambruogiuolo, "but since you want me to go on and say more about it, then that's just what I'll do. For I can tell you that under her left breast, Madonna Zinevra, your wife, has a largish mole, surrounded by maybe six fine, golden blonde hairs."[5]

When Bernabò heard this, he felt as if someone had taken a knife and stabbed him through the heart, such was the pain he experienced. His whole countenance changed, so that even if he had not uttered a word, it was clear that what Ambruogiuolo had said was true. After a while, Bernabò finally responded: "Gentlemen, what Ambruogiuolo says is true. Therefore, since he's won the wager, he can come whenever he likes and collect what he's owed." And the next day, Ambruogiuolo was paid in full.

Bernabò left Paris and went to Genoa filled with murderous rage against his wife. As he was approaching his destination, he decided he would not go into the city, but would stay at an estate of his some twenty miles outside it. He then sent one of his servants, a man he trusted implicitly, to Genoa with two horses and a letter telling his wife that he had returned and asking her to come and meet him under this man's escort. He also secretly instructed the servant that on reaching what seemed to him the most suitable spot, he should kill her, showing her no mercy, and then return to him. When the servant arrived in Genoa, he gave Madonna Zinevra the letter and delivered his master's message, receiving a truly joyous welcome from her in return, and the following morning they mounted their horses and set off down the road toward the estate.

As they were riding together, chatting about various subjects, they came to a deep, secluded valley, enclosed on all sides by steep crags and trees. To the servant this seemed like the ideal spot to carry out his master's orders without any danger to himself. He therefore took out his knife, grabbed the lady by the arm, and declared: "My lady, commend your soul to God, because you're going to die right here and not go another step forward."

On seeing the knife and hearing his words, the lady was absolutely terrified. "Have mercy," she cried, "for the love of God! Before you put me to death, tell me how I've offended you so much that you want to kill me."

"My lady," said the servant, "you haven't done anything at all to me, but you must have done something to offend your husband, for he ordered me to kill you without mercy here along this road. And if I didn't do it, he threatened to have me hanged by the neck. You must know how much I depend on him and how impossible it is for me to refuse to obey his orders. God knows I feel sorry for you, but I don't have an alternative."

"Oh, for the love of God, have mercy!" replied the lady, in tears. "Don't murder a person who has never wronged you just for the sake of carrying out somebody's orders. God, who knows everything, knows that I never did anything to merit such treatment from my husband. But let's forget about that for now. If you were willing, you have it within your power to satisfy God, your master, and me, all at the same time. Here's how to do it: you give me your doublet and a cloak, and take my clothes instead. Then you return with them to your master—who is mine as well—and tell him you've killed me. And I swear to you by the life you'll have given me that I'll disappear and go to some place from which no news of me will ever reach him or you or anyone else in these parts again."

Since the servant had no real desire to kill her, he was easily moved to feel compassion. After taking her garments, he gave her an old tattered doublet of his and a cloak in exchange, let her keep the money she had on her, and begged her to get out of the country.[6] Then he left her on foot in the valley and rode back to his master, to whom he reported not only that his orders had been carried out, but that when he had left her dead body, it was surrounded by a pack of wolves. A little while later, Bernabò returned to Genoa, but once the story got out, he was severely condemned for what he had done.

Abandoned and disconsolate, the lady disguised herself as best she could, and after nightfall, she walked to a tiny hamlet nearby, where she obtained some things she needed from an old woman so she could alter the doublet, shortening it to fit her. Then she turned her shift into a pair of knee-length breeches, cut her hair, and having thus transformed her whole appearance so that she looked like a sailor, headed down to the sea. There, by chance, she encountered a Catalan gentleman named Segner En Cararh who had just come ashore from one of his ships, which was lying a short distance off the coast, in order to get a supply of fresh water from a spring at Alba.[7] She struck up a conversation with him and persuaded him to take her on as his servant, calling herself Sicurano da Finale. Once they were on board, the gentleman gave her better clothes to wear, and she was soon performing her duties so well and with such discretion that he was entirely satisfied with him in every way.[8]

Not long afterward, the Catalan sailed to Alexandria. His cargo included several peregrine falcons that he presented to the Sultan, who in return, on several occasions, invited the Catalan back to dine with him. Observing how Sicurano, who was always there in attendance on his master, conducted himself, the Sultan was so impressed that he asked the Catalan to give him the boy, and although he found it distressing, the Catalan agreed to do so. Nor did it take very long before Sicurano's most capable service had gained him the favor and affection of the Sultan just as it had won over his previous master.

At a certain time each year, it was the custom in the city of Acre, then under the sway of the Sultan, to hold a fair, where merchants, both Christian and Saracen, used to congregate in great numbers.[9] In order to protect them and their goods, the Sultan would normally send them, in addition to other officials, one of his grandees, accompanied by soldiers to serve as guards. As the time for the fair was then approaching, the Sultan thought about sending Sicurano, who was already quite fluent in the language, to perform this service for him there. And so, he dispatched Sicurano to Acre, appointing him ruler of the city and captain of the forces that were to guard the merchants and their merchandise.

After arriving in the city, Sicurano carried out all the duties pertaining to his office with skill and diligence. As he made his rounds, carefully inspecting everything, he came into contact with a large number of merchants from Sicily, Pisa, Genoa, Venice, and other parts of Italy, whom he readily befriended out of the nostalgia he was feeling for the

place where he was born. One day, he happened to dismount at the stall
of some Venetian merchants, where he noticed a purse and a belt, in
among a number of other valuables, which he immediately recognized
as having been his. Without ever changing his expression, however,
and revealing his surprise, he asked pleasantly who owned them and
whether they were for sale.

One of the merchants at the fair was Ambruogiuolo da Piacenza,
who had come on a Venetian ship with a large quantity of merchandise,
and when he heard the captain of the guard asking about the owner of
the two articles, he stepped forward and said, with a laugh: "Sir, these
things are mine, and they're not for sale. But if you like them, I'd be
happy to make you a present of them."

Seeing him laugh, Sicurano suspected that he had been recognized
because of something he had done, but he kept a straight face and said:
"Perhaps you're laughing because you see me, a soldier, asking about
these feminine trinkets."

"I'm not laughing about that, sir," replied Ambruogiuolo, "but about
the way I acquired them."

"Well, God bless you," said Sicurano, "if there's nothing improper
involved, go on and tell us how you got them."

"Sir," Ambruogiuolo responded, "these things were given to me,
along with some other trinkets, by a gentlewoman from Genoa named
Madonna Zinevra, the wife of Bernabò Lomellin. I had spent the night
with her, and she begged me to take them as a token of her love. I was
laughing just now because it reminded me of the foolishness of her husband, who was crazy enough to bet five thousand gold florins against
a thousand of mine that I wouldn't be able to seduce his wife. But I
did it and won the wager. And from what I learned later on, although
Bernabò should have punished himself for his stupidity instead of punishing his wife for having done what all women do, he returned from
Paris to Genoa and had her put to death."

Upon hearing these words, Sicurano understood in a flash why Bernabò had been so angry at his wife, and realizing that this was the man
who was the cause of all his troubles, he vowed to himself that he would
not let him get away unpunished.[10] Thus Sicurano pretended to have

really enjoyed the story and skillfully cultivated so close a friendship with him that when the fair was over, at Sicurano's urging Ambruogiuolo gathered up all his merchandise and accompanied him to Alexandria. There Sicurano had a warehouse built for him and placed a great deal of money at his disposal, so that when he saw how well he was doing, he was more than willing to stay.

Anxious to give Bernabò clear proof of her innocence, Sicurano did not rest until, with the help of several influential Genoese merchants in the city, and by devising a variety of imaginative pretexts, he got him to come to Alexandria. Since Bernabò was by now living in poverty, he secretly arranged for him to stay with some friends of his until the time seemed right to put his plan into action.

Sicurano had already induced Ambruogiuolo to tell his story to the Sultan, who had been very amused by it. But now that Bernabò had arrived, he saw no reason for any further delays and at the first opportunity got the Sultan to summon Ambruogiuolo and Bernabò to appear before him. He wanted Ambruogiuolo, in Bernabò's presence, to be forced by harsh means, if fair ones did not suffice, to confess the truth about the boast he had made concerning Bernabò's wife.

Once Ambruogiuolo and Bernabò had arrived, the Sultan, glaring sternly at Ambruogiuolo, ordered him, in the sight of all the people there, to tell the truth about how he had won five thousand gold florins from Bernabò. Among those present was Sicurano, whom Ambruogiuolo trusted more than anyone, but who was glaring even more fiercely at him and threatening him with the harshest tortures if he did not speak. Thus, no matter which way he looked, Ambruogiuolo was terrified, and after being pressed yet harder to speak, he gave a clear and complete account to Bernabò and all the others in attendance of what had occurred, believing that he would receive no punishment for his deed beyond having to restore the five thousand gold florins along with the trinkets he had taken.

No sooner had Ambruogiuolo stopped talking, than Sicurano turned to Bernabò, and acting as though he were the Sultan's minister, said to him: "And you, what did you do to your wife as a result of this lie?"

"I was overcome with anger, because of the loss of my money,"

Bernabò replied, "and with shame, too, because of the way my wife had disgraced me. And so, I had her killed by one of my servants, after which, according to what he told me, she was straightway devoured by a pack of wolves."

Sicurano then addressed the Sultan, who had listened to what had been said in his presence and understood every last word of it, but was still wondering what Sicurano, who had requested and arranged the meeting, wanted to achieve by means of it.

"My lord," said Sicurano, "now you can see clearly what a wonderful lover and a wonderful husband this good lady could boast of. For the lover deprives her of her honor, destroying her reputation with lies while at the same time ruining her husband. And the husband, more willing to believe another's falsehoods than the truth he should have known from long experience, has her put to death and eaten by wolves. What's more, the goodwill and love that both her friend and her husband feel for her are so great that after spending a long time in her company, neither one recognizes her. But just to make sure you have no doubts about what each one of them deserves, provided that you will grant me the special favor of punishing the deceiver and pardoning the dupe, I shall make the lady appear, here and now, in your presence and in theirs."

The Sultan, who was entirely disposed to defer to Sicurano's wishes in this business, gave his consent and asked him to produce the lady. Bernabò was completely dumbfounded since he was convinced that his wife was dead, while Ambruogiuolo, who had an inkling of the danger he was in and feared that something worse than paying back a sum of money would be involved, did not know whether the appearance of the lady was reason for him to feel hopeful or all the more frightened. In any case, as he awaited her arrival, he was even more dumbfounded than Bernabò.

No sooner had the Sultan granted Sicurano's request than he burst into tears and threw himself down onto his knees before him, at one and the same time losing both the masculine voice and the masculine appearance she had long yearned to cast off.

"My lord," she said, "I myself am the wretched, unfortunate Zinevra, who for six years has been toiling through the world, disguised as a man, because she was falsely, criminally defamed by this traitor Ambruogiuolo and because this cruel, wicked man handed her over to be killed by one of his servants and eaten by wolves."

Tearing open her clothes in front and displaying her breasts, she made it clear to the Sultan and to everyone else that she was indeed a woman. Then she rounded on Ambruogiuolo and asked him in scathing terms whether he had ever slept with her as he boasted he had done. In reply, he said nothing, for now that he recognized her, he was too ashamed to speak.

The Sultan, who had always taken Sicurano for a man, was so astonished when he saw and heard all this that he kept thinking it could not be real and he had to be dreaming. Once he got over his astonishment, however, and realized it was all true, he lavished the highest praise on Zinevra, commending the person, who up until then had been called Sicurano, for her virtuous life, her constancy, and her upright behavior. After that, he had them bring her the finest female attire and provided her with women to attend her. In response to the request she had made, he pardoned Bernabò, sparing him the death he deserved. The latter, upon recognizing that she was his wife, threw himself down at her feet, weeping and asking for her forgiveness, and although he was hardly worthy of it, she graciously conceded it to him as she raised him up again and gave him a tender, wifely embrace.

The Sultan then ordered that Ambruogiuolo should be immediately taken to some high place in the city, tied to a pole in the full sun, smeared with honey, and left there until he collapsed in a heap. With that done, the Sultan next decreed that all of his possessions, which were valued at more than ten thousand doubloons, should be given to the lady, after which he arranged for a most magnificent feast in honor of Bernabò, as the husband of Madonna Zinevra, and of Madonna Zinevra herself as the most courageous of women. Finally, he bestowed money, jewels, and both gold and silver plate on her, all of which were worth more than another ten thousand doubloons.

The Sultan then had a ship fitted out for them, and when the feast was over, he gave them leave to return to Genoa whenever they pleased.

And so, laden with riches and very happy indeed, they returned home, where a magnificent welcome had been prepared for them, and especially for Madonna Zinevra, whom everyone had thought to be dead, and who, for the rest of her life, was considered the worthiest and most virtuous of women.

As for Ambruogiuolo, on the very same day that he was tied to the pole and smeared with honey, he suffered the most excruciating agony from all the flies and wasps and horseflies that abound in that country. The result was that he did not merely die, but as he expired, they devoured every last bit of his flesh. For a long time afterward, his whitened bones, hanging from his sinews, remained there without being moved, bearing witness to his wickedness for whoever saw them. And that is how the deceiver wound up beneath the foot of his dupe.

Day 2, Story 10

Paganino da Monaco abducts the wife of Messer Ricciardo di Chinzica, who, after finding out where she is, goes and befriends her abductor. When he asks Paganino to give her back, the latter agrees to do so, provided that she wants to go. She refuses to return to Messer Ricciardo, however, and after his death, becomes Paganino's wife.[1]

Every member of the worthy company enthusiastically praised the beautiful story told by their Queen, and especially Dioneo, who was the only one left to speak that day. After he had finished commending it, he said:

Lovely ladies, there was one part of the Queen's story that has led me to change my mind and substitute a different tale for the one I had thought to tell. And that is the part about the stupidity of Bernabò and of all those other men who believe the same thing that he apparently did, namely, that when they go about the world, enjoying themselves with one woman here and another there, they imagine that the wives they left at home are just sitting on their hands. Albeit things turned out well enough for Bernabò, we, who are born and grow up and live our lives surrounded by women, know what it is they really hanker for. By telling this story, I will show you just how foolish such men are, and at the same time, I will reveal the even greater folly of those who not only think they are stronger than Nature and convince themselves by means of specious arguments that they can do the impossible, but actually work directly against Nature by striving to get others to be just like them.

In Pisa there was once a judge named Messer Ricciardo di Chinzica who was endowed with more intelligence than physical strength and may well have believed that he could satisfy a wife with the same sort of effort he used to put into his studies. Because he was also very rich, he went to a great deal of trouble to find himself a woman to marry who possessed both youth and beauty, although if he had been capable of giving himself the good counsel he normally gave others, those are two attributes he would have absolutely avoided in a bride. Well, success came his way, for Messer Lotto Gualandi let him marry one of his daughters, a girl named Bartolomea, who was one of the most beautiful and charming young women in Pisa, a city where most of the women are as ugly as little wormy lizards.[2] The judge brought her home with great festivity, and the wedding was grand and beautiful. However, on the first night, when he attempted to consummate their marriage, he barely managed to score one random hit, and even then, it came very close to being a complete stalemate. Moreover, the next morning, this skinny, feeble, dried-up old man had to drink a quantity of Vernaccia wine and eat lots of sweets as well as other restoratives before he could return to the land of the living.[3]

So now, this Messer Judge guy, having achieved a deeper understanding of his own strength than ever before, started teaching his wife about the kind of calendar that schoolboys like to consult and that may have once been used at Ravenna.[4] As he explained it to her, every single day in it was the feast day of at least one, if not more, saints, and out of reverence for them, he said, supplying her with a host of arguments, men and women ought to abstain from conjugal relations. Then, on top of those days, he added in all days of fasting, and the four Ember Days,[5] and the vigils held for the Apostles and for a thousand other saints, and the Friday, Saturday, and Sunday of Our Lord, and the whole of Lent, plus certain phases of the moon as well as many other special occasions, possibly because he thought that men should take a holiday from bedding their wives just as he sometimes used to take a holiday from pleading civil cases in the law courts. He adhered to this schedule for a long time, which made his wife profoundly depressed, since her turn came up perhaps just once a month, and all the while he kept a close watch on her in case someone else should try to teach her how to observe workdays the way he had taught her about holidays.

It just so happened that one day, during a hot spell, Messer Ricciardo was suddenly seized by a desire to go to a fine estate he had near Monte Nero and spend a few days there, relaxing and enjoying the fresh country air.[6] He took his lovely lady along with him, and after they had been there for a while, he decided to arrange a fishing excursion as a little diversion for her. They set out on two little boats in order to watch it, he on the one with the fishermen and she with several women on the other, and they got so absorbed in the delightful experience that, before they realized it, they had gone several miles out to sea.

At the precise moment when they were most intent on watching the fishermen, a small galley belonging to Paganino da Mare, a notorious pirate in those days, suddenly arrived on the scene.[7] Upon catching sight of the boats, he headed in their direction, and although they fled away, they were not fast enough to keep him from overtaking the one carrying the women. As soon as he spotted the lovely lady on it, he had no interest in anything else, and while Messer Ricciardo watched from the shore, which he had already managed to reach, Paganino took her on board his galley and sailed away. There is no need to ask if Messer Judge was distressed by what he saw, for he was such a jealous man that to him even the air around his wife was suspect. But although he went about Pisa and elsewhere, bemoaning the wickedness of pirates, it was all in vain, for he had no idea who had abducted his wife or where he had taken her.

When Paganino saw how truly beautiful the lady was, he felt he was a pretty lucky guy, and having no wife of his own, decided to keep her for himself permanently. Since she was weeping bitter tears, he immediately tried using sweet talk to comfort her, but by nightfall, he had reached the conclusion that the words he had been using all day long were getting him nowhere. Instead, he turned to consoling her with deeds, for this guy had lost his calendar and had long since forgotten about feast days and holidays.[8] In fact, he was so good at consoling her in this fashion that before they reached Monaco, she had completely forgotten about the judge and his laws, and was happier living with Paganino than anyone in the world could be. And once they were in

Monaco, not only did he console her both day and night, but he also treated her as honorably as if she were his wife.

Some time later, when news reached the ears of Messer Ricciardo concerning the whereabouts of his wife, he was filled with the most passionate desire and decided, since he did not think anyone else was truly capable of doing everything that would be necessary, to go and fetch her himself. Ready to spend whatever amount of money it took to ransom her, he set sail for Monaco, where he caught sight of her soon after his arrival. She also caught sight of him and later that same evening informed Paganino both about what had happened and about what her intentions were. The next morning, Messer Ricciardo ran into Paganino and started a conversation with him, becoming his bosom buddy in short order, although Paganino, who pretended not to know him, was just waiting to see what he would do. At the earliest opportunity, Messer Ricciardo revealed the real reason why he had come, and in his best, most polite manner, told Paganino that he could have whatever ransom he wanted if he would just give back the lady.

"You're most welcome here, sir," replied Paganino, with a smile on his face. "And as for what you are asking, I will answer you briefly and tell you this much. While it's true that I have a young lady at my house, I can't really say whether she's your wife or not, for I don't know you, and all I know about her is that she's been living with me here for some time now. Since you seem like an amiable gentleman, I'll take you to her, and if you are her husband, as you say, I feel certain she'll recognize you without difficulty. What's more, if she says your story is true and wants to go with you, then, because you're such an amiable man, you can give me whatever you like as her ransom. However, if your story's not true, it would be wicked for you to try and take her from me, because I'm a young man who's just as capable of keeping a woman as anyone else, and especially this woman, for she's the nicest one I've ever seen."

"Of course she's my wife," said Messer Ricciardo, "and you'll soon see that she is, because if you take me to her, she'll throw her arms about my neck right away. And that's why I'm perfectly happy to agree to what you yourself are proposing."

"In that case," said Paganino, "let's go."

And so off they went to Paganino's house. After entering one of its great halls, he sent for the lady, who came in from another room, elegantly dressed and completely composed, and walked over to join the two men where they were waiting. She said no more to Messer Ricciardo, however, than she would have said to some complete stranger who had come home with Paganino. On seeing this, the judge was dumbfounded, for he had expected her to make an enormous fuss over him when she saw him. "Perhaps," he thought to himself, "my melancholy and the prolonged suffering I've been through since I lost her have changed my appearance so much that she doesn't recognize me." Consequently, he said to her:

"Wife, taking you fishing has cost me plenty. Nobody's ever experienced so much grief as I have since I lost you, and now it appears, from the cool reception you've just given me, that you have no idea who I am. Don't you see that I'm your own Messer Ricciardo, and that I've come here, to this gentleman's house, willing to pay him whatever he wants to let me take you away and bring you back home with me again? And for his part, he's been kind enough to hand you over for whatever I choose to give him."

Turning to him, the lady replied, with just the faintest suggestion of a smile: "Are you speaking to me, sir? Be careful not to confuse me with somebody else, because as far as I'm concerned, I can't remember ever having seen you before."

"Watch what you're saying," replied Messer Ricciardo. "Just take a good look at me, and if you try really hard to remember, you'll see for sure that I'm your very own Ricciardo di Chinzica."

"You must forgive me, sir," said the lady, "but for me to stare at you may not be so proper as you think it is. Nevertheless, I have looked you over sufficiently to know that I've never seen you before."

Messer Ricciardo thought she was doing all this because she was afraid of Paganino, in whose presence she did not want to admit that she recognized him, and so, after a while, he asked Paganino to be so kind as to allow him to speak all alone with her in another room. Paganino said that they could do so, provided Messer Ricciardo did not try to kiss her against her will. Then he told her to go into her room with Messer Ricciardo, listen to what he had to say, and freely give him whatever answer she wished.

The lady and Messer Ricciardo went to the room by themselves and sat down.

"Oh, sweetheart, my soul mate, my angel," he said, "do you still not recognize your Ricciardo now, your Ricciardo who loves you more than life itself? How is it possible? Can I have changed so much? Oh, light of my life, just take another little look at me."

The lady started laughing and cut him off.

"Surely," she said, "you don't think I'm so scatterbrained that I don't know you're my husband Messer Ricciardo di Chinzica, even though you showed little sign of knowing me when I was living with you. Because if either now or then you were as wise as you want people to think you are, you should have been smart enough to see that fresh, lively young women like me need more than food and clothing, even if modesty prevents them from saying so. And you know what you did to take care of that.

"If studying the law appealed to you more than your wife did, you should never have gotten married. To my mind, though, you never really did seem like much of a judge, but more like a town crier whose job it was to announce feast days and holidays—now that's something you really knew all about—to say nothing of fasts and vigils. And let me tell you, if you had given the laborers who work on your estates as many holidays as you gave the guy who had the job of tending my little field, you would never have harvested a single grain of wheat.

"But God looked down with pity on my youth, and by His will I chanced upon the man I share this room with, in which holy days are unheard of—I mean those holy days, of course, that you used to celebrate so religiously, since you were always more devoted to the service of God than the servicing of women. And not only has that door over there remained shut to keep out Saturdays and Fridays and vigils and the four Ember Days, not to mention Lent, which just goes on and on and on, but inside we're always at work together, giving the wool a good whacking day and night.[9] In fact, from the time matins was rung early this morning, I can't begin to tell you how much wool we've whacked since we did it the first time.

"So that's why I intend to stay with him and to keep working away at it while I'm still young. I'll take holy days and fasting as well as making pilgrimages to obtain indulgences, and reserve them all for when I'm an old woman. As for you, be so good as clear out of here as soon as you can, and good luck to you. Go and celebrate as many holy days as you like, just so long as you're not doing it with me."

As he listened to these words, Messer Ricciardo was suffering an unbearable agony, and when he saw she had finished, he said: "Oh, sweetheart, do you realize what you're saying? Have you no concern for your parents' honor or your own? Do you want to live here in mortal sin as this guy's whore rather than come to Pisa where you'll be my wife? When this guy's tired of you, he'll humiliate you by tossing you out, whereas I will always cherish you, and you'll always be the mistress of my household, no matter what. Do you really mean to abandon not just your honor but me, too, someone who loves you more than life itself, for the sake of this unbridled, dishonorable appetite of yours? Oh, my angel, don't say things like that anymore. Just agree to come away with me, and since I know what you want, from now on I'll make a really big effort. Please, sweetheart, change your mind and come with me, for I've been miserable ever since you were taken from me."

"As for my honor," the lady replied, "no one's going to defend the little that's left of it more than I'm going to do. I just wish my family had taken greater care of it when they gave me to you! But since they weren't concerned about my honor in the past, I don't intend to worry about theirs in the present. Furthermore, if I'm living now in *mortar* sin, I guess I'll just have to live with the *pestle's-in*, too.[10] So don't you go getting any more concerned about it than I am. And let me tell you this: here I really do feel like Paganino's wife, whereas in Pisa I used to feel like your whore. There we were always using the phases of the moon and making geometrical measurements to determine whether we could bring our planets into conjunction with one another. By contrast, here Paganino holds me in his arms all night long, hugging me and giving me little love bites, and God alone can tell you how he services me.

"You say you'll make a really big effort. But how? By coming up empty after three feeble bouts and having to give it quite a whacking to make it stand up?[11] From what I can see here, you've become quite the sturdy rider since the last time I saw you! Go away, and put all that energy of yours into just staying alive, for it seems as if you're barely hanging on there, that's how run-down and droopy you look to me. And I'll tell you this as well: if this guy should ever leave me—and he doesn't seem inclined to do so, as long as I want to stay—I have no intention of ever returning to you. For if you were squeezed till you were dry, they couldn't get a spoonful of sauce out of you. My life with you amounted to nothing but one giant loss, including both principal and interest, so next time I'll go looking somewhere else for my profit. Once and for all, then, let me tell you that I intend to stay here where there aren't any holy days or vigils. Now, good-bye, and go away as quickly as you can, because if you don't, I'm going to scream that you're trying to rape me."

Seeing that the situation was hopeless and finally realizing what a fool he had been to have married a young woman when he was so feeble, Messer Ricciardo left her room feeling sad and forlorn, and although he talked for a long time with Paganino, it was just so much whistling in the wind.[12] Finally, having accomplished absolutely nothing, he left the lady there and returned to Pisa, where his grief caused him to fall into such a state of madness that whenever anyone greeted him or asked him about something as he was walking about the city, he would always reply with the same words: "The evil hole never takes a holiday."[13] Not long after that he died, and when the news reached Paganino, knowing how much the lady loved him, he took her as his lawful wedded wife. And without ever paying attention to holy days and vigils or observing Lent, the two of them had a jolly life together, working away at it as long as their legs could support them.

And that is why, dear ladies, in my opinion, when Ser Bernabò was arguing against Ambruogiuolo, he was making a complete fool of himself.[14]

Day 2, Conclusion

his story gave the entire company so much to laugh about that there was no one whose jaws did not ache, and all the ladies unanimously agreed that Dioneo was right and that Bernabò had been an ass. When the story was finished, the Queen waited awhile for the laughter to subside. Then, seeing that the hour was late, and realizing that since everyone had told a story, her reign had come to its end, she took the garland from her head and, according to the rules they had agreed on, placed it on Neifile's, saying with a happy smile: "Now, my dear friend, you are the ruler of this tiny nation." After that, she sat back down again.

Neifile blushed a little on receiving this honor, so that her face looked like a fresh rose blooming just at daybreak in April or May, while her beautiful eyes, which she had lowered slightly, glittered like the morning star.[1] Once the respectful round of applause from her companions, who were happy to show their approval of her as Queen, had died down, and she had regained her composure, she took her seat in a slightly more elevated position than her usual one, and said:

"I have no desire to depart from the ways of my predecessors whose rule you approve of as you have shown by means of your obedience. But since I am now indeed your Queen, I shall take just a few words to acquaint you with what I propose to do, and if it meets with your approval, then we shall put it into effect.

"As you know, tomorrow is Friday and the next day, Saturday, both of which most people consider to be rather tedious because of the food we normally eat then.[2] Moreover, since Friday should be revered by us because it is the day when He who died that we might live suffered His

Passion, I would consider it right and proper for us to honor God and set aside that day, devoting it to prayers rather than stories. As for Saturday, it is customary for women to wash their hair then and get rid of all the dust and grime that have accumulated from the work they did the preceding week. Besides, many of them also fast on Saturday in honor of the Virgin Mother of the Son of God, and for the remainder of the day they rest from their labors in honor of the approaching Sabbath. Since, therefore, it is impossible for us to lead our lives on Saturdays completely in accordance with the plan we adopted, I think it would be a good idea for us to take a break from storytelling on that day, too.

"Then, seeing as how we will have been here four days, if we want to avoid the possibility that other people might join us, I think it would be an opportune moment for us to leave and go elsewhere—and I have already thought about where that elsewhere would be and have made arrangements for us to go there.

"As we were telling our stories today, we had quite a wide field to wander in, but when we get together in our new location after our nap on Sunday, you will have had more time for reflection, and I have therefore decided that since it will be much nicer if we place some restrictions on the freedom we had in our storytelling today, we should focus on just one of the many facets of Fortune and think we should talk about people who have relied on their resourcefulness to acquire something they really desired or recover something they had lost.[3] On this topic each of us should think up a story that might be useful, or at least enjoyable, for the entire company to hear, an exception always being made for Dioneo and his privilege."

Everyone praised what the Queen had said and adopted her proposal. She then summoned the steward, and after deciding where to put the tables that evening, gave him detailed instructions about what to do during the course of her reign. That done, she rose to her feet, as did the rest of the company, and gave them leave to go and enjoy themselves however they wished.

Both the ladies and the men made their way down a path that led to a little garden where they amused themselves for a while until the hour for supper had arrived. They ate their meal amid laughter and merriment, and when they had risen from the table, at the Queen's request Emilia led them in a *carola,** while Pampinea sang the following song, joined by all the others for the chorus.

> What lady sings except for me alone,
>   Since each desire of mine is satisfied?
>   Come, then, O Love, source of my joy,
> Of all my hopes and every happiness,
> Let's jointly sing awhile,
> Though not of sighs or of love's suffering,
> Which now for me make sweeter your delights,
> But just of love's clear flame,
> In which I burn and revel joyfully,
> Adoring you as if you were my god.
>
>   It's you, O Love, who placed before my eyes,
> That day I started burning in your fire,
> A youth who did possess
> Such talent, ardor, and such valor, too,
> That no man greater ever could be found,
> Not one to equal him.
> For him I've burned so bright that now
> I gladly sing of him with you, my Lord.
>
>   And what in all this pleases me the most
> Is that I please him as he pleases me,
> For which I thank you, Love.
> Since in this world, I now have all I could
> Desire, and in the next I hope for peace
> Through that unbroken faith
> I bear for him—which God, who sees all this,
> Will grant us from His Kingdom up above.[4]

* *Carola:* a dance in which the dancers joined hands and moved in a clockwise direction, usually accompanied by music and the singing of the dancers themselves.

When Pampinea had finished, they sang many other songs, danced a number of dances, and played several tunes, until the Queen decided it was time for them to go to bed. Then, carrying torches to light their way, they went to their respective rooms, and for the next two days they attended to the matters the Queen had previously spoken of, although all of them were looking forward eagerly to Sunday.

a number of dances, and played several tunes, until the Queen decided

Day 3, Introduction

Here ends the Second Day of the Decameron, *and the Third begins, in which,
under the rule of Neifile, they speak of people who have relied on their resourcefulness to acquire something they really desired or recover something they had
lost.*

On Sunday, just as dawn was beginning to turn from vermilion to
orange at the approach of the sun, the Queen arose and had the
entire company awakened. Quite some time before then, the steward
had sent a great many of the things they would need on ahead to their
new residence, together with servants to make all the necessary preparations for them. When he saw that the Queen was already on her way,
he quickly had everything else loaded up, as though he were striking
camp, and set out behind the ladies and gentlemen with the baggage
and the rest of the servants.

Accompanied by the ladies and the three young men, all of whom
were following behind her, the Queen made her way westward at a leisurely pace, guided by the song of perhaps a score of nightingales and
other birds. As she chatted and joked and laughed with her companions, she walked down a little-used path over soft green grass in which
a host of flowers were all beginning to open in response to the rising
sun. When they had gone no more than two thousand paces, and it was
still well before even halfway to the hour of tierce, she brought them
to a most beautiful, ornate palace, situated slightly above the plain on
a little hill.[1]

Entering the palace, they went from one end of it to the other, filled
with admiration for its great halls as well as for its clean, elegant bedrooms, complete with all the necessary furnishings, which led them

to conclude that its owner knew how to live in the grand style.[2] Then, when they went below and observed the extremely spacious, cheery courtyard, the vaulted cellars stocked with the finest wine, and the spring bubbling up with an abundant supply of ice-cold water, they praised it even more. Finally, by way of repose, they seated themselves on a loggia covered with seasonal flowers and foliage that overlooked the entire courtyard below, and there the thoughtful steward came to receive them and to offer them the most delectable sweets and the choicest wines for their refreshment.

Afterward, a walled garden attached to the palace was opened up for them, and when they went inside, it seemed at first glance a thing of such wondrous beauty that they set out to explore it in detail. There were wide walks both running around the garden and intersecting one another in the middle, all straight as arrows and covered over with trellised vines that gave every promise of producing grapes in abundance that year. They were all then in flower and filled the garden with a fragrance that, mingling with the odors of the many other sweet-smelling plants that were growing there, made them feel as if they were standing in the midst of all the spices that ever grew in the East. The sides of the walks were almost completely enclosed by red and white rosebushes and by jasmine, so that one could walk along any of them in pleasant, sweet-smelling shade without ever being touched by the sun, not just in the morning, but even at high noon.

It would take a long time to describe how numerous and varied the plants were that grew in the garden, or how they were arranged, but all the most attractive ones that flourish in our climate were there in profusion. At its center was located not the least, but actually the most praiseworthy of its features, namely, a lawn of exceptionally fine grass, so intensely green that it seemed almost black. It was sprinkled all over with perhaps a thousand kinds of flowers and surrounded by luxuriantly growing, bright green orange and lemon trees that were covered with blossoms as well as both mature and ripening fruit, and that provided a pleasant shade for the eyes as well as delightful odors for them to smell.

In the middle of this lawn there stood a fountain of gleaming white marble, covered with marvelous bas-reliefs. Out of a figure placed on a column at its center, a jet of water shot high into the sky and then fell back down again into the limpid pool below with a delightful splashing sound. I do not know whether it came from some natural source or was conveyed there by artificial means, but it was powerful enough to have turned a water mill. The water that overflowed the brimming fountain was carried away from it through a hidden conduit and then rose to the surface in a series of beautiful, ingeniously contrived little channels that completely encircled the lawn. After that, it coursed along similar channels that ran through almost every section of the garden until it all eventually came together again in one single spot. From there it finally flowed out of that beautiful place in a crystal-clear stream, descending with such tremendous force toward the plain below that it turned two water mills situated along the way, to the considerable advantage of the owner.

The sight of this garden, so beautifully arranged, with its plants and its fountain and the little streams that flowed out of it, gave so much pleasure to the ladies and the three young men that with one voice they declared that they did not think the beauty of the place could be improved on, and that if Paradise could be created on earth, they could not imagine it having any other form. As they wandered contentedly through it, making the loveliest garlands for themselves from the foliage of various trees, and listening to perhaps twenty different kinds of songs sung by the birds who seemed to be having a singing contest among themselves, they became aware of yet another delightful feature of the garden, which, being wonder struck by all the others, they had not noticed before: they saw that it was filled with perhaps as many as a hundred varieties of beautiful animals, which they began pointing out to one another. There were rabbits coming into the open in one spot, hares running in another, deer lying here, and young fawns grazing there, and apart from these, they saw many harmless creatures of other sorts roaming about at leisure in pursuit of their own pleasures as if they were tame, all of which added immensely to their already abundant delight.

When, however, they had wandered about the garden for quite

some time, examining one thing and then another, they arranged for tables to be set up around the lovely fountain, where, having first sung half a dozen little songs and done a number of dances, at the Queen's command they sat down to eat. A series of choice and dainty dishes, all carefully prepared and beautifully presented, were served them in order, after which they got up, merrier than before, and devoted themselves once again to making music, singing, and dancing. Eventually, however, with the heat of the day approaching, the Queen thought that the hour had come for those who felt like it to take a nap. Some of them, accordingly, retired, but the rest were so taken with the beauty of the place that they did not want to leave, and while the others were sleeping, they stayed where they were and passed the time reading romances or playing chess and backgammon.

A little after nones they all got up, and having refreshed themselves by washing their faces in the cool water, at the Queen's command they assembled on the lawn next to the fountain, where they seated themselves in their customary manner and waited to start telling stories on the theme she had proposed. The first one to whom the Queen assigned this task was Filostrato, who began in this way.

Day 3, Story 1

Masetto da Lamporecchio pretends he is a deaf-mute and becomes the gardener in a convent where the nuns all race one another to get to sleep with him.[1]

Loveliest of ladies, there are many men and women who are so stupid as to really believe that when a young woman has the white veil placed on her head and the black cowl on her back, she is no longer a woman and no longer feels female cravings, as though when she became a nun, she was turned into a stone. And if they should hear anything that runs counter to this belief of theirs, they get as angry as they would if some enormous, horrific crime had been committed against Nature. They never stop to think about themselves and reflect on how they are never satisfied despite having complete freedom to do whatever they want, nor do they consider how potent the forces produced by idleness and confinement can be. Likewise, there are a whole lot of people who believe only too readily that the hoe and the spade, coarse food, and hard living eliminate all carnal desires in those who work the land and make them dim-witted and unperceptive. But now, since the Queen has ordered me to speak, I would like to tell you a tiny little story that is quite in keeping with the topic she has chosen and that will make it clear to you just how deluded all those people are who believe such things.

Here in this countryside of ours there was, and still is, a convent quite renowned for holiness, which I will not name in order not to diminish its reputation in any way. Not so long ago it housed only eight nuns and their Abbess, all of them still young women, as well as a good little guy who tended their resplendent garden. Not content with his salary, he settled his accounts with the nuns' steward and returned to

his native village of Lamporecchio.[2] Among the others who gave him a
warm welcome home, there was a young laborer named Masetto who
was strong and hardy and, for a peasant, quite handsome. He asked the
good man, whose name was Nuto, where he had been for such a long
time, and after Nuto told him, Masetto wanted to know how he was
employed in the convent.

"I used to work in a great big beautiful garden of theirs," replied
Nuto, "and besides that, I sometimes used to go to the forest for firewood, or I'd draw water and do other little chores of that sort, but the
women gave me such a small salary that I hardly had enough to pay
for shoe leather. And another thing, they're all young and I think they
all had the Devil inside them because no matter what I did, it never
suited them. Sometimes when I was working in the vegetable garden,
one of them would say, 'Put this here,' and another would say, 'Put that
here,' and yet a third would snatch the hoe from my hand and tell me,
'You're doing it all wrong.' And they'd make themselves such a pain
that I'd stop working and leave the garden. Well, what with one thing
and another, I decided it was time to quit. As I was about to set off to
come back here, their steward asked me to see whether I could find
somebody who did that sort of work when I got home, and if so, he
told me I should send the guy to him. Although I did promise him I'd
do it, I'm not going to, because unless God gives the guy one heck of a
constitution, you won't find me sending him there."[3]

As he listened to Nuto's story, Masetto was filled with such a desire
to go and spend time with those nuns that it completely consumed
him, for it was clear from what he had heard that he would have no
difficulty in getting just what he wanted out of them. But realizing
that his plan would go nowhere if he told Nuto anything about it, he
said: "It sure was a good idea of yours to come back here. What kind
of life can a man lead when he's surrounded by women? He'd be better
off with a pack of devils. Six times out of seven they themselves don't
know what they want."

Once they had finished talking, Masetto started thinking about
what he needed to do in order to get to stay in the nunnery. Since he
knew he was capable of doing the chores mentioned by Nuto, he had

no worries about being rejected on that score, but he was afraid that he would not be hired because he was too young and attractive. After having pondered a number of options, an idea occurred to him: "The place is pretty far away, and no one there knows me. If I pretend I'm a deaf-mute, they'll take me on for sure."

Having settled on this plan, he dressed himself like a poor man, slung one of his axes over his shoulder, and without telling anyone where he was going, set off for the convent. When he arrived and entered the courtyard, he chanced to come upon the steward, and by using signs the way deaf-mutes do, made a show of asking him, for the love of God, to give him something to eat in return for which he would chop whatever wood they happened to need. The steward was perfectly willing to feed him, after which he presented him with a pile of logs that Nuto had not been able to split, but that Masetto, who was quite strong, managed to take care of in no time at all. The steward had to go to the forest, and taking Masetto along with him, he had him cut some firewood, while he himself went to bring up the donkey and by making certain signs, got Masetto to understand that he was to haul it all back to the convent. Masetto acquitted himself so well that the steward kept him around for several more days in order to take care of some chores he needed to have done, and it was on one of those days that the Abbess saw him and asked the steward who he was.

"My lady," said the steward, "he's a poor deaf-mute, one of those who came here a day or two ago begging for alms, and not only did I give him some, but I've had him take care of a bunch of chores that needed doing. If he knew how to tend the garden and wanted to stay on, I'm convinced we'd get good work out of him, because he's just what we need, a strong man who could be made to do our bidding. Besides, you wouldn't have to worry about him joking around with these young ladies of yours."

"I swear to God," said the Abbess, "you're telling the truth. Find out if he knows how to garden, and do your very best to make him stay here. Give him a pair of shoes plus some old hood or other, and be sure to flatter him and pamper him and give him plenty to eat."

The steward said he would take care of it. Masetto was not very far away, and although he was pretending to sweep the courtyard, he was really eavesdropping on their entire conversation. "Once you put me inside there," he said to himself gleefully, "I'm going to work your garden for you better than it's ever been worked before."

After the steward had confirmed that Masetto really knew how to do the work, he asked him by means of gestures if he wanted to stay on, and Masetto, using gestures to reply, said he would do whatever the steward wanted. The steward therefore hired him and ordered him to go and work in the garden, showing him what he needed to do there, after which he left Masetto alone and went to attend to other business for the convent.

As Masetto worked there day after day, the nuns started pestering him and making fun of him, something people frequently do with deaf-mutes, and since they were certain he could not understand them, they did not hesitate to use the worst language in the world in front of him. For her part, the Abbess paid little or no attention to what they were doing, perhaps because she was under the impression that Masetto had lost his tail just as he had lost his tongue.

One day, after he had been working hard and was taking a rest, two young nuns, who were walking through the garden, happened to approach the spot where he was lying. Since he appeared to be asleep, they gave him a good looking over, and the bolder of the two said to the other: "If I thought you could keep a secret, I'd share an idea with you that's often crossed my mind and that might work out to our mutual benefit."

"Don't worry about telling me," the other replied, "because I'm certainly not going to reveal it to anybody else."

Then the bold one began: "I don't know if you've ever spent much time thinking about how strictly we're confined here and how the only men who ever dare to set foot inside the convent are the steward, who's elderly, and this deaf-mute. Now, I've often heard many of the women who come to visit us say that all the other pleasures in the world are a joke compared to the one women experience when they're with a man. That's why I've frequently thought about putting it to the test with this deaf-mute here, seeing as how nobody else is available. He's actually the best one in the world for it, because he couldn't reveal it even if he wanted to. In fact, he wouldn't even know how, since you can see he's just a big dumb clod whose body's grown a lot faster than his brain. Anyway, I'd be glad to know what you think about all this."

"Oh, my goodness," said the other, "what are you saying? Don't you know that we've promised our virginity to God?"

"Oh," replied the first, "think about how many promises are made to Him every day, and not one of them is ever kept. So what if we've made promises to Him? He can always find lots of others who will keep theirs."

"But what if we get pregnant?" said her companion. "What'll we do then?"

"You're beginning to worry about difficulties before they've even happened," replied the other. "If and when they occur, that'll be the time to think about them. And there are a thousand ways to keep people from getting wind of what's going on, provided we don't talk about it ourselves."

With every word, her companion's desire became ever greater to find out what sort of beast a man might be. "So, how will we do it?" she asked.

"As you see, it's just about nones," the other replied, "and I'm sure that all the sisters are sleeping except for us. Let's have a look around the garden to see if anyone's here, and if there isn't, all we have to do is to take him by the hand and lead him into this hut where he stays when he wants to get out of the rain. Then one of us can go inside with him while the other stands guard, and he's such a simpleton that he'll do whatever we want."

Having heard their entire conversation, Masetto was quite eager to obey and was only waiting for one of them to come and get him. Meanwhile, the nuns had a good look around, and when they were sure they could not be seen from any direction, the one who had initiated their conversation approached Masetto and woke him up. He got to his feet right away, at which point she seized his hand and with all sorts of seductive gestures led him, giggling like an idiot, to the hut, where he did not need an invitation to do her bidding. When she had gotten what she wanted, like the loyal friend she was, she made way for her companion, and Masetto, still playing the simpleton, did what they asked him to do. And before the two of them finally left, each one made additional trials of just how good a rider the deaf-mute was. Later on, talking it over with one another, they both agreed that the experience really was as sweet as people said it was, if not more so. And from then on, whenever the opportunity presented itself, they went and amused themselves with him.

One day it just so happened that one of their sisters saw what they were up to from a window of her cell and showed the spectacle to two others. At first they thought to denounce the pair to the Abbess, but then they changed their minds and worked out an arrangement with the first two nuns whereby they would all have a share in Masetto's farm. And at different times by a variety of routes the last three nuns came to join them.

Finally, on one particularly hot day, the Abbess, who was still unaware of these goings-on, was walking by herself through the garden when she came upon Masetto. Because of all the riding he had been doing at night, even the little bit of work he engaged in during the day was proving too much for him, and so there he lay, fast asleep, stretched out under the shade of an almond tree. The front part of his tunic was blown back by the wind, leaving him entirely exposed, and the Abbess, who found herself quite alone, kept staring at it, until she succumbed to the same carnal appetite that the first two nuns had experienced. Consequently, she awoke Masetto and took him with her back to her room, where she kept him for several days, thereby provoking serious complaints on the part of the nuns because the gardener had stopped coming to work in the garden.

After repeatedly sampling the very sweetness she used to criticize in other women before then, the Abbess finally sent Masetto back to his own room. Still, she wanted to have him return again and again and was getting more than her fair share out of him, until Masetto, who was unable to satisfy so many women, realized that his playing the deaf-mute could wind up causing him irreparable damage if he continued to do so much longer. Consequently, one night, when he was with the Abbess, he untied his tongue and began to speak:

"My lady, it's my understanding that one cock is enough for ten hens, but that ten men will have a hard time satisfying one woman, and yet, it's my job to offer my services to no fewer than nine of them. Well, there's no way in the world I can keep it up any longer, and as a matter of fact, from doing what I've been doing up to now, I've reached the point where I can't do just about anything anymore. So, you should either say good-bye to me and let me go, or find some way to solve this problem."

Since the Abbess had always thought he was a deaf-mute, she was completely dumbfounded when she heard him speak. "What's all this?" she asked. "I thought you were a deaf-mute."

"I really was, my lady," replied Masetto, "but I wasn't born that way. I lost the ability to speak because of an illness, and I thank God from the bottom of my heart that on this very night, for the first time, I've managed to recover it."

The Abbess believed his story and then asked him what he meant when he said he had to offer his services to nine of them. Masetto explained how things stood, and as the Abbess listened, she realized that all of her nuns were much smarter than she was. Being a prudent woman, she then decided that rather than let Masetto go, in which case he might say something damaging to the reputation of the convent, she would work out some sort of arrangement with her nuns.

Their old steward had recently died, and so, with Masetto's consent, now that they all knew what they had all been doing in the past, the nuns decided unanimously to persuade the people living thereabouts that although Masetto had long been a deaf-mute, his speech had been restored through their prayers and through the intervention of the saint for whom the convent was named. Furthermore, they made Masetto their steward, but divided up his labors in such a way that he could take care of them all, and although he sired quite a few monklets and nunlets, the whole matter was handled with such discretion that no one heard anything about it until after the death of the Abbess, at a time when Masetto, now pretty well off, was approaching old age and was eager to return home. And once they knew what he wanted, he easily obtained their permission to go.

Thus, because he was clever and had figured out how he could put his youth to good use, Masetto, who had come from Lamporecchio with nothing more than an axe on his shoulder, returned home a rich, old man who had fathered numerous children, but spared himself the trouble of feeding them and the expense of raising them. And this was the way, he maintained, that Christ treated anyone who set a pair of cuckold's horns on His crown.

Day 3, Story 2

A groom sleeps with the wife of King Agilulf. When the King finds out about it, he says nothing, but tracks down the guilty party and shears off some of his hair. The shorn one then shears all the others and thus escapes a terrible fate.[1]

Some parts of Filostrato's tale caused the ladies to blush a bit, while others made them laugh. When he finished, it was the Queen's pleasure to have Pampinea continue the storytelling, and she, with a smile on her face, began as follows:

Some people are so lacking in discretion that when they have discovered or heard about things that they were better off not knowing, they feel compelled to reveal their knowledge at any cost, with the result that they sometimes censure faults in others no one else would have noticed, and although their goal in doing so is to lessen their own shame, they actually increase it out of all proportion. And now, pretty ladies, what I propose is to prove the truth of this to you by actually describing the contrary state of affairs in which the wisdom of a worthy king was matched by the cleverness of a man whose social position may have been even lower than Masetto's.

When he became the King of the Lombards, Agilulf followed the example of his ancestors and chose Pavia, a city in Lombardy, as the seat of his reign, having meanwhile married Theodolinda, who was the widow of Authari, the former Lombard ruler.[2] An exceptionally beautiful woman, Theodolinda was both wise and very honest, but she had a stroke of very bad luck with a man who had fallen in love with her.

At a time when Lombardy had been enjoying a long period of peace and prosperity, thanks to the valor and wisdom of King Agilulf, it just so happened that one of the Queen's grooms, a man who was as tall and handsome as the King himself, fell for her and loved her to distraction. Though of exceedingly low birth, the groom was in other respects vastly superior to his base occupation, and since his lowly condition did not prevent him from seeing that this love of his went well beyond the bounds of propriety, he wisely refrained from disclosing it to anyone and did not even dare to cast revealing glances in the lady's direction. Nevertheless, although he lived without any hope of ever winning her favor, deep inside he gloried that he had raised his thoughts to such a lofty height.[3] Burning all over in Love's fire, he showed himself more zealous than any of his companions in doing whatever he thought would give the Queen pleasure. And thus it came about that because the Queen preferred to ride the palfrey that was in his care rather than any of the others whenever she was obliged to go out on horseback, on those occasions, the groom felt that she was doing him the greatest of favors and would stand close by her stirrup, thinking himself blessed if he was merely able to touch her clothing.

However, what we see all too often is that as hope diminishes, love increases, and that is what happened with the poor groom, to the extent that, without a shred of hope to sustain him, he had the utmost difficulty controlling the powerful desire he kept hidden inside him, and on more than one occasion, being unable to free himself from this passion, he felt like killing himself. As he pondered the ways and means to do just that, he concluded that the circumstances leading up to his death should be such as to make everyone understand that it was the result of the love he had always borne for the Queen. At the same time, he was resolved to try his luck and see if those circumstances might also offer him an opportunity to wholly, or at least partially, gratify his desires. He had no intention of saying anything to the Queen or declaring his love for her by means of letters, for he realized that speaking or writing to her would be in vain, and so, instead, he concentrated on getting into her bed by means of some stratagem or other. Since he knew that the King did not spend every single night with his wife, he concluded that the one and only stratagem with a chance of success was for him to find some way to impersonate the King so that he would be free to approach her and gain access to her bedroom.

With the aim of discovering how the King was dressed and the routine he followed when he visited the Queen, the groom hid himself for several nights in a great hall of the palace that was situated between the two royal bedchambers. On one of those nights he saw the King come out of his room wrapped up in a large cloak, carrying a small lighted torch in one hand and a rod in the other. He walked over to the Queen's chamber, and without saying a word, knocked once or twice at the entrance with the rod, whereupon the door was opened at once and the torch taken from his hand.

Having observed what the King had done, and having likewise seen him return to his room some time later, the groom decided he would adopt the very same procedure. He managed to acquire a cloak that resembled the King's as well as a torch and a stick, and after first washing himself thoroughly in a hot bath so that the odor of dung would not repel the Queen or make her suspect a trick, he took his things to the great hall and hid himself in the usual place.

When the groom thought that everyone was asleep and that the time had come for him either to gratify his desires or to find a noble path to the death he had long sought, he used a piece of flint and steel he had brought with him to make a small fire by means of which he lit his torch. Then, wrapping himself up tightly in his cloak, he walked over to the entrance to the bedroom and knocked twice with his rod. The door was opened for him by a chambermaid who, more asleep than awake, took his light and covered it up, after which, without saying a thing, he stepped inside the curtains, took off his cloak, and got into the bed where the Queen lay sleeping. Knowing that it was not the King's habit to engage in conversation whenever he was angry about something, the groom made a show of being irritated as he took the Queen lustfully in his arms, and then, without either one of them ever uttering a single word, he had carnal knowledge of her over and over again. Although he was very loath to leave her, he was afraid that if he stayed there too long, the joy he had experienced might be turned into sorrow. Consequently, he got up, and after he had retrieved his cloak and his torch, he went away, still without saying a word, and returned to his bed as quickly as he could.

The groom could scarcely have reached it when, to the Queen's utter amazement, the King showed up in her chamber and gave her a cheerful greeting as he got into bed with her. "O my lord," she said, encouraged by his good humor, "what's the meaning of this change tonight? You've only just left me after having enjoyed me more than you usually do, and here you are, coming back for more. You should be careful what you're doing."

On hearing these words, the King immediately inferred that the Queen had been deceived by someone who had looked and behaved like him. He was a wise man, however, and since neither she nor anyone else had noticed the substitution, he decided on the spot that he would not reveal it to her. Many a fool would have acted differently and said: "That wasn't me. Who was the man who was here? What happened? Who was it who came?" This would have given rise to a great many complications that would have upset the lady unnecessarily and might have given her a reason to want to repeat the experience she had just had. And besides, it allowed him to avoid disgracing himself by not talking about something that, as long as it remained unsaid, would never have been able to cause him shame.

Thus, giving no sign of his inner turmoil either by the way he spoke or by his facial expression, the King answered her: "Wife, don't you think I'm man enough to come back here a second time after having been with you once before?"

"Yes, my lord," the lady replied, "but nevertheless I beg you to be careful with your health."

"I'm happy to follow your advice," said the King, "and so, this time I'll go away and won't bother you any further."

As he picked up his cloak and left the room, the King was seething with rage, indignant over what he saw had been done to him and determined to go quietly and search for the culprit, operating on the assumption that the man had to be a member of his household and that, no matter who he was, he would not have been able to get out of the palace. Taking a little lantern that shed only a very faint light, he went to a long dormitory located over the palace stables where almost all of his servants were asleep, each in his own bed. And since he surmised that neither the pulse nor the heart rate of whoever had done the deed reported by the Queen could have returned to normal after all his exertions, the King started at one end of the room and began quietly walking along, feeling everyone's chest to see if it was still throbbing.

Although all the others were sound asleep, the one who had been with the Queen was still awake, and when he saw the King coming and realized what he was looking for, he became so frightened that the terror he felt made his heart, which was already pounding because of his recent exercise, beat even harder. He was absolutely convinced that if the King noticed it, he would be instantly put to death, and thoughts about various possible courses of action went racing through his mind. Upon observing, however, that the King was unarmed, he decided to pretend he was asleep and wait to see what the King would do.

Having already examined a large number of the sleepers and concluded that none of them was the man he was seeking, the King finally reached the groom. When he discovered how hard the man's heart was beating, he said to himself, "This is the one." However, he did not want to let anybody know what his intentions were, and so, the only thing he did was to take a small pair of scissors he had brought with him and cut off a lock of hair on one side of the groom's head. Since people wore their hair very long in those days, that would be a sign by which the King would be able to recognize the culprit the next morning. Then, once he was done, he made his exit and returned to his own room.

Having witnessed everything that had happened, the groom, who was very shrewd, had no doubt as to why he had been marked in this manner. Therefore, he did not hesitate for a moment, but got up, and having located one of several pairs of scissors they happened to keep in the stables for tending to the horses, he went through the room from one man to the next as they lay sleeping and quietly cut off their hair just above the ear in the same way his own had been. Having finished what he was doing without having been observed by anyone, he returned to his bed and went to sleep.

The moment the King arose in the morning, he gave orders that the palace gates should remain closed until the members of his household were assembled before him. When they had all arrived and were standing bareheaded in his presence, he began looking them over with the intention of identifying the man whose hair he had cut off. To his amazement, however, he discovered that the vast majority of them had had their hair sheared in exactly the same way. "The man I'm looking for may well be lowborn," he said to himself, "but he's demonstrated that he has quite a lofty intellect."

Then, since he realized that he could not achieve what he wanted without making a scene, he decided he would not expose himself to so great a disgrace in order to take his revenge on so petty a person. Instead, he contented himself with giving the man a stern word of warning to show him that his deed had not gone unobserved.

"Whoever did it," he said, addressing the entire assembly, "he'd better not do it ever again. Now go, and may God be with you."

Another man would have had them all put on the strappado, tortured, examined, and interrogated, but in doing so, he would have brought out into the open something that people should make every effort to conceal, for even if, by revealing the whole story, he had been able to revenge himself to the full, he would not have lessened his shame. On the contrary, he would have greatly increased it and would have sullied his lady's reputation to boot.

Those who heard the King's speech were amazed by it, and for a long time afterward they debated among themselves what he had meant. There was no one, however, who understood it except for the one person it really concerned, and he, wise man that he was, never revealed its meaning as long as the King was alive, nor did he ever put his life at risk by performing any such deed again.

Day 3, Story 3

Under the pretext of making her confession as someone with an exceptionally pure conscience, a lady who has fallen in love with a young man gets a solemn friar unwittingly to provide her with a means to achieve the complete satisfaction of her desires.[1]

When Pampinea was silent, many of her listeners praised the groom's daring and resourcefulness as well as the King's good sense, after which the Queen turned to Filomena and ordered her to continue. In reply, Filomena began to speak, charmingly, as follows:

It is my intention to tell you about a trick that was actually played by a beautiful woman on a sanctimonious churchman, a trick that every layperson should find all the more entertaining insofar as the clergy, for the most part, is made up of extremely foolish men who have strange manners and ways of behaving, but nevertheless consider themselves wiser and more competent than others. The truth, however, is that they are vastly inferior, for, like so many swine, they are too simpleminded to provide for themselves and consequently take refuge wherever they can get something to eat.

I shall tell you this story, charming ladies, not merely in obedience to the command I received, but also to make you see how even the clergy, in whom we overly credulous women place far too much trust, can be cleverly deceived, as indeed they occasionally are, both by men and by some of us as well.

Not so many years ago in our city, which abounds more in trickery than in love or loyalty, there lived a noble lady who was adorned with beauty and good manners as well as being endowed by Nature with as lofty a spirit and subtle an understanding as any woman has ever had. I have no intention of revealing her name or that of anyone else involved in this story, even though I know them all, because certain people who are still living would be extremely offended despite the fact that the whole thing should be passed off with a laugh.

Possessing a distinguished pedigree, and finding herself married off to a wool draper, the lady was incapable of laying to rest the contempt she felt for him by reason of his occupation, for she was firmly convinced that no man of low condition, however extraordinarily wealthy he might be, deserved to have a noble wife. And indeed, when she saw that for all his riches the only things he was capable of doing were telling one kind of cloth from another or setting up a loom or haggling about yarn with the woman who did the spinning, she decided that she would no longer tolerate his embraces, unless there were no way for her to deny him. Furthermore, she was determined to satisfy herself by finding someone worthier of her affection than she thought her wool draper of a husband was.

And so it was that she fell deeply in love with an extremely attractive man around thirty-five years old, so deeply in fact that if she did not see him during the day, she could get no rest the following night. The gentleman, however, who knew nothing about what was going on, paid no attention to her, and since she was very cautious, she did not dare to inform him about her feelings either by writing to him or by sending a maidservant as her emissary, for fear of the dangers this might entail. But having observed that he was often in the company of a certain clergyman, a fat, coarse friar who was nevertheless regarded by almost everyone as extremely worthy because of the very devout life he led, she decided that he would make an excellent go-between for her and the man she loved. And so, after having figured out the course of action she would take, at an appropriate hour she went to the church to which the friar was attached, and having sent for him, asked him if he would be willing to hear her confession.

Since the friar could tell at a glance that she was a gentlewoman, he was happy to listen to her confession. When it was done, she said:

"Father, as I shall explain to you, there's another matter about which I felt obliged to come to you for aid and counsel. I've told you who my husband and my family are, and I feel certain that you must know them. Now, my husband loves me more than life itself, and since he's a very rich man, he never has the slightest difficulty or hesitation in giving me whatever I happen to desire. Consequently, I love him more dearly than life itself, and if I ever thought about acting contrary to his honor or his wishes—let alone actually doing so—I would be more deserving of hellfire than the most wicked woman who's ever lived.

"Now, there's a certain person, who looks to me like a proper gentleman and who, unless I'm mistaken, spends a great deal of time in your company. I really don't know his name, but he's tall and handsome, dresses elegantly in dark brown clothing, and perhaps because he's unaware of my disposition, appears to have laid siege to me. I can't go to a window or look out a door, let alone take a step outside my house, that he doesn't immediately appear before me. In fact, I'm surprised that he's not here right now. In any case, all this really upsets me, especially because such behavior often gives an honest woman a bad name, no matter how innocent she is.

"There are times when I've had a mind to inform my brothers about him, but it occurred to me that men sometimes handle such matters in a way that turns out badly, for their reactions give rise to words, and words, eventually, lead to blows. So, in order to avoid such unpleasantness and scandal, I've kept quiet. But since you appear to be his friend, and since it would be perfectly proper for someone like yourself to censure such behavior in people, whether they're friends or complete strangers, I decided to tell you all about it, rather than go to someone else. In the name of the one and only God, therefore, I beg you to give him a sound scolding and persuade him to refrain from what he's been doing. There are plenty of other women who would welcome such things and would enjoy being ogled and courted by him, but as for me, I have no interest in it at all and find it exceedingly disagreeable." When the lady finished speaking, she bowed her head as if she were going to weep.

The holy friar realized immediately who it was she was talking about, and as he was firmly convinced that she was telling the truth, he praised her for her virtuous disposition and promised to handle things in such a way that she would never be bothered by that man again. Then, since he knew she was quite rich, he commended works of charity and almsgiving to her, telling her all about what he himself needed at the same time.

"Please do take care of this, for the love of God," said the lady, "and if your friend should deny it, be sure to tell him that I myself was the one who informed you and complained to you about what he was doing."

When she had finished her confession and received her penance, she remembered the exhortation the friar had given her concerning acts of charity, and so she discreetly filled his hand with money, asking him to say Masses for the souls of her dead relations. Then she got up from where she was kneeling at his feet and returned home.

It was not too long before the gentleman paid one of his usual visits to the holy friar, and after they had chatted for a while about this and that, the friar took him aside and reproached him, albeit quite politely, for all the courting and ogling that, as the lady had given him to understand, he was convinced his friend had been doing. The gentleman was amazed, since he had never even looked at her and only passed by her house on rare occasions. But when he started trying to excuse himself, the friar prevented him from speaking.

"Now don't you pretend to be surprised," he said, "and don't waste your words trying to deny it, because you can't. I didn't learn these things from people in the neighborhood. The lady herself revealed everything when she came to me and complained bitterly about your behavior. And apart from the fact that it's inappropriate for a man like you to engage in foolishness of this sort, what I can tell you about her is that I've never encountered any woman who is as repelled by such things as she is. And so, for the sake of your honor and the lady's peace of mind, please stop what you've been doing and leave her alone."

The gentleman was more perceptive than the holy friar, and it did not take him long to grasp just how clever the lady was. Consequently, he pretended to be somewhat ashamed and promised he would not bother her anymore, but as soon as he left the friar, he set off in the direction of the lady's house. She had been continually watching out from a little window so that she could catch sight of him if he happened to pass by, and when she saw him coming, she looked at him with such joy and affection that he no longer had any doubts about the true meaning concealed in the friar's words. And from that day on, always proceeding with caution and creating the impression that he was engaged in some other business there, he began to take walks through her neighborhood on a regular basis, deriving great pleasure from doing so and giving the lady considerable delight and satisfaction as well.

After a while, having ascertained that he liked her as much as she liked him, the lady was possessed by a desire to enflame him all the more and assure him of the love she felt for him. Consequently, having found time and opportunity to return to the holy friar, she went to his church, where she knelt down at his feet and began weeping. As he watched her tears, the friar asked her, with pity in his voice, what her new affliction was.

"Father," the lady replied, "my new affliction is none other than that goddamned friend of yours, the man I was complaining about to you the other day. I think he was born to be my greatest torment and to make me do something that I'll regret for the rest of my life and that will prevent me from ever daring to place myself here at your feet again."

"What!" said the friar. "He hasn't stopped bothering you?"

"He certainly hasn't," said the lady. "On the contrary, he seems to have been offended that I complained to you about him, and ever since then, as though out of spite, he's taken to walking by my house at least seven times more frequently than he ever did before. And yet, would to God that his passing by and staring at me were enough for him, because yesterday he was so bold and shameless as to send a serving woman to me in my own house with his stories and his nonsense, and as if I didn't have enough purses and belts already, he had her bring me one of each. This made me so angry—indeed, it still does—that if I hadn't been concerned about the scandal involved and about maintaining your good opinion, I truly believe I would have raised Hell about it. I managed to restrain myself, however, because I didn't want to say or do anything without having first informed you about it.

"As for the purse and the belt, initially I gave them back to the woman who had brought them, dismissing her rather curtly and instructing her to return them to him. But then I started worrying that she'd keep them for herself and tell him I'd accepted them, something I believe such women do on occasion, and so, I called her back and in a fury snatched them out of her hands. Now I've brought them here to you so that you yourself could return them to him and tell him that I don't need his stuff, because, thanks to both God and my husband, I've got so many purses and belts that I could bury him under them. And here's where I must really beg your pardon, father, because come what may, if he doesn't stop doing this, I am going to tell my husband and my brothers, for I'd much rather have them give him a rough time, if that's what's going to happen to him, than have my reputation suffer on his account. And that, father, is just the way things stand now!"

She finished her speech, and while she continued to weep bitterly, she drew a very beautiful, quite expensive purse and an elegant, costly little belt out from beneath her cloak, and threw both of them into the friar's lap. Fully taken in by what she had said, he was filled with the utmost indignation as he accepted them from her.

"My daughter," he said, "I'm not surprised that you're disturbed by what has happened, nor could I possibly reprimand you for your reaction. On the contrary, I commend you warmly for following my advice in this affair. I scolded my friend the other day, but he did a really bad job of keeping the promise he made to me, and so, partly for that reason and partly because of what he's done more recently, I'm going to warm his ears for him to such an extent that he won't give you any more trouble. And you, God bless you, you shouldn't let yourself get so carried away by your anger that you say something to your family about this, because something really bad could happen to him. Nor should you worry that your reputation could be harmed by any of this, for I will always be here to offer the staunchest testimony to your honesty before both God and men."

The lady made a show of being somewhat comforted by this, and then, knowing just how greedy the friar and his kind were, she switched the subject.

"Father," she said, "for the last few nights the spirits of various relatives of mine have been appearing to me. They all look as if they've been going through the worst torments, and they continually ask for alms, especially my mama, who seems in such a state of affliction and misery that it's a pity to see her. I think she's suffering terribly from watching the way I've been persecuted by this enemy of God. Therefore, I should like you to say, on my behalf, the forty Masses of Saint Gregory for their souls, together with some of your own prayers, so that God may release them from that penal fire."[2] And having said this, she slipped a florin into his hand.

The Holy Father was happy to take it, and after having served up many good words and exemplary tales to reinforce her piety, he gave her his blessing and sent her on her way.

Not realizing that he had been hoodwinked, the friar summoned his friend as soon as the lady was gone. When the gentleman arrived and saw how upset the friar was, he realized at once that he was about to receive some news from the lady, and waited to hear what the friar had to say. The latter repeated what he had said to his friend before, and once again rebuked him with angry words, scolding him severely for what the lady said he had done. The gentleman, who still did not see where the friar was going with all this, denied having sent the purse and the belt, albeit half heartedly, so as not to undermine the friar's faith in the story, just in case she had, in fact, given them to him.

But the friar, who was quite heated, exclaimed: "How can you deny it, you wicked man? Here, take a look at them—she brought them to me in tears—and see if you don't recognize them!"

"Yes, indeed, I do," replied the gentleman, pretending to be deeply embarrassed, "and I confess to you that what I did was wrong. But now that I see how she's inclined, I swear to you, you're never going to hear another word about this."

There was a great deal more discussion, and eventually that dumb sheep of a friar handed the purse and the belt over to his friend. Finally, after admonishing him repeatedly and getting him to promise never to meddle in such affairs again, he sent him on his way.

The gentleman was absolutely delighted, both because he now felt certain that the lady loved him and because he had been given such a beautiful gift. Upon leaving the friar, he went and stood in a place from

which he could discreetly allow the lady to see that the two objects were
in his possession, something that made her very happy, and all the more
so since it seemed to her that her plan was working better and better.
The only thing she was still waiting for in order to bring her work to
its conclusion was for her husband to go away on a trip, and not long
afterward, it just so happened that he was indeed obliged to travel to
Genoa on business of some sort.

   That morning, as soon as he had mounted his horse and ridden off,
the lady went to the holy friar, and after a great deal of complaining,
said to him between tears: "Father, listen, I really can't take it anymore.
But since I promised you the other day that I wouldn't do anything
without first speaking to you about it, I've come here to offer you my
excuses in advance. And just in case you should think that my weeping
and complaining are unjustified, let me tell you what your friend—or
rather, that Devil from Hell—did to me this morning a little before
matins. I don't know what piece of bad luck led him to discover that
my husband went to Genoa yesterday morning, but today, at the hour
I just mentioned, he got into our grounds and climbed up a tree to my
bedroom window, which looks out over the garden. He had opened it
and was about to enter the room when I awoke with a start. I got up
and was all set to scream—and I would have done so, too—but as I listened to him explain who he was and beg me for mercy, both in God's
name and in yours, I kept quiet because of my love for you. Since he was
still outside, however, I ran, naked as the day I was born, and shut the
window in his face, after which I suppose he made off—and bad luck
go with him!—because I didn't hear any more from him. Now, you can
judge for yourself whether such behavior is seemly or permissible, but
I personally don't intend to put up with it any longer. On the contrary,
I've already endured far too much from him for your sake."

   Upon hearing this, the friar was so very upset that he did not know
what to say except to ask her over and over again if she was sure it had
not been someone else.

   "Praise God," replied the lady, "as if I can't distinguish him from
another man! It was he, I'm telling you, and if he denies it, don't you
believe him."

"Daughter," said the friar, "all I can say here is that he's gone much too far with that bad behavior of his, and you did the right thing in sending him away. But since God has preserved you from shame, I implore you to take my advice this one more time just as you've taken it twice before. Instead of complaining to your family, leave everything to me, and I'll see if I can restrain this unbridled Devil who I used to believe was a saint. If I can succeed in stopping him from behaving like an animal, all well and good, but if not, I now give you my permission—indeed, you have my blessing—to do whatever seems best in your judgment."

"Well look now," said the lady, "this time I won't upset you or disobey you, but you'd better see to it that he takes care not to bother me again, because I promise you that I'm not going to be coming back here to you again because of this." And without saying another word, she left the friar, making a show of being furious.

She had hardly gotten outside the church when the gentleman arrived and was called over by the friar, who drew him aside and gave him the worst dressing-down a man has ever received, calling him a disloyal traitor and a liar. Since the gentleman had already seen twice what this friar's scoldings amounted to, he waited attentively and then did his best to draw him out by means of ambiguous responses.

"Why are you so angry, sir?" he began. "Have I crucified Christ or something?"

"Look at this shameless man!" cried the friar. "Listen to what he's saying! He speaks just as if a year or two had passed, and because of that lapse of time, he'd forgotten all about his wickedness and dishonesty. Has the injury you offered someone this morning between matins and now completely slipped your mind? Where were you earlier today, a little before daylight?"

"I don't know," said the gentleman, "but wherever it was, news of it reached you pretty quickly."

"That's right," said the friar, "news of it did reach me. I suppose you thought that because her husband was away, the good lady wouldn't hesitate to welcome you into her arms. Well, here's an honorable gentleman for you! He's turned into a night prowler, a guy who breaks into people's gardens and climbs their trees! Do you think you're going to conquer this lady's chastity by constantly soliciting her and clambering up trees at night in order to get in through her windows? There's nothing in the world she finds more disgusting than your behavior—and yet you won't stop trying! Well, leaving aside the fact that she's shown you her disapproval in so many ways, it's clear to me just how much you've profited from all my admonitions! But let me tell you this: so far, she's kept quiet about what you've done, not out of any love she feels for you, but because of all my entreaties. She won't do so any longer, however, for I've given her my permission to act as she thinks fit, if you should bother her again in any way. And just what are you planning to do if she tells her brothers?"

Having grasped enough of what he needed to know, the gentleman took his leave of the friar, after having done his best to calm him down by making him many fulsome promises. Then, the following night, at the stroke of matins, he entered her garden and climbed up the tree to her window. Finding it open, he entered her bedchamber, and as quickly as possible, threw himself into the arms of his lovely lady. As she had been waiting for him with the most intense longing, she gave him a joyous welcome.

"Many thanks to Messer Friar," she said, "for giving you such good instructions about how to get here."

Then, as they took their pleasure of one another, amusing themselves to the immense delight of both parties, they had a good laugh as they talked about the asinine stupidity of the friar and made all sorts of disparaging comments about distaffs full of wool and combing and carding.[3]

Later on, the couple arranged their affairs so that, without having further recourse to Messer Friar, they spent many more equally pleasurable nights in one another's company. And I pray to God in His holy mercy that He will lead me, and all those Christian souls who are similarly inclined, to the same happy conclusion.

Day 3, Story 4

Dom Felice teaches Frate Puccio how to achieve blessedness by performing an act of penance he devises for him, and while Frate Puccio is carrying it out, Dom Felice has a good time with the friar's wife.[1]

hen Filomena, who had concluded her story, fell silent, Dioneo offered up a few sweet words of praise for the lady's ingenuity as well as Filomena's closing prayer. The Queen, laughing, looked over in Panfilo's direction and said, "Now, Panfilo, you may add to our delight with some pleasant little trifle of your own." Panfilo immediately replied that he was happy to do so, and began as follows:

My lady, there are a great many people who, while they are striving mightily to get into Paradise, unwittingly send others there instead—which is what happened to a lady in our city not so very long ago, as you are about to hear.

According to what I have been told, there used to be a good man, and a rich one, too, living close by San Pancrazio who was called Puccio di Rinieri. In his later years, he devoted himself wholly to matters of the spirit and became a Tertiary of the Franciscan Order, taking the name of Frate Puccio.[2] Since his family consisted only of his wife and a single maidservant, which relieved him of the necessity of practicing a trade, he spent a great deal of time at church so that he could pursue that spiritual life of his. Being a simple, rather slow-witted person, he used to recite his Our Fathers, attend sermons, and go to Mass, nor would he ever fail to show up when the lay brothers were chanting lauds.* What

---

*Lauds: the second canonical hour (after matins) celebrated before daybreak. On the canonical hours, see Headnote 2.

is more, he would fast and mortify his flesh, and it was whispered about that he was one of the Flagellants.[3]

His wife, Monna Isabetta by name, was still a young woman of about twenty-eight to thirty, and she was as fresh and pretty and plump as an apple from Casole.[4] Because of her husband's holy life, and possibly also on account of his age, she frequently had to go on much longer diets than she would have liked, and when she was in the mood to sleep or perhaps to play around with him, he would rehearse the life of Christ to her, followed by the sermons of Frate Nastagio, or the Lament of the Mary Magdalene, or things of that sort.[5]

About this time, a good-looking young monk called Dom Felice, a conventual brother at San Pancrazio, who was sharp-witted and deeply learned, returned from Paris. Frate Puccio formed a close friendship with him, and since Dom Felice, who was quite good at resolving all his friend's doubts, knew what his character was like, he made a great show of holiness himself as well. Frate Puccio consequently started taking him home with him, offering him a dinner or a supper, depending on the time of day, and out of love for her husband, Frate Puccio's wife likewise became his friend and was happy to entertain him.

In the course of his visits to Frate Puccio's house, the monk observed how fresh and plump his friend's wife was, and realizing what it was that she lacked the most, he decided that he would do his best to save Frate Puccio the trouble by making up for that deficiency himself. And so, proceeding with great caution, he began giving her the eye from time to time until he kindled the same desire in her mind that was burning in his. Then, when he perceived it was working, he seized the first opportunity that came his way and spoke to her about what he wanted. Although he found her quite willing to put his proposals into effect, it was impossible to do so, since she would not risk having an assignation with him anywhere except in her own home, and they could not do it there because Frate Puccio never left town. All of this made the monk quite melancholy, but although it took quite a while, a plan finally occurred to him as to how he could spend time with the lady in her own house and not have to worry even though her husband happened to be there, too. And so, one day, when Frate Puccio had come to visit him, he spoke to him as follows:

"It's been my understanding for some time, Frate Puccio, that your one overwhelming desire is to achieve saintliness, but you seem to me to be trying to reach this goal by taking the long route to get there, even though there's a very short one that the Pope and his chief prelates know about and make use of themselves. They don't want it revealed to others, however, for the clergy, who live for the most part on charitable donations, would be instantly undone, in that laymen would no longer support them by means of alms or anything else. But since you're my friend and have given me such honorable entertainment, I'd be willing to teach you the way, although only if I were sure that you really wanted to give it a try and would never reveal it to anyone else."

Eager to hear all about it, Frate Puccio began earnestly begging his friend to tell him how to do it, and then went on to swear he would never talk about it to anyone without Dom Felice's permission, affirming at the same time that he would really apply himself to it, provided it were the sort of thing he could manage.

"Since you've given me your promise," said the monk, "I'll let you in on the secret. Be aware that the Doctors of the Church maintain that anyone who wishes to achieve blessedness must perform the penance I'm about to describe. But don't misunderstand me: I'm not saying that after your penance you will no longer be a sinner just as you are right now. Rather, what will happen is that all the sins you've committed up to the time you perform your penance will be purged and remitted because of it. And as for those you commit afterward, they won't be written down against you and lead to your damnation. On the contrary, they'll be removed with holy water the way venial ones are now.

"What's really essential for the man who's about to start his penance is to be extremely diligent in confessing his sins, after which he must begin a fast and practice a very strict form of abstinence that is to continue for forty days, during which time you must abstain from touching not just other women, but even your own wife. Moreover, you've got to have some place in your house from which you can see the heavens at

night and to which you will go at about the hour of compline.* There
you will have a broad plank set up in such a way that you can stand with
your back against it, and while keeping your feet on the ground, stretch
out your arms in the manner of the Crucifixion. Should you wish to
rest them on pegs of some sort, you may do so, but you must remain
absolutely immobile in that position, looking up at the heavens, until
matins. If you were a scholar, you would be obliged, in the course of the
night, to recite certain prayers I'd give you, but since you're not, you're
going to have to say three hundred Our Fathers and three hundred Hail
Marys in honor of the Trinity. And while you're gazing at the heavens,
you must always remember that God was the Creator of heaven and
earth, and be mindful of the passion of Christ, since you will be in the
same position he was in when he hung on the cross.

"As soon as matins is rung, you may, if you wish, go and throw yourself on your bed, dressed just as you are, and get some sleep. But later
that morning, you must go to church, listen to three Masses, and say
fifty Our Fathers and as many Hail Marys. Then, you may quietly go
about your own business, should you happen to have any, after which
you will have dinner and go to church again around vespers in order
to say certain prayers I'll give to you in writing, without which the
whole thing won't work. Finally, toward compline, you must go back
and begin all over again. Now, I've done this myself, and if you carry
it out with sufficient devotion, then I'm hopeful that even before your
penance comes to an end, you will experience a marvelous sensation
of eternal blessedness."

"This isn't a very difficult task," said Frate Puccio, "nor is it going
to last all that long. And so, since it should be fairly easy to manage, I
propose, in God's name, to start on Sunday."

After leaving Dom Felice, he returned home where, having first
obtained the monk's permission, he recounted everything in great
detail to his wife. The lady understood only too well what the monk

---

*Compline: the last canonical hour, celebrated after dark. On the canonical hours,
see Headnote 2.

meant, especially the part about his standing still and not moving at all until matins, and since it seemed like an excellent arrangement to her, she told him that she was pleased with it, as she was with whatever he did for the good of his soul. Furthermore, she said that in order to persuade God to make his penance profitable, she was willing to join in his fast, although that was as much as she would do.

Thus, it was all settled, and when Sunday came, Frate Puccio began his penance. As for Messer Monk, having made prior arrangements with the lady, on most nights he would show up at an hour when he could get inside unobserved, and would always bring plenty of good things to eat and drink along with him. Then, after the two of them had had their supper together, he would sleep with her until matins, at which point he would get up and go away before Frate Puccio returned to bed.

The place that Frate Puccio had chosen for his penance was next door to the bedroom in which the lady slept, separated from it by only the thinnest of walls. And one time, while Messer Monk was romping with her, having cast all restraints aside, just as she had with him, Frate Puccio thought he could feel the floor of the house shaking. When he finished reciting one hundred of his Our Fathers, he came to a stop, and without stirring from his spot, he called out to his wife and asked her what she was doing. The lady, who had a talent for making witty remarks, and who at the moment may have been riding Saint Benedict's ass or, even better, Saint Giovanni Gualberto's,[6] replied: "By gosh, husband, I'm tossing about here for all I'm worth."

"Tossing about?" asked Frate Puccio. "What's the meaning of all this tossing about?"

The lady started laughing, not only because she was a lively, jolly person, but also, most likely, because she had a pretty good reason to do so. "How is it possible you don't know what it means?" she replied. "Why, I've heard you say a thousand times, 'If you don't eat at night, you'll toss till daylight.'"

Frate Puccio was convinced that her fasting was the reason for her inability to sleep, which was, in turn, causing her to toss about in her bed, and so he said to her in good faith: "Wife, I told you, 'Don't fast.'

But since you've chosen to do so anyway, stop thinking about it, and concentrate, instead, on getting some rest. You're tossing about in bed so much that you're making the whole house shake."

"No, no, don't you worry about it," said the lady. "I know exactly what I'm doing. You just keep up your good work, and as for me, I'll do the best I can with mine."

So Frate Puccio said no more and turned his attention to his Our Fathers once again. From that night on, however, for as long as his penance lasted, the lady and Messer Monk, who had had a bed set up in another part of the house, would go there and have themselves a ball until it was time for the monk to take off and for the lady to return to her bed, where she was joined by Frate Puccio shortly after his nightly vigil came to an end. Thus, while he carried on with his penance this way, his wife carried on her pleasant affair with the monk, during which she would quip to him from time to time: "You made Frate Puccio do the penance, but we're the ones who've gained Paradise."

The lady thought that things had never been better for her, and since she had been kept on a very lengthy diet by her husband, she wound up getting so accustomed to the monk's fare that even when Frate Puccio's penance was done, she found a way to keep on feasting with the monk in another location, and she was sufficiently discreet in managing the affair that she was able to go on enjoying herself with him for a long time afterward.

And so, to make the last words of my story accord with the first, this is how it came about that Frate Puccio, who thought he was getting into Paradise by doing his penance, actually showed the way there both to the monk, who had revealed the shortcut to him, and to his own wife, who lived with her husband in a state of scarcity, wanting that which Messer Monk, who was the soul of charity, supplied her with in great abundance.

Day 3, Story 5

In exchange for giving one of his palfreys to Messer Francesco Vergellesi, Zima is granted permission to talk with his wife, but when she says nothing, Zima answers on her behalf, and what happens after that bears out the response he made.[1]

The ladies all laughed over the story of Frate Puccio, and when Panfilo was finished, the Queen, with womanly grace, asked Elissa to continue. In response, speaking in a somewhat acerbic manner, not out of malice, but because it was her long-established habit, Elissa began as follows:

Many people imagine that because they know a great deal, nobody else knows anything, and so it often happens that just when they think they are putting something over on others, they find out afterward that they themselves were the ones who have been duped. Consequently, I consider it the height of folly to put the power of another person's intelligence to the test when there is no need to do so. However, since some people may not share my opinion, I should like, without deviating from the subject we have agreed to speak on, to tell you what happened to a certain gentleman from Pistoia.

That gentleman, who was named Messer Francesco, was a member of the Vergellesi family of Pistoia. He was extremely wealthy and wise and shrewd, but he was also exceedingly avaricious. Having been appointed the *podestà* of Milan, he furnished himself with everything necessary for a person of his rank before setting off for that city, with the sole exception of a palfrey handsome enough to suit him, and this inability to find one to his liking left him in quite a quandary.

At that time there was a very rich young man of humble origins

234

living in Pistoia named Ricciardo who went about so well dressed and so spruced up that everyone called him Zima.* For a long time he had loved and courted, albeit in vain, Messer Francesco's extremely beautiful and virtuous wife. Now, it just so happened that Zima owned one of the finest palfreys in Tuscany, which he treasured because of its beauty, and since it was common knowledge that he was enamored of the wife of Messer Francesco, someone told the latter that if he asked for the horse, he was bound to get it simply on account of Zima's love for the lady. Moved by his greed, Messer Francesco sent for Zima and asked if he would sell the palfrey, fully expecting that Zima would offer it to him as a gift.

"Sir," said Zima, who was pleased with what he had heard, "even if you gave me everything you have in the world, there is no way you would be able to buy my palfrey. But you could certainly have it as a gift whenever you liked, on this one condition, namely, that before you take possession of it, you give me your permission to address a few words to your wife in your presence, but in a place far enough away so that she alone, and no one else, will be able to hear me."

Spurred on by avarice and hoping to hoodwink Zima, the gentleman responded that he liked the idea, adding that Zima could speak with her for as long as he wished. Then, having left him to wait in the great hall of his palace, Messer Francesco went to his wife's room, told her how easy it would be to win the palfrey, and ordered her to come and listen to Zima, but to be very careful not to utter anything at all in response to whatever he said to her. The lady condemned this arrangement in no uncertain terms, but since she felt she had no choice but to accede to her husband's wishes, she said she would do it, and followed him into the hall in order to hear what Zima had to say.

After reconfirming the agreement he had reached with the gentleman, Zima sat down beside the lady in a part of the hall at some distance from everyone else.[2] "Worthy lady," he began, "I am certain that someone as wise as you are must have been aware for quite some time

---

* Zima (actually, il Zima) comes from *azzimato*, which means "spruce, neat, dapper, fastidious, dressed in one's Sunday best"; hence, his name means "The Dandy."

now of just how much I love you, not only because of your beauty, which, without question, transcends that of any other woman I've ever seen, but also because of your admirable manners and the singular virtues you possess, which would be sufficient to capture the heart of the noblest man alive. Thus, it is not necessary for me to have recourse to words in order to prove to you that my love is the deepest and most fervent a man ever felt for a woman, or that it will last as long as life sustains this wretched body of mine—and even longer, for if people love one another in the Beyond as they do down here, then I will love you for all eternity. Because of this, you may rest assured that there is nothing you possess, whether precious or of little value, that you can consider so completely yours or can depend on with greater assurance than myself, such as I am, and the same applies to everything I own. But to give you the most unshakable proof of what I'm saying, I assure you that I would consider it a far greater honor to be asked by you to do something that would give you pleasure than to have the whole world at my command, ready to obey me without hesitation.

"Since I am yours, as I've told you, it is not without reason that I should make so bold as to address my pleas to your noble self, for you are the source, the only source, of all my peace, my every good, my very salvation. My dearest beloved, you who are my soul's one hope, from which it nourishes itself while it burns in love's fire, as your most humble servant, I beseech you to show me so much kindness as to miti-gate the harshness you have displayed toward me in the past, so that I, who am entirely your own, may find comfort in your compassion and may say that if I fell in love with you because of your beauty, I now owe my very life to it. For if your haughty spirit does not yield to my prayers, then it will surely decline until I die, and people will say you were, indeed, my murderer.

"Now, leaving aside the fact that my death would not redound to your honor, I believe, as well, that your conscience would occasionally gnaw at you because of it, making you feel sorry for what you've done, and that sometimes, when you were in a better frame of mind, you would say to yourself, 'Alas, how wrong it was for me not to take pity

on my Zima.' But since this regret would come too late to have any
effect, it would only worsen your distress.

"Consequently, to prevent that from happening, now, while you are
still able to come to my rescue, repent and take pity on me before I die,
for in you alone lies the power to make me the happiest or the most
miserable man alive. I hope that you will not be so ungracious as to
allow death to be my reward for loving you so passionately, but that
with a happy, merciful reply, you will bring comfort to my failing spirits, which are all trembling here in your presence."

At this point, he fell silent and heaved several profound sighs, after
which he allowed a few tears to fall from his eyes, while he waited to
see what the noble lady's answer would be. Although she had been
untouched by Zima's long courtship, by his jousting and his morning
serenades and all the other things he had done to show his love for her,
the lady was moved by the words of affection spoken by this most passionate of suitors, and she began to feel something she had never felt
before, namely, what it means to be in love. And despite the fact that
she remained silent in obedience to her husband's command, she could
not prevent a few little sighs from revealing what she would have willingly made clear to Zima had she been able to reply to him.

After having waited awhile, only to discover that no response was
forthcoming, Zima, who was initially puzzled, soon began to realize
just how clever the gentleman had been. Nevertheless, as he gazed on
her face, he noticed how her eyes would sparkle from time to time when
she glanced in his direction, and this, together with the only partially
suppressed sighs she let slip out from inside her breast, filled him with
fresh hope and inspired him to come up with a novel plan. And so,
assuming her part as she sat there and listened, he began to answer his
own plea in the following manner:

"My Zima, you may rest assured that I've been aware for a long time
of the depth and perfection of your love for me, and now, thanks to
what you've just said, I feel even more confident about it. This makes me
happy, as indeed it should. Still, although I've seemed harsh and cruel
toward you, I don't want you to believe that what I felt in my heart is

what I showed in my face. On the contrary, I've always loved and treasured you beyond any other man, but I was obliged to behave like that both out of fear of another and in order to preserve my reputation for honesty. Now, however, the time is coming when I will be able to show you clearly how much I love you and to reward you for your past and present devotion to me. Take comfort, then, and be of good cheer, for Messer Francesco is about to go off to become the *podestà* of Milan in a few days, a fact you must surely know since you gave him your handsome palfrey because of your affection for me. And once he's gone, I swear to you on my faith and on the true love I feel for you that in just a short while there will be nothing to prevent you from being with me and that we will bring our love to its perfect, joyous consummation.

"And so that I don't have to make you speak about this subject again, from this point on, whenever you see two towels hanging during the day in the window of my bedroom, which overlooks our garden, you are to come to me that evening after nightfall, entering by way of the door to the garden and taking great care not to let anyone catch sight of you. There you'll find me waiting for you, and we shall spend the whole night together, enjoying ourselves and taking from one another all the pleasure we could desire."

After having spoken thus in the person of the lady, Zima began speaking on his own behalf. "Dearest lady," he replied, "the immense joy your kind answer has given me has so overwhelmed my faculties that I can scarcely find the words to give you the thanks you deserve. But even if I could go on talking the way I wish I could, there would still not be enough time for me to express my gratitude as fully as I would like and as you deserve. I will therefore leave it to your wise judgment to imagine what I desire to say, but cannot put into words. This much only will I tell you: I intend to perform, without fail, precisely what you asked me to do, and at that time, perhaps, when I feel more assurance because of the great gift you have bestowed on me, I will do everything in my power to show you all the gratitude I am capable of. Since for the present, there is nothing more that remains to be said, I bid you farewell, my dearest lady, and may God grant you those joys and blessings you most ardently desire."

Through all this, the lady did not utter a single word, and at the end Zima arose and started moving in the direction of the gentleman, who walked over to him as soon as he saw him get up.

"So what do you think?" asked Messer Francesco with a laugh. "Did I make good on the promise I gave you?"

"No, sir," replied Zima, "for you promised you would allow me to speak with your wife, and you've had me talking to a marble statue."

This remark gave a great deal of pleasure to the gentleman, who, while he had had a good opinion of his wife before, now had an even better one. "From now on," he said, "the palfrey you used to own belongs to me."

"Yes, sir, it does," replied Zima, "but if I'd thought that the favor you bestowed on me was going to produce such fruit, I would not have asked for it, but would have simply let you have the horse as a gift. And I wish to God I'd done so, because you may have bought it from me, but I got nothing out of the sale."

The gentleman had a good laugh over this remark, and having been provided with a palfrey, set off a few days later down the road to Milan in order to assume his position there as *podestà*. Left at home to her own devices, the lady recalled Zima's words and thought about how much he loved her and how he had given away his palfrey because of his affection for her. Observing him from her house as he regularly passed back and forth, she said to herself:

"What am I doing? Why am I wasting my youth? This husband of mine has gone off to Milan, and he won't be coming back for six whole months. And when will he ever make up for them? When I'm an old woman? Besides, when will I ever find such a lover as Zima? Since I'm here all by myself, and I have no reason to fear because there's nobody about, I don't see why I shouldn't take advantage of such a good opportunity while I can. I won't always have a chance like the one I have right now. No one will ever know a thing about it, and even if it were to get out, it's really better to act and repent than to do nothing and repent about that instead."

Having reasoned thus with herself, she hung two towels one day in the window overlooking the garden, in the way Zima had indicated.

Overjoyed to see them there, he set off all alone as soon as night fell
and cautiously made his way to her garden door. Upon discovering that
it was open, he continued on to a second door leading into the house,
where he found the noble lady waiting for him. The moment she saw
him coming, she got up to meet him and gave him the warmest of welcomes. Hugging her and kissing her a hundred thousand times, he followed her up the stairs, and the two of them went straight to bed, where
they experienced the ultimate pleasures of love. And although this was
their first time, it was by no means their last, for not only while the
gentleman was in Milan, but even after his return, Zima came back
there on many occasions, to the immense delight of both parties.

Day 3, Story 6

Ricciardo Minutolo loves the wife of Filippello Sighinolfi, and upon learning how jealous she is, he makes her think that his own wife would be meeting with Filippello at the baths the next day and thus persuades her to go there herself, after which she discovers that she had really been there with Ricciardo although all along she thought he was her husband.[1]

Elissa had nothing more to say, and after they had praised Zima's cleverness, the Queen ordered Fiammetta to proceed with the next story. "Gladly, my lady," she replied, all smiles, and began as follows:

Although our city is as rich in stories on every sort of topic as it is in everything else, I should like to leave it behind for a while and, like Elissa, rehearse a story about what happened in another part of the world. Let us therefore pass on to Naples, and I will tell you how one of those prudes, who make such a show of their disdain for love, was brought by her lover's ingenuity to taste its fruits before she was even aware that it had flowered. You will thus, at one and the same time, learn how to deal prudently with things that might happen, and be entertained by those that already have.

In the most ancient city of Naples, which is perhaps as delightful as any in Italy—if not actually more so—there once lived a young man named Ricciardo Minutolo who was as celebrated for his noble blood as he was renowned for his immense fortune. Despite the fact that he had a charming, very pretty young wife, he fell for a lady who by common consent was far more beautiful than any other in Naples. Her name was Catella, and she was married to an equally noble young man named Filippello Sighinolfi whom she, a model of virtue, loved and cherished more than anything else in the world. Although Ricciardo Minutolo was in love with this Catella and did everything anyone would normally do in order to win a lady's favor and affection, he was unable, for all that, to satisfy his desires and was thus on the verge of despair. Even if he had known how to free himself from the bonds of love, he lacked the strength to do so, and yet, he could neither die nor see any reason to go on living.

One day, while he was languishing away in this condition, it happened that certain female relatives of his began earnestly entreating him to renounce his passionate attachment. All of his labors were in vain, they argued, for the only thing Catella cared about was Filippello, and she was so jealous of him that she thought the very birds flying through the air were trying to whisk him away from her. As soon as he heard about Catella's jealousy, it immediately occurred to Ricciardo that there was a way for him to obtain what he desired, and he began pretending that, since he despaired of his love for Catella, he had, as a result, transferred his affections to another lady. For her sake he started going to tournaments and jousting and doing all the things he had once done for Catella, and it did not take him very long to convince almost everyone in Naples, including Catella, that he was madly in love, not with her, but with this other lady. Moreover, he persevered with his act until this opinion was so firmly rooted in everyone's mind that Catella herself, not to mention many others, abandoned the reserve she used to display toward him because of his love for her and started giving him the same affable, neighborly greeting, whenever she ran into him, that she gave to everyone else.

Now it just so happened that during one particular warm spell, many companies of ladies and gentlemen, following the Neapolitan custom, went to the seashore, where they amused themselves and ate both dinner and supper. Knowing that Catella had gone there with her party, Ricciardo likewise took his and headed for the same place, where he was welcomed by Catella and her lady friends, although not before he had made them ask him repeatedly to join them and had acted as if he was not particularly interested in spending time with them.

When the ladies, joined by Catella, began teasing him about his new love, he pretended to be profoundly offended, thus giving them plenty of material to work with. Eventually, many of them wandered off by themselves in one direction or another, as people do in such places, leaving only Catella and a few of her friends behind with Ricciardo, who proceeded to toss off a witty quip in her direction about a certain love affair her husband Filippello was having. This instantly provoked a jealous fit in her, and she was soon burning up with desire to know what Ricciardo was talking about. For a while she managed to restrain herself, but in the end, incapable of controlling her feelings any longer, she begged Ricciardo, in the name of that lady whom he loved beyond all others, to be so good as to clarify what he had said about Filippello.

"Since you've implored me in the name of that person," he replied, "I dare not refuse anything you ask of me. Therefore I'm prepared to tell you all about it, but only if you promise me that you'll never utter a word on the subject either to him or to anyone else until you've actually confirmed that what I'm about to tell you is true. And whenever you like, I can actually show you how to do that."

The lady accepted his offer, which made her believe all the more that he was telling the truth, and swore that she would never say a word about it. They then went off to the side so that the others would not hear them.

"My lady," he began, "if I were still in love with you the way I used to be, I would not have dared to tell you something that I thought might distress you, but since that love is now in the past, I have fewer misgivings about revealing the entire truth to you. I don't know whether Filippello ever took offense at the love I bore you, or whether he believed that you returned it, but whatever the case may be, he never showed any sign of such feelings to me personally. Now, however, having waited perhaps for a time when he thought I would be less suspicious, he appears to be intent on doing to me what I'm afraid he fears I was doing to him, that is, having an affair with my wife. From what I've discovered, he's been courting her for some time now with the utmost secrecy, sending her messages, all of which she's shown to me, and she's been replying to them in accordance with my instructions.

"But just this morning, before I came here, I found a woman in my house having a private conversation with my wife, and immediately recognizing her for what she was, I called my wife and asked her what the woman wanted. 'It's that pest Filippello,' she replied. 'He keeps bothering me because you made me answer him and raise his hopes. Now he says that he wants to know once and for all what my intentions are, and he tells me that if I want to do it, he could make arrangements for us to meet in secret at one of the bathhouses in the city, and he just keeps begging and begging me to do it. If it weren't for the fact that you forced me to continue negotiating with him—and I have no idea why you did—I would have gotten rid of him in such a way that he would never have looked in my direction again.'

"That's when I felt the guy was going too far and was no longer to be put up with, and it seemed to me that I should tell you about it so that you could see how he rewards you for that unwavering fidelity of yours that at one time was almost the death of me. And to convince you that this is not just a lot of idle talk and gossip, and to let you see it clearly, and indeed, actually touch it, if you want to, I had my wife tell the woman, who was waiting around for her response, that she was ready to go to the baths tomorrow around nones, when everybody's asleep. After that, the woman left, quite pleased with the arrangement.

"Now I trust you don't believe I'd actually send my wife to the bath-house. But if I were in your place, I'd arrange for him to find me there instead of the woman he's expecting to meet, and after I'd spent some time with him, I'd let him see just who it was he'd been with, and then I'd give him precisely the kind of honorable treatment he deserves for what he did. If you take my advice here, I truly do believe he'd be put to such shame that at a single stroke we'd both be avenged for the injury he is trying to do to us."

As is the way with jealous people, Catella did not pause to consider who the speaker was or whether he might be deceiving her, but believed every word the moment she heard it. As she began connecting the story he was telling her to certain events that had happened in the past, all of a sudden she flared up in anger and declared that she would definitely do what he suggested, since it would not take much of an effort on her part. Furthermore, she insisted that if Filippello really did show up there, she would not fail to make him feel so ashamed of himself that he would never look at another woman without having this experience buzzing about in his brain.

Ricciardo was pleased with her reaction, and seeing as how he was making good progress with his plan, he said a great many other things to firm up her belief in his story, at the same time begging her never to reveal that she had heard it all from him. In response, she swore on her faith that she would never do so.

The next morning, Ricciardo went to the good woman who ran the baths he had told Catella about, explained what he wanted to do, and asked her to give him as much assistance as she could.[2] Since the good woman was very much in his debt, she said she would be happy to help and arranged with him what she was supposed to say and do. In the house where the baths were located, she had a room that was very dark, there being no window one could open to let in the light. Following Ricciardo's instructions, the good woman prepared the room for him and had the best bed available set up there, in which, after he had eaten, Ricciardo stretched out and began waiting for Catella to arrive.

The lady had returned home the previous evening, seething with anger because of the story Ricciardo had told her, to which she had given much more credence than she should have. As chance would have it, when Filippello turned up a little later, he was preoccupied with other thoughts and did not treat her with his usual show of affection. His behavior thus made Catella even more suspicious than she had been before, and she said to herself: "He's clearly thinking about that woman and about all the fun and games he'll be having with her tomorrow. Well, there's no way that's going to happen." And this thought, plus imagining what she would say to him after their encounter the next day, kept her awake most of the night.

But what more is there to say? When nones arrived, Catella fetched her maid and without giving the matter another thought, went to the baths that Ricciardo had told her about. Finding the good woman there, she asked her if Filippello had come around that day, and the good woman replied, as she had been instructed to by Ricciardo: "Are you the lady who is supposed to come here and speak with him?"

"Yes, I am," replied Catella.

"Then," said the good woman, "go right on in. He's waiting for you there."

In pursuit of something she would have been happy not to find, the heavily veiled Catella had the woman take her to the room where Ricciardo was waiting and then locked the door behind her once she had gone inside. The moment he saw her enter, Ricciardo joyfully got to his feet, took her in his arms, and whispered: "Welcome, my darling!"

Eager to convince him that she was the other woman, Catella kissed and hugged and made a great fuss over him, although all along she refrained from uttering a single word out of fear that he would recognize her if she spoke. The room was exceptionally dark, a circumstance that pleased both parties, so dark, in fact, that it was impossible for them, even after they had been there awhile, to see anything clearly at all. Ricciardo led her up onto the bed, where they remained for quite some time, never saying a single thing lest their voices give them away, although one of them found the experience there much more pleasant and enjoyable than the other one did.

Finally, however, Catella thought it was time to release her pent-up indignation, and blazing with passionate anger, she began speaking: "Ah, how wretched is the fate of women, and how misplaced the love that many of them bear their husbands! Poor me! For eight years now I've loved you more than my very life, and you, I've now found out, you are all on fire, burning up with love for another woman! What a base, evil man you are! Who is it that you think you've just been with? You've been with the woman you've been deceiving for ever so long with your phony expressions of affection, pretending you loved her when all the time you were in love with someone else.

"You faithless traitor, I'm not Ricciardo's wife, I'm Catella. Just listen to my voice, and you'll see who I really am. Oh, how I want to be out in the light again—it seems as if it'll be a thousand years before I can give you the shaming you deserve, you filthy, disgusting dog.

"Oh, poor me! For whom have I borne so much love for so many years? For this unfaithful dog who believes he's got some other woman in his arms and has lavished more caresses and loving affection on me in the little while I've spent with him here than in all the rest of the

time I've been his wife. You've sure been good and lusty today, you ren-
egade dog, as opposed to the way you are at home, where you're always
so feeble and worn out and incapable of keeping it up! But praise be to
God, you've been tilling your own field here rather than someone else's
as you thought you were doing. No wonder you didn't come near me last
night! You were waiting to discharge your load elsewhere and wanted
to arrive really fresh for your knightly battle, but thanks to God and
my wits, the water's run downhill in the proper direction!

"Why don't you answer, you evil man? Why don't you say something? Have my words struck you dumb? I swear to God I don't know
what's keeping me from sticking my hands into your eyes and plucking
them out! Did you think you could carry out your infidelity in secret?
Well, by God, you didn't succeed, because you're not the only one who
knows a thing or two, and I've had better hounds on your tail than
you thought."

Ricciardo was inwardly relishing these words, but instead of saying
anything in response, he hugged her and kissed her, caressing her more
passionately than ever, which only led her to continue her tirade.

"Oh yes," she said, "now you think you'll calm me down with your
phony caresses, you disgusting dog. Well, if you think you can pacify
me and console me like that, you're wrong. I'll never be consoled for
what you did until I've shamed you in front of our entire family as well
as every last one of our friends and neighbors. Am I not as beautiful
as Ricciardo Minutolo's wife, you evil man? Am I not just as much a
lady? Why don't you answer me, you dirty dog? What's she got that
I don't?

"Get away from me, and keep your hands to yourself. You've done
more than enough jousting for today. I'm well aware that since you
know who I am, from now on you could use force to have your way
with me, but with God's grace, I'll see to it that you go hungry. In fact,
I don't know what prevents me from sending for Ricciardo, who has
loved me more than his very life, even though he could never boast
that I gave him so much as a single look. Nor can I see any reason why
it would be wrong for me to do that, because, after all, you thought
you were having his wife here, and it's all just the same to you as if you

really did, since you didn't succeed for lack of trying. So, if I had him, you would have no right to hold it against me."

Now, there were many, many more words, and the lady's complaint went on and on. But in the end, thinking how much trouble might ensue if he let her go away believing what she did, Ricciardo decided to free her from the delusion she labored under by revealing who he was. He therefore caught her in his arms and held her so tightly that she could not escape.

"My sweet soul, don't be upset," he said. "What I was unable to achieve simply by loving you, Love himself has taught me to obtain by means of deception. I am none other than your Ricciardo."

As soon as Catella heard this and recognized his voice, she immediately tried to jump out of bed. Ricciardo prevented her from doing so, however, and then, when she attempted to scream, covered her mouth with one of his hands.

"My lady," he said, "it's impossible to undo what's been done, even though you were to go on screaming for the rest of your life. Moreover, if you do that, or if you do anything to reveal this to anyone, two things are going to happen. The first, which should cause you more than a little concern, is that your honor and your good name will be ruined, because no matter how much you insist that I tricked you into coming here, I shall respond that it's not true. Indeed, I shall maintain that I persuaded you to come by promising you money and gifts, and that you're just saying these things and making all this fuss because you got angry when I didn't give you as much as you were expecting.[3] Now, you know that people have a tendency to believe the worst rather than the best about others, which is why my version of what happened will be just as convincing as yours. In the second place, your husband and I will become mortal enemies, and it could just as easily reach the point where he would be killed by me as I would by him, and in either case you would be miserably unhappy for the rest of your life.

"Therefore, heart of my heart, do not at one and the same time seek to bring dishonor upon yourself and to place your husband and me in danger by setting us at odds. You're not the first woman who has ever been deceived, nor will you be the last, and in any case, I did not deceive

you in order to deprive you of anything, but because of the overwhelming love I feel for you. Indeed, I'm fully prepared to love you and to
remain your most humble servant forever. For a long while now, I and
my possessions have been yours, and all my power and influence have
been at your service, but from this time on, they will be, more than
ever, yours to command. You are a wise woman, and I feel certain that
you will show the same good sense in this case as you have in others."

While Ricciardo was talking, Catella wept bitterly, but although
she was very upset and complained a great deal, nevertheless her reason admitted that there was some truth in Ricciardo's words, and it
dawned on her that what he was talking about really could happen.
Consequently, she declared:

"Ricciardo, I don't know how the Lord God can ever give me the
strength to bear the injury you've done me and the deceit you practiced
here. Although I have no intention of making an outcry in this place, to
which my own simplemindedness and excessive jealousy have led me,
you may rest assured that I won't be happy until I see myself revenged
in some way or other for what you did to me. Now, let me go and get
out of here. Since you've got what you wanted and tortured me to your
heart's content, the time has come to release me, and so, I'm begging
you, please let me go."

Seeing just how disturbed she was, Ricciardo, who was determined
not to leave her until she forgave him, set about the task of appeasing
her, using the sweetest words he could think of, and he said so much
and begged so much and pleaded so much that she finally surrendered
and made peace with him. After that, by mutual consent, they stayed
there a good long time together, enjoying themselves enormously.

Now that the lady knew how much tastier the kisses of her lover
were than those of her husband, all her harshness toward Ricciardo
was transformed into sweet affection, and she loved him from that
day forward with the greatest tenderness in the world. Moreover, as
the two of them always acted with the utmost discretion, they were
able to go on enjoying that love of theirs time and time again. And may
God grant that we enjoy ours as well.

Day 3, Story 7

Angered by his lady, Tedaldo leaves Florence, but returns some time later disguised as a pilgrim, speaks with her, making her aware of her error, and not only liberates her husband, who has been convicted of having murdered him and been sentenced to death for it, but makes peace between the husband and his own brothers, after which he discreetly enjoys himself with his lady.[1]

Once Fiammetta was silent and everyone had congratulated her, in order not to lose time, the Queen promptly designated Emilia as the next speaker, who began as follows:

I intend to return to our city, from which the last two speakers chose to depart, and to show you how one of our fellow citizens got his lady back after having lost her.

There once lived in Florence a young nobleman named Tedaldo degli Elisei who fell madly in love with a lady called Monna Ermellina, the wife of a certain Aldobrandino Palermini.[2] Because of his many admirable qualities, Tedaldo deserved to have his desires gratified, but Fortune, the enemy of those who prosper, denied him this happiness, in that the lady, who had begun to bestow her favors on him, for some reason or other absolutely ceased to have any interest in doing so. Not only did she refuse to listen to his messages, but she would not see him under any circumstances, thus driving him into a state of fierce and painful melancholy. Since he had kept his love well hidden, however, no one guessed it was the source of his misery.

Feeling that he had lost the lady's love through no fault of his own, he tried to get it back in every conceivable way, but when he found that all his efforts were in vain, he decided to retire from society there in order to prevent the woman who was the cause of his grief from enjoying the spectacle of watching him waste away. Without saying a word to any of his friends or relations, except for one confidant of his who knew all about the affair, he took what money he had available and departed in secret for Ancona. There, under the assumed name of Filippo di San Lodeccio, he made the acquaintance of a rich merchant, accepted a position with him, and accompanied him to Cyprus on one of his ships.[3] Tedaldo's character and comportment impressed the merchant so much that not only did he pay him a good salary, but he also made him an associate in the business, placing him in charge of a large portion of his affairs. Tedaldo performed his duties so well and with such diligence that in a few years he became a successful, wealthy, well-regarded merchant himself.

In the midst of all these activities, Tedaldo's thoughts often returned to his cruel lady, but although he suffered ferocious pain from Love's wound and longed desperately to see her again, he was so strong-willed that for seven years he won this battle with his feelings. However, one day in Cyprus he happened to hear someone singing a song he himself had composed in which he told the story of the love he felt for his lady, her love for him, and the pleasure he derived from her, and thinking that it was impossible for her to have forgotten him, all of a sudden he found himself burning with such a desire to see her again that he could not endure it any longer and decided to return to Florence.

Having put his affairs in order, he traveled with a single servant to Ancona where he waited for all his belongings to arrive and then forwarded them to Florence, sending everything ahead to a friend of his business associate in Ancona, after which he himself, disguised as a pilgrim returning from the Holy Sepulcher, followed with his servant. When they reached Florence, he stopped at a little inn run by two brothers, which was close to where his lady lived. The first thing he did after that was to go and station himself before her house to see if he might catch a glimpse of her. What he discovered, however, was that the doors and windows and everything else were all locked up tight, which led him to fear that she might have died or moved away. Deeply disturbed, he went on to his family's house, in front of which he saw four of his brothers, all of whom were, to his great surprise, dressed in black. Knowing that people would have trouble recognizing him, because both his clothing and his physical appearance were very different from what they had been when he had gone away, he boldly walked up to a shoemaker and asked him why the men were wearing black.

"They're dressed like that," replied the shoemaker, "because within the past two weeks, a brother of theirs named Tedaldo, who's not been around here for a long time, was found murdered. And from what I've gathered, they've proved in court that the killer was someone by the name of Aldobrandino Palermini, who has now been arrested. Apparently, the murdered man was in love with Palermini's wife and had returned here in disguise to be with her."

Tedaldo was quite amazed that someone could resemble him so closely as to be mistaken for him, and at the same time he was very distressed to learn of Aldobrandino's misfortune. But he also managed to find out that the lady was alive and well, and since by then night had fallen, he returned to the inn, preoccupied with his thoughts on all these subjects. After eating supper together with his servant, he was shown to his sleeping quarters, which were located near the very top of the house. There, whether it was the result of all the thoughts that were bothering him, or the uncomfortable nature of his bed, or the meager supper he had had, Tedaldo spent half the night trying unsuccessfully to fall asleep. He was thus still awake, when, around midnight, he thought he could hear people entering the building from the roof, and shortly afterward, through the cracks in the door to his room, he saw a light coming up the stairs. Quietly making his way over to one of the openings, he looked out to see what was happening and caught sight of a rather pretty young woman who was holding the light. She was met there by three men, who had just come down from the roof.

After they had exchanged friendly greetings, one of them said to her: "We've got nothing more to worry about, thank God, because we've learned for certain that Tedaldo Elisei's brothers have proved he was killed by Aldobrandino Palermini, who's confessed that he did it. But even though the sentence has been recorded, we'd still better keep this thing quiet because if they ever found out that we were the ones who did it, we'd be in the same danger as Aldobrandino." The woman seemed quite delighted with what the man said, and when he finished speaking, they all walked downstairs and went to sleep.

Having overheard the entire exchange, Tedaldo started thinking about all the many different kinds of errors that are capable of lodging themselves in people's minds. First, he thought about his brothers who had mourned and buried some stranger in place of him, and then of the innocent man who had been accused because of false suspicions and was at the point of being executed on the evidence of lying witnesses. This led him to reflect on the blind severity of laws and magistrates who act as if they are eagerly seeking the truth, but frequently, relying on cruel means of persuasion, get falsehoods accepted as facts, and who call themselves the ministers of God's justice when they are really carrying out the mandates of wickedness and the Devil. Finally, however, Tedaldo turned his attention to how he could save Aldobrandino and decided on the plan of action he was going to adopt.

When he got up in the morning, he left his servant behind and made his way alone, at what seemed an appropriate hour, to his lady's house. Finding the door open by chance, he went in and saw her, all tears and bitter lamentations, sitting on the floor in a little room that was downstairs. Ready to weep himself because of the pity he felt for her, he approached her and said: "My lady, don't torment yourself; your peace is at hand."

On hearing his voice, the lady raised her head. "Good sir," she said through her tears, "you appear to be a pilgrim and a foreigner, so how can you know anything about my peace or my troubles?"

"My lady," he replied, "I'm from Constantinople, and I've just arrived here, sent by God to convert your tears into laughter and to deliver your husband from death."[4]

"If you're from Constantinople," said the lady, "and if you've only arrived just now, how can you know anything about me and my husband?"

Starting from the beginning, the pilgrim recounted the entire story of Aldobrandino's sufferings and then explained to her exactly who she was, how long she had been married, and many other details that were very well known to him concerning her affairs. The lady was thoroughly amazed by this, and taking him for a prophet, fell down on her knees at his feet, beseeching him, for God's sake, if he really had come to save Aldobrandino, to do so quickly because time was running out.

"Arise, my lady," said the pilgrim, putting on a very saintly air, "and weep no more. Listen closely to what I am about to tell you, and be really careful never to repeat it to anyone. According to what God has revealed to me, the tribulation you are enduring right now is the result of a sin you once committed. The Lord decided that you should purge it, at least partially, by means of this present affliction, but He still wants you to make amends for it in full, because if you don't, you will assuredly be plunged into even greater suffering."

"Sir," said the lady, "I have so many sins that I don't know which one the Lord God would want me to atone for out of all the rest. So, if you know what it is, tell me, and I'll do everything I can to make amends for it."

"My lady," replied the pilgrim, "I know precisely what it is, but I will nevertheless question you about it now, not for the sake of my own knowledge, but so that you may feel even more remorse when you speak of it. However, let's get to point. Tell me, do you recall ever having had a lover?"

On hearing this question, the lady heaved a deep sigh and was truly amazed since she thought that no one knew anything about it, even though on the day when the man was murdered, who was then buried as Tedaldo, there was some whispering about it because of certain indiscreet little words that Tedaldo's confidant had spoken.

"It's apparent that God reveals all the secrets of mankind to you," she said, "and I therefore see no reason why I should keep mine hidden any longer. In my youth I was indeed deeply in love with the unfortunate young man whose death has been blamed on my husband. I have been overwhelmed with grief since he died and have cried my eyes out over him, for even though I showed myself harsh and cruel toward him before he went away, neither his departure, nor his long absence, nor even his unfortunate death has ever been able to dislodge him from my heart."

"That unlucky youth who was killed was not the man you were in love with," the pilgrim replied, "but Tedaldo Elisei certainly was. Still, tell me: what was the reason that you fell out with him? Did he ever do anything to offend you?"

"Certainly not," said the lady. "He never gave me any offense. My harshness was caused by the words of an accursed friar who once heard my confession, for when I told him about the love I felt for Tedaldo and the intimacy we shared, he yelled at me, creating such a racket in my head that it frightens me to this very day. He said that unless I ended the affair, I'd go straight into the Devil's mouth at the bottom of Hell and from there be cast into the penal fire.[5] I was so terrified that I firmly resolved never to be on intimate terms with him again, and to make sure there would be no reason for that to happen, from then on I refused to accept any of his letters or messages. Now, I presume that when he went away, he was in despair, but if he had persevered a little while longer, I do believe that my hard resolve would have softened, for I could see he was already wasting away like snow in sunlight, and there was nothing in the world I wanted to do more than to relent."

"My lady," said the pilgrim, "it is this sin alone that is the source of all your tribulations. I know for a fact that Tedaldo did not coerce you in any way, and that when you fell in love with him, you did so of your own free will, because you found him attractive. It was in response to your wishes that he came to you and the two of you began an intimate affair, and your delight in him, which was evident in both your words and deeds, was so great that if he loved you before then, you increased his love a thousandfold.

"And if this was so—and I know it was—what reason could there possibly have been for you to separate yourself so definitively from him? This is something you should have thought through in advance, so that if you felt that what you were going to do was wrong and would cause you to repent, you would not have done it. For just as he became yours, so you became his. Had it simply been a matter of his being attached to you, then you could have acted on your own discretion and discarded him whenever you wished, but since you were attached to him as well, it was quite improper, indeed, it was a form of robbery, to take yourself away from him when that went against his will.

"Now, you should know that I'm a friar, and since I'm well acquainted with all their ways, it's not inappropriate for me, as it would be for someone else, to speak rather freely about them for your benefit. Actually, I'll do this quite happily so that you'll have a better understanding of them in the future than you seem to have had in the past.

"There used to be a time when friars were extremely pious and worthy men, but those who call themselves by that name today and want to be taken for such possess nothing in common with friars except their habits. In fact, their habits aren't real, because the founders of the orders all ordained that they should be close-fitting, humble garments made of coarse cloth, so that by swathing the body in base apparel, they would reveal the spirit's scorn for the things of this world. Today, by contrast, friars have ample habits that are well lined and cut from the finest, most smoothly textured material. They are, moreover, elegant and pontifical in style, so that their wearers can go strutting about like peacocks through churches and piazzas just as laymen do with the robes they wear. And like the fisherman who throws his net into the river trying to catch a large number of fish with a single cast, so these guys, wrapping themselves up in the ample folds of their fancy garments, do their best to take in as many sanctimonious old maids, and widows, and other fools of both sexes as they can, for that's the only thing they are concerned about. To tell the truth, they don't really wear friars' habits at all, just clothing of the same color.

"Moreover, whereas friars of old sought the salvation of mankind, the ones today desire women and wealth, and all their efforts have been aimed, as they still are, at striking terror into the souls of simple people by means of their noise and the pictures they make use of, and then to show them how sins may be purged by means of offering alms and Masses. Thus, these wretches, who have taken refuge in the mendicant orders more out of cowardice than true devotion and in order to avoid hard work, are given bread by one person, have another one send them wine, and get special meals from yet others to say Masses for the souls of their dearly departed.

"Now it's certainly true that sins are purged by almsgiving and prayers, but if the donors really got to know the sort of people on whom they were bestowing their largess, they'd either keep everything for themselves or cast it down before so many swine instead. And since these friars know that the fewer the people are who have shares in a great fortune, the better off they are, each one does his utmost, haranguing and terrifying his auditors, in order to deprive them of what he wants to have all for himself. They denounce men's lust so that once those who've been denounced are out of the way, the women will be left for those who did the denouncing. They condemn usury and ill-gotten gains, so that people will trust them to make restitution on their behalf, and then they take that which, they've claimed, will lead those who possess it to perdition and use it to procure grander habits for themselves and to purchase bishoprics and the other great offices in the Church.

"Whenever they are reproached for such actions and for the many other disgraceful things they do, they think they can unload the heaviest charges by replying, 'Do as we say and not as we do'—as if constancy and steadfast behavior came more easily to the sheep than to their shepherds. And yet a great many of them know that there are people to whom they make such a reply who hardly take it in the way they intend.

"Friars nowadays want you to do as they say, that is, to fill their purses with money, confide your secrets to them, remain chaste, practice patience, forgive injuries, and avoid speaking evil, all of which are good, honest, pious actions. But why these in particular? Simply so that they can do things they'd be prevented from doing if laymen did them, too. Who doesn't know that it takes money to maintain a life of sloth? If you're going to take what you have and spend it on your own pleasures, then the friar cannot idle away his time in the monastery. If you go around pursuing women, there'll be no room left for him to do so, too. If you don't practice patience and forgive injuries, he won't dare to come to your house and corrupt your family. But why am I going into such detail? Each time they make this excuse, they actually accuse themselves in the eyes of every intelligent person. If they don't think they can behave in a chaste and pious manner, why don't they just stay in their cloisters? Or if they really wish to live that way, why don't they follow that other holy saying of the Evangelist: 'Then Christ began to act and to teach'?[6] Let them first put things into practice themselves, and then let them offer instruction to others. In my day I've seen a thousand of them courting, making love, and paying visits not just to laywomen, but to nuns—and yet some of them are the biggest noisemakers in the pulpit. And we're supposed to follow the lead of such people? Anyone may do so if he likes, but God knows if he's acting wisely.

"Nevertheless, even supposing we granted that what the friar said who scolded you is right and that breaking one's marriage vows is a very serious fault, isn't robbing a man an even greater one? Isn't it far worse to kill him or send him wandering through the world in exile? Everyone would agree that it is, because for a woman to have an intimate relationship with a man is a natural sin, whereas to rob him or kill him or drive him into exile is a matter of malice aforethought.[7]

"I've already proved to you that you robbed Tedaldo when you tore yourself away from him after having given yourself to him of your own free will. I'll now go further and say that you did your utmost to murder him as well, because by your treating him with ever more cruelty, it's no thanks to you that he didn't wind up taking his life—and according to the law, the person who is the cause of a crime is as guilty as the person who actually commits it. Finally, it cannot be denied that you are responsible for his wandering the world in exile for seven years. So, truly, you've committed a much graver sin in each one of the three cases I've mentioned than you did by means of your intimate affair with him.

"But let's see: is it possible that Tedaldo deserved what happened to him? No, he certainly did not, as you yourself already confessed. And I also happen to know that he loves you more than his very own life, for nothing was ever so acclaimed, extolled, or exalted as you were by him above all other women whenever he was in a situation where he could speak honestly about you without giving rise to suspicion. He placed all his welfare, all his honor, all his liberty in your hands. Wasn't he a noble youth? Wasn't he as handsome as any of his fellow citizens? Wasn't he accomplished in performing all those things that are expected of young men? Wasn't he loved and cherished and well regarded by everyone?

You can't deny all this, either. So, how could you have decided to treat him with such cruelty, all because of the insane ravings of an asinine, envious little friar?

"I simply don't understand how some women can make the mistake of shunning men and looking down on them, for if they would only think about their own natures and how much more nobility God has bestowed on man than on the other animals, they would take pride in the fact that some man loved them, would hold him in the highest esteem, and would make every conceivable effort to please him so that he would never stop loving them. Now you yourself know exactly what you did, swayed by the words of a friar who was, without doubt, some gluttonous soup-swilling pie muncher and who may well have intended to install himself in the place from which he wanted to dislodge someone else.[8]

"This, then, is the sin that divine justice, which always maintains a perfect balance as it brings all its operations to completion, would not allow to remain unpunished. Since you did everything you could for no good reason to separate yourself from Tedaldo, in the same way, not only has your husband's life, for no good reason, been placed in danger and remains in danger on Tedaldo's account, but you yourself have been made to suffer. If you want to be released from these afflictions, here's what you must promise, or, even better, what you must do. If Tedaldo should ever happen to come back here from his long exile, you should restore him to your favor, your love, your goodwill, and your intimate friendship, and you should reinstate him once again in the position he occupied before you were foolish enough to give heed to that half-witted friar."

When the pilgrim finished his remarks, to which the lady had listened with rapt attention, feeling all along that his arguments were very sound, she was convinced, having heard him identify it as such, that all her suffering was the result of that one particular sin she had committed.

"Friend of God," she said, "I know only too well that the things you've said are true, and thanks largely to what you've taught me, I can now see friars for what they are, although I once used to regard all of them as holy men. I also recognize that I undoubtedly committed a serious fault in treating Tedaldo as I did, and if it were in my power, I would gladly make amends in the way you've described. But how can that be done? Tedaldo is dead and can never come back to us, so I don't know why I should make you a promise I can't possibly keep."

"My lady," said the pilgrim, "from what God has revealed to me, Tedaldo is not dead in the least; he's alive and well, and if only he enjoyed your favor, he'd be quite a happy man."

"Watch what you're saying," the lady replied. "I saw him lying dead outside my door, his body riddled with stab wounds, and I held him in these very arms and bathed his lifeless face with a flood of tears, which may have been the reason for all the malicious gossip that has been going about."

"No matter what you say, my lady," said the pilgrim, "I assure you that Tedaldo is alive, and if you'll just make me that promise, with every intention of keeping it, it's my hope that you'll soon be seeing him again."

"I'll do it," the lady replied, "and willingly, for nothing would make me happier than to see my husband freed unharmed and Tedaldo alive."

Tedaldo now felt that the moment had come to reveal himself to the lady and thus reassure her that there was every good reason to feel hopeful about her husband.

"My lady," he said, "to set your mind at ease with regard to your husband, I have to tell you an important secret that you must promise you'll never reveal for as long as you live."

Since the two of them were all alone in a fairly remote part of the house—the lady was clearly feeling quite assured by the pilgrim's appearance of holiness—Tedaldo took out a ring that she had given him on the last night they had spent together and that he had taken the greatest care of ever since.

"My lady," he said, holding it out for her to see, "do you know this ring?"

"Yes, sir," she replied, having recognized it at first sight. "I gave it to Tedaldo long ago."

In an instant, then, the pilgrim stood up, and having removed his cloak and taken his hat from his head, he said to her, speaking with a Florentine accent: "And now do you know me, too?"

When the lady looked up and realized that it was Tedaldo, she was completely petrified with fear, the way people are when they think they've seen some dead man walking about as though he were alive. And so, instead of rushing up to welcome him as a Tedaldo who had just come back from Cyprus, she was terrified and wanted to flee a Tedaldo who had seemingly just come back from the grave.

"Don't be afraid, my lady," he said. "I really am your Tedaldo, alive and well, and no matter what you and my brothers may think, I never died and was never murdered."

Somewhat reassured, but still a little frightened by the sound of his voice, the lady continued to stare at him for a while until she finally convinced herself that he was indeed Tedaldo. Then she threw her arms around his neck, and weeping as she kissed him, she said: "My sweet Tedaldo, how welcome back you are!"

"My lady," replied Tedaldo, after kissing and hugging her, "there is no time now for a more intimate reunion. I must go and arrange for Aldobrandino to be restored to you safe and sound, and I am hopeful that before tomorrow evening you'll get information that will cause you to rejoice. In fact, if I manage to get some good news about his safety myself, as I fully expect I will, then I'd like to come to your place tonight and tell you all about it at greater leisure than I have time for at present."

Putting his cloak and hat back on, Tedaldo kissed the lady once more, reassured her that all would be well, and took his leave of her. He then went directly to the prison where they were holding Aldobrandino who was brooding fearfully on his imminent death more than hoping for some sort of future deliverance. Playing the spiritual comforter, Tedaldo was let in by the jailors, went to Aldobrandino, and sat down beside him.

"I'm here as a friend, Aldobrandino," he said, "sent to save you by God Himself, who has been moved to pity by your innocence. Consequently, if out of reverence for Him you will grant me the small gift I'm about to ask you for, you may rest assured that before tomorrow evening, instead of the sentence of death you're expecting right now, you'll hear that you've been acquitted."

"Good sir," replied Aldobrandino, "since you are concerned for my safety, you must be a friend, as you say, even though I don't know you and can't remember ever having seen you before. The truth is that I didn't commit the crime for which it is said I must be put to death, but I have sinned in many other ways, which may well be what has brought me to this pass. In all reverence to God, however, let me tell you this: if He takes pity on me now, there is nothing, no matter how great it may be—let alone how small, as you insist—that I wouldn't be willing to do, and not just make promises about. So, ask of me whatever you please, and if I'm released from here, I will, without fail, keep my word to you."

"All I want you to do," said the pilgrim, "is to forgive Tedaldo's four brothers for having placed you in this predicament, because they thought you were guilty of having murdered their brother, and should they ask your pardon for what they did, I want you to treat them as your brothers and friends."

"No one knows better than a person who has been wronged how sweet revenge is," replied Aldobrandino, "or how intensely it may be desired. Nevertheless, so that God will provide for my deliverance, I'll forgive them willingly. Indeed, I'll do it right now, and if I get out of here with my life and liberty, I'll act in a way you'll find quite gratifying."

This answer pleased the pilgrim who had nothing more he wished to add, except to encourage Aldobrandino most heartily to be of good cheer and to assure him that he would definitely hear news of his release before the next day was over.

After taking leave of Aldobrandino, Tedaldo went to the Signoria and had a private interview with a gentleman who was in charge.

"My lord," he said, "all of us—and especially people in your position—have a duty to work zealously to ensure that the truth comes to light, so that those who have not committed a crime won't have to pay the penalty for it and the guilty parties may be punished. And that's why I've come here to you, both for the sake of your honor and to mete out retribution to those who deserve it. As you know, you have prosecuted Aldobrandino Palermini quite rigorously, and thinking you've found convincing proof that he murdered Tedaldo Elisei, you are now about to pass sentence on him. But the evidence is utterly false, and I believe I can prove it to you before midnight by placing that young man's actual murderers in your hands."

The worthy gentleman, who had already been feeling sorry for Aldobrandino, gladly lent an ear to the pilgrim's words, and after having been supplied with many more details concerning the case, on the basis of that information he arrested the two innkeeper brothers and their servant without a struggle just after they had gone to bed. He wanted to have them tortured in order to get the truth out of them about what had happened, but they could not handle such a prospect and openly confessed, first singly and then all together, that they had killed Tedaldo Elisei without having any idea who he was. When asked why, they said that he had been really bothering one of their wives while they were away from the inn and that he had tried to force himself on her.

Being apprised of all this, the pilgrim took his leave of the worthy gentleman and made his way, unobserved, back to Madonna Ermellina's house. Everyone else there had gone to bed, and he found her waiting for him all by herself, eager to hear some good news about her husband and to be fully reconciled with her Tedaldo. He went up to her with a smile on his face and said, "Cheer up, my dearest lady. It's a sure thing that you'll have your Aldobrandino back here tomorrow safe and sound." And in order to remove any doubts she might still have, he proceeded to give her a full account of what he had done.

Madonna Ermellina was the happiest women alive to learn of these two sudden and unexpected developments, that is, getting Tedaldo back alive after truly believing that she had wept for him as a dead man, and seeing Aldobrandino delivered from danger, when she thought that in just a few days she was going to have to weep for him as a dead man, too. And so, kissing and hugging Tedaldo with real passion, she went off to bed with him, where, to their mutual delight and happiness, with one accord they gladly, graciously made peace with one another.

Just before dawn, Tedaldo got up, and having already told the lady what he intended to do and repeated his plea that she should keep it all a deep secret, he left her house, still dressed in his pilgrim's clothing, so as to be ready, when the time was right, to take care of Aldobrandino's affairs. At daybreak, the Signoria, convinced that it now had all the relevant information, hastened to release Aldobrandino, and a few days later the murderers were beheaded on the spot where they had committed the crime.

Aldobrandino was overjoyed to find himself a free man, as were his wife and all of his friends and relations, and since he knew for certain that the whole thing was the result of the pilgrim's endeavors, they brought him to their house and invited him to stay there for as long as he chose to remain in the city. Nor could they get their fill of honoring and feting him, and especially the lady, because she knew who it was that they were doing it for.

A few days later, however, having learned that his brothers were being held up to public ridicule because of Aldobrandino's release, and that they had even armed themselves out of fear, Tedaldo decided that the time had come to reconcile them all with one another and asked Aldobrandino to make good on his promise. When Aldobrandino readily agreed that he would, the pilgrim had him arrange a sumptuous banquet for the following day, at which he wanted Aldobrandino and all his relatives, together with their wives, to welcome the four brothers, together with theirs, adding that he himself would go at once and invite the brothers to the peacemaking festivities on Aldobrandino's behalf.

Since Aldobrandino was content with what the pilgrim proposed, the latter set off immediately to find the four brothers. After speaking at sufficient length to tell them everything the case required and using a number of irrefutable arguments, he finally persuaded them, without too much difficulty, that they should beg Aldobrandino's forgiveness and seek to win back his friendship. This done, he invited them and their wives to dine with Aldobrandino the following morning, and they, convinced of his good faith, willingly accepted the invitation.

The next day, therefore, around dinnertime, Tedaldo's four brothers, still dressed in black and accompanied by a number of their friends, were the first to arrive at Aldobrandino's house where they found him waiting to welcome them. There, in the presence of all the people he had invited to join them for the occasion, they threw their weapons onto the ground and placed themselves in Aldobrandino's hands, begging his pardon for what they had done to him. Aldobrandino, in tears, received them with affection, kissed each one of them on the mouth, and with just a few words quickly forgave every wrong they had done him. They were then joined by their wives and sisters, all dressed in mourning, who were given a gracious welcome by Madonna Ermellina and the other ladies.

Then all the guests, gentlemen and ladies alike, were served a magnificent feast, which was praiseworthy in every way except one: the general reticence caused by the recent bereavement of Tedaldo's relatives to which their somber garments bore witness. For this reason some of the guests had been critical of the pilgrim's initiative and his invitation, and since he was well aware of what they were thinking, Tedaldo decided that the time had come to dispel the melancholy atmosphere. He therefore got to his feet, as he had been planning to do all along, and while the others were still eating their fruit course, he declared:

"The only thing lacking to make this banquet a truly happy event is the presence of Tedaldo. It just so happens that he's been here with you all along, but since you failed to recognize him, let me point him out to you."

Then, casting off his cloak and the rest of his pilgrim's costume, he stood there before them in his doublet of green taffeta. The guests all stared at him in complete astonishment and had to scrutinize him a long time before anyone dared to believe it was actually Tedaldo. Noting their reaction, he told them all about their family connections, described various events in their lives, and recounted his own adventures, until finally his brothers and the other men, all of them weeping tears of joy, rushed to embrace him. They were soon followed by the women, whether they were related to him or not, all except for Madonna Ermellina.

"What's this, Ermellina?" said Aldobrandino, when he noticed her behavior. "Why aren't you greeting Tedaldo like the other ladies?"

As everyone listened, she replied: "I'd welcome him more willingly than any of the ladies here have done already or are doing right now, for it is through his efforts that I got you back again, and I am thus more beholden to him than anyone else is. But I've been restraining myself because of the scurrilous things that were said when we were all mourning the man we took to be Tedaldo."

"Get away with you," replied Aldobrandino. "Do you think I pay any attention to all that barking? By obtaining my release, he more than proved such rumors to be false—not that I ever believed them in any case. So, get up quickly now, go over there, and embrace him."

Since this was just what the lady wanted, she was not slow to obey her husband's command, and rising from her place, she hugged him just as the other ladies had done, and gave him a joyous welcome. Tedaldo's brothers were deeply delighted by Aldobrandino's magnanimity, as were all the gentlemen and ladies who were there, and it succeeded in dispelling every last trace of suspicion that the rumor had once engendered in people's minds.

Now that everyone had given Tedaldo a warm welcome, he himself tore the black mourning clothes from off his brothers' backs, removed the somber robes that both their wives and his sisters were wearing, and ordered other garments to be brought for them. When they were all dressed again, there was no lack of singing and dancing and entertainment of all sorts, which gave the banquet, whose beginning had been fairly quiet, a resounding conclusion. Then, with the greatest joy, all of them went, just as they were, to Tedaldo's house, where they ate their supper that evening, and in this manner they continued their festivities for many more days to come.

It was a long time before the Florentines stopped looking at Tedaldo as a miracle, thinking he was a man come back from the dead, for many people, including his brothers, continued to harbor a slight doubt in their minds as to whether he was the real Tedaldo. Even at this point they were still not entirely convinced, and perhaps might not have been convinced for quite some time to come, if an event had not accidentally occurred that clarified who the murdered man really was.

Here is how it happened. One day some soldiers from Lunigiana were passing by in front of their house, and when they caught sight of Tedaldo there with his brothers, they came up to him and said: "We hope everything's going well for you, Faziuolo."

"You've mistaken me for somebody else," replied Tedaldo.

As soon as the soldiers heard him speak, they were embarrassed and begged his pardon. "The fact is," they said, "we've never seen a person look so much like another as you look like a buddy of ours called Faziuolo da Pontremoli.[9] He came here a couple of weeks or so ago, and we haven't been able to discover what's happened to him since then. We were, to be sure, surprised by the clothes you're wearing, because he was just an ordinary soldier like us."

When Tedaldo's oldest brother heard this, he stepped forward and asked how this Faziuolo had been dressed. What they told him was found to fit the facts so precisely that between this and other pieces of evidence, it became quite obvious that the man who had been murdered was Faziuolo, not Tedaldo. And so, from then on, neither his brothers nor anyone else had any further suspicions about him.

Thus, having come back home a very rich man, Tedaldo remained constant in his affection for the lady, who never fell out with him again, and as the two of them always acted with discretion, they went on enjoying their love together for a good long time. And may God grant that we enjoy ours as well.

Day 3, Story 8

Having consumed a certain powder, Ferondo is buried for dead, but the Abbot, who has been enjoying his wife, removes him from his tomb, imprisons him, and makes him believe he is in Purgatory, until he is finally resuscitated and then raises as his own a child his wife had with the Abbot.[1]

Emilia thus reached the end of her long story, which, despite its length, everyone found quite enjoyable. In fact, they all thought it short, considering the number and variety of incidents it contained. Then, the Queen, revealing her wishes to Lauretta by means of a single nod, induced her to begin as follows:

My dearest ladies, I find myself faced with the task of having to recount a true story that looks more like a lie than was actually the case and of which I was reminded when I heard about the man who had been mourned and buried in place of another. My story, then, is concerned with a living person who was buried because he was presumed dead, and who later, after he had emerged from the tomb, believed that he had been brought back to life, although he had actually been alive all along, a belief that was shared by many others who adored him as a saint when they should have blamed him for his folly.

In Tuscany, then, there was once—and there still is today—an abbey, situated, as we see so many of them are, in a place little frequented by people. Its newly created Abbot was a monk who was extremely saintly in every way except when it came to women, but he was so cautious with every move he made that hardly anyone suspected, let alone knew, what was going on, so that he was considered to be not merely just, but the holiest of men in every respect.

Now, the Abbot happened to develop a close relationship with a very wealthy peasant named Ferondo, an exceedingly coarse and dim-witted individual, whose friendship he enjoyed only because he was occasionally amused by the man's simplicity. During the course of his association with Ferondo, the Abbot discovered that he was married to a very beautiful woman, and he fell so passionately in love with her that day and night he thought of nothing else. When he found out, however, that although Ferondo was simpleminded and stupid in every other regard, he was as shrewd as can be when it came to loving his wife and always keeping a strict watch over her, the Abbot was close to despair, but since he was very shrewd himself, he managed to per-suade Ferondo to bring his wife on occasion to enjoy the pleasures of the abbey's garden. There, adopting an unassuming manner, the Abbot would talk to them about the blessedness of the life eternal and the most holy deeds of men and women from times past, until eventually the lady was seized by a desire to make her confession to him, and she asked and received Ferondo's permission to do so.

Thus, to the Abbot's boundless delight, the lady came to him in order to make her confession. Seating herself at his feet,[2] before she went on to say anything else, she began as follows: "Sir, if God had given me a proper husband, or none at all, perhaps it might be easy for me, with the help of your teaching, to start down the road you've told us about that leads to the life eternal. But considering the kind of person Ferondo is and his utter stupidity, I might as well call myself a widow, for even though I'm married, I can't have any other husband except that half-wit as long as he's alive, and he, for no good reason, is so extraordinarily jealous of me that my life with him amounts to endless suffering and misery. Therefore, before I get to the rest of my confession, I beg you in all humility to be so kind as to give me some advice on this subject, because if I can't find some means here for me to start improving my life, then confessions and other good deeds won't do me much good."

This declaration filled the Abbot's heart with glee and made him feel that Fortune had opened the way for him to fulfill his greatest desire. "My daughter," he said, "I do think it's a terrible affliction for a beautiful and delicate lady like you to have an idiot for a husband, but it's even worse, in my opinion, to have one who's jealous, and since you have both kinds in the same man, it's not hard for me to believe what you're saying about how much you suffer. But there's only one piece of advice, only one remedy, I can suggest, and that is, in a word, to cure Ferondo of his jealousy. Now, I know perfectly well how to make the medicine needed to do it, provided you have it in you to keep what I'm about to tell you a secret."

"Don't worry about that, father," said the lady, "because I'd sooner die than tell anyone something you've asked me not to repeat. So, how is this going to be done?"

"If we want to cure him," replied the Abbot, "he'll have to go to Purgatory."

"And just how can he do that, while he's still alive?" asked the lady.

"He's got to die," said the Abbot. "That's how he'll get there. And when he's suffered enough pain to purge him of his jealousy, we'll recite certain prayers and ask God to restore him to life, and God will do it."

"Then I'll be left a widow?" the lady declared.

"Yes, for a certain length of time," replied the Abbot, "but during that period you must really take care not to let them marry you off again, because God would take it badly. Furthermore, when Ferondo returned, you'd have to go back to him, and he'd be more jealous than ever."

"As long as he gets cured of this malady of his," said the lady, "and I don't have to spend the rest of my life living like a prisoner, it's fine with me. Do as you please."

"And I will," said the Abbot. "But what reward am I to have from you for such a service?"

"Whatever you want, father," she replied, "provided it lies within my power. But what gift can a woman like me give that would be suitable for a man in your position?"

"My lady," he said, "you can do as much for me as I am going to do for you. Just as I'm preparing to provide for your welfare and your happiness, you, too, can do something that will rescue me and save my life."

"If that's the case," said the lady, "I'm ready to do it."

"Then, give me your love," said the Abbot, "and let me enjoy you, for I'm all on fire, consumed with desire for you."

Completely dumbfounded by what she had heard, the lady exclaimed: "Oh no, father, whatever are you asking me to do? I always thought you were a saint—and is it really proper for saints to make such a request of ladies who come to them for advice?"

"Don't be so surprised, sweetheart," replied the Abbot. "This isn't something that diminishes saintliness, for that resides in the soul, and what I'm asking you for is a sin of the flesh. But in any case, your beauty is so ravishing, so powerful, that love forces me to act like this, and let me tell you, when you consider how pleasing your loveliness is to saints, who are used to seeing the beauties of heaven, you have more reason to be proud of it than any other woman. Furthermore, although I'm an Abbot, I'm still a man just like the others, and as you can see, not all that old. So, you shouldn't find this a burden; on the contrary, you should be looking forward to it, because while Ferondo's in Purgatory, I'll be keeping you company at night and providing you with the kind of consolation he should be giving you. No one will ever notice what's going on, either, because they all believe in my saintliness just as much as—in fact, more than—you did a short while ago. Don't reject the grace that God is bestowing upon you, for you've been offered something that plenty of women long for, and if you're sensible enough to follow my advice, it'll be yours. Besides, I have some beautiful jewels, expensive ones, and I don't intend to give them to anyone but you. Therefore, my sweet hope, don't refuse to do for me what I'll gladly do for you."

The lady kept her eyes fixed on the ground, for although she did not know how to refuse him, she still felt it was wrong for her to grant his request. As the Abbot observed her listening to his proposition and hesitating about how to respond to it, he felt she was already half converted. He therefore added a great deal to his former arguments, and by the time he stopped talking, he had gotten it into her head that it was all right for her to comply with his wishes. And so she said, rather bashfully, that she was ready to obey his every command, although she could not do so before Ferondo had gone to Purgatory.

"Well," said the Abbot gleefully, "we'll see to it that he goes there right away. Just arrange for him to come here and stay with me either tomorrow or the next day."

That said, he slipped a very beautiful ring into her hand on the sly and sent her away. Delighted by the gift, and looking forward to receiving others, the lady returned to her companions, and as they made their way home together, she told them all sorts of marvelous things about the Abbot's saintliness.

A few days later, Ferondo came to the abbey, and the moment the Abbot caught sight of him, he decided to send him off to Purgatory. Consequently, he went to get a wondrous powder he had, which had been given to him in the East by a great prince who maintained that the Old Man of the Mountain would use it whenever he wanted to send people to his Paradise in their sleep or to bring them back from it again.[3] The prince had also said that by varying the dose, one could make them sleep for longer or shorter periods without suffering any sort of harm, and that as long as the powder's effect lasted, nobody would ever think they were alive. The Abbot took a quantity of it sufficient to make a man sleep for three days, added it to a glass of somewhat cloudy wine, and gave it to the unsuspecting Ferondo to drink while they were in his cell. He then led him into the cloister where he and some of his monks began amusing themselves at Ferondo's expense and making fun of his foolishness. This had not gone on for long, however, before the powder began to work, and all of a sudden, Ferondo's faculties were overwhelmed by such a powerful sensation of drowsiness that he dozed off while he was still standing, then fell to the ground, fast asleep.

Pretending to be upset over what had happened, the Abbot had them loosen Ferondo's clothes, sent for cold water, and had them throw it in his face. He then had them try a variety of other remedies he knew, acting as if he wanted to restore the life and feeling that had been taken away from Ferondo by some expulsion of gas out of his stomach or by whatever else it was that might have afflicted him. But when the Abbot and the monks saw that despite all their efforts he did not come to and that when they felt his pulse, it did not seem to be beating, they all concluded that he was dead. Accordingly, they sent word to his wife and family, all of whom came rushing to the scene. A little later, after the lady and her female relations had finished weeping, the

Abbot had Ferondo placed in a tomb, dressed in the same clothes he had been wearing.

The lady returned home and announced that she would never part from the little boy she had had with Ferondo. And so, she remained there in the house, planning to take care of her child and to manage the fortune her husband had left her.

That night the Abbot got up quietly, and with the assistance of a monk from Bologna who enjoyed his full confidence and who had just come from there that very same day, he dragged Ferondo from his tomb and carried him to a lightless underground vault that had been built as a prison to punish monks for their transgressions. They removed his clothes, dressed him in one of their habits, and left him lying on a bundle of straw until he recovered his senses. In the meantime, unobserved by anyone else there, the monk from Bologna waited for Ferondo to come to, having been told everything he needed to do by the Abbot.

The next day the Abbot pretended he was making a pastoral visitation, and attended by a group of his monks, went to the lady's house, where he found her dressed in black and overcome with grief. He comforted her for a while, and when he was done, quietly reminded her of her promise. Realizing that she was now free, unhindered by Ferondo or anyone else, and spotting another fine ring on the Abbot's finger, the lady told him that she was ready to do it and arranged for him to pay her a visit that evening.

After dark, therefore, the Abbot disguised himself in Ferondo's clothes and went to her house, accompanied by his monk. There he lay with her in the utmost pleasure and delight all night long, returning to the abbey just before matins. And from then on, he frequently traveled down the same road to perform the same service. Although people occasionally encountered him on his way back and forth, they always believed it was Ferondo who was wandering about the area, doing penance of some sort, and before long, many strange stories sprang up among the simple people from the village, some of which were reported to his wife, who knew very well what was really going on.

When Ferondo regained consciousness, he did not have the faintest idea where he was, and at just that moment, the monk from Bologna

entered the room with a horrible roar, and clutching a bundle of sticks
in his hand, gave him a terrible beating.

As he wept and wailed, Ferondo kept on asking: "Where am I?"

"You're in Purgatory," said the monk.

"What? Am I dead, then?" asked Ferondo.

"You sure are," said the monk, at which point Ferondo started weeping for himself and for his wife and son, and saying some of the strang-
est things in the world as he did.

The monk then brought him something to eat and drink, and when
Ferondo saw it, he asked: "Oh, do dead people get to eat?"

"Yes," replied the monk. "In fact, the food I'm giving you here was
sent to the church this morning by the lady who was once your wife
in order to have Masses said for your soul. And the Lord God wants
you to have it."

"May God give her a year's worth of blessings!" said Ferondo. "I really
loved her a whole bunch before I died. Why, I used to hold her in my
arms all night long and never stop kissing her, and when I felt the urge,
I'd occasionally do something else as well."

Then, being very hungry, he began eating and drinking, but when
he discovered that the wine was not very good, he exclaimed: "Goddamn her! She didn't give the priest the wine from the cask that's next
to the wall."

When he finished his meal, the monk brandished his sticks again,
seized him a second time, and gave him another terrible beating.

"Hey," said Ferondo, after screaming for quite a while, "why are you
doing this to me?"

"Because the Lord God has decreed that you should get it twice a
day," said the monk.

"And for what reason?" asked Ferondo.

"Because you were jealous of your wife, even though you had the
finest woman in the area," answered the monk.

"Alas, you're telling the truth there," said Ferondo. "She was the sweetest, too—in fact, sweeter than a sugarplum. But I would never have been
jealous if I had known that God Almighty was offended by it."

"You should have thought of that yourself and mended your ways while you were still down there," said the monk. "If you should ever happen to return, make sure you remember what I'm doing to you now, and don't you ever be jealous again."

"Oh! Do the dead ever return to life?" asked Ferondo.

"Yes, the ones God chooses," replied the monk.

"Oh! Well, if I ever go back," said Ferondo, "I'll be the best husband in the world. I'll never beat her, never scold her, except about the wine she sent here this morning, and also for not sending me any candles so that I was forced to eat in the dark."

"Yes, she did send some," said the monk, "but they were used up during the Masses."

"Oh, yes," said Ferondo, "you must be right. Well, if I ever do get back there, I'll be sure to let her do whatever she wants. But tell me, who are you, and why are you treating me like this?"

"I'm dead, too," said the monk. "I used to live in Sardinia, and because I praised one of my masters to the skies for his jealousy, I've been condemned by God to be punished by giving you food and drink and these beatings until He decides otherwise about you and me."

"Isn't there anyone here besides the two of us?" asked Ferondo.

"Yes, thousands," replied the monk, "but you can't see or hear them any more than they can see or hear you."

"Oh, how far are we from our homes?" asked Ferondo.

"Oh my, oh my!" said the monk. "We're more miles away than we can crap."

"By gosh!" said Ferondo. "That's a lot! If we're that far away, I think we really must be out of the world."

Thus, what with discussions of this sort and others like them, they kept Ferondo there for ten months, alternately feeding and beating him, while the Abbot, being quite the enterprising type, paid countless visits to the lady and had himself the jolliest time in the world with her. But accidents will happen, and the lady got pregnant. She told the Abbot about it as soon as she was aware of her condition, and both of them concluded that Ferondo should be brought back to life from Purgatory without delay and reunited with her, and furthermore, that she should tell him that it was he who had gotten her with child.

Consequently, the following night, the Abbot went to Ferondo in his prison, and disguising his voice, spoke to him.

"Be of good cheer, Ferondo," he said, "for it is God's pleasure that you should go back to earth, where, after your return, your wife will present you with a son. And you shall name him Benedetto, for God is bestowing this grace on you in answer to the prayers of your reverend Abbot and your wife, and out of His love for San Benedetto."*

When he heard this, Ferondo was overjoyed.

"This really makes me happy!" he declared. "May God give a year's worth of blessings to Messer God Almighty and the Abbot and San Benedetto and my cheesy-weesy, sweet honeybun of a wife."

Having put enough of the powder in the wine he had sent Ferondo to make him sleep for four hours or so, the Abbot dressed him in his own clothes again, and aided by the monk, quietly carried him back to the tomb in which he had been buried. At daybreak the next morning, Ferondo came to his senses and saw that light was coming in through a chink in the tomb. Not having seen such a thing for a good ten months, he concluded that he had to be alive and began shouting, "Open up! Open up!" At the same time he pressed his head up against the lid of the sarcophagus, which was not very secure, and shoved it so hard that it began to move. He had just about pushed it off when the monks, who had finished reciting matins, rushed to the scene, recognized Ferondo's voice, and saw him emerging from the tomb. They were all so frightened by this unexpected event that they took to their heels and ran off to find the Abbot.

The Abbot pretended he was just rising up from prayer. "Be not afraid, my sons," he said. "Take up the cross and the holy water and follow me. Let's go and see what God Almighty wants to show us." And away he went.

In the meantime, Ferondo, who was deathly pale from having spent so much time without seeing the sky, had gotten out of the tomb. When he saw the Abbot, he threw himself at his feet and declared: "Father,

---

*I.e., Saint Benedict. The Abbot's words here distantly parody those of the angel to Zacharias, the father of John the Baptist (see Luke 1:13).

I've been rescued from the pains of Purgatory and brought back to life, and it's been revealed to me that your prayers, along with those of San Benedetto and my wife, were responsible for it. And so, I pray to God that He send you a good year, and good months, both now and forever."

"Praised be the power of God!" exclaimed the Abbot. "Now that He has sent you back here, my son, you should go and comfort your wife, who has done nothing but weep since you departed this life. And from now on may you live to serve God and preserve His friendship from this day forth."

"That's exactly what I've been told to do, sir," said Ferondo. "Just let me handle it. As soon as I find her, I'm going to give her a great big kiss. I love her so much."

The Abbot acted as if what had happened was a miracle, and as soon as he was alone with his monks, he had them devoutly sing the *Miserere*.*

When Ferondo returned to his village, everyone who caught sight of him fled away, as from some horrible vision, and his wife, too, seemed terrified, but he called them all back and assured them that he had, indeed, been restored to life. Then, once they all felt more comfortable being around him and saw that he really was alive, they plied him with questions, all of which he answered as if he were some sage returned from the grave, giving them news about the souls of their relatives, and inventing the most beautiful fables in the world about the goings-on in Purgatory. And he gave the assembled populace a full account of the revelation that he had received straight from the mouth of the Ark-Ranger Bagriel just before he came back to life.[4]

Having returned home with his wife and taken possession once again of his property, he proceeded to get her pregnant—or so he imagined. And by chance he happened to arrive not a moment too soon, for his wife, confirming the opinion of fools who believe that women carry their babies for precisely nine months, gave birth to a son, who was named Benedetto Ferondi.

---

* *Miserere* ("Have mercy upon me") is the opening of Psalm 51 that constitutes a prayer asking for God's forgiveness.

Since almost everyone believed that Ferondo had really come back from the dead, his return and the stories he told enhanced immeasurably the Abbot's fame for holiness. Moreover, Ferondo was cured of his jealousy by the countless beatings he had received, and never behaved like that toward his wife again, just as the Abbot had promised her he would not. The lady was pleased with this turn of events, and from then on she lived with Ferondo no less chastely than she had in the past, except that, whenever she could do so conveniently, she was always happy to spend time with the Abbot who had attended to her greatest needs with such skill and diligence.

Day 3, Story 9

Having cured the King of France of a fistula, Giletta of Narbonne asks for the hand of Beltramo of Roussillon, who marries her against his will and then, in disdain, goes away to Florence. There he courts a young woman, whom Giletta impersonates, sleeping with him and bearing him two children, as a result of which he finally comes to cherish her and acknowledge her as his wife.[1]

Now that Lauretta's tale was finished, the only person left to speak was the Queen, and since she had no wish to infringe on Dioneo's privilege, she did not wait to be asked by the others, but with all her charm began addressing them as follows:

How is anyone to tell a story as beautiful as the one we have just heard from Lauretta? It was certainly fortunate for us that hers was not the first, since few of the tales we would have heard after it would have pleased us—which is what I expect will happen with the two that remain to be told today. But for what it is worth, I will nevertheless tell you the one that occurs to me on the topic we proposed.

In the Kingdom of France there was once a nobleman named Isnardo, Count of Roussillon, who suffered from poor health and always kept a doctor, Master Gerardo of Narbonne, to attend him.[2] The Count had only one child, Beltramo, an exceptionally handsome, charming little boy, who was brought up with other children his age, one of whom was Giletta, the daughter of the physician I just mentioned. Giletta fell in love with this Beltramo and adored him with a boundless passion whose fervor was not really proper in one of her tender years, so that when, on the death of the Count, Beltramo became a ward of the King and had to go to Paris, the girl was plunged into the deepest despair. Her own father died shortly afterward, and if she could have found a plausible excuse, she would have gladly gone to visit Beltramo in Paris. But now that she was wealthy, being her father's sole heir, she was so closely watched over that she could see no honorable way of doing so. Even later, after reaching marriageable age, she was still incapable of getting Beltramo out of her mind, and without providing any explanation, she refused numerous suitors whom her relatives wanted her to marry.

Now, while she was burning more fiercely than ever with love for Beltramo—she had found out that he had become an extremely handsome young man—she happened to hear the news that the King of France, who had been suffering from a tumor on his chest, had not received adequate treatment for it and had been left with a fistula that was causing him extreme pain and anguish.[3] He had not been able to find a single doctor who could cure him of it, and although many had tried, they had all made things worse. As a result, the King had lost any hope of getting better and was refusing any further treatment or advice from anyone.

The young lady was overjoyed by this news, for not only did it give her a legitimate reason to go to Paris, but if this ailment was what she thought it was, she would not have much difficulty in obtaining Beltramo's hand in marriage. Consequently, having been extremely well taught by her father, she made up a powder from certain herbs she knew were good for treating the infirmity she believed she had diagnosed. Then, she mounted her horse, and off she rode to Paris.

Her first business there was to find a way to see Beltramo, after which, having obtained an audience with the King, she asked him if he would be so gracious as to show her what was wrong with him. Not knowing how to refuse so lovely and attractive a young woman, the King let her see it, and as soon as she did, she was confident that she could make him well. "My lord," she said, "if it please you, I trust that with God's help I will be able to cure you of this ailment in a week's time, without causing you any difficulty or discomfort."

Thinking her claim ridiculous, the King said to himself, "How could a young woman possibly know how to do something that has stymied the knowledge and ability of the greatest doctors in the world?" He therefore thanked her for her good intentions and answered that he had resolved never to follow the advice of physicians again.

"You look down on the skill I profess to have, my lord," said the young lady, "because I'm young and because I'm a woman. But I would have you bear in mind that when I practice medicine, I do not rely on my own knowledge so much as on the help of God and the expertise of Master Gerardo of Narbonne, my father, who was a famous physician during his lifetime."

"Perhaps she's been sent to me by God," thought the King to himself. "Why don't I find out what she can do, especially since she says she can cure me in short order without causing me any discomfort?" And so, he decided to put her to the test.

"Young lady," he said, "let's say you get us to break our resolve, but then fail to cure us. What do you think the consequences ought to be for you in that case?"

"Keep me under guard, my lord," she replied, "and if I don't cure you within a week, you can have me burned. But if I do make you better, what will I receive as my reward?"

"Since it appears that you're still unmarried," declared the King, "if you do succeed, then we'll provide you with a fine, noble husband."

"My lord," said Giletta, "I would be truly pleased to have you arrange a marriage for me, but I want to have a husband of my own choosing, although I wouldn't ask you for one of your sons or a member of the royal family."

The King gave her his promise there and then, after which she began the treatment, and in short, actually managed to restore him to health ahead of schedule. Once the King felt he was cured, he declared: "Young lady, you've certainly earned a husband for yourself."

"In that case, my lord," she replied, "I've earned Beltramo of Roussillon, whom I fell in love with back when I was a child and have been passionately devoted to ever since."

Letting her have Beltramo seemed a very serious matter to the King, but since he had given her his word and did not want to go back on it, he sent for the young man.

"Beltramo," he said, "not only have you come of age, but you've

finished your training here. And it is now our wish that you return
and govern your lands and that you take with you a young lady whom
we have chosen to be your wife."

"And who is the young lady, my lord?" asked Beltramo.

"She's the one who has used her medicine to restore us to health,"
replied the King.

Beltramo was quite aware of who it was because he had seen Giletta
there, but although he found her very beautiful, he knew that her lineage was by no means a match for his nobility. Filled with indignation,
he said: "So, my lord, you want to give me some she-doctor as my wife?
God forbid that I should ever marry a woman of that sort."

"Then," said the King, "you want us to break the promise we have
given the young lady who asked to have your hand in marriage as her
reward for restoring us to health?"

"My lord," replied Beltramo, "you have the power to take away everything I possess and to give me, as your vassal, to anyone you choose, but
let me assure you that I shall never be content with such a marriage
arrangement."

"Yes, you will," said the King, "for the girl is beautiful and intelligent,
besides being deeply in love with you, which is why we expect you'll
have a much happier life with her than with a lady of higher rank."

Beltramo fell silent, and the King gave orders for a great wedding
feast to be prepared. And so, even though it went directly against his
will, on the appointed day and in the presence of the King, Beltramo
did marry the girl who loved him more than her very own life. He had
already made up his mind about what he was going to do next, however,
and once the festivities were over, he asked the King for permission to
leave, saying that he wanted to return to his estates and to consummate his marriage there. Then he mounted his horse, but instead of
riding back home, he went to Tuscany, where he discovered that the
Florentines were at war with the Sienese and decided to offer them his
assistance. Accordingly, the Florentines gave him a warm welcome
and honored him by making him the captain of a company of men,
and since they also assigned him quite a liberal stipend, he remained
in their service for a good long time.

His new bride was quite unhappy with this turn of events, but hoping that she could get Beltramo to return to his estates if she took good care of them for him, she went to Roussillon, where all the people received her as their sovereign lady. Because the Count had been absent from the area for a long time, she was confronted with nothing but ruin and chaos. She was an intelligent woman, however, and applying herself with the utmost diligence and care, she managed to set everything right. Her subjects were very pleased with what she had done, and while they cherished her and loved her with real devotion, they were extremely critical of the Count for not being satisfied with her.

After having thoroughly restored order in the region, the lady sent two knights to convey this information to the Count, beseeching him to let her know if it was on her account that he was refusing to return to his lands, in which case she would gratify him by leaving. His reply to them was exceedingly harsh. "In this matter let her please herself," he said. "For my part, I'll only go back to live with her when she's wearing this ring on her finger and holding a child of mine in her arms." The ring was very dear to the Count, and he never took it off because he had been given to understand that it possessed certain magical powers.

The knights grasped just how difficult the Count was making it for her, what with these two virtually impossible conditions, but seeing that nothing they said could persuade him to change his mind, they returned to the lady and reported his answer to her. It filled her with sorrow, but after thinking long and hard about it, she decided to try and see if she could find a way to fulfill those two conditions and thus win her husband back.

Having devoted considerable thought to what she had to do, the Countess called together a number of the most important and distinguished men in her domain, gave them a detailed and quite moving account of what she had already done out of love for the Count, and explained what had happened as a result. Then, she told them that she had no intention of staying there if this meant perpetual exile for her husband. On the contrary, she planned to spend the rest of her life making pilgrimages and performing pious works for the salvation of her soul. Finally, she asked them to take over the defense and government of the county and to let the Count know that she had left it in his possession, free and unencumbered, and had gone away with the intention of never returning to Roussillon. As she spoke, the good men shed countless tears and begged her over and over again to be so good as to change her mind and stay, but it was all to no avail.

Having said good-bye to them, she furnished herself with money and precious jewels, and set off with a male cousin of hers and one of her chambermaids, all of them dressed like pilgrims. Without telling anyone where she was going, she made straight for Florence and did not stop until she reached the city. When she arrived, she chanced upon a little inn run by a respectable widow, and there she stayed, quietly playing the part of the poor pilgrim and hoping to hear news of her lord. And it just so happened that the very next day she saw Beltramo on horseback passing by the inn with his company. Although she certainly recognized him, she nevertheless asked the good woman from the inn who he was.

"He's a foreigner," replied the hostess, "a pleasant, courteous nobleman by the name of Count Beltramo who's quite the favorite in this city. He's head over heels in love with a neighbor of ours, a woman nobly born, but living in reduced circumstances. Truth to tell, she's a very honest young lady, but because of her poverty, she has not gotten married yet and still lives with her mother, a very wise and virtuous woman. And perhaps, if her mother weren't there, she would have already given this Count just what he would be pleased to get from her."

The Countess listened intently, taking in every last word, and after giving further thought to everything she had heard and getting it all clear in her mind, she decided what her course of action would be. And so, one day, having discovered the name and address of the lady whose daughter was loved by the Count, she made her way unobtrusively to their house, dressed in her pilgrim's garb. She found the two women living in great poverty, and after greeting them, asked the lady if she would object to their having a private conversation together.

The noblewoman got up, assuring her that she was ready to listen, and the two of them went into another room where they sat down by themselves. "My lady," the Countess began, "it seems that Fortune is as hostile to the two of you as she is to me, but if you're willing, there may perhaps be a way for you to help yourselves and to assist me at the same time." The lady replied that there was nothing she would like better, so long as it did not compromise her honor.

"I have to have your word on it," the Countess continued, "for if I rely on you and you betray me, you'll spoil things for yourselves as well as for me."

"You can tell me whatever you like," said the noblewoman, "for you may rest assured that I'll never deceive you."

The Countess then revealed who she was and what had happened to her from the first moment she fell in love up to that very day, recounting everything with such emotion that the noblewoman, who believed every last word of her story, having already heard parts of it from other people, began to feel pity for her. Having finished reciting all the facts, the Countess went on to say:

"Now you've heard the tale of my misfortunes. As I said, there are two things I must obtain if I want to get my husband back, and I know of no one who can help me obtain them except for you, provided it's true, as I've been told, that my husband the Count is passionately in love with your daughter."

"My lady, whether the Count loves my daughter, I really don't know," said the gentlewoman, "although he certainly puts on a great show as if he does. But what is it, exactly, that you want me to do?"

"I shall tell you, my lady," replied the Countess, "but first I want to explain to you what I propose you should get out of all this if you do this service for me. I see that your daughter is beautiful and old enough to get married, but from what I've heard, and from what I can see for myself, you're forced to keep her here at home because you don't have what is needed to arrange a marriage for her. Now, it's my intention to reward the service you'll perform for me by providing her immediately, out of my own funds, with whatever dowry you yourself think suitable so that she can make an honorable match."

Needy as the lady was, she felt attracted by this offer, but she also possessed a noble spirit and replied: "Tell me in what way I might be able to assist you, my lady, and if it is consistent with my honor, I'll be glad to do it. Afterward, you may do whatever you please."

"What I need," said the Countess, "is for you to have someone you trust take a message to my husband the Count, telling him that your daughter is ready to place herself entirely at his disposal, but only if she is convinced that he really loves her as much as he professes. And tell him as well that this is something she will never believe until he sends her the ring he wears on his finger that she's heard he's so attached to. If he does send it to you, give it to me, and let him know that your daughter is ready to do his bidding. Then you'll arrange for him to come here in secret and for me, surreptitiously, to take your daughter's place beside him. Perhaps by God's grace I'll become pregnant, and later on, with his ring on my finger and the child he begot in my arms, I'll get him back and live with him as a wife should live with her husband. And it'll all be thanks to you."

This seemed a serious matter to the gentlewoman who was afraid that her daughter's reputation might suffer in the process, but after reflecting awhile, she concluded that it was consistent with her honor to assist the good lady in getting her husband back, for in such an enterprise she would be pursuing a worthy goal. And so, relying on the goodness and honesty of the Countess's intentions, not only did she promise to do it, but within just a few days' time, always acting with great caution and secrecy in accordance with the instructions she had been given, she managed to acquire the ring, despite the Count's reluctance to give it up, and skillfully arranged for the Countess, rather than her daughter, to sleep with him.

In the course of their first couplings, which the Count sought with considerable ardor, it pleased God that the lady should become pregnant with two sons, as was made manifest in due course when she gave birth. Nor was this the only time that the gentlewoman managed the situation so that the lady could find happiness in her husband's embraces. Nevertheless, even though she did so on many other occasions, she used such secrecy that not a single word about it ever got out. And all the while the Count went on believing that he had been

with the woman he loved rather than his wife, and when it came time
for them to part in the morning, he would always give her beautiful,
expensive jewels, all of which the Countess took great pains to put in
safekeeping.

Once she knew she was pregnant, the Countess did not want to
trouble the noblewoman with such services any further and said to
her: "Thanks to God and to you, my lady, I've got what I wanted, and
therefore it's time for me to fulfill your wishes in whatever way you
want me to, after which I will be taking my leave of you."

The gentlewoman replied that if the lady was pleased with what
she had gotten, then she herself was satisfied, adding that she had not
acted in hope of a reward, but was merely doing a good deed because
she felt that was her duty.

"I'm quite pleased to hear you put it that way, my lady," said the
Countess. "And for my part, I likewise have no intention of giving you
what you ask of me to reward you, but rather, because I, too, will be
doing a good deed, which is, I think, the correct thing to do."

Forced by her needs, the gentlewoman, deeply embarrassed, asked
for one hundred *lire* so that she could arrange a marriage for her daughter. Hearing her ask for so modest a sum, the Countess sensed her
embarrassment and gave her, instead, five hundred *lire* as well as many
beautiful, expensive jewels that probably amounted to as much again in
value. The gentlewoman was more than satisfied and thanked her with
all the warmth she could muster, after which the Countess took her
leave and went back to the inn. To prevent Beltramo from having any
excuse to send her messages or visit her house again, the gentlewoman
took her daughter away with her to reside with some relatives of hers
in the country. And shortly after that, Beltramo, who had been recalled
by his vassals, returned home, though only after having learned that
the Countess had gone away.

When the Countess heard that he had left Florence and gone back
to his estates, she was quite pleased. She herself remained in the city
until the time came for her delivery, when she gave birth to two sons
who were the very image of their father. She took great care in putting
them out to nurse, and when the time seemed ripe, she took to the

road with them and reached Montpellier without being recognized by anyone.[4] There she rested for a few days, making inquiries concerning the Count and his whereabouts. Upon discovering that he was going to host a grand feast for his lords and ladies in Roussillon on All Saints' Day, she made her way there, still dressed in the pilgrim's garb she had been wearing from the start of her travels.

When she found that the lords and ladies who had come to the Count's palace were about to sit down to the table, she did not pause to change her clothes, but went right up into the great hall, carrying her two little sons in her arms. Going from one guest to the next, she finally reached the spot where she saw the Count standing and threw herself down at his feet.

"My lord," she said, dissolving in tears, "I am your unfortunate bride who has long wandered the world in misery so that you could return and live in your own home. I now beg you, in God's name, to abide by the conditions you imposed on me when you spoke with the two knights I sent to you. Look, here's your ring, and in my arms I'm holding not just one son of yours, but two. So, the time has come for you to keep your promise and accept me as your wife."

Thoroughly confounded by what she said, the Count had to admit not only that the ring was his, but that the two children were his as well, seeing how much they looked like him. The only thing he could find to say, however, was: "How can this have happened?"

Then, as the Count and all the others present listened in utter amazement, the Countess proceeded to recount her story from beginning to end. Conceding that she was telling the truth, and seeing both how persistent and intelligent she was, and in addition, what a handsome pair of children she had, the Count cast off the unshakable hostility he had felt toward her and kept the promise he had made, thus endearing himself to his lords and ladies, all of whom were begging him to accept the Countess and honor her now as his lawful wedded wife. Thus, after having raised her to her feet, he embraced her and kissed her, and recognized her as his wife, at the same time acknowledging that the two children were his own.

Once the Countess had been dressed again in more suitable attire, the Count held the most magnificent of celebrations, which went on not just for the rest of the day, but for many days after that as well, to the utter delight both of those who were present and of all his other vassals who came to hear of it. And from that time forth, always honoring the Countess as his lawful wedded wife, the Count loved her and cherished her more than anything else in the world.

the utter delight both of those who were present and of all his other
cherished her more than anything... ...in the world.

Day 3, Story 10

Alibech becomes a recluse, and Rustico, a monk, teaches her how to put the Devil
back in Hell. She is then led away from there and becomes the wife of Neerbale.[1]

Dioneo had listened carefully to the Queen's story, and when he
saw that it was finished and that he alone remained to speak, he
smiled, and without waiting to be ordered to do so, he began:

Gracious ladies, perhaps you've never heard anyone explain how
the Devil is put back in Hell, and therefore, without departing from
the topic you've all been talking about today, I want to tell you how to
do it. Perhaps you'll even be able to save your souls once you've learned
it. You'll also learn that although Love prefers to dwell in gay palaces
and voluptuous bedchambers more than in poor huts, for all that, he
sometimes makes his powers felt in dense forests, on rugged mountains,
and in desert caves—from which you'll be able to see that everything
is subject to his power.

Now, to get to the point: let me tell you that there once lived in the
city of Capsa in Barbary a very rich man who, among his many children, had a beautiful and graceful little daughter named Alibech.* She
was not a Christian, but having heard how greatly the Christian faith
and the service of God were praised by the numerous Christians living
in the city, one day she asked one of them how God could be served best
and with the least difficulty. He replied that those served God best who
fled farthest from the things of this world, as did the people who had
gone to live in the desert around Thebes. The young girl of about four-

---

*Barbary is the old name for Tunisia; Capsa was the name for the southern Tunisian
town now called Gafsa. The "desert around Thebes" mentioned later in the paragraph
is the Sahara.

teen was extremely naive, and the following morning, moved not by
a reasonable desire, but rather by a childish whim, she set out secretly
for the Theban desert all by herself without letting anyone know what
she was doing.

With great difficulty, but sustained by her desire, she reached that
solitary place several days later. Catching sight of a hut in the distance, she went up to it and found a holy man on the threshold who
was amazed to see her there and asked her what she was looking for.
She answered that, inspired by God, she wanted to enter His service
and was seeking someone who would teach her how to do that. Seeing how young and very beautiful she was, and fearing that the Devil
would tempt him if he kept her there, the worthy man praised her good
intentions, and after giving her some roots of herbs and wild apples
and dates to eat along with some water to drink, he said to her: "My
daughter, not very far from here there is a holy man who is much more
capable than I am of teaching you what you want to know. You should
go to him." And he sent her on her way.

When she reached the second man, she heard the same thing from
him, and so she went farther on until she reached the cell of a young
hermit, a truly good and devout person named Rustico, whom she
asked the same question she had asked the others. Eager to put the
firmness of his religious vow to a very demanding test, Rustico, unlike
the first two, did not send her away or direct her to go farther on, but
kept her with him in his cell. And when night came, he made her a
little bed out of palm fronds on one side of it and told her to sleep there.

Once these things were done, temptations did not wait long before
launching an attack on his powers, whose strength he found he had
greatly overestimated, so that after a very few assaults, he turned tail
and surrendered. Casting aside holy thoughts and prayers and peni-
tential discipline, he began contemplating her youth and beauty, and
beyond that, what ways and means he might employ in dealing with her
so that she would not see just how dissolute he was as he went about getting what he wanted from her. After first testing her by asking certain
questions that showed she had never had carnal knowledge of a man
and was just as naive as she appeared to be, he came up with a plan by

means of which, under the pretext of serving God, she would have to satisfy his desires. He started out with long speeches, demonstrating to her how great an enemy the Devil was to the Lord God, and finally giving her to understand that the most pleasing service she could offer Him would be to put the Devil back in the Hell to which the Lord God had damned him.

The young girl asked him how this might be done, and he replied: "You'll soon find out. Just do whatever you see me do." And he began to take off the few clothes he had on until he was completely naked, while the girl did the same thing. Then he knelt down as if he wanted to worship, and he made her position herself right in front of him. And as they knelt in this way, and Rustico felt his desire growing hotter than ever at the sight of her beauty, the resurrection of the flesh took place.[2] Staring at it in amazement, she said, "Rustico, what's that thing I see sticking out in front of you, the thing I don't have?"

"O my daughter," said Rustico, "this is the Devil I told you about, and now you can see for yourself how he's tormenting me so much that I can scarcely endure it."

Then the girl said, "Oh, praised be God, for I see I'm better off than you are, since I don't have any such Devil."

"That's the truth," said Rustico, "but you do have something else I don't have, and you have it in place of this."

"Oh," said Alibech, "what's that?"

"You've got Hell there," Rustico said to her. "And let me tell you, I believe God has sent you here for the salvation of my soul. For this Devil is giving me such pain that if you'll take pity on me and allow me to put him back in Hell, you'll give me the greatest relief. Plus, you'll please God by performing an immense service, if you really came here to do that, as you say."

"Oh, Father," replied the young girl in good faith, "since I've got that Hell, just do it whenever you please."

"Bless you, my daughter," said Rustico. "Let's go ahead and put him back in there so that he'll finally leave me in peace."

And with those words, he led her up onto one of their little beds and taught her what she should do to incarcerate that evil spirit cursed by

God. The young girl, who had never, ever put any Devil in Hell, felt a little pain the first time, and because of it she said to Rustico: "Surely, Father, this Devil must be a wicked thing and truly the enemy of God, for he not only hurts others, but he even hurts Hell when he's put inside it."

"My daughter," said Rustico, "it won't always be like that." And to ensure that it would not be, they put the Devil back in there a good six times before they got out of the bed, so that, when they were done, they had forced him to lower his proud head, and he was content to be quiet a while.

The Devil's pride often came right back up during the next few days, however, and the young girl, who was obedient and always willing to take it down for him, began to enjoy the game and would say to Rustico: "Now I certainly see that those worthy men in Capsa were telling the truth about how sweet a thing it is to serve God, for I'm sure I can't recall any other thing I've done that has been so delightful or given me so much pleasure as putting the Devil back in Hell. And for that reason, in my judgment, anyone interested in doing something other than serving God is an ass."

Repeatedly approaching Rustico with this purpose in mind, she would say to him, "Father, I've come here to serve God and not to remain idle. Let's go and put the Devil back in Hell." While they were engaged in doing it, she would sometimes remark, "Rustico, I don't know why the Devil wants to escape from Hell, for if he liked being inside it as much as Hell likes taking him in and holding him there, he'd never want to leave."

Thus, by inviting Rustico to play the game over and over again, always encouraging him to serve God in this way, she took so much padding out of his doublet that he started feeling cold whereas anyone else would have been sweating. Consequently, he tried telling her that the Devil was only to be punished and put back in Hell when he raised his head in pride: "And we have so humiliated him, by the grace of God, that he is begging the Lord to be left in peace."

In this way he was able to keep the girl quiet for a while. But one day, when she realized that Rustico was no longer asking her to put the

Devil back in Hell, she said to him, "Rustico, though your Devil has been punished and is no longer making you suffer, this Hell of mine is giving me no peace. So, you would do a good deed if you, with your Devil, helped to quench the fury of my Hell, just as I, with my Hell, helped you lower the pride of your Devil."

Now Rustico was living on the roots of herbs and spring water, so that her invitations could hardly get a rise out of him. He told her that it would take an awful lot of Devils to quench the fires of her Hell, but said that he would do what he could for her. Thus, he was sometimes able to satisfy her, but it was so seldom that it amounted to little more than tossing a bean into the mouth of a lion. Consequently, the young girl, feeling she was not getting to serve God as much as she wanted to, went around grumbling more often than not.

While this dispute went on between Rustico's Devil and Alibech's Hell, the result of too much desire on the one side and too little potency on the other, a fire happened to break out in Capsa that burned Alibech's father to death in his own house, together with all his children and the rest of his household, leaving Alibech the heir to his entire estate. Because of this, a youth named Neerbale, who had spent his entire substance in sumptuous living and who had heard that she was alive, set out in search of her and found her before the courts could confiscate her father's property because he had died without an heir. To the great relief of Rustico, though much against her will, Neerbale brought Alibech back to Capsa and took her as his wife, and together with her he became the heir to her enormous patrimony.

Before Neerbale slept with her, however, she was asked by some women how she used to serve God out in the desert. She replied that she served Him by putting the Devil back in Hell and that Neerbale had committed a great sin in taking her away from such a fine service. The women asked her how the Devil is put back in Hell, and when, between her words and her gestures, the girl showed them how, they laughed so much that they are still laughing to this day. Then they said, "Don't feel sad, child, no, for they do it pretty well here, too. Neerbale will serve the Lord God with you just fine."

Then one woman told this story to another throughout the city until they turned it into a common saying, namely that the most delightful service one could perform for God was to put the Devil back in Hell. This saying, which has crossed the sea from there, is still current. And so, young ladies, you who need God's grace, learn to put the Devil back in Hell, because this is greatly pleasing to God and a pleasure for those who are doing it, and much good may arise and come out of it.

Day 3, Conclusion

So apt and well chosen were Dioneo's words that his story moved the virtuous ladies to laughter a thousand times or more. When he reached the conclusion, the Queen, recognizing that the term of her reign had come to an end, took the laurel crown from her head and very graciously placed it on Filostrato's, saying: "We will soon see if the wolf knows how to guide the sheep better than the sheep did the wolves."

On hearing her remark, Filostrato laughed and said: "Had they listened to me, the wolves would have taught the sheep how to put the Devil in Hell no worse than Rustico did with Alibech. But you should not call us wolves, since you have not been acting like sheep. Still, now that you have entrusted the kingdom to my care, I will govern it to the best of my ability."

"Listen, Filostrato," replied Neifile, "if you men had tried to teach us to put the Devil in Hell, you might have learned a lesson from us the way Masetto da Lamporecchio did from the nuns, for you would have recovered your ability to speak at just about the time when the wind would have been whistling through your hollow bones."[1]

On perceiving that the ladies' scythes were as sharp as his arrows, Filostrato stopped making witty quips and addressed himself to the business of ruling the kingdom entrusted to him. Summoning the steward, he asked how matters stood, after which he discreetly gave him his orders, basing them on what he thought would be worthwhile and would give satisfaction to the company during the term of his reign. Then he turned to the ladies and said:

"Loving ladies, ever since I could distinguish good from evil, it has been my misfortune, because of the beauty possessed by one of your number, to be perpetually enslaved to Love. I have been humble and obedient and followed his rules, to the extent that I understood them, but all to no avail, for first I would be abandoned for another lover, and then things would always go from bad to worse for me—and I think they will continue to do so from now on until the day I die. Consequently, it is my pleasure that the subject for us to talk about tomorrow should be none other than the one that fits my situation best, namely, those whose love came to an unhappy end. For I myself expect a most unhappy one in the long run, and that is the reason why the name you use to address me was conferred on me by someone who certainly knew what it meant."* Then, having finished speaking, Filostrato got to his feet and dismissed everyone until suppertime.

The garden was so beautiful and delightful that no one chose to leave it in search of greater pleasures elsewhere. On the contrary, since the sun's heat had already abated, making it much less trouble to go hunting, some of the ladies set off in pursuit of the kids and the rabbits and the other animals that were in the garden and that had startled them perhaps a hundred times by jumping into their midst while they were sitting. Dioneo and Fiammetta began singing a song about Messer Guiglielmo and the Lady of Vergiù, while Filomena and Panfilo devoted themselves to a game of chess.² So intent were they on their various activities that the time flew by, and when the hour arrived for supper, it caught them unawares. Tables were then set up around the lovely fountain, and there, in the evening, they ate their meal with the greatest delight.

Once the tables were cleared away, Filostrato, not wishing to stray from the path taken by the ladies who had ruled as queens before him, ordered Lauretta to lead a dance and sing them a song.

"My lord," she said, "I only know songs I have composed myself, and I cannot recall any of mine that are really suitable for such a merry company. Still, if you are willing to accept those I know, I will be happy to sing one of them for you."

"Nothing of yours could be anything other than beautiful and

---

* Boccaccio thinks *Filostrato* means "he who is cast down or overcome by love." On the names of the storytellers, see Headnote 1.

pleasing," replied the King, "so sing whatever you have for us, just as it is."

Then, in very sweet, but rather doleful tones, Lauretta began as follows, while the other ladies joined her in the refrains.

No lady all forlorn
Could grieve more than I do,
Who sigh here all in vain, cast down by Love.³
He who moves heaven and all of its stars
Made me, for His delight,
Refined and charming, graceful, too, and fair,
To give to lofty spirits here below
A certain sign of that
Beauty abiding ever in His sight.
But mortals imperfect,
Who can't see what I am,
Find me unpleasing, nay, treat me with scorn.

There once was one who cherished me, was glad,
When I was young, to hold
Me in his arms and fix me in his thoughts,
And from my eyes he caught such searing heat
That he spent all his time,
Which lightly flies away, in wooing me.
And I, in courtesy,
Deemed him a worthy mate,
But now, alas! I've been bereft of him.

A youth did then present himself to me,
Presumptuous and proud,
Boasting himself a brave and noble man.
He took me captive and through false surmise
Succumbed to jealousy,
Which brings me almost to despair, alas!
For I see clearly how,
Although I'd come to earth
For all men's good, of one I'm now the slave.

And so I curse my luckless nuptial hour
When I said yes and changed
My widow's weeds, for dressed in garments black,
I was so fair and gay, but wearing these,
I lead a harsh life here
And others think me much less honest now.
O mournful bridal day,
I wish that I had died
Before I'd seen you in such dire straits.
      O dearest love, with whom I was content
Beyond all women once,
Since now you are in Heaven with the One
Who fashioned us, alas! take pity please
On me, for I cannot
Forget you for another. Make me see
How flames I kindled once
In you still burn unquenched:
Obtain for me my swift return above.[4]

Everyone had been listening attentively to Lauretta's song, and when she finished, they all interpreted it in different ways. Some wanted to take it in the Milanese fashion as meaning that it was better to have a good pig than a pretty gal, while others gave it a finer, more sublime, and truer sense, which need not be rehearsed at present.* Next, the King called for a large number of lighted torches to be set on the grass and in among the flowers, after which, at his command, the other ladies continued the singing until every star that had risen had begun its descent.[5] Then, thinking it was time to go to sleep, he bid them good-night and told them all to return to their rooms.

* To approach things in the "Milanese fashion" is to be very practical and down to earth. The saying about the good pig and the pretty gal means that it is better to have something like a pig that one can eat than a girl whose attractiveness offers no tangible benefit. In other words, it is better to have a live husband, though bad, than a good one who is up in Heaven.

Day 4, Introduction

Here ends the Third Day of the Decameron and the Fourth begins, in which, under the rule of Filostrato, they speak of those whose love came to an unhappy end.

Dearest ladies, both from what I have heard wise men say as well as from everything I have often read and seen for myself, I have always thought that the fierce, scorching wind of envy assaulted only lofty towers and the highest treetops.[1] I have found myself deceived in this judgment, however. For whenever I fled—and I have always done my best to flee—the wild buffetings of this furious storm, I have tried to go about my affairs quietly and unobtrusively, not just staying on the plains, but seeking out the deepest valleys. This should be patently clear to anyone who casts an eye on these little stories of mine, which lack a title and were written in the Florentine vernacular, in prose, and in the homeliest and lowest style possible.[2] Yet in spite of all this, I have not been able to avoid being violently shaken and almost uprooted by that wind and practically torn to pieces by the fangs of envy. Consequently, I now see clearly the truth of what wise men have frequently said, namely that misery alone is free of envy in this our present life.[3]

Discerning ladies, there are those who, upon reading these little stories, have claimed that I like you too much and that it is improper for me to take so much delight in entertaining and consoling you, and even worse, in praising you as I do. Others, wishing to make it seem as though their judgment were more mature, have said that it is inappropriate for someone of my years to occupy my time with such things, that is, with talking about women and finding ways to please them. There are many who present themselves as being very concerned about my renown and who say that it would be wiser for me to stay with the Muses in Parnassus than to be with you and to busy myself with this nonsense. And yet others, who speak more out of scorn than wisdom, have said that it would be more prudent for me to think about where I am going to obtain my daily bread than to pursue these trifles and feed myself on mere wind. Finally, there are certain people who, in order to disparage my efforts, endeavor to show that the things I have told you about did not happen in the way I said they did.

Thus, worthy ladies, while I have been fighting in your service, I have been blown about and battered by all these gusts, cut to the quick by these cruel, sharp teeth. God knows my mind has remained serene while I have listened to and made a record of their criticisms. Now, although I depend entirely upon you for my defense, nevertheless I have no desire to spare myself any pains, and so, while I will not respond to my critics as fully as they deserve, I intend to offer a few slight rejoinders to them in order to secure my ears from all their noise—and to do so right away. For if there are so many of them and they are already so presumptuous before I have even completed a third of my labors, I can only suppose that unless they encounter some resistance now, they will have multiplied to such an extent before I reach the end that they will be able to lay me low with only the slightest of efforts, and your power, great though it may be, will not suffice to withstand them.

Before responding to any of my critics, however, as a matter of self-defense I would like to recount not an entire story, lest it seem as though I would equate my own stories with those of the very distinguished company I have been telling you about, but merely part of one, whose very incompleteness will reveal that it is not one of theirs. Thus, for the benefit of my assailants, let me say that a man called Filippo Balducci once lived in our city quite some time ago.[4] His social position was rather modest, but he was rich and prosperous and knowledgeable about everything pertaining to his station in life. Furthermore, he had a wife whom he loved devotedly, as she loved him, and the two of them had a peaceful life together, their only desire being to make one another as happy as possible.

Now it so happened, as it will happen to all of us, that the good woman departed this life, leaving nothing of herself to Filippo except the single son whom she had had with him and who was about two years of age. No one has ever been more distressed by the loss of the thing he loved than Filippo was by the death of his wife. Seeing himself bereft of the companion who was so dear to him, he resolved to withdraw from the world in order to devote himself to the service of God, and to do the same thing with his little boy.

Having given away everything he owned for the love of God, Filippo went straightway up to the top of Monte Asinaio and installed himself in a little tiny cell with his son.* There he lived on alms, fasting and praying, and taking the greatest pains, whenever his son was present, never to discuss worldly matters, or to let him see such things, so that they would not distract him from his devotions. Instead, he always spoke to him about the glory of the life eternal and about God and the Saints, nor did he ever teach him anything other than holy prayers. And for many years he kept this up, never letting his son out of their cell or allowing him to see anything except his father.

From time to time the worthy man would come to Florence, and after various friends of God had supplied him with the things he needed, he would return to his cell. One day, when the boy was eighteen, he happened to ask his father where he was going, and Filippo, who had become an old man by this time, told him.

"Father," said his son, "since you're an elderly man now and have trouble dealing with such hardships, why don't you take me with you on one of your trips to Florence? Once you've introduced me to those friends of yours who are devout followers of God, then, seeing as how I'm young and better able to put up with such toil than you are, I can go to Florence and get what we need whenever you like, while you stay here."

Thinking that his son, who was now grown up, was so accustomed to serving God that the things of this world would have difficulty attracting him, the worthy man said to himself, "He's got a point." And since he had to go to Florence anyway, he took his son along with him.

---

* *Monte Asinaio*, "Mount Donkeyman," is a playful corruption of *Monte Senario*, whose many grottos served as cells for Florentine hermits.

When the young man saw the palaces, the houses, the churches, and all the other things that abound in the city, he could not remember ever having seen such things before and was truly amazed by them. He questioned his father about many of them and wanted to know what every one of them was and what it was called. His father told him, and once the boy heard each explanation, he was content, but then went on immediately to ask about something else.

As the pair walked along thus, the son asking questions and the father answering them, by chance they came upon a company of beautiful, well-dressed young women who were returning from a wedding somewhere. As soon as the boy saw them, he asked his father what they were.

"My son," replied his father, "keep your eyes on the ground and don't look at them, for they are evil."

"Oh," asked his son, "what are they called?"

In order to avoid awakening some less than useful desire from among his son's carnal appetites, the father was unwilling to give them their proper name, that is, women, and answered instead: "They're called goslings."*

How wonderful! He who had never before set eyes on a woman was no longer interested in the palaces, the oxen, the horses, the asses, the money, or any of the other things he had seen, but said straight out: "Father, please arrange it so that I can have one of those goslings."

"Oh no, my son!" said his father. "Be quiet. They're evil."

"Is that what evil things are like?" asked his curious son.

"Yes," replied his father.

"I don't understand what you're saying," his son replied, "or why they're evil. As far as I know, I've never seen anything so beautiful or attractive. They're lovelier than the painted angels you've frequently pointed out to me. Oh, if you care for me at all, arrange it so that we can bring one of these goslings back up there with us, and I'll take care of feeding it."

---

*Filippo calls them *papere*, which means "(female) adolescent geese." In many of the versions of this story recounted before the *Decameron*, women are dubbed "demons" instead.

"No, I won't do it," said his father. "You don't know how they do their pecking." And right then and there he realized that his wits were no match for Nature, and he regretted that he had ever brought his son to Florence.

But let what I have told of the present story suffice, so that I may return to those for whose sake I recounted it.

Now, many of my detractors say that I am wrong for doing my best to entertain you, O my young ladies, and for being too fond of you. I confess this most freely, for I am indeed fond of you, and I do take pains to please you. But what, I ask, do they really find so astonishing about this, when you consider that a young man, who was nurtured and reared on top of a savage, solitary mountain, grew up within the limits of a tiny cell, and had no company other than his father, no sooner caught sight of you than you became the only thing he wanted, the only thing he asked for, the only thing he pursued with passion? As for us, my sweetest ladies, even if we set aside the amorous kisses, the pleasant embraces, and the blissful couplings we have frequently enjoyed with you, one need only think about how we are continually exposed to the vision of your refined manners, your charming beauty, and your elegant grace, not to mention your womanly decorum, to understand our affection for you.

Will they reproach and bite and tear me if I am fond of you and strive to please you, when Heaven has given me a body fit for loving you, and when I have devoted my soul to you from my childhood, having felt the power that comes from the light shining in your eyes, from the sweetness of your mellifluent speech, and from the fire kindled by your compassionate sighs—especially considering how you first pleased a young hermit, a witless youth, in fact a savage animal, more than anything else ever did? Those who scold me are surely people who, being entirely ignorant about the pleasures and power of natural affection, neither love you nor desire your love in return, and about such people I care very little.

As for those who keep harping on my age, they simply reveal what they do not know, namely that although the head of the leek is white, its tail is still green.[5] But joking aside, I will respond to them by saying

that to the very end of my life I will never be ashamed of seeking to
give pleasure to those whom Guido Cavalcanti and Dante Alighieri,
when they were already old men, and Messer Cino da Pistoia, when
he was very aged indeed, found it an honor to serve and whose beauty
was so dear to them.[6] And if it did not require that I depart from the
customary mode of debate, I would turn to history and show how it
is filled with countless examples of worthy men from antiquity who
even in their most mature years still strove with all their might to give
pleasure to the ladies. And if my critics are ignorant of such things, let
them go and learn about them.

That I should dwell with the Muses on Parnassus is good counsel, I
agree, but we cannot always live with the Muses, any more than they
can live with us. And so, if a man sometimes happens to leave them, he
is not to be blamed if he delights in seeing that which resembles them,
for the Muses are women, and although women are not as worthy as the
Muses, yet at first sight they do look like them, so that if they pleased
me for no other reason, they should do so on this score. Besides, women
have been the occasion of my composing a thousand lines of poetry,
whereas the Muses never caused me to write anything. To be sure, they
have assisted me and shown me how to compose those thousand lines,
and perhaps in writing these stories here, no matter how very humble
they may be, the Muses have stayed with me on several occasions possibly because they acknowledge and honor the likeness that women
bear to them. Consequently, as I go weaving these tales together, I do
not stray so far away from Mount Parnassus or from the Muses as
many may chance to think.

But what shall we say to those who feel so much pity for me because
of my supposed hunger that they advise me to make provision for my
daily bread? I certainly do not know how to answer them except to
say that when I try to imagine how they would respond if I, were I in
need, should ask them for food, I conclude that their answer would be:
"Go look for it among the fables." And yet, poets have always found
more to nourish them among their fables than many rich men have
among their treasures, and quite a few have lived to a ripe old age by
pursuing their fables, whereas, on the contrary, many who sought more

bread than they needed have died young. But what more is there to say? Let them chase me away if ever I ask them for food, although in any case, I thank God that I still have no need of it. And even if I did, I know, in the words of the Apostle, both how to abound and to suffer need, and therefore, let no one worry more about me than I do about myself.[7]

As for those who say these stories never happened the way I have narrated them, I would appreciate it if they would produce the original versions, and if the latter proved to be different from what I have written, then I would grant that this criticism is just and would do everything in my power to mend my ways. But since thus far I have seen nothing but words, I will leave them to their opinion and will stick to my own, and I will say precisely the same thing about them that they have been saying about me.

For the time being, since I think I have supplied a sufficient response to my critics, let me say that with God's assistance, and with yours, my most noble ladies, in which I place all my hope, I will go forward with my work, fortified with good patience, turning my back to this storm and letting it blow as much as it likes. For I do not see that anything can happen to me that is different from what happens to fine dust in a whirlwind. Either it remains where it is on the ground, or if it is moved, it is carried aloft and often deposited on the heads of men, on the crowns of kings and emperors, sometimes even on high palaces and lofty towers, from which, if it falls, it cannot go lower than the place from which it was lifted up.

And if I have ever been disposed to use all my strength in order to serve your pleasure in any way, I am now more inclined to do so than ever, because I know that no one can justly say anything about me or any of the others who love you except that we are acting naturally. In order to oppose the laws of Nature, one has to have exceptional powers, and they are often employed not only in vain, but to the greatest harm of the person who makes use of them. Such strength I confess I lack, nor do I have any desire to acquire it for such a purpose. In fact, even if I did possess it, I would lend it to others rather than use it myself. Therefore, let my detractors be silent, and if they cannot find any warmth in themselves,[8] let them live in their cold rancor, and while they pursue their own delights, or rather, their corrupt appetites, may they allow me to pursue mine during the brief life that is granted to us.

But we have wandered quite far afield, O my lovely ladies, and now it is time for us to return to our point of departure and continue along our preestablished course.

The sun had already chased all the stars from the sky and had driven the humid shadow of night from the earth, when Filostrato arose and had the entire company awakened. They then went off to the fair garden, where they proceeded to entertain themselves until the hour for dinner arrived, which they ate in the same spot where they had taken their supper the previous evening. While the sun was at its highest, they took their nap, after which, having gotten up, they went and seated themselves in their usual order beside the lovely fountain. There Filostrato ordered Fiammetta to begin the storytelling, and without waiting for him to say another word, she displayed all her feminine grace and began to speak as follows.

Day 4, Story 1

Tancredi, Prince of Salerno, kills his daughter's lover and sends her his heart in a golden chalice. Sprinkling it with poison, she drinks it down and thus dies.[1]

Our King has certainly given us a harsh topic to speak about today, especially when we consider that, having come together in order to cheer ourselves up, we are obliged to recount stories about others' tears, stories that cannot be told without awakening feelings of pity in speaker and listener alike. Perhaps he chose this topic to temper somewhat the gaiety of the past few days. However, no matter what moved him to do so, since it is not appropriate for me to alter the topic that it is his pleasure to have chosen, I will recount an incident that was not only pitiful, but disastrous, and entirely worthy of our tears.

Tancredi, Prince of Salerno, was a man of benevolent character and a ruler known for his humanity, except that in his old age he sullied his hands with the blood of lovers. In the entire course of his life, he had only a single daughter, and he would have been happier if he had never had her at all. He loved the girl more tenderly than any daughter was ever loved by her father, and not knowing how to part with her because of this tender love, he refused to arrange a marriage for her, even when she was well beyond the age when she should have wed. At long last, he gave her away in marriage to one of the sons of the Duke of Capua, but she lived with him for only a short while before she was left a widow and returned to her father.

Her face and her body were as beautiful as those of any other woman who has ever lived. Youthful and vivacious, and wiser than might have been appropriate in a woman, she lived like a great lady with her doting father in the midst of real luxury. When she saw, however, that because of his devotion to her, he was not giving much thought to arranging a new marriage for her, and since she thought it unseemly for her to ask him to do so, she decided that she would try to find a clandestine lover for herself who was worthy of her affection.

After looking over all the men, both noble and non-noble, who frequented her father's court, men of the sort we see in courts everywhere, and after considering the manners and conduct of quite a number of them, she found herself attracted to one of her father's young valets above all the rest. He was named Guiscardo, and although his origins were humble, his virtues and his manners sufficed to ennoble him. By dint of seeing him often, she soon became secretly inflamed with the most passionate love for him, and her admiration for the way he comported himself grew greater every day. As for the young man himself, he was by no means unperceptive, and from the moment he noticed her interest in him, he took her so deeply into his heart that he thought of virtually nothing else except his love for her.

In this way, then, the two of them went on secretly loving one another. The young girl wished for nothing more than to be together with her beloved, but since she was unwilling to make anyone her confidant in the matter, she thought up a new trick by means of which she could communicate her plan to him. She composed a letter in which she explained what he had to do in order to be with her on the following day, and then she inserted it into the hollow center of a reed, which she gave to Guiscardo, telling him in a joking manner: "Make a bellows of this for your servant girl, and she'll rekindle your fire with it this evening."

Guiscardo took it, and thinking that she would not have given it to him and spoken to him as she did without good reason, he left the room and returned to his lodging with it. When he examined the reed and discovered that there was a crack in it, he opened it up and found her letter inside. As he read it and noted what she wanted him to do, he was the happiest man who ever lived, and he immediately set about making preparations to meet with her, following all the details of the plan she had laid out for him.

Next to the Prince's palace there was a mountain containing a grotto

that had been formed in the distant past and that was faintly illumi-
nated by an air shaft, which had been dug out of the solid rock. The
grotto, however, had been abandoned, and the mouth of the shaft was
almost completely blocked by the brambles and weeds growing over
it. From one of the ground-floor rooms of the palace that were occupied by the lady, a hidden stairway led into the grotto, although its
entrance was barred by a very strong door. So much time had passed
since the stairway had been used that there was virtually no one who
still remembered it. Love, however, from whose eyes nothing can be
concealed, had reminded the enamored lady of its existence.

To keep anyone else from noticing what was going on, she spent several days working hard on the door with various implements until she
finally got it open. Once she had done so, and had climbed down alone
into the grotto and seen the shaft, she sent word about it to Guiscardo,
letting him know approximately how high its mouth was from the
ground and telling him he should make every effort to get in by that
route. With this end in mind, Guiscardo lost no time in obtaining a rope
and tying knots and loops in it so that he could use it to descend and
climb back out again. Then, without arousing anyone's suspicion about
what was going on, the next night he went to the shaft, wearing a leather
suit to protect himself from the brambles. After securely tying one end
of the rope to a sturdy bush growing out of its mouth, he used the rope
to lower himself into the grotto and waited there for the lady to appear.

The next day the lady sent her ladies-in-waiting away on the pretext
that she wanted to take a nap, and having locked herself alone in her
bedroom, she opened the door to the stairway and descended into the
grotto where she found Guiscardo waiting for her. The two of them
greeted one another with wonderfully warm affection and then went
to her bedroom together where they spent the greater part of the day
enjoying themselves in utter delight. After they had agreed on the most
prudent plan for keeping their love affair a secret, Guiscardo went back
to the grotto, while the lady locked the door and came out to rejoin her
attendants. Then, after nightfall, Guiscardo used the rope to climb out
of the shaft, exited from the place where he had come in, and returned
to his lodging.

Having mastered this route, Guiscardo made the return journey many times after that. Fortune, however, was envious of such great and long-lived happiness, and made use of a calamity to transform the two lovers' joy into tears of sorrow.

From time to time, Tancredi was in the habit of going alone to his daughter's bedroom, with whom he would stay and chat for a while before he left. One day he went down there after dinner, and having entered her room without being seen or heard by anyone, he discovered that the lady, whose name was Ghismunda, was out in one of her gardens with all of her ladies-in-waiting. Not wishing to deprive her of her recreation, he sat down to wait on a stool located at the foot of the bed near one of its corners. The windows of the room were closed and the bed curtains drawn aside, and after a while Tancredi pulled one of them over him almost as if he were deliberately trying to hide, lay his head against the bed, and fell asleep.

Unfortunately, Ghismunda had arranged to have Guiscardo meet her that day, and as Tancredi was sleeping, she left her ladies-in-waiting in the garden and quietly returned to her room. Without noticing that anyone was there, she locked herself in and opened the door for Guiscardo who was waiting for her. The two of them got into bed as they usually did, and while they were playing and enjoying themselves together, Tancredi happened to wake up. When he saw and heard what Guiscardo and his daughter were doing, his grief overwhelmed him. His first impulse was to scream at them, but then he decided to hold his peace and, if possible, remain hidden, because a plan had already taken shape in his mind and he wanted to proceed with more caution, and with less shame to himself, as he put it into effect.

The two lovers remained together a long time, as they usually did, without ever once noticing Tancredi. When they felt it was time to part, they got out of bed, after which Guiscardo returned to the grotto, and the lady left her room. Despite his advanced age, Tancredi then lowered himself down from a window into the garden, and without being seen, returned to his room, sick to death with grief.

At Tancredi's orders, that night around bedtime two of his men seized Guiscardo, who, encumbered by his leather suit, was just coming out of the shaft. They then brought him in secret to Tancredi, who said to him, practically in tears:

"Guiscardo, the kindness I've shown you did not deserve the outrage and dishonor that you've done to what belongs to me, and that I witnessed today with my very own eyes."

All that Guiscardo offered by way of reply was to say: "Love is much more powerful than either you or I."[2]

Tancredi ordered his men to take Guiscardo to an inner room, where he would be guarded in secret, and they took him away.

Ghismunda knew nothing of all this, and after dinner the next day, Tancredi, who had spent time thinking up all sorts of strange and terrible possibilities, went to his daughter's room just as he usually did. Having sent for her, he locked her in with him and began weeping.

"I never doubted your virtue and honesty, Ghismunda," he sobbed, "and so, no matter what anyone might have said, it would never have occurred to me that you could have thought of yielding to any man other than your husband, let alone actually doing it. But now that I've seen it with my own eyes, I will be grief stricken whenever I recall it during the little bit of life that is left to me in my old age.

"I would to God that if you had to commit such a dishonorable act, you had chosen a man whose rank was suited to your nobility. Instead, from among all the people who frequent my court, you selected Guiscardo, a young man of the basest condition who has been raised in our court as an act of charity from the time he was a small child right up to the present. Your behavior has created the most distressing dilemma for me, in that I simply don't know what I'm going to do about you. As for Guiscardo, I had him apprehended last night as he was coming out of the grotto and put in prison, and I've already made up my mind what I will do about him. But God knows, I have no idea how I'm going to deal with you. I am moved, on the one hand, by the love I've always felt for you, a love greater than that which any father ever felt for his daughter. On the other, I'm filled with righteous indignation because of your folly. My love prompts me to pardon you, while my anger wants me to go against my nature and show you no pity. Still, before I reach any decision about you, I'd like to hear what you have to say in reply."

When he finished speaking, Tancredi, like a child who has just been given a sound beating, lowered his head and wept bitter tears.

As she listened to her father, Ghismunda realized not merely that her secret love had been discovered, but that Guiscardo had been captured. This filled her with such incalculable grief that she was frequently on the point of expressing it by screaming and weeping, as most women usually do. Her lofty soul enabled her to triumph over such base behavior, however, and instead, making a marvelous effort to keep her countenance unchanged, she decided that she would sooner die than make any sort of plea on her own behalf, convinced as she was that her Guiscardo was already dead. Thus, presenting herself not like a grief-stricken woman who had been rebuked for a fault, but like an undaunted figure of courage, she turned to her father with dry eyes and a fearless look on her face that did not betray the least hint of any distress.

"Tancredi," she said, "I am disposed neither to argue with you nor to beg, because the first won't help me and I don't want the second to do so. I intend no appeal to either your mercy or your love. Rather, I will tell you the truth, and after defending my reputation with sound arguments, I will then, by means of my actions, resolutely follow the lofty promptings of my heart. It's true that I have loved—and still love—Guiscardo. In fact, as long as I shall live, which will not be long, I shall continue to love him. And if there is love after death, my affection for him will never cease. I have been brought to act as I did not so much by my womanly frailty as by your lack of concern to see me married as well as by Guiscardo's own worth.

"It should have been clear enough to you, Tancredi, as a creature of flesh and blood, that you have produced a daughter of flesh and blood, not one of stone or iron. And even though you are now an old man, you should have been mindful all along of the nature and the strength of the laws of youth. As a man, you may have spent a portion of your best years in martial activity, but you should still be aware of the powerful effects that idleness and luxury can have on old and young alike.

"Being your daughter, I am a creature of flesh and blood, and what is more, I am still quite a young woman. Now, for both of those reasons

I am filled with carnal desires whose force has been enormously increased by the fact that I was once married and have known the pleasure that comes from satisfying them. Not being able to resist their force, I decided, being a woman in the prime of life, to follow where they led me, and as a result, I fell in love. But insofar as I was able, I certainly did everything in my power to prevent that to which I was being drawn by my natural sinfulness from conferring shame on either you or me. To that end I was assisted by compassionate Love and benevolent Fortune who found out and showed me how to satisfy my desires in perfect secrecy. No matter who revealed this to you or however you came to know about it, I do not deny that this is what happened.

"I did not take a lover at random, as many women do, but made a deliberate choice of Guiscardo, selecting him ahead of everyone else. With thoughtful planning I drew him to me, and by dint of prudence and persistence on both of our parts, I have been satisfying my desires with him for a long time now. What you are blaming me for with such bitterness, far more than for my carnal sin itself, is that I am consorting with a man of base condition, as if it wouldn't have bothered you for me to have chosen a nobleman as my lover. In doing this, you are following common opinion rather than the truth, for you fail to see that you are not really blaming my sin, but Fortune, who has very frequently raised the unworthy to great heights, while keeping the most deserving down low.

"But leaving all this aside, just consider the basic principles involved, and you will see that we are all made of one flesh and that the same Creator has created all our souls, giving them equal faculties, powers, and virtues. Since we are all born equal, and always have been, it is virtue that made the first distinctions among us, and those who not only had, but actually made use of a greater portion of it were the ones considered noble, while the rest were not. Since then, practices to the contrary have obscured this law, but it has never been erased from Nature or good manners, so that a person who behaves virtuously shows unmistakably that he is noble, and if anyone calls him something else, then that person, not the other, is in the wrong.

"Just take a look at your noblemen, and compare their lives, manners,

and general behavior with those of Guiscardo. If you judge them all
without prejudice, you will say that he is the true nobleman and the
rest of them are mere commoners. In estimating the virtues and valor
of Guiscardo, I did not trust the judgment of other people, but that
which was contained in your own words and which my own eyes have
confirmed. What person ever commended him as much as you did
for performing all those praiseworthy deeds for which men of valor
merit commendation? And you were certainly not wrong to do that,
because if my eyes have not deceived me, you have never praised him
for something I didn't actually see him do, and usually in a manner
more wonderful than your words could ever express. Thus, if I was ever
deceived at all in this, you were the one who deceived me.

   "Will you say, then, that I have allied myself with a man of base condition? Well, you're simply not telling the truth. Perhaps if you'd said
I'd done so with a poor man, that might be conceded—but it would be
conceded to your shame, because it reveals you have failed to reward
such a worthy servant with the advancement he deserves. In any case,
poverty does not take away a man's nobility of character; only wealth
can do that. There have been many kings, many great princes, who
were once poor, and many a farmer and many a shepherd were once
immensely wealthy and are so again.

   "As for the last doubt you entertain, namely, about what you should
do with me, banish it altogether. If you are ready in your extreme old
age to do what you were never accustomed to do when you were young,
that is, to treat me with savage cruelty, then go ahead and use all of
it on me, since I myself am the real cause of this supposed sin. I am
determined not to offer you any sort of plea for mercy, and I swear to
you that whatever you have done to Guiscardo, or are planning to do
to him, if you don't do the same thing to me, I will do it to myself with
my very own hands. Now get out of here. Go shed your tears with the
women. And then, when you are inclined to cruelty again, kill us both
with the same blow if you think we've merited it."

   The Prince recognized the lofty nature of his daughter's spirit, but
for all that, he doubted she was so resolute as to do what her words
suggested. As a result, once he left her, he lost any desire he had to take

out his anger on her and decided, instead, that he would cool off her fervent love by punishing her lover. Consequently, he ordered the two men who were guarding Guiscardo to strangle him noiselessly that night, and then to take out Guiscardo's heart and bring it to him. The two of them did as they were ordered, and the next day the Prince sent for a beautiful large chalice made of gold, into which he put the heart. Then he had one of his most trusted servants take it to her, bidding him to say the following words as he handed it over: "Your father sends you this to comfort you for the loss of the thing you love best, just as you have comforted him for the loss of what he loved best."

After her father had left her, Ghismunda, who was unflinching in her fierce resolve, had them bring her poisonous herbs and roots, which she distilled into a liquid so as to have it at the ready in case what she feared actually came to pass. When the servant then appeared and presented her with the cup and the Prince's message, she took it, and with her countenance unchanged, removed the cover. As soon as she saw what it contained, she understood the meaning of the Prince's words and had no doubt whatsoever that this was Guiscardo's heart. Raising her head, she looked straight at the servant.

"A heart like this," she said, "deserves nothing less splendid than a sepulcher of gold. At least in this case, my father has acted wisely." And having spoken, she raised the heart to her lips and kissed it.

"In every respect," she said, "right down to the very end of my life, I have always found my father's love for me to be most tender, and now it is more so than ever. Consequently, on my behalf, I ask you to give him the last thanks I shall ever give him for so great a gift." Having said this, she turned to the chalice, which she held firmly in her grip, and stared at the heart.

"Ah," she said, "sweetest vessel of all my pleasures, I curse the cruelty of the man who now compels me to look at you with the eyes of my body! It was enough for me to have beheld you at all hours with those of my mind. You have finished the course of the life that Fortune has allotted you, you have reached the end to which everyone hastens, and having left behind all the misery and weariness of the world, you have received from your enemy himself the sepulcher that your worth deserves. Your funeral rites lacked nothing but the tears of the woman you loved so dearly while you were alive, and God prompted my pitiless father to send you to me so that you might have them now. I shall weep for you, even though I intended to die with my eyes dry and my countenance completely unmarked by fear. But once I have paid you the tears I owe you, I will make no delay in sending my soul, with your help, to join the one that you have guarded so tenderly.[3] Is there another companion with whom I would be happier or more secure as I travel to that unknown place? I am certain that your soul is nearby right now, looking down on the scene of all the delights we shared, and since I am sure it loved me, I know that it awaits my soul, which loves it beyond all measure."

When Ghismunda finished speaking, she bent her head over the chalice, and suppressing all sounds of womanly grief, she began weeping in a way that was wondrous to behold. As her tears poured forth like water from some fountain in her head, all the while she gave the dead heart an infinite number of kisses. Her ladies, who were standing around her, did not understand whose heart it was or what her words meant, but overcome with pity, they, too, began to weep. Filled with compassion, they asked her to reveal the cause of her lamentation, but it was all in vain, nor could they comfort her, despite all their best efforts to do so.

When Ghismunda had wept her fill, she raised her head and dried her eyes.

"O my dearly beloved heart," she said, "now that I have discharged the duty I owe you, the only thing I have left to do is to send my soul to you and unite it with yours as your eternal companion."

Having made this pronouncement, she sent for the little vial containing the liquid she had made the day before, and poured it into the chalice where lay the heart she had bathed with so many of her tears. Then, without a trace of fear, she brought it to her lips and drained it dry, after which, with the chalice still in her hand, she climbed up onto her bed. There she arranged her body as decorously as she could, placed the heart of her dead lover next to her own, and without saying another word, waited for death.

When her ladies had seen and heard all these things, even though they did not know the nature of the liquid that she had drunk, they sent word of it to Tancredi. He was afraid of what was in fact transpiring and immediately descended to his daughter's room, arriving just as she was positioning herself on her bed. When he saw the condition she was in, he tried—too late—to comfort her with sweet words, and then dissolved in a flood of bitter tears.

"Tancredi," said the lady, "save your tears for some misfortune less desired than mine is. Just don't shed them for me, for I don't want them. Who ever heard of anyone, aside from you, weeping when he gets what he wanted? But if you still retain even a bit of the love you used to feel for me, grant me one last gift: since it displeased you that I lived quietly with Guiscardo in secret, let my body be publicly laid to rest beside his wherever it may be that you had them throw it after his death."

His anguished sobbing did not permit the Prince to respond, whereupon the young lady, who felt her end approaching, pressed the dead heart to her bosom, and said: "God be with you, for now I take my leave of you." Then, her vision grew blurry, her senses failed, and she left this life of sorrow behind her.

Thus, as you have heard, the love between Guiscardo and Ghismunda came to its sad conclusion. Tancredi grieved deeply over what had happened, and although his repentance for his cruelty came too late, he did have the couple honorably buried in the same tomb, to the universal mourning of all the people of Salerno.

Day 4, Story 2

Frate Alberto, having given a lady to understand that the Angel Gabriel is in love with her, assumes the angel's form himself and sleeps with her on numerous occasions, until, scared by her relatives, he throws himself out of her house and takes refuge in that of a poor man. The next day the latter leads him to the piazza dressed up like a wild man, where he is recognized and apprehended by his fellow friars who proceed to incarcerate him.[1]

More than once, Fiammetta's story had brought tears to the eyes of her companions, but when it was done, the King looked at them sternly and declared:

"I think it would be a small price to pay if I were to give up my life in exchange for even half the pleasure that Ghismunda had with Guiscardo. Nor should any of you find this surprising, seeing as how every hour of my life I die a thousand deaths without ever having received even a tiny morsel of pleasure. However, setting my affairs aside for the present, I want Pampinea to continue the storytelling with some savage tale that partly resembles my own predicament, and if she will just follow Fiammetta down the way she has set out on, I shall doubtless begin to feel some drops of dew falling upon the fire that burns within me."

Because of the way she felt herself, Pampinea was far more responsive to her companions' mood than to the King's after what he had just said, and so, when she heard herself ordered to speak, although she was perfectly willing to obey his command, she was more inclined to amuse them a bit than to satisfy him. Consequently, she decided that, without straying from the prescribed theme, she would tell them a tale that would make them laugh, and thus, she began:

The people have a proverb that goes like this:

A man who's wicked, yet thought to be good,
Can always do wrong: no one thinks that he would.

This proverb provides me not just with ample material to discuss in connection with the theme that has been proposed, but also with an opportunity to reveal both the nature and the extent of the clergy's hypocrisy. When they go about begging, they don long, flowing robes, make their faces look pale by artificial means, and keep their voices mild and low, but they become loud and haughty when they attack others for their own vices, or show how the people will achieve salvation by giving alms to them, while they do so by taking alms from the people. Furthermore, unlike the rest of us, they do not act as if they have to work to get into Paradise, but as if they already owned it and had been made its rulers, assigning everyone who dies a better or a worse place depending on the amount of money he has bequeathed to them. In this they make every effort to deceive, first, themselves, if they really believe what they say, and then, all those who put faith in their words. If I were permitted to reveal their tricks, I would soon open the eyes of many simple people and show them just what it is that they keep hidden underneath those ample habits of theirs.

But now, may it please God that what happened to a Franciscan should happen to them on account of all of their lies.[2] No longer a young man, that friar was considered to be among the most authoritative churchmen in Venice,[3] and it will give me the greatest pleasure to tell you a story about him so that your spirits, which have been filled with pity for the death of Ghismunda, may perhaps be lifted up to some degree if I can get you to laugh and enjoy yourselves.

In Imola, worthy ladies, there once lived a wicked, corrupt man by the name of Berto della Massa whose ignominious deeds were so well known to the people of the town that no one there was willing to believe anything he said, no matter whether he was lying or telling the truth.[4] When he perceived that his scams would no longer work in Imola, as a last resort he moved to Venice, that receptacle of every sort of filth, thinking he would find a different way to practice fraud there than he had anywhere else before then.[5] And so, pretending he was conscience stricken because of his past misdeeds, he gave everyone the impression that he was overcome by the utmost feeling of humility, and then, as if he were the most pious man alive, he went and became a Franciscan, adopting the name of Frate Alberto da Imola. Wearing the habit of that order, he put on a show of living an austere life, greatly commending both penance and abstinence, and never eating meat or drinking wine, at least when he did not find any to his taste.

Almost no one perceived that the man who had suddenly turned into a great preacher had been a thief, a pimp, a forger, and a murderer, let alone that he had never really abandoned any of his vices, which he would practice on the sly whenever he could. To top it off, after being ordained a priest, every time he went up to the altar to celebrate the Mass, provided that there were a lot of people present, he would weep over the Passion of Our Savior, for he was the kind of guy it cost very little to shed tears whenever he wanted. In short, between his sermons and his tears, he knew how to lure in the Venetians so successfully that not only was he made the trustee and executor of practically every will written in the city, but many people asked him to safeguard their money, and the vast majority of both men and women named him their confessor and advisor. Having thus changed from a wolf into a shepherd, he acted in such a way that he gained a reputation for holiness in those parts much greater than that which Saint Francis had ever enjoyed in Assisi.

Now it just so happened that a group of women went to this holy friar one day in order to be confessed, and among them there was a frivolous, empty-headed young lady named Madonna Lisetta da Ca' Quirino, the wife of an important merchant who had sailed away to Flanders with his galleys.[6] She was kneeling at his feet, and being a Venetian, all of whom are chatterboxes, she had only gotten through a few of the things she had done, when Frate Alberto asked her whether she had a lover.

"Hey, Messer Friar," replied Madonna Lisetta, giving him a black look, "don't you have eyes in your head? Do you think my charms are just like everybody else's? I could have lovers to spare if I wanted, but my kind of beauty is not something for just anybody who happens to be attracted to it. How many women have you seen whose good looks are anything like mine? Why, I'd be counted a beauty even in Paradise." And she added so much more about this beauty of hers that it was a pain to listen to her.

Frate Alberto saw immediately that this one was something of an idiot, and since she seemed like good soil for him to plow, he fell passionately in love with her then and there. He decided, however, to postpone any courtship until a more suitable moment. Instead, in order to keep up his saintly appearance for the time being, he began scolding her, telling her this was all vainglory and making her listen to a lot more of his nonsense. In reply, the lady told him that he was an ass and that he could not tell one woman's beauty from another's. Since he wanted to avoid irritating her unduly, Frate Alberto heard the rest of her confession and allowed her to go on her way with the other women.

A few days later, Frate Alberto went to Madonna Lisetta's house with a trusted companion, and withdrawing into a separate room with her where he could not be seen by anybody, he threw himself on his knees before her.

"My lady," he said, "I beg you for God's sake to forgive me for what I said to you on Sunday when you were talking to me about your beauty. I was punished so severely for it the following night that I have not been able to get out of my bed until today."

"And who was it who punished you like that?" asked Lady Blockhead.

"I'll tell you," replied Frate Alberto. "When I was praying that night, as I usually do, all of a sudden I was aware of a great light shining in my cell, and before I could turn around to see what it was, there was an incredibly beautiful young man standing over me with a large club in his hand. He grabbed me by my habit, pulled me down to the floor at his feet, and really let me have it until he'd bruised practically every bone in my body. When I asked him why he had treated me like that, he replied, 'Because today you presumed to disparage the celestial beauty of Madonna Lisetta, and except for God Himself, there is no one in the world I love more than her.'

"'Who are you?' I asked, and he replied that he was the Angel Gabriel.

"'O my lord,' I said, 'I beg you to forgive me.'

"'I forgive you on this condition,' he replied, 'that you go to her as soon as you can and persuade her to forgive you. And if she doesn't, I'm going to come back here and give it to you so soundly that you'll be sorry for the rest of your life.' What he said to me after that I don't dare to tell you unless you forgive me first."

Lady Pumpkinhead, who was somewhat lacking in wit, was enormously gratified upon hearing his words and took them all to be the utter truth.

"Well, Frate Alberto," she said, after a brief pause, "I told you that my beauty was celestial, didn't I? But so help me God, I do feel sorry for you, and in order to spare you any further injury, I will forgive you, but only on the condition that you tell me what else the angel said to you."

"Now that you've pardoned me, my lady," replied Frate Alberto, "I'll do so gladly. But let me ask you to bear one thing in mind, and that is never to tell anyone in the world what I'm about to say to you, if you don't want to ruin everything for yourself. Truly, you're the luckiest lady alive, for the Angel Gabriel told me to tell you how he'd taken such a liking to you that he would have come to spend the night with you on many occasions if he hadn't been worried about frightening you. Now he's sent me to inform you that he wants to come one night and spend time in your company, and because he's an angel and you would not be able to touch him in that form, he says that for your own pleasure he would like to come in the form of a man. Therefore, you should let him know when you want him to be here and in whose shape, and he'll do it. And so, now you know why you should consider yourself more blessed than any other woman alive."

Madonna Simple declared she was very pleased that the Angel Gabriel loved her, seeing how she certainly loved him and never let the opportunity go by to light a four-penny candle for him wherever she saw his image in a painting. And he would be very welcome to visit her whenever he pleased, and he would always find her all alone in her room. Nevertheless, there was this proviso, that he would not leave her for the Virgin Mary, whom, it was said, he loved very much, and it did appear that way because wherever she saw him, he was always on his knees in front of her.* For the rest, she said, it was up to him to come in whatever form he wanted as long as she would not be frightened.

"Spoken like a wise woman, my lady," said Frate Alberto. "I'll be sure to arrange everything with him just as you've suggested. But you can do me a great favor that will cost you nothing, namely, you should have him use this body of mine when he comes to you. Let me explain how you'll be doing me a favor: the moment he enters my body, he's going to remove my soul and place it in Paradise, where it will remain for as long as he's down here with you."

"What a good idea," said Madonna Noodlepate. "I'd really like you to have this consolation to compensate for all the blows he gave you on my account."

"You should make sure he'll find the door to your house open tonight so that he can get in," said Frate Alberto, "because he'll be coming in human form, and when he arrives, he'll have to enter that way."

The lady replied that she would take care of it, and after Frate Alberto left, she strutted around so high and mighty that her shift did not reach down to cover her butt. And still, to her it seemed like a thousand years before the Angel Gabriel arrived.

Thinking he was going to play the horseman, not the angel, that night, Frate Alberto fortified himself with sweets and other delicacies so that he would not be easily thrown from his mount. Then, at nightfall, after having obtained permission to leave the monastery, he went with a trusted companion to the house of a lady friend of his, a place he often used as a starting post for racing after his fillies, and when the time seemed right, from there he went on in disguise to the lady's house. Once inside, he transformed himself into an angel by putting on the gewgaws he had brought with him, after which he climbed up the stairs and entered the lady's room.

When she saw the brilliantly white object in front of her, she fell on her knees before it. The angel gave her his blessing, raised her to

---

*Madonna Lisetta is thinking about paintings of the Annunciation in which the Angel Gabriel typically kneels before the Virgin as he tells her she has been chosen by God to bear the Christ child.

her feet, and gestured to her to get into bed. Eager to obey, she did so immediately, and the angel lay down beside his devotee. Frate Alberto was a physically attractive man, quite robust, and with a more than sufficiently sturdy pair of legs on him, so that when he was with Madonna Lisetta, who was herself soft and fresh, he showed himself to be quite a different partner in bed than her husband. Many times that night he took flight without wings, causing the lady to cry out loud with satisfaction at what he did, which he supplemented by telling her all about the glories of Heaven. Then, as day approached, having made arrangements for his return, he took all his gear and went to rejoin his companion to whom the good lady of the house had offered her friendly company in bed so that he would not feel frightened if he had to sleep all by himself.

As soon as she had eaten, the lady went with her maidservant to see Frate Alberto and told him her news about the Angel Gabriel. She rehearsed what he had said about the glories of the life eternal and described his appearance, while adding to her account all sorts of marvelous inventions of her own.

"My lady," said Frate Alberto, "I don't know how you fared with him. What I do know is that when he came to me last night and I gave him your message, in an instant he transported my soul among so many more flowers and so many more roses than have ever been seen down here, and there, in one of the most delightful spots that ever existed, he permitted my soul to remain until matins this morning. As for what happened to my body, I just don't know."

"Isn't that what I've been telling you?" said the lady. "Your body, with the Angel Gabriel inside, spent the entire night in my arms. And if you don't believe me, take a look under your left breast where I gave the angel such a passionate kiss that its mark is going to be there for days to come."

"Well, then," said Frate Alberto, "today I'm going to do what I haven't done in a long time, and that is, I'm going to undress myself to see if you're telling the truth."

Finally, after a lot more chitchat, the lady returned home, which, from that day on, is where Frate Alberto also went to pay her many a visit, unimpeded, in the form of the angel.

One day, however, when Madonna Lisetta was talking with a close friend of hers,[7] engaged in a dispute about physical beauty, she was determined to place her own charms up above everyone else's, and having precious little wit in her pumpkinhead, she declared: "If you only knew who was taken with my beauty, you'd certainly stop talking about how attractive other women are."

Because her friend certainly understood the kind of woman she was dealing with, she was very curious about what Madonna Lisetta had to say.

"My lady," she said, "you may well be telling the truth, but still, since his identity remains unknown, it's difficult for one to change one's opinion."

"I shouldn't be telling you this, neighbor," replied Madonna Lisetta, who got all worked up very easily, "but my sweetheart is the Angel Gabriel, who loves me more than he loves himself, and according to what he tells me, it's all because I'm the most beautiful woman to be found anywhere in the world or in the Maremma."[8]

Her friend wanted to laugh, but held herself in check so that Madonna Lisetta would continue talking.

"I swear to God, my lady," she said, "if the Angel Gabriel is your sweetheart and tells you that, then it must be true. But I didn't think that the angels did such things."

"That's where you've got it wrong, neighbor," replied Madonna Lisetta. "By God's wounds, he does it better than my husband, and in fact, he tells me they all do it up there, too. And because he thinks I'm more beautiful than anyone in Heaven, he's fallen in love with me and frequently comes to stay with me. Now do you get it?"

After her friend left Madonna Lisetta's, it seemed like a thousand years before she found someone to whom she could repeat what she had heard. Finally, while attending a party where there was a large group of women, she told them the entire story from start to finish. These women told it to their husbands and to other women, and they told it to yet others, and thus in less than two days the news was all over Venice. But among those whose ears it reached were Madonna Lisetta's brothers-in-law. Without saying a word about it to her, they decided they would find that angel and discover if he really could fly, and for the next few nights in a row they lay in wait for him.

Some vague news about all this happened to reach the ears of Frate Alberto, and so he went one night to give her a scolding. No sooner had he undressed, however, than her in-laws, who had spotted him coming, were at the door to the room and in the process of opening it. When Frate Alberto heard them and realized what was up, he got out of bed, and seeing no other way to escape, opened a window overlooking the Grand Canal and threw himself into the water. Since the canal was deep there, and he was a good swimmer, he got away without suffering any harm. Having swum over to the other side of the canal, he hurried through the open door of a house and begged the good man he found inside, for the love of God, to save his life, making up some tall tale about how he had come there at that hour and why he was completely naked. The good man took pity on him, and since he was obliged to go off and tend to some affairs of his, he had Frate Alberto get into his bed and told him to stay there until he returned. Then, after locking him in the house, he went about his business.

When the lady's in-laws entered her room, they found that the Angel Gabriel had flown away, leaving his wings behind. Disconcerted, they directed a stream of verbal abuse at the lady, after which they took the angel's trappings and returned home, leaving her all alone in a state of utter dejection. By now it was broad daylight, and while the good man was on the Rialto,[9] he heard the story about how the Angel Gabriel had gone to bed that night with Madonna Lisetta and been discovered there by her brothers-in-law, how he had been terrified and thrown himself into the canal, and how no one knew what had become of him. He immediately realized that this was the guy he had in his house. Upon his return he confirmed his suspicions, and after listening to a lot more stories from Frate Alberto, he got him to send for fifty ducats if he wanted to avoid being handed over to the lady's in-laws. Once the money was taken care of, Frate Alberto was anxious to get away.

"There's only one way for you to do that," said the good man, "provided you're willing to go along with my plan. Today we're holding a festival in which people will be led about in various disguises, one dressed up like a bear, someone else like a wild man, and so on, and so on. Then they'll stage a hunt in the Piazza San Marco, and when that's over, the festival will come to an end, and everyone will be free to take the person he brought there with him and go wherever he wants.[10] So, if you're willing to have me lead you around wearing one of those disguises, I can take you away wherever you want to go before someone spots you. Otherwise, I can't see any way for you to get out of here without being recognized, because the lady's in-laws have concluded that you're somewhere in this quarter, and they've placed guards all over the place in order to capture you."

Although it seemed hard to Frate Alberto to go about in such a disguise, nevertheless his fear of the lady's relations persuaded him to do so, and he told the good man where he wanted to go, leaving the choice of a disguise up to him. The good man then smeared Frate Alberto from top to toe with honey, scattered downy feathers all over him, and after attaching a chain to his neck and putting a mask over his face, gave him a large club to hold in one hand and two huge dogs in the other that he had gotten from the slaughterhouse.[11] Then he sent a man ahead to the Rialto to announce that whoever wanted to see the Angel Gabriel should go to the Piazza San Marco—that was Venetian trustworthiness for you!

Once everything was ready, the good man waited a bit longer and then took Frate Alberto outside, making him lead the way while holding him from behind by the chain. As they went along, they stirred up a lot of commotion among the throngs of people there, all of whom were asking, "What's that? What's that?" The good man led Frate Alberto on toward the piazza, where, between those who were following them from behind and those who had heard the announcement and had come from the Rialto, the crowd had grown so large that it was impossible to count all the people in it. When they finally arrived at the piazza, the good man tied his wild man to a column in an elevated spot where everyone could see him. Then, he pretended to wait for the hunt to begin, while Frate Alberto, because he was smeared all over with honey, was suffering intense pain from all the gnats and gadflies.

When the good man saw that the piazza was almost completely full, he made as if he was going to unchain his wild man, but pulled off Frate Alberto's mask instead and declared:

"Gentlemen, since the boar is not going to make an appearance, there won't be any hunt today. However, I didn't want you to have come here in vain, and so I've decided to let you have a look at the Angel Gabriel who descends at night from Heaven to earth in order to console the women of Venice."

No sooner was his mask off than Frate Alberto was instantly recognized by everybody, who all started yelling at him, using the foulest words and the worst insults ever hurled at any scoundrel, at the same time throwing filth of every sort in his face. They kept this up for a very long time until, by chance, the news reached his fellow friars. As many as six or so of them came to the piazza, threw a cloak over his shoulders, and unchained him, after which, followed by a general hue and cry, they led him to their monastery where they locked him up. And there it is believed he finally died, having spent the remainder of his life in utter misery.

Thus this guy, whose evil deeds were never believed because he was thought to be a good man, had dared to turn himself into the Angel Gabriel. After being transformed into a wild man, however, he was put to shame as he deserved to be, and for a very long time he wept in vain for the sins he had committed. May it please God that the same thing should befall all the others like him.

Day 4, Story 3

Three young men fall in love with three sisters and run away with them to Crete, where the eldest sister kills her lover out of jealousy. The second, by giving herself to the Duke of the island, saves her sister from death, but she herself is killed by her own lover who then takes flight with the eldest sister. The murder is blamed on the third sister and her lover, who are arrested for it and confess, but fearing execution, they bribe their guards and flee, now destitute, to Rhodes, where they die in poverty.[1]

After listening to the end of Pampinea's story, Filostrato remained pensive for a while, then looked in her direction and said: "The conclusion of your tale contained a little something of merit, and I liked that part, but there was far too much to laugh about before then, which I would have preferred to do without." Then, turning toward Lauretta, he said: "Lady, follow it up with a better story if possible."

"You are too cruel to lovers," she replied with a laugh, "if all you ever want is for them to come to some unhappy end. Nevertheless, I will obey you and will tell one about three of them for all of whom things turned out badly before they had much of a chance to enjoy their loves." And having said that, she began:

Young ladies, as you must surely know, every vice is capable of doing the greatest harm to the person who practices it, and frequently, to other people as well. Furthermore, in my opinion, the one that we control the least as it leads us into danger is anger. For anger is nothing other than a sudden, thoughtless impulse, prompted by a feeling of resentment, that banishes reason, shrouds the eyes of the mind in darkness, and sets our souls on fire with raging fury.[2] And although this often happens to men, and to some men more than others, it has nevertheless been known to produce even more destructive effects in women, for not only do they catch fire more easily, but their anger burns in them with a fiercer flame, and meeting less resistance there, carries them away with it.

Nor is this surprising, for if we examine the matter closely, we will see that fire, by its very nature, catches more readily in objects that are soft and light than in those that are harder and denser, and I hope the gentlemen will not be offended if I say that we are more delicate than they are, as well as being much more capricious. Thus, bearing in mind that we have a natural propensity to get angry, and considering not only how pleasurable and soothing an effect our gentleness and mild manners have on the men with whom we spend our time, but also how much harm and anguish are the result of anger and fury, I would like to strengthen our hearts against this vice by telling you my story. As I have said, it is concerned with the love of three young men and an equal number of women, and it will show how, thanks to the ire of one of the latter, all their happiness was turned into absolute misery.

Marseilles, as you know, is an ancient and most noble city on the coast of Provence, and in the past it teemed with wealthy men and great merchants, containing many more of them then than one can find there nowadays. One of their number was a man of humble origins named N'Arnald Civada, a most trustworthy merchant of spotless integrity, who had accumulated an immense fortune in the form of both property and money.[3] He and his wife had a number of children, the three eldest being girls, and the rest, boys. Two of the girls were twins who were fifteen years old, while the third one was fourteen, and the only thing delaying the marriages their family had arranged for them was the return of N'Arnald from Spain, where he had gone to sell his merchandise. The names of the two older sisters were Ninetta and Magdalena, and the third one was called Bertella.

A young man named Restagnone, who was poor but of noble birth, was head over heels in love with Ninetta, as the girl was with him, and they had been able to arrange things so that they could consummate their love without revealing what was going on to a living soul. They had already been enjoying themselves this way for quite some time when two good friends, young men named Folco and Ughetto, whose fathers had died and left them very wealthy, happened to fall in love, the first with Magdalena and the second with Bertella. Restagnone, who had been told about this by Ninetta and had ascertained that it was indeed the case, thought that their love for the two sisters might serve him as a means to relieve his poverty. So, he struck up an acquaintance with them and started accompanying them, sometimes individually and sometimes together, on their visits to see their young ladies as well as to see his own.

One day, when he thought that he was on sufficiently intimate and friendly terms with the two young men, he invited them to his house and said to them: "My dear, dear young friends, we've now spent enough time in one another's company for you to have no doubts about the deep love I feel for you and to realize that I'll always work as hard for your interests as I would for my own. Because of my genuine affection for you, I want to share with you an idea that's occurred to me, after which the three of us together will pursue whatever course of action seems best to you. If I may believe what you've been saying, and if I'm right about what I've deduced from observing your behavior day and night, you are both burning with the most passionate desire for the two young ladies you love, just as I am for their sister. Now, provided that you agree to go along with my plan, I feel confident I've found a truly sweet, enjoyable remedy for the fiery torment from which we are all suffering. And here's what it is.

"The two of you are extremely wealthy young men, whereas I am not. If you were willing to combine your fortunes and give me a third share in them as your partner, and if you would then decide where in the world we might go in order to live in happiness with our ladies, I have no doubt that I can persuade the three sisters to come with us to any place we choose and to bring a large part of their father's wealth along with them as well. Then each of us will have the lady he loves, and we'll be able to live there like three brothers, more content than any other men in the world. So, that's my plan. Now it's up to you to decide whether you want to console yourselves in this way or, instead, to leave things just as they are."

Since the two young men were burning with a passion beyond belief, once they heard that they were to have their ladies, they had no difficulty in making up their minds and told Restagnone that if things would actually work out the way he said, they were ready to go along with his plan. A few days after receiving this answer from them, Restagnone found himself alone with Ninetta, whom he could only manage to see on occasion, and even then, with great difficulty. Having been there with her awhile, he got around to telling her about the discussion he had had with the young men, and using a variety of arguments, did his best to win her over to his plan. This, however, was not particularly difficult for him, since she was even more eager than he was to find a way for them to meet freely without fear of getting caught. And so, after telling him frankly that she liked his idea, she assured him that her sisters would do whatever she wanted them to, especially in this case, and asked him to make all the necessary arrangements as quickly as possible.

Restagnone returned to the two young men, who pressed him a great deal on the subject they had discussed before. As far as the ladies were concerned, he said, the matter was settled. Then, having decided among themselves that they should go to Crete, they sold some of the properties they owned on the pretext that they needed the money for a trading expedition. They converted everything else they had into cash, bought a brigantine, which they had lavishly provisioned in secret, and proceeded to wait for the appointed day to come.[4] For her part, Ninetta, who was well aware of what her sisters wanted, sweet-talked them into accepting the plan and got them so fired up with enthusiasm that they thought they would die before they saw it carried out.

When the night arrived for them to go aboard the brigantine, the three sisters opened up one of the large chests belonging to their father and took a vast amount of money and jewelry from it, which, according to plan, they carried quietly out of the house with them. Their three lovers were waiting for them, and without pausing for a moment, all six of them climbed onto the brigantine, which lowered its oars into the water and put out to sea. They arrived at Genoa the following evening, not having stopped at any other port along the way, and it was then and there that the new lovers experienced all the joys and pleasures of their love for the very first time.

Having replenished their stores as needed, they set off again, sailing unimpeded from one port to the next until, a week later, they arrived in Crete, where they purchased splendid, vast estates not far from Candia on which they built the most beautiful and delightful of mansions.[5] Then, with their large retinue of servants, their dogs, their birds, and their horses, they began to live like lords, banqueting and merrymaking and enjoying themselves with their ladies, the most contented men in the world.

As we all know from our daily experience, however, too much of even a very good thing will lead to revulsion, and so, while the three couples went on living in this fashion, Restagnone, who had once loved Ninetta dearly and could now have her whenever he pleased without fear of discovery, began to have regrets, with the result that his love for her began to wane. At the same time, he found himself powerfully attracted to a beautiful, young noblewoman from the island whom he had seen at a banquet, and whom he now began pursuing with all the zeal he could muster, paying her handsome compliments and putting on entertainments in her honor. When Ninetta perceived what was happening, she became so jealous of him that he could not make a move without her finding out about it and then, with her reproaches and accusations, making life miserable for him as well as for herself.

But in the same way that an overabundance of things generates disgust, the denial of what we desire increases our appetite for it, and so, the only thing Ninetta's reproaches did was to fan the flames of Restagnone's new love. Whether or not in the course of time he actually happened to gain the favors of his beloved, Ninetta was convinced by someone or other who reported it to her, that he had. As a result, she fell into a state of profound melancholy, which was replaced first by intense anger, and then by such a fury that all the love she felt for Restagnone was transformed into bitter hatred. Blinded by her wrath, she made up her mind to kill him and thus avenge the shame to which, she believed, he had exposed her.

Having called in an old Greek woman who was a great expert in the preparation of poisons, Ninetta persuaded her by means of promises and gifts to concoct a lethal potion. Some time later, without having given the matter any further thought, she offered it to Restagnone to drink one evening when he was hot and had no reason to be suspicious, and such was its strength that he was dead before matins. Folco, Ughetto, and their ladies soon heard about his demise, but having no idea that he had been poisoned, they came and joined Ninetta in weeping bitter tears over him, after which they arranged for him to be given an honorable burial.

Just a few days later, however, the old woman who had concocted the poisonous liquid for Ninetta happened to be arrested for some other wicked deed of hers. Under torture, she confessed to this crime, along with others she had committed, and provided a full account of what had happened. The Duke of Crete did not say a word about it to anyone, but went in secret one night and surrounded Folco's palace, then quietly arrested Ninetta without a struggle and took her away. There was no need for torture in this instance, and he very quickly learned everything he wanted to know from her about Restagnone's death.

Folco and Ughetto had been secretly informed by the Duke of the reason for Ninetta's arrest, and they, in turn, told their ladies. All of them were deeply upset and made every conceivable effort to save Ninetta from being burned at the stake, which was the punishment to which they realized she would be condemned, as she so richly deserved. All their efforts seemed in vain, however, for the Duke was firmly resolved to see justice done.

Magdalena was a beautiful young woman and had long been courted by the Duke. So far, she had not deigned to do anything that might give him the least satisfaction, but now, thinking that if she complied with his wishes, she just might save her sister from the fire, she informed him through a trusted messenger that she was his to command, provided that two conditions were met. The first was that her sister should be returned to her safe and sound, and the other, that everything should be kept secret. When he heard what she was proposing, the Duke was pleased, and after thinking long and hard about it, he agreed to Magdalena's terms and sent her word that he was ready to go. Accordingly, one evening, with the consent of the lady, he had Folco and Ughetto placed under arrest on the pretext that he wanted to get information from them about the case, and then went in secret to spend the night with Magdalena. First, however, he made a show of having Ninetta tied up in a sack as if she were going to be thrown into the sea that evening and drowned, instead of which he took her with him back to her sister and handed her over as payment for their night of pleasure. When he was leaving in the morning, he begged her that this, their first night of love together, might not be their last, although at the same time he also ordered her to send her guilty sister away so that he would not be criticized or feel obliged once more to proceed against her with the full rigor of the law.

That same morning, Folco and Ughetto were released. They had been told that Ninetta had been drowned in a sack during the night, and believing the story to be true, they returned home to console their ladies for the death of their sister. Although Magdalena made every effort to keep Ninetta completely concealed, Folco nevertheless discovered she was there. Not only was he very surprised by this, but he immediately became suspicious, for he had heard it said that the Duke was in love with Magdalena. How was it possible, he asked her, for Ninetta to be in the house? Although Magdalena spun out quite a tall tale for him in an effort to explain, he was too shrewd to give it much credit and kept pressing her to reveal the truth. She went on talking and talking, but in the end, she was forced to tell him. Overwhelmed with grief, Folco flew into a rage, drew out his sword, and slew her as she was begging him in vain for mercy.

Fearing the wrath and the justice of the Duke, Folco left her dead body in the room and went in search of Ninetta, to whom he said, putting on a phony air of cheerfulness:

"Let's go right now to the place where your sister said I should take you, so that you won't fall into the Duke's hands again."

Ninetta, who believed everything he said, was frightened and anxious to get away. Night had already fallen, and without stopping to say good-bye to her sister, she and Folco set out, taking with them all the money he could lay his hands on, which did not amount to much. On reaching the seashore, they got on board a boat, and since that time, no one has ever heard a word about what happened to them.

The next morning, when Magdalena was found dead, certain people who hated and envied Ughetto immediately brought the news to the Duke. Since he had been deeply in love with her, he rushed to the house, blazing with anger, and placed Ughetto and his lady under arrest. Although they were as yet ignorant about what had happened, knowing nothing, that is, about the flight of Folco and Ninetta, he nevertheless forced them to confess that they were jointly responsible with Folco for Magdalena's death.

Because of this confession, they were afraid—and not without reason—that they would be put to death, and so they very cleverly bribed their guards by giving them a certain sum of money that they kept hidden in their house for just such occasions. They did not have enough time to collect any of their possessions, however, but boarded a ship with their guards after nightfall and fled away to Rhodes, where it was not long before they died, poverty stricken, in misery.

This, then, was the end to which Restagnone's foolhardy love and Ninetta's rage brought not just them, but others as well.

Day 4, Story 4

Violating a pledge given by his grandfather King William, Gerbino attacks a
ship belonging to the King of Tunis in order to abduct his daughter, but when
she is slain by those on board, he kills them, after which he himself is beheaded.[1]

Upon reaching the end of her story, Lauretta remained silent as
various members of the company turned to one another and
bemoaned the sad fates of the lovers. Some of them were blaming it
all on Ninetta's anger, while others were offering different opinions on
the subject, when the King, who was deep in thought, roused himself,
and raising his head, gave Elissa the signal that she should speak next.[2]
Humbly, she began as follows:

Charming ladies, there are many who believe that Love shoots his
arrows only when kindled by the eyes, and they scoff at those who
maintain that people may fall in love purely on the basis of what they
hear. That they are mistaken will be made abundantly clear by a story I
plan to tell, in which you will see not only how rumor worked to make
two individuals fall in love without ever having seen one another, but
also how it led each of them to a miserable death.

As the Sicilians have it, William the Second, King of Sicily, had
two children, a son called Ruggiero and a daughter by the name of
Gostanza. Ruggiero died before his father, leaving behind a son named
Gerbino, who, having been carefully reared by his grandfather, grew
up to be a very handsome young man, renowned for his prowess and
his courtesy. His fame was not confined within the borders of Sicily,
however, but resounded throughout various parts of the world and
was most resplendent in Barbary, which at that time was a tributary to
the King of Sicily.[3] Gerbino's exalted reputation for courtesy and valor

reached the ears of many people, including a daughter of the King of Tunis, who was, according to what everyone said who had seen her, one of the most beautiful creatures ever fashioned by Nature, as well as being the most well mannered. She was, moreover, endowed with a lofty, noble spirit, and since it was her delight to hear tell of valiant men, she cherished the accounts she gathered from one person or another of Gerbino's courageous deeds. They pleased her to such an extent that she formed an image for herself of what he was like and fell so passionately in love with him that nothing gave her more happiness than to talk of him and to listen whenever anyone else mentioned his name.

On the other hand, glorious reports of her own beauty and worth had likewise spread to other lands, including Sicily, where they reached the ears of Gerbino, nor did they do so in vain, for they brought him such delight that he was soon burning with love for her as much as she was for him. Although he yearned desperately to see her, until such time as he might find some honest excuse to obtain permission from his grandfather to visit Tunis, he charged all those friends of his who went there to do everything in their power, and using whatever means they thought best, to acquaint her with his secret, passionate love for her and to bring news about her back to him. One of them found a very clever way to do it, for by posing as a merchant who was bringing her some jewelry to look over, he managed to give her a full account of Gerbino's love for her and to let her know that Gerbino had placed himself and everything he possessed at her disposal. The lady's face was positively glowing with happiness as she received both the messenger and his message, and having replied that the fervor of Gerbino's love was entirely equaled by her own, she sent him one of her most valuable jewels as a token of her affection. No precious object ever brought the person to whom it was given greater joy than that jewel did to Gerbino, who made use of the same messenger to send her frequent letters and the most costly gifts. And soon the two of them reached a secret understanding that if Fortune ever allowed them to do so, they would find an opportunity to see and, indeed, to touch one another.

Things had been going on in this fashion for somewhat longer than they would have liked, the young lady burning with desire for Gerbino in one place, and he for her in another, when the King of Tunis suddenly up and promised her in marriage to the King of Granada. She was terribly distressed by this development, for it meant not only that a vast distance would separate her from her lover, but that for all practical purposes, she would be entirely out of his reach. To prevent that from happening, she would have gladly run away from her father and gone to join Gerbino, if only she could have envisaged a way to do it.

When Gerbino found out about the marriage arrangement, he, too, was extremely upset and often thought to himself that if she happened to go to her husband by sea, and if he could find the means, he would resort to force and abduct her.

Rumors of their love and of Gerbino's plan reached the King of Tunis, who felt apprehensive because of the young man's strength and valor, and as the time for his daughter's departure approached, he sent word about his intentions to King William, saying that he would put them into effect as soon as he had the King's assurance that neither Gerbino nor anyone else acting on his behalf would stand in the way. Since the King of Sicily was an old man and had no inkling of Gerbino's love for the lady, he never imagined that this was the reason he was being asked for such a guarantee, and so he freely granted the King of Tunis's request, sending him his glove as a token of his word. Once the King of Tunis had received this pledge, he had a fine, large ship fitted out in the port at Carthage and saw that it was furnished with everything the people who were going to be sailing on it would need. Then, after it had been equipped and decked out in a style suitable for conveying his daughter to Granada, there was nothing left for him to do but wait for favorable weather.

The young lady observed all this, and knowing what it meant, sent one of her servants in secret to Palermo, instructing him to greet the gallant Gerbino on her behalf and to tell him that she was set to depart within a few days for Granada. Thus, it was now to be seen whether Gerbino was the courageous man everyone took him for and whether he loved her as much as he had so often told her he did.

The man to whom she had entrusted this task carried out her instructions to the letter, after which he returned to Tunis. Gerbino, who knew that his grandfather King William had pledged his word to the King of Tunis, had no idea what to do in response to the message he had just received. Nevertheless, prompted by Love and loath to appear a coward—for he had clearly grasped the lady's meaning—he set off for Messina, where in short order he had two light galleys put in fighting trim and manned with a valiant crew. He then sailed toward Sardinia, calculating that the lady's ship would have to pass by the island.

Nor was his prediction very far off the mark, for after he had been there just a few days, the lady's ship came sailing up on a light breeze, not far from the place where he was lying in wait. As soon as he caught sight of it, Gerbino said to his companions:

"Gentlemen, if you're as brave as I think you are, then there can't be a single man among you who is not in love or has not had some experience of love in the past, for it's my conviction that no mortal can possess true virtue or be capable of any good without first experiencing that emotion. And if you are, or if you have ever been, in love, then it will be easy for you to understand what it is that I desire.

"I am in love, and it is Love that has led me to assign you the task that lies ahead, for what I love is on the ship you see riding there before you. It does not merely contain the thing I most desire, however, but is heap full of treasure, and if you are courageous and fight like men, it won't be very difficult for us to make all those riches our own. Still, the only spoils I seek as my share in that victory is one sole lady, for whose love I have taken up arms. Everything else I freely concede to you here and now. So, let's go and launch our assault while Fortune's on our side, for God, who favors our enterprise, has stilled the wind and becalmed the ship here for us."

The gallant Gerbino had no need of so many words, for the crew from Messina that he had with him, eager for plunder, was already predisposed to carry out what he was exhorting them to do. Consequently, when he finished his speech, after giving him an enormous roar of approval, they sounded the trumpets, grabbed their weapons, and thrusting their oars into the water, headed for the ship.

The crew on board it could see the galleys approaching in the distance, and since they realized there was no way for them to flee, they prepared to defend themselves. Upon reaching the ship, the gallant Gerbino demanded that they send their officers over to his galleys if they wanted to avoid a fight, but when the Saracens, after identifying themselves, ascertained what it was that Gerbino and his men wanted, they protested that any attack on them would be a violation of the royal pledge they had been given, in token of which they displayed King William's glove. At the same time they declared in the most emphatic terms that they would never surrender and would never hand over anything they had on board, unless they were defeated in battle.

Gerbino had caught sight of the lady on the poop deck of the ship, looking much more beautiful than he had imagined her to be, and he was thus inflamed with a far greater desire for her than he had ever felt before. When they showed him the glove, he retorted that it was irrelevant since there were no falcons around just then, and he went on to say that if they refused to hand over the lady, they should get ready for a fight. Then, without further ado, they unleashed a fierce barrage of arrows and stones on one another, and they went on fighting in this way for quite some time, causing serious damage on both sides.

Finally, seeing that he was not getting very far, Gerbino took a small boat he had brought with him from Sardinia, set it ablaze, and used the two galleys to tow it up alongside the ship. When the Saracens saw them coming and realized that they had no choice but to surrender or die, they brought the King's daughter, who was weeping below, up onto the deck and led her to the ship's prow. Then they called over to Gerbino, and before his eyes, while the lady was begging for mercy and crying for help, they slaughtered her and threw her into the sea.

"Take her," they said. "This is the only way we'll give her to you—the way your trustworthiness deserves."

Upon witnessing this act of cruelty, Gerbino seemed eager to die himself. Indifferent to the stones and arrows, he had his men bring him right up alongside the ship, and he managed to climb on board despite the resistance of the entire crew. Just like a starving lion who falls upon a herd of bullocks, slashing this one with his teeth and that one with his claws, intent on satisfying his anger rather than his hunger, so Gerbino, sword in hand, cut down one Saracen and then another, slaughtering a host of them without mercy.[4] As the fire was now spreading through-out the entire ship, however, Gerbino ordered his sailors to carry away what they could as payment for their services, and then he climbed down off it himself, feeling little joy at the victory he had achieved over his enemies.

Gerbino saw to it that the body of the fair lady was recovered from the sea, and after mourning over it at length and shedding many a tear, he sailed back to Sicily. He had it given an honorable burial on the little island of Ustica, which is situated almost directly opposite Trapani, and from there he returned home, the saddest man alive.

Upon hearing the news of this event, the King of Tunis sent his ambassadors to King William, dressed all in black, to complain that he had not kept his word. When they explained to him exactly what had happened, the King was very upset, and seeing no way to deny them the justice they were demanding, he had Gerbino arrested. Then, while all of his vassals were attempting to persuade him to change his mind, he himself sentenced Gerbino to death and had him beheaded in his presence, preferring to lose his only grandson rather than to be considered a king whose word could not be trusted.

And so, in the miserable way I have described for you, and within the space of just a few days, the two lovers died a violent death, never once having tasted the fruits of their love.

Day 4, Story 5

After Lisabetta's brothers kill her lover, he appears to her in a dream and shows her where he is buried. She secretly digs up his head and puts it in a pot of basil, weeping over it for hours every day, but when her brothers take it away from her, shortly afterward she herself dies of grief.[1]

When Elissa's tale was finished and the King had bestowed a few words of praise on it, Filomena was told to speak next. Overwhelmed by compassion for poor Gerbino and his lady, she heaved a piteous sigh and thus began:

My story, gracious ladies, will not concern people of so lofty a rank as those Elissa has been speaking of, but it will, perhaps, arouse just as much pity in you. I was reminded of it by the mention that was just made of Messina, which is where it all occurred.

There once lived in Messina three young men who were brothers. All of them were merchants and had been left very rich after the death of their father, who had come there from San Gimignano.[2] They also had a sister named Lisabetta, but although she was a young woman who was quite beautiful and well mannered, for some reason or other, they had still not arranged for her to be married.

In addition to the three brothers, there was a young Pisan named Lorenzo in their trading establishment who oversaw and managed all of their operations, and who, being quite handsome and charming, had often caught Lisabetta's eye. Having noticed from time to time that she was unusually attracted to him, he abandoned all his other love relationships and in like fashion set his heart on her. And thus the business went on in such a way that with the two of them equally drawn to one another, it was not long before they took all the necessary precautions and did what each of them desired to do more than anything else.

As they continued their affair, to their mutual joy and pleasure, they did everything they could to keep it a secret, but one night, as Lisabetta was making her way to Lorenzo's sleeping quarters, she was observed, without knowing it, by her eldest brother. This young man was quite discreet, and however great the distress he felt over his discovery, he made the prudent decision, out of concern for their family honor, not to make a sound, let alone to say anything about it, and he bided his time all night long, turning over in his mind many possible responses to what had happened.

The next morning he told his brothers what he had seen of Lisabetta and Lorenzo the night before, and the three of them discussed the matter at great length. Determined to spare both themselves and their sister any loss of reputation, he decided they would pass it over in silence and act as if they had neither seen nor heard anything at all until such time as it would be safe and convenient for them to rid themselves of this shame before it went any further.

Keeping to their plan, the three of them chatted and joked around with Lorenzo just as they always used to do until one day came when they pretended they were going on an outing to the country and took Lorenzo along with them. Once they had reached a very remote and isolated spot, they saw their opportunity, and catching Lorenzo off guard, they killed him and buried his body, doing it all in such a way that no one had any idea what had happened. On their return to Messina, they put it about that they had sent Lorenzo away on business, something people readily believed, since the brothers frequently used to have him make such trips for them.

Lorenzo's failure to return weighed heavily on Lisabetta, and in her anxiety, she kept asking her brothers about him. One day, when she happened to be particularly persistent in questioning them, one of her brothers said to her:

"What's the meaning of all this? What do you have to do with Lorenzo that you keep asking about him all the time? If you question us any more on the subject, we'll give you the kind of answer you deserve."

This made the young woman sad and miserable, and from then on, filled with fear and foreboding, she refrained from asking them about him. At night, however, she would repeatedly call out to him in a pitiful voice and beg him to come to her, occasionally dissolving in a flood of tears because of her grief over his absence. Nor was anything capable of cheering her up, as she went on and on, waiting for him to return.

One night, after crying so much over Lorenzo's absence that she finally cried herself to sleep, he appeared to her in a dream, pallid and terribly disheveled, his clothes torn to shreds and rotting, and it seemed to her that he said: "Oh, Lisabetta, you do nothing but call out to me, bemoaning my long absence and cruelly accusing me with your tears. You should know that I can't ever come back here, because on the day when you saw me for the last time, I was killed by your brothers." He then described to her the place where they had buried him, told her not to call him or wait for him any longer, and disappeared. Lisabetta awoke, and believing that the vision she had seen was true, wept bitter tears.

When she got up the next morning, she decided to go to the place Lorenzo had shown her and seek confirmation of what she had seen in her dream. She did not dare to say anything about it to her brothers, but got their permission to go on a little outing in the country, accompanied by a maid who had served the two lovers at one time and was privy to all her affairs. She went to the spot as quickly as she could, and after clearing away the dry leaves, began digging where the soil seemed looser. Nor did she have to dig very deep before she uncovered her unfortunate lover's body, which as yet showed no sign of decay or decomposition and offered her clear proof that her vision had been true.

Lisabetta was the saddest woman alive, but knew that this was no time for tears. Although she would have willingly taken the entire body away and given it a proper burial if she had been able to do so, she realized how impossible that would be. And so, instead, she took out a knife, and after severing the head from the trunk as best she could, she wrapped it up in a towel and gave it to her maid to hold. She then covered the rest of the body with dirt, after which, unobserved, she left the scene and made her way home.

Taking the head to her room, she shut herself in and cried bitterly, weeping so profusely that she bathed it thoroughly with her tears, and at the same time planting a thousand kisses all over it. Then she wrapped it in a lovely piece of cloth and put it inside a beautiful large pot of the sort people use for growing marjoram and basil. Covering it with soil, she planted in it a number of sprigs of the finest basil from Salerno, and refused to sprinkle anything on it other than the water of roses or orange blossoms, or her own tears.[3] It became her custom to sit with this pot always by her side and to stare at it, concentrating all her desire on it, since her Lorenzo lay concealed within. After she had gazed at it raptly for a long period, she would bend over it and begin to weep, and would go on weeping until the basil was thoroughly watered by her tears.

Because of the constant, unremitting care she gave it, and because the soil was enriched by the decomposing head inside the pot, the basil grew luxuriantly and was exceptionally fragrant. And as the young woman maintained this routine consistently, on several occasions it came to the attention of her neighbors, who reported it to her brothers. "We've noticed," they said, "that she keeps doing the same thing every day."

The brothers had been puzzled by the fact that Lisabetta was losing her looks and that her eyes had become sunken in her head. When they heard their neighbors' account and then observed her behavior for themselves, they chided her for it several times, but to no avail, which prompted them to have the pot secretly removed from her room. Upon discovering that it was missing, she kept asking to have it back with the greatest insistence, but they refused to return it to her. And so, she went on crying and lamenting until she fell ill, and from her sickbed all she ever asked for was her pot of basil.

The brothers were very puzzled by her persistent entreaties and decided to find out what was inside the pot. When they dumped out the soil, they saw the cloth and the head wrapped inside it, which was not yet sufficiently decomposed that they could not help but identify it, from the curly hair, as being Lorenzo's. Utterly confounded by what they had discovered, and fearful that news of it would get around, they buried the head, after which, without saying another word, they made all the arrangements for an orderly departure from Messina, secretly left the city, and moved to Naples.

The young woman never stopped weeping and asking over and over again for that pot of hers. And so weeping, she died, thus bringing her ill-fated love to its end. In the course of time, however, people did learn the truth about the affair, and one of them composed the song that we still sing today, which goes:

Who was that wicked Christian man
Who stole my pot of herbs from me, etc.

Day 4, Story 6

After Andreuola, who is in love with Gabriotto, tells him about a dream she had, he tells her about one of his and then, suddenly, dies in her arms. While she is carrying him back to his house, assisted by one of her maids, they are arrested by the officers of the watch. She explains what happened to the podestà, who tries to rape her, but she fends him off. Her father learns of what has been going on, and since his daughter has been found innocent, he procures her release. She, however, absolutely refuses to go on living in the world any longer, and instead, becomes a nun.[1]

The ladies were quite taken with the story that Filomena had told, for they had listened to people sing that song on more than one occasion, but had never been able, no matter how often they asked, to ascertain the reason for its composition. As soon as the King had heard Filomena's final words, however, he ordered Panfilo to follow suit, and he began speaking as follows:

The dream described in the preceding tale prompts me to tell you another one that makes mention of two dreams, this time involving future events rather than something that had taken place in the past. Moreover, no sooner did the individuals involved finish their accounts of what they had seen while they were asleep than both of their dreams came true. Now, as you must surely know, dear ladies, every living being has had the experience of seeing various things in his sleep that seem, at the time, to be absolutely real. After he wakes up, however, he thinks only some of them are real, while judging others to be merely probable, and still others, totally incredible. Nevertheless, you will find that many dreams actually do come true, which is why lots of people have just as much faith in them as they do in the things they see when they are awake, and why their dreams, in and of themselves, will make them feel happy or sad, depending on whether they fill the dreamer with hope or fear. At the opposite extreme, there are those who do not believe in dreams at all until they find that they have fallen into the very difficulty of which they were forewarned. As for me, I do not approve of either view, since dreams are not invariably true, any more than they turn out to be false in every instance. That they are not always true, each of us knows from a great many experiences; that they are not always false is something that has already been demonstrated by Filomena's story and that I intend, as I said before, to show in my own. For it is my belief that if people live and act virtuously, there is no reason for them to fear a dream that encourages them to behave differently or to abandon their good intentions because of it. By contrast, in wicked and perverse enterprises, no matter how much one's dreams may seem to favor them and appear to offer auspicious omens, one should not believe in them, but should rather give full credence only to those dreams that point in the opposite direction. Now, however, let us get to the story.

In the city of Brescia there once lived a nobleman named Messer Negro da Ponte Carraro.[2] He had several children, including a daughter called Andreuola, who was young and very beautiful and as yet unmarried. Andreuola chanced to fall in love with a neighbor of hers named Gabriotto, a man of humble origins, but handsome, debonair, and endowed with many admirable qualities. Aided and abetted by her maid, the girl not only managed to apprise Gabriotto of her love for him, but to the mutual delight of both parties, she also had him repeatedly brought to pass the time with her in a lovely garden located on her father's estate. And to prevent anything from ever breaking up this happy love of theirs, except for death alone, they secretly became husband and wife.

The couple continued their clandestine love affair until one night, while she was sleeping, the girl happened to have a dream in which she seemed to see herself in the garden, holding Gabriotto in her arms. And as they were thus engaged in giving one another the most intense pleasure, it appeared to her that something dark and dreadful emerged from his body, the shape of which she could not make out. The thing seemed to seize Gabriotto and to tear him from her arms with tremendous force despite all her efforts to resist it. It then took refuge with him underground, and they never saw one another again.

The indescribable anguish Andreuola felt was so intense that it woke her up, and although, now that she was awake, she was glad to discover that what she had seen in her sleep had not occurred, she was nonetheless filled with terror because of her dream. Consequently, when Gabriotto wanted to visit her that night, she did everything she could to prevent him from coming. The following night, however, seeing how determined he was, and to prevent him from suspecting that there was some other reason for her behavior, she met with him again in the garden.

Having picked a large number of red and white roses, which were then in bloom, she went and joined him beside a beautiful fountain of clear running water.[3] There, after they had spent quite some time enjoying themselves to the full, Gabriotto asked her why she had forbidden him to come to her the day before, and in response, she told him all about the dream she had had the preceding night and the foreboding it had aroused in her.

When he heard what she had to say, Gabriotto laughed and told her that it was the height of folly to give any credence to dreams, for they were the result of eating too much or too little, and everyday experience showed how meaningless they all turned out to be.

"If I was the kind of man to attach any importance to dreams," he said, "I wouldn't have come here, not so much because of your dream as because of one that I, too, had last night. In it, I seemed to be in a lovely, pleasant forest, where I'd gone out hunting and captured the most beautiful, charming doe you've ever seen. She looked whiter than snow to me, and in no time she became so tame that she refused to leave my side. Moreover, I was apparently so fond of her that in order to keep her from straying, I'd put a golden collar around her neck and kept hold of her by means of a golden chain.

"After this, I dreamt that at one point, while the doe was resting with her head in my lap, I saw a greyhound, black as coal, suddenly appear out of nowhere, looking famished and quite terrifying. She came toward me, and I seemed incapable of resisting her as she thrust her muzzle into the left side of my chest and gnawed away at it until she reached my heart, which she then seemed to tear out and carry off with her. The pain was so great that it interrupted my sleep, and once I was awake, the first thing I did was to start feeling my side with my hand in order to see if anything was wrong. But when I failed to discover any injury there, I laughed at myself for having looked for one in the first place.

"And so, what is this dream trying to tell me? I've had many dreams like it before, and some that were even more terrifying, but nothing in the world has ever happened to me, one way or the other, as a result. So let's not pay any more attention to them and concentrate, instead, on how we can have a good time together."

The girl was already scared on account of her own dream, and her fears only increased when she learned about Gabriotto's. She did her best to conceal them, however, in order not to upset him. Still, although she took some solace from hugging and kissing him repeatedly, and being hugged and kissed in return, she was filled with an incomprehensible feeling of apprehension and kept looking into his face more often than she usually did, while occasionally glancing around the garden to see if some black thing were approaching them from one direction or another.

As they were thus engaged, Gabriotto heaved a great sigh, clutched her to him, and said, "Oh no, my soul, help me. I'm dying." And so saying, he fell to the ground and lay there on the grass that covered the little lawn.

Seeing this, the girl drew his fallen body to her bosom. "O my sweet lord," she said, verging on tears, "what is the matter?" Gabriotto did not reply, but gasping hard for breath and sweating all over, in no time at all he departed this life.

Each of you ladies can imagine how much pain and suffering the girl experienced, for she loved him more than her very own life. Weeping uncontrollably, she called out to him over and over again, but to no avail. Eventually, after she had felt his body all over and found it was cold wherever she touched it, she was forced to acknowledge that he was dead indeed. Overcome with anguish, at a loss as to what she could do or say, the tears streaming from her eyes, she went to find her maid, the one who was privy to this love affair of hers, and poured out all her grief and misery.

Gazing down in sorrow at Gabriotto's lifeless face, the two of them wept together for some time, until the girl turned and addressed her maid. "Now that God has taken this man from me," she declared, "I no longer have any desire to go on living. But before I proceed to kill myself, I'd like us to find some proper way to preserve my honor and to keep the love we shared a secret, while, at the same time, seeing to the burial of his body, from which his noble soul has departed."

"Don't talk about killing yourself, my child," replied the maid, "for though you've lost him here, by killing yourself you'd lose him in the other world as well, seeing as how you'd wind up in Hell, which, I'm convinced, is hardly the place where the soul of such a good young man has gone. It is far better for you to console yourself and to think about helping that soul of his by means of prayers and other pious works on the chance that he needs them because of some sin or other he may have committed. As for burying him, the quickest way is to do it right here in this garden. No one will ever find out about it, because no one knows that he's ever come here. Or if you don't want to do that, then let's take him from the garden and leave him outside. He'll be found there tomorrow morning and carried back home where his family will see to his burial."

Although she was grief stricken and crying the entire time, the girl nevertheless listened to her maid's advice, and after rejecting the first part of what had been suggested, she responded to the second part by saying:

"God forbid that I should allow such a precious young man, someone I've loved so deeply and accepted as my husband, to be buried like a dog or left lying on the ground out in the street. I have already given him my own tears, and I'll do everything I can to make sure he gets those of his family as well. In fact, I've already thought of what we have to do on that score."

She immediately sent the maid for a piece of silk cloth that she kept in one of her coffers, and when she returned with it, the two of them spread it out on the ground and laid Gabriotto's body on it. Shedding copious tears, the girl placed his head on a cushion, closed his eyes and mouth, and after making him a garland of roses from some of the ones they had gathered, filled the space all around him with the rest. Then she said to her maid:

"Since it's not very far from here to his house, you and I are going to carry him and place him right in front of his doorway, leaving him there in exactly the same way as we've just arranged him. It's not long until daybreak, and then they'll take him inside. Although that won't really console them, still to me, seeing as how he died in my arms, it will offer a certain gratification."

Then, as she finished speaking, she threw herself down on him once again and bathed his face with her tears. She went on weeping like that for a very long time, but finally, in response to her maid's urgent reminders that dawn was approaching, she stood up, took the very ring with which she had been wed to Gabriotto, removed it from her finger, and placed it on his. Still crying, she addressed him: "My dear lord, if your soul now sees my tears, or if, after it has departed, there is any sense or feeling left in the human body, receive with kindness this final gift from the woman you loved so passionately while you were alive." When she finished speaking, she fainted and fell down on top of his body yet again.

After a while she came to her senses and stood up. Then she and her maid picked up the cloth on which the body was lying and walked out of the garden with it, heading in the direction of his house. By chance, as they were going down the street with his dead body, they were discovered and taken into custody by the officers of the watch, who just happened to be on their way to investigate some other incident. Far more eager to die than to go on living, Andreuola had recognized the men as being in the service of the *podestà* and was utterly unintimidated in speaking to them.

"I know who you are," she said, "and realize that it would be futile for me to try to escape. I'm fully prepared to come with you and to explain what this is all about before the authorities. But as long as I continue to obey your orders, don't any of you dare to touch me or to remove anything from this body, unless you are prepared to have me bring charges against you." And in fact, no one laid a hand on her as they led her away with the body to the palace of the *podestà*.

As soon as they informed him about the situation, the *podestà* got out of bed and ordered the girl to be brought to his chambers. He questioned her there as to the facts of the case, and then had certain doctors carry out an investigation to see if the good man had been murdered either by poison or by some other means. They were unanimous in confirming that he had not been, however, and said that he had been asphyxiated after an abscess, located close to his heart, had burst.

When the *podestà* heard their report, he remained convinced that the girl was still guilty of some lesser crime, and so, he made a great show of offering her as a favor something that he was in no position to sell her, and let her know that he would free her in exchange for her consenting to gratify his desires. Upon finding that his words had no effect, however, he cast all decency aside and resorted to force, but Andreuola, who was seething with anger, her strength significantly amplified, defended herself with such virile energy that she drove him off, mocking him as she did so with haughty, scornful words.

By now it was broad day, and news of what had happened had reached Messer Negro. Worried sick about his daughter, he set right off for the palace, accompanied by a large number of his friends. There, after receiving a thorough account of the case from the *podestà*, he complained about how Andreuola had been treated and demanded that she be released to him. The *podestà*, thinking it preferable to accuse himself of having tried to rape her before she leveled that charge herself, began by praising her for her constancy, in proof of which he proceeded to explain what he had done. He went on to say that as a result of seeing how wonderfully resolute she had remained, he had fallen passionately in love with her, and in conclusion, declared that, if it was agreeable to Messer Negro, as her father, and also to the girl herself, he would gladly make her his wife, notwithstanding the fact that her previous husband had been baseborn.

While they were engaged in this discussion, Andreuola came into her father's presence, and weeping, threw herself down on her knees before him.

"Father," she said, "I suppose it's unnecessary for me to tell you the story of my recklessness and my tragedy, for I'm certain you've already heard it and now know everything. What I'm begging you for here—and I do it with all the humility I can muster—is to pardon my transgression for having married, without your knowledge, the man I preferred above all others. Nor am I asking you to forgive me so that my life may be spared, but rather, so that I may die as your daughter rather than your enemy." And with these words, Andreuola collapsed in tears at his feet.

Messer Negro, a rather elderly man who was kind and affectionate by nature, began crying himself as he listened to her words. Then, still weeping, he tenderly helped her to her feet.

"My child," he said, "it would have been my dearest wish for you to have married someone who was, in my judgment, suitable for you, and if you had chosen a man who pleased you, then he would have pleased me as well. But to think that you concealed your choice because you have so little trust in me, well, that saddens me, and all the more so, seeing as how you've lost him even before I knew anything about it. Still, since that's the way it is, now that he's dead, I want to treat him exactly as I would have been happy to have treated him, for your sake, while he was alive, and that is, to honor him as my son-in-law." Then, turning to his sons and other family members, he ordered them to see to it that a lavish, honorable funeral service be arranged for Gabriotto.

Meanwhile, news of what had happened had reached the young man's relatives, both male and female, and they all rushed to the scene together, followed by practically every last man and woman in the city. Gabriotto's body, laid out on Andreuola's silk cloth and surrounded by her roses, had been placed in the middle of the courtyard, where he was publicly mourned not only by the girl and by his female relatives, but by nearly all the women in the city and a large number of the men as well. After that, not like a commoner, but like a lord, he was taken from the courtyard, borne on the shoulders of the noblest men in the city, and carried with the greatest reverence to his tomb.

Some days later, the *podestà* pursued the offer he had made, but when Messer Negro discussed the matter with his daughter, she would hear none of it. Instead, it being her father's will that her wishes should be respected in this case, she and her maid entered a convent that was greatly renowned for its sanctity, and there, as nuns, the two of them lived out their long and virtuous lives.

Day 4, Story 7

Simona loves Pasquino, and while they are together in a garden, Pasquino rubs his teeth with a sage leaf and dies. Simona is arrested, and as she attempts to show the judge how Pasquino met his death, she rubs one of the leaves against her teeth and dies in the same manner.[1]

When Panfilo had dispatched his story, the King, who did not betray a hint of compassion for Andreuola, looked over at Emilia, giving her to understand that he would like her to add her tale to the ones already told, and she, without a moment's hesitation, began:

Dear companions, Panfilo's story leads me to recount one for you that in no way resembles his, except that just as Andreuola lost her lover in a garden, so did the girl of whom I am obliged to speak. Like Andreuola, she, too, was arrested, but managed to free herself from the authorities not by dint of her strength and her virtue, but through her unexpected death. As we have already had occasion to note among ourselves, although Love willingly comes to take up residence in the houses of the great, he does not, for that reason, refuse to govern those of the poor. On the contrary, at times he makes a show of his strength there so that he causes the wealthy to fear him just as they would the most powerful of lords. A large part, if not all, of what I am claiming will be confirmed by my story, which will also give me the pleasure of returning to our city, from which we have wandered very far away, passing through many different parts of the world today as we talked about a wide variety of subjects.

Not so very long ago, then, there lived in Florence a young woman by the name of Simona. The daughter of a poor man, she was very beautiful and refined for someone of her social condition, and although she was obliged to earn the bread she ate by working with her hands, supporting herself by spinning wool, she was not, for that reason, so lacking in spirit that she had failed to keep her mind open to Love, who for some time had been showing signs that he wished to gain entrance there through the agreeable words and deeds of a young man whose social position was no higher than her own and whose master, a wool merchant, employed him to go around and deliver wool for spinning.

Simona thus welcomed Love into her thoughts in the pleasing shape of the young man, who was named Pasquino, and who adored her. No matter how much she longed for him, however, she did not have the courage to act on her feelings. Instead, she would sit there and spin, recalling the man who had given her the wool and heaving a thousand sighs hotter than any fire with every length of thread she wrapped around her spindle.

For his part, Pasquino had developed quite an interest in seeing that his master's wool was properly spun, and acting as though all the cloth to be woven would come exclusively from what Simona was spinning, he showed much more concern about her work than anyone else's. As he went on devoting all his attention to her, and she was clearly enjoying it, eventually he became uncharacteristically daring, while she cast aside much of her usual modesty and shyness, and the two of them consummated their love in a mutually satisfying physical union. In fact, the experience proved so pleasurable for both of them that neither one would wait for an invitation from the other, but rather, whenever they got together, it was a contest to see who would be the first to make the offer.

With their pleasure thus continuing from one day to the next and their passion becoming ever more heated in the process, Pasquino happened to say to Simona that more than anything, he wanted her to find some way to meet him at a certain garden, because, he said, after he took her inside, they would feel more relaxed there and could spend their time together with less fear of arousing suspicion. Simona said she liked his proposal, and one Sunday after dinner, having given her father to understand that she wanted to go to the pardoning at San Gallo, she made her way to the garden Pasquino had told her about, accompanied by a friend of hers called Lagina.[2] She found him there with one of his friends, whose name was Puccino, but who was known generally as Kooky. Since he and Lagina took a fancy to one another from the start, Pasquino and Simona left them in one part of the garden while they retired to another in order to pursue their own pleasures.

In the part of the garden to which the couple had gone, there was a great big beautiful sage bush, at the foot of which they sat down and amused themselves for quite some time. Afterward, as they were engaged in a lengthy discussion about a picnic they intended to have at their leisure there in the garden, Pasquino turned to the large sage bush, plucked off a leaf, and began rubbing his teeth and gums with it, saying that sage was very good for cleaning off everything that remained stuck on them after a meal.[3] Having rubbed them awhile, he returned to the subject of the picnic, which they had been discussing before. He had not uttered very many words, however, before a change came over his features, such that in no time at all, he lost the ability to see and speak, and just a few moments after that, he was dead.

Simona, who had witnessed the entire episode, began crying and screaming and calling out to Kooky and Lagina, who promptly came running up to her. When Kooky saw that Pasquino was not just dead, but that his face and body were already swollen and covered with dark blotches, he shouted: "Oh, you evil woman, you've poisoned him!"

He made such a racket that a large number of people who lived near the garden heard him and raced over in the direction of the sound. There they discovered Pasquino's dead, swollen body, and as they listened to Kooky lamenting and accusing Simona of having tricked Pasquino into taking poison, while the girl, who was almost beside herself with grief because of the sudden accident that had deprived her of her lover, had no idea what to say in her own defense, they all concluded that Kooky's version of events had to be correct.

Simona was therefore arrested and led off to the palace of the *podestà*, shedding copious tears all along the way. By then, two other friends of Pasquino called Husky and Clumsy had shown up, and together with Kooky they made such a fuss that a judge immediately began interrogating Simona about the facts of the case.[4] But being unable to persuade himself that she had acted with malice or that she was guilty in any way, he decided he would take her with him when he went to examine the dead body and the site for himself, after which he would have her show him how it all happened according to the account she had given him, since he had not been able to get a very clear idea of what had occurred from her words alone.

Without causing any commotion, he therefore had her brought to the spot where Pasquino's body was still lying, swollen up like a barrel. When he himself arrived on the scene a bit later, he was astonished at the sight of the corpse and asked her to explain exactly what had taken place. The girl went over to the sage bush, and after recounting the story in some detail up to that point, in order to give him a full understanding of the case, she did what Pasquino had done and rubbed her teeth with one of the sage leaves.

The whole thing seemed frivolous and pointless to Kooky and Husky and Pasquino's other friends and acquaintances, all of whom ridiculed it in front of the judge, denouncing Simona's wickedness with greater vehemence and demanding that she be burned at the stake, since no lesser punishment would be appropriate for such a horrendous crime. While they went on talking, the poor girl just stood there, paralyzed both by her grief over the loss of her lover and by her fear of the punishment that Kooky was insisting on. But then, as a result of having rubbed her teeth with the sage, she succumbed to the same misfortune that had earlier befallen Pasquino, to the utter astonishment of everyone present.

O happy souls, whose fervent love and mortal existence both came to an end on the same day! And happier still, if you traveled together to the same destination! And happiest of all, if love is possible in the next life, and you love one another there just as much as you did down here! But the happiest soul beyond compare is Simona's—insofar as those of us who have survived her may judge—since Fortune did not permit her innocence to be destroyed because of the testimony of Kooky, Husky, and Clumsy, who were perhaps no better than wool carders or even lower than that. Instead, by means of a death identical to her lover's, Fortune found a more honorable way for her to free herself from their slanderous accusations and allowed her to follow after the soul of her Pasquino, whom she loved so passionately.

The judge, like everyone else there, was so completely stupefied by what had occurred that he had no idea what to say and did not budge from where he was standing for a long time. Finally, having recovered his wits, he declared:

"Evidently, this sage is poisonous, which is not typically the case with this plant. So, to prevent anyone else from being harmed in a similar manner, let it be cut down right to the roots and burned."

In the judge's presence, the caretaker of the garden undertook this task, but no sooner had he chopped through the bush and it had fallen to the ground than the reason for the deaths of the two poor lovers became apparent. For underneath it there was a toad of extraordinary size, whose venomous breath, they concluded, must have made the plant poisonous. Since no one dared to get any closer to the toad, they surrounded it with a huge palisade of firewood and burned it up together with the sage bush.

Thus ended His Honor the Judge's inquest into the death of poor Pasquino. His swollen body, together with Simona's, was buried by Kooky, Husky, Guccio the Slob, and Clumsy in the Church of San Paolo, which happened to be the parish to which they belonged.[5]

Day 4, Story 8

Girolamo loves Salvestra, but yielding to his mother's prayers, he goes to Paris, and when he returns, he finds that Salvestra has gotten married. After sneaking into her house, he lies down at her side and dies. His body is borne to a church, where she, too, dies at his side.[1]

W hen Emilia's story had come to an end, Neifile responded to the King's command by beginning as follows:

In my opinion, worthy ladies, there are some people who think they know more than others when they actually know less, and they consequently presume to set up this wisdom of theirs in opposition not only to the counsels of men, but also to the very nature of things. Not only has no one ever seen any good coming from such presumption, but it has sometimes been the occasion of very serious harm. Now, there is nothing in all of Nature that is less receptive to advice or contradiction than Love, whose character is such that it is more likely to burn itself out than be removed by any sort of counsel. And that is why it occurs to me to tell you a story about a lady who sought to be wiser than she was, wiser than she really had any right to be, indeed wiser than the situation in which she sought to manifest her intelligence actually warranted. For although she thought she could remove from a lover's heart the feelings that had perhaps been put there by the stars, instead, at one and the same time, she succeeded in driving life, as well as Love, from the body of her son.

According to the tales our elders tell, in our city there once lived a very powerful, wealthy merchant named Leonardo Sighieri, who had a son with his wife they called Girolamo.[2] After his birth, Leonardo passed away, but he had put his affairs in order, and the boy's guardians, together with his mother, skillfully and scrupulously managed his interests for him. Growing up with the children of the other families who lived nearby, the boy became friends with a girl his own age, the daughter of a tailor; in fact, he was far closer to her than to anyone else in the neighborhood. As they grew older, their friendship was transformed into a love so great and so fierce that Girolamo was miserable whenever he could not see her, and she was, without doubt, as much enamored of him as he was of her.

The boy's mother noticed what was going on, and she frequently scolded and even punished him for it. When she saw that she still could not make him refrain, she complained to his guardians, and in the belief that because of his immense wealth, she could, as it were, turn a plum into an orange tree,[3] she said:

"This boy of ours, who hasn't even reached his fourteenth birthday, is so infatuated with a local tailor's daughter named Salvestra that if we don't get him away from her, there's a chance that he'll up and marry her one day, without anyone knowing anything about it, and then I, personally, will never be happy again. If, on the other hand, he sees her getting married to someone else, he'll pine for her and simply waste away. So, it would seem to me that to avoid all this, you should send him away, far away from here, on business for the company, because if she's out of sight for a long time, she'll eventually be out of mind as well. Then, after that, we can arrange for him to marry some wellborn young lady."

The guardians told her that they approved of her plan and said they would do everything they could to realize it. Having sent for the boy to come to the warehouse, one of them started out by adopting a very affectionate manner.

"My boy," he said, "since you're now pretty much grown up, it would be a good idea for you to start looking after your own affairs in person. Consequently, we'd be very happy if you went and stayed in Paris for a while, where you'll see how a large part of your fortune is being put to work. What's more, by observing all those lords and barons and noblemen who are so abundant there and by studying their behavior, not only will you become a much better man, but you'll also acquire greater refinement and experience than you could by staying here. After that, you'll be free to come back home."

Having listened attentively, the boy gave them a curt answer, saying that he wanted none of it, since he thought he had just as much right to stay in Florence as anyone else. When the worthy men heard his reply, they spoke again at greater length in an attempt to persuade him, but being unable to get any other response out of him, they went and reported what had transpired to his mother. She became terribly angry and gave him a severe scolding, not because of his unwillingness to go to Paris, but because of his love for the girl. Then, however, soothing him with honeyed words, she turned to praising him and begging him sweetly to be so kind as to do what his guardians wanted. In fact, so skillful was she in speaking to him that he finally agreed to go and stay there for a year, though not for a moment longer. And in this way, it was all arranged.

Still passionately in love, Girolamo went to Paris, but his return was put off from one day to the next, and he wound up being detained there for two years. When he came back home, more in love than ever, he discovered that his Salvestra had gotten married to a fine young man who was a tent maker. Girolamo's grief knew no bounds, but seeing that there was nothing he could do about it, he tried to reconcile himself to the situation as best he could. He therefore found out where she lived and began walking back and forth in front of her house, the way young men in love usually do, in the belief that she could not have forgotten him any more than he had forgotten her. This was not the case, however, for as the young man quickly realized, to his infinite distress, she no more remembered him than if she had never seen him before, or if she did recollect anything at all, she never showed any sign of it. Nevertheless, he did everything he could to get her to recall him, until finally, feeling that he was getting nowhere, he decided to go and speak to her in person, even at the risk of his life.

After learning the layout of her house from someone who lived nearby, one evening when she and her husband had gone with some neighbors of theirs to attend a wake, he secretly got inside and hid himself behind some sheets of tent cloth that were hanging in her bedroom.

There he waited until the couple had returned and gone to bed, and as soon as he knew that her husband was asleep, he went over to where he had seen Salvestra lying down, placed his hand on her breast, and said in a whisper: "O my soul, are you asleep already?"

The girl, who was still awake, was about to yell, but the young man quickly blurted out: "For the love of God, don't scream. I'm your Girolamo." On hearing this, she started trembling all over.

"Oh, for God's sake," she said, "get out of here, Girolamo. Being in love was all right when we were children, but that time has come and gone. As you can see, I'm married now, which is why it's no longer proper for me to pay attention to any man except my husband. So, I'm begging you, in the name of the one and only God, to go away, because if my husband were to hear you, even supposing no other harm came from it, the result would certainly be that I'd never be able to live in peace and quiet with him again, whereas now he loves me, and I've got a happy, tranquil life with him."

To hear her say such things made the young man feel terribly depressed, but although he reminded her of their past together and of the fact that his love for her had not diminished despite the distance separating them, and although he begged and pleaded with her, making her the most extravagant of promises, he got nothing for all his efforts.

His only wish now was to die, and so he finally asked her, in the name of the immense love he bore her, if she would allow him to lie down by her side so that he could warm up some, for he had gotten thoroughly chilled while he was waiting for her. He promised her that he would neither talk to her nor touch her, and that he would go away as soon as he had gotten a little warmer.

Feeling somewhat sorry for him, Salvestra granted his wish, but only on the basis of the conditions he had proposed, after which the young man lay down by her side and neither touched her nor uttered another word. Instead, he concentrated all his thoughts on the long love he had borne her, her present cruelty, and his dashed hopes, and resolving to end his life, he clenched his fists, repressed his vital spirits, and died right there beside her.[4]

The girl wondered what he was doing, and after a while, fearful that her husband would wake up, she broke the silence. "Oh, Girolamo," she said, "why don't you get up and leave?" On receiving no answer, she assumed he had fallen asleep. Consequently, she stretched out her hand to wake him up and started nudging him, but found, to her great astonishment, that when she touched him, he felt as cold as ice. After prodding him more vigorously, and discovering that he did not move even though shaken repeatedly, she realized that he was dead. This filled her with dismay, and for a long time, she just lay there, not knowing what to do.

At last, she decided to tell her husband about the situation, but to pretend it concerned other people, in order to see what he would say they should do about it. And so, after waking him up, she described what had actually happened to Girolamo as if it had happened to someone else, and asked him what advice he would give, supposing that she herself was the one involved. The good man replied that in his opinion the dead man should be quietly brought back to his own house and left there, adding that no one would harbor any feelings of resentment against the woman since it did not seem to him that she had done anything wrong.

"And that's just what we should do," said the young lady, and taking his hand, she made him touch the dead body of the young man. Completely bewildered, her husband got to his feet and lit a lamp. Then, without exchanging another word with his wife, he proceeded to dress the dead body in its own clothes. After that, feeling quite confident about their own innocence in the affair, he quickly hoisted it onto his shoulders and carried it to the entryway of Girolamo's house, where he put it down and left it.

When morning arrived and Girolamo's dead body was discovered lying on his own doorstep, there was a huge outcry, especially from his mother. Several doctors examined the corpse, checking it all over, but when they were unable to find any sign of a wound or a blow, it was generally concluded that he had died of grief, as, in fact, he had. The body was then conveyed to a church, to which the sorrowing mother

came, accompanied by many other women, including both her relatives and neighbors, and they all began weeping and wailing without
restraint, as is our custom.

When the mourning was at its height, the good man in whose house
Girolamo had died said to Salvestra: "Look, wrap a mantle around your
head, and go to the church where they took Girolamo. While you min-
gle with the women there, and listen to what they're saying about this
business, I'll do the same thing among the men. That way we'll find out
if they're saying anything against us."

The girl was attracted by this idea, because now that it was too late,
she was actually feeling pity and was longing to see the body of the dead
man to whom she would not have condescended, while he was alive, to
have given even a single kiss. And so, off she went.

It is incredible when you think about it, and so difficult to understand, just how powerful Love can be! The girl's heart, which had
remained closed to Girolamo when Fortune favored him, was now
opened up by this misfortune of his. Indeed, the flames of Salvestra's
former love were rekindled, and from the moment she saw his dead
face, they were transformed into such a feeling of compassion that she
forced her way through the women, still wrapped up in her mantle,
and did not stop until she had reached the corpse. Once there, she let
out a piercing shriek and threw herself down on top of the dead youth.
She never had a chance, however, to bathe his face with her tears, for
she had scarcely touched him when, like Girolamo before her, she, too,
died of grief.

The women, who had still not recognized her, gathered round to
comfort her and coax her back up onto her feet, but since she was not
moving, they attempted to lift her themselves, only to find that she
was completely unresponsive. Finally, when they managed to raise her,
they discovered, at one and the same time, that she was Salvestra—and
that she was dead. Then all the women there, overcome by a two-fold
sorrow, began wailing again much louder than before.

The news got spread among the men outside the church, finally
reaching the ears of Salvestra's husband who was standing there with
them. For a long time he wept and wept, ignoring all the efforts the

others made to comfort and console him. Eventually, however, he told several of them the story of what had happened the night before between his wife and the young man. The reason for their deaths now being clear, everyone there grieved for them.

The dead girl was taken and adorned the way we usually do when we prepare the bodies of the dead. They then placed her on the same bier with the youth, laying her by his side, and wept over her for a good long while. Afterward, the pair were buried in a single tomb, so that those whom Love could not unite in life were joined inseparably to one another by death.

Day 4, Story 9

Messer Guiglielmo Rossiglione slays his wife's lover, Messer Guiglielmo Guardastagno, and gives her his heart to eat, but when she finds out about it later, she throws herself down to the ground from a high window, and after her death, is buried with her beloved.[1]

Neifile's story had inspired great feelings of pity in the entire company, and when it was finished, the King, who had no intention of infringing on Dioneo's privilege, saw that there was no one else left to speak. Consequently, he began as follows:

Considering how much you are saddened, my most compassionate ladies, by lovers' misfortunes, the tale that presents itself to me will make you feel at least as much pity as the last one did, since the people involved in the events I am about to relate were of loftier rank and met with a crueler fate than those of whom we have already spoken.

You must know, then, that according to the people of Provence, there were once two noble knights living in that region, each of whom had a castle and a large number of vassals under him. One was named Messer Guiglielmo Rossiglione and the other Messer Guiglielmo Guardastagno, and since both excelled in feats of arms, they used to arm themselves from head to toe,[2] and not only would they go together to tournaments and jousts and other contests involving martial prowess, but they would do so wearing exactly the same device.*

Although the castles in which the two of them resided were a good ten miles apart, Messer Guiglielmo Guardastagno chanced to fall madly

---

* A knight's "device" was an emblematic figure or design that he wore on his armor or carried as a banner; it had heraldic significance and enabled him to be recognized on the field of battle.

in love with Messer Guiglielmo Rossiglione's very beautiful and charming wife, and despite all the affection and camaraderie the men shared, he made use of one means and then another to make her aware of his feelings. The lady, knowing him to be a most gallant knight, was pleased by this and soon became so infatuated with him that there was nothing she burned and yearned for more, until the only thing she was still waiting for was to have him proposition her. Nor was it very long before he did, after which they met with some frequency and made passionate love together.

Since they were not very discreet in their encounters, one day her husband chanced to discover them and became so deeply incensed that the great love he felt for Guardastagno was transformed into mortal hatred. Better at keeping it hidden, however, than the two lovers had been with their affair, he decided, no matter what, that he would kill the man.

With Rossiglione in this frame of mind, a grand tournament happened to be announced in France. He immediately sent word of it to Guardastagno, asking him if he would like to come to his castle where the two of them could decide together whether they wanted to go and how they would get there. Quite delighted, Guardastagno replied that he would come without fail the next day and have supper with him.

When he received Guardastagno's message, Rossiglione thought the time had come to kill him. The next day, after arming himself, he got on his horse, and with a few of his men he went about a mile away from his castle, where he set up an ambush in a wood through which Guardastagno was bound to pass. After a long wait, he caught sight of him approaching, unarmed, followed by two servants, who were likewise unarmed, because he never thought for a moment that he might need to protect himself against his friend. When Rossiglione saw Guardastagno reach the spot he had chosen, he rushed out at him, with murder and vengeance in his heart, holding his lance above his head and shouting, "Traitor, you're a dead man!" And before the words were even out of his mouth, he thrust his lance straight through Guardastagno's chest.

Unable to defend himself, let alone even utter a word, Guardastagno fell, impaled on the lance, and died almost instantly, at which point his servants, without waiting to see who had killed him, turned their horses' heads around and fled back to their master's castle as fast as they could.

After dismounting from his horse, Rossiglione cut open Guardastagno's chest with a knife, tore out the heart with his own hands, and wrapping it up in a banderole, told one of his men to take it with him. Having given them all strict instructions not to dare to say so much as a word about what had happened, he got back on his horse and returned to his castle, by which time it was nightfall.

The lady, who had heard that Guardastagno was supposed to come to supper, was waiting for him with the greatest impatience. When he did not show up with her husband, she was quite surprised and asked him: "How is it, sir, that Guardastagno hasn't arrived?"

"Wife," replied her husband, "I've received word from him that he can't be here until tomorrow"—a statement that left her feeling somewhat perturbed.

After he had dismounted, Rossiglione had his cook summoned and said to him: "Take this boar's heart and make sure that you prepare the finest, most delectable dish you can with it. Then, when I'm seated at table, send it to me on a silver serving plate." The cook took the heart, and calling upon all his knowledge and all his skill, he minced it, seasoned it with a number of savory spices, and made a very tasty dish out of it indeed.

When it was time to eat, Messer Guiglielmo sat down at the table with his wife. The meal was served, but he was preoccupied with the crime he had committed and ate very little. The cook then sent him the special dish, and he had it placed before the lady, saying he had no appetite that evening. He heartily commended the dish, however, and the lady, who did have an appetite, started to eat it, and finding it quite tasty, consumed every last morsel.

When the knight saw that his wife had finished the whole thing, he asked her: "Wife, what did you think of the dish?"

"In good faith, my lord," she replied, "I liked it very much."

"So help me God," said the knight, "I do believe you did. But I'm really not surprised that you liked it dead, because you liked it when it was alive more than anything else in the world."

Upon hearing these words, the lady hesitated a moment. Then she asked: "How's that? What's this thing you've had me eat?"

"What you ate," said the knight, "was actually the heart of Messer Guiglielmo Guardastagno, whom you, like the faithless woman you are, were so infatuated with. And you may rest assured that it really was his, because I ripped it out of his chest myself, with these hands, just a little while before I came back here."

When she heard what had happened to the man she loved more than anything else in the world, there's no need to ask if she was grief stricken. After a brief pause, she said: "In doing what you did, you've behaved like a wicked, faithless knight, for if I was not forced into it by him, but freely chose to abuse you by making him the master of my love, then you should have punished me for it, not him. But now that I've eaten such a noble dish, made from the heart of so gallant and courteous a knight as Messer Guiglielmo Guardastagno, God forbid that any food should ever pass my lips again."

Then she stood up, and going to a window right behind her, without the slightest hesitation she let herself fall backward out of it. Because it was so high above the ground, the lady did not merely die, but was completely dashed to pieces.

Messer Guiglielmo was profoundly shaken by what he had witnessed and conscience stricken over having done wrong. Moreover, he feared what his fellow countrymen and the Count of Provence might do. Consequently, he had his horses saddled and rode away.[3]

By the next morning, news of what had happened had spread throughout the entire region, and people came from both Messer Guiglielmo Guardastagno's castle and that of the lady's family to gather up the two bodies, which were taken, amid a great outpouring of grief and lamentation, to the chapel inside the lady's castle and buried there in a single tomb together. Upon it there was an inscription in verse, indicating who was buried inside and the manner as well as the cause of their deaths.

Day 4, Story 10

The wife of a doctor assumes that a lover of hers, who has taken an opiate, is dead and puts him in a chest, which two usurers carry off to their house with the man still inside. When he comes to, he is arrested as a thief, but the lady's maid tells the Signoria that she was the one who stuck him in the chest, which the usurers stole, thus enabling the lover to escape the gallows, while the moneylenders are condemned to pay a fine for having taken the chest.[1]

Once the King had finished his story, only Dioneo still had his task to perform. Knowing this to be the case, and having already been asked by the King to proceed, he began as follows:

These sorry accounts of unhappy love have brought such sadness to my eyes and my heart, to say nothing of yours, my ladies, that I have been fervently longing for them to come to an end. Unless I were minded to make a sorry addition to this wretched fare—and Heaven forbid that I should do so—they are now all finished, thank God. Instead of pursuing such a sad topic, I will make a start on a better and much happier one, which may well provide a good suggestion as to what we should talk about tomorrow.

You should know, then, fairest of ladies, that not so long ago there lived in Salerno a doctor who was a very great surgeon and whose name was Master Mazzeo della Montagna.[2] Having reached a ripe old age, he had taken to wife a beautiful, young gentlewoman of the same city, and he kept her better supplied than any other woman there with elegant and expensive clothing, jewelry, and everything else that can give pleasure to a lady. But the truth is that most of the time she felt pretty chilly, since the Master did not keep her sufficiently covered in bed. Like Messer Ricciardo di Chinzica, of whom we have previously spoken, the doctor also taught his wife to observe all the holy feast days.[3] He would demonstrate to her how, after sleeping with a woman just once, you needed I do not know how many days to recover, and would tell her similar kinds of nonsense, all of which made her life utterly miserable.

Since she was an intelligent, high-spirited woman, she decided to save the goods she had at home and to use up, instead, what others had to offer her. Thus, she took to the street where she checked out a large number of young men, finally finding one to her liking, to whom she entrusted all her hopes, all her heart, and all her happiness. Noticing her interest in him, he found himself profoundly taken with her and, in similar fashion, wholeheartedly returned her love.

His name was Ruggieri d'Aieroli, and although he was of noble birth, he was so wicked and disreputable that he did not have a friend or relative left who wished him well or really wanted to have anything to do with him.[4] He was notorious throughout all of Salerno for the robberies he committed and for other crimes of the vilest sort. The lady cared little about all that, however, because she liked him for something else, and with one of her maids, she arranged it so that the two of them could get together. But then, after they had been taking their pleasure of one another for a while, the lady began to criticize him for his past life and to beg him, out of love for her, to change his ways. What is more, in order to provide him with the means to make that change, she took to supplying him with various sums of money on occasion.

Behaving with great discretion, the two of them had been carrying on in this manner for some time, when a sick man with an ulcerated leg happened to be placed in the doctor's hands. Once he had examined the malady, Master Mazzeo told the man's relatives that unless he removed a gangrenous bone from the man's leg, it would be necessary to have the entire thing amputated, because otherwise he would die. The doctor went on to say that although the man might recover if the bone were removed, he would take on the case only if they accepted the fact that the man might not survive. His relatives agreed to this condition and left him in the doctor's care.

The operation was to be performed around vespers, and since the doctor realized that the sick man would not be able to withstand the pain and thus not allow himself to be treated unless he were first given an opiate, that morning he had a quantity of liquid distilled according to one of his special prescriptions that would suffice to make the man sleep, after drinking it, for as much time as he estimated it would take him to perform the operation. He then had them deliver it to his house, where he stored it in the bedroom, without telling anyone what it was.

The hour of vespers had come, and just as Master Mazzeo was about to go off to see his patient, a messenger arrived from some very close friends of his in Amalfi, telling him that he should drop what he was doing and come at once because there had been a violent brawl in which a great many people had been injured. Postponing the treatment of the leg until the next morning, the doctor got into a little boat and sailed off for Amalfi. Since his wife knew he would not return home that night, she did what she usually did in such cases and sent in secret for Ruggieri. When he arrived, she took him to the bedroom and locked him inside until certain other people in the house had gone to sleep.

Perhaps Ruggieri had done a lot of hard work that day, or had eaten salty food, or perhaps it was a matter of his constitution, but for whatever reason he became terribly thirsty as he waited for the lady there in her room. He caught sight of the vial of liquid, which the doctor had prepared for the sick man and had left on the windowsill. In the belief that it was drinking water, Ruggieri raised it to his lips and drank the whole thing down. An immense lethargy instantly overcame him, and he fell fast asleep.

As soon as she could get free, the lady came back to her room, and when she found Ruggieri sleeping there, she started nudging him and telling him in a whisper to get up. But it was no use, for he did not answer her, did not, in fact, make any sort of movement at all. Feeling slightly irritated, she shook him even harder. "Get up, slugabed," she said. "If you wanted to sleep, you should have gone home instead of coming over here." As a result of her pushing, Ruggieri fell off the chest on which he was lying and landed on the floor, showing no more sign of life than if he had been a corpse. Now rather alarmed, the lady tried lifting him up and shaking him even harder, she tried tweaking his nose and pulling him by his beard, but it was all pointless, for he was sleeping like a log.[5]

Beginning to fear that he was dead, the lady started pinching his skin really hard and even tried singeing him with a lighted candle, but nothing worked. And so, being no doctor herself although she was married to one, she was utterly convinced that Ruggieri had died. There is no need to ask if this distressed her, for she loved him more than anything else in the world, and since she did not dare to make a sound, she began silently weeping over him and lamenting her terrible misfortune.

After a while, however, fearing to add shame to the loss she had already experienced, the lady realized that she had to act quickly and find some means to get his dead body out of her house. Having no idea where to turn for advice, she quietly called her maid, showed her the awful problem she had, and asked her what she should do. The maid was quite astonished, and she, too, tried tugging Ruggieri and pinching him, but when she saw that he was completely unresponsive, she agreed with what her mistress had said, namely that he was dead, and advised her to get him out of the house.

"And just where can we put him," asked the lady, "so as to prevent people from suspecting, when they discover him tomorrow morning, that he was brought out from in here?"

"My lady," replied the maid, "late this evening I saw a chest outside the shop of our neighbor the carpenter. It's not too big, and if he hasn't taken it back into the house, it'll be just right for our purposes, because we could put the body inside, stab him two or three times with a knife, and leave him there. If anyone finds him, there's no reason why they'd believe he came from here rather than from somewhere else. In fact, he's been such a bad guy they're going to think one of his enemies killed him while he was on his way to commit some crime or other, and then stuck him inside the chest."

The lady liked her maid's suggestion, except for the part about stabbing Ruggieri, saying that she did not have the heart to do it, no, not for anything in the world. And so, she sent the maid to ascertain whether the chest was still in the place where she had seen it. Upon her return, the maid confirmed that it was still there, after which, being a sturdy young woman, she proceeded, with the help of her mistress, to hoist Ruggieri up onto her shoulders. Then, with the lady walking on ahead to make sure no one was coming, the two of them made their way to the chest, dumped him inside, and after having closed it up, left him there.

A few days earlier, two young men, who made their living as usurers, had moved into a house a bit farther down the street. They were eager to make lots of money, while spending very little, and since they were in need of furniture and had seen the chest the day before, they had agreed between them that if it was still there that night, they would take it back home with them.

At midnight the pair left their house, located the chest, and picked it up at once, without stopping to give it much of an examination. Although it seemed somewhat heavy to them, they quickly carried it back to their home, where they put it down next to the room in which their wives were sleeping, and there they left it, without bothering to position it very securely, after which they went off to bed.

Ruggieri slept for a very long time, but just a little before matins, when he had digested the drink and its effects had worn off, he woke up. But although he was done sleeping and had recovered his senses, his mind still remained fuzzy, and he was left feeling somewhat bewildered not just through the following night, but for several days after that.

Having opened his eyes and finding himself unable to see a thing, he stretched out his hands, and by feeling around here and there, he discovered that he was inside the chest. Utterly dumbfounded, he started muttering to himself: "What's this? Where am I? Am I asleep or awake? I do remember coming to my lady's room this evening, and now I seem to be inside a chest. What's this all about? Can it be that the doctor's returned, or has something unexpected occurred, and that's what made her hide me in here while I was sleeping? Why, I'm sure that's the explanation."

Having reached this conclusion, Ruggieri tried to keep still and listened to see if he could hear anything. He was rather uncomfortable in the chest, which was quite small, and after he had been waiting there for quite some time, the side on which he was lying began hurting him so much that he decided to turn over onto the other one. He did this with great dexterity by pressing his back against one of the sides of the chest, but since it had not been set down on a level surface, he caused it to tip over and fall to the ground with a tremendous crash, waking up the women who were sleeping in the room next door and giving them such a fright that it left them completely incapable of uttering a word.

Ruggieri was very scared when the chest toppled over, but upon discovering that it was now open as a result, he preferred to climb out rather than remain inside, just in case something else should happen to him. Then, what with his not knowing where he was and what with one thing and another, he began groping around the house to see if he could find a stairway or a door that would offer him a way to get out. When the women, who were wide awake, heard him fumbling about, they began shouting, "Who's there?" Since he did not recognize their voices, Ruggieri made no reply, and so the women started calling out to the two young men. They, however, had stayed up very late and were consequently sleeping so soundly that they did not hear a thing that was going on.

More frightened than ever, the women got up, ran over to the windows, and started screaming, "Thieves! Thieves!" At this, many of their neighbors came rushing into the house from different directions, some crossing over the roof and others getting in through one door or another. They made such a racket that even the young men were awakened by it and got out of bed.

When Ruggieri saw the situation he was in, he was almost beside himself with sheer bewilderment. He had no idea how he could possibly escape them, nor was he really in any condition to do so. Consequently, he was captured and turned over to the officers who served the chief magistrate of the city and who had come on the run when they heard all the commotion. Ruggieri was brought up before the magistrate, and because he had a very bad reputation, he was immediately subjected to torture, which led him to confess that he had broken into the money-lenders' house with the intention of robbing them. Accordingly, the magistrate decided to have him hanged by the neck as soon as possible.

In the course of the morning the news spread all over Salerno that Ruggieri had been caught in the act of burgling the moneylenders' house. When the lady and her maid heard about it, they were in such a strange state of bewilderment, so utterly astonished, that they came close to convincing themselves that what they had done the night before had not really happened and that they had merely dreamed the whole thing up. Beyond that, the lady was almost out of her mind with anxiety over Ruggieri because of the danger he was in.

Just a little after half tierce,[6] the doctor returned from Amalfi and sent for his potion, so that he could go and treat the sick man who was his patient. When the vial was found to be empty, he made a huge hullabaloo about it, complaining that in his own house he could never find anything where he had left it. The lady, who had a very different reason for being upset, got angry herself and said: "What would you say if something serious had happened, Master, when you make such a fuss over a little bottle of water that's been spilled? Do you really believe we'll never find another drop of it anywhere in the world?"

"Wife," replied the doctor, "you seem to think this was pure drinking water, but it wasn't. It was a potion I prepared for putting people to sleep." And he went on to explain to her why he had prepared it.

When the lady heard this, she immediately realized that Ruggieri must have drunk the potion, which was why they had thought he was dead. "Master," she said, "we didn't know anything about all that. You'll have to prepare some more of it for yourself." Seeing that he had no alternative, the doctor had an additional quantity of it made up.

A little later, the maid, who had been sent on the lady's instructions to find out what was being said about Ruggieri, returned to her mistress with her report.

"They're all bad-mouthing Ruggieri, my lady," she said, "and from what I've been able to learn, he doesn't have a single friend or relation who's turned up to help him, or has any intention of doing so, and everyone's absolutely convinced that the judge is going to have him hanged tomorrow. But there's something else: I want to tell you about a surprising discovery I've made, because I think I've figured out how he wound up in the moneylenders' house. Just listen to this.

"You remember the carpenter outside of whose shop we found the chest that we put Ruggieri in. Well, he was having the most heated argument in the world just now with some guy to whom the chest apparently belongs. He was demanding the money he was owed for it, while the carpenter kept insisting that he hadn't sold it and was saying, on the contrary, that it had been stolen from him during the night. The other guy then replied, 'That's not so. You sold it to two young money-lenders, and they told me all about it last night when I spotted the chest in their house at the time that Ruggieri was arrested.' 'They're lying,' said the carpenter, 'because I never sold it to them. In fact, they're the ones who must have stolen it from me last night. Let's go and see them.' And so they all agreed to go to the moneylenders' house, while I myself came back here. As you can see, I really do think I know how Ruggieri got taken to the place where they found him. But I still don't see how he came back to life again."

Since the lady now understood exactly what had happened, she informed her maid about what she had heard from the doctor, and begged her to help rescue Ruggieri, telling her that she was in a position, if she wished, not only to save him, but also to preserve her mistress's honor at one and the same time.

"Just tell me how to take care of it, my lady," said the maid, "and I'll be glad to do anything you want me to."

The lady, who was really in a bind,[7] came up with a plan on the spot and described it in detail to her maid, who first of all went off to the doctor and began crying the moment she started speaking to him.

"Sir," she said, "I must ask you to forgive me for a great wrong I've done you."

"And what is that?" he asked.

"You know the kind of man that young Ruggieri d'Aieroli is," replied the maid, continuing to weep. "Well, sir, he took a fancy to me a little while ago, and what with my fear of him on the one hand and my love for him on the other, I felt I had no choice but to become his mistress. When he found out that you weren't going to be here last night, he coaxed me into letting him into your house so that he could sleep with me in my room. Then he got thirsty, but there was no way for me to bring him any water or wine, because I didn't want to be seen by your wife, who was in the great hall. Then I remembered noticing a little bottle of water in your bedroom, so I ran to get it, gave it to him to drink, and afterward, put it back where I'd found it. Since then, I've discovered that you made a terrible fuss here in the house about it. Well, I've come to confess to you that what I did was wrong, but is there anyone who doesn't make a mistake from time to time? I'm truly sorry both because of what I did, and because Ruggieri is now about to lose his life as a result of my mistake and what happened afterward. So, I'm begging you with all my heart to pardon me and to give me permission to go and see what I can do to help him."

Angry though he was as he listened to her story, the doctor's response to it was quite witty. "You've already imposed your own penance on yourself for this," he said, "seeing as how you thought you were going to be having a young man last night who would have really given your fur a good shaking, and instead, you got yourself a sleepyhead. Well, be off with you, and go see about saving your lover. But from now on, take care not to bring him to the house again, because then I'll make you pay for this time as well as that one."

Thinking that she had come off pretty well in the first of her encounters, the maid went as quickly as she could to the prison where they were holding Ruggieri and wheedled the jailor into letting her speak with him. After telling him the answers he needed to give the judge if he wanted to get out, she managed to arrange a hearing with the judge for herself.

Observing how fresh and lusty she was, the judge decided that before giving her an audience, he would have a go at casting his grappling hook aboard this nice little piece of God's creation, and since she knew that she would get a better hearing as a result, the maid was by no means disinclined to accommodate him.[8] When they were done grinding away at it, and she had picked herself up, she said: "My lord, you're holding Ruggieri d'Aieroli here on a charge of theft, but it's not true."

Then, starting from the beginning, she rehearsed the entire story for him right down to the end, explaining how she was Ruggieri's mistress, how she had let him into the doctor's house, how she had given him the opiate to drink without knowing what it was, and how she had put him into the chest because she thought he was dead. Next, she told him what she had heard the carpenter and the owner of the chest saying to one another and thus showed him exactly how Ruggieri had wound up in the moneylenders' house.

Seeing that it would be easy to verify her story, the judge first asked the doctor if what she said about the potion was true, and discovered that it was. He then summoned the carpenter, the owner of the chest, and the moneylenders, and after listening to a lot of tall tales told by the last two, he determined that they had stolen the chest during the night and brought it to their house. Finally, he sent for Ruggieri and asked him where he had lodged the previous evening. Ruggieri told him that he did not know where he had been, but that he certainly remembered having gone to spend the night with Master Mazzeo's maid, and that he had drunk some water in her bedroom because he had gotten really thirsty, but what had happened to him after that, he did not know, except that when he woke up, he found himself inside a chest in the moneylenders' house.

The judge was much amused by what he had heard, and made Ruggieri and the maid and the carpenter and the moneylenders repeat their stories several times over. Finally, acknowledging Ruggieri's innocence, he freed him and condemned the moneylenders who had stolen the chest to pay a fine of ten gold florins. There is no need for anyone to ask how welcome all this was to Ruggieri, and as for his mistress, her happiness knew no bounds. Later on, as she celebrated his release, she had a good laugh about it with him as well as with her precious maid, who had been all set to stab him with a knife. The couple's love continued to flourish, and the pleasure they derived from it grew ever greater—all of which is just what I wish would happen to me, except for the part about being stuffed inside a chest.

Day 4, Conclusion

If the earlier stories had saddened the hearts of the pretty ladies, this last one of Dioneo's made them laugh so hard—especially what he said about the judge getting his grappling hook aboard the maid—that they were able to recover from the compassion they had felt in response to the others. But perceiving that the sun was fading to yellow and the end of his reign had come, the King offered the lovely ladies the most courteous apology for what he had done, that is, for having made them speak on so harsh a subject as the misfortunes of lovers. Having thus excused himself, he got to his feet and removed the laurel wreath from his head. Then, as the ladies waited to see whom he would bestow it on next, he set it graciously on Fiammetta's brilliantly blonde hair, and said to her: "I now place this crown upon you because you will know better than anyone how to console our companions tomorrow for the disagreeable experience we have had today."

Fiammetta, who had long, golden curls that tumbled down over her delicate, white shoulders, a softly rounded face resplendent with the authentic hues of white lilies and crimson roses, a pair of eyes in her head that were like those of a peregrine falcon, and a dainty little mouth with lips like two tiny rubies, answered him with a smile:

"I am happy to accept it, Filostrato. And to make you even more aware of just what it is that you have done, I desire and decree forthwith that each of us should be ready tomorrow to recount the stories of lovers who, after terrible accidents or misfortunes, finally found happiness."

Everyone liked Fiammetta's proposal, and after summoning the steward and making all the necessary arrangements with him, she got up from her seat and gaily dismissed the entire company until suppertime.

All of them went off to amuse themselves in whatever ways they wished, some of them strolling through the garden, whose beauties never seemed stale to them, while others walked in the direction of the mills, which were grinding away outside. When the hour for supper arrived, they reassembled as usual next to the beautiful fountain and had their meal, which was very well served and which they ate with the greatest pleasure.

After getting up from the table, they devoted themselves, as was their custom, to singing and dancing. As Filomena took the lead, the Queen said:

"Filostrato, I have no intention of departing from the ways of my predecessors. Just like them, I intend to have a song performed at my command, and since I am certain that your songs are just like your stories, it is our pleasure that you should choose the one you like best and sing it for us now. Thus we will not have any more days, other than this one, that will be disturbed by your woes."

Filostrato replied that he was quite willing to do so, and immediately began a song that went this way:

> By weeping I can show
> How very much my heart is right to grieve,
> Betrayed, O Love, despite your promises.
>
> When first you found within my heart, O Love,
> A special place for her for whom I sigh
> In vain, deprived of hope,
> You made her seem so full of virtue then
> That I considered all those torments light
> With which you filled my breast
> Whose suffering still goes on
> Unchecked today. But I have gravely erred
> And realize it now in all my pain.
>
> You made me recognize her treachery
> And understand that she, my only hope,
> Had then abandoned me
> Just when I thought that I for sure enjoyed

Her favor and was held her servant true.
I could not see what pain
And suffering I would have,
When finding she'd embraced another's worth
Within her heart, and cast me out of it.

    And when I knew that I'd been spurned by her,
A sad lament welled up within my heart,
And there it lingers on.
That day and hour I curse and curse again
When first I saw that lovely face of hers,
With lofty beauty graced,
Radiant beyond compare.
And so, my faith, my ardor, and my hope,
My dying soul will go on cursing you.

    Just how bereft of comfort in my woe
I am, my Lord, you know, for calling you,
My voice is filled with grief.
I tell you that I burn with so much pain
The death I seek's the lesser martyrdom.
Come, Death, and take from me
My cruel, my wretched life,
And end as well my madness with your stroke;
Wherever I may go, I'll feel it less.

    No other course than death remains for me,
No other comfort's left for all my grief.
Then grant it to me now,
And with it put an end, Love, to my woes—
From such a wretched life release my heart.
Since wrongly I'm deprived
Of joy and solace, too,
Ah, do it, Lord; let my death give her joy
As did the new love whom you sent to her.

    O song of mine, I do not care if no
One ever learns to sing you, for they could
Not sing you as I do.

There's one sole task I wish to give to you:
May you find Love and unto him alone
Explain how little worth
My sad and bitter life
Still has for me, and for his honor's sake,
Beg him to steer me to a better port.

The words of this song quite clearly revealed Filostrato's state of mind as well as what was causing it, and perhaps the face of a certain lady among the dancers would have revealed even more if the darkness of the night, which had come upon them, had not concealed the blush that was spread across it. When his song was done, they sang many another until it was time to go to bed, at which point, in response to the Queen's command, they all retired to their own individual rooms.

Day 5, Introduction

※

*Here ends the Fourth Day of the Decameron and the Fifth begins, in which,
under the rule of Fiammetta, they speak of lovers who, after terrible accidents
or misfortunes, finally found happiness.*

The whole of the east was already white and the rays of the rising
sun were illuminating every part of our hemisphere when Fiammetta was roused from sleep by the sweet songs of the birds in the trees
that were warbling their merry greeting to the dawn. She got up, and
after summoning all the other ladies and the three young men, she set
off at a leisurely pace with her companions, descending to the fields
below, where she walked across the dew-covered grass of the broad
plain and amused herself by chatting with them about one thing and
another until the sun had risen well into the sky. When she felt the
heat from its rays was becoming too intense, however, she retraced her
steps, and on reaching the place where they were staying, she saw to it
that her companions were refreshed from their light exercise with the
finest of wines and a variety of sweets, after which they entertained
themselves in the delectable garden until it was time for dinner.

Every detail of their meal had been seen to by their extremely
resourceful steward, and in due course, after they had sung a few
*stampite** and a little song or two, at the Queen's bidding they happily
sat down to eat. They enjoyed their meal as they consumed it course
by course, and then, mindful of their usual routine, they did a number
of little dances, some accompanied by musical instruments and others
by songs. When they were finished, they were dismissed by the Queen

---

* A *stampita* was a rhythmic instrumental composition accompanying a poem.

388

until after their nap, at which point some of them went off to sleep, while others stayed in the lovely garden and amused themselves there.

Shortly after nones, however, at the Queen's command, they all reassembled as usual beside the fountain. Having taken her seat *pro tribunali,** Fiammetta looked over at Panfilo, smiled, and ordered him to begin telling the first of the day's stories with happy endings. Quite willing to address himself to this task, he began as follows.

* "In a position of honor," as a judge would have in a courtroom.

Day 5, Story 1

Cimone acquires wisdom through his love for his lady Efigenia, whom he then
abducts at sea. Imprisoned in Rhodes, he is freed by Lisimaco, with whom he
once again abducts both Efigenia and Cassandrea during their wedding. They
then flee with their ladies to Crete, where they get married, after which they
are summoned to come back to their homes with their wives.[1]

There are many tales I can think of telling you, delightful ladies,
which would make an appropriate beginning for so happy a day as
this is going to be. There is one, however, that is, to my mind, especially
appealing, for not only will it enable you to perceive the happy goal at
which all the storytelling we are now about to begin is aimed, but it
will allow you to see just how divine, how powerful, and how beneficial
the forces of Love can be, even though many people, who speak out of
ignorance, mistakenly condemn and revile them. All of this, if I am
not mistaken, you ladies should find quite agreeable, for I believe that
you are yourselves in love.

As we have read in the ancient chronicles of Cyprus, there was once
a very noble gentleman by the name of Aristippo living on that island
who was far richer in worldly possessions than any of his countrymen,
and who might have considered himself the happiest man alive if Fortune had not given him one particular source of grief. And this was
that among his children, he had a son, taller and much better looking
than all the other young men, who was, for all intents and purposes, an
imbecile. His case appeared hopeless, and neither his tutor's efforts, nor
his father's cajoling and whippings, nor the ingenious stratagems others
devised had been able to beat one jot of learning or good manners into
his head. On the contrary, they left him with a coarse, uncouth mode of

speech and manners more suitable to a wild beast than a man, so that although his real name was Galeso, he was contemptuously referred to as Cimone by everyone, because in their language that meant the same thing as "stupid ass" in ours.[2] His waste of a life was a matter of the gravest concern to his father, but since he had by now given up all hope for his son and did not wish to have the source of his grief constantly in front of him, he ordered him to go and live among the peasants on his country estate. Cimone was overjoyed to do so, for he found the customs and practices of rustics more to his liking than those of city dwellers.

And so, off to the country went Cimone, where he busied himself with whatever work needed doing on the estate. One day in the early afternoon, while he was walking from one farm to another with his staff slung over his shoulder, he chanced to enter a little wood, the most beautiful in the area, where, since it happened to be the month of May, everything was in full leaf. As he went along, seemingly guided there by Fortune, he came upon a clearing surrounded by extremely tall trees, in a corner of which there was a very lovely, cool fountain. Beside it, sleeping on the green grass, he saw an exquisitely beautiful young lady who was wearing a dress made of such sheer fabric that it concealed almost nothing of the white flesh beneath it. From the waist down, she was covered by a pure white quilt of equally transparent material, and at her feet, likewise fast asleep, lay two women and a man, who were her attendants.

On catching sight of her, Cimone stopped, leaned on his staff, and without saying a word, began staring at her with the greatest intensity, utterly rapt in admiration, as though he had never before seen a woman's form. And within his rustic breast, on which, despite a thousand lessons, no touch of civilized pleasure had been able to make the slightest impression, he felt the awakening of a sentiment that spoke to his gross, uncouth mind and informed it that she was the most beautiful thing any mortal had ever seen. Cimone then proceeded to examine her features, admiring her hair, which he thought was made of gold, her brow, her nose and mouth, her neck and arms, and especially her breasts, still not fully developed. Having been instantaneously transformed from a peasant into a connoisseur of beauty, he desired more than anything to see her eyes, which she kept closed under the weight of a profound slumber. More than once he was moved to wake her up in order to observe them, but as she seemed far more beautiful to him than any other woman he had ever seen before, he feared that she might be some goddess, and he had enough sense to know that divine things merit greater respect than those of this world. He therefore refrained, waiting for her to wake up of her own accord, and even though the wait seemed to go on forever, he was so taken by the unfamiliar pleasure he felt that he was incapable of tearing himself away.

It took a long while before the young lady, whose name was Efigenia, woke up. Her servants were still sleeping as she raised her head and opened her eyes, and when she caught sight of Cimone standing there before her, leaning on his staff, she was utterly astonished.

"Cimone," she said, "what are you going about looking for in these woods here at this hour?"

Cimone, who was known to practically everyone in the area by reason of his good looks and his coarse manners as well as his father's nobility and wealth, said nothing in reply to Efigenia's question. But seeing that her eyes were now open, he proceeded to gaze into them with great intensity, for it seemed to him that there was a sweetness emanating from them that filled him with a pleasure he had never experienced before.

When the young lady noticed how fixedly he was staring at her, she began to worry that his rusticity might move him to do something that could bring dishonor upon her. Consequently, after calling her women, she got to her feet and said: "God keep you, Cimone, farewell."[3]

"I'm going to come along with you," he replied.

Still afraid of him, the young lady refused his company, but she was unable to get rid of him until he had escorted her all the way back home. From there, he went to his father's house, where he announced that he would on no account ever go back to the country again. Although his father and his family were upset by this, they nevertheless allowed him to stay and waited to see what might have caused him to change his mind.

Now that Cimone's heart, which no amount of schooling had been able to penetrate, had been pierced by Love's arrow through the medium of Efigenia's beauty, he underwent a swift mental development, coming up with one new idea after another that simply astonished his father, his whole family, and everyone else who knew him. First, he asked his father if he could wear the same type of clothing and all the other kinds of ornaments as his brothers, and his father was only too happy to oblige. He then started spending time with worthy young men, observing the manners appropriate to gentlemen, especially gentlemen in love, and to everyone's absolute amazement, in a very short space of time not only did he acquire the rudiments of learning, but he was more than able to hold his own with students of philosophy. The next thing he did—and this, too, was the result of the love he bore for Efigenia—was to transform his coarse, rustic mode of speech into one that was more seemly and civilized, while also becoming an accomplished singer and musician, and he soon distinguished himself in horsemanship and the martial arts, whether on sea or land, by means of his great skill and daring. In brief, without going into all the particulars of his many virtues, it took less than four years from the day he had first fallen in love for him to turn into the most refined, well-mannered, multitalented young man on the island of Cyprus.

What then, charming ladies, shall we say about Cimone? Surely, nothing except that the lofty virtues instilled by Heaven in his valiant spirit had been tied tightly together and locked away by envious Fortune in a tiny little corner of his heart, and that Love, who is by far the mightier of the two, had burst those bonds and torn them asunder. As the awakener of sleeping talents, Love had taken Cimone's virtues out of the cruel darkness in which they lay concealed, and with his power he had forced them into the light, clearly showing from what sort of place he will extract those spirits who are subject to his rule and where he will lead them with his radiant beams.

Although with his passion for Efigenia Cimone went to extremes in some respects, as young men in love often do, nevertheless Aristippo thought of how Love had transformed him from a muttonhead into a man and did not merely bear his extravagances with patience, but

encouraged him to pursue Love and all of its pleasures. Cimone, however, who refused to be called Galeso because he remembered how
Efigenia had used that name when she spoke to him, was determined
to bring his desires to an honorable conclusion and tried on many
occasions to persuade Cipseo, Efigenia's father, to allow him to marry
her. Every time, however, Cipseo replied that he had promised her to
Pasimunda, a young nobleman from Rhodes, and he had no intention
of going back on his word.

When the time arrived for Efigenia's arranged marriage to take
place, and her husband had sent to fetch her, Cimone said to himself:
"O Efigenia, now is the time for me to show you just how much I love
you. Because of you I've become a man, and if I can make you mine,
then I have no doubt I will achieve a glory greater than that of any god.
What's certain is that I'll have you, or else I'll die."

Thus resolved, he quietly went about recruiting a number of young
noblemen who were friends of his and had a ship fitted out in secret
with everything necessary for a naval battle. He then put out to sea
where he lay in wait for the vessel that was supposed to convey Efigenia
to her husband in Rhodes.

After Pasimunda's friends had been lavishly entertained by her
father and had taken her on board, they aimed their prow in the direction of Rhodes and departed. Ever on the alert, Cimone overtook them
the next day, and from up on the bow of his ship, he shouted in a loud
voice to the sailors over on Efigenia's: "Strike your sails and heave to,
or prepare to be captured and sunk."

Since Cimone's opponents had brought weapons up on deck and
were preparing to defend themselves, he followed up his words by seizing a grappling iron, which he threw onto the poop deck of their vessel
as it was rapidly pulling away, and thus secured it tightly to the prow
of his own. Spurred on by Love, he did not wait for anyone to follow
him, but leaped aboard the Rhodians' ship as if he took no account of
any opposition they might offer. Then, like a ferocious lion, he fell upon
his enemies in an amazing display of force, and sword in hand, struck
them down one after the other, slaughtering them like so many sheep.

Seeing this, all the Rhodians threw down their weapons, and, practically with one voice, declared themselves his prisoners.

Cimone then addressed them. "Young men," he said, "it was not any
desire for plunder, or any hatred I feel toward you, that made me leave
Cyprus and subject you to an armed assault here on the high seas. My
only motive was to acquire something that I value very highly, and that
you can easily, and peacefully, surrender to me. And that something is
Efigenia, whom I love more than anything in the world. Since I could
not obtain her from her father by friendly and pacific means, Love has
compelled me to take her from you as your enemy and by force of arms.
And now I intend to be for her what your Pasimunda was to have been.
So, give her to me, and may God's grace go with you."

Yielding to force more than acting out of generosity, the young men
handed the weeping Efigenia over to Cimone. "Noble lady," he said,
seeing her in tears, "don't be upset. I am your own Cimone, and my
long love for you has given me a much greater right to have you than
anything Pasimunda has because of the pledge that was made to him."

Having watched her taken aboard his ship, Cimone returned to his
comrades himself, and without touching anything else that belonged
to the Rhodians, he allowed them to depart. The acquisition of so dear
a prize made him the happiest man alive, and after spending quite a
while consoling his tearful lady, he and his comrades decided not to
return to Cyprus for the time being. Instead, they all agreed together
that they would turn the prow of their ship in the direction of Crete,
where they believed they would be safe with Efigenia, for almost all
of them, and especially Cimone, had both long-established and more
recent family ties there as well as a large number of friends.

But Fortune is fickle, and although she was quite happy to let Cimone
acquire the lady, all of a sudden she transformed the young lover's
incalculable joy into sadness and bitter weeping. Scarcely four hours
had passed since he had parted company with the Rhodians when, as
night approached, from which Cimone was expecting more pleasure
than he had ever experienced before, an extremely violent storm arose,
filling the sky with clouds and sweeping the sea with furious winds. It

was impossible for those on board to see what they were doing or where they were going or even how they could manage to stay on their feet long enough to carry out any of their duties on the ship.

There is no need to ask how much this turn of events upset Cimone. It seemed as if the gods had granted his desire, but only to make him feel all the more distressed at the prospect of his death, which before, without Efigenia, would have mattered very little to him. Although his comrades were equally downcast, the most disconsolate of all was Efigenia, who was weeping violently and shuddering with fear every time they were battered by the waves. Between her tears she bitterly cursed Cimone's love and condemned his rash behavior, proclaiming that the furious storm had arisen because his wish to marry her was contrary to the will of the gods, and that they were determined not merely to prevent him from deriving any joy from his presumptuous desire, but to make him witness her death before coming to a miserable end himself.

The laments went on and on, including some that were even more vehement, until, with the wind growing ever stronger, the sailors not knowing what to do, and no one having the slightest idea of their location and how they should direct their course, they finally arrived off the coast of Rhodes. Failing to recognize the island, they did everything they could possibly do to reach land and thus save their lives.

Fortune favored their efforts and led them into a little bay that the Rhodians who had been released by Cimone had entered with their own vessel just a little while before. Dawn was breaking, and as the sky grew lighter, not only did they realize that they were at the island of Rhodes, but they saw they were no more than a bow shot away from the ship they had parted from the previous day. Distressed beyond measure by this discovery, and fearing the very fate that did in fact befall him, Cimone ordered his crew to make every effort to get out of there and let Fortune carry them wherever she wished, since they could not be in a worse place than the one they were in. Although they strove with might and main to escape, it was all to no avail, for a violent gale was blowing against them with such force that not only did it prevent them from getting out of the little bay, but it drove them relentlessly, against their will, toward the shore.

The moment they reached it, they were recognized by the Rhodian sailors who had by now disembarked from their ship. One of them immediately ran off to find the young noblemen from Rhodes, who had gone earlier to a nearby village, and told them that, as luck would have it, the ship carrying Cimone and Efigenia had, like their own, arrived in the little bay. Overjoyed to hear this news, the young Rhodians assembled a large number of the villagers and were back down at the shore in no time. In the meantime, although Cimone and his men had left their ship and were intent upon fleeing into some neighboring woods, they were all seized, together with Efigenia, and brought back to the village. From there, Cimone and his entire crew were taken by Lisimaco, the chief magistrate of the island for that year, who had come up from the city, and they were led away to prison under the escort of a very large company of men-at-arms, all of which had been arranged by Pasimunda who had gone and lodged a complaint with the Senate of Rhodes as soon as he had heard the news.

And so it came about that the wretched Cimone lost his beloved Efigenia only a little while after winning her, without ever getting anything more than a kiss or two out of her. As for Efigenia, she was welcomed by numerous Rhodian noblewomen who helped her recover from the painful experience of being abducted as well as from the fatigue she had endured during the storm. And with them she remained until the day appointed for her wedding.

Pasimunda did everything in his power to have Cimone and his comrades executed, and although their lives were spared because they had set the young gentlemen from Rhodes free the day before, they were still condemned to life in prison. And there, it is easy to believe, they led a wretched existence, with little hope of ever knowing happiness again.

While Pasimunda was doing all he could to hasten the preparations for his upcoming marriage, Fortune, as if repenting of the sudden blow she had dealt Cimone, came up with a novel way to save him. Pasimunda had a brother named Ormisda, a younger but no less worthy man, who had long sought the hand of a beautiful young noblewoman from the city called Cassandrea, with whom Lisimaco was also very deeply in love. The wedding had been postponed many times, however, thanks to a variety of unexpected events.

Seeing that he was now about to have an extremely lavish banquet in order to celebrate his own wedding, Pasimunda thought it would be an excellent idea to arrange for Ormisda to get married as well on the same occasion, thus allowing him to avoid a repetition of the festivities and all the expenses involved. Consequently, he reopened negotiations with Cassandrea's family and came to an understanding with them, after which all the parties agreed that Ormisda should marry Cassandrea on the same day that Pasimunda married Efigenia.

When Lisimaco heard about this plan, he was desperately unhappy, because he saw himself deprived of the hope he had preserved, namely, that if Ormisda did not marry Cassandrea, he would surely be able to have her himself. He was wise enough, however, to keep his suffering hidden, and began thinking of ways to prevent the wedding, ultimately concluding that the only possible solution was to abduct her. This course of action seemed quite feasible to him because of the office he held, although he would have considered it a far less dishonorable thing to do if he were not the chief magistrate. But finally, after a great deal of deliberation, honor gave way to love, and he resolved that, come what may, he would carry off Cassandrea. Moreover, as he was thinking about the companions he needed to do this and about the strategy he would adopt, he remembered that he had imprisoned Cimone, together with his men, and it occurred to him that for an undertaking like this one, he could not find a better or more loyal confederate.

And so, that night, he had Cimone secretly brought to his chamber and proceeded to speak with him in this fashion:

"Cimone, not only are the gods extraordinarily free and generous in bestowing their gifts on men, but they are also extremely wise when they put men's virtues to the test. And those whom they find to be firm and constant in all circumstances, since they are the most valiant, are considered worthy of receiving the greatest rewards. The gods wanted a surer proof of your mettle than what you could display while confined to the house owned by your father, whom I know to be immensely rich. And so, having first transformed you, as I've been told, from a senseless beast into a man through the bittersweet stimulus of Love, now they wish to see whether, after the harsh misfortune you've suffered and the pain of your present imprisonment, your spirit has been changed from what it was when you were made happy for a brief time with the spoils you'd won. So, if it is indeed what it once was, they are preparing to bestow a boon on you that will make you even happier than anything they gave you before. And I intend to explain what it is in order to help you recover your former strength and regain your courage.

"Pasimunda, who rejoices over your misfortune and has been zealously urging that you be put to death, is doing everything he can to advance the date for the celebration of his marriage to your Efigenia, so that he may enjoy the prize that Fortune was originally happy to grant you and then suddenly snatched away again in anger. If you are as much in love as I think you are, then I know from my own experience just how much pain this would cause you, for his brother Ormisda is preparing to do a similar wrong to me on the very same day by marrying Cassandrea, whom I love more than anything else in the world. Nor do I see how we can prevent Fortune from dealing us such a painful blow except to take the only way she has left open for us, and that is to rely on our stout hearts and our strong right hands, with which we must seize our swords and force open a path to our ladies, so that you may abduct yours for the second time, and I may carry off mine for the first. Consequently, if you value the recovery of—I won't say your freedom, because I believe that would mean little to you without your lady—but the recovery of your lady herself, then the gods have placed her within your grasp, provided you are willing to second me in my enterprise."

These words completely restored any spirits Cimone had lost, and with scarcely a moment's hesitation, he replied: "Lisimaco, if the reward you speak of really does come my way, you cannot have a hardier or more trustworthy comrade than I will be in such an undertaking. Therefore, impose on me whatever task you think I should perform, and you'll marvel at the vigor I'll display in carrying it out."

"Two days from now," Lisimaco replied, "the new brides will go to their husbands' homes for the very first time. As evening is approaching, we'll enter the house ourselves, fully armed, you with your comrades, and I with those of mine whom I trust the most. Then we'll seize the ladies right in the midst of all the guests and carry them off to a ship I've had fitted out in secret, killing anyone who should dare to stand in our way." Cimone liked the plan and remained quietly in prison, waiting for the appointed time.

When the wedding day arrived, it was celebrated with so much pomp and splendor that every corner of the house belonging to the two brothers resounded with their joyous revelry. Having completed all his preparations, Lisimaco delivered a lengthy harangue to Cimone and his comrades, as well as his own friends, in order to fire them up with enthusiasm for his plan. Then, when the time seemed right, he divided the men, all of whom came carrying arms concealed beneath their clothing, into three groups. One of the three he prudently sent to the port so that no one could prevent them from getting on the ship when it was time to leave. Arriving at Pasimunda's house with the other two, he left one group posted at the main entrance to prevent anyone inside from closing it behind them or barring their retreat, and with the rest, including Cimone, he climbed the stairs. In the hall the new brides were already seated at their allotted places with a large number of other ladies and were preparing to dine, when Pasimunda's company arrived and forced their way in. Hurling the tables to the floor, each man seized his lady, handed her over to his comrades, and ordered them to carry the two women off at once to the waiting ship.

The new brides began crying and screaming, as did the other women and the servants, and in an instant the entire place was in an uproar, filled with the sound of their wailing. But Cimone, Lisimaco, and their comrades drew out their swords, and as everyone stood aside to let them pass, they made their way over to the stairs unopposed. They were just in the process of descending, when they were met by Pasimunda, who had been attracted by all the noise and came carrying a large staff in his hand, but Cimone gave him such a vigorous blow on the head that a good half of it was sliced off and he fell dead at Cimone's feet. Rushing up to his brother's assistance, the wretched Ormisda was likewise killed by Cimone with a single blow, while a handful of others who ventured to approach were driven back, wounded, by his followers and by those of Lisimaco.

Leaving the house full of blood and noise, tears and sorrow, they made their way unimpeded to the ship, maintaining a tight formation as they carried their booty along with them. After getting the ladies on board, Cimone, Lisimaco, and their comrades followed, and then, just as the shore was filling up with armed men who were coming to rescue the ladies, they put their oars into the water and cheerfully made their escape.

When they arrived in Crete, they were given an ecstatic welcome by their many friends and relations, and after they had married their ladies and held a grand wedding feast, they happily enjoyed the spoils they had taken.

In Cyprus and Rhodes their deeds gave rise to a great deal of clamor and commotion that continued unabated for quite some time. Finally, however, their friends and relations, interceding for them on the two islands, found a way for Cimone, after a period of exile, to make a joyful return to Cyprus with Efigenia and for Lisimaco, similarly, to go back to Rhodes with Cassandrea. And each of them lived a good long life, happy and contented with his lady in the country of his birth.

Day 5, Story 2

Gostanza is in love with Martuccio Gomito, but when she hears that he has died, in her despair she sets off alone in a boat, which is carried by the wind to Susa. Upon finding him alive in Tunis, she reveals herself to him, and he, who was a great favorite of the King's because of the advice he had given him, marries her and then, having become a rich man, returns with her to Lipari.[1]

Seeing that Panfilo's story had come to an end, the Queen gave it high praise, after which she ordered Emilia to follow his lead and tell another one. Emilia thus began:

It is only right for people to rejoice when they see an undertaking obtain rewards appropriate to the emotions that inspired it, and since love deserves to be crowned with happiness in the long run, rather than with misery, it gives me much greater pleasure to obey the Queen and speak on the present topic than it did yesterday when I obeyed the King and spoke on the one he chose.

You must know then, gentle ladies, that there is a little island near Sicily called Lipari, where, not so very long ago, there lived a very beautiful girl named Gostanza who was born into one of its noblest families. There was also a young man living on that island, a certain Martuccio Gomito, who was a skilled craftsman as well as being both well mannered and exceptionally handsome.[2] Now, Martuccio fell in love with Gostanza, and she likewise burned for him, so much so that she felt miserable whenever he was out of her sight. Wishing to make her his wife, Martuccio asked her father for her hand, but was told he was too poor to have her.

Indignant at seeing his offer rejected on the grounds of his poverty, Martuccio fitted out a little ship with certain friends and relations of

his, and swore never to return to Lipari until he was rich. After leaving
the island, he proceeded to become a pirate and sailed up and down
the Barbary coast, robbing anyone whose forces were weaker than his
own. In this endeavor Fortune was quite favorably disposed to him,
had he only known how to place some sort of limit on his successes.
Not satisfied, however, with having grown extremely wealthy in just a
short time, Martuccio and his companions went on seeking to become
even wealthier, when they chanced to run into a Saracen fleet, by which,
after a lengthy defense, they were captured and plundered. The vast
majority of the crew were then thrown into the sea, their ship sunk,
and Martuccio himself taken to Tunis where he was held in prison for
a long time under miserable conditions.

The news was brought back to Lipari, not just by one or two, but
by many different people, that every last man on board the little ship
with Martuccio had drowned. Upon hearing that her beloved and his
companions were dead, Gostanza, whose grief over his departure had
known no bounds, wept and wept, until she finally resolved to take
her own life. Since she did not have the courage to lay violent hands
on herself, she came up with a novel but seemingly infallible way to
procure the death she desired. Slipping secretly out of her father's
house one night, she went down to the port, where by chance she
found a little fishing boat lying some distance away from the other
ships. The owners had just gone ashore, and Gostanza discovered that
the boat was still equipped with its mast as well as its sails and oars.
Since she had some knowledge of the rudiments of seamanship, as all
the women living on the island generally do, she quickly climbed on
board, rowed a little way out to sea, and raised the sail, after which
she threw the oars and the rudder overboard, abandoning herself to
the mercy of the wind. She was convinced that one of two things was
bound to happen: either the boat, having neither ballast nor steers-
man, would capsize because of the wind, or it would be driven onto
the rocks somewhere and smashed to pieces. And in both cases she
would necessarily wind up drowning, for she would not be able to save
herself even if she wanted to. Then, having wrapped a cloak around
her head, she lay down, weeping, in the bottom of the boat.

Everything turned out differently, however, than she had imagined. For the wind blew so gently from the north that there was hardly a wave, the boat maintained an even keel, and the next day around vespers it brought her ashore near a city called Susa, a good hundred miles beyond Tunis.³ The girl was not aware that she was now more on land than at sea, for nothing had occurred to make her raise her head from the position in which it was lying, nor did she have any intention of doing so, no matter what happened.

By chance, when the boat ran aground on the shore, there was a poor woman down by the seaside gathering up the nets that had been left in the sun by the fishermen she worked for. Seeing the boat, she wondered how anyone could have allowed it to run up onto the beach under full sail, and thinking that some fishermen were sleeping on board, she went over to it and discovered that the only person there was this young lady, fast asleep. By calling to her repeatedly, she finally got her to wake up, and since she could see from her clothing that the girl was a Christian, she asked her in Italian how she had managed to get there, and in that boat, all by herself. When the girl heard the woman speaking her language, she wondered whether a shift in the wind had taken her back to Lipari. She got to her feet at once and looked all around her, and seeing that she was on land, but in unfamiliar territory, she asked the good woman where she was.

"My daughter," the woman replied, "you're in Barbary, not far from Susa."

When she heard these words, the girl, dismayed that God had refused to allow her to die, began to fear for her honor, but since she had no idea what to do, she simply sat down by the keel of her boat and began to cry. Upon seeing this, the good woman took pity on her and got her, after a great deal of begging and pleading, to accompany her to her little hut where she coaxed her into explaining how she had come to be there. Realizing that the girl had to be hungry, the woman set some dry bread, water, and a few fish before her, and eventually persuaded her to eat a little.

Gostanza then asked her who she was and how she spoke Italian like that, to which the woman replied that she came from Trapani, her

name was Carapresa, and she worked for certain fishermen who were
Christians.* Although the girl was generally feeling very sad, when she
heard the woman say "Carapresa," she took it, without knowing why,
as a good omen. Indeed, for reasons she could not comprehend she
began to feel hopeful and was no longer quite so intent on dying. Without revealing who she was or where she had come from, she earnestly
begged the good woman to have pity on her youth for the love of God
and to advise her as to what she could do in order to protect her honor.

Responding to the girl's request like the good woman she was, Carapresa left her in the hut while she quickly gathered up her nets, but the
moment she returned, she wrapped the girl up in her own cloak from
top to bottom, and then took her with her to Susa. When they arrived
in the city, she said: "Gostanza, I'm going to take you to the home of
a very nice, elderly Saracen lady, who frequently employs me to do
various chores for her. She's an extremely compassionate person, and
since I'm going to recommend you to her as warmly as I can, I feel quite
certain that she'll be glad to take you in and treat you like a daughter.
For your part, while you stay with her, you must serve her to the best
of your ability so as to win and retain her favor until such time as God
sends you better luck."

Carapresa was as good as her word, and when the lady, who was
indeed well on in years, had heard Gostanza's story, she looked the
girl in the face and started weeping. Then, taking her by the hand, she
kissed her on the forehead and led her into her house, where she lived
with several other women, no men being allowed to reside on the premises. The women did various types of work with their hands, producing
articles of all kinds from silk and palm leaves and leather, and within
a few days, having learned how to make some of those things herself,
the girl began working right there alongside them. It was marvelous to
see with what kindness and affection the lady and the other women
treated her, and thanks to their instruction, in a relatively short space
of time, Gostanza also managed to learn their language.

*Carapresa is made up of two words: *cara*, which means "dear," and *presa*, which
means "taken" or "acquired." Thus, the name means something like "dear (or precious)
acquisition," which is why Gostanza will take it as a good omen in the next sentence.

Now, while the girl was living in Susa, having long since been mourned by her family, who considered her dead and gone forever, it just so happened that the King of Tunis, whose name was Meriabdela, was threatened by a young man of considerable power, the scion of an important family in Granada.[4] Having decided that the Kingdom of Tunis belonged to him, he had assembled a vast army and was marching on the King, intent upon driving him from his realm.

News of this development reached the ears of Martuccio Gomito where he lay in prison, and since he knew the language of Barbary quite well, when he heard that the King of Tunis was making enormous efforts to prepare his defenses, he spoke to one of the men who were guarding him and his companions. "If I might speak with the King," he said, "I feel confident I can give him the advice he needs to win this war of his."

The guard repeated these words to his superior, who immediately relayed them to the King. In response, the King ordered them to bring Martuccio to him and asked him what his advice might be.

"My lord," he replied, "I used to visit this country of yours in the past, and if I've correctly observed the tactics you employ in your battles, it seems to me that you rely on your archers more than anything else to do the fighting. Consequently, if you can find a way to deprive your adversaries of arrows, while your own troops have more than enough, I know you'd win the battle."

"If this could be done," said the King, "I have no doubt but that I'd be victorious."

"My lord," replied Martuccio, "if you so desire, it certainly can be done. Listen, and I'll tell you how. You must equip your archers' bows with much finer strings than those that are normally used, and then have arrows made with notches that will only fit these finer strings. All of this must be done in secrecy so that your enemy doesn't get wind of your plan, because otherwise, he'll find a way to get around it. Now, here's the reason why I'm making this recommendation. As you know, when your enemy's archers have used up all their arrows, and ours have shot theirs, for the battle to continue, they'll have to collect all the arrows your troops have shot, just as ours will have to collect theirs. But the enemy won't be able to use what your men shot at them because their bowstrings will be too thick to fit into the narrow notches of your arrows, whereas just the opposite will happen for us, since our fine strings will easily fit into the wide notches of theirs. Thus, your troops will have a plentiful supply of arrows, and the others won't have any."

A wise ruler, the King approved of Martuccio's plan, and by following it to the letter, he managed to win his war. As a result, Martuccio became one of the King's greatest favorites, and consequently acquired wealth and a position of considerable importance.

News of these events spread throughout the country, and when it reached Gostanza's ears that Martuccio Gomito, whom she had long believed dead, was actually alive, the love she felt for him, which had cooled off in her heart, instantly flared up again, burning with a hotter flame than ever and bringing all her dead hopes back to life. She therefore gave the good woman with whom she was staying a full account of all the events she had been through, and then told her that she wanted to go to Tunis so that she might feast her eyes with looking on that which she longed to see because of the report she had heard with her own ears. The lady approved her request with enthusiasm, and acting as if she were Gostanza's mother, embarked with her for Tunis, where the two of them were honorably received in the home of one of the lady's relatives. She then sent Carapresa, who had accompanied them there, to find out what she could about Martuccio. When she reported back that he was alive and occupied a high place in the kingdom, the gentlewoman decided that she would be the one to have the pleasure of telling Martuccio about the arrival of his Gostanza. And so, one day she went around to where he was living and said to him: "Martuccio, a servant of yours from Lipari has turned up in my house and would like to speak with you there in private. And since he didn't want me to entrust this to anyone else, I've come here to tell you about it myself." Martuccio thanked her and followed her back to her house.

When the girl saw him, she almost died of happiness. Overcome by her emotions, she ran right up to him, flung her arms about his neck, and embraced him. Then, incapable of uttering a word, she gently began to weep, both because of her sorrowful memories of the misfortunes she had been through and because of all the joy she felt in the present moment.

When Martuccio recognized who it was, for a while he was struck dumb with amazement and did not make a move. But at last he heaved a sigh and said, "O Gostanza, are you really alive? I was told a good long time ago that you had vanished, and since then, no one at home has heard anything about you." Then, having managed to say this much, he, too, shed gentle tears as he held her in his arms and kissed her.

Gostanza told him about everything that had happened to her and about the honorable treatment she had received from the gentlewoman with whom she had been staying. Martuccio spent a long time talking with her, after which he went to the King, his master, and gave him a full account both of his own ups and downs and of those the girl had endured, adding that he intended, with the King's permission, to marry her in accordance with the laws of our religion.

Truly amazed by what he heard, the King summoned the girl, and when he discovered that everything was exactly the way Martuccio had described it, he said to her, "Well, then, you've certainly earned the right to have him as your husband." The King proceeded to send for the most opulent and noble of gifts, some of which he bestowed on her, and some on Martuccio. He then gave the couple permission to arrange their affairs between them in whatever way they pleased.

After lavishly entertaining the gentlewoman with whom Gostanza had been staying, not only did Martuccio thank her for what she had done to assist the girl, but he gave her presents suitable for a person of her station. Then, while Gostanza shed many a tear, he said good-bye to the lady and departed. Finally, with the King's leave, the couple embarked on a small boat, taking Carapresa with them, and thanks to a favorable breeze, they quickly returned to Lipari, where the rejoicing was so great that no words could ever describe it.

There, Martuccio and Gostanza were married and celebrated their nuptials with great pomp and splendor, after which, for many a day, the two of them enjoyed the love they bore one another in peace and tranquility.

Day 5, Story 3

Fleeing with Agnolella, Pietro Boccamazza runs into a gang of thieves, and while the girl escapes through a forest and is led to a castle, Pietro is captured by them. He manages to get out of their clutches, however, and after one or two more adventures, he happens upon the castle where Agnolella is staying, gets married to her, and returns with her to Rome.[1]

There was no one in the company who did not praise Emilia's story, and when the Queen saw that it was finished, she turned to Elissa and told her to continue. Eager to obey, Elissa began:

The tale that presents itself to me, charming ladies, concerns a terrible night spent by two somewhat indiscreet young people, but since it was succeeded by many days of happiness, it fits our topic, and I should like to tell you about it.

Not long ago, in Rome—once the head of the world, but now its tail—there lived a young man named Pietro Boccamazza, a member of an illustrious Roman family, who fell in love with a very beautiful, charming girl named Agnolella, the daughter of a certain Gigliuozzo Saullo, who, though a plebeian, was held in high repute by his fellow citizens.[2] Having fallen for the girl, Pietro was so skillful in courting her that she soon came to love him as much as he did her. Spurred on by his burning passion, and no longer willing to endure the harsh pain of his desire for her, he asked for her hand in marriage. But when his relations found out about it, they all came to him and gave him a good scolding for what he wanted to do, at the same time letting Gigliuozzo Saullo know that he should on no account take what Pietro said seriously, because if he did, they would never acknowledge him as a friend or a kinsman.

When Pietro saw that the only way he could think of to obtain what he desired was blocked, he was ready to die of grief. If he could have just obtained Gigliuozzo's consent, he would have married the girl, even if it displeased every last one of his relations. But in any case, he made up his mind that he would do whatever was necessary to achieve his goal, provided the girl was willing, and when he learned through a third party that she was, he got her to agree to elope from Rome with him.

Having made all the preparations, Pietro arose very early one morning, saddled up a pair of horses, and the two of them took off down the road toward Anagni, where Pietro had certain friends of his whom he trusted implicitly.[3] Since they were afraid of being pursued, they had no time to stop and get married, so they simply talked together about their love for one another, exchanging the occasional kiss as they went riding along.

Now, Pietro did not know the route very well, and when they were about eight miles away from Rome, they happened to take a road that went off to the left when they should have gone to the right. They had only ridden a little more than two miles when they saw a small castle from which, the moment they were sighted, about a dozen soldiers sallied forth. Just as they were about to intercept the couple, the girl spotted them and yelled, "Pietro, let's get out of here, we're being attacked!" To the best of her ability, she turned her nag's head in the direction of a vast forest nearby, grabbed onto the saddle horn, and dug her spurs into his flanks. When the animal felt her jabbing him, he took off at a gallop and carried her into the woods.

Pietro, who had been riding along looking at Agnolella's face more than the road, was not as quick as she had been to notice the approaching soldiers, and so, he was still looking around to see where they were coming from and was unable to locate them, when he was overtaken, captured, and forced to get down off his horse. They asked him who he was, and as soon as he told them, they began conferring among themselves.

"This guy's one of the friends of the Orsini," they said. "What better way to spite our enemies than to take his clothes and this nag of his, and to string him up on one of these oaks?"[4]

They all agreed on this plan and ordered Pietro to take his clothes off. Well aware of what was in store for him, he began undressing, when all of a sudden, a good twenty-five soldiers, who had been waiting in ambush, fell upon them with shouts of "Kill them! Kill them!" Taken by surprise, Pietro's captors abandoned him and turned to defend themselves, but seeing that they were greatly outnumbered, they took to their heels, with their attackers in hot pursuit. When Pietro saw this, he quickly picked up his things, jumped on his horse, and fled as fast as he could down the road he had seen the girl taking.

Upon reaching the woods, however, and finding no sign there of a road or a path, or even a horse's hoofprints, let alone the girl, Pietro was the saddest man alive, and as soon as he thought he was safely beyond the reach of his captors and their assailants, he began weeping. He continued to wander through the woods, calling her name here, there, and everywhere, but no one answered him, and since he did not dare to turn back, he rode on without having the slightest idea of where he was going. What is more, he was afraid, both for his own sake and for that of his beloved, of the wild animals that generally lurk in the forest, and at every moment he imagined some bear or wolf seizing her and ripping open her throat.

Thus the unfortunate Pietro spent the entire day meandering through the forest, shouting and calling her name, sometimes going backward just when he thought he was going forward, until at last, what with his yelling and his weeping and his fear and his lack of food, he was so exhausted that he could go no farther. Seeing that night had fallen, and not knowing what else to do, he found a large oak, got off his nag, and tied him to the tree. Then he climbed up into the branches to avoid being devoured by wild animals during the night. Afraid of falling, Pietro did not dare to let himself go to sleep, although that would have been impossible in any case because of all his grief and anxiety about Agnolella. And so, after the moon rose a little later in the cloudless sky, he remained awake, sighing and weeping and cursing his misfortune.

Meanwhile, the girl, who, as we said before, had fled with no idea where she was going, simply allowed her horse to carry her wherever he wanted until she had gone so far into the forest that she could no longer see the spot where she had entered it. Thus, she spent the entire day just as Pietro had done, wandering round and round that wilderness, now pausing and now moving on, weeping and calling his name and bemoaning her misfortune. Finally, as evening was falling and Pietro had still not come, she stumbled upon a little path that her horse turned into and began to follow, until after riding more than two miles, she caught sight of a cottage up ahead of her in the distance. She made her way to it as quickly as she could, and there she found a good man, well along in years, with a wife no younger than he was.

When they saw she was by herself, they said: "Oh, child, where are you going in these parts, all alone, at this hour?" Weeping, the girl replied that she had lost her escort in the woods, and asked them how far it was to Anagni.

"My child," said the good man, "this isn't the road to Anagni. It's more than twelve miles away from here."

"Then how far is it to the nearest house where I could find lodging?" asked the girl.

"There's nothing around here that's close enough for you to reach before nightfall," he answered.

"Since I have nowhere else to go," said the girl, "would you, for the love of God, be so kind as to let me stay here tonight?"

"Young lady," replied the good man, "we would be delighted to have you stay the night with us, but all the same, we must warn you that these parts are overrun by gangs of bandits, some of whom are allied to one another, while others are mortal foes, and all of them go about day and night doing us injuries and causing a great deal of damage. If we were unlucky enough to have one of those gangs come here while you're staying with us, and they were to see how young and beautiful you are, they might harm you and dishonor you, and there'd be no way for us to help you. We wanted to tell you this so that if something like that should happen, you wouldn't blame us for it."

The old man's words terrified her, but seeing how late the hour was, Agnolella said: "God willing, He will protect all of us from such harm, but even if such a thing should happen to me, it's much better to be mistreated by men than torn to pieces by wild beasts in the forest."

Having said this, she got off her horse and went into the poor man's house. There she supped with them on what little food they had, after which, fully clothed, she threw herself down on their little bed where she lay with them, sighing and weeping all night long over both her own misfortunes and Pietro's, to whom she could only suppose that the very worst must have happened.

Just a little before matins, she heard a loud sound of people walking around, which led her to get up and make her way into a large yard at the rear of the cottage. On one of its sides, she spied a big pile of hay and went over to hide in it, thinking that if those people were to come in, this would make it more difficult for them to find her. Scarcely had she finished concealing herself than the men, a large gang of bandits, were at the door of the cottage. After forcing the old people to open it, they came inside, where they discovered the girl's horse still fully saddled and demanded to know who was there.

Seeing no sign of the girl, the good man answered: "There's nobody here except us. But this nag, which must have run away from somebody, showed up here yesterday evening, and we brought him into the house to keep the wolves from devouring him."

"In that case, since he doesn't belong to anyone else," said the leader of the gang, "he'll do quite well for us."

Then the men spread out all over the cottage, some of them finding their way into the yard, where they put down their lances and wooden shields. One of them, having nothing better to do, happened to toss his lance into the hay where it came within an inch of killing the girl who was hiding there and who almost gave herself away when the head of the lance went right by her left breast, so close to her body that it tore her clothing. Fearing that she had been wounded, she was at the point of screaming out loud, when she remembered where she was, and getting a grip on herself, she kept quiet.

The gang cooked kid as well as some other meat they had with them, and after having eaten and had something to drink, they took the girl's horse with them and went about their business, some going one way, some another. Once they were fairly far away, the first thing the good man did was to ask his wife: "Whatever happened to that young lady of ours who showed up here yesterday evening? I haven't seen her since we got out of bed." The good woman replied that she did not know and went off to look for her.

When the girl realized that the gang had gone, she climbed out from under the hay. The old man was greatly relieved to see that she had not fallen into their hands, and since it was then getting light, he said to her: "Now that day is breaking, we'll accompany you, if you like, to a castle just five miles from here where you'll be safe. But you're going to have to go there on foot, because that gang of bandits who just left here took your horse with them." Resigning herself to the loss, the girl asked them in God's name to lead her to the castle, for which they set out at once, reaching it halfway between prime and tierce.

The castle belonged to a member of the Orsini family named Liello di Campo di Fiore, whose wife, a very good and pious woman, just happened to be staying there at the time.[5] On seeing Agnolella, she recognized the girl right away and gave her a hearty welcome, after which she insisted on knowing precisely how she came to be there. In response, the girl told her the entire story. The lady, who also knew Pietro because he was a friend of her husband's, was distressed to learn what had happened, and when she was told where Pietro had been captured, she was convinced he must have been killed. So she said to the girl: "Since you don't know what's happened to Pietro, you must stay here with me until such time as it's possible for me to send you safely back to Rome."

Meanwhile, Pietro had been sitting in the oak tree, as sad as sad could be, and at just about the time he would normally have fallen asleep, he saw a good twenty wolves approaching. When they caught sight of the horse, they came up on him from all sides, but he heard them coming, and yanking his neck, he snapped his reins and made an attempt to flee. Since they had him surrounded, he could not get away, and although he defended himself for quite some time with his teeth and hooves, they finally brought him down, ripped out his throat, and quickly gutted him. Then, they all gorged themselves on him until they had picked him clean, after which they took off, leaving nothing but his bones behind. Pietro was utterly dismayed by what he saw, for to him the horse had been a companion and a prop in his troubles, and now he began to think that he would never succeed in getting out of the woods.

He continued to keep a lookout in every direction, however, and a little before dawn, when he was dying from the cold up there in the oak, he caught sight of a huge fire perhaps a mile from where he was sitting. Consequently, as soon as it was completely light out, he climbed down from the tree, even though he felt pretty apprehensive as he did so, and set off in that direction. When he reached the spot, he saw a band of shepherds who were sitting around the fire, eating and making merry. The shepherds took pity on him and invited him to join them.

Once Pietro had eaten and warmed himself, he gave them an account of his misadventures and how he had come there all by himself, after which he asked them if there was a village or a castle in those parts to which he might go. The shepherds said that about three miles away there was a castle belonging to Liello di Campo di Fiore whose wife was staying there at present. Overjoyed, Pietro asked if any of the shepherds would accompany him to the castle, and two of them did so with a ready will.

When Pietro reached the castle, he ran into a few people he knew, and as he was trying to make arrangements with them to go out and search for the girl in the forest, he was told that Liello's wife wanted to see him. He went to her at once, and on finding that she had Agnolella with her, there has never been a man whose happiness was equal to his. He longed to take her in his arms, but he refrained because he felt too embarrassed to do so in the presence of the lady. And if he was ecstatic, the girl was no less delighted to see him.

The noble lady gave him a warm welcome and took him in, although after listening to what had happened to him, she rebuked him sternly for seeking to defy the wishes of his family. But when she saw that he was determined to do so anyway, and that it was what the girl wanted, too, she said to herself: "Why should I give myself all this trouble? The two of them are in love, they understand one another, they're both friends of my husband, and their intentions are honorable. Besides, I believe that what they want must be pleasing to God, seeing as how the one of them was saved from a hanging, the other from being killed by a lance, and both of them from being devoured by wild beasts. So, let them do as they wish." Then, turning to the couple, she said: "If it's still your desire to be joined together as husband and wife, well, so be it. I'm in favor of it, too, and in fact, we can celebrate your wedding right here at Liello's expense. After that, you can safely leave everything to me, and I'll make peace between you and your families."

The jubilant Pietro and his Agnolella, who was even happier, got married then and there, and the noble lady gave them the most honorable wedding one could have in the mountains. And that is where they tasted the incomparable sweetness of the first fruits of their love.

Several days later, accompanied by a substantial escort, they and the lady set off on horseback and returned to Rome. Although she found that Pietro's relatives were very angry with him for what he had done, she managed to restore him to their good graces. And after that he lived with his Agnolella to a ripe old age in perfect peace and pleasure.

Day 5, Story 4

Ricciardo Manardi is discovered by Messer Lizio da Valbona with his daughter, whom Ricciardo marries, thus remaining on good terms with her father.[1]

Having fallen silent, Elissa listened as her companions praised her tale, after which the Queen ordered Filostrato to tell a story, who laughed and began as follows:

I have been scolded so often, and by so many of you, because I imposed the topic of sad stories on you and made you weep, that I feel myself obliged to make amends to some extent for the sorrow you experienced by telling you a tale that will make you laugh a little. Consequently, I am going to recount a very short love story in which the only unpleasant things are the lovers' sighs and their brief experience of fear and shame before the tale proceeds directly to its happy ending.

Not so very long ago, worthy ladies, there was a quite reputable, well-bred knight living in Romagna who was called Messer Lizio da Valbona.[2] When he was at the threshold of old age, it was his good fortune that his wife, named Madonna Giacomina, gave birth to a daughter who, as she grew up, turned out to be more beautiful and charming than any other girl in those parts. And since she was the only daughter left to her father and mother, not only did they love and cherish her very dearly, but they took extraordinary care in guarding her, for they hoped to be able to arrange a great match for her.

Now, there was a handsome, lively young man named Ricciardo, from the Manardi da Brettinoro family, who used to frequent Messer Lizio's house and spend a great deal of time in his company, and neither Messer Lizio nor his wife kept watch on Ricciardo any more than they would have if he had been one of their own sons. On more than one occasion, Ricciardo noticed the girl, who he knew was of marriageable age, and as he observed how beautiful and graceful she was, and how admirable her manners and comportment, he fell passionately in love with her. Although he took the greatest care to keep his love hidden, the girl perceived it, and making no effort to ward off the emotion, she fell for him as well, to Ricciardo's great delight.

Ricciardo had often wanted to say something about his feelings to her, but he remained silent out of fear, until one day, summoning up the courage, he seized the opportunity to speak. "Caterina," he said, "I implore you, don't let me die of love."

"May God grant that you don't let me die of it first!" she promptly replied.

This response only served to increase Ricciardo's love and desire, and he said to her: "There's nothing I wouldn't undertake to do if it would give you pleasure, but it's up to you to find a way to save both your life and mine."

"Ricciardo," the girl replied, "you see how closely I'm being watched, so closely that I can't really imagine any way for you to come to me. But if you can think up something I can do without exposing myself to shame, tell me, and I'll do it."

After considering a number of options, all of a sudden Ricciardo declared: "My sweet Caterina, I don't know of anything better except for you to go and sleep on the balcony that overlooks your father's garden, or at least to find some means to get out onto it. For although it's very high up, if I knew you were going to be spending the night there, I would certainly find a way to reach you."

"If you have the courage for such a climb," replied Caterina, "I'm sure I can arrange things so that I can get to sleep there."

Ricciardo swore he would do it, after which they gave one another a quick kiss on the sly and parted.

It was already close to the end of May, and the next day, the girl began complaining to her mother about how she had not been able to sleep the night before because of the stifling heat.

"Daughter of mine," said her mother, "what's this heat you're talking about? It wasn't hot at all."

"Mother of mine," replied Caterina, "you should say 'in my opinion,' and then you might be speaking the truth. But you should remember how much hotter girls are than older women."[3]

"My child," the lady answered, "that's certainly true. But I can't make it hot or cold at my whim, as you might want me to do. You just have to take whatever weather comes with the seasons. Maybe it'll be cooler tonight, and you'll sleep better."

"Now, God grant that may be the case," said Caterina, "but it's not normal for the nights to get cooler as summer approaches."

"Well," said the lady, "what do you want us to do about it?"

"If you and my father wouldn't object," replied Caterina, "I'd like to have a little cot made up out on the balcony that is next to his room and overlooks his garden, and I'll go to sleep there. I'll certainly be better off in that nice cool place, listening to the song of the nightingale, than I would be in your bedroom."

"Cheer up, my child," said her mother. "I'll speak to your father, and we'll do whatever he decides."

Perhaps because Messer Lizio, as an old man, was inclined to be somewhat surly, he listened to what his wife had to say and then remarked: "What's this nightingale she wants to listen to when she goes to sleep? I'll make her go to sleep listening to the song of the cicadas."

When Caterina found out what he had said, not only did she not go to sleep the following night, but acting more out of spite than because of the heat, she kept complaining about how hot it was, thus preventing her mother from sleeping as well. In response to her daughter's complaints, the next morning her mother went to Messer Lizio and said:

"Sir, you can't be very fond of this young daughter of yours. What difference does it make to you if she sleeps out on the balcony? All night long she didn't get any rest because of the heat. And besides, why are you surprised that she should take pleasure in hearing the nightingale sing? She's just a little girl, and young people like things that are just like them."

"All right, then," replied Messer Lizio, after he had heard her out. "Have whatever kind of bed you want set up for her out there, and have them hang a light curtain around it. She can sleep there and listen to the song of the nightingale to her heart's content."

Once the girl heard what her father's decision was, she promptly had a bed made up for herself on the balcony, and since she was planning to sleep there that night, she waited until she saw Ricciardo, at which point she gave him the signal they had arranged between themselves to let him know what he had to do.

As soon as Messer Lizio heard his daughter getting into bed, he locked the door that led from his bedroom to the balcony, and then he, too, retired for the night.

When Ricciardo saw that all was quiet, he got up onto a wall with the aid of a ladder, from which, with great difficulty and always in danger of falling, he climbed up another wall by holding on to certain stones that jutted out from it. Finally, he reached the balcony where he was received by the girl in silence, but with the greatest joy imaginable. After a multitude of kisses, the two of them lay down together, and for virtually the entire night, they took their pleasure of one another, delightedly making the nightingale sing over and over again.

The nights were so short at that time of year, and their enjoyment of one another lasted such a long time, that it was almost daybreak before they fell asleep, completely unaware of what time it was. They did not have a stitch of clothing on, for they had gotten heated up both by the weather and by all the fun they had been having together, and as she slept, Caterina cradled Ricciardo's neck in her right arm, while with her left hand she held him by that thing which you ladies are too embarrassed to name when you are in the presence of men.

They went on sleeping in that position and did not wake even after dawn arrived. Messer Lizio, however, did get up, and when he recalled that his daughter was sleeping out on the balcony, he quietly opened the door, saying to himself as he did so: "Let's just see how the nightingale helped Caterina sleep last night." He walked over to the bed, and when he lifted up the curtain that surrounded it, he saw his daughter and Ricciardo, naked and uncovered, fast asleep there, embracing one another in the way that has just been described. Having clearly recognized Ricciardo, he left them there and went to his wife's bedroom, where he called her and said: "Quick, woman, get up. Come see how fond your daughter is of the nightingale, for she's captured it, and she's holding it in her hand."

"How is that possible?" the lady replied.

"You'll see," said Messer Lizio, "if you come quickly."

The lady got dressed in a hurry and quietly followed Messer Lizio until they reached the bed. When the curtain was raised, she saw plainly enough how her daughter had captured and was still holding on to the nightingale whose song she had so wanted to hear.

Feeling herself terribly deceived by Ricciardo, Madonna Giacomina wanted to shout insults at him, but Messer Lizio said to her: "Woman, if you value my love, don't make a sound, because now that she's caught him, he's going to be hers for keeps. Ricciardo is young and rich and noble, so a match with him can only be to our advantage. If he wants to part with me on good terms, he's going to have to marry her first, and this way he'll discover that he's put the nightingale into his own cage, not into somebody else's."

The lady was reassured to see that her husband was not upset about what had happened, and when she considered that her daughter had had a good night, was now well rested, and had caught the nightingale, Madonna Giacomina held her peace.

They did not have to wait long after this exchange before Ricciardo woke up. As soon as he saw that it was broad daylight, he thought he was as good as dead, and calling to Caterina, he said, "Oh, my darling, day has come and caught me here. What are we going to do?"

At these words, Messer Lizio approached the bed, raised the curtain, and replied: "We are going to do just fine."

When Ricciardo saw him, he felt as though his heart had been ripped out of his body, and sitting up straight in bed, he said: "My lord, I beg you, in God's name, have mercy on me. I know that I deserve to die because of my wickedness and disloyalty, so you should do whatever you want with me. And yet, I implore you to spare my life, if it's possible. Please don't let me die."

"Ricciardo," said Messer Lizio, "this deed was not worthy of the love I bore you and the trust I placed in you. But what's done is done, and since it's your youth that moved you to commit such a fault, there's a way for you to save yourself from death, and me from dishonor: you must take Caterina as your lawful wedded wife. That way, for the rest of her life she'll be yours just as she has been yours tonight, and as a result, you'll be able to secure both my pardon and your own safety. But if you don't agree to do this, then you'd better commend your soul to God."

While the two men were speaking, Caterina let go of the nightingale, and after covering herself up, she burst into tears and begged her father to forgive Ricciardo, at the same time beseeching her lover to do as Messer Lizio wished so that the two of them could spend many more nights like this one together in perfect safety.

All this pleading was not really necessary, however, for Ricciardo readily agreed, without so much as a moment's hesitation, to accept Messer Lizio's proposal, being moved to do so not just by his shame over his misdeed and his desire to make amends for it, but also by his fear of death and his desire to escape with his life, to say nothing of the ardent love he felt and his yearning to possess the object of his affections.

Consequently, Messer Lizio borrowed one of Madonna Giacomina's rings, and Ricciardo did not budge from the bed, but took Caterina as his wife right there and then in the presence of her parents. With the marriage thus sealed, Messer Lizio and his wife left the young couple, saying as they went: "You should get some rest now, for you probably need that more than you need to get up."

As soon as they were gone, the two young people embraced one another again, and since they had only traveled six miles that night, they went two more before they finally got out of bed—which is how they brought their first day together to a close.

Once they were up, Ricciardo discussed things in greater detail with Messer Lizio, and a few days later, as was proper, he went through the full ceremony of marrying the girl again in the presence of all their friends and relations. Then, with great pomp, he brought her to his house where their nuptials were celebrated in splendor and dignity. And for many years after that he lived with her in peace and happiness, catching nightingales both day and night to his heart's content.

Day 5, Story 5

Before he dies, Guidotto da Cremona entrusts a young girl to the care of Giacomino da Pavia. Later, in Faenza, Giannole di Severino and Minghino di Mingole fall in love with her and come to blows on her account, but when she is identified as Giannole's sister, she is given in marriage to Minghino.[1]

In listening to the tale of the nightingale, all the ladies had laughed so much that even after Filostrato stopped, they still could not contain themselves. Finally, however, when their merriment had died down, the Queen said: "Although you did make us suffer yesterday, Filostrato, you have certainly tickled us so much today that no one has the right to hold it against you any longer." Then, addressing herself to Neifile, she asked her to tell a story, and Neifile cheerfully began, as follows:

Since Filostrato went into Romagna for the subject matter of his tale, I shall likewise feel free to wander about there for a while as I tell you my own.

Let me say, then, that there were once two men from Lombardy living in the city of Fano, one of whom was named Guidotto da Cremona and the other, Giacomino da Pavia. Both of them were getting on in years, after having spent almost their entire youth as soldiers, continually engaged in feats of arms. On his deathbed, Guidotto, who had no son, let alone any other friend or relation whom he trusted more than Giacomino, left a young girl he had who was about ten years old in his comrade's care. Guidotto also bequeathed to him all his worldly possessions, and after having told him many of the particulars of his life, he died.

Around that time, it happened that the city of Faenza, which had long suffered from war and other misfortunes, was restored to a condition of greater stability, and anyone who wished to return was freely granted permission to do so. Because of this, Giacomino, who had once lived in the city and had enjoyed his stay there, also returned, bringing with him all of his possessions, including the girl who had been left to him by Guidotto and whom he loved and treated as if she were his very own daughter.

Growing up, she turned into quite a beauty, far lovelier than any other girl living in the city at that time, and she was no less well mannered and virtuous than she was beautiful. She thus began to attract the interest of many different suitors, and in particular, two young men named Giannole di Severino and Minghino di Mingole. They were both quite handsome and equally well situated, and they fell so passionately in love with her that in their jealousy they developed a hatred for one another that knew no bounds. Since the girl was now fifteen years old, the two of them would have gladly married her if their families had only given their consent. But seeing as how they were prevented from obtaining her in this honorable manner, each of them devoted himself to finding a way to have her by whatever means seemed best to him.

In his house Giacomino had an elderly maid as well as a manservant named Crivello, a very jovial and sociable person, with whom Giannole had become quite friendly. When the time seemed right, Giannole revealed his love for the girl to the servant, begging him to help him obtain his desire and promising him great things in return.

"Look," said Crivello, "the only thing I can do for you is this. If Giacomino should go out someplace to have supper, I can let you in where you can meet her, because if I tried to tell her something on your behalf, she'd never stick around to listen to me. Now, if you like this plan, I promise to carry it out, and I'll be as good as my word. But then it's up to you to decide to do what you think will best suit your purpose." Declaring that he wanted nothing more, Giannole thus reached an understanding with Crivello.

For his part, Minghino had made friends with the maid and had worked on her so successfully that she had already delivered messages to the girl on several occasions and had gone a long way toward setting her on fire in response to Minghino's love. What is more, the maid had promised that she would take him to see the girl if Giacomino chanced to leave the house in the evening for any reason.

And thus, not so very long after these discussions, Crivello managed to maneuver Giacomino into going out to have supper at a friend's house. After informing Giannole of what he had done, Crivello arranged that when he gave him a certain signal, Giannole should come to the front door, which he would find unlocked. For her part, the maid, who knew nothing about all this, let Minghino know that Giacomino was not eating supper at home and told him to position himself nearby so that when he saw the sign she would make for him, he could come to the house and be let in.

Although neither lover knew anything about what the other was up to, once night had fallen, each one, suspicious of his rival, set out with a group of friends, all of them armed, determined to take possession of the place. Minghino stationed himself at a house belonging to a friend of his who was the girl's neighbor and waited there with his men for the signal, while Giannole and his companions took up a position a short distance away from where she lived.

With Giacomino out of the way, Crivello and the maid did their best to get rid of one another.

"How is it you haven't gone to bed yet?" said Crivello. "Why are you still wandering all about the house?"

"And you," the maid retorted, "why don't you go and wait for your master? What're you hanging around here for, now that you've had your supper?"

Thus neither one could get the other to budge until Crivello realized that the hour he had agreed upon with Giannole had come and said to himself: "Why am I worried about her? If she won't keep her mouth shut, she'll get hers." At that, he gave the prearranged signal, after which he went and opened the main door to the house for Giannole, who rushed up with two of his companions and came inside. Finding the girl in the great hall, they grabbed her with the intention of carrying her off, but she began to struggle and scream at the top of her voice, and the maid did likewise. Hearing the noise, Minghino immediately came racing to the spot with his men, and when they saw the girl already being dragged through the doorway, they all drew their swords and shouted: "Ah, traitors, you're as good as dead! You're not going to get away with this. What's the meaning of this outrageous violence?" And the moment they finished speaking, they started hacking away at them.

Meanwhile, because of all the noise, the neighbors had come outside, carrying lanterns and weapons, and started hurling abuse at Giannole for what they saw he was trying to do. With their assistance, Minghino, after a lengthy struggle, finally managed to tear the girl away from his rival and get her back inside Giacomino's house. The fray was still going on, however, when the officers who served the *podestà* of the city arrived on the scene.[2] They arrested many of the combatants, including Minghino, Giannole, and Crivello, and marched all of them off to prison.

By the time Giacomino had returned home, things had quieted down, and although he was very distressed about what had happened, once he had looked into it and discovered that the girl was in no way to blame, he felt somewhat relieved. All the same, he vowed to himself that he would prevent anything like that from ever happening again by arranging a marriage for her as soon as possible.

The next morning, he received a visit from the two young men's families, who had found out precisely what had happened and knew only too well how badly it might go for the prisoners if Giacomino decided to press charges, as he had every right to do. And so, they sweet-talked him, begging him to give more weight to the love and goodwill that they were convinced he bore to them, who had come there to plead with him, than to the injury he had received because of the young men's thoughtlessness. In addition, they offered, both on their own account and on that of the two young men who had committed the crime, to make whatever amends he saw fit to ask of them.

Giacomino, a good-hearted man who had seen a great many things in his time, answered them in short order. "Gentlemen," he said, "even if I were in my hometown and not in yours, as I am right now, I really do consider myself your friend, the kind who would never do anything that would displease you, either in this case or in any other. Besides, I am bound all the more to comply with your wishes in that you've actually wronged one of your own. For this girl here is not from Cremona or Pavia, as many people suppose, but from Faenza, although neither she, nor I, nor the person who entrusted her to my care ever discovered whose daughter she was. Therefore, with regard to what you are asking me to do, I'm prepared to give you exactly what you want."

The worthy men were quite surprised to learn that the girl was from Faenza, and after thanking Giacomino for being so generous in response to their request, they asked him if he would be so kind as to tell them how she had come into his hands and how he knew she was from their city.

"Guidotto da Cremona was a friend and comrade of mine," said Giacomino, "and he told me as he was about to die that when the city had been captured by the Emperor Frederick and pillaging was going on in every quarter of it, he and his men entered one particular house, which they found full of booty. All of the inhabitants had abandoned it, except for this girl, who was then two years old or thereabouts. She called Guidotto 'father' as he was climbing up the stairs, which made him feel sorry for her, and so, together with everything else in the house, he carried her off with him to Fano. When he was dying there, he bequeathed all his possessions to me, including the girl, and charged me, when the time came, to arrange for her to get married and to give her everything that had been his as her dowry. Although she's now of an age to wed, I've still not succeeded in finding a husband I approve of for her, and I'd be really happy to do that before another incident like the one that occurred yesterday happens to me again."

One of the people present was a certain Guiglielmino da Medicina, who had been with Guidotto at the capture of Faenza and who knew very well whose house it was that he had looted.[3] Spotting the owner standing there among the others, he went over to him and said: "Bernabuccio, do you hear what Giacomino's saying?"

"Yes, indeed," replied Bernabuccio, "I was just thinking about it, especially because I remember how, in all that confusion, I lost a little daughter who was the same age as the one Giacomino's been talking about."

"Then this has got to be the girl," said Guiglielmino, "for when I was once with Guidotto, I heard him describe the location of the house that had been sacked, and I realized that it was yours. So, try and remember if the child had any mark by which you could identify her. Then have her examined, and I'm sure you'll find that she's your daughter."

After giving it some thought, Bernabuccio recalled that she ought to have a little scar above her left ear in the shape of a cross, the remains of a growth he had had cut off shortly before Faenza was captured. And so, without a moment's hesitation, he went right up to Giacomino, who was still there, and asked to be taken into his house and allowed to see the girl. Giacomino was quite happy to bring him inside and to present the girl to him, and as soon as Bernabuccio laid eyes on her, it seemed to him that he was looking at the very face of her mother, who was still a beautiful woman. Not content with this, however, he asked Giacomino if he would be so gracious as to allow him to pull back her hair a little from above her left ear. Giacomino consented, and Bernabuccio walked over to the girl, who was standing there looking rather embarrassed. When he lifted up her hair with his right hand and saw the cross, he knew for certain that she was his daughter, and gently weeping, he began to embrace her, although she kept trying to fend him off.

"Brother, this is my daughter," he said, turning to Giacomino. "It was my house that was looted by Guidotto, and in all the sudden commotion, my wife, the child's mother, completely forgot about her. Until now we've always assumed that she perished in the flames when the house burned down that day."

On hearing this, the girl, who had noted that he was a somewhat elderly man and had sensed the truth in his words, was moved by some occult power to yield to his embraces and also began gently weeping, mingling her tears with his own.

Bernabuccio immediately sent for her mother and for some other female relatives of hers as well as for her sisters and brothers, and having presented the girl to everyone, he told them the entire story. Then, after they had all embraced one another a thousand times, he brought her back home with him amid great rejoicing, leaving Giacomino feeling very satisfied indeed.

The *podestà*, worthy man that he was, found out about this

development, and knowing that Giannole, whom he had in custody, was Bernabuccio's son and thus the girl's brother, bound to her by blood, he decided to be lenient and to overlook the offense he had committed. Moreover, he took on the role of intermediary, and acting in concert with Bernabuccio and Giacomino, he got Giannole and Minghino to make peace with one another. Then, to the immense satisfaction of Minghino's entire family, he announced that the girl, whose name was Agnesa, would be married to him, and he freed the two young men as well as Crivello and all the others who had been involved in the affair.

Some time later, a very happy Minghino celebrated his wedding with great pomp and splendor, after which he brought Agnesa home, where he lived with her in peace and prosperity for a great many years to come.

Day 5, Story 6

Having been found with the girl he loves, who had been given to King Frederick, Gianni di Procida is tied to a stake with her, and they are about to be burned when he is recognized by Ruggieri de Loria. He is then released and becomes her husband.[1]

The ladies had really enjoyed Neifile's story, and when it was finished, the Queen asked Pampinea to get ready to tell another one. She raised her face, glowing serenely, and began at once:

Immense indeed, charming ladies, are the powers of Love, which can induce lovers to endure great hardships and expose themselves to extraordinary, unheard-of dangers, something that can be seen in many of the stories we have already told, both today and on other occasions. Nevertheless, it would be my pleasure to prove it to you once again with a tale about the courage of a young man in love.

On Ischia, which is an island not very far from Naples, there once lived an extremely beautiful, charming young girl named Restituta, the daughter of Marin Bolgaro, a local nobleman.[2] A young man by the name of Gianni, who hailed from Procida, a little island close to Ischia, loved her more than life itself, and the girl fully returned his feelings. Not only did he come over from Procida to Ischia every day in order to see her, but he did so frequently at night as well, and when he could not find a boat, he would swim all the way from one island to the other so that, even if he managed to do nothing else, he could at least gaze upon the walls of her house.[3]

In the course of this passionate love affair, one summer's day when the girl happened to be down at the seashore all by herself, going from rock to rock and prying shellfish from them with a little knife, she chanced upon a cove hidden among the crags, where a group of young Sicilians, on their way back from Naples, had taken refuge with their frigate because it provided them with shade and the opportunity to obtain some wonderfully cool water from a nearby spring. They caught sight of the exquisitely beautiful young girl before she was aware of their presence, and observing that she was all alone, they decided among themselves to seize her and carry her off. They wasted no time in putting their plan into action, and grabbing the girl, they got her aboard their ship even though she kept shrieking at the top of her lungs. They then sailed away, but upon arriving in Calabria, they began arguing about who was going to have her, and to make a long story short, each man wanted her for himself. Since they were unable to reach any sort of agreement and were afraid of making matters worse and ruining their business over her, they decided to give the girl to Frederick, King of Sicily, who was then a young man and delighted in things of that sort. And as soon as they reached Palermo, that is just what they did.

Seeing how beautiful she was, the King treasured the gift, but because he was somewhat physically indisposed, he ordered that until such time as he regained his strength, she should be lodged in a luxurious villa called La Cuba, which he had in one of his gardens, where she would be waited on by his servants, who proceeded to carry out all his instructions.[4]

There was a great outcry in Ischia over the abduction of the girl, but what disturbed them the most was that they could not discover who was responsible for having taken her. Gianni, however, who had more at stake in the affair than anyone else, did not wait around in Ischia for news of her. Instead, having ascertained the direction that the frigate had taken, he had a similar ship fitted out for himself, and after getting on board, he proceeded to scour the entire seacoast as quickly as possible from Minerva down to Scalea in Calabria, making inquiries about the girl everywhere he went.[5] Finally, having been told in Scalea that she had been carried off to Palermo by some Sicilian sailors, he made his way there with all the speed he could muster and went searching for her throughout the city. Upon discovering that she had been given to the King and was being kept by him in La Cuba, he was deeply distressed and almost gave up all hope that he would ever see her again, let alone get her back.

Nevertheless, Love would not let him leave, and so, he sent the frigate away and stayed on in Palermo, it being clear that no one in the city recognized who he was. He then began taking frequent walks around La Cuba, and one day by chance, to his and the girl's great delight, they caught sight of one another as she was standing at a window. Seeing that the place was deserted, Gianni got as close to her as he could so that he would be able to speak to her, and she told him exactly what he needed to do if he wanted to talk with her in greater privacy. He left her, but only after having first carefully surveyed the layout of the area, and biding his time until well after nightfall, he returned and managed to get up and over into the garden by hanging on to places where a woodpecker would have scarcely been able to find a perch. Once inside, he found a pole, which he leaned against the window as the girl had instructed him to do, and by its means he climbed up without any difficulty.

Feeling as if she had already lost her honor, the girl, who had attempted to preserve it in the past by coyly refusing his advances, now decided that she would gratify his every desire, for she thought there was no one worthier to whom she could give herself, and furthermore, she reckoned that she would be able to persuade him to carry her off with him. Accordingly, she had left the window unlocked so that he could quickly get inside. Finding it open, Gianni climbed silently into the room and lay down beside the girl, who was by no means asleep. Before they got around to anything else, however, she informed him fully of her plan, begging him with all her heart to get her out of there and carry her off with him. Gianni responded that nothing would give him greater pleasure and that by the time he left her, he would without fail have worked out all the details so that he could spirit her away the next time he visited her. Then, after rapturously embracing one another, they shared together the greatest delight that Love can offer, repeating the experience many, many times until they unwittingly fell asleep in one another's arms.

A little before daybreak, the King, who had been attracted to the girl from the first time he saw her and was now feeling in better shape, just happened to remember her and decided that despite the hour, he would go and spend some time with her. Consequently, accompanied by a few of his servants, he quietly made his way to La Cuba. Having entered the building, he went to the room in which he knew the girl was sleeping and had them open it for him without making a sound. Proceeded by a large, blazing torch, he walked in, only to see, when he looked down at the bed, that the girl was lying there fast asleep with Gianni, the two of them naked in one another's arms.

This spectacle drove the King instantly into a fierce rage that rendered him speechless, and his anger grew so intense that he could scarcely refrain from taking out a knife he had at his side and slaying them. But upon reflecting how very cowardly a thing it would be for any man, let alone a king, to kill two naked people in their sleep, he kept himself in check and decided instead to have them publicly executed by being burned at the stake. Turning to the single companion he had in there with him, he said, "What do you think of this wicked woman in whom I'd once placed my hopes?" He then went on to ask if his companion knew the young man who had been so presumptuous as to come into his house and offer him such an outrageous affront, to which the man replied that he could not remember ever having set eyes on him.

Leaving the chamber in a rage, the King ordered that the two lovers should be taken and tied up, naked as they were, and that when it was broad daylight outside, they should be brought to Palermo, where they were to be bound back-to-back to a stake in the piazza, there to remain until the hour of tierce so that everyone could see them, after which they were to be burned, as they so richly deserved. Having delivered these instructions, the King then returned to Palermo and retired to his room, grief stricken and furious.

The moment the King was gone, a group of men descended on the pair of lovers, woke them up, and then, without pity, swiftly seized them and tied them up. It is easy to imagine how distressed the two young people were when they saw what was happening to them, how they feared for their lives, and how they wept and bitterly reproached themselves. In accordance with the King's command, they were taken to Palermo and bound to a stake in the piazza, where before their eyes the wood was heaped up and the fire made ready so that they could be burned at the hour appointed by the King.

All the inhabitants of Palermo, both men and women, immediately flocked to the piazza in order to see the two lovers, and while the men, without exception, pressed in to take a look at the girl, admiring her beautiful face and shapely figure, in a similar fashion all the women ran over to see the young man and were full of praise for his good looks and splendid physique. The hapless lovers, however, hung their heads down low, both of them deeply ashamed, and wept over their misfortune, expecting at any moment to be put to a cruel death in the fire.

While the two of them were thus being held until the hour fixed for their execution, news of the crime they had committed was cried throughout the city, eventually reaching the ears of Ruggieri de Loria, a man of inestimable worth who was at the time the Admiral of the Royal Fleet. Intent upon seeing the pair for himself, he made his way to the place where they were bound. When he arrived, the first thing he did was to have a look at the girl, whom he found rather attractive, after which he went to observe the young man and without difficulty recognized him at once. Drawing nearer, he asked him if he were Gianni di Procida.

Gianni raised his head, and recognizing the Admiral, replied: "My lord, I was indeed the man you're asking about, but I won't be that man for very much longer."

The Admiral then asked him what had brought him to such a pass, and Gianni replied: "Love, and the King's wrath."

The Admiral got him to recount the story in greater detail, and when he had heard the entire thing and was at the point of leaving, Gianni called him back. "Oh, my lord," he said, "if it's possible, would you procure a favor for me from the person who is responsible for my being here?"

"What favor?" asked Ruggieri.

"I realize that I must die, and very soon," said Gianni, "which is why I'm begging this favor. Since I've been placed here back-to-back with this girl, whom I've loved more than life itself, just as she's loved me, let us be turned to face one another, so that when I die, I'll have the consolation of seeing her face as I expire."

Ruggieri laughed and declared that he would be happy to do it: "I'll arrange for you to see so much of her that you'll wind up sick and tired of doing so."

After leaving Gianni, the Admiral ordered the men who were charged with carrying out the sentence to do nothing more than what they had already done without further instructions from the King, to whom he then immediately made his way. Although Ruggieri saw how angry he was, he did not hesitate to speak his mind.

"Your Majesty," he said, "how have you been injured by the two young people you've sentenced to be burned down there in the piazza?"

The King told him, and Ruggieri continued: "They certainly deserve to be punished for the crime they committed—just not by you. For although misdeeds merit punishment, good works ought to receive a reward, in addition to a pardon and clemency. Those two people you wish to have burned at the stake, do you know who they are?"

When the King replied that he did not, Ruggieri went on: "Well, I want you to know who they are so that you can see just how very prudent it was for you to let yourself get carried away by a fit of anger! The young man is the son of Landolfo di Procida, who is the blood relative, the brother, of Messer Gianni di Procida, by whose means you became king and lord of this island. The girl is the daughter of Marin Bolgaro, whose power is what currently keeps you from losing control of Ischia. What's more, these two youngsters have loved one another for a long time, and it was not out of any desire to show disrespect to Your Majesty, but rather because they were driven to it by their passion, that they committed this sin—if what young people do in the name of love should be called a sin. So, why do you wish to have them put to death when you ought to be entertaining them lavishly and honoring them with the greatest gifts you have to offer?"

After the King had heard him out and was certain that he was telling the truth, not only did he regret what he had already done, but he felt terrible that he was about to do something even worse. He therefore immediately ordered that they should be untied from the stake and brought into his presence. His orders were carried out, and after being fully informed about their situation, he decided that he should compensate them through his largess and his hospitality for the wrong that had been done to them. Accordingly, he had them dressed anew in courtly attire, and after determining that it would be by their mutual consent, he arranged for Gianni and the girl to get married. Finally, having given them magnificent presents, he sent the two of them, quite content, back to their home, where they received the most festive of welcomes, and where they lived together for a long time afterward in pleasure and happiness.

Day 5, Story 7

Teodoro falls in love with Violante, the daughter of his master, Messer Amerigo, and gets her pregnant, for which he is condemned to be hanged. While he is being whipped along the way to the gallows, however, he is recognized by his father and set free, after which he takes Violante as his wife.[1]

The ladies were all in suspense, anxiously wondering whether the lovers would be burned, and on learning that the two of them had escaped, they rejoiced and gave thanks to God. Then, since they had heard the end of the story, the Queen assigned the task of telling the next one to Lauretta, who happily proceeded to say:

Loveliest of ladies, during the time when the good King William ruled Sicily, there was a nobleman living on the island by the name of Messer Amerigo Abate da Trapani, who was well supplied with worldly goods, including a large number of children. He was therefore in need of servants, and when some galleys arrived from the eastern Mediterranean belonging to Genoese pirates who had captured a great many children while scouring the coast of Armenia, he purchased a few of them, thinking they were Turks.[2] Although all the others looked like shepherds, there was one named Teodoro who seemed better bred and was less rustic in appearance than the rest.

Despite being treated as a slave, Teodoro was brought up in the household right alongside Messer Amerigo's children, and as he grew older, prompted more by his innate character than by the condition he accidentally found himself in, he acquired such poise and grace that he impressed Messer Amerigo who proceeded to grant him his freedom. Moreover, thinking he was a Turk, he had him baptized and renamed

437

Pietro, and placed him in charge of all of his affairs, taking the young man deeply into his confidence.

Growing up side by side with Messer Amerigo's other children, there was a daughter of his named Violante, a dainty young beauty, who, because her father was in no hurry to arrange a marriage for her, chanced to fall in love with Pietro.[3] But although she adored him and had the greatest esteem for his conduct and accomplishments, she was too shy to reveal her feelings to him. Love, however, spared her the trouble, for Pietro, who had cast more than one furtive glance in her direction, had fallen so hard for her that he felt miserable whenever she was out of his sight. Since it seemed to him that what he was doing was less than proper, he was terribly afraid that someone might notice, but the girl, who took great pleasure in his company, divined what he was going through, and to bolster his confidence, she let it appear that she was quite delighted with it, as indeed she was. And so, for a good long while, that was how their relationship remained, neither one daring to say anything to the other, however much they both desired to do so. But while the two of them were burning with equal intensity in the flames of Love, Fortune, acting as though she had actually decided to bring it about, found a way for them to get rid of the fears and timidity that held them back.

Perhaps a mile outside of Trapani, Messer Amerigo had a very lovely property to which his wife and daughter, together with various other ladies and their maidservants, frequently went as a form of recreation. They had gone there one day when the weather was extremely hot, taking Pietro along with them, and as they were whiling away the time, all of a sudden the sky, as we see it occasionally does in summertime, became overcast with dark clouds. The lady had no desire to be caught out there in the storm, and so she set off to return to Trapani with her party, moving along just as quickly as they could. But Pietro and Violante, who were younger than her mother and the rest of the women, soon outstripped them, perhaps being driven on as much by Love as by any worry they had about the weather. When they had gotten so far ahead of the group as to be almost out of sight, there were several thunderclaps, followed immediately by a very heavy hailstorm, from which the lady and her party took refuge in the house of a peasant.[4] For lack of any other shelter nearby, Pietro and the girl entered a little old church that had been abandoned and was almost entirely in ruins. There, as the two of them squeezed in under the tiny piece of the roof that still remained intact, they were forced by necessity, because of the limited cover they had, to huddle close together, and that physical contact made them pluck up their courage enough to reveal their amorous desires to one another. Pietro was the first to speak:

"Would to God this hailstorm might never stop so that I could stay here like this forever!"

"That'd be great for me, too!" replied the girl.

Then, as the hail continued to fall, they went from talking to holding and pressing hands, and from that to embracing one another and kissing. To cut a long story short, by the time the weather improved, the two of them had experienced Love's ultimate delights and made arrangements to meet again in secret for their mutual pleasure.

The city gate was not far away, and when the storm abated, they went there to wait for the lady and then returned home with her. From time to time, using the utmost secrecy and discretion, they would meet in the same place as before, enjoying themselves there to the full. And in this way, things went on until the girl became pregnant, much to the dismay of both parties, and although she took a number of measures to resist the course of Nature and produce a miscarriage, none of them had any effect.

Afraid for his life, Pietro made up his mind to flee and told her so. But on hearing this, she said: "If you leave, I'm going to kill myself for sure."

To this remark, Pietro, who was deeply in love with her, replied: "O my lady, how can you possibly want me to stay here? Your pregnancy will reveal our offense, and although you may be easily forgiven for it, I'm the poor wretch who'll have to pay the penalty for both your sin and my own."

"Pietro," said the girl, "my sin will certainly be obvious to everyone, but you may rest assured that yours will never be discovered unless you're the one to reveal it."

"Since you've given me this promise, I'll stay," said Pietro, "but you'd better make sure you keep it."

The girl did everything she could to keep her pregnancy concealed, but one day, when she saw that she could hide it no longer because of the way her body had grown, she revealed everything to her mother, and weeping profusely, begged her for her help. The lady was utterly distraught and reprimanded her daughter severely, insisting that she be told how it had all come about. Intent upon protecting Pietro from harm, the girl concocted a tall tale containing a disguised, garbled version of the truth, which her mother believed, and in order to conceal her daughter's problem, she sent her away to one of their country estates.

Since Messer Amerigo was not in the habit of visiting the place, the girl's mother never imagined that he would show up there, but just as the time arrived for the girl to give birth, he happened to stop at the estate on his way back from hawking. As he walked by the room where his daughter lay, he was astonished to hear her screaming, as women usually do at such times, and immediately went in to ask what was going on.

When she saw her husband enter the room, the lady got to her feet and ruefully explained what had happened to their daughter. Less credulous than his wife, he insisted that it was not possible for the girl to have no idea who had gotten her pregnant, and being absolutely determined to find out who it was, he said that by revealing the truth, she might regain his favor, and that otherwise, she should expect to be put to death without mercy.

His wife did everything in her power to persuade him to rest content with the story their daughter had told, but all in vain. Drawing out his sword, he rushed over in a towering rage toward the girl, who had, in the meantime, while her mother was talking with her father, given birth to a baby boy. "Either tell me who fathered this child," he exclaimed, "or you're going to die right now."

Afraid of being killed, the girl broke the promise she had made to Pietro and revealed everything that had passed between them, although this only served to send the knight into a paroxysm of rage so great that he barely managed to keep himself from slaying her. After giving vent to everything his anger dictated, however, he got back on his horse and returned to Trapani where he went straight to a certain Messer Currado, the Captain put in charge of the local militia there by the King, and told him about the injury that he had received from Pietro. The Captain immediately had the unsuspecting young man arrested, and when he was subjected to torture, he made a full confession.

A few days later, Pietro was condemned by Messer Currado to be whipped through the city and then hanged by the neck. In order to rid Trapani of the two lovers and their child, all at the same time, Messer Amerigo, whose anger had not been appeased by Pietro's death sentence, poured poison into a goblet of wine and gave it to one of his servants together with an unsheathed dagger.

"Go take these two things to Violante," he said, "and tell her in my name that she must choose the means by which she prefers to die, either by poison or by steel. Say that she must do it at once, and that if she refuses, I'll have her burned to death, as she deserves, in the presence of all the citizens in the town. And when you've done this, you will take the child she gave birth to a few days ago, smash its head against a wall, and throw it away to be eaten by the dogs."

When the cruel father finished pronouncing this vicious sentence on his daughter and his grandson, the servant, who was more inclined to do evil than good, set off.

Meanwhile, as the condemned Pietro was being whipped on his way to the gallows by a troop of soldiers, their leaders decided to take a route that passed in front of an inn where three noblemen from Armenia were staying. Their king had sent them to Rome as his ambassadors in order to negotiate with the Pope about certain extremely important matters concerning a Crusade that was about to be launched, and having disembarked at Trapani for a few days' rest and relaxation, they had been lavishly entertained there by the local nobility, and by Messer Amerigo in particular. When they heard Pietro's escort passing by, they came over to a window to have a look.

One of the three ambassadors was an elderly gentleman of great authority named Fineo, and as he observed Pietro, who was completely naked from the waist up and had his hands tied behind him, he noticed a large red spot on the young man's chest, not painted on the skin, but imprinted there by Nature, just like the ones that the women here call "roses." The moment he saw it, he immediately called to mind a son of his who had been kidnapped by pirates from the seashore at Laiazzo some fifteen years earlier and had never been heard of since.[5] After estimating the age of the poor wretch who was being whipped, he figured that his son would be just about that old if he were still alive, and because of the mark on Pietro's body, he began to suspect that that was indeed who it was. Then he thought to himself that if it were his son, he should still remember his own name and that of his father as well as the Armenian language. Consequently, when the boy passed close by, he shouted: "O Teodoro!"

Upon hearing this cry, Pietro immediately raised his head, and Fineo addressed him directly in Armenian: "Where do you come from? Whose son are you?"

Out of respect for the worthy gentleman, the guards who were leading Pietro came to a halt, allowing him to reply: "I'm from Armenia, my father's name was Fineo, and I was brought here as a little boy by a bunch of complete strangers."

When he heard this, Fineo now knew for certain that this was the son he had lost, and in tears he descended with his companions and ran through the entire group of guards to embrace him. He took off the exquisite silk cloak he was wearing, threw it over Pietro's shoulders, and asked the leader who was taking him to be executed if he would be so good as to wait there until such time as he received an order to bring the prisoner back again. The man replied that he would be happy to do so.

Fineo already knew the reason why his son was being led away to his death, for the news had spread all over the town, and so he hurried off to see Messer Currado, accompanied by his companions and their entourage.

"Sir," he declared, "the person you've condemned to death as a slave is actually my son, a free man, and he's ready to marry the girl he is said to have robbed of her virginity. Therefore, I beg you to delay his execution until we can find out whether she'll accept him as her husband, because that way, if she does want him, you won't find that you yourself have gone and broken the law."[6]

Messer Currado was amazed to hear that the prisoner was Fineo's son, and feeling rather ashamed of the injustice that Fortune had perpetrated, he confessed that what Fineo had just said was correct and ordered Pietro to be taken home at once.

Messer Currado then sent for Messer Amerigo and explained what had transpired. Believing that his daughter and his grandson were already dead, Messer Amerigo was the sorriest man in the world for what he had done, since he now knew that if his daughter were still alive, everything could have been easily set to rights. But nevertheless, just in case his instructions had not yet been carried out, he sent a man racing off to the place where his daughter was being held with a new order to countermand the old one. The messenger found that the servant who had been sent earlier by Messer Amerigo had placed the dagger and the poison in front of the girl, and was attempting to force her to choose between the two, all the while berating her for not acting quickly enough. The moment he heard his master's command, however, he left her alone, returned to Messer Amerigo, and told him how things stood. Greatly relieved, Messer Amerigo went to Fineo's lodging, and on the verge of tears, he apologized to the best of his ability for what had happened, asking Fineo to pardon him and declaring that if Teodoro were willing to marry his daughter, he would be very happy to give her to him.

Fineo readily accepted his apologies and replied: "I fully intend to have my son marry your daughter. And if he doesn't want to, then let them carry out the sentence that has been passed upon him."

With Fineo and Messer Amerigo thus in agreement, they went to Teodoro, who, though happy to have found his father again, was still utterly terrified of being put to death, and they asked him what his own wishes were in this case. When he heard that Violante would be his wife if that was what he wanted, his joy was so great that he felt as if he had leaped from Hell all the way up to Paradise, and he told them that he would consider it the greatest possible favor, if the two of them were willing to grant it. Next, they sent someone to ascertain the wishes of the girl, who was at that moment the saddest woman alive, fully expecting to be put to death. When she heard what had happened to Teodoro and what was yet in store for him, it took her quite a while, but she finally allowed herself to believe a little in what the messenger was saying, and feeling somewhat more optimistic, she replied that if she could indeed do what she wanted, nothing would make her happier than to become Teodoro's wife, although in any case, she would do whatever her father ordered. And so, since they were now all in accord with one another, the girl was betrothed to Teodoro, and a great feast was held, to the immense delight of all the townspeople.

Putting her little son out to nurse, the girl recovered her strength, and before long she appeared more beautiful than ever. After rising from her confinement, she presented herself to Fineo, whose return from Rome everyone had been expecting, and greeted him with all the respect due to a father. Overjoyed to have acquired such a beautiful daughter-in-law, Fineo arranged for the marriage to be celebrated with the greatest festivity and merrymaking, and from that moment on he always looked upon Violante as his daughter. A few days later, he embarked on a galley with her, his son, and his little grandson, taking them back with him to Laiazzo, where the two lovers lived in peace and quiet for the rest of their days.

Day 5, Story 8

In love with a lady from the Traversari family, Nastagio degli Onesti spends all his wealth without obtaining her love in return. At the urging of his friends and family, he goes away to Chiassi where he sees a young woman being hunted down and killed by a knight and devoured by two dogs. Nastagio then invites his relations as well as his beloved to a banquet where she sees that same young woman being torn apart and, fearing a similar fate, accepts Nastagio as her husband.[1]

When Lauretta fell silent, at the Queen's command Filomena began as follows:

Amiable ladies, just as we are commended for our pity, so our cruelty is also punished rigorously by divine justice. In order to prove this to you and to give you a reason for ridding yourselves of every last trace of cruelty, I would like to tell you a story that is no less moving than delightful.

In Ravenna, a very ancient city in Romagna, there once lived a great many noblemen and gentlemen, among whom was a youth named Nastagio degli Onesti who had been left rich beyond all measure by the deaths of his father and one of his uncles.[2] He was as yet unmarried, and as often happens to young men, he fell in love with one of the daughters of Messer Paolo Traversari, a young lady much more noble than he was, whom he hoped to persuade to love him by virtue of his accomplishments. But no matter how magnificent, splendid, and commendable his deeds, not only did they not help him, but they actually seemed harmful, so cruel and hard and unyielding did the girl he loved show herself to him. In fact, perhaps because of either her singular beauty or her noble rank, she became so haughty and disdainful that she took a dislike both to him and to everything he cared for. This was so hard for Nastagio to bear that at times, after having wallowed in grief, he would be filled with despair and be seized by a desire to kill himself. Nevertheless, he repressed this urge and instead frequently resolved to give her up altogether or, if he could manage it, to hate her the way she hated him. But he made such resolutions in vain, for it seemed that the more his hope dwindled, the more his love increased.

The young man persisted in both loving and spending lavishly, until it seemed to certain of his friends and relations that he was in danger of exhausting both himself and his fortune. Consequently, they offered him their counsel over and over again, imploring him to leave Ravenna and to go and stay somewhere else for a while, in the expectation that if he did so, both his love and his expenditures would decrease. Nastagio repeatedly rejected their advice with scorn, but he was solicited so earnestly that, finally, he could no longer say no to them and agreed to do as they suggested. After having had enormous preparations made, as if he were intending to go to France or Spain or some other faraway land, he mounted his horse and left the city, accompanied by many of his friends. Having arrived at a place some three miles outside of Ravenna called Chiassi, he sent for his tents and pavilions, and informed those who had accompanied him that he intended to stay there and that they were free to return to the city. Once he had set up his camp, he began living in as elegant and magnificent a style as any man ever did, inviting different groups of friends to come and have dinner or supper with him, as he had been accustomed to doing.

Now it happened that one Friday near the beginning of May, when the weather was very fine, Nastagio fell to brooding about the cruelty of his lady, and having ordered all his attendants to leave him alone so that he could meditate without being disturbed, he wandered, lost in thought, and was transported, step-by-step, into the pine forest.[3] The fifth hour of the day had almost passed, and he had gone a good half mile into the woods, oblivious of food or anything else, when all of a sudden he seemed to hear the loud wailing and earsplitting shrieks of a woman.* His sweet reverie thus interrupted, he raised his head

---

* The fifth hour of the day is sext, or noon. On the canonical hours, see Headnote 2.

to see what was happening and was surprised to discover himself in the woods. But then, when he looked straight ahead of him, he caught sight of a very beautiful young woman, stark naked, who was running through a dense thicket of bushes and brambles toward the very spot on which he was standing. Her hair was disheveled, her flesh was all torn by the branches and the briars, and she was weeping and screaming for mercy. Nor was this all, for he saw two huge, fierce mastiffs chasing after her in a fury, one on either flank, who would catch up to her every so often and bite her savagely. Behind her he saw a swarthy knight, his face contorted with anger, come riding on a black courser. He held a sword in his hand and was threatening her with death in the most terrifying and abusive language.

This sight filled Nastagio's mind with both wonder and terror at once and then moved him to feel compassion for the unfortunate lady, which engendered, in turn, a desire to save her, if he could, from such horrible suffering and the threat of death. On finding himself unarmed, he ran and took up a branch from a tree to use in place of a cudgel, preparing to ward off the dogs and set himself in opposition to the knight. When the latter saw this, he shouted to him from the distance: "Don't get in the way here, Nastagio. Leave it to me and the dogs to give this wicked woman what she deserves."

And even as he was speaking, the dogs seized the woman so hard by the flanks that they halted her in her flight. When the knight had come up and dismounted from his horse, Nastagio approached him and said: "I don't know who you are or how you know me by name, but I'll say this much, that it's base cowardice for an armed knight to seek to slay a naked woman and set his dogs on her as if she were a wild beast. I'm certainly going to do all I can to defend her."

"Nastagio," the knight replied, "I lived in the same city as you do, and my name was Messer Guido degli Anastagi. You were still a little boy when I fell far more passionately in love with this woman than you did with that Traversari girl. Her pride and cruelty reduced me to such a miserable state that one day I took this sword, which you see in my hand, and in despair I killed myself with it, for which I have thus been condemned to eternal punishment. Nor was it long before she, who derived immeasurable happiness from my death, died as well, and for her cruelty and the joy she got from my torments, sins for which she never repented since she thought her behavior meritorious rather than sinful, she, too, has been condemned to the pains of Hell.[4]

"No sooner had she been cast down there than it was ordained for our punishments that she was to flee from me, and I, who once loved her so dearly, was to pursue her as my mortal enemy rather than the woman I once loved. And every time I catch up to her, I kill her with this same sword with which I slew myself. Then I rip open her back, and as you are about to see for yourself, I tear from her body that cold, hard heart of hers, which neither love nor pity could ever penetrate, and together with the rest of her inner organs, I give it to these dogs to eat. In a short space of time, as the justice and power of God ordain, she rises up as if she had never died and begins her woeful flight all over again, with the dogs and me in pursuit.

"Now it just so happens that every Friday around this hour I overtake her in this spot where I slaughter her in the way you are about to observe. Do not imagine, however, that we are resting on the other days, for then I hunt her down in different places where she either practiced her cruelty against me or thought up ways to do so. As you can see, I have now been turned from her friend into her enemy, and I must go on like this for a number of years equal to the number of months she treated me with such cruelty. Now allow me to carry out the decree of divine justice, and do not think to oppose what you could never prevent."

On hearing these words, Nastagio was so frightened that there was scarcely a hair on his head that was not standing on end, and stepping back, he stared at the wretched young woman in terror as he waited to see what the knight would do. Having finished speaking, the latter, with sword in hand, pounced like a mad dog upon the girl who was kneeling before him, held tightly by the two mastiffs, and crying for mercy. With all his strength he stabbed her right in the middle of her chest, causing his blade to pass right through her body and come out the other side. After receiving this blow, she fell down face forward, still weeping and screaming, at which point the knight, having laid hold of a knife, slit open her back, ripped out her heart and everything else around it, and threw it all to the two famished dogs who devoured it at once. Before very long, however, the young woman suddenly rose to her feet as though none of this had happened, and began fleeing toward the sea, with the dogs right after her, tearing at her flesh. Having picked up his sword and gotten back on his horse, the knight set off in pursuit, and a short while later they were so far away that Nastagio could no longer see them.

Nastagio stood there meditating for a long time on what he had seen, divided between pity and fear, but after a bit it occurred to him that since this scene was enacted every Friday, it might well be very useful for him. Consequently, once he had marked the spot, he returned to his attendants, after which, when the time seemed ripe, he sent for a number of his friends and relations.

"For a long time now," he said to them, "you've been urging me to stop loving this enemy of mine and to put an end to all my expenditures on her. Well, I'm ready to do it, provided that you obtain a favor for me, which is this: that you arrange for Messer Paolo Traversari, his wife and daughter, and all their female relations, as well as any other women you like, to come here and dine with me next Friday. You'll see for yourselves later on why I want you to do this."

To all of them this seemed like a small enough commission to carry out, and they promised him they would do it. After returning to Ravenna, in due course they invited all those whom Nastagio wanted as his guests. Although it was no easy matter to persuade the girl he loved to go there, in the end she went along with the others.

Nastagio had them prepare a magnificent feast and had the tables set under the pine trees around the spot where he had witnessed the slaughter of the cruel lady. Moreover, when the men and women were being seated at the tables, he arranged to have his beloved seated directly in front of the spot where the spectacle was going to take place.

They had just been served the last course when they all began to hear the despairing cries of the young woman as she was being chased. Everyone was greatly astonished and asked what it could be, but since no one seemed to know the answer, they all got to their feet in order to see what was happening and caught sight of the weeping girl, the knight, and the dogs who in no time at all arrived in their midst. The spectators made a loud outcry against the dogs and the knight, and many of them rushed forward to help the girl, but the knight, speaking to them just as he had spoken to Nastagio, not only got them to fall back, but terrified every last one of them and filled them with amazement. When he then did to the girl what he had done to her before, all the women present, many of whom were related to either the suffering young woman or the knight, recalled both his love for her and his death, and began to weep as piteously as though what they were witnessing were happening to them.

When the spectacle had come to an end, and the lady and the knight had departed, they all started talking and offering different opinions about what they had seen. Among those who had been the most terrified, however, was the cruel young woman loved by Nastagio, for she had seen and heard everything distinctly, and as she recalled the cruelty with which she had always treated him, she realized that what had happened applied to her more than to anyone else there. And it made her feel as though she was already fleeing from her furious lover, with the two mastiffs at her flanks.

So great was the fear engendered in her by this spectacle that in order to prevent a similar fate from happening to her, she transformed her hatred into love, and seizing the earliest opportunity, which was granted to her that very evening, she secretly sent a trusted chambermaid of hers to Nastagio, asking him on her behalf to be so kind as to come to her, for she was ready to do everything he desired. Nastagio replied to her that this was very gratifying, but that, if she agreed, he preferred to take his pleasure of her in a way that would be consistent with her honor, in other words, by marrying her. Knowing that it was no one's fault but her own that she had not already become Nastagio's wife, the young lady replied to him that she consented. And so, acting as her own intermediary, she told her father and mother that she was happy to become Nastagio's bride, which made the two of them quite happy as well.

The following Sunday Nastagio married her, and after celebrating their nuptials, he lived happily with her for a very long time. Nor was this the only good that came from that fearful spectacle, for indeed, all the women of Ravenna were so frightened because of it that from then on they were far more willing to yield themselves to men's pleasures than they had ever been before.

Day 5, Story 9

In love with a lady who does not return his affection, Federigo degli Alberighi consumes his fortune, spending it all on courting her, until the only thing he has left is a single falcon. When she comes to call on him at his house, he serves it to her to eat because he has nothing else to offer her. Upon discovering what he has done, she has a change of heart, takes him as her husband, and makes him a rich man.[1]

Once Filomena had stopped speaking, the Queen saw that no one else was left except for Dioneo, who had his privilege, and so she said, with a cheerful expression on her face:

Since it is now my turn to speak, dearest ladies, I shall do so gladly and shall tell you a story that partly resembles the preceding one. I do not do so just to make you realize what an effect your charms have on noble hearts, but to teach you how you should, when it is fitting, decide for yourselves how to bestow your favors rather than always allowing Fortune to direct you, for she, as it happens, almost always distributes her gifts with more abundance than discretion.

You should know, then, that Coppo di Borghese Domenichi, who used to live in our city, and perhaps lives there still, was one of the most distinguished and highly respected men of our times, an illustrious person who deserved eternal fame more because of his character and abilities than his noble lineage.[2] When he was well advanced in years, he often derived great pleasure from talking with his neighbors, and with others as well, about incidents from the past. In this he excelled other men, for he had a good sense of how to order things, possessed a capacious memory, and was quite eloquent. Among his many fine stories, there was one he used to tell about a young man who once lived in Florence named Federigo, the son of Messer Filippo Alberighi, who for feats of arms and courtly manners was more highly spoken of than any other squire in Tuscany.[3]

As often happens with gentlemen, Federigo fell in love with a noble lady named Monna Giovanna, who was in her time considered to be one of the most beautiful and refined women in Florence. In an attempt to earn her love, he participated in jousts and tournaments, held banquets, lavished gifts on people, and spent his wealth without restraint. She, however, who was no less honest than beautiful, took no notice of either the things that were done for her or the person who did them.

As Federigo continued to spend money well beyond his means, while acquiring nothing from his lady in return, he went through his entire fortune, as can easily happen, and wound up a poor man, left with nothing except a tiny little farm, the income from which was just enough for him to live very frugally, and a single falcon, which was among the finest in the world. More in love with the lady than ever, but knowing that he could no longer live in the city in the style he preferred, he moved out to Campi where his little farm was located.[4] There he would go hunting with his falcon whenever he could, and without asking assistance from anyone, he bore his poverty with patience.

One day, while Federigo was living in these extremely straitened circumstances, Monna Giovanna's husband, who was very rich, happened to fall ill, and seeing death approach, drew up his will. In it he left his entire estate to his son, who was still a growing boy, and since he also loved his wife very dearly, he made her his heir in the case that his son should die without lawful issue. Then, shortly after that, he passed away.

Monna Giovanna was left a widow, and as our women normally do every year, she went to the country during the summer, taking her son with her to an estate of theirs not far from Federigo's farm. Consequently, the little boy happened to strike up a friendship with Federigo and developed a passionate interest in birds and dogs. He had often seen Federigo's falcon in flight and was so taken with it that he longed to have it for his own, but since he realized how dear it was to Federigo, he never dared to ask him for it.

So things stood, when, to his mother's deep distress, the boy happened to fall ill. Since he was her only child and she loved him as much as one possibly could, she hovered about him all day long, never ceasing to comfort him. Every so often she asked him if there was anything he wanted, imploring him to tell her, because if it was possible to acquire it, she would see about getting it for him.

Finally, after hearing her make this offer over and over again, the boy said: "Mother, if you could arrange for me to have Federigo's falcon, I think I'd soon get better."

When she heard his request, the lady pondered it a great while as she tried to figure out what she should do in response. Knowing that Federigo had been in love with her for a long time and had not received even a single passing glance from her, she said to herself: "How can I send someone to him, let alone go there myself and ask him for his falcon, which is, from everything I've heard, the finest that ever flew, and more than that, the only thing keeping him alive? How can I be so insensitive as to want to deprive such a noble man of his one remaining pleasure?"

Stuck in this quandary, she remained silent, not knowing what to say in answer to her son's request, even though she was certain the falcon was hers for the asking. Finally, however, her love for her son got the better of her, and she decided to satisfy him, come what may, not by sending someone for the falcon, but by going there herself to get it and bring it back to him. "Cheer up, my son," she said, "and just think about getting better. I promise you I'll go to fetch it first thing in the morning, and I'll bring it back here to you for sure." The boy was overjoyed, and that very same day, began showing signs of improvement.

The next morning, taking another woman along with her as company, the lady went over to Federigo's little cottage and asked for him just as though it was nothing more than a casual visit. Since the weather had not been right for hawking for several days, Federigo was in his kitchen garden taking care of one or two little chores, but the moment he heard, to his utter astonishment, that Monna Giovanna was at the door and wanted to see him, he was so happy that he ran there at once to meet her.

When she saw him coming, she got up to meet him with womanly grace. After receiving his respectful greeting, she said, "I hope you are well, Federigo." Then she continued: "I have come to make amends for the harm you have suffered on my account in loving me more than you should have. What I offer you by way of compensation is that I and my companion should like to have a simple dinner here at home with you this morning."

"My lady," replied Federigo in all humility, "I cannot recall ever having suffered any harm on account of you. On the contrary, I have received so much good that if I have ever proved myself worthy in any way, it was entirely due to your merit and to the love I bore you. Moreover, let me assure you that this visit, which is such a generous gesture on your part, is even more precious to me than it would be if I were once again able to spend as much as I have in the past, although on this occasion you have come to a very poor host indeed."

When he finished speaking, he humbly welcomed her into his house and from there led her into his garden, where, not having anyone to keep her company, he said: "My lady, since there is no one else available, this good woman, who is the wife of this farmhand here, will keep you company, while I go to see about having the table set."

Although his poverty was dire, until then Federigo had not realized how desperately needy he had made himself by squandering all his wealth. That morning, however, when he discovered that he had nothing with which he could honor the lady, for whose love he had entertained countless people in the past, he was forced to realize just what it was that he had done. Distressed beyond measure, he silently cursed his fortune, as he ran here and there like a man out of his senses, but he had no success in finding either money or something to pawn. It was already late in the morning, and he was still determined to honor the noble lady with a meal of some sort without asking for assistance from his own farmhand, let alone anyone else, when his eye happened to fall upon his precious falcon sitting on its perch in the little room where he kept it. Since he had no other recourse, he seized the bird, and finding it nice and plump, decided it would make a worthy dish for such a lady. So, without giving the matter a second thought, he wrung its neck and promptly gave it to a maidservant to be plucked, dressed, and care-fully roasted on a spit. Then, when the table was laid with the whitest linen—for he still had some of that in his possession—he returned to the lady in the garden and with a smile on his face told her that their dinner, such as he could prepare for her, was ready.

The lady and her companion arose and came to the table. Then, together with Federigo, who served them with the greatest devotion, they ate the fine falcon without knowing what it was they were eating.

After they had finished dining and the two women had chatted pleasantly with Federigo for a while, the lady felt it was the right time to tell him her reason for coming. Thus, in an affable manner, she began speaking to him:

"Federigo, I haven't the slightest doubt but that you are going to marvel at my presumption when you hear the principal reason for my coming here, especially when you recall your past life and my honesty, which you may have interpreted as harshness and cruelty. But if you had children, or if you had ever had any, you would recognize just how powerful the love one bears for them can be, and on that account, I feel certain you would, to some extent, forgive me.

"Although you have no children, I, who do have a son, am not exempt from the laws common to all other mothers, and since I have no choice but to obey them, I am forced, against my will and contrary to all the rules of decency and decorum, to ask you to make me a gift of some-thing to which I know you are deeply attached—and with good reason, for it is the only delight, the only recreation, the only consolation left you after the loss of your entire fortune. And that gift is your falcon, for which my son has such a longing that if I do not bring it back to him, I fear his sickness is going to get so much worse that I might well lose him. And therefore, not because of the love you bear me, which places you under no obligation to me, but because of your nobility, by which you have shown yourself superior to everyone else in performing acts of courtesy, I implore you to be so kind as to give it to me so that I may be able to say I have preserved my son's life by means of this gift and have thereby placed him forever in your debt."

When he heard what the lady wanted from him and realized that there was no way for him to be of service to her because he had given her the falcon to eat, Federigo began weeping in her presence before he could so much as utter a word in reply. The lady at first believed his tears arose more from his grief over having to part with his prized falcon than from any other motive, and she was on the point of telling him she no longer wanted it. She held herself back, however, and waited to see how Federigo would respond once he stopped crying.

"My lady," he said, "ever since it pleased God that I should make you the object of my love, I have repeatedly complained that Fortune has been my enemy, but everything she did is trivial in comparison with what she has done to me just now. Nor shall I ever be able to forgive her, for I cannot help thinking of how you have come here to my poor house, which you never deigned to visit when it was rich, and how you want only a trifling gift from me, but she has arranged things so that I cannot give it to you. Why I cannot do so, I will explain to you in just a few words.

"When you did me the kindness of saying you wished to dine with me, I deemed it right and proper, in consideration of your distinction and your merit, to honor you by doing all I could to provide you with choicer fare than that which I generally serve other people. Calling to mind the excellence of the falcon you asked me for, I decided it would make a worthy dish for you, and so, this morning I had it roasted and served to you on a trencher, which was, I thought, the best way to present it. But now, I realize that you wanted to have it in a different sense, and I am so distressed by my inability to be of service to you that I do not believe I shall ever forgive myself."

After he finished speaking, he had the feathers, the talons, and the beak placed before her as evidence. On seeing and hearing all this, although the lady initially reproached him for having killed such a falcon simply in order to feed a woman, she then began commending him to herself and was soon filled with admiration for his magnanimity, which his poverty had not been able to diminish, nor ever would. Now, however, that she could not hope to obtain the falcon, she feared that her son's health was therefore in jeopardy, and so, after thanking Federigo for both his hospitality and his good intentions, she took her leave of him, utterly despondent, and returned to her child. To the immeasurable grief of his mother, in the space of a few days, whether it was the result of his depression because he could not have the falcon, or simply the case that his illness would have inevitably led him to such a pass, the boy departed from this life.

After a period of bitter mourning and endless tears, the lady was urged by her brothers on more than one occasion to remarry, since she had been left very rich and was still a young woman. Although she would have preferred to remain a widow, they importuned her so insistently that finally, recalling Federigo's great worth and his last act of generosity, that is, his having killed such a splendid falcon in her honor, she said to them: "I would gladly abstain from marriage, if only that would please you, but since you really want me to choose a husband, you may be certain that I shall never take any man other than Federigo degli Alberighi."

"What are you saying, you silly woman?" said her brothers, making fun of her. "How can you want someone who doesn't have a thing in the world?"

"My brothers," she replied, "I am well aware of the truth of what you're saying, but I'd rather have a man without riches than riches without a man."

Seeing that her mind was made up and knowing Federigo to be a very worthy gentleman, despite his poverty, the brothers acceded to her wishes and gave her to him, together with all her wealth. And so, Federigo, finding himself not just married to the great lady he had loved so dearly, but a very rich man to boot, managed his fortune more prudently than he had before and lived with her happily to the end of his days.

Day 5, Story 10

After Pietro di Vinciolo goes out to have supper, his wife invites a young man to come to her house, but hides him underneath a chicken coop when her husband returns. Pietro tells her that while he was eating at Ercolano's place, they discovered a young man who had been brought there by his wife. Pietro's wife criticizes her severely, but then an ass unfortunately steps on the fingers of the young man underneath the coop, and when he screams, Pietro runs out and sees him, thus discovering his wife's deception. In the end, however, because of his own perversion, he reaches an understanding with her.[1]

W hen the Queen's story had come to its conclusion, and every-one had praised God for having given Federigo the reward he deserved, Dioneo, who never waited around to be asked, began speaking:

I do not know whether to term it an accidental failing stemming from our bad habits, or a defect in our nature as human beings, but the fact is that we are more inclined to laugh about bad behavior than about good deeds, and especially when we ourselves are not involved. And since the sole purpose of the task I am about to undertake, as I have undertaken it on previous occasions, is to dispel your melancholy, loving ladies, and to provide you with laughter and merriment, I am going to tell you the following story, for even though the subject matter is a little unseemly, it may well give you pleasure. As you listen to it, you should do what you would normally do when you go out into your gardens, where you stretch out your delicate hands to pluck the roses, but leave the thorns alone. This you will do if you leave the wicked husband to his ill-fated, degenerate behavior, while laughing merrily

at the amorous tricks of his wife, and feeling compassion, as need be,
for the misfortunes of others.

There once lived in Perugia, not so very long ago, a rich man named
Pietro di Vinciolo who got married, perhaps to deceive his fellow citizens and to improve the low opinion they all had of him, more than
because of any desire he had to take a wife.[2] And Fortune showed
herself to be in such conformity with his proclivities that the wife he
chose for himself was a buxom young woman with red hair and a fiery
complexion who would have preferred to have two husbands rather
than one, and who now found herself with a man whose inclinations
led him elsewhere rather than in her direction.

In the course of time the wife came to understand the way things
stood, and since she was well aware of just how fresh and lovely she
was, and how lusty and lively she felt, she got so upset about it that
every once in a while, she would quarrel with her husband and call
him filthy names. She was miserable practically every moment until it
finally dawned on her that if she went on like this, it might well lead
to her prostration rather than any reformation of her husband's vice,
and so, she said to herself:

"Since this sorry pervert abandons me to go up the dry path in his
clogs, I'll do my best to get others to board my boat and carry them
through the rain.* I took him as my husband and brought him a fine
large dowry, acting on the assumption that he was a man and believing he was interested in the kind of thing men generally like, as they
certainly should. After all, if I hadn't thought he was a man, I would
never have married him. Furthermore, he knew I was a woman, and
if women weren't to his taste, why did he ever take me as his wife? I'm

---

*The two expressions in this sentence were proverbial: *andare in zoccoli per l'asciutto*
("go in [his] clogs up [lit., through, along] the dry [path]") for homosexual love; and for
heterosexual love, *portare altrui in nave per lo piovoso* ("get others to board my boat and
carry them through the rain"). The first saying may involve the idea that since clogs had
high soles, there was no need for them when walking on a dry surface—i.e., homosexual
love is superfluous or irrelevant. But clogs, in and of themselves, generally evoked homosexual love in the period, perhaps through their association with friars. "The dry path"
is suggestive in its own right, of course, and the second saying about heterosexual love,
involving carrying people on board one's boat when it is raining, should need no comment.

not going to put up with this. Had I wanted to turn my back on the world, I would have become a nun, but in choosing to live in it as I do, if I expect any fun and games out of this guy, I'll probably still be waiting in vain for that when I'm an old woman. And what good will it do me, in my old age, to look back and grieve over having wasted my youth, especially since this husband of mine here has actually been a really good teacher and shown me precisely how I ought to console myself? I should get my pleasure from the same thing he delights in, but whereas that pleasure will be strongly condemned in his case, in mine it will be commendable, for I will merely be breaking the laws of marriage, while he breaks those of Nature as well."

These, then, were the good lady's thoughts, to which she probably returned on more than one occasion, and in order to put them into effect on the sly, she made the acquaintance of an old woman who gave every indication of being a Saint Verdiana feeding the serpents, for she would go around to every pardoning service at church, always carrying her rosary in her hand, and never talking about anything except the lives of the Holy Fathers and the wounds of Saint Francis, with the result that virtually everyone considered her a saint.* When the time seemed right, the wife revealed her intentions in full to the old woman, who said in reply:

"My child, God knows—and He knows everything—that what you'll be doing is right, because even if you had no other reason, you're bound to do it, you and every other young woman, rather than fritter away your youth. To anyone who's had any experience of such matters, there's no grief equal to that of having let your time go to waste. After all, what the devil are we women good for in our old age except to sit around the fire and stare at the ashes? If there are any women who know this and can prove it to you, I'm certainly one of them. Now that I'm old, I experience the sharpest, most bitter pangs of regret in

---

*According to popular legends recounting the life of Saint Verdiana Attavanti (1182–1242), the most venerated saint in Castelfiorentino, Tuscany, two serpents entered the nun's cell there, and since she thought they were sent by God to tempt her, she fed them and took care of them. The saint's name was thus synonymous with devotion and asceticism.

my heart whenever I realize, all to no avail, how many opportunities I let slip by. Actually, I didn't waste all of them—I wouldn't want you to think me a complete idiot—but I still didn't do as much as I could have. And so, when I recall the past and then contemplate the state you see me in today, God only knows how sorry I feel that I can't find anyone nowadays to light my fire for me.[3]

"It's not like that for men. They're born with a thousand different talents besides this, and for the most part, the older ones are worth much more than the young. But women are born just to do this single thing, and to make babies, and that's the only reason why they're cherished. Now, if nothing else will convince you of this, then you ought to consider the fact that we women are always ready for it, which is not the case with men. What's more, one woman could exhaust a host of men, whereas a host of men can't tire out a single woman. And since this is the purpose for which we are born, I repeat that you'll be doing the right thing if you give your husband tit for tat, for that way, when you grow old, your heart won't have any reason to lodge a complaint against your flesh.

"In this world, you only get what you grab for, especially in the case of women, so it's far more important for them than for men to make the best use of their opportunities while they've still got some, because as you can see for yourself, when we get old, neither our husbands nor any other man can bear the sight of us. On the contrary, they chase us away into the kitchen to tell tales to the cat and to count the pots and pans. What's worse, they make up rhymes about us and sing:

For young gals, all the best mouthfuls in town;
For old ones, stuff that gets stuck halfway down.

And they have lots of other sayings just like that.

"But to avoid detaining you any longer with my chatter, let me tell you that you couldn't have revealed your thoughts to anybody else in the world who was better able to help you. For there's no man so refined that I would hesitate to tell him what's required of him, nor is there anyone so hard and churlish that I couldn't really soften him up and get him to do what I want. All you have to do is to show me which one you like, and then leave the rest to me. But let me ask one thing of you, my child, and that is to always keep me in mind, for I'm a poor old woman, and from now on I want you to take a share in all of my indulgences and all the Our Fathers I recite, so that God may turn them into so many lights and candles for your own dear departed ones."

When the old woman had had her say, the young lady came to an understanding with her, telling her that if she ever happened to see a certain young fellow who often walked through that part of the city and whose features the young lady described to her in great detail, she would know what she had to do. She then gave the old woman a piece of salted meat and sent her on her way with God's blessings.

It only took a few days for the old woman, acting on the sly, to get the guy the young lady had been talking about into her bedroom, and then, a little after that, another one and yet another one, as they happened to catch the young lady's fancy. And although she lived in constant fear of her husband, she never failed to take advantage of any opportunity that presented itself to her.

One evening, when her husband was supposed to go out to have supper with a friend of his named Ercolano, the wife gave the old woman the order to bring her one of the prettiest, most agreeable youths in Perugia, an order that she carried out with alacrity.[4] But the wife had just sat down at the supper table with young man when, lo and behold, there was Pietro at the entrance shouting for her to open the door.

When she heard her husband's voice, the lady thought she was as good as dead, but all the same, she wanted to conceal the young man if she could, and since she did not see how she could send him away or think of any other place for him to hide, she got him to take refuge underneath a chicken coop in the shed adjoining the room in which they were having supper. Then she took the cover of a straw mattress, whose contents had been emptied out earlier that day, and threw it over him. This done, she rushed to the door and opened it for her husband, saying to him as he entered the house: "You sure gulped down that supper of yours in a big hurry."

"We didn't even get to taste it," he replied.

"How come?" the lady asked.

"I'll tell you how come," he said. "We'd just sat down at the table, Ercolano, his wife, and I, when we heard someone sneezing nearby. We took no notice of it the first time, or the second, but when the guy who had sneezed did it again a third and then a fourth and a fifth time, and a good many more times after that, it got us all to wondering. Already a little irritated by his wife because she'd left us standing in the entryway for ages before opening the door, Ercolano just about flew into a rage and blurted out, 'What's the meaning of this? Who's doing all that sneezing?' Then he got up from the table and walked over to some stairs nearby, which had an enclosure made of wooden boards at the bottom, the sort of thing we often see people use for storage when they're tidying up their houses.

"Since it seemed to Ercolano that the sneezing was coming from inside there, he opened the little door, and the moment he did, out flew the worst smell of sulfur in the world. We had actually gotten a whiff of the stench before then, but when we had complained about it, Ercolano's wife had said, 'That's because I was using sulfur earlier to bleach my veils, and even though I sprinkled it over them in a large pan so they would absorb the fumes and then placed it under the stairs, it's still giving off an odor.'

"Since Ercolano had opened the closet door and the fumes had now dispersed to some extent, he looked inside and caught sight of the guy who'd been sneezing. In fact, he was still doing it because of the over-powering stench of the sulfur, and despite all his sneezing, the sulfur was choking him to the point that if he'd stayed in there much longer, he wouldn't have sneezed, or done anything else for that matter, ever again.

"The moment he saw the guy, Ercolano yelled: 'Now I see, woman, why you made us wait so long outside the door just now before you got around to opening it. But I'm going to pay you back for this, if it's the last thing I do!' When his wife heard this threat and realized that her sin had been discovered, she got up from the table without saying a word to excuse herself and fled away, nor do I have the slightest idea where she went. Not noticing that she'd taken off, Ercolano repeatedly told the guy who was sneezing to come out, but he was on his last legs and didn't budge no matter what Ercolano said. So, Ercolano grabbed him by one of his feet, dragged him out, and then ran off for a knife with the intention of killing him. But I was afraid we'd be arrested by the watch, myself included, and so I got up and wouldn't let him murder the guy or even do him any harm. In fact, as I was defending him from Ercolano, it was my shouting that brought some of the neighbors to the scene, and they picked up the young man, who was now more dead than alive, and carried him to some place out of the house, although I have no idea where. Because of all these goings-on, our supper was disrupted, and as I said before, not only did I not gulp it down, I didn't even get to taste it."

When the wife heard her husband's story, she realized that there were other women who were just as clever as she was, even though some of their plans occasionally met with misfortune. She would have been glad to speak out in defense of Ercolano's wife, but thinking that if she condemned someone else's misdeeds, she would have a freer scope for her own, she said:

"What fine goings-on! What a good, saintly person that woman must be! What a faithful, honest spouse! Why, I was practically ready to make my confession to her, she seemed so devout! And the worst part of it is that someone her age should be setting such a fine example for young women! I curse the hour she came into the world, and curse the wicked, deceitful woman for allowing herself to become a universal figure of shame and scorn for all the women in the city! Not only has she thrown away any concern for her honor, the vow of fidelity she made when she got married, and her reputation in society, but she felt no remorse at involving her husband in her disgrace, despite the fact that he's treated her very well and is such a proper man and a well-respected citizen—and all for the sake of some other guy! So help me God, women of that sort should be shown no mercy. They should be killed. In fact, they should be burned alive until they're reduced to ashes!"

Then, recollecting that she had concealed her lover underneath the chicken coop next to the room they were in, she began coaxing Pietro to go to bed, telling him that it was time to do so. But he was much more interested in food than in sleep and kept asking her whether there was anything for supper.

"Sure, we've got something for supper!" she replied. "We always go ahead and make supper when you're not here! What do you take me for, Ercolano's wife? So, why don't you just go off to bed for tonight? It would be a lot better for you!"

Now, that evening, it just so happened that some of the farmhands who worked for Pietro had brought him a load of provisions from his farm and had tethered their asses in a little stable located next to the shed. They had not bothered to give the animals anything to drink, and one of them, desperately thirsty, had slipped its head out of its halter, strayed away from the stable, and gone sniffing around everywhere to see if it could find water. As it went roaming about, it wound up, by chance, bumping into the chicken coop under which the young man was hiding. Since he was forced to crouch there on all fours, the fingers of one of his hands, which he had stretched out on the ground, were protruding slightly from underneath the coop, and it was just his luck—or rather, his bad luck, we should say—that the ass stepped right on them with his hoof, causing the young man such excruciating pain that he started shrieking at the top of his lungs.

When he heard the noise, Pietro was astonished, and realizing that it was coming from the interior of the house, he went outside the room, where the guy was still howling, for the ass had not yet lifted up its hoof from off his fingers and was continuing to press down on them just as hard as ever. "Who's that there?" yelled Pietro, and he ran right over to the coop, lifted it up, and discovered the young man who was not only suffering from the pain of having his fingers crushed by the ass's hoof, but was shaking all over with fear that Pietro might do him some injury. Recognizing the young man as someone he had long pursued for his own wicked purposes, Pietro asked him, "What are you doing here?" The young man said nothing in reply to this question, but instead, begged Pietro, for the love of God, not to harm him.

"Get up," said Pietro. "There's no reason to worry. I'm not going to hurt you. Just tell me how you wound up in here, and why."

The young man told him everything, and Pietro, who was as happy to have discovered him there as his wife was upset about it, took him by the hand and led him back into the room where she was waiting for him, just as frightened as she could be. Pietro sat down right in front of her and said: "When you were cursing out Ercolano's wife just now, saying that she should be burned and that she was a disgrace to all you women, why didn't you say the same things about yourself? Or if you wanted to avoid speaking about yourself, how did you have the gall to talk about her since you knew you'd done exactly what she did? The only reason you said it, of course, is that you women are all alike: you're always looking to use other people's faults to cover up your own transgressions. I wish that Heaven would send down a fire and burn up the whole disgusting lot of you!"

Seeing that in the first flush of his anger Pietro had done nothing worse than abuse her verbally, and sensing that he was thoroughly delighted to be holding such a good-looking youth by the hand, his wife took heart and said: "I'm not surprised that you'd like to have a fire come down from Heaven and burn us all up, because you're the kind of guy who's as fond of women as a dog is of a cudgel, but by God's Cross, you're not going to see that wish of yours fulfilled. Still, I'd like to discuss this with you a bit more, because I want to know what it is you're complaining about. As far as I'm concerned, it would certainly be fine with me if you wanted to put me on an equal footing with Ercolano's wife, because at least that breast-beating old hypocrite gets what she wants out of her husband, and he's as fond of her as any man is of his spouse—which is more than can be said in my case. Sure, I grant you do a good job of providing me with clothes and shoes, but you know only too well how I'm doing in another respect and how long it's been since the last time you slept with me. I'd rather go around barefoot and in rags, and have you treat me well in bed, than to have all that stuff and to be treated by you the way I am. Now, you need to understand me clearly here, Pietro: I'm a woman just like the rest, and I want the same thing they do. And if I can't get it from you, you have no cause to bad-mouth me just because I go and find it for myself somewhere else. At least I do you the honor of not getting involved with stable boys and other riffraff."

Pietro realized that she could go on talking like this all night long, and since he was not particularly interested in her anyway, he said: "All right, woman, that's enough. I'll make sure that you get what'll really satisfy you. But now, will you be so kind as to arrange for us to have something to eat, because it seems to me that this young man here hasn't had any more supper than I have."

"Of course he hasn't had any supper yet," said the lady, "because we were just sitting down at the table to eat when you showed up, damn you."

"Well go then," said Pietro, "and see to it that we get some food. After that, I'll take care of things so that you won't have any more reason to complain."

Seeing that her husband was content, the lady got up and soon had the table set again. Once it was spread with the food that she had prepared, she ate supper merrily with her pervert of a husband and the young man.

What exactly Pietro had worked out to satisfy all three of them after supper has slipped my mind, but this much I do know. When the young man was escorted back to the piazza the next morning, he was not entirely sure whether he had been more of a wife or a husband that night. And that's why my advice to you, dear ladies, is to do unto others as they do unto you. And if you can't do it right then and there, bear it in mind until you can. That way, just like that ass bumping into the wall, you'll give as good as you get.*

---

*Dioneo's final comment repeats almost exactly a comment made by one of the merchants when they are talking together at the start of 2.9. The point of the comment is that when an ass bumps into a wall, he is, in a sense, bumped back by the wall. In short, Dioneo's advice is that it is a game of tit for tat: women should feel free to cheat on their husbands since their husbands feel free to cheat on them.

Day 5, Conclusion

If the ladies restrained their laughter at Dioneo's story, they did so more out of modesty than because they failed to find it amusing. When he was finished, the Queen realized that her reign had come to its end, and so she got up, took the laurel crown, and as she placed it gracefully on Elissa's head, said to her: "It is now your turn to command us, my lady."

Having accepted the honor, Elissa did exactly what they had all done in the past: first, she gave the steward orders for what would be needed during the course of her reign, and then, to the general satisfaction of the company, she said:

"We have already heard many times how all sorts of people, by dint of clever quips or ready retorts or prompt stratagems, have been able to make use of a biting response of their own in order to take the edge off the teeth of their opponents' attacks or to avert impending dangers. And since this is such a splendid topic, and one that may well prove useful, it is my desire that, with God's help, we should stay within these bounds tomorrow and speak about those who, having been provoked by some elegant witticism, have replied in kind, or who, with a prompt retort or a strategic maneuver, have managed to avoid danger, loss, or ridicule."

Everyone applauded this decision, after which the Queen got to her feet and dismissed them all until suppertime. When the honorable company saw the Queen arise, they all stood up, and, following their usual routine, turned their attention to whatever they enjoyed doing the most.

But when the cicadas had stopped their singing, everyone was called back, and they all sat down to supper, which they ate happily, fully enjoying one another's company. They then proceeded to sing and play music, and while Emilia was leading a dance at the Queen's behest, Dioneo was ordered to sing them a song. He promptly started in with "Monna Aldruda, lift up your tail, For wonderful tidings I bring you," which made all the ladies start laughing, and especially the Queen, who ordered him to stop and sing another.[1]

"My lady," replied Dioneo, "if I had a tambourine, I'd give you 'Hike up your skirts, Monna Lapa' or 'There's grass beneath the little olive tree.' Or would you like me to sing 'The waves of the sea make me so sick'? But I don't have a tambourine, so take your pick from among all these others. Would you prefer 'Come on out, and you'll get cut down, Like a May-pole in the country'?"

"No," said the Queen, "sing us something else."

"Well, then," said Dioneo, "I'll give you 'Monna Simona, fill up your cask, fill it up. But it's not yet the month of October.'"[2]

"Now, darn you," said the Queen with a laugh, "give us a pretty one, if you want to sing. We do not want that one."

"No, my lady, do not take offense," replied Dioneo. "Which one do you prefer? I know more than a thousand. How about 'This is my shell if I don't prick it well,' or 'Take it easy, husband dear,' or 'I bought me a cock worth a hundred *lire*'?"

Although all the other ladies were laughing, the Queen was getting a little exasperated.

"Stop your joking around, Dioneo," she said, "and sing us a nice one. Because if you do not, you will find out just how angry I can get."

When he heard this, Dioneo stopped wisecracking and immediately began a song that went like this:

> O Love, the charming light
> That issues from those gorgeous eyes of hers
> Has made me now her slave and yours as well.
> The splendor shining from her lovely eyes
> Passed through my own, and entering my heart,
> Set your flames there alight.

The beauty of her face made manifest
How overwhelming your true worth might be,
And contemplating it,
I felt I'd gathered all
The virtues, bound them up and gave her them,
Which gives me yet new reasons for my sighs.

  One of your servants have I thus become,
Dear Lord, and now await obediently
What grace your might may give.
But yet I do not know if she's aware
Of my unbroken faith, or of the high desire
You lodged within my breast,
For she possesses all
My thoughts so utterly that I can't find,
Nor would I seek, my peace except in her.

  Thus I beseech you, sweetest Lord of mine,
That you will show her this and make her feel
A little of your fire
On my behalf, because you see that I
Consume myself in loving, bit by bit,
And martyred, waste away.
So, when the time is ripe,
Commend me to her, as indeed you should,
Though to do that I'd gladly come with you.

When Dioneo showed by his silence that he had finished his song, the Queen, after conferring high praise on it, had them sing many others. By then, a good part of the night had passed, and since she could feel that the cool of the evening had quenched the heat of the day, the Queen ordered all of them to go and sleep for as long as they liked until the next morning.

Day 6, Introduction

Here ends the Fifth Day of the Decameron and the Sixth begins, in which, under the rule of Elissa, they speak of those who, having been provoked by some elegant witticism, have replied in kind, or who, with a prompt retort or a strategic maneuver, have managed to avoid danger, loss, or ridicule.

The moon, which was still in the middle of the sky, had lost its radiance, and the new light of dawn was already shining brightly everywhere in our hemisphere, when the Queen got up and had her companions summoned. After leaving the beautiful palace, they strolled for a while at a leisurely pace through the dewy grass, conversing together on a variety of topics, debating which of the stories they had heard were the most beautiful and which the least, and laughing anew over the many different incidents recounted in them, until, as the sun climbed higher and it was starting to get warm, they all decided they needed to go back. Consequently, they retraced their steps and returned to the palace, where the tables had already been set and fragrant herbs and beautiful flowers had been strewn all about. At the Queen's command they all addressed themselves to their dinner before the heat of the day set in, and then, having finished their merry meal, they first of all sang a number of beautiful, sprightly little songs, after which some of them went to take a nap and others played chess and dice games, while Dioneo, together with Lauretta, began singing about Troilus and Cressida.[1]

When the hour arrived for them to reassemble, the Queen had them summoned, and in their usual way they all sat down around the fountain. As she was about to call for the first story, however, something happened that had never happened before: namely, she and all the others heard a huge racket coming from among their maids and serving men in the kitchen.[2] She sent for the steward and asked him who was doing the screaming and what the uproar was all about. He replied that Licisca and Tindaro were having an argument, but that he did not know what had caused it, for just as he had arrived on the scene to make them quiet down, he had been summoned to appear before the Queen. Consequently, she ordered him to have Licisca and Tindaro brought before her at once, and when they arrived, she asked them to explain what they had been arguing about.

Tindaro was about to reply, when Licisca, who was no spring chicken and was rather full of herself, and who had, besides, gotten heated from all the yelling, turned on him and gave him a withering look. "Look, you ass of a man," she said, "how dare you, in my presence, speak before I do! Just let me talk." Then, turning back to the Queen, she went on:

"My lady, this guy wants to teach me all about Sicofante's wife, and just as if I wasn't acquainted with her at all, he would have me believe that the first night Sicofante went to bed with her, Messer Mace entered Black Mountain by force and with much bloodshed.[3] But let me tell you, that's not true: he entered it peacefully and to the general contentment of those inside. What's more, this guy is such an ass that he really believes young women are all so foolish that they're willing to waste their time waiting around for their fathers and brothers to marry them off, which six times out of seven takes them three or four years longer than it should. Brother, they'd be in a fine state if they postponed it that long! I swear to Christ—and I should really know what I'm talking about when I swear like that—I don't have a single neighbor who was a virgin when she got married, and as for the married ones, I sure know about all the different kinds of tricks they play on their husbands and how often they play them. Yet this muttonhead wants to teach me about women as if I were born yesterday!"

While Licisca was talking, the women were laughing so hard that you could have reached in their mouths and yanked out all their teeth. The Queen imposed silence on her a good half-dozen times, but all to no avail, for she would not stop until she had had her say.

When she was finally done, the Queen turned to Dioneo with a laugh and said: "Dioneo, this is a dispute for you to settle, and so, when our storytelling is over, I want you to pronounce the final judgment on it."

"My lady, there's no need for another word," replied Dioneo without hesitation. "Judgment has already been given. I declare that Licisca is in the right, and not only do I believe that things are the way she says, but I also agree that Tindaro is an ass."

When Licisca heard this, she burst out laughing, and turning to Tindaro, she said: "Didn't I tell you so? Now get along, and God be with you. Do you really think you know more than I do, when you're still wet behind the ears? Thank goodness, I haven't lived for nothing, no, not me."

With a stern look that by itself imposed silence on her, the Queen commanded Licisca not to utter another sound, let alone a word, unless she wanted to be whipped, and then sent her and Tindaro away. Indeed, had she not done so, the company would not have had anything else to do for the rest of the day but listen to Licisca talk. Then, when the two servants were gone, the Queen ordered Filomena to start the storytelling, which she cheerfully began as follows.

Day 6, Story 1

A knight offers Madonna Oretta a horseback ride in the form of a story, but he tells it in so disorderly a fashion that she begs him to set her down on foot.[1]

Young ladies, just as heaven is decorated with stars on cloudless nights and in the spring the green meadows are brightened with flowers and the hills with saplings dressed in their new foliage, so good manners and pleasant conversation are adorned with clever quips. These, because they are brief, are much better suited to women than to men, whereas it is much less becoming for the former than the latter to give elaborate speeches. Truth to tell, for whatever reason, whether because of the defectiveness of our wits or the singular hatred that the heavens bear toward our age, to our universal shame, there are few, if any, women left who know how to deliver a quip at the right time or are able to grasp one correctly after it has been delivered. Since Pampinea has already spoken at length on this subject, however, I do not intend to say any more about it. But in order to show you how beautiful a witticism can be when delivered at the right moment, I would like to tell you about the courteous way a gentlewoman once imposed silence on a knight.

As many of you know, having either met her or heard about her, not long ago there lived in our city a lady who was not only wellborn and well bred, but well-spoken, too, and who, for all her fine qualities, deserves to be identified by name. She was called Madonna Oretta and was the wife of Messer Geri Spina. Like us, she happened to be in the country at one point, where, as a form of recreation, she was going from one spot to another with a party of ladies and knights whom she had had to dinner at her house earlier that day. Since the trip between the place from which they had just come and the one to which they all wanted to go was rather long on foot, one of the knights in the company said to her: "Madonna Oretta, if you like, I'll carry you through most of what remains of our journey by giving you a horseback ride there astride one of the finest stories in the world."

"Sir," the lady replied, "I beg you most earnestly to do so, for I would look upon it as a great favor."

Consequently, this Messer Knight, who was perhaps no better at using the sword by his side than he was at using his tongue to tell stories, began reciting one of his tales to her. It was, admittedly, very beautiful in itself, but by repeating the same word three, four, or even six times, and going back to start sections over again, and sometimes declaring "I haven't got it right," and often getting lost in all the names, and confusing one person with another, he was well on his way to ruining it completely. Besides, his mode of delivery was terribly unsuited to the different characters and incidents he was describing.[2]

As Madonna Oretta listened to the knight's narration, she repeatedly broke out in a sweat and experienced heart palpitations, as if she had become ill and was almost at the point of death. When she finally could not endure it anymore, seeing that the knight had gotten bogged down in the mire[3] and was not about to extract himself from it, she said to him in a pleasant manner: "Sir, this horse of yours has too hard a trot. Please be so good as to set me down."

The knight, who was apparently better at taking a hint than at telling a tale, understood her quip, and treating it as a joke, took it in good humor. He then began rehearsing other stories and left unfinished the one he had begun and was narrating so badly.

Day 6, Story 2

By means of a single phrase, Cisti the baker makes Messer Geri Spina see how he has made an inappropriate request.[1]

Madonna Oretta's remark received high praise from all the women as well as the men. When the Queen then ordered Pampinea to follow suit, she began as follows:

Lovely ladies, for my part I am unable to decide which sin is greater, that of Nature in assigning a noble spirit to an inferior body, or that of Fortune in assigning a body endowed with a noble spirit to an inferior profession. The latter happened in the case of our fellow citizen Cisti, as well as in many others we have had occasion to observe, for although Cisti was endowed with a most exalted spirit, Fortune made him a baker.

I would certainly curse Nature and Fortune alike if I did not know that the former is very discerning and the latter has a thousand eyes, albeit fools picture her as being blind. I am convinced that since both are very shrewd, they do what mortals do when they are unsure about the future. For they often bury their most precious belongings in the most unprepossessing places in their homes, places where one would least expect to find them, so that then, when the need is greatest, they can be brought out again, the humble nature of their hiding place having kept them safer than if they had been in some elegant chamber. In the same way, the two arbiters of all worldly things often hide their most precious treasures beneath the shadow of the basest professions, so that when the need arises for them to be brought forth, their splendor will be all the more apparent. I will prove this to you by means of a very short tale, which I was reminded of by the last story we heard. It involves an episode, in itself of no great importance, in which Cisti the baker got Geri Spina, who was Madonna Oretta's husband, to open the eyes of his mind and see the truth.

Let me say, then, that when Pope Boniface, who held Messer Geri Spina in the highest esteem, sent certain noblemen as his ambassadors to Florence on urgent papal business, they stayed at Messer Geri's house.[2] He joined them in their negotiations, and almost every morning, for one reason or another, it just so happened that they would all walk past Santa Maria Ughi where Cisti the baker had his shop and plied his trade in person.

Although Fortune had assigned Cisti to a very humble profession, she had been sufficiently kind to him as he practiced it that he had become extremely wealthy, and while he felt no desire to change his profession for any other, he nevertheless lived in the most splendid style and had, among all the other fine things he called his own, the best white and red wines to be found in Florence or the surrounding region. As he watched Messer Geri and the Pope's ambassadors walking past his door every morning, it occurred to him that it would be very courteous on his part, seeing how hot the weather was, to offer them a drink of his good white wine. But being conscious of the difference in social rank between himself and Messer Geri, he felt it would be an unseemly act of presumption for him to make such an invitation, and so he thought up a plan, instead, by means of which he could induce Messer Geri to make the proposal himself.

Accordingly, every morning, Cisti would always put on the whitest of doublets and a freshly washed apron, which made him look more like a miller than a baker, and around the time he thought Messer Geri was going to walk past with the ambassadors, he would station himself near the entrance to his shop where a shiny tin pail of fresh water had been set up alongside a new little Bolognese pitcher filled with his good white wine and two goblets so luminous they seemed made of silver. There he would sit, and as they passed by, after clearing his throat once or twice, he would start drinking this wine of his with such gusto that he would have made the dead feel thirsty.

After Messer Geri had observed this two mornings in a row, on the third he asked: "How is it, Cisti? Is it good?"

"Yes, sir," replied Cisti, springing to his feet, "but I can't really make you understand just how good it is unless you taste some of it."

Whether it was the weather, or his having exerted himself more than usual, or maybe the sight of Cisti drinking with so much relish, Messer Geri had developed such a thirst that he turned to the ambassadors with a smile and said: "Gentlemen, we would do well to sample this worthy man's wine. Perhaps it's such that we won't regret having done so."

Messer Geri and the ambassadors all walked over to Cisti, who immediately had an attractive bench brought out from inside the shop and invited them to have a seat. He then turned to their servants, who were already coming up to wash the glasses, and told them:

"Stand aside, friends, and leave this duty for me to take care of, because I know as much about serving wine as I do about baking. As for you, just don't you think that you're going to taste a drop of this yourselves!"

After he had spoken, Cisti washed four beautiful new goblets with his own hands, had a little pitcher of his good wine brought out for them, and with meticulous care, poured some of it for Messer Geri and his companions, none of whom had drunk anything that fine in years. Messer Geri was enthusiastic in his praise of the wine, and for the rest of the time that the ambassadors were in Florence, he went there with them almost every morning to drink it.

When the ambassadors had finished their business and were about to depart, Messer Geri held a magnificent banquet for them to which he invited a number of the most prominent citizens. He also sent an invitation to Cisti, who could not be persuaded to come under any circumstances. Whereupon Messer Geri ordered one of his servants to go for a flask of Cisti's wine and to give half a glass of it to each person during the first course.

The servant, who was perhaps annoyed that he had never been allowed to taste the wine, took a large flagon with him, and as soon as Cisti saw it, he said: "Son, Messer Geri's not sending you to me."

The servant kept insisting that Messer Geri had indeed done so, but when he could not extract any other answer from Cisti, he returned to his master. After the servant explained what Cisti had said, Messer Geri told him: "Go back to him and tell him that I really did send you to him, and if he still responds like that, ask him to whom I'm sending you."

The servant returned and said: "Cisti, I assure you that Messer Geri really is sending me to you."

"And I assure you, son," replied Cisti, "he's really not."

"Then," said the servant, "to whom is he sending me?"

"To the Arno," replied Cisti.[3]

When the servant reported this exchange to Messer Geri, the eyes of his mind were immediately opened, and he said to the man: "Let me see the flask you're taking to him." The instant he saw it, Messer Geri declared, "Cisti's right," and then, after giving the servant a scolding, he had him take a flask of a suitable size.

When he saw the flask, Cisti said, "Now I'm certain he's sending you to me," and happily filled it up for him.

Later the same day, Cisti had a little cask filled with a wine of the same vintage and had it carefully transported to Messer Geri's house. He followed right behind, and upon encountering Messer Geri in person, he said to him: "I wouldn't want you to think, sir, that I was taken aback by that large flagon this morning. It's just that I thought you'd forgotten what I've shown you over the last few days with the help of my little pitchers, namely that this is no wine for servants. All I wanted to do this morning was to refresh your memory. Now, since I don't intend to be the guardian of this wine for you any longer, I've had it all brought here, and from this point forward, you may dispose of it as you please."[4]

Deeply appreciative of Cisti's gift, Messer Geri thanked him in an appropriate manner, and from that time forth he held Cisti in high esteem and considered him his friend forever.

Day 6, Story 3

With a ready retort, Monna Nonna de' Pulci silences the unseemly banter of the Bishop of Florence.[1]

When Pampinea had finished her story, and everyone had heaped praise on Cisti's reply as well as on his generosity, it was the Queen's pleasure to make Lauretta the next speaker, who gaily began as follows:

Charming ladies, there is a great deal of truth both in what Filomena said just now, and in what Pampinea was saying before, about the beauty of repartee and our lack of skill with it. Consequently, while it is not necessary to repeat their arguments, I want to remind you that, in addition to what has already been said about witticisms, their nature is such that they should bite the listener like a sheep and not like a dog, because if a clever quip bit the way a dog does, it would no longer be a quip, but an insult. Madonna Oretta's remark and Cisti's reply were both excellent illustrations of how to do this. Now it is true in the case of repartee that if the speaker bites like a dog after having first been bitten that way himself, his response does not seem as reprehensible as it would have been otherwise. One must therefore consider carefully how, when, with whom, and likewise where one makes a clever remark. These are matters to which a certain prelate of ours once paid so little attention that he received as much of a bite as the one he gave, something I should like to tell you about now in this little story.

When Messer Antonio d'Orso, a wise and worthy prelate, was Bishop of Florence, there came to the city a Catalan nobleman named Messer Dego della Ratta, who was King Robert's Marshal.[2] Physically quite attractive, Messer Dego was very much the ladies' man, and among all the women in Florence, there was one, a stunning beauty, whom he fancied in particular and who happened to be the niece of the Bishop's brother. Having learned that the lady's husband, although he came from a good family, was extremely avaricious and corrupt, he made a bargain with him to the effect that he would give him five hundred gold florins in exchange for being allowed to sleep for one night with his wife. What the Marshal went and did was to take some silver coins called *popolini*, which were then in circulation, and have them gilded, after which, having slept with the man's wife against her will, he gave them to her husband.* Subsequently, the story became common knowledge, and what the wicked husband finally got out of it was not just his financial loss, but his being turned into a public laughingstock. The Bishop, wise man that he was, feigned total ignorance of the affair.

The Bishop and the Marshal used to spend a great deal of time in each other's company, and one day, it being the feast day of Saint John, they happened to be riding side by side, looking over the ladies who were lining the street where the *Palio*† is run, when the Bishop spotted a young woman named Monna Nonna de' Pulci, whom this present pestilence has taken from us as an adult.[3] You must all know whom I mean—she was Messer Alesso Rinucci's cousin. In those days Monna Nonna was a fresh, beautiful girl, well-spoken and high spirited, who had just recently gotten married in the Porta San Piero quarter. The Bishop pointed her out to the Marshal, and then, when they got up close to her, he put his hand on the Marshal's shoulder and said: "Nonna, how does this fellow strike you? Do you think you could make a conquest of him?"

It seemed to Nonna that his words impugned her honor to some degree, or that they would at least tarnish it in the minds of the people who heard what he said—and there was quite a crowd of them

---

* The *popolino* was a silver coin first minted in 1305. It was the same size as the florin, but was worth a great deal less.

† On June 24, the feast day of Saint John (San Giovanni), the patron saint of Florence, there used to be a famous horse race, *Il Palio*, named for the prize, the *palio* or "banner," awarded to the winner. The race is no longer run in Florence, but Siena continues to host its own version of the *Palio* on July 2 and August 16.

there. She was less intent upon purging her honor of any stain it might have received, however, than upon returning blow for blow, and so she promptly replied:

"It's unlikely that he'd ever make a conquest of me, sir, but in any event, I'd want to be paid in good coin."

Both the Marshal and the Bishop were equally cut to the quick by her remark, the first as the author of the dishonorable deed involving the niece of the Bishop's brother, and the second as the victim insofar as it had been done to a member of his own family. Shamed and silenced, the two of them rode away without so much as looking at one another, and they did not say another thing to Monna Nonna that day.

In this case, then, since the young lady had been bitten first, it was not inappropriate for her to bite back with a clever quip of her own.

Day 6, Story 4

Chichibio, Currado Gianfigliazzi's cook, saves himself by means of a prompt retort that converts his master's anger into laughter, allowing him to escape the unpleasant fate with which Currado had threatened him.[1]

When Lauretta was silent and everyone had heaped praise on Nonna, the Queen ordered Neifile to follow suit, and she said:

Affectionate ladies, although a ready wit will often supply a speaker with things to say that are useful, beautiful, and appropriate for the circumstances, it sometimes happens that Fortune will come to the aid of people who are scared and will suddenly put words in their mouths that they would never have been able to come up with if they were not under pressure—which is what I want to show you with this story of mine.

As all of you ladies will have heard and seen for yourselves, Currado Gianfigliazzi has long been a noteworthy citizen of Florence, a generous and magnanimous individual who always led the life of a gentleman and delighted in hawks and hounds, to say nothing for the moment of his more significant activities. One day a falcon he owned brought down a crane in the vicinity of Peretola,[2] and finding it to be young and plump, he sent it to an accomplished cook of his, a Venetian named Chichibio, ordering him to dress it well and then roast it for supper.*

Chichibio, who was as much of a birdbrain as he looked, prepared the crane, set it over the fire, and began to cook it with great care. When it

---

* Chichibio's name is derived from an onomatopoetic Venetian word for the song of the chaffinch: *cicibìo*. The implication is, of course, that he is a birdbrain.

was almost done and was giving off a most appetizing smell, a little gal from the country named Brunetta, with whom Chichibio was utterly infatuated, happened to come into the kitchen. On catching sight of the crane and sniffing its aroma, she pleaded lovingly with him to give her one of its thighs.

Chichibio replied to her in his singsong way and said: "You're not a-goin' a get it from me, Donna Brunetta, you're not a-goin' a get it from me."*

Donna Brunetta was rather peeved and said, "I swear to God, if you don't give it to me, you'll never get what you want out of me ever again." In short, they went on exchanging words like this until finally Chichibio, not wishing to anger his ladylove, cut off one of the crane's legs and gave it to her.

A little later, when the crane was set before Currado and his guests, he was surprised to find that one of its legs was missing. He had Chichibio summoned and asked him what had happened to it, and the lying Venetian promptly replied: "My lord, cranes only have one thigh and one leg."

"What the devil do you mean they have only one thigh and one leg?" said Currado in a rage. "Do you think I've never seen any cranes except this one?"

"It's just the way I'm telling you it is, sir," continued Chichibio. "If you like, we can go and see some live ones, and I'll show you."

Out of consideration for his guests, Currado decided not to pursue the argument any further, but said: "I've never seen or even heard of any one-legged cranes, but since you've said you'll show me some live ones, I want to see them tomorrow morning for myself, and then I'll be satisfied. But I swear by the body of Christ that if you don't prove it,

---

*Making fun of Chichibio's Venetian dialect, Boccaccio has him "sing" his response and use Venetian forms of Italian words, which must have made the dialect sound somewhat songlike to a Florentine. Chichibio is also satirized for his use of a courtly vocabulary with his ladylove: he uses *donna* for her, meaning "lady," calling her *donna Brunetta*, and addresses her as *voi*, employing the plural and more polite form for "you," rather than the singular, more familiar *tu*.

I'll have them take care of you in such a way that you'll feel sorry every time you call my name to mind for the rest of your life."

Thus, the discussion was closed for that evening, but the next morning, as soon as it was light, Currado, whose anger had not abated while he slept, got out of bed, and still seething with rage, ordered them to bring the horses. After making Chichibio mount an old nag, he led him toward a riverbank where cranes could always be spotted at daybreak, and said to him: "We'll soon see which one of us was lying last night."

Perceiving that Currado was still angry and that he was going to have to make good on his lie, Chichibio, who had no idea how to manage it, was in a state of absolute terror as he rode along behind his master. If he could have run away, he would have done so gladly, but since that was impossible, he kept looking ahead of him and behind him and on either side, and everywhere he turned, the cranes he saw all seemed to be standing on two legs.

But just as they were approaching the river, Chichibio spotted a dozen cranes or more on its bank well before anyone else did, and all of them were standing on one leg as they normally do when they are sleeping. Chichibio immediately pointed them out to Currado and announced: "Now, if you'll take a look at those cranes over there, sir, you can see quite clearly that I was telling you the truth last night when I said that they have only one thigh and one foot."

Currado looked at them and said, "Wait a bit, and I'll show you they have two." Then, moving a little closer to them, he shouted, "Ho, ho!" At this outburst, the cranes put down their other feet, and after taking a couple of steps, they all began flying away. After that, Currado turned to Chichibio and said: "What do you say to that, you gluttonous rogue?[3] Do they have two legs, or not?"

Chichibio was utterly confounded, but managed to come up with a reply even though he did not have the slightest idea where the words were coming from.

"They do indeed, sir," he said, "but you didn't cry 'Ho, ho!' to the one last night. Had you yelled like that, it would have stuck out its other thigh and its other foot just the way these here did."

Currado enjoyed this answer so much that all his anger was transformed into merry laughter.

"You're right, Chichibio," he said. "That's exactly what I should have done."

Thus, by means of his prompt and amusing reply, Chichibio made peace with his master and avoided an unpleasant fate.

Day 6, Story 5

Messer Forese da Rabatta and Master Giotto the painter, returning from Mugello, cleverly mock one another's disreputable appearance.[1]

The ladies were greatly amused by Chichibio's retort, and as soon as Neifile fell silent, Panfilo, in deference to the Queen's wishes, began speaking:

My dearest ladies, just as Fortune sometimes hides the most precious virtues in those who practice humble trades, which is what Pampinea showed us just a little while ago, so, too, one often discovers that Nature has located the most marvelous intelligence in the ugliest of men.[2]

This was plainly to be observed in two of our fellow citizens, about whom I intend to tell you a short tale. One of them, Messer Forese da Rabatta by name, had such a small, deformed body and such a flat, snub-nosed face that he would have been considered repulsive next to the ugliest of the Baronci, although he was so knowledgeable a jurist that people considered him a veritable encyclopedia of civil law.[3] The other, named Giotto, possessed a genius so lofty that there was nothing he could not represent with his lead stylus, his pen, or his paintbrush. Indeed, whatever Nature might produce—and she is the mother and mover of all things, determining their operations through the continual revolutions of the heavens—he was able to imitate it, or rather, to make his work resemble the thing itself so closely that he often deceived men's eyes, making them think that what he painted was real.

Hence, by virtue of the fact that he brought back into the light of day an art that had been buried for many centuries beneath the errors of those who painted more to delight the eyes of the ignorant than to please the understanding of the wise, Giotto may justly be considered one of the shining glories of Florence—and all the more so because, despite his having achieved that glory and having been the master of other artists while he lived, he always displayed the utmost humility by refusing to be called "Master." In fact, this title, which he rejected, shone all the more resplendently in him when one compares his modesty to the overweening ambition and greed that led not just those who knew less than he did, but his very own pupils, to usurp it. However great his art may have been, nevertheless, he did not, for all that, have a body or a face that were any more attractive than those of Messer Forese.

Turning now to our story, I should tell you that both Messer Forese and Giotto had property in the region of Mugello. One summer, during the period when the law courts are suspended for the holidays, Messer Forese went there to visit his estates. As he was returning to Florence on a wretched nag he had rented, he ran into the Giotto I have been speaking of, who was also on his way back from a similar visit and whose horse and clothes were in no way any better than Messer Forese's. The two of them fell in together, and like the old men they were, they jogged along toward home at a very slow pace.

As chance would have it, they were caught by surprise in a sudden rainstorm of the sort we often see during the summer, and they took shelter as soon as they could in the house of a peasant, who was an acquaintance, indeed a friend, of both men. After a while, however, as the rain showed no sign of letting up, and they wanted to get back to Florence before nightfall, they borrowed two shabby old woolen cloaks and two hats, threadbare with age, from their host, who had nothing better to offer them, and set off again on their journey.

After they had traveled some distance, they found themselves thoroughly soaked and covered with vast quantities of mud that their nags' hooves had kicked up—things that normally do not make people appear more reputable to others. When the sky brightened a little, the two of them, having gone on in silence for quite some time, began to chat. As Messer Forese rode along, listening to Giotto, who was quite a wonderful talker, he began looking him over, going from one side to the other and from head to foot, taking him in from every direction.

When he saw how disreputable and unkempt his companion seemed, he started laughing and said, without thinking once about his own appearance:

"Giotto, what if we were to meet some stranger who had never seen you before, do you think he'd ever believe that you were the greatest painter in the world, as you really are?"

"Sir," Giotto promptly replied, "I think he'd believe it if, after looking you over, he gave you credit for even knowing your ABCs."

On hearing this, Messer Forese recognized his mistake, and perceived that he had gotten as good as he gave.[4]

Day 6, Story 6

Michele Scalza proves to certain young men that the Baronci are the noblest family in the whole wide world or even in the Maremma, and wins a supper.[1]

The ladies were still laughing over the beauty of Giotto's prompt retort, when the Queen ordered Fiammetta to continue, and she began speaking as follows:

Young ladies, Panfilo's mention of the Baronci, whom you perhaps may not know as well as he does, has brought to mind a story that will show just how great their nobility is, and since it does not require that I deviate from today's topic, I would like to relate it to you.

Not so very long ago there was a young man in our city named Michele Scalza who was the most agreeable, most entertaining person in the world. He always had the weirdest stories at hand, and for that reason the young men in Florence loved to have him in their company whenever they got together. One day, when he happened to be with a group of them in Montughi, they began having a debate among themselves as to which was the noblest and most ancient family in Florence.[2] Some said it was the Uberti, and others, the Lamberti, while yet others argued for this family and for that family, depending on whichever one came to mind.

As Scalza listened to them, he began grinning and said: "Go on, get out of here, you blockheads, you don't know what you're talking about. The noblest, most ancient family not only in Florence, but in the whole wide world or even in the Maremma, is the Baronci. All the philosophers are in agreement on this point, as is everyone who knows them as well as I do. But just in case you think I mean somebody else,

I'm speaking about the Baronci who are your neighbors in Santa Maria Maggiore."

The young men were expecting him to say something entirely different, and when they heard his comment, they all made fun of him and said: "You're just putting us on. Why, we know the Baronci as well as you do."

"I swear by the Vangelists, I'm not trying to do that," replied Scalza. "On the contrary, I'm telling you the truth. And if there's anyone here who's willing to wager a supper to be given to the winner and any six friends of his choosing, I'll be glad to take him up on it. In fact, I'll go you one better, because I'll abide by the decision of any person you select as judge."

There was a young man in the group named Neri Vannini, who said, "I'm ready to win this supper," and after he and Scalza agreed together that they should ask Piero di Fiorentino, in whose house they were meeting, to serve as the judge, off they went to find him, followed by the entire group, who were eager to see Scalza lose so that they could make fun of him about it.[3]

The pair told Piero what the argument was all about, and then Piero, who was a discreet young man, after having listened first to Neri's side of it, turned to Scalza and said: "And you, how are you going to be able to prove the claim you're making?"

"How?" replied Scalza. "Why, I'll prove it with so compelling an argument that not just you, but even this guy who denies it, will admit I'm telling the truth. As you know, the older the family, the nobler, which is what they were all saying just now among themselves, and since the Baronci are more ancient than anyone else, they must necessarily be the noblest. Consequently, if I show you that they really are the oldest family, then I shall have won the debate beyond any shadow of a doubt.

"What you need to know is that the Lord God created the Baronci at the time when He had just begun learning how to paint, whereas He made all the rest of humanity after He had mastered the art. If you don't believe I'm telling the truth, all you have to do is to picture the Baronci alongside other people, and you'll see that while everybody else has a face that is well shaped and properly proportioned, the Baronci sometimes have faces that are long and narrow, and sometimes exceptionally wide. Some will have very long noses; others, short ones; and still others, protruding, turned-up chins with huge jaws that look like those of an ass. Plus, there are some who have one eye that's much larger than the other, and even a few who have one eye that's lower than the other. In general, their faces look like the ones that children make when they're first learning how to draw. Hence, as I've already said, it seems abundantly clear that the Lord God made them when He was just learning to paint, and since they're more ancient than all the rest, they must be the noblest family."[4]

As they listened to Scalza's amusing argument, Piero, who was the judge, and Neri, who had wagered the supper, indeed the entire company—they all recalled what the Baronci looked like, and as a result, they began laughing and declaring that Scalza was right, that he had won the supper, and that without a doubt the Baronci were the noblest, most ancient family that existed, not just in Florence, but in the whole wide world or even in the Maremma.

And that is why, when Panfilo wanted to describe how hideous Messer Forese's face was, he was justified in saying that it would have looked ugly alongside one of the Baronci's.

Day 6, Story 7

When Madonna Filippa's husband discovers her with a lover, she is called before a judge, but secures her freedom by means of a prompt and amusing reply, while also getting the statute changed at the same time.[1]

Fiammetta had stopped talking, and everyone was still laughing about the novel argument used by Scalza to demonstrate the pre-eminent nobility of the Baronci, when the Queen charged Filostrato to tell a story, and so he began:

Worthy ladies, it is a fine thing to be able to speak well in all circumstances, but it is even better, I think, to know how to do so when necessity requires. A noblewoman I am going to tell you about knew this art so well that she did not merely entertain her auditors and make them laugh, but as you are about to hear, she extricated herself from the snare of a shameful death.

In the city of Prato there was once a statute, no less reprehensible than harsh, that condemned women taken in adultery to be burned alive, making no distinction between one whose husband caught her with her lover and one who was doing it with somebody for money. And while this statute was in force, a case occurred in which a gentlewoman named Madonna Filippa, who was not just beautiful, but exceptionally amorous by nature, was discovered one night in her own bedroom by her husband, Rinaldo de' Pugliesi, in the arms of Lazzarino de' Guazzagliotri, a handsome, young nobleman from that city, whom she loved as much as life itself.[2] When Rinaldo saw the two of them together, he was so deeply disturbed that he could scarcely keep himself from rushing upon them and killing them, and if he had not been afraid of what could happen to him, he might have given in to his angry impulse and done it. Although he kept this urge under control, however, he could not be restrained from seeking the death of his wife, and as it was unlawful for him to kill her, he was determined to use the city's statute in order to get what he wanted.

Since Rinaldo had more than sufficient evidence to prove that Madonna Filippa was guilty, he sought no further counsel, but denounced her the next morning and had a summons issued for her. Like most women who are truly in love, the lady was possessed of a lofty spirit, and even though many of her friends and relations discouraged her from doing so, she was firmly resolved to appear in court, confess the truth, and die bravely rather than flee like a coward and live in exile because she had defied the law, thus showing herself unworthy of such a lover as the man in whose arms she had been the night before.

Escorted by a large group of men and women, all of whom were encouraging her to deny the charge, she went before the *podestà* and with a steady gaze and a firm voice asked him what he wanted to question her about. As he gazed at her and noted that she was not only very beautiful and extremely well mannered, but possessed a lofty spirit, to which her words bore witness, he began to feel pity for her and was afraid that she would confess to something for which, if he wanted to do his duty as a judge, he would have to condemn her to death.

Since he could not, however, refuse to interrogate her about what she was charged with, he said: "My lady, as you can see, your husband Rinaldo is here, and he's lodged a complaint against you, alleging that he caught you committing adultery with another man. Consequently, he's demanding that I punish you according to the requirements of a statute that's in force here and have you put to death. I can't do that, however, unless you confess. So, be very careful now about how you reply, and tell me if what your husband accuses you of is true."

In no way intimidated, the lady replied in a pleasant voice:

"Sir, it's true that Rinaldo is my husband and that he found me last night in Lazzarino's arms, where I have been many times because of the deep and perfect love I bear him. Nor is this something I would ever deny. But as I'm sure you know, laws should be impartial and should only be enacted with the consent of those affected by them. In the present case, these conditions have not been met, because this law applies only to us poor women who are much better than men at giving satisfaction to a whole host of lovers. Moreover, when it was passed, not only were there no women present to give their consent to it, but since then, not once have they ever been consulted about it. And that's why, for all these reasons, it could with justice be called a bad law.

"If, however, to the detriment of my body and your soul, you choose to implement it, that's your business. But before you arrive at any sort of verdict, I beg you to grant me a small favor, and that is to ask my husband whether or not I ever told him no and refused to give myself fully and completely to him whenever, and however many times, he liked."

Without waiting for the *podestà* to ask the question, Rinaldo promptly replied that without doubt, she had always satisfied his every desire and given herself to him whenever he requested it.

"Then I ask you, Messer *Podestà*," she continued without a pause, "if he's always obtained what he needed from me and was pleased with it, what was I supposed to do—in fact, what am I to do now—with the leftovers? Should I throw them to the dogs?[3] Isn't it much better to serve some of them up to a gentleman who loves me more than his very own life than to let them go to waste or have them spoil?"

The nature of the case and the lady's fame were such that practically all the citizens of Prato had flocked to the trial, and when they heard her amusing questions, they had a good laugh over them, after which they immediately shouted with one voice that she was right and that it was all well said. Then, at the suggestion of the *podestà*, before they left, they modified their cruel statute, restricting it so that it only applied to those women who betrayed their husbands for money.

Thus, having made a fool of himself with what he had tried to do, Rinaldo left the courtroom feeling utterly abashed, whereas his wife was now happy and free, and having been, as it were, resurrected from the flames, she returned to her house in triumph.

Day 6, Story 8

Fresco urges his niece not to look at herself in the mirror, if, as she has said, she is annoyed by the sight of disagreeable people.[1]

As they listened to Filostrato's story, at first the ladies felt a slight twinge of embarrassment within, which was revealed in the modest blushes that spread over their faces, but soon they started exchanging glances with one another, and barely able to contain their laughter, they snickered as they heard the rest of it. When he reached the end, however, the Queen turned to Emilia and ordered her to follow suit. Acting as if she had just been aroused from sleep, Emilia heaved a sigh and began:

Pretty ladies, since I have been absorbed for a while in thoughts that have kept me far, far away from here, I shall now hasten to obey our Queen and tell you a tale that is perhaps much shorter than it would have been if I had had greater presence of mind. It concerns the foolish error of a young lady, and how that error was corrected by an amusing quip of her uncle's, had she only been intelligent enough to understand it.

There was once a man called Fresco da Celatico, who had a niece with the pet name of Cesca.[2] While she had a good figure and a lovely face, though not equal to those angelic faces we have often seen, she thought herself so high and mighty that she got into the habit of criticizing men and women, indeed everything, she saw, without giving any thought to her own behavior, even though she was the most disagreeable, ill-tempered, peevish young woman around, such that nothing anyone ever did could please her. In addition to all this, she had so much pride that it would have been excessive even if she had been a member of the royal house of France. And whenever she walked down the street, she was constantly wrinkling up her nose the way people do when they smell a burning rag as if she was greeted by a terrible stench every time she saw or met anyone.

Now, setting aside her many other tiresome, disagreeable mannerisms, one day she happened to come back home, and finding Fresco there, she sat down next to him and started making all sorts of pouty faces while she huffed and puffed. Fresco was curious and asked her: "Cesca, what's this all about? You've come home so early, and it's a holiday today."

"The truth is," she simpered, brimming over with affectation, "I've come home early because I doubt whether there has ever been such a collection of tiresome, disagreeable people in this town as there is today. Every man and woman who passes by me in the street is as repellent to me as bad luck itself. I don't think there's another woman in the world who is as annoyed by the sight of disagreeable people as I am, and so, I came back early in order to avoid seeing them."

Fresco hated his niece's disgustingly fastidious airs with a passion and said to her:

"My girl, if you dislike disagreeable people as much as you say, for your own peace of mind you should never look at yourself in a mirror again."

But Cesca, whose head was as hollow as a reed, even though she thought her wisdom rivaled Solomon's, had no more understanding of what Fresco's quip really meant than a sheep would have, and she told him that, on the contrary, she was going to look in her mirror the same way other women did. Thus she remained as foolish as before—and she still is, to this very day.

Day 6, Story 9

With a clever quip, Guido Cavalcanti justly puts down a group of Florentine gentlemen who had taken him by surprise.[1]

Perceiving that Emilia had dispatched her tale, and that apart from the person who had the privilege of going last, there was no one else left to speak except her, the Queen began as follows:

Graceful ladies, although you deprived me of at least two of the stories I intended to tell today, I still have one I can recount, which ends with a clever quip that is more profound, perhaps, than any we have heard so far.

Let me remind you that in the past we used to have a number of truly splendid and commendable customs in our city, all of which have now disappeared thanks to the avarice that has grown right along with our wealth and has driven them all away.[2] One of these customs was that in various places throughout Florence the gentlemen living in different quarters of the city used to get together in fairly exclusive companies, taking care to include in their number only those who could, without difficulty, support the expense of offering a banquet to the entire group, one of them doing so today, another tomorrow, and then all the rest of the company in turn. At these banquets they often honored foreign gentlemen who visited the city as well as their fellow citizens. Moreover, at least once a year they would all wear the same kind of clothing, and on holidays they would ride in procession through the city, sometimes holding tournaments, especially on the greater feast days or when the city had received the happy news of a victory or something of that sort.

Among these companies there was one led by Messer Betto Brunelleschi, who, together with his companions, had made every effort to get Guido, the son of Messer Cavalcante de' Cavalcanti, to join them.[3] Nor did they do so without reason, for leaving aside the fact that he was one of the best logicians in the world and an excellent natural philosopher—things that did not much interest the company—he was the most refined man, both well-mannered and well-spoken, and he exceeded all the rest in any gentlemanly activity he set his mind to undertake. Finally, to top it all off, he was extremely rich and capable of entertaining anyone he thought deserved it in as lavish a fashion as you can imagine.

Messer Betto, however, had never succeeded in getting him to join his group, a resistance that he and his companions thought was due to Guido's sometime engagement in philosophical speculation, which would cut him off from his fellow human beings. Moreover, because Guido was somewhat inclined to the opinions of the Epicureans, it was said among the common people that all his speculating had no other goal than to see whether he could show that God did not exist.

One day it just so happened that Guido had left Orsanmichele, and taking his usual route, was walking along the Corso degli Adimari heading for San Giovanni, around which there were many large marble sarcophaguses, including those that are located today in Santa Reparata.[4] Guido had reached a spot among the tombs, in between the porphyry columns that have been placed there and the door of San Giovanni, which was locked, when Messer Betto and his company came up on horseback through the Piazza of Santa Reparata. As soon as they caught sight of him, they said, "Let's go give him a hard time," and spurring on their horses in a mock assault, they were upon him almost before he noticed them.

"Guido," they said, "you can refuse to be part of our company, but look, when you've discovered that God doesn't exist, what will you have accomplished?"

Seeing himself hemmed in by them, Guido promptly replied, "Gentlemen, you may say whatever you please to me in your own house." Then, he placed his hand on one of the tombs, which were quite high, and being very nimble, he leaped up and vaulted over it onto the other side. Thus, having freed himself from them, he went on his way.

The others were left staring at one another. Then they started saying that he was out of his mind and that his remark was meaningless since the spot they were on had no more to do with them than with any of their fellow citizens, and least of all with Guido. But Messer Betto turned on them and said:

"You're the ones who are out of your minds, if you didn't understand him, for in just a few words, he has justly given us the greatest putdown in the world. If you think about it, these tombs are the houses of the dead, for this is where they are laid to rest and where they reside. When he said that this is our house, what he wanted to show us was that in comparison to him and the rest of the learned, all men who are as ignorant and uneducated as ourselves are worse than the dead. Thus, when we're here, we really are in our own house."

Now that they all understood what Guido had meant, they were quite abashed and never gave him a hard time again. And what is more, from that time forward, they considered Messer Betto to be a gentleman of subtle, discerning intelligence.

Day 6, Story 10

Frate Cipolla promises a group of peasants that he will show them a feather belonging to the Angel Gabriel, but when he finds lumps of coal in its place, he declares that they were the ones used to roast Saint Lawrence.[1]

Now that each member of the company had told a story, Dioneo knew that it was his turn to speak, and so, without waiting for a formal command, he imposed silence on those who were praising Guido's pithy retort and began as follows:

Charming ladies, although it is my privilege to speak about whatever I please, today I do not propose to depart from the topic that all of you have spoken about so very fittingly. On the contrary, following in your footsteps, I intend to show you how one of the friars of Saint Anthony, with a quick bit of thinking, found a clever way to avoid a humiliating trap laid for him by two young men. And if I speak at greater length in order to tell you the whole story as it should be told, you should not feel this is a burden, for if you take a look at the sun, you will see that it is still in mid-heaven.

Certaldo, as you may perhaps have heard, is a fortified town in the Val d'Elsa, located in our territory, and although it is small, the people living there were once noble and pretty well-to-do.[2] Because it offered him such rich pickings, one of the friars of Saint Anthony used to go to Certaldo once a year to collect the alms that all the people were simpleminded enough to donate to his order. His name was Frate Cipolla, and the people used to give him a warm welcome there perhaps as much for his name as for any pious sentiment they felt, since the soil in those parts produced onions that are famous all over

Tuscany.* Small of stature, this Frate Cipolla had red hair and a merry face, and was really the most sociable scoundrel in the world. What is more, although he was not learned, he was such a fine speaker and had such a ready wit that someone unacquainted with him would have concluded not just that he was a grand master of rhetoric, but that he was Cicero himself or maybe Quintilian.[3] And there was almost no one in those parts who did not consider him a good buddy, a friend, or at least a nodding acquaintance.

As was his custom, he went there for one of his visits in the month of August, and on a Sunday morning, when all the good men and women from the surrounding villages had gathered in the parish church to hear Mass, he waited for a suitable moment and then came forward.

"Ladies and gentlemen," he said, "it is, as you know, your yearly custom to send some of your wheat and oats to the poor of our Lord and Master Saint Anthony,[4] some of you giving more and some of you less, according to your ability and your devotion, in exchange for which the Blessed Saint Anthony will keep your oxen, asses, pigs, and sheep from harm. It's also customary, especially for those of you who are enrolled as members in our confraternity, to pay the small sum that constitutes your annual dues. Now, I've been sent to collect this money on behalf of my superior, that is, Messer Abbot. And so, with God's blessing, I want you to come outside after nones, when you hear the bells ring, and assemble in front of the church where I will, as usual, preach my sermon and you will kiss the cross. What's more, because I know how deeply devoted you all are to our Lord and Master Saint Anthony, I will, as an act of special grace, show you a beautiful and extremely sacred relic that I myself brought from the Holy Land across the sea, and that is nothing less than one of the Angel Gabriel's feathers that was left behind in the Virgin Mary's bedchamber when he came to Nazareth to perform the Annunciation." And having said all this, he fell silent and then returned to celebrating the Mass.

*Frate Cipolla's name means "Brother Onion," a vegetable whose many layers with no real "center" and whose particular odor are quite suggestive when one considers what Frate Cipolla does in the story.

Among the large number of people present in the church while Frate Cipolla was speaking were two very clever young men, one of them named Giovanni del Bragoniera and the other, Biagio Pizzini.[5] After having had a good laugh between themselves about Frate Cipolla's relic, they decided, even though they were very close friends and cronies of his, to make use of the feather in order to play a practical joke on him.

They knew that Frate Cipolla was going to dine that morning up in the citadel with one of his friends, and as soon as they knew he was at the table, they went down into the street and made their way to the inn where he was staying. Their plan was for Biagio to keep Frate Cipolla's servant occupied in conversation while Giovanni looked through the friar's belongings for the feather, or whatever it was, and stole it so that they could see later on how he was going to explain what had happened to the people.

Frate Cipolla had a servant whom some called Guccio the Whale, others Guccio the Slob, and yet others Guccio the Pig.[6] He was such a bad character that Lippo the Mouse never came close to being his match. When chatting with his cronies, Frate Cipolla would often make jokes about him.

"My servant," he would say, "has nine failings, and if any one of them had been found in Solomon or Aristotle or Seneca, it would have been sufficient to ruin all the ingenuity, all the wisdom, and all the sanctity they possessed. So, just think what sort of man he must be, who not only lacks these three qualities, but has nine failings altogether!"

On occasion, someone asked him what the nine were, and he would respond with a rhyme he had made up.

"I'll tell you," he would say. "He's slothful, untruthful, and crude; neglectful, disrespectful, and lewd; careless and witless and rude.[7] Apart from this, he has some other little black marks it would be better not to talk about. But the funniest thing about him is that wherever he goes, he's always looking to find a wife and rent a house, and since he has a big, black, greasy beard, he thinks he's very handsome and attractive, and that every woman who sees him is in love with him. In fact, if you let him have his way, he'd be chasing after all of them so hard that he wouldn't even notice it when his pants fell down. Truth to tell, though, he's very helpful to me because whenever anyone wants to impart something in secret to me, he always wants to hear his share of it, and if I'm ever asked a question, he's so afraid I won't be able to answer it that he immediately replies yes or no, just as he sees fit."

When Frate Cipolla had left his servant at the inn, he had been told that on no account was anyone to be allowed to touch any of his master's belongings, and especially his saddlebags, which contained the sacred objects. But Guccio the Slob was fonder of the kitchen than any nightingale is of the green branches, especially if he smelled out some serving girl there, and he had indeed caught sight of one about the inn. She was fat and coarse, short and deformed, with a pair of boobs that looked like two big dung baskets and a face like one of the Baronci's, all sweaty and greasy and covered with soot.[8] And so, Guccio did not bother to lock the door behind him, but left Frate Cipolla's room and all of his things to take care of themselves, and like a vulture pouncing on carrion, swooped down on the kitchen. Even though it was August, he took a seat next to the fire and struck up a conversation with the girl, whose name was Nuta, telling her he was a gentleman by proxy, that he had more than a gazillion and nine florins, not counting those he owed others, which were greater in number, and that he knew how to say and do more stuff than his master could.[9]

Despite the fact that his cowl was covered with so much grease it would have served as seasoning for the soup caldron of Altopascio, and that his doublet was torn and patched, glazed with filth around the neck and under the armpits, and stained in more colors than cloth from Tartary or India, and that his shoes were falling apart and his stockings all in tatters—despite all this, he told her, as though he were the Lord of Châtillon, that he wanted to buy her some new clothes, set her up properly, release her from this servitude of always waiting on others, and while she would not have much of her own, put her in hope of a better fortune.[10] Nevertheless, although he said all this, and much more besides, with great emotion, everything turned out to be as insubstantial as the wind, and like most of his undertakings, it came to nothing.

Upon discovering Guccio the Pig thus occupied with Nuta, the two young men were quite pleased because it meant that half their work was done for them. With no one to get in their way, they entered Frate Cipolla's room, which had been left open, and the first thing they came upon in their search was the saddlebag containing the feather. When they opened it, they found a tiny casket inside wrapped up in many folds of taffeta, and when they opened that in turn, they found one of the tail feathers of a parrot inside, which they concluded had to be the one he had promised to show the people of Certaldo.

And without a doubt, in those days he could have easily made them believe what he said about it, because the luxuries of Egypt had only just begun to make their way into Tuscany, as they have since done in great quantities everywhere, to the ruin of the whole of Italy. And if such things were little known elsewhere, in that town the people were not acquainted with them at all. In fact, since the rough, honest ways of their forefathers were still followed there, the vast majority had never seen a parrot, let alone heard people mention one.

Delighted to have found the feather, the young men took it out, and to avoid leaving the casket empty, filled it with some lumps of coal they saw in a corner of the room. Then they shut the lid, and after arranging everything the way it had been, went off gleefully with the feather, unnoticed by anyone, after which they waited to see what Frate Cipolla was going to say when he found the coals in its place.

The simple men and women who were in the church, hearing that they were going to see one of the Angel Gabriel's feathers after nones, returned home when Mass was over and spread the news from friend to friend and neighbor to neighbor.[11] Then, once they had all finished eating, they thronged the citadel in such numbers that it could scarcely hold them, men and women both, every last one of them desperate to see that feather.

Having had a good dinner and taken a short nap, Frate Cipolla arose a little after nones. When he learned that a huge crowd of peasants had come to see the feather, he ordered Guccio the Slob to come up to him and to bring the bells and the saddlebags with him. Tearing himself away from the kitchen and from Nuta with difficulty, Guccio struggled up with the things he was asked to bring. His body was so bloated from all the water he had drunk that when he arrived, he was completely out of breath. Still, at Frate Cipolla's command, he went to the church door and began vigorously ringing the bells.

Once all of the people were assembled, Frate Cipolla began his sermon and said a great deal to serve his own purposes, never noticing that any of his things had been tampered with. As he was approaching the moment to show them the Angel Gabriel's feather, first he recited the *Confiteor* with great solemnity and had two large candles lit.* Then, having thrown back his cowl, he slowly unfolded the taffeta wrapping, brought out the casket, and after reciting a short, laudatory speech in praise of the Angel Gabriel and his relic, proceeded to open it. When he saw it was filled with lumps of coal, he did not suspect that Guccio the Whale had done this to him, because he did not think the man capable of rising to such heights, nor did he blame him for having done a bad job of preventing others from playing such a trick. Instead, he silently cursed himself for having trusted Guccio to safeguard his belongings since he knew the man was neglectful, disrespectful, careless, and witless. Without changing color, however, he raised his hands and his eyes to heaven and said in a voice that all could hear, "O God, blessed be Thy power forever and ever." Then he closed the casket and turned to the people.

"Ladies and gentlemen," he said, "I want you to know that when I was still quite young, I was sent by my superior into those parts of the world where the sun rises, and at his express command I was charged to seek out the Privileges of the Porcellana, which, although they cost nothing to seal, are much more useful to others than to us.[12] I set out on my journey to find them, departing from Venice and going through Greekburg, after which, riding from there through the Kingdom of Algarve and Baghdad, I arrived in Parione, from which I made it to Sardinia after a while, though not without suffering great thirst.

"But why should I go through every particular country I visited? After having passed the Straits of Saint George, I came to Conland and Clownland, which are populous countries inhabited by a great many

---

* The *Confiteor* ("I confess") is a prayer recited at the beginning of the Mass.

people, and from there I went to Liarland, where I found a large number of friars, including many who belonged to our own order, all of whom were bent on forsaking a life of discomfort for the love of God, and cared little about others' troubles wherever they saw they could pursue their own advantage.[13] And in all of those countries I only spent money that had not been minted. Next I came to the Land of Abruzzi, where men and women climb up the mountains in clogs and clothe pigs in their own guts, and a little farther on I found a people who carry bread on sticks and wine in a sack, after which I arrived at the Basqueworm Mountains where all the water flows downhill.[14] In short, I went so far in those parts that I even reached India Parsinippia where I swear to you by the habit I'm wearing that I saw pruningbills fly, which is quite unbelievable if you haven't seen it—and Maso del Saggio will second me on this, for I met him there and he's a great merchant who cracks nuts and sells their shells retail.[15]

"But because I couldn't find what I was sent for, and because from that point on you have to go by water, I turned back and came to the Holy Land where in summertime cold bread costs you four pennies, but when it's hot, it doesn't cost you a thing. There I met with the Reverend Father Messer Dontblameme Ifyouplease, the most worshipful Patriarch of Jerusalem, who, out of respect for the habit of our Lord and Master Saint Anthony, which I've always worn, wanted me to see all the relics he had about him.[16] They were so numerous that if I tried to count them all, it would take me miles till I got to the end. Still, since I don't want to disappoint the ladies, I'll tell you about a few of them.

"First of all, he showed me the finger of the Holy Spirit, as whole and sound as it ever was; then the forelock of the seraphim who appeared to Saint Francis; and one of the fingernails of the cherubims; and one of the ribs of the Word-made-flesh-go-right-out-the-window; and the vestments of the Holy Catholic Faith; and some of the rays from the star that appeared to the three Magi in the East; and a vial of Saint Michael's sweat from when he fought with the Devil; and the jawbone of the Death of Saint Lazarus; and lots of others as well.[17]

And because I freely gave him *The Dingle of Mount Morello* in the vernacular and several chapters from the *Oldgoatius*, which he had long been seeking, he made me a part-sharer in his holy relics. He gave me one of the teeth of the Holy Cross, and in a little vial a bit of the sound of the bells from the temple of Solomon, and the feather of the Angel Gabriel, which I've already told you about, and one of the clogs of Saint Gherardo da Villamagna, which a little while ago I gave to Gherardo di Bonsi in Florence, who is particularly devoted to the saint.[18] Finally, he let me have some of the coals on which the most blessed martyr Saint Lawrence was roasted. With the greatest devotion, I brought these things back from over there, and I still have them all in my possession.

"True, my superior has never allowed me to display them until such time as they were verified as authentic, or not, but now that this has been established to his satisfaction by means of certain miracles they have wrought, and by letters sent to us from the Patriarch, he's given me permission to show them. But I'm afraid to entrust them to anyone else and always keep them with me.

"Now, as a matter of fact, I carry the Angel Gabriel's feather in one casket to prevent it from being damaged, and I have the coals on which Saint Lawrence was roasted in another. The two caskets are so much alike that I often mistake one for the other, and that's what happened to me today, for although I thought I was bringing you the casket with the feather, I actually brought the one with the coals.

"I don't think this was a mistake, however. On the contrary, it's clear to me that it was the will of God and that He Himself placed the casket containing the coals in my hands, for I've only now remembered that the Feast of Saint Lawrence is just two days away.* And since God wanted me to show you the coals on which the saint was roasted and thus rekindle the devotion you should feel for him in your hearts, He had me bring here, not the feather I intended to take, but those blessed coals, which were extinguished by the humors that came from the saint's most sacred body.† Therefore, my blessed children, you should take off your caps, and then you may, with reverence, come

---

* The Feast of Saint Lawrence takes place on August 10. Tradition has it that he was martyred by being burned to death on a gridiron, which served as his symbol throughout the Middle Ages.

† Humors: fluids, such as blood or sweat.

forward to behold them. But first, I want you to know that whoever is marked with the sign of the cross by these coals may rest assured that for an entire year he won't be burned by fire he doesn't feel."

When Frate Cipolla was finished speaking, he chanted a hymn in praise of Saint Lawrence, opened the casket, and displayed the coals. For a little while, the foolish multitude gazed at them in reverent wonder, after which they all pressed forward in a huge crowd around Frate Cipolla, and giving him much better offerings than usual, begged him to touch each one of them with the coals. Accordingly, Frate Cipolla picked up the coals with his hand and began making the largest crosses he could manage on their white smocks and doublets and on the women's veils, declaring that, as he had seen it happen many times, no matter how much the coals were worn away from making those crosses, they would grow to their former size again in the casket.

Thus, thanks to his quick-wittedness, Frate Cipolla not only profited enormously by scrawling crosses on the people of Certaldo, but made fools of those who thought they had made a fool of him. The two young men had attended his sermon, and as they had listened to the ingenious and truly far-fetched verbal display he used to turn the situation to his advantage, they had laughed so hard they thought their jaws would break. Then, after the crowd had dispersed, they went up to him, as merry as could be, and revealed what they had done, after which they gave him back his feather, which proved no less lucrative to him the following year than the coals had been that day.

Day 6, Conclusion

The entire company was greatly pleased and entertained by Dioneo's story, and they all laughed heartily about Frate Cipolla, especially about his pilgrimage and his relics, both the ones he had seen and those he had brought back with him. When the Queen realized that the tale was finished and that her reign had likewise come to an end, she got to her feet, removed her crown, and placed it on Dioneo's head.

"The time has come, Dioneo," she declared, laughing all the while, "for you to find out what a burden it is to have ladies to govern and guide. Therefore, you will be our King, and may your rule be such that when it has come to an end, we will all have reason to praise it."

After taking the crown, Dioneo responded with a laugh: "I am pretty sure you have had many opportunities to see kings who are worth a lot more than I am—kings on a chessboard, I mean. But I have no doubt that if you were to obey me as a real king should be obeyed, I would make sure that you had a chance to enjoy that without which no entertainment can ever be truly happy and complete. But enough of such talk. I shall rule over you to the best of my ability."

Then, in accordance with their usual practice, he sent for the steward and gave him orders about what his duties would be during the course of his reign, after which he said:

"Worthy ladies, we have already talked so much and spoken in so many different ways about both the resourcefulness of our fellow human beings and the vicissitudes of Fortune that if Madonna Licisca had not come here just a little while ago and said something that provided me with material for our discussions tomorrow, I suspect it would have been very difficult for me to have found a topic to speak on. As you heard, she claims that none of the girls in her neighborhood was a virgin when she got married, and she added that she knew all about the many different tricks wives play on their husbands. Now, if we set aside the first thing she said, which is a subject that concerns children, I reckon the second one should be a pleasant topic to discuss, and therefore, taking our cue from Madonna Licisca, tomorrow I want us to talk about the tricks that women, either for the sake of love or for their self-preservation, have played on their husbands, whether those tricks were ever discovered by them or not."[1]

Speaking about such a subject seemed quite unsuitable to some of the ladies, and they asked him to change the topic he had proposed.

"Ladies," said the King in reply, "I am just as aware as you are of what it is that I have chosen as our theme, but the objection you have raised would not have prevented me from selecting it, for I think that as long as men and women take pains to ensure that their behavior is honest, the times we are going through permit all subjects to be freely discussed. Are you not aware that since everything has been turned upside down nowadays, judges have forsaken their tribunals, the laws, divine as well as human, have fallen silent, and everyone has been granted ample license to preserve his life however he can? Consequently, if you go somewhat beyond the bounds of decorum in speaking, not with the intention of behaving indecently, but only of providing pleasure for yourselves and others, I do not see what plausible argument anyone in the future could make to criticize you.

"Furthermore, from the first day up to now our company has been the epitome of honesty, for no matter what we have said, our honor has never been sullied by anything we did—nor, with God's help, will it ever be. Besides, is there anyone who is unaware of your virtue? I doubt that even the fear of death, let alone these pleasant discussions of ours, could ever shake it.

"The truth of the matter is that if anyone were to discover that you had refrained at some point from talking about these trifles, he might suspect that you did not want to discuss them because you were actually guilty of having misbehaved. Not to mention the fact that you would be paying me quite a pretty compliment if now, after I have been so obedient to you all, and after you have chosen me as your King and made me your lawgiver, you refuse to talk about the subject I proposed. So, set aside these scruples, which are more appropriate for the wicked than for us, and may you all have the good fortune to think up some beautiful tale to tell."

After listening to Dioneo's arguments, the ladies agreed to do what he wished, at which point he gave them all permission to pursue their own pleasures until suppertime.

The sun was still high in the sky, because their storytelling had been brief, and so, once Dioneo and the other young men had started playing a game of backgammon, Elissa called the other ladies aside.

"From the day we arrived here," she said, "I have been wanting to take you to a place called the Valley of the Ladies where I think none of you has ever been. Although it is not very far away, I did not see an opportunity until today, the sun being still very high, to take you there. So, if you would like to come, I am completely confident that once you are there you will be very happy to have made the journey."

The ladies replied that they were ready to go, and without telling the men a thing about it, they summoned one of their maids and set out, reaching the Valley of the Ladies before they had traveled much more than a mile. They entered it by way of a narrow path on one side of which there flowed a crystal-clear stream, and they found what they saw there to be as lovely and delightful, especially then when it was so very hot, as could possibly be imagined. According to what one of them told me afterward, the floor of the valley was as round as if it had been drawn with a compass, although it looked more like Nature's artwork than something from the hand of man. A little more than half a mile in circumference, the valley was surrounded by six little hills, none of them very high, and on each of the summits there was a palace built more or less in the form of a lovely little castle.[2]

The sides of those hills sloped gradually down toward the floor of the valley in a regular sequence of terraces, arranged like the tiers in an amphitheater, their circumferences steadily decreasing in size as one went from top to bottom. The slopes that faced the southern sky were so full of grapevines and of olive, almond, cherry, fig, and many other species of fruit trees, that there was scarcely a handsbreadth of land left uncultivated between them. The slopes that looked toward the North Star were covered over with groves of oak saplings, ashes, and other trees, all as green and straight as could be. The plain below, which had no entrances other than the one through which the ladies had come, was filled with firs, cypresses, and laurels, plus a small number of pines, which were all so neatly arranged and symmetrically disposed that it seemed as if they had been planted there by the most skillful forester. And when the sun was high overhead, very little, if any, of its light shone through their foliage and reached the ground below, which was one continuous meadow of the finest grass abounding in flowers of every description, many of them purple in color.

Besides all this, what gave them just as much pleasure was a stream that cascaded down over the living rock of a gorge separating two of the little hills, for it made a most delectable sound to hear, and from a distance it looked as if its waters were being sprayed under pressure into a mist of fine quicksilver. When the stream finally reached the floor of the valley, it was collected into a lovely little channel along which it flowed quite swiftly toward the center of the small plain where it formed a diminutive lake like one of those fishponds that townspeople sometimes construct in their gardens when they can afford to do so.

The lake was not very deep, for its waters came up only chest high, and since it had no impurities in it, its bed of exceptionally fine gravel was so crystal clear that a man with nothing else to occupy him could have counted every last grain of it, had he wanted to do so. But in addition to the bed of the lake, on looking down into the water, one could see a large number of fish darting here and there, a sight not just delightful, but marvelous to behold. Nor was the lake enclosed by any bank other than the soil of the meadow that was all the more luxuriant around it because there was so much more moisture there. And the water that flowed out of the lake was collected in another little channel through which it issued from the valley and ran down into the lowlands.

This, then, was the place to which the ladies had come. After gazing all around at everything and heaping praise on it, they found themselves looking at the little lake that was right there in front of them, and since it was very hot, and they were in no danger of being observed, they decided to go for a swim. First, they ordered their maid to station herself above the path by which they had entered the valley, so that she could keep watch over it and warn them if someone was coming. Then, all seven of them got undressed and went into the lake, which concealed their pure white bodies no better than a thin sheet of glass would conceal a bright red rose.

Once in the water, which nevertheless remained as crystal clear as before, they started swimming as best they could, going in every direction after the fish, which had trouble finding a place to hide, and attempting to grab them with their bare hands. After they had spent some time amusing themselves this way and had caught some of the fish, they got out and put their clothes on again. Unable to praise the spot any more highly than they had already done, they decided it was time for them to go back. Consequently, they set off down the path at a leisurely pace, talking all the while about how beautiful the place was.

It was as yet quite early when they reached the palace and found the young men still playing there just as they had left them. With a laugh, Pampinea said to them: "We really managed to trick you today."[3]

"What?" said Dioneo. "Have you started off by doing precisely what you are going to be talking about later on?"

"Yes, Your Majesty," replied Pampinea. And she gave him a lengthy description of the place they had come from, telling him how far away it was and what they had been doing there.

When the King heard her describe the beauty of the spot, he was so eager to see it that he had supper served at once. They all ate it with great pleasure, and the instant they were done, the three young men and their servants left the ladies and went off to the valley. None of them had ever been there before, and after examining every aspect of it, they praised it as being one of the most beautiful sights in the world. Then, after they had gone for a swim and had gotten dressed again, since it was getting late, they returned to the palace, where they found the ladies dancing a *carola* to an air sung by Fiammetta. Once it was finished, they entered into a discussion of the Valley of the Ladies, saying many good things in praise of it. Consequently, the King sent for the steward and ordered him to have everything set up in the valley the following morning and to have beds carried there in case anyone wanted to lie down for a while or take a nap in the middle of the day. Then he had them bring lights, wine, and sweets, and when everyone had taken a little refreshment, he ordered them all to join in the dancing. At his request, Panfilo began the first dance, after which the King turned to Elissa and said to her pleasantly:

"My fair young lady, today you honored me with the crown, and now, this evening, I want to honor you by asking you to sing. So, give us a song, and make it one about the person you like the best."

Smiling, Elissa replied that she would do so gladly, and in a sweet voice thus she began:

> If ever I escape your claws, O Love,
> I never will be caught,
> I do believe, on any other hook.
>   When still a girl, I went to join your wars.
> Thinking to find there sweet and perfect peace,
> Upon the ground I laid down all my arms,
> Naively trusting your assurances,
> But you, rapacious tyrant, harsh and false,
> With cruel claws outstretched,
> And bearing arms, pounced on me instantly.
>   Then after I'd been fettered in your chains,
> You gave me, bound and weeping bitter tears,
> To him who for my very death was born.
> Now full of pain, I'm living in his power,
> And over me his rule has been so cruel
> That he could not be moved
> By sighs and tears that wear me quite away.
>   My prayers to him the winds all carry off;
> To none of them he listens, never will,
> Which makes my torment grow relentlessly.
> My life's reduced to pain, yet I can't die.

Ah, Lord, take pity on my suffering
And do what I cannot:
Give him to me bound tightly in your chains.
      If this you will not do, at least release
Me from the bonds of hope that tie me down.
Ah, Lord, I beg you, grant me this one gift,
For if you do, then I shall still have hope
To be again the beauty I once was,
And when my grief is gone,
To deck myself with flowers red and white.[4]

Elissa brought her song to an end with a very plaintive sigh, and although everyone wondered about her words, no one could guess what caused her to sing as she did. The King, however, who was in a merry mood, sent for Tindaro and ordered him to produce his bagpipe. To its strains he then had them all do a fair number of dances, after which, since a good part of the night had already passed, he told them, each and every one, that they should go to sleep.

Day 7, Introduction

Here ends the Sixth Day of the Decameron *and the Seventh begins, in which, under the rule of Dioneo, they speak about the tricks that women, either for the sake of love or for their self-preservation, have played on their husbands, whether those tricks were ever discovered by them or not.*

All the stars had vanished from the eastern skies except for the one we call Lucifer,* which was still gleaming in the increasingly white light of dawn, when the steward arose and went with a large baggage train to the Valley of the Ladies, intent upon arranging everything there in accordance with the orders and instructions he had received from his master. After his departure, it was not long before the King, who had been awakened by the noise of the animals and of the servants who were loading them, got out of bed himself. Once up, he had them rouse all the ladies as well as the young men.

The rays of the sun had not yet quite begun to shine when they all took to the road, and it seemed to them that the nightingales and the other birds had never sung so gaily as they did that morning. Those songs accompanied them all along the way to the Valley of the Ladies, where they were greeted by many more, who sang to them and seemed to rejoice at their coming.

After they had roamed around the place, examining it in detail once again, they thought it even lovelier than the day before, inasmuch as the hour was better for showing off its beauties. Then, when they had broken their fast with some good wine and assorted sweets, so as not

---

*Lucifer ("light bearer") is another name for the morning star Venus. This may be a suggestion that love, or sex, will play a large role in the stories to come.

to be outdone by the birds, they, too, began a song, which the valley took up with them, repeating the very strains they were singing, and to which all the birds added their sweet, new notes, as though they were determined not to be bested.

When the dinner hour arrived, they went and sat down at the tables that had been set at the King's command under the verdant laurels and the other fair trees beside the pretty little lake. As they ate, they watched the fish swimming through it in great shoals, which not only attracted their attention, but prompted discussion from time to time. With their meal at an end, and the food and tables removed, they began to sing even more merrily than before, after which they played music on their instruments and danced.

The prudent steward had arranged for beds to be set up in various locations throughout the little valley, all of them surrounded by curtains and covered by canopies of French serge, in which those who were so inclined were given permission by the King to go and take a nap, while those who had no interest in sleeping were free to entertain themselves to their hearts' content with any one of their usual pastimes.

Finally, when the hour had come for them to assemble and turn their attention again to storytelling, they all got up and took their seats on the carpets that, at the King's command, had been spread on the grass beside the lake, not very far from the place where they had eaten. The King then asked Emilia to start them off, and with a smile, she gaily began as follows.

Day 7, Story 1

Gianni Lotteringhi hears a knocking at his door during the night and awakens his wife. She makes him believe it is the bogeyman, and after they go and exorcise it with a prayer, the knocking stops.[1]

My lord, had it been your pleasure, I would have greatly preferred for you to have asked someone else to introduce so splendid a topic as the one we are supposed to speak on, but since it is your desire that I should provide an encouraging example for all the other women, I shall gladly do so. Moreover, I shall try my best, dearest ladies, to say something that might be useful to you in the future, for if other women are like me, they are all easily frightened, and especially of the bogeyman. Now, even though God knows I have no idea what sort of creature that is, nor have I ever met any woman who does, all of us are afraid of him just the same. But if you want to chase him away when he comes to visit you, you should pay attention to my story, for it will teach you a good, holy, and extremely effective prayer for the purpose.

There once lived in Florence, in the quarter of San Pancrazio, a wool dealer named Gianni Lotteringhi, who was more successful in his trade than sensible in other matters, for despite being something of a simpleton, he was frequently made the leader of the Laud Singers of Santa Maria Novella,* was charged with overseeing their performances, and had many other trivial duties of the same sort.[2] The result was that he had a very high opinion of himself, although all these offices came his way simply because, being a man of substance, he frequently treated the

---

*The Laud Singers of Santa Maria Novella was a confraternity officially called the *Società delle Laudi di Santa Maria Novella*, one of whose functions was to sing lauds, that is, hymns of praise, particularly during Lent.

friars to a good meal. Since they often used to get a pair of stockings, or a cowl, or a scapular out of him, in return they taught him a few good prayers and gave him a copy of the Lord's Prayer in the vernacular as well as the Song of Saint Alexis, the Lament of Saint Bernard, the Laud of the Lady Matilda, and lots of other nonsense like that.[3] He, however, considered all these things very precious and exercised great care in keeping them safe for the sake of his soul's salvation.

Now, this man had a very beautiful, charming wife, an intelligent, perceptive woman called Monna Tessa who was the daughter of Mannuccio dalla Cuculia.[4] Knowing how simple her husband was, and having fallen for Federigo di Neri Pegolotti, a handsome, lusty young man, who was likewise in love with her, she made arrangements through one of her maids for Federigo to come and see her at a very lovely villa Gianni had in Camerata.* She used to stay there the entire summer, and Gianni would occasionally join her to have supper and spend the night before going back to his shop in the morning or sometimes to his laud singers.

Federigo, who desired nothing better than to spend time with Gianni's wife, seized the opportunity to do so one day, when she had sent for him, and went up to Camerata a little before vespers. Since Gianni was not coming that evening, Federigo felt entirely at his ease, and after having eaten a very enjoyable supper there, he spent an equally enjoyable night with the lady, who lay in his arms and taught him how to sing a good half-dozen of her husband's hymns.

Neither she nor Federigo intended this to be their first and last time together, and since they did not want to have her constantly sending the maidservant for him, they worked out the following arrangement. Every day, on his way to or from a place he had that was a little farther up the road, he would keep his eye on a vineyard next to her house, where he could see the skull of an ass set on one of the stakes that held up the vines.[5] When he saw its muzzle turned in the direction of Florence, that meant it was safe, and so, he would not fail to come and see her that evening after dark. If he discovered that the door was

*Camerata is a village just north of Florence on the road leading up to Fiesole.

locked, he would knock softly three times, and she would open it for him. When he saw the muzzle of the ass turned toward Fiesole, however, he would stay away because this meant that Gianni would be there. Thus, by using this system, they managed to get together with some frequency.

But one time, when Federigo was supposed to have supper with Monna Tessa and she had arranged to have two fat capons cooked for him, it just so happened, much to the lady's distress, that Gianni showed up unexpectedly when it was already quite late. She had a little salted meat boiled separately and supped on it with her husband. Meanwhile, she ordered her maidservant to wrap the two cooked capons in a white tablecloth and carry them, together with a quantity of fresh eggs and a good flask of wine, into her garden that could be reached without going through the house and where she occasionally used to have supper with Federigo. She told the maidservant to leave everything at the foot of a peach tree that grew next to a little meadow, but she was so upset because of what had happened that she forgot to tell the maidservant to wait until Federigo showed up so that she could let him know that Gianni was inside and that he was to take the things in the garden away with him.

Not long after she, Gianni, and the maidservant had gone to bed, Federigo arrived and knocked once softly at the door. It was so close to the bedroom that Gianni heard it immediately, as did the lady, although she pretended to be asleep so that her husband would have no reason to suspect her of anything. After waiting a short while, Federigo knocked a second time. This really puzzled Gianni, who gave his wife a little poke and asked her: "Tessa, do you hear what I'm hearing? It sounds like somebody's knocking at our door."

The lady, who had heard it much better than he had, pretended to be waking up, and muttered: "What's that you say? Huh?"

"I'm saying," replied Gianni, "that it sounds like somebody's knocking at our door."

"Knocking?" said the lady. "Oh no, Gianni dear, don't you know what it is? It's the bogeyman. He's been giving me the fright of my life these last few nights. And every time I heard him, I stuck my head under the covers and didn't dare take it out again until it was broad daylight."

"Come on, woman," replied Gianni, "if that's what it is, there's no need to be afraid, because I said the *Te lucis* and the *'Ntemerata* and lots of other good prayers before we got into bed—plus, I made the sign of the cross from one corner of it to the other in the name of the Father and the Son and the Holy Ghost—so there's no reason to fear he can harm us, no matter how powerful he may be."[6]

To make sure there was no chance that Federigo would become suspicious and get angry with her, the lady decided that she absolutely had to get out of bed and let him know that Gianni was in the house. Consequently, she said to her husband: "That's all very well. You just go ahead and say those words of yours. But as far as I'm concerned, I'll never feel safe and secure until we exorcise him, and now that you're here, that's just what we're going to do."

"How are we going to perform an exorcism?" asked Gianni.

"I know exactly what to do," replied the lady, "because the other day, when I went to the pardoning service at Fiesole, one of those hermit women, who's the saintliest creature, Gianni dear, as God is my witness, saw how frightened I was and taught me a good, holy prayer. She said she'd used it many times before becoming a hermit and that it had always worked for her. Still, God knows, I would never have had the courage to go and try it out all by myself, but now that you're here, I want us to go and exorcise him."

Gianni said he really liked her idea, after which the two of them got out of bed and crept quietly to the door. On the other side of it Federigo was waiting and beginning to get suspicious. When they had reached a spot right next to the door, Gianni's wife said to him: "Now you go ahead and spit when I tell you to."[7]

"All right," replied Gianni.

Then the lady began the exorcism, saying:

Bogeyman, bogeyman, who goes walking by night,
Tail erect you came here, tail erect take your flight.

Go into the garden to the foot of the tree,
Where the peaches are growing, and here's what you'll see:
Greasy grease plus the droppings, five score, from my hen.
Put the flask to your lips, and just go away then.
And don't do any harm to my Gianni or me.

When she finished speaking, she told her husband, "Now spit, Gianni," and Gianni spat.

Federigo, who was listening to her words on the other side of the door, had stopped feeling jealous, and despite all his disappointment, he had such an urge to laugh that he thought he was going to burst. Then, just as Gianni spat, Federigo muttered under his breath, "Your teeth!"[8] Finally, after the lady had exorcised the bogeyman three times this way, she went back to bed with her husband.

Federigo had not yet eaten because he had expected to have supper with her, but since he understood exactly what the words of the exorcism meant, he went right into the garden where he found the two capons at the foot of the great peach tree together with the wine and the eggs. He took it all home with him and had his supper there in complete comfort. On many later occasions when he was with the lady, they used to have a good laugh together about this exorcism of hers.

Truth to tell, some people say that the lady had turned the skull of the ass toward Fiesole, but a farmhand, passing through the vineyard, had poked a stick up inside it and made it spin around and around until it wound up facing in the direction of Florence, which is why Federigo, believing he had been summoned, had come to her house. They also claim that the lady's prayer went this way:

Bogeyman, bogeyman, in God's name leave us be,
For the head of the ass was not turned 'round by me.
It was somebody else, and may God make him pine,
While I stay here in bed with this Gianni of mine.

In response, Federigo went away, losing his supper as well as his lodging there for the night.

However, a neighbor of mine, a very old woman, tells me that from everything she had learned as a girl, both stories are true, although the second one did not involve Gianni Lotteringhi, but a certain Gianni di Nello, who lived at Porta San Piero and who was no less a pea brain than Gianni Lotteringhi.[9]

It is therefore up to you, my dear ladies, to choose which exorcism of the two you like best, or to use both of them if you prefer, for as you have heard, experience shows they are extremely effective in such cases. You should learn them by heart, then, for they may be able to help you in times to come.

Day 7, Story 2

It is therefore up to you, my dear ladies, to choose which exorcism

*When her husband returns home unexpectedly, Peronella stashes her lover in a
barrel. Her husband has sold it, but she says that she herself had already done
so to a man who had climbed inside to see if it was in good condition. Leaping
out of the barrel, the lover gets the husband to scrape it out and then to carry
it back home for him.[1]*

Emilia's story was received with gales of laughter. When it was
finished, and everyone had praised the prayer as being indeed a
good and holy one, the King asked Filostrato to continue, who began
as follows:

My dearest ladies, so numerous are the tricks that men, and husbands in particular, play on you that when a woman sometimes happens to play one on her husband, you should not only be glad to have
heard about what had occurred, but you should go around telling the
story everywhere yourselves, so that men will come to realize that if
they know how to do such things, for their part, women know how to
do them, too. All of this cannot help but be advantageous to you, for
when a man recognizes that others are equally in the know, he will not
lightly undertake to deceive them. Who, then, can doubt that if men
could hear what we are going to say today on this topic, they would have
every reason to refrain from deceiving you, knowing that you also are
capable of tricking them if you want to? It is therefore my intention
to tell you about what a young woman, though of low birth, did to her
husband on the spur of the moment in order to save herself.

Not so very long ago in Naples, a poor man took to wife a beautiful,
charming young girl named Peronella.[2] Although they did not earn
very much, the two of them, he by plying his trade as a mason, and she

by spinning, supported themselves as best they could. One day this
Peronella caught the eye of a young man-about-town who, finding her
very attractive, fell in love with her, and by soliciting her one way and
another, soon managed to get on familiar terms with her. In order to
be able to spend time together, the two of them came up with this plan:
since her husband got up early every morning either to go to work or
to look for a job, the young man would station himself in a place from
which he could see him leaving the house, and as the neighborhood
where she lived, which is called Avorio, was pretty deserted, the young
man would go to her house as soon as the husband left. And that is just
what they did on many occasions.

One particular morning, however, when the good man was out of the
house and Giannello Scrignario—for that was the young man's name—
had gone inside to spend some time with Peronella, the husband, who
was usually away all day, happened to return after just a short absence.[3]
Upon finding the door locked from within, he knocked on it, and after
doing so, he said to himself: "O God, praised be Your name forever, for
although You've ordained that I should be poor, at least You've given
me the consolation of having a good, honest young woman as a wife!
You see how quickly she locked the door from the inside as soon as I
left so that nobody could get in and cause her trouble."

Peronella knew it was her husband from the way he was knocking, and said: "O no, Giannello my love, I'm a dead woman! Look, it's
my husband there, goddamn him. He's come back home, and I really
don't know what that means, because he's never returned at this hour.
Maybe he caught sight of you when you came in! But no matter what
the reason may be, for the love of God, get into this barrel you see here,
while I go and open the door. Then we'll find out what's brought him
back home so early this morning."

Giannello promptly climbed into the barrel, after which Peronella
went to the door and opened it for her husband. Giving him a withering look, she said: "What's the story here? Why have you come back
home so early like this? It seems to me, seeing you here with your tools
in your hands, that you want to take the day off. If you carry on like
this, how are we going to live? Where are we supposed to get our bread

from? Do you think I'm going to let you pawn my gown and the other rags I have for clothing, when I do nothing all day and night but spin until I've worked my fingers to the bone, just so there's enough oil to keep our lamp burning? Husband, husband, there's no woman in the neighborhood who doesn't marvel at it and make fun of me for all the work I put up with, and you, you come home with your hands dangling uselessly by your sides when you should be out working."

After she finished, she started to cry, but then she started up all over again: "Oh, alas, poor me! In what an evil hour was I born! Under what evil star did I come into the world! I could have had a proper young man, but turned him down and came instead to this guy who never gives a second thought to the woman he's taken into his home! Other women have a good time with their lovers—and there's no one around here who doesn't have two or three of them—and they enjoy them-selves while they make their husbands think the moon is the sun. But me, poor little me, because I'm a good girl and don't get involved in such hanky-panky, I'm the one who gets to suffer, I'm the one with all the bad luck. I don't know why I don't get me one of these lovers the way other women do! Listen up, husband of mine, if I wanted to be bad, I'd soon find someone to do it with, for there are plenty of good-looking guys here who are in love with me and are my admirers. They've sent me offers of lots of money, or dresses and jewels if I prefer, but my heart's never allowed me to do it, because I'm not the daughter of that kind of lady. And here you come home to me when you should be out working!"

"Oh, for God's sake, woman," replied her husband, "don't get down in the dumps about it. Believe me, I know you and the kind of woman you are, and as a matter of fact, I saw proof of it this very morning. Now, it's true that I went out to work, but what you don't seem to real-ize, any more than I did, is that today is the festival of Saint Galeone, and since everyone's taking a holiday, that's why I came back home at this hour.[4] But even so, I've been a good provider and found a way to keep us in bread for more than a month, for I've sold the barrel, which you know has been cluttering up our house for some time now, to the man you see here with me, and he'll give me five silver ducats for it."[5]

"Well, that really makes me mad," said Peronella. "You'd think that since you're a man and you get around, you'd know how the world works, and yet here you've gone and sold the barrel for five ducats. Now, I'm merely a woman, and I've hardly ever gone beyond our threshold, but I, too, could see that the barrel was cluttering up our house, and so I sold it to a good man here for a full seven ducats. In fact, when you came home, he had just climbed inside to see if it was in good condition."

Upon hearing this, her husband was overjoyed and turned to the man who had come with him for the barrel.

"God be with you, my good man," he said. "You heard my wife. She's sold it for seven, and the most you offered me for it was five."

"All right, then," replied the good man, and away he went.

"Now that you're home," said Peronella to her husband, "come on up here and take care of this business with him yourself."

While he was waiting, Giannello had been keeping his ears open in case there was anything he had to fear or needed to prepare himself to deal with. On hearing Peronella's words, he immediately leaped out of the barrel, and then, as if he had not heard anything about her husband's return, he said: "Where are you, my good woman?"

"Here I am," said the husband, who was just coming up. "What can I do for you?"

"Who are you?" asked Giannello. "I'd like to see the lady who was selling me this barrel."

"Don't worry," the good man answered, "you can deal with me, because I'm her husband."

"The barrel seems in pretty good condition to me," said Giannello, "but I think you let the lees from the wine remain in it, because it's entirely crusted over with something or other that's dried onto it, and it's so hard I can't get it off even if I use my nails. Now, unless it's cleaned out first, I'm not going to take it."

"Our bargain's not going to fall through just because of that," said Peronella. "My husband will clean the whole thing for you."

"That I will," declared her husband, who laid his tools down and stripped to his shirt. Then, after asking for a lighted lamp and a scraper, he got into the barrel and started working away at it. Pretending she wanted to watch what he was doing, Peronella leaned her head over the edge of the barrel, which was not very wide, along with one of her arms and shoulders.

"Scrape here, and here, and over there," she said to him, and "Look, there's still a little bit left here."

While she was standing there, giving her husband directions and telling him where to scrape, Giannello, who had not fully satisfied his desires that morning before the husband had arrived, and realizing that he could not do it the way he wanted to now, decided to take care of things as best he could. So, he came up behind Peronella, who was blocking off the entire mouth of the barrel, and just as the unbridled stallions of Parthia, burning with love, assail the mares in the open fields, so he satisfied his youthful appetite, which reached its climax almost at the very same moment that the scraping of the barrel was finished, at which point he backed off, Peronella removed her head from the barrel, and her husband climbed out.[6]

"Take this light, my good man," said Peronella to Giannello, "and see if it's all been cleaned out to your satisfaction."

After taking a look inside, Giannello said that everything was fine and that he was indeed satisfied. He then gave the husband seven ducats and got him to carry the barrel home for him.

Day 7, Story 3

Frate Rinaldo goes to bed with the mother of his godson, but when her husband discovers them in her room, they get him to believe that he was using an incantation to cure the little boy of worms.[1]

Filostrato could not veil his reference to the Parthian horses sufficiently to prevent the perceptive ladies from laughing over it, although they pretended they were responding to something else. But then, when the King saw that his story was finished, he asked Elissa to continue, and she, fully prepared to obey him, began as follows:

Charming ladies, Emilia's description of how the bogeyman was exorcised made me recall a story about another incantation, and although my story may not be as good as hers, I am going to tell it to you because nothing else comes to mind at the moment that suits our topic for today.

You should know that there once lived in Siena a quite charming young man by the name of Rinaldo who came from an honorable family and who was deeply in love with the very beautiful wife of a rich neighbor of his. Hoping that if he could just get to talk with her in private, he would be able to obtain everything he desired from her, he decided that since the lady was pregnant, and he could see no other way to do it, he would offer to become the child's godfather. And so, having become friends with her husband, he broached the subject to him in the most tactful manner he could think of, and it was all arranged.

Having thus become godfather to Madonna Agnesa's child, Rinaldo was provided with a slightly more plausible pretext for speaking with her, and he now felt confident enough to explain to her what he wanted in so many words, something that she had understood long before then

from the looks he gave her with his eyes. But it hardly got him anywhere with the lady, even though she did not dislike listening to what
he had to say.

Not long afterward, for some reason or other, Rinaldo happened to
become a friar, and whatever the pickings were that he got from the
profession, he stuck with it. Although from the time he became a friar,
he had, for a while, set aside the love he felt for his godchild's mother as
well as certain other worldly vices of his, still, in the course of time, he
took them all up again, without ever abandoning the habit he wore. He
began to take pleasure in his appearance, in wearing garments of fine
cloth, in doing everything in a gallant, refined manner, in composing
songs and sonnets and ballads, in singing, and in spending his time in
many other activities just like these.

But why do I go on talking about this Frate Rinaldo of ours? Are
there any of them who do not behave like that? Oh, the scandal of this
corrupt world! They are not ashamed to appear so fat, to have ruddy
faces, to be so dainty in their dress and in all their actions, and yet
they do not go about like doves, but like proud cocks, with their chests
puffed out and their crests erect. And yet, what is worse—let us set
aside the fact that their cells are filled with little bottles of elixirs and
ointments, boxes full of sweets, little jars and vials of essences and oils,
and flasks brimming over with Malvasia and Greco and other precious
wines, to such an extent that to any observer they look more like the
shops of apothecaries and perfumers than the cells of friars—what is
worse, I say, is that they are not ashamed to let others know they suffer from gout, believing people are completely unaware that frequent
fasts, a simple, meager diet, and sober living should actually make men
lean and slender, and, for the most part, healthy. Or if such things do
make them sick, then, at least it is not with gout, for which the usual
remedy is chastity and everything else that pertains to the lifestyle
of a humble friar. Indeed, they think people are ignorant of the fact
that long vigils, prayer, and strict self-discipline, together with a life of
poverty, will normally give men a pale, drawn appearance, and that
neither Saint Dominic nor Saint Francis had four cloaks apiece, or
dressed themselves in richly dyed, finely woven clothing, but rather

in garments of coarse wool in its natural color, made to keep out the cold and not for show. May God see to it that they, no less than the simpleminded people who provide for their nourishment, get what they deserve!

Anyway, having reverted to his original cravings, Frate Rinaldo began paying regular visits to his godchild's mother, and with his audacity on the increase, he started urging her more insistently than ever to grant him what he wished. One day, he pestered her so much that the good lady, finding herself under such pressure and thinking that he was, perhaps, more handsome than he had seemed in the past, had recourse to the expedient that all women resort to when they really want to grant what is being asked of them.

"Come now, Frate Rinaldo," she said, "is it possible friars really do that sort of thing?"

"My lady," replied Frate Rinaldo, "from the moment I take off this habit, which I can remove with the greatest of ease, I won't look like a friar to you anymore, but like a man who is made the same way all the rest of them are."

The lady grinned at this and said:

"O poor me! You're the godfather of my child. How could we do it? It would be terribly wrong. In fact, I've often heard tell that it's a most heinous sin. Otherwise, I'd certainly do what you want."

"If that's the only reason you pass this up," said Frate Rinaldo, "then you're being very foolish. I'm not saying it's not a sin, but God forgives greater ones in those who repent. But tell me this: to whom is your child more closely related, to me who held him at his baptism, or to your husband by whom he was begotten?"

"He's closer to my husband," said the lady.

"That's right," said the friar, "and doesn't your husband sleep with you?"

"Of course he does," she replied.

"Then, I," said the friar, "since I'm less closely related to your child than your husband is, I should be able to sleep with you just as he does."

The lady, who was no logician and needed very little to be persuaded, either believed, or pretended to believe, that what the friar was saying was true, and replied: "How could anyone possibly refute such words of wisdom?"

After that, despite his being the godfather of her child, she allowed him to fulfill his desires. Nor did they stop with just that one encounter, but got together again many, many times under the cover of his being the child's godfather, which made it easier for them to do it without arousing much suspicion.

But on one of those occasions, having come to her house and discovered that the only other person there was the lady's pretty, charming little maid, Frate Rinaldo sent the companion who had accompanied him upstairs to the pigeon loft with her to teach her the Lord's Prayer, while he and the lady, who was holding her little boy by the hand, went into her bedroom. After locking up behind them, they settled down on a little divan that was there and began fooling around.

As they were thus occupied, the child's father happened to return home, although no one heard him until he had arrived at the bedroom door and started knocking and calling his wife.

When Madonna Agnesa heard his voice, she said: "I'm as good as dead. Look, my husband's here. Now he's sure to discover what's behind this friendship of ours."

Frate Rinaldo was undressed down to his tunic, having taken off his hooded cloak and his scapular, and hearing the noise, he said: "You're right. If only I had my clothes on, we might find some way out of this, but if you open the door, and he finds me like this, there'll be no excuse for us."

Suddenly a bright idea occurred to the lady. "Now you get dressed," she said, "and when you're done, take your godson in your arms and listen carefully to what I'm going to tell my husband so that you can back me up later on with what you say. Just leave it all to me."

The good man was still knocking when his wife said, "I'm coming," and getting up, she put on a cheerful countenance, went over to the bedroom door, and opened it.

"Oh, husband," she said, "let me tell you, it was God who sent our child's godfather over to us today, for if he hadn't come, then we would have lost our son for sure."

When the pious fool heard this, he just about passed out. "What happened?" he asked.

"Oh, husband," said his wife, "a little while ago, the child suddenly fainted, and I thought he was dead. I didn't know what to say or do, but just at that moment his godfather Frate Rinaldo arrived, took him in his arms, and said to me, 'Neighbor, he's got worms inside his body, and if they get any closer to his heart, they'll kill him for sure. But don't be afraid, because I'm going to cast a spell on them and kill them all, and before I leave here, you'll see your child's just as healthy as he's ever been.' He needed to have you recite certain prayers, but because the maid couldn't find you, he had his companion say them in the highest part of our house. Then he and I came in here, and since no one except the child's mother can assist in matters like this, we locked ourselves in so that we wouldn't be disturbed by anyone. He's still got the child in his arms, and all he's waiting for now, I think, is for his companion to finish saying his prayers, and then the spell will be complete, because the boy is already his old self again."

The simpleton believed every last word, being so overwhelmed by his affection for his son that he did not give a thought to the possibility that his wife might be tricking him. Instead, heaving a great sigh, he said: "I want to go and see him."

"Don't go there," said his wife, "or you'll ruin what's been done. Just wait here while I go and see whether you can come in, and then I'll call you."

Frate Rinaldo, who had heard the entire exchange and had gotten dressed again at his leisure, took the child up in his arms, and as soon as he had arranged things to his satisfaction, he called out: "O neighbor, isn't that his father's voice I hear out there?"

"Yes, sir, it is," the simpleton replied.

"Well then, come right in," said Frate Rinaldo. And when the simple soul entered the room, Frate Rinaldo said to him: "Here, take your son. He's been restored to health by the grace of God, although there was a time when I thought you wouldn't get to see him alive at vespers. Now you go and order a figure of wax about the same size as your son, and have it placed, for the glory of God, in front of the statue of

Messer Saint Ambrose, through whose merits God has granted you this grace."[2]

When the boy saw his father, he ran up to him and made a fuss over him the way little children will do. His father picked him up in his arms, weeping as if he were lifting him up out of the grave, and began kissing him and thanking his godfather for having cured him.

In the meantime, Frate Rinaldo's companion had taught the little maid not just one Lord's Prayer, but perhaps as many as four, and had made her a present of a white linen purse given to him by a nun, thus turning her into his devotee. When he heard the simpleton calling to his wife from outside the bedroom, he quietly went and positioned himself so that he could see and hear what was going on. Upon observing how nicely everything was proceeding, he came downstairs and entered the room.

"Frate Rinaldo," he said, "those four prayers you asked me to say, I've recited them all."

"Well done, brother," replied Frate Rinaldo, "you've got real stamina. For my part, I'd only said two of them before my neighbor here arrived, but between your efforts and my own, the Lord God has bestowed His grace on us and the child's been cured."

The simpleton then sent for some choice wines and sweets, and with them he honored his child's godfather and his godfather's companion by giving them the refreshments they both really needed more than anything else. Then, accompanying them to the door, he commended them to God, after which, without the slightest delay, he had the wax image made and sent it to be hung up with the others in front of the statue of Saint Ambrose, but not, of course, the one in Milan.

Day 7, Story 4

Tofano locks his wife out of the house one night, and when she cannot get back in despite all her pleading with him, she pretends to throw herself down a well, but drops a large rock into it instead. Tofano comes out of the house and rushes over to the spot, at which point she slips back inside, locks him out, and screams insults at him.[1]

As soon as the King perceived that Elissa's story had reached its conclusion, he immediately turned to Lauretta, indicating that he wanted her to speak next. Without hesitation, she began as follows:

O Love, how great and varied are your powers, how wonderful your counsels and insights! What philosopher, what artist could have ever imagined the stratagems, the subterfuges, and the arguments that you supply in an instant to those who follow in your footsteps? There can be no doubt but that everyone else's teaching is slow in comparison with yours, as may clearly be deduced from the cases that have already been brought to our attention. And to those cases, dear ladies, I will now add yet another, this one involving a woman of quite ordinary intelligence who came up with a stratagem that only Love could have revealed to her.

In Arezzo, then, there once lived a rich man by the name of Tofano, who took an exceptionally beautiful woman called Monna Ghita to wife and then promptly became jealous of her for no particular reason.[2] When she found out about it, she got angry, and repeatedly asked him to explain why he felt as he did. Since the only explanations he came up with were vague and unconvincing, however, she resolved to make him die from the very illness that up to then he had had no real cause to fear.

Having noticed that a young man, a very agreeable person to her way

537

of thinking, was quite attracted to her, the lady discreetly arranged to make his acquaintance, and when things between them had advanced to the point that nothing remained for them to do but to translate words into deeds, she turned her attention to devising a way to bring this about as well. Since she knew that one of her husband's bad habits was his fondness for drink, not only did she start commending it to him, but she would cleverly encourage him to indulge as often as she could. In fact, she became so expert at doing this that practically any time she wanted to, she got him to drink himself into a stupor, after which, once she saw that he was good and drunk, she would put him to bed and go off to meet her lover. After their first time together, she felt secure enough to go on seeing him again and again. Indeed, she became so confident, because of her husband's weakness for drink, that she made bold not merely to bring her lover into the house, but on occasion to spend a large part of the night with him at his place, which was not very far away.

The amorous lady had been carrying on like this for some time, when her wretched husband happened to notice that although she encouraged him to drink, for all that, she never touched a drop herself. This made him suspect what was indeed the case, namely that his wife was getting him drunk so that afterward she could do what she wanted while he was asleep. Wishing to put this supposition to the test, he returned home one evening, having refrained from drinking all day long, and pretended by the way he spoke and acted that he was as drunk as could be. She was taken in by his show, and concluding that he did not need another drop to make him sleep soundly, she quickly put him to bed, after which, just as she had done on many other occasions, she left her house and went to her lover's place, where she remained until the middle of the night.

Once he no longer heard his wife about the place, Tofano got up, went over to the door, and after locking it from the inside, stationed himself at the window so he could see her when she came back and let her know that he was well aware of what she was up to. And there he stayed until she returned.

His wife eventually came home, and when she found herself locked out, she got very upset and started trying to force the door open. After putting up with this for a while, Tofano said: "You're wasting your energy, woman, because there's no way you can possibly get in. Go back to wherever it is you've been staying until now, and rest assured that you're never going to return to this house until I've honored you just as you deserve for this affair right in front of your family and neighbors."

The lady began pleading with him, for the love of God, to please open the door for her, saying that she was not coming from the place where he thought she had been. Instead, she had been sitting up with a neighbor of hers, who could not sleep the whole night through because it lasted so long and who did not want to sit up in her house all alone. The lady's prayers were completely unavailing, however, because the stupid brute was perfectly willing to have all of Arezzo learn about their shame, even though, so far, no one knew anything about it.

When she saw that her pleading was getting her nowhere, the lady resorted to threats. "If you don't open up for me," she said, "I'm going to make you the sorriest man alive."

"And just what can you possibly do to me?" asked Tofano.

Love had sharpened the lady's wits with his counsel, and she replied: "Before I'll allow myself to suffer the shame that you wrongly wish to inflict on me, I'll throw myself down this well here, and when they find me dead inside, they'll all think that you got drunk and threw me into it. Then, either you're going to have to run away, and you'll forfeit all your possessions and live in exile, or they'll wind up chopping off your head for having murdered me, which is, in effect, what you really will have done."

When all of her words failed to make Tofano budge one bit from his stupid decision, she said: "Look here, I'm not going to let you torment me like this any longer. May God pardon you! I'm leaving my distaff behind here, and you can put it back where it belongs."

The night was so dark that people could hardly see one another passing in the street, and having uttered these words, the lady made her way over to the well, picked up a huge rock that was lying next to it, and shouting "God forgive me!" let it fall in.

When Tofano heard the enormous splash the rock made as it struck the water, he was firmly convinced that she had thrown herself in, and snatching up his bucket and rope, he flung himself out of the house and rushed over to the well to help her. His wife had hidden herself near the front door, and the moment she saw him running to the well, she slipped inside the house, locked herself in, and went over to the window.

"You should add water to your wine when you're drinking it," she said, "and not later on in the middle of the night."

When Tofano heard what she said, he realized that she had made a fool of him and went back to the front door. On finding that he could not open it, he told her to let him in. Although she had been talking quietly up to that point, now, however, she began shrieking.

"By God's Cross, you repulsive drunk," she said, "you're not getting in here tonight. I won't put up with your antics anymore. I'm going to show everybody the kind of a man you are and let them see just what time of night it is when you come back home."

Now Tofano got angry, too, and began screaming insults at her, with the result that the neighbors, men and women alike, hearing all the noise, got up, went over to their windows, and demanded to know what the matter was.

The lady began crying and said: "The matter is this wretch of a husband of mine who comes home drunk every evening, or else he falls asleep in some tavern and only gets back at this hour. I've put up with this for years without being able to make him change, and I just can't take it anymore. So I decided to shame him by locking him out of the house to see whether he'll mend his ways."

The asinine Tofano, for his part, told them what had actually happened, while continuing to threaten her in the worst way. His wife then turned to the neighbors and said: "Now you see the kind of man he is! What would you think if I were out in the street like him, and he were in the house like me? I swear to God, I have no doubt you'd believe he was telling the truth. So, you can see just how clever he is! For here he is, saying that I did the very thing I'm pretty sure he did himself. He thought he could frighten me by throwing something or other into the well, but I would to God he'd really thrown himself down there and drowned, so that all that wine he's drunk far too much of would be well and truly diluted with water."

Without exception, all the neighbors who were present, both the men and the women, began scolding Tofano, blaming him for what had happened and reviling him because of what he was saying about his wife, and in short, they created such an uproar that it spread from one person to another until it eventually reached the lady's family. They hurried to the scene, and after they had put together the story from the accounts several of the neighbors gave them, they grabbed Tofano and beat him until he was completely covered with bruises. Then they went into the house, gathered up all the lady's belongings, and took her back home with them, threatening Tofano with even worse to come.

Seeing that he had gotten the worst of it and that his jealousy had brought him to a sorry pass, Tofano, who was really very fond of his wife, got some friends to act as intermediaries, and thanks to them he managed to make peace and arrange for her to come back home. And not only did he promise her that he would never be jealous again, but what is more, he gave her permission to do whatever she liked, as long as she was so discreet that he never found out anything about it. Thus, just like the peasant who was a dunce, having been beaten, he made peace at once. So, long live Love, and death to Avarice and all his company![3]

Day 7, Story 5

Disguised as a priest, a jealous man hears his wife's confession and is given to understand that she is in love with a priest who comes to see her every night. Then, while her husband is secretly keeping watch by the front door, the wife has her lover come to her across the roof and passes the time with him.[1]

Lauretta had ended her tale, and after everyone had praised the lady for treating that bad husband of hers just as he deserved, the King, who did not want to waste time, turned to Fiammetta and graciously assigned her the task of telling the next story, which she began as follows:

Noblest of ladies, the preceding tale prompts me to tell a similar one about a jealous husband, for in my opinion, whatever their wives do to them is well done indeed, especially when they become jealous for no reason at all. And if lawgivers had taken everything into consideration, then I think that the punishment they established for wives in such cases would not have differed from the one they prescribed for a person who attacks another in self-defense. For jealous men plot against the very lives of their young wives and will stop at nothing in seeking their deaths.

Like everyone else, after spending the entire week cooped up in their houses attending to the needs of their families and taking care of domestic chores, those wives long for peace and relaxation on holidays and want to have a little fun, just like the workers in the fields, the artisans in the cities, and the magistrates in the courts, indeed, just as God Himself did when He rested on the seventh day from all His labors. Both canon and civil law, which seek to promote the honor of

God and the general welfare of the people, want there to be a distinction between workdays and days of rest.

Jealous men will have none of this, however, but on precisely those days when other women are enjoying themselves, they keep their wives under lock and key not just in their houses, but in their rooms, making those days even more wretched and miserable for them, and only those poor creatures who have had to endure such treatment know how wearing it is. To sum it all up: whatever a wife does to a husband who is jealous without cause is surely to be praised rather than censored.

There was once a very wealthy merchant and landowner living in Rimini, who, having married an extremely beautiful woman, became inordinately jealous of her. And the only reason for it was that, since he loved her passionately, thought she was simply gorgeous, and knew that she did everything in her power to please him, he imagined that all the men were in love with her, that she seemed beautiful to every last one of them, and that she would do as much as she could to please them just as she did for him. This was the thinking of a wicked, insensitive man, who, in his jealousy, watched her so carefully and placed such restraints on her that I doubt whether prisoners sentenced to death are guarded so closely by their jailors. It was not merely that she was unable to attend weddings or parties, or go to church, or even set foot beyond her door at all, but she did not dare to show herself at a window or look outside her house for any reason. As a result, her life was pure misery, and she endured her suffering with less and less patience insofar as she knew she was innocent.

To console herself, seeing how unjustly her husband was persecuting her, she decided to find some way, if any could be found, to provide him with a real reason for treating her as he did. Since she could not appear at a window, she had no means of giving any sign of encouragement to a potential lover who might be passing through the neighborhood. Knowing, however, that a handsome, agreeable young man lived next door, she thought that if she could find a hole in the wall that divided her house from his, she could go on peeping through it until she caught sight of him. She would then have an opportunity to speak with him and offer him her love, if he were prepared to accept it, after which, should a way be found to do so, they could get together from time to time. And in this fashion she would be able to get through her unhappy life until the demon who possessed her husband left him.

And so, when her husband was not around, she went from one spot to another in her house examining the wall, until she discovered, in a fairly remote location, a place where there was a crack. Peering through it, she had a hard time making out what was on the other side, but she finally determined that it was a bedroom, and said to herself, "If this were Filippo's room"—that being the name of the young man who was her neighbor—"I'd be halfway there."

The wife got one of her maidservants, a woman who felt sorry for her, secretly to keep watch by the crack, and discovered that it was indeed the young man's bedroom and that he slept there all by himself. By paying frequent visits to the crack, and dropping pebbles and little pieces of straw through it whenever she heard the young man on the other side, she finally managed to get him to come over and see what was going on. Then she quietly called out to him, and when the young man, recognizing her voice, replied, she seized her opportunity and in short order told him everything that was on her mind. Overjoyed, the young man began to enlarge the hole from his side of the wall, but always in such a way that no one would notice what he was doing. And there, on numerous occasions, the two of them would talk and touch one another's hands, although they could go no further because of the strict surveillance maintained by her jealous husband.

Now, seeing as how Christmas was approaching, the lady told her husband that, if he approved, she would like to attend church on that morning so that she could go to confession and take Communion just like every other Christian.

"And what sins have you committed," asked the jealous husband, "that you want to go to confession?"

"What!" she replied. "Do you think I'm a saint just because you keep me locked up? You know very well that I commit sins like everyone else down here, but I have no intention of telling them to you since you're no priest."

His suspicions being aroused by her words, the jealous husband decided he would try to discover just what those sins were that she had committed. Having thought up a way to do it, he responded to her request by saying that he approved of it, but that he wanted her to go to their own chapel rather than some other church. Moreover, she was to get there early in the morning and make her confession to their chaplain, or to whatever priest the chaplain assigned her, and to no one else, after which she was to return home straightway. The lady had an inkling that he was up to something, but without saying anything further on the subject, she replied that she would do as he wished.

When Christmas morning arrived, the lady arose at daybreak, put on some nice clothes, and went to the church her jealous husband had insisted on. As for him, he, too, had gotten up and gone to the same church, arriving there ahead of her. He had already arranged things with the chaplain and quickly put on one of his robes. It had a large hood that covered his cheeks, like the ones we see priests wearing nowadays, and after pulling it forward a bit over his head, he took a seat in the choir stalls.

Upon entering the church, the lady asked for the chaplain, and when he arrived and heard that she wanted to make her confession, he told her he could not hear it himself, but would send her one of his fellow priests. Then away he went and sent the jealous husband, unfortunately for him, to speak with her instead. But even though he walked up to her with great solemnity, and the day was not particularly bright, and he had pulled the hood down well over his eyes, he was still unable to disguise himself so completely as to prevent the lady from recognizing him at once. The moment she realized who it was, she said to herself: "Praise be to God, this guy's turned from a jealous husband into a priest! But never mind, I'm going to see that he gets what he's looking for."

Pretending not to recognize him, she sat down at his feet.[2] Messer Jealous had put some pebbles in his mouth so that they would interfere with his speech a bit in order to keep his wife from identifying him by his voice, and he thought his disguise was otherwise so perfect that she would not be able to make him out.

But to come now to the confession: having first explained that she was married, the lady told him, among other things, that she was in love with a priest who came to sleep with her every night. When her jealous husband heard this, he felt as though someone had taken a knife and stabbed him through the heart, and if it were not for the fact that he was driven by his desire to know more about it, he would have abandoned the confession and gone away. Instead, he stayed put and asked her: "How's that? Doesn't your husband sleep with you?"

"Yes, father," replied the lady.

"Well, then," said the jealous man, "how can the priest sleep with you, too?"

"Father," said the lady, "I don't know what art the priest makes use of, but there's not a door in the house so securely locked that it won't open the instant he touches it. What's more, he tells me that when he arrives at the one to my bedroom, he recites certain words before unlocking it that immediately make my husband doze off, and as soon as he hears him sleeping, he opens the door, comes inside, and lies down with me. And this procedure of his never fails."

"My lady," said the jealous husband, "this is very wrong, and you must give it up completely."

"Father," said the lady, "I don't think I could ever do that because I love him too much."

"Then I won't be able to give you absolution," replied the jealous husband.

"I'm sorry about that," she said, "but I didn't come here to tell you lies. If I thought I could do what you ask, I'd tell you so."

"I am truly sorry for you, my lady," he said, "for I see you losing your soul by taking this course of action. But I will do you a favor and go to the trouble of saying some special prayers of mine to God on your behalf, which may possibly do you some good. Also, I'll be sending you one of my young clerks from time to time.* You're to report to him

---

* Clerk (Lat. *clericus*) is another word for clergyman or priest, and since the text specifies that he is a *cherichetto*, "a young clerk," the husband is probably referring to a boy who was training to become a priest and who assisted the priest in church services.

whether or not the prayers are helping you, and if they are, then we'll take it from there."

"Don't do it, father," she replied. "Don't send anyone to me at the house, because if my husband found out about it, he's so insanely jealous that nothing in the world would ever dislodge the idea from his head that the boy had some evil design in going there, and he'd give me no peace for the rest of the year."

"Don't worry about that, my lady," he said. "I'll make sure to arrange things in such a way that you'll never hear a word about it from him."

"If you're confident you can do that," said the lady, "then it's all right with me." And having recited the *Confiteor* and received her penance, she got to her feet and went to hear Mass.*

Fuming with jealousy, the hapless husband headed off as well, and after removing his priest's robes, he returned home, determined to find a way to catch the priest and his wife together and to do the pair of them a bad turn. When the lady came back from church, she saw quite clearly from the look on her husband's face that she had spoiled his holiday for him, although he did his best to conceal what he had done and what he thought he knew.[3]

Having made up his mind to spend the following night waiting near the front door to see whether the priest would show up, he said to his wife: "Tonight I have to go out for supper, and I'll be sleeping elsewhere as well, so be sure you do a good job of locking up not just the front door, but the one on the landing and the one to the bedroom. Then, whenever you feel like it, you can go to bed."

"Very well," replied the lady.

As soon as she had the chance, she went to the hole in the wall and gave the usual signal. When he heard it, Filippo came at once, and the lady told him what she had done that morning as well as what her husband had told her after they had eaten.

"I'm certain he won't leave the house," she said. "Instead, he's going to

---

* The *Confiteor*, which means "I confess," was a special prayer that penitents said when they had finished confessing their sins. It was also recited in the Mass.

keep watch by the front door. So, find some way to get in here tonight by climbing up over the roof, and then we can be together."

"Leave it to me, my lady," said the young man, who was thoroughly delighted by this development.

At nightfall, the jealous husband quietly concealed himself with his weapons in one of the rooms on the ground floor, while his wife locked up all the doors, and especially the one on the landing, so that he could not come back up, and in due time, the young man appeared, having made his way to her very cautiously by climbing over the roof from his side of it. Then the two of them went to bed, where they took their pleasure of one another, enjoying themselves until daybreak, at which point the young man returned to his house.

The jealous husband, freezing to death, aching, and supperless, spent practically the entire night with his weapons next to the front door, waiting for the priest to show up, but as dawn approached, incapable of staying awake any longer, he fell asleep in the ground-floor room. It was close to tierce when he awoke, and finding that the front door was now open, he acted as if he were just coming back home, went upstairs, and had something to eat. A little later he sent a servant boy of his, pretending to be the young clerk of the priest who had heard his wife's confession, to ask her if a certain person she knew about had come around again. The lady, who recognized the messenger quite easily, replied that he had not been there that night and that if he continued to behave like this, she might just wind up forgetting all about him, even though she did not particularly want to.

Now, what more is there to tell you? While the lady was having a good time with her lover, her jealous husband spent night after night at the front door trying to catch the priest, until he finally could not take it any longer, and with a look of fury on his face, demanded to know what his wife had said to the priest on the morning when she had gone to confession. The lady answered that she did not want to tell him because doing so was neither right nor proper.

"You wicked woman," said the jealous husband, "whether you like it or not, I know what you said to him, and I absolutely insist that you tell me, because unless you give me the name of the priest whom you're so much in love with and who uses incantations every night so he can sleep with you, I'll slit your throat."

The lady said it was simply not true that she was in love with a priest. "What?" asked her husband. "Didn't you say thus and such to the priest who was hearing your confession?"

"Yes, I sure did," she said, "not that he would have ever told you about it. All that would have really been required was for you to have been present and to have heard it for yourself."

"Then, tell me who this priest is," said the jealous man, "and be quick about it."

The lady began to smile, and said: "It's really very gratifying for me to see a simple woman lead a wise man around in the same way that a ram is led by the horns to the slaughter—not that you're a wise man, nor have you ever been one since the hour you allowed the evil spirit of jealousy to enter your breast, without there being any reason for it. And the more foolish and asinine you are, the less my accomplishment amounts to.

"Husband, do you really believe that the eyes in my head are as blind as the ones in your brain? They sure aren't. Because at first glance I recognized the priest who was hearing my confession and knew it was you, but I made up my mind to give you exactly what you were looking for—and that's just what I did. However, if you'd been as smart as you think you are, you would never have tried to find out your good wife's secrets by that means, and instead of succumbing to baseless suspicion, you would have realized that she was confessing the truth to you and hadn't committed a sin at all.

"I told you I was in love with a priest, and you, whom I'm greatly at fault for loving as I do, hadn't you turned yourself into a priest? I told you that no door in my house would remain locked when he wanted to sleep with me, and which door in your house was ever closed to you when you wanted to come to me, wherever I might happen to be? I told you that the priest slept with me every night, and was there ever a night when you didn't sleep with me? And every time you sent your clerk to me, you know it was always when you were not sleeping with me, and so, I sent him to tell you that the priest had not been here.

"How could anyone except you, a man who's let himself be blinded by jealousy, have been so foolish as to have failed to understand these things? And you, you've been in the house every night keeping watch by the front door, and you actually think you made me believe that you'd gone elsewhere to have supper and spend the night!

"It's time you took a good look at yourself and went back to behaving like a man the way you used to do. Stop allowing yourself to be made a fool of by someone who knows you as well as I do. And give up all this strict surveillance of yours, because I swear to God that if I had any desire to make you a cuckold, I'd find a way to enjoy myself without your ever noticing it, even though you had a hundred eyes instead of just a single pair."[4]

After listening to what she had to say, the jealous wretch, who thought he had been so very clever in discovering his wife's secret, realized that he had been made a laughingstock, and without saying another word by way of reply, he concluded that she was not only sagacious, but virtuous as well. And so, now that he really needed it, he divested himself completely of his jealousy, just as he had put it on before, when it was unnecessary. Consequently, his clever wife, having acquired, as it were, a license to pursue her pleasures, no longer had her lover come over the roof like a cat in order to visit her, but ushered him right straight in through the front door. And from then on, always acting with discretion, she had lots of good times with him and spent many a merry hour in his company.

Day 7, Story 6

While she is with Leonetto, Madonna Isabella is visited by a certain Messer Lambertuccio, who has fallen in love with her. When her husband then returns, she sends Messer Lambertuccio out of the house with a dagger in his hand, and her husband winds up escorting Leonetto home.[1]

Everyone enjoyed Fiammetta's tale enormously, and they all declared that the lady had done a superb job in giving that asinine man exactly what he deserved. Now that the story was over, however, the King ordered Pampinea to continue, and she proceeded to say:

There are many who speak like simpletons when they say that Love diminishes people's intelligence and that anyone who falls in love is more or less turned into a fool.[2] I think this notion is stupid, as has been amply shown by the stories we have already told, and as I now propose to demonstrate once again.

In our city, where all the good things of life can be found in abundance, there was once a young woman, both gently born and exceptionally beautiful, who was married to a very worthy and distinguished gentleman. And just as it often happens that people grow tired of always eating the same food and occasionally wish to vary it, so this lady, finding her husband less than completely satisfying, fell in love with a young man named Leonetto who did not come from a noble family, but was quite pleasant and well mannered. He likewise fell for her, and since it is unusual, as you know, for nothing to happen when each of the parties involved wants the same thing, it was not long before they consummated their love.

Now, seeing as how she was a beautiful and charming woman, a gentleman called Messer Lambertuccio also happened to fall passionately in love with her, but as she found him a tiresome, disagreeable man, she could not bring herself to return his affection for anything in the world. He kept attempting to win her favor with a steady stream of messages, and when they failed him, being a man who had considerable influence, he sent her one in which he threatened to ruin her reputation if she did not satisfy his desires. The lady was terrified, knowing the sort of man he was, and brought herself around to do his bidding.

Having gone to stay in a beautiful country estate of hers, as is our custom in the summer, the lady, whose name was Madonna Isabella, happened to send for Leonetto, inviting him to come and spend time with her, since her husband had ridden off somewhere that morning and would be away for several days. Leonetto was overjoyed and went there at once.

Meanwhile, Messer Lambertuccio, hearing that the lady's husband was not at home, mounted his horse, rode unaccompanied to her place, and knocked at the door. When the lady's maid saw him, she immediately went to her mistress, who was in her bedroom with Leonetto, called her out, and said: "My lady, Messer Lambertuccio is down below, and he's all by himself."

The lady was terribly distressed to hear of his arrival, but since she was absolutely terrified of him, she begged Leonetto not to be upset if she asked him to hide behind the curtains of her bed until such time as Messer Lambertuccio had departed. Leonetto, who was as scared of the man as she was, hid himself there, after which the lady told her maid to go and open the door for Messer Lambertuccio. She did so, and as soon as he was inside the courtyard, he dismounted, tied his palfrey to a hook, and went up into the house. Putting on a smile, the lady came to the head of the stairs, from which she greeted him as cheerfully as she could and asked him what had brought him there. Having embraced her and kissed her, he said: "Sweetheart, I heard your husband wasn't here, and so I've come to spend some time with you." After these words, they went into the bedroom, where they locked themselves in, and Messer Lambertuccio proceeded to have his way with her.

While he was thus engaged with the lady, quite contrary to her expectations, her husband happened to return. No sooner did the maid spot him approaching the villa than she ran immediately to her mistress's bedroom and said: "My lady, look, it's the master, he's come back. I think he must be down there in the courtyard by now."

Finding herself with two men in the house, and knowing it was impossible to conceal the gentleman since his palfrey was down in the courtyard, the lady thought she was as good as dead. Nevertheless, in response to her maid's warning, she quickly hit upon a plan and leaped out of bed.

"Sir," she said to Messer Lambertuccio, "if you have the slightest affection for me and wish to save my life, then you'll do what I tell you. Take out your dagger, hold it in your hand, and with a look of outrage on your face, rush down the stairs in a fury, yelling, 'I swear to God, I'll catch him somewhere else.' And if my husband should try to stop you, or ask you what's going on, don't say anything except what I've just told you. Then, once you've mounted your horse, don't hang about there with him for any reason."

Having agreed to her plan with a ready will, Messer Lambertuccio drew out his dagger, and with his face flushed fiery red both because of his recent exertions and because of his anger over the husband's return, he did everything the lady had instructed him to do. The husband, who had already dismounted in the courtyard, was puzzled at seeing the palfrey there. Just as he was about to go up the stairs, he saw Messer Lambertuccio coming down. Marveling at the man's words and at the look on his face, he said: "Sir, what's the meaning of this?"

Messer Lambertuccio, having put his foot in the stirrup and mounted his horse, said nothing but, "By God's body, I'll get ahold of him somewhere else." And away he rode.

The gentleman then climbed up the stairs and found his wife at the top, thoroughly dismayed and terrified. "What's going on here?" he asked her. "Why is Messer Lambertuccio so angry, and who's the person he's threatening?"

Drawing back toward the bedroom so that Leonetto would hear her, the lady replied: "Sir, I've never, ever had a fright like this one. Some

young man I don't know came running in here, pursued by Messer
Lambertuccio holding his dagger in his hand. By chance he found this
room open, and trembling all over, he said to me, 'My lady, help me for
God's sake, or I'm going to be killed and die right here in your arms.' I
stood up at once and was about to ask him who he was and what it was
all about, when lo and behold, there was Messer Lambertuccio coming
up the stairs, saying, 'Traitor, where are you?' Planting myself in the
doorway to the room, I held him back as he tried to come inside, and
he was enough of a gentleman that when he saw I had no intention of
letting him in, after a lot of rigamarole he went back down again, as
you saw for yourself."

"Wife, you did the right thing," said the husband. "It would have been
a terrible dishonor for us if somebody had been killed in our house. Not
that it wasn't very shameful for Messer Lambertuccio to have pursued
a person who'd taken refuge here."

Then he asked where the young man was, and his wife replied: "Sir,
I don't know where he went and hid himself."

"Where are you?" her husband called out. "It's safe for you to come
out now."

When Leonetto, who had heard everything, emerged from his hiding
place, he was shaking all over with fear, for he had indeed been utterly
terrified. The gentleman then asked him: "What have you got to do
with Messer Lambertuccio?"

"Not a thing in the world, sir," replied the young man, "and that's
why I'm thoroughly convinced that either he's not in his right mind,
or he's mistaken me for someone else, because as soon as he spotted me
in the street not far from this villa, he put his hand to his dagger and
said, 'Traitor, you're a dead man!' I didn't stop to ask him the reason
why, but started running away as fast as I could and wound up here,
where, thanks be to God and to this kind lady, I managed to escape."

"Come now, don't be afraid," said the gentleman. "I'll see you back
home safe and sound, and later on you can make some inquiries and
try to discover what this is all about."

And so, after they had eaten supper, he got a horse for the young
man to ride, escorted him back to Florence, and left him at his house.

That very evening, in accordance with the lady's instructions, Leonetto spoke in private to Messer Lambertuccio and arranged everything with him in such a way that, even though there was a great deal of talk about what had happened, the gentleman never discovered the trick his wife had played on him.

Day 7, Story 7

When Lodovico reveals to Madonna Beatrice how much he loves her, she persuades her husband Egano to dress up like her and sends him out into a garden. She then sleeps with Lodovico, who gets up afterward, goes into the garden, and gives Egano a beating.[1]

Everyone marveled at Madonna Isabella's astuteness, as described by Pampinea, but then the King asked Filomena to follow her, and she said:

Dear ladies, unless I am mistaken, I think I can tell you an equally fine story, and in short order.

You should know that there once lived in Paris a noble Florentine who had become a merchant because of his poverty, but had been so successful with his business that he had managed to acquire a vast fortune. His wife had borne him only a single son, whom he had named Lodovico. To ensure that he would be more inclined to grow up as a nobleman like his father, rather than a merchant, the latter had decided against placing him in a commercial establishment, and instead had arranged for him to join other noblemen in the service of the French King, where he acquired a great deal in the way of good manners and refinement.

While he was living there, a group of knights who had just returned from the Holy Sepulcher happened to come in upon a discussion he was having with several other young men about the fair ladies to be found in France and England and other parts of the world, and after listening to it for a while, one of the knights began to argue that of all the women he had ever seen in any of the numerous places he had visited, he had never encountered anyone whose beauty matched that of

Madonna Beatrice, the wife of Egano de' Galluzzi of Bologna.[2] And
with this judgment, all of his companions, who had been with him in
Bologna and had seen her, concurred.

Lodovico had not yet fallen in love with anyone, but as he listened to
what the knight was saying, he became inflamed with such a powerful
desire to see the lady that he could think of nothing else.[3] Fully intent
upon going all the way to Bologna in order to see her and to stay there
for a while if he did indeed find her attractive, he gave his father to
understand that he wanted to go to the Holy Sepulcher, and only with
great difficulty finally obtained his permission.

Having assumed the name of Anichino, he arrived in Bologna, and
as luck would have it, the very next day he caught sight of the lady at a
banquet. Finding her even more beautiful than he had imagined, he fell
head over heels for her and resolved that he would never leave Bologna
until he had won her love. He considered a variety of ways to achieve
his goal, but rejected all except one of them, concluding that he might
just have a chance of getting what he wanted if he could find service
with her husband, who had a large household staff. He therefore sold
his horses and made suitable arrangements for his servants to be taken
care of, having first ordered them to act as if they did not know who
he was, after which he got on friendly terms with his innkeeper and
told him that he would like, if it were possible, to enter the service of
some well-respected nobleman. To this the innkeeper replied: "You
are precisely the kind of person who would appeal to a nobleman in
this city named Egano, for he's got a house full of servants and wants
every last one to be as presentable as you are. I'll talk to him about it."
The innkeeper was as good as his word, and by the time he had taken
his leave of Egano, he had managed to place Anichino with him, which
suited Anichino to a tee.

Now that he was living with Egano and had ample opportunities to
see his lady on more than one occasion, he proceeded to serve his master so well and earned such a place in his esteem that Egano could do
nothing without him, and wound up putting himself and all his affairs
under Anichino's control.

One day, when Egano had gone out hawking and left Anichino

behind, Madonna Beatrice happened to engage him in a game of chess.[4] Up to that point, she still had no knowledge of Anichino's love for her, although she had often observed him and his manners, and being highly pleased with them, had come to admire what she saw. Wishing to make her happy, Anichino very cleverly contrived to let her win, which thrilled her to no end. But then, after all of her ladies-in-waiting, who had been watching the game, had gone out and left them to play alone, Anichino heaved an immense sigh. Staring at him, the lady asked: "What's the matter, Anichino? Does it grieve you so much that I'm winning?"

"My lady," said Anichino, "I'm sighing about something far more significant than that."

"Well, if you have any regard for me, tell me what it is," she said.

When he heard the lady qualify her entreaty with "if you have any regard for me," Anichino, who loved her more than anything else in the world, heaved another sigh even greater than the first, which made the lady ask him all over again if he would please tell her the reason why.

"My lady," said Anichino, "I'm terribly afraid that you'll be offended if I tell you what it is, and what's more, I'm worried that you might repeat it to someone else."

"I shall certainly not let it upset me," she said, "and you may rest assured that no matter what you say to me, I'll never utter a word about it to anyone else against your wishes."

"Since I have your promise," said Anichino, "I'll tell you what it is."

Scarcely able to keep his eyes from brimming over with tears, he told her who he was, what he had heard about her, where and how he had fallen in love with her, and why he had entered her husband's service. Then he humbly asked her if there were any way she might take pity on him and gratify the secret desire that burned so fervently within him. Or if she were unwilling to do this, he begged her to allow him to continue in his present position and to be content that he should go on loving her.

Ah, how singularly sweet is the blood of Bologna![5] How praiseworthy have you always proved in cases like this! You have never craved tears or sighs, but have always been responsive to prayers and yielded to lovers' desires. If I could find worthy words to commend you as you deserve, I would never grow tired of singing your praises.

While Anichino spoke, the gentlewoman watched him closely, and as she believed what he was saying without question, his prayers managed to impress the love he felt for her so forcefully upon her heart that she, too, began to sigh. After having done so several times, she replied: "O my sweet Anichino, don't be discouraged. I've been pursued by many men—and I still am to this day—but neither gifts, nor promises, nor the courtship of gentlemen or lords or anyone else was ever able to move my heart enough to make me love a single one of them. But in the brief space of time it took you to utter these words, you've made me feel that I belong to you far more than to myself. I consider that you have well and truly won my love, and I therefore give it to you and promise that before this night is over, it will be yours to enjoy. In order to bring this about, come to my bedroom around midnight. I'll leave the door open, and since you know which side of the bed I sleep on, make your way to me over there. If I'm asleep, just nudge me to wake me up, and I'll provide you with the consolation you have so long desired. And to make you believe what I'm saying, let me give you this kiss as my pledge." And with that, throwing her arms around his neck, she gave him a passionate kiss, and he replied in kind.

Their conversation thus ended, Anichino left her and went off to attend to certain duties of his, all the while waiting with the greatest joy imaginable for the night that was approaching. In the meantime, Egano returned from hawking, and after he had eaten supper, feeling tired, he went to bed. The lady soon followed him, and as she had promised, she left the door to the bedroom open.

Anichino arrived at the appointed hour, and having quietly entered the room and locked the door behind him, he went over to the side of the bed where the lady usually slept. Placing his hand on her breast, he found that she was awake, for as soon as she felt Anichino's presence, she seized his hand in both of hers, and holding it tightly, she turned and twisted about in the bed until she woke up the sleeping Egano. Then she said to him: "I didn't want to mention anything to you yesterday evening, because you seemed tired, but tell me Egano, so help you God, among all the servants you have in the house, which one do you consider the best, the most loyal, and the most devoted to you?"

"What's this, wife, that you're asking me about?" replied Egano. "Don't you know who it is? There's no one I trust or love more than I do Anichino, nor have I ever had anyone I trusted or loved like that. But why are you questioning me about this?"

Hearing that Egano was awake and that he himself was the subject of the conversation, Anichino, afraid that the lady intended to betray him, made several attempts to withdraw his hand and escape, but she was clutching it so tightly that he could not get away.

"I'll tell you why," she said, replying to her husband's question. "I thought that he was just the way you've described him and that he was more faithful than any of the others, but he has undeceived me, for when you went out hawking today and he stayed here, he had the gall, thinking the time was right for it, to ask me if I would consent to yield to his desires. Wishing to avoid having to gather a lot of evidence in order to convince you of this, I decided, instead, to provide you with visible, tangible proof. So I told him I'd be happy to do it, and said that tonight, some time after midnight, I'd go into our garden and wait for him by the foot of the pine tree. Now, personally, I have no intention of going there, but if you want to find out how loyal this servant of yours is, you can easily put on one of my gowns, cover your head with a veil, and go down there to see whether he shows up, as I'm sure he will."

"I must definitely go and have a look," said Egano. And so, he got up, and doing the best he could in the dark, put on one of her gowns and covered his head with a veil. Then he went into the garden and positioned himself by the foot of the pine tree, waiting for Anichino to arrive.

As soon as the lady heard him get up and leave the room, she got up herself and locked the door from the inside. After having experienced the worst scare he had ever had in his life and struggled with all his might to get out of her hands while calling down a hundred thousand curses on her and on his love and on himself for having trusted her, Anichino was the happiest man alive now that he finally realized what she had been doing. As soon as the lady returned to bed, she invited him to take off his clothes and get in beside her, and there the couple spent a good long time together in mutual pleasure and delight.

When the lady thought the moment had come for Anichino to go, she made him get up and put his clothes back on. "Sweet lips," she said, "I want you to get yourself a stout stick and go down to the garden. Then, pretending that you'd asked me to go there in order to test me, I want you to heap abuse on Egano just as if you thought you were talking to me, and after that, I want you to play a nice tune on him with your stick for me. Just think of the amazing pleasure and delight we'll get out of that!"

Anichino stood up and went off into the garden carrying a willow switch in his hand. Just as he approached the pine tree, Egano spotted him coming, got to his feet as if preparing to give him the warmest of welcomes, and walked over toward him. "Oh, so you actually came here, you wicked woman?" said Anichino. "And did you think it was ever my intention, then or now, to wrong my master like this? A thousand curses on you!" Then he raised the stick and began beating him.

The moment he heard this outburst and caught sight of the stick, Egano started running away without uttering a word, closely pursued by Anichino, who kept saying: "Get out of here, you evil woman, and may God damn you. Have no doubt, I'm going to tell Egano about this tomorrow morning."

Having received quite a few good ones, Egano returned to the bedroom as quickly as he could, and his wife asked him if Anichino had come to the garden. "If only he hadn't," said Egano, "because he took me for you and beat me black and blue with a stick, calling me the foulest names any wicked woman was ever subjected to. I must say, it certainly seemed puzzling to me that he had spoken to you the way he had with the intention of dishonoring me. But since he finds you so merry and sociable, he just wanted to put you to the test."

"Praise God, that he put me to the test with words and you with deeds," said the lady. "And I think he may say that I was able to bear those words of his with greater patience than you bore what he did to you. But since he's so loyal to you, we should cherish him and do him honor."

"You're absolutely right," replied Egano.

After pondering what had happened, Egano thus came to the conclusion that he possessed the most faithful wife and the most loyal servant any nobleman ever had. As a result, although on many future occasions he and his wife laughed with Anichino over the events of that night, the lady and her lover found it a great deal easier than it might otherwise have been to do the thing that brought them pleasure and delight, at least for as long as Anichino was content to remain with Egano in Bologna.

Day 7, Story 8

A man becomes jealous of his wife when he discovers that she has been tying a piece of string to her toe at night so that she will know when her lover has arrived. While her husband is off pursuing him, the lady gets another woman to take her place in bed. The husband beats the woman, and having cut off some of her hair, goes to fetch his wife's brothers, but when they discover that his story is untrue, they direct a stream of insults at him.[1]

Madonna Beatrice's cleverness in making a fool of her husband struck everyone as being quite peculiar, and they all agreed that Anichino must have been terribly afraid while the lady was holding him so tightly and he heard her saying that he had propositioned her. But then, when the King saw that Filomena was silent, he turned to Neifile and said, "You go ahead and speak." After smiling a little at first, she began:

Lovely ladies, if I am to entertain you with a story as fine as the ones that my predecessors have already produced, I am facing quite a heavy responsibility, but with God's help, I hope to carry it off successfully.

You must know, then, that in our city there once lived an extremely wealthy merchant named Arriguccio Berlinghieri who foolishly thought to ennoble himself by marrying into the aristocracy, as his counterparts have been doing continuously down to this very day, and who took to wife a young noblewoman, quite unsuited to him, by the name of Monna Sismonda.[2] Since her husband was often on the road, as merchants commonly are, and spent little time at home with her, she fell in love with a young man called Ruberto, who had been courting her for a long time.

Soon on intimate terms with him, Monna Sismonda took such

delight in his company that she possibly became somewhat careless, and Arriguccio, whether he had by chance gotten wind of the affair or for some other reason, became the most jealous man in the world. He stopped traveling about, abandoned every single one of his other concerns, and devoted all his care to keeping his wife under close surveillance, nor would he ever go to sleep until after he had felt her climb into bed. She was, as a result, in the deepest distress, for there was no possible way for her to get together with her Ruberto.

But having devoted a great deal of thought to finding some means to be with him, and being eagerly urged on by him to do so as well, she finally hit upon the following plan: since her bedroom overlooked the street, and she had frequently noticed that Arriguccio slept very soundly once he overcame the difficulty he had in getting to sleep, she decided that she would ask Ruberto to come to the front door of the house around midnight, and she would go and open it for him. In this way, she could spend time with him while her husband was sound asleep. And so that she would know when he had arrived, she came up with the idea of dangling a thin string out of the bedroom window in such a way that no one would notice it. Allowing one of its ends to almost touch the ground, she would run it low across the floor of the room until it reached the bed, where she would bring its other end up under the covers, and as soon as she was in bed, she would tie it to her big toe. She sent word of this plan to Ruberto, telling him that when he came, he was to pull the string, and if her husband were sleeping, she would release it and go to open the door for him, but if her husband were awake, she would hold it taut and pull it in to let him know that he was not to wait for her. Ruberto liked the plan and stopped by her house quite frequently, sometimes being able to spend time with her, and sometimes not.

They continued to make use of this elaborate stratagem until finally, one night, while the lady was sleeping, Arriguccio just happened to stretch his foot down in the bed and discovered the string. Reaching down for it with his hand, he found it was attached to his wife's toe and said to himself, "This must be some sort of trick." When he then noticed how the string went out through the window, he was sure of it, and so he quietly cut it off from his wife's toe, tied it to his own, and waited vigilantly to see what would happen next. It did not take long for Ruberto to arrive, and when he tugged on the string as usual, it gave Arriguccio quite a start. He had not tied it properly to his toe, however, and since Ruberto had given it a hard jerk and the string had come down into his hands, he assumed he was to wait. And so he did.

Leaping out of bed and grabbing his weapons, Arriguccio ran to the front door to see who it was, intent upon doing him some injury. Now, for all that he was a merchant, Arriguccio was a strong, savage man, and when he reached the front door, he did not open it quietly the way his wife always did. Ruberto was waiting outside, and the moment he heard the noise, he divined what it meant, namely that Arriguccio was the one who had opened the door, and he instantly took off, with Arriguccio in hot pursuit. At last, after running quite some distance without managing to shake off his pursuer, Ruberto, who was armed as well, drew out his sword and turned around, and the two of them began to fight, with Arriguccio on the attack and Ruberto defending himself.

Meanwhile, when Arriguccio opened the bedroom door, the lady woke up to find that the string attached to her toe had been cut, and she immediately realized that her ruse had been discovered. Hearing Arriguccio running after Ruberto, she got out of bed in haste, and anticipating what was likely to happen, she called to her maid, who knew the entire story, and prevailed upon her to take her own place in the bed, begging her not to reveal her identity, but to patiently endure all the blows that Arriguccio might inflict on her, in exchange for which she would receive such a reward that she would have no cause for complaint. Then, having extinguished the light that was burning in the bedroom, she went and hid herself in another part of the house, waiting to see what was going to happen.

While Arriguccio and Ruberto were scuffling, the people in the neighborhood heard the noise, got out of bed, and started cursing them out. Afraid that he might be recognized, Arriguccio stopped the fight and returned home, full of rage and indignation, without having been able to discover who the young man was or to inflict the slightest injury on him. When he reached the bedroom, he started shouting angrily:

"Where are you, you evil woman? You put out the light to prevent me from finding you, but you've got that one wrong!"

Going over to the bed, he grabbed the maid, thinking he had hold of his wife, and hit her and kicked her, giving her as many blows with his hands and feet as he could manage, until he had completely smashed in her face. Finally, he cut off her hair, all the while calling her the foulest names that were ever directed at an unchaste woman.

The maid was weeping bitterly, as she had every reason to, and although now and again she said, "Alas! For God's sake, have mercy!" or "No more!" her speech was so broken up by her sobbing, and Arriguccio was so blinded by his fury, that he did not realize that the voice belonged to some other woman, not his wife. Having thus beaten the living daylights out of her and cut off her hair, as we said before, he exclaimed: "You wicked woman, I have no intention of laying another hand on you, but I'll go fetch your brothers and tell them about the fine way you behave. Furthermore, I'll tell them to come for you and to do with you whatever they think their honor requires. Then I want them to take you away from here, for let me assure you, you're not going to stay in this house any longer." When he was finished speaking, he left the bedroom, locked it from the outside, and set off down the road all by himself.

Monna Sismonda had heard everything, and as soon as she knew that her husband had left the house, she opened the bedroom door, and having lit the lamp again, she found her maid there, bruised all over and weeping bitterly. She consoled her as best she could and led her back to her own bedroom, where, afterward, she secretly arranged for her to be waited on and given medical treatment, compensating her with Arriguccio's own money so handsomely that the maid declared she was quite satisfied.

Once the maid had been reinstalled in her own room, the lady quickly tidied up her bedchamber, remade the bed, and arranged everything as if no one had slept there that night. Having relit the lamp, she got dressed and fixed herself up to make it appear that she had not yet gone to bed, after which she lit another lamp, picked up her sewing, and sitting down at the head of the stairs, she began working on it as she waited to see how things would turn out.

Meanwhile, after leaving his house, Arriguccio had gone as quickly as possible to that of his wife's brothers, and once there, knocked away on the door until someone heard him and let him in. When the lady's brothers, all three of them, and her mother learned that Arriguccio was in the house, they got out of bed, called for lamps to be lit, and came down to see him and ask him what had brought him there, all alone, and at such an hour.

Beginning with the string he had found tied to Monna Sismonda's toe, Arriguccio went on to tell them the entire story about what he had discovered and what he had done. To supply them with conclusive proof of what had happened, he took the hair that he thought he had cut off his wife's head and handed it over to them, adding that they should come to get her and should deal with her in a way they thought consistent with their honor, for he had no intention of keeping her in his house any longer.

Believing every word of Arriguccio's story, the lady's brothers got very upset about what they had been told, and filled with rage at their sister, they called for torches to be lit and set out to accompany Arriguccio to his house with the intention of really giving her a bad time. Upon seeing their reaction, their mother started out after them, weeping and begging them, each in turn, not to be in such a rush to believe these things without seeing more evidence or learning more about what had happened. She noted that the husband might have had some other reason to be angry with their sister, and having treated her badly, he could now be blaming her in order to excuse his own behavior. She also said that she was truly amazed how such a thing could have happened, knowing her daughter as well as she did, and having raised her from the time she was a little girl. And she went on making many more remarks in a similar vein.

Upon reaching Arriguccio's house, they went inside and began climbing the stairs. When Monna Sismonda heard them coming, she asked, "Who's there?"

"You're going to find out soon enough who it is, you evil woman," replied one of her brothers.

"God help us! What's this all about?" she said, and getting to her feet, she went on: "Brothers, how nice to see you. But what can have brought the three of you here at this hour?"

When they saw her sitting there and sewing, without any sign of a beating on her face, although Arriguccio had said he had really pummeled her, they were initially somewhat taken aback, and restraining the vehemence of their anger, they asked her for an explanation in response to the complaint that Arriguccio had made about her, threatening her with dire consequences if she did not tell them the whole story.

"I don't know what I'm supposed to say to you," the lady replied, "or why Arriguccio should have complained to you about me."

Arriguccio was looking at her, staring like someone who had lost his mind, for he recalled having punched her maybe a thousand times in the face and having scratched her and given her the world's worst beating, but now she looked as though nothing had happened to her.

In brief, the brothers told her what Arriguccio had said to them about the string, the beating, and all the rest. Turning to her husband, the lady exclaimed: "Alas, husband, what's this I'm hearing? Why are you bringing so much shame on yourself by presenting me as some evil woman even though I'm nothing of the sort, while making yourself out to be a cruel, wicked man, even though you're not like that, either? And when were you ever in this house tonight until just now, let alone with me? And when was it that you gave me a beating? For my part, I have no recollection of it."

"What, you evil woman," Arriguccio started to say, "didn't we go to bed together? Didn't I come back here after giving chase to your lover? Didn't I punch you repeatedly and cut off your hair?"

"You didn't go to bed in this house last night," replied the lady. "But let's leave that be, since I have nothing but my own words to prove it's true, and let's come to what you said about beating me and cutting off my hair. You never hit me, and I ask everyone here, including you, to observe whether I have any sign of a beating anywhere on my body. Nor would I advise you to be so bold as to lay a hand on me, for by God's Cross, I'd scratch your face to pieces. And you didn't cut off my hair, either, as far as I felt or saw anything, although perhaps you did it without my noticing it. Let me see whether it's cut or not." Then, lifting her veils from off her head, she showed that her hair was all there and that not a single strand of it had been cut.

When her brothers and her mother saw and heard all this, they turned on Arriguccio and started in with: "What are you saying, Arriguccio? This doesn't jibe with what you came and told us you'd done, and we have no idea how you can possibly prove the rest of it." Arriguccio stood there like someone lost in a dream, and although he wanted very much to say something, on seeing that what he had thought he could prove true was not the case, he did not dare to utter a single word.

Turning back to her brothers, his wife said: "Now I see, brothers, what he's been looking for. He wants me to do something that I, myself, have never had any desire to do, which is to tell you all about his wicked, dishonorable behavior. And I'll do it, for I firmly believe that the story he told you about what happened to him is actually true and that he did do all the things he said he did. Just listen, and I'll explain how.

"This worthy man, to whom it was my misfortune to have been given by you in marriage, and who calls himself a merchant and wishes to be thought creditworthy—which means he should be more temperate than a monk and chaster than a maid—well, there are few evenings when he doesn't go from tavern to tavern getting drunk and consorting with one harlot after another. And he keeps me waiting up for him, just the way you saw me now, for half the night and sometimes all the way to matins.

"I'm sure that when he was good and drunk, he went to sleep with one of his trollops and that when he woke up and found the string on her foot, he did all those brave feats he told you about, after which he returned to her, beat her up, and cut off her hair. And since he was still in his cups, he believed—and I'm sure he still does—that he'd done those things to me. In fact, if you take a good look at his face, you'll see he's still half drunk. But all the same, whatever he may have said about me, I want you to think of it as nothing more than the words of a lush, and since I forgive him myself, you must do so, too."

In response to her speech, her mother started raising a stink and said: "By God's Cross, my daughter, that's not what should be done. Instead, this obnoxious cur, this nobody, who was completely unworthy of having a girl like you, he ought to be killed. Brother, this is just great! You'd think he'd picked you up out of the mud! May he rot in Hell before you have to put up with the foul slander of some petty dealer in donkey droppings. These yokels come up here from some country lord's gang of thugs and go around dressed in cheap clothes and baggy breeches with their quill pens stuck in their butts.[3] As soon as they've got three *soldi,* they want the daughters of noblemen and fine ladies for their wives, and they make up coats of arms for themselves, and they go around saying, 'I'm one of the so-and-sos,' and 'The people from my house did thus and such.'

"I really wish my sons had followed my advice, for they could have set you up just as honorably in the house of one of the Guidi counts even though you had no more than a piece of bread for your dowry.[4] Instead, they wanted to give you to this lovely jewel, this guy who's got the best, most virtuous girl in Florence, but who's not ashamed, and in the middle of the night, to say that you're a whore, as if we didn't know you. By God, if they took my word for it, he'd get such a beating that he'd be stinking from it for days."

Then she turned to the lady's brothers and said: "Boys, I told you all along that this couldn't be true. Have you been listening to how your sister is treated by this fine brother-in-law of yours? By this two-bit peddler here, which is what he is. Because, if I were you, after hearing what he says about her and what he's doing to her, I'd never rest content or consider myself satisfied until I'd wiped him off the face of the earth. And if I were as much of a man as I am a woman, I'd take care of this mess myself and wouldn't let anyone get in my way. God, damn him to Hell, the miserable, shameless drunk!"

Having taken everything in, the young men turned to Arriguccio and gave him the worst tongue-lashing any bad man has ever received.

They then concluded, however, by saying: "We forgive you this time because you were drunk, but as you value your life, from now on you better watch out that we never hear any more stories like this, for if another one ever reaches our ears, you may rest assured we'll pay you back for that one, and for this one as well."

Having said their piece, away they went, leaving Arriguccio standing there like someone who had lost his mind, unsure if what he had done was real or if he had been dreaming, and without uttering another word on the subject, from then on he left his wife in peace. Thus, thanks to her quick-wittedness, not only did Monna Sismonda manage to escape her imminent peril, but she opened the way to enjoy herself as much as she liked and never had to fear her husband again.

Day 7, Story 9

Nicostrato's wife, Lidia, is in love with Pirro, who asks her to do three things to persuade him that she is sincere, and not only does she do all of them, but in addition, she makes love to him while Nicostrato is watching and gets her husband to believe that what he saw was unreal.[1]

The ladies enjoyed Neifile's story so much that they simply could not stop laughing and talking about it, even though the King, who had ordered Panfilo to tell his own tale, repeatedly called for them to be silent. Once they finally quieted down, however, Panfilo began as follows:

I do not believe, esteemed ladies, that there is any enterprise, no matter how difficult or dangerous, that someone passionately in love would not dare to undertake. Although this has been shown in many of our stories, nevertheless, I believe I can offer even better proof with the one I intend to tell you. In it you will hear about a lady whose deeds were far more favored by Fortune than guided by reason, which is why I do not advise any of you to risk following in her footsteps, because Fortune is not always so well disposed, nor are all the men in the world equally gullible.

In Argos, that most ancient Greek city, whose former kings brought it great renown despite its small size, there once lived a nobleman by the name of Nicostrato, on whom, as he was approaching old age, Fortune bestowed a wife of distinction, a woman who was no less bold than beautiful, and who was called Lidia.[2] As befits a man both rich and noble, he maintained a large household, owned numerous hawks and hounds, and took the greatest delight in hunting. One of his retainers was a lively, elegant young man named Pirro, who was handsome and adept at whatever activity he chose to pursue, and Nicostrato loved and trusted him above all the others.

Lidia fell so passionately in love with this Pirro that she could think of nothing else day and night. Pirro, however, showed no interest in her passion, either because he did not notice it, or because he did not want to, and this filled the lady's heart with unbearable pain. Fully determined to make him aware of her feelings, she summoned one of her chambermaids, a woman named Lusca, who was her close confidante, and said to her:

"Lusca, all the favors you've had from me in the past should have earned me your loyalty and obedience, and therefore, you must take care that no one ever hears what I am about to tell you, except for the man to whom I will ask you to repeat it. As you can see, Lusca, I'm young and vigorous, as well as being abundantly supplied with everything a woman could desire. In short, I have nothing to complain about, with one exception, which is that my husband is much too old for me, so that I have been getting far too little of that which gives young women the greatest pleasure. And because I desire it no less than others do, I made up my mind long ago that since Fortune didn't show herself my friend when she bestowed such an elderly husband on me, I should at least avoid being my own worst enemy and try to find another way to obtain my happiness and my salvation. Now, to make sure that my enjoyment in this should be as complete as it is in everything else, I've decided that our Pirro is the one to take care of my needs with his embraces, for he is worthier in this regard than any other man, and such is the love I bear him that I feel sick whenever I'm not gazing at him or thinking about him. In fact, unless I can be with him very soon, I truly believe I'm going to die. Therefore, if you value my life, you must acquaint him with my love for him in whatever way you think best, and beg him on my behalf to be so good as to come to me whenever you go to fetch him."

The maid said she would be happy to do it, and as soon as she found a convenient time and place, she took Pirro aside and, to the best of her ability, delivered her mistress's message. Pirro was completely taken by surprise when he heard it, for such a thing had never occurred to him, and he was worried that the lady might have sent him the message in order to test him. Consequently, speaking harshly, he gave quite an abrupt reply: "Lusca, I can't believe these words come from my lady, so you'd better be careful about what you're saying. Even if they really did come from her, I don't believe she was sincere when she spoke with you. And even if she was, my lord has done me so much more honor than I deserve that I would never, on my life, commit such an outrage against him. So, you watch out and never talk to me about such things again."

"Pirro," said Lusca, undeterred by the severity of his speech, "if my lady orders me to speak to you about this, or about anything else, I'll do so as often as she tells me to, whether you like it or not. But you now, you really are an ass!"

Somewhat chagrined by what Pirro had said, Lusca returned to her mistress, who simply wanted to die when she heard his answer. A few days later, however, she spoke to her chambermaid about the matter once more.

"You know, Lusca," she said, "it's not the first stroke that fells the oak. So it seems to me you should go back again to this man who has such a strange way of wanting to prove his loyalty at my expense. Find a convenient time to give him a full account of my passion, and do your best to make sure you succeed. For if things remain as they are, I'm going to die, and he'll just think we were making a fool of him, so that instead of the love we're seeking, we'll wind up earning his hatred."

After comforting her mistress, the maid went in search of Pirro, and when she found him in a cheerful and agreeable mood, she said to him: "Pirro, a few days ago I explained to you how your lady and mine was being consumed by the flames of the love she feels for you, and I'm here to assure you yet again that if you remain as unyielding as you were the other day, she won't be alive much longer. I therefore implore you to be so kind as to provide her with the solace she desires. I used to consider you very wise, but if you persist in being stubborn like this, I will take you for an utter fool.

"What greater glory can you have than to be loved above everything else by such a lady, who's so beautiful and noble and rich? Furthermore, don't you realize how grateful you should be to Fortune for having given you quite a valuable prize, a woman who is perfectly suited to your youthful desires and who will also provide you with a secure refuge from all your material needs? How many of your peers will have a life more blissful than yours, if you'll just act and use your intelligence here? Which of them will be your equal when it comes to arms and horses, clothing and money, if you will just grant her your love? So, open your heart to my words, and return to your senses. Remember that Fortune greets a man only once with a smiling face and open arms, and if he does not know how to accept what she gives him and later on winds up an impoverished beggar, he has only himself, not her, to blame.

"Besides, there doesn't have to be the same sort of loyalty between servants and masters as that which exists between friends and family. On the contrary, to the extent that they can, servants ought to treat their masters the same way their masters treat them. If you had a beautiful wife, or a mother or daughter or sister, and Nicostrato took a liking to her, do you really believe he'd spend as much time thinking about loyalty as you are doing with regard to his wife? You're a fool if you give it a moment's thought, for you can be sure that if his flattery and entreaties weren't sufficient, he'd make use of force on her, no matter what you might think about it. So let's treat them and their belongings the same way they treat us and ours. Make the most of what Fortune's offering you, and don't chase my mistress away. Go out and meet her halfway as she approaches, because you may be sure that if you don't do that, not only will her death be inevitable, but you'll wind up reproaching yourself so often for what you did that you, too, will want to die."

Pirro had spent a great deal of time mulling over what Lusca had said to him during their previous exchange, and he had already made up his mind that if she ever approached him again, he would give her a different answer and would do everything he could to satisfy the lady, provided that it could be proved she was not simply testing him. And so, he replied by saying: "Look here, Lusca, I recognize the truth in everything you've said to me, but on the other hand, I also know that my master is not merely very wise, but very shrewd as well, and since he has placed the managing of all of his affairs in my hands, I'm really afraid that Lidia is doing all this with his advice and consent so as to put me to the test. However, if she's willing to do three things I'll ask of her in order to reassure me, then you may depend on me to do whatever she wishes without a moment's hesitation. And these are the three things I want her to do: first, she must kill Nicostrato's fine sparrow hawk right in front of his eyes; then she should send me a tuft of hairs from his beard; and finally, she should get me one of the soundest teeth he has left."

These terms seemed hard to Lusca and much, much harder to her mistress, but Love, that great provider of comfort and excellent teacher of cunning, made her resolve to attempt it. Consequently, she sent Pirro word through her maid that she would do everything he asked, and soon. Furthermore, since he thought Nicostrato was so smart, she told him that she would arrange for them to make love right in front of him and get him to believe that it was not really happening.

Pirro therefore waited to see what the lady would do, and a few days later, when Nicostrato was entertaining certain gentlemen at one of the great banquets he used to give with some frequency, the tables had no sooner been cleared away than the lady came out of her room, wearing a green velvet dress richly adorned with jewels, and entered the hall where the gentlemen had been dining. Then, as Pirro and all the others watched, she went over to the perch where the sparrow hawk that Nicostrato treasured so much was sitting, untied it as if she intended to set it on her hand, and having seized it by the jesses, dashed it against the wall and killed it.*

Nicostrato shouted at her, "Oh no, woman, what have you done?" She, however, said nothing in response, but turned instead to the gentlemen with whom he had been dining and said: "My lords, I'd hardly be able to revenge myself on a king who insulted me if I lacked the courage to take it out on a sparrow hawk. What you need to know is that this bird has long deprived me of the attention that men should devote to their ladies' pleasure, for Nicostrato always gets up at the crack of dawn, mounts his horse, and with his sparrow hawk on his hand, rides

---

*Jesses were strips of silk or leather fastened to the legs of a falcon to which a leash could then be attached.

off to the open plains in order to watch it fly, leaving me behind in my bed, just as you see me here, all alone and discontent. That's why I have often wanted to do what I did just now, and all I was waiting for was a chance to do it in the presence of men who would judge my cause justly, as I trust you will do."

Supposing that her feelings for her husband were exactly what her words implied, the gentlemen all started to laugh, and turning to the angry Nicostrato, they said, "Come on now, your wife did the right thing to avenge her wrongs by killing the sparrow hawk!" And with a host of witty remarks on the subject—the lady having returned to her room in the meantime—they managed to transform Nicostrato's irritation into laughter.

Pirro, who had observed all this, said to himself: "My lady has given my happy love a noble start. May God let her stay the course!"

Not many days after killing the sparrow hawk, Lidia found herself in her bedroom with Nicostrato, and when she began caressing and joking around with him, he gave her hair a playful little tug, which provided her with an opportunity to fulfill the second of Pirro's demands. She then promptly took hold of a little tuft of hairs in his beard, and laughing all the while, pulled it so hard that she tore it right out of his chin. In response to Nicostrato's complaints, she said: "Now what's the matter with you that you're making such a face? Just because I tore maybe half a dozen hairs out of your beard? That's nothing compared to what I felt when you were yanking at my hair just a moment ago." And so, they continued jesting and playing around with one another. Meanwhile, the lady carefully preserved the tuft of hairs she had pulled from his beard and sent it to her precious beloved the very same day.

The third task gave the lady a lot more to think about, but since she was a person of superior intelligence and Love had made her wits even sharper, she figured out a way to take care of it.

In his house Nicostrato had two young boys of gentle birth who had been entrusted to him by their fathers so that they might learn proper manners, and when he was dining, one of them used to carve for him, while the other poured him his drink. Having sent for them, the lady gave them to understand that their breath stank, and taught them that whenever they served Nicostrato, they were to hold their heads as far back as possible, and also, that they were never to mention the subject to anyone.

The boys believed her and began acting as she had told them to, until eventually, one day, she asked Nicostrato: "Have you noticed what these boys do when they're waiting on you?"

"I certainly have," said Nicostrato, "and in fact, I've been meaning to ask them why they do it."

"Don't bother," said the lady, "because I myself can tell you why. I've kept quiet about it for quite some time because I didn't want to upset you, but now that I see others are starting to notice, there's no reason to hide it from you any longer. This is all happening to you simply because your breath smells atrocious. Now, I don't know why it does, because it never used to, but it really is terrible, and since you spend your time in the company of gentlemen, we've got to figure out some way to cure it."

"What could be causing it?" said Nicostrato. "I wonder if one of the teeth in my mouth is rotten."

"Perhaps it is," replied Lidia, and leading him to a window, she made him open his mouth. After having inspected both sides of it, she said: "Oh, Nicostrato, how can you have put up with it for so long? You've got one on this side, and as far as I can see, it's not just decayed, but rotten through and through. If it stays in your mouth much longer, it'll be sure to ruin the teeth on either side. So, my advice to you is to have it out before it gets any worse."

"If that's what you think," said Nicostrato, "well, then, I agree. Send for a surgeon right away and have him extract it for me."*

"God forbid that we should have a surgeon come here and do that," replied the lady. "The way your tooth looks to me, I think I can do a very good job of pulling it out myself and won't need help from anyone else. Besides, those surgeons are so cruel when they perform such operations that I'd be utterly heartsick and couldn't bear to see and hear you suffering at their hands. No, I absolutely insist on doing it myself, because

---

*Surgeons were socially placed well beneath doctors in the period, handling minor injuries, setting fractures, pulling teeth, and even cutting hair.

then, if you're in too much pain, I'll stop at once, which is something a surgeon would never do."

She then had them bring her the necessary instruments and sent everyone out of room except for Lusca, whom she kept right by her side. After locking the door, they made Nicostrato stretch out on a table, put the pincers in his mouth, and grabbed one of his teeth with them. And although he roared out loud because of the pain, one of the women held him firmly down, while the other, using all her might, yanked out a tooth, which she hid away and replaced with another one, horribly decayed, that she had been holding in her hand. She showed it to Nicostrato, who was whimpering, practically half dead, and said to him: "Look at what you've had in your mouth for all this time."

Nicostrato did not doubt her story, and although the pain he was suffering was excruciating and he was still complaining bitterly about it, now that the tooth was out, he felt as if he were cured. And so, after he had been consoled in one way and another, and his pain had diminished, he left the room. The lady then took the tooth and promptly sent it to her lover who was now completely convinced of her affection for him and declared that he was prepared to minister to her every pleasure.

The lady wanted to reassure him even more, however, and although every hour she was not with him seemed like a thousand to her, she was determined to keep the promise she had made to him. Consequently, she pretended to be sick, and one day, when Nicostrato came to visit her after dinner, and she saw that there was no one with him except Pirro, she asked him if they would help her down to the garden in order to give her some relief in her illness. And so, with Nicostrato supporting her on one side and Pirro on the other, they carried her into the garden and placed her on the lawn at the foot of a lovely pear tree. After sitting there for a while, the lady addressed herself to Pirro, to whom she had already sent word about what he was to do. "Pirro," she said, "I have a great longing for a couple of those pears, so would you climb up there and throw down some of them."

Pirro immediately scampered up and began tossing down the pears, and as he was doing so, he said: "Hey, what are you doing there, sir?

And you, my lady, aren't you ashamed to permit it in my presence? Do you two think I'm blind? Up until a moment ago you were terribly sick: how did you get well so quickly that you can do such things? Really, if you want to carry on like that, you've got plenty of fine bedrooms. Why don't you go and do it in one of those? That would be much more decent than doing it in front of me!"

The lady turned to her husband and said: "What's Pirro talking about? Has he gone crazy?"

"No, my lady, I'm not crazy," replied Pirro. "Do you think I can't see you?"

"Pirro," said Nicostrato, who was completely baffled, "I really do think you're dreaming."

"No, my lord," Pirro replied, "I'm not dreaming, not one little bit, and neither are you. In fact, you're doing it with so much vigor that if this tree were shaking like that, there wouldn't be a single pear left on it."

"What can this mean?" said the lady. "Can he really be seeing what he says he's seeing? God help me, if my health were what it was before, I'd climb up there and see these marvels that he claims to be observing."

Meanwhile, from up in the pear tree, Pirro kept talking and telling them the same strange story, until Nicostrato said, "Come down." When Pirro was on the ground, Nicostrato asked him, "Now what is it you say you saw?"

"I do believe that you two take me for a madman or a dreamer," replied Pirro, "but since you force me to tell you, I saw you there on top of your wife, and then, when I was descending, you got off and sat down here where you are now."

"You really were out of your mind," said Nicostrato, "because from the time you climbed into the pear tree, we haven't budged from this spot."

"What's the point of having this debate?" said Pirro. "I really did see you, and if I did, then what I saw was you there on top of yours."*

---

*Pirro says he saw Nicostrato *in sul vostro*, which means literally "on top of yours." This most likely refers to the notion that a man's wife was considered his belonging or property; ironically, Nicostrato is sitting in his garden and in that sense is thus quite literally *on* his property.

Nicostrato grew more and more astonished. Finally, he declared: "I want to find out for myself if this pear tree is enchanted and what kind of marvels you can see from it!"

So up he went, and no sooner was he in the tree than his wife and Pirro started to make love together.[3] Nicostrato saw it and began yelling at them: "Oh, you vile woman, what are you doing? And you, Pirro, whom I trusted more than anyone else?" And as he was speaking, he started to climb down again.

"We're just sitting here," said Pirro and the lady at first, but upon seeing him descend, they went and seated themselves the way they had been before. The moment that Nicostrato reached the ground and saw them sitting where he had left them, he fell to berating them.

"Nicostrato," said Pirro in response, "now I must confess that what you were saying before was right, that my eyes were, in fact, deceiving me when I was up in the pear tree. And my only reason for saying this is that I now know for a fact that you, too, have had the same experience I did. Moreover, to convince you that I'm telling the truth, just stop and think about your wife for a moment. If a woman of such unequaled honesty and wisdom as she is wished to commit an outrage in this way against your honor, do you really think she would ever bring herself to do it right before your eyes? Of myself I say nothing, except that I would sooner allow myself to be drawn and quartered than even contemplate such a thing, let alone come and do it in your presence.

"Hence, whatever is causing our faulty perception must surely be emanating from the pear tree. For nothing in the world would have kept me from believing that you were having carnal relations with your wife here, until I heard you say that I myself appeared to be doing something that I know for sure I never did, let alone even thought of doing."

At this point the lady pretended to be terribly upset and got to her feet. "Damn you," she said, "for thinking me so stupid that, if I had wanted to engage in that disgusting behavior you claim to have seen, I'd come and do it right before your eyes. But there is one thing you can be certain of: should I ever feel such a desire, I wouldn't come out here to satisfy it. On the contrary, I think I'd be capable of finding one of our bedrooms and arranging to do it there in such a way that I'd be very surprised if you ever found out about it."

Nicostrato believed that the two of them were telling the truth and that they would never have brought themselves to commit such a deed in front of him. Consequently, he stopped shouting and berating them the way he had been doing, and instead began talking about the strangeness of what had happened and about the miraculous way people's eyesight was transformed when they climbed into the tree.

But his wife, who was still pretending to be upset over the opinion Nicostrato supposedly had of her, said: "If I can help it, there's absolutely no way this pear tree will ever put me or any other woman to shame again. Go, run and fetch an axe, Pirro, and at one stroke you can avenge both of us by chopping it down, although it would be much better if you took the axe and hit Nicostrato on the head with it for not giving the matter a second thought and allowing the eyes of his intellect to be blinded so easily. For although things may have appeared the way you said they did to those eyes in that head of yours, you should never have allowed the judgment of your mind to imagine, let alone admit, that they were true."

Pirro went for the axe as fast as he could and cut down the pear tree. And as soon as she saw it on the ground, the lady turned to Nicostrato and said: "Now that I've seen the fall of my honor's enemy, I'm not angry anymore." Then, she graciously pardoned Nicostrato, who had been begging her to do so, charging him never again to presume to think such thoughts about the woman who loved him more than her own life.

And so, the poor, deluded husband returned with his wife and her lover to the palace, where from that time on, it became much easier for Pirro to get together with Lidia at frequent intervals for their mutual pleasure and delight. And may God grant as much to all of us.

Day 7, Story 10

A woman is loved by two Sienese, one of whom is the godfather of her child, and after he dies, he returns to his companion, as he promised he would, to tell him all about what people do in the Beyond.[1]

The only one left to tell a story was the King, and as soon as the ladies, who were mourning for the innocent pear tree that had been chopped down, grew quiet, he began:

It is perfectly clear that a just king must observe the laws he himself has made, and if he fails to do so, he should not be considered a king, but a slave who deserves to be punished. And yet, as your King, I find I am left with almost no choice except to commit this error and receive your censure for having done so. Yesterday, when I laid down the law governing the discussions we have had today, I really did intend to forego my privilege, submit to the rules just like you, and address the theme on which you have all been speaking. But the story I thought to share with you has been told, and what is more, our subject has inspired you to recount so many other, truly fine ones, that for my part, although I have ransacked my memory, I cannot think of anything on this particular topic that would stand in comparison with the things you have already said. Since, therefore, I am obliged to violate the law that I myself have made, I am certainly worthy of being punished for it, and I am prepared right now to make whatever amends may be demanded of me, as I once again have recourse to my usual privilege.

Now, dearest ladies, taking my cue from the compelling story Elissa related about the godfather and the mother of his godchild as well as from the downright stupidity of the Sienese, I will tell you a little tale about them.[2] Although it will require me to set aside the subject of the tricks cunning women play on their foolish husbands, and a great deal of what I will say should not be believed, nevertheless, there are parts of my story, at least, that you should find quite entertaining to hear.

There once lived in the Porta Salaia neighborhood of Siena two young men from the lower classes named Tingoccio Mini and Meuccio di Tura who spent practically all their time together and seemed quite devoted to one another.[3] Like most men, they would go to church and attend sermons where they often heard about the glory as well as the misery awaiting the souls of the dead, according to their merits, in the next world. Since the two of them were eager to find out for sure about such matters and could think of no other way to do so, they promised one another that whoever died first would return, if he could, to the one who was still alive, and give him all the information he wanted on the subject. And this they then confirmed with an oath.

After making this promise to one another, and while the two of them were still going around together, as we said before, Tingoccio happened to stand godfather to the son of a certain Ambruogio Anselmini who lived with his wife, Monna Mita, in the Camporeggi neighborhood.[4] Now, Monna Mita was a charming and very beautiful woman, and despite the fact that he was her son's godfather, Tingoccio, who used to visit her from time to time with Meuccio, fell in love with her. And since Meuccio found her attractive and often heard Tingoccio singing her praises, he fell for her, too.

Each man kept his feelings hidden from the other, but not for the same reason. Tingoccio was careful not to reveal anything to Meuccio because it seemed wicked for him to be in love with the mother of his godchild and he would have been ashamed if anyone had found out about it.

Meuccio's reason for keeping his love a secret was quite different, namely, that he realized how much Tingoccio liked her, and he told himself: "If I reveal this to him, he'll be jealous of me, and since he can speak to her whenever he likes because he's her child's godfather, he'll do what he can to make her hate me, and then I'll never get what I want from her."

Now, the two young men went on loving Monna Mita in the way we have described, until Tingoccio, who had more of an opportunity to reveal his desires to her, managed to press his suit by means of word and deed with such success that he was able to have his way with her. Although Meuccio was well aware of what was going on and was hardly pleased about it, nevertheless, since he was hoping to fulfill his own desires someday, and since he did not want to provide Tingoccio with even the slightest excuse to ruin his chances or interfere with any of his plans, he went on acting as if he had not noticed a thing.

And so, the two companions went on loving the lady, albeit one more happily than the other. But the richness of the soil in Monna Mita's field led Tingoccio to spade it up and work it with such vigor that he was taken with an illness he simply could not shake off. In fact, it became so serious that in just a few days, he departed this life.

On the night of the third day following his death, perhaps because he could not get there any sooner, Tingoccio kept his promise and appeared in Meuccio's bedroom. He called out to his friend, who was sound asleep, and woke him up.

"Who are you?" asked Meuccio.

"I am Tingoccio," he replied, "and I've come back to bring you news of the other world, as I promised you I would."

Though initially somewhat frightened at the sight of his friend, Meuccio soon recovered his composure and said: "You're welcome here, my brother!" Then he asked him if he was among the lost.

"What is lost cannot be found again," replied Tingoccio, "so how would I be right here if I were among the lost?"

"No," said Meuccio, "that's not what I meant. I was asking you whether you are among the souls of the damned in the penal fires of Hell."

"As for that, no," said Tingoccio, "but I am, nevertheless, enduring the most painful torments and profound anguish because of the sins I committed."

Then Meuccio questioned him in detail about the punishments that were meted out up there for each of the sins committed down here, and

Tingoccio described every last one to him. After that, Meuccio asked if there was anything he could do for him in this world, and Tingoccio replied that there was. He wanted his friend to have Masses and prayers said for him, and for alms to be given as well, because those things helped a great deal in the Beyond. All of this Meuccio said he would be happy to do.

As Tingoccio was about to leave, Meuccio recalled Monna Mita, and raising his head up a little, he said: "O Tingoccio, I just remembered: what punishment were you given up there for sleeping with the mother of your godchild when you were down here?"

"My brother," replied Tingoccio, "as soon as I arrived up there, I was met by someone who seemed to know all my sins by heart, and who told me to go to the place where I now lament my misdeeds in the most agonizing pain. There I found myself in a large company who were condemned to the same punishment as I was myself, and standing in their midst, I remembered what I had done with the mother of my godson. Since I expected an even more severe penalty for that than the one I'd been given, I began trembling with fear, even though I was then in a great fire that was burning fiercely. Someone next to me noticed this, and said: 'Why are you shivering here in the middle of the fire? Have you done something worse than the rest of us?' 'Oh, my friend,' I replied, 'I'm absolutely terrified of the judgment I expect to receive for a dreadful sin I committed.' He then asked me what the sin might be, and I said: 'My sin was that I slept with the mother of my godchild. In fact, I went at it with such a vengeance that I wore myself down to the bone.'[5] He laughed scornfully at that and said, 'Get away, you fool. Don't worry about it. Nobody's really concerned about the mothers of godchildren up here.' Once I'd heard that, I felt totally relieved."

As Tingoccio finished his account, day was about to break, and so he said: "God be with you, Meuccio, I can't stay here any longer." And then, all of a sudden, he was gone.

Now that Meuccio had learned how little concern they felt up there about the mothers of people's godchildren, he laughed scornfully at his foolishness for having spared quite a few women of that sort in the past.

But from then on, shedding his former ignorance, he became a much wiser man in dealing with such affairs. And if only Frate Rinaldo had known about these things, it would not have been necessary for him to have had recourse to syllogisms when he persuaded the good mother of his godchild to serve his pleasures.[6]

Day 7, Conclusion

The sun was descending in the west and a gentle breeze had risen, when the King, who had finished his story and realized that there was no one else left to speak, removed the crown from his head and set it on Lauretta's. "My lady," he said, "with this, your namesake, I crown you Queen of our company.* And now, as our sovereign mistress, you may give orders for whatever you think will provide us all with pleasure and entertainment."

He then returned to his seat, and Lauretta, having become Queen, summoned the steward and ordered him to arrange to have the tables set up in the pleasant valley at a somewhat earlier hour than usual, so that they could return to the palace at their leisure. Next, she told him what he needed to do during the rest of her reign, after which she turned to the company and said:

"Yesterday, Dioneo proposed that we talk today about the tricks that women play on their husbands, and if it were not for the fact that I do not want to be thought of as belonging to that breed of snapping little curs who immediately want to retaliate for everything, I would insist that tomorrow we talk about the tricks men play on their wives. But letting that go, I want each of you, instead, to think up a story about the tricks that women are always playing on men, or men on women, or men on other men. This, without doubt, will be a topic just as pleasant to talk about as the one we had today." Having finished speaking, Lauretta got to her feet and dismissed the company until suppertime.

And so they all arose, the ladies and the men alike, and while some

---

*Lauretta, whose name means "little laurel tree," is being crowned with a wreath of laurel.

of them began wading barefoot through the clear water, others entertained themselves by roaming through the green meadow in among
the lovely tall, straight trees, and Dioneo sang a lengthy song about
Arcite and Palamon together with Fiammetta.* Thus, they all amused
themselves in their several different ways, passing the time very agreeably until the hour for supper. When it arrived, they took their places
at the tables next to the little lake, where they happily ate their meal
at their ease, with never a fly to bother them, while they listened to
the songs of a thousand birds and were cooled by a gentle breeze that
flowed down continuously from the surrounding hills.

The tables were then cleared away, and since it was only halfway
between nones and vespers and the sun was still up, they took a walk
around the pleasant valley for a while, until the Queen gave the word
and at a leisurely pace they went back down the road toward their
usual lodging. Joking and chatting not only about what they had discussed that day, but about a thousand other things as well, they finally
reached their lovely palace a little before nightfall. There they dispelled
the fatigue of their brief journey with the coolest of wines and a variety
of sweets, after which they immediately fell to dancing carole† around
the fair fountain, sometimes to the sound of Tindaro's bagpipes and
sometimes to that of other instruments.

At the end, however, the Queen ordered Filomena to sing a song,
which she began this way:

> Alas, my life's forlorn!
> Oh, shall it ever be that I'll regain
> The place from which I had to part in grief?
>   I'm far from sure I can return, alas,
> Where I once was, despite the great desire
> That burns within my breast.
> O you, my precious Good, my sole Repose,

* Arcite and Palamon are characters who appear in Boccaccio's long narrative poem
Teseida (1340–41), which Chaucer reworked as *The Knight's Tale*.

† *Carole*: dances in which the dancers joined hands and moved in a clockwise direction,
usually accompanied by music and the singing of the dancers themselves.

Who hold my heart bound tight,
Please answer me, for I don't dare to ask
Elsewhere, or know whom I
Might question. Oh, my Lord, please give me hope
So that my wandering soul may find relief.

    I can't describe how great the pleasure was
That has inflamed me so
That neither night nor day can I find rest.
For hearing, sight, and touch, my senses all,
With unfamiliar force,
Did kindle then new fires on their own,
So I burn everywhere.
There is no one but you to comfort me
Or to restore my shaken faculties.

    Please tell me if and when the time will come
I'll ever find you there
Where once I kissed those eyes that murdered me.
Tell me, my precious Good, O Soul of mine,
When you will come back there.
Please comfort me a little and say, "Soon."
May all the time be brief
Until you come, but then stay on, how long
I do not care—Love's wound's so deep in me!

    If I should happen once again to hold you,
I'll not be such a fool
As once I used to be and let you go.
I'll hold you fast, and then, let come what may,
For I must satisfy
All my desire on that sweet mouth of yours.
For now I'll say no more:
Come quickly therefore, come embrace me soon,
For just the thought of that moves me to sing.

This song made the entire company suspect that some pleasurable new love might have held Filomena in its grip. Indeed, the words

seemed to imply to them that she had tasted more of love than just exchanging glances, and if they considered her all the happier for it, some of those present could not help but feel envious. When her song was finished, however, the Queen, remembering that the next day was Friday, graciously addressed the whole group:

"You know, noble ladies, and you young men as well, that tomorrow is the day consecrated to the Passion of Our Lord, and you will surely remember that we observed it devoutly when Neifile was Queen by refraining from these delightful discussions of ours, just as we did the following Saturday. Therefore, since I want to imitate the excellent example Neifile has given us, I think that for tomorrow and the day after, it would be proper for us to abstain from our pleasant storytelling, just as we did in the past, and to meditate instead on what was done on those two days for the salvation of our souls."

Everyone approved the devout words of their Queen, and since a good portion of the night had already passed, she dismissed them, and off they all went to take their rest.

Day 8, Introduction

Here ends the Seventh Day of the Decameron and the Eighth begins, in which, under the rule of Lauretta, they speak of the tricks that women are always playing on men, or men on women, or men on other men.

On Sunday morning, when the Queen and her company arose, the rays of the rising sun had already appeared on the summits of the highest mountains, the shades of night had departed, and all things were clearly visible. After walking for a while on the dewy grass, in between prime and tierce they all paid a visit to a nearby church, where they heard divine service.[1] Having returned to their lodging, they ate a happy, festive meal together, and then they sang and danced for a time until they were dismissed by the Queen so that those who wanted to rest could do so. When the sun was well past the meridian, however, in accordance with the Queen's wishes, they all seated themselves next to the fair fountain in order to tell stories as usual, and at her command, Neifile began as follows.

Day 8, Story 1

Gulfardo borrows a sum of money from Guasparruolo after having agreed to pay his wife exactly that amount in order to let him sleep with her. He gives it to her, but later tells Guasparruolo, in her presence, that he returned it, and she admits that he did.[1]

I f God has ordained that I should tell the first story on this day, then I am pleased to do so, and seeing as how we have spoken so much, dear ladies, about the tricks that women have played on men, I should like to tell you about one that a man played on a woman, not because I intend to criticize what the man did or to claim that the woman did not get what she deserved, but on the contrary, to praise the man and condemn the woman, and to prove that men are just as capable of tricking those who trust them, as they are of being tricked by those they trust. Strictly speaking, however, what I am about to tell you should not be called a trick, but rather a matter of justice. For a woman should be the epitome of honesty and should guard her chastity like her life, on no account permitting herself to defile it. Although it is not always possible for us to observe this rule because of our frailty, I nevertheless insist that a woman who permits herself to sacrifice her chastity for a price deserves to be burned at the stake, whereas one who gives in to the forces of Love, knowing how immensely powerful they are, ought to be pardoned by a lenient judge—which, as Filostrato showed us a few days ago, is what happened to Madonna Filippa in Prato.[2]

There was once a German mercenary living in Milan, a valiant man named Gulfardo, who, unlike most of his fellow countrymen, was quite loyal to those in whose service he was enrolled. And because he was most dependable in paying back the money he borrowed, he could

593

always find any number of merchants willing to lend him whatever sums he wanted at a low rate of interest.

During his stay in Milan, he became enamored of a very beautiful woman called Madonna Ambruogia, the wife of a rich merchant, one Guasparruolo Cagastraccio, with whom he was on the most friendly and familiar terms, but since Gulfardo was the model of discretion, neither the lady's husband nor anyone else was ever aware of what he felt. One day he sent her a message, imploring her to be so kind as to look with favor on his love and saying that, for his part, he was ready to do whatever she wanted.

After a great deal of discussion, the lady finally made up her mind and said that she was ready to do what Gulfardo wanted, provided that two conditions were met: first, he would never reveal what had happened to anyone; and second, since he was rich and there was something she needed to buy, he would give her two hundred gold florins, and then she would always be at his service.

When he saw how greedy she was, Gulfardo, who had always thought her a worthy lady, was outraged at her lack of honor, and his fervent love turned into something quite close to hatred. Determined to make a fool of her, he sent her word that he would be happy to do not just what she wanted, but everything else in his power, if it would make her happy. Consequently, she merely had to let him know when she would like him to come to see her, and he would bring her the money. Finally, he assured her that no one would ever hear a word about it except for a comrade of his whom he trusted implicitly and who always accompanied him in everything he did.

The lady, or rather, the vile woman, was quite pleased with his reply and sent him word that in a few days' time Guasparruolo, her husband, would be going to Genoa on business and that she would let Gulfardo know when he left and would invite him to come to see her then.

Gulfardo waited until the time seemed right, at which point he went to Guasparruolo and said to him: "I'm about to conclude a business deal for which I need two hundred gold florins, and I'd like you to lend them to me at the rate of interest you usually charge me." Guasparruolo said he would be happy to oblige and counted out the money on the spot.

When Guasparruolo went to Genoa a few days later, as his wife had said he would, she sent word to Gulfardo that he should come to see her and bring the two hundred gold florins along with him. After collecting his companion, Gulfardo went to her house, where he found her waiting for him, and the first thing he did was to hand her the two hundred gold florins while his friend was watching. As he did so, he said: "Take this money, my lady, and give it to your husband when he returns."

Having no idea what Gulfardo's words meant, the lady took the money in the belief that he spoke as he did in order to prevent his companion from guessing that he was giving it to her by way of payment. Consequently, she replied, "I'm happy to take it, but first let me see how much is there." Then she dumped the florins out on a table, and on finding that they came to the full two hundred, she felt quite pleased with herself and put them away. After that, she returned to Gulfardo and led him to her bedroom where she placed her person at his disposal not just on that night, but on many others before her husband came back from Genoa.

As soon as Guasparruolo returned home, Gulfardo paid him a visit, having first made sure that his wife would be with him, and said to him in her presence: "Guasparruolo, I didn't need the money, I mean the two hundred gold florins, you lent me the other day because I wasn't able to close the deal for which I borrowed them. Since I brought them straight back here and gave them to your wife, you'll cancel my debt for me, won't you?"

Turning to his wife, Guasparruolo asked her if she had received the money, and since she saw there was a witness present, she could not think of any way to deny it. "Of course I got them," she said. "I just forgot to tell you."

"Well, that's fine by me, then," said Guasparruolo. "Good-bye, Gulfardo. I'll make sure your account gets closed."

Having made a fool of the lady, Gulfardo left, and she gave her husband the ill-gotten gains of her wickedness. And thus the clever lover enjoyed the favors of his avaricious lady free of charge.

Day 8, Story 2

The priest of Varlungo sleeps with Monna Belcolore in exchange for a cloak he leaves her by way of payment, although then, after borrowing a mortar from her, he sends it back and asks her for the cloak he left behind as a pledge. The good woman returns it, while directing a witty jibe his way.[1]

Both the men and the women were still praising Gulfardo's treatment of the greedy woman from Milan, when the Queen turned to Panfilo, smiled, and asked him to continue. In response, he began as follows:

Lovely ladies, it occurs to me to tell you a little story criticizing that group of people who wrong us constantly without our ever being able to retaliate. I mean a story about priests, who have proclaimed a Crusade against our wives, and who think, when they have succeeded in getting one down underneath them, they have gained nothing less than remission for their sins, just as surely as if they had dragged the Sultan back from Alexandria to Avignon, bound in chains.* By contrast, we poor little laymen cannot do the same thing to them, although we are as hot to revenge ourselves and take out our anger on their mothers, sisters, mistresses, and daughters, as the priests are to assault our wives. And that is why I intend to tell you a tale about a love affair between a couple of hicks. Although it is not very long, it will give you a great deal to laugh about at the end, and from it you may draw this moral, namely, that you should not believe everything a priest says.

Let me tell you, then, that in Varlungo, which, as all of you know or may have heard, is a village not very far from here, there was a worthy

---

* Avignon was the seat of the Papacy from 1305 to 1378.

priest who was quite a lusty guy when it comes to servicing the ladies.[2] Although he was not particularly proficient at reading, he nevertheless had a ready supply of good and holy sayings to entertain his parishioners of a Sunday underneath the elm tree. And whenever the men went away somewhere, he was more assiduous in calling on their wives than any priest who had ever served before him, and he would bring them religious trinkets and holy water and the odd candle end, as well as giving them his blessing right in their very own homes.

Now it just so happened that among the female parishioners to whom he was attracted from the start, there was one he liked more than all the others called Monna Belcolore who was married to a farmworker named Bentivegna del Mazzo. To tell the truth, she was a good-looking, lively gal, brown and buxom, and she really knew the art of grinding at the mill better than any other girl around.[3] Furthermore, when it came to playing the tambourine, singing "The water runs down the ravine," and taking the lead in a round or a jig, while holding a fine, dainty little kerchief in her hand, she had no equal among the women in the village.[4]

All of these things made Messer Priest desire her so much that it simply drove him crazy, and he would spend the entire day hanging around merely in the hope of seeing her. When he spotted her in church on a Sunday morning, he would intone a *Kyrie* and a *Sanctus*, trying very hard to show himself a master singer when he actually sounded like a braying ass.* By contrast, if he did not happen to see her, he would pass lightly over that part of the service. Nevertheless, he was generally so clever in managing such affairs that neither Bentivegna del Mazzo nor any of the women in the neighborhood ever had an inkling of what was going on.

In order to get to know Monna Belcolore better, every now and then he would give her presents. Occasionally, he would send her some knobs of fresh garlic, of which he had the finest in the area growing in a garden of his that he worked with his own hands. At other times it

---

* The *Kyrie*, short for *Kyrie eleison* ("Lord, have mercy"), is sung at the start of the Mass; the *Sanctus* ("Holy") is the hymn sung just before taking Communion.

would be a big basket of beans, and at yet others, a bunch of chives or shallots. And whenever he saw an opportunity, he would look slightly askance at her and make her some sort of lover's complaint, but she, being a coy little thing, would pretend not to notice and would pass by him with a haughty air. The result was that Messer Priest could never get anywhere with her.

Now, one day at high noon, as the priest was strolling aimlessly here and there around the neighborhood, he happened to run into Bentivegna del Mazzo who was driving an ass loaded with goods before him. After hailing him, the priest asked him where he was going.

"By gosh, your Reverence," Bentivegna replied, "to tell the honest truth, I'm a-goin' to the city on some bidness of mine, and I'm taking these things to Ser Bonaccorri da Ginestreto so that he'll help me with—well, I just don't know what to make of it—for the persecuting judge had his provoker give me a parentstory summons to appear before him."[5]

The priest was delighted and said: "You're doing the right thing, my son. Now go, with my blessing, and come back soon. And if you should catch sight of Lapuccio or Naldino,[6] remember to tell them that they should bring me those leather thongs for my flails."*

Bentivegna said he would, and as he went off in the direction of Florence, the priest decided that now was the time to call on Belcolore and try his luck with her. And so, he set right off down the road and never stopped to rest his feet once until he reached her place.

"God bless this house," he said, as he came in. "Is anyone at home?"

Belcolore was up in the loft, but when she heard his voice, she said: "Oh, your Reverence, you're very welcome. But what are you doing traipsing about in this heat?"

"By the grace of God," replied the priest, "I've come to keep you company for a while, because I ran into your man as he was on his way to town."

---

* A flail was an implement used for threshing wheat. It consisted of two sticks fastened together at the ends by means of leather straps or chains; one of the sticks served as a handle.

Belcolore came downstairs, took a seat, and began picking over some cabbage seeds that her husband had threshed just a little while before.

"Well then, Belcolore," said the priest, starting right in, "are you going to keep killing me like this forever?"

She began laughing and replied: "What is it that I'm doing to you?"

"You're not doing anything to me," said the priest. "It's just that there's something I'd like to do to you, something that God has commanded, but that you won't let me do."

"Oh, get out of here!" said Belcolore. "Do priests really do that sort of thing?"

"Of course we do, and much better than other men," he replied, "and why shouldn't we? Let me tell you: the job we do is a lot better than theirs, and do you know why? Because we only do our grinding when the millpond's full.* But listen, I'll really make it worth your while, if you'll just stop talking and let me get on with it."

"What could you possibly do to make it worth my while?" said Belcolore. "All of you priests are stingier than the Devil."

"I don't know," replied the priest, "so why don't you tell me? Do you want a pretty little pair of shoes or a silk headband or a nice wool waistband—or whatever you might have a hankering for?"

"Oh, brother, that's some choice!" said Belcolore. "I've already got all those things. But if you really like me so much, why don't you do me one little favor, and then I'll do whatever you like?"

"Just tell me what you want," said the priest, "and I'll be happy to do it."

"I've got to go to Florence on Saturday," replied Belcolore, "so that I can deliver some wool I've spun and get my spinning wheel fixed. Now, if you'll lend me five *lire*—and I know you've got them—I'll be able to go to the pawnbroker's and get back my dark skirt and my Sunday-best waistband, the one I brought as part of my dowry, because you see,

---

* The reference here is to the pond, typically created by damming a stream, in which water is stored and directed down a channel called a millrace, to power a water mill. Since priests would not be having sex on a regular basis—theoretically, not at all—they would have stored up a great deal of "water" to do the "grinding."

without them, I can't go to church or anywhere decent in public—and then I'll do whatever you want, always."

"So help me God," said the priest, "I don't have any money on me. But believe me, I'll be only too glad to see that you get it before next Saturday."

"Sure," replied Belcolore, "you all make these big promises, and then you don't keep any of them. Do you think you're going to treat me the way you treated Biliuzza, who went off empty-handed?[7] I swear to God you won't do any such thing to me, because that's what turned her into a streetwalker. So, if you haven't got the money on you, you can just go and get it."

"Come on!" said the priest. "Don't make me walk all the way home, not right now when my luck is looking up—as you can see it is there—and nobody's around. By the time I got back, there might be someone or other here who'd mess up our plans, and I don't know when it would work out as well as it would right now."

"Fine by me," she said. "If you want to go, go; if not, you can do without."

When the priest saw that she would not do anything to please him unless she had a *salvum me fac*, whereas he wanted it *sine custodia*,* he said to her: "Look, since you don't believe I'll bring you the money, will you trust me if I leave this blue cloak of mine with you as a guarantee?"

Belcolore glanced up at him and said: "Yeah, this cloak here? How much is it worth?"

"Really, what's it worth?" said the priest. "I want you to know that it's made from genuine cloth of Douai, not to say Three-ay, and that some of the people in our parish consider it Four-ay.† I bought it less than two weeks ago for seven whole *lire* from Lotto, the used-clothes dealer, and I saved myself a good five *soldi* according to what Buglietto

---

Salvum me fac: with a guarantee (lit., [God] help me); *sine custodia*: without a guarantee.

† Cloth from Douai in Flanders was made from the finest wool. The priest assumes Belcolore does not know anything about Douai and proceeds to play on the name, which is *Duagio* in Italian and thus sounds like the word for two, *due*.

d'Alberto told me—and you know he really is an excellent judge of fabrics like this."

"Oh, is that so?" said Belcolore. "So help me God, I would never have believed it. But all right, for starters, hand it over."

Messer Priest, whose had his crossbow all loaded up, removed the cloak and gave it to her. After she had put it away safely, she said to him: "Now, Father, let's go out to that shed. Nobody ever comes near it."

And so they went to the shed, where the priest gave her the sweetest smooches in the world and made her a kinswoman of Messer God Almighty. After he had enjoyed himself with her a good long time, he went back to the church, wearing only his cassock, which made him look as if he had just officiated at a wedding.

Once he was home, he fell to thinking that all the candle ends he collected from the offerings in the course of an entire year were not worth half as much as five *lire*, and he came to the conclusion that he had made a really bad bargain. Filled with regret about leaving his cloak behind, he immediately began casting about for a way to retrieve it without having to pay anything, and because he was a bit of a swindler, he came up with a great plan of action for getting it back, which worked out just fine for him.

On the next day, which happened to be a holiday, he sent a neighbor's boy to Monna Belcolore's house, asking her if she would be so kind as lend him her stone mortar, because Binguccio dal Poggio and Nuto Buglietti were dining with him that morning and he wanted to make a sauce. Belcolore sent it to him, and when it was just about time to eat and the priest reckoned that Bentivegna del Mazzo and Belcolore would be dining, too, he summoned his clerk* and said: "Take this mortar back to Belcolore, and tell her the following: 'The Reverend Father says thank you very much and asks you to send him back the cloak the boy left with you as security.'"

The clerk took the mortar to Belcolore's house, where he found her sitting at the table with Bentivegna eating their dinner. He set the

---

* A clerk (Lat. *clericus*) was a priest-in-training who assisted a parish priest.

mortar down on it and delivered the priest's message. When Belcolore heard him ask for the cloak, she started to say something, but Bentivegna gave her an angry look and said: "So, you ask for security from the Reverend Father? I swear to Christ I have half a mind to give you a great big punch in the mouth. A pox on you, woman, go and give it back to him at once! And you'd better make sure that whatever else he wants—I'm telling you that even if he asks for our ass—you'll never tell him no."

Belcolore got up, and grumbling all the way, went to the chest by her bed, from which she extracted the cloak. Then, as she was handing it over to the clerk, she said: "Give his Reverence this message from me: 'Belcolore says that she swears to God you'll never pound any more sauce in her mortar again, considering how much you honored her with the one you made this time.'"

The clerk went off with the cloak and delivered her message to the Reverend Father, who responded with a laugh: "The next time you see her, tell her that if she won't lend us her mortar, I'm not going to let her have my pestle. And so, it'll be tit for tat."

Since Bentivegna believed that his wife had spoken as she did because he had scolded her, he did not give what she had said another thought. But Belcolore was furious with the Reverend Father and refused to speak to him right up to the grape harvest. Then, however, after the priest threatened to have her taken down and put into the very mouth of Great Lucifer himself, she got good and scared, and made peace with him over some new wine and roasted chestnuts. From then on, they had more than one good guzzle together, and to make up for the five *lire*, the priest not only had her tambourine re-covered with a new skin, but had a little bell hung on it, and then she was happy.

Day 8, Story 3

Calandrino, Bruno, and Buffalmacco go down along the banks of the Mugnone in search of the heliotrope. Believing he has found it, Calandrino returns home with a load of stones, and when his wife scolds him, he gets angry and beats her. Finally, he tells his friends the story, which they know better than he does.[1]

Panfilo's story made the ladies laugh so hard that they have not stopped laughing about it to this very day. When it was finished, the Queen ordered Elissa to follow him, and she, still chuckling over it, began this way:

My most pleasant ladies, I do not know whether, with a little story of mine, which is both true and entertaining, I will be able to make you laugh as much as Panfilo has done, but I will certainly try my best.

Not so very long ago, there lived in our city, where there has never been a lack of unusual customs and bizarre characters, a painter named Calandrino, a simpleminded man with some strange habits.[2] He used to hang out with two other painters named Bruno and Buffalmacco, a pair who were very merry, but who, being quite perceptive and shrewd, spent time with Calandrino because they often found his antics and his simplicity really funny.[3] At the same time there also lived in Florence a marvelously entertaining, astute, and capable young man named Maso del Saggio, who, having heard tales of Calandrino's simplicity, decided to go and amuse himself at Calandrino's expense by playing a practical joke on him or by getting him to believe some far-fetched notion.[4]

One day he came upon Calandrino by chance in the Church of San Giovanni where he was staring intently at the paintings and the bas-reliefs on the canopy that had recently been placed above the altar.* Maso felt that it was the right time and place for him to carry out his plan, and having informed a companion about what he intended to do, the two of them approached the place where Calandrino was sitting all by himself. Pretending not to see him, they started talking with one another about the powers of various stones, of which Maso spoke as authoritatively as if he were some important, well-known expert on the subject.

Hearing them talk, Calandrino pricked up his ears, and after a while, concluding that their conversation was not really private, he got to his feet and went over to join them, much to the delight of Maso, who was still holding forth when Calandrino asked him where these magical stones were to be found. Maso replied that most of them were in Gluttonia, the country of the Basques, which can be found in Gourmandistan, where the vines were tied up with sausages and a goose could be had for a penny, with a gosling thrown in for good measure.[5] In those parts they had a mountain made entirely of grated parmesan cheese where people did nothing except make gnocchi and ravioli that they cooked in capon broth. Then they would toss them down below, and the more you picked up, the more you had. And nearby there was a stream flowing with Vernaccia wine, the best you ever drank, without a single drop of water in it.[6]

"Oh!" said Calandrino. "What a wonderful country! But tell me: what happens to the capons they cook?"

"They're all eaten by the Basques," replied Maso.

"Were you ever there?" asked Calandrino.

"Was I ever there, you say?" Maso responded. "Why, if I've been there once, I've been there a thousand times."

"And how many miles away is it?" asked Calandrino.

"Of miles you count a thousandfold, which all the livelong night are told," replied Maso.[7]

---

*The Church of San Giovanni is the Baptistery in Florence, which stands opposite the Duomo, or Cathedral. A contract was signed for the decoration of the canopy in 1313 with Lippo di Benivieni, a Tuscan painter (active 1296–1327).

"Then," said Calandrino, "it must be even farther away than Abruzzi."

"Sure is farther," Maso responded, "but it's really nothing."[8]

As he watched Maso say all this with a straight face, never laughing once, the simpleminded Calandrino believed absolutely everything Maso said, giving his words the kind of credence usually reserved for the most manifest of truths.

"As far as I'm concerned," Calandrino said, "that's just too far away. But if it were closer, you can bet I'd go there with you one of these days just to see those gnocchi come tumbling down and to get myself a bellyful of them. But tell me, God bless you, aren't any of those magical stones to be found in these parts?"

"Yes," replied Maso, "you can find two sorts of stones here that have extraordinary powers. They are the sandstones of Settignano and Montisci, by virtue of which, when they are turned into millstones, flour gets made, which is why they say in those parts over there that blessings come from God and millstones from Montisci.[9] But we've got so many of those sandstones around here that they're worth as little to us as emeralds are to them over there, where they have mountains of them higher than Monte Morello, and how they shine in the middle of the night, well, good-night to you.[10] And you should know that if someone had the ability to make beautiful millstones and tie them together in a ring before the holes were bored in them, and then take them to the Sultan, he could get whatever he wanted for them.

"The other type is what we lapidaries call a heliotrope, a stone of such enormous power that no one can see you when you're not there, provided you keep it in your possession at all times."

"What amazing powers!" said Calandrino. "But this second one, where can you find it?"

Maso replied that they were commonly found in the valley of the Mugnone.

"How big is the stone?" asked Calandrino. "And what color is it?"

"They come in various sizes," replied Maso, "some bigger and some smaller, but all of them are nearly black in color."

Having made a mental note of all these details, Calandrino pretended he had other business to attend to and left Maso, determined to go and look for one of these stones. He did not want to do that, however, until he had informed Bruno and Buffalmacco about it, since they were his very closest friends. He therefore set out to find them so that they could all go and search for the stones at once before anyone else was able to do so, and he spent the rest of the morning hunting them down. Finally, some time after the hour of nones, he remembered that they were working in the convent at Faenza, so he dropped everything else he was doing, and although it was extremely hot, ran practically all the way there to find them.[11]

"Friends," he said, calling out to them, "if you'll trust me, we can become the richest men in Florence. Because I've heard it from a trust-worthy guy that there's a stone in the valley of the Mugnone and that whoever has it on him will be completely invisible, so I reckon we should go and look for it right away before anybody else does. And since I know what it looks like, we're sure to find it, and once we do, what's to stop us from putting it in our purses, going to the money changers' tables, which are, you know, always loaded with groats and florins, and helping ourselves to as many as we want? No one's going to see us, and we'll be able to get rich quick and not have to spend every day sliming the walls like a bunch of snails."

As they listened to him, Bruno and Buffalmacco began laughing to themselves, but looking at one another, they pretended to be completely astonished and praised Calandrino's plan. Then Buffalmacco asked him what the stone was called, but like the dough-head he was, he had already forgotten its name.

"What does the name matter to us," he replied, "as long as we know about its powers? I think we should get a move on and go look for it rather than hang around here."

"All right, then," said Bruno, "so what does it look like?"

"They come in all shapes and sizes," Calandrino answered, "but since they're all more or less black, what we have to do, in my opinion, is to pick up all the black ones we see until we come across it. So let's get going and not waste any more time."

"Just wait a minute," replied Bruno and turned to Buffalmacco. "I think Calandrino's got a good idea," he said, "but it strikes me that this isn't the right time for it. The sun is high at this hour, and since it's shining straight down on the Mugnone, it will have dried out all the stones there, so that the ones that looked black this morning before the sun got to them will now appear to be white. Besides, since it's a workday, there are going to be a lot of people with business of one sort or another along the Mugnone, and if they see us, they might be able to guess what we've gone there to do. Then maybe they'll do it as well, and if they should get their hands on the stone, we would have wasted all our efforts.[12] So if you agree, it seems to me that this is a job we should do during the morning, when it will be easier to distinguish the black stones from the white ones, and on a holiday, when there won't be anyone around to see us."

After Buffalmacco praised Bruno's advice, Calandrino accepted it as well, and the three of them arranged to go together the following Sunday morning to look for the stone. Calandrino, however, begged them on no account to mention this to a living soul, as it had been imparted to him in the strictest confidence. After this, he went on to tell them what he had learned about the Gourmandistan, swearing an oath that it was all true. Once he had gone, the pair took time to work out the details of their plan together.

Calandrino waited impatiently for Sunday morning to arrive, and when it did, he got up near the crack of dawn and went to call on his friends. They left by the Porta San Gallo and went down to the Mugnone, where they followed its course as they began their search for the stone. The most eager of the three, Calandrino rushed on ahead, hopping nimbly from one place to the next. Whenever he spotted a black stone, he would throw himself to the ground, pick it up, and stuff it down the front of his shirt, while his companions followed behind, collecting the odd stone here and there. Calandrino had not gone very far before his shirt was filled to the brim with stones. He therefore pulled up the hem of its skirt—for it was not cut in the style of Hainault*—and tucking it securely into his leather belt all around,

---

* Hainault is a city in present-day Belgium, which was an important center for making cloth and clothing in the late Middle Ages. Shirts cut in the "style of Hainault" would have been short and tight fitting, thus not having a skirt that hung down below the belt.

he made a large pouch out of it, which he filled up with stones in no time. After that, in the same way, he made another pouch out of his cloak and soon had it filled up as well.

Bruno and Buffalmacco could see that Calandrino was now loaded down with stones, and since the hour for dinner was approaching, Bruno set the plan they had agreed on in motion by asking Buffalmacco: "Where's Calandrino?" Although Buffalmacco could see Calandrino right there beside him, he turned around in one direction and then another, looking for him.

"I don't know," he replied. "He was right here in front of us just a little while ago."

"A little while ago, yeah!" said Bruno. "I'll bet he's at home now eating dinner and has left us here like a couple of idiots to go hunting for black stones down along the Mugnone."

"Well," said Buffalmacco, "it serves us right for him to play this practical joke on us and leave us here, since we were stupid enough to have believed him. Look, who besides us would've been so dumb as to have imagined you could find such a magical stone by the Mugnone?"

Hearing their words, Calandrino imagined that he had gotten his hands on the stone and that because of its power they were unable to see him although he was right there just a short distance away. Overjoyed at such a stroke of luck, he decided to go home without saying a word to them, and turning on his heel, he started to walk back.

Buffalmacco observed this and said to Bruno: "What'll we do now? Why don't we leave, too?"

"Let's go," replied Bruno, "but I swear to God that Calandrino's never going to play another trick on me again. If I were as close to him now as I was this morning, I'd hit him so hard on the heels with this stone that he'd remember this practical joke for the next month or so."

And even as he spoke, he drew back his arm and threw a stone that hit Calandrino right on the heel. When he felt the pain, Calandrino jerked his foot high in the air and started panting and blowing, but he said nothing and kept on walking.

Buffalmacco took one of the stones they had gathered between his fingers and said to Bruno, "Just look at this nice sharp one. How I'd

like to catch Calandrino in the back with it now just like this," and he
let it fly, smacking Calandrino hard, right in between the kidneys. To
make a long story short, they kept hurling stones at him in this fashion,
now saying one thing and now another, all the way back up from the
Mugnone to the Porta San Gallo. There, after they had dumped all
the stones they had collected on the ground, they stopped to chat
with the customs guards whom they had let in on the joke earlier and
who allowed Calandrino to pass, pretending not to see him, though all
the while they were roaring with laughter.

Without stopping, Calandrino went straight to his house, which was
near the Canto alla Macina.[13] And Fortune favored the joke to such an
extent that while he was walking along the river and then across the
city, no one said anything to him, although he actually encountered
very few people since almost everyone was home eating dinner.

When Calandrino entered his house with the load he was carrying,
by chance his wife, a beautiful, virtuous woman named Monna Tessa,[14]
was at the head of the stairs, and as she was rather irritated because
he had stayed out so long, no sooner did she see him come in than she
began to scold him.

"Hey, brother, where the devil have you been?" she said. "Everybody
else has finished dinner, and you're just getting home."

When Calandrino heard this and realized she could see him, he was
filled with anger and dismay. Then he started shouting: "Oh no, you
damned woman, why did you have to be there? You've ruined me. But
I swear to God I'm going to pay you back for it."

He went upstairs, where he dumped the huge load of stones he had
brought home in a little room, after which he ran at his wife in a rage.
Grabbing her by the hair, he threw her to the ground at his feet, and
then, for as long as he could move his arms and legs, he let her have it
from head to foot. She cried to him for mercy and prayed to him with
clasped hands, but it was all in vain, and he went on hitting her and
kicking her until she did not have a hair left on her head that had not
been torn or a bone that remained unbruised.

After having had a good laugh with the customs men at the gate,
Bruno and Buffalmacco set off to follow Calandrino, walking at a

leisurely pace and always staying some distance behind him. When they reached the steps leading up to his front door and heard the savage beating he was giving his wife, they called out to him, pretending they had just arrived. Soaked in sweat, red faced, and out of breath, Calandrino appeared at the window and invited them to come on up. Acting as though they were somewhat annoyed, they climbed the stairs and found the room full of stones, with the woman sobbing pitifully in a corner, her hair disheveled, her clothes torn, and her face all livid and bruised. On the opposite side sat Calandrino, whose belt was unfastened and who was panting with exhaustion.

After surveying the scene awhile, they said, "What's going on, Calandrino? Are you planning to build a wall with all these stones we see here?" And to this, then, they added: "And what's the matter with Monna Tessa? It looks as though you've given her a beating. What's the story here?"

Worn out by the weight of the stones he had carried, and the fury with which he had assaulted his wife, and the despair he felt over losing the fortune he thought he had acquired, Calandrino was unable to catch his breath and utter a single word in reply. So, after pausing a moment, Buffalmacco started in again.

"Calandrino," he said, "you shouldn't have played such a mean trick on us the way you did just because you were angry about something or other. First, you seduced us into looking for that precious stone with you, and then, without saying 'God be with you,' let alone 'the Devil take you,' you came back here, leaving us behind down by the Mugnone like a couple of jerks. We're pretty unhappy about the way you treated us, but you can be sure, this is the last time you're ever going to do such a thing to us."

Calandrino had to make quite an effort to respond, but finally he managed to say: "Don't be angry, friends. It's not the way you think. Poor unlucky me, I'd actually found the stone. Now, you just give a listen, and I'll prove to you that I'm telling the truth. When you two started asking one another where I'd gone, I was less than ten yards away from you. Then I noticed how you started walking home and didn't see me, so I got out in front of you and always stayed a little ahead of you all the way back here."

After that, he gave them a detailed account of everything they had said and done, beginning at the beginning and taking it right down to the end. He also showed them the welts the stones had made on his back and heel.

"And I'm telling you," he continued, "when I came through the gate, my shirt was filled with all these stones you see here, but nobody said a thing to me, and you yourselves know how unpleasant and annoying those customs men are, with their habit of demanding to inspect every last thing. And besides, I ran into lots of my friends and neighbors along the way, and they can always be depended on to say hello to me and invite me to go for a drink, yet none of them uttered a word to me, not so much as a syllable, just as though they didn't see me. Finally, when I arrived home, this devil of a woman, damn her, appeared in front of me and looked at me—and you know how everything loses its special power in the presence of women. So, where before I'd been thinking myself the luckiest man in Florence, I wound up becoming the unluckiest, and that's why I beat her until I couldn't move my hands anymore. In fact, I don't know what's keeping me from slitting her throat right now. I curse the hour I first laid eyes on her and the day she came into this house." And blazing with fresh anger, he was about to get up and start beating her all over again.

Bruno and Buffalmacco made a great pretense of being astonished as they listened to Calandrino's story, and repeatedly confirmed what he was telling them, though all the while they had such a desire to laugh that they almost burst. But when they saw him getting up in a fury to beat his wife a second time, they also stood up in order to block his way and hold him back, telling him it was not the lady's fault, but his, because he knew that things lose their power in the presence of women, and yet he had not told her to keep out of sight that day. It was God, they said, who had kept him from taking that precaution either because he did not deserve to have such good luck or because it had been his intention to deceive his friends, to whom he should have revealed his discovery as soon as he realized that he had found the stone. After much discussion, they finally managed, though not without a great deal of difficulty, to reconcile him and his grieving spouse. They then departed, leaving him in a melancholy state, with his house full of stones.

Day 8, Story 4

The Rector of Fiesole is in love with a widow, who does not return his affec-
tion, but while he is in bed with one of her maids, thinking he is sleeping with
the widow, her brothers contrive to have him discovered there by his Bishop.[1]

When Elissa had reached the end of her tale, which had given
great pleasure to the entire company, the Queen turned to
Emilia and indicated that she wanted her to tell the next story, which
she began without a moment's hesitation:

Worthy ladies, a fair number of the tales we have told have shown,
as I recall, how priests and friars and other clerics force their attentions
on us, but since we cannot exhaust this topic no matter how much
we may say about it, I want to supplement those stories with another
one about a Rector who was determined, come what may, to obtain
the favors of a widow, whether she wanted to grant them or not. This
noblewoman, however, was very wise and treated him in precisely the
way he deserved.

As you all know, Fiesole, whose hill we can see from here, is a city of
immense antiquity. It was once quite large, and although today it is in
ruins, there has never been a time, including the present, when it was
without a bishop of its own. A widow of noble birth named Monna
Picarda had an estate close to the cathedral, and since she was not the
most well-to-do woman in the world, she used to live there practically
all year long in a modest house with her two brothers, both of them
very respectable and courteous young men.[2]

This lady regularly attended services at the cathedral, and seeing as
how she was still quite a beautiful, pleasant young woman, it just so
happened that the Rector there fell in love with her, so passionately in

613

fact that he could think of nothing else. After some time, he finally became so bold as to tell the lady himself what it was he wanted, begging her to be content that he should love her and to requite his passion with her own.

Although this Rector was already old in terms of years, he had the intelligence of a child, and he was arrogant and presumptuous to boot. Possessing an extremely high opinion of himself, he had a habit of jeering at others and making himself unpleasant, and he was so tiresome and insufferable that everybody disliked him. And if there was anyone who truly did not care for him, that person was Monna Picarda, who not only thoroughly detested him, but found him more hateful than a migraine. Nevertheless, she was quite discreet when she replied to the proposition he had made her.

"Sir," she said, "I consider your love something very precious, and not only do I feel bound to love you in return, but I will do so quite willingly, provided that the love we share never involves anything dishonorable. Since you are my spiritual father and a priest, and you are now getting well on in years, these things should induce you to lead a chaste and virtuous life, whereas I, on the other hand, am no longer a girl, to whom such love affairs might still be acceptable. In fact, I'm a widow, and you know how widows are expected to be models of chastity. I therefore ask you to excuse me, for I'll never love you in the manner you request, nor do I have any desire to be loved by you that way."

Incapable of extracting anything else out of her on this occasion, the Rector was not the type to be dismayed or defeated at a first encounter, but with his usual arrogance and effrontery, he solicited her repeatedly with letters and messages, and would even accost her in person when he saw her coming into the church. Finding his constant prodding an intolerable burden, the lady decided to get him off her back in the way he truly deserved since she could not see any other alternative.

She did not want to do anything, however, without consulting her brothers about it, and so, after first explaining the way the Rector had been behaving toward her, she told them what she proposed to do. Having received their full consent, a few days later she went to the church as she usually did, and as soon as the Rector caught sight of her, he came straight over and began chatting with her in his customary, overly familiar manner.

When the lady saw him approaching, she looked up in his direction and gave him a cheerful smile. Then the two of them went a little way off to the side, and after the Rector had treated her to a great deal of his usual patter, she sighed deeply and declared: "Sir, I've often heard it said that there's no castle strong enough to avoid being taken some time or other if it's under continual siege, and I now see clearly that this is what has happened to me. For you have come at me from every direction with your sweet words and with one courteous gesture after another so that you've forced me to break my resolve, and seeing just how much you like me, I am now disposed to give myself to you."

Ecstatic, the Rector replied: "Thank you so much, my lady. To tell you the truth, I was rather amazed that you held out for so long, considering that such a thing has never happened to me with any other woman before. In fact, I've sometimes said, 'If women were silver, you couldn't make coins out of them, for they wouldn't be able to hold up against the hammering.'³ But enough of this for now. When and where can we get together?"

"Sweet my lord," replied the lady, "the when can be whenever you like, since I have no husband to whom I have to give an account of my nights. But as for the where, I haven't the slightest idea."

"You don't?" asked the Rector. "Why not in your house?"

"Sir," she said, "as you know, I have two young brothers who bring groups of their friends home with them day and night, and besides, my house isn't very large. So, we couldn't do it there unless we were willing to remain completely silent, not uttering a single word as if we were deaf-mutes, and going about in the dark as if we were blind. Should you be willing to do it like that, however, then it'd be feasible, because my brothers don't meddle with things in my bedroom. Still, theirs is so close to mine that you can't whisper the least little word in it without being overheard."

"My lady, this won't be a problem for a night or two," replied the Rector, "and meanwhile I'll think of a place where we can meet with less difficulty."

"I'll leave that to you, sir," said the lady, "but there is one thing I will ask of you, and that's to let this be our secret and never allow a word about it to get out."

"Don't you worry about that, my lady," he replied. "In fact, if it's possible, will you arrange things so that we can get together this evening?"

"With pleasure," said the lady, and after explaining to him how and when he was to come, she left him and returned home.

The lady had a maid who was not, however, all that young, and who had the ugliest, most misshapen face you ever saw. She had a flat, squashed nose, a mouth twisted awry, thick lips, and huge, crooked teeth. Furthermore, she squinted, had bleary, watery eyes, and her complexion was greenish yellow, as though she had spent the summer not in Fiesole, but in Sinagaglia.* Besides all this, she limped and was a little crooked on the right side. Her name was Ciuta, but because she had such a discolored face, everybody called her Ciutazza, and although her body was misshapen, she was nevertheless always ready for a bit of mischief.[4]

His mistress summoned her and said: "Ciutazza, if you're willing to perform a service for me tonight, I'll give you a fine new shift."[5]

At the mention of the shift, Ciutazza replied: "My lady, if you give me a shift, I'll throw myself into the fire, or even worse."

"Now then," said the lady, "what I want you to do is to sleep with a man in my bed tonight and make love to him. But be careful never to utter a single sound so that my brothers don't hear you, since, as you know, they sleep in the next room. After that, I'll give you the shift."

"Sure," said Ciutazza. "If I have to, I'll sleep with six of them, let alone one."

When evening came, Messer Erectum made his appearance as had been arranged, and the two young men carried out the lady's plan by stationing themselves in their bedroom where they made a fair amount of noise.[6] The Rector quietly entered the lady's bedroom in the dark

---

*Sinagaglia (now Senigallia) is a modern port on the Adriatic across the peninsula from Florence. It was in decline during the late Middle Ages and was in a mosquito-infested area so that people spending the summer there tended to come down with malaria and their skin might well be greenish yellow.

and went over to her bed, as she had told him to do, while Ciutazza got in on the other side, having been well coached by the lady as to how she should act. Thinking he had his lady beside him, Messer Erectum took Ciutazza in his arms and began to kiss her without saying a word, to which Ciutazza responded in kind. Then the Rector proceeded to console himself with her, taking possession of the goods he had coveted for so long.

Having accomplished this much of her plan, the lady ordered her brothers to carry out the rest of it. Quietly leaving their room, they made their way to the piazza, and Fortune was more favorable to their enterprise than they themselves had hoped. For the weather was very hot and the Bishop had been searching for the two young men, intending to stroll back to their house in their company and to relax and have a drink with them there. As soon as he saw them coming in his direction, he told them what he had in mind and set off down the street with them. Entering their cool little courtyard, which was well lit up by a host of lamps, he drank one of their fine wines with great pleasure. When he was finished, the young men said: "My lord, since you have been so gracious in deigning to visit this humble little abode of ours, which we were just on our way to invite you to do, we'd be gratified as well if you would be so kind as to take a look at a little something we wish to show you."

The Bishop replied that he would be happy to go with them, and so one of the young men took a lighted torch in his hand, and leading the way, headed for the bedroom in which Messer Erectum was sleeping with Ciutazza, followed by the Bishop and all the others. In a great hurry to get where he was going, the Rector had done a lot of hard riding, and before the group arrived, he had already covered more than three miles, with the result that he was somewhat tuckered out, and despite the heat, had fallen asleep, holding Ciutazza in his arms.

Thus, when the young man bearing the torch entered the bedroom, followed closely by the Bishop and all the others, what greeted them was the sight of the Rector with Ciutazza in his embrace. At precisely that moment Messer Rector woke up, and upon seeing the people standing around him in the torchlight, he hid his head under the covers, thoroughly ashamed and terrified. The Bishop proceeded to give him a terrible tongue-lashing and forced him to uncover his head so that he would see the person he had been sleeping with.

Both because of the trick he realized that the lady had played on him, and because of the disgrace he now saw himself exposed to, the Rector instantly became the saddest man who has ever lived. The Bishop ordered him to get dressed, and when he had put on his clothes once again, he was sent back to his house under close guard, there to undergo severe penance for the sin he had committed.

As the Bishop wanted to know how it had come about that the Rector had gone to bed with Ciutazza in the young men's house, they told him the entire story from start to finish. After hearing it, he was full of praise for the lady, and for the young men as well, who, not wishing to sully their hands with the blood of a priest, had treated the Rector exactly as he deserved.

The Rector was forced by the Bishop to do penance for his sin, weeping and wailing over what he had done for forty days, but between his love and his humiliation he bewailed it for more than nine-and-forty, not to mention that for a very long time afterward he could not walk down the street without having boys point their fingers at him and say: "Look, there's the guy who slept with Ciutazza"—which bothered him so much that it almost drove him crazy.

This, then, was how the worthy lady got the annoying Rector with his shameless propositions off her back, and how Ciutazza earned herself a shift.

Day 8, Story 5

Three young men pull down the breeches of a judge from The Marches while he is sitting on the bench and administering justice in Florence.[1]

After Emilia had brought her story to an end and the widow had been praised by everyone, the Queen looked at Filostrato and said, "Now it is your turn to speak." He responded promptly by saying he was ready, and began as follows:

Delightful ladies, the young man Elissa mentioned just a short while ago, that is, Maso del Saggio, has prompted me to pass over a story I intended to tell you in order to recount another one about him and some of his companions. Although the tale itself is not indecent, certain words do appear in it that you would be ashamed to use. Nevertheless, since it is so funny, I am going to tell it anyway.

As all of you may well have heard, the chief magistrates of our city very frequently come from The Marches, and they are generally mean-spirited men who lead such wretched, beggarly lives that everything they do looks like chicanery. And because of their innate miserliness and avarice, they bring judges and notaries along with them who seem to have been brought up behind the plow or taken from the cobbler's shop rather than from the law schools.

Now, one of them had come here as *podestà*, and among the numerous judges he brought with him, there was a man called Messer Niccola da San Lepidio who looked more like a smith than anything else, and he was assigned to go with the other judges and hear criminal cases.

It often happens that people go to the law courts although they have no business there at all, which is just what Maso del Saggio was doing one morning, for he had gone there to look for one of his friends. When

619

he arrived, he happened to glance over to where this Messer Niccola was sitting, and thinking him a weird birdbrain, surveyed him from top to bottom. He noticed that the vair in the cap the man was wearing had been completely blackened by smoke,* that he had a pen case hanging down from his belt, that his gown was longer than his robe, and many other strange things that would be unbecoming in a proper, well-bred gentleman. The most noteworthy thing of all, in his opinion, was the pair of breeches the judge was wearing, for their crotch was halfway down his legs, something that Maso could easily see because the man's outer garments were so tight that when he sat down, they opened up all the way in the front.

Having seen all he needed to, Maso abandoned his first search for his friend, and setting out on a new one, ran into two of his buddies, named Ribi and Matteuzzo, both of whom loved to have fun as much as Maso did.[2]

"If you value my friendship," he said to them, "come with me to the courthouse, and I'll show you the weirdest jerk you've ever seen."

So off they went to the courthouse where Maso showed his friends the judge and his breeches. What they could see from a distance already got them laughing, and when they were closer to the platform on which Messer Judge was sitting, not only did they realize that it would be a very easy matter to crawl underneath it, but they also noticed that the plank on which Messer Judge was resting his feet was broken and had an opening in it through which someone could easily stick his hand and arm.

Accordingly, Maso said to his friends: "Let's go and pull his breeches all the way down. It'll be a snap to do it."

The other two had already figured out how it could be managed, and having arranged with one another what they were going to say and do, they returned there the next morning. The courtroom was crowded, allowing Matteuzzo to crawl under the platform without being seen by anyone and position himself right beneath the spot where the judge was resting his feet.

---

*The ceremonial caps and gowns of physicians and lawyers in the Middle Ages were normally lined with vair, the fur of a gray and white squirrel.

Then Maso approached Messer Judge from one side and seized the hem of his robe, while Ribi came up to him from the other and did the same thing.

"Your Honor, your Honor," Maso started to say, "I beg you in God's name, don't let that petty thief, the one over there on the other side of you, get away from here before you make him give me back the pair of boots he stole from me. He says he didn't do it, but I saw him getting them resoled less than a month ago."

On the other side, Ribi was yelling at the top of his lungs: "Your Honor, don't you believe him, the lousy crook. Just because he knows I've come to file a complaint against him for stealing a saddlebag of mine, he shows up here with this story about the boots, which I've had in my house for I don't know how long. And if you don't believe me, I can call up plenty of witnesses, like the lady from next door who's a fruit seller, and Fatty the tripe woman, and a street sweeper from around Santa Maria a Verzaia who saw him coming back from the country."[3]

Maso for his part was not prepared to let Ribi do all the talking, and started shouting, prompting Ribi to shout right back at him. Then, while the judge was standing up, leaning closer to them in order to hear them better, Matteuzzo seized the opportunity to stick his hand through the opening in the plank, grabbed the seat of the judge's breeches, and gave them a tremendous yank. Down they came in a flash, for the judge was a skinny guy, and he had really scrawny shanks. He felt his breeches slip, but had no idea how this had happened, and he tried to cover himself up by sitting back down and pulling his robe around in front of him. Maso and Ribi, however, were holding it tight on either side and yelling with all their might: "Your Honor, it's outrageous for you to refuse to listen to me and try to get away before giving me justice. Surely, you don't need to get written evidence in this town for a little case like this one."

While they were saying all this, they held him by his robe long enough for everyone in the tribunal to see that he did not have his breeches on. Matteuzzo, however, who had clung to them for some time, let them go and slipped outside without being seen, while Ribi, who thought he had done quite enough, exclaimed: "I swear to God I'm going to appeal this to the superior court!"[4] On the other side, Maso let go of the robe and declared: "Not me. I'm just going to keep coming back here until I find you less distracted than you seem to be this morning." And then, the two of them went off in opposite directions, leaving the tribunal as quickly as they could.

Only at this point, after Messer Judge had pulled up his breeches in front of everyone, as if he were just getting out of bed, did he realize what had happened and demanded to know the whereabouts of the two men who had been arguing about the boots and the saddlebag. Since they were nowhere to be found, he started swearing by God's guts that he would have liked it if somebody had told him it was the custom in Florence for people to pull down a judge's breeches when he was sitting on the seat of justice.

When the *podestà*, for his part, heard what had happened, he made a real stink about it, but his friends explained to him that it had only been done to show him that the Florentines knew how he had tried to save money by bringing stupid fools to town with him, instead of real judges. Consequently, he thought it best to say nothing more on the subject, and so, for the time being, that was as far as it went.

Day 8, Story 6

Bruno and Buffalmacco steal a pig from Calandrino, and then, pretending to help him recover it, they get him to undergo a test involving ginger pills and Vernaccia wine. They give him two of the pills, one after the other, consisting of dog ginger seasoned with aloes, which make it appear as though he himself had stolen it. Finally, they force him to pay them blackmail if he does not want them to tell his wife about it.[1]

Filostrato's tale, which caused a great deal of laughter, had no sooner reached its conclusion than the Queen ordered Filomena to follow it with another one, and she began in this manner:

Gracious ladies, just as Filostrato was led by the mention of Maso's name to rehearse the story about him you just heard, I, too, have been led in exactly the same way by the one concerning Calandrino and his buddies to tell you another, which I believe you are really going to enjoy.

I do not have to explain to you who Calandrino, Bruno, and Buffalmacco were, since you have already heard quite a lot about them in the earlier tale. So, I shall get right on with my story and tell you that Calandrino had a little farm not very far from Florence that he had received from his wife as part of her dowry. Among many other things, it provided him with a pig every year, and it was his regular custom to take his wife and go to the country some time around December in order to slaughter the animal and have it salted.

It happened that one of those years, when Calandrino's wife was not feeling very well, he went there by himself to slaughter the pig. Bruno and Buffalmacco heard he was going to the country, and when they found out that his wife would not be with him, they set off to spend a few days with a priest, a very close friend of theirs, who was one of Calandrino's neighbors.

Calandrino had killed the pig the very morning of the day they arrived, and on seeing them with the priest, he called out to them, saying: "A hearty welcome to you all. I want to show you what a terrific farmer I am." And he took them into the house, where he showed them the pig.

It was a very fine animal, as they could see for themselves, and when they understood from Calandrino that he wanted to have it salted for his family, Bruno said to him: "Hey, you must be nuts! Sell it, and let's have a good time on what you get for it. You can always tell your missus somebody stole it from you."

"No," replied Calandrino, "not only wouldn't she believe it, but she'd chase me out of the house. So, stop interfering, because I'm never going to do it."

They talked with him at great length, but it was all to no avail. Calandrino then invited them to have supper with him, but he did so with such reluctance that they decided not to accept and took their leave of him instead.

Bruno asked Buffalmacco: "What would you say to stealing that pig of his tonight?"

"But how could we do that?" said Buffalmacco.

"I've already got the how of it all worked out," said Bruno, "provided he doesn't move it from where it was just now."

"Let's do it, then," said Buffalmacco. "After all, why shouldn't we? And later on, we could enjoy the proceeds together with the *padre* here."

The priest declared he was all for it, after which Bruno said: "This will call for some cunning on our part. Now, you know, Buffalmacco, how stingy Calandrino is and how happy he is to have a drink when somebody else is paying. So, let's go and take him to the tavern, where the priest can pretend to be the host and offer free drinks to all of us. When Calandrino sees that he doesn't have to pay for a thing, he'll get drunk out of his mind, and then we can manage it easily enough because there's no one else with him in the house."

They all did just what Bruno suggested. When Calandrino saw that the priest would not let him pay for anything, he started doing some serious drinking, and although it normally did not take much to get him drunk, in this case he really got a load on. By the time they left the tavern, it was already the wee hours of the night, and Calandrino, who had no interest in having any other kind of supper, returned home and went to bed. As he came in, he left the door wide open, although he thought he had locked it up tight.

Buffalmacco and Bruno went off to have supper with the priest, and when they were finished, they quietly made their way to Calandrino's house, having collected the tools they needed so that they could break into it at the spot Bruno had decided on earlier. Upon discovering the door was open, however, they just walked in, took the pig down from its hook, and carried it over to the priest's house. Then, having stowed it away there, off they went to bed.

The next morning, after his head had cleared from the effects of the wine, Calandrino got up and went downstairs, where he looked around only to discover that the pig was gone and the door was standing wide open. He asked one person after another if they knew of anybody who might have taken it, and when he failed to find it, he started creating a ruckus, complaining about how miserable he was, alas! and lamenting that his pig had been stolen.

Meanwhile, Bruno and Buffalmacco got up and went over to Calandrino's to hear what he would say about the pig. As soon as he saw them, he called out to them, almost in tears, and said: "Alas, my friends, somebody's stolen my pig from me!"

Bruno sidled up to him and whispered, "It's a miracle! Here you are actually using your brains for a change!"

"Oh, woe is me," said Calandrino. "I'm telling you the absolute truth."

"That's the way to talk," replied Bruno. "Go ahead and shout, so people will think it really did happen."

"God's body, I'm telling you the truth," said Calandrino, howling even louder. "Somebody stole it from me."

"That's good, well said," replied Bruno. "You really need to talk like that. Yell it so loud that everyone can hear you, and that way they'll all believe it's true."

"You're going to drive me to perdition!" exclaimed Calandrino. "I say it, and you don't believe me. May I be hanged by the neck if my pig hasn't been stolen!"

"Come on! How is it possible?" said Bruno, "I saw the pig here myself only yesterday, and you think you can convince me that it's just flown away?"[2]

"It's exactly the way I've been telling you," said Calandrino.

"Really, is it possible?" asked Bruno.

"Yes, it sure is," replied Calandrino, "and I'm ruined because of it. I don't know how I can go back home, because my missus won't believe me, and even if she does, there'll be no peace between us for all of next year."

"God save me," said Bruno, "this is serious stuff if you're telling the truth. But you know, Calandrino, just yesterday I was advising you to say something like this, and I wouldn't want to think you were making fools of both your missus and us at the same time."

"Oh, you're driving me to despair," Calandrino started shouting. "You'll have me cursing God and the Saints and everything else. I'm telling you somebody stole the pig from me last night."

"If that's the case," said Buffalmacco, "then we'll have to see if we can't find some way to get it back again."

"Find a way?" asked Calandrino. "How can we do that?"

"Well, if anything's certain," replied Buffalmacco, "it's that the guy who took your pig didn't come here all the way from India. It must have been one of your neighbors. So, if you could manage to round them up, I know how to do the bread and cheese test, and then we'll see right away who took it."[3]

"Oh yes," said Bruno, "what a great idea, to use bread and cheese on the fine folks who live around here! It's certain that one of them took it, but he'd just see through what we're doing and refuse to come."

"So, what's to be done, then?" asked Buffalmacco.

"What we ought to do," said Bruno, "is to make use of some nice ginger pills along with some good Vernaccia wine and then invite them to come here for a drink.[4] That way they wouldn't suspect a thing, and they'd all come. And we could have the ginger pills blessed the same way the bread and cheese are."

"That's the way to do it, all right," said Buffalmacco. "And you, Calandrino, what do you say? Shall we give it a try?"

"Yes, for the love of God," said Calandrino, "I beg you to do it. If only I knew who took the pig, I wouldn't feel half so bad about it."

"Well, then," said Bruno, "just to oblige you, I'm ready to go all the way to Florence to get the things you need if you'll give me the money for them."

Calandrino had perhaps forty *soldi* on him,[5] and he gave them to Bruno, who went to a friend of his in Florence, an apothecary, from whom he bought a pound of good ginger pills, but also had him make up two others out of dog ginger, seasoning them with fresh hepatic aloes.[6] Then he had the apothecary coat those two with sugar just like the other ones, and to keep them from being misplaced or getting confused with the good ones, he had him put a certain little mark on them so that he would have no trouble telling them apart. Finally, after purchasing a flask of good-quality Vernaccia wine, Bruno returned to Calandrino's place in the country and said to him: "See to it that you invite every-body who's a suspect to have a drink with you tomorrow morning. Since it's a holiday, they'll all be happy to come. Tonight, along with Buffalmacco, I will recite a spell over the pills, and bring them to your house in the morning. Because we're such good friends, I'll hand the pills out myself, and I'll do and say everything necessary."

Calandrino issued the invitations, and the next morning, a sizable group of people, including farmhands and young men from Florence who happened to be staying in the country, had already assembled around the elm in front of the church, when Bruno and Buffalmacco appeared, carrying the box of pills and the flask of wine. Then they made everyone stand around in a circle.

"Gentlemen," said Bruno, "it's my job to explain to you why you're here so that if something happens that's not to your liking, you'll have no cause to blame me for it. The night before last, Calandrino, who's right here, had a fine pig of his stolen from him and has been unable to discover who took it. Considering that it could only have been taken by someone here, he wants to find out who it was by having each of you in turn eat one of these pills and then have a drink. Now, let me explain right away that the one who took the pig will not be able to get it down. In fact, he'll find it's more bitter than poison, and he'll spit it out. So, before subjecting himself to such shame in the presence of so many people, it might be better for the person who took the pig to confess what he did to the *padre,* in which case I won't proceed any further with this business."

Everyone there declared that he was ready to eat the pills, after which Bruno made them stand in a line, placing Calandrino in among them, and then, starting at one end, he gave each person his pill. When he came up in front of Calandrino, he took out one of those containing dog ginger and put it in his hand. Without a moment's hesitation, Calandrino popped it into his mouth and started chewing on it, but as soon as he felt the aloes on his tongue, he could not stand the bitter taste and spat it out.

All the people were staring one another in the face to see if anyone would spit it out, when Bruno, who had not finished giving out the pills and was pretending not to notice what was going on, heard someone behind him say, "Ah, Calandrino, what's this all about?" Bruno quickly whirled around, and when he saw that Calandrino had spit his pill out, he said: "Hold on. Maybe he spat it out for some other reason. Here, have another one." And picking up the second pill, he put it in Calandrino's mouth, after which he continued distributing those that were left.

If the first pill had seemed bitter to Calandrino, this one appeared far, far worse. But since he was ashamed to spit it out, he kept it in his mouth for a while. As he chewed on it, he began shedding tears as big as hazelnuts, until finally, he could not stand it any longer and sent it flying out just like the first one.

Meanwhile, Buffalmacco was in the process of pouring drinks for everyone in the group, as was Bruno, and when they and all the others saw what happened, they all agreed that it had to be Calandrino who had stolen the pig himself. In fact, there were even some of them who criticized him harshly for having done so.

When the crowd had gone, however, leaving Bruno and Buffalmacco alone with Calandrino, Buffalmacco said to him: "I knew all along that you were the one who'd taken it and that you wanted to make us believe it had been stolen so you wouldn't have to stand us to a round of drinks with the money you were paid for it."

Calandrino, who had still not gotten all the bitter taste of the aloes out of his mouth, started swearing that he had not taken it. "On your honor, now, buddy," said Buffalmacco, "how much did you get for it? Did it amount to six florins?"[7] When he heard this, Calandrino felt close to despair.

"Now you just listen and get this straight, Calandrino," said Bruno. "There was a guy in the group of people who were eating and drinking with us, and he told me that you had some girl around here you were keeping at your disposal and that since you gave her whatever you could scrape together, he was certain that you'd sent her this pig of yours. You've become quite the trickster, haven't you? There was that time you led us down along the Mugnone to collect black stones, but after sending us on a wild-goose chase, you took off back home and tried to make us believe you'd found the thing. And now that you've given away the pig, or, what's more likely, sold it, once again you think that with all those oaths of yours you'll persuade us that it was actually stolen. We've caught on to your tricks, and now we know them when we see them, so you're never going to be able to pull one on us again. And to tell you the truth, that's why we took so much trouble with the magic spell, because unless you give us two pairs of capons for it, we're going to tell Monna Tessa everything."

Seeing that they would not believe him, and thinking that he had had enough grief already without getting a scolding from his wife on top of it, Calandrino gave them the two pairs of capons. Then, after they had salted the pig, they carried everything back with them to Florence, leaving Calandrino behind with nothing but his losses and his humiliation.[8]

Day 8, Story 7

A scholar falls for a widow who is in love with someone else and gets the scholar to spend a winter's night waiting for her in the snow. Later on he persuades her to follow his counsel and spend an entire day in the middle of July, naked atop a tower, exposed to flies and gadflies and the sun.[1]

The ladies had a good laugh about the hapless Calandrino and would have laughed even harder if they had not felt sorry for him because the people who had stolen his pig relieved him of his capons as well. But when the story came to an end, the Queen ordered Pampinea to tell hers, and she promptly began as follows:

Dearest ladies, since it often happens that one person's cunning makes someone else's seem ridiculous, it is unwise to take delight in causing others to look like fools. Although many of our little stories have made us laugh a great deal over the pranks that people have played, we have never talked about how any of the victims avenged themselves. I, however, intend to make you feel sympathy for an act of just retribution that was meted out to a woman from our city who almost died when the trick she played got turned around and used against her. Nor will this tale be unprofitable, for when you have heard it, you will be more hesitant about deceiving others and will thereby show your splendid good sense.

Not so many years ago there was a young woman living in Florence named Elena who was physically attractive, proud of spirit, well bred, and rather generously supplied with the goods of Fortune.[2] Having been left a widow by her husband's death, she decided never to marry again, having fallen in love with a handsome, charming young man of her own choosing. Now that she was free of all other cares, she managed, with the help of her maid, whom she trusted implicitly, to spend many wonderfully pleasurable hours with him to their mutual delight.

At that time it just so happened that a young nobleman of our city named Rinieri came back to Florence from Paris. He had been studying there for many years, not in order to sell his knowledge for profit, as many do, but to understand the nature of things and their causes, a most fitting pursuit for the well born. Greatly honored in Florence for both his nobility and his learning, he settled down to lead the life of a gentleman there.

It is often the case, however, that those who have the keenest understanding of life's profundities are the soonest caught in the halter of Love, and that is just what happened to Rinieri. For one day, seeking to amuse himself, he had gone to a banquet where who should appear before his eyes but this Elena, dressed all in black as our widows usually are. She seemed more beautiful and charming than any woman he had ever seen, and he said to himself that the man to whom God granted the grace of holding her naked in his arms might consider himself truly blessed. As he glanced at her cautiously over and over again, he thought to himself that things great and precious cannot be acquired without an effort, and he therefore made up his mind to devote all his care and attention to pleasing her, hoping that he would acquire her love in that way and thus be able to enjoy her to the full.

The young woman, who admired herself for all she was worth, if not more, was not in the habit of keeping her eyes directed down toward the nether regions.[3] Instead, she would dart coy glances in all directions, being quick to spot anyone who took pleasure in looking at her. Thus, when she noticed Rinieri, she laughed to herself and thought, "My coming here today wasn't a waste of time, because unless I'm mistaken, I'll soon be leading this gull around by the nose." She then started glancing at him every so often out of the corner of her eye and did her best to make it appear that she was interested in him, since it was her view that the more men she allured and captured with her charms, the more highly her beauty would be prized, and especially by the man on whom, together with her love, she had actually bestowed it.

The learned scholar, setting his philosophical speculations aside, devoted all his thoughts to the lady, and after discovering where her house was located, he invented a variety of pretexts to begin taking frequent walks by it, thinking he would please her. For the reason already mentioned, the lady was vain, and glorying in this, she pretended she was very happy to see him. Accordingly, the scholar found a way to strike up a friendship with her maid, revealed his love to her, and begged her to use her influence with her mistress in order to help him obtain her favor.

The maid was lavish with her promises and then went and reported everything to her mistress who had the heartiest laugh in the world about it.

"Have you noticed how he's managed to lose all the wisdom he brought back here from Paris with him?" said the lady. "Well, anyhow, let's give him what he's looking for. The next time he speaks to you, tell him I'm even more in love with him than he is with me, but that I have to safeguard my honor if I want to be able to hold my head up when I'm in the company of other women. And if he's as wise as people say he is, then that ought to make him value me even more."

Ah, the wretched, wretched woman! She really had no idea, dear ladies, what it means to tangle with scholars.

When the maid next encountered him, she carried out her mistress's orders, and the scholar, overjoyed, proceeded to make even warmer entreaties, writing letters and sending gifts to the lady, all of which she accepted. The only responses he got back from her were vague generalities, however, and thus she kept him feeding on hope for quite some time.

When the lady revealed everything that was going on to her lover, he got rather angry at her and was sufficiently jealous that she finally decided she had to do something to prove to him that his suspicions of her were wrong. Since the scholar was becoming ever more insistent with his entreaties, she sent her maid to tell him, on her mistress's behalf, that although from the time he had declared his love for her, she had not had a single opportunity to give him satisfaction, she hoped to spend time with him during the Christmas holidays, which were fast approaching. If, therefore, he were willing to come to her courtyard after nightfall on the day after Christmas, she would go to meet him there as soon as she could. The scholar was the happiest man in the world, and having gone to her house at the time specified, he was taken by the maid to a courtyard, where he was locked in and began waiting for the lady to appear.

The lady had sent for her lover that evening, and after the two of them had happily eaten their supper, she told him what she was planning to do that night, adding: "And so, now you'll be able to see the true nature and intensity of the love I've felt—and still feel—for the guy you were foolish enough to be jealous of." These words filled the lover's heart to the brim with happiness and made him eager to see how the lady would make good on what she had said.

By chance they had had a heavy snowfall during the day that had covered everything, and as a result, the scholar was not in the courtyard for very long before he started to feel colder than he would have wished. Because he was expecting relief, however, he suffered it all with patience.

After a while, the lady said to her lover: "Let's go over to the little window in the bedroom and watch the guy you're so jealous of. From there we'll be able to see what kind of answer he'll give the maid I just sent to have a chat with him." So off they went to the little window, through which they could look out without being seen, and heard the maid talking to the scholar from another window.

"Rinieri," she was saying, "my lady is the unhappiest woman there ever was, because one of her brothers came by this evening, and after talking and talking to her, he decided to stay for supper, and although I think he'll be going pretty soon, he still hasn't left, which is why she hasn't been able to make it here to see you. She'll be coming down soon enough, though, and begs you not to get upset for having to wait."

Believing the maid's story to be true, the scholar replied: "Tell my lady not to give another thought to me until it's convenient for her to come, but do ask her to come as soon as she can."

The maid drew her head back inside and went to bed. Then the lady said to her lover: "So, what do you say to that? Do you think I'd keep him down there, freezing in the cold, if I really cared for him, as you suspect I do?"

Her lover was now pretty well satisfied, and after she got into bed with him, the two of them amused themselves there for quite a long stretch, taking their pleasure of one another, while laughing and making fun of the hapless scholar.

Since there was no place for the scholar to sit down or find shelter from the open air, he kept moving in order to stay warm, and as he walked around the courtyard, he repeatedly cursed the lady's brother for staying with her for so long. Every time he heard a sound, he imagined it was his lady opening the door for him, but all his hopes were in vain.

After amusing herself with her lover until almost midnight, the lady said to him: "What do you think about this scholar of ours, my darling? Which do you think's greater, his wisdom or my love for him? Will the cold I'm making him suffer expel the cold that entered your heart because of the remarks I made about him in jest to you the other day?"

"Yes, indeed, sweetheart," replied her lover, "now I see clearly that you really are my treasure, my repose, my bliss, my every hope, just as I am yours."

"Then give me a thousand kisses at least," said the lady, "so I may see whether you're telling the truth." And in response, her lover held her tight in his embrace and kissed her not a thousand, but more than a hundred thousand times.

After they had carried on like that for quite a while, the lady said: "Come on, let's get up and take a moment to see if the fire, which this strange, new lover of mine says in his letters is always burning inside him, has been partly extinguished by now." And so, they got up and went over to the little window they had used before. Looking out into the courtyard, they saw the scholar down in the snow doing a brisk dance to the accompaniment of his chattering teeth. Because of the extreme cold, his movements were so lively and quick that they had never seen anything like it.

"What do you say to that, my sweet hope?" said the lady. "Wouldn't you agree that I can make men do a dance without hearing the sound of trumpets or bagpipes?"

"I do indeed, my darling," replied her lover with a laugh.

"Let's go down to the courtyard door," said the lady. "You keep quiet while I do the talking, and let's hear what he has to say. Perhaps we'll get as much fun out of it as we've had in watching him from up here."

Then they quietly left the bedroom and made their way down to the door, which the lady kept shut up tight. There was a tiny hole in it, however, and speaking through it, she called out to the scholar in a low voice. When he heard her summons, he believed all too readily that she was about to let him in, and thanking God, he walked over to the door. "Here I am, my lady," he said. "Open up, for the love of God, because I'm dying from the cold."

"Oh yeah," said the lady, "I'm sure you're awfully chilly! It must be really cold out there, all because of that little bit of snow! Well, I happen to know the snow's much worse in Paris. In any case, I can't open the door for you yet because this damned brother of mine, who came to have supper with me yesterday evening, still hasn't left. But he'll be going soon, and then I'll be down in a jiffy and let you in. I had a hard enough time slipping away from him just now so that I could come here to comfort you and tell you not to be upset over all the waiting you've had to do."

"Oh, my lady," replied the scholar, "I beg you, for God's sake, open the door and let me take shelter inside, for there's never been such a heavy snowfall as the one that started just a little while ago, and it's still coming down. I'll wait for you in there just as long as you please."

"Alas, my sweet, I can't do it," said the lady. "This door makes so much noise when it's opened that my brother would be sure to hear it. Anyway, what I want to do now is to go and tell him he has to leave. After that, I'll come back and let you in."

"Go quickly, then," said the scholar, "and I beg you, have them make up a good fire so that I can warm myself up when I come inside, for I've gotten so cold I scarcely have any feeling left in my body."

"I don't see how that's possible," replied the lady. "You've said over and over again in your letters that you're all on fire because of your love for me. But I feel certain you're just kidding me. In any case, I'm going now. Wait for me, and don't give up."

The lady's lover, who had heard everything, was as pleased as he could be and went right back to bed with her, although the two of them did not do much sleeping there that night. Instead, they spent almost the entire time, when they were not satisfying their desires, making fun of the scholar.

Finally realizing that he had been duped, the wretched scholar, whose teeth were chattering so badly that it sounded as if he had been turned into a stork, tried repeatedly to open the door while he looked around everywhere for another way to get out. When he could not find one, he began pacing up and down like a caged lion, cursing the state of the weather, the treachery of the lady, and the length of the night as well as his own simplemindedness. So intense was the anger he felt at her that his long-standing, fervent love was instantly transformed into bitter, unrelenting hatred, and he began mulling over a wide variety of schemes for revenge, which he now desired far more than he had ever longed to be with the lady in the past.

Although the night went on forever and ever, day eventually drew near, and when dawn began to appear, the maid, following her mistress's instructions, came down to the courtyard and opened the door.

"Curse that guy for coming here yesterday evening!" she said, pretending to feel sorry for the scholar. "He kept us on tenterhooks all night long while you were left to freeze out here. But you know what? Don't be discouraged, because if it didn't work out for you last night, it'll work out some other time. I know for a fact that nothing could have occurred that would have upset my lady as much as that."

The scholar was furious, but like the wise man he was, he knew that threats only serve to arm those who are threatened. Consequently, he kept his feelings locked up tight within his breast, feelings that would surely have burst out if he had not used all his willpower and done everything he could to restrain them.

"Truth to tell," he said in a low voice, without revealing the least hint of the anger he felt, "it was the worst night I've ever had, but I could certainly see that my lady was in no way to blame for what happened, inasmuch as she herself felt so sorry for me that she came down here to apologize and try to cheer me up. And since, as you say, what didn't work out for me last night will surely work out some other time, commend me to her, and may God be with you."

Almost completely numb from the cold, the scholar did what he could to make his way back to his own house, where, exhausted and dying from lack of sleep, he flung himself down on his bed to rest. When he awoke and discovered that he could hardly move his arms and legs, he sent for physicians, and after telling them about the cold he had been exposed to, he placed himself in their care. Although they gave him the most quick-acting and potent medicines, it was a long time before they managed to get his muscles to heal sufficiently so that he could straighten out his limbs once again, and if it had not been for his youth and the arrival of warm weather, the experience would have been too much for him to have borne. He did regain his health and vigor, however, and keeping his hatred down deep inside him, he pretended to be much more in love with his widow than ever before.

After a certain amount of time had passed, it just so happened that Fortune provided the scholar with an opportunity to get what he really desired. For the young man who was the object of the widow's affection, paying no heed whatsoever to her feelings for him, fell in love with another woman. Because he no longer had much interest in talking with the widow or doing anything else to please her, she pined away in tears and bitter sorrow. Her maid pitied her, but could find no way to assuage the grief her mistress felt over the loss of her lover. Then, however, she came up with the foolish idea that they could use some sort of necromantic spell to make the lover return to his former passion. Since she thought that the scholar, whom she would see walking through their neighborhood the way he used to, had to be a grand master of the art of magic, she explained all this to her mistress.

The lady, who was not very bright, did not once stop to think that if the scholar had known anything about necromancy, he would have used it on his own behalf. Therefore, taking her maid's advice, she told her to go at once and find out if he would be willing to do it, and to assure him that, in return for his help, her mistress would do whatever he wanted.

The maid was quite diligent in delivering the message. When he had heard it, the scholar was overjoyed and said to himself: "Praise be to God, for with Your assistance, the time has now come for me to punish that wicked woman for the harm she did to me as my reward for all the love I bore her." Then he said to the maid: "Tell my lady not to worry about it, for even if her lover were in India, I would make him come back at once and ask her to pardon him for what he's done to displease her. As for the course she has to take in this affair, however, I will wait to explain that to her at a time and place of her choosing. Say all this to her, and tell her, from me, not to worry."

The maid brought back his answer, and arrangements were made for them to meet in the Church of Santa Lucia near the Prato Gate. When they arrived there, the lady and the scholar went and spoke together in private. Forgetting that this was the man she had almost led to his death, she freely told him everything about her situation, explained what she wanted, and begged him to come to her rescue.

"My lady," the scholar said in reply, "it's true that necromancy was one of the subjects I studied in Paris, and you may rest assured that I know everything there is to know about it. But because that art is most displeasing to God, I've sworn never to practice it either for my own benefit or for anyone else's. Nevertheless, the love I bear for you is so strong that I find myself incapable of refusing to do anything you ask of me, and so, even though this deed alone would be enough to send me down to the Devil's domain, I'm ready to perform it since that is your pleasure. Let me warn you, however, that this thing is harder to do than you may perhaps realize, especially when a woman wants to regain a man's love, or a man wants to regain a woman's, because it can't be done except by the person involved. Moreover, this person has to be very brave, for the ceremony must be performed at night in a solitary spot when no one else is around, and I don't know whether you are ready to do such things."

The lady, who was more in love than wise, replied: "I am spurred on by Love so hard that there's nothing I wouldn't do to get back the man who has wrongfully forsaken me. But tell me, please, how will I have to show that I'm brave?"

"My lady," said the scholar with diabolical cunning,[4] "it'll be my job to make a tin image of the man you wish to get back. Once it's been delivered to you, take it, and when the moon is on the wane, go all by yourself to a flowing stream, in which, about the time you would first go to sleep, you must immerse yourself seven times, completely naked. After that, still naked, you must climb up to the top of a tree or of some deserted house, where, facing north and still holding the image in your hand, you are to repeat seven times certain words that I'm going to give you in writing. Once you've said them, you'll be approached by two of the fairest damsels you've ever seen who'll greet you and ask you graciously what you want them to do. See that you explain your wishes to them as fully and as clearly as possible, taking care not to confuse the names. When you've told them everything, they'll depart, and you may descend to the spot where you left your clothes, get dressed again, and return home. And then, without a doubt, before the following night is half over, your lover will come to you in tears, asking for your forgiveness and begging you for mercy. From that moment on, I can assure you, he will never again leave you for another woman."

Believing wholeheartedly in everything she had heard, the lady felt as if she were already holding her lover in her arms again and that half her troubles were over.

"Never fear," she said. "I'll do everything you tell me down to the last detail. What's more I have the best place in the world to do it, for I own a farm in the upper valley of the Arno that is very close to the riverbank, and since it's only the beginning of July, it'll actually be a pleasure to go bathing in it. In fact, now I remember, there's a little tower not very far from the river that's been abandoned, except that every so often the shepherds will climb up a ladder made out of chestnut wood and get on a platform to look around for their lost sheep. It's all quite solitary and out of the way, and by going up there, I'll be able to carry out your instructions to perfection."

The scholar, who knew exactly where the lady's property and the little tower were located, was delighted that things were going according to plan.

"My lady," he said to her, "I've never been in those parts, so I'm not familiar with the farm or the little tower, but if everything's the way you describe it, then there couldn't be a better place in the whole world. Consequently, when the time is ripe, I'm going to send you the image and the spell. But I beseech you, when you've got what you desire and realize how well I've served you, do think of me and remember to keep the promise you've made me."

The lady said she would do so without fail, and, after taking her leave of him, returned home.

Delighted that his plan seemed about to produce results, the scholar created an image, marking it with various characters, and wrote some nonsense he made up by way of a spell. In due course he sent these things to the lady and told her not to wait, but to carry out the instructions he had given her the very next night. Then, taking one of his servants with him, he went in secret to a friend's house, which was not very far from the little tower, in order to put his plan into action.

For her part, the lady set out with her maid and went to the farm. As soon as night had fallen, pretending that she was about to go to sleep herself, she sent the maid off to bed, and in the dead of night, she quietly left the house and made her way to a spot on the bank of the Arno that was quite close to the tower. Having first looked about with great care and having neither seen nor heard anyone, she got undressed and hid her clothes under a bush. Then, she took the image and immersed herself in the river with it seven times, after which, still naked and holding the image in her hand, she walked up to the little tower.

Meanwhile, the scholar was watching everything from the clump of willows and other trees near the tower where he had been hiding with his servant since nightfall. When the lady passed by right next to him, naked as she was, he was struck by the way the whiteness of her form overcame the gloom of the night, and as he stared at her bosom and the other parts of her body, impressed by just how beautiful they were, he thought to himself about what was going to happen to them in just a short while and began to feel a twinge of pity for her. At the same time, he suddenly found himself assailed by the prickings of the flesh, which made a certain something that had been lying down stand right up, so that he was tempted to leave his hiding place, seize her, and take his pleasure of her. Between them, these two promptings almost got the better of him, but when he remembered who he was, the injury he had received, and why, and at whose hands, his wrath was rekindled, dispelling both his pity and his carnal appetite. The result was that he clung firmly to his original resolve and allowed her to go on her way.

Having climbed to the top of the tower, the lady turned to the north and began reciting the spell given to her by the scholar, who had come in right behind her and was quietly dismantling the ladder, piece by piece, that led up to the platform where she stood. Then he waited to see what she would say and do.

The lady finished reciting the spell seven times and expected the two damsels to appear at any moment, but her wait went on so long that she started feeling far chillier than she would have liked, and she was still standing there when dawn arrived. Upset that things had not turned out as the scholar had told her they would, she said to herself: "I suspect he was trying to give me a night like the one I gave him. But if that was his intention, he had a pretty bad idea about how to go about avenging himself, because the night he spent was three times as long as this one, and the cold he had to deal with was really something else altogether."

Since she had no desire to be caught up there in broad daylight, she decided to climb down from the tower, only to discover that the ladder was gone. Feeling as though the earth beneath her feet had disappeared, she fell down in a faint onto the platform of the tower. As soon as she came back to her senses, she started weeping and wailing in the most pitiful fashion, and since she knew only too well that this had to be the work of the scholar, she began to regret the harm she had done as well as her willingness to trust someone she had had every good reason to consider her enemy. And thus she remained, meditating on all this, for a very long time.

After looking around for another way to get down and finding none, she began weeping again and thought bitterly to herself: "Oh, you unlucky woman, what are your brothers and relatives and neighbors, indeed what are people generally in Florence, going to say when they learn that you were found naked up here? They'll all know that your supposedly unimpeachable honesty was phony, and even if you tried to come up with some lying excuses for this—assuming you could find any—you'll be prevented from using them by that damned scholar who knows everything about you. Oh, you poor wretch, at one and the same time you've lost not only the young guy you stupidly chose as a lover, but your honor into the bargain." Having reached this conclusion, she felt so overcome with grief that she very nearly threw herself down from the tower onto the ground below.

Since the sun had already risen, the lady moved closer to the wall on one side of the tower, looking out in the hope that she might see some boy approaching with his flock of animals whom she could send to fetch her maid. Just then, the scholar, who had gone to sleep for a while underneath a bush, happened to wake up and catch sight of her at the very moment she caught sight of him.

"Good-day, my lady," he said to her. "Have the damsels arrived yet?"

When she saw him and heard what he said, she burst into tears once more and begged him to come inside the tower so that she could speak to him. With the utmost courtesy, the scholar granted her request, while the lady went and lay down prone on the platform in such a position that only her head showed through the opening.

"Rinieri," she said, sobbing, "if I gave you a bad night, surely you've gotten even with me. Even though it's July, I was convinced, standing naked up here last night, that I was going to freeze to death, not to mention the fact that I've wept so much over the trick I played on you and over my being such a fool as to believe you, that it's a miracle I still have any eyes left in my head. So, not for love of me, whom you have no reason to love, but for your self-esteem as a gentleman, I beseech you to let what you've done up to this point suffice as revenge for the injury I did you, and to have my clothes brought to me and allow me to climb down from here. Please don't deprive me of the one thing you could never restore to me later even if you wanted to, namely, my honor, because although I did prevent you from spending a night with me, I can offer you many others in exchange for it whenever you please. So, let this suffice for you, and like a gentleman, be satisfied that you were able to avenge yourself and make me fully aware of it. Don't employ all your strength against a woman: the eagle gets no glory from having defeated a dove. Therefore, for the love of God and for the sake of your own honor, have mercy on me."

His heart filled with hatred, the scholar had been brooding on the injury he had received, but when he perceived her tears and listened to her entreaties, he felt both pleasure and sorrow simultaneously, pleasure in his revenge, which he had longed for above all else, and sorrow because his sense of humanity moved him to feel compassion for her. His humanity, however, could not overcome his fierce desire for vengeance.

"Madonna Elena," he said to her in reply, "if my prayers, which, it is true, I did not know how to bathe with tears and coat with honey the way you do yours, had been able to persuade you to give me the slightest bit of shelter on that night when I was freezing to death out in your snow-filled courtyard, then it would be an easy matter for me now to answer your prayers. But if you are more concerned about your honor at present than you were in the past, and if it bothers you to be up there completely naked, why don't you direct your prayers to the man in whose arms, as you well remember, you did not mind being naked that night while you listened to me tramping back and forth, my teeth chattering, through the snow in your courtyard? Go get him to help you, get him to bring you your clothes, get him to put the ladder in place so that you can climb down. In fact, do everything you can to make him feel some concern for your good name even though you yourself never hesitated to place it in danger for his sake, not just now, but on a thousand other occasions.

"Why don't you call him to come to your rescue? What could be more fitting, since you are his, and if there's anything he's going to protect, it would have to be you? When you were enjoying yourself with him, you asked him what he thought was greater, my folly or your love for him, so go ahead and call him now, you silly woman, and find out whether the love you bear him, and your intelligence, combined with his, can save you from this folly of mine.[5] And don't think you can make me a generous offer now of something I no longer desire, although if I did want it, there's no way that you could refuse to give it to me. Save your nights for your lover, if you should happen to get out of here alive. The two of you are welcome to them. One night was more than enough for me, and I have no intention of being made a fool of a second time.

"What's more, with those cunning words of yours, you do your best to flatter me, calling me a gentleman and a man of honor, all in order to get my goodwill and quietly dissuade me from punishing you for your wickedness by appealing to my sense of magnanimity. But your flattering words will not cloud the eyes of my mind the way your treacherous promises once did. I really know myself now, for you taught me more about that subject in a single night than I ever learned during the whole of my stay in Paris.

"But even supposing I were a magnanimous man, you are not the kind of person who deserves to be treated with magnanimity. For a savage beast like you, the only fit punishment, the only just revenge must be death, whereas if I were dealing with a human being, what I've already done, as you mentioned before, would suffice. Furthermore, I'm no eagle, and you're certainly no dove. No, you're a poisonous serpent, and I intend to hunt you down with all my hatred and all my strength as if you were our oldest enemy.* Nevertheless, what I've done to you cannot properly be called revenge, but rather, retribution, for revenge should exceed the offense, and this will fall short of it. In fact, when I consider the peril you exposed me to, it would not suffice for me to take your life by way of revenge, nor a hundred lives just like yours, since I'd only be killing a vile, wicked, worthless little woman.

"Except for that tolerably pretty face of yours, which will be ruined and covered with wrinkles in just a few years, how the devil do you differ from any other poor, worthless serving girl? It was not for lack of trying that you almost caused the death of a gentleman, as you called me just a moment ago, who could be of more use to the world in a single day than a hundred thousand of your kind could be for as long as the earth shall last. Therefore, through the pain you're suffering now, I'm

---

*The "oldest enemy" is Satan.

going to teach you what it means to make fun of men who have feelings, and especially scholars, and should you manage to escape from here with your life, I'll give you good cause never to stoop to such folly again.

"But if you are so anxious to come down, why don't you just throw yourself onto the ground here? That way, with God's help, you'll break your neck, and at one and the same time, you'll escape the pain you seem to be suffering while making me the happiest man in the world. That's all I have to say to you for the time being. I was smart enough to get you to climb up there; now let's see if you're as smart about getting down as you once were about making a fool of me."

As the scholar spoke, the wretched woman wept incessantly. Meanwhile, time was passing, and the sun was climbing higher and higher in the sky. When he finally stopped talking, she said: "Ah, what a cruel man you are! If you suffered so much on that damned night and if my fault seemed so serious to you that neither my youthful beauty, nor my bitter tears, nor my humble prayers can make you feel a touch of pity, at least you should be a little moved to treat me with less remorseless severity by the fact that I eventually trusted in you and revealed all of my secrets to you, thus giving you the means to satisfy your desire and show me how I've sinned. For if I hadn't trusted you, you wouldn't have had any way to avenge yourself on me, as you seemed so passionately intent upon doing.

"Ah, put aside your anger now and forgive me. Should you deign to pardon me and let me get down from here, I'm ready to abandon that faithless young man forever and to take you alone as my lover and my lord even though you disparage my beauty and say it's fleeting and of little value. Whatever it may be worth when you compare it to the beauty of other women, yet this much I do know: it should be prized, if for no other reason than that it is a joy and a plaything and a delight for men in their youth—and you're by no means an old man.

"However cruelly I've been treated by you, I still can't believe that you would want to see me die so shameful a death as to throw myself down there in despair right before your eyes, eyes which, if you were not a liar in the past as you have since become, once found me so very attractive. Ah, for the love of God, have mercy on me, for pity's sake!

The sun is becoming unbearably hot, and it's beginning to make me feel as miserable now as the intense cold did last night."

"My lady," replied the scholar, who was only too delighted to chat with her, "you didn't place your trust in me just now because of the love you felt for me, but to get back the lover you'd lost, and that's why you deserve to be treated even more harshly. Furthermore, you're crazy if you think this was the one and only way I had to obtain the revenge I desired. I had a thousand others. Indeed, while I was pretending to love you, I had spread a thousand snares around your feet, so that if it hadn't happened now, you would have inevitably been caught in one of them.[6] Although you could have been snagged by many others that would have meant more suffering and shame than this one does, I did not choose it to make things easier for you, but because I wouldn't have to wait so long to be happy like this.

"Moreover, should all of my tricks have failed, I would still have had my pen, and with it I would have written such things about you in such profusion and in such a style that when they came to your notice, as they most certainly would have, you would have wished, a thousand times a day, that you had never been born. The power of the pen is very much greater than those people suppose who have not proved it by experience. I swear to God—and may He make my revenge as sweet right down to the end as He has made it here at the beginning—I would have written things about you that would have shamed you so much not only in others' sight, but in your own, that you would have gouged out your eyes so you would never have had to look at yourself again. Therefore, don't go blaming the sea because a tiny little stream has added to its waters.

"As for your love and your claim that you are mine, I couldn't care less, as I've already said. Go ahead and stay with the guy you belonged to before, if you can. Because of what he's done to you, I now love him as much as I once used to hate him. You women are always falling for young men and longing for them to love you in return, because you see their fresher complexions and blacker beards, their strutting about and dancing and jousting. Men who are more mature have been through all that, and now they know things that those others have yet to learn.

"What's more, you believe that the young are better riders and can do more miles in a day than men of riper years. But whereas I certainly confess that they can give your fur-trimmed gown a more vigorous shaking, older men, being more experienced, are superior when it comes to finding out where the fleas are hiding. Besides, it's far better to have a small portion that's tasty than a large one that's bland, and although a fast trot will tire and weaken a man, even if he's young, an easy gait may bring another somewhat later to the inn, but at least he'll be in good shape when he gets there.

"Witless creatures that you are, you women don't realize how much evil is hidden under that handsome appearance of theirs. Young men are never content with just a single woman, but want every one they see, thinking they deserve to have them all. Consequently, their love can never be stable, something to which you yourself can now testify as an expert witness, thanks to the experience you've had. Moreover, they think they have a right to be worshipped and pampered by their women, and believe there's no greater glory than bragging about all the ones they've had, a fault that has caused many women to go and spread themselves underneath some friar simply because he'll keep mum about it. Although you claim nobody knew anything about your love affairs except your maid and me, you are badly misinformed. You deceive yourself if that's what you believe, for in his neighborhood, they talk about almost nothing else, just as they do in yours, although the people most involved are usually the very last to have news about such things reach their ears. Moreover, young men will steal from you, whereas the older ones will give you presents. Consequently, since you've made a bad choice, you may stay with the guy you gave yourself to, and leave me, whom you've spurned, for another, because I've found a woman who's worth a lot more than you are and who has understood me better than you ever did.

"Now, because it seems you don't believe what I've been telling you in the here and now, if you want to get a better idea of my feelings about you, you can do so the next world. Just throw yourself down onto the ground here, and then your soul, which I truly believe is already in the Devil's arms, will be able to see whether or not your headlong fall will trouble these eyes of mine in any way. Still, since I don't believe you'll consent to make me such a happy man, let me say this to you, that if you find yourself beginning to burn up, just think back to the cold you made me endure, and then, if you mix it with this heat, you will, without doubt, make the sun feel more temperate."

On seeing that the scholar's words were always directed at the same cruel end, the disconsolate lady began weeping again. "Look," she said, "since there's nothing about me that is capable of making you feel pity, at least be moved by the love you bear that woman you've found who's wiser than I am and who, you say, returns your affection. Forgive me out of love for her, bring me my clothes so that I can get dressed again, and let me climb down from here."

This made the scholar burst out laughing, and observing that it was already well past the hour of tierce, he replied: "Well, there's no way I can refuse your request now that you've appealed to me in the name of my lady. So, if you'll tell me where your clothes are, I'll go fetch them and arrange for you to get down from there."

The lady believed him, and feeling somewhat reassured, she gave him precise directions to the place where she had put her clothes. Upon emerging from the tower, the scholar ordered his servant not to leave the area, but to stay close by and do all he could to keep anyone else from getting in until he himself had returned. After he finished speaking, he walked over to his friend's house where he dined, completely at his ease, and then, in due course, went to take a nap.

Left atop the tower, the lady may have felt reassured to some degree because of her foolish hope, but since she was still terribly uncomfortable, she went over and sat next to that part of the wall that offered a little shade. There she settled down to wait, with nothing but her own exceedingly bitter thoughts as company, by turns brooding and weeping, now buoyed by hope and now in despair that the scholar would ever return with her clothes. As her mind flitted from one thought to another, she was finally overcome by her grief, and since she had been awake all night, fell fast asleep.

The sun was blazing hot, and when it reached its zenith, it beat straight down on the lady's tender, delicate body and her unprotected

head, striking them with such intensity that it produced blisters on
every last bit of her exposed flesh, causing countless tiny cracks to open
up all over it. In fact, she was burned so badly that the pain forced her
awake even though she was in a deep sleep.

Feeling her flesh on fire, she tried to move just a little, but when she
did, it seemed that her scorched skin was cracking and bursting open
all over, as if someone had taken a burned piece of parchment and was
stretching it. Besides—and this was hardly surprising—her head hurt
her so badly that she felt it was going to split in two. Since the floor of
the platform atop the tower was so hot that she could not find a place
to put her feet or any other part of her body, she was unable to stand
still and kept shifting her position constantly, weeping with every step
she took. Even worse, there was not a breath of wind, which allowed
swarms of flies and gadflies, which had arrived in large numbers, to
settle down inside the fissures in her flesh where they stung her so
fiercely that every sting felt as if she were being stabbed with a spear. In
response, she went flailing about with her hands, while she continually
cursed herself, her life, her lover, and the scholar.

Being thus tormented and goaded and pierced to the quick by the
incalculable heat, by the sun, by the flies and gadflies, and by her hunger, too, though much more by her thirst, and on top of all that, by a
thousand distressing thoughts, the lady got to her feet, and standing
up straight, she began looking everywhere she could, hoping to see or
hear someone nearby, for she was ready to call out and ask for help, no
matter what might happen to her as a result.

Even this, however, her enemy Fortune denied her. For the farmhands had all left the fields because of the heat, and in any case no one
had actually gone to work anywhere near there that day, for they were
all staying close to their houses in order to thresh their wheat. Consequently, the lady heard nothing but the cicadas and saw only the Arno,
which filled her with a desire for its waters that only served to increase
her thirst rather than diminish it. Here and there she saw woods and
patches of shade and houses, all of which similarly caused her anguish
because of the longing she felt for them.

Is there anything more for us to say about the hapless widow? What with the sun overhead and the hot platform beneath her, the stings of the flies and gadflies on every side, she was in such a sorry state that her skin, whose whiteness had overcome the gloom on the previous night, had now turned as red as madder* and was so spotted everywhere with blood that she would have seemed to anyone who saw her the ugliest thing in the world.

There she remained, bereft of counsel and hope, fully expecting to die, until halfway to the hour of nones. At that point, the scholar woke up, and calling his lady to mind, he returned to the tower to see how she was doing. When he spoke to his servant, who had not yet had his dinner, and told him to go and eat, the lady heard him, and even though she was weak and suffering terribly from the pain, she went over and sat down next to the opening.

"Rinieri," she said to him in tears, "surely you've taken your revenge beyond any conceivable limit. If I made you freeze in my courtyard all night, you didn't just stop at giving me a roasting, but you've had me burning up on this tower all day long, not to mention the fact that I'm dying from hunger and thirst. That's why I implore you, if only for the love of God, to climb up here, and since I don't have the heart to take my own life, to kill me yourself, for the torment I'm suffering is so horrible that what I want more than anything else is to die. Or if you won't bestow this grace on me, at least have someone bring me a cup of water so that I can moisten my mouth, for it's so parched and scorched that my tears aren't sufficient to do that."

The scholar could tell from her voice just how weak she was, and since he could also see part of her body that had been completely burned by the sun, he was moved by those things as well as by her humble prayers to feel a little pity for her. But nevertheless, he replied: "You wicked woman, you won't die at my hands, but at your own if that's what you really want. You're going to get just as much water from me to relieve you from the heat, as I got fire from you to relieve me from the cold. What I most regret is that the illness I suffered on account of the cold

---

*Madder (*Rubia tinctorum*) is a plant whose root was used to make a range of red dyes up through the nineteenth century.

had to be treated with the warmth of stinking dung, whereas they'll heal the injuries you got from the heat by means of cool, sweet-smelling rose water. And while I practically lost my life as well as the use of my limbs, you will merely be flayed by this heat, and will wind up no less beautiful than a serpent who has shed her old skin."

"Oh, woe is me!" cried the lady. "May God take such beauty, acquired in such a way, and give it to all my worst enemies. But you, who are crueler than any wild beast, how could you bear to torture me this way? Is there a worse punishment you or anyone else could have inflicted on me if I had killed everyone in your family after subjecting them to the direst of torments? I certainly don't know what greater cruelty could have been used against a traitor who had put an entire city to the slaughter than the one you subjected me to. I've been roasted by the sun and devoured by the flies, and on top of that, you refuse to offer me a cup of water, although even condemned murderers on their way to be executed are often given wine to drink if they merely ask for it. But look, now that I see you are unwavering in your savage cruelty and my suffering is in no way capable of moving you, I will prepare myself to meet my death with resignation. May God have mercy on my soul, and may He look down, I pray, on what you are doing with the eyes of justice."

When she finished speaking, she dragged herself in agonizing pain, filled with despair that she would ever be able to survive the fiery heat, toward the middle of the platform, where, quite apart from her other torments, she felt she was going to faint from thirst, not once, but a thousand times. And all the while she wept bitter tears as she bemoaned her misfortune.

Finally, when vespers arrived, it seemed to the scholar that he had done enough. He therefore had his servant take her clothes and wrap them up in his cloak, and they set off for the hapless lady's house, where he found her maid, sad and forlorn, sitting on the doorstep, unable to determine what she should do.

"My good woman," he said to her, "what's become of your mistress?"

"Sir," replied the maid, "I don't know. This morning I expected to find her in her bed, where I thought I saw her going last night, but I didn't find her there or anywhere else, and since I don't know what's happened to her, I'm really very worried. But you, sir, is there anything you can tell me about her?"

"I just wish," replied the scholar, "that I'd had you up there where I put her so that I could have punished you for your sins the way I've punished her for hers! But you can bet you're not going to escape my clutches until I've made you pay such a price for what you did that you'll never make a fool of any man again without remembering me." And having said this, he told his servant: "Give her those clothes and tell her she can go for her mistress if she wants to."

The servant did as he was told and gave the clothes to the maid. When she recognized whose they were, she was so terrified that she could scarcely keep herself from screaming, for she was convinced, in light of what had been said, that they had killed her mistress. Then, as soon as the scholar had left, she burst into tears and immediately set off at a run for the tower, carrying the clothes along with her.

That same day, one of the lady's swineherds had had the misfortune to lose two of his pigs and had gone in search of them, arriving at the little tower just a short time after the scholar's departure. As he went looking for them all over the place, he heard the hapless lady's woeful moans, and climbing up as high as he could go, he shouted: "Who's that crying up there?"

Recognizing the farmhand's voice, the lady called to him by name. "For pity's sake," she said, "go find my maid and have her come to me up here."

The farmhand realized who it was and replied: "Oh no, my lady, who carried you up there? Your maid's been running around searching for you all day long. But who'd ever have guessed you were here?"

Taking the two uprights of the ladder, the peasant set them up in the proper position and began tying the rungs in place with bands of willow. As he was doing this, the maid arrived, and when she entered the tower, unable to restrain herself any longer, she cried out, while beating her head with the palms of her hands: "Alas, my sweet lady, where are you?"

On hearing her, the lady called out as loudly as she could: "Oh, my sister, I'm up here. Don't cry. Just bring me my clothes, and do it quickly."

Greatly relieved to hear her mistress's voice, the maid started climbing up the ladder, which the peasant had just about finished repairing, and with his help she managed to reach the platform. When she saw her mistress lying naked on the floor, utterly exhausted and defeated, looking less like a human being than a half-burned log, she dug her nails into her face and wept over her as if she were dead.

The lady begged her to be quiet, for God's sake, and to help her get dressed. Then, when she learned from the maid that no one else knew where she had been except the peasant and those who had brought her clothes, she felt somewhat relieved and begged them for God's sake never to say a word about this to anyone. Since the lady could not walk on her own, after much discussion the farmhand lifted her onto his shoulders and carried her safely down and out of the tower. The wretched maid, who had stayed behind, was less careful as she climbed down the ladder, with the result that her foot slipped and she fell to the ground, breaking her thigh.

Because of the pain she was experiencing, the maid began roaring like a lion, so that the farmhand, after having set the lady down on a plot of grass, went back to see what was wrong with her. Upon discovering that she had broken her thigh, he also brought her to the same spot and placed her on the grass beside her mistress. When the lady saw that, on top of all her other misfortunes, the person on whose assistance she most depended had broken her thigh, she felt unspeakably sad and began weeping once again so bitterly that not only was the swineherd incapable of consoling her, but he actually started crying himself.

Since the sun was already beginning to set, however, and the disconsolate lady did not want to be caught out there when night fell, she prevailed upon the farmhand to go back to his house. There he found his wife and two of his brothers who returned to the tower with him, carrying a plank on which they placed the maid and brought her home. The farmhand himself, having comforted the lady with words of sympathy and given her fresh water to drink, lifted her onto his shoulders and carried her to his wife's room, who gave her some sops of bread to

eat, undressed her, and put her to bed. After that, they made arrangements for the lady and her maid to be taken to Florence that very night.
And so they were.

Once she was back in the city, the lady, who had a plentiful supply
of tricks,[7] made up a yarn about herself and her maid that had nothing to do with what had actually happened, and managed to persuade
her brothers and sisters and everyone else that it was all the result of
diabolical spells. The doctors lost no time in curing her of her raging
fever and other ills, but since she shed her skin more than once in the
process, leaving it stuck to the sheets, she suffered the greatest anguish
and torment imaginable. They also took care of the maid with her
broken thigh. As a result of her experience, the lady forgot all about
her lover, and from then on she wisely refrained both from playing any
more tricks and from falling in love with anyone. As for the scholar,
once he found out that the maid had broken her thigh, he decided that
his revenge was complete, and happy to leave it at that, he never said
another word about it.

This, then, is what happened to the foolish young woman with all of
her tricks, for she thought she could trifle with a scholar the way she
could with anyone else, not realizing that scholars—not all of them, I
say, but the vast majority—know where the Devil keeps his tail. Consequently, ladies, take care not to play such tricks yourselves, especially
when you are dealing with scholars.

Day 8, Story 8

Two men are close friends, and when one of them sleeps with the other's wife, and he finds out about it, he arranges with his wife to have his friend locked up in a chest on top of which he then makes love with his friend's wife while he is inside.[1]

Grievous and painful though Elena's misfortunes were for the ladies to hear, they felt only a moderate degree of compassion as the story unfolded because they thought she had partly deserved them, although they did judge the scholar to be inflexible and uncompromisingly fierce, if not downright cruel. But now that Pampinea had reached the end of her story, the Queen called upon Fiammetta, who, eager to obey, proceeded to say:

Charming ladies, since it seems to me that you have been distressed by the offended scholar's severity, I think it would be appropriate to soothe your bitter feelings with something more cheerful, and I therefore intend to tell you a brief story about a young man who had a milder response to an injury he had received and devised a less extreme way to avenge himself. Through this you can see that when someone wishes to get revenge for some wrong he has suffered, it ought to be sufficient for him to behave like the ass and to give just as good as he gets, without seeking to inflict harm that exceeds any appropriate measure of vengeance.[2]

You should know, then, that in Siena, as I have been given to understand, there once lived two fairly prosperous young men from respectable, though common, families, one of whom was named Spinelloccio Tavena, and the other, Zeppa di Mino.[3] Next-door neighbors in the Camollia quarter, they spent a great deal of time in one another's company, and to all appearances, they loved one another as if they had been brothers, or even more.

Both were married to very beautiful women, and since Spinelloccio used to spend a great deal of time at Zeppa's house, whether his friend was there or not, he happened to grow so close to Zeppa's wife that he eventually started sleeping with her. He continued to do so for some time before anyone discovered it, but in the long run, one morning when Zeppa was at home and his wife was unaware that he was in the house, Spinelloccio came to call on him. On being told by Zeppa's wife that her husband was not around, Spinelloccio went upstairs where he found her in the main room, and seeing that there was no one else about, he took her in his arms and began kissing her, to which she responded in kind.

Zeppa saw the whole thing, but did not make a sound and remained hidden so that he could see how the game was going to end, and in short order, he saw his wife and Spinelloccio, still embracing one another, go into the bedroom and lock themselves inside. Although he was terribly upset, he realized that neither by creating an uproar, nor by intervening in any other way, was he going to diminish the injury he had received, but, on the contrary, he would only increase his shame. And so, he applied his mind to devising some sort of revenge he might pursue that would satisfy his own feelings while keeping the affair from becoming public knowledge. Finally, having pondered the matter a long while, he thought he had discovered a way to do it.

Zeppa remained in hiding the entire time Spinelloccio stayed there with his wife, but as soon as his friend had left, he went into the bedroom, where he found she had not yet finished the process of rearranging the veils she wore on her head, which had fallen off when Spinelloccio was playing around with her.

"Wife," he asked, "what're you doing?"

"Don't you see?" she replied.

"Yes, indeed I do," he said, "and I've seen some other things I would have preferred not to!" He then had words with her about what she had done, and after making up a whole lot of stories as excuses, she confessed, in a terrible fright, that there was no decent way for her to deny the intimate relationship she had with Spinelloccio, and in tears, she began begging him to forgive her.

"Look here, wife," said Zeppa, "you've done wrong, and if you want me to pardon you, concentrate on doing exactly what I'm about to order you to do, which is this. I want you to tell Spinelloccio tomorrow around the hour of tierce that he should find some excuse to leave me so that he can come over here to see you. Then, while he's in the house, I'm going to return, and as soon as you hear me coming, get him to climb into this chest and lock him inside. After you've done that, I'll tell you what else you have to do. And there's no need for you to be afraid if you do this, because I promise you I'm not going to harm him in the least." In order to satisfy her husband, the lady agreed to do what he asked, and gave Spinelloccio the message.

The next day, when Zeppa and Spinelloccio were hanging out together, at the hour of tierce, Spinelloccio, who had promised the lady that he would go to see her then, announced: "I have to go to dinner with a friend this morning, and I don't want to keep him waiting. So, farewell for now."

"But it's not time to eat yet," said Zeppa.

"That doesn't matter," replied Spinelloccio. "I also have to speak with him about some business of mine, so I need to get there on the early side."

After leaving, Spinelloccio took a roundabout route and had soon joined Zeppa's wife in her house. But they had barely entered the bedroom when Zeppa returned, and the moment his wife heard him, she made a show of being very frightened, and having gotten Spinelloccio to take refuge in the chest her husband had been speaking about, she locked him inside and left the bedroom.

"Wife, is it dinnertime?" asked Zeppa, when he arrived upstairs.

"Yes," she said, "it is."

"Spinelloccio has gone to eat with a friend of his this morning," said Zeppa, "and he's left his wife all by herself. Go to the window and call her. Tell her she should come over and eat with us."

Fearful of what might happen to her, his wife was quite ready to obey her husband and carried out all his instructions. It took a great deal of coaxing, but after learning that her husband would not be dining at home, Spinelloccio's wife finally came and joined them. When she arrived, Zeppa gave her an extremely warm welcome, and taking her familiarly by the hand, he ordered his wife, in a whisper, to go into the kitchen. He then led his guest into the bedroom, and the moment they were inside, he turned around and locked the door. When Spinelloccio's wife saw him do this, she said: "Oh no, Zeppa, what's the meaning of this? Is this the reason you had for inviting me to come here? Is this the kind of love you have for Spinelloccio and your loyalty to him as your friend?"

Holding her tight, Zeppa sidled over toward the chest where her husband was locked up inside. "My lady," he said, "before you start complaining, listen to what I have to tell you. I've loved Spinelloccio like a brother, and I still do, but yesterday, without his knowing it, I discovered that the trust I'd placed in him had come to this, that he's been sleeping with my wife the same way he does with you. Now, since I love him, I don't want to take any more revenge on him than the offense merits, and seeing as how he's had my wife, I intend to have you. And if you're not cooperative, make no mistake about it, I'm going to catch him in the act, and since I have no intention of letting this affront pass unpunished, I'll serve him such a turn that you and he will rue it for the rest of your lives."

Having listened to his story and been given repeated reassurances to confirm it, the lady was persuaded he was telling the truth. "My dear Zeppa," she said, "if I'm the one who must bear this revenge, then I'm all right with that, but only so long as you see to it that I'm still on good terms with your wife after what we're about to do, just as I myself intend to remain on good terms with her in spite of what she's done to me."

"You may rest assured, I'll take care of it," replied Zeppa, "and what's more, I'll give you as beautiful and costly a jewel as any other one you own." And that said, he embraced her and began kissing her, and having laid her out on the chest in which her husband was locked up, he enjoyed himself with her on top of it to his heart's content—and she did the same with him.

Inside the chest, Spinelloccio, who had heard every word that Zeppa had said as well as his wife's reply, and had then felt the jig they were dancing over his head, was filled with such anguish for so long that he thought he was going to die, and if it had not been that he was afraid of Zeppa, he would have given his wife a terrible tongue-lashing, locked up though he was.[4] But then he recalled that he was the one who had given the first offense, that Zeppa was in the right to have done what he had done, and that he had not only displayed humanity in dealing with him, but had treated him like a friend. Consequently, he resolved that if Zeppa permitted it, he would be a better friend to him than ever.

Having had as much fun with the lady as he wanted, Zeppa got down off the chest, and when she asked him for the jewel he had promised, he opened the bedroom door and summoned his wife, whose only words were, "Lady, you've given me tit for tat." And as she said this, she laughed.

"Open this chest," commanded Zeppa, and when his wife did so, he showed the lady her Spinelloccio inside.

It would be hard to say which of the two was the more ashamed, Spinelloccio, on seeing Zeppa there and realizing that his friend knew what he had done, or Spinelloccio's wife, on seeing her husband and realizing that he had heard and felt what she had been doing to him right over his head.

"Look, here's the jewel I have to give you," said Zeppa.

Spinelloccio then climbed up out of the chest, and without manufacturing a lot of stories, he said: "Zeppa, now that we're quits, it's a good idea for us to remain friends the way we used to be, as you were saying to my wife just a moment ago, and since we've always held everything in common before this except for our wives, let's share them, too."

Zeppa agreed to his proposal, after which the four of them all dined together in perfect amity, and from that day forth, each of the ladies had two husbands, and each of the husbands, two wives, nor did this arrangement ever give rise to any dispute or conflict among them.

Day 8, Story 9

Eager to be made a member of a company of privateers, Master Simone, a physician, is persuaded by Bruno and Buffalmacco to go one night to a certain spot, where he is thrown into a ditch by Buffalmacco and left to wallow in filth.[1]

hen the ladies had chatted awhile about the communal sharing of wives practiced by the two Sienese men, the Queen, not wishing to wrong Dioneo and finding that she was the only one left to speak, began as follows:

Dear ladies, Spinelloccio richly deserved the prank that Zeppa played on him, and that is why, as Pampinea was trying to show just a little while ago, I believe we should not judge people too harshly who play tricks on others if the victim is asking for it or is getting his just deserts. Spinelloccio got what he deserved, and so, now I intend to tell you about someone who went around looking for it and whose deceivers, in my opinion, are consequently to be praised rather than blamed. The man in question was a physician who came to Florence from Bologna, covered in vair, like the stupid sheep he was, from head to toe.*

Every day we see our fellow citizens returning from Bologna, this one a judge, that one a physician, and yet another a notary, all sporting long, flowing robes of scarlet and vair as well as a host of other things designed to make a grand impression—and we likewise see every day just how much all this really amounts to in practice. A certain Master Simone da Villa was one of this sort, for his patrimony was far greater than his learning. He came here, not all that many years ago,

*The ceremonial caps and gowns of physicians and lawyers in the Middle Ages were normally lined with vair, the fur of a gray and white squirrel. During this period, the University of Bologna was celebrated for its medical school throughout Europe.

dressed in a scarlet robe with a large hood, proclaimed himself a doctor of medicine, and rented a house in the street we now call Via del
Cocomero.[2] Having just recently arrived, as I said, this Master Simone
made it a practice, among his many other remarkable habits, of asking whomever he was with to identify all the people he saw passing in
the street, and he would observe and remember everything they did
as though he were going to make up the medications he had to give his
patients on that basis.

Among those he eyed most intently were his two neighbors Bruno
and Buffalmacco, the two painters about whom we have already told
two stories today. The pair of them were constantly in one another's
company, and since they seemed to him to be the most carefree people in the world and to lead happier lives than anyone else, as indeed
they did, he made lots of inquiries about their situation and was told
by everyone that they were just a couple of poor painters. Unable to
comprehend how they could possibly lead such merry lives if they did
not have much money, he concluded, having heard how clever they
were, that they had to be extracting enormous profits from some source
people knew nothing about. He was therefore very eager to strike up a
friendship with one of them at least, if not with both, and finally managed to do so with Bruno.

It only took a few meetings with Master Simone for Bruno to conclude that he was an ass and to begin having a grand old time with
him thanks to his very eccentric behavior. The doctor likewise found
Bruno's company wonderfully entertaining, and after having invited
him to dinner on several occasions, from which he assumed they could
talk on familiar terms, Master Simone expressed his amazement at
how the two painters could lead such merry lives despite being so very
poor, and he asked Bruno to teach him how they did it.

Thinking that this was another one of the doctor's usual stupid,
senseless questions, Bruno started to laugh. But then he decided he
would reply to him as his asininity deserved.

"Master," he said, "I wouldn't tell many people how we manage it,
but as you're my friend and I know you won't reveal it to anyone else,
I won't keep it all to myself. Now it's true that the life I lead with my

buddy is just as happy and contented as you suppose. Actually, it's even better than that. Still, we don't get enough money from our work or from the property we own even to pay for the water we consume. Not that I want you to think we're a couple of robbers; no, we simply go about privateering, and from that, without harming anyone, we don't just obtain the necessities of life, but many of the extras that give us pleasure as well. And that's how, as you've noticed, we've been able to lead such merry lives."

The doctor took in everything Bruno said, and since he believed him without knowing what he was really talking about, he was filled with amazement and promptly conceived an intense, burning desire to discover what it meant to go privateering, swearing to Bruno that he would never, ever tell anyone else about it.

"Oh no, Master," said Bruno, "what are you asking me to do? The secret you want me to reveal is so serious that if anyone were to find out about it, I'd be ruined, driven right off the face of the earth. I could even wind up in the jaws of the Lucifer at San Gallo.[3] Still, the love I bear your qualitative melonosity of Legnaia and the faith I have in you are so great that I feel myself obliged to grant your every wish.[4] So, I'll reveal the secret to you, but on this condition, that you swear to me by the cross at Montesone to keep your promise and never tell anyone."

The doctor swore he would not.

"Know then, my dull-cified Master," said Bruno, "that not long ago there was a grand master of necromancy in this city named Michael Scot, so-called because he came from Scotland.[5] He was received with the greatest hospitality here by many gentlemen, of whom only a few remain alive today. When the time came for him to depart, he was moved by their urgent entreaties to leave behind two quite capable disciples, charging them to grant, without a moment's hesitation, every wish those very noble men might have who had given him such an honorable reception.

"The disciples freely assisted the gentlemen I've referred to in certain love affairs of theirs as well as in other trifling matters, and after a while, having taken a liking to the city and its people's ways, they decided to settle down here permanently. They managed to form good, close friendships with a number of people, showing no concern for whether they were gentlemen or commoners, rich or poor, provided only that they all shared the same interests. And in order to please the friends they had made, they formed a company of some twenty-five men who were to meet at least twice a month in whatever place the pair selected. When they are all assembled, each man tells them what he wants, and the two of them immediately see about granting his wish that very night.

"Since Buffalmacco and I are on the most friendly and intimate terms with the pair, they made us members of their company, and we've belonged to it ever since. And let me tell you that whenever we get together, it's a wonderful thing to see the hangings all around the hall where we eat, the tables set for a king, and the noble array of handsome servants, both men and women, who are at the beck and call of everyone in the company, not to mention the bowls and pitchers, the flasks and cups, and the rest of the vessels we use for eating and drinking, all of them made of gold and silver. Finally, no less marvelous, there is the abundance and variety of the dishes that they set before us in their proper order, each one prepared according our own individual preferences. I couldn't begin to describe the range and variety of the sweet sounds coming from countless instruments and the melodious songs that we hear there, nor could I tell you how many wax candles are burned at those suppers, or the number of sweets consumed, or how costly the wines are that we drink. And I wouldn't want you to imagine, my dear sweet pumpkin, that we show up there in the same clothes you see us wearing right now. The poorest person at the dinner would look like an emperor to you, for we are decked out, each and every one of us, in expensive robes and other finery.

"But over and above all these delights, there are the beautiful women who are brought in from all over the world the moment anyone asks for them. Not only would you see the Lady of the Barbanichi, the Queen of the Basques, and the Consort of the Sultan, but also the Empress of Osbech, the Chitterchatterer of Norwega, the Semistanding of Gluttonia, and the Scapulathedral of Narsia. But why do I go on enumerating them to you? All the queens of the earth are there, I'm telling you, down to the Skinkimurra of Prester John.[6] Now, there's a sight for you! And once they've had something to drink and eaten some of the sweets, they do a dance or two, and then each of them goes off to her bedroom with the guy who wanted her brought to him there.

"And let me tell you, those rooms are so beautiful you'd think you were in Paradise, and they're as fragrant as the spice jars in your shop when you're grinding the cumin.[7] When we all lie down to rest, we do it in beds that would seem to you more beautiful than the one the Doge has in Venice. And I'll leave it to your imagination just how those lady weavers push your treadles and tug on your shuttle, pulling it toward them in order to make your fabric nice and tight![8]

"But in my opinion, among the people who have the best time there you've got to count Buffalmacco and me, because he usually has them bring him the Queen of France, and I send for the Queen of England. They're two of the most beautiful women in the world, and we know how to handle them so they don't have eyes for anyone else but us. So, now you can decide for yourself whether we have good reason to be happier than other men as we go about our lives, considering that we have the love of two queens like that—not to mention the fact that whenever we want a thousand florins or two from them, it's because we haven't got them.

"And that's what, in our way of speaking, we call going about privateering. Just as pirates take everybody's goods, so do we, except that there's this much of a difference between us: they never give anything back, whereas we return what we've taken once we're finished with it. Now that you know what we mean, my good and simple Master, when we say we go about privateering, you can surely see for yourself how closely you've got to guard this secret, so there's no need for me to say anything more on that subject or ask you not to talk about it, either."

The doctor, whose knowledge of medicine most likely did not extend beyond treating babies for thrush infections, trusted Bruno's words as if they were truth itself, and was enflamed with an intense longing to be made a member of their company as though that were the most desirable thing in the world. Accordingly, while he told Bruno that he was no longer surprised that the two of them went about as happy as could be, it was only with the greatest difficulty that he could restrain himself from asking to be made a member of the company right then and there, rather than waiting until such time as he had shown Bruno more of his hospitality, after which he could plead his case with greater confidence that he would succeed. Having thus held himself in check, he began assiduously cultivating Bruno's friendship, inviting him over to eat both mornings and evenings, and displaying boundless affection toward him. In fact, they spent so much time with one another and got together so often that the doctor seemed incapable of living without him, indeed, that he could not even imagine doing so.

Bruno felt he was doing pretty well, and so, in order not to seem ungrateful for the hospitality the doctor had shown him, he painted the figure of Lent for him in his dining room, an *Agnus Dei* at the entrance to his bedroom, and a urine flask over the door to the street so that those people who needed a consultation could distinguish his house from the others. Moreover, in a small loggia of his, Bruno painted the battle of the cats and the mice, which seemed to the doctor beautiful beyond description.[9]

Bruno would sometimes say to him, when the two had not had supper together the previous evening: "Last night I was with the company, and since I'd gotten a little tired of the Queen of England, I had them send me the Gumedra of the Great Khan of Altarisi."[10]

"Gumedra," said the doctor, "what does that mean? I don't understand these names."

"I'm not surprised, my dear Master," said Bruno, "because I've been told that Hoggiphates and Avadinner don't say anything about it."[11]

"You mean Hippocrates and Avicenna," replied the doctor.

"By gosh," said Bruno, "I just don't know, for I'm as bad at your names as you are at mine. However, 'gumedra' in the language of the Great Khan means the same thing as 'empress' in ours. Oh, you'd really find her one good-looking gal! She'd make you forget all about your medicines and your enemas and your poultices, let me tell you."

Bruno went on talking to him like this from time to time in order to get him all fired up, until one evening, when he was painting the battle of the cats and the mice, with Simone holding up a light for him to see by, Messer Doctor decided that, thanks to all his hospitality, he had Bruno sufficiently in his debt, and could open up and freely reveal his feelings. Since the two of them were all alone, he said: "Bruno, God knows there's no one alive today for whom I'd do all the things I'd be willing to do for you. If you asked me to go from here to Peretola, I don't think it would take much to get me to do it.[12] So, don't be surprised if I speak to you as a friend and ask you a favor in strict confidence. As you know, not so long ago you spoke to me about the activities of that merry company of yours, and it's filled me with a desire to become a member that's stronger than anything I've ever felt in my life. I have good reason for wanting to join, as you'll see for yourself if I should ever happen to get in, for I assure you here and now that if I don't have them bring me the prettiest serving girl you've seen in a long, long time, you can make me the butt of all your jokes from then on. I only caught sight of her just last year at Cacavincigli, but I fell passionately in love with her, and I swear by Christ's body that I offered her ten Bolognese groats if she'd consent to give herself to me, but she didn't want to.[13]

"And so, I beg you from the bottom of my heart to tell me what I have to do in order to join the company, and also, to use whatever influence you have to help me get in, for I can assure you that you'll never have a better, more loyal member, nor one who'll bring you more credit. First of all, you can see how handsome a guy I am, what a fine pair of legs I've got under me, and that this face of mine is just like a rose. Besides, I'm a doctor of medicine, and I doubt you have any of them in your company. On top of that, I know lots of good stories as well as some lovely little songs. In fact, let me give you one of them right now"—and all of a sudden he started singing.

Bruno had such a tremendous urge to laugh that he could hardly contain himself, although he nevertheless managed to do so. Then, when the song was done, the Master asked him: "What do you think of it?"

"Your barbartistic caterwarbling would sure put all the reed whistles to shame," replied Bruno.[14]

"You would never have believed it," said the doctor, "if you hadn't heard me yourself, would you?"

"You're certainly right about that," said Bruno.

"I know a whole lot of other ones," said the doctor, "but let's let that be that for now. What you see here in me is what you get. My father was a nobleman, although he lived in the country, and on my mother's side I was born into a family from Vallecchio.[15] Furthermore, as you may have observed yourself, I've got the finest books and the most beautiful wardrobe of any doctor in Florence. I swear to God, I have a robe that cost me, all told, about a hundred *lire* in small change more than ten years ago! And that's why I'm begging you from the bottom of my heart to have them make me a member, and I swear to God that if you do get me in, I'll never take a penny from you for my services, no matter how sick you are."

Having listened to him run on, Bruno was as convinced as ever that the man was a pea brain, and said to him: "Master, give me a little more light over here, and if you'll just be patient until I've finished the tails of these mice, I'll give you your answer then."

When the tails were done, Bruno pretended he was very worried about the doctor's request. "I know all about the great things you'd do for me, Master," he said, "but nevertheless, what you're asking of me, although it may seem insignificant to a great mind like yours, is still a very big deal as far as I'm concerned. Now, even if I were in a position to grant it, I don't know of another person in the world for whom I'd do it except for you, not only because I love you as a good friend should, but also because your words are seasoned with so much wisdom that they would draw pious old ladies right out of their boots, let alone make me change my mind.[16] In fact, the more time I spend with you, the wiser you seem to me. And let me tell you this as well: even if I had no other reason to love you, I am bound to do so because you've fallen for such a beautiful creature as the one you described.

"I must point out, however, that I don't have as much influence in these matters as you think, which is why I can't do what's necessary for you. But if you'll promise me, on your solemn and tainted word,[17] to keep it a secret, I'll explain how you can take care of it yourself, and since you have all those fine books and the other things you were telling me about earlier, I feel certain you'll succeed."

"You can speak freely," said the doctor. "If you knew me better, then you'd know that I'm really good at keeping secrets. When Messer Guasparuolo da Saliceto was serving as a judge for the *podestà* of Forlimpopoli, there were very few things he did not tell me, because he found me such a good secretary.[18] And if you want proof, well, I was the first man he told that he was about to marry Bergamina. Now, what do you think of that?"

"Well, that settles it," said Bruno. "If a man like that confided in you, I can certainly do the same. Here's how you should go about it. In our company we always have a captain as well as two counselors who are replaced every six months, and we know for certain that on the first of next month, Buffalmacco is to be captain, and I'll be one of the counselors. Now, whoever becomes captain has a lot of influence over who gets to be admitted as a member, so, in my opinion, you should do everything you can to strike up a friendship with Buffalmacco and start entertaining him on a lavish scale. He's the kind of man who'll take a real liking to you from the moment he sees how intelligent you are, and once you've managed to advance your friendship with him by means of your wit as well as all those fine things you own, you can ask him to do it, and he won't know how to tell you no. I've already spoken to him about you, and he feels as well disposed toward you as can be, so, as soon as you've accomplished what I've told you to do, you can leave all the rest to the two of us."

"I'm really, really pleased with your plan," said the doctor, "for if he's a man who takes pleasure in the company of the wise, he has only to talk with me for a while, and I promise you he'll never want to let me out of his sight. I've got enough intelligence to supply an entire city, and I'd still remain as wise as they come."

Having arranged everything with the doctor, Bruno recounted the whole story in all its particulars to Buffalmacco, who was so eager to provide this Master Sappyhead with what he was looking for that every moment passing seemed like a thousand years to him.[19]

The doctor, who wanted more than anything to go privateering, did not rest until he had struck up a friendship with Buffalmacco, which, of course, he had no difficulty doing. He then began treating him, both morning and night, to the finest meals in the world, and always invited Bruno to join them as well. For their part, knowing that Simone had an excellent wine cellar and many fat capons, not to mention a host of other good things, Bruno and Buffalmacco were happy to indulge themselves and live like lords, never needing much of an invitation to spend time in his company, although they constantly assured him that they would not have done such a thing for anyone else.

But eventually, when the time seemed right to the doctor, he made the same request to Buffalmacco that he had made before to Bruno. Upon hearing it, Buffalmacco pretended to be absolutely furious and blew up at Bruno.

"I swear by the High God of Passignano," he said, "I can barely keep myself from giving you such a wallop on your head that it'd knock your nose down to your heels, you traitor, because you're the only one who could've revealed these things to the Master."[20]

Simone, however, did his utmost to excuse Bruno, saying on his oath that he had learned everything from another source, and after many of those wise words of his, he finally managed to mollify Buffalmacco, who then turned to him and said: "My dear Master, it's pretty clear that you've been in Bologna and that you've been keeping your mouth shut since you came back to this town. And let me tell you something else: you didn't learn your ABCs by writing them on an apple, the way many fools try to do it, but instead, you used that great big, long melon of yours, and in fact, unless I'm badly deceived, you were baptized on a Sunday.* Bruno told me you studied medicine up there, but in my opinion you were really studying how to attract men to you, for what with your wisdom and your fine talk you do that better than any other man I've ever seen."

Cutting him off in midsentence, the doctor turned to Bruno and said: "What a thing it is to talk with wise men and to pass the time

---

*Boys were sometimes taught the alphabet by having letters carved on apples. The reference to Simone's "great big, long melon" is, of course, a satirical remark about his stupidity, his empty "melon" or "pumpkin" of a head. The remark that he was baptized on a Sunday has the same function, since salt was not available for sale on that day, meaning that there was no salt, no "wit," available for Simone on the day of his christening.

in their company! Who would've been able to read my mind down to the last little thought as promptly as this worthy man just did? You were not nearly so quick to perceive my true value as he was. But you might at least tell him what I said to you when you informed me that he takes pleasure in the company of the wise. Do you think I've been as good as my word?"

"Better," replied Bruno.

The Master then said to Buffalmacco: "You would have had even more to say, if you had seen me in Bologna, for there was no one, high or low, professor or student, who didn't think the world of me, because I could keep them entertained with my wit and wisdom. And I'll tell you something else: I never uttered a word there without making them all laugh, that's how much they enjoyed my company. As a result, when it was time for me to leave, they complained bitterly, and every last one of them begged me to stay, until it reached the point that to keep me there, they offered to let me alone do all the lecturing in the faculty of medicine. But I didn't want to, because I'd already decided to come here where I've got some very substantial estates that have been in my family forever. And that's just what I did."

"Now what do you think?" said Bruno to Buffalmacco. "I told you what he was like, but you wouldn't believe me. I swear on the Holy Gospel, there's not a doctor in these parts who knows his way around ass's urine in comparison to him. In fact, you wouldn't find his equal between here and the gates of Paris. Now just see if you can prevent yourself from doing whatever he wants!"

"Bruno's telling the truth," said the doctor, "but people don't give me the recognition I deserve around here. You all are a bunch of dummies. I just wish you could see me in my natural element, among my fellow doctors."

"Truly, Master," replied Buffalmacco, "you know far more than I would have ever imagined. Therefore, speaking frankastically—to use here the kind of language one should employ with wise men like yourself—let me tell you that without fail, I'll arrange for you to become a member of our company."[21]

After receiving this promise, the doctor lavished even more

hospitality on the pair, who enjoyed themselves at his expense, persuading him to believe the most nonsensical things in the world, and promising that he would have as his mistress the Contessa di Crappa, who was the most beautiful thing to be found in the whole ass-sembly of the human race.[22]

When the doctor asked who this Countess was, Buffalmacco replied: "O my seed-filled cucumber, why she's so great a lady that there are few houses in the world that do not, at least to some extent, come within her jurisdiction. Indeed, even the Franciscans, to say nothing of all the others, pay her tribute to the sound of the kettledrum. And let me assure you that whenever she goes about, you'll certainly have some scents of her presence, albeit most of the time she keeps herself shut up tight inside. Although her usual residence is in Laterina, nevertheless, not so very long ago she passed right by the entrance to your house when she was making her way one night to the Arno to wash her feet and get a whiff of fresh air.[23] You can frequently see her servants making their rounds, carrying her staff and pail as the sign of her authority, and everywhere you look, you'll find her noble retainers, such as Sir Dingleberry, Lord Turd, Viscount Broomhandle, Baron Squirts, and others with whom you are intimately acquainted, even if you may not recall them at the present moment.[24] So, you can forget all about that woman from Cacavincigli, for unless we're deceiving ourselves, we'll soon have you in the sweet embraces of that very great lady."

The doctor, who had been born and bred in Bologna, did not understand the meaning of their words, and told them that the lady would suit him to a tee. Nor did he have to wait very long after hearing their tall tales before the two painters brought him the news that he had been accepted into the company. On the day before the group's next evening get-together, Simone invited the pair to dinner, and when they were finished, asked them how he was supposed to get to the meeting.

"Look, Master," said Buffalmacco, "for reasons you are now about to hear, you've got to be very brave, because if you aren't, you might run into trouble, and you could make things very difficult for us as well. Tonight, around bedtime, you must find a way to get up onto one of those raised tombs they've recently erected outside of Santa Maria

Novella, and be sure to wear one of your finest robes so that your first appearance before the company will be an honorable one, and also because the Countess is proposing, in light of the fact that you're a gentleman, to make you a Knight of the Bath at her own expense—or so we've been told, for we weren't actually there at the time.[25] And you're to wait at the tombs until we send someone to get you.

"Now, so you'll know exactly what to expect, let me tell you that a black beast with horns on its head is going to come for you, and though it isn't particularly large, it'll try to scare you by going up and down before you in the piazza, leaping high into the air and making loud hissing noises. When it sees you aren't afraid, however, it'll quiet down and come over to you. As soon as it's close enough, don't be frightened or call on God and the Saints, but get down from the tomb and climb right up onto its back. After you've firmly seated yourself there, fold your arms across your chest the way courtiers do, and don't touch the beast again with your hands. Soon, it will set off at a slow pace and bring you right to us. But let me tell you, if you invoke God or the Saints, or show any sign of fear before you've arrived, it might throw you off or knock you into something, and then you'd be in a big stinking mess. So, unless you're sure you'll be brave, don't come, because you'd just make trouble for us and not do yourself the least bit of good."

"You still don't know me," replied the doctor. "Perhaps you're worried about me because of the gloves and the long robes I wear, but if you knew what I used to do in Bologna when I went around at night with my buddies on the lookout for women, you'd be amazed. I swear to God, I remember a night when there was one of them, a skinny gal, and what's worse, no taller than my fist, who didn't want to come with us. So, after giving her a few good punches to start with, I picked her up and carried her, I think, about as far as a crossbow shot, and finally made her agree to join us. Then, there was another time when I was all alone, except for one of my servants, and shortly after the "Ave Maria," I was passing by the Franciscans' cemetery, where they had just buried a woman that very day, and I wasn't the least bit afraid. So, you don't have to worry on that score: I've got courage and vigor to spare. As for my making an honorable appearance before you all, let me tell you, I'll

put on the scarlet robe I wore when I graduated, and you'll soon see
how happy the whole company will be the moment they catch sight of
me and how they'll be making me their captain before too long. Just
wait till I get there, and you'll see how things will go. After all, without
ever having laid eyes on me, the Countess is already so in love with me
that she wants to make me a Knight of the Bath. But perhaps you think
knighthood won't suit me and that I won't know what to do with it
once I've got it. Well, just leave it to me!"

"That's all very well said," replied Buffalmacco. "Only make sure
you don't play a trick on us, either by not showing up or by not being
around there when we send for you. I'm saying this because it's cold
outside, and that's something you medical men are very sensitive to."

"God forbid!" said the doctor. "I'm not one of those chilly guys, so I
don't really mind it. In fact, whenever I get up at night to relieve myself,
as we men do sometimes, I almost never put anything on over my doublet except a fur gown. So rest assured, I'll be there."

The two men left, and as night began to fall, Master Simone found
some excuse or other to make to his wife at home, and having secretly
taken his splendid robe with him, he put it on when the time seemed
right and made his way to one of the tombs. After climbing up on top,
he sat down, all huddled together on the marble surface because of the
bitter cold, and began waiting for the beast to show up.

Buffalmacco, who was tall and sturdily built, managed to get one
of those masks that they used to wear in certain festivals we no longer
celebrate nowadays, and having put on a black fur gown turned inside
out, he got himself up to look exactly like a bear, except that his mask
had the face of a devil and horns on top.[26] Thus disguised, off he went
to the new piazza at Santa Maria Novella, with Bruno following right
behind to see what was going to happen. As soon as Buffalmacco perceived that Messer Doctor was there, he began leaping madly up and
down all around the piazza, hissing and howling and screeching like
a man possessed.

When the Master, who was more fearful than a woman, saw and
heard all this, every hair on his body stood on end, and he began shaking all over. For a moment he wished he had stayed at home, but now

that he had come so far, he forced himself to buck up his courage, so great was his desire to see all the marvels that the two painters had told him about.

After raging around for a while in the manner just described, Buffalmacco pretended to calm down and moved toward the tomb on which the doctor was sitting, where he finally came to a stop. Master Simone was shaking all over from fear and could not make up his mind whether to climb up onto the beast or to stay put. Finally, since he was afraid that it would hurt him if he did not get on its back, this second fear drove out the first, and having slid down from the tomb, he mounted the creature, saying "God help me!" under his breath as he did so. Once he was securely seated there, still trembling all over, he folded his arms across his chest in a courtly fashion, just as he had been told to do.

Heading off in the direction of Santa Maria della Scala, Buffalmacco slowly crawled along on all fours until he had carried Master Simone almost as far as the nunnery at Ripoli.[27] In those days there were ditches in that quarter into which the farmhands would pour their offerings to the Contessa di Crappa in order to enrich their fields. When Buffalmacco reached the spot, he walked right up to the edge of one of them, and choosing his moment, he put his hand under one of the doctor's feet, used it to push him up off his back, and hurled him headfirst into the ditch. Then he began to snort ferociously, leaping about like a man possessed, as he made his way back past Santa Maria della Scala toward the meadow of Ognissanti. There he met up with Bruno, who had fled the scene because he could not contain his laughter, and after slapping one another on the back in glee, the two of them went and watched from a distance to see what the filthbespattered doctor was going to do.

Finding himself in such a loathsome place, Messer Doctor struggled to his feet and tried to climb out, but he kept falling back down in one place after another until, finally, he managed to extricate himself from it. Grieving and miserable, he stood there covered in filth from head to foot, having swallowed several drams of the stuff and left his hood behind in the ditch. He proceeded to clean himself off with his hands as best he could, and then, not knowing what else to do, he made his

way back home where he knocked on the door again and again until
he was let in.

No sooner had he entered the house, stinking all over, and had
the door shut behind him, than Bruno and Buffalmacco showed up
to hear what kind of welcome the Master would get from his wife.
As they stood there listening, they heard her giving him the worst
tongue-lashing any wretch ever received. "Well, it serves you right!"
she said. "Went to see some other woman and wanted to make a big
impression with your scarlet robe, did you? So, I'm not enough for you?
Brother, I could satisfy an entire parish, let alone you. Well, I wish
they'd drowned you instead of just dumping you where you deserved
to be put! Just look at the honorable physician here who has a wife of
his own, but goes around at night chasing after other people's women."
To these words she added many others, while the doctor was washing
himself from head to foot, and she did not stop tormenting him until
well into the middle of the night.

The next morning, Bruno and Buffalmacco painted bruises all over
the parts of their bodies that were covered by their clothes to make it
look as if they had been given a beating, after which they made their
way to the doctor's house where they found him already up and about.
From the moment they set foot inside, they were greeted by a foul
stench coming from everything, because there had not been enough
time to clean it all up and get rid of the smell.

When the doctor was told that they had come to see him, he went
to greet them, bidding them a very good morning. By way of response,
the two of them glared at him in anger, as they had planned to do. "We
can't say the same to you," they replied. "On the contrary, we pray to
God to give you years and years of misery and that you end up with
your throat cut, because you're the most disloyal, vilest traitor alive.
Although we did everything we could to make sure you were honored
and entertained, it's no thanks to you that we barely escaped being
killed like a couple of dogs. As a result of your treachery, we were
punched so many times last night that you could have driven an ass
from here to Rome with fewer blows, not to mention the fact that we
were in danger of being kicked out of the company that we'd arranged

for you to join. And if you don't believe us, take a look at our bodies and see what shape they're in." At this point they bared their chests in the dim light long enough for him to see all the bruises they had painted there, after which they hastily covered them up again.

The doctor attempted to apologize and tell them about his misfortunes and about how he had been dumped into a ditch, but Buffalmacco broke in with: "I wish he'd thrown you off the bridge into the Arno. Why did you call on God and the Saints? Didn't we warn you beforehand about that?"

"I swear to God," replied the doctor, "I did no such thing."

"What?" said Buffalmacco. "You weren't thinking about them? Well, here's something you should really remember: the man we sent for you told us you were shaking like a reed and had no idea where you were. Anyway, you've really put one over on us, but we're never going to let anyone ever do that to us again. And as for you, from now on we're going to give you precisely the kind of honorable treatment you deserve."

The doctor pleaded with them to pardon him and did his best to mollify them, using all the eloquence at his command. He begged them for God's sake not to shame him, and out of fear that they would make him into a public laughingstock, from then on he treated them to dinners and pampered them in even more lavish ways than he had ever done in the past.

So now you have heard how wisdom is learned by those who did not acquire very much of it in Bologna.

Day 8, Story 10

A Sicilian woman masterfully relieves a merchant of the goods he has brought to Palermo, but when he later returns, pretending he has much more merchandise than before, he borrows money from her and leaves her with nothing but water and tow instead.[1]

There is no need to ask how much the ladies laughed over certain parts of the Queen's story; indeed, they laughed so much that there was no one whose eyes were not filled with tears a dozen times. But when the tale was over, Dioneo knew that it was his turn and said:

Gracious ladies, it is clear that the more cunning someone is, the more pleasure we take in those tricks by means of which that person is himself cleverly deceived. And therefore, although you have all recounted the most splendid stories, I propose to tell you one that should please you more than any of the others we have heard, for the woman who was tricked was a greater mistress in the art of deception than any of the dupes, whether men or women, you have told us about so far.

In all the maritime cities that have ports, it used to be the custom—and perhaps it still is today—for any merchant arriving there with his goods to unload them and have them all transported to a warehouse, which in many places is called the customshouse and is maintained either by the commune or by the local ruler.[2] There, once those in charge have been presented with a bill of lading describing the entire cargo and its value, they assign the merchant a storeroom where it is kept under lock and key. The men, who are called customs officers, then record all the goods belonging to the merchant in their register, after which they make him pay a duty on what he retrieves from the customshouse, whether he takes all or just a portion of his goods at a time. It is by using this register that brokers, more often than not, obtain information about the amount and value of the goods that are being stored there, together with the names of the merchants involved, with whom they later make arrangements to exchange, barter, sell, and otherwise dispose of the merchandise when a suitable opportunity presents itself.

Among the many places where this system obtained was Palermo, in Sicily, which used to have, as it still does today, a large number of women who were physically quite beautiful, but hostile to virtue, and who, to anyone who does not know them, would be considered great ladies of impeccable honesty. Since their whole purpose is not merely to give men a shave, but to skin them alive, as soon as they spot a foreign merchant, they use the customshouse book to get information about what he had deposited there and how much he is worth. Then, employing their alluring, amorous charms and the sweetest of words, they do their best to draw their victims into their love traps, and in this way they have caught a large number from whom they have taken the better part of their merchandise out of their hands, and gotten many others to give them the entire lot, while there are some who have left behind not just their ship and its cargo, but even their flesh and bones, so deftly did the lady barber know how to wield her razor.[3]

To Palermo, then, not so very long ago, there came one of our fellow Florentines, a young man named Niccolò da Cignano, who was generally known as Salabaetto and who had been sent there by his principals with a large quantity of woolen cloth, probably worth some five hundred gold florins, that was left over from the fair at Salerno.[4] Having given his bill of lading to the customs officers, he put his goods in a storeroom, and not being in any great hurry to dispose of them, he took to going into the city from time to time, looking for ways to entertain himself.

Since Salabaetto was a good-looking man, with a fair complexion, blond hair, and an elegant figure, one of these lady barbers, who styled herself Madama Iancofiore, happened to hear something about his affairs and began giving him the eye.[5] He noticed what she was doing, and assuming her to be some great lady who was taken with his good looks, he thought that if he had an affair with her, he would have to be extremely cautious in managing it. Consequently, without uttering a word on the subject to anyone, he began walking back and forth in front of her house, where she soon spotted him, and after she had spent several days inflaming his passion by casting glances in his direction and making it seem as though she were languishing away for him, she secretly sent one of her maidservants to him. This woman, who was a past mistress in the arts of the procuress, entertained him for a long while with her chitchat before she told him, her eyes practically brimming over with tears, that her mistress was so taken with his good looks and his pleasant manners that she could find no rest, day or night, and that it was her most ardent desire that he should meet with her in secret at some bathhouse whenever it would please him to do so.[6] Finally, the woman took a ring from her purse and gave it to him on behalf of her mistress. When he heard her proposal, Salabaetto was the happiest man who had ever lived, and taking the ring, he drew it across his eyes, kissed it, and put it on his finger, telling the good woman that if Madama Iancofiore loved him, her feelings were indeed reciprocated, for he loved her more than life itself and was prepared to go anywhere to meet her at whatever hour she wished.

The messenger returned to her mistress bearing this response, and soon afterward Salabaetto was informed that he was to wait for her at a certain bathhouse after vespers on the following day. Without informing a single person of his plans, he went there swiftly at the appointed hour and found that the lady had already rented it for them. He did not have to wait long before two slave girls arrived loaded down with all manner of things, the first one carrying a lovely large cotton mattress on her head, and the other, an enormous basket filled with goods. Having placed the mattress on a bed in one of the rooms of the bathhouse, over it they spread a pair of extremely fine sheets, edged with silk, upon which they placed a coverlet of the whitest Cyprus linen and two exquisitely embroidered pillows. They then took their clothes off, got into the bath, and washed and scrubbed it all over to perfection.

Nor was it long before the lady herself appeared at the bath, accompanied by two more slave girls. At the first opportunity she came forward and gave Salabaetto an ecstatic welcome, hugging and kissing him repeatedly, after which she heaved several tremendous sighs and declared: "Except for you, there's no other man in the world who could have led me to do this, my darling Tuscan. You've set my soul on fire."

At her request the two of them took their clothes off and entered the bath naked, attended by two of the slave girls. Refusing to allow either one of them to lay a hand on him, she herself washed Salabaetto from head to foot with marvelous care, using soap scented with musk and cloves, after which she had the slave girls wash her and rub her down. When they were done, they fetched two finely woven sheets, brilliantly white, which emitted such an odor of roses that it seemed as if the entire room were filled with them. After wrapping Salabaetto in one of the sheets and the lady in the other, they lifted them up and carried them to the bed that had been prepared for them. When the couple had finished perspiring, the sheets wound about them were removed, and they found themselves lying naked on the ones covering the bed. Beautiful little vials of silver were then taken from the basket, some filled with rose water, others with the waters of orange blossoms and jasmine flowers, and yet others with the oil of oranges, which the slave girls sprinkled all over them. Finally, boxes of sweets and the most precious wines were produced, with which the couple refreshed themselves for a while.

Salabaetto was convinced he was in Paradise, and as he looked the lady up and down a thousand times—for she was certainly very beautiful—every hour seemed like a hundred years to him until the slave girls would go away and he might find himself in her arms. When, at the lady's command, they finally withdrew, leaving a little light burning in the room, she and Salabaetto embraced one another passionately. And there the two of them passed a very long hour together, to Salabaetto's immense delight, for he imagined she was being utterly consumed by her love for him.

When the lady decided it was time to get up, she summoned the slave girls, and after the couple was dressed and had taken more refreshments, eating a variety of sweets and drinking some wine, they washed their hands and faces in the sweet-scented waters. Finally, as they were about to depart, the lady said to Salabaetto: "If it would please you, I would consider it the greatest of favors if you came to have supper at my house this evening and spent the night with me."

Since Salabaetto was already captivated by her beauty and her calculated charm, firmly believing that she loved him as dearly as the very heart in her body, he replied: "Seeing as how your every pleasure, my lady, gives me the greatest delight, I will gladly do whatever you ask of me if it will make you happy, not only this evening, but at any other time you like."

Upon returning home, the lady saw to it that an array of her gowns as well as some of her other belongings were ornately displayed around her bedroom, and having given orders for a splendid supper to be prepared, she waited for Salabaetto's arrival. The moment it started to get dark, he showed up at her house where he was welcomed with open arms and ate a convivial supper, that was extremely well served. When they then entered her bedroom, he smelled the marvelous fragrance of aloeswood and Cyprian birds,* and looking around, observed the luxurious bed she had as well as the multitude of beautiful gowns that were hanging on pegs. All of these things, both taken together and considered individually, convinced him that she had to be a great lady with a substantial fortune, and although he had heard rumors quite to the contrary about the life she led, there was nothing in the world that would make him believe them. Furthermore, even if he did lend some credence to the suspicion that she had tricked others in the past, nothing in the world could persuade him that such a thing might happen to him.

There is no way to describe the pleasure Salabaetto experienced as he slept with her that night, the flames of his passion burning all the more fiercely with every passing hour. When morning finally arrived, the lady fastened a lovely, elegant little silver belt around his waist, to which a beautiful purse was attached. "My sweet Salabaetto," she said,

---

* Aloeswood is the fragrant resin of a tree from the Far East. Cyprian birds were actually incense made in the shape of birds, perhaps originally imported from Cyprus, that gave off a pleasant odor when burned.

"don't forget me, and always remember that just as my person is yours to enjoy, so everything I have here and all that I can do are yours to command."

After embracing her and kissing her, the happy Salabaetto left her house and went to the part of the city where it was customary for the other merchants to congregate. And as he continued to spend time with her on a regular basis, all at no cost whatsoever to himself, he became increasingly caught up in her snares.

Eventually, he happened to sell his cloth for ready cash, making a tidy profit on the deal, and the good lady was immediately informed about it, though by someone else, not by Salabaetto himself. Consequently, one evening when he had gone to her place, she began to joke around and romp with him, hugging and kissing him with such a show of being on fire for him that it seemed as if she were going to die of love in his arms. Furthermore, she kept insisting that he accept two exquisite silver goblets of hers, which he refused, since on more than one occasion he had received things from her worth a good thirty gold florins without ever being able to get her to take anything from him that was worth so much as a tiny silver coin. At last, when she had gotten him absolutely red hot with her show of passion and generosity, one of her slave girls called her away from the room, as she had been ordered to do earlier. After a long while, the lady returned, and weeping, threw herself facedown on the bed, where she began to give vent to the most pitiful lamentation a woman has ever uttered.

Astonished, Salabaetto took her in his arms and was soon weeping right along with her. "Oh, sweetheart," he said, "what's this that's happened to you all of a sudden? What's the cause of all this grief of yours? Ah, please tell me about it, my darling."

After allowing him to coax her for quite some time, she replied: "Alas, my sweet lord, I don't know what to say or what I'm going to do. Just now I received letters from my brother in Messina, who writes to me that I must send him a thousand gold florins in the next week without fail, even if I have to sell or pawn everything I have, because otherwise, he's going to have his head cut off. I have no idea what I could do to get that much money on such short notice. If only I had a couple of weeks, I'd find a way of procuring it from a certain source who owes me a great deal more than that, or I could sell one of our estates. But since that's not possible, I wish I'd died before this bad news had ever reached me"—at which point she broke off, appearing to be in deep distress, and would not stop crying for anything.

Since the flames of love had already eliminated a substantial portion of Salabaetto's usual good sense, he believed that her tears were absolutely genuine, and that her words were even more so. "My lady," he said, "although I couldn't supply you with a thousand gold florins, I can certainly give you five hundred, if you're sure you'll be able to repay me within the next two weeks. Luckily for you, I sold my entire consignment of cloth just yesterday, because if I hadn't, I wouldn't be able to lend you as much as a groat."*

"Oh no," said the lady, "have you yourself been short of cash? Why didn't you ask me for some? I may not have a thousand, but I could certainly have given you a hundred, or even two. Now you've made it so that I no longer have the heart to accept your offer of assistance."

Taken in more than ever by these words, Salabaetto replied: "My lady, I would not have you refuse it on that account, because if my need had been as great as yours, I would certainly have asked for your help."

"Oh, my Salabaetto," said the lady, "now I see how true and perfect your love for me is, since you didn't wait to be asked for such a large sum of money before freely offering to help me out in my hour of need. Although I was already entirely yours without this gesture, with it, from now on, I shall belong to you even more than before, nor will I ever fail to acknowledge that I owe my brother's life to you. But God knows how reluctant I am to accept your offer, considering the fact that you're a merchant and merchants do all their business with money. Nevertheless, I'll take it, since I'm forced to do so by necessity, and besides, I have every hope of being able to repay you in the near future. As for the rest of the sum, if I don't quickly find it some other way, I'll pawn everything I own here." And having said this, she let herself fall down on Salabaetto, and weeping, lay there cheek to cheek beside him.

* Groat (*grosso*): a silver coin of relatively modest worth.

Salabaetto set about consoling her, and after having spent the night with her, in order to prove how generous and devoted he was, he brought her five hundred fine gold florins without waiting to be asked for them. She accepted his money with tears in her eyes—and laughter in her heart—while he contented himself with nothing more than the simple promise she made to repay it.

The moment the lady had his money, she began making revisions in their schedule, for whereas Salabaetto used to have free access to her any time he pleased, now she started coming up with all sorts of excuses so that he did not get in to see her six times out of seven, and on those occasions when he did, he was not received with the same smiling face and the same embraces or given the same warm welcome as before.

Soon the date passed for the return of his money—and then a month, and then another month went by as well—but words were all he got by way of payment when he asked to have it back. Having finally come to see the wicked woman's cleverness as well as his own lack of good sense, Salabaetto was exceedingly distressed and wept inwardly over his folly. There was nothing he could say against her, however, unless she were willing to confirm it, for he had no written evidence of their arrangement, nor had there been any witnesses to it. Moreover, he was ashamed to go and complain about her to anyone, not just because he had been warned about her beforehand, but because of the well-deserved ridicule he expected to be exposed to because of his stupidity. As he had received a number of letters from his principals, instructing him to exchange the money he had and send it to them, in order to prevent his fault from being discovered when he failed to do so, he decided to leave. Consequently, he boarded a small ship, but instead of sailing to Pisa, where he should have gone, he went to Naples.

At that time there was a compatriot of ours living in Naples named Pietro dello Canigiano, a man of great intellect and subtle wit, who was treasurer to Her Highness the Empress of Constantinople and a very close friend of Salabaetto and his family.[7] Since he was a model of discretion, the disconsolate Salabaetto gave him an account, a few days after his arrival, of what he had done and of his wretched misfortune. He went on to ask him for his assistance and advice in finding some sort of livelihood for himself there in the city, declaring that he had no intention of ever returning to Florence.

Saddened by what he had heard, Canigiano said: "What you did was terrible! Your behavior's been terrible! The way you've carried out your employers' orders is terrible! Plus, you've squandered entirely too much money at one stroke in easy living! But what's done is done, and we must now look for some way out of it."

Clever man that he was, Canigiano quickly saw what they needed to do and explained it to Salabaetto, who was pleased with the plan and accepted the risk involved in carrying it out. He had some money himself, and after supplementing it with a loan from Canigiano, he ordered a fair number of bales to be packed and tied up good and tight, and then, having bought and filled about twenty oil casks, he had everything loaded on board a ship and returned to Palermo. There he presented the invoice for the bales to the customs officers, along with his declaration of the value of the casks, and making sure it was all registered in his account, he had it put in some storerooms, saying that he did not want to touch any of it until some other merchandise he was expecting had arrived.

Upon learning of his return and hearing that what he had brought with him was worth a good two thousand gold florins or more, not counting what he was expecting, which was valued at more than three, Iancofiore felt she had set her sights too low and decided to return the five hundred to him in the expectation that she would be able to get the greater part of his five thousand for herself. Accordingly, she sent for him, and when Salabaetto came to see her, she pretended to know nothing about what he had brought with him and gave him a wonderfully warm welcome. "Look," she said, "if you were angry with me because I didn't give you back your money on time…?"

Salabaetto, who had now grown cunning, began by laughing and said: "To tell the truth, my lady, I was indeed a little upset, considering that I would have plucked out my heart and given it to you if I thought it would please you. But now I want you to listen, and you'll see just how angry I am with you. So intense and so special is the love I feel for you that I've sold the greater part of my possessions, and I've brought a huge quantity of merchandise with me here that's valued at more than two thousand florins. Plus, I'm expecting another shipment from the West that's worth more than three. It's my intention to start a business in this city and to settle here so that I can always be near you, since I feel happier with this love of yours than I believe any lover has ever been with his."

"Look, Salabaetto," she said, "whatever success you have makes me very happy, for I love you more than my very own life, and I'm quite delighted that you've decided to return here with the intention of staying, because I'm hoping we will still have plenty of good times together. But I'd also like to offer you a little apology for those occasions, just before your departure, when you wanted to come here and you weren't allowed to, as well as for those times when you were let in, but were not greeted so cheerfully as you used to be. And beyond all that, I want to say how sorry I am for not giving you back your money on the date I promised.

"You must know how terribly sad and deeply distressed I was at the time, and that for a person in such a condition, no matter how much she may love another, there is no way she can put on as cheerful a countenance and be as attentive toward him as he would like her to be. Furthermore, you must also know how difficult it is for a woman to find a thousand gold florins, for all day long people tell us lies and fail to keep their promises to us, so that we, too, are forced to lie to others. And it was for this reason alone, and not because of some other failing on my part, that I didn't pay you back. I did obtain the money shortly after your departure, however, and if I'd known where to send it, I would have certainly done so, but since I didn't know your address, I've kept it safe for you here." Then, having sent for a purse that contained the very coins he had brought to her, she placed it in his hand and said, "Count them and see if there are five hundred there."

Salabaetto had never been so happy, and after counting the money and finding that it came to exactly five hundred florins, he put it all away. "I know you're telling the truth, my lady," he said. "Indeed, you've done more than enough to prove it, and both because of this and because of the love I bear you, let me tell you that if you should ever be in need of money, and it were in my power to supply it, there wouldn't be any sum you could ask me for that I would refuse to give you. And as soon as I've got myself set up here, you may put my promise to the test."

Salabaetto thus reestablished his love for her by means of these declarations, and he began treating her to various displays of affection, while for her part, she did everything she could to entertain him and give him pleasure, pretending she felt the most intense passion for him. Salabaetto, however, was determined to deceive her and thus punish her for the trick she had played on him, and one day, when she had invited him to come for supper and to spend the night with her, he showed up looking so distraught and melancholy that it seemed as if he wanted to die. Hugging and kissing him, she began to question him as to why he was so depressed, and after allowing her to go on begging him for a while, he finally replied to her.

"I'm utterly ruined," he said, "for the ship carrying the merchandise I was expecting has been captured by pirates from Monaco, and the ransom for it is ten thousand gold florins.[8] My share comes to a thousand, and I don't have a penny, because as soon as you gave me the five hundred, I sent the money to Naples to be invested in cloth, which they're going to be shipping to me here. If I were to sell the goods I have on hand at the moment, I'd hardly get half price for them because it's not the right time to put them on the market, and there's nobody around here who knows me well enough yet to help me out. So I have no idea what to do or what to say, but if I don't send the money soon, my merchandise will be taken to Monaco, and I'll never get any of it back."

The lady was very annoyed by this development since it seemed to her as if she were about to lose everything, but she soon figured out what she had to do to keep the goods from winding up in Monaco. "God knows I'm terribly concerned because of my love for you," she said. "But what's the use of getting so upset over it? If I had the money, God knows I'd lend it to you on the spot, but I just haven't got it. On the other hand, it's true that there's a certain person here who does— the one who supplied me with the five hundred I needed that other time. He, however, charges a high rate of interest, and if you want to borrow money from him, he won't accept less than thirty percent, and he'll insist that you pledge something substantial as a guarantee. For my part, in order to help you, I'm ready to put up everything I own, myself included, for as much as he's willing to lend us for it. But what security do you have for the rest of the loan?"

Salabaetto was delighted, because he knew the motive that prompted her to offer him this service, being well aware that she was going to be lending him the money herself. So, after thanking her, he told her that despite the exorbitant interest rate, his need was too pressing to allow him to pass up the opportunity. He then went on to say that he would secure the loan with the merchandise he had in the customshouse, registering it in the name of the person who was to lend him the money. However, he wanted to retain the key to the storerooms, so that he would be able to display his merchandise if someone asked him to do so and to make sure that none of his goods would be tampered with or moved elsewhere or exchanged.

The lady said that his plan was good, and his collateral, more than adequate. And so, the next morning, she sent for a broker who enjoyed her complete confidence, and having explained the arrangement to him, she gave him a thousand gold florins, which he, in turn, lent to Salabaetto, after having everything that Salabaetto had stored in the customshouse put under his own name. Then, once they had signed and countersigned a number of receipts for one another, and everything was concluded between them, they both went off to attend to other business.

At the first opportunity, Salabaetto boarded a little ship and returned to Pietro Canigiano in Naples with the fifteen hundred gold florins, from which he made a full remittance of what he owed his principals in Florence for the cloth they had originally sent with him. Once he had paid Pietro, as well as everyone else to whom he owed anything, he spent many days making merry with his friend over the trick he had played on the Sicilian woman, after which he left Naples and went to Ferrara, having resolved never to be a merchant again.

When Iancofiore discovered that Salabaetto was no longer in Palermo, she was surprised at first, but then grew suspicious, and after waiting two months for him to return and still seeing no sign of him, she got the broker to force open the storerooms. First, they sounded the casks, which they thought were full of oil, and found they were filled with seawater, except for a small quantity of oil floating on top near the spouts. Then they untied the bales to discover that all except two of them, which actually contained cloth, were packed with tow.* In short, when the whole lot was added together, it was not worth more than two hundred florins.

Realizing she had been outwitted, for a long time Iancofiore lamented the five hundred florins she had given back to Salabaetto, and for even longer, the thousand she had lent him, often saying as she did:

If with Tuscans you vie,
Don't you dare close an eye.[9]

And so, she was left with nothing but loss and scorn, having discovered that some people know their way around just as well as others do.

---

*Tow is the term for the rough fibers of flax or hemp that have been given a first combing but have not yet been finished in order to be spun into cloth or rope.

Day 8, Conclusion

No sooner had Dioneo finished his story than Lauretta, realizing that the end of her reign had come, praised the advice given by Pietro Canigiano, which to judge by its results appeared quite sound, as well as Salabaetto's wisdom, which was no less commendable for his having put that advice into practice. Then, removing the laurel wreath from her head, she placed it on Emilia's and said, with womanly grace: "My lady, I do not know how agreeable a Queen you will be, but we will certainly have a lovely one in you. See to it, then, that your deeds are in keeping with your beauty."

Lauretta sat back down, leaving Emilia feeling somewhat embarrassed, not so much from having been made Queen as from seeing herself praised in public for possessing something that women normally want more than anything else. Her face turned the color of roses, new blooming at dawn, but after having kept her eyes lowered for a while until her blushes had faded, she gave orders to the steward about everything the company was going to be needing. Then she addressed them as follows:

"Delightful ladies, we may readily observe that when oxen have labored for a portion of the day, confined under the yoke, they will be released from it, unhitched, and allowed to wander freely through the woods, seeking their pasture wherever they wish. Likewise, we have all seen that gardens containing plants with different kinds of foliage are not less, but actually more beautiful than forests composed exclusively of oaks. Therefore, considering how many days we have carried on our conversations while working under the constraint of a fixed rule, I think it would be not only useful, but appropriate for us, like all those in such need, to wander about for a while, because in this way we will recover our strength and be able to place ourselves once again under the yoke.

"Accordingly, when we continue our delightful storytelling tomorrow, I do not intend to restrict you to any particular subject; on the contrary, I want each of you to speak about whatever you like, it being my firm conviction that we will find it no less entertaining to hear you discourse on a variety of topics than talk about just a single one. Moreover, by doing it this way, we will be all the more energized, and the ruler who succeeds me can, with greater confidence, confine us within the limits of our customary laws."

After Emilia had finished speaking, she set the entire company at liberty until suppertime. Everyone praised her for the wisdom of what she had said, and then, rising to their feet, they went off in pursuit of their various pleasures, the women making garlands and otherwise amusing themselves, while the young men played games and sang songs. In this fashion they passed the time until the hour for supper had arrived, at which point they came together about the fair fountain and ate their meal with festive good cheer. Once they were done, they entertained themselves as they usually did by singing and dancing.

Finally, the Queen, wishing to imitate the style of her predecessors, ordered Panfilo to give them a song, notwithstanding the fact that many members of the company had already, of their own accord, sung quite a few of them. Nevertheless, without hesitation, Panfilo began as follows:

> So great, Love, are the good,
> The joy, and the delight I feel through you
> That I am happy, burning in your fire.
>   The boundless gaiety within my heart,
> Derived from that high joy
> And dear you've given me,
> Cannot be kept inside; it issues forth,
> And shining in my face,
> Reveals my happy state.
> Only to be in love

With one who holds so high and venerable a place
Makes all the burning I endure feel light.
    I know not how to show you with my song,
Or with my finger sketch
The bliss I feel, O Love.
Though if I could, concealing it's still best,
For were it known, it would
Become my torment now.
But my content is such
That words would all fall short, inadequate,
Before I'd shown you one small part of it.
    Could anyone conceive these arms of mine
Would ever reach so high
As to embrace her there,
Or that I would have brought my face to touch
That place from which I gained
Salvation and my grace?
My luck would never be
Believed by anyone; that's why I burn,
For I conceal what brings me joy and bliss.

Panfilo's song came to an end, and while all of them had joined fully in singing the refrain, there was no one who did not give the words more than the usual amount of attention, striving to guess what it was that he felt himself obliged to conceal. Although various members of the company came up with their own individual interpretations, for all that, they never managed to hit on the truth of the matter.

Finally, when the Queen saw that Panfilo had finished singing and that the young men and women would be glad to get some rest, she ordered them all to go to bed.

Day 9, Introduction

Here ends the Eighth Day of the Decameron *and the Ninth begins, in which, under the rule of Emilia, they all speak as they wish on whatever topic they like the most.*

The light, whose splendor puts the night to flight, had already changed the color of the entire eighth heaven from azure to pale blue,* and the little flowers scattered throughout the meadows had started lifting up their heads, when Emilia arose and had both her companions and the young men summoned to her. Once everyone had arrived, they set off, following the Queen's leisurely steps, and made their way to a little wood no great distance from the palace. On entering it, they spotted roebucks and stags and other wild animals, who, as though sensing they were safe from hunters because of the widespread plague, stood waiting for them there as if they had been tamed and rendered fearless. By approaching the animals one after the other and pretending they were about to touch them, the members of the company made them run and leap, and in this way they amused themselves for a while until the sun had risen well into the sky, at which point they all agreed that it was a good time to return.

The members of the company were wearing garlands made of oak leaves, their hands full of either fragrant herbs or flowers, so that if anyone had encountered them, the only thing he could possibly have said was: "Either these people will not be vanquished by death, or they will die happy." And so back they came, step by leisurely step, singing

---

*In the Ptolemaic universe, the eighth heaven is the heaven of the fixed stars; it is surrounded by the ninth heaven, or *Primum mobile*, and the *Empyrean*, neither of which is visible to us on earth.

and chatting and engaging in witty banter with one another, until they reached the palace, where they found everything set out in order and their servants in a gay and festive mood. The young men and the ladies rested there for a while, and would not go to the table before they had sung half a dozen songs, each one merrier than the last. But then, having washed their hands, on the Queen's instructions, they were seated by the steward, and when the food came, they happily ate their meal. Getting up from the table, they next devoted themselves for some time to dancing *carole** and making music until the Queen told those who wanted to rest that they had her permission to go and do so.

When the customary hour arrived, however, they all went to the place where they usually gathered to tell stories. The Queen, looking over at Filomena, asked her to tell the first one of the day, and with a smile, she began in the following manner.

Carole: dances in which the dancers joined hands and moved in a clockwise direction, usually accompanied by music and the singing of the dancers themselves.

Day 9, Story 1

Madonna Francesca is courted by a certain Rinuccio and a certain Alessandro, but is not in love with either man, and since neither one can complete the task she assigns him, the first being required to enter a tomb and pose there as a corpse, while the second must climb inside and carry out the supposedly dead man, she discreetly rids herself of both of them.[1]

Since it is your pleasure, my lady, I am delighted to be the first to joust in this free and open field for storytelling to which you, with your generosity, have brought us, and if I acquit myself with distinction, I have no doubt that those who come after me will do as well as I, and even better.

In the course of our discussions, charming ladies, although we have often seen how great and how varied Love's powers can be, I still do not believe that we have exhausted the topic or that we would be able to do so even if we were to speak of nothing else for an entire year. And since it not only leads lovers to risk their lives in perilous situations of every sort, but has even induced them to enter the houses of the dead by playing dead themselves, I should like to recount a story on the subject, in addition to all the others that have already been told, which will enable you not merely to comprehend Love's power, but to appreciate the ingenuity a worthy lady made use of in ridding herself of two unwanted suitors.

Let me say, then, that in the city of Pistoia there once lived a very beautiful widow, with whom, as chance would have it, two of our fellow citizens, who had settled there after having been exiled from Florence, had fallen very deeply in love. Their names were Rinuccio Palermini and Alessandro Chiarmontesi, and while they remained ignorant of

one another's existence, each of them cautiously went on doing everything in his power to win her affection.[2]

The lady, who was named Francesca de' Lazzari, was constantly
being pestered with their messages and entreaties, and having been fool
enough, on occasion, to lend them a willing ear, she found she could
not extricate herself from her relationship with them, which she now
wisely wished to do, until a thought finally occurred to her as to how
she might stop them from importuning her.[3] Her idea was to request
that they perform a service for her, one that would not be impossible,
but that they would be unable to do, so that when they failed, she would
have an honorable, or at least a plausible, excuse for refusing to accept
their advances. And this was her plan.

On the day the idea came to her, a man had died in the city who,
despite having had noble ancestors, was reputed to be the worst person
who had ever lived, not just in Pistoia, but in the whole wide world.
Moreover, when he was alive, he was so deformed and had so hideous a
face that anyone who did not already know him would have been filled
with terror upon seeing him for the first time. He had been interred in
a tomb outside the church of the Franciscans, which the lady felt would
be quite useful in carrying out her scheme, and so she said to one of her
maids: "As you know, I'm annoyed and tormented all day long by the
messages that those two Florentines, Rinuccio and Alessandro, keep
sending me. Since I have no intention of gratifying either one of them
with my love, in order to get rid of them, I've decided to respond to the
great protestations of affection they're always making by setting them a
task that I'm certain they can't accomplish, and that way I'll stop them
from pestering me. Now just listen to how I'll do it.

"You know that this morning Scannadio—for that was the name of
the evil man we just mentioned—was buried at the monastery belonging to the Franciscans and that the mere sight of him, while he was
alive, let alone now that he's dead, was enough to frighten the bravest
men in this town.[4] So first, I want you to go in secret to Alessandro and
say to him: 'Madonna Francesca sends me to tell you that the time has
come for you to enjoy the love that you have so ardently desired, and
that you can get to be with her, if you wish, in the following way. For

reasons you'll be informed about later on, a relative of hers is supposed to fetch the body of Scannadio, who was buried this morning, and bring it to her house tonight. But since she's still terrified of him, even though he's dead, and she doesn't want him in the place, she implores you to do her a great favor. Namely, at bedtime this evening she wants you to be so good as to enter the tomb in which Scannadio has been interred, to put on his clothes, and to lie there impersonating him until someone comes to get you. Then, without saying a word or making a sound, you are to allow yourself to be taken out of it and carried to her house. She'll be there to welcome you, and you can stay with her for as long as you like, leaving the rest of the details for her to take care of.' Now, if he says he'll do it, well and good, but if he refuses, then tell him from me that he should stay out of my sight, and if he values his life, he shouldn't send me any more of his messages or entreaties.

"After that, you'll go to Rinuccio Palermini and tell him: 'Madonna Francesca says she's ready to comply with your every desire, provided that you do her a great favor. Namely, around midnight tonight you are to go to the tomb where Scannadio was interred this morning, and without saying a word in response to anything you see or hear, you are to remove the body ever so gently and bring it to her at her house. There you'll discover why she wants you to do this, and you'll be able to satisfy your desires with her. But if you're not willing to do this, then from now on she orders you never to send her any messages or entreaties again.'"

When the maid went to the two young men and delivered the messages exactly as she had been instructed to do, in both cases they replied that they would go as far as Hell itself, let alone climb down into a tomb, if that would please her. The maid conveyed their response to the lady who waited to see if the two of them would be truly crazy enough to do it.

After nightfall, around the time when people have just gone to sleep, Alessandro Chiarmontesi stripped down to his doublet and left his house in order to go and take Scannadio's place inside the tomb. As he went on his way, a terrifying thought entered his head, and he began talking to himself: "Oh, why am I such an ass! Where do I think I'm going? How do I know her relations haven't discovered that I'm in love with her? Perhaps they believe things that aren't true about what we've done, and they've forced her to have me do this so they can murder me inside the tomb. If that were to happen, I'd be the one to get the blame, since no one in the world would know a thing about what happened, and they'd escape scot-free. Or for all I know, perhaps one of my enemies has set this up for me, and because she may be in love with him, she wants to do this for him as a favor."

"But let's suppose," he continued, "that neither of these things is the case, and that her relations really do intend to carry me to her house. I can't believe they want to take Scannadio's body there so they can clasp it in their arms, let alone put it in hers. The only conclusion I can draw is that they want to do violence to it because of some wrong he did to them. She says I shouldn't make a sound no matter what happens to me, but where would I be if they were to pluck out my eyes or yank out my teeth or cut off my hands or play some other trick like that on me? How could I keep quiet? And if I speak, they'll recognize me, and perhaps they'll hurt me. But even if they don't, I won't have accomplished anything, for they're not going to leave me there with the lady in any case. And then she'll say I've disobeyed her orders, and she'll never do anything to please me."

Talking to himself this way, he was at the point of turning around and heading home, but the immense love he felt drove him on, providing counterarguments so strong that they brought him eventually right up to the tomb. Having opened it, he climbed inside, stripped off Scannadio's clothes, and dressed himself in them. Then, closing the tomb over his head, he lay down in Scannadio's place. As he began thinking about the kind of person the dead man had been and dwelling on the stories he had heard people tell concerning what happened at night not just among the tombs of the dead, but even outside them, pretty soon every hair on his body was standing on end, and he felt sure that at any moment Scannadio was going to rise up and slit his throat. But fortified by his fervent love, he overcame these as well as other terrifying thoughts, and lying there as if he were the corpse, he waited to see what was going to happen to him.

As midnight approached, Rinuccio left his house in order to carry out the orders that the lady had given him, and as he was walking along, he began mulling over the various things that could possibly happen to him, such as falling into the hands of the watch while he was carrying Scannadio's body on his shoulders, for which he would be condemned to be burned as a sorcerer, or incurring the wrath of the dead man's relations if they found out what he was doing. Several other thoughts of the same sort occurred to him, and he was almost deterred from going on, but then he changed his mind and said to himself: "What, shall I say no to the first request I've gotten from this gentlewoman, whom I love as deeply as ever, and especially when I'm going to win her favor if I do it? No, even if I should die for it, I'm determined to honor the promise I made her." And so, he continued walking on until he arrived at the tomb, which he then opened with ease.

As Alessandro heard the lid being moved, he was absolutely terrified, but managed nevertheless to remain perfectly still. Rinuccio climbed inside, and thinking he was picking up Scannadio's body, he grabbed Alessandro by the feet, dragged him out of the tomb, hoisted him up onto his shoulders, and began walking in the direction of the gentlewoman's house. Since the night was pitch black, he could not see where he was going, and as he went along, not taking much care with the body he was carrying, he frequently banged it against the edges of one or another of the benches that lined the street.

Waiting to see if he was actually going to bring Alessandro to her house, the gentlewoman was standing there at the window with her maid, already armed with an excuse to send the pair of them away, but just as Rinuccio was about to reach the first step leading up to her front door, the officers of the watch happened to hear the noise he was making with his feet as he went shuffling along. They had been placed on guard in the neighborhood, where they were quietly lying in wait in order to catch an outlaw, and they immediately produced a lantern to see what was going on and which direction they had to take. Picking up their shields and lances, they shouted, "Who goes there?" Rinuccio recognized who they were, and having no time to compose his thoughts, he dropped Alessandro and ran away as fast as his legs would carry him. Alessandro quickly leaped to his feet, and despite being hampered by the dead man's shroud, which was very long, he, too, took off.

By the light the watch was holding out, the lady had clearly observed Rinuccio carrying Alessandro on his shoulders, noting as well that the latter was dressed in Scannadio's clothing, and she was amazed at the courage displayed by the two men. For all her amazement, however, she had a good laugh when she saw Alessandro being dropped and then watched the two men take to their heels. Overjoyed at this turn of events, and praising God for having freed her from the awkward situation the pair had put her in, she turned from the window and went back to her room, agreeing with her maid that both of the men certainly loved her very much, for, as it appeared, they had done precisely what she had ordered them to do.

Heartbroken and cursing his bad luck, Rinuccio did not return home despite everything that had happened, but as soon as the watch had left the neighborhood, he returned to the spot where he had dumped Alessandro and groped around on all fours to see if he could find him and thus complete the task the lady had assigned him. But when he failed to locate the body, he supposed that it had been carried off by the watch, and sadly made his way back home.

Alessandro had no idea what else he could do, and so, without ever having discovered who had been carrying him, he likewise returned to his house, grief stricken over his terrible misfortune.

When Scannadio's tomb was found open the next morning and there was no sign of his body—for Alessandro had rolled it down to the bottom of the vault—the whole of Pistoia came up with various explanations for what had happened, the fools among them concluding that he had been carried off by devils. Each of the lady's lovers informed her of what he had done, and using the events that had occurred as an excuse for why he had not carried out her instructions to the full, he demanded her forgiveness and her love. But she pretended she did not believe either one, and by curtly responding that she had no desire to do anything for them since they had not completed the tasks she had assigned them, she managed to get the pair of them off her back.

Day 9, Story 2

Arising hurriedly in the dark, an Abbess rushes out to catch one of her nuns who was reported to be in bed with her lover, but the Abbess herself was with a priest at the time and places his breeches on her head, thinking she is putting her veils there, with the result that when the accused nun sees them and points them out to the Abbess, she is acquitted and from then on is able to spend time with her lover at her leisure.[1]

When Filomena was silent, the entire company praised the lady's intelligence in getting rid of the men she did not love, while, on the contrary, they all judged the men's daring presumption to be madness rather than love. Then, turning to Elissa, the Queen graciously said, "Continue, Elissa," and she promptly began speaking as follows:

My dearest ladies, as we have heard, Madonna Francesca certainly knew how to get rid of a nuisance by using her wits. Now, however, I am going to tell you about a young nun who, with Fortune's help, freed herself from imminent danger by means of a clever remark. You all know that there are plenty of very foolish people who take it upon themselves to instruct and correct others, but as you will learn from my story, from time to time Fortune justly puts them to shame—which is precisely what happened to the Abbess who was the superior of the nun I am going to tell you about.

You should know, then, that in Lombardy there used to be a convent, widely renowned for the holiness and religious zeal of its nuns, one of whom was a young woman of noble birth, endowed with wondrous beauty, who was named Isabetta. One day, having come to the grating to speak with a relative of hers, she fell in love with a handsome young man who was with him, and who, when he saw how very beautiful she was and understood what she was feeling from the look in her eyes, began burning with just as fierce a passion for her.

The two of them suffered intense anguish for quite some time because of this unfulfilled love of theirs, but it kept spurring them on until, finally, the young man thought of a way he could get together with his nun in secret. From that time on, with her full consent, he visited her not once, but many, many times, always to their mutual delight.

Things went on in this manner until one night, unbeknownst to him or Isabetta, he happened to be spotted by one of the nuns after he had taken his leave and was going on his way. The nun communicated her discovery to several others, and their first thought was to denounce Isabetta to the Abbess, a certain Madonna Usimbalda, who was a good and pious woman in the opinion of the nuns and of everyone else who knew her.[2] On second thought, however, they decided to arrange for the Abbess to catch the girl with the young man so that there would be no room for her to deny it. Consequently, they held their peace and secretly took turns keeping her under close surveillance in the hope of taking her by surprise.

Now, Isabetta, who had no idea what was going on and was not on the lookout, happened to arrange one night for her lover to join her. The nuns who were keeping watch spotted him at once, but waited to act until the wee hours of the night. Then, when they thought the time was right, they divided themselves into two groups, the first standing guard by the entrance to Isabetta's cell while the second ran off to the Abbess's room. There they knocked on the door, and as soon as they heard her voice, they said: "Get up, Reverend Mother, and hurry. We've discovered Isabetta has a young man in her cell."

That night the Abbess was keeping company with a priest whom she often had brought to her inside a chest. When she heard all the racket, she was afraid that the nuns, in their haste and excessive zeal, would force the door open. Consequently, she got up in a rush and dressed herself as best she could in the dark. Thinking that she had picked up the pleated veils that nuns wear on their heads and are called psalters,*

---

*Psalter (It. *saltero*): an arrangement of veils worn by nuns on their heads that had a triangular shape like the musical instrument of the same name (also called a psaltery).

she happened to grab the priest's beeches, and she was in such a hurry that without realizing what she was doing, she clapped them onto her head in place of her veils. She exited the room, quickly locking the door behind her and exclaiming: "Where is that goddamned girl?"

Accompanied by the nuns, who were so fired up, so eager to see Isabetta caught in the act, that they took no notice of what the Abbess had on her head, she arrived at the entrance to the cell, and all of them together managed to push down the door. Upon entering the room, they found the two lovers in bed together, lying in one another's arms, so confused by this sudden and surprising turn of events that they had no idea what to do and just stayed where they were, unable to move.

The nuns immediately seized the girl and at the Abbess's orders led her to the chapterhouse. Meanwhile, the young man, who had stayed where he was, got dressed and waited to see what the outcome would be, fully resolved, if his young lady were harmed in any way, to make all the nuns he could get his hands on pay dearly for it, after which he would take her away with him.

Having assumed her seat in the chapterhouse surrounded by the nuns, all of whom had their eyes fixed on the accused, the Abbess launched into the severest scolding any woman has ever received, telling the girl that by her reprehensible, disgusting conduct—if people outside ever found out about it—she had sullied the sanctity, the honor, and the good reputation of the convent. And to these insults, the Abbess added the worst threats imaginable.

Knowing she was at fault, the girl had no idea how to respond, and as she stood there, fearful and ashamed, her silence was actually beginning to make the others feel sorry for her. After a while, however, as the Abbess went on and on multiplying her insults, the girl happened to raise her head and caught sight of what the Abbess had on her head, with its straps dangling down on either side. Realizing what was up, she completely recovered her composure and said: "God help you, Reverend Mother, would you tie up your cap, and then you may tell me whatever you want."

The Abbess had no idea what she meant and replied: "What cap, you

vile woman? Do you have the cheek to make jokes now? Does it really
seem to you that what you've done is some laughing matter?"

"Reverend Mother, I beg you," said the girl a second time, "tie up
your cap. Then you can say anything you please to me."

At this point, several of the nuns raised their eyes and looked in the
direction of the Abbess's head, while she simultaneously raised her
hands up to it. And then all of them realized just what it was Isabetta
had been referring to.

Recognizing that she was equally guilty, and that there was no way
for her to cover things up since everyone was staring at her, the Abbess
changed her tune and began telling a very different story than she had
before. When she reached the conclusion that it was impossible to
defend oneself from the goadings of the flesh, she told them all that
they should enjoy themselves whenever they could, provided it was
done discreetly, as it had been up until then.

After setting Isabetta free, the Abbess returned to sleep with her
priest, while the girl went off to rejoin her lover. And from then on,
regardless of the envy felt by the nuns, Isabetta had him come back to
see her at frequent intervals, and the others, who lacked lovers, did their
best to find some sort of consolation for themselves in secret.

Day 9, Story 3

Egged on by Bruno, Buffalmacco, and Nello, Master Simone makes Calandrino believe he is pregnant. Calandrino then gives them all capons and money in return for medicine, and he is cured without having to give birth.[1]

When Elissa had finished, everyone thanked God for the young nun's happy escape from the fangs of her envious companions. At that point the Queen ordered Filostrato to continue, and he, without waiting to be asked again, began:

Loveliest of ladies, that boorish judge from The Marches about whom I spoke to you yesterday took a story about Calandrino that I was all prepared to tell you and snatched it right out of my mouth. We have, to be sure, heard quite a bit about him and his comrades, but since everything we say about him can only serve to increase the fun we are having, I am going to recount the story now that I intended to tell you then.

From what was previously said, you should have a very clear picture of Calandrino and of the others who are going to be the subject of this story. Consequently, I will get right to the point and tell you that one of Calandrino's aunts happened to die and leave him two hundred *lire* in small change, which prompted him to start talking about how he was going to buy himself a farm.[2] Acting as if he had ten thousand gold florins to spend, he entered into negotiations with all the brokers in Florence, although the deals always fell through as soon as they mentioned the asking price for the property. Bruno and Buffalmacco, who knew what had happened, had told him many times that it would be better for him to use the money in order to have a good time with them than to go and buy just enough land to make mud pies out of it.[3] But

705

far from getting him to do what they proposed, they had never managed to persuade him to stand them to a single meal.

As they were griping about this one day, they were joined by a buddy
of theirs, a painter named Nello, and the three of them decided they
just had to find a way to stuff their snouts at Calandrino's expense.[4] It
did not take them very long to work out a plan of action among themselves, and the next morning they were lying in wait for Calandrino as
he left his house. Before he had gone even a short distance, Nello came
up to him and said, "Good-day, Calandrino."

Calandrino replied by saying that God should give him a good day,
and a good year, too, after which Nello paused for a moment and began
looking Calandrino hard in the face.

"What are you staring at?" asked Calandrino.

"Did anything happen to you last night?" replied Nello. "You don't
seem like your usual self."

Calandrino immediately started worrying and said, "Oh no! How's
that? What do you think I've got?"

"Well, I'm not saying that you've got something," said Nello. "It's just
that you look very different to me. Maybe it's nothing at all."

Nello let him go, and as Calandrino continued on his way, he was
terribly upset, although he did not sense that there was anything at all
wrong with him. Buffalmacco, however, was not far off, and when he
saw Calandrino leave Nello, he walked up to him, greeted him, and
asked him if he was feeling all right.

"I don't know," said Calandrino, "but just now Nello was telling me
that I looked all different to him. Is it possible I could have come down
with something?"

"Yes, you could well have a little something or other," replied Buffalmacco. "You look half dead."

Calandrino had already started to feel feverish when lo and behold,
Bruno appeared on the scene, and the first words out of his mouth
were, "Calandrino, what a face! You look like death itself! How are
you feeling?"

Having heard all of them say the same thing, Calandrino was now absolutely convinced that he was sick, and completely dismayed by the prospect, he asked them, "What shall I do?"

"In my opinion," said Bruno, "you should go right home, get into your bed, and cover yourself up good and tight. Then you should send a specimen of your urine to Master Simone who, as you know, is a very good buddy of ours and will soon tell you what you have to do.[5] Plus, we'll come with you, and if anything has to be done, we'll take care of it."

Nello soon joined them, and the three of them accompanied Calandrino back to his house where he made his way, utterly exhausted, to his bedroom. "Come and pile the covers over me," he said to his wife. "I'm feeling terribly ill."

After he got settled in his bed, he sent a serving girl with a specimen of his urine to Master Simone, who in those days had set up his practice in the Mercato Vecchio at the sign of the Melon.[6] Bruno turned to his buddies and said: "You stay here with him, while I go and see what the doctor has to say. If it's necessary, I'll escort him back here with me."

"Ah, yes, my friend," said Calandrino, "do go there and bring me back word about how things stand, because I'm feeling I've got something, I don't know what, inside me."

Bruno set off for Master Simone's, getting there ahead of the serving girl who was carrying the specimen, and explained to the doctor what they were up to. Thus, when the girl arrived, Master Simone examined the urine and said to her: "Go back and tell Calandrino that he should keep himself good and warm. I'm coming to see him right away to let him know what's wrong with him and what he has to do about it."

After the girl delivered the message, it was not long before the doctor, accompanied by Bruno, showed up. Sitting down beside Calandrino, he began taking his pulse, and then, after a pause, in the presence of Calandrino's wife, he said to him: "Look here, Calandrino, speaking to you as a friend, I'd say there's nothing wrong with you except for the fact that you're pregnant."

When Calandrino heard this, he began wailing in despair. "Oh no, Tessa," he exclaimed, "you did this to me. You always want to be on top, and I've told you clearly all along what would come of it." When she heard him say this, Calandrino's wife, who was a very modest woman, turned scarlet with shame, and lowering her gaze, left the room without saying a word.

Meanwhile, Calandrino went on with his lament. "Oh, poor me," he said, "what shall I do? How am I going to give birth to this child? Where will he come out? Now I see only too clearly that this wife of mine, what with that insatiable lust of hers, has been the death of me. May God make her as miserable as I wish to be happy. If I were well— which I'm not—I'd get up and give her such a beating I'd break every bone in her body. It does serve me right, though, because I should never have let her get up on top. Anyway, one thing's for certain: if I manage to get out of this alive, she can die of frustration before she ever gets to do it that way again."

As they listened to Calandrino, Bruno, Buffalmacco, and Nello had such a desire to laugh that they were ready to explode. They managed to contain themselves, however, but Master Simonkey guffawed, opening his mouth so wide that you could have pulled out every one of his teeth.[7] After a long while, Calandrino finally threw himself on the doctor's mercy and begged him for his advice and assistance.

"Calandrino," Master Simone told him, "there's no reason for you to get upset. God be praised, we diagnosed the problem early enough for me to set you right quite easily in just a few days. However, you're going to have to spend a little money on it."

"Oh yes, doctor," said Calandrino, "do it, for the love of God. I've got two hundred *lire* here that I thought of using to buy a farm. If you need them, you can have them all, just so long as I don't have to give birth. I don't know how I'd manage it, because I hear women making so much noise when they're having a baby, despite the fact that they have such a great big thing to use for it to come through, that I'm afraid if I suffered so much pain, I'd die before I got it out."

"Don't give it another thought," said the doctor. "I'll have a certain potion made up for you, a distillation that's good for such cases and very pleasant to drink. It'll take care of everything by the third morning and make you as healthy as a horse.[8] But see to it that you're wiser in the future and don't get into such foolish situations. Now, to prepare this medicine, we'll need three pairs of good, fat capons, and you must give one of your buddies here five of those *lire* to buy all the other ingredients that are needed. Then make sure that everything is taken around to my shop, and tomorrow morning, in God's name, I'll send you that distilled potion, which you should start drinking, a nice, big glassful at a time."

When Calandrino heard what Master Simone had to say, he declared, "Doctor, it's in your hands," and he gave Bruno the five *lire* as well as enough money for three pairs of capons, asking him to purchase everything and thanking him profusely for going to so much trouble on his behalf.

The doctor went away and had a little bit of spiced wine prepared, which he sent around to Calandrino.[9] As for Bruno, he went out and bought the capons as well as everything else necessary for a good meal, which he then proceeded to eat in the company of his two buddies and the doctor.

Calandrino drank the wine for three mornings in a row, after which the doctor came to see him, accompanied by his three comrades. Having taken Calandrino's pulse, he announced: "You're cured, Calandrino, no doubt about it. You may safely attend to your affairs today and don't have to stay home any longer."

The happy Calandrino got up and went about his business, and whenever he ran into anyone to talk to, he was full of praise for the wonderful way that Master Simone had cured him, because in just three days he had terminated his pregnancy with absolutely no pain at all. Bruno, Buffalmacco, and Nello were pleased to have found a clever plan to get around Calandrino's stinginess, but Monna Tessa had figured it out and did nothing but grumble to her husband about it.

Day 9, Story 4

At Buonconvento, Cecco, the son of Messer Fortarrigo, gambles away not only everything he possesses, but the money belonging to Cecco, the son of Messer Angiulieri, as well. He then runs after him, clad only in his shirt, saying that he has been robbed, and causes Angiulieri to be seized by some peasants, after which he puts on Angiulieri's clothing, mounts his palfrey, and rides away, leaving him behind in nothing but his shirt.[1]

The entire company laughed uproariously on hearing what Calandrino said about his wife, but when Filostrato fell silent, Neifile, at the Queen's request, began to speak:

Worthy ladies, if it was not more difficult for people to display their wisdom and virtue to others than to exhibit their folly and vice, it would be a wasted effort for many of them to place a bridle on their tongues. All of this is something that Calandrino's foolishness has made abundantly clear, for there was no need for him to reveal in public the secret pleasures of his wife in order to be cured of the malady that his simplicity made him believe he suffered from. His story has brought to mind a tale pointing in the opposite direction, for it shows how one man's cunning triumphed over another man's wisdom, to the severe distress and embarrassment of the latter. And this is what it will now be my pleasure to relate to you.

Not many years ago, there lived in Siena two young men, both of whom had come of age and were named Cecco, although one was the son of Messer Angiulieri, and the other, of Messer Fortarrigo.[2] Although they did not share the same attitudes on many issues, there was one subject—namely, the hatred the two of them felt for their fathers—on which they were so fully in accord that they became friends and often wound up spending time in one another's company.

Angiulieri, who was a handsome, well-mannered man, found it hard to live in Siena on the allowance he was given by his father, and when he heard that a certain cardinal, who was a great patron of his, had been sent by the Pope as a legate to The Marches of Ancona, he decided to go and join him there, in the belief that he would better his situation by such a move.[3] Having made his intentions known to his father, he arranged with him to receive six months' worth of his allowance in a single payment so that he could buy clothes, furnish himself with horses, and go there in suitable style.

As he was looking around for someone to come along as his servant, word of his plan reached Fortarrigo who immediately went to Angiulieri and begged him, using all the eloquence at his command, to take him with him. Although Fortarrigo offered to be his serving man and his valet and his general factotum without requiring any salary beyond his living expenses, Angiulieri rejected his offer, not because he judged the man incapable of performing such services, but because Fortarrigo was a gambler and sometimes got drunk as well. In response, Fortarrigo assured him that he would be on his guard against both weaknesses, and swearing oath upon oath, begged him over and over again until Angiulieri finally surrendered and agreed to hire him.

The two of them set out one morning, reaching Buonconvento in time to dine, and since the weather was very hot, once Angiulieri was finished eating, he asked the innkeeper to have a bed prepared for him.[4] With Fortarrigo's assistance, he got undressed, and as he lay down to rest, told his servant to wake him at the stroke of nones.

While Angiulieri was sleeping, Fortarrigo repaired to the tavern, and after having had a few drinks, he started gambling with some people there who managed in a short space of time to beat him, winning not just all the money he had on him, but practically every last stitch of clothing he was wearing. Dressed now only in his shirt and anxious to recoup his losses, he went back to the room in which Angiulieri was taking his nap, and seeing that his master was sound asleep, he took all

the money out of his purse and returned to the game, where he managed to lose everything just as he had done before.

Angiulieri woke up, and after getting out of bed and putting on his
clothes, he called for Fortarrigo. Unable to find him, he assumed that he
had gotten drunk and was sleeping it off somewhere, just as he used to
do from time to time in he past. He thus decided to leave him behind,
and feeling confident that he could furnish himself with a servant in
Corsignano, he had his saddle and saddlebag put on his palfrey, and
prepared to depart. When he sought to pay the innkeeper, however,
he found himself without a red cent. There was a huge scene, and the
entire inn was thrown into turmoil, as Angiulieri went about claiming that he had been robbed, and threatening to have them all arrested
and taken to Siena. At just that moment, lo and behold, who should
show up but Fortarrigo, dressed only in his shirt, who had come to
steal his master's clothes just as he had taken his money. When he saw
Angiulieri about to mount his horse and ride off, he said: "What's all
this, Angiulieri? Do we have to go so soon? Just wait a little longer. I
pawned my doublet for thirty-eight *soldi*, and the guy who has it should
be bringing it back here any moment now. I'm certain he'll let us have
it for thirty-five if we pay him cash down."

While they went on talking, a man appeared on the scene who made
it clear to Angiulieri that Fortarrigo was the one who had taken his
money by showing him the precise sum he had lost. Beside himself
with rage, Angiulieri gave Fortarrigo a tongue-lashing and would have
done him in if he had not feared the laws of man more than those of
God. Then, threatening to have him hanged by the neck, or to see him
banished from Siena under pain of death, he got up on his horse.

Responding as if Angiulieri had not been talking to him but to somebody else, Fortarrigo said: "Come on, Angiulieri, we've had enough of all
this talk that doesn't amount to a hill of beans. Here's the deal: we can
get it back for thirty-five *soldi*, cash down, but if we wait even just till
tomorrow, he won't accept anything less than the thirty-eight he lent
me for it. And he's doing this favor for me because I wagered the money
on his advice. So why don't we take the opportunity to save ourselves
these three *soldi*?"[5]

Hearing Fortarrigo go on this way drove Angiulieri to distraction, especially because he saw everyone around them staring at him suspiciously as if they did not believe that Fortarrigo had gambled away Angiulieri's money, but that he was holding some of Fortarrigo's. "What's your doublet got to do with me?" he said to Fortarrigo. "I hope they string you up by the neck! Not only have you robbed me and gambled away my money, but on top of that, you've prevented me from leaving. And now here you are, making fun of me!"

Fortarrigo was undeterred, however, and kept responding as if Angiulieri's words were not directed to him. "So," he said, "why don't you want me to save those three *soldi*? Don't you think I'll be able to let you have them back again? Come on, do it, if only for the sake of our friendship. Why are you in such a rush? We'll still reach Torrenieri in plenty of time this evening. Go and find your purse. You know I could ransack all of Siena and not find another one of them that fits me as well as this one did—and to think that I let the guy have it for thirty-eight *soldi*! It's actually worth forty or more, so you're making me a loser twice over here."

Exasperated beyond measure that Fortarrigo, after having robbed him, was now holding him up with his chatter, Angiulieri said nothing more to him by way of response, but turned his horse's head and set off down the road to Torrenieri. A cunning little trick occurred to Fortarrigo, however, and he began trotting along behind him, still wearing nothing but his shirt. He had already gone a good two miles, pleading with him all along the way about his doublet, when, just as Angiulieri was picking up the pace in order to get beyond earshot of his pestering servant, Fortarrigo spotted some peasants working in a field close to the road up ahead of them and started shouting to them at the top of his lungs, "Grab him! Grab him!" In response, the peasants, some of them clutching their spades, and others their hoes, blocked the road in front of Angiulieri, and supposing that he had robbed the guy in the shirt who came running and screaming after him, they seized him in order to stop him from going any farther. And no matter how often he told them who he was and how things actually stood, it was of little use to him.

When Fortarrigo reached them, he looked angrily at Angiulieri and said, "I don't know what keeps me from killing you, you sneak thief, for running off with my belongings this way!" Then, turning to the peasants, he declared, "You can see for yourselves, gentlemen, the state he left me in back there at the inn, after first going and gambling away everything he possessed! But thanks be to God, and to you, I can now say that I've salvaged this much at least, and for that I'll be eternally grateful to you."

Angiulieri also told his side of the story, but no one listened to what he had to say. So Fortarrigo, with the help of the peasants, dragged him down to the ground from off his palfrey, stripped him of his clothes, and put them on himself. Then he mounted the horse, and leaving Angiulieri there barefoot and dressed in nothing but his shirt, he returned to Siena, telling everyone he met that he had won Angiulieri's palfrey and clothing in a wager.

Thus, instead of presenting himself as a rich man before the cardinal in The Marches, as he had planned to do, Angiulieri returned impoverished to Buonconvento, clad only in his shirt. Feeling deeply ashamed, he did not dare to go back to Siena for the time being, but rather, having borrowed a suit of clothes, he mounted the nag that Fortarrigo had been riding and went to Corsignano, where he stayed with some relatives of his until his father once again came to his assistance.

Although Fortarrigo's malicious trick spoiled Angiulieri's well-laid plans, it did not go unpunished, for Angiulieri got him back when the proper time and place presented themselves.

Day 9, Story 5

When Calandrino falls in love with a young woman, Bruno makes a magic scroll for him, with which he no sooner touches her than she goes off with him. Then, however, he gets caught by his wife and finds himself in a very serious and unpleasant predicament.[1]

When Neifile's relatively brief story was finished, the company passed over it without much laughter or discussion, and the Queen, turning to Fiammetta, ordered her to go next. Thoroughly delighted, she replied that she was happy to do so and began as follows:

Noblest of ladies, as I believe you already know, there is no subject, no matter how much has already been said about it, that will fail to provide even more pleasure if the person who wants to discuss it knows how to choose the right time and place to speak. Now, since the reason we are here is to enjoy ourselves and have some fun, then I reckon this is the proper time and place for any subject that would entertain us and give us pleasure, for even though the subject had been discussed a thousand times already, we could return to it a thousand times more and still find it delightful.

Now, despite the fact that we have talked quite a lot about Calandrino's antics, when you consider that everything he does is amusing, as Filostrato observed just a little while ago, then I shall be so bold as to add yet one more tale to the others we have heard about him. Had I wanted to depart from the truth, I could have easily disguised things with fictitious names, and I could still do so now. However, since a storyteller greatly diminishes the delight he gives his audience by departing from the truth of what really happened, I shall, for the reason I have just mentioned, tell you my story as it actually happened.

A wealthy fellow citizen of ours named Niccolò Cornacchini had, among his many possessions, a fine piece of property at Camerata, on which he had a beautiful, stately mansion built for himself.[2] He arranged with Bruno and Buffalmacco to paint the entire building with frescoes, but since it was a very substantial job, they enlisted Nello and Calandrino to help them, and then the four of them got down to work. Although a few rooms in the house contained beds and other furnishings, none of the members of the household lived on the premises except for an old serving woman who stayed there to keep watch over the place. Consequently, from time to time, one of Niccolò's sons, a young bachelor named Filippo, was in the habit of bringing some woman or other there who would tend to his pleasures for a day or two before she was sent away.

On one of those occasions he happened to bring with him a certain Niccolosa who was kept by an unsavory character named Mangione at a house in Camaldoli from which he used to let her out for hire.[3] She had a beautiful figure and was nicely dressed, and for a woman of her sort she was polite and well-spoken. One day around noon she left the bedroom, wearing a white shift with her hair tied up around her head, and went to a well located in the courtyard of the house, where she was washing her hands and face when Calandrino happened to come by to get some water. He gave her a friendly greeting, and after replying, she started to stare at him, not because she found him attractive, but because he seemed to her a very strange man indeed. Calandrino returned her gaze, and on seeing how beautiful she was, he came up with any number of excuses not to take the water back to his buddies. Since he did not know who she was, however, he could not pluck up the courage to address her. Noticing how he was staring at her, she decided to play a trick on him and started glancing over at him from time to time, heaving little sighs as she did so, with the result that Calandrino instantly fell head over heels for her and did not leave the courtyard until Filippo called her back to the bedroom.

Upon returning to work, Calandrino did nothing but breathe out one huge sigh after another. Bruno took great delight in whatever Calandrino did and always kept his eye on him, and when he noticed this, he said: "What the devil's the matter with you, Calandrino, my friend? You do nothing but sigh all the time."

"If I could only find someone to help me, buddy," replied Calandrino, "I'd be all right."

"What do you mean?" asked Bruno.

"Don't tell anyone," said Calandrino, "but there's a young woman down there who's more beautiful than a fairy, and she's so much in love with me that it would astonish you.⁴ I spotted her just now when I went for the water."

"Uh-oh," said Bruno, "you'd better be careful it isn't Filippo's wife."

"I think she is," said Calandrino, "because when he called her from his room, she went right in to him. But what difference does that make? In affairs like this, I'd put one over on Christ Himself, to say nothing of Filippo. Truth is, buddy, I couldn't begin to tell you how much I'm attracted to her."

"I'll find out who she is for you, buddy," said Bruno, "and if she's Filippo's wife, it'll only take me two words to fix things up for you, because she's a good friend of mine. But how will we manage it so that Buffalmacco doesn't find out? I never get a chance to speak with her except when he's around."

"I'm not worried about Buffalmacco," replied Calandrino, "but we've got to watch out for Nello, because he's one of Tessa's relatives and he'd ruin everything."*

"That's true," said Bruno.

Now, Bruno knew exactly who the girl was because he had seen her arrive, and besides, Filippo had told him all about her. Consequently, when Calandrino interrupted his work for a while in order to go and see if he could catch a glimpse of her, Bruno told everything to Nello and Buffalmacco, and together they secretly agreed on what they were going to do about this infatuation of his.

Upon his return, Bruno asked Calandrino in a whisper: "Did you get to see her?"

"Oh yes, alas," replied Calandrino, "and she's knocked me dead!"

---

* Tessa is Calandrino's wife.

"I'll just go and see if she really is the one I think she is," said Bruno. "And if that's the case, you can just leave everything to me."

Bruno went downstairs, and when he found Filippo and the girl, he explained precisely what kind of man Calandrino was and told them what he had said. Then Bruno arranged with each of them what they should say and do to have fun and enjoy the spectacle of Calandrino's infatuation. Afterward, returning to Calandrino, he said to him: "It's her, all right, and that's why we're going to have to proceed with great caution in this business, because if Filippo gets wind of it, all the water in the Arno won't wash us clean of it. But what do you want me to tell her from you if I should have a chance to speak with her?"

"By gosh," said Calandrino, "the very, very first thing to tell her is that I wish her a thousand bushels of that good stuff you get pregnant with, and then say that I'm her obedient server, and if there's anything she wants—you get my meaning?"[5]

"Yes," replied Bruno. "Leave it all to me."

When the hour for supper arrived, they stopped working for the day and went down into the courtyard where they found Filippo and Niccolosa and stayed awhile for Calandrino's benefit. Staring continually at Niccolosa, Calandrino began performing the oddest antics in the world. In fact, there were so many of them, and they were so weird, that even a blind man would have noticed them. As for Niccolosa, in light of what Bruno had told her, she did everything she thought would set Calandrino on fire, having the best time in her life because of his strange behavior. Meanwhile, Filippo pretended to be talking with Buffalmacco and the others, unaware of what was going on.

After a while, however, to Calandrino's very great disappointment, they left, and as the painters made their way back to Florence, Bruno said to him: "I have to tell you, you're making her melt like ice in the sun. By God's body, if you bring your rebeck* here and sing some of those love songs of yours, you'll make her throw herself out the window and right down to the ground in order to get to you."

---

* The rebeck, a relative of the viola, was a three-stringed, pear-shaped instrument played with a bow.

"Do you think so, buddy?" said Calandrino. "Do you think I should bring it?"

"Yes, I do," replied Bruno.

"You didn't believe me today when I told you about it," said Calandrino. "But there's no doubt about it, buddy: I know better than any man alive how to get what I want. Who besides me would have discovered the way to make such a woman fall in love with him so quickly? Not these young guys. They're just a bunch of blowhards who go parading up and down all day long and wouldn't be able to pick up three handfuls of nuts in a thousand years. Just you watch me with my rebeck for a little while. I'll show you a trick or two! And I'll have you know I'm not as old as you think. She's certainly noticed it, she has, but in any case, I'll really prove it to her once I get my paws on her. I swear by the true body of Christ, I'm going to play such a game with her that she'll follow me around everywhere like the mad mother doting on her son."[6]

"Oh," said Bruno, "you'll stick your snout right into her. In fact, I can see you now, with those lute-peg teeth of yours, biting her little red mouth and those cheeks that look like two roses, and then devouring every last bit of her."

As he listened to Bruno's words, Calandrino thought he was already doing the deed, and he went around singing and skipping with such glee that he practically jumped right out of his hide. Moreover, the next day, he brought his rebeck along, and accompanying himself with it, he sang a number of songs, to the great delight of the entire group.

To cut the story short, Calandrino took so many breaks to go and see the girl as often as he could that he stopped working altogether. Instead, a thousand times a day, he would dash to the window, and then to the door, and then into the court, all in order to catch a glimpse of her, while she astutely followed Bruno's instructions and provided him with every opportunity to do so. For his part, Bruno would answer Calandrino's messages in her name and would sometimes carry notes to him as if they came from her. When she was not around, which was mostly the case, he would have letters sent to Calandrino from her in which she filled him with the hope that he was going to be able to satisfy his desires, but explained that she was then staying at the house of some relatives and that he could not come to see her there.

In this way, Bruno and Buffalmacco managed the affair, deriving the greatest pleasure in the world from Calandrino's antics. Sometimes, they got him to give them gifts, pretending that she was asking for them. At one time it was an ivory comb, at another a purse, and at yet another a little knife, plus other trifles of that sort, in exchange for which they gave him some worthless little counterfeit rings, which made him deliriously happy. In addition, they got some nice meals out of him, and he showed them other little favors to encourage them to work diligently on his behalf.

They kept him on tenterhooks like this for a good two months without his making any more progress. When Calandrino saw that their work was at the point of completion, and realized that if he did not satisfy his desires before it was finished, he was never going to be able to do so, he started pressing Bruno as hard as possible for his help. Consequently, the next time the girl was there, Bruno made arrangements with her and Filippo about what they were to do.

"Look, buddy," he said to Calandrino, "this lady has promised me at least a thousand times that she's ready to give you what you want, and every time she does absolutely nothing about it. I think she's leading you around by the nose. So, if you're willing, seeing as how she isn't keeping her promises, we'll make her do it whether she wants to or not."

"Ah yes, for the love of God," replied Calandrino, "let's do it right away."

"Are you brave enough to touch her with a scroll I'll give you?" asked Bruno.

"Yes," answered Calandrino, "I sure am."

"Then," said Bruno, "go and fetch me a little piece of parchment from a stillborn lamb, a live bat, three grains of incense, and a candle that's been blessed. You can leave the rest to me."

Calandrino spent the whole of that evening trying to catch a bat by means of various contrivances. Finally, he managed to snag one and brought it to Bruno along with the other things. Withdrawing into another room, Bruno wrote some nonsense in made-up characters on the parchment and took it back to Calandrino.

"Now be aware, Calandrino," he said, "if you touch her with this scroll, she'll come with you immediately and do whatever you want. So, if Filippo should go off anywhere today, find some way to get close to her and touch her with it. Then go to the barn that's off to the side of the house. It's the best place for your purposes because no one ever goes there. You'll see that she'll come, too, and when she does, you know exactly what it is you have to do."

Calandrino was the happiest man in the world as he took the scroll. "Buddy," he said, "just leave it to me."

Nello, against whom Calandrino was constantly on guard, was enjoying the affair as much as the others, and like them, he had his hand in the trick they were playing. Thus, following Bruno's instructions, he went down to see Calandrino's wife in Florence.

"Tessa," he said to her, "you remember the terrible beating that Calandrino gave you, for no reason at all, the day he came back home from the Mugnone with all those stones? Well, I want to give you a chance now to get even with him, and if you don't take it, don't you ever call me your kinsman or your friend again. He's really fallen for some woman up there, and she's such a slut that she's been regularly shutting herself up in some room or other with him. As a matter of fact, just a little while ago, they arranged to get together very soon, and that's why I want you to come and see him, and then punish him the way he deserves."

When Monna Tessa heard this, it did not seem like a joke to her, and leaping to her feet, she blurted out: "Oh no, you common thief, you. So, this is how you treat me, is it? By God's Cross, you won't get away without paying for it."

Then she grabbed her cloak, and accompanied by a little maidservant, set off with Nello, rushing to the mansion at a furious pace. Bruno saw her coming in the distance and said to Filippo, "Look, here comes our friend." So Filippo went up to where Calandrino and the others were working and said to them, "Masters, I have to go to Florence immediately. Keep up the hard work." As soon as he left them, he went and hid himself in a place from which, without being seen, he could observe what Calandrino would do.

When Calandrino thought that Filippo had gotten far enough away, he went down into the courtyard where he found Niccolosa alone and started chatting her up. She knew exactly what she was supposed to do, and sidling over to him, she treated him with greater familiarity than usual, at which point Calandrino touched her with the scroll. As soon as he had done so, without saying a word he turned and directed his steps toward the barn, with Niccolosa following right behind him. Once she had gotten inside and had closed the door behind them, she took him in her arms and threw him down on the straw that was lying on the floor. Then she climbed on top and straddled him. Placing her hands on his shoulders to hold him down and keep his face away from hers, she gazed at him as if he were her utmost desire.

"O my sweet Calandrino," she said, "heart of my body, my soul, my treasure, my comfort, how long have I wanted to have you all for myself and to clasp you to me like this! Your charms have got me wound around your little finger! You've chained up my heart with that rebeck of yours! Is it really possible that I'm here, holding you in my arms?"

"Ah, my sweet soul," said Calandrino, who was scarcely able to move, "let me kiss you."

"Oh, you're in such a rush!" said Niccolosa. "Let me first have my fill of gazing upon you! Let me sate my eyes with looking at that sweet face of yours!"

Bruno and Buffalmacco had gone to join Filippo, and the three of them were watching and listening to everything that was going on, when lo and behold, just as Calandrino was about to give Niccolosa a kiss, who should arrive but Nello and Monna Tessa.

"I swear to God the two of them are in there together," said Nello, as they approached the door to the barn. Fuming with rage, Monna Tessa gave it a shove with her hands that flung it wide open. When she entered the barn, she saw Calandrino lying there, straddled by Niccolosa, who no sooner caught sight of her than she sprang to her feet and ran off to join Filippo.

Before Calandrino could get up, Monna Tessa ran at him with her nails and clawed him all over his face. Then she seized him by the hair and started dragging him up and down. "You damned filthy dog, you!" she said to him. "So this is how you treat me? You old fool, I curse all the love I ever felt for you! Don't you think you've got enough to take care of at home, instead of going around lusting after other women? Just look at this fine lover! Don't you know who you are, you wretch? Don't you know yourself, you sad sack? Why, if you were completely squeezed dry, there wouldn't be enough juice to make a sauce. I swear to God, the woman who was getting you pregnant just now, that wasn't Tessa.[7] Whoever she is, may God make her suffer, because she must really be pretty pathetic to be attracted to a precious jewel like you!"

When he first saw his wife coming, Calandrino did not know whether he was alive or dead, and he did not have the courage to do anything to defend himself against her. But later, all scratched and scraped and disheveled, he gathered up his cloak, got to his feet, and began humbly begging her not to shout, unless she wanted to see him all cut up into little pieces, because the woman who had been with him was the wife of the master of the house.

"I don't care who she is," said Monna Tessa. "May God punish her!"

Bruno and Buffalmacco, who, along with Filippo and Niccolosa, had had their fill of laughing at this scene, came in, pretending they had been attracted there by all the noise. After a lot of talk back and forth, they managed to pacify the lady, and advised Calandrino to return to Florence and never come up there again, because if Filippo ever found out about the affair, he would certainly do him some harm.

Thus, the miserable, forlorn Calandrino, all scratched and scraped, made his way back to Florence and never dared to go up to Camerata again. Vexed and tormented night and day by his wife's reproaches, he put an end to his fervent love, having made himself a complete laughingstock not only for his companions, but for Niccolosa and Filippo as well.

Day 9, Story 6

Two young men find lodging overnight, and while one of them goes to bed with their host's daughter, the host's wife inadvertently sleeps with the other. Then the youth who was with the daughter gets into bed with her father, and thinking he is talking to his companion, tells him everything. A great commotion ensues, at which point the wife, realizing her mistake, gets into bed with her daughter and by means of a few choice words restores the peace.[1]

Just as he had done before, Calandrino made the entire company laugh once again. Then, when the ladies finally stopped talking about his antics, the Queen ordered Panfilo to speak, and he said:

Praiseworthy ladies, the name of Calandrino's beloved has brought to mind a story about another Niccolosa that I would like to recount for you, because in it you will see how a good woman's presence of mind enabled her to avert a great scandal.

Not so long ago, in the valley of the Mugnone there lived a worthy man who earned money by supplying travelers with food and drink, and although he was poor and his house tiny, he would sometimes put them up, but only in cases of urgent need and only if he knew who they were. The man was married to a most attractive woman, who had borne him two children, a lovely, charming young girl fifteen or sixteen years old who was still unmarried, and a tiny baby boy not yet one whom his mother was breast-feeding herself.

The girl had caught the eye of a young gentleman from our city, a lively, attractive youth who spent a lot of time in the countryside, and he fell passionately, fervently, in love with her. For her part, she took great pride in having won the affection of such a young man, and making every effort to keep his love for her alive by behaving with the greatest affability toward him, in the process she likewise fell in love with him. Now, on more than one occasion they would have consummated their love for one another, to the great delight of both parties, if Pinuccio—for that was the youth's name—had not been worried about exposing both the girl and himself to censure. His ardor, however, grew from day to day until he was simply overwhelmed by his desire to be with her. It therefore occurred to him that he just had to discover a way to find lodging at her father's house, for he knew its layout and thought that if he could just get inside, he and the girl could be together, and no one would be any the wiser. And in fact, no sooner did this idea enter his head than he promptly proceeded to put it into effect.

Late one evening, Pinuccio and a trusted companion of his named Adriano, who knew about his love for the girl, hired a couple of pack-horses, placed a pair of saddlebags on them, which may have been filled with straw, and set out from Florence. After riding around in a large circle, they arrived at the valley of the Mugnone, reaching it some time after nightfall. There, after turning their horses around as if they were returning from Romagna, they rode up to the worthy man's house and knocked on the door, which he opened right away since he was well acquainted with the pair.

"Look, you have to put us up for the night," Pinuccio told him. "We thought we would've reached Florence by this time, but as you can see, we couldn't ride fast enough to get any farther than here."

"Pinuccio," replied the host, "you must know how poorly provided I am to offer lodging to gentlemen like yourselves, but still, since you've been caught here at this hour, and there's no time for you to go anywhere else, I'm happy to do what I can to put you up for the night."

The two young men dismounted, and after having first seen to their horses, they entered the cottage where they got out the generous supper they had brought with them and ate it with their host. Now, the latter had only one tiny little bedroom, in which he had set up three small beds to the best of his ability, leaving so little space that it was a tight squeeze indeed to maneuver around them. Two of the beds were next to one of the walls, while the third one stood on the opposite side of the room. The host then had the least uncomfortable bed made up for the two companions and invited them to sleep there. A little later, while the two of them were still wide awake, although they were pretending to be asleep, the host had his daughter settle down in one of the other beds, and he got into the third one with his wife, who placed the cradle holding their little baby son next to where she was sleeping.

After everything had been arranged in the room, Pinuccio made a mental note of it all and waited a little while until he thought everyone was asleep. At that point, he quietly got up, went over to the little bed where the girl he loved was sleeping, and lay down beside her. Although she was frightened, she gave him a joyous welcome, and there he stayed, taking his fill of that pleasure for which they had both been yearning for such a long time.

While Pinuccio was in bed with the girl, a cat happened to knock some things over. The noise woke up the wife, who was afraid that it was something else. She got out of bed in the dark, naked as she was, and headed for the place from which the sound had come.

By chance, Adriano also happened to get up, not for the same reason, but in response to a call of nature, and as he was going to take care of his business, he bumped into the cradle where the wife had placed it on the floor. Since he could not get past without moving it out of the way, he grabbed it, lifted it up from where the wife had set it, and put it down next to the bed in which he himself had been sleeping. Then, having finished what he had gotten up to do, he came back, and without giving any further thought to the cradle, climbed into bed.

After having searched the house for a while, the wife concluded that nothing of importance had fallen down, and having no desire to light a lamp in order to inspect things more closely, she yelled at the cat and then returned to the little bedroom, groping her way right up to the bed where her husband was sleeping. But when she failed to find the cradle there, she said to herself: "Oh no, stupid me! See what I was about to do! For God's sake, I was heading right for the bed where my guests are sleeping!" Moving forward a bit, she found the cradle, and then lay down with Adriano in the bed beside it, thinking she was lying down with her husband. Adriano had not yet gone back to sleep, and when he realized what had happened, he gave her a warm reception, after which, without uttering a single sound in the process, he yanked his rope until it was taut and his sail was all swollen out, much to the wife's great satisfaction.[2]

This was how matters stood when Pinuccio, who had enjoyed himself with the girl as much as he had wanted, started worrying that sleep might surprise him there with her. Consequently, he rose from her side in order to go back and rest in his own bed. When he got there, however, only to run into the cradle, he moved on, thinking it was the host's bed, and wound up getting in beside the host himself, who was awakened by his arrival. Being under the impression that the man who lay beside him was Adriano, Pinuccio said: "About that Niccolosa, I have to say, there's nothing could be sweeter, in any way.[3] By God's body, I've had more fun with her than any man's ever had with a woman. And let me assure you, since I left here, I've managed to get into her country house six times."

When the host heard this bit of news, he was not exactly pleased. First, he asked himself: "What the devil is this guy doing here?" Then, allowing his anger to get the better of his prudence, he said: "Pinuccio, what you've done is shameful. I don't know why you had to do it to me, but by God's body, I'm going to pay you back for it."

Pinuccio was not the smartest young man in the world, and when he realized his mistake, instead of trying to find the best remedy he could for it, he replied: "How're you going to pay me back? What could you do to me?"

The host's wife, who thought she was sleeping with her husband, said to Adriano: "Uh-oh! Just listen to the way our guests are quarreling with one another."

"Let 'em go ahead," said Adriano, with a laugh, "and to Hell with 'em. They had too much to drink last night."

The wife was thinking it was her husband's voice when she heard him cursing them, but as soon as she heard Adriano's words, she immediately realized where she was and with whom. Wise woman that she was, however, she got up at once without saying another word and grabbed her baby son's cradle. Since there was absolutely no light in the room, she felt her way along, carrying the cradle to the side of the bed in which her daughter was sleeping. There she put it down and got into the bed with her. Then, pretending to have been awakened by the noise her husband was making, she called to him and asked him what he was having words with Pinuccio about.

"Didn't you hear what he says he did to Niccolosa tonight?" her husband replied.

"He's lying through his teeth," she said. "He didn't sleep with Niccolosa, because I've been lying here all this time and haven't slept a wink since I got in. You're a fool to believe him. You men drink so much in the evening that at night you do nothing but dream and walk about all over the place in your sleep without knowing where you are and imagine you've performed all sorts of miracles. It's a pity you don't break your necks! But what's Pinuccio doing over there? Why isn't he in his own bed?"

For his part, seeing how adroitly the woman was covering up both her own shame and her daughter's, Adriano added: "Pinuccio, I've told you a hundred times that you shouldn't be wandering about, because this vice of yours of sleepwalking and then recounting the fantasies that you've dreamed as though they were true is going to get you into trouble one of these days. Come back here, goddamn you."

When the host heard what his wife and Adriano were both saying, he started to think that Pinuccio really was dreaming. Consequently, taking him by the shoulders, he began to shake him and yell at him. "Wake up, Pinuccio," he said. "Get back in your own bed."

Having taken in everything they had said, Pinuccio began raving like someone who was dreaming, provoking the host to the heartiest laugh in the world. Finally, as if in response to the shaking he was being given, Pinuccio pretended to wake up, and shouting over to Adriano, he said: "Why are you calling me? Is it day already?"

"Yes, it is," said Adriano. "Come over here."

Feigning ignorance of what had happened and acting as if he were very drowsy, Pinuccio finally left the host's side and went back to bed with Adriano. When day came and everyone was up, the host started laughing and making fun of Pinuccio and his dreaming. And so, between one jest and another, the two young men got their horses ready and strapped on their saddlebags. Then, after having had a drink with the host, they mounted up and rode off to Florence, no less content with the way things happened than with the outcome of their night's adventures.

From then on, Pinuccio found other ways to spend time with Niccolosa, and since she swore to her mother that he had unquestionably been dreaming, her mother, who certainly recalled Adriano's embraces, was left with the conviction that she had been the only one awake that night.

Day 9, Story 7

Talano d'Imolese dreams that a wolf rips up his wife's throat and face, but when he tells her to be on her guard, she ignores him, and that is exactly what happens to her.[1]

Once Panfilo was finished and everyone had praised the wife's presence of mind, the Queen asked Pampinea to tell another story, and she began as follows:

On previous occasions, my most pleasant ladies, we have spoken about how truths are revealed in dreams, a notion many of us women scoff at, and therefore, although the subject has been discussed before, I cannot leave it before telling a little tale in just a few short words about what happened to a neighbor of mine not so long ago because she did not believe a dream her husband had in which she appeared.[2]

I do not know whether you were ever acquainted with Talano d'Imolese, but he was a very worthy man who had married a young woman named Margherita.[3] She was more beautiful than all the rest, but surpassed them even more in being irritable, obstinate, and ill tempered to the point that she utterly refused to follow other people's advice and never approved of anything anyone else ever did. All this was a heavy burden for Talano to bear, but he put up with it since he had no choice in the matter.

Now it happened one night that when Talano was staying with this Margherita of his at an estate they had in the country, he went to sleep and dreamed that he saw her wandering through a very lovely forest they owned that was located not far from their house. While he watched her walking about, a huge, ferocious wolf seemed to emerge from one corner of the woods, leap at her throat, and drag her to the ground. Screaming for help, she struggled mightily to free herself from its jaws, and when she finally managed to escape, her entire face and throat appeared to have been torn to shreds.

The moment he awoke the next morning, Talano turned to his spouse and said to her: "Wife, although I've never had even one good day with you because of your ill temper, all the same I'd still be sorry if anything bad happened to you, and therefore, if you'll take my advice, you won't leave the house today."

Upon being asked why, he told her all about his dream. But his wife just shook her head and said: "Evil wishes beget evil dreams.[4] You pretend to be very concerned about my welfare, but you dream about what you'd like to see happen to me. Well, you may rest assured I'll take care to prevent you from gloating over me today—or at any other time in the future—because of some such misfortune as the one you describe."

"I knew that's what you'd say," Talano replied, "because that's the thanks one gets for combing a scabby head. But believe whatever you like. For my part, what I said to you was for your own good, and once again, I advise you to stay home today, or at least to avoid going into those woods of ours."

"Very well," said his wife, "I'll do what you say."

But then she began thinking to herself: "Did you see how cunning this guy is, thinking he's scared me out of going into our woods today? I'm sure he's arranged to meet with some harlot or other there and doesn't want me to catch him at it. Ah, he'd do well for himself if he were eating dinner with the blind, but since I know him for what he is, I'd be a real fool to take him at his word![5] He certainly won't get away with this. I'm going to see what sort of business he's planning to conduct in the woods now, even if I have to stay there all day long."

No sooner had she reached this conclusion than her husband left the house by one door, at which point she, too, left it by another, and doing everything she could to keep from being seen, she headed off for the woods without a moment's delay. Upon entering it, she hid herself in a spot where the cover was thickest and kept a sharp lookout on all sides to see if anybody was coming.

The thought never crossed her mind that she faced any sort of danger from wolves, but as she was standing there in the way we have described, lo and behold a huge, ferocious beast jumped out of a dense thicket that was right next to her. From the moment she saw it, she hardly had time to say "God help me!" before the wolf had leaped at her throat, seized her firmly in its jaws, and started dragging her away as though she had been a little baby lamb.

So tight was the wolf's grip on her throat that she could neither cry out nor help herself in any other way, and as it carried her off, it would have throttled her for sure, if it had not run into some shepherds who started yelling at the beast and forced it to release her. The poor, unfortunate woman was recognized by the shepherds, who took her back home, where, after being treated at length by a number of physicians, she was eventually healed. Her recovery was not complete, however, for her entire throat and part of her face were so disfigured that whereas she had formerly been a beautiful woman, from then on she looked utterly ugly and repulsive.

And so, ashamed to show herself in public, she shed many a bitter tear over her surly behavior and her refusal to give any credence, though it would have cost her nothing, to her husband's truthful dream.

Day 9, Story 8

When Biondello plays a trick on Ciacco about a dinner, Ciacco cleverly avenges himself by arranging for Biondello to get a shameful beating.[1]

Every single member of the merry company declared that what Talano had seen while he was sleeping was not a dream, but a vision, because it corresponded so precisely, without exception, to what had actually occurred. But when they all fell silent, the Queen ordered Lauretta to continue, and she said:

Wisest of ladies, just as those storytellers who preceded me today have almost all been prompted to speak by something that was mentioned earlier, I, too, am moved by the account Pampinea gave us yesterday of the scholar's uncompromising revenge to tell you about an act of vengeance that was quite painful for the person who suffered through it, but was nevertheless, for all that, much less savage.

Let me tell you, then, that there was once in Florence a man everyone called Ciacco who was the greatest glutton that ever lived. A very sophisticated individual, he always had a wealth of witty, amusing things to say, and since he lacked the means to meet the expenses his gluttony required, he developed a reputation for himself not exactly as a court entertainer, but as someone good at making clever cutting remarks, and he took to spending time in the company of rich men who enjoyed good food. With them he would regularly eat both dinner and supper, even though they did not always invite him.

In those days there was also a man living in Florence named Biondello, who practiced the same profession as Ciacco. This Biondello was short of stature, a sharp dresser, and cleaner than a fly, and he went around wearing a close-fitting cap on his head over his long blond locks,

which were always done up with such care that there was never a strand
out of place.²

One morning during Lent, Biondello had gone to the fish market
where he was in the process of purchasing two impressively large lampreys* for Messer Vieri de' Cerchi, when he was spotted by Ciacco who
came right over to speak to him.³

"What's this all about?" he asked.

"Yesterday afternoon," replied Biondello, "three lampreys even finer
than these, together with a sturgeon, were sent to Messer Corso Donati,
but since he didn't think they were enough to feed a group of gentlemen he'd invited, he sent me to buy two more. Won't you be coming
to join us?"

"You can count on my being there," said Ciacco.

And so, at what seemed like the appropriate time, Ciacco went to
Messer Corso's house where he found him with several of his neighbors. They had not yet sat down to dinner, and when he was asked
what he was up to, he answered: "Sir, I've come to dine with you and
your company."

"You're most welcome," said Messer Corso, "and since it's time now,
let's go and eat."

Upon sitting down, they were first served a course of chickpeas
with tuna belly, followed by some fried fish from the Arno, and that
was it. Realizing that Biondello had played a trick on him, Ciacco got
really upset and resolved to pay him back for it. Just a few days later,
he bumped into Biondello, who had, in the meanwhile, amused quite
a few people with the story of his practical joke. As soon as he caught
sight of Ciacco, he greeted him and asked him with a laugh how Messer
Corso's lampreys had tasted.

"Before a week's gone by," replied Ciacco, "you'll be able to answer
that question much better than I can."

As soon as he left Biondello, Ciacco did not wait a moment before
getting to work, and having agreed on a fee with a clever little huckster,
he supplied the man with a large glass flask, led him to the Loggia de'

---

*Lampreys are eel-like fish.

Cavicciuli, and pointed out a gentleman there called Messer Filippo Argenti, a huge, powerful, muscular individual who was not only the haughtiest, but the most irascible and pugnacious man alive.[4]

"Go up to him with this flask in your hand," said Ciacco, "and say to him: 'Sir, I've been sent to you by Biondello who asks if you would be so kind as to rubify this flask for him with some of your fine red wine because he wants to have a good time with his little drinking buddies.'[5] But be careful he doesn't get his hands on you because he'd really ruin your day, and you'd wind up spoiling my plans."

"Is there anything else I need to say?" asked the huckster.

"No, just go on now," said Ciacco, "and after you've finished your errand, come back here to me with the flask, and I'll give you your pay."

So, away went the huckster and delivered the message to Messer Filippo. No sooner did he hear it than he knew that Biondello, with whom he was well acquainted, was playing a trick on him. Short tempered by nature, Messer Filippo got all red in the face. "What's this stuff about 'rubifying the flask' and 'little drinking buddies'?" he said. "May God curse both you and him!" Then leaping to his feet, he stuck out his arm with the intention of grabbing the huckster, but the latter was on his guard and quickly fled away. Taking a roundabout route, he returned to Ciacco, who had witnessed the entire exchange, and reported what Messer Filippo had said to him.

Ciacco was pleased, and after he had paid the huckster, he went in search of Biondello, never resting for a moment until he found him.

"Have you been at the Loggia de' Cavicciuli recently?" he asked.

"No, not at all," replied Biondello. "Why do you ask?"

"Because I've heard that Messer Filippo's been looking for you," said Ciacco, "though I don't know what he wants."

"All right," said Biondello, "I'm going in that direction, and I'll have a word with him about it."

Biondello set off, with Ciacco following right behind him to see how things would turn out. Meanwhile, Messer Filippo, having been unable to catch the huckster, was left in an absolute fury and was fuming and fretting because the only sense he could make of the man's words was that Biondello had been set on by someone or other to make fun of him.

And while he was gnawing away at himself with rage, lo and behold, Biondello appeared on the scene. As soon as Messer Filippo spotted him, he strode right up to him and gave him a really hard punch in the face.

"Oh no, sir," cried Biondello, "what's this for?"

"Traitor," yelled Messer Filippo, who proceeded to grab him by the hair, tear off his cap, and throw his hat onto the ground. Then, he began laying into him with all his might, adding as he did: "You're sure going to see what it's for. Why did you send somebody to me talking about 'rubifying the flask' and 'little drinking buddies'? Do you think you can make a fool out of me as if I were some kid?" And as he spoke, he smashed in Biondello's face with his fists, which seemed to be made out of iron, and did not leave a single hair on his head in place. Then he rolled him over in the mud and ripped all the clothes he had on to shreds, applying himself to all of these tasks with such zeal that after Biondello's first utterance, he was unable to say another thing, let alone ask Messer Filippo why he was doing all this to him. He had clearly heard Messer Filippo saying something about "rubifying the flask" and "little dinking buddies," but he had no idea what these expressions meant.

By the time Messer Filippo had finished giving him a terrible beating, a large crowd had gathered around them, and they finally managed, with the utmost difficulty, to get Biondello, all bruised and bedraggled, out of his hands. They explained why Messer Filippo had done this to him and scolded him for having sent such a message, telling him that he should have known Messer Filippo better by then and that he was not the sort of man to joke around with. The weeping Biondello protested his innocence, denying that he had ever sent anyone to Messer Filippo asking him for wine. In the end, however, after straightening himself out a bit, he returned home, sad and forlorn, with a full awareness that the entire thing was Ciacco's doing.

It took a number of days, but when the bruises on Biondello's face had finally faded and he began going out of his house once again, Ciacco happened to run into him.

"So, Biondello," he asked with a laugh, "how did you like the taste of Messer Filippo's wine?"

"I wish Messer Corso's lampreys had struck you the same way!" Biondello replied.

"Well, from now on, it's up to you," said Ciacco. "Whenever you want to treat me to a nice meal the way you did, I'll treat you to as nice a drink as the one you got."

Recognizing that it was easier for him to wish Ciacco ill than to do him any real harm, Biondello bid him good-day and from then on took care never to play tricks on him again.

Day 9, Story 9

When two young men ask Solomon's advice, one wanting to know what he must do to gain people's love and the other how he should punish his obstinate wife, Solomon tells the first to love and the second to go to Goosebridge.[1]

Wishing to preserve Dioneo's privilege, the Queen saw that she alone remained to tell a story, and so, as soon as the ladies had had their fill of laughing about the unfortunate Biondello, she cheerfully began as follows:

Amiable ladies, if the order of things is viewed from a sound perspective, it will quite quickly become apparent that Nature, custom, and the laws have decreed that the vast majority of women are subservient to men and must be controlled and governed by them at their discretion. Therefore, any woman who wants to have a quiet, pleasant, untroubled life with the men to whom she is attached should be humble, patient, and obedient, in addition to being chaste, a quality every wise woman considers her greatest, most treasured possession.

Even if we were not taught this by the laws, which aim at the common good in every case, and by usage, or rather custom, as we prefer to call it, whose power is both immense and venerable, Nature proves it to us very plainly, for not only has she made our bodies soft and delicate, our spirits timid and fearful, and our minds benign and compassionate, but she has given us little corporal strength, pleasing voices, and graceful bodily movements—all of which testify to the fact that we need to be ruled by others. Now, it stands to reason that those who need to be assisted and governed should be obedient, submissive, and deferential to those who govern them. And whom do we have to assist us and govern us except men? Therefore, we must submit to them and pay them every conceivable honor, and in my opinion, any woman who deviates from this rule fully deserves not just to receive a stern rebuke, but to be severely punished.

I have been led to make these observations—though this is not for the first time—by what Pampinea said a little while ago about Talano's obstinate wife to whom God meted out the punishment her husband was unable to visit upon her.[2] And so, it is my conclusion, as I said before, that all those women deserve to be punished firmly and harshly whose behavior is not pleasant, benign, and compliant, as Nature, custom, and the laws require.

Now, it is my pleasure to tell you about a piece of advice that Solomon once handed out, for it will serve as useful medicine to cure those who are afflicted with the disease I have just been describing. To be sure, no woman who considers herself undeserving of such a cure should conclude that his counsel applies to her, although men do have a proverb that goes:

Good horses or bad require the spur;
Good woman or bad, the rod's right for her.[3]

Although some might want to interpret these words as a kind of joke, all women would readily grant the truth in them, but I suggest that if you simply take them in their direct moral sense, you must concede the point being made. For all women are pliant and yielding by nature, and hence, in order to correct those who allow themselves to stray too far beyond their prescribed limits, the rod is needed to punish their wickedness. And to bolster the virtue of the others, who do not let themselves transgress, the rod is needed both to sustain and to frighten them.

But setting aside this preaching for now, and coming to what I want to tell you about, let me say that at a time when Solomon's exalted reputation for miraculous wisdom had spread to practically every corner of the earth, and it was well known that he was incredibly liberal in sharing it with anyone wishing to verify it in person, many people would flock to him from all over the world in order to ask his advice about their most pressing and perplexing problems. And one of those who set out to go and consult him was a very wealthy young nobleman named Melisso from the city of Laiazzo, in which he had been born and bred.[4]

Having just left Antioch on his way to Jerusalem, he happened to fall in with another young man named Giosefo, who was going in the same direction, and after the two of them had ridden some distance together, Melisso struck up a conversation with him, as travelers are wont to do. Having learned about Giosefo's background and where he was coming from, Melisso asked him where he was going and what his purpose was in doing so. Giosefo replied that he was off to seek Solomon's advice about how to deal with his wife, for she was the most stubborn, most perverse woman alive, and he could not make her budge from her contrary ways by means of prayers or flattery or anything else.

Then Giosefo in turn asked Melisso where he was coming from, where he was going, and why.

"I'm from Laiazzo," replied Melisso, "and like you, I, too, have a serious problem. I'm a rich young man, and I spend my money giving banquets and entertaining my fellow citizens. And yet, the strange and curious thing about it is that despite all this, I've never found anyone who wishes me well. And that's why I'm going where you are, to get advice about what can be done to make people love me."

The two companions continued their journey together, and upon reaching Jerusalem, through the good offices of one of Solomon's courtiers, they were admitted into the presence of the King, to whom Melisso briefly explained what he needed. Solomon's response was, "Love."

This said, Melisso was immediately ushered out of the room, after which Giosefo explained his reason for coming. The only response he got from Solomon, however, was, "Go to Goosebridge." And in the same way, once the King had spoken, Giosefo was immediately dismissed from his presence. Outside, he found Melisso waiting for him and told him about the answer he had received.

The two of them pondered Solomon's words, but could not divine their meaning or derive anything from them to solve their problems, and so, feeling as though they had been mocked by the King, they started back down the road heading for home. After they had traveled for several days, they came to a river spanned by a fine bridge, and since a long caravan of mules and packhorses loaded with merchandise was going over it, they had no choice but to wait until the entire train had crossed.

When almost all of the animals were on the other side, by chance, a single mule took fright, as we often see them do, and would not move ahead for anything. So, a muleteer took a stick and began beating him, albeit with some restraint at first, in order to make him cross over. But the mule, swerving from one side of the road to the other, and sometimes turning back, utterly refused to go forward. This made the muleteer so furious that he started hitting the animal as hard as is humanly possible, now on the head, now on the flanks, and now on the hindquarters, but all to no avail.

Melisso and Giosefo, who were standing there watching, addressed the muleteer repeatedly.

"Hey, you brute," they said, "what are you doing? Do you want to kill him? Why don't you try being kind and gentle when you lead him? He'll come along more quickly than by beating him the way you're doing."

"You know your horses, and I know my mule," replied the muleteer. "Let me handle it." And having said this, he started in on the animal again, giving him so many blows to each of his flanks that the mule did at last move on, and the muleteer won the contest.

As the two young men were about to continue on their way, Giosefo asked a good man sitting at the head of the bridge what the place was called, and he answered: "Sir, it's called Goosebridge."

The instant Giosefo heard the name, he recalled Solomon's words and turned to Melisso. "I'm telling you, my friend," he said, "the counsel Solomon gave me may yet prove good and true, for now it's perfectly clear to me that I didn't know how to beat my wife, and this muleteer has shown me just what I need to do."

A few days later they reached Antioch, and Giosefo invited Melisso to stay with him and rest up for a while. After receiving a rather cold welcome from his wife, he told her to have whatever Melisso ordered fixed for supper, and since Melisso saw that this would please his friend, he explained what he wanted in just a few words. The wife, however, remained true to her former habits, and instead of following Melisso's orders, did almost the exact opposite.

When Giosefo saw what she had done, he became furious and said: "Weren't you told what kind of supper you were supposed to make?"

Turning to him, his wife replied arrogantly: "Now what's that supposed to mean? Hey, why don't you eat your supper if you want to? Even if I was told to prepare it differently, this is what I felt like making. If you like it, that's fine; if not, you can go without."

Melisso was astounded by the wife's response and was highly critical of it, while Giosefo, on hearing it, said: "Woman, you're still the same as ever, but believe you me, I'm going to make you change your ways."

Then he turned to Melisso and said: "My friend, we'll soon see what Solomon's advice was worth. But please be so good as to stay and watch what I'm about to do, and look on it as a game. Furthermore, to keep yourself from interfering, remember the answer the muleteer gave us when we were feeling sorry for his mule."

"Seeing as how I'm in your house," said Melisso, "I have no intention of opposing your wishes."

Having located a stout cudgel that had been made out of an oak sapling, Giosefo set off for his wife's room to which she had gone, grumbling all the way, after having gotten up from the table in a fit of pique. Grabbing her by the hair, he threw her down to the floor at his feet and began beating her ferociously with his stick. At first she started out by screaming, and then she threatened, but when she saw that no matter what she did, Giosefo would not stop, she began, battered as she was from top to bottom, to cry for mercy, begging him for God's sake not to kill her and saying that she would never again act against his wishes.

None of this, however, got Giosefo to stop. On the contrary, with ever-increasing fury, he went on thrashing her all over the place, hitting her on the ribs and the hips and the shoulders, and only stopping when he was completely exhausted. To sum it up, there was not a bone or a bit of flesh left on the good woman's back that remained unbruised.

When he was finished, Giosefo came over to Melisso and said, "Tomorrow we'll see how the advice about going to Goosebridge stood up to the test." Then, after he had rested awhile and washed his hands, he ate supper with Melisso, and in due course the two of them went to sleep.

Meanwhile, the miserable wife got up off the floor with great difficulty and threw herself onto her bed where she did her best to get some rest. The next morning she rose very early and sent to ask Giosefo what he wanted to have for dinner. Laughing over this with Melisso, he gave his instructions. Then, when it was time to eat, the two men came back and found that an excellent meal had been prepared for them exactly as Giosefo had ordered it. Consequently, the two of them now gave the highest praise to the counsel they had initially failed to understand.

A few days later, after taking leave of Giosefo, Melisso returned home, where he told a wise man he knew about the answer he had received from Solomon, and the man said: "He could not have given you a truer or a better piece of advice. You yourself know that you don't really love anyone and that you do all that entertaining and all those favors for others not because of any love you feel for them, but simply to show off. You should love, therefore, as Solomon told you, and then you, too, will be loved."

So that was how the shrewish woman was punished, and how the young man, by learning to love others, came to be loved himself.

Day 9, Story 10

Donno Gianni is prevailed upon by compar *Pietro to use an incantation in order to turn his wife into a mare, but when the priest comes to stick on the tail,* compar *Pietro says he did not want one and completely ruins the spell.*[1]

The story the Queen had told provoked some murmuring among the ladies while giving the young men a bit of a laugh, but when they grew quiet, Dioneo began to speak as follows:

Graceful ladies, the beauty of a flock of white doves is enhanced more by a black crow than by a pure white swan, and in the same way, among many wise people, on occasion the presence of someone less wise will not only add splendor and beauty to their mature wisdom, but will be a source of delight and entertainment as well.

Now, you are all ladies of exceptional discretion and modesty, whereas I feel myself to be more the fool than not, and since I therefore make your virtue shine all the brighter in comparison with my deficiency, I ought to be dearer to you for that reason than if my superior worth made yours seem dimmer. Consequently, in telling the tale I am about to relate to you, I should have greater license to reveal myself such as I am, and you should display greater patience in tolerating me than if I were wiser. In any case, I am going to tell you a story that is not especially long, but that will teach you how carefully one must follow the instructions of those who do things by means of incantations and how making even one tiny mistake will ruin everything the magician has done.

A year or two ago in Barletta there was a priest called Donno Gianni di Barolo,* who, because his church was poor, was forced to eke out a

---

*Donno is the southern Italian version of *don*, which derives from the Latin *dominus*, an honorific meaning "lord" or "master" and used for religious as well as secular figures.

living for himself by carrying goods on his mare to fairs all over Apulia, and by buying and selling things.[2] In the course of his travels, he struck up a close friendship with a certain Pietro da Tresanti who plied the same trade, albeit in his case, he made use of an ass he owned. As a sign of their love and friendship, the priest adopted the Apulian custom of calling him *compar* Pietro,* and every time the man came to Barletta, the priest always took him to his church, where he gave him lodging and entertained him to the best of his ability.

Since *compar* Pietro, for his part, was exceedingly poor and had only a little cottage in Tresanti that scarcely sufficed for him, his beautiful young wife, and his ass, every time Donno Gianni showed up in town, he would take him to his house and entertain him there as well as he could, in recognition of the hospitality he had received from the priest in Barletta. With regard to lodging, however, *compar* Pietro could not take care of him in the way he would have liked, because he only had a tiny bed in which he slept with his pretty wife. Instead, Donno Gianni was obliged to go into the little stable where his mare was quartered next to the ass and to lie down beside her on a pile of straw. Knowing all about the hospitality the priest showed her husband, *compar* Pietro's wife had volunteered on more than one occasion, when he had come to stay with them, to go and sleep with a neighbor of hers named Zita Carapresa, the daughter of Giudice Leo, so that he would have been able to pass the night in the bed with her husband.[3] However, although she frequently said as much to him, Donno Gianni would never hear of it.

On one occasion like that, among many others, he said to her: "Comar Gemmata, don't trouble yourself about me. I'm doing just fine, because whenever I like, I change this mare into a beautiful gal and pass the time with her. Then, whenever I want to, I turn her into a mare again. And that's why I would never part from her."

The young woman was amazed, and believing every word of it, she told her husband what the priest had said, adding: "If he's such a good

* *Compare* (*compar*) technically meant godfather, but it often simply designated a close male friend, a gossip, as it does here. The female equivalent is *comare* (*comar*) and is applied to *compar* Pietro's wife in the story.

friend as you say, why don't you get him to teach you that magic spell so you can turn me into a mare, and then you can run your business with a mare as well as an ass? That way we'll earn twice as much, and when we got home, you could turn me back into a woman again just as I am now."

Compar Pietro, who was something of a dunce, believed the story, and taking his wife's advice, started begging Donno Gianni for all he was worth to teach him how to do it. Although the priest tried his best to talk him out of this foolishness, he was ultimately unable to do so. "Look," he said, "since that's what you want, we'll get up tomorrow before daybreak as usual, and then I'll teach you how it's done. However, to tell the truth, as you'll see for yourself, the most difficult thing to manage in this business is to stick on the tail."

Compar Pietro and *comar* Gemmata were looking forward so eagerly to what was going to happen that they hardly slept a wink that night, and when day was finally just about to dawn, they got out of bed and called Donno Gianni who, having just risen and still in his nightshirt, came to *compar* Pietro's little room. "I wouldn't do this for anybody else in the world," he said, "except for the two of you, and since you're so insistent, I'll go ahead with it for you. But if you really want it to work, you've got to obey my every order."

After the pair of them assured him that they would, Donno Gianni took a light, and said, as he was handing it to *compar* Pietro: "You should watch what I'm about to do very closely, and memorize carefully what I say. Furthermore, unless you want to ruin everything, make sure you don't utter a single word yourself, no matter what you see or hear. And pray to God that the tail really sticks on tight." Taking the light, *compar* Pietro promised to do as he was told.

Then, Donno Gianni made *comar* Gemmata strip off her clothes until she was completely naked and stand with her hands and feet on the ground just like a mare, similarly instructing her not to utter a sound no matter what happened. After that, he began passing his hands over her face and head, while saying:

"Let this be a fine mare's head."

Then, stroking her hair, he said:

"Let this be a fine mare's mane."

Next, he touched her arms, saying:

"Let these be a fine mare's legs and hooves."

When he came to her breasts, he found they were so firm and round that a certain uninvited something or other awoke and stood up, and he said:

"And let this be a fine mare's chest."

He then did the same thing to her back, her stomach, her hindquarters, her thighs, and her legs. Finally, having nothing left to take care of but the tail, he whipped up his shirt, grabbed hold of the stick he used for planting men, and quickly stuck it into the furrow that was designed for it, saying:

"And let this be a fine mare's tail."

Up to this point, *compar* Pietro had been watching everything with the greatest attention, but when he saw this last bit, he took it amiss and exclaimed:

"Oh, Donno Gianni, no tail! I don't want a tail there!"

The vital fluid that all plants need to take root had already come by the time Donno Gianni pulled it out.

"Oh no, *compar* Pietro," he said, "what have you done? Didn't I tell you not to say a word no matter what you saw? The mare was just about finished, but now you've gone and ruined everything by talking, and there's no way for us to do it over ever again."

"That's all right," said *compar* Pietro, "I didn't want that tail there, no, not me. Why didn't you tell me, 'Do it yourself'? And besides, you were sticking it on too low."

"I didn't tell you because it was your first time," replied Donno Gianni, "and you wouldn't have known how to stick it on as well as I do."

After listening to their exchange, the young woman stood up and said to her husband in all seriousness:

"What a dope you are! Why did you have to go and ruin everything for the two of us? When did you ever see a mare without a tail? So help me God, you may be poor now, but you deserve to be even poorer."

Now that there was no longer any way for the young woman to be turned into a mare, thanks to the words that her husband had spoken, she got dressed, feeling downcast and melancholy, while *compar* Pietro prepared to ply his old trade again, taking with him his single ass, as usual. Then off he went to the fair at Bitonto together with Donno Gianni, and he never asked him for such a favor again.[4]

Day 9, Conclusion

How the company laughed at this story, which the ladies understood better than Dioneo had intended, can be left to the imagination of that lady who has read it and is laughing at it still. But since their storytelling was now over and the sun's heat had started to abate, the Queen rose to her feet, and aware that her rule had come to an end, she took her crown and placed it on the head of Panfilo, who was the last one left to be granted this honor.

"My lord," she said, with a smile, "you are left with a great burden, for as the last ruler, you must make amends not just for my shortcomings, but for those of all the others who have held this office before you. May God grant you His grace in this undertaking, just as He has granted it to me in proclaiming you King."

Panfilo happily accepted the honor and replied: "Your own excellence and that of my other subjects will ensure that my reign will be as praiseworthy as all the others have been." And following the custom of his predecessors, he made all the necessary arrangements with the steward, after which he turned to the ladies who were waiting for him to address them.

"Loving ladies," he said, "the prudent Emilia, who has been our Queen today, gave you the freedom to talk about whatever you pleased so that you might rest your faculties awhile. But now that you have done so, I think it would be good to return to our customary rule, and I therefore want each of you to think up something to say tomorrow on the subject of those who have acted with liberality or magnificence, whether in matters of love or otherwise.

"Both the description of those actions and the actions in and of themselves will assuredly enflame you, well disposed as your spirits already are, to perform worthy deeds. And thus our lives, which cannot help but be brief in these mortal bodies of ours, will be preserved through the fame of our praiseworthy achievements—a goal that those who do not serve their bellies, like brute beasts, should not only desire, but zealously pursue and make every effort to attain."

The merry company approved of the theme, and with the new King's permission, they all got up from their seats and devoted themselves to their usual pleasures, all of them going wherever their desires led them, until it was time for supper, to which they returned in a festive mood. At the end of the meal, which had been served with care and in the proper order, they rose and danced as they normally did, and after they had sung perhaps a thousand little songs, more entertaining for their words than distinguished by their music, the King asked Neifile to sing one on her own account. And without a moment's hesitation, in a clear and joyful voice, she began singing pleasantly, as follows:

A youthful maiden, I'm so happy now
To sing and take delight in early spring,
All thanks to Love and the sweet thoughts he brings.

I walk through verdant meadows, looking at
The white and yellow flowers and the red,
The roses with their thorns, the lilies white,
And I compare them, each and every one,
Unto his face whose love has conquered me
And keeps me his forever, so that I
Now have no wish but to serve his delight.

Whenever I find one among these blooms,
That to my mind is similar to him,
I pluck it, kiss it, and then speak to it,
And as I can, I open up my soul
Entirely and all my heart's desires.
I make a garland of it with the rest,
And bind them with my dainty golden hair.

The pleasure that a flower naturally
Provides the eyes, that one bestows on me:

It's just as if I see him here himself,
The man who's fired me with his sweet love.
What more he does to me with his perfume
I never could express by means of words:
My sighs, though, bear true witness to its power.

    Those sighs will never issue from my breast
As other women's do, so sad and harsh,
But rather, warm and soft they come from me
And make their way into the presence of
My love, who, hearing them, moves instantly
To bring me pleasure, and arrives as I'm
About to say, "Ah, come, lest I despair!"

The King and all the ladies bestowed lavish praise on Neifile's song, after which, since much of the night was already spent, the King ordered everyone to go and rest until morning.

Day 10, Introduction

Here ends the Ninth Day of the Decameron and the Tenth and Last begins, in which, under the rule of Panfilo, they all speak of those who have acted with liberality or magnificence, whether in matters of love or otherwise.

A few small clouds in the west were still crimson, while the fringes of those in the east, struck by the rays of the approaching sun, were already shining like bright gold, when Panfilo got up and had the ladies and his comrades awakened. As soon as the entire company was assembled, he deliberated with them as to where they could go to amuse themselves, and he then set out at a leisurely pace, accompanied by Filomena and Fiammetta, and followed by all the rest. While they were walking, they entertained themselves for a long time discussing all the details of their future life together and answering one another's questions, until, having gone a considerable distance, they found that the sun was already getting too hot, and returned to the palace. Gathering about the fountain, they had their glasses rinsed out in its clear waters so that those who were thirsty could have something to drink, after which they wandered about the garden, enjoying themselves in its pleasant shade until it was time to eat. Then, when they had finished their meal and taken a nap, as they usually did, they reassembled at a spot chosen by the King, who asked Neifile to tell the first story, which she cheerfully began as follows.

Day 10, Story 1

A knight in the service of the King of Spain feels he is being inadequately rewarded, so the King offers him irrefutable proof to demonstrate that it is not his fault, but that of the knight's own malevolent Fortune, and in the end bestows quite a handsome gift on him.[1]

Honorable ladies, I cannot help but account it a very great favor on the part of the King that he has singled me out to speak on so lofty a theme as magnificence, which, just as the sun embellishes and adorns the whole of the heavens, gives light and splendor to every other virtue. I shall therefore tell you a little story that, in my opinion, is quite charming and surely cannot be anything but profitable to recall.

You should know then that among the many gallant knights who have lived in our city from time immemorial, there was one, Messer Ruggieri de' Figiovanni, who was perhaps the finest of them all.[2] He was both rich and high spirited, and seeing that the style of life and the customs in Tuscany were such that as long as he remained there he would have little or no opportunity to demonstrate his worth, he made up his mind to go and live for a time at the court of Alfonso, King of Spain, whose reputation for valor surpassed that of any other ruler in those days.

Quite honorably equipped with an array of weapons and horses, and accompanied by a large retinue, Messer Ruggieri set off for Spain, where he was given a gracious welcome by the King, and while he resided there, his lifestyle was marked by such splendor and he accomplished so many amazing feats of arms that he quickly gained a reputation for himself as a man of valor.

After he had been there for quite some time, it seemed to him, through close observation of the King's behavior, that he was acting with very little discretion in bestowing castles, cities, and baronies on one man after another who did not particularly deserve them. Messer Ruggieri knew his own worth, and since he had received nothing, he felt that his reputation was greatly diminished as a result and therefore made up his mind to leave. When he went to the King and asked for his permission to do so, the King granted his request and gave him a fine-looking mule, one of the best that anyone had ever ridden, which Messer Ruggieri deeply appreciated because of the long journey he had ahead of him.

The King next commanded a tactful servant of his to use whatever means he thought best and arrange matters in such a way that he could accompany Messer Ruggieri without appearing to have been sent there by the King. He was, furthermore, ordered to make a mental note of everything Messer Ruggieri said about the King so that he could report it all back to him, and the morning after that, he was to order Messer Ruggieri to return to the King.

The servant kept watch, and as soon as Messer Ruggieri left the city, he deftly maneuvered to attach himself to the knight's entourage, giving him the impression that he, too, was going to Italy.

Messer Ruggieri went riding along on the mule the King had given him, conversing on one topic and then another with the servant, until around the hour of tierce, when he announced, "I think it would be a good idea for us to allow these animals to relieve themselves." Accordingly, they were put in a stable, where all of them, except for the mule, did so. The party then rode on, the King's servant paying close attention to everything Messer Ruggieri said, until they came to a river, in which, as they were watering their mounts, the mule finally defecated. On seeing this, Messer Ruggieri exclaimed:

"Ah, God curse you, you beast, you're just like the lord who gave you to me."

The King's servant noted his words, but although he took in a great many others during the course of their journey that day, he never heard him say anything else that was not extremely complimentary about the King. Consequently, the next morning, when they had mounted their horses and were about to ride off in the direction of Tuscany, the servant delivered the King's order, and Messer Ruggieri turned back immediately.

Having been informed about the comment the knight had made concerning the mule, the King had him summoned, welcomed him with a smile on his face, and asked him why he had likened him to his mule, or rather, the mule to him.

"My lord," replied Messer Ruggieri with complete candor, "I likened it to you because just as you bestow your gifts where it's not appropriate and don't give them where it is, in the same way, the mule didn't relieve itself where it should have and did so where it should not have."

"Messer Ruggieri," replied the King, "if I did not bestow my bounty on you as I have on many others, who are worthless in comparison with yourself, that did not happen because of my failure to recognize that you are a truly valiant knight, deserving of all the most lavish rewards. Rather, in this matter the fault lies not with me, but with your Fortune, which did not present me with an opportunity to do so. And I will offer you clear proof that what I'm saying is the truth."

"My lord," said Messer Ruggieri, "I'm not upset that you haven't given me any gifts, since I've never desired to be richer than I am now, but rather, that my valor has never received a single sign of recognition from you. Nevertheless, I consider your explanation both sound and honorable, and although I'm prepared to take a look at whatever you wish to show me, I accept what you say without proof."

The King then led him into a great hall where he had arranged ahead of time for there to be two large coffers, both of which were locked, and in the presence of a large group of onlookers, he said:

"Messer Ruggieri, one of these coffers contains my crown, the royal orb and scepter, and a large number of my belts, buckles, rings, and every other precious jewel I possess. The other is filled with earth. Choose one of them, and the one you've chosen will be yours to keep, and in this way you'll be able to see whether it is I or your Fortune who failed to acknowledge your worth."

Seeing that it was the King's pleasure, Messer Ruggieri chose one of the coffers, and when it was opened at the King's command and found to be full of earth, the King laughed and said:

"As you can see for yourself, Messer Ruggieri, I was telling you the truth about Fortune, but your worth is such that you certainly deserve to have me do something to oppose her powers. I realize that you have no inclination to become a Spaniard, and for that reason I don't want to bestow a castle or a city on you here, but that coffer that Fortune deprived you of, I wish to make it yours in defiance of her, so that you may carry it back to your country and justifiably boast among your fellow citizens of your valor, to which my gifts will bear witness."

Messer Ruggieri took the coffer, and having thanked the King in a manner befitting such a grand present, he happily returned with it to Tuscany.

Day 10, Story 2

After having captured the Abbot of Cluny, Ghino di Tacco cures him of a stomach ailment before releasing him, and when the Abbot returns to the court of Rome, he effects a reconciliation between Ghino and Pope Boniface and makes him a friar in the Order of the Hospitallers.[1]

After the company finished praising the generosity that King Alfonso had displayed toward the Florentine knight, the King, who had been very pleased with Neifile's account of it, asked Elissa to continue, and she began at once:

It cannot be denied, delicate ladies, that for a king to have acted munificently, and to have bestowed his munificence upon someone who had served him, is all very fine and commendable, but what are we to say when we hear a story about a churchman who displayed amazing generosity toward a person whom no one would have blamed him for treating as an enemy? Surely, our only conclusion is that whereas the king's magnificence was a virtue, the cleric's was a miracle, considering the fact that the whole lot of them are even greedier than women and stand with swords drawn in opposition to every kind of liberality. Moreover, although all men naturally hunger to revenge offenses committed against them, everyone knows that the members of the clergy, however much they may preach patience and especially commend the pardoning of wrongs, pursue vengeance with more fiery zeal than other men do. Nevertheless, in the story you are about to hear from me, you will plainly discover just how magnanimous a churchman can be.

Ghino di Tacco, whose ferocious deeds and countless robberies gained him a great deal of notoriety after he had incurred the enmity

of the counts of Santafiore and been banished from Siena, staged a
rebellion in Radicofani against the Church of Rome, and using the
town as his base, he sent out his highwaymen to rob anyone who passed
through the surrounding region. At that time, Boniface VIII was Pope,
and to his court in Rome there came the Abbot of Cluny, reputed to
be one of the richest prelates in the world. During his stay, the Abbot
developed a terrible stomach ailment, and his physicians advised him
to go to the baths at Siena where he was certain to be cured. Consequently, he obtained the Pope's permission to leave, and heedless of
Ghino's reputation, he set out on his journey with great pomp, taking
with him a large baggage train loaded with goods as well as a great many
horses and servants.

Upon learning of his approach, Ghino di Tacco spread out his nets,
and without allowing so much as a single little servant boy to escape,
he managed to trap the Abbot and his entire retinue, together with all
of his belongings, inside a narrow pass. This done, Ghino sent one of
his ablest men, accompanied by a suitable escort, to the Abbot, with
whom he spoke on his master's behalf, asking him quite courteously
if he would be so kind as to go to Ghino's castle and dismount there.
Upon hearing this request, the Abbot, completely infuriated, replied
that he would do nothing of the sort, for he had no business whatsoever
with Ghino. He was going to continue his journey, he said, and would
like to see anyone try to stop him.

"Sir," responded the envoy, speaking in a humble manner, "you're here
in a place where we fear nothing but the power of God, and where all
excommunications and interdicts have themselves been excommunicated.[2] And so, if you please, it would be best for you to comply with
Ghino's wishes in this matter."

While they were engaged in this exchange, the whole place had been
surrounded by bandits, and since the Abbot now saw that he and his
men were trapped, he set off, beside himself with anger, accompanying Ghino's envoy down the road toward the castle, followed by his
entire company and all his goods. Having dismounted at a large building, he was lodged, on Ghino's orders, all by himself in a rather dark,
uncomfortable little room, whereas all the others were given quite cozy

accommodations, each according to his rank, in various parts of the castle. Meanwhile, all the horses and the baggage were put in a safe place, where they were left untouched.

When all this had been taken care of, Ghino went to see the Abbot and said to him: "Sir, you are Ghino's guest, and he sends me to ask you if you would be so good as to inform him where you were going and for what reason."

By this time, the Abbot, who was a wise man, had set his haughtiness aside and explained where he was going and why. Having heard him out, Ghino left the room and decided that he would try to cure the Abbot without having any recourse to the baths. Accordingly, after giving orders for the little room to be closely guarded and for a great fire to be kept burning in it, he left the Abbot alone until the next morning, at which point he returned, bringing him two slices of toast wrapped in a spotless white napkin along with a large glass of Vernaccia di Corniglia from the Abbot's own stores.[3]

"Sir," he said, "when Ghino was younger, he studied medicine, and he says that there's no better treatment for stomach ailments than what he's going to give you. The things I've brought you here are just the beginning. Take them, then, and be of good cheer."

The Abbot, whose hunger was greater than any desire he had to bandy words, did indeed eat the bread and drink the Vernaccia, albeit he did so with an ill will. Afterward, he made many haughty remarks, asked a number of questions, and gave lots of advice, demanding in particular that he be allowed to see Ghino. Since much of what he said was beside the point, Ghino chose to let it ride, but he replied quite courteously to some things, assuring the Abbot that Ghino would visit him as soon as he could. With these words, he left him and did not return until the following day, bringing him the same quantities of toast and Vernaccia wine as before.

Ghino thus kept him on this regimen for several days until he saw that the Abbot had eaten some dried beans, which he had brought there on the sly and left behind on purpose. He then asked the Abbot on behalf of Ghino how his stomach was feeling.

"It would seem all right to me," replied the Abbot, "if only I were out of his hands. Other than that, my greatest desire is to eat, that's how well his remedies have cured me."

Ghino therefore had the Abbot's servants fix up a splendid chamber for him, furnished with the Abbot's own things, and made arrangements for a grand banquet to be prepared to which the Abbot's entire retinue as well as many men from the castle were invited. The next morning Ghino went to see the Abbot and said to him: "Sir, since you're now feeling well again, it's time for you to leave this sickroom of yours." And taking him by the hand, he led him to the chamber that had been prepared for him and left him there with his men while he himself went to make sure the banquet would be truly magnificent.

The Abbot relaxed for a while with his attendants, giving them an account of the sort of life he had been leading there, whereas, by contrast, they all said that the treatment they had received from Ghino had been wonderful. By then, the time having arrived for them to eat, the Abbot and all the others were served a series of excellent dishes accompanied by fine wines, although Ghino still refrained from revealing his identity to the Abbot.

After the Abbot had spent several days there in this fashion, Ghino eventually gave orders for all his possessions to be brought into one of the great halls and had all his horses, down to the sorriest nag, led into a courtyard located below it. He then went to the Abbot and asked him how he was feeling and whether he thought he was well enough to ride. In reply, the Abbot said that he was certainly strong enough, that his stomach ailment was cured, and that he would be just fine once he got out of Ghino's hands.

Then Ghino led him into the hall in which his entire retinue and his goods were located, after which he motioned the Abbot over to a window from which he could see all his horses.

"My lord Abbot," he said, "you should know that Ghino di Tacco, who is the very man you see here before you, was driven to become a highwayman and an enemy of the Roman court in order to defend his life and his honor, not out of some instinctive attraction to evil, but because he is an impoverished gentleman who has been banished from his home and is forced to contend with many powerful enemies. But since you seem to me a worthy lord, now that I've cured you of your stomach ailment, I have no intention of treating you as I would any other person who fell into my hands the way you did and from whom I would take as much of his goods as I saw fit. On the contrary, what I propose is that you should take my need into consideration and give me whatever portion of your property you yourself wish to leave with me. It's all here, untouched, right in front of you, and you can see your horses down there in the courtyard from this window. So go ahead and take a part of it, or all of it, as you wish, and from now on, you should feel free to stay here or leave, according to your pleasure."

Amazed that a highwayman should speak in such generous terms, the Abbot was so pleased by what he heard that he promptly shed his anger and disdain, or rather, they were transformed into a feeling of goodwill for Ghino, whom he now loved as a friend with all his heart. Rushing over to embrace him, he said: "I swear to God that to win the friendship of such a man as I now judge you to be, I'd be willing to suffer an even greater injury than anything you appear to have inflicted on me up till now. A curse on Fortune for having forced you into such an infamous profession!"

When he finished speaking, the Abbot had his men take just a very few necessities from among his many belongings, and then do something similar with his horses, after which, leaving all the rest to Ghino, he made his way back to Rome.

The Pope had heard the news of the Abbot's capture, but even though he was seriously upset about it, the first question he asked when he saw him again was whether the baths had done him any good. "Holy Father," replied the Abbot with a smile, "before I even reached the baths, I came upon an excellent physician who cured me completely." The Pope laughed as the Abbot explained how, and in the course of telling his story, he was moved by a feeling of magnanimity to ask for a favor.

Thinking it would involve something quite different, the Pope freely offered to grant his request.

"Holy Father," said the Abbot, "what I intend to ask of you is to restore my doctor, Ghino di Tacco, to your good graces, for he is assuredly one of the finest and worthiest men I've ever encountered. As for his evil deeds, I believe that Fortune is much more to blame than he is, and if you change his Fortune by giving him the means to live according to his station, I have no doubt whatsoever that in a very short time you will come to have the same opinion of him that I do."

Upon hearing this, the Pope, who possessed a lofty spirit himself and was well disposed toward men of worth, said that he would gladly grant such a boon if Ghino was as fine a man as the Abbot claimed. He then told the Abbot to arrange for Ghino to be granted a safe-conduct and summon him to come to Rome.

Once he had received that guarantee, in accordance with the Abbot's wishes, Ghino came to the court, nor had he been there very long before the Pope acknowledged his worthiness, and as a gesture of reconciliation, gave him a large priory belonging to the Hospitallers, having first made him a knight of that order, an office he held, as a friend and servant of the Holy Church and the Abbot of Cluny, for the rest of his life.

Day 10, Story 3

Envious of Nathan's reputation for courtesy, Mithridanes sets out to murder him. After accidentally coming across him without recognizing him, and being informed by him as to how he might do the deed, he finds him, just as Nathan had arranged it, in a little wood. When Mithridanes realizes who it is, he is filled with shame and becomes Nathan's friend.[1]

To everyone it certainly seemed as though what they had heard was close to miraculous, namely that a cleric would have performed an act of generosity, but when the ladies finally stopped discussing it, the King ordered Filostrato to continue, and he began immediately:

Noble ladies, although the munificence of the King of Spain was great and that of the Abbot of Cluny possibly unheard of, you will perhaps be no less amazed to hear about a man who, intent upon bestowing his generosity on a person who did not merely thirst for his blood, but for his very life, cleverly arranged to give it to him. Furthermore, as I intend to show you in a little story of mine, he would have done so if his adversary had desired to take it.

It is beyond doubt, if the reports of various men from Genoa and elsewhere who have been to those parts may be trusted, that in the region of Cathay there once lived a man of noble lineage named Nathan who was rich beyond compare.[2] He owned an estate close to a road along which everyone who wanted to go from west to east or east to west was more or less forced by necessity to pass, and since he had a lofty and magnanimous spirit, and wanted to be known for his deeds, he assembled a host of master builders there who in a short space of time erected one of the largest, most beautiful, and most luxurious palaces for him that had ever been seen, which he then had excellently furnished with everything suitable for the reception and honorable entertainment of gentlemen. Having engaged a large group of splendid servants, he saw to it that everyone passing by in either direction was received and made welcome there in a most agreeable and festive manner, a laudable practice he kept up until his reputation had soon spread not only throughout the East, but throughout most of the West as well.

When Nathan had already reached a ripe old age, without ever tiring of displaying such courtesy, his fame happened to reach the ears of a young man named Mithridanes who lived in a country not far from his. Knowing that he was just as rich as Nathan, he grew envious of Nathan's renown and his virtue, and he resolved that through an even greater display of liberality he would either obliterate the old man's renown or overshadow it. And so, after having had a palace built similar to Nathan's, he began to bestow the most extravagant courtesies ever seen on everyone who passed by, going in either direction, and there is no doubt that in a short time he became very famous.

Now one day, while the young man was all alone in the courtyard of his palace, a poor woman happened to come in through one of its gates and ask him for alms. Not only did she get them, but then, returning to him through a second gate, she received them yet again. This occurred twelve times in succession, and when she came back for the thirteenth, Mithridanes remarked, "My good woman, you're very persistent with this begging of yours," although he gave her alms just the same.

In response to his comment, the little old woman said: "Ah, Nathan's generosity, how wonderful you are! For his palace has thirty-two gates, just like this one, and even though I came in through every single one of them and asked for alms, I always got them without his ever giving any sign that he knew who I was. Here, by contrast, I've only come in through thirteen, and not only have I been recognized, but I've been given a scolding." Then, having said her piece, she left, never to return.

Mithridanes felt that the words he heard the old woman speak about Nathan's reputation only served to diminish his own, and they ignited a raging fury in him. "Oh, poor me!" he exclaimed. "How can I ever match Nathan's greatest acts of generosity, let alone surpass him as I've sought to do, when I can't come close to him in the smallest things? All my efforts will truly be in vain unless I wipe him off the face of the earth, and since old age isn't carrying him away all by itself, I'll have to do the job with my own hands, and that without delay."

Driven by this emotion, he leaped to his feet, and without communicating his plan to anyone, he set out on horseback, accompanied by only a small entourage. In three days they reached the place where Nathan lived, arriving there toward evening. Mithridanes instructed his followers to pretend that they were not with him and had no idea who he was, telling them to find somewhere to stay until they received further orders from him. Left alone, he came upon Nathan not far from his magnificent palace, taking a leisurely stroll, unattended and dressed in simple clothing. Not realizing who it was, Mithridanes asked him if he could tell him where Nathan lived.

"My son," Nathan replied cheerfully, "nobody in these parts can show you the way better than I can, and so, whenever you wish, I'll take you there myself."

The young man said that he would like that very much, but that, if possible, he did not want Nathan to see him or to know that he was there.

"And this, too, I will do," replied Nathan, "since that's the way you want it."

Mithridanes then dismounted, and as they walked along, Nathan soon engaged him in the most pleasant conversation, until he reached his lovely palace. There Nathan got one of his servants to take Mithridanes's horse, and drawing close to the servant, he whispered in his ear, telling him to pass the word immediately that no one in his household should tell the young man that he himself was Nathan. His order was carried out, and once the two men had entered the palace, he had Mithridanes lodged in a very handsome room where no one saw him except those who were delegated to be his servants. And to make sure that the young man was entertained in the most honorable fashion, Nathan himself kept him company.

After they had spent some time together, although Mithridanes treated Nathan with all the reverence due to a father, he finally could not refrain from asking him who he was.

"I'm one of Nathan's menial servants," he replied, "but despite having been with him since my childhood and grown old in his service, he has never raised me above my present station, so, however much everyone else may praise him, I myself have little cause to do so."

These words raised Mithridanes's hopes that he could carry out his wicked plan with greater safety and assurance. When Nathan then asked him very politely who he was and what business brought him to that part of the world, offering to advise and assist him in whatever way he could, Mithridanes hesitated for a while before responding. Eventually, he decided to take Nathan into his confidence, and after much beating about the bush, he began by swearing the old man to secrecy, then asked him for his help and his counsel, and finally revealed everything about who he was, his purpose in coming there, and what had motivated him to do so.

Upon hearing Mithridanes speak and learning of his savage plan, Nathan was deeply disturbed, but he had a resolute spirit, and without changing the expression on his face, he scarcely paused a moment before replying.

"Mithridanes," he said, "your father was a noble man, and your desire to live up to his example is revealed by the lofty enterprise you have undertaken of bestowing your generosity on all comers. Moreover, I greatly commend the envy you have of Nathan's virtue, because if there were a great deal of that sort of feeling around, the world, which is quite a miserly place, would soon change for the better.[3]

"I shall certainly keep the plan you've revealed to me a secret, and although I can't offer you any substantial assistance with it, I can give you some useful advice, which is this. About half a mile from here you can see a little wood where practically every morning Nathan takes a long, leisurely walk all by himself. It'll be easy for you to find him there and deal with him as you please. If you kill him, however, and want to be able to return home without encountering any obstacles, you must leave the wood not by the road you took when you went there, but by the one you see over there to your left, because although it may be a bit rougher, it'll bring you out closer to your house and be safer for you."

Once he had given this information to Mithridanes, Nathan took his leave, and the young man secretly informed his companions, who were likewise staying in the palace, where they were to wait for him the following day. Nathan had no second thoughts about the advice he had given Mithridanes, and when the new day dawned, with his mind still unchanged, he set off alone for the little wood, there to meet his death.

Mithridanes had no other weapons other than his bow and his sword, and after he awoke, he collected them, mounted his horse, and rode off toward the little wood, where, from a distance, he caught sight of Nathan taking a stroll all by himself. Mithridanes raced toward him, but having decided that he would take a good look at him and hear him speak before attacking him, he seized him by the turban he had on his head and exclaimed: "Old man, you're as good as dead!"

To this, Nathan's only response was, "Then I must deserve it."

Upon hearing his voice and looking him in the face, Mithridanes instantly recognized him as the man who had received him with such kindness, had kept him company like a friend, and had advised him so faithfully. Consequently, his fury immediately subsided, and his anger was transformed into shame. Hurling away the sword, which he had already drawn out in order to strike his adversary, he dismounted and flung himself down in tears at Nathan's feet.

"Your generosity is only too clear to me now, dearest father," he said, "considering how prudently you arranged to come here in order to offer me your life, which I, despite having no reason to do so, wanted to take from you, as I told you myself. But at the point when my need was greatest, God showed He was more concerned about where my duty lay than I was myself, and opened the eyes of my mind that wretched envy had sealed. Indeed, considering how ready you've been to comply with my desires, I am all the more cognizant of the debt of penance I owe you because of my fault. Therefore, take your revenge on me in whatever way you think appropriate for the sin I've committed."

After raising Mithridanes to his feet, Nathan embraced him and kissed him tenderly. "As far as your design here is concerned, my son," he said, "call it evil or not as you will, there's no need to ask for my forgiveness or for me to grant it, because you didn't pursue it out of hatred, but in order to be held in greater esteem. Live, then, and have no fear of me, for you may rest assured that there's no other man alive who loves you as much as I do, considering the lofty nature of your spirit, in that you have dedicated yourself not to the amassing of wealth, which is what misers do, but to spending what you have accumulated. Nor should you feel ashamed of having wanted to enhance your reputation by slaying me or imagine that I am surprised by it. In order to increase their realms, and thus their fame, the most illustrious of emperors and the greatest of kings have practiced almost no art other than killing, not just one man as you wanted to do, but an infinite number of them, as well as putting entire countries to the torch and razing cities to the ground. And so, if, to achieve renown, I was the only person you wanted to kill, you were not doing anything extraordinary or unusual, but something actually quite commonplace."

Without attempting to exculpate himself for his perverse desire, Mithridanes praised the honorable way Nathan had found of excusing it, and in the course of conversing with him finally reached the point of expressing his utter astonishment that Nathan had accepted it and was prepared not only to supply him with the means, but also with advice for carrying out his plan.

"Mithridanes," replied Nathan, "neither my compliance nor my advice should astonish you, for ever since I've been my own master and had a mind to pursue the same goal that you, too, have been aiming at, I have always sought to satisfy anyone who showed up at my house, to the extent that I could, by giving him whatever he asked of me. You came here seeking my life, and as soon as I heard what it was that you wanted, I immediately resolved to give it to you, so that you wouldn't be the only person ever to leave my home unsatisfied. With that end in mind, I gave you advice I thought would be good for taking my life without losing your own. Therefore, I say to you yet again that if that's what you want, I implore you to give yourself the satisfaction of taking my life, for I can't think of how it might be better spent.

"I've had the use of my life now for some eighty years, spending it all on my own pleasures and comforts, and I know that as I follow the course of Nature just like other men, indeed like everything else in the world, it will only be mine to have for a little while longer. And that's why I think it's much better to give it away, just as I have always given away and spent my treasures, than to try to hold on to it until Nature takes it from me against my will.

"To give away even a hundred years is a trifle, and if so, how much less is it to give away six or eight of the ones remaining to me down here? Take my life, then, if you want it, I beg you, for during all the years I've been alive, I've never yet found anyone who wanted it, and if you don't take it, you who are actually asking for it, I have no idea when I'd ever be able to find someone who would. But even if I should happen to find such a person, I realize that the longer I keep it, the less value it will have. So take it, I implore you, before it depreciates even more."

"God forbid," said Mithridanes, feeling profoundly ashamed of himself, "that I should deprive you of so precious a thing as your life, let alone contemplate such a deed, which is what I was doing just a little while ago. In fact, far from wanting to shorten the years you have left, I'd gladly add some of my own to them if I could."

"And if you could," Nathan promptly replied, "would you really seek to add some of your years to mine? Why, then, you'd have me serve you in a way I've never served another human being, for you'd make me take something you possessed away from you, when I've never taken anything from anyone?"

"Yes," said Mithridanes, without a moment's hesitation.

"In that case, you must do what I tell you," said Nathan. "Remain here in my house, young as you are, and assume the name of Nathan, while I go to yours and from now on have myself called Mithridanes."

"If I knew how to comport myself as well as you do now, and as you've always done," replied Mithridanes, "I'd take your offer without giving it a second thought, but because I feel quite certain that my actions would only serve to diminish Nathan's fame, and because I have no intention of marring in another what I cannot make perfect in myself, I won't accept it."

After they had conversed agreeably on these and many other topics, the two of them returned together, as Nathan wished, to his palace, where for many days he entertained Mithridanes in the most honorable fashion, using all the wit and wisdom at his disposal to encourage the young man to pursue his grand and lofty enterprise. And when Mithridanes finally wanted to go back home with his companions, Nathan, having made it abundantly clear that his own liberality could never be surpassed, gave his guest leave to depart.

Day 10, Story 4

Messer Gentile de' Carisendi comes from Modena and takes the lady he loves out of the tomb in which she had been buried for dead. After she is revived and gives birth to a male child, Messer Gentile restores both her and her little boy to Niccoluccio Caccianemico, her husband.[1]

It seemed miraculous to all of them that any person could be so liberal with his own blood as Nathan had been, and everyone agreed that his generosity had truly surpassed that of the King of Spain and the Abbot of Cluny. But then, after they had discussed the matter awhile, the King looked over in Lauretta's direction, indicating that he wished her to speak. In response, Lauretta began immediately:

Young ladies, we have been told about such beautiful and magnificent things, and heard stories that are filled with such lofty examples of magnanimity, that for those of us who have yet to speak, there is, I think, little terrain left for us to explore, unless we turn to the deeds of lovers, which will always provide a most copious supply of material on any topic. Consequently, for this reason, and also because our youth especially inclines us in that direction, I would like to tell you about a generous deed performed by a man who was in love. And if it is true that in order to obtain the object of their affections, men will give away fortunes, set aside enmities, and expose their very lives, their honor, and what is even more important, their reputation to a thousand dangers, then you may possibly conclude, all things considered, that this man's actions were in no way inferior to some of those already described.

In Bologna, then, that most noble city in Lombardy, there once lived a gentleman called Messer Gentile de' Carisendi who was quite noteworthy for his virtue and the nobility of his blood.[2] In his youth, he became enamored of a gentlewoman named Madonna Catalina, the wife of a certain Niccoluccio Caccianemico, and because his love for her was ill requited, he almost despaired of it, and went off to Modena, where he had been appointed the *podestà*.

At that time, Niccoluccio was away from Bologna, and his wife, being pregnant, had gone to stay on one of his estates about three miles outside the city. There she had the misfortune to be stricken all of a sudden by a terrible malady so virulent that it extinguished every sign of life in her, and she was pronounced dead by several different doctors. Since her closest female relations said that from what she had told them, she had not been pregnant long enough for her child to have been completely formed, they did not reflect further on that subject, but after a great deal of weeping, buried her in a tomb, just as she was, in a nearby church.

The news of her death was immediately reported to Messer Gentile by one of his friends, and despite the fact that he had never been the recipient of her favors, he was overcome with grief. At length, however, he said to himself: "So there you are, Madonna Catalina, you're dead. Well, I never managed to get as much as a single glance from you while you were alive, but now that you're dead and can't defend yourself, it's only right that I should take a kiss or two from you."

Night had already fallen as he said these things to himself, and so, after making arrangements to keep his departure a secret, he mounted his horse, accompanied by just one of his servants, and did not stop until he had reached the place where the lady was buried.[3] Having opened up the tomb, he cautiously went inside, and lying down beside her, he drew his face close to hers and kissed her again and again, all the while weeping profusely. But as we know, men's appetites—and especially those of lovers—are never content to stay within bounds, but always want to go further, and so, just as he was deciding that it was time to leave, he said to himself: "Ah, why don't I fondle her breast a little, seeing as how I'm here? I never touched her in the past, and I will never have the opportunity to do so again."

Thus, overcome by this desire, he placed his hand on her breast, and after keeping it there for some time, he thought he could sense her heart faintly beating. Having subdued his fears, he began examining her with greater care and discovered that she was in fact still alive, although the signs of life in her were minimal and very weak. Consequently, as gently as he could, he removed her from the tomb with the aid of his servant, and having set her across his horse in front of him, he carried her in secret to his house in Bologna.

His mother, a wise and worthy woman, was living there, and after she had heard her son's lengthy account of what had happened, she was moved to compassion and skillfully brought the lady back to life again with the aid of a series of warm baths and a good hot fire. When she came to, she heaved a great sigh and said: "Alas! Where am I now?"

"Don't worry," replied the worthy woman. "You're in a good place."

Having recovered her senses, the lady looked all around her and discovered, to her amazement, that she had no idea where she was, but seeing Messer Gentile standing before her, she asked his mother to tell her how she came to be there, which prompted Messer Gentile to give her a detailed account of everything that had happened. She was distressed over what she heard, but after a while, she thanked him as best she could and begged him, out of the love that he had borne for her and his own sense of honor, to do nothing to her in his house that would impair her honor or that of her husband, and to let her return home at daybreak.

"My lady," replied Messer Gentile, "whatever my desire may have been like in the past, seeing as how God has bestowed this grace on me of bringing you back to life because of the love I once bore you, I do not intend, either now or in the future, to treat you as anything other than a dear sister, whether here or elsewhere. But since the service I did for you tonight deserves some sort of reward, I hope you will not deny me the favor I'm about to ask of you."

The lady responded graciously that she was ready to grant his wish, provided that it lay in her power to do so and that there was nothing improper about it.

"My lady," said Messer Gentile, "since all of your relations, indeed, all the people in Bologna believe with utter certainty that you're dead, there's no one expecting you at your house any longer. Consequently, the favor I would ask of you is to be so good as to stay here quietly with my mother until I return from Modena, which will be fairly soon. And the reason I'm making this request of you is that I propose to stage a solemn ceremony in which I will make a precious gift of you to your husband in the presence of all the leading citizens in the town."

The lady truly longed to cheer up her family by showing them she was still alive, but realizing that she was in Messer Gentile's debt and that his request was honorable, she decided to do what he wanted and gave him her word of honor to that effect.

She had scarcely finished giving him her answer when she felt that she was about to have her baby, and not long afterward, with the tender assistance of Messer Gentile's mother, she gave birth to a handsome boy, which doubled and redoubled the joy both she and Messer Gentile felt. After ordering that she should have everything she needed and that she was to be treated as though she were his own wife, Messer Gentile then returned in secret to Modena.

When the term of his office there was finished and he was about to go back to Bologna, he arranged that on the morning of his return a grand, sumptuous banquet should be given at his house, to which he invited a host of gentlemen from the city, and among them, Niccoluccio Caccianemico. Upon his arrival, he dismounted and went to join his guests, although he first called on the lady and found that she was more beautiful and in better health than ever and that her little boy was thriving. Then, with a joy beyond compare, he showed his guests to their tables and offered them a magnificent feast served in multiple courses.

When they were close to the end of the meal, he began speaking to the group, after having first told the lady what he intended to do and having arranged with her how she should comport herself.

"Gentlemen," he said, "I remember having once been told that in Persia they have a custom, most agreeable in my opinion, which is that whenever someone wants to confer a special honor on one of his friends, he invites him to his house and shows him the thing he holds most dear, whether it's his wife or his mistress or his daughter or whatever it may be, declaring that just as he has shown him this thing, he would show him his heart even more readily if he could. Now this is a custom I would like us to observe here in Bologna. You have been so good as to honor my banquet with your presence, and I would like to honor you in the Persian fashion by showing you the most precious thing I have in the world or am ever likely to have.

"However, before I do so, I would ask you to tell me what you think about a problem I am going to place before you. A certain person has in his house a good and extremely faithful servant who becomes gravely ill; this person, without waiting for the servant to die, has him carried out into the middle of the street and takes no further interest in him; then a stranger comes along, and moved by compassion for the sick man, takes him to his house where, with much care and at great expense, he restores him to his former healthy condition. Now, what I should like to know is this: if the second master retains him and makes use of his services, does the first one have any right to complain or to blame the other one, should he refuse to give the servant back when he's asked to do so?"

After they had discussed the question from a variety of viewpoints among themselves, the gentlemen all reached the same conclusion, and since Niccoluccio Caccianemico was an eloquent and polished speaker, they entrusted him with their response.

Niccoluccio began by praising the Persian custom and then declared that he and the others were all of the same opinion that the first master no longer had any claim on his servant since in such a desperate situation he had not merely abandoned him, but cast him away. Moreover, because of the benefits conferred on him by the second master, they thought it just if he claimed the servant as his own, for in refusing to give him up, he was neither doing any harm, nor offering any insult or injury to the first master. All the others who were sitting around the tables—and there were many worthy gentlemen among them—all of them seconded the opinion that Niccoluccio had given.

Delighted with this answer and with the fact that it had come from Niccoluccio, Messer Gentile affirmed that he, too, shared their opinion, after which he declared: "Now it's time for me to honor you as I promised I would." And calling two of his servants, he sent them to the lady, who, at his command, had been decked out in magnificent clothing and jewelry, charging them to ask her if she would be so good as to come and gladden the gentlemen with her presence.

Taking her extraordinarily beautiful little boy in her arms, the lady entered the hall, accompanied by the two servants, and at Messer Gentile's bidding, sat down next to one of his distinguished guests.

"Gentlemen," he said, "this is the thing I value above all others and intend to treasure forever. Look for yourselves and see whether you think I'm right to do so."

The gentlemen welcomed her, praised her enthusiastically, and assured Messer Gentile that he was indeed right to cherish her. As they were gazing at her, there were quite a few of them who would have said that she was the very woman she was, except for the fact that they thought she was dead. No one scrutinized her so closely, however, as Niccoluccio, who was seized by a burning desire to find out who she was. As soon as Messer Gentile stepped aside for a moment, he was no longer able to contain himself and asked her whether she was from Bologna or a foreigner. On hearing this question being put to her by her husband, it was quite difficult for her to keep from responding, but she followed the instructions she had been given and remained silent. One of the other gentlemen asked her if the child were hers, and yet another, if she were Messer Gentile's wife or related to him in any way, but to both of them she made no reply.

When they were rejoined by Messer Gentile, however, one of his guests said to him: "Sir, this treasure of yours is a beauty, but she seems to be mute. Is that so?"

"Gentlemen," said Messer Gentile, "the fact that she has not spoken up to now is no small proof of her virtue."

"Then you must tell us who she is," replied the other.

"I'll do so gladly," said Messer Gentile, "but only if you promise me not to budge from your places, no matter what I say, until I've finished my story."

When they had all promised they would and the tables had been cleared away, Messer Gentile sat down beside the lady and said:

"Gentlemen, this lady is that loyal and faithful servant to whom I was referring in the question I put to you just now. Little prized by her own people, she was thrown out, like something vile and worthless, into the middle of the street from which I retrieved her, and through my care, I saved her from death with my own hands. Recognizing my pure affection, God has transformed her from a fearsome corpse into the beauty you see before you. But to give you a clearer understanding of what happened to me, I shall briefly explain it all to you."

Then, to the great amazement of his listeners, he narrated every detail of what had occurred, from his first falling in love with the lady up to the present moment, after which he added: "Consequently, unless you, and especially Niccoluccio, have changed the judgment you reached just a little while ago, I'm the one who deserves to have this lady, and no one can legitimately ask me to give her back."

To this no one offered a reply. Instead, all of them waited to see what he would say next. While Niccoluccio was weeping for pity, being joined in that by a few of the others as well as by the lady herself, Messer Gentile got to his feet, took the little boy in his arms, and led the lady by the hand over to where Niccoluccio was sitting.

"Stand up, *compare*," he said.* "I'm not giving you back your wife whom your family as well as hers threw away. Instead, I want to make you a gift of both this lady, my *comare*, and this little boy of hers, of whom you are assuredly the father and whom I held at his baptism and named Gentile.⁴ And I beg you to prize her as much as ever, even though she has been in my house for almost three months, for I swear to you—by that God who perhaps made me fall in love with her so that my love might be, as indeed it has been, the cause of her salvation—she has never led a more virtuous life either with her father and mother or with you than she has with my mother here in my house."

Having said this, he then turned to Catalina and declared: "My lady, I now release you from every promise you made me and leave you free to return to Niccoluccio." And having left her and the baby in Niccoluccio's arms, he returned to his seat.

---

*Gentile identifies Niccoluccio as his *compare* and later calls Catalina his *comare*. These terms mean "godfather" and "godmother," but could also designate something like a close friend or what was once called a "gossip," which is how Gentile uses them here.

Niccoluccio eagerly embraced his wife and son, his present happiness being far greater than his hopelessness had been before, and he did the very best he could possibly do to thank the knight, while all the others, who were weeping for pity, were full of praise for what he had done, as was everyone else who came to hear about it. The lady was given a wonderfully festive reception upon her return home, and for a long time afterward the people of Bologna regarded her with awe as someone who had returned from the dead. As for Messer Gentile, for the rest of his life he remained a good friend of Niccoluccio, his family, and the lady's family as well.

So, what do you say now, gentle ladies? Do you think that a King's giving away his crown and scepter, or an Abbot's reconciling a malefactor with the Pope at no cost to himself, or an old man's exposing his throat to the knife of his enemy—can any of these match the deed performed by Messer Gentile? For he was a lusty young man who felt he had a legitimate claim to that which the negligence of others had thrown away and that he had had the good fortune to retrieve. Nevertheless, not only did he behave honorably in tempering his glowing ardor, but upon obtaining the object that he had always desired with all his heart and had long sought to steal for himself, he generously returned it. Surely, none of the acts of magnanimity about which we have spoken seems to me the equal of this one.

Day 10, Story 5

Madonna Dianora asks Messer Ansaldo for a garden in January as beautiful as it would be in May, and he provides it for her by hiring a magician. Her husband then gives her permission to satisfy Messer Ansaldo's desires, but upon hearing of her husband's generosity, Messer Ansaldo releases her from her promise, and the magician releases Messer Ansaldo from his, refusing to accept any sort of payment from him.[1]

Every member of the merry company praised Messer Gentile to the skies, after which the King ordered Emilia to continue, and as if she just could not wait to speak, she boldly began as follows:

Delicate ladies, no one can reasonably deny that Messer Gentile acted with generosity, but if anyone should argue that doing more than he did is impossible, it will perhaps not be all that difficult to prove that his accomplishments can indeed be surpassed, as I propose to show you in a little story of mine.

In Friuli, which is a cold province, but one happily endowed with beautiful mountains, numerous rivers, and clear springs, there is a town called Udine where there once lived a beautiful, noble lady called Madonna Dianora, the wife of a very wealthy man named Gilberto who was exceptionally pleasant and amiable.[2] Such was this lady's worth that she attracted the most fervent love of a noble lord named Messer Ansaldo Gradense, an important man of exalted station who was known everywhere for his feats of arms and his courtesy. Although he loved her passionately and did everything he could to get her to return his affection, sending her frequent messages to this end, all his efforts were in vain. Eventually, the lady found the gentleman's solicitations wearisome, and realizing that despite refusing everything he asked of her, he nevertheless persisted in loving her and would not stop importuning her, she came up with a novel and, to her mind, impossible request as a way to get rid of him. So one day she spoke to a woman who often came to her on his behalf.

"My good woman," she said, "you've assured me many times that Messer Ansaldo loves me more than anything else, and you've frequently offered me marvelous gifts on his behalf, which I'd prefer he kept for himself, because they could never induce me to love him or satisfy his desires. Were I certain, however, that he really did love me as much as you say he does, then I should undoubtedly bring myself to return his affection and do whatever he wished. Consequently, if he were willing to provide me with proof by doing what I intend to ask of him, I shall be only too ready to obey his commands."

"And just what is it, my lady, that you want him to do?" said the good woman.

"What I desire is this," she replied. "In the month of January that is now approaching, I want a garden, close to town here, that will be full of green grass and flowers and leafy trees just the way it would be in May. And if he can't produce it, then he's not to send you or anyone else to me ever again, because if he bothers me any more, I won't keep it a secret, as I have up to now, but instead, I'll seek to rid myself of him by complaining to my husband and my relatives."

When the gentleman heard what his lady was demanding as well as what she was offering in return, he felt that she was really asking him to do something quite difficult, indeed virtually impossible, and realized that the only reason she had for making such a request was to dash his hopes. Nevertheless, he resolved to try everything he could to fulfill it and had inquiries made throughout many parts of the world to see whether anyone could be found who might provide him with assistance or advice. Finally, he got hold of a man who offered to do what he wanted by means of necromancy, provided he was well paid for his services.

Having agreed to pay the magician a very large sum of money, Messer Ansaldo waited contentedly for the appointed time to arrive.

On the night before the calends* of January, when it was extremely cold and everything was covered with snow and ice, the worthy man went to work with his arts, and the very next morning, in a quite lovely meadow not far from the town, there appeared, according to the testimony of those who saw it, one of the most exquisite gardens anyone has ever seen, with grass and trees and fruit of every kind.

After the ecstatic Messer Ansaldo had looked over it, he arranged for some of the finest fruit and the most beautiful flowers growing there to be picked and presented in secret to the lady, along with an invitation for her to come and see the garden that she had asked for. Thus she would not only realize how much he loved her, but she would remember the promise she had given him, which she had sealed with an oath, and would thus, as a woman of honor, find a way to keep her word.

The lady had already heard many reports about the wonderful garden, and when she saw the flowers and fruit, she began to repent of the promise she had made. Nevertheless, for all her repentance, being curious to see such novelties, she set off with a large group of ladies from the town to have a look at the garden, and after according it great praise and expressing no small astonishment over it, she returned home, the saddest woman alive as she thought of what it obliged her to do. So intense was her grief that she was unable to conceal it, and her husband, noticing how she looked, insisted on knowing the reason why. Deeply ashamed, she maintained her silence for a long time, but finally felt compelled to tell him everything down to the last detail.

As he listened to her story, Gilberto was initially enraged, but then, upon mature reflection, considering the purity of his wife's intentions, he cast off his anger and said: "Dianora, it's not the part of a discreet and honorable lady to listen to messages of that sort, or to make a bargain about her chastity with any man, under any condition. The power of words that the heart receives by way of the ears is greater than many people believe, and for those who are in love there's almost nothing they can't accomplish.[3] Thus, you did wrong, first of all by listening to

---

* The calends is the first of the month.

him, and then by making that bargain. But because I know how pure your heart is, I'll allow you to do something to fulfill the promise you made, something that perhaps no other man would permit, albeit I'm also moved by my fear of the magician, for Messer Ansaldo might ask him to harm us if you played him for a fool. I therefore want you to go to him, and using any means at your disposal, I want you to do what you can to preserve your chastity and get him to release you from your promise. However, if that's not possible, then just this once you may yield your body, but not your heart, to him."

As she listened to her husband, the lady wept and insisted that she did not want such a favor from him. But no matter how vehemently she refused it, Gilberto remained adamant, and so, the next morning around dawn the lady set out, not having bothered to get especially dressed up, and made her way to Messer Ansaldo's house, preceded by just two of her servants and followed by a single chambermaid.

Messer Ansaldo was utterly astonished when he heard that his lady had come to him, and as soon as he got out of bed, he sent for the magician. "I want you to see for yourself what a wonderful prize your art has procured for me," he said. The two of them then went to meet her, and far from displaying anything like unbridled passion, Messer Ansaldo welcomed her with courtesy and reverence. After that, they went into a lovely room where a great fire was burning, and having offered her a place to sit, he said: "My lady, if the long love I have borne for you merits any sort of reward, I beseech you to do me the kindness of revealing the truth about what has brought you here at such an hour and with such a small escort as this."

Ashamed, her eyes welling up with tears, the lady replied: "Sir, I have not been led here because of any love I feel for you or because of the promise I gave you, but rather, because I was ordered to do so by my husband, who has more regard for the labors you've undertaken to satisfy your unbridled passion than he does for his own honor or for mine. And it is at his command that I am furthermore disposed, just this once, to satisfy your every desire."

If Messer Ansaldo had been astonished by the lady's coming to his house, his astonishment was much greater when he heard what she had to say, and he was so moved by Gilberto's liberality that his ardor gradually changed into compassion.

"My lady," he said, "things being the way you say they are, God forbid that I should mar the honor of a man who takes pity on my love. And so, for as long as you choose to stay here, you will be treated as if you were my sister, and whenever you please, you shall be free to depart, provided that you convey to your husband such thanks as you deem appropriate for the immense courtesy he has displayed and that from now on you always look upon me as your brother and servant."

Upon hearing his words, the lady was happier than she had ever been. "From what I've noted of your conduct," she replied, "nothing could ever make me believe that my coming here would have produced any result other than the response I see you've made to it, and for that, I will be eternally in your debt." The lady then took her leave and returned, now with an honorable escort, to Gilberto. She told him what had occurred, with the result that he and Messer Ansaldo became faithful friends, attached to one another by the closest of bonds.

The magician had observed Gilberto's liberality toward Messer Ansaldo as well as Messer Ansaldo's toward the lady, and so, just as Messer Ansaldo was preparing to give him the reward he had been promised, he declared: "Now that I've seen how generous Gilberto has been with regard to his honor and you with regard to your love, God forbid that I shouldn't also be equally generous as far as my remuneration is concerned. And considering how you deserve it, I intend to let you keep it for yourself."

This embarrassed the gentleman, who did everything he could to make him take either the entire sum, or at least part of it, but all his efforts were in vain. Consequently, when the magician, having removed his garden on the third day, expressed a wish to depart, Messer Ansaldo bid him Godspeed. And from then on, any carnal desire he felt for the lady having been extinguished in his heart, Messer Ansaldo burned only with honorable affection for her.

What, then, shall we conclude, loving ladies? Shall we take the case of a lady who was almost dead and a man's love for her that had already grown lukewarm because his hopes had waned, and shall we place it above the generosity of Messer Ansaldo, whose love was more fervent than ever, who burned, as it were, with even more hope than before, and who held the prey he had pursued for so long right there in his hands? It strikes me as foolish to believe that first example of generosity could be compared to this one.[4]

Day 10, Story 6

The victorious King Charles the Old, having fallen in love with a young girl, feels shame over his foolish fancy and arranges honorable marriages for her and her sister.[1]

It would take too long to give a full account of all the varied discussions among the ladies as to whether Gilberto, Messer Ansaldo, or the necromancer had displayed the greater liberality in the case of Madonna Dianora. After the King had allowed them to debate the question for a while, however, he looked over at Fiammetta and ordered her to put an end to their dispute by telling her story. Without a moment's hesitation, she began as follows:

Illustrious ladies, I have always been of the opinion that in companies like ours, we should talk in such general terms that what one person says never gives rise to arguments among the others because of its excessive subtlety, something that is much more appropriate for scholars in the schools than for us, since we have quite enough to do just to manage our distaffs and spindles. Consequently, although I have been thinking about a certain story, it is perhaps a trifle ambiguous, and seeing as how you are at odds over the ones we have already heard, I shall set it aside and tell you another that concerns the chivalrous deed, not of some man of little account, but of a valiant king whose reputation was in no way diminished by what he did.

Each of you must have heard tell many times of King Charles the Old, or King Charles the First, through whose magnificent campaign and the glorious victory he later achieved over King Manfred, the Ghibellines were driven out of Florence and the Guelfs allowed to return.[2] As a result, a knight named Messer Neri degli Uberti left the city, taking his entire household and a great deal of money with him, intent upon finding a refuge somewhere under the protection of King Charles.[3] Wishing to retire to a secluded spot where he could live out his life in peace, he went to Castellammare di Stabia, and there, perhaps a crossbow shot away from the other houses in the area, amid the olives and hazelnuts and chestnuts that abound in those parts, he purchased an estate on which he built a fine, comfortable mansion. Next to it he laid out a delightful garden, in the middle of which, there being a plentiful supply of fresh water, he constructed a beautiful, clear fishpond in our Florentine style, which he stocked in his own good time with an abundant supply of fish.[4]

While he went on dedicating himself every day to the task of making his garden more attractive, it just so happened that King Charles, in the heat of the summer, came to Castellammare for a bit of relaxation. Upon hearing how beautiful Messer Neri's garden was, he was quite eager to see it. Once he discovered who its owner was, however, he decided that since the knight belonged to the party opposed to his own, he would make his visit more informal. Consequently, he sent word to Messer Neri that on the following evening he and four of his companions desired to have a private supper with him in his garden.

Messer Neri was deeply appreciative of this gesture, and having made preparations for a magnificent feast and given instructions to his household about what was to be done, he received the King in his lovely garden as cordially as he possibly could. The King inspected the entire garden as well as Messer Neri's house, lavishing praise on everything he saw, after which he washed up and seated himself at one of the tables, which had been placed next to the fishpond. He ordered Count Guy de Monfort, one of his companions, to sit on one side of him, and Messer Neri on the other, and then he directed the other three who had come with him to wait upon them according to Messer Neri's instructions.[5] Exquisite dishes were then set before them, as were wines both costly and rare, all of which elicited great praise from the King, as did the service, which was fine and quite commendable, free from any noise or unpleasantness.

The King was happily eating his meal and enjoying the solitude of the place, when lo and behold, two young girls, both around fifteen years old, entered the garden. Their hair was a mass of ringlets that were as blonde as spun gold and crowned with a dainty garland of periwinkle blossoms, and their features were so delicate and lovely that it made them seem more like angels than anything else. They were wearing gowns of sheer linen, that had close-fitting bodices and bell-shaped skirts stretching down to their feet, and that looked white as snow up against their skin. The girl in front had thrown a pair of fishnets over her shoulders, which she was holding on to with her left hand, while in her right she carried a long pole. The girl behind had a frying pan on her left shoulder, a bundle of sticks under her left arm, and a trivet in her left hand, while in the other, she held a flask of oil and a small lighted torch. The King was surprised by their appearance and waited in some suspense to see what it meant.

The girls came forward, chaste and modest in their bearing, and bowed before the King. Then they went over to the edge of the fishpond, where the one carrying the frying pan put it down along with the other things she had brought and took the pole from her companion, after which the two of them waded out into the water until it just came up to their breasts. One of Messer Neri's servants quickly lit a fire beside the pool, and pouring oil into the frying pan, he placed it on the trivet and waited for the girls to throw him some fish.

While the first girl poked around in places where she knew the fish were hiding, the other prepared her nets, and in no time at all, to the great delight of the King, who was watching them attentively, they had caught a large number of them. They threw some of their catch to the servant, who took them, still alive, and put them directly into the frying pan, after which the pair began picking out some of the finest specimens, as they had been instructed to do, and tossing them onto the table in front of the King, the Count, and their father.

The sight of the fish flopping about pleased the King to no end, who picked them up in his turn and politely tossed them back again to the girls. And in this fashion they went on playing for some time until the servant had finished cooking the ones that had been thrown to him. At Messer Neri's command the grilled fish were then placed before the King as an entremets or side dish rather than as a really fancy, delectable main course.

When the girls saw that the fish had been cooked and that there was no need for them to catch any more, they got out of the pond, their thin white garments clinging to their skin all over and revealing practically every last detail of their delicate bodies. After picking up the things they had brought with them, they walked shyly past the King and went back into the house.

The King, the Count, and the other gentlemen who were serving the meal had observed the young girls closely, and each one had secretly admired them for their beauty and shapeliness as well as for their charm and good manners. But they had made the deepest impression on the King, for when they had come out of the water, he had stared at their bodies up and down with such intensity that if someone had pricked him then, he would not have felt a thing.

The more the King's thoughts dwelt on the girls, without knowing who they were or how they had come to be there, the more he felt awakening in his heart the most fervent desire to please them, and because of this he knew full well that unless he was careful, he was going to fall in love with them. Nor could he decide which of the two he preferred, so closely did they resemble one another in every way. After brooding on this question for a while, however, he finally turned to Messer Neri and asked him who the two maidens were.

"My lord," replied Messer Neri, "these are my twin daughters, one of whom is called Ginevra the Fair and the other, Isotta the Blonde."[6]

The King heaped praise on them and encouraged him to arrange marriages for them, to which Messer Neri replied apologetically that he no longer had the wherewithal to do so.

At that moment, when the supper was almost over and there was nothing left but the fruit course to bring to the table, the two girls returned. Wearing stunning gowns of fine silk, they carried two enormous silver trays piled high with every kind of fruit then in season. After the trays had been placed on the table before the King, the girls withdrew a short distance and started in on a song, which began with these words:

> O Love, the state that I have reached
> Could not be told in many, many words. . . .

They sang it so sweetly and pleasantly that to the King, who was watching and listening with delight, it seemed as if all the hierarchies of the angels had come down there to sing.[7] When they were finished, they knelt down and respectfully asked the King for permission to leave, and although he was sorry to see them go, he granted it, making a show of cheerfulness as he did so. Since supper was now over, the King and his companions mounted their horses, took their leave of Messer Neri, and returned to the royal residence, talking of various subjects as they rode along.

Still harboring his secret passion, the King was unable, even when important affairs of state supervened, to forget the beauty and charm of Ginevra the Fair, for whose sake he also loved the sister who resembled her. So entangled did he become in the snares of Love that he could scarcely think of anything else, and he invented various pretexts to cultivate a close relationship with Messer Neri and to visit him frequently in his lovely garden, all in order to catch a glimpse of Ginevra. Finally, unable to endure it any longer, he came to the conclusion that, for lack of any other alternative, he had to take not one, but both girls away from their father. He then revealed his love and his intention to Count Guy who, being the honorable man he was, said to him:

"My lord, I am utterly astonished by what you've told me, indeed, more astonished than someone else would be because I think I have a greater familiarity with your ways than any man alive, having known you intimately from your childhood up to the present day. I do not recall your ever having experienced such a passion in your youth, when it would have been easier for Love to have gotten its talons into you. To hear that you've actually fallen in love, now when you're on the verge of old age, seems so new and strange that it's nothing less than miraculous. And if the task of reprimanding you for it fell to me, I know exactly what I'd say to you, considering that you're still bearing arms in a realm you've just recently acquired, that you live among an alien people who are extremely wily and treacherous, and that you have been so completely preoccupied with the gravest concerns and the loftiest affairs of state that you have not yet been able simply to sit securely in the seat you occupy—and nevertheless, in the midst of all this, you've succumbed to the flattering allure of Love. This is not the behavior of a magnanimous king, but of a weak-willed youth.

"What's far worse is that you say you've decided to abduct the two girls from the poor knight, who went beyond his means to honor you by entertaining you in his own home, indeed, who honored you even more by showing his daughters off to you practically naked, thereby demonstrating the great faith he has in you and how firmly he believes you to be a king and not a rapacious wolf. Have you forgotten so soon how the gates of this kingdom were opened to you because Manfred violated the women here? Has anyone ever committed an act of betrayal worthier of eternal punishment than this deed of yours would be: to deprive the man who honored you not only of his own honor, but of his hope and his consolation? What would people say of you if you did this?

"Perhaps you think it would be a sufficient excuse for you to say: 'I did it because he's a Ghibelline.' Now, is it consistent with a king's justice that those who turn to him for protection, whoever they may be, should receive this kind of treatment? Let me remind you, my King, that although you achieved the greatest glory in conquering Manfred and defeating Conradin, it is far more glorious to conquer oneself.[8] Therefore, since it is your task to rule over others, you must triumph over your feelings and curb this appetite of yours, lest such a blemish mar all the splendor of your achievements."[9]

These words pierced the King to the heart, affecting him all the more profoundly because he knew they were correct. And so, after breathing one or two fervent sighs, he said: "Count, it's certainly true that for the well-trained warrior, all other enemies, however powerful, are actually quite weak and easy to defeat in comparison with his own appetites. Nevertheless, even though I am going to suffer horribly, and even though the strength I will need is incalculable, your words have spurred me on to such an extent that before too many days have passed, I am determined to show you by my actions that just as I know how to conquer others, I am likewise capable of mastering myself."

Just a few days after this exchange, the King returned to Naples, both in order to deprive himself of any opportunity to behave dishonorably and in order to prepare a reward for the knight in recognition of the honorable entertainment he had been given. Even though it was hard for the King to allow someone else to possess what he ardently desired for himself, he nevertheless determined to arrange marriages for the two young girls, not as Messer Neri's daughters, but as his own. Thus, to Messer Neri's delight, after having provided magnificent dowries for the two of them, he gave Ginevra the Fair to Messer Maffeo da Palizzi and Isotta the Blonde to Messer Guiglielmo della Magna, both of whom were noble knights and great lords.[10] After consigning the girls to their husbands, he departed, utterly grief stricken, for Apulia where, by dint of constant effort, he mortified his fierce appetite to such a degree and in such a way that the chains of Love were snapped apart and broken into bits, and for the rest of his life he was never enslaved by that passion again.

Perhaps some will say that it was a trifling matter for a king to arrange the marriages of two young girls, and I will grant their point. Still, if we consider that this was done by a king who was himself in love and who arranged to marry off the person he had fallen for without his ever having taken or plucked a single leaf, flower, or fruit from this love of his, then I would say that this was a very great feat, if not the greatest one of all.

So, that is how this magnanimous King behaved, generously rewarding the noble knight, laudably honoring the girls he loved, and using his strength to triumph over himself.

Upon learning that a young woman named Lisa had become ill because of her fervent love for him, King Peter goes to comfort her, after which he weds her to a young nobleman, and having kissed her on the brow, from then on always calls himself her knight.[1]

When Fiammetta had come to the end of her story, and the manly magnanimity of King Charles had received lavish praise, except from one of the ladies who was a Ghibelline and did not wish to commend him, Pampinea, at the King's command, began speaking:

Distinguished ladies, no sensible person would disagree with what you have said about good King Charles, unless she had some other reason for speaking ill of him, but since his deed reminds me of another one, perhaps no less commendable, that was performed by an adversary of his for the sake of one of our Florentine girls, I would like to tell you about it.

At the time when the French were expelled from Sicily, there was a very rich apothecary from our city living in Palermo named Bernardo Puccini, whose wife had borne him only one child, an exceptionally beautiful daughter, who was then of marriageable age.[2] King Peter of Aragon, having become the ruler of the island, staged a spectacular celebration in Palermo with all of his noblemen, and it just so happened that while he was jousting in the Catalan fashion, Bernardo's daughter, whose name was Lisa, was viewing the activities from a window along with some other ladies.[3] Having caught sight of the King riding in the lists, she found him so wonderfully attractive that after watching him perform once or twice more, she fell passionately in love with him.

When the festivities had come to an end, and Lisa was back in her father's house, she could not think of anything except this magnificent, exalted love of hers, and what grieved her the most about it was the knowledge of her own inferior rank, which left her with hardly any hope that it was going to have a happy ending. Although she could not bring herself to stop loving him, still, for fear of making matters even worse, she did not dare to reveal what she felt.

The King neither knew nor cared about what was going on, which made Lisa's suffering intolerable, worse than anything that can be imagined. And thus it happened that, as her love continued to grow within her, her melancholy was doubled by a yet greater melancholy until the beautiful young girl, incapable of bearing it any longer, became ill and started visibly wasting away day by day, just like snow in sunlight. Heartbroken because of these developments, her father and mother did what they could to help her, continually comforting her, bringing in doctors, and supplying her with various kinds of medicine. It was all to no avail, however, for the girl, despairing of her love, had reached the point where she no longer wanted to go on living.

Now, since the girl's father kept offering to do whatever she wanted, one day the thought occurred to her that if some suitable means could be found, she would like to have the King informed, before she died, about her love as well as her intention to end her life, and she therefore asked Bernardo to arrange for Minuccio d'Arezzo to come and see her.[4] Minuccio, who was considered a very fine singer and musician in those days, was a welcome guest at King Peter's court, and Bernardo, thinking that Lisa wanted to hear him sing and play for her, sent him an invitation to that effect. An obliging man, Minuccio promptly came to pay her a visit, and after cheering her up a little with words of affection, he played a number of dance tunes sweetly for her on his viol[5] and then sang some songs, although they all only served to stir up the fire and flames of her love rather than providing her with the consolation he intended.

When he had finished, the girl told him that she would like to have a few words with him in private, and once all the others had withdrawn, she said: "Minuccio, I've chosen you as the most trustworthy guardian of a secret of mine, hoping first that you'll never, ever reveal it to anyone except the person whose name I'm about to tell you, and second that you'll do everything in your power to help me. Indeed, I'm begging you to do this for me.

"What you need to know, my dear Minuccio, is that on the day when our lord King Peter staged the grand festival in honor of his accession, I happened to see him at a fateful moment while he was jousting, and such was the fiery passion he kindled in my heart that it's brought me to the state you see me in here. I know how inappropriate it is for me to love a king, but I've had no success in moderating, let alone expelling, my passion, and since continuing to bear it is sheer agony for me, I've chosen to die as the lesser evil—and that is precisely what I'm going to do.

"Still, the truth is that I'll be utterly inconsolable when I go if he hasn't learned about my love before then, and since I don't know of anyone better than you to inform him about what I intend to do, I wish to entrust you with this task, and I implore you not to refuse it. Then, when you've carried it out, you are to let me know, so that I may thus find release from these torments and die in peace."

Having said all this through her tears, she fell silent. Amazed as much by the loftiness of her spirit as by the fierce nature of her resolve, Minuccio was feeling a terrible sense of distress when, all of a sudden, a thought occurred to him as to how he might honorably be of service to her.

"Lisa," he said, "I pledge you my word, by which you may rest assured you will never be deceived, and as a token of my admiration for your lofty aspiration in having set your heart on so great a king, I shall indeed offer you my assistance. If you'll keep up your courage, my hope is to take such steps as I think will enable me, before three days have passed, to bring you news that will make you exceedingly happy. And to avoid losing time, I intend to go and get started at once."

Lisa promised him that she would take comfort from what he had said, and having repeated her requests all over again, she bade him farewell.

As soon as he left her, Minuccio went off to find a certain Mico da

Siena, an extremely talented writer of verse in those days, and by dint of many earnest entreaties Minuccio prevailed upon him to compose the following little song:[6]

> Bestir thyself, O Love, go to my Lord,
> And tell him of the pains that I endure;
> Tell him I'm close to death,
> Because I hide my longing out of fear.
> I cry thee mercy, Love, with claspéd hands,
> That thou mayst go where'er my Lord doth dwell.
> Tell him how much I love and long for him,
> So sweetly is my heart enamoréd;
> How by the fire, which hath me all aflame,
> I fear I'll die, and yet I ardently
> Desire to leave behind the pain so fierce
> And fell, which I endure in fear and shame
> Through my desire for him:
> Oh! Let him know, for God's sake, of my woe.
>
> Since first I fell in love with him, O Love,
> Thou didst not give me daring, but instead
> Didst make me fear to show him openly
> A single time how desperately I yearn
> For one who keepeth me in grievous pain.
> If thus I die, such death is hard to bear!
> Perhaps he would not be displeased to know
> About the dreadful anguish that I feel—
> If only I'd been giv'n
> The courage to reveal my state to him.
>
> Yet since it hath not been thy pleasure, Love,
> To grant such bold self-confidence to me
> As to lay bare my heart unto my Lord
> Through messages, alas, or through my looks,
> I beg thee, sweet my master, of thy grace,
> To go to him and make him call to mind
> The day I saw him bearing lance and shield

In tourney with the other cavaliers:
On him I fixed my gaze,
So smitten that my heart now perisheth.

Minuccio immediately set these words to music, providing as sweet
and sorrowful a melody as the material required, and on the third day,
he went to the court where King Peter, who was in the midst of his
dinner, asked him to sing something to the accompaniment of his viol.
He therefore began singing this song, playing it so sweetly that every
single person present in the royal hall seemed entranced by it, the King
perhaps more than the others, so quiet and absorbed were they all as
they paused to listen to it. When Minuccio finished his song, the King
inquired as to where it had come from, for he could not recall ever having heard it before.

"My lord," said Minuccio, "the words and the music were composed
less than three days ago." And when the King asked for whom, Minuccio replied, "I dare not reveal that to anyone but you."

The King was eager to hear the secret, and as soon as the tables were
cleared away, he took Minuccio with him to his chamber, where the
poet recounted everything he had been told, down to the last detail.
The King was overjoyed by the story, and lavishing great praise on the
girl, he declared that such a worthy young lady deserved to be treated
with compassion. Consequently, he told Minuccio to go to her on his
behalf, to comfort her, and to tell her that he himself would, without
fail, come to visit her that very same day a little before vespers.

Delighted to be the bearer of such happy news, Minuccio went
directly to the girl, taking his viol along with him, and once he was
alone with her, he told her the entire story, after which he sang her the
song, accompanying himself on his instrument. The girl felt so happy
and contented because of all this that she immediately, visibly, started
to show marked signs of improved health, and without anyone else in
the house knowing, or even suspecting, what was going on, she began
eagerly waiting for vespers when she would get to see her lord.

A kind and generous ruler, the King devoted a great deal of thought
to what Minuccio had told him, and recalling the girl and her beauty

quite well, he felt even more pity for her than before. Around the hour of vespers, he got on his horse, and pretending he was going out for a jaunt, he rode to the place where the apothecary's house stood. Bernardo had a very fine garden there, and the King, having requested that it be opened for him, went inside and dismounted. After talking with Bernardo awhile, he asked him how his daughter was doing and if he had as yet given her to anyone in marriage.

"My lord," replied Bernardo, "she's not married. As a matter of fact, she's been very sick, and she still is, although the truth is that from nones on she has miraculously improved."

The King immediately understood what this improvement meant and said: "In truth, it would be a shame if the world were to be deprived so soon of such a beautiful creature. Let us go and pay her a visit."

A little while later, accompanied by just two of his retainers, the King went with Bernardo to Lisa's chamber, and once inside, walked right over to the bed, where the girl, sitting up a bit, was waiting for him with eager anticipation.

"What is the meaning of this, my lady?" said the King, taking her by the hand. "You're young and should be comforting other women rather than allowing yourself to become ill. We would ask you to be so kind as to cheer up, for our sake, so that you may make a speedy recovery."

When she felt herself being touched by the hands of the man whom she loved above all else, the girl may have been a little embarrassed, but in her heart she experienced such pleasure that she thought she was in Paradise.

"My lord," she said, doing her best to compose an answer, "my infirmity was caused by my attempt to bear a burden that was far too heavy for my feeble strength, but you'll soon see that I'll be free of it, thanks to your gracious assistance."

Only the King grasped the hidden meaning of the girl's words, and as she thus rose still higher in his esteem, he inwardly cursed Fortune more than once for having made her the daughter of such a man as Bernardo. He stayed there with her for a while longer, comforting her even more, and finally took his leave.

The King's humane gesture was accorded the highest praise, being regarded as a singular honor for the apothecary and his daughter, who was as contented with her lover as any woman has ever been. Within a few days, aided by the revival of her hopes, she not only recovered her health, but became more beautiful than ever.

Now that she was well again, the King, having taken counsel with the Queen about the reward he would bestow on the girl for so grand a passion, mounted his horse one day and rode to the apothecary's house, accompanied by a large group of his lords. Having entered the garden, he sent for the apothecary and his daughter. In the meantime, the Queen arrived with many of her ladies-in-waiting, all of whom received the girl in their midst with such festive cheer that it was a wonder to behold. At length, the King, with the Queen at his side, summoned Lisa to him and said:

"Worthy young lady, the great love you have borne for us has led us to grant you a great honor, with which, for our sake, we trust you will be content. And the honor is this, that since you are as yet unmarried, it is our wish that you should accept as your husband the man we will bestow on you, it being nevertheless our intention always to style ourself your knight, without requiring from you, out of all that love of yours, anything more than a single kiss."

The girl was so embarrassed that her entire face turned scarlet, and in a low voice, adopting the King's pleasure as her own, she replied: "My lord, I'm quite certain that if people knew I'd fallen in love with you, most of them would consider me mad, for they'd think I'd taken leave of my senses and didn't recognize the difference between your rank and my own. But God, who alone sees inside the hearts of mortals, knows that from the hour I was first attracted to you, I knew full well that you were a king, that I was the daughter of Bernardo the apothecary, and that it did not become me to direct my soul's ardent affection toward such lofty heights. But you know far better than I do that when people here below fall in love, they are not making a considered choice, but are guided by appetite and sensual attraction. I repeatedly fought against this law with all my might until, no longer able to resist, I fell in love with you—and I continue to love you now and will do so forever.

"The truth is that as soon as I felt myself overcome by my affection for you, I resolved to make your will my own, and for that reason, not only shall I gladly accept and treasure any man it pleases you to bestow on me as my husband, who will bring me honor and dignity, but if you ordered me to walk through fire, I would be happy to do so if I thought it would give you pleasure. With regard to having you, a king, as my knight, you know how appropriate such a thing would be for a person of my condition, and so, on that score I will say nothing more, nor will I grant you the single kiss you request of my love without the permission of my lady, the Queen. Nevertheless, for the great kindness that you and my lady, the Queen, who has accompanied you here, have shown me, may God give you thanks and may He recompense you on my behalf, since I myself have nothing with which to repay you."

At this point she stopped talking, but her answer, which the Queen found very satisfying, convinced her that the girl was every bit as wise as the King had said. King Peter then summoned Lisa's father and mother, and once he knew that they approved of what he was planning to do, he sent for a young man named Perdicone, who was of gentle birth, though poor, placed some rings in his hand, and had him marry the girl, something he was by no means unwilling to do. Then, in addition to the many precious jewels that the King and Queen bestowed on Lisa, the King gave Perdicone Cefalú and Calatabellotta, two excellent, very lucrative fiefs.[7]

"These we give you as a dowry for your wife," declared the King. "What we have in store for you yourself, that you shall see in the time to come."

Then King Peter turned to the girl and said, "Now we wish to gather the fruit of your love that is our due." And taking her head between his hands, he kissed her on the brow.

Perdicone, along with Lisa's father and mother, and Lisa herself were all quite delighted, and they celebrated the happy marriage with a enormous feast. Furthermore, as many people affirm, the King was most faithful in honoring the compact he had made with the girl, always styling himself her knight for the rest of his life, and whenever he engaged in feats of arms, he never bore any favor* other than the one she sent him.

It is by deeds such as these that one captures the hearts of one's subjects, provides occasions for others to do good, and acquires eternal fame. But nowadays, this is a target at which few, if any, rulers have bent the bow of their minds, most of them having become pitiless tyrants.

---

* A favor was a token, such as a kerchief or ribbon, given to a knight by his lady and carried by him when he fought in a tournament or battle.

Day 10, Story 8

Sophronia thinks she is marrying Gisippus, but she actually becomes the wife of Titus Quintus Fulvius with whom she travels to Rome, where the impoverished Gisippus eventually turns up. Believing that he has been slighted by Titus, Gisippus claims to have killed a man so that he will be put to death, but Titus recognizes him, and in order to save him, says that he himself committed the crime. Upon witnessing this, the real murderer reveals himself, at which point they are all released by Octavianus, and Titus not only gives his sister to Gisippus in marriage, but shares everything he possesses with him.[1]

When Pampinea had stopped talking and King Peter had been praised by all the ladies, but especially by the one who was a Ghibelline, at the King's command, Filomena began speaking:

Magnificent ladies, who does not know that kings are capable of performing grand feats if they are so inclined, and that they, above all others, are obliged to be magnanimous? Those people do well, then, who possess the means and carry out what is expected of them, but we should not marvel so much at their deeds or extol them to the skies to the same extent that we would a person who behaves just as magnanimously, but from whom less is expected since his means are more limited. Therefore, if you found the deeds of kings so fair and were so voluble in commending them, I have no doubt whatsoever that you would take more delight in those performed by our peers that match or surpass the accomplishments of kings, and that they would elicit far more praise from you. Accordingly, I propose to tell you a story about two citizens, who were friends, and about the laudable magnanimity they displayed toward one another.

In the time when Octavianus Caesar, before he was called Augustus, held the office of Triumvir and ruled the Roman Empire, there was a gentleman living in Rome named Publius Quintus Fulvius.[2] He had an astonishingly intelligent son called Titus Quintus Fulvius whom he sent to study philosophy in Athens, doing all he could to recommend him to a very old friend of his, a nobleman named Chremes, who lodged him in his own house with Gisippus, one of his sons, and sent the two young men to study together under the guidance of a philosopher called Aristippus.

As they went on spending time in one another's company, the pair discovered they shared a great deal in common, and as a result there sprang up between them a feeling of brotherliness and friendship so powerful that it lasted until their dying day. Indeed, neither one felt happy or at ease unless they were together. Since they were equally endowed with the highest intelligence, once they began their studies, they ascended the glorious heights of philosophy side by side, receiving marvelous acclaim as they did so. And in this way of life, to the enormous delight of Chremes, who treated both of them alike as his sons, they continued for a good three years. At the end of that time Chremes, who was already an elderly man, happened to pass from this world, just as all things must eventually do, and his friends and relations could not determine which of the young men was more in need of consolation because of the misfortune that had occurred, for he had been a father to both of them, and they were equally grief stricken as a result.

After several months had passed, Gisippus's friends and relations came to see him, and joined by Titus, they encouraged him to get married, having found him a fifteen-year-old girl of astonishing beauty by the name of Sophronia, who was a citizen of Athens and came from one of the noblest families in the city.[3] One day, as the time appointed for the nuptials was drawing near, Gisippus asked Titus to go with him to see the girl, since he had not yet laid eyes on her. After they arrived at her house, the pair sat down with the girl in between them, and Titus began scrutinizing her very attentively, as though he were appraising the beauty of his friend's bride-to-be. So great was the boundless pleasure he got from viewing every part of her, however, that as he went on contemplating her in silent admiration, without showing any sign of what he was feeling, he soon started burning for her with a passion as fervent as that which any lover has ever experienced for his lady. Then, after having spent a little more time with her, they took their leave and returned home.

When they got back to the house, Titus went to his room all by himself where he began meditating on the young woman's charms, and the more he continued to brood on her, the hotter his ardor became. Perceiving the condition he was in, he heaved many a burning sigh and began communing with himself.

"Ah, Titus," he said, "what a wretched life you lead! Where and on whom are you setting your heart and your love and your hopes? Don't you realize that the honorable reception you've gotten from Chremes and his family, and the perfect friendship that exists between you and Gisippus, who is going to be her husband, oblige you to treat this girl with the same respect you'd show a sister? Who is it, then, that you love? Where are you letting yourself be carried away by the deceptions of passion? By the delusions of hope? Open the eyes of your mind, you wretch, and see yourself for what you are. Make way for reason, bridle your carnal appetites, temper those unhealthy desires of yours, and direct your thoughts elsewhere. Struggle against this lust of yours now at the beginning, and conquer yourself while you still have time.[4] It's unseemly for you to desire this; it's dishonorable. That which you are inclined to pursue, even though you were sure—which you are not—of obtaining it, is something you ought to flee from if you had any regard for what true friendship requires and what your duty entails. So what are you going to do, then, Titus? If you want to do what's proper, you'll abandon this unseemly love of yours."

But then, recalling Sophronia, he would turn in the opposite direction, and rejecting every argument he had made, he would say: "The laws of Love are more powerful than any others: they not only override those of friendship, but divine laws as well. How often before now has a father loved his daughter, a brother his sister, a stepmother her stepson? Things much more monstrous than a man's falling for the wife of his friend have occurred a thousand times before now. Besides, I'm a young man, and youth is entirely subject to the laws of Love, so that whatever Love finds pleasing must necessarily be pleasing to me as well. Honorable deeds are well enough for older men, but the only things I can desire are what Love wishes. Since my lady is so beautiful that she deserves to be loved by everyone, who can justly blame me if I, a young man, have fallen for her? It's not because she belongs to Gisippus that I love her, but for herself; in fact, I'd love her no matter whose she was. Fortune is at fault here for having given her to my friend Gisippus rather than to another man, and if she ought to be loved, as she rightly deserves to be because of her beauty, Gisippus should be happier to discover that I'm the person, instead of someone else, who's taken with her."

Then mocking himself for the argument he had just made, he would adopt the contrary position, and as he went from this one back to the other, and vice versa, not only did he consume the rest of the day and the following night, but many others after that, until finally, having long gone without food and sleep, he grew so weak that he was forced to take to his bed.

Gisippus was very upset when, after having observed Titus lost in thought day after day, he now discovered that he was sick. Refusing to leave his friend's side, he utilized all his art and skill, doing his very best to comfort him, and repeatedly asking him, with some insistence, the reason for his pensiveness and his illness. Titus kept telling him one unbelievable story after another by way of reply, but Gisippus saw through all of them, until Titus finally found himself constrained to speak, and with sighs and tears, answered his friend in this manner:

"Gisippus, if it had pleased the gods, I would have been much happier to have died than to live any longer, seeing as how Fortune has brought me to a pass where my virtue has been put to the test, and where, to my very great shame, it has been found wanting. But I certainly expect to receive, before long, the reward I deserve in the form of death, and this will be dearer to me than to go on living with the memory of my baseness, which, since there is nothing I can and should hide from you, I will reveal, even though I'll blush with shame when I do so."

Then, starting from the beginning, Titus disclosed the reason for his brooding, describing the thoughts consuming him and the battle that had been raging among them, which ones had been victorious, and how he was wasting away out of love for Sophronia. He went on to declare that since he knew how improper his passion was, he had decided to die by way of penance, an end he imagined would soon occur.

As he listened to his friend's story and watched him weep, Gisippus vacillated for a while, because even though his feelings were more tempered, he, too, was taken with the charms of the beautiful girl. Nevertheless, he quickly decided that his friend's life ought to be dearer to him than she was, and so, moved by the tears his friend was shedding, he began to weep himself.

"Titus," he said, "if you were not in need of comfort the way you are, I would take you to task for having violated our friendship by keeping the terrible burden of this passion of yours hidden from me for so long. Although such feelings may have seemed improper to you, they should not be concealed from a friend any more than proper ones should be, for just as a true friend delights in sharing honorable things with his friend, so he will do everything in his power to remove that which is dishonorable from his friend's heart. But setting this aside for the present, let me come to that which is of greater moment.

"That you have fallen passionately in love with Sophronia, who is betrothed to me, does not surprise me. Actually, it would have surprised me if you hadn't done so, considering her beauty and the nobility of your spirit, which is all the more susceptible to passion, the finer the object that attracts you. And as much as it's perfectly reasonable for you to love Sophronia, it's unjust of you to complain—albeit you do not say this in so many words—that Fortune has given her to me, as though your love for her would be proper had she been anyone else's but mine. But if you're the wise man you've always been, you should be thanking Fortune for having bestowed her on me, and not on someone else. For had she belonged to another, no matter how honorable your love might have been, he would have desired to keep her for himself rather than for you, whereas, if you consider me your friend—and I truly am—you need not fear any such thing from me.

"Now, the reason for this is that since the time we first became friends, I can't remember ever having had anything that wasn't as much yours as it was mine. And so, even if things had advanced to the point where there was no other possible course of action, I'd still be willing to do with her what I've done with everything I possessed in the past, but as the matter stands at present, I can ensure that she'll be yours alone—and that is precisely what I'm going to do. For I don't know why you would value my friendship if I were incapable of forgoing my desire in favor of yours when it involves something that can be done with honor. Now, it's true that Sophronia is engaged to me, that I love her very much, and that I was eagerly looking forward to our wedding, but since you are far more intent upon having her and you desire to possess such a dear creature with much greater fervor than I do, rest assured that when she enters my chamber, it will not be as my wife, but as yours.[5] So, stop brooding, cast off your melancholy, recover the health you've lost along with your comfort and your gaiety, and from this moment on, look forward cheerfully to obtaining the reward you deserve for your love, a love far worthier than mine ever was."

To hear Gisippus speak this way, Titus was both pleased because of the flattering hope being held out to him and ashamed because of his consciousness of his duty, which told him that the greater the generosity of his friend, the more unseemly it appeared for him to benefit from it. Thus, weeping continuously, he struggled to reply.

"Gisippus," he said, "your true and generous friendship shows me with utter clarity what my own obliges me to do for you. God forbid that I should ever accept as my wife the woman whom he has given to you as the worthier person.[6] If he had judged it fitting for her to be mine, neither you nor anyone else can believe that he would have ever bestowed her on you. Rejoice, therefore, in his great wisdom, in the fact that he has selected you, and in the gift you have received from him. In the meanwhile, leave me to waste away in the tears that he has allotted to me as being unworthy of such a boon, for either I will conquer my grief, which will make you happy, or it will conquer me, and I will be put out of my misery."

"Titus," replied Gisippus, "if our friendship would allow me sufficient license not merely to compel you to entertain one of my wishes, but to induce you to carry it out, then this is the time when I intend to exploit it to the full, and since you won't willingly yield to my entreaties, I shall have recourse to the force one may use to advance the interests of one's friends and ensure that Sophronia shall be yours. I know what the powers of Love can do and that not just once, but on many occasions, they've led lovers to an unhappy death. Furthermore, I see you're now so close to it that there's no longer any question of your turning back or overcoming your tears. If you were to go on like this, you would perish, and I myself, without a doubt, would follow you shortly afterward. Therefore, even if I had no other reason to love you, your life is dear to me because my own depends on it. Sophronia, then, shall be yours, for you won't easily find another creature you'll like nearly so much, whereas in my case, I'll have no difficulty in directing my love elsewhere, and this way I'll succeed in satisfying both of us.

"I wouldn't be so generous in this situation, perhaps, were wives as scarce and as hard to find as friends are, but since I can, with the greatest of ease, find another wife for myself, but not another friend, I prefer, rather than to lose you, not to lose her exactly, since I won't be doing that in giving her to you, but instead, to transfer her, as it were, to my other—and better—self.[7] So, if my prayers mean anything to you, I beg you to cast off this affliction of yours and thus bring solace to both of us at the same time. And with good hope, prepare yourself to enjoy the happiness that your ardent passion seeks in the object of your affection."

Feeling ashamed to consent that Sophronia should become his wife, Titus resisted the idea for quite some time, but finally, with Love pulling him on one side and Gisippus's exhortations pushing him on the other, he said: "Look here, Gisippus, I don't know which of us would be the most contented were I to do what you implore me to do, seeing as how you tell me it would give you so much pleasure, but since your liberality is such that it overcomes any shame I ought to feel, I'll do it. Nevertheless, you may rest assured that I'll do it as a man who recognizes that I am receiving from you not merely the woman I love, but along with her, my very life as well. May the gods grant that if I'm given the chance, I may yet find the means to pay you back with honor and demonstrate to you the gratitude I feel for what you've done on my behalf, considering how you've shown more compassion for me than I have for myself."

"Titus," said Gisippus, when his friend had finished, "if we want to succeed in this affair, I think this is the way for us to go. As you know, Sophronia was betrothed to me only after protracted negotiations between her people and mine, so if I went now and announced that I no longer had any desire to marry her, it would produce a terrible scandal, and I would upset both of our families. This wouldn't bother me in the least if I was sure that she was going to become your wife as a result of it, but I'm afraid that if I gave her up at this juncture, her relatives would immediately give her to someone else—someone else who will not necessarily be you—in which case you will have lost her, and I will have gained nothing. Therefore, if you're amenable to it, I think that I should continue what I've begun. I'll bring her back home with me as my bride and celebrate the wedding here, after which we'll find some secret means for you to sleep with her as your wife. Then, at the right time and place, we'll make the matter public. If they all like it, well and good, but if they don't, it'll be a done deal, and since there'll be no going back, the only choice they'll have is to make their peace with it."

Titus liked the plan, and as soon as he was healthy and strong again, Gisippus brought the girl back to his house as his wife. They put on a grand wedding feast, and as night fell, the women withdrew, leaving the new bride in her husband's bed.

Titus's room was located right next to Gisippus's, enabling them to pass easily from one to the other, and so, after Gisippus had entered his and extinguished all the lights there, he stealthily made his way over to his friend and told him he should go to bed with his wife. Overcome with shame at hearing his friend's invitation, Titus began to have second thoughts and refused to go, but Gisippus, who sincerely desired to serve his friend's pleasure and had meant every single word he had said, finally, after a lengthy argument, managed to send him in to her.

As soon as Titus was in bed with the girl, he took her in his arms and asked her in a whisper, almost as if he were playing a game, whether she wanted to be his wife. Thinking it was Gisippus, she replied in the affirmative, at which point he took a beautiful, costly ring, placed it on

her finger, and said to her: "And I want to be your husband." The marriage was then consummated, after which Titus continued taking his
amorous pleasure of her for quite some time, although neither she nor
anybody else ever suspected that someone other than Gisippus was
sleeping with her.

This, then, was the marital situation in which Sophronia and Titus
found themselves when his father Publius departed this life, at which
point Titus received letters telling him to return to Rome without delay
so that he could tend to his affairs. After consulting with Gisippus,
he decided to leave Athens and take Sophronia with him, a course of
action that would be inappropriate, not to say impossible, unless he
revealed to her how things stood. Accordingly, one day they called
her into the room with them and explained the entire situation to her,
Titus confirming the story by recounting many details for her of what
had passed between the two of them.

After casting disdainful looks first at the one, and then at the other,
Sophronia poured forth a flood of tears and complained bitterly about
the trick that Gisippus had played on her. Rather than say another
word on the subject while she was still in his house, however, she went
off to her father's, where she told him as well as her mother about how
she and they had all been deceived by Gisippus, declaring that she was
not his wife, as they had supposed, but Titus's. Sophronia's father took
a very dim view of the business and complained loud and long about
it to both his own relations and those of Gisippus, which led to a great
deal of discussion and gossip. Gisippus incurred the hatred of his own
family as well as Sophronia's, and everyone said he deserved not only to
be reprimanded, but severely punished. He, however, maintained that
he had acted honorably and that he ought to be thanked by Sophronia's family since he had given her in marriage to someone better than
himself.

For his part, Titus, who had heard about everything, managed to put
up with it for a while, albeit under great duress, but eventually, knowing that the Greeks had the habit of making a lot of noise and threats
until there was someone to answer them back, at which point they
would become not merely humble, but quite abject, he decided their

prattle could no longer be tolerated and that he needed to respond to it.[8] Having the spirit of a Roman and the wits of an Athenian, he adroitly contrived to get the families of Gisippus and Sophronia to gather together in a temple, and having gone there accompanied by Gisippus, he addressed the group waiting inside it as follows:

"It's the belief of many philosophers that all human actions are ordained and decreed by the immortal gods, and consequently, some would have it that what happens down here either now or in the future is the result of necessity, although there are others who claim that this necessity applies only to that which has already occurred. If these opinions are considered with any care, then it will become apparent that our disapproval of things that cannot be undone amounts to nothing less than an attempt to demonstrate that we are more intelligent than the gods, who, we must suppose, control and govern us and our affairs with eternal, infallible wisdom. Therefore, you can see quite easily how senseless, brutish, and presumptuous it is to criticize what the gods bring about, just as you will appreciate with how many heavy chains those people deserve to be bound who get carried away by such boldness. Now, in my judgment, you all belong in that group, if there's any truth in what I hear you've been saying, and continue to say, about Sophronia's becoming my wife after you'd given her to Gisippus, for you're ignoring how it's been ordained *ab eterno** that she should belong to me rather than to him, as we now know from the outcome.[9]

"But since speaking about the secret providence and intentions of the gods seems too difficult and weighty a subject for many people to understand, let's suppose that they remain utterly uninvolved in our affairs. Instead, I'm happy to descend to the level of human judgment, speaking of which obliges me to do two things quite contrary to my customary practices. The first is to praise myself a little, and the second, to criticize or disparage others to a certain extent. But since I have no intention of departing from the truth in either case, and since the present occasion requires it, this is nevertheless what I'm going to do.

"Moved more by rage than reason, you complain about Gisippus, and

---

* *Ab eterno*: "from eternity."

you abuse, attack, and condemn him with your endless murmuring—
or rather, your clamoring—because he decided to bestow upon me the
wife whom you had decided to bestow upon him. But in this case, I
think he deserves the highest praise, and for these reasons: first, because
he's done what a friend should do; and second, because he's acted more
wisely than you did. I have no intention of explaining to you at present
what the sacred laws of friendship require one friend to do for another,
being content merely to remind you that the tie of friendship is more
binding than that of blood or kinship, in that our friends are of our
own choosing, whereas our relations are allotted to us by Fortune. And
so, none of you should marvel that Gisippus valued my life more than
your goodwill, since I am his friend, as I consider myself to be.

"But let's come to the second reason, which, if I'm to prove to you
that he's wiser than you are, I must unfold at greater length, for it
seems to me you know nothing about the providence of the gods, and
still less about the consequences of friendship. What I will say is that
it was your judgment, your counsel, and your resolve that Sophronia
should be given to Gisippus, a young man and a philosopher, and that
it was Gisippus who then decided to give her to a young man and a
philosopher in his turn. It was your decision to bestow her on an Athenian; that of Gisippus, on a Roman. It was yours to give her to a noble
youth, Gisippus's to a nobler one; yours to a rich young man, Gisippus's
to one much, much richer; yours to someone who not only didn't love
her, but scarcely knew her, whereas Gisippus decided to bestow her on
a young man who loved her above all his other blessings, indeed, more
than life itself.

"And to see that what I'm saying is true and that Gisippus's actions
are more praiseworthy than yours, let's examine it all point by point.
That I'm a young man and a philosopher just like Gisippus, my face
and my intellectual endeavors can demonstrate without my making a
longer speech on the subject, for we're the same age, and we've always
kept pace with one another as we advanced in our studies. Although
it's true that he's an Athenian and I'm a Roman, if we argue about the
merits of our cities, let me say that I come from one that is free, while
his pays tribute; that mine is the mistress of the entire world, while his

remains its subject; and that soldiers, statesmen, and the arts are all flourishing in mine, while his has only the last to commend it.

"Furthermore, although you see me here a rather humble student, I was not born from the dregs of the Roman masses. My houses as well as the public places in Rome are filled with the ancient images of my ancestors, and the annals of Rome abound with records of the triumphs celebrated by the Quintii on the Capitoline Hill. Nor has the glory of our name fallen into decay because of its antiquity, but flourishes today more than ever. Modesty makes me refrain from speaking of my wealth, since I am mindful that the noble citizens of Rome have always considered honorable poverty to be their ancient and most ample patrimony, but if poverty is to be condemned, following the opinion of the common herd, who value riches, then of those I do possess an abundance, not because I'm avaricious, but because I've been befriended by Fortune. And while I'm fully aware of how much value you've placed on having Gisippus as your kinsman here—something you should have done and should still be doing today—there's no reason why I would be worth less to you in Rome, considering that you would find in me there the best of hosts and a useful, solicitous, and powerful patron, both in public matters and where private needs are concerned.

"Who, then, setting passion aside and considering everything from the standpoint of reason, would rate your counsels above those of Gisippus? No one, assuredly. Sophronia is thus rightly married to Titus Quintus Fulvius, a noble, wealthy citizen of Rome from an ancient house, as well as being a close friend to Gisippus, and anyone who laments or complains about this situation is acting improperly and out of complete ignorance.

"There may be some who'll say they're not upset that Sophronia was wedded to Titus, but because of the way in which she became his wife, secretly, furtively, without her friends and relations knowing anything about it. But there's nothing miraculous about this, nor is it the first time that such a thing has happened. I'll gladly set aside those women who got married against the wishes of their fathers, and those who eloped with their lovers, having been their mistresses before becoming their wives, and those who revealed their marriages through pregnancy or childbirth before doing so verbally, thereby forcing their fathers to give their consent. This is not what happened with Sophronia, who, on the contrary, was bestowed upon Titus by Gisippus in an orderly, discreet, and honorable manner.

"Although there are yet others who will say that he had no right to give her away in marriage, these are foolish, womanly complaints, the result of shallow reasoning. Doesn't Fortune make use of strange, unheard-of ways and means to achieve her predetermined ends? What do I care if a shoemaker rather than a philosopher takes care of some affair of mine according to his own judgment, whether openly or on the sly, as long as the end result is good? If the shoemaker is indiscreet, then I should certainly see to it that he can never meddle in my business again and yet thank him all the same for his services.[10] If Gisippus has done a good job in marrying off Sophronia, then to go around complaining about him and the manner in which he did it is a piece of gratuitous folly; if you don't have any confidence in his judgment, thank him for what he's done, and make sure he never has the chance to do it again.

"Still, I would have you know that I never sought by means of cunning or fraud to stain the honor and nobility of your blood in the person of Sophronia. Although I married her in secret, I did not come to ravish her and despoil her of her virginity, nor did I intend to possess her on dishonorable terms, acting like your enemy and rejecting any alliance with your family. Rather, being passionately enflamed by her enchanting beauty and her virtue, I knew that if I had courted her in the way you might have wished, I would not have obtained her, because, loving her as much as you do, you would have feared that I would take her away to Rome. Accordingly, I had recourse to secret measures that can now be openly revealed to you, and I made Gisippus, acting on my behalf, consent to that which he himself was not disposed to do. After that, despite loving her passionately, I didn't seek to unite myself with her as a lover, but as her husband. For as she herself can truthfully testify, I kept my distance from her until I had wedded her with the required words and the ring, and when I asked her if she would accept me as her husband, she replied that she would. If she feels she's been deceived, she shouldn't blame me, but herself, for failing to ask me who I was. So, the great crime, the great sin, the great wrong committed by Gisippus as a friend and by myself as a lover was that Sophronia got married to Titus Quintus in secret, and this is why you tear him apart and threaten him and plot against him. What more would you have done if Gisippus had given her to a peasant, a scoundrel, a slave? What chains, what dungeon, what crosses would be sufficient punishment for that?

"But let's set this aside for the present. An event has now occurred that I was not expecting just yet, for my father has died, obliging me to return to Rome, and since I wish to take Sophronia along with me, I've revealed to you that which I might otherwise have continued to conceal. If you're wise, you will cheerfully accept it, for if I had wanted to deceive and insult you, I might have left her behind with you, an object of scorn, but God forbid that such baseness might ever find lodging in a Roman heart!

"Sophronia then is mine, not only by the consent of the gods and the force of the laws of men, but also by virtue of my Gisippus's good sense and my own lover's guile. But you condemn this, perhaps because you think you're wiser than the gods and the rest of mankind, and you brutishly persist in doing two things I find particularly offensive. First, you're holding on to Sophronia, which you have no right to do without my consent, and second, you're treating Gisippus, to whom you owe a great debt, as your enemy. I have no intention at present of proving to you still further just how foolish your behavior is, but I advise you as friends to let go of your grievances, set all the anger you feel aside, and see that Sophronia is restored to me, so that I may happily leave here as your kinsman and continue to live as such. Whether you like what has happened or not, you may be certain that if you refuse to do what I've suggested, I'll take Gisippus away from you, and if I manage to reach Rome, I'll make sure that I get the girl back who rightfully belongs to me, no matter how much you may object. And treating you as lifelong enemies, I will see to it that you learn through experience just what Roman hearts, once roused to anger, are capable of."

After he had finished speaking, Titus got to his feet, his features completely contorted by the anger he felt. Taking Gisippus by the hand, he left the temple, turning his head from side to side and casting menacing looks all about him, as if to show he was not intimidated by the number of people who were present there. Those who remained inside, part of whom were persuaded by his arguments about accepting him as a family member and a friend, and part of whom were frightened into doing so by his final words, all decided, of one accord, that it was better to have him as a kinsman, since Gisippus declined to become one himself, than to have lost the latter as a kinsman and to have acquired Titus as an enemy. And so they went to find Titus and told him how pleased they were that Sophronia should be his, adding that they were glad to have him as a dear family member and Gisippus as a good friend. Once they were done celebrating both their friendship and their kinship together, they went their separate ways and sent Sophronia back to Titus. Being a sensible woman, she quickly made a virtue of necessity by bestowing on him the love she had once felt for Gisippus, after which she accompanied him to Rome where she was received with great honor.

Meanwhile, Gisippus remained in Athens, where he was held in low esteem by practically all the people there, and because of certain factional quarrels among them, it was not long before he was expelled from the city, poor and destitute, and condemned to perpetual exile along with everyone else in his house. Having been thus banished, Gisippus did not merely become a pauper, but a beggar, and he made his way to Rome, avoiding as many difficulties as he could along the way, in order to see if Titus would remember him. Having discovered not only that his friend was alive, but that he was well regarded by all the Romans, and having found out where his dwelling was located, Gisippus went and stationed himself in front of it, waiting for Titus to appear. Because of his beggarly condition, Gisippus did not dare to say a word to his friend, but did everything he could to catch his eye, hoping that he would be recognized and that Titus would then have him sent for. But when Titus passed right by him, it seemed to Gisippus that his friend had seen him, but had deliberately shunned him, and calling to mind everything he had done on Titus's behalf, he left the scene, both furious and in despair.

Night had fallen, and as the hungry, penniless Gisippus wandered on, having no idea where he was going and desiring death more than anything else, he came upon a very solitary place in the city. Spotting a large grotto, he went inside with the intention of spending the night, and there, ill clad and worn out by his prolonged weeping, he fell asleep on the bare ground.

Around matins a pair of men who had committed a robbery that night came into the grotto with their loot, and after squabbling over it awhile, the stronger of the two killed the other one and took off. Gisippus had seen and heard everything, and it now seemed to him that he had found a way to achieve the death he longed for without resorting to suicide. He consequently stayed put until the officers of the watch, who had already gotten wind of the affair, showed up and angrily led him away as their prisoner. During the examination, he confessed that he had killed the man, but had not been able to escape from the grotto, and so the praetor, who was named Marcus Varro, sentenced him to death by crucifixion, as was the custom then.[11]

By chance Titus had come to the praetor's court at that very hour, and as he was staring into the face of the wretched condemned man, having already heard the reason for his punishment, all of a sudden he recognized that it was Gisippus. Though amazed to see that his friend's fortunes had fallen so low, and puzzled as to how he had come to be in Rome, Titus was moved by the most fervent desire to help his friend, and since he could see no other way to do so except to accuse himself and thus excuse Gisippus, he quickly came forward.

"Marcus Varro," he exclaimed, "recall the poor man you've just condemned because he's innocent. I myself have already given offense to the gods with one blow that killed the man your officers found murdered this morning, and I don't want to wrong them yet again with the death of another innocent."

Varro was astonished at these words, and even more disturbed that the entire court had heard them, but since he could not, for the sake of his honor, refrain from following the course prescribed by the laws, he had Gisippus brought back and addressed him in Titus's presence:

"How could you be so foolish as to confess, without being subjected to any form of torture, to a crime you never perpetrated when your life was at stake? You said you were the one who'd committed the murder last night, and now this other man has come and says that he was the one who killed him, not you."

When Gisippus looked up and saw that it was Titus, he knew only too well that his friend was acting to save his life out of gratitude for the favor that Gisippus had done for him in the past. And so, weeping for pity, Gisippus said: "Varro, the truth is that I killed him, and the pity that Titus feels is too late to save me now."

For his part, Titus responded: "Praetor, as you see, this man is a foreigner, and when he was found next to the body of the victim, he was unarmed. Furthermore, you can also see that his poverty is the reason he wants to die. Therefore, you ought to free him and give me the punishment I deserve."

Marveling at the way the two of them kept insisting on their guilt, Varro had already reached the point of thinking that both were innocent and was casting about for a way to acquit them when, lo and behold, a young man named Publius Ambustus stepped forward. A hardened criminal who was well known throughout Rome as a thief, he was, in fact, the real murderer, and since he knew that neither man was guilty of the charge of which they were both accusing themselves, his heart was so softened because of their innocence that, moved by the most intense feeling of compassion, he went and stood before Varro.

"Praetor," he said, "my Fates compel me to resolve the difficult debate between these two men, although I do not know what god inside me is spurring me on, tormenting me, in order to make me reveal my crime to you. I want you to know that neither of these men is guilty of the crime they are both confessing to. I am, in fact, the one who murdered that man around daybreak, and while I was dividing the loot we'd stolen with him, I noticed that this poor wretch was sleeping there. As for Titus, there's no need for me to say anything to clear him. His reputation is unsullied, and everyone knows he's not the sort of man who would do such a thing. Release him, therefore, and impose the punishment on me that is prescribed by the law."

By this time, news of the affair had already reached Octavianus, and summoning all three to appear before him, he demanded to know what it was that made each one so eager to condemn himself. After they had all told their stories, Octavianus freed the first two because they were innocent, and the third one as well out of love for the others.

Taking his Gisippus aside, Titus initially reprimanded him sternly for having reacted to him in so lukewarm and diffident a manner, but he then made a great fuss over his friend and led him away to his home where Sophronia, shedding tears of compassion, welcomed him as a brother. After Titus had restored his friend's spirits to some extent and had clothed him anew, dressing him in garments consistent with his worth and his nobility, the first thing he did was to make his friend the joint owner of all his wealth and possessions, after which he gave him one of his sisters, a young girl named Fulvia, as his wife. Then he said: "Gisippus, it's up to you whether you want to stay here with me or return to Achaea with all the things I've given you."*

Prompted on the one hand by the exile that his city had imposed on him, and on the other by the love he rightly felt in response to Titus's cherished friendship, Gisippus consented to become a citizen of Rome, where the pair lived a long and happy life together in the same house, Gisippus with his Fulvia and Titus with his Sophronia, becoming ever closer friends, if that were possible, with each passing day.

Friendship, then, is a most sacred thing, not merely worthy of singular reverence, but of being accorded eternal praise as the most discerning mother of magnanimity and honorable behavior, the sister of gratitude and charity, and the enemy of hatred and avarice, ever prepared, without waiting to be asked, to do virtuously unto others what she would have them do unto her.[12] Nowadays, only on the rarest of occasions do we find a pair in whom her most hallowed effects are to be seen, this being the fault of the shameful, wretched cupidity of mankind, which is concerned solely with its own advantage and has sent friendship into perpetual exile, banishing it beyond the farthest limits of the earth.

---

*Achaea was the Roman province that consisted of central Greece and the Peloponnesus and included Athens. In the late Middle Ages, the name was used interchangeably with Morea, but applied to the Peloponnesus alone.

Except for friendship, what love, what riches, what familial bond would have had so powerful an effect upon the heart of Gisippus as to make him respond to the ardor, the tears, and the sighs of Titus by giving him the beautiful, gracious lady to whom he was betrothed and with whom he himself was in love? Except for friendship, what laws, what threats, what fear would have persuaded Gisippus to abstain from embracing with his youthful arms the fair young girl when they were all alone and in the dark, or even in his very own bed—embraces that she, on occasion, perhaps invited? Except for friendship, what honors, what rewards, what benefits would have induced Gisippus to remain indifferent to the alienation of his own family as well as Sophronia's, to the muttering of the masses, and to all the mockery and the jeers, simply for the sake of satisfying his friend?

On the other side, except for friendship, what would have induced Titus, when no one would have blamed him for pretending not to have noticed Gisippus, to have sought his own death so eagerly, without pausing to give the matter a second thought, in order to save his friend from the crucifixion he himself was seeking? Except for friendship, what would have moved Titus, without hesitation, to share his most ample patrimony with Gisippus, whom Fortune had deprived of the one that had been his own? And except for friendship, what would have prompted Titus to be so trusting and so zealous in giving his own sister to Gisippus when he could see that his friend had been reduced to extreme poverty and utter destitution?

Let men therefore go on wishing for throngs of kinsmen, hordes of brothers, and swarms of children, and let them use their wealth to increase the number of their servants. But what they continue to ignore is that every single one of these people, no matter who he may be, is more worried about the least little danger to himself than concerned to ward off the great perils faced by his father, his brother, or his master, whereas what we see happening between friends is precisely the opposite.

Day 10, Story 9

Disguised as a merchant, Saladin is honorably entertained by Messer Torello, who, when a Crusade is launched, establishes a time period for his wife to wait before she remarries. He is taken prisoner, but because of his skill in training falcons, he comes to the attention of the Sultan, who recognizes him, reveals himself in turn, and entertains him lavishly. Having fallen ill, Messer Torello is transported by magic in a single night to Pavia, where his wife's second marriage is about to be celebrated. She recognizes him, and he then returns with her to his house.[1]

Filomena had brought her story to a close, and when one and all had finished heaping praise on Titus for his magnificent act of gratitude, the King, who was reserving the last place for Dioneo, began speaking as follows:

Pretty ladies, not only is what Filomena says about friendship undoubtedly true, but she was right to complain in her final comments about how little regard people have for it nowadays. If we had come here to correct the errors of the world, or even to criticize them, I would follow up on what she said with a substantial discourse of my own. But since our purpose is different, it occurs to me to tell you a story, long perhaps but enjoyable from start to finish, that concerns one of the generous deeds performed by Saladin.[2] Thus, even though our defects may prevent us from winning the deepest sort of friendship with another person, by imitating the things you will hear about in my tale, we may at least derive a certain delight from being courteous to others and hope that sooner or later we will receive our reward for doing so.

Let me begin by saying, then, that during the reign of Emperor

Frederick I, according to a number of accounts, the Christians launched a great Crusade to recover the Holy Land. Saladin, a most worthy lord who was then the Sultan of Babylon,* having heard about what was happening sometime in advance, decided to go in person and see what preparations the Christian leaders were making so that he would be better prepared to protect himself from them. Consequently, having settled all his affairs in Egypt, he pretended he was going on a pilgrimage and set out disguised as a merchant, taking with him only three servants and two of his wisest senior counselors.[3] After they had inspected many Christian kingdoms, one evening close to vespers, as they were riding through Lombardy on their way to cross the mountains, they happened to come upon a gentleman on the road between Milan and Pavia. He was named Messer Torello di Stra da Pavia, and he was going, together with his servants, his dogs, and his falcons, to stay at a beautiful estate he owned on the banks of the Ticino.[4]

As soon as Messer Torello caught sight of them, he concluded that they were foreigners of gentle birth and was eager to offer them some sort of honorable entertainment. So, when Saladin asked one of Messer Torello's servants how much farther it was to Pavia and whether they could still reach it in time to enter the city, Messer Torello prevented the man from saying a word by replying himself: "Gentlemen, by the time you reach Pavia, it'll be too late for you to get in."

"Then," said Saladin, "since we're strangers here, would you be so kind as to tell us where we can find the best lodging."

"I'll do so gladly," said Messer Torello. "I was thinking just now that I would send one of these servants of mine on an errand to a spot not too far from Pavia. I'll have him go with you, and he'll take you to a place where you'll find quite suitable accommodations."

Messer Torello then went up to the most discreet of his servants, told him what to do, and sent him off with Saladin's party. Meanwhile, he himself quickly rode on to his estate where he arranged for the best possible supper to be prepared and for tables to be set up in one of his gardens, after which he went to wait for his guests at the entrance. The

*Babylon: the medieval name for Cairo.

servant, conversing with the gentlemen about various subjects, took them on a roundabout route, leading them along various byroads, until he had brought them, without their suspecting it, to his master's estate. As soon as Messer Torello saw them, he went out on foot to meet them and said with a laugh: "Gentlemen, you are very welcome here, indeed."

An extremely astute man, Saladin realized that the knight had not invited them there when they first met, for fear they would have turned him down, and that he had cleverly arranged to have them brought to his house so they could not refuse to spend the evening with him. Thus, after returning Messer Torello's greeting, he said: "Sir, were it possible to lodge a complaint against courteous people, we would lodge one against you, for even leaving aside the fact that you have taken us somewhat out of our way, you have more or less constrained us to accept this noble courtesy of yours when the only thing we did to deserve your goodwill was to exchange a single greeting with you."

"Gentlemen," replied the knight, who was both wise and well-spoken, "if I may judge from your appearance, the courtesy you are going to receive from me is a poor thing in comparison with what you deserve. Truth to tell, however, you could not have found decent lodging outside of Pavia, and that's why I hope you won't be upset to have gone somewhat out of your way in exchange for a little less discomfort here."

While he was speaking, his servants gathered around Saladin's party, and as soon as they had dismounted, took charge of the horses. Messer Torello then led the three gentlemen to the rooms that had been prepared for them. There, after they had been helped off with their boots, he offered them some deliciously cool wine as a refreshment and detained them with pleasant conversation until such time as they might go to supper.

Since Saladin and his companions and servants all knew Italian, they had no difficulty understanding Messer Torello or making themselves understood, and they were all of the opinion that this knight was the most agreeable and well-mannered gentleman and a better conversationalist than anyone they had ever encountered. For his part, Messer Torello concluded that they were all quite eminent men, much more distinguished than he had originally thought, and he regretted deeply that he could not entertain them in company that evening or offer them a more elaborate banquet. He therefore resolved to make amends the next morning, and having told one of his servants what he wanted him to do, he sent the man off to Pavia, which never locked its gates and was not that far away, bearing a message for his wife, a woman of great intelligence and exceptional spirit. This done, he led his guests into the garden and politely asked them who they were, where they had come from, and what their destination was.

"We are Cypriot merchants," replied Saladin. "We've just arrived from our country, and now we're heading to Paris on business."

"Would to God," said Messer Torello, "that this country of ours bred gentlemen comparable to the merchants I see coming from Cyprus."

On these and other matters they chatted for a while until it was time for supper. Messer Torello then asked them if they would do him the honor of being seated at his table, and although it was an impromptu meal, the food was quite good and the service, excellent. Nor had the tables long been cleared away before Messer Torello, seeing how tired his guests were, showed them to the very comfortable beds that had been prepared for them to sleep in, following which, a little while later, he too retired for the night.

Meanwhile, the servant sent to Pavia delivered his message to Messer Torello's wife, who, in a spirit more like a queen's than an ordinary woman's, promptly summoned a large number of his friends and servants, and had all the preparations for a magnificent banquet set in motion. She had invitations delivered by torchlight to many of the most important nobles in the city, saw to it that a supply of fine clothes and silks and furs was at the ready, and took care of everything else, down to the last detail, that her husband had asked her to do.

The next day, after the gentlemen had risen, Messer Torello set out on horseback with them, and having called for his falcons, he led the group to a nearby stretch of shallow water where he showed off how his birds could fly. Then, when Saladin asked if there was someone who could escort them to Pavia and direct them to the best inn in the city, Messer Torello replied, "I'll do it myself, because I'm obliged to go there anyway." They took him at his word and happily set off down the road together, reaching the city just after tierce. Thinking they were being escorted to the finest inn available, they arrived, instead, at Messer Torello's mansion where they found a good fifty of the leading citizens of Pavia who had assembled to receive them and who immediately gathered around them in order to hold their reins and stirrups for them.

When Saladin and his companions saw this, they realized only too well what it all meant. "Messer Torello," they said, "this isn't what we asked you to do for us. You treated us so very well last night, much better than we deserve, which is why it would have been quite proper for you to have just let us go on our way."

"Gentlemen," replied Messer Torello, "with regard to the service that was done for you last night, I am more indebted to Fortune than to you, for it was she who overtook you on the road at a hour when you had no choice but to come to my humble abode. However, with regard to the service that will be done for you this morning, I will be beholden only to you, as will all these gentlemen you see here about you, although if you think it courteous to decline an invitation to dine with them, then you are certainly at liberty to do so."

Acknowledging defeat, Saladin and his companions dismounted and were welcomed by the gentlemen who happily led them to a richly furnished set of rooms that had been prepared for them. After they had removed their traveling clothes and taken a little refreshment, they made their way to the great hall, where everything was magnificently arranged. Having washed their hands, they were seated at the table with great pomp and circumstance and were served so many courses in such splendid style that if the Emperor himself had been present, it would have been impossible to honor him more highly. In fact, even though Saladin and his companions were great lords and were accustomed to the grandest displays of opulence, they were nevertheless overcome with wonder at their treatment here, which, considering the position of the knight, whom they knew to be no ruler, but just a private citizen, seemed to them about as fine as anything they had ever experienced.

Once the meal was over and the tables cleared away, they discussed serious affairs for a while until, at Messer Torello's suggestion, the weather being quite hot, the gentlemen from Pavia all went off to take a nap, leaving him alone with his three guests. To make sure they got to see all of his most precious possessions, he escorted them into another room and sent for his good lady. A tall, strikingly beautiful woman, she presented herself before them, decked out in her rich garments and flanked by her two little children, who looked like a pair of angels, and welcomed them cordially to her home. The moment the three men saw her, they rose to their feet, gave her a most respectful greeting in return, and invited her to sit down with them, all the while making a great fuss over her beautiful little children. After starting a pleasant conversation with them, during which Messer Torello left the room for a while, she graciously asked them where they were from and where they were going, to which they gave her the same answer they had given her husband.

"Then I see that my woman's intuition may well be useful," said the lady, with a smile, "for I want to ask you a special favor, namely that you will neither refuse nor look down on the little trifling gift I'm going to have them bring for you. Instead, you should bear in mind that women, with their tiny hearts, give tiny presents, and consequently, you should judge what you are going to get more by the good intentions of the giver than the size of the gift."

She then sent for two pairs of robes for each of the guests, one lined with silk and the other with fur—all of them more suitable for lords than for private citizens or merchants—as well as three doublets of taffeta and a number of undergarments.

"Take these robes," she said. "They're just like the ones I've always dressed my husband in. As far as the other things are concerned, although they're of no great value, you may find they'll come in handy, considering how far away you are from your wives, not to mention the fact that you've come a long way and still have a long way to go, and I know how you merchants always like to be neat and trim."

The gentlemen were astonished, for it had become abundantly clear that Messer Torello was intent upon showing them every conceivable courtesy. Considering how magnificent the robes were and how unlike the ones any merchant would wear, they were afraid that he had recognized who they really were, but one of them nevertheless replied to his wife: "My lady, these things are exquisite and should not be accepted lightly, but we feel compelled to do so because of your prayers, to which we cannot say no."

Thus they took her gifts, and since Messer Torello had now returned, the lady, having said good-bye to them, left the room and went away to see that their servants were supplied with similar gifts according to their rank. In response to Messer Torello's repeated entreaties, the gentlemen agreed to spend the entire day with him, and after they had slept for a while, they got dressed in their robes and rode through the city with him until it was time for supper, at which point they sat down to a magnificent feast in the company of many noble guests.

In due course they went to bed, and when they arose at daybreak, they discovered that they now had three fine, sturdy palfreys in place of their tired old nags and that their servants had likewise been provided with fresh, strong horses. Upon seeing all this, Saladin turned to his companions and said: "I swear to God there's never been a more perfect gentleman than this, or one who is more courteous and considerate. If the kings of Christendom are as good at being kings as this man is at being a knight, the Sultan of Babylon will be unable to resist even one of them, let alone all those we've seen preparing to descend on him." Knowing there was no way for them to refuse Messer Torello's gifts, they thanked him most politely and mounted their horses.

Messer Torello, together with many of his companions, escorted them quite some distance down the road leading out of the city. Finally, even though it weighed heavily on Saladin that he had to part company from his host, to whom he had formed a deep attachment, he felt he could not delay his departure any longer and begged him to turn back. Messer Torello, who found it just as hard to part from his guests, said:

"Since you want me to go, gentlemen, that's what I'll do. But there's one thing I must tell you: I don't know who you are, nor do I wish to know more than you care to reveal, but whoever you may be, you cannot make me believe you are merchants. Now, that said, I bid you Godspeed."

Saladin, who had already taken leave of Messer Torello's companions, turned to face him. "Sir," he said, "we may yet have the chance to show you some of our merchandise and make a believer out of you. In the meantime, may God be with you."

Saladin then rode off with his companions, utterly determined that, if he managed to survive the war he was facing and avoid defeat, he would show Messer Torello no less hospitality than Messer Torello had shown him. As they went on, he talked to his companions about the gentleman and his wife and about all his gifts and favors and acts of kindness, praising them ever more highly each time he returned to the subject. But finally, when he had with no little labor surveyed all of the West, he put to sea and returned with his companions to Alexandria, where, now that he had all the information he needed, he prepared his defenses. As for Messer Torello, he went back to Pavia, and although he pondered at length who the three men might be, he never arrived at the truth or even came anywhere near it.

When the time came for the Crusade to begin and great preparations for it were under way everywhere, Messer Torello, despite the tears and entreaties of his wife, was fully determined to go. He therefore got everything ready, and just as he was about to ride off on his horse, he said to his wife, whom he loved deeply: "As you can see, my lady, I'm joining this Crusade, both for the sake of my personal honor and for the salvation of my soul. I'm placing our good name and our possessions in your care. And since I feel less assurance about my return than about my departure, considering the thousand accidents that can occur, I would ask this favor of you: no matter what happens to me, even if you don't have any trustworthy news that I'm still alive, I nevertheless want you to wait for a year and a month and a day before you get married again, starting from this, the day of my departure."

"Messer Torello," replied the lady, who was weeping bitterly, "I don't know how I'm going to bear the sorrow you'll be leaving me in after you're gone, but if I'm strong enough to survive it, and if anything should happen to you, you may live and die in the certain knowledge that for the rest of my days, I shall remain wedded to Messer Torello and his memory."

"My lady," said Messer Torello, "I feel confident that you'll do every-thing in your power to keep your promise, but you're a beautiful young woman who comes from an important family, and everyone knows what a wonderful person you are. Consequently, I haven't the slightest doubt that if there's the least suspicion of my death, many fine gentle-men will come asking your brothers and kinsmen for your hand, and that no matter how much you try to resist, they'll subject you to so much pressure that you'll eventually be forced to comply with their wishes. And that's the reason why I'm not asking you to wait any longer than the time limit I've set for you."

"I'll do whatever I can to keep my promise," said the lady, "and even if I'm forced to act otherwise, I'll certainly follow those instructions you've given me. But I pray to God that neither you nor I ever have to deal with such extremities."

When she finished speaking, the lady wept and embraced Messer Torello. She then removed a ring from her finger and gave it to him, saying: "If I should happen to die before I see you again, remember me whenever you look at it."

Messer Torello took the ring, and having mounted his horse, he said farewell to everyone and went on his way. Upon reaching Genoa with his company, he boarded a galley and set sail, arriving at Acre in short order, where he met up with the rest of the Christian forces.[5] Almost immediately, however, a deadly epidemic broke out that over-whelmed the army, in the course of which, whether because of his skill or his good fortune, Saladin had no difficulty in capturing almost all the Christians who survived, and whom he divided up and sent away to be incarcerated in various cities. Among those taken was Messer Torello, who was led off to prison in Alexandria. No one recognized him there, and being afraid to reveal his true identity, he had no choice but to apply himself to the training of hawks. Since he was a past mas-ter of this art, his abilities soon brought him to the notice of Saladin, who had him released from prison and appointed him his falconer.

Neither man recognized the other, and Messer Torello, whom Sala-din referred to simply as "the Christian," thought of nothing except Pavia and tried many times to escape, but always without success.

Consequently, when a group of emissaries from Genoa, who had come to Saladin to ransom certain fellow citizens of theirs, were about to depart, Messer Torello decided he would write to his wife, letting her know that he was alive and would return to her as soon as possible, and asking her to wait for him. When he finished the letter, he earnestly begged one of the emissaries, whom he knew, to see that it got into the hands of his uncle, who was the Abbot of San Pietro in Ciel d'Oro.[6]

This, then, is how things stood with Messer Torello until one morning, as Saladin was speaking with him about his birds, he just so happened to smile, moving his mouth in a way that the Sultan had noted in particular when he was staying at Messer Torello's house in Pavia. It put Saladin in mind of his former host, and after staring intently at him for a while, he felt pretty sure he knew who it was. He thus dropped the subject they had been discussing, and said: "Tell me, Christian, what country do you come from in the West?"

"My lord," answered Messer Torello, "I'm a poor man of humble condition, and I come from a city in Lombardy called Pavia."

When Saladin heard this, he was now almost completely certain that what he suspected was correct, and he happily said to himself, "God has given me a chance to show this man how much I appreciated his hospitality." He did not say another word on the subject, however, but had them put all of his robes on display in another room, and took Messer Torello there to see them.

"Have a look at these clothes, Christian," he said, "and tell me whether you've ever come across any of them before?"

Messer Torello began inspecting them, and albeit he spotted the garments his wife had given to Saladin, it was inconceivable to him that they could possibly be the same ones. Nevertheless, he replied: "My lord, I don't recognize any of them, although it's certainly true that these two look like robes I once wore myself, as did three merchants who happened to come to my house."

Saladin could no longer restrain himself and embraced Messer Torello tenderly. "You are Messer Torello di Stra," he said, "and I am one of the three merchants to whom your wife gave these robes. And the time has now come for me to show you exactly what kind of merchandise I have, something I said, when I left you, might well happen one day."

Upon hearing this, Messer Torello felt both overjoyed and ashamed, overjoyed to have had such a distinguished guest, and ashamed because he thought he had entertained him poorly. But then Saladin went on: "Messer Torello, since God has sent you to me, from now on you should consider yourself, and not me, the master here."

After much mutual rejoicing at their reunion, Saladin had him dressed in regal robes, and having presented him to a gathering of his greatest lords, and spoken at length in praise of him as a most worthy gentleman, he ordered all those who valued his favor to honor Messer Torello's person as they did his own. And from then on, that is what everyone did, and especially the two lords who had accompanied Saladin when he stayed at Messer Torello's house.

For a while Messer Torello's sudden elevation to the heights of glory took his mind off his affairs in Lombardy, all the more so because he had no doubt that his letters had reached his uncle.

On the day that the crusaders had been captured by Saladin, however, there was a Provençal knight of little account named Messer Torello di Dignes who had died and been buried on the battlefield, or rather in the Christian camp itself, and since Messer Torello di Stra was well known for his nobility throughout the army, whenever anyone heard people saying "Messer Torello is dead," it was assumed they were referring to Messer Torello di Stra and not the man from Dignes.[7] Before those who had been deceived had a chance to be undeceived, however, Messer Torello was taken prisoner, and as a result, many Italians returned home bearing the news of his death with them, including some who were so presumptuous that they did not hesitate to say they had seen his corpse and been present at the burial. When the story finally reached his wife and family, it was the cause of the most intense, inexpressible sorrow not just for them, but for everyone who had known him.

It would take a long time, indeed, to describe the nature and the depth of the lady's grief, the sadness and the woe she experienced. After she had mourned for several months straight in utter misery, however, her sorrow showed signs of abating, and since many of the most influential men in Lombardy were seeking her hand, her brothers and the rest of her relatives began urging her to get married. Although she repeatedly refused to do so, always amid floods of tears, her resistance was overcome in the end, and she agreed to give them what they wanted, but only on the condition that she could refrain from taking a husband until the period of time she had promised to wait for Messer Torello was up.

This, then, was how things stood with the lady in Pavia when, about a week or so before the date when she was supposed to be married, Messer Torello happened to catch sight one day in Alexandria of a man he had seen embarking with the Genoese emissaries on the galley that was taking them home. He therefore sent for him and asked him how their trip had been and when it was that they had reached Genoa.

"My lord," the man replied, "I was left behind in Crete, where I later learned that the galley had had a disastrous voyage. As it was approaching Sicily, a furious northerly gale arose, driving it onto the Barbary reefs, so that no one managed to escape, including two of my brothers who perished along with the rest."

Messer Torello had no reason to doubt the man's account, which was only too true, and when he realized that there were just a few days left until the end of the time period he had asked his wife to wait and that nothing was known in Pavia about his present situation, he was absolutely convinced that she was going to be getting married again. So deep was the despair into which he fell that he lost his appetite, lay down on his bed, and resolved to die.

As soon as Saladin, who loved Messer Torello with great tenderness, heard what had happened, he came to see him. Having discovered, after earnest and repeated entreaties, the reason for his grief and his sickness, he scolded him severely for not having told him about it before. Then, however, the Sultan begged him to take heart, assuring Messer Torello that if he did so, he would arrange for him to be in Pavia on the date prescribed. Saladin then went on to explain how this would be done.

Messer Torello took him at his word, and since he had often heard that such things were possible and had actually happened on numerous occasions, he began to feel more optimistic and urged Saladin to take care of it at once. The Sultan therefore ordered one of his necromancers, a man whose skill he had already tested, to find a way to transport Messer Torello on a bed to Pavia in a single night. The magician replied that it would be done, but that for Messer Torello's own good, he would first put him to sleep.[8]

When all this was arranged, Saladin returned to Messer Torello, whom he still found fully determined either to be back in Pavia by the date prescribed, if it were possible, or to die, if it were not. "Messer Torello," he said, "God knows I can't blame you in the least for loving your wife so passionately and being so fearful of losing her to another. For I believe that of all the women I've ever seen, she's the one whose way of life, whose manners, and whose demeanor—to say nothing of her beauty, which will fade like a flower—seem to me most precious and commendable. Since Fortune has brought you here to me, I should have liked nothing better than for the two of us to have spent the rest of our lives together, ruling as equals over this realm of mine. God has not granted me this wish, however, and now that you've made up your mind to die unless you can return to Pavia by the appointed date, I really would have preferred to have known about all this in time for me to have sent you home with all the honor and pomp, as well as the splendid escort, your virtues deserve. But since even this has not been granted to me, and you, moreover, are set upon going there at once, I will do what I can to get you to Pavia in the manner I've described to you."

"My lord," replied Messer Torello, "apart from your words, your actions have given me sufficient proof of your goodwill toward me, which is far, far above anything I've merited, so that even if you'd said nothing, I should have lived and died utterly convinced that what you say is true. But seeing as how my mind's made up, I beg you to act quickly and do what you promised me, because tomorrow is the last day she's still going to be waiting for me."

Saladin assured him that everything had been taken care of, and the next day, it being his intention to send Messer Torello off that same night, he had a very beautiful, luxurious bed set up in one of his great

halls. Its mattresses were all covered in the Eastern fashion with velvet and cloth of gold, and on top of them there lay a quilt embroidered
with enormous pearls and the rarest of precious stones arranged in oval
patterns—the quilt was later considered a priceless treasure in these
parts—as well as two pillows selected to match the bedding. When this
was ready, he ordered them to dress Messer Torello, who had by now
recovered his strength, in a robe of the Saracen fashion, the richest and
most beautiful thing anyone had ever seen, while they took one of his
longest turbans and wrapped it around his head in their usual style.

It was already late when Saladin, with many of his lords in attendance, went to Messer Torello's room and sat down beside him. "Messer
Torello," he began, practically in tears, "the hour is approaching for you
to be separated from me, and since I cannot accompany you myself or
send anyone with you, because the nature of the journey you have to
make won't permit it, I must take my leave of you here in this room
to which I've come for that purpose. But before I bid you Godspeed,
I beg you, in the name of the love and friendship that exists between
us, not to forget me, and if it's possible, before our days have ended, to
come and see me at least one more time after you've taken care of your
affairs in Lombardy. For not only will I rejoice to see you again, but I'll
be able to compensate then for the delight I must now forego because
of your hasty departure. Until such time as that should occur, I hope
it won't be a burden for you to visit me by means of your letters and to
ask me for whatever you please, because there is certainly no man alive
I would serve more gladly than you."

Unable to hold back his own tears, Messer Torello only managed to
utter a few words, declaring that it would be impossible for him ever to
forget Saladin's kind deeds and noble spirit and that he would, without
fail, do what Saladin requested if he were given the opportunity. Saladin embraced him and kissed him tenderly. Then, weeping copiously,
he said "Godspeed" and left the room, after which the other lords all
took their leave of him and accompanied Saladin into the hall where
the bed had been set up.

It was getting late, and since the magician was anxious to send him
quickly on his way, a doctor arrived with a potion that he got Messer

Torello to drink, persuading him that it would enable him to keep up his strength. Soon afterward he fell asleep, and as he slept, he was carried at Saladin's command and laid upon the beautiful bed where the Sultan placed a large, exquisite, and extremely valuable crown, which he marked in such a way that later on everyone saw clearly that it was a present from him to Messer Torello's wife. Then, onto Messer Torello's finger he slipped a ring containing a ruby that gleamed like a lighted torch and whose value could scarcely be assessed. Next, he had him girded with a sword so richly ornamented that its value, too, would be difficult to determine, and in addition, he had them fasten a brooch on his chest that was studded both with pearls, the like of which had never been seen, and with many other precious stones. Finally, Saladin had them fill two enormous golden bowls with doubloons and set them on either side of him, while all around him were strewn numerous strings of pearls, plus rings and belts and other things that would take too long to describe. When they were done, he kissed Messer Torello one more time, and he had hardly finished telling the magician to hurry up when the bed and Messer Torello were suddenly whisked away right before his eyes, leaving Saladin behind still talking with his lords about his departed friend.

As he requested, Messer Torello was set down in the Church of San Pietro in Ciel d'Oro in Pavia, with all the jewels and finery that have been mentioned, and he was still fast asleep when the hour of matins was rung and the sacristan entered the church with a light in his hand. He immediately caught sight of the opulent bed, and after his initial amazement, he was so terrified that he turned on his heels and fled back the way he had come. The Abbot and the other monks were equally amazed to see him running away, and they asked him for an explanation, which he then produced.

"Come on," said the Abbot, "you're not a child anymore, and you're hardly a newcomer to this church, either, so you shouldn't get frightened so easily. Let's all go now and see what gave you such a scare."

After lighting a number of lanterns, the Abbot entered the church with his monks, where they saw this amazing, luxurious bed on which the knight lay sleeping. Then, as they were casting a wary and timorous eye over all the princely jewels, the effect of the potion just happened to wear off, Messer Torello woke up, and a great sigh escaped his lips. Upon seeing this, the monks were terrified, as was the Abbot, and they all ran away screaming "Lord, help us!"

When he opened his eyes and looked about him, Messer Torello discovered, to his immense satisfaction, that he was in the very place where he had asked to be taken. Although he had been aware of Saladin's generosity in the past, after he sat up and observed, one by one, the treasures around him, he was all the more conscious of it and judged it now to be even greater than he had thought it was before. He could hear the monks running away, however, and divining the reason why, he did not make another move, but began calling the Abbot by name, telling him not to be afraid, as it was only Torello, his nephew.

Hearing these words, the Abbot became even more frightened, because for many months he had thought that Messer Torello was dead. But after a while, reassuring himself with rational arguments, as he continued to hear his name being called, he made the sign of the cross and went up to him.

"O my father," said Messer Torello, "what are you afraid of? I'm alive, by the grace of God, and I've come back here from across the sea."

Although Messer Torello had a full beard and was dressed in Arab clothing, after a little while the Abbot managed to recognize him. Now, feeling thoroughly reassured, he took him by the hand and said, "Welcome home, my son."

"Our fear shouldn't surprise you," he continued, "because there's no one in this city who isn't firmly convinced that you're dead. What's more, I can tell you that your wife, Madonna Adalieta, has been overcome by the threats and the pleading of her relatives, and has been forced to remarry against her will.[9] In fact, this is the very morning when she's to go to her new husband, and they've made all the necessary preparations there for the nuptials and the wedding feast."

Messer Torello got up off the luxurious bed, and after warmly embracing the Abbot and the monks, he begged them, each and every one, to say nothing about his return to anybody until he had taken care of some business of his. Next, having put all of the rich jewels in a safe place, he gave the Abbot an account of everything that had happened to him up to then. Delighted by his good fortune, the Abbot joined him in giving thanks to God. When they were done, Messer Torello asked him for the name of his wife's new husband, and the Abbot told him what it was.

"Before anyone learns of my return," said Messer Torello, "I intend to see how my wife conducts herself at these nuptials. And so, even though it's not customary for the religious to attend such festivities, I'd ask you, for my sake, to make arrangements for the two of us to go there."

The Abbot said he would be happy to oblige him, and right after daybreak, he sent a message to the new bridegroom, saying that he wished to attend the nuptials with a companion of his. In reply, the gentleman declared he would be quite delighted to see them.

When the hour for the banquet arrived, Messer Torello, still wearing the clothes he had arrived in, went with the Abbot to the bridegroom's house, where everyone who saw him stared at him in amazement, although none of them managed to recognize who he was. The Abbot told them all that Messer Torello was a Saracen who was being sent by the Sultan as his ambassador to the King of France. Accordingly, Messer Torello was seated at a table directly across from his wife, whom he gazed at with the utmost pleasure, thinking that, from the look on her face, she was none too happy about this marriage. From time to time, she, too, glanced over at him, not because she recognized him in any way—for his great beard, his foreign dress, and her own firm belief that he was dead made this impossible—but because of the unusual clothes he had on.

Finally, when Messer Torello felt the time was right to put his wife to the test and see if she remembered him, he took the ring she had given to him at his departure, and holding it in his hand, called over a young man who was waiting on her.

"Tell the new bride on my behalf," he said, "that in my country, whenever a stranger, like me, is attending the wedding feast of a newly married woman, like her, it's customary for the bride to take a cup from which she herself has been drinking, fill it with wine, and send it to him as a token of her appreciation for his coming there to dine with her. Then, when the stranger has drunk his fill, he puts the cover back on, and the bride drinks up what remains."

The young man delivered this message to the lady, who, being both wise and well mannered, and believing that she was dealing with an important dignitary, hastened to show him how pleased she was that he had come. Accordingly, she ordered that a large gold cup, which stood on the table before her, should be washed, filled with wine, and taken over to the gentleman.

They carried it to Messer Torello, who had placed his wife's ring in his mouth, and he drank in such a way as to let it fall into the cup without anyone noticing. Then, when there was only a tiny bit of wine left in it, he replaced the cover and sent it back to the lady. In deference to the custom of his country, she took it, removed the lid, and put it to her lips. At that moment, she caught sight of the ring. After gazing at it for some time without saying a word, she identified it as the one she had given Messer Torello when he left her. She then picked it up and stared intently at the man she had assumed was a stranger. Now that she could see who it really was, she seized the table in front of her and hurled it to the ground, shouting as if she had gone mad:

"This is my lord, this is really Messer Torello."

Then she dashed over to where he was sitting, and without giving a thought to her clothing or any of the things on the table, she flung herself across it as far as she could and hugged him to her in a tight embrace. Nor could she be induced to let go of his neck, for anything the people there could say or do, until Messer Torello himself told her to exercise a little self-control, for she would have plenty of time to embrace him later on.

The lady accordingly stood back up, and although by now the wedding feast was in total disarray, the return of so distinguished a knight actually made it happier than ever. Then, at Messer Torello's request, everyone grew silent, and he told them the story of what had happened to him from the day of his departure up to that very hour. He concluded by saying that the gentleman who, in the belief that he was dead, had married his wife could hardly take offense if he now reclaimed her as his own, since he was alive after all.

Though somewhat embarrassed, the bridegroom freely replied in a friendly manner that Messer Torello was at liberty to dispose of that which belonged to him in whatever way he pleased. The lady accordingly returned the ring and the crown her new bridegroom had given her and put on the ring she had taken from the cup as well as the crown that the Sultan had sent her. They then left the house they were in, and with all the pomp of a wedding procession, they made their way to Messer Torello's estate, where the merrymaking went on for hours, lifting the spirits of his unhappy friends and relations and all the townspeople, who considered his return something verging on a miracle.

After giving away some of his precious jewels to the gentleman who had paid for the wedding feast as well as to the Abbot and to numerous others, Messer Torello sent more than one messenger to Saladin with word of his happy homecoming, declaring himself to be the Sultan's friend and servant. And for many years after that, he lived with his worthy wife, behaving in a more courteous manner than ever.

This, then, was how the tribulations of Messer Torello and his beloved wife came to an end, and how they were rewarded for their prompt and cheerful acts of courtesy. There are many people who strive to do the like, but although they have the wherewithal, they perform such deeds so ineptly that before they are finished, those who receive them wind up paying more for them than they are worth. And so, if such people get no credit for what they do, neither they nor anyone else should be surprised.

Day 10, Story 10

Induced by the entreaties of his vassals to take a wife, the Marquis of Saluzzo, wanting to choose one his own way, selects the daughter of a peasant. After he has had two children with her, he makes it look to her as though they have been put to death. Later on, pretending to have grown weary of her, he claims he has married another woman and arranges to have his own daughter brought home as though she were his bride, meanwhile having turned his wife out of doors wearing nothing but her shift. On finding that she has borne everything with patience, however, he takes her back home again, dearer to him than ever, shows her their grown-up children, and honors her as Marchioness and causes everyone else to do so as well.[1]

When the King had finished his long story, which everyone seemed to have really enjoyed, Dioneo laughed and said: "The good man who was looking forward to raising and lowering the bogeyman's tail the next night would have given less than two cents for all the praise you are bestowing on Messer Torello."[2] But then, knowing that he was the only one left to speak, he began as follows:

My gentle ladies, the way I see it, we have given this entire day over to kings and sultans and people of that ilk, and therefore, lest I stray too far away from the path you are on, I want to tell you about a Marquis whose behavior was not an example of magnanimity, but of senseless brutality.[3] And even though things turned out well for him in the end, I would not recommend that you follow his lead, because it is a real shame that he derived any benefit from it at all.

A long time ago, there was a young man named Gualtieri who, as the head of the family, had succeeded to the Marquisate of Saluzzo, and being unmarried and childless, spent all of his time out hawking and hunting. He never gave a thought to finding a wife and starting a family, for which he should have been considered very wise, but his vassals were not content with this and repeatedly begged him to get married so that he would not be left without an heir and they without a lord. Moreover, they offered to find him a woman whose character and parents were such that there would be every reason to feel hopeful about the match and he could expect to be quite happy with her. In response Gualtieri said:

"My friends, you are forcing me to do something I had absolutely resolved never to do, considering how hard it is to find a person whose character will be a fit for your own, how very many of the other sort there are out there, and how miserable life will be for a man if he stumbles upon a wife who is not well suited to him. Furthermore, it's foolish of you to believe that you can figure out what daughters will be like by considering how their fathers and mothers behave and on that basis to argue that you are going to find one who will please me. For I don't know how you can get any information about the fathers, let alone find out the secrets of the mothers, and even if you could, daughters are often very different from either one of their parents. But look, since you want to bind me in these chains, I'm willing to do it. Nevertheless, so that I won't have anybody to blame except myself if it turns out badly, I want to be the one who's responsible for finding her. And let me assure you that no matter what woman I choose, if you fail to honor her as your lady, you will learn to your great misfortune just how serious a matter it was for you to have begged me to take a wife against my will."

The gentlemen replied that they were satisfied, as long as he was amenable to taking a wife.

For quite some time Gualtieri had been impressed with the behavior of a poor girl who lived in a village not far from his home, and since she was also very beautiful, he thought that life with her ought to be rather agreeable. Thus, without searching any further, he resolved to marry her, and having summoned her father, who was very poor indeed, he made arrangements with him to take her as his wife.

This done, Gualtieri called all his friends in the area together and said to them: "My friends, since it continues to be your pleasure that I should agree to take a wife, I'm prepared to do it, though more to gratify you than from any interest I have in getting married. You know what you promised me, namely, that you would be content with whatever woman I chose and would honor her as your lady. Now the time has arrived for me to keep my promise to you and for you to keep yours to me. I've located a young woman after my own heart who lives quite close by, and just a few days from now I intend to marry her and lead her home as my bride. So, see to it that the wedding feast is splendid and that you give her an honorable reception. That way I'll be able to pronounce myself satisfied that you've kept your word to me just as you'll be satisfied that I've kept mine to you."

The gentlemen all replied joyfully that they were very pleased with this decision and that no matter whom he chose, they would accept her as their lady and would honor her as such in every way they could. After that, they got everything ready so that the feast would be as grand and lavish and happy as possible, and Gualtieri did likewise, arranging for the most magnificent and beautiful wedding, to which he invited a host of his friends and relations as well as many great noblemen and others from the area round about. In addition, he had them make a fair number of beautiful dresses out of expensive material, all tailored to fit a girl who seemed to him the same size as the one he intended to marry. Finally, he ordered belts and rings, a lovely, costly crown, and everything else a new bride would require.

On the day set for the wedding, halfway between prime and tierce, Gualtieri mounted his horse, as did all those who had come to honor him, and after everything necessary had been seen to, he announced, "Gentlemen, it's time to go and fetch the new bride." Then off he rode with the entire company. Before long they reached the little village, and when they got to the house belonging to the girl's father, they spotted her carrying water back from the spring, hurrying so that she could go with the other women to see Gualtieri's spouse as she arrived. The moment Gualtieri saw her, he called her by her name, which was Griselda, and asked her where her father was, to which she bashfully replied, "He's in the house, my lord."

Gualtieri dismounted and told everyone to wait for him while he

went into the hovel by himself. There he found her father, whose name
was Giannucole, and said to him: "I've come to marry Griselda, but
first, here in your presence, there are certain things I need to find out
from her."[4] Then he asked her whether, if he were to wed her, she would
do her best to please him and never get upset at anything he ever said
or did, and whether she would be obedient, and many other things of
this sort, to all of which she replied that she would.

At this point Gualtieri, taking her by the hand, led her outside and
in the presence of his entire company as well as all the other people
living there, he had her stripped naked. Then he called for the clothing
and shoes he had ordered for her and quickly had them dress her, after
which he had them place a crown on her hair, disheveled though it was.
And as everyone looked on in wonder, he proclaimed: "My lords, this
is the woman I intend to take as my wife, provided that she wants to
marry me." Then, turning to her as she stood there, feeling stunned
and quite embarrassed, he asked her: "Griselda, will you have me as
your husband?"

"Yes, my lord," she replied.

"And I," he said, "will take you as my wife." Then, right there, in the
presence of the entire assembly, he married her, after which he had her
seated on a palfrey and led her, honorably attended, to his house where
the wedding was celebrated in as beautiful, festive, and magnificent a
style as if he had married the daughter of the King of France.

The young bride appeared to change her mind and her manners
along with her clothes. As we have already said, she had a fine figure
and lovely features, and in keeping with her beauty, she now became
so charming, so pleasant, and so well mannered that she did not seem
like a shepherdess and the daughter of Giannucole, but like the child of
some noble lord, leading everyone who had known her earlier to marvel at her transformation. Moreover, she was so obedient and attentive
to her husband that he thought himself the happiest, most contented
man in the world. At the same time she was so gracious and kind to her
husband's subjects that they all loved her with utter devotion, honored
her of their own free will, and prayed for her well-being, her prosperity, and her advancement. And whereas they used to say that Gualtieri

had shown some lack of discretion in marrying her, now they declared him to be the wisest, most discerning man on earth because no one else could have ever perceived her lofty virtues, which were hidden under the poor rags of her peasant's clothing. In short, she comported herself so well that before long she had everyone talking, not only in her husband's domain, but far and wide, about how fine her character was and how virtuous her behavior, and she got people to change their minds if they had ever criticized her husband on her account at the time of his marriage.

She had not lived with Gualtieri very long before she became pregnant and in time, to his great happiness, gave birth to a little girl. But a little while later the strange idea popped into his head to test her patience by subjecting her to constant tribulations and generally making life intolerable for her. Consequently, he started by goading her with words, pretending to be angry and telling her that his vassals were thoroughly disgruntled with her because of her base origin, especially now that they saw her bearing children, and that, furthermore, they were upset about the little girl who had just been born and were doing nothing but grumbling about it.

The lady did not change her expression or show the least resentment when she heard these words. "My lord," she said, "do with me whatever you think best for your honor and your peace of mind, and I will be entirely content with it, for I know that I'm socially inferior to your vassals and that I'm unworthy of the honor that you have so graciously bestowed on me."[5] This reply was very gratifying to Gualtieri, for he realized that she had not gotten puffed up with pride because of the honors that he or the others had paid her.

Some time later, having already given her to understand in general terms that his subjects could not endure the little girl she had given birth to, he gave certain instructions to one of his servants and sent him to her. "My lady," said the servant, with the most sorrowful expression on his face, "if I don't want to be put to death, I have to do what my lord has commanded, and he has commanded me to take this daughter of yours and to . . ." And at this point he could say no more.

When the lady heard the servant's words and saw his face, and when she recalled what her husband had said to her, she concluded that the man had been ordered to put her child to death. In response, although she was desperately sick at heart, she immediately took her daughter from the cradle, and without ever changing her expression, she kissed her and blessed her and placed her in the servant's arms. "There," she said to him, "do exactly what your lord, who is my lord as well, has ordered, but don't leave her to be devoured by the beasts and the birds unless he's told you to do so."

The servant took the child and reported what the lady had said to Gualtieri, who, marveling at her constancy, sent him away with the baby to one of his relatives in Bologna, asking her to raise and educate the child with some care, but never to reveal whose daughter she was.

Shortly afterward, the lady became pregnant once again, and when she came to term, she gave birth to a baby boy, which made Gualtieri very happy. Nevertheless, not content with what he had already done, he wounded his wife even more deeply. One day, glowering at her with feigned fury, he said: "Woman, ever since you gave birth to this boy, I've found it completely impossible to live with my vassals, so bitterly do they complain that one of Giannucole's grandsons is to succeed me as their lord. So, if I don't want to be deposed by them, I'm afraid that I'll have to do in this case what I did in the other one, and that I'll also eventually have to leave you and find another wife."

The lady listened patiently, and her only reply was: "My lord, you should think about your own happiness and about how to satisfy your desires. Don't waste another thought on me, for nothing is of any value to me unless I see that it gives you pleasure."

Not many days after that, Gualtieri sent for his son the same way he had for his daughter, and having likewise pretended to have him put to death, he sent him to be brought up in Bologna just as he had done with the girl. In response, his wife said nothing more and did not change the expression on her face any more than she had in her daughter's case, all to Gualtieri's great astonishment, who told himself that no other woman could do what she did. And if it were not for the fact that he saw her treat the children with the utmost tenderness as long as he permitted her to do so, he would have concluded that she acted as she did because she had stopped caring for them. He knew, however, that her behavior was the product of her wisdom.

Since Gualtieri's subjects believed he had arranged to have his two children murdered, they condemned him, blaming it all on his cruelty, whereas they felt nothing but the most profound pity for his wife. But to the women who mourned with her for her children because they had suffered such a death, she never said anything except that if such was the pleasure of the man who had conceived them, then it was her pleasure as well.

Finally, many years after the birth of his daughter, Gualtieri decided the time had come to put his wife's patience to the ultimate test. Accordingly, he spoke with a large company of his vassals and told them that under no circumstances could he put up with Griselda as his wife any longer. He said that he had come to realize just how bad and immature a decision he had made when he chose her, and that he would therefore do everything he could to procure a dispensation from the Pope so that he could leave Griselda and take another wife. A large number of the worthy men took him to task over this plan, but his only reply was that it had to be done that way.

Upon learning of her husband's intentions, the lady grieved bitterly inside, for it seemed to her that what she had to look forward to was returning to her father's house and perhaps tending his sheep as she had done before, while being forced to see the man she loved with all her heart in another woman's embrace. But still, just as she had borne all of Fortune's other afflictions, she was determined to keep her countenance unchanged and endure this one as well.

A little later Gualtieri arranged to have counterfeit letters sent to him from Rome and led his subjects to believe that they contained the Pope's dispensation, which allowed him to leave Griselda and take another wife. Hence, he summoned her to appear, and in the presence of a large number of people, he said to her: "Woman, through the concession granted me by the Pope I am now free to leave you and choose another wife. Since my ancestors have always been great noblemen and rulers in these parts, whereas yours have always been peasants, I no longer want you as my wife. You should return to Giannucole's house with the dowry you brought me, and I will bring home another woman I've found who is a more appropriate match for me."

When she heard these words, the lady managed to hold back her tears only by making an enormous effort that went well beyond the normal capacity of women.

"My lord," she said, "I have always known that my lowly condition and your nobility were in no way suited to one another, just as I have acknowledged that the position I have held with you was a gift from you and from God, nor have I taken what was given to me and treated it as if it were my own rather than as something lent to me. So, if it pleases you to have it back, then it must also please me—and it does—to return it to you. Look, here's the ring with which you married me: take it. As for your ordering me to carry away the dowry I brought here, to do that will not require a paymaster on your part, nor a purse, let alone a packhorse on mine, for I haven't forgotten that I was completely naked when you took me.[6] And if you think it proper to let everybody see this body that bore the children you sired, I will depart naked as well, but I beg you, in return for the virginity I brought here and cannot take away again, that it may please you to let me take away at least one single shift in addition to my dowry."

Although Gualtieri had a greater desire to weep than anything else, he maintained his stony expression and said: "You may take a shift with you."

The people standing about there begged him to give her a dress so that the woman who had been his wife for thirteen years or longer should not suffer the shame of leaving his house wearing only a shift like a pauper. All their pleading was in vain, however, and thus she left the house in her shift, barefoot, and with nothing to cover her head. After having said good-bye to them all, she returned to her father's home, accompanied by the weeping and wailing of everyone who saw her.

Since Giannucole never really believed it possible for his daughter to last very long as Gualtieri's wife, he had been expecting just such a development every day and had kept the clothes that she had taken off the morning Gualtieri married her. He brought them to her, and after she had put them on, she devoted herself to all the menial chores in her father's house just as she had been accustomed to do, bravely enduring the fierce assault of a hostile Fortune.

As soon as he had sent Griselda away, Gualtieri led his vassals to believe that he had chosen as his wife a daughter of one of the counts of Panago.[7] And having ordered great preparations to be made for the wedding, he sent for Griselda to come to him. When she appeared, he said to her:

"I'm going to bring home the lady whom I have recently chosen to marry, and I want her to be given an honorable reception the moment she arrives. Since you know that I don't have any women in my house who can prepare the rooms properly and do many of the things that a festive occasion of this sort requires, and since you understand such household matters better than anyone else, I want you to see to it that all the arrangements are taken care of and that you invite as many ladies as you think necessary and receive them as though you were the mistress of the house. Then, when the wedding celebration is over, you can return home."

Gualtieri's words pierced Griselda's heart like so many knives, for she had not been able to put aside the love she bore him in the same way that she had relinquished the good fortune she once had. Nevertheless, she replied: "My lord, I am ready and willing."[8] And so, clad in homespun garments of coarse wool, she entered the house, which only a little while before she had left in a shift. Then she began sweeping and tidying up the rooms, had bed curtains and bench coverings put in place throughout the great halls, got the kitchen ready to go, and turned her hand to everything just as if she were some little household serving wench, never stopping until it was all as neat and trim as the occasion called for. Finally, after having invitations sent to all the women in those parts on Gualtieri's behalf, she stopped and waited for the celebration to begin. When the wedding day arrived, though the clothes she had on were poor, she displayed the spirit and bearing of a lady, receiving, with a happy smile on her face, all the women who came to the feast.

Gualtieri had seen to it that his children were brought up with care in Bologna by his kinswoman, who had married into the house of the counts of Panago. His daughter, who had now reached the age of twelve, was the most beautiful creature ever seen, and his son was six. Gualtieri sent word to his kinswoman's husband, asking him if he would be so kind as to accompany his daughter and her brother to Saluzzo, to arrange a noble, honorable escort for her, and not to reveal to anyone who she was in reality, but simply to tell them that he was bringing her there as Gualtieri's bride.

The nobleman did everything the Marquis requested, and a few days after he set out on his journey with the girl and her brother and their noble retinue, he reached Saluzzo, arriving around the dinner hour, where he found that all the people there, as well as many others from neighboring communities, were waiting for Gualtieri's new bride. She was received by the ladies, and as soon as she entered the hall where the tables were set up, Griselda, dressed just as she was, happily went to meet her, and said: "You are welcome here, my lady."

The ladies had begged Gualtieri, earnestly but in vain, either to have Griselda remain in another room or to lend her one of the dresses that had once been hers, so that she would not appear in front of the guests looking as she did. But she was nevertheless seated at the tables along with all the rest of them, after which dinner was served. As everyone stared at the girl, they said that Gualtieri had done well by the exchange, and Griselda joined in, praising her warmly, and her little brother, too.

It seemed to Gualtieri that he had now seen as much as he could have ever desired of his wife's patience, for he had observed that no event, however outrageous, had produced any sort of change in her at all. Moreover, he felt sure that her reaction was not the result of obtuseness, since he knew just how wise she was. He therefore decided that it was time to deliver her from the bitter sorrow he guessed she was keeping hidden beneath her impassive exterior, and having summoned her, he smiled and asked her in the presence of all the assembled people: "What do you think of our bride?"

"My lord," replied Griselda, "she seems very fine to me, and if, as I believe, her wisdom matches her beauty, I have no doubt whatsoever that living with her will make you the happiest gentleman in the world. However, I beg you with all my heart not to inflict on her the same wounds you once gave the other spouse you used to have, because I find it hard to believe she'll be able to endure them, considering how much younger she is and also how refined an upbringing she has had, whereas the other one experienced continual hardships from the time she was a little girl."

Seeing that she firmly believed the girl was going to be his wife, and yet had nothing but good things to say, Gualtieri had her sit down beside him.

"Griselda," he said, "the time has finally come both for you to taste the fruit of your long patience, and for those who have thought me cruel, unjust, and brutish to realize that what I've done I've done with a deliberate end in view. For I wanted to teach you how to be a wife, to teach them how to manage one, and at the same time to beget for myself perpetual peace and quiet for the rest of my life with you. When I was at the point of taking a wife, I really feared I'd have no peace, and that's why I decided to choose one by means of a test and have, as you know, inflicted so much pain and suffering on you.

"And since I've never seen you deviate from my wishes in either word or deed, and since it seems to me that you will provide me with all the happiness I've desired, I intend to restore to you in an instant that which I took from you over such a long time, and with the sweetest of cures to heal the wounds I gave you. Receive this girl, then, with a glad heart, the one you believed to be my wife, along with her brother, for they are, in fact, our children, yours as well as mine, the very ones whom you and many others believed for a long time I had cruelly ordered to be put to death. And I am your husband, who loves you more than anything else, since I believe I may boast that there is no one else who could be as content with his wife as I am with you."[9]

When he finished speaking, he embraced her and kissed her, and while she wept for joy, they both got up and went over to where their daughter sat, listening in amazement to what they were saying. Both of them embraced her and her brother tenderly, thus dispelling any confusion that they, like many others present, were feeling. The ladies were overjoyed, and getting up from the tables, they went with Griselda into a chamber where, with a more auspicious view of her future, they divested her of her old clothes and dressed her in one of her own stately gowns. Then, like the lady of the castle, which she always appeared to be even when clad in rags, they led her back into the hall, where her rejoicing with her children was simply wonderful. Indeed, everyone was so happy about what had happened that the feasting and the celebrating were redoubled and continued unabated for many more days. They all declared that Gualtieri was very wise, although they thought that the tests to which he had subjected his wife were harsh and intolerable, but they considered Griselda to be the wisest of them all.

A few days later the Count of Panago returned to Bologna, and Gualtieri, having taken Giannucole away from his drudgery, set him up in a position befitting the man who was his father-in-law, so that he was treated with honor and lived in great comfort during his last remaining years. As for Gualtieri himself, having arranged a noble match for his daughter, he lived a long, contented life with Griselda, always honoring her in every way he could.

What more is there left to say except that divine spirits may rain down from the heavens even into the houses of the poor, just as there are others in royal palaces who might be better suited to tending pigs than ruling men. Who, aside from Griselda, would have suffered, not merely dry eyed, but with a cheerful countenance, the cruel, unheard-of trials to which Gualtieri subjected her? Perhaps it would have served him right if, instead, he had run into the kind of woman who, upon being thrown out of the house in her shift, would have found some guy to give her fur a good shaking and got a nice new dress in the bargain.

Day 10, Conclusion

When Dioneo's story was done, the ladies inclined to one side or the other in their responses, some criticizing one detail in it, some praising another. After they had discussed it at length, the King glanced up at the sky, and seeing that the sun was already quite low and the hour of vespers was at hand, he began, without getting up from his seat, to speak to them as follows:

"Elegant ladies, as I believe you know, the wisdom we mortals possess does not merely consist of remembering things past and apprehending the present, but on the basis of these two activities being able to predict the future, which is considered by serious men to be the highest form of human intelligence.[1] Tomorrow, as you are aware, will be the fifteenth day since we left Florence in pursuit of recreation, seeking both to preserve our health and our lives, and to avoid the melancholy, grief, and anguish that have been inescapable in our city ever since the plague first began. In my estimation, we have managed to achieve this goal without any loss of honor, because as far as I have been able to observe, although the merry stories we have told could have been conducive to arousing carnal desire, and although we have continually enjoyed good food and drink as well as playing music and singing songs—all of which are apt to incite weak minds to less than proper behavior—I have never noted a deed or a word or anything else that is blameworthy, either on your part or on that of us men. Considering what I have seen and heard, it seems to me that our activities have been marked from start to finish by a sense of propriety, harmony, and fraternal friendship, all of which certainly gives me great pleasure and redounds to your honor and credit as well as to my own.

"Accordingly, to keep things from becoming tedious because of an established custom too long observed, and to prevent people from being able to raise frivolous objections to our having stayed here all this time, I think it proper, since all of us have had a day's share of the regal honor I still possess, that with your approval we should go back to the place from which we came. Furthermore, if you examine the matter carefully, there is also the fact that our company has already become known to many people around here, with the result that our numbers could increase to such an extent that it would take away all our pleasure. And so, if my advice meets with your approval, I will keep the crown that was given to me until our departure, which I propose should take place tomorrow morning. But if you should decide otherwise, I already have someone in mind to bestow it on for the next day."

The ladies and the young men debated the matter at great length, but finally, having judged the King's counsel to be both sensible and proper, they decided to do what he had recommended. He therefore summoned the steward and spoke with him about the arrangements for the following morning. Then, after dismissing the company until suppertime, he got to his feet.

The ladies and the other two men rose as well, and just as they always did, they devoted themselves to a variety of different pastimes. When the hour for supper arrived, they attended to it with the greatest pleasure, after which they started singing, playing music, and dancing *carole*,* and while Lauretta was leading them in a round, the King called for a song from Fiammetta, which she began singing very pleasantly, as follows:

If Love could come unmixed with jealousy,
There'd be no lady born
So glad as I, whoever she may be.
    If youth and gaiety,
Good looks and virtue, too, could satisfy

---

* *Carole*: dances in which the dancers joined hands and moved in a clockwise direction, usually accompanied by music and the singing of the dancers themselves.

A lady in her love,
If daring, prowess proved,
Intelligence, good manners, eloquence,
Or perfect gracefulness,
Then I'm the one who's pleased, for I'm in love
And see those qualities,
For certain, in the one who is my hope.
      But since I'm well aware
That other women's wisdom equals mine,
I tremble, terrified,
And always fear the worst,
Convinced those others want to take the one
Who stole my soul from me.
Thus Fortune's greatest gift, bestowed on me,
Makes me disconsolate,
Sigh deeply, and live on in misery.
      Yet if I knew my lord's
Fidelity were equal to his worth,
I'd not be jealous then.
But nowadays one sees
So many women lead men on that I
Hold all men culpable.
This breaks my heart and makes me long to die,
For I suspect each one
Who eyes him, fearful she'll take him away.
      For God's sake, then, I pray
No woman in the world would ever dare
To do me such a wrong,
For should some one of them,
By using words or signs or flattery,
Attempt in this affair
To do me harm, and should I learn of it,
Then mar my looks if I
Don't make her weep her folly bitterly.

As soon as Fiammetta had finished her song, Dioneo, who was right beside her, said with a laugh: "My lady, you would be doing all your companions a great service by revealing who he is, lest they take him from you out of ignorance, considering how angry that is bound to make you."

After Fiammetta's song, the company sang many another until the night was already almost half gone. Then, at the King's command, they all went off to rest.

The next day, they arose at dawn, by which time the steward had already sent all their baggage on ahead, and following the lead of their prudent King, they all walked back to Florence. There, taking their leave of the seven women in Santa Maria Novella, from which they had all set out, the three young men went off to pursue other pleasures of theirs, while the ladies in due course returned to their homes.

THE AUTHOR'S CONCLUSION

Most noble young ladies, for whose consolation I have undertaken this protracted labor, I believe that with the aid of divine grace, which has been granted to me, I think, more because of your prayers than because of any merits of my own, I have completely fulfilled what I promised to do at the start of the present work. Consequently, after giving thanks first to God and then to you, it is time for me to allow my pen and my weary hand to rest. Before doing so, however, I intend to respond briefly to a few trifling, though unspoken, objections that might have occurred to some of you as well as to others. For what seems absolutely clear to me is that these tales do not enjoy the special privilege of being immune to criticism more than anything else is, a fact I remember actually having noted at the start of the fourth day.

There may be some of you who will perhaps claim that I have employed too much license in writing these stories, because sometimes I had ladies say things, and quite often had them listen to things, that are not very suitable for virtuous women to say or hear. This I deny, for there is no story so unseemly that it may not be told, provided it is couched in seemly language, as I think I have done very well here.[1]

But supposing you are correct—for I do not want to get into a dispute with you, which you would certainly win—I still say, when asked to explain why I did what I did, that many reasons come quite readily to mind. First, if liberties were taken in a few cases, it was required by the nature of the stories, something that will be abundantly clear to any perceptive individual who examines them with an unprejudiced eye, for unless I had wished to deform them, they could not have been recounted in any other manner. And if perhaps there is some tiny expression in them, some little word, that is freer than might seem appropriate to prudish women who attach more weight to speech than to deeds and make more of an effort to seem good than to be good, then I say that it was no more improper for me to have written them than for men and women generally to go around all day long saying "hole" and "rod" and "mortar" and "pestle" and "sausage" and "mortadella" and lots of other things like that. Besides, my pen should have as much latitude as that which is given to the brush of the painter who, without incurring any, or at least any just, censure not only depicts Saint Michael striking the serpent with either a sword or a lance, and Saint George wounding the dragon wherever he pleases, but also makes Christ male and Eve female, and takes Him who, for the salvation of the human race, was willing to die on the cross, and has his feet fastened to it sometimes with one nail and sometimes with two.[2]

Moreover, it is perfectly clear that these stories were not told in a church, about whose affairs we should speak with the greatest reverence both in our hearts and in our words, although one can find many things in its sacred stories that go well beyond what you encounter in mine. Nor were they rehearsed either in the schools of philosophy where decency is required no less than anywhere else, or in any locale frequented by clergymen and philosophers. Rather, they were told in gardens, places designed for pleasure, among people who were young, but sufficiently mature so as not to be led astray by stories, and at a time when it was acceptable for even the most virtuous to go about with their breeches on their heads if they thought it would preserve their lives.[3]

Like everything else, these stories, such as they are, may be harmful or helpful, depending upon the listener. Who does not know that wine is a very fine thing for the healthy, as Cinciglione and Scolaio* and many others affirm, but that it is harmful for people suffering from a fever? Shall we say it is bad because it does harm to those who are feverish? Who does not know that fire is extremely useful, in fact downright necessary, for mankind? Shall we say it is bad because it burns down

---

*Both Cinciglione and Scolaio were proverbial drunkards (the former is also mentioned in 1.6).

houses and villages and cities? In the same way, arms are the safeguard of those who wish to live in peace, and yet they also kill men on many occasions, not because of any wickedness inherent in them, but because of the wickedness of those who use them wrongfully.

No single word has ever been wholesomely construed by a corrupt mind. And just as proper language can do nothing for such a mind, that which is improper cannot contaminate one that is well disposed, any more than mud can sully the rays of the sun, or earthly filth, the beauties of the heavens. What books, what words, what letters are holier, worthier, more to be revered than those of the Holy Scriptures? And yet there have been many who, by interpreting them in a perverse manner, have led themselves and others to perdition. All things, in themselves, are good for some purpose, but if they are wrongly used, they will cause a great deal of harm. And I say the same thing about my tales. Anyone who wishes to extract some wicked counsel from them or to come up with some wicked plan will not be prevented from doing so by the tales themselves if by chance they contain such things and can be twisted and distorted to such an end. But anyone seeking profit and utility in them will not be prevented from finding it either, nor will these stories ever be thought of or described as anything other than useful and seemly if they are read at the proper time and by the people for whom they were composed. As for the lady who is forever saying her rosary or baking cakes and pies for her holy confessor, she can just leave them be. These stories will not run after anyone demanding to be read, even though they are no more improper than certain little things pious hypocrites both talk about and actually do, if offered the opportunity.

There will also be those who will say that it would have been better to have omitted some of the stories that are included here. I grant you that, but still, I had to write down—indeed, I had an obligation to write down—what was actually said, which means that the speakers should have made their stories truly beautiful, and then I could have written them down that way. But even if people assumed that I was not just the writer, but the inventor of the stories—which I was not—then I would still reply that I am not ashamed if some of them were less than beautiful, because there is no craftsman other than God who has made everything perfect and complete. Even Charlemagne, who first created the Paladins, did not know how to make a sufficient number to form an army.[4]

In a multitude of things one will necessarily find many differences in quality. No field was ever so well cultivated that nettles and thistles and brambles were not found mixed in with the better plants. Besides, since I have to speak to unaffected young ladies, as most of you are, it would have been foolish of me to have exhausted myself by looking everywhere for the most exquisite material and to have taken great pains to speak about it in the most carefully measured style. Still, whoever reads through these stories can skip over those that give offense and read only those that promise delight, for lest anyone should be deceived, each story bears a sign on its brow of that which it keeps hidden within its bosom.*

I suppose there are also people who will say that some of the stories are too long. To them I will say, again, that if anyone has something better to do, it would be foolish to read them, even if they were brief. Although a great deal of time has passed from the day I started writing until this present hour, in which I am now approaching the end of my labors, it has not slipped my mind that I offered this effort of mine to ladies living in idleness rather than to anyone else, and nothing will seem long to those who read in order to pass the time, if it serves the purpose for which they chose it. Brevity is much more fitting for students, who undertake their labors not to pass the time, but to put it to good use, than it is for you ladies who have all that spare time left over that you do not spend in the pleasures of love. And besides, since none of you is going to be a student in Athens or Bologna or Paris, I need to speak to you here at greater length than to those whose wits have been sharpened by their studies.

I have no doubt but that there will be yet other women who will say that the matters I have related are overly full of clever quips and jests, and that it is unbecoming for a serious and substantial man to

---

*The "sign on its brow" is the summary of each story, the "rubric," that Boccaccio has placed at its beginning.

have written such things. To these women I feel obliged to express my gratitude, and I do so, indeed, because, moved by a well-intentioned zeal, they feel so tender a concern for my reputation. But I also want to respond to their objection this way: I confess that I am a man of some substance and that in my day I have been weighed on many occasions, but speaking to those women who have no experience of my weight, let me assure them that I am not heavy—in fact, I am so light that I float on the surface of the water.[5] Moreover, since the sermons preached by friars nowadays in order to rebuke men for their sins are, for the most part, filled with clever quips and jests and gibes, I concluded that such things would not be out of place in my stories, which were written, after all, to dispel the melancholy with which ladies are afflicted. Still, if they should laugh too hard because of them, the Lamentations of Jeremiah, the Passion of Our Savior, and the Complaint of Mary Magdalene will easily be able to cure them.[6]

And who can doubt that there are still others who will say that I have an evil and venomous tongue because in certain places I have told the truth about friars? Nevertheless, women who say such things ought to be pardoned, for there is no question but that they are moved by the best of motives, seeing as how friars are truly good men who flee hardship for the love of God, do their grinding when the millpond is full, and never blab about it afterward. And if it were not for the fact that they all give off a faint odor of billy goat, their company would be most agreeable.[7]

I acknowledge, however, that the things of this world are completely unstable and endlessly changing—which could explain what happened with my tongue. For not so long ago, distrusting my own judgment, which, in matters concerning myself, I avoid as much as possible, I was told by one of the women next door that I had the best and sweetest tongue in the world, and in all honesty, this occurred when only a few of the stories I have been talking about still remained to be written. As for those other ladies who speak of me so spitefully, let what I have just said suffice as my reply to them.

And now I leave it up to every lady to say and think whatever she wishes, for the time has come to bring these remarks to an end and give humble thanks to Him who, after aiding me in my immense labor, has brought me to the goal I pursued. As for you, charming ladies, may His grace and peace be with you always, and may you remember me if perhaps any of you have benefited in any way from having read these stories.

Here ends the Tenth and final Day of the book called Decameron, *also known as* Prince Galeotto

ACKNOWLEDGMENTS

Anyone producing a book like this one has incurred debts almost too
numerous to mention. In the first place, there are all the hundreds of
students with whom I have read Boccaccio over many, many years
as well as all the scholars in Italy, England, the United States, and
elsewhere whose work has made my understanding of the *Decameron*
possible. I am especially grateful for the careful editorial work on the
Italian text done by the great Italian scholar Vittore Branca, whose
Einaudi edition (Turin, 1980, 1987, 1992) has been the primary basis
of my translation, although I have also profited from that of Carlo
Salinari for Laterza (Bari, 1966) and from the edition of the Hamilton
codex, a transcription of Boccaccio's own copy of the *Decameron* done
by Charles S. Singleton and published by the Johns Hopkins University Press (Baltimore, 1974). I have learned a great deal from previous
translators of Boccaccio's book, including those of John Payne from
1886 (edited and annotated by Charles S. Singleton in 1982 for the University of California Press), of J. M. Rigg from 1903, of Mark Musa and
Peter Bondanella from 1982, of Guido Waldman from 1993, of G. H.
McWilliam from 1995 (second edition), and of J. G. Nichols from 2008.
I should also mention "The *Decameron* Web," a project that was started
in 1995 at Brown University, and contains materials I found invaluable
during the course of my work.

I am particularly grateful to three colleagues here at the University
of Texas at Austin for their help with various matters historical and
with occasional problems in translation: Alison Frazier of the Department of History, Louis Waldman of the Department of Art and Art
History, and Andrew Dell'Antonio of the Butler School of Music. I
owe an additional debt for help with translation matters to my friend

in Italy, Francesca Piviotti. I am also grateful to the University of Texas at Austin for having awarded me two semester-long leaves (Faculty Research Assignments) to complete my work on this project.

I am deeply appreciative of all the support that Peter Simon, my editor at Norton, has given this project from the very beginning. What I thought would be done in three or four years wound up taking close to seven, and Pete has been patient and understanding throughout the entire process. I am also grateful to Quynh Do, an assistant editor at Norton, who has been extremely helpful with many aspects of this project, and to my copy editor, David Stanford Burr, who carefully and conscientiously read through the entire manuscript, catching errors and inconsistencies, not just once, but twice.

Finally, my greatest debt of gratitude is owed to the two individuals to whom I have dedicated this book. The first is my wife Marlette, who has read every word of it, sometimes more than once, and always made sure that what I wrote was clear and fully idiomatic. The second is my good friend and colleague here in the Italian Department, Douglas Biow, who has read the entire book and has offered a vast amount of useful advice on my work in the Introduction and notes as well as on matters of translation. I could not have brought this work to completion without their assistance and support. If there are any mistakes or infelicities, whether they are in my translation, the Introduction, or the notes, they are, of course, my responsibility.

Wayne A. Rebhorn
The University of Texas at Austin
2013

NOTES

Preface

1 Boccaccio follows the principles of medieval rhetoric and opens his work with a proverb: "misery loves company." He also personalizes the idea, for earlier in his career he had memorialized his suffering for the love of Maria d'Aquino, referring to her by the pseudonym of Fiammetta, in his work of the same name. Fiammetta ("little flame") will reappear as one of the ten narrators of the *Decameron*. In the next sentences, he acts out one of the conventional tropes of courtly love by stressing his low condition in relationship to the beloved and to love itself (although the experience of loving was also thought in the Middle Ages to be so ennobling that it compensated for whatever degradation the lover might experience).

2 Melancholy ("black humor") meant more than just an unhappy mood, as it does today. In the medical theory of Boccaccio's time, the body contained four "humors" (blood, choler, and phlegm, in addition to melancholy) that determined both its physical functions and the mental states accompanying those functions. Good health required that all four humors be in balance, so that to have one, such as melancholy, become dominant was to suffer a serious disease.

3 Boccaccio's different names for the narratives comprising his collection are not synonyms, nor can they be applied individually to distinct subsets of them. Furthermore, all of these names are, to some degree, approximations, since the genres they label were rather fluid in the period. Nevertheless, some distinctions can be made among them. "Story" (Italian: *novella*) was a late medieval descriptive term, fairly new in Boccaccio's lifetime, that defined a story focused on a single incident. "Fable" probably refers less to something like the moralizing tales of Aesop than to what the French called a *fabliau*, a short tale usually concerned with lower-class characters in which the main action involved their tricking one another in pursuit of money or sex. A "parable," by contrast, was a story with an explicit, usually conventional moral, like the parables recounted by Christ in the New Testament, or like similar tales told throughout the Middle Ages and typically called *exempla*. Finally, "history" (or "story," *istoria* in Italian) identifies a narrative involving elevated and important historical persons or incidents.

4 In insisting that his stories will offer readers both "pleasure and useful advice," Boccaccio is rephrasing the well-known and widely endorsed dictum of the Roman writer Horace who said that art should be both *dulce* ("sweet") and *utile* ("useful"); see his *Ars poetica* (*The Art of Poetry*) 343.

Day 1, Introduction

1 Boccaccio's image of the reading of his work as the making of a journey up a difficult mountain recalls the opening of the *Divine Comedy* in which Dante is trying without success to climb a mountain (Purgatory). In the next sentence, Boccaccio rephrases *Proverbs* 14:13.

2 For Florentines in this period, the year began on March 25, the date of the Incarnation or Annunciation, and in fact, the plague did appear for the first time in Florence in April 1348. As Boccaccio's next sentence explains, it had started in Asia—to be precise, in the Crimea—from which it was brought by sea to Sicily in 1346. In that same sentence Boccaccio offers two conventional explanations for the disease: the influence of the stars, and God's anger at the sins of humans. Boccaccio's description of the plague, although pretending to be an eyewitness account, is generally based on earlier accounts such as that by Paulus Diaconus in his eighth-century *Historia Longobardorum* (*History of the Lombards*).

3 Boccaccio is, of course, being ironic in this sentence. Those "things," which the wise, like the simple, must learn to bear, are the suffering and death that are part of the "natural course of events," that is, the human condition.

4 Aesculapius (in Gk., Asclepios) was the Greco-Roman god of medicine; Galen (2nd c. CE) and Hippocrates (5th c. BCE) were the two most famous doctors of the ancient Greek world.

5 Elissa's opening remark alludes to Ephesians 5.23.

6 Although some scholars have attempted to identify this palace with a specific country villa Boccaccio owned, the ensuing description is so general and so idealized—and is so similar to the description of the palace to which the group goes at the start of Day 3—that it makes more sense to see it as being inspired not by Boccaccio's recollection of a specific place, but by the literary tradition of the *locus amoenus*, the "pleasant place" that serves as a setting for pastoral poetry. This tradition lies behind similar descriptions in Boccaccio's earlier works and in such medieval classics as *The Romance of the Rose*.

7 Crowning a victorious athlete or a poet with leaves from the laurel tree, which was sacred to Apollo, was an ancient Greek custom; the Romans awarded such a wreath to a victorious general. The custom of crowning writers and poets with laurel wreaths was revived in 1315 by the citizens of Padua for the humanist scholar Albertino Mussato, and then, more famously, when, on April 8, 1341, Petrarch was crowned poet laureate by the Roman Senate on the Capitoline Hill.

8 The names of all the servants who accompany the group into the countryside have Greek roots, although they are taken by Boccaccio, for the most part, from Roman comedy and satire. They function generically as "names for lower-class servants" rather than pointing, through their etymologies, to specific qualities the individual servants might possess.

9 "News" in this sentence translates Boccaccio's *novelle*, which can also mean "stories."

10 The viol (Boccaccio writes *viuola*; the more common French name was *vielle*) was a stringed instrument like the modern violin, but with a longer, deeper body, and

an indeterminate number of strings; it could be bowed or plucked and was used to
accompany singing or dancing.

Day 1, Story 1

1   There is no specific source for this story, although hypocrisy is frequently a subject
of satire in the Middle Ages, and there were occasional cases in various countries
of criminals and the like actually being venerated as saints.

2   Musciatto di Messer Guido Franzesi (d. 1310) was a merchant from Tuscany who
grew rich in France where he served as a counselor to the French King Philip the Fair
(Philippe le Bel, b. 1268, ruled 1285–1314), who did, in fact, make Musciatto a "gentleman." The latter wickedly advised the king to falsify his coinage and to plunder the
Italian merchants living in France; and he also had a close business relationship with
a certain Cepparello da Prato. King Philip's brother, Charles Sans Terre (Charles
"Lackland," 1270–1325), was the third son of Charles III. Although the Count of
Valois, Maine, and Anjou, he owed his nickname of "Lackland" to his failure to
acquire a kingdom. In 1301 he was invited by Pope Boniface VIII (b. ca. 1235; pope
1294–1303) to bring an army to Italy in order to support papal forces fighting the
Florentines. Note that "Tuscany," like "Lombardy" (the usurers mentioned later in
the story are identified as Lombards), was often used in this period to refer to all of
northern Italy.

3   Cepparello da Prato (or Ciapperello Dietiaiuti da Prato) was a historical person-
age whose name appears in documents from the period as a receiver of taxes and
tithes for King Philip and Boniface VIII. Although he did have business relations
with Musciatto Franzesi, he was not, as Boccaccio says, a notary; moreover, he was
married and had children. The "Ser" before his name is short for "Messer" and is
an honorific, like calling someone "sir," but without the implication of aristocratic
status. On titles and forms of address, see Headnote 3.

4   Like other Italian cities of the time, Florence had *fossi,* "garbage pits," on its outskirts.
However, *fossi* could also refer to pits dug in unconsecrated ground where suicides,
heretics, the excommunicated, and even usurers were dumped. According to the
chronicler Giovanni Villani (ca. 1275–1348), such bodies were thrown into the *fossi,*
that is, the *fossati* or (dry) moat, outside the walls of Florence. The specific meaning
of Boccaccio's term is thus hard to determine even if the general meaning of what
will happen to Ciappelletto is clear enough.

5   Ciappelletto's last words here echo a line from the *Te Deum: quos pretioso sanguine
redemisti* ("whom Thou hast redeemed with Thy precious blood").

6   The friar begins by asking Ciappelletto about sins of incontinence (lust, gluttony,
sloth, avarice, and anger).

7   According to Church law, the celebration of the Sabbath began at vespers on the
preceding Saturday, and since nones (midafternoon) was the canonical hour before
vespers (sunset), it was not officially part of the Sabbath. Out of feigned religious
scrupulousness, however, Ciappelletto extends the observance of the Sabbath back
to nones as well.

8   Panfilo begins the final paragraph of his story by echoing the formulas used at the ends of medieval saints' lives.

9   This is the only case in the *Decameron* in which the narrator of the story is mentioned, albeit briefly, at the end.

Day 1, Story 2

1   Although there is no specific source for this story, arguments like the one that Abraham makes at the end can be found in a variety of medieval sermons and stories.

2   In French, the last name of Giannotto di Civignì could be Souvigny, Chauvigny, Chevigny, or Chovigny, all typically French names. His first name would be Jehannot or Jeannot in French, and both it and the Italian variant Boccaccio uses are diminutives, meaning "Little John." Since Giannotto could be a form of Boccaccio's own first name, and Giovanni is the new name that Abraham will adopt later in the story, Boccaccio may be encouraging readers to see both characters as projections of the author himself.

3   Popes typically address the cardinals as "fratres," "brothers."

4   In the late Middle Ages, the University of Paris was an intellectual center celebrated for the study of philosophy and theology.

5   I.e., there was nothing to lose because if Abraham stayed home, he would not become a Christian any more than if he went to Rome and saw how decadent it was.

6   Boccaccio's Italian for the first of the clergy's euphemisms, "procurement," is *procureria*, which means simply to obtain the means to live. His second, "daily rations," is *substentazioni*. *Substentatio* (or *susstentatio*) was a late Latin word that referred to a monk's meager daily allowance of food. Both terms are clearly ironic, and the second one in particular deepens Boccaccio's religious satire in the story.

7   Abraham's repeated architectural metaphors for the Church recall the biblical notion that Saint Peter, the first bishop of Rome, was the rock on which the Church was built (see Matthew 16:18). His counterintuitive argument here is not Boccaccio's invention; it exists in many of the sources of the story.

Day 1, Story 3

1   Stories of the wise Jew and the three rings were widespread in the Middle Ages, including a version that appeared in the *Novellino* (73), sometimes leading to the conclusion that Christianity was the true ring and at other times endorsing a notion of skeptical tolerance. Similar stories continued to appear after the *Decameron* as well, and included, most famously, Gotthold Ephraim Lessing's Enlightenment play *Nathan der Weise* (*Nathan the Wise*, 1779). The name Melchisedech (or Melchizedek) means "king of justice" and was common among the ancient Hebrews; see, for example, Genesis 14.18 and Psalms 110.4. Saladin (Salah al-Din, 1138–93) was the Sultan of Cairo, and he was most famous for the reconquest of Jerusalem from the crusaders in 1187. A popular figure in medieval literature, he was celebrated for his knowledge, his chivalry, his military leadership, and his generosity. Dante placed

him among the great pagan figures in Limbo (*Inferno* 4.129), Petrarch exalted him in his *Trionfo della Fama* (*Triumph of Fame* 2.148–50), and Boccaccio speaks glowingly of him in his earlier work, the *Amorosa visione* (12.28ff.) as well as here in this story and in *Decameron* 10.9, where his generosity in particular is on display.

2 Lending money at interest (*prestare a usura*, in Boccaccio's Italian) was widely practiced in the Middle Ages by Jews and by many Christians as well. Although it was classified by the Church as a sin, the sin of usury, which is the term (*usura*) Boccaccio employs here, it seems unlikely that he considered it one.

Day 1, Story 4

1 Versions of this story were widely diffused in the Middle Ages, appearing in French *fabliaux* as well as in the *Novellino* (54), which was one of Boccaccio's models.

2 In his first story, Dioneo lives up to his name by focusing on the body and, in particular, on illicit sexuality, as he will do repeatedly in the stories he tells on the other nine days. In fact, when he is made King on the seventh day, he chooses as its topic the (sexual) tricks that women play on their husbands. And, starting on Day 2, he is allowed to tell the last story, thus ending almost every day on a note of sexual license that often parodies what goes on in the preceding stories.

3 Lunigiana is a mountainous region in northwest Tuscany extending from Emilia-Romagna down to the sea. It had two Benedictine monasteries in the fourteenth century, that of Montelungo near Pontremoli and that of the Priory of Santa Croce del Corvo near Lerici. The latter is the more likely candidate for the one in this story, since it was the scene of an encounter between Dante and a monk named Frate Ilaro whose letter describing their encounter Boccaccio had transcribed in his *Zibaldone* (*Notebook*).

4 The narrator calls him "Messer l'abate" in this sentence. I have retained this Italian title "Messer," as I have done generally throughout this translation, rather than replace it with something like "Mister" or "Master." In most cases, it is used before a person's name as a sign of his status, but in satirical stories, like this one, it is clearly ironic. An abbot might well deserve such an honorific, but this one clearly does not, especially at this point when he is doing a sexual appraisal of the girl. On titles and forms of address, see Headnote 3.

5 This last clause (in Italian: *peccato celato è mezzo perdonato*) was a proverbial saying in the fourteenth century, as was its contrary, "a sin confessed is half forgiven" (*peccato confessato è mezzo perdonato*), a saying still current in Italian.

6 Monasteries typically had rooms to incarcerate monks who violated the rules.

Day 1, Story 5

1 There are various versions of this story in Eastern collections such as *The Book of the Seven Sages* and *The Thousand and One Nights* as well as in popular traditions of storytelling in Europe. Monferrato is a region of Italy to the south of Turin lying along the roads running between France and Genoa.

2 By referring to specific historical figures, Boccaccio dates his story to the time of
   the Third Crusade (1189–92), which attempted unsuccessfully to retake Jerusalem
   from Saladin who had conquered it in 1187. The Crusade was led by the French
   King Philippe Auguste, known as "le Borgne" ("the One Eyed"), together with the
   Holy Roman Emperor Frederick Barbarossa and the English King Richard the Lion-
   Hearted. The Marquis of Monferrato, Corrado degli Aleramici, was a successful
   commander who was named the Defender of Constantinople and of Tyre and then
   the King of Jerusalem before he was assassinated on April 28, 1192. In the story, he
   is called a "Gonfalonier (i.e., Standard-bearer) of the Church," an honorific title that
   popes bestowed on various kings and noblemen between the thirteenth and the seventeenth centuries. He had succeeded to the title of Marquis of Monferrato upon
   the death of his father Guiglielmo in 1190, and he had already been in Palestine for
   several years before he was joined there by the crusaders in 1189. Boccaccio's story is
   thus set sometime in the months before March 1191, when Philippe signed a treaty
   of alliance with Richard in Sicily while they were on their way to the Holy Land.
   However, Boccaccio departs from the historical record in two important details.
   First, the Marquis did not leave a wife behind him in Monferrato. A widower when
   he went to the Holy Land, he married Theodora, the sister of the Byzantine emperor
   in 1187, but then abandoned her and married Isabella, Princess of Jerusalem, in 1192;
   neither of his wives was ever in Monferrato. Second, Philippe did not stop in Monferrato on his way to Genoa to sail to the Holy Land. This interweaving of history
   and fiction is typical of Boccaccio's stories.

3 Falling in love with a lady from afar, merely on the basis of her description, was a
   commonplace in medieval romance. This motif is consistent with other suggestive
   details in the story that seek to create an idealized portrait of a courtly and chival-
   ric society of the past. The Marchioness's final quip to the king works, of course, to
   undercut this idealization to some extent.

Day 1, Story 6

1 There were several Inquisitors who served in Florence during the fourteenth century
   and of whom Boccaccio may have been thinking when he composed this story. In
   general, they were disliked for their decadent lifestyles, for trumping up charges of
   heresy, and for taking bribes in exchange for reducing the charges they would make.

2 Contrary to popular opinion, there was no papal institution, no tribunal, known as
   the Inquisition during the late Middle Ages (although there would be such official
   tribunals later: the Spanish Inquisition, established under Ferdinand and Isabella
   in 1478, and the Holy Office, established by Pope Paul III to fight Protestantism in
   1542). In a papal bull of 1231, however, Gregory IX instituted the practice of appointing special investigating judges called *Inquisitores haereticae pravitatis* to investigate
   heresy and bring heretics to trial. (Boccaccio uses a vernacular translation of this
   official title for the Inquisitor in his story.) The ultimate punishment for unrepen-
   tant heretics was burning at the stake.

3 Nothing is known of the historical Cinciglione whose name appears in this sentence; he was apparently a famous drinker.

4 Epicurus (341–270 BCE) was a Greek philosopher who saw pleasure as the end of life. Although the pleasure he advocated was simple and relatively innocent, he came to be associated with sensual excess in the Middle Ages and was also believed to have denied the immortality of the soul. Dante accordingly places him in the circle of Hell reserved for the heretics (see *Inferno* 10.14–15).

5 According to the rule of their order, the lives of the friars were to be modeled on that of their founder, Saint Francis of Assisi. They were to wander from town to town, preaching and aiding the poor and the sick, while living in poverty themselves and avoiding any contact with money.

6 The largest Franciscan convent in Florence was attached to the Church of Santa Croce.

7 This is a slight paraphrase of the beginning and end of Matthew 19:29: *Et omnis... centuplum accipiet, et vitam aeternam possidebit* ("And everyone...shall receive a hundredfold, and shall inherit everlasting life").

8 The leftover broth is the watery liquid that remains after one has eaten the meat and vegetables cooked in it. The implication is that the friars eat gluttonously while not giving the poor much in the way of substantial nourishment.

Day 1, Story 7

1 There is no source for this story, although some critics see similarities with *Novellino* 44 and Peter Alphonsi, *Disciplina clericalis* (*A School for Clerics*) 4.

2 Messer Can della Scala is said to be a *magnifico signore*, which I have translated as "great lord." However, the adjective really means "grand," "magnificent." It defines the idealized lifestyle of the secular and religious elite as being one of splendor and lavish expenditures and also of generosity and hospitality. Avarice or miserliness is clearly opposed to this set of characteristics. The noun form of *magnifico*, namely *magnificenza*, which is applied to both Can della Scala and to the Abbot of Cluny in the story, has sometimes been translated as "magnificence" and sometimes as "munificence," that is, generosity.

3 Messer Can della Scala is also referred to more simply as Messer Cane in the story. He is usually called Cangrande (or Can Grande) della Scala (1291–1329) who was the ruler of Verona. His magnificence and generosity were well known and had been celebrated by Dante (*Paradiso* 17.76–93). The liberality of Frederick II (1197–1250), King of Sicily and Holy Roman Emperor, was also well known. One sign of such lordly munificence was to arrange for elaborate festivals, as Cangrande does in this story. Scholars have not, however, been able to identify the festival in the story with any particular one Cangrande organized.

4 Nothing is known about this Bergamino who was most likely a storyteller by profession. His name may simply mean that he came from the town of Bergamo. Boccaccio groups him with the other *uomini di corte*, a phrase translated as "court entertainers"

to avoid suggesting that they were "courtiers," that is, individuals, often aristocrats, who were more permanent residents in the courts that were attached to powerful rulers and noblemen. In Boccaccio's time, the word *corte* meant such a body of individuals, but it also referred to a festival like the one Cangrande della Scala plans to hold, and to which "court entertainers" such as Bergamino would flock from all over the peninsula.

5 During the first half of the twelfth century, Hugh d'Orléans, who was called "Primas," "the Primate," by his friends at the University of Paris, was a canon in Cologne. He may have been the author of numerous satirical poems and drinking songs in Latin, writing under the name of Golias. He was imitated by many other poets, known consequently as Goliards, whose works were often critical of the Church and eventually provoked it to attempt to suppress them. The *Carmina Burana* is the best-known collection of verse produced by these poets.

6 The Benedictine Abbey of Cluny, located in Burgundy, was founded in 910 by Duke William the Pious of Aquitaine. It controlled a number of abbeys elsewhere, including one in Paris, and by the late Middle Ages its wealth had become legendary. It is not clear which abbot is the one involved in this story. Note that another abbot from Cluny appears in 10.2.

7 A poem in which wine is celebrated as being superior to water is attributed to the historical Primas.

8 This last clause rehearses a formula used by rulers welcoming ambassadors to their courts; it is used again at the end of the story, and essentially means something like, "you have the run of the place."

Day 1, Story 8

1 There is no source for this story. The Grimaldi was among the oldest and most powerful families in Genoa and was often allied with the Florentines. Since no Ermino Grimaldi has been found, it is likely that Boccaccio invented him as a representative of the proverbial miserliness of the Genoese. Guiglielmo Borsiere (d. ca. 1300) appears to be a historical figure, and his witty remark was recorded as historical by various fourteenth-century writers, including Boccaccio himself, when commenting on Dante's *Inferno* 16.70–72, where Guiglielmo is placed in the circle reserved for the sodomites. In this canto of his poem Dante also denounces the nouveaux riches of Florence in his own time for their pride and materialism, and this denunciation may inform Boccaccio's own critique (through Lauretta) of his contemporary society in this story. Note that Guiglielmo's last name means "purse maker" and may thus not be a true surname. He is assumed to have had that profession and then abandoned it to become a denizen of various courts in Italy. On his characterization as a "court entertainer," see 1.7, note 4.

Day 1, Story 9

1   A version of this story can be found in the *Novellino* (51). The first King of Cyprus was Guy de Lusignan (b. ca. 1129, ruled 1192–94). He had been installed as king by Richard the Lion-Hearted, who conquered the island on his way to the Holy Land during the Third Crusade. Guy's insufficiency and weakness were well known. There is no record, however, of the personal transformation he underwent that is described in this story. Godfrey of Bouillon, who is mentioned in the story, was actually the leader of the First Crusade and had taken Jerusalem in 1099; Boccaccio's reference to him here is anachronistic.

Day 1, Story 10

1   There is no source for this story. The leek image used in it may well have been proverbial, and Boccaccio himself employs it in the Introduction to Day 4.

2   Master Alberto is probably Alberto de' Zancari (b. ca. 1280) who was a professor of medicine at the University of Bologna and was still alive in 1348. He was indeed famous, and his second wife was called Margherita. The protagonist of the story is named Malgherida (the Bolognese form of Margherita), and her surname, Ghisolieri, was, in fact, that of a prominent family in the city, although no Malgherida Ghisolieri has been found in the historical record.

3   In describing Master Alberto's infatuation—the "flames of love," his inability to sleep, the beauty of his beloved's face, etc.—Boccaccio employs the language of courtly love, which had been used by the poets of the so-called *Dolce Stil Novo* ("Sweet New Style"), including Dante, Guido Cavalcanti, and Guido Guinizelli, in the preceding century. Dante is, of course, a constant presence in the *Decameron*, and Cavalcanti is the protagonist of 6.9.

Day 1, Conclusion

1   Pampinea is paraphrasing a medieval proverb: *providus est plenus, improvidus extat egenus* ("the provident one will be full, the improvident will wind up needy"). The moment she has chosen to name the next Queen is the canonical hour of vespers, which marks the end of one liturgical day and the start of the next. Her decision heightens the ritual-like nature of what they are doing, as does her use of the proverb here and her reference to the deity in the next sentence, which echoes Luke 20.38.

2   Filomena was the one who worried at the start about the women going off into the countryside without any men along to guide them. Hence, Pampinea is pronouncing "prudent" here.

3   Emilia's song invites allegorical interpretation, as Boccaccio's next sentence suggests. Some critics see the "good that makes the mind content" (*ben che fa contento lo 'intelletto*) as God, who is contained within the beauty she sees in her mirror. Dante speaks of the damned in Hell as having lost *il ben dell'intelletto* (*Inferno* 3.18: "the good of the intellect"; cf. *Purgatorio* 27.103 and *Paradiso* 26.16). Dante took this concept from

Aristotle (*Nicomachean Ethics* 6.2), for whom the "good of the intellect" meant the truth that the intellect has as its proper object; Dante then redefined it as the truth that is the proper object of all human striving and knowing, namely, God. Other critics, however, have imagined the good of which Emilia sings as wisdom or one of the liberal arts.

Day 2, Story 1

1 Although there is no literary precedent for this story, its characters appear to be historical. Stecchi and Martellino were lower-class professional entertainers (*buffoni*), whom Sacchetti also mentions in his *Trecentonovelle* (*Three Hundred Stories*) 144. There was a Saint Arrigo who worked as a humble porter (or perhaps a wood carrier) while he was alive. When he died on June 10, 1315, the church bells rang of their own accord, and after a reverent crowd had taken his body into the cathedral, it became the source of miracles, one of the first being the curing of a cripple. The tomb of the Blessed Arrigo can still be seen in the Cathedral of Treviso. Also lying behind the story is the episode in the New Testament in which a man stricken with palsy cannot be brought before Christ because of a crowd and has to be lowered down to him from the roof (see Mark 2:3–12 and Luke 5:18–26).

2 The "Germans" here are probably compatriots of Arrigo rather than mercenaries and most likely hailed from Bolzano in the far north of Italy where German is still spoken.

3 In the early fourteenth century, Treviso was in fact governed by a Ghibelline *podestà* from Gubbio named Manno della Branca. *Podestà* was the name given to the chief magistrate, usually functioning as a judge, in the towns of northern and central Italy during the late Middle Ages. On titles and forms of address, see Headnote 3.

4 Boccaccio's phrase, which I have translated as "a thorough shellacking," is *senza pettine carminato*; it means literally that Martellino was being "carded without a comb." Wool was carded in Boccaccio's time by means of heavy iron carding combs that were drawn through it to straighten out the fibers and remove dirt and debris. Such combs were also used as torture devices to tear off the skin of their victims. Saint Blaise, the governor of Sebastea (Sivas in modern Turkey), was martyred by being carded and then having his head cut off, and in representations he often appears holding such combs in his hands. In Boccaccio's day, "being carded" was slang for being beaten.

5 The strappado was an instrument of torture that consisted of a rope running through a pulley affixed to the ceiling. The victim's hands, tied behind his back, were attached to the rope, and he was hauled up into the air by them, then suddenly released, his fall being stopped with a jerk before he hit the ground. Such jerks, which would have dislocated most people's shoulders, were supposed to make the victim confess the truth.

6 The Agolanti was a noble Florentine family that was exiled from the city in the thirteenth century, and some of its members were in Venice and Treviso where they probably worked as bankers. A certain "Bernardus de Agolantis de Florentia" appears in a document concerning a miracle performed by the Blessed Arrigo on

June 20, 1315, and at least one critic thinks that this member of the family may have told the tale in Florence that Boccaccio is reworking here.

Day 2, Story 2

1 There are precedents for Boccaccio's *novella* in Asian story collections such as the *Panchatantra* (4.1) as well as in the *Novellino* (99). However, its true origins can be found in the widely known legend of Saint Julian the Hospitaller, also known as Saint Julian the Poor, the patron saint of travelers. Probably of French origin, the legend is romantic fiction rather than historical fact. It concerns a nobleman who killed his parents unintentionally and then performed various acts of penance, which included building a hospice, taking care of the poor, and offering hospitality to travelers, until an angel, disguised as a traveler, told him he had been forgiven. Well into the Renaissance, travelers did, in fact, offer a variety of prayers to Saint Julian, and it is worth noting that in Boccaccio's time, the "hospitality" of Saint Julian often included the furnishing of one's guest with a bed companion. There is a Castel Guiglielmo in the province of Rovigo not far from Ferrara, and it is possible, considering the accuracy of the details Boccaccio supplies about the setting of the story, that he might have traveled there at some point.

2 Filostrato's claim that his story will be merely "profitable" echoes the Horatian dictum that poetry should be *dulce*, "sweet," and *utile*, "useful" or "profitable"; see the *Ars poetica* (*The Art of Poetry*), 343. Although he implies that his story may not be particularly "sweet," most readers would disagree.

3 Marquis Azzo VIII d'Este da Ferrara (1263–ca. 1308) is the most likely candidate for the figure to whom Boccaccio is referring. Dante identifies him as a patricide (*Inferno* 12.109–11).

Day 2, Story 3

1 This story has no literary source, but is a development of the widespread folktale about a youth who makes his fortune by conquering the heart of a princess. The motif of a noble man or woman traveling in disguise as a member of a religious order was also well known in medieval literature.

2 There are historical records documenting the existence of the Lamberti and Agolanti families in Florence in the thirteenth and fourteenth centuries. The former were merchants and the latter moneylenders. Note that a Sandro Agolanti appears in 2.1.

3 There was, in fact, a community of Italian merchants and moneylenders in England during the late Middle Ages. There was also one in Bruges, a city through which the brothers' nephew Alessandro will travel later on in the story.

4 It is difficult to determine the exact historical event Boccaccio is thinking of here. A struggle broke out in 1173, pitting Henry II (1154–89) against his sons who were led by the eldest one, also named Henry. Peace was made in 1174, but the rebellion was renewed in 1181, and only ended in 1183 with the death of Prince Henry.

5 The fact that the Abbot is dressed in white means that he belonged to one of the orders of the Cistercians.

6 In order to avoid the marriage her father has arranged for her, the "Abbot" has come to ask the Pope to use his ecclesiastical authority and marry her to someone else of her choosing. The Pope in question may be Alexander III (b. 1100/1105, pope 1159–81) who had close ties to Henry II of England.

7 It is difficult to say which King of Scotland Boccaccio has in mind. William I (1143–1214) is a possibility, but he was not very old at the time the story supposedly takes place.

8 There were, in fact, three kings of Scotland named Alexander (Alessandro in Italian): Alexander I (1078–1124), Alexander II (1198–1249), and Alexander III (1241–86). Alexander III married the daughter of Henry III of England. Moreover, one of the daughters of Henry II of England married an Italian, Guiglielmo di Sicilia. All of these historical details resonate with the story, but their exact relevance is uncertain.

Day 2, Story 4

1 Although this story has no literary source, it generally recalls Greek romances, such as Longus's *Daphnis and Chloe* and Achilles Tatius's *Leucippe and Clitophon*, works whose heroes experience the highs and lows of Fortune as they wander around the Mediterranean world, often over a period of many years.

2 There are records of the Rufolo family living in Naples and Ravello in the thirteenth and fourteenth centuries. The branch in the latter city was extremely wealthy and cultured, as can be seen today from the palace it possessed there and from the pulpit dedicated to the family in the city's cathedral. A certain Matteo and his son Lorenzo, who managed a lucrative trade with Greece and Egypt, were condemned to prison by the Angevin rulers of Naples in 1283 for having joined in the uprising against their rule called the Sicilian Vespers. Lorenzo was later pardoned, but after becoming a pirate, he was captured and died in a Calabrian stronghold in 1291. In the story, Boccaccio is clearly recollecting the time he himself spent in Naples and the surrounding region as well as the story of Lorenzo, although he has given his version of it a happy ending.

3 Cephalonia is the largest island in the Ionian Sea off the west coast of Greece. Corfu, to which Landolfo will eventually drift, is a small island to the north close to the southern tip of present-day Albania.

4 Trani is a town on the Adriatic coast of Italy about twenty-five miles west-northwest of Bari.

Day 2, Story 5

1 There are many literary and folkloric antecedents for various aspects of this story, although it is difficult to speak here of "sources." The story contains, however, quite

specific references to places in Naples, where Boccaccio spent a substantial time in his youth, as well as to individuals associated in different ways with the city. A certain Andreuccio da Perugia appears in a fourteenth-century document, although he was not a horse trader by profession and for that reason does not seem a model for Boccaccio's character.

2 This story is unique in the *Decameron* in that it begins quite directly, with scarcely any mention of the reaction of the listeners to the previous story or anything more than a passing reference to the rules of the storytelling game they are playing. Nor does the narrator supply a moralizing framework within which to place the narrative she is about to present.

3 Malpertugio was a commercial area of Naples near the port and the arsenal in which many foreign merchants, including those from Sicily, located their businesses. Not far away was the Bardi bank in which Boccaccio had worked when he was in Naples. Needless to say, the district also attracted prostitutes, thieves, and all sorts of riffraff.

4 The houses of Anjou and Aragon were struggling in the later Middle Ages for control of the kingdoms of Naples and Sicily. Charles I of Anjou, supported by the Papacy— thus making him a Guelf—took control of the two kingdoms in the 1260s. His harsh rule, however, led to an uprising against him in 1282 known as the Sicilian Vespers. The French and their Guelf supporters were expelled from the island, and in 1296, the Guelfs' opponents there, the Ghibellines, had Frederick II of Aragon proclaimed king of the island, over which he reigned until 1337. Boccaccio's story is set some time after the Treaty of Caltabellotta in 1302, by which Charles II of Anjou, then King of Naples, gave up all claims to Sicily after a series of unsuccessful attempts to restore the Angevins to power there. The lady's fictitious husband presumably took part in one of those attempts.

5 Greco is the name of a wine grape, originally from Greece, that is grown in southern Italy. Although there is a red variety, when people speak of "Greco," they usually mean the white wine, which is most likely what Andreuccio and the lady are drinking here.

6 The Ruga Catalana ("Catalan Street") was named for the numerous Catalan expatriates living there who were attached to the Angevin court. By turning left and going up this street, Andreuccio is heading away from the sea.

7 Boccaccio calls this character Scarabone Buttafuoco. His last name was—and is— common in Sicily; it means "throws fire," and hence, perhaps, could be translated as "Spitfire" or "Belchfire." His first name is probably a common noun, not a name. *Scarabuni* meant "thief" in Sicilian and may thus identify him as the leader, the "boss," of one of the gangs of criminals who terrorized Naples in the period (their modern successor is the Camorra, the Neapolitan equivalent of the Mafia). *Scarabone* also suggests *scarafuni*, which means "scrounger" and derives from *scarafaggio*, "cockroach."

8 There was an archbishop named Filippo Minutolo who had been an important figure in the Kingdom of Naples and who had died, not during the heat of the summer as Boccaccio's story suggests, but on October 24, 1301. His tomb can still be seen in the chapel of the Minutolo family in the Cathedral of Naples.

Day 2, Story 6

1   Although many parallels to the events in this story may be found in various saints'
    lives, in collections such as *The Thousand and One Nights*, and in popular romances,
    no single text can be claimed as its source. Moreover, the historical context evoked—
    the struggle among the Hohenstaufens, the Aragonese, and the Angevins for con-
    trol of the Kingdom of Sicily, which included all of southern Italy from Naples on
    down—plays only the most general role in the story, even though certain events in
    that struggle are relevant at particular junctures in the plot.

2   Frederick II (1194–1250), a Hohenstaufen, was King of Sicily from 1198 and Holy
    Roman Emperor from 1220. After his death, he was succeeded by his son Conrad
    IV (1228–54), following whose death a period of conflict ensued until Manfred (ca.
    1232–66), Frederick's illegitimate son, was crowned king in 1258 (he claimed the title
    of Holy Roman Emperor in 1263). As a Ghibelline, he was opposed by the Papacy,
    which supported the Guelf Party and which unsuccessfully offered the throne of
    Sicily to various rulers until Charles of Anjou accepted it in 1263. Charles invaded
    Italy two years later and defeated and killed Manfred on February 25, 1266, at the
    battle of Benevento. Both the Capece and the Caracciolo were prominent aristo-
    cratic families in Naples, and although there is no record of an Arrighetto Capece,
    a Corrado Capece was the governor-general of Sicily under Manfred. After the
    latter's death, Corrado led an uprising against the Angevin rulers of Sicily, but was
    captured and hanged. He had a wife whom various historical sources name Bianco-
    fiore or Beritola of the Caracciolo family, which was also firmly opposed to Angevin
    rule in Sicily. Boccaccio includes a Beritola of the Caracciolo-Carafa family in his
    early poem, the *Caccia di Diana* (*Diana's Hunt*), 1.23. Throughout the story, Beritola
    Capece is referred to as *madama*, the dialectal equivalent of *madonna*, or "my lady."

3   Lipari is about twenty-five miles north of Sicily. Ponza, mentioned in the next para-
    graph, is some seventy miles west of Naples. Contrary to what the narrator says, it
    was not uninhabited in Boccaccio's time.

4   Currado (Conrad) II Malaspina (d. 1294) was the Marquis of Villafranca and ruled
    over Lunigiana, a region that consisted of portions of Tuscany and Liguria in north-
    ern Italy. Currado was celebrated by Dante and others for his love of his family
    and his generosity (see *Purgatorio* 8.109–39). As Ghibellines, the Malaspina family
    would have welcomed fugitives such as Madama Beritola and her family who had
    been chased out of Sicily by the Angevins. The Kingdom of Apulia (or Puglia) was
    another name for the Kingdom of Naples.

5   The Doria family played an important role in the economic, military, and political
    life of Genoa from the twelfth century onward. There is no record of any of its mem-
    bers having the surname of Guasparrino (a Genoese dialectal variant of Gasparino,
    the diminutive form of "Gasparo," or Casper, the name of one the three Magi).

6   Boccaccio has invented a daughter for Currado, perhaps deriving her name, Spina,
    from the last two syllables of her family name, Malaspina. By contrast, her husband
    was a historical character: a certain Niccolò, a dependent of the Malaspina, lived in

the Val di Gragnano, the Valley of the Gragnano River (hence, Niccolò da Grignano, as Boccaccio spells the name of the river).

7　Boccaccio is alluding to the rebellion called the Sicilian Vespers. Its name derives from the fact that a riot, which broke out at the hour of vespers in the Church of the Holy Spirit outside of Palermo on Easter Monday, March 30, 1282, resulted in the killing of a band of French soldiers inside the church and led to the massacre of two thousand Frenchmen in Palermo itself. The rule of the Angevin King Charles I had been very unpopular in Sicily, and the rebellion, later called the War of the Sicilian Vespers, soon spread from Palermo to the rest of the island. Giovanni da Procida (1210–98) was a Ghibelline who had been with Manfred when he was defeated by Charles in 1266. Giovanni had fled the island and spent the next years attempting to drum up support to oust Charles until finally enlisting Peter III of Aragon (1239–85), who had married Manfred's heir. Peter was, in fact, attempting to foment a rebellion when the Sicilian Vespers occurred. Giovanni then came to the island, as did an Aragonese army later in 1282, and the war continued until a peace treaty was signed in 1295, followed by yet another in 1302, at which time Frederick III (1272–1337), Peter's son, was finally accepted as the island's king, thus beginning a long period of Spanish rule in Sicily. Note that the "fourteen years" referred to in the next paragraph would put Beritola's flight from Sicily in 1268; it should be sixteen years, since Manfred was defeated by Charles in 1266.

8　Boccaccio echoes a remark made by Peisistratos, whose wife was demanding capital punishment for a youth who had kissed their daughter in public, to which Peisistratos replied that if he put those who loved him to death, he did not know what he would do with those who hated him. This anecdote appears in Valerius Maximus, *Factorum et dictorum memorabilium libri IX* (*Nine Books of Memorable Deeds and Sayings*), 5.1.2, and was rehearsed throughout the Middle Ages, including by Dante in *Purgatorio* 15.94–105.

9　Giannotto and Spina are engaging in a type of marriage called *per verba de presenti* (or just *verba de presenti*), an extra-ecclesiastical practice or custom that involved the exchanging of vows, usually in front of a witness. The Church recognized such a marriage as valid, although it insisted, with only limited success, that the couple had to wait to consummate it until after a wedding ceremony in a church.

10　The opening of this sentence is a direct quotation of the first two lines of Canto 7 of Dante's *Purgatorio*, which recounts in elevated style how Dante's guide, the Roman poet Vergil, embraced the medieval Italian troubadour Sordello.

11　Lerici is a port in the Gulf of La Spezia not far from the mouth of the Magra River where travelers coming from Genoa or elsewhere usually disembarked before going on to the provinces of Tuscany and Emilia-Romagna.

Day 2, Story 7

1　Alatiel, the heroine of the story, actually sleeps with just eight men; the first ship's captain who seizes her is prevented by his wounds from taking her to bed. This story

has some general plot similarities to *The Tale of Anthia and Habrocomes*, a romance
by the third-century Greek writer Xenophon of Ephesus. There are also parallels
to stories in *The Thousand and One Nights*, to various versions of the Tristan story
in medieval romances, and at the most general level, to stories of wandering about
the Mediterranean, including those of Odysseus and Aeneas.

2 Boccaccio is quoting a line from Seneca that had become quasi-proverbial: *venenum
in auro bibitur* (*Thyestes* 453: "poison is drunk from a golden cup").

3 The Sultan's name is fictitious, although an Amminadab appears in the Bible as the
father of Nahshon, one of the followers of Moses (Numbers 1:7 and 7:12), and as one
of the ancestors of Christ (Matthew 1:4). His daughter's name, Alatiel, is likewise
fictitious, although it might be an anagram for "La Lieta," "The Happy One." The
different parts of her name are particularly suggestive: "ala" is the word for "wing"
and thus evokes the heroine's "flight" around the Mediterranean, while the ending of
the word, "tiel," points to the names of angels, such as Raphael and Michael, which
end in "el," the Hebrew word for "God," thus ironically underscoring the un-angelic
character of Alatiel's earthly experience.

4 In Boccaccio's time, the Kingdom of Algarve was an Islamic state that included
most of the Mediterranean coast of North Africa as well as a portion of the Iberian
Peninsula (the southernmost province of Portugal is still called by that name); *el
Gharb* was the Arabic name for "the West."

5 Pericone da Visalgo is a purely fictitious character. His first name is a diminutive
of the Catalan *Pere* (Peter); his last is the name of a castle in Majorca, a large island
off the east coast of Spain almost directly south of Barcelona and east of Valencia.

6 The notion that wine functions as "Venus's assistant" (or minister or companion)
has been a commonplace since antiquity and can be found in several of Boccaccio's
favorite classical authors, including Horace, *Odes* 3.18.6–7 and 3.21.21, and Apuleius,
Metamorphoses 2.11 and 2.15.

7 The Duke of Athens, like the Prince of Morea, is a fictional character. However,
Boccaccio had known a real Duke of Athens, Walter of Brienne, who had been made
the ruler of Florence in 1342–43. The Duchy of Athens, which included Attica and
Boeotia, was created in 1205 during the Fourth Crusade, when the territory was
taken from the Byzantine Empire. It was then held by a variety of European rulers
until it fell to the Turks in 1456.

8 The notions of love as a poison and as a snare or trap were commonplaces in the
courtly love tradition. For some examples of the former, see Petrarch, *Canzoniere*
(*Song Book*) 152.8 and 207.84; of the latter, see 55.15 and 165.5–8.

9 There was, in fact, a Constantine who was the son of the Byzantine emperor
Andronikos II (1259–1332, ruled 1282–1328) and whom Boccaccio may have known
about. However, the name, like Manuel, may simply be generic for Byzantine rulers.
Constantinople was the capital of the Byzantine Empire until it fell to the Turks in
1453 and was renamed Istanbul.

10 Aegina is the name of both a city and the island on which it is located. It is about
twenty miles southwest of Athens. Chios, mentioned in the next paragraph, is a
Greek island just off the coast of Turkey.

11 Smyrna, the modern Izmir, is a city on the east coast of Turkey not very far across the Aegean Sea from the island of Chios.

12 Osbech, or Uzbek (ruled ca. 1312–ca. 1342), was a Mongol who was the Khan of the Golden Horde in what is now southern Russia. He had good relations with both Christians and Muslims and encouraged the Black Sea trade of the Venetians and the Genoese. Boccaccio turns him into the King of the Turks and has him engage in a fictional struggle against the Byzantine Empire.

13 Like Osbech, Basano is a fictional character. By the early fourteenth century, Cappadocia, a province in Asia Minor, was not an independent state, but was ruled by the Turks. The name of Boccaccio's character may be a reflection of that of Baudon Bassian (in Italian, Baldon Bassano) who was the chamberlain of King Robert of Naples (ruled 1309–43). His Italian-sounding name might also be meant to suggest that he is a Christian.

14 Rhodes is an island strategically located off the southwest coast of Turkey, to the south of both Chios and Smyrna. Now a part of Greece, it was much disputed in the Middle Ages by the Byzantine Empire, the Arabs, the Genoese, and others, until it was captured by the Knights Hospitaller in 1309 who held it until it was taken by the Turks in 1522.

15 Currently an independent republic, Cyprus is a large island south of Turkey and west of Syria and Lebanon that was part of the Byzantine Empire until it was conquered by crusaders in 1191 and ruled by various Europeans states until it was annexed by Venice in 1489 and eventually fell to the Turks in 1570.

16 Paphos was a major center on Cyprus for the worship of Aphrodite in classical times. The Greek goddess of love was said to have been engendered in the Mediterranean Sea when the god Chronos cut off Uranus's testicles and threw them into the water. Some versions of the myth have Aphrodite coming ashore at Paphos; others, on the island of Cythera.

17 Antigono's name, like Antioco's, is generic and is meant to evoke the Hellenistic eastern Mediterranean. His full name is Antigono di Famagosto, which means that he is from the town of Famagosto, which, like Paphos, is located on Cyprus. Although the King of Cyprus is not identified by name, the island was, in fact, a kingdom. It had been part of the Byzantine Empire until 1192, when it became an independent state ruled by the crusader Guy de Lusignan. During the period in which Boccaccio sets his story, the early fourteenth century, the relevant kings would have been Henry II of Jerusalem (ruled 1310–24) and Hugh IV (ruled 1324–59).

18 Aigues-Mortes, a walled city on the coast of Provence to the east of Montpellier, had a flourishing commerce with Florence and Genoa. Its name means literally "Dead [i.e., stagnant] Waters," referring to the marshes on which the city was built. The name suggests a contrast with the literal and sexual storms of Alatiel's Mediterranean odyssey.

19 Although Alatiel's saint seems her, or Antigono's, clever invention, there was, in fact, a sanctuary dedicated to San Cresci in Valcava ("Saint Grows-in-the-Deep-Valley") that was located in Mugello, a river valley about fifteen miles north of Florence. "Cresci" is short for Crescenzio, or, to use his more usual Latin name, Crescentius,

an eleven-year-old Christian martyr who was brought to Rome during the persecutions of Diocletian in the early fourth century, CE, and was tortured and beheaded after he refused to deny Christ. The appellation "Valcava," which I have translated as "Deep Valley," really means something like "the valley of the mine," most likely because a mine of some sort was located in the Mugello valley.

20 Boccaccio's story is the first recorded instance of this Italian saying: *Bocca basciata non perde ventura, anzi rinnova come fa la luna*. It is composed of two clauses, each of which is a perfect hendecasyllabic line (the standard Italian verse line in Petrarchan sonnets and the *Divine Comedy*), and the two clauses are also almost rhymed (*ventura* and *la luna*). What I have translated as "charm" (*ventura*) means, literally, "adventure" or "luck," which is the central theme of the story. The saying has a romantic quality that Verdi famously brings out by means of his wonderful musical setting of the words when they are sung by the young lovers in *Falstaff*, his last opera. Boccaccio's story is, of course, anything but romantic—it is, indeed, a satire of romance—and the saying is, instead, witty and ironic.

Day 2, Story 8

1 The initial plot element in this story, the false accusation of a spurned woman, is widespread in world literature: it can be found in various Eastern collections, such as *The Thousand and One Nights* as well as in the myth of Phaedra and the story of Joseph and Potiphar's wife in the Bible (Genesis 39). Boccaccio probably also knew about Pierre de la Brosse, a surgeon at the court of Philip III of France, who was executed for treason in 1278 after having been accused of attempted rape by the queen, Mary of Brabant. Dante alludes to Pierre in a passage of *Purgatorio* (6.19–24), and his story was told at length by various commentators on the passage. The story of the love between Giannetta and Giachetto, which appears later in this tale, may be modeled on that of Antiochus I of Babylonia and Stratonice, which is recounted by Plutarch in his *Life of Demetrius* (38) and in Valerius Maximus, *Factorum et dictorum memorabilium libri IX* (*Nine Books of Memorable Deeds and Sayings*), 5.7. Note that the rubric, or title, to the story has the Count going to Scotland; in the story itself, it is clear that he goes to Ireland.

2 The Roman Empire had been re-created in 799 as the Holy Roman Empire, and Charlemagne was crowned the first Holy Roman Emperor the following year. Then, in 962 it was transferred from France to Germany when Otto I of Saxony was crowned Emperor in Rome. When Boccaccio speaks of the power of the Empire being "transferred" (*transportato*) from one country to the other, his verb echoes the medieval notion of *translatio imperii* (transfer of rule), which saw world history as a linear movement from the Roman Empire to its successor under Charlemagne. Although Boccaccio thus inserts his story into history, many of the specific events he recounts, such as the war launched by the French King's son after his coronation, have no historical basis.

3 Boccaccio is echoing the notion of courtly love, codified in a treatise such as Andreas Capellanus's *De amore* (*On Love*), which presents it as something more suited to the

upper classes than the lower (although Boccaccio does see the latter as experiencing some form of love, as Masetto the peasant does in 3.1).

4 It was customary to tear down the houses belonging to traitors.

5 Violante was the name of one of Boccaccio's children who died at the age of six or seven in 1355. The new names given to the children are Italianized versions of French names: Perotto from Pierrot ("Little Peter") and Giannetta from Jeanette ("Little Jean"). Boccaccio would have encountered the first name frequently at the Angevin court of Naples, while Giannetta was a name he used for his mother (see, for instance, *Il Filocolo* 5.8), and he jokingly called himself Giannetto in a letter to a friend. The "French tramps" mentioned in the next sentence is probably an allusion to friars belonging to the Dominican Order that had been founded in France in the thirteenth century and had established itself in Italy by the time Boccaccio was writing.

6 Strangford Lough is an inlet on the Irish Sea in Ulster. It was a frequent point of entry into Ireland during the Middle Ages.

7 When Giannetta refers to herself as a "maiden," she uses the word *damigella*, a Gallicism (from *demoiselle*) meaning "damsel," which also contributes to the French atmosphere of the story.

8 The Count is referred to both in this sentence and in subsequent ones as a *prod'uomo*, a word that I have consistently translated as "worthy man." The term is actually an Italianization of the French *prod'homme* or *prud'homme*, which meant "valiant [*preux*] man," but also "man of discretion" because of the connection between *prud-* and *prudent*. Thus, a more accurate, though wordy, translation would be "man of valor and discretion." Boccaccio's use of an Italianized French term is clearly meant to contribute to the French atmosphere of the tale, which is also suggested by other words, such as the use of *madama* (Fr. *madame*) for the more standard Italian *madonna*.

9 The text mistakenly has the King lavishing honors on Giachetto here.

Day 2, Story 9

1 There are many medieval and Renaissance stories in various languages in which a husband makes a wager on his wife's fidelity. Boccaccio has replaced the kings and noblemen, who were the subjects of the stories preceding this one, with merchants from Genoa and Florence. This replacement is a testimony not just to his actual acquaintance with Italian merchants in Paris (and elsewhere), but to his celebration throughout the *Decameron* of the *ingegno* of his heroes and heroines. *Ingegno* is the kind of practical intelligence, wit, or cleverness that may be found in people of all kinds, but is a major requirement in those who are engaged in commerce. Boccaccio's story influenced other stories in its turn and eventually found its way to England, to become one of the plot strands in Shakespeare's late romance *Cymbeline*.

2 I have rendered Boccaccio's Italian proverb (*lo 'ngannatore rimane a piè dello 'ngannato*) as closely as I can. Unfortunately, it has no exact equivalent in English. There is a large group of folktales, including many from the Middle Ages, that involve a

trickster who is eventually fooled and defeated by his dupe. They are sometimes called "biter-bit" tales, using a slightly archaic expression ("biter" once meant "trickster" or "deceiver"), which nicely captures the inversion implied by Boccaccio's proverb. The Italian proverb can also be found in Sacchetti, *Trecentonovelle* (*Three Hundred Stories*) 198.

3 A number of rich merchants and noblemen from Liguria, the province in which Genoa is located, shared the family name of Lomellin. Boccaccio was familiar with merchant circles in Paris, and the rivalry between Florentine and Genoese merchants there was well known. Ambruogiuolo, who will appear a little later in the story, comes from Piacenza, a city in the region known as Emilia-Romagna in north-central Italy. Merchants from that city were also quite active in France during the late Middle Ages.

4 Ambruogiuolo's sententious remark echoes a famous line in Ovid's *Amores* (*Loves*): *casta est quam nemo rogavit* (1.8.43: "she is chaste whom no one has propositioned").

5 This is the first time the story supplies the name of Bernabò's wife. Zinevra is Genoese for the more standard Italian Ginevra, a fairly common name in the Middle Ages because of the fame of Saint Geneviève, who lived in Paris during the fifth century and was celebrated for her austerity and piety. She is credited with having saved the city from destruction by the Huns under Attila in 451 and for passing through enemy lines to bring food to the city when it was under siege in 464. In the story, Zinevra clearly shares a number of the virtues of her namesake, including her virtue and her energy.

6 Women disguising themselves as men was a common motif in the folklore and literature of the Middle Ages and Renaissance.

7 Segner En Cararh is a typical Catalan name: "Segner" is an honorific coming from the archaic Catalan "senyer," equivalent to the Spanish "Señor"; and "En" is the equivalent of the Spanish "Don" (from Lat. *dominus*, "lord"). In the fourteenth and fifteenth centuries, the Catalans were often allies of the Genoese against the Venetians. Alba, the name of the town where the Catalan captain has gone for water, may be either the modern Albisola or Albenga, both of which are on the Ligurian coast not far from Genoa, but also not far from the town of Finale, from which Zinevra takes her new last name.

8 At this point in the narrative, once Madonna Zinevra has disguised herself as a man, Boccaccio's pronouns referring to her change their gender from feminine to masculine (with one exception later on). They change back again near the end of the story when she finally reveals herself in public to be a woman. In translating the text, I have respected the specific gender of each reference to her.

9 Acre was a fortified coastal city in Syria (now in Israel) that was held for the most part by various crusaders from 1104 until it fell to the Arabs in 1291, marking the end of the crusaders' presence in the Holy Land. Its fall, widely lamented in Europe, did not prevent the city from being a trading center between the Christian West and the Muslim East. Boccaccio's story thus takes place some time after 1291.

10 Boccaccio briefly reverts to using the feminine pronoun for Madonna Zinevra at the start of this paragraph, perhaps because he is dealing with her inner thoughts

and feelings rather than her actions and the impressions she makes on others in her role as Sicurano. By the end of the paragraph, the masculine pronoun has displaced the feminine one.

Day 2, Story 10

1 This story of a May–December marriage has so many antecedents in world literature that identifying any one of them as its source would be a mistake. There was a quarter in Pisa called Chinzica, but there is no record of a Ricciardo ever having lived there. His wife comes from the Gualandi family, which was well established in the city, but there is, likewise, no record of a Bartolomea among its members.

2 The ugliness of Pisan women was proverbial among Florentines. In the Italian, Dioneo speaks of *lucertole verminare* ("wormlike lizards"), an expression that is Neapolitan in origin and refers to a small greenish lizard found in the Campagna.

3 Vernaccia wine is a white wine made from a varietal of the same name that is grown throughout Italy. The name derives from a word meaning "vernacular," i.e., "local." Nowadays, when people say Vernaccia, they are usually referring to the Tuscan white wine, Vernaccia di San Gimignano, but in Boccaccio's time that was not necessarily the case.

4 Ravenna was famous for having almost as many churches as there are days of the year, thus making practically every day a saint's day. Calendars made there would have been attractive to schoolboys because they contained nothing but holidays.

5 Ember Days is the English name (Lat. *quater tempora*) for the periods of fasting to be observed in the four seasons of the year, specifically on the Wednesday, Friday, and Saturday following four specific holy days: the first Sunday in Lent; Whitsunday or Pentecost; Holy Cross Day (September 14); and St. Lucia's Day (December 13). They are also referred to as Ember Weeks.

6 Monte Nero is a promontory located some twenty miles south of Pisa.

7 Although he is called Paganino da Monaco (Paganino of Monaco) in the rubric that serves as the title for the story, here Boccaccio supplies his family name *da Mare*, which was that of a well-known noble family in Genoa. There are no historical records concerning this figure, although there are many instances of members of important Italian families becoming pirates or bandits in the late Middle Ages. Boccaccio features such figures in 2.4 (Landolfo Rufolo), 2.6 (Guasparrino Doria), and 10.2 (Ghino di Tacco). The Monaco from which Paganino hails was a notorious haven for pirates at the time.

8 Boccaccio writes *essendo a lui il calendaro caduto da cintola*, which I have translated as "he had lost his calendar." More literally, the phrase means that the calendar had fallen off his belt, which is apparently where people would carry it.

9 After being sheared, raw wool had to be cleaned, a process that involved washing it and then beating it. Boccaccio clearly uses beating, or "whacking," wool as a metaphor for sexual intercourse here.

10 The lady's sexual wordplay in this sentence is brilliant. First, she replaces Ricciardo's *in peccato mortale* ("in mortal sin") with *in peccato mortaio* ("in mortar sin"). Then,

as she looks to her future with Paganino, she transforms the phrase even more cleverly into *imbeccato pestello*, which I have translated as a matter of living "with the *pestle's-in*," a pun on "*pestle sin*." More literally, the phrase means a "pestle [that has been] put in a [baby bird's] mouth [to feed it]." Boccaccio will later see mortar and pestle in such sexualized terms in his Introduction to Day 4, in 8.2, and in the Author's Conclusion.

11 Another untranslatable set of plays on words. The first of the phrases is: *di farla in tre pace*. This contains a play on the expression *fare patta*, meaning "to finish a card game in a stalemate," and thus, "to accomplish nothing." The entire phrase would mean something like "to accomplish nothing three times in a row." But there's also a play on *patta* and *pace* ("peace"), suggesting that the matches were not all that energetic. The second phrase *rizzare a mazzata* means "to straighten [something] by dint of blows [as with a *mazza*, a mace]." However, the phrase can also refer to lifting up a fishing rod to see if any fish are dangling there. I can see no way to work this second meaning into my translation. Note that in her next sentence the lady will refer mockingly to Ricciardo as a *pro' cavaliere*. I have rendered this as "sturdy rider" to bring out the latent sexual meaning, but it meant something more like "valiant or worthy knight," a phrase suggesting that *rizzare a mazzata* may be less about fishing than about wielding a mace, as knights were wont to do.

12 Dioneo's phrase here is *non montavano un frullo*, which could be rendered: "[his words] did not amount to anything," i.e., they made no difference. However, a *frullo* is a bone that has been hollowed out and tied to a cord, and that when whirled in the air makes a sound like the sound of the word itself. *Frullo* was also used for the sound certain birds make when they take off in flight.

13 Boccaccio's original reads: *Il mal furo non vuol festa*. The word I have translated as "hole," *furo*, is a parody of the Pisan pronunciation of *foro*. Although *foro* means "hole," it could also mean "the bar" or "the law courts," a meaning that is ironic in context, since Messer Ricciardo is, after all, a judge. However, the word Boccaccio actually supplies, *furo*, also suggests "thief" (Lat. *fur*), a meaning that likewise seems to fit the context, since Ricciardo's wife has been stolen from him. In fact, the "evil thief" could be the lady herself as well as Paganino since she prefers to remain "stolen."

14 Referring to the dispute at the start of 2.9 between Bernabò and Ambruogiuolo concerning the chastity of Bernabò's wife, Dioneo uses an Italian saying that is untranslatable in any direct way: *Bernabò ... cavalcasse la capra inverso il chino* (lit.: "Bernabò ... was riding a she goat down a slope [or toward a precipice]"). The Italian saying *cavalcare la capra* (lit., "to ride a she goat") means to do something stupid, deceive oneself, get things all wrong. Dioneo develops the saying by having the rider go *inverso il chino* ("down the slope" or "toward the precipice"). His having Bernabò ride a she goat rather than a horse is also in keeping with his conception of women (and men) as driven by their sexual appetites, since goats were well known for their randiness.

Day 2, Conclusion

1 The younger women in the company—Filomena, Neifile, and Emilia—frequently blush as a sign of their modesty and innocence. Sparkling or glittering eyes were an attribute of Dante's Beatrice (see, for example, *Purgatorio* 12.89–90), but they were also a cliché in courtly love and popular poetry more generally, as was the association of women's faces with roses. The "morning star" is Venus.

2 Both Fridays and Saturdays were days for fasting. Note that the Sabbath was celebrated in Florence between noon on Saturday and noon on Sunday.

3 Neifile's topic focuses on the *industria* displayed by people in getting what they want. I have translated that key word as "resourcefulness," but it actually has a range of meanings from industriousness and hard work at one extreme, through resourcefulness and inventiveness, down to cleverness and trickiness at the other.

4 Pampinea's song reflects her general serenity and happiness. Its motifs can be traced back to Petrarch's *Canzoniere* (*Song Book*). For examples, see poems 14, 26, 59, and 70.

Day 3, Introduction

1 This new palace is very much like the first one the company stayed in, the only exception being the walled garden next to it that is accorded an elaborate description that evokes the Garden of Eden. Halfway to the hour of tierce would make it in between sunrise and midmorning. On the canonical hours, see Headnote 2.

2 Boccaccio's narrator says that the members of the company considered the owner of the palace to be *magnifico*. Although that word started being used as a substantive in the fifteenth century to mean a great and noble person (Lorenzo de' Medici was known as *il Magnifico*), when Boccaccio was writing it was an adjective that meant someone endowed with greatness, nobility, and especially, generosity or liberality. In the Aristotelian tradition, it was one of the defining features of aristocrats and referred to a liberality of expenditure combined with good taste. That Boccaccio is thinking of just such an aristocratic sense of the word is evident in his use of *signore* ("lord") when speaking of the owner of the palace.

Day 3, Story 1

1 There are antecedents for this story in the *Novellino* (62) as well as, more generally, in the *fabliau* tradition.

2 Lamporecchio is a small village near Pistoia to the north of Florence.

3 Nuto's oath in this sentence ("unless God gives...") is *il faccia Idio san delle reni*, which means literally, "May God make him sound in his loins." It may reflect the fact that the Bible frequently connects God with the loins (see Psalms 16:7, 26:2 and 73:21).

Day 3, Story 2

1 Although there are many antecedents for the groom's cleverness and the King's prudence in tale collections that appeared before the *Decameron*, no particular story can be identified as the source for this one.

2 Agilulf, who had been the Duke of Turin, ruled over the Lombards from 590, the year in which he married Theodolinda, the widow of King Authari, until his death in 616. The Lombards had taken Pavia in 572 and controlled most of Italy north of the Po River. Boccaccio's source for this historical information is the third book of the eighth-century *Historia Longobardorum* (*History of the Lombards*) of Paulus Diaconus. This work was also a source for Boccaccio's description of the plague in the Introduction to the first day.

3 According to the conventions of courtly love, even though the lover is rejected or ignored by his beloved, the very fact that he loves such a worthy object serves to ennoble him.

Day 3, Story 3

1 There is no source for this story.

2 After Saint Gregory the Great celebrated thirty Masses for the soul of the monk Justus in 590, the "Gregorian Thirty," as they were called, would be offered on thirty consecutive days for a specific soul in Purgatory, after which that soul would be released into Heaven. The "forty" in the text may either be Boccaccio's mistake or the lady's exaggeration.

3 They are making comments here at the expense of the lady's husband.

Day 3, Story 4

1 There is no source for this story, which was also told by Chaucer, in a very different way, in *The Miller's Tale* and by Giovanni Sercambi in *Il novelliere* (111 and 117). The figure of the gullible religious devotee appears frequently in the *Decameron*; see, for instance, 3.3 and 7.1. "Dom" was a title (from Lat. *dominus*, "lord") given to monks who had earned some sort of distinction, such as, in this case, having completed theological studies at the prestigious University of Paris. Felice means "happy, fortunate." Puccio is a pet name; it derives from Giacopuccio and means "Jimmy."

2 San Pancrazio is a church in the center of Florence not far from Santa Maria Novella. Tertiaries (from Lat. *tertius*, "third") were lay members of the "third order" of the Franciscans (after the Friars Minor and the Poor Clares); they did not have to follow all the rules of the order or live in the monastery, but took simple vows and were allowed to wear the habit.

3 The Flagellants were organized bands of the devout who whipped themselves in public. They started appearing in the twelfth century and became quite numerous after the outbreak of the plague in 1348.

4 Casole: a town in the Val d'Elsa some seventeen miles to the west of Siena.

5 "Frate Nastagio" (Anastasius) here is probably meant as a generic name for preachers, since there is no collection of sermons attributed to such a person. There were many versions of the Lament of Mary Magdalene circulating in late medieval culture.

6 Both Saints Benedict and Giovanni Gualberto were frequently depicted in the Middle Ages as riding on an ass. The image here is, of course, sexual in nature.

Day 3, Story 5

1 There is no source for this story. The Vergellesi, or Vergiolesi, was a prominent family in Pistoia, and one of its members, named Francesco, was sent on a political mission to France in 1313 and became a *podestà* in Lombardy in 1326.

2 When Zima speaks, he uses the conventional, hyperbolic language of courtly love, thus demonstrating that his linguistic skill is as refined as his taste in clothing and personal adornment.

Day 3, Story 6

1 There are many precedents for this kind of story in Eastern collections. Ricciardo Minutolo came from an important family in Naples, one of whose members, an archbishop named Filippo Minutolo, who died in 1301, is mentioned in 2.5. There was a Filippo (Filippello is the diminutive) Sighinolfi who held various administrative positions under Queen Giovanna I of Naples (b. 1328, ruled 1344–82); Boccaccio was on friendly terms with the family. Catella, the name of Filippello's wife, is an endearing form of Caterina. The baths were notorious as places where lovers met for trysts and prostitution was regularly carried on.

2 Since the woman who manages the baths is essentially arranging romantic trysts and illicit sexual liaisons, the narrator's references to her as "the good woman" are obviously ironic. The Minutolo family actually owned a bathhouse in Naples in the early thirteenth century, which may explain why the next sentence says that the good woman was very much in Ricciardo's debt.

3 Ricciardo's arguments here are the same ones that Tarquin used after raping the Roman matron Lucretia; Boccaccio rehearses them in his *De mulieribus claris* (*On Famous Women*), 48, and could have found them in Livy, *Ab urbe condita* (*From the Founding of the City*), 1.58, and Valerius Maximus, *Factorum et dictorum memorabilium libri IX* (*Nine Books of Memorable Deeds and Sayings*), 6.1.

Day 3, Story 7

1 There is no source for this story.

2 The two families of the Elisei and the Palermini were among the oldest and most prominent in Florence. There were no Tedaldos, Aldobrandinos, or Ermellinas in either of them, however, although those first names were rather common in the city.

3 Ancona is a seaport on the Adriatic somewhat more than a hundred miles to the east and slightly south of Florence. Not far away there is a town called San Lodeccio

(or Saludeccio), which explains the name Tedaldo assumes when he arrives in Ancona.

4 Tedaldo's statement about converting her tears into laughter inverts biblical notions in both the Old and New Testaments emphasizing how laughter will—and should—be turned into sadness; see Proverbs 14:13 and James 4:9. But at the same time, Tedaldo is also bringing the lady a secular version of the "good news" Christ brings to humanity in the New Testament.

5 Satan was frequently depicted as eating sinners in medieval art, such as in the Baptistery in Florence. Dante's three-headed Satan has three mouths with which he chews for eternity on those whom Dante saw as the ultimate betrayers: Judas, Brutus, and Cassius.

6 The closest parallel to this quotation in the Bible is Acts 1:1: *coepit Jesus facere et docere* ("Jesus began both to do and teach"). For more general parallels, see Matthew 4:23, Mark 1:21, and Luke 4:18.

7 Tedaldo's distinction here between lust, on the one hand, and robbery and murder, on the other, follows the usual Aristotelian and Thomistic distinction, which Dante also uses in the *Inferno*, namely that between sins of incontinence, such as lust and gluttony, which involve defective appetite, and those of violence, such as murder, which involve a perverted will (i.e., malice).

8 Compare this attack on the gluttony of friars to that at the end of 1.6.

9 Faziuolo is the diminutive of Bonifazio (Boniface). His full name identifies him as coming from Pontremoli, which is in Lunigiana, the northernmost part of Tuscany.

Day 3, Story 8

1 This story has, at best, vague antecedents in French *fabliaux* and tales from the East.

2 Penitents typically kneeled at the feet of their confessors; the confessional booth was only introduced after the Council of Trent met to reform the Catholic Church (1545–63).

3 The Old Man of the Mountain was Rashid ad-Din As-sinan (d. 1192), leader of the Syrian branch of a Shiite sect known as the Assassins that was active between the eleventh and thirteenth centuries. He got his name from the fact that his stronghold was a fortress at Masyaf in the mountains of northern Syria. His followers were called Assassins (Hashishim) from the hashish they smoked, which induced visions before they were sent off to murder their enemies. In his *Il milione* (*The Million*, known in English as *The Travels of Marco Polo*), from the late thirteenth century, Marco Polo described how the Old Man of the Mountain supposedly had a beautiful garden in the mountains that he identified as Paradise. He attracted a following of young people, would put them into a deep sleep, and have them transported there, after which he had them consume a drug before sending them off on their murderous enterprises. Boccaccio actually transcribed this passage from *Il milione* in his notebooks and wrote in the margin *il veglio della montagna* ("The Old Man of the Mountain").

4 The "Ark-Ranger Bagriel" (*Ragnolo Braghiello* in Italian) is Ferondo's corruption of either "Archangel" or "Angel Gabriel" (*Arcagnolo* or *Agnolo Gabriele*), revealing a verbal deficiency he shares with other dupes in the *Decameron*. His linguistic confusion is especially funny in the original, since he is conflating the high with the low, the word for archangel or angel with that for spider (*ragno*), and the name Gabriel with the word for breeches (*le brache*) to which a diminutive ending has been added.

Day 3, Story 9

1 The bed trick, which is central to Boccaccio's plot, was a widely diffused motif in both Eastern and Western story collections during the Middle Ages. Shakespeare's *All's Well That Ends Well* is based on this tale, which he may have read in Antoine de Maçon's French version of the *Decameron* of 1545 or in William Painter's translation, in his *Palace of Pleasure*, of 1575. All the characters in the story appear to be fictitious. The names Beltramo (Bertram) and Giletta (the Italianized form of the French Gillette, itself the feminine form of Gilles) were widely diffused in the Middle Ages.

2 Roussillon, whose capital city is Perpignan, is a region in southwestern France bordered by the Mediterranean to the east, the Pyrenees to the south, and Andorra to the west; in the late Middle Ages it was part of Aragon and was controlled by the rulers of Catalonia. Narbonne was a port town on the Mediterranean to the east of Roussillon, some thirty-five miles from Perpignan.

3 A fistula is an abnormal connection between an organ or a blood vessel and some other part of the body; it is often caused by surgery as well as infection and inflammation.

4 Montpellier was an important trading center in the late Middle Ages and had a famous medical school. It lies approximately halfway between Italy and Spain and is about six miles from the Mediterranean and sixty miles from Roussillon.

Day 3, Story 10

1 There are only the vaguest of antecedents for this story. Throughout history there were a number of holy men named Rustico who were known for their continence, including several saints, the most famous of whom was probably Saint Rustico of Narbonne (d. 461). Rustico's name was probably meant to recall such figures, but it is clearly ironic in the story and was most likely chosen because of its "meaning": Rustico is a "rustic," a rube, who badly overestimates his ability to satisfy Alibech. The latter's name is equally suggestive. It is meant to sound Arabic: the name Ali was well known in western Europe during the Middle Ages as being that of Mohammad's follower who founded the Shiite branch of Islam (see Dante, *Inferno* 31–33). However, "Ali" could also suggest the idea of nourishment (*alimentare* means "to feed"), and "bech" might evoke the idea of eating (*beccare* means "to peck at [like a bird]"). These meanings of Alibech's name may be relevant at the climax of the

story when the exhausted Rustico can no longer handle his all-too-willing pupil, and the narrator makes a joke about a bean and a lion's mouth.

2   This last phrase also occurs in Apuleius, *Metamorphoses* (2.7), where it has a similar sexual meaning.

Day 3, Conclusion

1   Neifile's last phrase is, in Italian, *l'ossa senza maestro avrebbono apparato a sufolare*, which could be rendered more literally as: "your bones, without a teacher, would have learned how to whistle." The essence of her gibe is that Filostrato, like Masetto with the nuns, would have been so worn out from having served the "sheep" sexually that he would have been reduced to nothing but hollowed-out bones emptied of their marrow. That they would be making a whistling sound allows for two different interpretations. One is that the men would be reduced to a heap of hollow bones that had been turned into flute- or pipe-like instruments through which the wind could whistle. This meaning derives from the fact that *sufolare* (*zufolare* in modern Italian) means not just to whistle, but to play an instrument, such as a pipe or a flute, a *zufolo*, that makes a whistling sound. Another possible interpretation has Neifile compounding her insult by implying that Filostrato would be reduced to a skeleton hanging on a gibbet, the fate usually meted out to lower-class criminals, through which the wind would whistle as it blows.

2   The song of Messer Guiglielmo and the Lady of Vergiù was evidently an Italian version of the fourteenth-century French poem *La Chastelaine de Vergi* ("The Mistress of the Garden").

3   Lauretta's phrase here, *lassa innamorata* ("cast down, tired out, or exhausted by Love"), seems intended to echo the meaning of Filostrato's name ("cast down, or overcome, by Love"). The third line of the song is based on the last line of Dante's *Commedia*, which describes God as *L'amor che move il sole e l'altre stelle* (*Paradiso* 33.145: "The love that moves the sun and the other stars").

4   Lauretta's melancholy song anticipates the sad tales that will be told on Day 4. Critics have attempted to link it to Boccaccio's own life and to allegorize it in various ways, but with little success.

5   The reference to the setting of the stars indicates that the group has stayed up past midnight.

Day 4, Introduction

1   Boccaccio's image of a fierce wind striking the tops of trees is taken from Dante, *Paradiso* (17.133–34). In what follows, Boccaccio will defend the artistic value of the low genre of vernacular prose. He will also deal with potential critics of the perspectives and themes he adopts in his works, anticipating their objections and responding to them one by one. It is possible that the thirty stories of the first three days of the *Decameron* were already in circulation at this point, but there is no hard evidence that that was the case.

2 Boccaccio's reference to his work as being *senza titolo*, "without a title," is clarified by what he wrote in his commentary on Dante, in which he says that Ovid's love lyrics, his *Amores* (*Loves*), were often dubbed *Sine titulo* (*Without Title*), because of the diversity of the work's contents. A similar statement might be made about the *Decameron*, which offers many different kinds of stories. Note that Boccaccio's claim about his humble and low style is an example of false modesty; he is extremely capable of manipulating many different stylistic registers in his work.

3 Boccaccio is citing Valerius Maximus, *Factorum et dictorum memorabilium libri IX* (*Nine Books of Memorable Deeds and Sayings*), 4.7.2: *sola miseria caret invidia*.

4 The partial tale that Boccaccio recounts here has antecedents in the Indian epic the *Ramayana*, as well as in *Barlaam and Josaphat*, a Christianized version of the life of the Buddha that came to the West through a variety of intermediaries. The story was widely diffused thanks to translations of this last work, and it appeared in the *Novellino* (14), among other texts. Note that several members of the Balducci family were employed by the Florentine banking firm of the Bardi, for which Boccaccio's father also worked.

5 This image of the leek also appears in 1.10.

6 Guido Cavalcanti (ca. 1259–1300), Dante Alighieri (1265–1321), and Cino da Pistoia (ca. 1265–1336) were the three greatest practitioners of the *Dolce Stil Novo* ("Sweet New Style"), a type of courtly love lyric celebrating women's beauty and linking it to philosophical truths. Guido appears in the *Decameron* as the protagonist of 6.9, and Dante is a constant, though implicit, presence in Boccaccio's work. Cino was a lawyer as well as a poet, and Boccaccio apparently attended his lectures on law in Naples.

7 The Apostle is Paul. See his letter to the Philippians 4:12: *Scio et humiliari et abundare ubique et in omnibus institutus sum et satiari et esurire et abundare et penuriam pati* ("I know both how to be abased, and I know how to abound: everywhere and in all things I am instructed both to be full and to be hungry, both to abound and to suffer need").

8 Boccaccio's "warmth" may be referring to the "heat" of love and passion, or to some warm feeling of sympathy his critics might have for his work.

Day 4, Story 1

1 Although there is no specific source for this story, one of the most popular in the *Decameron*, a poisoned chalice does appear in a love story in Paulus Diaconus's *Historia Longobardorum* (*History of the Lombards*), 2.28, as well as in the French *Roman du Châtelain de Couci* (*The Romance of the Lord of the Castle of Couci*). The characters in Boccaccio's story are not historical, but their names are those of various Norman princes, who did, in fact, control Salerno, although none of its rulers was named Tancredi in the period before Boccaccio wrote his story.

2 Note that this is Guiscardo's only speech in the story. His words may be seen as echoing Vergil's in the tenth eclogue (69: *Omnia vincit Amor*: "Love conquers all") and perhaps those of the tragic lover Francesca in Dante's *Inferno*: *Amor, che a nessun*

amato amar perdona (5.103: "Love, that does not pardon someone who is loved for not loving").

3 Ghismunda is addressing Guiscardo's heart, and it was a common belief in Boccaccio's time that the soul of an individual was lodged in that organ.

Day 4, Story 2

1 Boccaccio was familiar with several versions of this story that were circulating in the Middle Ages. They are all traceable back to Greek antiquity to such works as Chariton of Aphrodisias's romance *Chaereas and Callirhoe*, the *Romance of Alexander* of the Pseudo-Callisthenes, and the story of Mundus and Paulina in Flavius Josephus's *Antiquities of the Jews* (18.7).

2 According to the rule of their order, the lives of the Franciscans were to be modeled on that of their founder, Saint Francis of Assisi. They were to wander from town to town, preaching and aiding the poor and the sick, while living in poverty themselves and avoiding any contact with money. On the basis of topographical references in the story, one may imagine that the protagonist joins the convent of Franciscans that was attached to the Venetian Church of Santa Maria Gloriosa dei Frari that is located to the south of the Grand Canal and the Rialto bridge.

3 What I have translated as one of the "most authoritative churchmen" in Venice appears in Boccaccio's Italian as one of the greater *cassesi*. This word comes from Arabic and appears in Turkish as well, and in the sixteenth century it was used to denote a particularly important Christian priest. The fact that Boccaccio employs it here suggests that it had already gained some currency by the fourteenth century, and perhaps especially in Venice, which had substantial communities of Middle Eastern traders. If so, then Boccaccio is using it for the sake of providing something like local color.

4 No historical figure has been found with whom Frate Alberto may be identified. His name, Berto (short for Alberto) della Massa, suggests he may be imagined as having come from Massa Lombarda, a town close to Imola, which lies to the southeast of Bologna in the province of Emilia-Romagna.

5 Boccaccio gives vent to anti-Venetian sentiments here and throughout this story. He may have been motivated by the fact that Venice was a great political and commercial rival to Florence in the fourteenth century (as it would continue to be for the next two hundred years).

6 Madonna Lisetta's name is given in the Venetian fashion: she is Lisetta (short for Elisabetta, "Elizabeth") from the House ("Ca'") of the Quirini (or, more usually, Querini), an important family in the city. In the late Middle Ages, there were many women in that family whose first names were variants on Elisabetta. The reference to "lover" in the next sentence is my translation of *amadore*, the variant that Boccaccio uses for *amatore* (lover) and whose spelling is intended to suggest Venetian dialect.

7 Boccaccio's word for "good friend" here is *comare*. Technically, this means godmother, but it often simply designated a close female friend, a neighbor, and a gossip, as it does here.

8   The Maremma was a sparsely populated, marshy, desolate, inhospitable area in the southwestern part of Tuscany. Madonna Lisetta's reference to it as being something on a par with the world suggests, again, the limits of her knowledge and intelligence.

9   The Rialto was one of the business centers of Venice where the only bridge spanning the Grand Canal was located. It was on the opposite side of the canal from Lisetta's house.

10 Although it is not clear which festival is occurring here, the activities associated with it in the story were shared with many festivals throughout the year, and especially with carnival. Among those activities were dressing people up as wild animals or wild men and staging a hunt, which typically involved tying a boar up with a chain and then setting dogs on it, dogs like the two Frate Alberto will be leading. The dogs were normally chained as well. In the story, Frate Alberto himself becomes a version of the chained animal, and he is physically and symbolically punished by the crowd for his mockery of religion and his violation of marriage. Festival times were often used by the populace of towns and cities to visit such unofficial justice on those who broke the largely unwritten rules of the community.

11 Frate Alberto is being dressed as a wild man. In medieval and Renaissance folklore, such figures were believed to dwell in the woods and were usually represented as hairy, naked or semi-naked, and carrying a stick or club. Since they were symbolic of everything opposed to civilization, Frate Alberto's being dressed up like one is certainly suggestive.

Day 4, Story 3

1   There is no specific antecedent for this story, although it contains many motifs that can be found in Greek romance.

2   Lauretta's definition of anger is derived from Aristotle (*Rhetoric* 2.2.2 [1378a–1380a]), by way of Saint Thomas Aquinas (*Summa Theologica* 2.2, question 158).

3   In Provençal, "N'" is an honorific, the equivalent of the Spanish "Don."

4   A brigantine was a fast, sleek sailing vessel often used for piracy or espionage in the Mediterranean.

5   Candia, the modern Heraklion, was the largest city on Crete, which the Venetians had purchased from the Byzantine Empire in 1204; its name came from the Arabic word for the city, Khandaq ("Moat"). The Peruzzi family of Florence had a branch of their bank there.

Day 4, Story 4

1   There is no specific antecedent for this story, although some scholars want to relate it to a supposed historical event reported by a medieval chronicler, Roberto di Torigny, namely the capture of a galley containing a princess, the daughter of a king who ruled over North Africa and Spain, by ships belonging to William II of Sicily in 1179 or 1180. William II ruled from 1166 to 1189, but contrary to what Boccaccio says in the story, he had no children and was succeeded by his aunt Gostanza (Constanza).

Gerbino is an entirely fictitious character, as is the King of Granada, whose country was not established as such until the thirteenth century. His name could be Sicilian, deriving from *sgirbinu*, meaning "light blue," or from *gerbo*, meaning "uncultivated land." He could also be named after the island of Djerba (*Gerba* in Italian), which lies just off the Tunisian coast.

2 Elissa, who is named after Dido, the Queen of Carthage, in Vergil's *Aeneid* tells the only tale on Day 4 that has a North African connection.

3 Barbary usually refers to the entire northern coast of Africa west of Egypt, including the modern countries of Libya, Tunisia, Algeria, and Morocco, but here it seems limited to Tunisia, which is called the Kingdom of Tunis.

4 Vergil is the likeliest source for the epic simile being used here; see, for example, *Aeneid* 9.339–42.

Day 4, Story 5

1 There is no specific source for this story, although the tragic ghost of a former lover does appear in Apuleius, *Metamorphoses*, 8.8 and 9.31. The beginning of the song cited at the end of the story resembles that of a song in Neapolitan dialect that has been preserved in several different versions, although none recount the tale that Boccaccio provides to explain why a woman would be weeping over a pot of basil. The sexual innuendo involved in the song, in which a woman complains about a man's having stolen her pot of basil, has been considerably transformed in Boccaccio's story. This story is the source of Keats's poem *Isabella; or, The Pot of Basil*.

2 In the thirteenth and fourteenth centuries Messina actually had various "colonies" composed of merchants from San Gimignano, the celebrated "City of a Thousand Towers" in Tuscany, that was an important center of the wool trade in the period. There were also close connections among traders in Messina and Naples, to which the three brothers move at the end of the story.

3 Since Salerno is not especially known for its basil, this could be a slip of the pen on Boccaccio's part, who might have been thinking of the basil of Benevento, which was famous for its powerful aroma.

Day 4, Story 6

1 There is no specific source for this story.

2 This name is probably a deformation of da Ponte Carali, or Poncarale, the name of an important family in Brescia, one of whose members had been the *podestà* in Florence and later in Siena during the 1340s. There was also a Brescian named Paolo di Negro who held a military position in Florence in 1347–48. Gabriotto, the name of Andreuola's lover, who is mentioned two sentences later, is a Brescian version of Gabriele.

3 Traditionally, red roses were associated with the passion of love, while white ones signified regeneration and resurrection after death, thus linking together the two motifs of love and death, which the roses continue to evoke throughout the story.

Day 4, Story 7

1 There is no specific source for this story. However, the Florentine setting is rendered with great historical accuracy. Simona and Pasquino are the first tragic working-class heroes in European literature.

2 Just beyond the San Gallo gate on the north side of Florence stood the church of the same name, together with its convent and hospital, all of which dated back at least to the early thirteenth century. According to Franco Sacchetti (ca. 1330–1400), people would go there to the pardoning on the first Sunday of every month both to obtain indulgences (pardons) for their sins and to enjoy a day in the countryside. Lagina is the diminutive form of Lagia, itself short for Adalagia (Adelaide), then a popular name in the city. Puccino, the first name of Pasquino's friend, who is mentioned in the next sentence, is the diminutive of Jacopo (Jacopino), or Jimmy. His nickname, lo Stramba, is pejorative and means "the odd or eccentric one," which I have turned into "Kooky."

3 Since antiquity, medical authorities thought that sage had various curative and health-giving qualities. But there was also a superstition in the Middle Ages that toads were venomous and would leave traces of their venom behind when they chewed on the leaves of plants.

4 Pasquino's two other friends are l'Atticciato and il Malagevole. The first nickname means someone who is husky or stocky. The second means someone who is awkward: hence, Clumsy.

5 Guccio the Slob (Guccio Imbratta) also makes an appearance as the servant of Frate Cipolla in 6.10. The Church of San Paolo is today that of San Paolino.

Day 4, Story 8

1 There is no specific source for this story.

2 The Sighieri family lived in the quarter of San Pancrazio, and many of its members belonged to the guilds of the merchants and the money changers. According to his will, a certain Giovannone di Michele Sighieri owned property in France, albeit in the southern part of the country.

3 Boccaccio says that the boy's mother believed she could fare del pruno un melrancio, which I have translated as "turn a plum into an orange tree," meaning that she thought she could transform something less valuable into something of greater worth. Pruno could mean "thorn" or "thornbush" here, but "plum (tree)" seems likelier.

4 Boccaccio says that Girolamo died, ristretti in sé gli spiriti. The phrase means that he repressed or held back his (vital) spirits in sé, that is, either inside himself or in themselves. In Galenic medicine, which dominated the Middle Ages, the human organism lives because the lungs transfer pneuma, that is, air or vital spirits, to the heart, which heats them and distributes them throughout the body. Girolamo has supposedly stopped this process, possibly suffocating himself by holding his breath.

Day 4, Story 9

1 Versions of this story can be found in romances throughout the late medieval period. Boccaccio's narrator indicates that his story is based on some Provençal account of a (fictitious) love triangle involving the troubadour Guilhem de Cabestaing (1162–1212), his lord Raimon de Castel-Rossillon (d. 1209), and the latter's wife Saurimonda de Pietralata who married Raimon in 1197, was remarried in 1210, a year after Raimon's death, and was still alive as late as 1221. The motif of the eaten heart can also be found in the courtly love tradition immediately preceding Boccaccio. In his *Vita nuova* (*The New Life*), 3, for instance, Dante has a dream in which his heart is eaten by a woman.

2 The preceding clause is a translation of *s'armavano assai*. This is the reading in the most important manuscript of Boccaccio's work, the Hamilton codex, although there is a variant in other manuscripts: *s'amavano assai*. In this case, the clause would read: "they loved one another very deeply."

3 In the Provençal versions of the story, Rossiglione is in fact punished by King Alfonso II of Aragon (b. 1152, ruled 1162–96), who inherited the County of Roussillon in 1172. Note that he died before the events in the story could have taken place.

Day 4, Story 10

1 This story has no specific antecedent, except for the motif of the lover hidden in a chest, although in most cases, the lover gets inside it of his own volition in order to avoid detection by the lady's husband.

2 This is Matteo Selvatico from Mantua (Lat. *Mantuanus*, often corrupted as *Montanus*; hence, It. *della Montagna*: "of the Mountain") who dedicated a huge encyclopedic work on medicine to King Robert of Naples (b. 1277, ruled 1309–43) in 1317 and died, a very old man, some time after 1342.

3 Messer Ricciardo di Chinzica appears in 2.10.

4 Boccaccio is probably thinking of Ruggiero Meli or Mele, who lived a dissolute life and eventually became a bandit during the reign of Queen Giovanna of Naples (b. 1328, ruled 1343–82). Aieroli (or Agerola) was the name of a tract of land that was owned by Ruggiero's family and that he often used in his escapades.

5 This last clause is an Italian saying, meaning that someone was fast asleep or dead to the world: *egli aveva a buona caviglia legato l'asino*. A literal translation would be: "he had tied his ass to a good peg (or post)."

6 Half tierce means halfway between prime and tierce, i.e., between dawn and midmorning.

7 In Italian, Dioneo says she was someone *alla quale strignevano i cintolini*. Literally, this means that her laces—usually the ones holding up one's stockings—were too tight. In modern English we might say that her shoes were pinching her feet.

8 What I have translated in this sentence as "nice little piece of God's creation" is Boccaccio's *cristianella di Dio*, a phrase that means literally "God's little Christian woman (or girl)." *Cristianella*, the diminutive of *Cristiana*, occurs nowhere else in

Italian literature according to Salvatore Battaglia's *Grande Dizionario della Lingua Italiana* (*Great Dictionary of the Italian Language*), which defines it as *povera donna,* "poor woman," and goes on to specify that "poor" implies both scorn and affection. My sense is that in this context it implies the former more than the latter since the judge is about to take advantage of the maid and the word reflects his (and Dioneo's) perspective on the matter.

Day 5, Story 1

1 Although this story contains many motifs from Greek romance, there is no single source for it. The theme of its first half—the educational and transformative power of love and beauty—made it quite popular, and it was both imitated by later writers and made the subject of paintings by Botticelli, Veronese, Rubens, and others.

2 Cimone's real name, Galeso, comes from a Greek word meaning "milk," but Boccaccio's etymology for "Cimone" is misleading. It could be related to the Greek words for goat or for the muzzle of an animal, but is more likely meant to recall the historical Cimon (510–450 BCE), who was the son of Miltiades, the hero of the battle of Marathon. Cimon himself became a famous political leader and general in Athens who was celebrated for his bravery in the naval battle of Salamis, but who was said to have been somewhat simpleminded when he was a young man by both Valerius Maximus, *Factorum et dictorum memorabilium libri IX* (*Nine Books of Memorable Deeds and Sayings*), 6.9.3, and Plutarch in his *Life of Cimon.* The name might also suggest the Italian word *scimmione,* which means "large monkey" or "ape." The name of Cimone's father, Aristippo, is also Greek and may have been chosen simply for that reason, although there was a famous philosopher named Aristippus (ca. 435–366 BCE) who was a follower of Socrates and founder of what was known as the Cyrenaic school of hedonism. Efigenia, Cimone's beloved, is Boccaccio's Italianized version of Iphigenia ("wellborn"), but it is hard to see much of a connection between her and the tragic Greek heroine. All the other characters likewise have Italianized versions of Greek names, which seem chosen primarily to suit the setting of the story.

3 In Italian, she says, *Cimone, rimanti con Dio,* which means, literally, "Cimone, abide [remain] with God." Although she is essentially saying "good-bye," her phrase is a variant of the more usual *va' con Dio* (nowadays: *addio*), and she has no doubt chosen it because she really does want Cimone to *remain* where he is and to let her get away.

Day 5, Story 2

1 There are a few antecedents for the advice that Martuccio offers the King and even more for Gostanza's voyage at sea, but there is no specific story on which this one is modeled. Lipari is the largest of the Aeolian islands off the northern coast of Sicily. During the late Middle Ages it was often used as a base by pirates, which is what the hero of this story becomes. Note that Lipari also figures in the story of Madama Beritola (2.6).

2 Although there is no historical record of a Martuccio Gomito, there were many people named Gomito living in the Kingdom of Naples in Boccaccio's day. Martuccio is the diminutive of Martino; Gostanza is a variant of Costanza (Constance).

3 Boccaccio is usually quite accurate about geography, but a light, northerly wind would have driven Gostanza's boat to the shore of Sicily, not to Susa (which does indeed lie about a hundred miles south of Tunis).

4 Meriabdela may be a mistake for Muliabdela. *Muli-* derives from an Arabic word meaning "my lord," and *-abdela* is an Italianized version of Abd Allah, which was the actual name of several kings who ruled in Tunis during Boccaccio's lifetime.

Day 5, Story 3

1 There is no antecedent for this story, although the protagonists of medieval romances typically wander through landscapes filled with surprises and adventures.

2 There were two families named Boccamazza living in Rome in the fourteenth century, one of which had an Angela in it who was still alive in 1394 and may have been a descendant of Agnolella. There were no Pietros, however, in either branch of the family, and nothing is known about the family of Gigliuozzo Saullo. Boccaccio's complaint here about the decadence of contemporary Rome is not an isolated one in his works and is a sentiment he shared with Petrarch. Both were reacting to the decay of the city during the period known as the Babylonian Captivity, when the Papacy was transferred to Avignon between 1305 and 1377 and was under the thumb of the French kings, leaving Rome to be overrun by gangs of bandits. Boccaccio's reference to Rome as being once "the head of the world" is a translation of a common inscription found on Roman coins, *Roma caput mundi*.

3 Anagni is a town about thirty miles southeast of Rome. To get there, the couple plans to follow the ancient *via Latina* that continued on to Naples. Scholars have suggested that they make a wrong turn at Casale Ciampino, about nine miles outside of the city, and then get lost in the forest of Aglio near Frascati.

4 The Orsini was a powerful, aristocratic Roman family who, as Guelfs, supported the Church in its struggle with the Holy Roman Empire in the thirteenth and fourteenth centuries. Their enemy was the Colonna family, who, as Ghibellines, backed the Empire. Presumably, the soldiers who capture Pietro are members of the Colonna faction.

5 One branch of the Orsini family had taken its name from the properties it owned near the Campo dei Fiori in Rome, and one of its members, who was, in fact, named Liello (most likely a diminutive of Raffaello), lived around the end of the thirteenth century and the start of the fourteenth. His wife was Banna di Tolomea de' Leoni di Montanea, and she was still alive in 1352. The family actually did have a castle east of Grottaferrata. Note that one of Boccaccio's friends and patrons was Niccolò Orsini who often entertained the writer in his castles.

Day 5, Story 4

1 Although a number of different stories have been proposed as sources for this one, none of them is sufficiently close to merit that label. However, the nightingale, which is central to the story, was frequently associated with sex throughout medieval European literature.

2 Lizio da Valbona is a historical character, a Guelf lord who was a minor military and political figure in the second half of the thirteenth century, and who was celebrated for his nobility and generosity. Lizio appears as a character in the *Novellino* (47) and is mentioned by Dante in *Purgatorio* 14.97, a line that also contains a reference to Arrigo Mainardi. In Boccaccio's story, the family name appears as Manardi, and there was no Ricciardo among its members.

3 According to ancient and medieval medical theory, women became colder (i.e., colder humors such as melancholy became more dominant in them) as they aged.

Day 5, Story 5

1 This story has many touches that recall Roman comedy, especially the recognition scene in Plautus's *Epidicus*. Most of it takes place in Faenza, a northern Italian city southwest of Ravenna, thirteen years after the Holy Roman Emperor Frederick II captured it in 1241. Fano, which is also mentioned in the story, is, like Ravenna, on the Adriatic, but farther south. Giannole di Severino and Minghino di Mingole were common names in medieval Faenza.

2 What I have rendered as *podestà* here is actually called the *capitano della terra* ("Captain of the Town") in the text, a figure who was also identified as the *capitano di giustizia* ("Captain of Justice"), and whose functions resembled those of the *podestà*.

3 There is a town named Medicina quite close to Bologna, and there were several families in the province of Emilia with that surname, but Boccaccio's character has not been identified with any specific historical figure from the area.

Day 5, Story 6

1 This story is a reworking of a central episode from Boccaccio's own *Il Filocolo*, but it is adapted here to a very specific historical context. The Hohenstaufen family of Germany had controlled Sicily in the early thirteenth century as part of the Holy Roman Empire, but had been ousted from it by Charles of Anjou, who, with papal support, became king of the island in 1265. The Sicilians disliked his rule, however, and in 1282, a group of French soldiers were killed in Palermo around the time of vespers, thus beginning the War of the Sicilian Vespers, which the House of Anjou and the Papacy lost to the House of Aragon, whose rulers were related to the Hohenstaufens, and thus to the Empire, by marriage. Frederick III (or II) of Aragon, the King Frederick of the story, was named regent for the Aragonese monarchy in 1291 and became King of Sicily in 1296, ruling the island until 1337. Ruggieri de Loria (or di Lauria) (ca. 1245–1305) was, in fact, his Admiral, and since he would leave Sicily

in 1297 or 1298 and begin serving the House of Anjou (although he was eventually reconciled with Frederick), the incidents described in the story would have occurred in 1296–97. Moreover, the girl in the story is identified as the daughter of Marin Bolgaro, and although there is no evidence that this nobleman helped hold Ischia for Frederick, that island did remain under his control until 1299. Finally, the young man, Gianni di Procida, is later revealed to be the son of Landolfo di Procida, the supposed brother of Gianni di Procida (or Giovanni da Procida) (1210–98), a doctor and diplomat who worked for the Aragonese cause in Sicily and was made Lord Chancellor of the island in 1283.

2   Restituta was apparently a popular name on Ischia because the people of the island were especially devoted to Saint Restituta, a North African saint and martyr who died in either 255 or 304.

3   Gianni's swimming from one island to the other recalls the classical tale of Hero, whose lover Leander would swim across the Hellespont to be with her until he accidentally drowned one night (and she killed herself in response). Boccaccio could have read the story in the third book of Vergil's *Georgics* or in Ovid's *Heroides* 18 and 19, and had already told it at greater length in his *Filocolo* earlier in his career.

4   La Cuba was a building, surrounded by gardens, that William II, King of Sicily, had constructed outside Palermo in 1180. The name may refer to its cubical shape or, more likely, came from a Moorish word meaning a recessed place. The building survives to this day.

5   Gianni sails from Punta Campanella, here called Minerva, which is across from the island of Capri at the southern tip of the Gulf of Naples, to the town of Scalea, which is in Calabria about halfway between Naples and the Straits of Messina.

Day 5, Story 7

1   There is no specific source for this story. It takes place during the reign of William II, the Norman King of Sicily (b. 1155, ruled 1166–89). The Abate (Abbate) family, to which Amerigo supposedly belongs, were *capitani,* that is, leaders of the local militia, in Trapani under the Normans and, after them, under the Aragonese. There is no Amerigo among its members, although there is an Arrigo who was a privy counselor to King Frederick II in the next century.

2   The Armenia in question here is what historians refer to as Lesser Armenia, which was founded in the twelfth century by Armenians fleeing from their homeland in what is now the northeastern part of Turkey (as well as in areas to the east) and settling in Cilicia, which lies on the Mediterranean in the southeastern part of Turkey just north of present-day Syria and Lebanon. The Armenians had actually been Christians since the fourth century, and Lesser Armenia, being the easternmost Christian country on the Mediterranean in the later Middle Ages, was an important way station for Italian merchants trading with the East as well as a staging ground for various Crusades. The Crusade that is mentioned later in the story is presumably the Third, which was launched in 1189, although Boccaccio also refers there to the "King" of Armenia, which is anachronistic, since Lesser Armenia only

became a kingdom in 1199. Note that the kidnapped boy's name, mentioned in the next sentence, is Greek and means "God's gift."

3 The daughter of the Count of Antwerp in 2.8 is also named Violante, as was Boccaccio's own daughter who died in 1355.

4 The storm here is modeled on the one in Vergil's *Aeneid* (4.100ff.), which leads Dido and Aeneas to take refuge in a cave, with the same result as for Boccaccio's young couple.

5 Laiazzo (Ayas), a port city in Lesser Armenia, was an important center of trade between East and West in the second half of the thirteenth century.

6 Messer Currado would be guilty of breaking the law by punishing Pietro either because Violante's acceptance of him would mean that he was not guilty of raping her, or because it was customary for a condemned man to be freed if a woman agreed to marry him.

Day 5, Story 8

1 Tales of diabolic hunts were widespread in ancient and medieval literature and folklore, and theologians used them to describe the punishments of the damned. For Nastagio's astute use of the scene for his own ends, there are also precedents, such as Peter Alphonsi's *Disciplina clericalis* (*A School for Clerics*) 14, a work with which Boccaccio was certainly familiar. However, the most important influences on Boccaccio's tale were the punishments described in Dante's *Inferno* (e.g., those meted out to the profligate in *Inferno* 13 and to the sowers of discord in *Inferno* 28) as well as Boccaccio's various sojourns in Ravenna where his tale is set (he lived there at least four, and possibly five, times between 1346 and his death in 1375). Chiassi, or Classi, to which Nastagio retires, is a forested spot on the shore of the Adriatic outside of Ravenna; the name is recalled in that of the modern town Sant'Apollinare in Classe.

2 The Onesti was a noble family in Ravenna, although no Anastagio can be found among its members in the fourteenth century. Boccaccio could have learned about the family from commentators on Dante who, in *Purgatorio* 14.107–10, has Guido del Duca, a member of the family, lament the dying out of other notable families in Ravenna such as the Traversari and the Anastagi. Paolo Traversari, who is mentioned in the next sentence, served as the patron for various poets; he died in 1240, leaving behind a single daughter named Aica. Guido degli Anastagi appears later in the story, but there is no historical record of any Guido in the family.

3 Boccaccio echoes Dante here in his selection of the date (April was traditionally a month associated with visions and with both the Annunciation and the Crucifixion); the location (at the very start of the *Commedia* Dante finds himself in a dark wood); and Nastagio's being transported into the forest (Dante is similarly transported into the forest of the Earthly Paradise; see *Purgatorio* 28.22–23). Note that some medieval commentators identified pine trees as symbols of immortality because they remained green throughout the year.

4 In many of the sources of this story, the woman is being punished in Purgatory, not Hell.

Day 5, Story 9

1 Although there are several Eastern tales involving birds who sacrifice themselves for people, and several medieval stories vaguely rehearse a similar motif, there really is no precedent for Boccaccio's tale except perhaps for Ovid's story of Baucis and Philemon, who sacrifice their only goose for guests who turn out to be gods and reward them for their generosity (*Metamorphoses* 8.611–724). In the Middle Ages, the falcon was considered a symbol of the triumph over lust and over the passions more generally, and it was, of course, a hunting bird trained and used by the mem-. bers of the upper classes.

2 Hailing from a prominent family that lived in the Santa Croce quarter of Florence, Coppo (Giacopo, or Jacopo: James) held numerous important civic positions during the first four decades of the fourteenth century, including that of Gonfaloniere (Mayor) in 1315; he died sometime before April 1353. Sacchetti features him in two of his stories in his *Trecentonovelle* (*Three Hundred Stories*), 66 and 137.

3 The Alberighi, one of the oldest families in Florence, lived in the Porta San Piero quarter near the church bearing their name, the Chiesa di Santa Maria degli Alberighi, and not far from the home in which Dante had grown up. By the early fourteenth century, they had fallen on hard times, as Dante notes in *Paradiso* 16.88–93.

4 Campi, or Campi Bisenzio, is a tiny town a few miles to the northwest of Florence not far from Prato.

Day 5, Story 10

1 The source of this story is Apuleius's *Metamorphoses* (9.14–28), one of Boccaccio's favorite works, which he was actually making a copy of at the time he wrote the *Decameron*.

2 The story is set in Perugia, which apparently had a reputation for homosexuality in the period and was otherwise one of Florence's mercantile rivals. The Bardi bank, for which Boccaccio's father worked, had a branch there. There was, in fact, a Pietro from the well-known family of the Vincioli who held various administrative positions in and around the city at the end of the thirteenth and start of the fourteenth centuries.

3 The old woman's phrase is *mi desse fuoco a cencio*, which means literally "he would give me fire for my rag." She is referring to the fact that in the Tuscan countryside, people would take a rag and go to their neighbors for a light to start their fires with back home, since a rag would burn longer than glowing coals or a lighted brand.

4 Ercolano was a common name in Perugia, since San Ercolano (Saint Herculanus) was the patron saint of the city. He had been a bishop there and had been martyred by the Ostrogoths in 549.

Day 5, Conclusion

1 Although none of the songs Dioneo mentions is extant, all of them have a generic similarity to the kinds of popular songs that were sung during carnival and on other festive occasions. Some of the titles are clearly equivocal and sexual in character, while others remain obscure. That all had some sort of erotic content, however, can be inferred from the reaction they provoke among the ladies.

2 A few scholars want to assign "But it's not yet the month of October" to either Elissa or Dioneo, but most think it is part of the title of the song. If so, then the song involves, hypothetically at least, two speakers, a man who invites a woman to fill up her cask (with wine), and the woman who protests that it is not yet October, the month in which wine-making would occur. The sexual double entendre in the title is unmistakable in this case.

Day 6, Introduction

1 During his youth Boccaccio had himself composed a long romance on the ill-fated love of Troilus for Cressida called *Il Filostrato*, whose title is constantly recalled in the *Decameron* by the name Filostrato that Boccaccio gives to one of the three young men in the company whose lovelorn condition matches that of Troilus. Since *Il Filostrato* also features an unfaithful heroine, their singing the poem at this point anticipates the dispute between the servants that is about to occur.

2 This is the only time in the *Decameron* when the idyllic retreat of the ten young storytellers is interrupted by any sort of external reality. The servants' argument rehearses one of the main themes of the text, the ubiquity of sexual desire and, in particular, its importance for women, as well as touching on the themes of this day, namely quick retorts and witticisms, as well as that of trickery, which will become the chosen topic for the next day. This is also the only place after the start of Boccaccio's work where the servants' names are mentioned (except for when Tindaro is said to play the bagpipes), and it is the only place where they actually speak.

3 Although *Sicofante* sounds like the English "sycophant," it is not connected with that word. Rather, it is a Greek-based name, like those of the servants in the *Decameron*, and since the etymology of the word is uncertain, it is impossible to know if Boccaccio means anything by it other than to say that Sicofante belongs to the same class of characters as Licisca and Tindaro.

Day 6, Story 1

1 Boccaccio's story has an antecedent in the *Novellino* (89), but can also be counted more generally as one of a host of stories that are told during trips, including those in Sercambi's and Chaucer's collections. Boccaccio is, of course, actually equating horseback riding and storytelling here. The Madonna Oretta of the story was the wife of Geri Spina, who appears in the next story. She was left a widow by him in 1332 and was apparently considered something of a wit. *Oretta* is short for *Lauretta*,

which is the diminutive of *Laura*, but it also suggests the meaning "little, or brief, hour" (*ora* means "hour"), thus underscoring one of the faults of the knight's narrative, its long-windedness. Note that in the opening sentences of the story, Filomena deliberately reprises Pampinea's framing statement at the start of 1.10.

2 In this story, Boccaccio offers a commentary on the art of storytelling itself. By having the knight make a mess of his narration, Boccaccio implies that his own stories are free of the particular flaws the knight's displays. Coming roughly at the halfway point in the collection, the story thus focuses readers on the issue of proper and improper modes of storytelling as one of the main themes of the collection. In this way, the *Decameron* also parallels the *Divine Comedy*, which devotes its central canto (*Purgatorio* 17) to the poem's chief concern, love.

3 Boccaccio's word here is *pecoreccio*, which means "sheepfold," the muddy, mucky place where the sheep sleep at night.

Day 6, Story 2

1 There is no literary source for this story, which may be a retelling of a well-known anecdote. Cisti (short for Bencivenisti) was a fairly common name in Florence in the fourteenth century, and a certain *Cisti fornaio* (Cisti the baker) does appear in a document of 1300 from the Chiesa di Santa Maria Ughi next to which Cisti's bakery is located in the story. Geri Spina was Geri (short for Ruggeri) di Manetto Spina (d. 1321 or 1322) who was a merchant and a figure of some political importance in Florence.

2 The ambassadors sent by Pope Boniface VIII (b. ca. 1235, pope 1294–1303) were attempting (unsuccessfully) to negotiate peace between the White and the Black Guelfs. After defeating the (imperial) Ghibellines at the battles of Campaldino and Caprona in 1289, the Guelf (papal) Party had itself split into these two factions, the Blacks continuing to support the Papacy, while the Whites allied themselves with the Empire. Messer Geri was one of the heads of the Blacks.

3 Cisti is saying that the flagon is large enough to contain the water of the Arno, the river that flows through Florence.

4 Cisti is being extremely polite and deferential, essentially saying that from the time Messer Geri started tasting the wine, it became his, and that since Cisti was now merely its guardian, he wanted to give up that role and hand the wine over to its rightful owner.

Day 6, Story 3

1 There is no literary source for this story.

2 Antonio degli Orsi di Biliotto degli Orsi was made Bishop of Fiesole in 1301 and served as Bishop of Florence from 1309 until his death in 1322. He held the office of Privy Counselor to the English King Edward II in 1310, helped to defend Florence from a siege by the Holy Roman Emperor Henry VII in 1312, and was a widely

cultured individual who owned a large library. Despite being described here as a "wise and worthy prelate" by Lauretta, he was, however, also renowned for his avarice, and that may be why Boccaccio thought of him for this story. Dego della Ratta, or Diego de la Rath (d. 1343), first came to Naples in the retinue of Violante of Aragon, the bride-to-be of King Robert (b. 1277, ruled 1309–43). Dego served the King in various capacities and was his representative in Florence in 1305, 1310, and 1317–18.

3   A certain Nonna de' Pulci was mentioned briefly in a Florentine document of 1340, as was the Rinucci family, to whom the Bishop was in fact related. Porta San Piero, in which Nonna was living, was a quarter of the city named after a gate on its eastern side; it lay along the route where the Florentine *Palio* was run.

Day 6, Story 4

1   There is no literary source for this story, although Apuleius's *Metamorphoses* contains an episode involving a cook who makes off with a haunch of venison (8.31). Currado di Vanni di Cafaggio Gianfigliazzi, who lived around the turn of the fourteenth century and was known for his lavish lifestyle, was a member of an important family associated with prominent Florentine bankers, including the Peruzzi. Dante places one of the Gianfigliazzi in the circle of Hell reserved for the usurers (*Inferno* 17.58–60). Boccaccio knew several members of the family in his own day and celebrates at least two of them in his minor works.

2   Peretola is a small town in Tuscany just a short distance from Florence in the direction of Prato. Currado Gianfigliazzi actually owned property in the area.

3   Currado calls Chichibio a *ghiottone*, which meant "glutton," but also had the extended meaning of "rogue, rascal, knave, or scoundrel," all of which fit Chichibio well, since Currado thinks his cook cut off the crane's leg in order to eat it.

Day 6, Story 5

1   Although there is no extant source for Boccaccio's story, later Renaissance writers treated it as historical. Forese da Rabatta (d. 1348) was a well-known jurist who was a professor at Pisa (1338–39), held various political offices in Florence, including those of Prior and Gonfaloniere (Mayor) between 1320 and 1340, and served as the city's ambassador to Pisa in 1343. Although it is generally agreed that he died in 1348, he is mentioned in historical records as late as 1359. Giotto di Bondone (1266/67–1337) was, of course, the famous painter whose innovative works have been seen as inaugurating the Renaissance from at least 1549–50, when Vasari's *Le vite de' più eccellenti architettori, pittori, e scultori italiani* (*Lives of the Most Eminent Italian Painters, Sculptors, and Architects*) appeared. He was greatly admired by both Petrarch and Boccaccio who celebrated him in several other works beside the *Decameron*. Mugello is an area northeast of Florence; both Forese and Giotto were born there.

2   Pampinea's story is that of Cisti the baker (6.2).

3   The Baronci were proverbial for their ugliness. See 6.6 for more details.

4   A more literal rendering of the final clause in the story would be that Messer Forese perceived that "he had been paid in coin equal in value to the merchandise he had sold."

Day 6, Story 6

1   There is no extant source for Boccaccio's story. The Maremma was a large marshy region about thirty-five or forty-five miles southwest of Florence. Sparsely populated, infested with brigands, and a breeding ground for malaria, it was a place to which numerous Florentines were exiled. Guido Cavalcanti, a leader of the Guelf faction, was sent to it in 1300 and died there, most likely of malaria. When Michele Scalza, who is celebrated for his wit in the story, couples it with "the whole wide world," he is parodying a kind of provincialism: he is speaking like someone who does not really have any idea how large the world truly is, someone who thinks that Florence is huge and the area around it in Tuscany is practically the entire world, although he has some sense that there is also an enormous, scary place called the Maremma that is even farther away. Scalza's parody here is consistent with the clever argument (including its false logic) by which he wittily "proves" the Baronci to be the noblest family in Florence. The Baronci was an actual middle-class family who lived near the Cistercian-run Church of Santa Maria Maggiore, where one of its members, a certain Tommaso Baronci, served as Prior in 1346, 1354, and 1361. The Baronci's awkwardness and ugliness were apparently proverbial. As for the witty Michele Scalza who is the protagonist of the story, nothing is known about him.

2   Montughi was a pleasant hill to the north of Florence beyond the Porta San Gallo and overlooking the valley of the Terzolle River; a number of Florentine families had built villas there. The Uberti and Lamberti, who are mentioned in the next sentence, were indeed among the oldest, most distinguished families in the city.

3   The Vannini (named after San Giovanni, the patron saint of the city) was a prominent Florentine family; Neri is short for Rinieri. There were any number of families named Fiorentino in the city, so it is impossible to identify precisely who this particular Piero was.

4   Scalza's argument here was scandalous, indeed blasphemous, to Catholics in Italy after the Counter-Reformation, since it presented a less than perfect God, and for centuries Italian editors of the *Decameron* either changed this part of the tale or replaced the tale entirely. English translators followed suit until John Payne returned to Boccaccio's original text in 1886.

Day 6, Story 7

1   There is no precedent for this story.

2   The Pugliesi and Guazzagliotri families were important families in Prato who were also notorious enemies; the latter played a principal role in the expulsion of the former from the town in 1342. Prato is about seventeen miles northwest of Florence.

3 The lady's remark echoes Matthew 7:6: *Nolite dare sanctum canibus* ("Give not that which is holy unto the dogs"). In Boccaccio's time, the words *sanctum* and *sacrum* could refer to a woman's body.

Day 6, Story 8

1 There is no precedent for this story, although throughout his career Boccaccio often satirized women for being vain and admiring themselves in the mirror. Looking into the mirror was also, however, associated with the virtue of prudence and with the contemplative life, and it was a conventional metaphor for seeing the truth, which is what Fresco means when he uses it later in the story.

2 Fresco da Celatico is Francesco from Celatico, a town in the Arno valley where he could have had a villa or a farm, but since he is not given a family name, his precise identity has not been determined. Cesca is short for Francesca and is a pet name.

Day 6, Story 9

1 Guido Cavalcanti (ca. 1255–1300) was, along with Dante, the leading poet of the *Dolce Stil Novo* ("Sweet New Style") as well as being Dante's close friend. His poetry justifies his being termed a logician and natural philosopher by Boccaccio. In the tenth canto of the *Inferno* Dante places Guido's father in the circle of Hell reserved for those, including the Epicureans, who did not believe in the immortality of the soul. This was the most likely source of the notion that Guido was also an Epicurean. The quip attributed here to Guido had been assigned to other figures earlier in the Middle Ages and first appeared in the *Dialogues* of Pope Gregory the Great (4.3) in which a passage from Psalm 48 in the Bible was cited to condemn the Epicureans for denying the immortality of the soul: *domus suas in saeculo tabernacula sua* (12: "their sepulchers shall be their houses forever"). (The King James Bible identifies this as Psalm 49:11 and translates it rather differently.)

2 Boccaccio denounces avarice and greed throughout the *Decameron*. See, for example, 1.8, 3.5, 6.3, and 8.1.

3 Betto (short for Brunetto) Brunelleschi came from a Ghibelline family, but was a White Guelf for a short time and a friend of both Guido Cavalcanti and Dante, who dedicated a sonnet (99) to him. However, after the defeat of the White Guelfs in 1301, which led to Dante's exile, Betto became one of the leaders of the Black Guelfs. In 1311, after having caused the death of another leader, Corso Donati, he was himself assassinated by two of Corso's young kinsmen.

4 The Cavalcanti family lived in Orsanmichele, an area in the center of Florence named after the *orto* (kitchen garden) of the monastery of San Michele. A building designed to be a grain market was built there in 1337, and between 1380 and 1404, it was converted into the church we see today. The Corso degli Adimari, which Guido is taking as he walks from Orsanmichele to the Baptistery of San Giovanni, is now called the Via Calzaiuoli. The Baptistery was the second-oldest building in the city and had been rebuilt in its present octagonal form around 1059;

it was surrounded by a cemetery containing Roman sarcophaguses that Florentine families had moved there and were using as tombs. The Church of Santa Reparata was located on the site next to the Baptistery where the Duomo, or Cathedral of Florence, to be named Santa Maria del Fiore, would be built, starting in 1294. By the middle of the fourteenth century, when Boccaccio was writing the *Decameron*, the old Church of Santa Reparata had not yet been demolished, although a great deal of work had been done on the new cathedral, which locals would continue to call Santa Reparata for quite some time. The porphyry columns mentioned in the next sentence still flank Lorenzo Ghiberti's *Gates of Paradise* on the east side of the Baptistery. The columns were given to Florence by the Pisans in 1117 in gratitude for the city's assistance in their fight against Lucca; the Pisans had originally taken them from the island of Majorca.

Day 6, Story 10

1   There is no direct source for this story, although analogues may be found in Eastern collections such as the *Panchatantra*, and in the Middle Ages there was an abundant literature concerned with the abuse of relics, such as a swindle involving the "arm" of Saint Reparata that occurred in Florence in 1352.

2   Certaldo, which is about eighteen miles southwest of Florence, was probably Boccaccio's birthplace, and although he often referred to it elsewhere with warmth, here it is viewed more critically. Boccaccio spent the last years of his life there, living in his house in the citadel (the upper part of the town); he was buried there as well. The friars of Saint Anthony, mentioned both earlier and in the next sentence, were members of the oldest monastic order, which was founded by Saint Anthony of Egypt (ca. 251–ca. 356) around 313. (This Saint Anthony should not be confused with the Franciscan friar Saint Anthony of Padua.) Saint Anthony was venerated for protecting animals from diseases and was often represented with a pig at his feet. By Boccaccio's time, however, friars in the order were condemned for their greed, which Dante denounces in *Paradiso* (29.124) where he identifies them with their own pigs that were allowed to wander freely in the streets.

3   Marcus Tullius Cicero (106–43 BCE) and Marcus Fabius Quintilian (35–96 CE) were, of course, the two most important Roman writers on rhetoric. Although Quintilian did give speeches in the law courts, his greatest fame was as a teacher and writer. By contrast, Cicero was so celebrated for his public oratory that his name (often in the form of "Tully," or *Tulio*, as it is in Boccaccio's story) became a byword for eloquence.

4   Cipolla refers to the saint as the *baron messer Santo Antonio*, which could be translated as the "Baron Messer Saint Anthony." *Baron*, though normally a title for men in the secular hierarchy, was also used as an honorific for saints.

5   Both Bragoniera and Pizzini are the names of families that lived in Certaldo in Boccaccio's day. The Pizzini owned property that adjoined Boccaccio's, and a Biagio Pizzini was a close friend of Boccaccio's father.

6   Guccio's three nicknames in Italian are, in order: *Balena*, *Imbratta*, and *Porco*. The first one translates directly as "Whale" and the last as "Pig," while *Imbratta* means

"he who makes a mess": hence, the Slob. Historical records from the years between 1318 and 1335 mention the existence of someone variously referred to as Guccio Aghinetti, Guccio Porcellana, and Frate Porcellana, who lived in the quarter of San Paolo in Florence and worked in the Hospital of San Filippo. There is also a document dating from 1305 that mentions a Guccio Imbratta (a Guccio Imbratta makes an appearance as a gravedigger in the *Decameron* at the end of 4.7). Lippo (short for Filippo) the Mouse (*Topo*), who is mentioned in the next sentence, was a proverbial character to whom various eccentricities and jokes have been attributed.

7 It is impossible to duplicate Boccaccio's triple rhymes: *tardo, sugliardo e bugiardo; negligente, disubediente e maledicente; trascutato, smemorato e scostumato.* A more literal translation would be: "slothful, filthy, and untruthful; neglectful, disobedient, and foul mouthed; careless, witless, and ill mannered."

8 The Baronci were proverbial for their ugliness. Boccaccio refers to them in this way in 6.5 and 6.7.

9 A possible alternative translation for the last part of this sentence might be: "he knew how to say and do more than God ever could." The serving girl's name, which is mentioned earlier in the sentence, is short for Benvenuta. The phrase translated as "gentleman by proxy" is *gentile uomo per procuratore*, which means "gentleman through, or by way of, the procurator (or prosecutor)." In other words, he enjoys a title that does not attach to his person, just as someone delivering a warrant for a prosecutor may possess the title and authority of the prosecutor, though only temporarily. In bragging of his wealth, Guccio says he has *de' fiorini piú di millantanove*, "of florins more than *millanta* and nine" (*millanta* is a fanciful derivative from *mille*, "thousand," and refers to any very large, indeterminate number).

10 The monks of the Abbey of the Hospitallers in Altopascio near Lucca were renowned for the generous portions of soup they prepared for the poor twice a week. The cloth, most likely silk, of the East was famous for its wealth of colors, as Boccaccio himself noted in his *Esposizioni* on Dante's *Inferno* (17.8); Tartary here is probably China. The Lord of Châtillon is a fictional title meant to suggest great wealth.

11 The "friends" referred to here are male; the "neighbors" are *comari*, technically, a term identifying the godmothers of someone's child, but often used for close female friends from the neighborhood, or gossips, as it is here.

12 Frate Cipolla's sermon is a brilliant performance, filled with words designed to impress and mystify the people of Certaldo that have much less exalted meanings a more sophisticated audience would "get." He also uses truisms and tautologies and sometimes seems to produce sheer nonsense. "Parts of the world where the sun rises" in this sentence is meant to suggest the East (the direction in which we see the sun rise), but the phrase literally means all countries, because the sun rises everywhere. The "Privileges of the Porcellana" is a nonsense phrase, whose literal meaning is obscure. It may be linked to Frate Cipolla's servant, who was called Guccio Porco and whose real last name may have been Porcellana, or it may refer to the sodomitical practices often associated with the clergy. However, this name and most of the following ones, while suggesting faraway places, also designate streets and quarters in Florence, and they take us on a journey, generally from east to west, through the

city. There was thus both a street and a hospital named Porcellana near the Arno to the east of the Ponte Vecchio. In the next sentence, Venice (*Vinegia*) and Greekburg (*Borgo de' Greci*, the "burg or suburb of the Greeks") were quarters lying between the Piazza della Signoria and Santa Croce; they were also the names of streets. Algarve (*Garbo*) was a street of that name (now via Condotta), while Baghdad (*Baldacca*) was a street near Orsanmichele, although both names are meant to suggest exotic lands (Algarve was the name of a kingdom in the southern part of the Iberian Peninsula). Parione, perhaps meant to suggest "Paris," is the present-day via da Santa Trinità alla Carraia, and Sardinia (*Sardigna*) was a deserted stretch of shoreline on the Arno. Although Saint George (*San Giorgio*) was the name of a quarter near the Dogana, or customshouse, as well as one in the Oltrarno (the part of Florence on the left bank of the Arno), the Straits of Saint George (*Braccio di San Giorgio*) may suggest something like the Bosphorus.

13 Conland and Clownland are *Truffia* and *Buffia*. *Truffia* comes from the verb *truffare*, "to deceive, con," whereas *Buffia* suggests *buffone*, "clown," as well as *beffare*, "to trick, play a practical joke on." Liarland is the *terra di Menzogna* (*menzogna* means "lie"). The denunciation of the clergy in this sentence is focused on abuses generally associated with the Order of Saint Anthony whose members Dante accused not merely of fattening themselves on the offerings they received, but also of mystifying others with the empty language of their sermons ("money that has not been minted").

14 To clothe pigs in their own guts is to make sausages, while carrying bread on sticks can be done with *ciambelle*, ring-shaped buns, and wine can be put in a sack if the sack is a wineskin. All three expressions have phallic overtones. Abruzzi, an actual region in southern Italy, is sufficiently far away to appear exotic. The Basqueworm Mountains translates *montagne de' bachi*, literally, "Mountains of the Worms," but *bachi* also suggests Basques, another faraway people.

15 Parsinippia is *Partinaca*, which means "parsnip," perhaps to suggest the spices and delicacies of the East; it may also mean a "fantastic, unbelievable story," for which modern Italians would say *carota* ("carrot"). Pruningbills is my punning translation of *pennati*, the pruning hooks or tools with curved blades that were used to prune vines; the word contains a play on *pennuti*, "feathered ones," i.e., birds. Maso del Saggio was a Florentine, by profession a broker or middleman, who was known in his own time for his tricks and his mocking humor. He makes an appearance as a trickster in 8.3 and 8.5.

16 The Patriarch's name is a translation of the Old French *Nemeblasmez Sevoiplait*, which echoes the kinds of allegorical names one finds in such works as *Le Roman de la Rose* (*The Romance of the Rose*).

17 Boccaccio is satirizing the cult of holy relics here by assigning material parts to spiritual entities. The "whole and sound" finger of the Holy Spirit is bawdy and blasphemous as well. There is no adequate way to translate *Verbum-caro-fatti-alle-finestre* ("Word-flesh-made/get-you-out-the-windows"), which plays on the biblical *Verbum caro factum est* ("the Word was made flesh," John 1:14).

18 The two "books" Frate Cipolla gives the Patriarch are part of a complex set of puns. What he says is that *gli fece copia* of them, a phrase that I rendered as "I . . . gave him,"

and which means both that "I gave him a gift of" and "I gave him plenty of." Moreover, both of the book titles suggest sodomy, a practice with which the cloistered male clergy were frequently associated in Boccaccio's time. The first of the "books" is *le piagge di Monte Morello*, the slopes (or, as I rendered it, the "dingle") of Mount Morello, while the second one is *il Caprezio*, a made-up word that plays on the Italian *capro*, or male goat, and that may also contain a pun on the name of a Latin author such as Lucretius (*Lucrezio* in Italian, although the *-tius* ending in Latin was pronounced as though it started with the letter z). The "teeth of the Holy Cross" contains a play on the notion of the "arms" of the cross. Gherardo di Bonsi was an important member of the *Arte della lana*, the Wool-Workers Guild, and was devoted to the saint after whom he was named, Saint Gherardo (1174–1267), who was one of the earliest followers of Saint Francis and was frequently represented wearing *zoccoli*, or sandals. Note that *zoccoli* had associations with sodomy as well in the period.

Day 6, Conclusion

1 The word for "tricks" in this sentence is *beffe*, which can also be translated as "practical jokes" or "pranks" or "con games." Moreover, the verb *beffare* not only meant "to play a trick on," but also "to mock or make fun of," thus underscoring the potentially sadistic element in such tricks and the way they "put down" the one who is their victim.

2 The Valley of the Ladies is a literary fiction, an idealized description of a natural spot that presents a perfect balance of Nature and Art. It is a version of the *locus amoenus* ("pleasant place"), a commonplace that goes back to the Garden of Eden in the Bible and to the ancient tradition of pastoral. To some degree, all the settings in which the ten young men and women tell their stories are examples of such an idealized natural spot, although Boccaccio heightens the idealization in this particular case. It is noteworthy that he produces this description just after Dioneo has suggested a topic for storytelling that has met with resistance from the women in the group and that they retreat to a valley that is, as its name would suggest, their natural place.

3 The word that Pampinea uses here for "tricked" is the slightly less charged *ingannati*, which lacks some of the scornfulness that would have been implied by *beffati*. Dioneo's reply, however, suggests that he sees the two terms, for his purposes, as interchangeable.

4 Elissa's song, like most of the others in the *Decameron*, is a love lament, and it should also be remembered that Elissa is another name for the love-stricken, tragic figure of Dido in Vergil's *Aeneid*. Her reference to red and white flowers at the end of the poem alludes to the marriage ceremony in which women were adorned with orange blossoms, lilies, and roses.

Day 7, Story 1

1 This tale has no literary antecedent, but seems to be one of many such popular stories current in Florence during Boccaccio's life.

2 A number of men named Lotteringhi worked at different times as agents for the Bardi bank during the fourteenth century. Some of them were connected to the confraternity of the Laud Singers. There was no Gianni (short for Giovanni) among them, however.

3 There were many popular religious texts in the vernacular such as the ones named here. Saint Alexis was a Florentine mystic who, with six companions, founded the Order of the Servites, or Servants of Mary, some time after 1233. The text may be referring to the *Ritmo de Sant'Alessio,* one of the earliest examples of Italian verse. There were many laments attributed to Saint Bernard of Clairvaux (1090–1153) who was a key figure in the spread of the austere Cistercian Order during the twelfth century. Finally, the Laud of the Lady Matilda was one of many hymns of praise for the German mystic Mechtilde of Magdeburg (ca. 1210–ca. 1285), whose fame was spread in Italy by the Dominicans who also happened to own the monastery at Santa Maria Novella.

4 There was a real Monna Tessa who was a member of the Mannuccio family that lived in the quarter of San Frediano on the far side of the Arno; she was born in 1307 and was married to Neri (short for Rinieri) Pegolotti. The name Tessa, short for Contessa, was common in Tuscany because of the fame of Matilde di Canossa (1046–1115), the Countess (*Contessa*) of Tuscany, who supported the Papacy against the Holy Roman Emperor Henry IV, sometimes even donning armor and leading troops into battle. Mannuccio is a nickname used as a family name; it is derived from Alamanno, a name adapted from that of a group of Germanic tribes (the *Alamani*). One of the districts in the San Frediano quarter was called Cuculia ("Cuckoo"), because it had a chapel containing a painting of the Virgin with a cuckoo in it. Tessa's father's name may thus symbolically foreshadows the cuckolding Gianni is about to receive.

5 Putting the skull of an ass on a stake in order to protect one's crops was a practice going back to Etruscan times.

6 Gianni names two popular medieval hymns. The first was a prayer to God said at the end of the day: *Te lucis ante terminam* ("To Thee before the light has ended"). The second was to the Virgin: *O intemerata* ("O unspotted [Virgin]"). It was also mentioned by a robber in 2.2. In the first of the hymns appear the words *procul recedant … noctium phantasmata*: "may the phantoms of the night stay far away." In his *Specchio della vera penitenza* (*The Mirror of True Penitence*), Jacopo Passavanti (1302–ca. 1357) defined what Monna Tessa calls a *fantasima* as a kind of satyr or a bogeyman (*gatto mammone*) that went about at night disturbing people. While it is possible to translate the Italian word, which is derived from the Latin *phantasmas,* as *phantom,* Passavanti's description makes *bogeyman* a better choice, in that it is an old English word for Satan who was traditionally imagined as being part animal with cloven hooves and a tail just like a satyr. Moreover, since Boccaccio's tale expresses some skepticism about such creatures, even though the credulous and extremely pious Gianni does not, it seems appropriate to use a word that in modern English has a slightly old-fashioned character and is chiefly employed when talking with children. Finally, Boccaccio's own drawing of the figure in the Hamilton codex is clearly the portrait of (the top half of) the Devil.

7 Spitting was a common practice in rites of exorcism.

8 Federigo actually says *I denti!* meaning "the teeth." There are two explanations for his words. The first is that he wishes Gianni would expel his own teeth when he spits. The second is that Federigo is pretending to be the bogeyman and is saying that his own teeth are being drawn out by the magic spell. In my translation, because Federigo says this "under his breath" (*pianamente*), I selected the first possibility as the more likely.

9 There was a Giovanni di Nello who was a successful apothecary and who was buried in Santa Maria Novella in 1347 where he had had a chapel built at his own expense. He did not live in the quarter around the Porta San Piero, however. Emilia condemns Gianni di Nello as being *non meno sofficiente lavaceci* than Gianni Lotteringhi; her phrase, which I have rendered as "no less a pea brain," literally means he was "just as good at washing chickpeas," i.e., not good for very much at all.

Day 7, Story 2

1 This story, like 5.10, derives from a tale told in Apuleius's *Metamorphoses* (9.5–7), one of Boccaccio's favorite authors, occasionally following it word for word.

2 Peronella was a common name in Naples at the time. It comes from the French Peronnelle ("little Peter," with a feminine ending).

3 In 1324 the brothers Giovanni (Giannello is a diminutive) and Niccolò Scrignario were living on or near the Piazza Portanova, which is not far from the harbor in the Avorio neighborhood where the story is set. Their family was an important one in the city at that time.

4 Not far from the neighborhood in which Peronella and her husband live there was a chapel dedicated to Saint Galeone (San Galione in Neapolitan), also known as Saint Eucalione.

5 The man who wants to buy the barrel is offering five silver *gigliati*, coins minted in Naples around 1300. They got their name from the *gigli* ("lilies") with which they were decorated. I have turned these coins into the more familiar *ducats*.

6 With the image of the Parthian stallions and mares, Boccaccio is recalling not just Apuleius, but several passages in Ovid's *Ars amatoria* (*The Art of Love*), 1.209–10 and 3.785–86. The Parthians, an Iranian people in central Asia, were famed for turning their backs and feigning retreat on their horses before bringing their enemies down by shooting arrows expertly behind them. Boccaccio may have been thinking of Parthian horses in particular because of this trait.

Day 7, Story 3

1 Although there are many stories in medieval collections that have one spouse being discovered by the other in bed with a lover and yet managing to salvage the situation with some clever trick, there are no precedents for the particulars of Boccaccio's tale. Frate Rinaldo serves as *il compare*, the sponsor or godfather, for the couple's child. In the Middle Ages, the relationship between a child's parents and its godparents was

so sacred that any sort of sexual relationship between them was considered incestu-
ous. Throughout the story, the woman Frate Rinaldo sleeps with is called *la comare*,
which could mean "godmother," but here it means the mother of Frate Rinaldo's
godchild. Both words, *compare* ("godfather") and *comare*, were also used as familiar
terms of address—as they still are in southern Italy—for people who had not spon-
sored a child at baptism, but were simply one's good friends and neighbors. There is
no exact modern English equivalent for the words; although "gossip" once had the
same set of meanings, the word is now pejorative and primarily means a woman
who talks about people behind their backs. I have thus chosen to use "neighbor" in
preference to "gossip."

2 This is not the Saint Ambrose who is the patron saint of Milan, but the Blessed
Ambrogio (Ambrose) Sansedoni of Siena (1220–86) who had a chapel dedicated to
him after his death in his native city, where the story takes place. There may be a
pun, suggested by the name of the saint, on the old word *brogio*, which meant fool
or simpleton, thus reinforcing the characterization of the husband in the story.

Day 7, Story 4

1 This story is a reworking of an exemplary tale (14) from the *Disciplina clericalis*
(*A School for Clerics*) of Peter Alphonsi. Stories about women's deceptiveness were,
however, widespread in medieval literature.

2 Tofano is short for Cristofano (an alternative version of Cristoforo: Christopher).
There is a record of a Tofano, the son of a notary, living in Arezzo in the mid-
fourteenth century. The town also has a *pozzo di Tofano* ("Tofano's well"), but it
was probably called that because of Boccaccio's story. Tofano's wife is named Ghita,
which is short for Margherita.

3 In her next-to-last sentence, Lauretta has recourse to a rhymed proverbial saying: *E
così, a modo del villan matto, dopo danno fé patto.* A more literal translation would be:
"And so, just like a crazy (or stupid) peasant, after (his) defeat (or harm or damage),
he made a pact (or treaty)." Lauretta's last sentence echoes her praise of Love at the
start of the story, although why she condemns Avarice (*soldo*: money, pay) is unclear.
The structure of the sentence itself is puzzling, for she first says "long live Love,"
then "death to Avarice," and then adds *e tutta la brigata*, which I have translated as
"and all his company," meaning all those associated with Avarice. But some editors
and translators feel that this last phrase is actually the object, like "Love," of "long
live." Thus, what Lauretta may be saying is: "So, long live Love and all his company,
and death to Avarice!" Or even: "So, long live Love, and all our company, and death
to Avarice!"

Day 7, Story 5

1 Although the theme of this story was widely diffused in medieval literature, no
specific source has been found for it.

2 Penitents typically kneeled at the feet of their confessors; the confessional booth was only introduced after the Council of Trent (1545–63) met to reform the Catholic Church.

3 For "spoiled his holiday," the text says that *ella gli aveva data la mala pasqua,* which literally means, "she had given him a bad Easter." However, *pasqua* in this phrase was used to mean any holiday, and the general sense is that she spoiled things for him.

4 What the wife really says here is that she would *porti le corna,* "put horns on his head," i.e., make him a cuckold. The horns metaphor is still actively used by contemporary Italians. To make the sign of the horns by extending the index and fifth fingers, while clenching all the rest, remains the Italian equivalent of "giving someone the finger" in American culture. The mention of a hundred eyes may well be an allusion to the mythological figure of Argos, a giant possessing many eyes (his epithet was *Panoptes,* "all seeing"), who was tasked with guarding a sacred white heifer by Hera. The heifer was in actuality the nymph Io, and Zeus sent Hermes to blind and then kill Argos so that he could sleep with her.

Day 7, Story 6

1 Although the theme of this story can be found in a number of tales from the Middle Ages, including those in collections such as *The Thousand and One Nights,* no individual story can be identified as its source.

2 There were various Latin sayings in the Middle Ages to the effect that Love and Wisdom were incompatible with one another.

Day 7, Story 7

1 Stories about deceived husbands who get beaten by their wives' lovers were widespread in medieval European literature, especially in French *fabliaux.* There are no precedents in those texts, however, for the more courtly elements that appear in the first part of this story.

2 The Galluzzi was a prominent family in Bologna, but none of its members was ever named Egano. The wife's name, of course, means "blessed" (*beata*) and thus suggests a contrast with—if she is not a parody of—the Beatrice who was described by Dante in elevated terms as his beloved in *La vita nuova* (*The New Life*) and whom he made into his heavenly intercessor and guide in the *Divine Comedy.*

3 Falling in love at a distance (*amor de lonh* in Provençal) was a convention of courtly love literature and was assumed to be a trait distinguishing the refined people of the upper classes in the Middle Ages. The motif has already appeared in other stories in the *Decameron* (1.5 and 4.4).

4 A game of chess by means of which the players reveal their love for one another was a commonplace in courtly romances; losing at it was often a preliminary move in a seduction.

5 The women of Bologna are generally regarded positively in the *Decameron* (see also
   1.10 and 10.4), unlike those of Pisa (2.10), Venice (4.2), and Milan (8.1). Of course,
   the narrator may be speaking ironically here.

Day 7, Story 8

1 There are many tales in Eastern collections such as *The Thousand and One Nights*, as
   well as in French *fabliaux*, which involve an unfaithful wife tricking her husband by
   putting another woman in her place.

2 The Berlinghieri was a merchant family that rose to prominence in the middle of
   the fourteenth century; none of them was named Arrigo or Arriguccio, however.
   This story, like 3.3, may be read as an implicit warning to the nouveaux riches, the
   gente nuova, in Boccaccio's world about their excessive social ambition.

3 The mother's comment alludes to the fact that merchants and notaries used to carry
   their quill pens and inkwells around in holders that they attached to their belts or
   put in the back pockets of their pants. Her diatribe against Arriguccio is generally
   filled with insults that associate him with filth and excrement, and in this particular
   example, she actually uses the word *culo*, which I have translated as "butt," but could
   be rendered as "ass." The mother's speech gives voice to the hostility that Florentine
   aristocrats not only felt to the nouveaux riches, the *gente nuova*, in their society, but
   also to country lords who had once controlled the city and were now associated with
   lawless violence, as the reference to Arriguccio's having "come up here from some
   country lord's gang of thugs." The word she uses here for what I have translated as
   "gang of thugs" is *troiata*, which is defined as the band of men-at-arms who served a
   feudal lord. It is an unusual word, and there is good reason to think that she chooses
   it because it echoes *troia*, the word for "sow," which was beginning to acquire in Boccaccio's time its modern slang meaning of "whore."

4 The Guidi family was a byword for aristocratic status.

Day 7, Story 9

1 This story is a retelling of the *Comoedia Lydiae* (*The Comedy of Lydia*), a work written by the twelfth-century French poet and theorist Matthieu de Vendôme, which
   Boccaccio had transcribed with his own hand. The two motifs that make up the
   story—the trickery used by a woman on her husband to prove herself to her lover,
   and the enchanted pear tree—were widespread in medieval literature.

2 Nicostrato is the only name that Boccaccio changes from his source, in which the
   character is called Decius. This change may have been dictated by a desire to make
   the name fit the Greek setting, but since it means "triumphant warrior," the change
   can also be seen as ironic. Boccaccio retains the name of Lidia's maid, Lusca, from his
   source, where it is the Latinized version of the French *louche*, which means "squint
   eyed" or "disreputable."

3 Chaucer's *The Merchant's Tale*, which generally follows Boccaccio's story quite closely, but may not be directly derived from it, has Pirro and Lidia, somewhat improbably, making love together in the tree rather than on the ground.

Day 7, Story 10

1 Although there are many examples in medieval religious literature of people returning from the grave to admonish those still alive, this story expresses a definite skepticism on the subject. It is also critical of the Sienese, archrivals of the Florentines throughout the late Middle Ages and the Renaissance. Finally, it satirizes what was called *il comparatico*, the quasi-sacred relationship between the godparent and parent of a child, which forbade any sexual relationship between them.

2 Elissa's story is 7.3.

3 The Mini and the Tura were lower-class families in Siena, and while no Tingoccio Mini appears in the historical record, there were two men named Meuccio di Tura. The endings of both men's first names are diminutives and express endearment. Tingoccio comes from Lotterringo, which is in turn derived from the Germanic Lother or Lutherr, which means "brave warrior." Meuccio is the diminutive of Meo, which is short for Bartolommeo (Bartholomew). The Porta Salaia neighborhood is in one of the *contrade* ("quarters"), that of the *Selva* ("Forest"), into which Siena is famously divided to this day.

4 The Anselmi was also a lower-class family, but nothing is known of this particular branch. The wife's name Mita is short for Margherita. The Camporeggi neighborhood is in another one of the *contrade* of Siena—namely that of the *Draco* ("Dragon").

5 More literally: "I skinned myself by doing it" (*io me ne scorticai*). Even while being tormented in the afterlife because of his sin, Tingoccio cannot resist making an erotic joke of sorts.

6 Frate Rinaldo appears in 7.3.

Day 8, Introduction

1 The company did not go to church the preceding Sunday. This is thus their only contact with the outside world during their sojourn in the country.

Day 8, Story 1

1 Boccaccio could have found versions of this story in various French *fabliaux*, and after him it was reworked by Giovanni Sercambi in *Il novelliere* (32) and by Chaucer in *The Shipman's Tale*. Gulfardo may be an Italianized version of the German name Wolfard; Guasparruolo means Little Caspar; and his wife Ambruogia is named after the patron saint of Milan, Saint Ambrose (Ambruogio in Italian). None of these characters appears in the historical record, although their names, including Guasparruolo's family name, Cagastraccio, were typical in the period. That Boccaccio

makes Ambruogia rapacious may indicate his low opinion of the Milanese more generally, something that is perhaps suggested as well by his reference to the "Milanese fashion" at the end of Day 3.

2   See 6.7.

Day 8, Story 2

1   There is no specific source for this story, although its theme, like that of the preceding story, was widespread in medieval literature.

2   Varlungo was a village in the Valdarno just a short distance from Florence; it has long since been incorporated into the city. In such towns throughout Tuscany, it was the custom to plant an elm tree, like the one mentioned in the next sentence, near the local church in order to provide shade for the parishioners when they gathered there on Sunday afternoons in the summer.

3   The names of husband and wife were fairly common in Tuscany, and historical records document the existence of a Belcolore in Varlungo and of a Bentivegna, who was an associate of Boccaccio's, in Certaldo. Her name means "Fair colored," and his, more suggestively, "May you have joy of the club" (or, alternatively, "may you get a good drubbing from the club, or mace"). A large number of other characters with typically rustic Tuscan names make brief appearances in the story as well. "Grinding at the mill" means having sex; the metaphor also appears in 4.10 and the Author's Conclusion.

4   "The water runs down the ravine" (*L'acqua corre la borrana*) was a popular dance song that was very sexually suggestive. The peasant dances Monna Belcolore leads are the *ridda*, a round dance, and the *ballonchio*, a type of *saltarello*, a dance featuring jumping and leaping.

5   Bentivegna mangles the legal terminology, confusing such words as *parentorio* for *perentorio* (peremptory); *pericolatore* for *procuratore* (solicitor, attorney); and *giudice del dificio* for *giudice del maleficio* (judge of the criminal court). There was an actual Buonaccorso di Ginestreto whose presence in Florence has been documented between 1341 and 1354.

6   Lapuccio is the diminutive of Lapo, a nickname for Giacopo (James or Jacob). Naldino is a diminutive nickname for Rinaldo or Arnaldo. Nothing is known about these two characters.

7   Belcolore's comment here is untranslatable. She says that Biliuzza *se n'andò col ceteratoio*: she "went off with the *ceteratoio*." Scholars think this word may be a corruption of *eccetera* ("etcetera") to be found in legal documents; it is as though Belcolore sees Biliuzza as the victim of some legal arrangement containing special clauses and technical language that confused her and led to her impoverishment. Or the word may be a corruption of *cetera* (*chitarra*: guitar), suggesting either that she wound up with a belly swollen like a guitar, or that she was left with nothing but a bit of music.

Day 8, Story 3

1 This story, set in a working-class milieu, has no specific literary antecedent. The heliotrope was a name for a sandstone, green with blood-red streaks, that some medieval thinkers believed could render its bearer invisible; such a power was mentioned by Pliny, *Istoria naturalis* (*Natural History*), 37.60.165. The Mugnone is a stream that flows into the Arno near Florence; in the hot months of summer, it is usually just a dry bed. The protagonist of the story will be featured again in 8.6, 9.3, and 9.5, and by the sixteenth century his name had become a byword in Italy for someone who was a pathetic simpleton and dupe.

2 Calandrino was the nickname of the painter Nozzo (short for Giannozzo) di Perino who lived in Florence in the early part of the fourteenth century. He was probably a pupil of Andrea Tafi and thus a member of a school that resisted the new realism associated with Giotto. There are some frescoes of no great importance that he painted in a villa at Camerata, but his real claim to fame is his simplemindedness and gullibility. His nickname may refer to a square with hinged arms used by stonecutters and painters to measure angles or, more likely, to a kind of lark, since birds in general were frequently seen as being gullible, as the verb *uccellare* (to catch birds, to make a fool of) suggests. The word is also a diminutive of Calandro (Lark), a fairly widespread name in the period. Note that in this sentence Florence is said to be full of *nuove genti*, which I have translated as "bizarre characters." Although the phrase could be rendered more literally as "new people," the word *nuovo* had a range of meanings from the more positive, such as unfamiliar, strange, or unusual, to the more negative, such as bizarre or weird. The same adjective is applied later in the sentence to Calandrino himself, who is said to be a man *di nuovi costumi*, a phrase that I have rendered as "strange habits." At the end of the paragraph, Maso del Saggio is said to be planning to make Calandrino believe *alcuna nuova cosa*, "some far-fetched (i.e., novel) notion." Finally, near the end of the story, Bruno and Buffalmacco ask Calandrino, *che novelle son queste?* which I have translated as "What's the story here?" It would have been more accurate, though less idiomatic, to have said, "What are all these strange goings-on about?"

3 Bruno was Bruno di Giovanni d'Olivieri, a minor painter who was active in the first decades of the fourteenth century, and who worked along with Buffalmacco, an acknowledged master artist. Buffalmacco's real name was Bonamico (ca. 1262–1340), and like Calandrino, he was a pupil of Andrea Tafi. He was a more accomplished artist, however, and the remains of his paintings can still be seen in the Badia in Florence, the Cathedral of Arezzo, and, perhaps, the Camposanto in Pisa (*The Triumph of Death*). He was reputed to be quite a prankster, and writers after Boccaccio, including Sacchetti and Vasari, told stories about him. The nickname Buffalmacco comes from a combination of *buffo*, an alternate for *beffa*, meaning "trick" or "prank," and *macco*, the name of a soup made from shelled fava beans, thus suggesting the character's pleasure in eating, but also his relatively slender income, since bean soup was the food of the poor.

4 Maso del Saggio is also remembered as a prankster by later writers. Although he was, by profession, a broker or middleman, he was known in his own time for his tricks and his mocking humor. He was mentioned by Frate Cipolla in 6.10 and will appear again as a trickster in 8.5.

5 Maso's discourse conjures up a magical land of plenty for Calandrino. This was a fantasy place that appears in various kinds of popular literature throughout the Middle Ages (and after). Maso calls it *Berlinzone,* which I have translated as "Gluttonia," since Florentines at the time referred to someone who stuffed food into his mouth as a *berlingaio.* He places it in the land of the Basques, which was "beyond beyond" for fourteenth-century Italians, and he also says it is in the *contrada che si chiamava Bengodi. Bengodi* is made up of *godi* (enjoy) and *bene* (well), and thus means something like the "land of real enjoyment, or pleasure," but since food is the central feature of Maso's fantasy country, I have turned *Bengodi* into "Gourmandistan."

6 Vernaccia wine is a white wine made from a varietal of the same name that is grown throughout Italy. The name derives from a word meaning "vernacular," i.e., "local." Nowadays, when people say Vernaccia, they are usually referring to the Tuscan white wine, Vernaccia di San Gimignano, but in Boccaccio's time that was not necessarily the case.

7 Not only does Maso fool Calandrino by talking of fantastic places and using equivocal expressions, but like Frate Cipolla, he sometimes comes close to talking nonsense, although he uses an impressive style as he does so in order to dupe his listener. In this sentence he says, *Haccene più di millanta, che tutta notte canta,* which means, literally, "There are more than a thousand (miles) to there, which sing all night long." Maso renders his statement impressive by using the variant *millanta* for *mille* (it means "a thousand," but also refers to any very large number) and by rhyming that word with *canta* (sings). *Millanta* also suggests *millantare,* a verb meaning to boast or brag. That Calandrino is appropriately impressed is indicated by his response that the place is farther away than Abruzzi, the name for a province in Italy that at the time belonged to the Kingdom of the Two Sicilies and that was used proverbially, like the country of the Basques, to mean a land "at the other end of the earth."

8 Maso is punning here when he says *Sì é cavelle.* It can be translated as "It's really nothing" in the sense that the extra distance to Gluttonia is nothing at all, but also that Gluttonia itself is nothing at all, that is, a complete fiction.

9 Settignano and Montisci (more correctly, Montici) are hills (and towns) near Florence, just as Monte Morello is.

10 This is another bit of linguistic foolery on Maso's part. Speaking of the emeralds, he says *rilucon di mezzanotte vatti con Dio.* The first part of this clause speaks of how the stones shine in the middle of the night, but the word *mezzanotte* (middle of the night) is followed by a standard locution for "good-bye," *vatti con Dio* ("God go— or be—with you"), which I have rendered as "good-night to you," perhaps because Maso's clause is structured by a process of association: speaking about the middle of the night leads him to say good-bye, since it is long past bedtime.

11 Faenza is a reference to the old Faenza Gate that was located less than half a mile to the west of the present-day train station of Santa Maria Novella in Florence. There was a convent just outside it in Boccaccio's day.

12 Boccaccio's Italian here reads: *noi avremmo perduto il trotto per l'ambiadura*. Literally, this means, "we would have lost the trot for the sake of the amble." The proverb involves two different gaits of horses. The amble is a leisurely pace that is more comfortable for the rider, whereas the trot is faster, but less comfortable. Also, the trot is a natural gait for horses, whereas they must learn to amble, and they may lose the ability to trot if they do. Thus, Buffalmacco's proverb means essentially that they will potentially be losing a sure thing (the natural gait of the trot that is sure to lead them to the prize of the heliotrope) by doing something that promises to be easier (ambling, or going to the Mugnone right away), but is less sure (because ambling has to be learned and may keep them from getting to their goal as they could by trotting there).

13 Canto alla Macina means "Millstone Corner" and actually exists at the intersection of Via Ginori and Via Guelfa. Having Calandrino live at a place associated with another stone (probably because there was a mill there once) makes sense in terms of the imagery in the story.

14 The name Tessa, short for Contessa, was common in Tuscany because of the fame of Matilde di Canossa (1046–1115), the Countess (*Contessa*) of Tuscany who supported the Papacy against the Holy Roman Emperor Henry IV, sometimes even donning armor and leading troops into battle.

Day 8, Story 4

1 There are multiple classical sources for this story, including Plautus's *Casina*, Ovid's *Fasti* (*On the Roman Calendar*) 3.667–96, and one of Quintilian's *Declamationes* (*Declamations*), 363, as well as the French *fabliau* entitled *Du prestre et d'Alison* (*Of the Priest and Alison*) by Guillaume le Normand. The Rector was the chief ecclesiastical dignitary in a cathedral or a collegiate church.

2 Picarda was a very common name in Florence during Boccaccio's time, so it is impossible to identify the woman with any particular historical figure. It is equally impossible to identify the Rector in the story.

3 The Rector's derogatory comment here means that women are so soft, so pliable, that they could be easily moved ("hammered") to do any man's bidding, whereas true silver is resistant enough so that a hammer is able to impress the design of a coin on it. He is implying both that women are not worth much (they cannot be turned into real coins) and that they are malleable and thus superficial and easily persuaded. The hammering metaphor has an additional sexual suggestiveness that puts women down even further.

4 Ciuta is short for Ricevuta, an unusual given name, which is probably itself short for *per grazia ricevuta*, which means "for a received grace," suggesting that Ciuta's parents may have prayed to have a child and then named her as they did because God

chose to grant her to them as an expression of His grace. Boccaccio's explanation for Ciuta's nickname is incomprehensible in English. In Italian we are told that she had a *cagnazzo viso* ("*cagnazzo* face"), so that everyone called her Ciutazza, adding the ending of *cagnazzo* to Ciuta to create her derogatory nickname. There is some debate about the meaning of *cagnazzo*. Dante uses the word to describe the faces of the damned who are stuck in the ice at the center of Hell (see *Inferno* 32.70), which suggests that the word means "livid," that is, discolored, perhaps purplish red, from the cold. But *cagna* means "bitch," leading some translators to read *cagnazzo* as an adjective deriving from that noun and thus seeing Ciuta's face as being "doglike." Since we are told she has a bad complexion, and since there is nothing else doglike about her face, I have chosen to translate *cagnazzo* as "discolored," without, however, ruling out the canine association.

5 Ciutazza's mistress is offering her a *camiscia* (*camicia* in modern Italian), which now means "shirt" or "blouse," but in the Middle Ages referred to the long, shirt-like undergarment worn by both sexes (which has since been replaced by bras and slips for women and undershirts for men). In this context I have called it a "shift," although "smock" would work equally well.

6 The narrator refers to the Rector, the *proposto*, here as *messer lo ploposto*, ridiculing him by playing nonsensically on his title. Since "rector" and "provost" are virtually equivalent terms to render the Italian *proposto*, half of modern translations using the one and half the other, my choice of rector allows for the pun I use in this sentence for his title, a pun that Boccaccio, admittedly, did not intend, but that nicely captures both the sexual appetite of the character and his general stupidity.

Day 8, Story 5

1 There is no specific antecedent for this story, although Florentines were well known for playing practical jokes on outsiders. The judge in this story is named Niccola da San Lepidio, which means he comes from the town of San Lepidio, now known as Sant'Epidio al Mare, which is located in the southern part of the province known as *Le Marche* (The Marches). Florence frequently found its *podestà* and the magistrates who worked with them in that region, which is west and slightly south of Tuscany.

2 Although Matteuzzo has not been identified, Ribi was a well-known professional entertainer, according to the writer Sacchetti, who recounts several of the clever quips he was supposedly responsible for making; see his *Trecentonovelle* (*Three Hundred Stories*), 49 and 50. Matteuzzo is a pet name for Matteo (Matthew); Ribi, a nickname for Garibaldo, Ribaldo, or Riberto.

3 Santa Maria a Verzaia was a church near the Porta San Frediana, a gate in the walls of Florence on the south side of the Arno.

4 Ribi actually says he will appeal the matter to the *sindacato*, which is really short for *il momento del sindacato*. The "moment of the *sindacato*" was the moment when all the magistrates in Florence ended their tenure in office and delivered a report (the *sindacato*) about their activities. At that moment, citizens could appeal their cases to the magistrates, known as *sindacatori*.

Day 8, Story 6

1 There is no specific antecedent for this story, although it has some general points of contact with a number of medieval tales involving trickery where the prize pursued is bacon, which is precisely what Calandrino would turn his pig into.

2 There is an untranslatable pun here: Calandrino has been complaining that his pig has been "stolen" (*imbolato*), to which Bruno replies that he cannot believe it has "flown away" (*volato*).

3 The bread and cheese test was a widespread magical rite in the Middle Ages in which people suspected of theft were given a portion of bread and cheese to eat over which a magical formula had been recited. Their inability to swallow it was assumed to be proof of their guilt.

4 Vernaccia wine is a white wine made from a varietal of the same name that is grown throughout Italy. The name derives from a word meaning "vernacular," i.e., "local." Nowadays, when people say Vernaccia, they are usually referring to the Tuscan white wine, Vernaccia di San Gimignano, but in Boccaccio's time that was not necessarily the case.

5 Forty *soldi* were worth about half a florin, which was a reasonably valuable coin at the time.

6 There is a debate about what exactly "dog ginger" (*zenzero canino*) is. Some scholars think the phrase refers to an inferior type of ginger, while others argue that it is a name for "water pepper" (*Persicaria hydropiper*), a marsh weed with an acrid juice. Yet another school of thought believes that "dog ginger" was a euphemism for "dog excrement," which was, in fact, occasionally used in medieval medicine. "Hepatic aloes" (*Liliacea amarissima*) was a bitter, nauseating drug used as a purgative. "Hepatic" ("pertaining to the liver") refers to its dark red color.

7 Since the florin was a fairly valuable coin, and "six" was used in the period to mean something like "a large, indefinite sum," Buffalmacco is suggesting that Calandrino made a killing when he sold the pig.

8 A more literal translation of the last words of the story—*col danno e con le beffe*—would be that Calandrino is left "with the loss and with the tricks (that had been played on him)," or "with the loss and the ridicule (he had been subjected to)."

Day 8, Story 7

1 There is no specific literary antecedent for this story, although it is clearly related to a long tradition of misogynistic writing throughout the Middle Ages. Many scholars also see it as being autobiographical, the reworking of an unhappy episode in Boccaccio's life, which he also wrote about in his *Corbaccio* (1354–55), a virulently misogynistic work about a widow who had jilted him.

2 Elena is Helen, and her name cannot help but evoke that of Helen of Troy. The scholar's name Rinieri is less suggestive.

3 My "nether regions" is a compromise. Boccaccio writes *in inferno*, "in the direction of Hell." Most translators see this as an emphatic way of saying that she did not stare

down at the ground and translate the phrase accordingly. But in the context of a story filled with allusions to devils, serpents, Hell, and Dante's *Inferno*, Boccaccio's phrase is quite suggestive.

4 What Boccaccio actually says here is: *che di mal pelo avea taccata la coda*. A literal translation would be: "who had attached to him a tail with (tufts of) bad hair." The clause connects the scholar to traditional images of the devils, such as the ones who appear in Cantos 21–22 of Dante's *Inferno*, one of whom is named *Malacoda* ("Bad Tail"). The devils were traditionally supposed to be cunning and malicious, as Dante's are, and as the scholar is.

5 This may be a slip on Boccaccio's part in that the scholar could not have known about the question the lady had asked her lover. Or perhaps she may have revealed this in some way when she was asking Rinieri for his assistance.

6 The scholar's "snares" (*lacciuoli*) here may be an ironic reference to the snares that courtly love poetry said women used with men and that were frequently identified, metaphorically, with their hair. The word also looks forward to the end of the story where the lady is said, in a phrase alluding to Dante's *Inferno*, to have a plentiful supply of snares or tricks.

7 The lady's "plentiful supply of tricks" (*a gran divizia lacciuoli*) echoes the scholar's boast about having many snares or tricks (*lacciuoli*) earlier in the story and also constitutes an allusion to the anonymous Navarese, a con man appearing in Dante's *Inferno*, who *avea lacciuoli a gran divizia* (22.109: "had snares [or tricks] in abundance") and uses one of them to escape the clutches of the devils who are about to punish him.

Day 8, Story 8

1 There is no specific literary antecedent for this story, although many medieval *fabliaux* feature husbands and wives doing the sorts of things that happen here.

2 The comment about the ass recalls the one made at the end of 5.10, which in turn goes back to one made by a merchant who is talking with his colleagues at the start of 2.9. The point of the comment is that when an ass bumps into a wall, he is, in a sense, bumped back by what he has run into. In other words, he gets a blow from the wall equal to the one he gave it. Fiammetta's advice is clear: in matters of revenge, do not seek an excessive retribution, but go "tit for tat." The story thus becomes something of a parody of the serious punishments meted out to the damned in Dante's *Inferno* where their suffering was God's perfectly calibrated "revenge" for the sins they had committed.

3 Both the Tavena and the Mino (actually, the Tolomei) were real families in Siena, and there are documents from the fourteenth century that mention a Spinello from the former and a Zeppa from the latter. Spinelloccio is a double diminutive derived from Crispino, the name of the saint who was the patron of shoemakers, tanners, and leather workers (Crispino might also suggest that the character has curly—*crespo*—hair). Zeppa is short for Giuseppe (Joseph), the husband of the Virgin Mary, who was a carpenter by trade and became the patron saint of workers and craftsmen.

The names of both characters thus speak to the social position assigned them in the story as well-to-do *popolani* ("commoners"). The Tolomei were actually a cut above that status, however. As we see in the next sentence, the two men are neighbors in the Sienese *contrada* ("quarter") located near the Porta Camollia, one of the eight gates of the city on its northern side; the gate has been preserved to this day.

4 Boccaccio refers to the couple as doing a *danza trevisana* ("Trevisan dance"), which I have translated as a "jig." The Trevisan dance was apparently quite lively and possibly obscene. Its equivocal meaning here does not need further commentary.

Day 8, Story 9

1 There is no specific literary antecedent for this story, although it reflects a belief in magic that is a staple of many classical and medieval stories.

2 There was, in fact, a da Villa family: a Messer Simone da Villa is mentioned in a history of Pistoia as living between 1315 and 1326; and a Messer Simone Medico ("Doctor") was buried in Santa Croce in Florence around the middle of the fourteenth century. The doctor's family name means, essentially, that he is from the country, reinforcing the notion that he is simpleminded, something of a bumpkin. Via del Cocomero corresponds to a section of the present-day Via Ricasoli near the Mercato Vecchio, which is where the house of Boccaccio's two trickster painters, Bruno and Buffalmacco, is located (cf. 9.3). *Cocomero* means "watermelon," and thus, like the earlier reference to the sheep, constitutes a comment on Messer Simone's intelligence: his head is as (relatively) empty as a melon.

3 The hospital of San Gallo had a devil's head painted on its façade with multiple mouths, each devouring a sinner. This iconography was widespread in the late Middle Ages. Dante's *Inferno*, for example, features a three-headed Satan, whose three mouths are devouring those whom Dante saw as the most sinful traitors in the history of the world: Judas, Brutus, and Cassius.

4 Bruno refers to Simone as *vostra qualitativa mellonaggine da Legnaia*, which I have rendered as "your qualitative melonosity of Legnaia." *Qualitativo* was an adjective used in contemporary philosophical writing; it has no precise meaning here, but is designed to make what Bruno is saying sound impressive. The reference to *mellonaggine*, "melonosity," like later ones to pumpkins and cucumbers, is a comment on Simone's lack of intelligence, his empty-melon-headedness. Legnaia is a village not far from Florence that was famous for its watermelons. Montesone (or Montisoni) in the next sentence is a hill near Florence with a famous cross on its summit.

5 Bruno addresses Simone as *maestro mio dolciato*, "my sweet (or, more accurately, sweetened) Master." "Sweet" here is an antonym for "salty," meaning witty or clever; hence, my "dull-cified," i.e., sweet means dull or stupid. Bruno will repeatedly use this opposition between sweet and salty, that is, between stupid and witty, in addressing Simone. Michael Scot (ca. 1175–ca. 1235) was a scholar and mathematician whose translations of Aristotle from Arabic and Hebrew initiated the late medieval vogue for the Greek philosopher. Scot wrote works on philosophy, astrology, and alchemy, and served as the court astrologer for Holy Roman Emperor

Frederick II. Although he has been praised for his learning, Dante placed him in Hell with the magicians and soothsayers (see *Inferno* 20.116–18). Commentaries on the *Divina commedia* speak of the magical banquets Scot supposedly held for his followers.

6   Bruno's list of famous women veers between real people and places, on the one hand, such as the Basques, the Sultan, Osbech, and Norwega (*Norrueca* is, perhaps, a corruption of *Norvegia*, "Norway"), and pure fantasy, on the other. *Barbanicchi*, which has been left as it is in Italian, may suggest "barbarians"; "Chitterchatterer" is *ciancianfera*, the "bearer of *ciancia*," which means "chitchat"; and *semistante*, which I have rendered as "Semistanding" (*semi-* means "half," and *stante* is the present participle of *stare*, "to stay, stand, or be") also distantly suggests *almirante* ("admiral") or *amorante* ("lover"). *Scalpedra di Narsia* suggests both *scalpitare* ("to claw") and *puledra* ("female colt") to Italian scholars. However, Bruno's *Narsia* may be a reference to the Umbrian town of Norcia (Lat. *Nursia*), which was the birthplace of Saint Benedict, the founder of Western monasticism, who was known in the Middle Ages as Saint Benedict of Narsia (as well as of Nursia, Norsia, and Norcia). If so, then *Scalpedra* may be a play on words on both *scapolare* ("scapular"), the hooded cloak worn by monks over their shoulders (Lat. *scapula*), and *cattedra* (Lat. *cathedra*), the name for a bishop's seat in a church that was accordingly called a cathedral. Hence my decision to make her the "Scapulathedral of Narsia." Legends concerning Prester John were brought back to Europe by crusaders after about 1200, identifying him as the legendary Christian ruler of an empire in Asia or Africa, sometimes specified as Ethiopia, who was going to retake Jerusalem for Christendom. He supposedly signed himself simply as Prester John, i.e., John the Priest. Florentines called him Presto Giovanni ("Quick John"). His wife Skinkimurra (It.: *Schinchimurra*) is, of course, a pure fabrication; her name is possibly intended to suggest the exotic language Prester John was imagined as speaking.

7   Cumin seeds are very aromatic and were used not only to flavor dishes, but also in medicines, including those to control flatulence.

8   Bruno is making a bawdy play on the actions involved in weaving.

9   The figure of Lent would have been that of an emaciated woman. An *Agnus Dei*, the "Lamb of God," was the figure of a lamb bearing a cross or having a small cross above it; it was a symbol of Christ. Since doctors diagnosed diseases by examining patients' urine, it would make sense for Master Simone to have a urine flask painted over his front door. Cats and mice were frequently represented in medieval painting and sculpture, although there are few examples of actual battles between groups of them. Cats were usually associated with the Devil; mice sometimes had similar associations, but were also linked to weakness and hence to frail humanity.

10 *Gumedra* seems sheer nonsense, but Marco Polo had spoken of the Genghis Khan who lived in a region called *Altai*. *Altarisi* could thus be seen as a conflation of that place-name with the word for "altar," *altare*, although it could also be a comical corruption of *Tartary*.

11 Bruno is caricaturing the names of two medical authorities in the Middle Ages, the Greek physician Hippocrates, and the Arabic philosopher Avicenna. Bruno's

Porcograsso (for Hippocrates) means "Fat Hog"; his *Vannaccena* (for Avicenna) means "Vain [or empty] Supper."

12 Peretola is only a few miles from Florence.

13 Cacavincigli is the name of a street or alley in Florence associated with lowlifes. The first part of the word, *caca*, means "crap" and thus anticipates the end of the story. Simone offered the woman ten Bolognese *grossi*, the early modern equivalent of which was the Dutch or English groat, a silver coin of relatively modest worth.

14 Bruno's nonsense, which sounds impressive and which he is counting on Simone not to understand, can only be approximated in translation. Bruno first tells the doctor that his singing would beat *le cetere de' sagginali*, literally, "the lyres (or harps or whistles) made from sorghum stalks." The word *cetere* can also refer to the mumbo jumbo of doctors and lawyers who were given to saying *etcetera* a great deal. Then Bruno says to the doctor: *sí artagoticamente stracantate*, literally, "you sing beyond the limits (*stra-*) in so super (*arta-*, or *arci-* in modern Italian) Gothic a manner." "Gothic" was clearly already a pejorative term for the art and architecture of the late Middle Ages. However, since the word begins with *arta-*, Simone is meant to hear it as praise for his *artfulness*.

15 Vallecchio is a small town in Tuscany near Castelfiorentino about eighteen miles southwest of Florence.

16 When Bruno says that Simone's wise words would "draw pious old ladies right out of their boots," his term for them is *pinzochere*, which meant the pious laywomen who associated themselves with various religious orders, but who did not take vows, did not live in convents, and could choose to marry. Many went around barefoot—hence the humor of Bruno's comment, which is another bit of the deliberate obscurity that he uses to make fun of the linguistically challenged Simone. Boccaccio seems to have thought such women were generally hypocrites.

17 Bruno refers to his *grande e calterita fede*, his "great and *calterita* faith (or word)." *Calterita* is the past participle of *calterire*, which means "to bruise" or "to damage," and thus really means *bad* faith. It is another bit of verbal mumbo jumbo on Bruno's part.

18 There was a professor of medicine named Guiglielmo da Saliceto who was active in the late thirteenth and early fourteenth centuries, although it cannot be certain that Boccaccio is thinking of him here. Forlimpopoli is a town located between Forlí and Cesena; the name has farcical overtones. Simone calls himself a good *segretaro*, using a word that could mean in the late Middle Ages both a "keeper of secrets" and the person who was entrusted with his master's secrets, as well as with correspondence and the like, that is, a secretary. *La Bergamina* (the "Woman from Bergamo"), who is mentioned in the next sentence, has not been identified.

19 The narrator refers to Simone as *maestro sapa*, which I have translated as "Master Sappyhead." Since *sapa* is actually concentrated grape juice, once again Simone's lack of wit, his lack of "salt," is the point of the joke.

20 High up on the façade of the church at Passignano there is a painting of God the Father. Buffalmacco's playing on the word "High" (*alto* in Italian) works on the assumption that the parochial Simone has never seen the image.

21 Buffalmacco uses a word Boccaccio appears to have made up here: *frastagliatamente.* The verb *frastagliare* means to cut an intricate design or cut something into pieces, and by extension, to confuse or deceive by talking in a grandiose and extravagant manner. Simone is supposed to hear, perhaps, the idea of "intricate detail" as a form of sincere praise. Hence, I have translated it as "frankastically," conflating "frankly," "fantastically," and "sarcastically."

22 Here begins a series of scatological puns inspired by the countess's name. In Italian she is the *contessa di Civillari,* the name of a spot in Florence near the monastery of San Jacopo a Ripoli that was used as an open sewer and an outhouse of sorts. Buffalmacco says the Countess is the most beautiful thing in *tutto il culattario dell'umana generazione.* The key word here is *culattario,* an Italianized play on a late Latin word such as *collectarium* (*collecta,* or "assembly," plus *-arium,* "place of"). The initial part of the word has been replaced with *cul-,* from *culo,* meaning "butt." Hence, "ass-sembly."

23 The Countess's trip to the Arno refers to the practice of taking household waste to be dumped into the river at night. There actually is a town near Arezzo called Laterino that had existed since Roman times and had been the source of jokes as early as the *Curculio* (*The Weevil,* 4.4) of Plautus (254?–184 BCE).

24 "Her staff and pail," *la verga e 'l piombino,* is an untranslatable pair of puns. *Verga* means both the staff or rod a ruler held and a cleaning instrument, while *piombino* (from *piombo:* "lead") could mean a (lead) seal or a pail or bucket. The Countess's retainers all refer to different sizes and forms of human excrement. They are called *il Tamagnin dalla Porta, don Meta, Manico di Scopa, lo Squacchera,* which mean, respectively: the little old man who keeps, or stays by, the door; don turd; broom-handle; and the loose one (*Squacchera* comes from a verb meaning "to squirt"), i.e., diarrhea.

25 The tombs outside of Santa Maria Novella were erected around 1314, thus suggesting a possible date for the story. Although "Bath" will have a special meaning in the story, there was an actual "ceremony of the bath" in which knights-to-be were washed of their imperfections.

26 The festival they no longer celebrate is probably the *Gioco del Veglio* ("Game of the Old Man") in which someone would impersonate the Devil. It was banned in 1325.

27 Buffalmacco is going along the present-day Via della Scala. His route takes him by the hospital of Santa Maria della Scala (founded 1316; later the monastery of San Martino) toward the nunnery of San Jacopo di Ripoli, which had been founded in 1300–01 and contained paintings by Bruno and Buffalmacco, according to Vasari.

Day 8, Story 10

1 There are multiple antecedents for what happens in this story both in Eastern and Western collections, although Boccaccio's rendering of the mercantile environment is unique. The theme of the "biter bit," the trickster who gets tricked, has appeared before in the *Decameron;* see, for example, 2.9 and 8.7.

2 "Customshouse" translates Boccaccio's *dogana*, which was a word of Arabic origin, as are several others in this opening paragraph, all of which enhance the exotic feel of the story.

3 In Boccaccio's time there were many women who worked as barbers, thus explaining his recourse to such imagery in this paragraph.

4 The Cignano was an important Florentine family, and there are archival records attesting to the existence of a Niccolò di Cecco da Cignano from the mid-fourteenth century. He may have been a member of the Compagnia Scali, a firm that dominated the cloth trade in the Kingdom of Naples, which included Salerno (as well as Palermo, except for a brief period in the late fourteenth century when the island of Sicily was ruled by the House of Aragon). Salabaetto means something like "the fast liver" or "the happy one"; both meanings could apply to the protagonist of the story.

5 Iancofiore is Sicilian for Biancofiore, the Italian equivalent of the French Blanche-fleur ("white flower"), the name of the heroine who appears in the eponymous French romance; the heroine of Boccaccio's earlier prose romance *Il Filocolo* was called Biancofiore. Iancofiore is referred to as *Madama* on several occasions in the story, a linguistic equivalent for *Madonna* ("my lady") in keeping with the Sicilian setting; I have accordingly kept her title as it is.

6 Baths were not places to wash oneself in the late Middle Ages, but to bathe, relax, and socialize, as one does today in a spa. However, they also served as popular locations for romantic trysts and functioned as houses of prostitution. The Italian word for the place, *bagno*, would enter English as *bagnio* in the seventeenth century and became a standard euphemism for brothel. Note that a bathhouse serves as a setting for a romantic tryst in 3.6. Salabaetto's drawing the ring across his eyes two sentences later indicates how precious it is to him (i.e., as precious as his eyesight).

7 Pietro Canigiano was Boccaccio's rough contemporary who held various positions of responsibility both in the Kingdom of Naples and in Florence, although after 1378 his houses in the latter were destroyed, he was forbidden to hold office, and he died in prison in 1381. Caterina di Valois-Courtenay (1301/1303–46) was titled the Empress of Constantinople in that she was the descendant of one of the French noblemen who, along with the Venetians, had captured the city in 1204 during the Second Crusade and had created the Latin Empire of Constantinople (it was eventually retaken by the Byzantines in 1261). Caterina was married to Philip I of Taranto (1278–1331), the fourth son of Charles II of Anjou, "the Lame," King of Naples (1254–1309). It was said that she was responsible for the initial worldly success of Niccolò Acciaiuoli (1310–65), a member of an important banking family and a close friend to both Boccaccio and Pietro Canigiano. I have Dioneo refer to him as "a compatriot of ours," but in Italian he is said to be *nostro compare*. *Compare* technically meant godfather, but it often designated a close male friend, a gossip, and so, Dioneo's term indicates that Canigiani has a somewhat closer social connection to them than "compatriot" might suggest.

8 Monaco was a notorious haven for pirates, as can be seen in 2.10.

9 Boccaccio is citing a widely diffused proverb: *Chi ha far con tosco, non vuole esser losco.* Translated literally: "He who has to do with a Tuscan does not want to be squinting."

Day 9, Story 1

1 There are many stories in medieval literature in which women impose virtually impossible tasks on would-be lovers in order to keep them at bay, but there is no particular tale that is the source for this one.

2 The Palermini was a noteworthy Ghibelline family from the quarter of San Pancrazio in Florence who had been exiled in 1267; another member of the family appears in 3.7. The Chiarmontesi was an important Florentine family living near the Orsanmichele that had originally been Ghibelline and had likewise been exiled in 1267; it later switched political allegiance and turned Guelf.

3 The Lazzari was a powerful Guelf family in Pistoia and included among its members Dante's Vanni Fucci, who is punished among the thieves in Hell (see *Inferno* 24.122–51), as well as a famous lawyer named Filippo de' Lazzari. There is no record of any Francesca de' Lazzari.

4 The name Scannadio means literally "he slits the throat of God."

Day 9, Story 2

1 Versions of this story can be found in devotional works, such as Jacobus de Voragine's *Legenda aurea* (*The Golden Legend*), 146, as well as in several French *fabliaux*.

2 The Abbess's name is unusual, but the family name Usimbardi did exist at the time.

Day 9, Story 3

1 The theme of the pregnant man is very ancient and was widespread in classical and medieval literature, from the Greek geographer Strabo's *Geography* (3.4) through Marie de France's fable *Du vilain et de l'escarbot* (*The Peasant and the Beetle*) to the *Legenda aurea* (*The Golden Legend*), 89.

2 The joke here is that Calandrino's "two hundred *lire* in small change" (*dugento lire di piccioli contanti*) are not worth all that much, although he fantasizes about buying a farm with them.

3 The original speaks of Calandrino going about *comperando terra come se egli avesse avuto a far pallottole*: "buying earth (or land) as if he had to make pellets." The pellets in question were clay projectiles shot out of crossbows. The point here is that the only "farm" Calandrino has enough money to buy would be a tiny plot just large enough to obtain clay for making pellets; there would not be not enough land, in other words, for a proper farm, which was what anyone with social ambitions would have wanted to purchase in Boccaccio's time.

4 Nello di Dino (or Bandino) is mentioned in several documents at the start of the fourteenth century, and like Bruno and Buffalmacco, he may have been a disciple

of Andrea Tafi, a painter who is best known for his work on the mosaics in the Florentine Baptistery. Nello is said to be a relative of Calandrino's wife in 9.5. Nello is short for Antonello or another name ending in *nello*.

5 Master Simone da Villa appeared in 8.9, where he was identified as a particularly stupid doctor from Bologna and was the object of a complex practical joke that Bruno and Buffalmacco played on him.

6 In 8.9, Master Simone is said to live on the Via del Cocomero (the present via Ricasoli), which was near the Mercato Vecchio where Bruno and Buffalmacco also lived. Note that "Cocomero" means "watermelon," and that here Master Simone lives "at the sign of the Melon," that is, he advertises his practice by means of a sign with a melon painted on it. Both watermelon and melon are, of course, images of his (empty) head.

7 Here Boccaccio replaces *Simone* with *Scimmione*, deforming the name only slightly (in pronunciation), while turning it into the word for monkey or ape.

8 In the original, Simone assures Calandrino he will be *più sano che pesce* ("healthier than a fish").

9 Master Simone sends Calandrino a little bit of *chiarea*, which critics have glossed in various ways. The word may derive from the French *clarée*, meaning "liquor." Since Calandrino finds it inoffensive, "spiced wine" seems a reasonable translation, since it was often used as a cure itself or as a base for other medicines.

Day 9, Story 4

1 There is no known source for this story, although some of its motifs can be found in various popular narratives.

2 These are both historical characters from prominent Sienese families. Cecco Angiulieri, or Angiolieri (ca. 1260–ca. 1312), was a poet, who wrote burlesque verse, addressing one of his sonnets to Dante. It is recorded that Cecco di Fortarrigo Piccolomini was condemned to death for murder in 1293, although the sentence was apparently never carried out. Another one of Angiulieri's sonnets was addressed to him. Note: Cecco is short for Francesco.

3 Scholars have suggested several candidates for the cardinal in question, but none of them convincingly. Ancona is a seaport on the Adriatic and was one of three Marches (borderlands) that owed allegiance to the Papacy in the Middle Ages. It is now the capital of the Italian province known as *Le Marche* (The Marches), which lies directly to the east of Tuscany and Umbria.

4 Buonconvento is a small town about twenty-five miles southeast of Siena. Seven miles farther on, heading east (toward The Marches), lies the town of Torrenieri, which is mentioned later in the story, and Torrenieri, in turn, is almost halfway to Corsignano (now known as Pienza), which is also mentioned later on.

5 I have used colloquialisms in this passage to reflect the fact that Fortarrigo's speech, here in particular, is larded with Sienese expressions. Indeed, Boccaccio uses them throughout the story, such as consistently replacing the more standard *giocare* or *giuocare* ("to play, gamble") with the Sienese *giucare*.

Day 9, Story 5

1 This story has no literary antecedents.

2 The Cornacchini was a important family of merchants in Florence in the fourteenth and fifteenth centuries and owned a house in Via del Cocomero, which is close to where Bruno, Buffalmacco, and the others lived. Camerata, a hill just below Fiesole where many suburban estates were located, has been mentioned before in 7.1.

3 Niccolosa was a common name in Tuscany at that time. Her pimp is referred to as *il Mangione*. *Mangione* may possibly be his last name, which is how I have translated it, even though it is preceded by the definite article, since such a procedure was—and still is—common enough in the Tuscan dialect of Italian. It is also possible, however, that *il Mangione* may be a sobriquet, so that his "name" is "The Glutton." Camaldoli was a lower-class quarter in Florence.

4 Calandrino called Niccolosa a *lammia*. The word had been used since classical antiquity for a female monster with the body of a snake and the head of a woman who supposedly came out at night to kill children and drink their blood. The word could also have the less threatening meaning of an enchanting nymph or fairy or siren. Calandrino intends it in this second sense, but the other meaning may resonate in context.

5 Calandrino is mangling the conventional language of courtly love here.

6 This last comparison is simpler in Boccaccio's Italian: *come va la pazza al figliuolo*. Literally, it means "as the madwoman goes for her child (or son)." It was a proverbial expression for anyone who pursued without restraint the person whom he or she loved passionately.

7 See 9.3.

Day 9, Story 6

1 There are several *fabliaux* that narrate versions of this story, including Jean de Boves's *De Gombert et des deux clers* (*Gombert and the Two Clerks*) and the anonymous *Le meunier et les deux clers* (*The Miller and the Two Clerks*). Chaucer's *The Reeve's Tale* does so as well and may have been influenced by Boccaccio's version of the story. Note that the valley of the Mugnone, which provides the setting for the story, also appears in 8.3; the Mugnone flows from Fiesole south to Florence, and at one time entered the Arno near the Ponte Vecchio.

2 In this sentence, Boccaccio writes simply that Adriano *caricò l'orza* ("he yanked his rope"). The *orza* was the rope or cable attached to the yardarm of a sailing ship. The expression *caricare l'orza* meant to make or keep the line taut (so that the sail attached to the yardarm would swell out in the prevailing breeze). I have had to fill out Boccaccio's phrase in order to bring out the obscene double entendre it contains.

3 Pinuccio's enthusiasm expresses itself as a rhyming couplet in the Italian original.

Day 9, Story 7

1 Although there is no direct precedent for this story, there are a number of tales in European literature concerning obstinate wives who ignore warnings and die as a result.

2 Several stories earlier in the *Decameron* concern prophetic dreams; see 4.5 and 4.6 for examples.

3 There are records of a family called Imolese (or da Imola or Imole) that lived in Florence during Boccaccio's lifetime, although the name suggests that at some point it had come from Imola, a city in Romagna. Talano is short for Catalano, apparently a relatively common name at the time. (Catalano was actually a family name that was widespread in Italy, especially in the south, and indicates that its ancestors had most likely come originally from the region of Catalonia in Spain.)

4 This was apparently a proverbial saying. The Italian reads *Chi mal ti vuol, mal ti sogna,* and could be translated more literally as: "He who wishes you ill has bad dreams about you."

5 The wife's comment that her husband would "do well for himself if he were eating dinner with the blind" is another proverbial statement, the gist of which is that one who eats with the blind can easily take advantage of them by helping himself to whatever food he wishes to have.

Day 9, Story 8

1 Although there is no direct precedent for this story, the Ciacco who is featured in it was clearly taken by Boccaccio from Dante's *Inferno* where he is punished for the sin of gluttony (see 6.38–57). There have been attempts to identify him with the minor poet Ciacco d'Anguillaia, but unconvincingly. Ciacco is short for Giacomo or Jacopo (James), although the name was also slang for "hog." There is no record whatsoever of the Biondello ("little blond guy") who appears in the story.

2 Biondello is said to be "cleaner than a fly," because flies always seem to be cleaning themselves off with their legs. Biondello wears a tight-fitting *cuffia,* a kind of skullcap, a head covering usually worn by women, over which one might place a hat. These details, together with his long blond locks, suggest that he is something of a dandy.

3 A prominent and extremely wealthy merchant who was celebrated for the open house he kept, Vieri de' Cerchi was the leader of the party of the White Guelfs in Florence. He was exiled from the city in 1300, but soon returned, only to see his party defeated the next year by its enemies, the Black Guelfs, after which he went into exile and died in Arezzo around 1305. Corso Donati, whom Biondello mentions in his next comment, was, by contrast, of noble origin and the head of the Blacks, and he, too, must have kept a great table. Corso had also been exiled from Florence in 1300, but returned to the city in 1301 with the aid of Pope Boniface VIII and Charles de Valois, King of Naples, defeating his enemies and sending not only Vieri into exile, but Dante Alighieri, who had married Gemma Donati, a distant relative of Corso's, as well. Corso was finally assassinated in 1308 by an angry mob after having been

accused of conspiring to become the head of the state. The political feud between Vieri and Corso forms the background for the practical joke that Biondello plays on Ciacco.

4   "Huckster" is my translation of *barattiere*, which means a person who sold cheap goods in the public market or had some sort of (low-end) gaming table there. The word was also used for those who sold public offices for money, which is how most Italians know it from Dante's *Inferno*, where it identifies a particular group of sinners who are punished for their fraudulent behavior by being boiled in pitch (see Cantos 21 and 22). In translations of Dante, *barattiere* is often rendered as "grafter," but since the man in this story is willing to participate in Biondello's practical joke for a presumably small sum of money, it is unlikely that he would have been engaged in the sale of public offices. The Loggia de' Cavicciuli to which he is taken was located in the Corso degli Adimari, now the via Calzaiuoli, where the family Cavicciuli-Adimari owned various properties. Filippo Argenti degli Adimari, who is mentioned later in the sentence, was immortalized by Dante in the eighth canto of the *Inferno* as epitomizing the sin of wrath. So angry is he there that he winds up biting himself in his rage, an action that Boccaccio's story recalls later on just before Filippo runs into Biondello.

5   The two Italian words used by Ciacco here, *arubinare* ("rubify," i.e., turn ruby colored) and *zanzeri* ("little drinking buddies"), are made-up words—made up by Boccaccio as well as by Ciacco—and are seemingly designed to irritate Filippo by taunting him simply because they are unfamiliar. The word *zanzeri* actually could have two quite distinct meanings according to Italian lexicographers: there is the more neutral "drinking buddies or companions," and the more scandalous "catamites or boy prostitutes." Although this second meaning became the dominant one several centuries after Boccaccio wrote, there is no firm evidence that it would have meant that for Boccaccio. Nevertheless, since that meaning cannot be excluded here, I have attempted to capture both senses of the word with my translation by making the "drinking buddies" little ones.

Day 9, Story 9

1   Although there is no specific source for this story, there are many precedents in both Eastern and Western literature for the figure of Solomon as a sage as well as for the punishment given to the shrewish wife.

2   See 9.7.

3   Versions of this proverb were widely diffused in the late Middle Ages.

4   Melisso is the Italianized form of the name of the pre-Socratic Greek philosopher Melissus of Samos who lived in the fifth century, BCE. Giosefo, whom he meets in the next paragraph, is a variant of the name Giuseppe (Joseph). In Boccaccio's day, Laiazzo, or Lajazzo (Ayas), was a prosperous port in what was called Little Armenia, or Cilicia, a kingdom founded by Armenians fleeing from the Turks; it was located on the eastern coast of the Mediterranean in what is now the country of Turkey.

Day 9, Story 10

1 There are many stories in which human beings are turned into animals in both antiquity and the Middle Ages, including one of Boccaccio's favorites, Apuleius's *Metamorphoses*.

2 Barletta was a coastal city northwest of Bari in the southern Italian province of Apulia (Puglia) where the Bardi bank, for which Boccaccio's father worked, had a branch. This is the only story in the *Decameron* set in this region of Italy. Gianni di Barolo, who is introduced in this sentence, means Gianni from Barletta, Barolo deriving from the Italianized version of the Latin name of the town. Pietro da Tresanti means Pietro from the town of Tresanti.

3 Zita (which means "little girl" in the Tuscan dialect) was a common name in southern Italy, and there was a Saint Zita (ca. 1212–72) from Tuscany who was the patron saint of maids and domestic servants. Carapresa ("dear—or precious—acquisition") is the name of the woman from the island of Trapani off the northern coast of Sicily who appears in 5.2. Giudice ("Judge") was also a common southern Italian name, and an actual Giudice Leo appears in chancellery records from the town of Bitonto. The wife's name, which appears a little later in the story, is Gemmata, which means "one adorned with gems."

4 Bitonto was a market town ten miles west of Bari and held a famous fair on All Saints' Day, just eleven days before a similar fair at Barletta. Boccaccio chooses the name, however, for its suggestiveness, since it could be read as *bi-* (or *bis*) + *tonto*, "twice stupid." Pietro is twice stupid, first for being tricked by the priest, and then, according to his wife, for having to return to his ordinary life. That we are repeatedly told he uses an *ass* to carry his goods is also suggestive.

Day 10, Story 1

1 There are many stories in classical, Eastern, and medieval literature that turn on the protagonist's choice between two or more objects, often coffers as in this case, that are seemingly identical, but only one of which actually contains a treasure. This plot device appears in English literature most famously in Shakespeare's *The Merchant of Venice*, in which Bassanio wins Portia's hand in marriage by choosing the right casket.

2 The Figiovanni was a noble Florentine family that also owned property in Certaldo, some of which may have been adjacent to the house where Boccaccio spent his last years. The Spanish King Alfonso, who is mentioned in the next sentence may have been Alfonso III of Castile (b. 1155, ruled 1158–1244), who was celebrated by many, including Dante, for his liberality as well as for the wars he waged against the Moors. He has also been identified with Alfonso X, the Wise, King of Castile (b. 1221, ruled 1252–84), whose generosity was proverbial.

Day 10, Story 2

1 There is no precedent for this story, which is treated as historical fact by several medieval chroniclers as well as by commentators writing on Dante's *Purgatorio*, which mentions Ghino in passing (6.13–14); Boccaccio's story is, however, the ultimate source for all of their accounts. Ghino di Tacco, who died in either 1303 or 1313, was a Sienese nobleman who, from his youth, had been a bandit like the rest of his family. After being banished from Siena by the counts of Santafiore in the 1290s, he captured the stronghold of Radicofani, which was located near a main road between Siena and Rome, and from there he preyed on travelers passing to and from the Holy City. Ghino murdered a judge in Rome, which is what Dante mentions about him, and for which he was condemned by Pope Boniface VIII (b. ca. 1235, pope 1294–1303), who eventually pardoned him (as he does in this story). Ghino was famous as a kind of "Robinhood" character, a view that Boccaccio seems to accept, although he was clearly also a brutal, violent man who was eventually assassinated himself. His first name is probably short for "Borghino," a family name that identifies someone as a town dweller (*borgo* means "town") and that appears frequently in late medieval documents from central Italy; Ghino was also a family name in the period. The Benedictine Abbey of Cluny, located in Burgundy, was founded in 910 by Duke William the Pious of Aquitaine. It controlled a number of abbeys elsewhere, including one in Paris, and by the late Middle Ages its wealth had become legendary. There were many Benedictine monasteries in the region around Siena. Note that another unidentified Abbot of Cluny is mentioned in 1.7. The Hospitallers, also called the Knights Hospitaller, were members of the Order of Saint John of Jerusalem, which was originally attached to a hospital founded in Jerusalem around 1023, but became a religious and military order in 1099 during the First Crusade and was charged with defending the Holy Land. In Boccaccio's time, they had established themselves as the rulers of Rhodes, the Holy Land having been recaptured by Islamic forces in 1291.

2 Excommunications are directed at individuals, banning them from participation in the sacraments of the Church. Interdicts are wholesale bans on religious activities in an entire region.

3 Corniglia is one of *le Cinque Terre* ("The Five Towns") perched on cliffs overlooking the Mediterranean that are located in Liguria between Genoa and La Spezia. The town is surrounded by vineyards to this day, although the grape varietal called Vernaccia is not produced there. However, Vernaccia derives from a word meaning "vernacular," i.e., "local," and is a white wine made from a varietal of the same name that is grown throughout Italy. Nowadays, when people say Vernaccia, they are usually referring to the Tuscan white wine, Vernaccia di San Gimignano, but in Boccaccio's time that was not necessarily the case.

Day 10, Story 3

1 There are some antecedents for this story in Persian and Arabic literature, and especially in Arab legends concerning Hatim Tai, a heroic character from the pre-Islamic period who was celebrated for his courage, wisdom, and unmatched generosity. A story in Arabic about this figure may have shaped elements in the life of Saint John the Merciful (also known as Saint John the Almsgiver), which is included in Jacobus de Voragine's *Legenda aurea* (*The Golden Legend*), 27; Saint John, who was the Patriarch of Alexandria from 606 to 616, was famous for his liberality, especially toward the poor. In Hebrew, the name Nathan means "he who has given." The name Mithridanes (Boccaccio writes "Mitridanes") seems to be Boccaccio's invention. It may have been meant to echo Mithra or Mithras, a Persian god who was the center of a mystery religion practiced in the Roman Empire from the first to the fourth century, CE, but since the character in the story has little or nothing in common with the Persian god and the religious practices he inspired, Boccaccio may simply intend to evoke the exotic by means of his name, just as he does by situating the story in faraway China.

2 Both Nathan and the palace he has built (which is referred to in the next sentence) seem to echo what the Venetian Marco Polo reported about Kublai Khan and his residences in Cathay (i.e., northern China), but Boccaccio has deliberately named the Genoese, not the Venetians, as the source of his story, perhaps because of a typical Florentine sense of rivalry with Venice. That rivalry may also be seen in the story of Frate Alberto (4.2).

3 Nathan says that the world is "miserissimo," which I have translated as "quite a miserly place," but the word could also mean that the world is "quite a wretched place."

Day 10, Story 4

1 Various antecedents for this story can be found in Eastern tale collections as well as in classical and medieval literature in the West. Boccaccio had already told a version of this story in his early prose work, *Il Filocolo*.

2 Bologna is not in what is now identified as the province of Lombardy, but in Boccaccio's time the entire region north of the Apennines was referred to as Lombardy. The Carisendi, like the Caccianemico mentioned in the next sentence, was actually a noble family in the city, and there is still a leaning tower there named after them. Catalina is the Bolognese form of Caterina (Catherine).

3 Modena and Bologna are about twenty-four miles apart.

4 Gentile's name means "noble" or "gentle," and the word designates both a class position and a set of ethical attributes. In some ways, the story identifies its protagonist's magnanimous behavior as the epitome of gentility or gentle behavior, but there are moments, such as this one, in which Gentile makes himself into the godfather of Niccoluccio's child and names the child after himself, that may give one pause.

Day 10, Story 5

1   As with the preceding story, Boccaccio had told a version of this one in *Il Filocolo*. It
    has Eastern antecedents in Chinese, Indian, Persian, and other literatures as well as
    in that of medieval France. Chaucer's *The Franklin's Tale* resembles it, although schol-
    ars are not sure that Chaucer knew the *Decameron* the way he knew (and translated
    or adapted) many of Boccaccio's earlier works. It is more likely that both writers
    were working from a common, probably French, source.

2   Friuli, a province located in the northeastern part of Italy, was—and is—known for
    its severe winters. Udine is its main city. Neither Dianora nor her husband have last
    names in the story, and thus their identities cannot be determined. Nor can that of
    Ansaldo Gradense, who is mentioned in the next sentence, although his last name
    means his family probably came from the town of Grado, which was also located
    in Friuli.

3   Boccaccio is echoing a classical notion, formulated by Cicero as *Nil difficile amanti*
    (*Orator* 10: "Nothing is difficult for a lover").

4   In her conclusion, Emilia is referring, of course, to the previous story.

Day 10, Story 6

1   There is no literary source for this story. Its principal figure, Charles the Old, usu-
    ally referred to as Charles I (1226–85), was Charles of Anjou who ruled as the King
    of Sicily from 1266 to 1282, when he was expelled from the island; he was known
    thereafter as the King of Naples, which he controlled until his death. Charles, who
    also appears in the tale of Madama Beritola (2.6), is generally treated sympatheti-
    cally by Boccaccio. He was actually a notorious womanizer, and since the story is
    set just after 1266, he can hardly be called "the Old."

2   Manfred (1232–66), a Hohenstaufen and son of the Holy Roman Emperor Fred-
    erick II, had usurped the throne of Sicily from his nephew Conradin (1252–68) in
    1258. The Papacy wished to detach the Kingdom of Sicily (which included Naples
    and southern Italy) from the Holy Roman Empire, and enlisted Charles of Anjou
    to conquer it, which he did by winning the battle of Benevento on February 26,
    1266, at which Manfred was killed. This led to the expulsion from Florence of the
    Ghibellines, who supported the Empire, and the reinstatement of the Guelfs, who
    supported the Papacy.

3   This character cannot be identified with any specific historical figure, although
    the Uberti was a powerful Ghibelline family in Florence. Its most famous member
    was Farinata degli Uberti, immortalized by Dante in *Inferno* 10, who had served
    with Manfred in his victory over the Florentine Guelfs at the battle of Montaperti
    in 1260. Farinata died in 1264, but after defeating Manfred in 1266, Charles had
    Farinata's children hunted down, imprisoned, and murdered. Boccaccio's Charles
    is a very different ruler. Note that some critics have found it strange for Boccaccio
    to have Messer Neri, a Ghibelline, elect to live anywhere in Charles's realm.

4   Castellammare di Stabia is a resort on the southeast side of the Bay of Naples. The Angevin rulers of the city had a summer palace built there in 1310.

5   Guy de Montfort, one of Charles's most loyal followers, was appointed his vice-regent in Tuscany in 1270. During that same year, in revenge for the killing of his father, he murdered Prince Henry, the nephew of Henry III of England, in the Cathedral of Viterbo during High Mass. Dante places him in the part of Hell reserved for those who committed acts of violence against their neighbors (see *Inferno* 12.119–20).

6   Ginevra and Isotta (or Isolde) were common names in courtly romances.

7   Medieval theologians believed there were nine (in some cases, seven) orders of angels arranged in a hierarchy. The most influential classification was that of Pseudo-Dionysius the Areopagite from the fifth century, whose hierarchy included (ranging from the from lowest to the highest): Angels, Archangels, Principalities, Powers, Virtues, Dominions, Thrones, Cherubim, and Seraphim.

8   Conradin I, Manfred's nephew, led an army to Italy in an attempt to retake Sicily from Charles in 1267. He was defeated at the battle of Tagliacozzo in August 1268, and after he fled, he was captured and turned over to Charles, who had him tried and beheaded in Naples on October 29. With Conradin's death, the legitimate branch of the Hohenstaufens became extinct.

9   In the preceding sentence, Count Guy rehearses a well-known saying of Publilius Syrus: *Bis vincit qui se vincit in victoria* ("he conquers twice who, when victorious, conquers himself"). In this sentence, he echoes the argument, though not the exact words, that the Roman general Scipio Africanus used to persuade Massinissa, a Roman ally, to give Sophonisba, the beautiful wife of the defeated African king Syphax, up to the Romans rather than to ravish her; see Livy, *Ab urbe condita* (*From the Founding of the City*), 30.14.

10 The Palizzi family was one of the most powerful in Messina and had ties to the Uberti; Matteo was a common name among its male members. There was a Guiglielmo d'Alemagna (William of Germany) in the retinue of Charles's son in 1306, and the family was still flourishing in Boccaccio's time.

Day 10, Story 7

1   Several chronicles recount the story of a certain Macalda di Scaletta who fell in love with King Peter of Aragon after he entered her town as a conqueror. There was also a now-lost poem on the subject, from which the poetical material in the center of this story may derive. Boccaccio's story thus seems an unfolding of the kind of biographical scenario that courtly love lyrics often seem to be alluding to. Since Peter of Aragon was a Ghibelline (and thus a supporter of the Holy Roman Empire's claims in Italy), while the protagonist of the previous story was a Guelf (and thus a supporter of the Papacy), the two stories balance one another nicely.

2   There were seven distinct families named Puccini living in Florence during this period, but none of them had a Bernardo among its members. The King Peter mentioned in the next sentence was Peter III of Aragon (b. 1239, ruled 1276–85). Famed

for his great stature and physical strength, he became ruler of Sicily in September of 1282, after the French, who had held the island since 1266, were expelled during the revolt known as the Sicilian Vespers, which began on March 31, 1282.

3 To joust "in the Catalan fashion" meant to follow the rules established in Catalonia, which had been united with the Kingdom of Aragon in the twelfth century.

4 There was a Mino d'Arezzo (Minuccio is a diminutive) who was a minor thirteenth-century poet active in Sicily during this period. King Peter was also a poet and welcomed poets and musicians in his court.

5 The viol (Boccaccio writes *viuola;* the more common French name was *vielle*) was a stringed instrument like the modern violin, but with a longer, deeper body, and an indeterminate number of strings; it could be bowed or plucked and was used to accompany singing or dancing. "Dance tunes" is my translation of *stampita,* a rhythmic instrumental composition accompanying a poem.

6 A Mico da Siena is named by Dante in his *De vulgari eloquentia (On Vernacular Eloquence),* 1.13, and a song directly attributed to him is preserved in a Vatican codex. The name Mico was short for either Michele or Amico ("Friend") and was quite common in Sicily in the period. It is most likely, however, that the poem is Boccaccio's and represents his attempt to compose verse in the then somewhat archaic style of the so-called Sicilian School, a group of poets who were attached to the courts of Frederick II and his son Manfred. These poets wrote during the middle third of the thirteenth century and included Tuscans and Sicilians as well as King Frederick himself. In keeping with the archaic flavor of Boccaccio's poem, I have elected to translate it using at times slightly older forms of English.

7 Cefalú is located in the province of Palermo; Calatabellotta, in that of Agrigento. I have translated Boccaccio's *terre* (lit. "lands") as "fiefs" in order to reflect the emphatically medieval character of this story. Even though fiefs and the feudal system are usually thought of as being typical of northern rather than southern Europe, Sicily had been conquered by the Normans in the eleventh century and was later ruled by the Hohenstaufens, the Angevins, and the Aragonese, all of whom maintained versions of the feudal system in the island.

Day 10, Story 8

1 The earliest direct antecedent for the first portion of this story is the second exemplary tale found in the fourteenth-century *Disciplina clericalis (A School for Clerics)* of Peter Alphonsi, which influenced a number of later works, any one of which may also have been known to Boccaccio. The celebration of friendship in the second portion of the story as a force that can triumph over love and even the fear of death is mostly a retelling of the legend of Damon and Pythias, but it echoes themes found in various Eastern story collections as well as in a host of classical texts from the West, ranging from Cicero's *De amicitia (On Friendship)* through Quintilian's *Declamationes (Speeches)* to Valerius Maximus's *Factorum et dictorum memorabilium libri IX (Nine Books of Memorable Deeds and Sayings).* Boccaccio's story, frequently translated into Latin, enjoyed great popularity in Europe over the next several centuries.

2 Octavianus (or Octavius) was a member of the Second Triumvirate, along with
   Mark Antony and Marcus Aemilius Lepidus, between 43 and 30 BCE. Boccaccio
   is using "generic" Roman names for both the father Publius and his son Titus, and
   although there was, in fact, a quite important Roman clan at the time called Quintus, none of the families in it was named Fulvius. Chremes, who is mentioned in the
   next sentence, is named after a character in one of Boccaccio's favorite comedies,
   Terence's *Phormio*; his son's name is entirely Boccaccio's invention; and the philosopher Aristippus, who is mentioned later, is named after Aristippus of Cyrene,
   a Greek philosopher who lived in the fourth century, BCE. Sending one's sons to
   Greece in order to study philosophy was a common practice among Roman aristocrats, something Cicero comments on in the introduction to his well-known *De
   officiis* (*On Duties*).

3 In Florence the legal age at which girls might marry was twelve. Sophronia's name
   comes from a Greek word meaning "soundness of mind" and hence "wisdom," thus
   suggesting that the story can be read as an allegory in which the two friends both
   embody the art they are studying: they are "lovers of wisdom," which is what the
   word "philosophy" means in Greek.

4 Boccaccio is echoing a sentiment to be found Ovid's well-known *Remedia amoris*
   (*The Remedies for Love*): *principiis obsta* (91: "oppose [things] at the start").

5 Gisippus tells his friends that he should have the girl because he is *molto più intendente di me*, which I have translated as "more intent upon having her." *Intendente*
   here means Titus is more focused on the girl, more taken with her, but the word can
   also mean that he has a superior understanding of her (and her worth?), since the
   verb *intendere* can mean "to understand," or that, in other words, he is something
   of a connoisseur. Elsewhere in the *Decameron*, *intendente* can mean "wise," so while
   that meaning is probably not the main one here, it is not to be excluded altogether.

6 Being a Roman, Titus's "god" in this case must be Jupiter, not the Christian God,
   and hence I have not capitalized the pronouns referring to him in the following
   sentences.

7 Boccaccio's text admits two possible readings here, although the one I have chosen
   seems the more likely. Gisippus says that giving up Sophronia will not be a loss for
   him, because *a un altro me la transmuterò di bene in meglio*. In addition to meaning
   "I'll be transferring her, as it were, to my other—and better—self," this could be
   rendered as: "I'll be transferring her to my other self, thereby changing her lot for
   the better."

8 Titus's opinion of the Greeks reflects a belief that was current in Boccaccio's time.

9 Titus has argued that it is presumptuous for people to claim they know what the
   gods ordain, but that is precisely what he is doing here.

10 In an anecdote Boccaccio may well have known that was recorded by Pliny the
   Elder, *Historia naturalis* (*Natural History*), 36.85, and Valerius Maximus, *Factorum
   et dictorum memorabilium libri IX* (*Nine Books of Memorable Deeds and Sayings*), 8.12.3,
   the painter Apelles (late fourth century, BCE) would hide behind a curtain while
   people viewed his paintings. Once a shoemaker remarked that a sandal Apelles
   had drawn lacked a loop, and Apelles corrected it, but when the shoemaker later

criticized Apelles's drawing of the subject's leg, Apelles looked out and told him he had gone too far.

11 Marcus and Varro are, again, generic Roman names. A praetor was an elected magistrate who was subordinate to the two consuls who together had supreme military, administrative, and judicial authority in the Roman Republic.

12 Boccaccio's text here rehearses the so-called Golden Rule, which can be found in many religions, including various places in the New Testament, such as in the Book of Luke: *et prout vultis faciant vobis homines et vos facite illis similiter* (6:31: "And as ye would that men should do to you, do ye also to them likewise"). Boccaccio's text echoes the sentiments involved, but not exactly the words of the Vulgate Bible.

Day 10, Story 9

1 The first part of this tale has antecedents in stories concerning Saladin that spread his legend throughout Europe, including some that had him going about among Christians in disguise. One such story appears in the *Novellino* (23), for example. There are even more antecedents in the literature of the Middle Ages for elements in the second half of Boccaccio's tale (Messer Torello's magical voyage and his appearance at the wedding of his wife).

2 Saladin (Salah al-Din, 1138–93) was the Sultan of Cairo and was most famous for the reconquest of Jerusalem from the crusaders in 1187. A popular figure in medieval literature, he was celebrated for his knowledge, his chivalry, his military leadership, and his generosity. The Frederick I (1122–90) who is mentioned in the next paragraph—also known as Frederick Barbarossa ("of the Red Beard")—was a German King and Holy Roman Emperor (from 1152 on). One of the leaders of the Third Crusade, with Richard the Lion-Hearted of England and Philip II of France, which began in 1189, he drowned in the Saleph River, which is in modern-day Turkey, the following year.

3 Since both Muslims and Christians made pilgrimages in the Middle Ages, Saladin's doing so would not have been perceived as unusual.

4 There are records of a Torello who was Frederick II's *podestà* in various cities during the early thirteenth century; he may also have been a poet who wrote works in Provençal. Torello was a popular name in Tuscany in the late Middle Ages and is a nickname (with a diminutive ending) probably derived from Salvatore; *torello* in Italian means "little bull," although how that could apply to Boccaccio's character is uncertain. The last part of his name means that he comes from Strà (or Strada, "Street") in the province of Pavia, which is about twenty miles south of Milan and lies on the east bank of the Ticino River.

5 Boccaccio is following inaccurate contemporary accounts of the battle of Acre. The city, called Saint John of Acre, had been captured by crusaders in 1104, but was taken back by Saladin's army in 1187, only to be attacked two years later by members of the Third Crusade. Saladin attempted to lift the siege unsuccessfully, and the crusaders eventually captured the city in 1191. During the siege, disease ravaged the camps of both the armies. Acre was finally recaptured by the Muslims in 1291.

6 The Church of San Pietro in Ciel d'Oro ("Saint Peter in the Sky of Gold") stands in the center of Pavia.

7 Dignes (more accurately, Digne) is a town in the French Alps at one time controlled by the Angevin rulers of Naples.

8 Although magic has a significant presence in medieval literature, Boccaccio is skeptical about it, as he clearly is in 8.7, and he rarely accords it much of a place in the *Decameron*. On this day, however, which is devoted to examples of magnanimity, his narrators sometimes include magical elements, thus giving their stories an increasingly exalted—if implausible—character.

9 Adalieta is a diminutive of Adelaide, a popular name among noble families.

Day 10, Story 10

1 Although there are many examples of faithful wives put to harsh tests in medieval literature, the clearest "source" for this story is that of Job in the Bible. No scholar has been able to find anyone in the historical record who resembles Griselda. Indeed, her name seems to have been invented by Boccaccio, possibly as an ironic variation of Criseida, the notably unfaithful lover of Troilo (Troilus) in his romance *Il Filostrato*. Saluzzo is a town south of Turin lying in the foothills of the Alps. It was ruled by a series of marquises between 1142 and 1548, one of whom named Gualtieri was mentioned in a document dating from 1174 to 1175.

2 Dioneo is alluding to the language used by the heroine in 7.1.

3 Dioneo's phrase here, *matta bestialità* (lit.: "insane bestiality"), echoes Dante, who uses it to sum up the two types of sins in the lowest regions of Hell (see *Inferno* 11.82–83). The concept was developed by Saint Thomas Aquinas in his commentary on Aristotle's *Nicomachean Ethics*, 7.1.1.

4 Giannucole is a diminutive of Giovanni and means "Johnny" or "Little John."

5 Griselda's response here echoes what Mary says to the Angel Gabriel: *Fiat mihi secundum verbum tuum* (Luke 1:38: "be it unto me according to thy word").

6 Compare Job's words: *nudus egressus sum de utero matris meae et nudus revertar illuc Dominus dedit Dominus abstulit sit nomen Domini benedictum* (Job 1:21: "Naked came I out of my mother's womb, and naked shall I return thither: the Lord gave, and the Lord hath taken away; blessed be the name of the Lord").

7 Panago (or, more correctly, Panico) was located near Bologna and was ruled by counts of the Alberti family.

8 Another biblical allusion, this time to Mary's *Ecce ancilla Dei* (Luke 1:38: "Behold the handmaiden of the Lord").

9 Gualtieri's "I believe I may boast" (*credendomi poter dar vanto*) is a formula used by medieval knights who would boast, often at the dinner table, of some heroic deed they had done or some extraordinary possession they had, challenging the others present to match their claim.

Day 10, Conclusion

1 Boccaccio is here paraphrasing Dante's *Convivio* (*The Banquet*): *Conviene adunque essere prudente, cioè savio: e a ciò essere si richiede buona memoria de le vedute cose, buona conoscenza de le presenti e buona provedenza de le future* (4.27.5: "Thus one must be prudent, that is, wise, for which it is necessary for one to have a good memory of things seen in the past, good knowledge of those in the present, and good foresight with regard to those in the future").

The Author's Conclusion

1 Boccaccio's self-defense here was a commonplace in medieval poetics.
2 In the early Middle Ages, Christ was depicted on the cross with four nails hammered into his two hands and feet. A new tradition arose in the late twelfth century of their being just three nails (one for the two feet together), because of the symbolic significance of the number three. Boccaccio's references to Christ as male and Eve as female, like his reference to Christ on the cross, may also evoke the image of the naked body, which has particular resonance at this point in his text.
3 Boccaccio's last comment here refers to a common saying about how topsy-turvy the world is, but it also recalls an earlier story (9.2) in which the crime of an adulterous Abbess is discovered because she has mistakenly placed her lover's breeches on her head.
4 In medieval literature concerned with Charlemagne (the so-called "Matter of France"), the Paladins were his twelve peers; the term was later extended to mean all knights. It originally designated the Roman emperor's chamberlain and personal guards who lived with him in his palace in Rome on the Palatine Hill (from which the word is derived). The term was later used for high officials in the Catholic Church, the Holy Roman Empire, and various countries throughout Europe.
5 Aside from the sexual banter in this passage, Boccaccio is doubtless joking about the fact that he was actually quite corpulent.
6 The Lamentations of Jeremiah were sung during Holy Week; there were several medieval poems on the Passion of Christ; and there were several other poems called The Complaint (or Lament) of Mary Magdalene to which Boccaccio may be alluding, although his reference in this case may simply be generic. (The Lament is also mentioned in 3.4.)
7 Boccaccio is, of course, being ironic in praising friars for avoiding hard work. His image of their "grinding when the millpond is full" is a reference to their sexual behavior, suggesting that they have sex, but only at infrequent intervals (i.e., "when the millpond is full"). That they smell like billy goats may refer both to their filthiness and to their randiness, since goats have been credited with excessive sexual appetites since antiquity. Note that all of these statements about friars have appeared before, sometimes verbatim, in the *Decameron* (see Cipolla's comments in his sermon in 6.10 for the references to friars avoiding hard work and the allusion to goats, and a comment about the priest of Varlungo in 8.2 for the millpond image).

SUGGESTIONS FOR
FURTHER READING

Since this book is primarily aimed at an Anglophone reading audience, these suggestions for further reading are limited to books and articles in English. The list is not intended to be exhaustive, but to point readers toward studies of the *Decameron* that I have found rewarding in a variety of ways. For many other materials concerning the *Decameron*, including the text of the work in Italian and English as well as a more extensive bibliography, the reader might consult the website "The *Decameron* Web," created by scholars at Brown University (http://www.brown.edu/Departments/Italian_Studies/dweb/index.php).

Almansi, Guido. *The Writer as Liar: Narrative Technique in the* Decameron. London: Routledge, 1975.

Ascoli, Albert. "Pyrrhus's Rules: Playing with Power in Boccaccio's *Decameron*." In *A Local Habitation and a Name: Imagining Histories in the Italian Renaissance*, 80–117. New York: Fordham University Press, 2011.

Auerbach, Erich R. *Mimesis: The Representation of Reality in Western Literature*. Trans. Willard R. Trask. Princeton: Princeton University Press, 1953. See chapter 9, "Frate Alberto."

Barolini, Teodolinda. "'Le parole son femmine e i fatti sono maschi': Toward a Sexual Poetics of the *Decameron* (*Decameron* II, 10)." *Studi sul Boccaccio* 21 (1993): 175–97.

_____. "The Wheel of the *Decameron*." *Romance Philology* 36 (1983): 521–39.

Bergin, Thomas G. *Boccaccio*. New York: Viking Press, 1981.

Bernardo, Aldo S. "The Plague as Key to Meaning in Boccaccio's *Decameron*." In *The Black Death: Papers of the 11th Annual Conference of the Center for Medieval and Early Renaissance Studies*, ed. Daniel Williman, 39–64. Binghamton, NY: Center for Medieval and Early Renaissance Studies, 1982.

Branca, Vittore. *Boccaccio: The Man and His Works*. Trans. Richard Monges and Dennis J. McAuliffe, with a foreword by Robert C. Clements. New York: New York University Press, 1976.

Cottino-Jones, Marga. *Order from Chaos: Social and Aesthetic Harmonies in Boccaccio's* Decameron. Washington, DC: University Press of America, 1982.

Durling, Robert M. "Boccaccio on Interpretation: Guido's Escape (*Decameron*, VI, 9)." In *Dante, Petrarch, and Boccaccio: Studies in the Italian Trecento in Honor of Charles S. Singleton*, ed. Aldo S. Bernardo and Anthony L. Pellegrini, 273–304. Binghamton, NY: Center for Medieval and Early Renaissance Studies, State University of New York at Binghamton, 1983.

Ferrante, Joan M. "The Frame Characters of the *Decameron*: A Progression of Virtues." *Romance Philology* 19 (1965): 212–26.

Fido, Franco. "Boccaccio's 'Ars Narrandi' in the Sixth Day of the *Decameron*." In *Italian Literature, Roots and Branches: Essays in Honor of Thomas Bergin*, ed. Giose Rimanelli and Kenneth John Atchity, 225–42. New Haven: Yale University Press, 1976.

Forni, Pier Massimo. *Adventures in Speech: Rhetoric and Narration in Boccaccio's Decameron*. Philadelphia: University of Pennsylvania Press, 1996.

Greene, Thomas M. "Forms of Accommodation in *The Decameron*." *Italica* 45 (1968): 297–313.

Hastings, Robert. *Nature and Reason in the Decameron*. Manchester: Manchester University Press, 1975.

Hollander, Robert. *Boccaccio's Dante and the Shaping Force of Satire*. Ann Arbor: University of Michigan Press, 1997.

Kirkham, Victoria. *The Sign of Reason in Boccaccio's Fiction*. Florence: Olschki, 1993.

Marcus, Millicent. *An Allegory of Form: Literary Self-Consciousness in the Decameron*. Saratoga, CA: Anma Libri, 1979.

———. "Misogyny as Misreading: A Gloss on *Decameron* VIII, 7." *Stanford Italian Review* 4 (1984): 23–40.

———. "Seduction by Silence: A Gloss on the Tales of Masetto (*Decameron* III, 1) and Alatiel (*Decameron* II, 7)." *Philological Quarterly* 58 (1979): 1–15.

———. "The Sweet New Style Reconsidered: A Gloss on the Tale of Cimone (*Decameron* V, 1)." *Italian Quarterly* 81 (1980): 5–16.

Marino, Lucia. *The Decameron "Cornice": Allusion, Allegory, and Iconology*. Ravenna: Longo, 1979.

Mazzotta, Giuseppe. *The World at Play in Boccaccio's Decameron*. Princeton: Princeton University Press, 1986.

Migiel, Marilyn. "Beyond Seduction: A Reading of the Tale of Alibech and Rustico (*Decameron* III, 10)." *Italica* 75 (1998): 161–77.

———. *A Rhetoric of the Decameron*. Toronto: University of Toronto Press, 2003.

Ó Cuilleanáin, Cormac. *Religion and the Clergy in Boccaccio's Decameron*. Rome: Edizioni di Storia e Letteratura, 1984.

Olson, Glending. *Literature as Recreation in the Later Middle Ages*. Ithaca: Cornell University Press, 1982.

Scaglione, Aldo. *Nature and Love in the Late Middle Ages: An Essay on the Cultural Context of the Decameron*. Berkeley: University of California Press, 1963.

Sherberg, Michael. *The Governance of Friendship: Law and Gender in the Decameron*. Columbus: Ohio State University Press, 2011.

Smarr, Janet. *Boccaccio and Fiammetta: The Narrator as Lover*. Urbana: University of Illinois Press, 1986.

Stillinger, Thomas, and F. Regina Psaki (eds.). *Boccaccio and Feminist Criticism*. Chapel Hill, NC: Annali d'Italianistica, 2006.

Wallace, David. *Giovanni Boccaccio: Decameron*. Cambridge: Cambridge University Press, 1991.

Weaver, Elisa B. (ed.). *The Decameron First Day in Perspective*. Toronto: University of Toronto Press, 2004.

Wofford, Susanne L. "The Social Aesthetics of Rape: Closural Violence in Boccaccio and Botticelli." In *Creative Imitation: New Essays on Renaissance Literature in Honor of Thomas M. Greene*, ed. David Quint, Margaret W. Ferguson, G. W. Pigman III, and Wayne A. Rebhorn, 189–238. Binghamton, NY: Medieval and Renaissance Texts and Studies, 1992.

